PENGUIN BOOKS

STRANGERS AND BROTHERS

VOLUME TWO

To Her
Who After The First Volume Was Part Of It
This Work
With Gratitude And Love

C. P. SNOW

STRANGERS

AND

BROTHERS

Volume Two

The Masters (1937)
The New Men (1939–47)
Homecomings (1938–51)
The Affair (1953–54)

PENGUIN BOOKS

Penguin Books Ltd, Harmondsworth, Middlesex, England
Penguin Books, 40 West 23rd Street, New York, New York 10010, U.S.A.
Penguin Books Australia Ltd, Ringwood, Victoria, Australia
Penguin Books Canada Ltd, 2801 John Street, Markham, Ontario, Canada L3R 1B4
Penguin Books (N.Z.) Ltd, 182–190 Wairau Road, Auckland 10, New Zealand

The Masters first published by Macmillan 1951
Published in Penguin Books 1956
Copyright © the Estate of C. P. Snow, 1951

The New Men first published by Macmillan 1954
Published in Penguin Books 1959
Copyright © the Estate of C. P. Snow, 1954

Homecomings first published by Macmillan 1956
Published in Penguin Books 1962
Copyright © the Estate of C. P. Snow, 1956

The Affair first published by Macmillan 1960
Published in Penguin Books 1962
Copyright © the Estate of C. P. Snow, 1960

Published by Macmillan as *Strangers and Brothers*, Volume 2, 1972
Published in Penguin Books 1984
Revised text © the Estate of C. P. Snow, 1972
All rights reserved

Reproduced, printed and bound in Great Britain by
Hazell Watson & Viney Limited,
Member of the BPCC Group,
Aylesbury, Bucks

Except in the United States of America,
this book is sold subject to the condition
that it shall not, by way of trade or otherwise,
be lent, re-sold, hired out, or otherwise circulated
without the publisher's prior consent in any form of
binding or cover other than that in which it is
published and without a similar condition
including this condition being imposed
on the subsequent purchaser

CONTENTS

The Masters

1937

CONTENTS

PART ONE. A LIGHT IN THE LODGE

PART TWO. WAITING

Contents

PART THREE. NOTICE OF A VACANCY

PART FOUR. MORNING IN THE CHAPEL

REFLECTIONS ON THE COLLEGE PAST

PART ONE

A LIGHT IN THE LODGE

CHAPTER I

NEWS AFTER A MEDICAL EXAMINATION

THE snow had only just stopped, and in the court below my rooms all sounds were dulled. There were few sounds to hear, for it was early in January, and the college was empty and quiet; I could just make out the footsteps of the porter, as he passed beneath the window on his last round of the night. Now and again his keys clinked, and the clink reached me after the pad of his footsteps had been lost in the snow.

I had drawn my curtains early that evening and not moved out. The kitchens had sent up a meal, and I had eaten it as I read by the fire. The fire had been kept high and bright all day; though it was nearly ten o'clock now, I stoked it again, shovelling coal up the back of the chimney, throwing it on so it would burn for hours. It was scorchingly hot in front of the fire, and warm, cosy, shielded, in the zone of the two armchairs and the sofa which formed an island of comfort round the fireplace. Outside that zone, as one went towards the walls of the lofty medieval room, the draughts were bitter. In a blaze of firelight, which shone into the sombre corners, the panelling on the walls glowed softly, almost rosily, but no warmth reached as far. So that, on a night like this, one came to treat most of the room as the open air, and hurried back to the island in front of the fireplace, the pool of light from the reading lamp on the mantelpiece, the radiance which was more pleasant because of the cold air which one had just escaped.

I was comfortable in my armchair, relaxed and content. There was no need to move. I was reading so intently that I did not notice the steps on the staircase, until there came a quick repeated knock on my door, and Jago came in.

'Thank the Lord I've found you,' he said. 'I'm glad you're in!'

Outside, on the landing, he kicked the snow from his shoes and then came back to the armchair opposite mine. He was still wearing his gown, and I guessed that they had sat a long time in the combination room.

He apologised for disturbing me. He apologised too much, for a man who was often so easy.

But sometimes he found the first moments of a meeting difficult; that was true with everyone he met, certainly with me, though we liked each other. I had grown used to his excessive apologies and his over-cordial greetings. He made them that night, though he was excited, though he was grave and tense with his news.

He was a man of fifty, and some, seeing that he had gone both bald and grey, thought he looked older. But the first physical impression was deceptive. He was tall and thick about the body, with something of a paunch, but he was also small-boned, active, light on his feet. In the same way, his head was massive, his forehead high and broad between the fringes of fair hair; but no one's face changed its expression quicker, and his smile was brilliant. Behind the thick lenses, his eyes were small and intensely bright, the eyes of a young and lively man. At a first glance, people might think he looked a senator. It did not take them long to discover how mercurial he was. His temper was as quick as his smile; in everything he did his nerves seemed on the surface. In fact, people forgot all about the senator and began to complain that his sympathy and emotion flowed too easily. Many of them disliked his love of display. Yet they were affected by the depth of his feeling. Nearly everyone recognised that, though it took some insight to perceive that he was not only a man of deep feeling, but also one of passionate pride.

At this time – it was 1937 – he had been Senior Tutor of the college for ten years. I had met him four years before, in 1933, when Francis Getliffe, knowing that I wished to spend most of my time in academic law, proposed to the college that they should give me a fellowship. Jago had supported me (with his quick imagination, he guessed the reason that led me to change my career when I was nearly thirty), and ever since had borne me the special grateful affection that one feels towards a protégé.

'I'm relieved to find you in, Eliot,' he said, looking at me across the fireplace. 'I had to see you tonight. I shouldn't have rested if I'd had to wait until the morning.'

'What has happened?'

'You know,' said Jago, 'that they were examining the Master today?'

I nodded. 'I was going to ask at the Lodge tomorrow morning.'

'I can tell you,' said Jago. 'I wish I couldn't!'

He paused, and went on:

'He went into hospital last night. They put a tube down him this morning. The results came through just before dinner, and they've sent him home. It is utterly hopeless. At the very most – they give him six months.'

'What is it?'

'Cancer. Absolutely inoperable.' Jago's face was dark with pain. He said: 'I hope that when my time comes it will come in a kinder way.'

We sat silent. I thought of the Master, with his confidential sarcasms, his spare and sophisticated taste, his simple religion. I thought of the quarrels he and Jago had had for so many years.

Though I had not spoken, Jago said:

'It's intolerable to me, Eliot, to think of Vernon Royce going like this. I can't pretend that everything has always been easy between us. You know that, don't you?'

I nodded.

'Yet he went out of his way to help me last term,' said Jago. 'You know, my wife was ill, and I was utterly distracted. I couldn't help her, I was useless, I was a burden to everyone and to myself. Then one afternoon the Master asked me if I would like to go for a walk with him. And he'd asked me for a very definite reason. He wanted to tell me how anxious he was about my wife and how much he thought of her. He must have known that I've always felt she wasn't appreciated enough here. It's been a grief to me. He said all he'd set out to say in a couple of dozen words on the way to Waterbeach, and it touched me very much. Somehow one's dreadfully vulnerable through those one loves.' Suddenly he smiled at me with great kindness. 'You know that as well as anyone alive, Eliot. I felt it when you let me meet your wife. When she's better, you must ask me to Chelsea again. You know how much I enjoyed it. She's gone through too much, hasn't she?' He went on: 'That afternoon made a difference to all I felt for Royce. Do you wonder that it's intolerable for me to hear this news tonight?'

He burst out:

'And do you know? I went for another walk with him exactly a month ago. I was under the weather, and he jogged along as he always used to, and I was very tired. I should have said, I believe anyone would have said, that he was the healthier man.'

He paused, and added: 'Tonight we've heard his sentence.'

He was moved by a feeling for the dying man powerful, quick, imaginative and deep. At the same time he was immersed in the drama, showing the frankness which embarrassed so many. No man afraid of expressing emotion could have been so frank.

9

'Yes, we've heard his sentence,' said Jago. 'But there is one last thing which seems to me more ghastly than the rest. For there is someone who has not heard it.'

He paused. Then he said: 'That is the man himself. They are not going to tell him yet.'

I exclaimed.

'For some reason that seems utterly inhuman,' said Jago, 'these doctors have not told him. He's been given to understand that in two or three months he will be perfectly well. When any of us see him, we are not to let him know any different.'

He looked into my eyes, and then into the fire. For a moment I left him, opened my door, went out into the glacial air, turned into the gyp room, collected together a bottle of whisky, a syphon, a jug of water. The night had gone colder; the jug felt as though the water inside had been iced. As I brought the tray back to the fireside, I found Jago standing up. He was standing up, with his elbows on the mantelpiece and his head bent. He did not move while I put the tray on the little table by my chair. Then he straightened himself and said, looking down at me:

'This news has shaken me, Eliot. I can't think of everything it means.' He sat down. His cheeks were tinged by the fire. His expression was set and brooding. A weight of anxiety hung on each of those last words.

I poured out the whisky. After he took his glass, he held it for an instant to the firelight, and through the liquid watched the image of the flames.

'This news has shaken me,' he repeated. 'I can't think of everything it means. Can you,' he asked me suddenly, 'think of everything it means?'

I shook my head. 'It has come as a shock,' I said.

'You haven't thought of any consequences at all?' He gazed at me. In his eyes there was a question, almost an appeal.

'Not yet.'

He waited. Then he said:

'I had to break the news to one or two of our colleagues in hall tonight. I hadn't thought of it myself, but they pointed out there was a consequence we couldn't put aside.'

He waited again, then said quickly:

'In a few weeks, in a few months at most, the college will have to elect a new Master.'

'Yes,' I said.

'When the time arrives, we shall have to do it in a hurry,' said Jago. 'I suppose before then we shall have made up our minds whom we are going to elect.'

I had known, for minutes past, that this was coming: I had not wanted to talk of it that night. Jago was longing for me to say that he ought to be the next Master, that my own mind was made up, that I should vote for him. He had longed for me to say it without prompting; he had not wanted even to mention the election. It was anguish to him to make the faintest hint without response. Yet he was impelled to go on, he could not stop. It harassed me to see this proud man humiliating himself.

Yet that night I could not do as he wanted. A few years before I should have said yes on the spot. I liked him, he had captured my imagination, he was a deeper man than his rivals. But my spontaneity had become masked by now; I had been too much knocked about, I had grown to be guarded.

'Of course,' I said, 'we've got a certain amount of time.'

'This business in the Lodge may go quicker even than they threaten,' said Jago. 'And it would be intolerable to have to make a rush election with the college utterly divided as to what it wants.'

'I don't see,' I said slowly, 'why we should be so much divided.'

'We often are,' said Jago with a sudden smile. 'If fourteen men are divided about most things, they're not specially likely to agree about choosing a new Master.'

'They're not,' I agreed. I added: 'I'm afraid the fourteen will have become thirteen.'

Jago inclined his head. A little later, in a sharp staccato manner, he said:

'I should like you to know something, Eliot. It was suggested to me tonight that I must make a personal decision. I must decide whether I can let my own name be considered.'

'I've always taken it for granted,' I said, 'that whenever the Mastership fell vacant you'd be asked that.'

'It's extraordinarily friendly of you to say so,' he burst out, 'but, do you know, before tonight I've scarcely thought of it for a single moment.'

Sometimes he was quite naked to life, I thought; sometimes he concealed himself from his own eyes.

Soon after, he looked straight at me and said:

'I suppose it's too early to ask whether you've any idea whom you prefer yourself?'

Slowly, I raised my glance to meet his.

'Tonight is a bit too early. I will come and tell you as soon as I am certain.'

'I understand.' Jago's smile was hurt, but appeasing and friendly. 'I understand, I shall trust you to tell me, whoever you prefer.'

After that we talked casually and easily; it was not till the college clock struck midnight that Jago left. As he went down the stairs, I walked across to my window and pulled the curtains. The sky had cleared, the moon was shining on the snow. The lines of the building opposite stood out simple and clear; on the steep roofs the snow was brilliant. All the windows were dark under the moon, except for the great bedroom of the Lodge, where the Master lay. There a light glowed, warm, tawny, against the stark brightness of the night.

The last chimes of twelve were still falling on the court. On the ground the snow was scarcely marked. Across it Jago was walking fast towards the gate. His gown blew behind him as he moved with light steps through the bitter cold.

CHAPTER II

THE MASTER TALKS OF THE FUTURE

WHEN I woke next morning, the bedroom seemed puzzlingly bright. Round the edges of the blind a white sheen gleamed. Then, half-awake, I felt the chill against my face, remembered the snow, drew the bed-clothes higher. Like a pain returning after sleep, the heavy thought came back that that morning I was obliged to call at the Lodge.

The quarters chimed, first from a distance away, then from Great St Mary's, then from the college clock, then from a college close by. The last whirr and clang were not long over when, soft-footedly, Bidwell came in. The blind flew up, the room was all a-glare; Bidwell studied his own watch, peered at the college clock, uttered his sacramental phrase:

'That's nine o'clock, sir.'

I muttered. From beneath the bedclothes I could see his rubicund face, open and yet sly. He said:

'It's a sharp old morning, sir. Do you lie warm enough in bed?'

'Yes,' I said. It was true. That bedroom, niche-like and narrow as a monastic cell, had not been dried or heated in five hundred years. When I returned to it from some of our food and wine, it seemed a curious example of the mixture of luxury and bizarre discomfort in which the college lived. Yet, in time, one missed the contrast between the warmth in bed and the frigid air one breathed, and it was not so easy to sleep elsewhere.

I put off ringing up the Lodge until the middle of the morning, but at last I did so. I asked for Lady Muriel and soon heard her voice. It was firm and loud. 'We shall be glad to see you, Mr Eliot. And I know my husband will be.'

I walked across the court to the Lodge, and in the drawing-room found Joan, the Royces' eldest daughter. She interrupted me, as I tried to sympathise. She said: 'The worst thing is this make-believe. Why don't they tell him the truth?'

She was nearly twenty. In girlhood her face had been sullen; she was strong and clever, and longed only to be pretty. But now she was just at the age when the heaviness was lifting, and all but she could see that her good looks would soon show through.

That morning she was frowning in her distress. She was so direct that it was harder to comfort her.

Her mother entered; the thick upright figure bore towards us over the deep carpet, past the Chinese screens, past the Queen Anne chairs, past the lavish bric-à-brac of the long and ornate drawing-room.

'Good morning, Mr Eliot. I know that we all wish this were a happier occasion.'

Her manner was authoritative and composed, her eyes looked steadily into mine. They were tawny, full and bold; in their boldness lay a curious innocence.

'I only learned late last night,' I said. 'I did not want to bother you then.'

'We only learned ourselves before dinner,' said Lady Muriel. 'We had not expected anything so drastic. There was a great deal to decide in a short time.'

'I don't suppose there is anything I can do,' I said. 'But if there is—'

'You are very kind, Mr Eliot. The college is being most kind. There may be matters connected with my husband's manuscripts where Roy Calvert could help us. In the meantime, you can do one great service. I hope you've already been told that my husband does not realise the true position. He believes that the doctors have overhauled him and found him pretty sound. He has been told that he has the trace of an ulcer, and he believes he will soon be well. I ask you to think before every word, so that you leave him with the same conviction.'

'It won't be easy, Lady Muriel,' I said. 'But I'll try.'

13

'You will understand that I am already acting as I ask you to act. It is not easy for me.'

There was grandeur in her ramrod back. She did not budge. 'I am positive,' she said, 'that we are doing right. It is the last comfort we can give him. He can have a month or two in peace.'

'I completely disagree,' Joan cried. 'Do you think comfort is all he wants? Do you think he would take comfort at that price?'

'My dear Joan, I have listened to your views—'

'Then for God's sake don't go on with this farce.' The girl was torn with feeling, the cry welled out of her. 'Give him his dignity back.'

'His dignity is safe,' said Lady Muriel. She got up. 'I must apologise to you, Mr Eliot, for forcing a family disagreement upon you. You will not wish to hear more of it. Perhaps you would care to see the Master now.'

As I followed Lady Muriel upstairs, I thought about her as I had often done before: how she was strong and unperceptive, snobbish and coarse-fibred, downright and brave. Beneath the brassy front there lingered still an inarticulate desire for affection. But she had not the insight to see why, even in her own family, she threw it away.

She went before me into the bedroom, which was as wide, and nearly as long, as the drawing-room below. Her words rang loudly in the great room. 'Mr Eliot has come to pay you a visit. I'll leave you together.'

'This is nice of you,' came the Master's voice from the bed. It sounded exactly as I had last heard it, before his illness – brisk, cheerful, intimate. It sounded like the voice of a gay and healthy man.

'I've told Mr Eliot that you ought to be back at college meetings by the end of term. But he mustn't tire you this morning.' Lady Muriel spoke in the same tone to me. 'I shall leave you with the Master for half an hour.'

She left us. 'Do come and sit down,' said the Master, and I brought a chair by the bedside. He was lying on his back, looking up at the ceiling, where there was embossed a gigantic coloured bas-relief of the college arms. He looked a little thinner, but the cheeks were full; his dark hair was only just turning grey over the ears, his comely face was not much lined, his lips were fresh. He was sixty-two, but that morning he looked younger. He was in extraordinarily high spirits.

'It is a relief, you know,' he said. 'I'd imagined this might be something with an unpleasant end. I may have told you that I don't think much of doctors – but I distinctly enjoyed their conversation last night.'

He smiled. 'As a matter of fact, I feel a little more tired than you'd imagine. But I take it that's natural, after those people have been rummaging about. And I suppose this ulcer has been tiring me and taking away my appetite. I've got to lie here while it heals. I expect to get a little stronger every day.'

'You may get some intermissions.' From my chair I could see over the high bed rail, out of the single window; from the bed there was no view but the cloudless sky, but I could see most of the court under snow. My eyes stayed there. 'You mustn't worry too much if you have setbacks.'

'I shan't worry for a long time,' he said. 'You know, when I was nervous about the end of this, I was surprised to find how inquisitive one is. I did so much want to know whether the college would ever make up its mind about the beehives in the garden. And I did want to know whether our old friend Gay's son would really get the job at Edinburgh. It will be remarkable if he does. It will reflect the greatest credit on Mrs Gay. Between you and me' – he passed into his familiar, intimate whisper – 'it's an error to think that eminent scholars are very likely to be clever men.'

He chuckled boyishly. 'I shouldn't have liked not to know the answers. And I shouldn't have liked not to finish that little book on the early heresies.'

The Master had spent much of his life working on comparative religion. It seemed to have made not the slightest difference to his faith, which had stayed unchanged, as it were in a separate compartment, since he first learned it as a child.

'How long will it take you?'

'Only a couple of years. I shall ask Roy Calvert to write some of the chapters.' ·

He chuckled again. 'And I should have hated not to see that young man's *magnum opus* come out next year. Do you remember the trouble we had to get him elected, Eliot? Some of our friends show a singular instinct for preferring mediocrity. Like elects like, of course. Or, between you and me,' he whispered, 'dull men elect dull men. I'm looking forward to Roy Calvert's new book. Since the Germans dined here, our friends have an uncomfortable suspicion that he's out of the ordinary. But when this book appears, they will be told that he's the most remarkable scholar this society has contained for fifty years. Will they be grateful to you and me and good old Arthur Brown for backing him? Will they be grateful, Eliot?'

His laugh was mischievous, but his voice was becoming weaker as he went on talking about Roy.

When I got up to go, he said:

'I hope you'll stay longer next time. I told you, I expect to get a little stronger every day.'

After I had said goodbye to Lady Muriel and Joan, I let myself out of the Lodge into the sunny winter morning. I felt worn out.

In the court I saw Chrystal coming towards me. He was a very big man, both tall and strongly muscled. He walked soft-footed and well balanced.

'So you've seen him this morning?'

'Yes,' I said.

'What do you think of it?'

'I'm sorry.'

'I'm sorry myself,' said Chrystal. He was crisp and brusque, and people often thought him hectoring. This morning he was at his sharpest. From his face alone one would have known that he found it easy to give orders. His nose was beak-like, his gaze did not flicker.

'I'm sorry myself,' he repeated. I knew that he was moved. 'Did you talk to him?'

'Yes.'

'I shall have to do the same.' He looked at me with his commanding stare.

'He's very tired,' I said.

'I shouldn't think of staying.'

We walked a few steps back towards the Lodge. Chrystal burst out:

'It's lamentable. Well, we shall have to find a successor, I suppose. I can't imagine anyone succeeding Royce. Still, we've got to have some-one. Jago came to see me this morning.'

He gave me a sharp glance. Then he said:

'It's lamentable. Well, it's no use our standing here.'

I did not mind his rudeness. For, of all the college, he was the one most affected by the news of the Master. It was not that he was an intimate friend; in the past year, apart from the formal dinners at the Lodge, they had not once been in each other's houses; it was a long time, back in the days when Chrystal was Royce's pupil, since they spent an evening together. But Chrystal had hero-worshipped the older man in those days, and still did. It was strange to feel, but this bustling, dominating, success-ful man had a great capacity for hero-worship. He was a power in the college, and would have been in any society. He had force, decision, the liking for action; he revelled in command. He was nearly fifty now, successful, within the modest limits he set himself, in all he undertook.

In the college he was Dean (a lay official of standing, though by this time the functions were dying away); in the university he was well known, sat on the Council of the Senate, was always being appointed to committees and syndicates. He made a more than usually comfortable academic income. He had three grown-up daughters, and had married each of them well. He adored his wife. But he was still capable of losing himself in hero-worship, and the generous, humble impulse often took the oddest forms. Sometimes he fixed on a business magnate, or an eminent soldier, or a politician; he was drawn to success and power on the grand scale – to success and power, which, in his own sphere, he knew so well how to get.

But the oldest and strongest of his worships was for Royce. That was why he was uncontrollably curt to me in the court that morning.

'I must get on,' he said. 'We shall have to find a successor. I shall have to think out who I want. I'll have a word with Brown. And I should like five minutes with you.'

As we parted, he said:

'There's something else Brown and I want to talk to you about. The way I see it, it's more important than the next Master.'

CHAPTER III

A SMALL PARTY IN THE COMBINATION ROOM

THE combination room glowed warm when I entered it that evening. No one had yet come in, and the lights were out; but the fire flared in the open grate, threw shadows on to the curtains, picked out the glasses on the oval table, already set for the after-dinner wine. I took a glass of sherry and an evening paper, and settled myself in an armchair by the fire. A decanter of claret, I noticed, was standing at the head of the table; there were only six places laid, and a great stretch of the mahogany shone polished and empty.

Jago and Winslow came in nearly together. Winslow threw his square into one armchair and sat in another himself; he gave me his mordant, not unfriendly grin.

'May I pour you some sherry, Bursar?' said Jago, not at ease with him.

'*If* you please. *If* you please.'

'I'm dreadfully afraid I've spilt most of it,' said Jago beginning to apologise.

'It's so good of you to bring it,' said Winslow.

Just then the butler entered with the dining-list and presented it to Winslow.

'We are a very small party tonight,' he said. 'Ourselves, the worthy Brown and Chrystal, and young Luke.' He glanced at the decanter on the table. He added:

'We are a small party, but I gather that one of us is presenting a bottle. I am prepared to bet another bottle that we owe this to the worthy Brown. I wonder what remarkable event he is celebrating now.'

Jago shook his head. 'Will you have more sherry, Bursar?'

'If you please, my dear boy. *If* you please.'

I watched him as he drank. His profile was jagged, with his long nose and nutcracker jaw. His eyes were hooded with heavy lids, and there were hollows in his cheeks and temples that brought back to me, by contrast, the smooth full face of the Master – who was two or three years younger. But Winslow's skin was ruddy, and his gangling body moved as willingly as in his prime.

His manners were more formal than ours, even when his bitter humour had broken loose. He was wealthy, and it was in his style to say that he was the grandson of a draper; but the draper was a younger son of a county family. Lady Muriel was intensely snobbish and Winslow had never got on with the Master – nevertheless, he was the only one of the older fellows whom she occasionally, as a gesture of social acceptance, managed to call by his Christian name.

He had a savage temper and a rude tongue, and was on bad terms with most of his colleagues. The Master had quarrelled with him long before – there were several versions of the occasion. Between him and Jago there was an absolute incompatibility. Chrystal disliked him unforgivingly. He had little to his credit. He had been a fine classic in his youth and had published nothing. As Bursar he was conscientious, but had no flair. Yet all the college felt that he was a man of stature, and responded despite themselves if he cared to notice them.

He was finishing his second glass of sherry. Jago, who was trying to placate him, said deferentially:

'Did you get my note on the closed exhibitions?'

'Thank you, yes.'

'I hope it had everything you wanted.'

Winslow glanced at him under his heavy lids. For a moment he paused. Then he said:

'It may very well have done. It may very well have done.' He paused again. 'I should be so grateful if you'd explain it to me some time.'

'I struggled extremely hard to make it clear,' said Jago, laughing so as not to be provoked.

'I have a feeling that clarity usually comes when one struggles a little less and reflects a little more.'

At that Jago's hot temper flared up.

'No one has ever accused me of not being able to make myself understood—'

'It must be my extreme stupidity,' said Winslow. 'But, do you know, when I read your notes – a fog descends.'

Jago burst out:

'There are times, Bursar, when you make me feel as though I were being sent up to the headmaster for bad work.'

'There are times, my dear Senior Tutor, when that is precisely the impression I wish to make.'

Angrily, Jago snatched up a paper, but as he did so Brown and Chrystal came through the door. Brown's eyes were alert at once behind their spectacles; the spectacles sat on a broad high-coloured face, his body was cushioned and comfortable; his eyes looked from Jago to Winslow, eyes that were sharp, peering, kindly, and always on the watch. He knew at once that words had passed.

'Good evening to you,' said Winslow, unperturbed.

Chrystal nodded and went over to Jago; Brown talked placidly to Winslow and me; the bell began to ring for hall. Just as the butler threw open the door, and announced to Winslow that dinner was served, Luke came rapidly in, and joined our file out of the combination room, on to the dais. The hall struck cold, and we waited impatiently for the long grace to end. The hall struck more than ever cold, when one looked down it, and saw only half-a-dozen undergraduates at the far end; for it was the depth of the vacation, and there were only a few scholars up, just as there were only the six of us at the high table.

Winslow took his seat at the head, and others manœuvred for position; Jago did not want to sit by him after their fracas, so that I found myself on Winslow's right hand. Jago sat by me, and Luke on the same side: opposite was Brown and then his friend Chrystal, who had also avoided being Winslow's neighbour.

Brown smiled surreptitiously at me, his good-natured face a little pained, for though he could master these embarrassments he was a man who liked his friends to be at ease: then be began to talk to Winslow about the college silver. My attention strayed. I found myself studying one of the portraits on the linenfold. Then I heard Jago's voice, unrecognisably different from when he replied to Winslow, talking to young Luke.

'You look as though things are going well in the laboratory. I believe you've struck oil.'

I looked past Jago as Luke replied:

'I hope so. I had an idea over Christmas.' He had been elected a fellow only a few months before, and was twenty-five. Intelligence shone from his face, which was fresh, boyish, not yet quite a man's; as he talked of his work, the words tripped over themselves, the west-country burr got stronger, a deep blush suffused his cheeks. He was said to be one of the most promising of nuclear physicists.

'Can you explain it to a very ignorant layman?'

'I can give you some sort of notion. But I've only just started on this idea.' He blushed again cheerfully. 'I'm afraid to say too much about it just yet.'

He began expounding his subject to Jago. Chrystal made an aside to Brown, and asked across the table if I was free next morning. Winslow heard the question, and turned his sardonic glance on to Chrystal.

'The college is becoming quite a hive of activity,' he said.

'Term starts next week,' said Chrystal. 'I can't leave things till then.'

'But surely,' said Winslow, 'the appearance of the young gentlemen oughtn't to obstruct the really serious purposes of our society? Such as rolling a log in the right direction?'

'I'm sure,' Brown intervened, quickly but blandly, 'that the Dean would never roll a log across the table. We've learned from our seniors to choose a quieter place.'

We were waiting for the savoury, and someone chuckled.

'By the way,' Winslow looked down the table, 'I noticed that a bottle of claret has been ordered in the combination room. May I enquire whom we are indebted to?'

'I'm afraid I'm responsible.' Brown's voice was soothing. 'I ought to have asked permission to present a bottle, but I rather anticipated that. And I ought to have asked whether people would have preferred port, but I found out from the kitchens who were dining, and I thought I knew everyone's taste. I believe you always prefer claret nowadays?' he said to Winslow.

'If you please. If you please.' He asked, the astringent note just on the edge of his voice: 'And what remarkable event do you wish to celebrate?'

'Why, the remarkable event I wish to celebrate,' said Brown, 'is the appearance of Mr R. S. Winslow in the Trial Eights. I don't think anyone has got in before me. And I know we should all feel that when the Bursar has a son at the college, and the young man distinguishes himself, we want the pleasure of marking the occasion.'

Winslow was taken right aback. He looked down at the table, and gave a curiously shy, diffident smile.

'I must say this is handsome of you, Brown,' he said.

'It's a privilege,' said Brown.

We returned to the combination room, and took our places for wine. The table could hold twenty, and we occupied only one end of it; but the room was intimate, the glasses sparkled in the warm light, the silver shone, the reflection of the decanter was clear as it passed over the polished table. Luke filled our glasses, and, since Winslow's health was to be drunk, it was the duty of Jago, as the next senior, to propose it. He did it with warmth, his face alight. He was full of grace and friendliness. Brown's steady cordiality had infected him, he was at ease within this group at the table as he never could be with Winslow alone. 'The Bursar and his son,' he said.

'Thank you, Senior Tutor. Thank you all. Thank you.' Winslow lifted his glass to Brown. As we drank Brown's health, I caught his dark, vigilant eye. He had tamed Winslow for the moment: he was showing Jago at his best, which he very much wanted to do: he had brought peace to the table. He was content, and sipped his claret with pleasure. He loved good fellowship. He loved the arts of management. He did not mind if no one noticed his skill. He was a very shrewd and far-sighted man.

He was used to being thought of as just a nice old buffer. 'Good old Brown', the Master called him. 'The worthy Brown', said Winslow, with caustic dismissal: 'uncle Arthur' was his nickname among the younger fellows. Yet he was actually the youngest of the powerful middle-aged block in the college. Jago was just over fifty; Chrystal, Brown's constant friend and ally, was forty-eight, while Brown himself, though he had been elected a fellow before Chrystal, was still not quite forty-six. He was a historian by subject, and was Jago's junior colleague as the second tutor.

Winslow was talking, with a veneer of indifference, about his son.

'He'll never get into the boat,' he said. 'He's thought to be lucky to have gone as far as this. It would be pleasant for his sake if they made another mistake in his favour. Poor boy, it's the only notoriety he's ever likely to have. He's rather a stupid child.'

His tone was intended to stay bleak – it turned indulgent, sad, anxiously fond. Brown said:

'I'm not prepared to agree. One might say that he doesn't find examinations very congenial.'

Winslow smiled.

'Mind you, Tutor,' he said with asperity, 'it's important for the child that he gets through his wretched tripos this June. He's thought to stand a chance of the colonial service if he can scrape a third. Of course, I'm totally ignorant of these matters, but I can't see why our colonies should need third-class men with some capacity for organised sports. However, one can forgive the child for not taking that view. It's important for his sake that he shouldn't disgrace himself in June.'

'I hope we'll get him through,' said Brown. 'I think we'll just about manage it.'

'We'll get him through,' said Jago.

'I'm sorry that my family should be such a preposterous nuisance,' said Winslow.

The wine went round again. As he put down his glass, Winslow asked: 'Is there any news of the Master tonight?'

'There can't be any,' said Chrystal.

Winslow raised his eyebrows.

'There can't be any,' Chrystal repeated, 'until he dies. It's no use. We've got to get used to it.'

The words were so curt and harsh that we were silent. In a moment Chrystal spoke again:

'We've got to get used to him dying up there. That is the fact.'

'And him thinking he will soon be well,' Jago said. 'I saw him this evening, and I tell you, I found it very hard to sit by.'

Chrystal said:

'Yes. I've seen him myself.'

'He's quite certain he'll soon be well,' Jago said. 'That is the most appalling thing.'

'You would have told him?'

'Without the shadow of a doubt.'

'I'm surprised that you're so convinced,' said Winslow, ready to disagree.

'I am utterly convinced.'

'I don't like to suggest it, but I'm inclined to think that Dr Jago may be wrong.' Winslow glanced round the table. 'If I'd had to make Lady Muriel's decision, I think I might have done the same. I should have thought: this will mean for him a few days or weeks of happiness. It's the last happiness he'll get – he ought to have it if it's in my power. Do any of you share my view?' Winslow's eyes fell on Chrystal, who did not reply: then on Brown, who said:

'I haven't thought it out.'

'No,' said Jago. 'You're presuming where no one has a right to presume.' His tone was deep and simple, no trace of awkwardness left. 'There are a few things no one should dare to decide for another man. There are not many serious things in a man's life – but one of them is how he shall meet his death. You can't be tactful about death: all you can do is leave a man alone.'

We were all watching him.

'Winslow,' Jago went on, 'you and I do not often see things with the same eyes. Neither you nor I have been friendly with Royce through most of our lives. We know that, and this is not a good time to pretend. But there is one thing we should never have disagreed about. We had a respect for him. We should have admitted, shouldn't we? that he always faced the truth, even when it was grim. We should have said that he was the last man among us to be drugged by lies when he was coming near his death.'

Winslow was staring at his empty glass. Chrystal broke the silence: 'You've said things I should like to have said myself.'

Silence came to the table again. This time Brown spoke:

'How long will it be before they have to tell him?'

'Three or four months,' I said. 'It may be sooner. They say it's certain to be over in six months.'

'I can't help thinking of his wife,' said Brown, 'when she has to break the news.'

'I'm thinking of the Master,' said Chrystal, 'the day he hears.'

The coffee was brought in. As Winslow lit a cigar, Brown took the chance of bringing them to earth.

'I suppose,' he said, 'that the position about the Master will have to be reported to the next college meeting?'

'I'm clear that it must,' said Chrystal.

'We have one, of course,' said Brown, 'on the first Monday of full term. I feel that we're bound to discuss the Mastership. It's very painful and delicate, but the college has to face the situation.'

'We can't elect while the Master is alive. But the college will have to make up its mind in advance,' said Chrystal.

Winslow's temper was not smoothed. He was irritated by Jago's effect on the party, he was irritated by the competence with which Chrystal and Brown were taking charge. He said, the edge in his voice just audible:

'There's a good deal to be said for discussing the wretched business this term. We can bring it to a point in some directions.' His eyes flickered at Jago, then he turned to Brown as though thinking aloud. 'There are one or two obvious questions we ought to be able to decide. Are we going outside for a Master, or are we going to choose one of ourselves?' He paused, and continued in his most courteous tone: 'I think several of the society will agree that there are good reasons for going outside this time.'

I caught sight of Luke leaning forward, his face aglow with excitement. He was a sanguine young man who so far at high table kept his thoughts to himself: he had scarcely spoken at the table that night, he was not going to intervene now of all times, when Winslow was deliberately, with satisfaction, undermining Jago's hopes. But I thought that little had escaped young Luke: as acutely as anyone there, he was feeling the antagonism that crackled through the comfort-laden room.

'I didn't mean,' said Brown, roundly but with a trace of hurry, 'that the college could go nearly as far as that at the present time. In fact I'm very dubious whether it would be proper for a college meeting to do more than hear the facts about the Master's condition. That gives us a chance to talk the matter over privately. I'm afraid I should deprecate doing more.'

'I agree with Brown,' said Chrystal. 'I shall propose that we take steps accordingly.'

'You believe in private enterprise, Dean?' Winslow asked.

'I think the Dean and I believe,' said Brown, 'that, with a little private discussion, the college may be able to reach a very substantial measure of agreement.'

'I must say that that is a beautiful prospect,' said Winslow. He looked at Jago, who was sitting back in his chair, his lips set, his face furrowed and proud.

Winslow rose from the head of the table, picked up his cap. made off in his long loose stride towards the door. 'Goodnight to you,' he said.

CHAPTER IV

A PIECE OF SERIOUS BUSINESS

I CALLED at Brown's rooms, as we had arranged with Chrystal, at eleven
o'clock next morning. They were on the next staircase to mine, and not
such a handsome set; but Brown, though he went out each night to his
house in the West Road, had made them much more desirable to live in.
That day he stood hands in pockets in front of the fire, warming his
plump buttocks, his coat-tails hitched up over his arms. His bright
peering eyes were gazing appreciatively over his deep sofas, his ample
armchairs, his two half-hidden electric fires, out to the window and the
snowy morning. Round the walls there was growing a set of English water
colours, which he was collecting with taste, patience, and a kind of modest
expertness. On the table a bottle of madeira was waiting for us.

'I hope you like this in the morning,' he said. 'Chrystal and I are rather
given to it.'

Chrystal followed soon after me, gave his crisp military good-morning,
and began at once:

'Winslow gave a lamentable exhibition last night. He makes the place a
perfect bear-garden.'

It seemed to me a curious description of the combination room.

'He's not an easy man,' said Brown. 'And he doesn't seem to be
mellowing.'

'He won't mellow if he lives to be a hundred,' said Chrystal. 'Anyway,
it's precisely because of him that we want to talk to you, Eliot.'

We sat down to our glasses of madeira.

'Perhaps I'd better begin,' said Brown. 'By pure chance, the affair
started in my direction. Put it another way – if I hadn't been tutor, we
mightn't have got on to it at all.'

'Yes, you begin,' said Chrystal. 'But Eliot ought to realise all this is
within these four walls. Nor a word outside.'

I said yes.

'First of all,' Brown asked me, sitting back with his hands folded on his
waistcoat, 'do you happen to know my pupil Timberlake?'

I was puzzled.

'I've spoken to him once or twice,' I said. 'Isn't he a connection of Sir
Horace's?'

'Yes.'

'I know the old man slightly,' I said. 'I met him over a case, I'm not sure when it was.'

Brown chuckled.

'Good,' he said. 'I was almost sure I remembered you saying so. That may be very useful.

'Well,' he went on, 'he sent young Timberlake to the college – he's a son of Sir Horace's cousin, but his parents died and Sir Horace took responsibility for him. The boy is in his third year, taking Part II in June. I hope to God he gets through. It will shatter everything if he doesn't. He's a perfectly decent lad, but a bit dense. I think he's just a shade less stupid than young Winslow – but it's a very very near thing.'

'It's not a near thing between their seniors,' said Chrystal. 'I'll trade Winslow for Sir Horace any day.'

'I was very much taken with Sir Horace when I met him.' Brown liked agreeing with his friend. 'You see, Eliot, Sir Horace came up for a night just about three weeks ago. He seemed to be pleased with what we were doing for the boy. And he specially asked to meet one or two people who were concerned with the policy of the college. So I gave a little dinner party. The Master was ill, of course, which, to tell you the truth, for this particular occasion was a relief. I decided it was only prudent to leave out Winslow. I had to ask Jago, but I dropped him a hint that this wasn't the kind of business he's really interested in. Naturally, I asked the Dean.' He gave Chrystal his broad, shrewd, good-natured smile. 'I think the rest of the story's yours. I left everything else to you.'

'Sir Horace came up,' said Chrystal, 'and Brown did him well. There were only the three of us. I should have enjoyed just meeting him. When you think what that man's done – he controls an industry with a turnover of £20,000,000 a year. It makes you think, Eliot, it makes you think. But there was more to it than meeting him. I won't make a secret of it. There's a chance of a benefaction.'

'If it comes off,' Brown said, cautiously but contentedly, 'it will be one of the biggest the college has ever had.'

'Sir Horace wanted to know what our plans for the future were. I told him as much as I could. He seemed pleased with us. I was struck with the questions he asked,' said Chrystal, ready to make a hero of Sir Horace. 'You could see that he was used to getting to the bottom of things. After he'd been into it for a couple of hours, I'd back his judgment of the college against half our fellows. When he'd learned what he came down to find out, he asked me a direct question. He asked straight out: "What's the most useful help any of us could provide for the college?"

There was only one answer to that – and when there's only one answer, I've found it a good rule to say it quick. So I told him: "Money. As much money as you could give us. And with as few conditions as you could possibly make." And that's where we stand.'

'You handled him splendidly,' said Brown. 'He wasn't quite happy about no conditions—'

'He said he'd have to think about that,' said Chrystal. 'But I thought it would save trouble later if I got in first.'

'I'm not ready to shout till we've got the money in the bank,' Brown said, 'but it's a wonderful chance.'

'We ought to get it – unless we make fools of ourselves,' said Chrystal. 'I know that by rights Winslow should handle this business now. It's his job. But if he does, it's a pound to a penny that he'll put Sir Horace off.'

I thought of Sir Horace, imaginative, thin-skinned despite all his success in action.

'He certainly would,' I said. 'Just one of Winslow's little jokes, and we'd have Sir H. endowing an Oxford college on a very lavish scale.'

'I'm glad you confirm that,' said Chrystal. 'We can't afford to handle this wrong.'.

'We mustn't miss it,' said Brown. 'It would be sinful to miss it now.'

These two were the solid core of the college, I thought. Year by year they added to their influence; it was greater now than when I first came four years before. It had surprised me then that they should be so influential; now that I had lived with them, seen them at work, I understood it better.

They were both genuinely humble men. They were profoundly different, at the roots of their natures, but neither thought that he was anything out of the ordinary. They knew that others round them were creative, as they were not; Chrystal had once been a competent classic, was still a first-rate teacher, but had done nothing original – Brown wrote an intricate account of the diplomatic origins of the Crimean war soon after he graduated, and then stopped. They did not even think that they were unusual as men. Either would say that the Master or Jago or one or two others were the striking figures in the college. All they might add was that those striking figures did not always have the soundest judgment, were not the most useful at 'running things'.

For, though they were the least conceited of men, they had complete confidence in their capacity to 'run things'. Between them, they knew all the craft of government. They knew how men in a college behaved, and the different places in which each man was weak, ignorant, indifferent, obstinate or strong. They never overplayed their hand; they knew just how to take the opinion of the college after they had settled a question in private. They knew how to give way. By this time, little of importance happened in the college which they did not support.

They asked very little more for themselves. They were neither of them ambitious; they thought they had done pretty well. They were comfortable and happy. They accepted the world round them, they believed it was good the college should exist, they had no doubt they were being useful in the parts they played. As they piloted their candidate through a fellowship election, or worked to secure this benefaction from Sir Horace, they gained the thrill that men feel at a purpose outside themselves.

They were both 'sound' conservatives in politics, and in religion conforming and unenthusiastic churchmen. But in the college they formed the active, if sometimes invisible, part of a progressive government. (College politics often cut right across national ones: thus Winslow, an upper-class radical, became in the college extremely reactionary, and Francis Getliffe and I, both men of the left, found ourselves in the college supporting the 'government' – the Master, Jago, Chrystal, Brown – with whom we disagreed on most things outside.) To that they devoted their attention, their will, their cunning, and their experience. They had been practising it for twenty years, and by now they knew what could be done inside the college to an inch.

I had never seen a pair of men more fitted for their chosen job. They were loyal to each other in public and in private. If they brought off a success for the college, they each had a habit of attributing it to the other. Actually most men thought that, of the two, Chrystal was the dominating spirit. He had a streak of fierceness, and the manifest virility which attracts respect – and at the same time resentment – from other men. He also possessed the knack of losing his temper at the right moment, which made him more effective in committee. He was urgent and impatient and quick to take offence. He gave an immediate impression of will, and many of the college used to say: 'Oh, Chrystal will bring Brown along with him.'

I did not believe it. Each was shrewd, but Brown had the deeper insight. I had seen enough of both to be sure that, in doubt or trouble, it was Chrystal who relied on the stubborn fortitude of his friend.

'How much is it likely to be?' I asked. They glanced at each other. They thought I knew something about men, but was altogether too unceremonious in the way I talked of money.

'Sir Horace hinted,' said Chrystal, with a suspicion of hush in his voice, 'at £100,000. I take it he could sign a cheque for that himself and not miss it.'

'He must be a very hot man,' said Brown, who was inclined to discuss wealth in terms of temperature.

'I wonder if he is?' I said. 'He must be quite well off, of course. But he's an industrial executive, you know, not a financier. Isn't it the financiers who make the really big fortunes? People like Sir H. don't juggle with money and don't collect so much.'

'You put him lower than I do,' said Chrystal, somewhat damped. 'You're under-rating him, Eliot.'

'I'm not letting myself expect too much,' said Brown. 'But if Sir Horace decided to raise £50,000 for us, I dare say he could.'

'I dare say he could,' I said.

They had asked me to join them that morning in order to plan the next move. They had heard nothing from Sir Horace since his visit. What could we do? Could we reach him again? Were any of my London acquaintances any use?

I thought them over, and shook my head.

'Is it a good idea anyway to approach him from the outside?' I asked. 'I should have thought that it was very risky.'

'I've felt that all along,' said Brown.

'You may be right,' said Chrystal sharply, irritated but ready to think again. 'What do we do? Do we just wait?'

'We've got to rely on ourselves,' said Brown.

'What does that mean?' said Chrystal.

'We've got to get him down again,' said Brown. 'And let him see us as we really are. Put it another way – we must make him feel that he's inside the picture. I don't say we wouldn't make things decent for the occasion. But we ought to let him realise the difficulty about Winslow. The more we take him into our confidence, within reason, the more likely he is to turn up trumps.'

I helped him persuade Chrystal. Chrystal was brusque, he liked his own ideas to prevail, he liked to have thought of a plan first; but I noticed the underlying sense which brought him round. He could have been a moody man; his temper was never equable; but he wanted results so much that he had been forced to control his moods.

They agreed to try to attract Sir Horace to the feast in February. Brown was as realistic as usual. 'I don't suppose for a moment that anything we can do will make a pennyworth of difference. once he's made up his mind. But it can't do any harm. If he's forgetting us, it might turn out useful to remind him that we're glad to see him here.'

He filled our glasses again. Chrystal gave a satisfied sigh. He said:

'Well, we can't do any more this morning. We've not wasted our time. I told you, Eliot, I regard this as more important than the Mastership. Masters come and Masters go, and whoever we elect, everyone will have forgotten about it in fifty years. Whereas a benefaction like this will affect the college for ever. Do you realise that the sum I've got in my mind is over ten per cent of our capital endowment?'

'It would be a pity to miss it,' said Brown.

'I wish we hadn't got this Mastership hanging over us,' said Chrystal. 'One thing is quite clear. There's no reason to go outside. That's just a piece of Winslow's spite. We can find a Master inside the college easily enough. Jago would do. I was impressed with the way he spoke last night. He's got some of the qualities I want in a Master.'

'I agree,' said Brown.

'Other names will have to be considered, of course. I expect some people will want Crawford. I don't know about him.'

'I agree,' said Brown. 'I'm not keen on him. I don't know whether Eliot is—'

'No,' I said.

'He'll certainly be run. I don't know whether anyone will mention Winslow. You haven't seen a Master elected, have you, Eliot? You'll find some people are mad enough for anything. I'm depressed,' said Chrystal, 'at the whole prospect.'

Soon afterwards he left us. Brown gave a sympathetic smile. 'He's upset about poor Royce,' he said.

'Yes, I thought that.'

'You're very observant, aren't you?'

Brown added:

'I think Chrystal will get more interested when things are warming up a bit. I think he will.' He smiled again. 'You know, I don't see how this can possibly be an easy election. Chrystal says that there may be support for Crawford, and I suppose there's bound to be. But I should regard him as a disaster. He wouldn't lift a finger for any of us. I don't know what you feel, but I shall be inclined to stick in my heels about him.'

'He wouldn't do it well,' I said.

'I'm glad we're thinking alike. I wonder whether you've come down definitely for anyone yet?'

His eyes were fixed on me, and I hesitated. Easily he went on:

'I should value it if you would keep me in touch, when you do know where you're coming down. My present feeling, for what it's worth, is that we ought to think seriously about Jago. I know people criticise him; I'm quite prepared to admit that he's not ideal; but my feeling is that we can't go far wrong with him.'

'Yes.'

'Do you agree, really?'

'Yes.'

'Might you consider supporting him?'

'I'm not sure, but I think I shall.'

His glance had stayed on me. Now he looked away, and said:

'I very much wanted to know how you would respond to his name. I'm not committed to him myself, of course. I've been held up a little by a personal matter which you'll probably think a trifle far-fetched.'

'Whatever's that?'

'Well,' said Brown, 'if Jago were to be elected Master, the college would need a new Senior Tutor. And it seems to me possible that some people would want me to follow him in the job.'

'It's a complete and utter certainty,' I said. That was the truth.

'It's nice of you to say so, but I don't believe it's as certain as that. There are plenty who don't think much of me.' Brown chuckled. 'But I can't pretend it's not a possibility. Well then, you see the problem. Am I justified in trying to get Jago in as Master, when I may provide myself with a better job out of it?'

'There's no doubt of the answer—'

'Yes', said Brown. 'I've arrived there myself, after thinking it over. If one always stopped supporting people whose election could bring one the slightest advantage, it would be remarkably silly. Put it another way – only a crank could really be stopped by such scruples.' He burst into his whole-hearted, fat man's laughter.

'So I'm quite easy in my conscience about supporting Jago,' he finishing up. 'But I'm still not ready to commit myself. He'd be a good Master, in my judgment. I'd put it a bit stronger, and say that he's the best Master in view. We don't want to run him, though, unless he's got plenty of support. It would do no good to anyone.

'Well,' he said, with a smile good-natured, cunning and wise, 'that's what I've been thinking. That's as far as I've got.'

CHAPTER V

SUCCESS AND ENVY

JAGO came to see me that afternoon. He made no reference to our first talk, nor to the conversation about the Mastership the night before; but he had manufactured an excuse to call on me. He had thought up some questions about my law pupils; neither he nor I was interested in the answers.

He had been driven to see me – so that, if I had anything to say, he would know at once. His delicacy revolted, but he could not prevent himself from spinning out the visit. Was I going to Ireland again? He talked, with unaccustomed flatness, about his native town of Dublin. Not that he showed the vestigial trace of an Irish accent. He was born in the Ascendancy, his stock was as English as any of ours; he had – surprisingly, until one knew his origin – the militant conservatism of the Anglo-Irish. His father had been a fellow of Trinity, Dublin, and Jago was the only one of the present college who had been born into the academic life.

He went on talking, still tied to my company, unable to recognise that I could say nothing that day. I thought that no one else in his position would have kept his dignity so well: whatever his excesses, that remained. Before he went away, he had to ask:

'Did I hear that you and Chrystal and Brown were colloguing this morning?'

'Yes. It was just a financial matter. They wanted a legal opinion.'

He smiled off his disappointment.

'You three work much too hard,' he said.

The college was slowly filling up. I heard that Nightingale and Pilbrow were back from vacation, though I had not yet seen them. And the next evening, a few minutes before hall, I heard a familiar step on my staircase, and Roy Calvert came in.

He had been working for three months in Berlin. With relief I saw that he was looking well, composed and happy. I had not needed the Master to tell me that he was the most gifted man the college had produced for years. But, by this time, I had had to take responsibility which others didn't know. They had not seen the attacks of melancholy, so intense that no one could answer for his actions.

That night, though, I knew at a glance that he was rested. He was more as I first knew him, cheerful, lively, disrespectful and kind. Thinking of the life he had led, the work he had got through, one found it hard to remember that he was not yet twenty-seven; yet in that mood, his eyes sparkling with malicious fun, he still looked very young.

We arrived a little late in the combination room, just in time to see Gay, with slow, shuffling steps, leading the file into hall. He was wearing an overcoat under his gown, so as to meet the draughty hall, and under the long coat there was something tortoise-like about his feet; but, when one looked at his face, there was nothing pathetic about him. His cheeks were red, his beard white, trimmed and sailor-like, his white hair silky and abundant; he carried his handsome head with arrogance and panache. He was getting on towards eighty, and the oldest fellow.

As he sat at the head of the table, tucking with good appetite into his food, Brown was trying to explain to him the news about the Master. Gay had not heard, or had forgotten: his memory was beginning to flicker and fade, he forgot quickly about the weeks and months just past. Brown was having some trouble in making it clear which Master he meant; Gay seemed to be thinking about the last Master but one.

'Ah. Indeed,' said Gay. 'Very sad. But I have some recollection that he had to live on one floor some little time ago.'

'That wasn't the present Master,' said Brown patiently. 'I mean Royce.'

'Indeed. Royce. You didn't make that clear,' Gay reproved him. 'He's surely a very young man. We only elected him recently. So he's going, is he? Ah well, it will be a sad break with the past.'

He showed the triumph of the very old, when they hear of the death of a younger man. He felt half his age. Suddenly he noticed Roy Calvert, and his memory cleared.

'Ah. Do I see Calvert? Haven't you been deserting us?'

'I got back to England this morning.'

'Let me see. Let me see. Haven't you been in Germany?'

'Yes,' said Roy Calvert.

'I hadn't forgotten you,' said Gay victoriously. 'And where in Germany, may I ask?'

'Berlin.'

'Ah. Berlin. A fine city. A fine university. I was once given an honorary degree by the university of Berlin. I remember it to this day. I remember being met at the Zoo station by one of their scholars – fine scholars they have in that country – and his first words were: "Professor M. H. L. Gay, I think? The great authority on the sagas." Ah. What do you think of that, Calvert? What do you think of that, Brown? The great authority on the sagas. They were absolutely the first words I heard when I arrived at the station. I had to demur to the word "great" of course.' He gave a hearty laugh. 'I said: "You can call me the authority on the sagas, if you like. The authority, without the great." '

Brown and Chrystal chuckled. On Chrystal's left, Nightingale looked polite but strained. Roy Calvert's eyes shone: solemn and self-important persons were usually fair game to him, but Gay was too old. And his gusto was hard to resist.

'That reminds me,' Gay went on, 'about honorary degrees. Do you know that I've now absolutely collected fourteen of them? What do you think of that, Calvert? What do you think of that, Chrystal?'

'I call it pretty good,' said Chrystal, smiling but impressed.

'Fourteen honorary degrees. Not bad, eh? From every civilised country except France. The French have never been willing to recognise merit outside their own country. Still, fourteen isn't so bad. And there's still time for one or two more.'

'I should think there is,' said Chrystal. 'I should think there is. And I shall want to present a bottle in honour of every one of them, Gay.'

Gay said the final grace in a ringing voice, and led us slowly back to the room. On the table, a bottle of port was ready for him; though the rest of us preferred claret, it was a rule that the college should drink port on any night when he came in to dine. As Chrystal helped him off with his overcoat, Gay's eye glittered at the sight of walnuts in a silver dish.

'Ah. Nuts and wine,' he said. 'Splendid. Nuts and wine. Is the Steward here? Congratulate him for me.'

He rolled the port on his tongue and cracked nut after nut. His teeth were as sound as in youth, and he concentrated vigorously on his pleasure. Then he wiped his lips and said:

'That reminds me. Are any of us publishing a book this year?'

'I may be,' said Roy. 'If they can finish cutting the type for—'

'I congratulate you,' said Gay. 'I congratulate you. I have a little work of my own coming out in the summer. I should not absolutely rank it among my major productions, but I'm quite pleased with it as a *tour de force*. I shall be interested to see the reception it obtains. I sometimes think one doesn't receive such a fair hearing when one is getting on in years.'

'I shouldn't have thought you need worry,' said Brown.

'I like to insist on a fair hearing,' Gay said. 'I'm not vain, I don't mind what they say against me, but I like to be absolutely assured that

34

they're being fair. That's all I've asked for all along, ever since my first book.

'Ah. My first book.' He looked down the table. His eyes had been a bright china blue, but were fading now. 'That was a great occasion, to be sure. When the Press told me the book was out, I went round to the bookshops to see for myself. Then I walked out to Grantchester to visit my brother-in-law Dr Ernest Fazackerley – my wife was his youngest sister, you know. And when I told him the great news, do you know that cat of his – ah, that was a cat and a half – he put up his two paws, and I could imagine for all the world that he was applauding me.'

In a few minutes the butler brought a message that the Professor's taxi was waiting at the porter's lodge. This was part of the ritual each Thursday and Sunday night, for on those nights, in any weather, he left his house in the Madingley Road, and was driven down to the college for dinner. There was more of the ritual to come: Chrystal helped him into his overcoat again, he replaced his gown on top of it, and said goodnight to each of us one by one. Goodnights kept coming back to us in his sonorous voice, as he shuffled out of the room, with Roy Calvert to help him over the frozen snow.

'Those old chaps were different from us,' said Chrystal, after they had gone. 'We shan't do as much as that generation did.'

'I'm not quite convinced that they were so wonderful,' said Nightingale. There was a curious carefulness about his manner, as though he were concealing some pain in order not to embarrass the party. About his face also there was a set expression: he seemed to be disciplining himself to behave well. His lips were not often relaxed, and lines of strain etched the fine skin. He had a mane of fair wavy hair, brushed across his brow. His face was drawn, but not weak, and when he was pleased there was charm in his looks.

'No one has ever explained to me,' said Nightingale, 'what there is original about Gay's work.'

'I'll take you up on that, Nightingale,' Chrystal said. 'He's better known outside the college than anyone we've got. It will be time enough for us to talk when we've done as much.'

'I agree,' said Brown.

'If anyone sat down to his sagas for four hours a day for sixty years, I should have thought they were bound to get somewhere,' said Nightingale.

'I wish I could feel sure there is one man among us,' Chrystal retorted, 'who'll have as much to his credit – if he lives to be Gay's age.'

'From what the German professors have written,' Brown put in, 'I don't think there's any reasonable doubt that Calvert will make as big a name before he's done.'

Nightingale looked more strained. 'These gentlemen are lucky in their subjects,' he said. 'It must be very nice not to need an original idea.'

'You don't know anything about their subjects,' said Chrystal. He said it sharply but amicably enough, for he had a hidden liking for Nightingale. Another thought was, however, troubling him. 'I don't like to hear old Gay criticised. I've got as great a respect for him as anyone in the college. But it is lamentable to think that we shall soon have to elect a Master, and the old chap will have his vote. How can you expect a college to do its business, when you've got people who have lost their memories but are only too willing to take a hand?'

'I've always thought they should be disfranchised,' said Nightingale.

'No,' said Brown. 'If we cut them off at sixty-five or seventy, and didn't let them vote after that, we should lose more than we gained.'

'What do you mean?'

'I think I mean this: a college is a society of men, and we have to take the rough with the smooth.'

'If you try to make it too efficient,' I said, 'you'll suddenly find that you haven't a college at all.'

'I thought you were a man of advanced opinions,' said Nightingale.

'Sometimes I am,' I said.

'I don't know where I come down,' said Chrystal. He was torn, torn as he often was, torn as he would have hated anyone to perceive. His passion to domineer, his taste for clean efficiency, all his impulses as a party boss with the college to run, made him want to sweep the old men ruthlessly away – take away their votes, there would be so much less dead wood, they impeded all he wanted to do. Yet there was the other side, the soft romantic heart which felt Gay as larger than life-size, which was full of pious regard for the old, which shrank from reminding them that they were spent. 'But I don't mind telling you that there are times when I consider the college isn't a fit body to be entrusted with its money. Do you really mean to tell me that the college is fit to handle a capital endowment of a million pounds?'

'I'll give you an answer,' said Brown cheerfully, 'when I see how we manage about electing a Master.'

'Is anything being done about that?' Nightingale asked.

'Nothing can be done yet, of course,' said Brown. 'I suppose people are beginning to mention names. I've heard one or two already.' As he talked blandly on, he was watching Nightingale. He was usually an opponent, he was likely to be so now, and Brown was feeling his way. 'I think that Winslow may rather fancy the idea of Crawford. I wonder how you'd regard him?'

There was a pause.

'I'm not specially enthusiastic,' said Nightingale.

'I'm interested to hear you say that,' said Brown. His eyes were bright. 'I though it would be natural if you went for someone like Crawford on the scientific side.'

Suddenly Nightingale's careful manner broke.

'I might if it weren't Crawford,' he said. His voice was bitter: 'There's not been a day pass in the last three years when he hasn't reminded me that he is a Fellow of the Royal, and that I am not.'

'That's ridiculous', said Brown consolingly. 'He's got a good many years' start, hasn't he?'

'He reminds me that I've been up for election six times, and this year is my seventh.'

Nightingale's voice was harsh with envy, with sheer pain. Chrystal left all the talk to Brown.

'Well, I might as well say that at present I don't feel much like going for Crawford myself,' said Brown. 'I'm beginning to doubt whether he's really the right man. I haven't thought much about it so far, but I have heard one or two people speak strongly for someone else. How do you regard the idea of Jago?'

'Jago. I've got nothing against him,' said Nightingale.

'People will feel there are certain objections,' Brown reflected.

'Some people will object to anyone.'

Brown smiled.

'They'll say that Jago isn't so distinguished academically as – for instance, Crawford. And that'a a valid point. The only consideration is just how much weight you give to it. Put it another way – we're unlikely to get everything we want in one man. Do you prefer Jago, who's respectable on the academic side but not a flyer -- but who seems admirably equipped in every other way? Or do you prefer Crawford, who has other limitations that you've made me realise very clearly? Wouldn't those limitations be unfortunate in a Master?'

'I'm ready to support Jago,' said Nightingale.

'I should sleep on it if I were you,' said Brown. 'But I value your opinion—'

'So do I,' said Chrystal. 'It'll help me form my own.'

He and Brown went off together, and Nightingale and I were left alone.

'Come up to my rooms,' said Nightingale.

I was surprised. He was the one man in the college whom I actively disliked, and he disliked me at least as strongly. There was no reason for it; we had not one value or thought in common, but that was true with others whom I was fond of; this was just an antipathy as specific as love. Anywhere but in the college we should have avoided each other. As it was, we met three or four nights a week at dinner, talked across the table, even spent, by the force of social custom, a little time together. It was one of the odd features of a college, I sometimes thought, that one lived in social intimacy with men one disliked: and, more than that, there were times when a fraction of one's future lay in their hands. For these societies were always making elections from their own members, they filled all their jobs from among themselves, and in those elections one's enemies took part – for example, Jago disliked Winslow far more intensely than I Nightingale, and at that moment he knew that, until the election was over, he was partially in Winslow's power.

We climbed a staircase in the third court to Nightingale's rooms. He was a teetotaller, the only one in the college, and he had no drink to offer, but he gave me a cigarette. He asked a few uninterested questions about my holidays. But though he tried, he could not keep to his polite behaviour. Suddenly he broke out:

'What are Chrystal and Brown up to about the Mastership?'

'I thought Brown had been telling us – at some length.'

'I know all about that. What I want to hear is, has one of those two got his eye on it for himself?'

'I shouldn't think so for a moment,' I said.

'We're not going to be rushed into that, are we?' he asked. 'I wouldn't put it past them to try.'

'Nonsense,' I said. He was irritating me. 'They made it clear enough – they'll run Jago.'

'I'll believe that when I see it. I've never noticed them exert themselves much for anyone else. I've not forgotten how they squeezed Brown into the tutorship. I was two or three years junior, but there's no doubt I had the better claim.'

Suddenly he snapped out the question:

'What are you going to do?'

I did not reply at once.

'Are you going to propose Chrystal as a bright idea at the last minute?'

He was intensely suspicious, certain that there was a web of plans from which he would lose and others gain. If I had told him I too was thinking of Jago, he would have seen meanings behind that choice, and it might have turned him from Jago himself. As it was, Jago's seemed the one name that did not arouse his suspicion and envy that night.

I looked round his sitting-room. It was without feature, it was the room of a man concentrated into himself, so that he had nothing to spend outside; it showed nothing of the rich, solid comfort which Brown had given to his, or the eccentric picturesqueness of Roy Calvert's. Nightingale was a man drawn into himself. Suspicion and envy lived in him. They always would have done, however life had treated him; they were part of his nature. But he had been unlucky, he had been frustrated in his most cherished hope, and now envy never left him alone.

He was forty-three, and a bachelor. Why he had not married, I did not know: there was nothing unmasculine about him. That was not, however, his abiding disappointment. He had once possessed great promise. He had known what it was to hold creative dreams: and they had not come off. That was his bitterness. As a very young man he had shown a spark of real talent. He was one of the earliest theoretical chemists. By twenty-three he had written two good papers on molecular structure. He had, so I was told, anticipated Heitler-London and the orbital theory; he was ten years ahead of his time. The college had elected him, everything seemed easy. But the spark burnt out. The years passed. Often he had new conceptions; but the power to execute them had escaped from him.

It would have been bitter to the most generous heart. In Nightingale's, it made him fester with envy. He longed in compensation for every job within reach, in reason and out of reason. It was morbid that he should have fancied his chances of the tutorship before Brown, his senior and a man made for the job; but it rankled in him after a dozen years. Each job in the college for which he was passed over, he saw with intense suspicion as a sign of the conspiracy directed against him.

His reputation in his subject was already gone. He would not get into the Royal Society now. But, as March came round each year, he waited for the announcement of the Royal elections in expectation, in anguish, in bitter suspiciousness, at moments in the knowledge of what he might have been.

CHAPTER VI

STREETS IN THE THAW

It began to thaw that night, and by morning the walls of my bedroom carried dank streaks like the tracks of a snail. Lying in bed, I could hear the patter of drops against the window ledge. 'Dirty old day underfoot, sir,' Bidwell greeted me. 'Mr Calvert sends his compliments, and says he'd send his goloshes too, if he could persuade you to wear them.'

I had scarcely seen Roy Calvert alone since he returned; he called in for a new minutes after breakfast on his way to pay visits round the town. 'They'd better know I am alive.' He grinned. 'Or else Jago will be sending out a letter.' It was one of Jago's customs to 'send out a letter' whenever a member of the college died; it was part of the intimate formality which, to Roy Calvert, was comic without end. He went out through the slush to pay his visits; he had a great range of acquaintances in Cambridge, and he arranged to visit them in an order shaped partly by kindness, partly by caprice. The unhappy, the dim, the old and passed over, even those whom anyone else found tedious and ordinary, could count on his company; while the important, the weighty, the established – sometimes, I thought in irritation, anyone who could be the slightest use to him – had to wait their turn.

Before he went out, he arranged for us both to have tea in the Lodge, where he was a favourite. He would go himself earlier in the afternoon, to talk to the Master. So at teatime I went over alone, and waited in the empty drawing-room. The afternoon was leaden, the snow still lay on the court, with a few pockmarks at the edges; the fire deep in the room behind me was reflected in the heavy twilight. Roy Calvert joined me there.

It had been worse than he imagined, and he was subdued. The Master had been talking happily of how they would collaborate – the 'little book on the heresies'. This was a project of the Master's which Roy had been trying to avoid for years. Now he said that he would do it as a memorial.

When Lady Muriel came in, she began with her inflexible greetings, as though nothing were wrong in the house. But Roy took her hand, and his first words were:

'I've been talking to the Master, you know. It's dreadful to have to pretend, isn't it? I wish you could have been spared that decision, Lady Mu. No one could have known what to do.'

She was taken aback, and yet relieved so that the tears came. No one else would have spoken to her as though she were a woman who wanted someone to guide her. I wished that I had been as straightforward.

She was already crying; she said that it was not easy.

'No one could help you,' said Roy. 'And you'd have liked help, wouldn't you? Everyone would.'

He took care of her until Joan joined us, and then they began to argue about the régime in Germany. 'Just so,' said Roy, to each of Joan's positive statements. Both women knew that he had no liking for disputation; both laughed at the precise affirmative, which had once been affected but now was first nature.

Joan's tenderness for Roy was already near to open love, and her mother indulged him like a son. She must have known something of his reputation, the 'vineleaves in his hair' (as the Master several times quoted), the women who pursued him. But she never said to Joan, as she had said about any other man whom her daughter brought to the Lodge, 'My dear Joan, I can't imagine what you can possibly *see* in him.'

I talked about Joan as we walked out of the Lodge into the dark, rainy night.

'That girl,' I said, 'is falling more in love with you.'

He frowned. Like many of those who attract passionate love, there were times when he wanted to forget it altogether. And that night, despite his sadness over the Master, he felt innocent and free of the shadows.

'Come and help me do some shopping,' he said. 'I need to buy some presents at once.'

We walked along Sidney Street in the steady rain. Water was swirling, chuckling, gurgling in the gutters; except by the walls, the pavements were clear of snow by now, and they mirrored the lights from the lamps and shop-fronts on both sides of the narrow street.

'We shall get much wetter.' He smiled. 'You always looked remarkable in the rain. I need to get these presents off tonight.'

We went from shop to shop, up Sidney Street, down John's Street, Trinity Street, into the market place. He wanted the presents for his disreputable, unlucky Berlin acquaintances who lived above his flat in the Knesebeckstrasse, and he took great care about choosing them.

'That might do for the little dancer.' I had heard of 'the little dancer', by the same title before. 'She weighs 35 kilos,' Roy commented. 'Light. Considerably lighter than Arthur Brown.'

In one shop, he suddenly asked, quietly, with complete intimacy, about Sheila. He knew the whole story of my marriage, and what I had to expect when I went each Tuesday to the Chelsea house. I was glad to talk. In the street, he looked at me with a smile full of affectionate sharp-edged pity. 'Yet you go on among those comfortable blokes – as though nothing was the matter,' he said. 'I wish I could bear as much.'

Without speaking, we walked past Great St Mary's into the market place. He could say no more, and, with the same intimacy, asked:

'About those comfortable blokes, old boy. Who are we going to have for Master?'

We were loaded with parcels, our coats were heavy with the damp, rain dripped from our faces.

'I think I want Jago,' I said.

'I suppose there's a move for Crawford.'

'I'm against that,' I said.

'Crawford is too – stuffed,' said Roy Calvert. 'He'll just assume the job is due to him by right. He's complacent. I'd never vote for a man who was complacent.'

I agreed.

'You know,' he said, 'old Winslow is the most unusual man among that lot. He bites their heads off, he's a bit of a bully, he's frightfully ill-adjusted. But no one on earth could call him tug. They wouldn't have him at any price.'

'No one on earth could call Jago tug,' I said. 'He's the least common-place of men.'

'There are plenty of things in favour of Jago,' said Roy. 'But they're not the things we're going to hear.'

'He stands a fair chance,' I said.

'He's not a commonplace man, is he?' said Roy. 'Won't he be kept out because of that? They'll never really think he's "sound".'

'Arthur Brown is for him.'

'Uncle Arthur loves odd fish.'

'And Chrystal,' I said, 'thinks he can manage him. By the way, I'm very doubtful whether he's right.'

'It will be extremely funny if he isn't.'

We turned down into Petty Cury, and Roy said:

'The ones who don't want Jago won't take it quietly. They'll have a good deal to say about distinguished scholars – and others not so distinguished.

'I know more about that than they do,' he added. I smiled at the touch of arrogance, unusual in him. I saw his face, clear in the light from a shop. He shook his head to get rid of some raindrops, he smiled back, but he was in dead earnest. He went on quietly: 'Why won't they see what matters? I want a man who knows something about himself. And is appalled. And has to forgive himself to get along.'

CHAPTER VII

DECISION TO CALL ON JAGO

ROY CALVERT and I kept coming back to the Mastership, as we talked late into the night. Before we went to bed, we agreed to tell Brown next day that we were ready to support Jago. 'Sleep on it, sleep on it,' said Roy, mimicking Brown's comfortable tones. The next morning Bidwell, after announcing the time and commenting on the weather, said: 'Mr Calvert's compliments, sir, and he says he's slept on it and hasn't changed his mind.'

At five that afternoon, we found Brown in his rooms. His tea was pushed aside, he was working on some lists: but, continuously busy, he was always able to seem at leisure. 'It's a bit early for sherry,' he said. 'I wonder if you feel like a glass of chablis? I opened it at lunch-time, and we thought it was rather special.'

He brought out some glasses, and we sat in his armchairs, Brown in the middle. His eyes looked from one of us to the other. He knew we had come for a purpose, but he was prepared to sit there all evening, drinking his wine with enjoyment, and leave the first move to us.

'You asked me,' I said, 'to let you know, when I'd decided about the next Master.'

'Why, so I did,' said Brown.

'I have now,' I said. 'I shall vote for Jago.'

'I shall also,' said Roy Calvert.

'I'm very glad to hear it,' Brown said. He smiled at me: 'I had a feeling you might come round to it. And Roy—'

'It's all in order,' said Roy, 'I've slept on it.'

'That's just as well,' said Brown. 'Because if not I should certainly have advised you to do so.'

I chuckled. In his unhurried, ponderous fashion he was good at coping with Roy Calvert.

'Well,' said Brown, sitting back contentedly, 'this is all very interesting. As a matter of fact, I can tell you something myself. Chrystal and I had a little talk recently, and we felt inclined to put Jago's name forward.'

'Without committing yourselves, of course?' Roy enquired.

'Committing ourselves as much as it's reasonable to do at this stage,' said Brown.

'There's one other thing I think I'm at liberty to tell you,' he added. 'Nightingale told me definitely this morning that he was of the same way of thinking. So at any rate we've got the nucleus of a nice little party.'

How capably he had managed it, I thought. He had not pressed Jago on any one of us. Chrystal had been undecided, but patiently Brown drew him in. With Chrystal, with me, with Nightingale, he had waited, talking placidly and sensibly, often rotundly and platitudinously, while our likes and dislikes shaped themselves. Only when it was needed had he thrown in a remark to stir one of our weaknesses, or warm our affection. He had given no sign of his own unshakeable resolve to get the Mastership for Jago. He had shown no enthusiasm, he had talked with his usual fairmindedness. But the resolve had been taken, his mind had been made up, the instant he heard that the Master was dying.

Why was he so resolved? Partly through policy and calculation, partly through active dislike of Crawford, partly through a completely uncalculating surrender to affection; and, as in all personal politics, the motives mixed with one another.

Most of all, Brown was moved by a regard for Jago, affectionate, indulgent and admiring; and Brown's affections were warm and strong. He was a politician by nature; since he was set on supporting Jago he could not help but do it with all the craft he knew – but there was nothing politic about his feeling for the man. Jago might indulge his emotions, act with a fervour that Brown thought excessive and in bad taste, 'let his heart run away with his head', show nothing like the solid rational decorum which was Brown's face to the world. Brown's affection did not budge. In some part of his secret self he loved Jago's wilder outbursts, and wished that he could have gone that way himself. Had he sacrificed too much in reaching his own robust harmony? Had he become too dull a dog? For Brown's harmony had not arrived in a minute. People saw that fat contented man, rested on his steady strength, and thought he had never known their conflicts. They were blind. He was utterly tolerant, just because he had known the frets that drove men off the rails, in particular the frets of sensual love. It was in his nature to live them down, to imbed them deep, not to let them lead him away from his future as a college worthy, from his amiable wife and son. But he was too realistic, too humble, too genuine a man ever to forget them. 'Uncle Arthur loves odd fish', said Roy Calvert, whom he had helped through more than one folly. In middle age 'Uncle Arthur' was four square in himself, without a crack or flaw, rooted in his solid, warm, wise and cautious nature. But he loved odd fish, for he knew, better than anyone, the odd desires that he had left behind.

'We've got the nucleus of a nice little party,' said Brown. 'I think the time may almost have come to ask Jago whether he'll give us permission to canvas his name.'

'You don't think that's premature?' said Roy, anxiously solemn.

'He may find certain difficulties,' said Brown, refusing to be put out of his proper rhythm. 'He may not be able to afford it. Put it another way – he'd certainly drop a bit over the exchange. With his university lectureship and his college teaching work, as Senior Tutor he must make all of £1800 a year, and the house rent free. As Master he'll have to give up most of the other things, and the stipend of the Master is only £1500. I've always thought it was disgracefully low, it's scarcely decent. Of course, he gets the Lodge free, but the upkeep will run him into a lot more than the Tutor's house. I really don't know how he's going to manage it.'

I was smiling: with Roy present, I found it harder to take part in these stately minuets. 'Somehow I think he'll find a way,' I said. 'Look, Arthur, you know perfectly well that he's chafing to be asked.'

'I think we might be able to persuade him,' Brown said. 'But we mustn't be in too much of a hurry. You don't get round difficulties by ignoring them. Still, I think we've got far enough to approach Jago now.'

'The first step, of course,' he added, 'is to get Chrystal. He may think we're anticipating things a bit.'

He telephoned to Chrystal, who was at home but left at once for the college. When he arrived, he was short-tempered because we had talked so much without him. He was counter-suggestible, moved to say no instead of yes, anxious to find reasons why we should not go at once to Jago. Brown used his automatic tact; and, as usual, Chrystal was forming sensible decisions underneath his short pique-ridden temper (he had the kind of pique which one calls 'childish' – though in fact it is shown most clearly by grave and adult men). Suddenly he said:

'I'm in favour of seeing Jago at once.'

'Shall I fix a time tomorrow?' said Brown.

'I'm against waiting. There's bound to be talk, I want to get our feet in first. I'm in favour of going tonight.'

'He may be busy.'

'He won't be too busy for what we're coming to say,' said Chrystal, with a tough, pleasant, ironic smile.

'I'll ring up and see how he's placed,' said Brown. 'But we mustn't forget Nightingale. It would be nice to take him round as well.' He rang up at once, on the internal exchange through the porter's lodge: there was no answer. He asked for a porter to go to Nightingale's rooms: the report came that his rooms were shut.

'This is awkward,' said Brown.

'We'll go without him,' said Chrystal.

'I don't like it much.' Brown had a slight frown. 'It would be nice to bring everyone in. It's important for everyone to feel they're in the middle of things. I attach some value to taking Nightingale round.'

'I'll explain it to Nightingale. I want to get started before the other side.'

Reluctantly, Brown rang up the Tutor's house. He was sure it was an error of judgment not to wait for Nightingale – whom he wanted to bind to the party. On the other hand, he had had trouble bringing Chrystal 'up to the boil'. He did not choose to risk putting him off now. He rang up, his voice orotund, confidential, cordial; from his replies, one could guess that Jago was welcoming us round without a second's delay.

'Yes, he'd like to see us now,' said Brown, as he hung the receiver up.

'I can't say I'm surprised,' said Chrystal, rising to go out.

'Wait just a minute,' said Brown. 'The least I can do is send a note to Nightingale, explaining that we tried to find him.'

He sat down to write.

'It might help if I took the note round to Nightingale.' said Roy Calvert. 'I'll drop the word that I'm going to vote for Jago, but haven't gone round on the deputation.'

'That's very thoughtful of you,' said Brown.

'Not a bit of it,' said Roy. 'I very much doubt whether the next but one junior fellow ought to be included in such a deputation as this.'

Chrystal did not know whether he was being serious or not.

'I don't know about that, Calvert, I don't know about that,' he said. 'Still, we can tell Jago you're one of us, can we?'

'Just so,' said Roy. 'Just so.'

The Tutor's house lay on the other side of the college, and Brown, Chrystal and I begun walking through the courts. Chrystal made a remark about Roy Calvert:

'Sometimes I don't know where I am with that young man.'

'He'll be a very useful acquisition to our side,' said Brown.

CHAPTER VIII

THREE KINDS OF POWER

In Jago's house we were shown, not into his study, but into the drawing-room. There Mrs Jago received us, with an air of *grande dame* borrowed from Lady Muriel.

'Do sit down, Dean,' she said to Chrystal. 'Do sit down, Tutor,' she said to Brown. 'A parent has just chosen this time to call on my husband, which I feel is very inconsiderate.'

But Mrs Jago's imitation of Lady Muriel was not exact. Lady Muriel, stiff as she was, would never have called men by their college titles. Lady Muriel would never have picked on the youngest there and said:

'Mr Eliot, please help me with the sherry. You know it's your duty, and you ought to like doing your duty.'

For Mrs Jago wanted to be a great lady, wanted also the attention of men, and was never certain of herself for an instant. She was a big, broad-shouldered woman, running to fat, physically graceless apart from her smile. It was a smile one seldom saw, but when it came it was brilliant, open, defenceless, like an adoring girl's. Otherwise she was plain.

That night, she could not keep up her grand manner. Suddenly she broke out:

'I'm afraid you will all have to put up with my presence till Paul struggles free.'

'That's very nice for us all,' said Arthur Brown.

'Thank you, Tutor,' said Mrs Jago, back for a second on her pedestal again.

She had embarrassed Jago's friends ever since he married her. She became assertive in any conversation. She was determined not to be overlooked. She seized on insults, tracked them down, recounted them with a masochistic gusto that never flagged. She had cost her husband great suffering.

She had cost him great suffering, but not in the way one might expect. He was a man who gained much admiration from women. With his quick sympathy, his emotional power, he could have commanded all kinds of love. He liked the compliment, but he wanted none of them. He had loved his wife for twenty-five years. They had had no children. He loved her still. He could still be jealous of that woman, who, to everyone outside, seemed so grotesque. I had seen her play on that jealousy and give him pain.

47

But that was not his deepest suffering about her. They had married when he was a young don, and she his pupil. That relation, which can always so easily fill itself with emotion, had never died. He wanted people to recognise her quality, how gifted she was, how much held back by her crippling sensitiveness. He wanted us to see that she was gallant, and misjudged; he was burning to explain that she went through acuter pain than anyone, when the temperament she could not control drove his friends away. His love remained love, and added pity: and the sight of her in a mood which others dismissed as grotesque still had the power to rend him right through.

He suffered for her, and for himself. He loathed having to make apologies for his wife. He loathed all his imagination could invent of the words that were spoken behind his back – 'poor Jago. . . .' But even those wounds to his pride he could have endured, if she had been happier. He would still, after twenty-five years, have humbled himself for her as for no one else – just to see her content. As he told me on the night we first knew the Master was dying, 'one is dreadfully vulnerable through those one loves'.

When Jago came in, his first words were to his wife.

'I'm desperately sorry I've been kept so long. I know you wanted to get back to your book—'

'It doesn't matter at all, Paul,' she said with lofty dignity, and then cried out: 'It only means that the Dean and the Tutor and Mr Eliot have had to make conversation to me for half an hour.'

'If they don't get a greater infliction than that this term,' he said, 'they'll be very lucky men.'

'It's wretched for them that because of parents who haven't the slightest consideration—'

Gently Jago tried to steer her off, and show her at her best. Had she talked to us about the book from which we had drawn her? Why hadn't she mentioned what she told him at teatime?

Then Chrystal said:

'You'll excuse us if we take your husband away, won't you, Mrs Jago? We have a piece of business that can't wait.'

'Please do not think of considering me,' she retorted.

This was a masculine society, and none of us would have considered discussing college business in front of our wives, not even in front of Lady Muriel herself. But, as we went out to Jago's study, I caught sight of his wife's face, and I knew she had embraced another insult. Jago would hear her cry 'they took the opportunity to say I wasn't wanted'.

Once in Jago's study, with Jago sitting behind his big tutorial desk, crowded with letters, folders, dossiers, Reporters, copies of the Ordinances, Chrystal cleared his throat.

'We've come to ask you one question, Jago,' he said. 'Are you prepared to be a candidate for the Mastership?'

Jago sighed.

'The first thing I want to say,' he replied, 'is how grateful I am to you for coming to speak to me. It's an honour to be thought of by such colleagues as you. I'm deeply touched.'

He smiled at us all.

'I'm specially touched, if I may say so, to see Eliot with you. You two are old friends – we've grown up together. It isn't so much a surprise to find you're indulgent towards me. But you don't know how flattering it is,' he said to me, 'to be approved of by someone who's come here from a different life altogether. I'm so grateful, Eliot.'

He was the more pleased, I thought, because I had hesitated, because I had not been easy to convince: it is not the whole-hogging enthusiasts for one's cause to whom one feels most gratitude.

'We shouldn't ask you,' said Chrystal briskly, 'unless we could promise you a caucus.'

'I think it's only fair to tell you, before you give us your answer, that we haven't made any attempt to discover the opinion of the college,' said Brown. 'But I don't think we're going beyond our commission in speaking for one or two others besides ourselves. Calvert specially asked us to tell you that he will give you his vote, and, though I'm not entitled to bring a categorical promise from Nightingale, I regard him as having pledged his support.'

'There's no doubt of that,' said Chrystal.

'Roy Calvert, that's nice of him!' cried Jago. 'But Nightingale – I'm astonished, Brown, I really am astonished.'

'Yes, we were a bit surprised ourselves.' Brown went on steadily: 'There are thirteen of us, not counting the present Master. If we leave you out, and assume that another member of the society will be the other candidate, that gives eleven people with a free vote. It needs seven votes to get a clear majority of the society, and a Master can't be elected without, of course. Personally, I should regard five as a satisfactory caucus to start with. Anyway, it's all we're entitled to promise tonight, and if you think it's not enough we shall perfectly understand.'

Jago rested his elbows on the desk, and leant forward towards us.

'I believe I've told each one of you separately that this possibility came to me as an utter shock. I still feel that my feet aren't quite firm under me. But since it did seem to become a possibility I've thought it over until I'm tired. I had serious doubts as to whether I ought to do it, whether I wanted to do it, whether I could do it. I've had several sleepless nights this week, trying to answer those questions. And there's one thing I've become convinced of, even in the small hours – you know, when one's whole life seems absolutely pointless. I'm going to tell you without modesty, between friends. I believe I can do it. I believe I can do it better than anyone within reach. So, if you want me, I've got no choice.'

'I'm glad to hear it, Jago,' said Chrystal.

'Splendid,' said Brown.

'As for the campaign,' said Jago, with a brilliant smile, 'I put myself at your disposal, and no one could be in better hands.'

Chrystal took charge. 'There'll be opposition,' he said.

'You don't think I mind that, do you?' said Jago.

'You don't mind, but we do,' said Chrystal sharply. 'We're bound to, as we're taking the responsibility of running you. The opposition will be serious. It will come from an influential part of the college. They're the people I call the obstructors.'

'Who are they, when it comes to the point?' said Jago, still exhilarated.

'I haven't started counting heads,' said Chrystal. 'But there's Winslow, for certain. There's old Despard—'

'Crawford, if he isn't a candidate,' Brown put in.

'I don't believe he's in a particularly good position to be impartial,' said Jago. 'And as for the other two, I'm not depressed by their opposition. They're just two embittered old men.'

'That's as may be,' said Chrystal. 'But they're also two influential old men. They get around, they won't let you in by default. I didn't mean to say we shan't work it. I think we've got a very good chance. But I wanted to warn you, this isn't going to be a walk-over.'

'Thank you, Dean, thank you. Don't let me run away with myself.' Jago was friendly, gracious, full of joy. 'But I'm glad that we have the younger men on our side. I wouldn't exchange those two old warriors for Calvert and Eliot here. If we can call on the young men, Dean, we can do something with the college. It's time we took our rightful place. We can make it a great college.'

'We shall need money,' said Chrystal, but his own imagination was stirred. 'We're not rich enough yet to cut much of a dash. Perhaps we can get money. Yes—'

'It's inspiring to listen to you,' Brown said to Jago. 'But, if I were you, I shouldn't talk too much in public about your plans. People might think you were too ambitious. We don't want to put their backs up. I'm anxious that nothing you say in the next few months shall give them a handle against you.'

I watched their heads, grouped round the desk, their faces glowing with their purpose – Brown's purple-pink, rubicund, keen-eyed, Chrystal's beaky, domineering, Jago's pale, worn with the excesses of emotion, his eyes intensely lit. Each of these three was seeking power, I thought – but the power each wanted was as different as they were themselves. Brown's was one which no one need know but himself; he wanted to handle, coax, guide, contrive, so that men found themselves in the places he had designed; he did not want an office or title to underline his power, it was good enough to sit back amiably and see it work.

Chrystal wanted to be no more than Dean, but he wanted the Dean, in this little empire of the college, to be known as a man of power. Less subtle, less reflective, more immediate than his friend, he needed the moment-by-moment sensation of power. He needed to feel that he was listened to, that he was commanding here and now, that his word was obeyed. Brown would be content to get Jago elected and influence him afterwards, no one but himself knowing how much he had done. That was too impalpable a satisfaction for Chrystal. Chrystal was impelled to have his own part recognised, by Jago, by Brown and the college. As we spoke that evening, it was essential for Chrystal that he should see his effect on Jago himself. He wanted nothing more than that, he was no more ambitious than Brown – but irresistibly he needed to see and feel his power.

Jago enjoyed the dramatic impact of power, like Chrystal: but he was seeking for other things besides. He was an ambitious man, as neither Brown nor Chrystal were. In any society, he would have longed to be first; and he would have longed for it because of everything that marked him out as different from the rest. He longed for all the trappings, titles, ornaments and show of power. He would love to hear himself called Master; he would love to begin a formal act at a college meeting 'I, Paul Jago, Master of the college . . .' He wanted the grandeur of the Lodge, he wanted to be styled among the heads of houses. He enjoyed the prospect of an entry in the college history – 'Dr P. Jago, 41st Master'. For him, in every word that separated the Master from his fellows, in every ornament of the Lodge, in every act of formal duty, there was a gleam of magic.

There was something else. He had just said to Chrystal 'we can make it a great college'. He believed that there were things that only he could do. Money did not move him in the slightest; the joys of office moved him a great deal; but there was a quality pure, almost naïve, in his ambition. He had dreams of what he could do with his power. These dreams left him sometimes, he became crudely avid for the job, but they returned. With all his fervent imagination, he thought of a college peaceful, harmonious, gifted, creative, throbbing with joy and luminous with grace. In his dreams, he did not altogether know how to attain it. He had nothing of the certainty with which, in humility, accepting their limitations, Chrystal and Brown went about their aims, securing a benefaction from Sir Horace, arranging an extra tutorship, making sure that Luke got a grant for his research. He had nothing of their certainty, nor their humility; he was more extravagant than they were, and loved display far more; in his ambition he could be cruder and more predatory; but perhaps he had intimations which they could not begin to hear.

CHAPTER IX

QUARREL WITH A FRIEND

WHEN I arrived in the combination room that evening, Winslow, Nightingale and Francis Getliffe were standing together. They had been talking but as they saw me at the door there was a hush. Winslow said:

'Good evening to you. I hear you've been holding your adoption meeting, Eliot?'

Nightingale asked:

'Did you all get the reception you wanted?'

'It was very pleasant. I'm sorry you weren't there,' I said. It was from him, of course, that they had heard the news. There was constraint in the air, and I knew that Francis Getliffe was angry. He had returned from Switzerland that day, deeply sunburned; his strong fine-drawn face – I thought all of a sudden, seeing him stand there unsmiling – became more El Greco-like as the years passed.

'Aren't you even going to see your candidate?' I asked Winslow. 'Do you prefer to do it all by correspondence?' Sometimes he liked to be teased, and he knew I was not frightened of him. He gave an indulgent grin.

'Any candidate I approved of would be fairly succinct on paper,' he said. 'Your candidate, if I may say so, would not be so satisfactory in that respect.'

'We are appointing a Master, you know, not a clerk,' I said.

'If the college is misguided enough to elect Dr Jago,' said Winslow, 'I shall beg to be excused when I sometimes fail to remember the distinction.'

Nightingale gave a smile – as always when he heard a malicious joke. He said:

'My view is, he will save us from worse. I don't object to him – unless someone better turns up.'

'It should not be beyond the wit of men to discover someone better,' said Winslow.

'I don't see this college doing it. It always likes to keep jobs in the family. That being so, I'm not displeased with Jago,' said Nightingale.

I heard the door open, and Chrystal walked up to shake hands with Francis Getliffe, who had not spoken since I came in.

'Good evening to you, Dean,' said Winslow.

I said, in deliberate candour:

'We were just having an argument about Jago. Two for, and two against.'

'That's lamentable.' Chrystal stared at Francis. 'We shall have to banish the Mastership as a topic in the combination room. Otherwise the place won't be worth living in.'

'You know what the result of that would be, my dear Dean?' said Winslow. 'You would have two or three knots of people, energetically whispering in corners. Not but what,' he added, 'we shall certainly come to that before we're finished.'

'It's lamentable,' said Chrystal, 'that the college can't settle its business without getting into a state.'

'That's a remarkable thought,' said Winslow. As Chrystal was replying tartly, the butler announced dinner: on the way in, Francis gave me a curt word: 'I want a talk with you. I'll come to your rooms after hall.'

We were sitting down after grace when Luke hurried in, followed by Pilbrow, late as he had been so often in his fifty years as a fellow. He rushed in breathlessly, his bald head gleaming as though it had been polished. His eyes were brown and sparkling, his words tumbled over each other as he apologised: he was a man of seventy-four, with the spontaneity, the brilliance, the hopes of a youth.

Chrystal had not been able to avoid Winslow's side, but he talked diagonally across the table to Francis.

'Have we fixed the date of the next feast, Getliffe?' he asked.

'You should have written it down in your pocket book, my dear Dean,' said Winslow. Chrystal frowned. Actually, he knew the date perfectly well. He was asking because he had something to follow.

'February the 12th. A month tomorrow,' said Francis, who had during the previous summer become Steward.

'I hope you'll make it a good one,' said Chrystal. 'I'm asking you for a special reason. I happen to have a most important guest coming.'

'Good work,' said Francis mechanically, preoccupied with other thoughts. 'Who is he?'

'Sir Horace Timberlake,' Chrystal announced. He looked round the table. 'I expect everyone's heard of him.'

'I am, of course, very ignorant of these matters,' said Winslow. 'But I've seen his name occasionally in the financial journals.'

'He's one of the most successful men of the day,' said Chrystal. 'He controls a major industry. He's the chairman of Howard & Hazlehurst.'

From the other side of the table, Francis Getliffe caught my eye. The name of that company had entered his wife's life, and I knew the story. In the midst of his annoyance, he gave a grim, intimate smile of recognition.

Nightingale smiled.

'I suppose,' he said, 'he might be called one of these business knights.'

'He's none the worse for that,' retorted Chrystal.

'Of course he's none the worse for that,' Pilbrow burst out from the lower end of the table. 'I've never been much addicted to businessmen, but really it's ridiculous to put on airs because they become genteel. How else do you think anyone ever got a title? Think of the Master's wife. What else were the Bevills but a set of sharp Elizabethan businessmen? It would be wonderful to tell her so.' He exploded into joyful laughter. Then he talked rapidly again, this time to Winslow, several places away at the head of the table. 'The trouble with your ancestors and mine, Godfrey, isn't that they made money, but that they didn't make quite enough. Otherwise we should have found ourselves with titles and coronets. It seems to me a pity whenever I order things in a shop. Or whenever I hear pompous persons talking nonsense about politics. I should have liked to be a red Lord.'

'Of course, ' he said, following his process of free association, 'snobbery is the national vice. Much more than other things which foreigners give us credit for.' He often talked so fast that the words got lost, but phrases out of Havelock Ellis bubbled out – '*le vice anglais*', I heard.

Pilbrow was delighted with the comparison. When he had quietened down, he said:

'By the way, I've hooked an interesting guest for the feast too, Getliffe.'

'Yes, Eustace, who is it?'

Pilbrow produced the name of a French writer of great distinction. He was triumphant.

In matters of art, the college's culture was insular and not well informed. The name meant nothing to most men there. But nevertheless they wanted to give Pilbrow the full flavour of his triumph. All except Chrystal and Nightingale. Chrystal was piqued because this seemed to be stealing Sir Horace's thunder; Sir Horace had been jeered at by Nightingale that night, and Chrystal was sensitive for his heroes; he also liked solid success, and a French writer, not even one he had heard of, not even a famous one, was flimsy by the side of Sir Horace. He was huffed to notice that I took this Frenchman seriously, and told Pilbrow how much I wanted to meet him.

Nightingale did what seemed impossible, and detested Pilbrow. He was full of envy at Pilbrow's ease, gaiety, acquaintance with the cultivated world. He knew nothing of Pilbrow's artistic friends, but hated them. When Pilbrow announced the French writer's name, Nightingale just smiled.

The rest of us loved Pilbrow. Even Winslow said:

'As you know, Eustace, I understand these things very little – but it will be extremely nice to see your genius. I stipulate, however, that I am not expected to converse in any language but my own.'

'Would you really like him next to you, Godfrey?'

'If you please. If you please.'

Pilbrow beamed. All of us, even the youngest, called him by his Christian name. He had been a unique figure in the college for very long. He would, as he said, have made a good red Lord. And, though he came from the upper middle classes, was comfortably off without being rich (his father had been the headmaster of a public school), many people in Europe thought of him in just that way. He was eccentric, an amateur, a connoisseur; he spent much of his time abroad, but he was intensely English, he could not have been anything else but English. He belonged to the fine flower of the peaceful nineteenth century. A great war had not shattered his feeling, gentlemanly and unselfconscious, that one went where one wanted and did what one liked.

If nostalgia ever swept over him, he thrust it back. I had never known an old man who talked less of the past. Long ago he had written books on the Latin novelists, and the one on Petronius, where he found a subject which exactly fitted him, was the best of its kind; all his books were written in a beautifully lucid style, oddly unlike his cheerful incoherent speech. But he did not wish to talk of them. He was far more spirited describing some Central European he had just discovered, who would be a great writer in ten years.

He went round Europe, often getting dazzled by a tiny gleam of talent. One of his eccentricities was that he refused to dress for dinner in a country under a totalitarian régime, and he took extreme delight in arriving at a party and explaining why. Since he was old, known in most of the salons and academies of Europe, and well connected, he set embassies some intricate problems. He did not make things easier for them by bringing persecuted artists to England, and spending most of his income upon them. He would try to bring over anyone a friend recommended – 'everything's got to be done through nepotism', he said happily. 'A pretty face may get too good a deal – but a pretty face is better than a committee, if it comes to bed.'

He had never married, but he did not seem lonely. I believed that there were days of depression, but if so he went through them in private. In public he was irrepressible, an *enfant terrible* of seventy-four. But it was not the exuberant side of him that I most admired; it was not that no one could think of him as old; it was that he, like other people who do good, was at heart as tough as leather, healthily self-centred at the core.

Chrystal came back to the feast.

'There's one thing we can't overlook. I've already warned my guest. I don't know how others feel, but I can't bring myself to like having a feast here with the Master dying in the Lodge. Still, we've got no option. If we cancel it, it gives the show away. But, if they've told the Master the truth before the time of the feast, we should have to cancel it. Even at an hour's notice. I shouldn't have much patience with anyone who didn't agree.'

'I think we should all agree,' said Winslow. 'Which is a very surprising and gratifying event, don't you think so, Dean?'

He spoke with his usual caustic courtesy, and was surprised to find Chrystal suddenly rude. He had not realised, he still did not, that Chrystal had spoken with deep feeling and was shocked by the sarcastic reply. In turn, Winslow became increasingly caustic, and Nightingale joined in.

I noticed young Luke watching this display of conflicts, and missing nothing.

There was no wine that night. Pilbrow left for a party immediately after hall; cultivated Cambridge parties were not complete without him, he had been attending them for over fifty years. Between the rest of us there was too much tension for a comfortable bottle. Winslow gave his 'Goodnight to you', and sauntered out, swinging the cap, which, in his formal style, he was the only one of us to bring into the room. I followed, and Francis came after me.

He said, the moment we were inside my sitting-room:

'Look, I'm worried about this talk of Jago.'

'Why?'

'It's bloody foolish. We can't have him as Master. I don't know what you can be thinking about.'

We were still standing up. A vein, always visible when he was angry, stood out in the middle of Francis's forehead. His sunburn made him look well, on the surface; but under the eyes the skin was darkened and pouched by strain. He had been doing two men's work for months – his own research, on the nature of the ionosphere, and his secret experiments for the Air Ministry. The secret was well kept, neither I nor anyone in the college knew any details until three years later, but he was actually busy with the origins of radar. He was tired and overloaded with responsibility. His fundamental work had not received the attention that he looked for, and his reputation was not yet as brilliant as we had all prophesied. He was seeing some of his juniors overtake him; it was hard to bear.

Now he was throwing every effort into a new research. It had not yet started smoothly. It was an intolerable nuisance for him to come back to this trouble over the Mastership. He did not want to think about it, he was overtaxed already. Plunged into the middle of this human struggle, he felt nothing but goaded irritation and impatience.

We had been friends since we first met, nearly ten years before. We were about the same age: he was now thirty-four and I thirty-two. We had much the same views, and a good deal of experience in common. I owed him a debt of gratitude. In my three years in the college, we had been allies, trusting each other, automatically on the same side in any question that mattered. This was the first time we had disagreed.

'I don't know what you can be thinking about,' said Francis.

'He'd be a goodish Master,' I said.

'Nonsense. Sheer bloody nonsense,' said Francis. 'What has he done?'

It was a harsh question, and difficult to answer. Jago was an English scholar, and had published articles on the first writings produced by the Puritan settlers in New England. The articles were sound enough: he was interesting on William Bradford's dialogue; but it was no use pretending to Francis.

'I know as well as you that he's not a specially distinguished scholar,' I said.

'The Master of this college must be a distinguished scholar,' said Francis.

'I don't mind that as much as you,' I said. 'I'm not a perfectionist.'

'What has he done?' said Francis. 'We can't have a man who's done nothing.'

'It's not so much what he's done as what he is,' I said. 'As a human being there's a great deal in him.'

'I don't see it.'

He had lost his temper; I was trying to keep mine. But I heard an edge coming into my voice.

'I can't begin to explain the colour red,' I said, 'to a man who's colour blind. You'd better take my word for it—'

'You get more fun out of human beings than I do,' he said, 'But I don't want to choose someone who gives you the maximum amount of fun. I just want a decent Master of this college.'

'If you're trying to secure that by cutting out all human judgment,' I said, 'you'll make the most unforgivable mistake.'

Francis walked three strides, three of his long, plunging strides, to the fire and back. His steps fell heavy in the quiet room.

'Look,' he said, 'how much are you committed?'

'Completely.'

'It's sheer utter irresponsibility. It's the first time I've seen you lose your balance. You must have gone quite mad.'

'When I say completely,' I said, 'I could get out of it if there were a reason. But there won't be one. Jago satisfies what I want better than anyone we shall find.'

'Have you given a second's thought to the fact that he's an absurd conservative? Do you think this is a good time to elect conservative figureheads, when we might get a reasonable one?'

'I don't like that any more than you—'

'I wish you showed more sign of not liking it in practice,' Francis said.

'For this particular job,' I said, 'I can't believe it's vitally important.'

'It's vitally important for every job where men can get into the public eye,' said Francis. 'You oughtn't to need me to tell you. Things are balanced so fine that we can't give away a point. These conservative

fools are sticking out their chests and trying to behave like solid responsible men. I tell you, they'll either let us drift lock, stock and barrel to the
fascists; or they'll get us into a war which we shall be bloody lucky
not to lose.'

Francis spoke with a weariness of anger. He was radical, like many
scientists of his generation. As he spoke, he was heavy with the responsibility that, in two or three years at most, he and his kind would have to
bear. He looked so tired that, for a second, I was melted.

'You needn't tell me that, you know, Francis,' I said. 'I may be voting
for Jago, but I haven't changed altogether since we last met.'

His sudden creased smile lit up his face, and then left him stern again.

'Whom do you want?' I asked.

'The obvious man. Crawford.'

'He's conceited. He's shallow. He's a third-rate man.'

'He's a very good scientist. That's understating the case.'

I had never heard a contrary opinion. Some people said that Crawford
was one of the best biologists alive.

Francis went on:

'He's got the right opinions. He isn't afraid to utter them.'

'He's inconceivably self-satisfied—'

'There aren't many men of his standing with radical views. Anything
he says, he says with authority behind him. Can't you see that it might
be useful to have a Master of a college who is willing to speak out like
that?'

'It might be very useful,' I said. The quarrel had died down a little;
I was listening to his argument. 'It might be very useful. But that isn't
all we want him for. Think what Crawford would be like inside the
college.'

I added: 'He'd have no feeling. And no glow. And not a scrap of
imagination.'

'You claim all those things for Jago?'

'Yes.'

'One can't have everything,' said Francis.

I asked:

'Will Crawford be a candidate?'

'If I have anything to do with it.'

'Have you spoken to Winslow yet?'

'No. I count him in for Crawford. He's got no option,' said Francis.

Yes, I thought. Winslow had talked vaguely of 'going outside', he had
ostentatiously mentioned no name. Those were the symptoms of one

who hoped against hope that he would be asked himself: even Winslow, who knew how much he was disliked, who had been rejected flatly at the last election, still had that much hope. But everyone knew that he must run Crawford in the end.

'I don't see any other serious candidate,' said Francis. He asked, suddenly and sternly: 'Lewis, which side are you on?'

It was painful to quarrel. There was a silence.

'I'm sorry,' I said. 'I can't manage Crawford at any price. I see your case. But I still think this is a job where human things come first. So far as those go, I'm happy with Jago.'

Francis flushed, the vein was prominent.

'It's utterly irresponsible. That's the kindest word I can find for it.'

'We've got to differ,' I said, suppressing the first words that came.

'I can't for the life of me understand why you didn't wait before you decided. I should have expected you to discuss it with me.'

'If you'd been here, I should have done,' I said.

'No doubt you've talked to other people.'

'Of course.'

'It will be hard,' he said, 'for me to think you reliable again.'

'We'd better leave it,' I said. 'I've stood as much as I feel like standing—'

'You're going on with this nonsense?' he shouted.

'Of course I'm going on with it.'

'If I can find a way to stop it,' he said, 'I promise you I shall.'

CHAPTER X

FIRST COLLEGE MEETING OF TERM

TRUNKS piled up in the college gateway, young men shouted to each other across the court, the porters' trucks groaned, ground and rumbled on their way round the stone paths. The benches in hall were filled, there was a surge of noise before and after grace; feet ran up and down stairs, all evening long. At night the scratchings behind the walls were less insistent; the kitchens were full of food now, and the rats, driven out to forage in the depth of the vacation, were going back. A notice came round, summoning a college meeting for next Monday, the first Monday of full term.

The meeting was called for 4.30, the customary time, just as each alternate Monday was the customary day; the bell pealed, again according to custom, at four o'clock, and Brown came down his staircase, Francis Getliffe and Chrystal walked through the gate, I looked round for my gown, all of us on our way to the combination room. The room itself looked transformed from when it was laid for wine at night; a blotter, a neat pile of scribbling paper, an inkwell, pens and pencils, stood in each place instead of glasses; covered with paper, the table shone white, orderly, bleak; the curtains were not drawn, though the wall lights were switched on, and through the windows came the cold evening light. The room seemed larger, and its shape was changed.

Its shape was changed partly because another table, almost as long as the main one, was brought in specially for these occasions. This table was covered with a most substantial tea – great silver teapots and jugs, shining under the windows, plates of bread and butter, white, brown, wholemeal, bread with currants in it, bread with raisins in it, gigantic college cakes, black with fruit and already sliced, tarts, pastries, toasted teacakes under massive silver covers. It was for this tea that the bell pealed half an hour before the meeting; and it was for this tea that we came punctually when we heard the bell.

Old Gay was already there. He seemed to have been there a considerable time. The rest of us stood round the table, holding our cups, munching a teacake, reaching out for a tart; but Gay had drawn up a chair against the table, and was making a hearty meal.

'Ah. How are you getting on, Chrystal?' he said, looking up for a moment from his plate. 'Have you had one of these lemon curd tarts?'

'I have,' said Chrystal.

'I congratulate you,' said Gay.

In a moment he looked up again.

'Ah, I'm glad to see you, Calvert. I thought you'd left us. Have you had any of this excellent stickjaw cake?'

'I was wondering whether it was too heavy for me,' said Roy Calvert.

'I must congratulate the Steward. Winslow, I congratulate you on the remarkably fine tea you've given us.'

'My dear Professor,' said Winslow, 'I was a most uninspired Steward: and I gave up being so five-and-twenty years ago.'

'Then congratulate the new Steward for me,' said Gay, quite un-abashed, picking out a chocolate éclair. 'Tell him from me that he's doing splendid work.'

We stood round, occupied with tea. Everyone was in the room except Crawford; snatches of conversation kept reaching me and fading away. Chrystal and Brown had a quiet word, and then Chrystal moved to the side of the Master's Deputy, Despard-Smith, who was listening with a sombre, puzzled expression to Roy Calvert. Chrystal plucked the sleeve of his gown, and they backed into the window: I heard a few words in Chrystal's brisk whisper – 'Master . . . announce the position . . . most inadvisable to discuss it . . . dangerous . . . some of us would think it improper.' As in all the whispered colloquies before meetings, the s's hissed across the room.

The half-hour struck. Despard-Smith said, in his solemn voice – 'It is more than time we started,' and we took our places in order of seniority, one to the right, and one to the left of the chair. Round the table clockwise from Despard-Smith's left hand, the order became – Pilbrow, Crawford (whose place was still empty), Brown, Nightingale, myself, Luke, Calvert, Getliffe, Chrystal, Jago, Winslow, Gay.

There was one feature of this curious system of seating: it happened at that time to bring side by side the bitterest antipathies in the college, Jago and Winslow, Crawford and Brown, Nightingale and me.

Despard-Smith looked round the table for silence. His face looked grey, lined, mournful above his clerical collar, grey above his black coat. He was seventy, and the only fellow then in orders, but he had never held a living; in fact, he had lived continuously in college since he entered it as a freshman fifty-one years before. He had been second wrangler in the days of the old mathematical tripos, and had been elected immediately after, as was often the practice then. He did no more mathematics, but became bursar at thirty and did not leave go of the office until he was over sixty. He was a narrow, competent man who had saved money for the college like a French peasant and, at any attempts to spend, predicted the gravest catastrophe. He had the knack of investing any cliché with solemn weight. At seventy he still kept a curious brittle stiff authority. He prided himself on his sense of humour: and, since he was also grave and self-assured, he accordingly become liable to some of Roy Calvert's more eccentric enquiries.

It lay in the Master's power to name his own deputy: and Despard-Smith had been appointed by the Master under seal in December, at the beginning of his illness – probably because the Master, like all the older fellows, could not struggle free from the long years in which Despard-Smith as bursar had held the college down.

'I shall now ask for the minutes,' he said. He stuttered on the 'm': he sometimes stuttered slightly on the operative word: it added to his gravity and weight.

Everyone there was anxious to come to the question of the Mastership. Some were more than anxious: but we could not do it. Customs ordained a rigid order of business, and custom was unbreakable. So we settled down to a desultory discussion about who should be offered a country living worth £325 a year. It carried with it a rectory with fourteen bedrooms. In the eighteenth century it had been worth exactly the same figure, and then it had been a prize for which the fellows struggled. Now it was going to be hard to fill. Despard-Smith considered that a contemporary of his might listen to the call; Roy Calvert wanted it for a young Anglo-Catholic friend.

The college was inclined to think that Despard-Smith's contemporary might be a trifle old. As for Roy's nominee, he never stood a chance, though Roy pressed him obstinately. Roy never got the ear of a college meeting. He became too ingenious and elaborate; *tête-à-tête* with any of these men, he was perceptive, but when they were gathered together he became strangely maladroit. But Arthur Brown himself could not have manoeuvred a job for an Anglo-Catholic. At the bare mention Jago, who was in fact an eloquent agnostic, invariably remembered that he had been brought up an Irish protestant. And all the other unbelievers would follow him in a stampede and become obdurate low churchmen.

Thus it happened that afternoon. The college would not take either of the names.

At that point, Crawford came in, and slipped quietly but noticeably into his place. He moved sleekly, like a powerful man who has put on weight.

'My apologies, Mr Deputy,' he said. 'As I informed you, I had to put in an appearance at the faculty board.'

Despard-Smith gloomily, competently, recapitulated the arguments: it appeared to be 'the sense of the college' that neither of these men should be offered the living, and the question would have to be deferred until next meeting: it was, of course, deplorable: had Dr Crawford any advice to give?

'No, Mr Deputy, I have no observations to make,' said Crawford. He had a full, smooth voice, and a slight Scottish accent. He assumed that he would be listened to, and he had the trick of catching the attention without an effort. His expression stayed impassive: his features were small in a smooth round face, and his eyes were round and unblinking.

His hair was smoothed down, cut very short over the ears; he had lost none of it, and it was still a glossy black, though he was fifty-six. As he spoke to the Deputy, he wore an impersonal smile.

The financial business did not take long. The college was selling one of its antique copyholds at twenty years' purchase; the college owned property in all the conceivable fashions of five hundred years; some early gifts had, by their legal form, kept their original money value and so were now more trouble than they were worth. When it came to property, the college showed a complete lack of antiquarian sentimentality.

'If that is all,' said Despard-Smith with solemn irritation, 'perhaps we can get on. We have not yet dealt with our most serious piece of business. I cannot exaggerate the catastrophic consequences of what I have to say.'

He stared severely round from right to left. Luke, for one moment free from scribbling notes for the minutes, had been whispering to Roy Calvert. He blushed down to his neck: he, and the whole room, became silent.

Despard-Smith cleared his throat.

'The college will be partly prepared for the announcement which it is my painful duty to make. When the Master asked me to act as his deputy less than two months ago, I fully expected that before this term was over he would be back in the s-saddle again. I little imagined that it would fall to me to announce from this chair the most disastrous news that I have been informed of in my long association with the college.' He paused. 'I am told,' he went on, 'upon authority which cannot be denied that the Master will shortly be taken from us.'

He paused again, and said:

'I am not qualified to express an opinion whether there is the f-faintest hope that the medical experts may be proved wrong in the event.'

Crawford said:

'May I have permission to make a statement, Mr Deputy?'

'Dr Crawford.'

'Speaking now not as a fellow but as one who was once trained as a medical man, I must warn the society that there is no chance at all of a happy issue,' Crawford said. He sat impassively, while others looked at him. I saw Jago's eyes flash at the other end of the table.

'You confirm what we have been told, Dr Crawford, that the Master's days on earth are n-numbered?'

'I must confirm that,' said Crawford. He was a physiologist, best known for his work on the structure of the brain. His fingers were short and thick, and it was surprising to be told that he was an experimenter of the most delicate manual skill.

'We are all bound to be impressed by Dr Crawford's statement,' said Despard-Smith.

'I must add a word to it,' said Crawford. 'The end cannot be long. The college must be prepared to have lost its head by the end of the Easter term.'

'Thank you for telling us the worst.'

'I considered it my duty to tell the college all I knew myself,' said Crawford.

He had said nothing novel to most of us; yet his immobile certainty, Despard-Smith's bleak and solemn weight, the ritual of the meeting itself, brought a tension that sprang from man to man like an electric charge.

After a silence, Winslow said:

'Dr Crawford's statement brings the whole matter to a point. I take it that with your permission, Mr Deputy, the college will wish to discuss the vacancy we shall soon be faced with.'

'I don't understand,' said Chrystal at his sharpest.

'I thought I made myself fairly clear,' said Winslow.

'I don't understand,' said Chrystal. This kind of obstinate pretence of incomprehension was one of his favourite techniques at a meeting. 'I should like us to be reminded of the statute governing the election of a Master.'

'I wonder,' said Brown, 'if you would be good enough to read it, Mr Deputy?'

'I'm in the hands of the m-meeting,' said Despard-Smith.

'Why are we wasting time?' said Francis Getliffe.

'I should like the statute read,' snapped Chrystal.

Winslow and Crawford exchanged glances, but Despard-Smith opened his copy of the statutes, which lay in front of him on the table, and began to read, half-intoning in a nasal voice:

'When a vacancy in the office of Master shall become known to that fellow first in order of precedence he shall summon within forty-eight hours a meeting of the fellows. If the fellow first in order of precedence be not resident in Cambridge, or otherwise incapable of presiding, the duty shall pass to the next senior, and so on. When the fellows are duly assembled the fellow first in order of precedence attending shall announce to them the vacancy, and shall before midnight on the same day authorise a notice of the vacancy and of the time hereby regulated for the election of the new Master, and cause this notice to be placed in full sight on the chapel door. The time regulated for the election shall be ten o'clock on the morning on the fifteenth day from the date of the notice if the vacancy occur in term, or on the thirtieth day if it occur out of term.'

When he had finished, Gay said sonorously:

'Ah. Indeed. Very interesting. Very remarkable. Fine piece of draughtsmanship, that statute.'

'It makes my point,' said Chrystal. 'The college as a college can't take any action till the Mastership is vacant. There's no question before us. I move the next business.'

'This is formalism carried to extreme limits,' said Winslow angrily. 'I've never known the Dean be so scrupulous on a matter of etiquette before—'

'It's completely obvious the matter must be discussed.' said Francis.

'I'm sure the Dean never intended to suggest anything else, Mr Deputy,' said Brown with a bland and open smile. 'If I may take the words out of his mouth, I know the Dean hopes – as I feel certain we all do – that we shall discuss every possible element in the whole position, so that we finally do secure the true opinion and desire of the college. The little difference of opinion between us amounts to nothing more than whether our discussion should be done in a formal college meeting or outside.'

'Or, to those of us who haven't the gift for softening differences possessed by Mr Brown, whether we shall dissolve immediately into cabals,' said Winslow with a savage grin, 'or talk it out in the open.'

'Speaking now as a fellow and not as a former medical man,' said Crawford, 'I consider that the college would be grossly imprudent not to use the next few months to resolve on the dispositions it must make.'

'But that's agreed by everybody,' I put in. 'The only question is, whether a formal college meeting is the most suitable place.'

'Cabals versus the open air,' said Winslow, and Nightingale smiled.

Despard-Smith was not prepared for the waves of temper that were sweeping up.

'I cannot remember any p-precedent in my long association with the college,' he said.

Suddenly Pilbrow began speaking with great speed and earnestness:

'The college can't possibly have a meeting about a new Master. . . . When the man who ought to be presiding is condemned. . . . I've never known such an extraordinary lack of feeling.'

He finished, after his various starts, with complete lucidity. But the college had a habit of ignoring Pilbrow's interventions, and Chrystal and Winslow had both begun to speak at once when Jago quietened them. His voice was not an orator's: it was plummy, thick, produced far back in his throat. Yet, whenever he spoke, men's glances turned to him. He had his spectacles in hand, and his eyes, for once unveiled, were hard.

'I have no doubt,' he said, 'that we have just listened to the decisive word. This is not the first time that Mr Pilbrow has represented to some of us the claims of decent feeling. Mr Deputy, the Master of this college is now lying in his Lodge, and he has asked you to preside in his place. We know that we must settle on someone to succeed him, however difficult it is. But we can do that in our own way, without utterly offending the taste of some of us by insisting on doing it in this room – in a meeting of which he is still the head.' When he sat back the room stayed uncomfortably still.

'That settles it,' said Roy Calvert in a clear voice.

'I moved the next business ten minutes ago,' said Chrystal, staring domineeringly at Despard-Smith. 'I believe Mr Brown seconded it. Is it time to vote on my motion? I'm ready to wait all evening.'

The motion was carried by seven votes to four. For: Pilbrow, Jago, Brown, Chrystal, myself, Calvert, Luke. Against: Winslow, Crawford, Nightingale, Getliffe.

Neither Despard-Smith nor Gay voted.

CHAPTER XI

VIEW FROM ROY CALVERT'S WINDOW

At hall after the meeting, Winslow was grumbling about Jago's last speech – 'high-minded persons have a remarkable gift for discovering that the requirements of decent feeling fit in exactly with what they want to do'. I thought about how we had voted. The sides were sorting themselves out. Nightingale had voted with the opposition: was that merely a gesture of suspiciousness against Chrystal and Brown? He was the most uncomfortable of bedfellows. Despard-Smith would presumably vote for Crawford. What about old Gay? He might do anything. I fancied Pilbrow would decide for Jago. It looked encouraging.

Two days afterwards, a note went round:

'Those who are not disposed to vote for the Senior Tutor may like to discuss candidates for the Mastership. I suggest a meeting in my rooms at 2.30 on Friday, 22 Jan. G.H.W.'

Winslow had had his note duplicated in the bursary, and sent it to each fellow. There was a good deal of comment. 'The man's got no manners,' said Chrystal. 'He's always doing his best to make the place a beargarden.' Brown said: 'I've got a feeling that the college won't be a very happy family for the next few months.' Jago said: 'I shall manage to hold my tongue – but he's being needlessly offensive.'

Although the same servant waited on me and Roy Calvert, his rooms were to be found not in the first court proper, but in a turret over the kitchen. His sitting-room commanded a view of the second court and the staircase up which Winslow's visitors must go. I arrived there after lunch on the Friday afternoon; Roy was standing at his upright desk, reading a manuscript against a light opalescent screen.

'I've kept an eye across the way,' he said. 'No one has declared himself yet.'

'I need to finish this,' he went on, looking back at the screen. 'There's a new martyr in this psalm.'

He read for a few minutes, and then joined me by the windows. We looked across, through the mist of the raw January afternoon, to the separate building which contained the sets not only of Winslow, but also of Pilbrow and Chrystal. It was a building of palladian harmony; Eustace Pilbrow had lived in it for fifty years, and said that it was still as tranquil to look at as when he saw if for the first time.

It was twenty-five past two.

'High time the enemy appeared,' said Roy.

Just then Winslow came lounging along the path from the first court. He wore no overcoat, but, as usual when in college on business, a black coat and striped trousers. As he lounged along, his feet came down heavily at each step; one could guess from his gait that he had unusually big feet.

'He's declared himself, anyway,' said Roy. 'He'd be sold if no one else turned up.'

Roy was on edge in his own fashion, though he was not given to anxiety. Waiting for critical news of his own, he felt instead of anxiety a tingle of excitement. He felt it now, watching for news of Jago's chances.

We saw Winslow disappear in the mouth of his staircase.

'He's extremely tiresome.' Roy smiled. 'But I like the old stick. So do you.'

A moment later, Despard-Smith, in clerical hat and overcoat, walked across the front of the building from the third court.

'That was only to be expected,' I said.

'If he weren't able to express his view,' said Roy, 'it would be nothing short of catastrophic.'

Francis Getliffe came quickly the way Winslow had come, in his long plunging strides.

'Now *he* ought to know better,' said Roy.

'He's got some good reasons.'

'He's getting stuffier as he gets older.'

The half-hour struck. Very slowly, along the same path, came Gay. One foot shuffled slowly in front of the other; he was muffled up to the throat, but his cheeks shone very red, his beard very white.

'How in God's name did he decide?' I cried in disappointment.

He took minutes to make his way across the court. He was almost there when we saw Nightingale come along from the third court and join him.

'Judas?' said Roy.

They talked for a moment; we saw Nightingale shake his head, and walk away in our direction.

'Apparently not,' I said.

Then, from the first court, Crawford walked smoothly into view. He was late, he was moving fast, but he gave no appearance of hurry. Roy whistled 'Here comes the bride' until he slipped up Winslow's staircase.

'I wonder,' said Roy suddenly, 'if old Winslow is still hoping. I wonder if he expects to be asked to stand this afternoon.'

'People hope on,' I said, 'long after they admit it to themselves.'

'Just so,' said Roy. 'In this case until they're seventy.' (Under the statutes, seventy was the retiring age for the Master.)

No one else came. The court was empty.

'Is that the whole party?' said Roy. 'I believe it is.'

We waited, and heard the quarters chime. We waited again.

'If this is all, old boy,' cried Roy, 'it's in the bag.'

We still stood there, looking over the court. The mist was deepening. An undergraduate brought in a girl, and they passed out of sight towards the third court. All of a sudden a light shone from Winslow's room. It made the court seem emptier, the afternoon more raw.

'They've only collected five,' said Roy. 'Not many. They've lost face.'

Crawford came out again into the court. Again quickly but without hurry, he walked towards the first court. We could see down on to his face as he approached. He looked utterly impassive.

'Asked to retire,' I said.

'I wonder what he thinks his chances are,' said Roy. He added: 'One thing – Winslow knows the worst now. His last chance has gone.'

'I'm sorry for some of our friends,' I said, 'if they sit next to him to-night.'

'I'd better get there early,' said Roy. 'I can look after myself.'

I smiled. We gazed, as the afternoon darkened, at the one window lighted in the quiet building. At last Roy turned away. 'That is that,' he said. 'It's pretty remarkable. We seem to be home.'

'I think I'd better tell Arthur Brown,' I said. Roy's telephone stood by his bedside, and I went there and talked to Brown. 'How do you know how many turned up?' I heard Brown saying, cautious and inquisitive as ever. 'How can you possibly have found out?'

I explained that we had been watching from Roy Calvert's window. Brown was satisfied, and asked for the names again. 'Our party seems to be hanging together,' he said. 'But I think, to be on the safe side, I'll give a little luncheon soon. I say, Eliot, I'm sorry about old Gay. I should like to know who got at him. We've let them steal a march on us there.'

'But it's pretty good,' I said.

'I must say it looks perfectly splendid.' For a second Brown had let himself go. Then the voice turned minatory again: 'Of course, you'll remember it's much too early to throw your hats in the air. We haven't even got a paper majority for Paul Jago yet. We must go carefully. You mustn't let people feel that we think it's safe. It would be a wise precaution if you and Calvert didn't let on that you know who turned up this after-noon.'

I told Roy, who gave a malicious chuckle.

'Good old Uncle Arthur,' he said. 'He must be the only person on this earth who regards you as an irresponsible schoolboy. It gives me great pleasure.'

He rang down to the kitchens for tea and crumpets, and we ate them by the fire. When we had finished and I was sitting back with my last cup of tea, Roy glanced at me with a secretive grin. From a drawer he produced, as though furtively, a child's box of bricks. 'I bought these yesterday,' he said. 'I thought they might come in useful. They won't be necessary unless Winslow shows us a new trick or two. But I may as well set them out.'

He always had a love for the concrete, though his whole professional life was spent with words. Another man would have written down the fellows' names, but Roy liked selecting fourteen identical bricks, and printing on them the names from Royce to Luke. The brick marked Royce he put by itself without a word. His expression lightened as he placed the two bricks Jago and Crawford together. Then he picked out Gay, Despard-Smith, Winslow and Getliffe, and arranged them in a row. He left the other seven in a huddle – 'until everyone's in the open. It ought to be a clear majority.'

I had to give two supervisions from five to seven, and when the second was over went straight to the combination room. There Crawford was sitting by the fire alone, reading the local paper. He nodded, impersonally cordial, as I went over to the sherry table. When I came back, glass in hand, to the armchairs, Crawford looked at me over the top of his paper. 'I don't like the look of the war, Eliot,' he said. 'The war' was the civil war in Spain.

'Nor do I,' I said.

'Our people are getting us into a ridiculous mess. Every Thursday when I go up to the Royal I try to call on someone or other who is supposed to be running our affairs. I try to make a different call each week and persuade them to see a little military sense. It's the least one can do, but I never come away feeling reassured. Speaking as one liberal to another, Eliot, and without prejudice to your subject, I should feel happier if we had a few men of science in the House and the Foreign Office.'

For a few minutes he talked about the winter campaign in Spain. He had made a hobby of military history, and his judgment was calm and steady. Everything he said was devastatingly sensible.

Then Jago entered. He started as he saw Crawford, then greeted him with effusiveness. He was more uncomfortable than I had ever seen him – more uncomfortable, I suddenly realised, because he had heard the good news of the afternoon. He felt guilty in the presence of the less lucky one.

Crawford was unperturbed.

'I think we'd better abandon our military researches for tonight, Eliot,' he said. 'I believe the Senior Tutor isn't specially interested in war. And certainly doesn't share our sympathies about the present one. He'll realise we were right in time.'

He got up from his chair, and stood facing Jago. He was several inches shorter, but he had the physical presence that comes through being able to keep still.

'But I am glad of the chance of a word with you, Jago,' he said. 'I was thinking of sending you a note. That won't be necessary if we can have three minutes. I understand that Eliot is committed to support you, and so I can speak in his presence.'

'By all means,' said Jago. 'I am in your hands. Go ahead, my dear man, go ahead.'

'This afternoon,' said Crawford, 'I was asked to let myself be a candidate for the Mastership. Those who asked me did not constitute a numerical majority of the college, but they represent a sound body of opinion. I saw no reason to hesitate. I don't approve of people who have to be persuaded to play, like the young woman who just happens to have brought her music. I told them I was ready to let my name go forward.'

He was confident, impervious, conceited, self-assured. On the afternoon's showing he was left without a chance, but he seemed in control of the situation.

'I'm very grateful to you for telling me,' said Jago.

'It was the least I could do,' said Crawford. 'We are bound to be the only serious candidates.'

'I wish both the candidates,' said Jago, with a sudden smile, 'reached the standard of distinction set by one of them.'

'That's as may be,' Crawford replied. 'There will be one question for us two to decide together. That is, what to do with our own personal votes. We ought to reach a working agreement on that. It is conceivable that the question may become important.'

Then he said that he was dining in another college, and left us, with a cordial, impersonal goodnight.

Jago sighed and smiled.

'I'd give a good deal for that assurance, Eliot!'

'If you had it,' I said, 'you'd lose something else.'

'I wonder,' Jago cried, 'if he's ever imagined that he could possibly be wrong? Has he ever thought for a minute that he might possibly disgrace himself and fail?'

Not in his world of professional success, power, ambition, influence among men, I thought. Of his mastery in this world Crawford was absolutely and impenetrably confident. Nothing had ever shaken him, or could now.

But I guessed that in his nature there was one rift of diffidence. He had a quiet, comely wife and a couple of children – while Jago would go home after dinner to his tormented shrew. Yet I guessed that, in time past, Crawford had been envious of Jago's charm for women. Jago had never been frightened that he might not win love; he had always known that it would come his way. It was an irony that it came in such a form; but he stayed confident with women, he was confident of love; in fact, it was that confidence which helped him to devote such tenderness and such loving patience upon his wife. Whereas Crawford as a young man had wondered in anguish whether any woman would ever love him. For all his contented marriage – on the surface so much more enviable than Jago's – he had never lost that diffidence, and there were still times when he envied such men as Jago from the bottom of his heart.

CHAPTER XII

JAGO WALKS ROUND THE COURT

THE evening after Winslow's caucus, Brown asked me to join him and Chrystal, and when I went into Brown's room, they were busy talking. Brown said to me:

'I suggested we should meet here because it's a bit more private than the combination room. And I happen to have a glass of manzanilla waiting for you. We think it's rather helpful to a bit of business.'

Brown gave me my glass, settled himself, and went on:

'I regard it as desirable to strike while the iron's hot. I can't forgive myself for letting them snatch old Gay from in front of our noses. We must have our little luncheon before we lose anyone else.'

'I'm with you,' said Chrystal.

'I think they've shown more enterprise than we have,' said Brown, 'and we've got out of it better than we deserved.'

'If I were Crawford, I shouldn't thank Winslow much,' said Chrystal. 'He's just run amok. He's done them more harm than good. If Crawford had us to look after him, there'd be no need to have an election.'

'Well,' said Brown, 'I shall be happier when we've got our party round a luncheon table.'

'We must make them speak,' said Chrystal.

'You'll preside,' said Brown, 'and you can make everyone say that he's supporting Jago.'

'Why should I preside?'

'That's your job. I regard you as the chairman of our party.' Brown smiled. 'And we ought to have this lunch on Sunday. The only remaining point is whom do we ask. I was telling the Dean' – he said to me – 'that I haven't been entirely idle. I haven't let the other side get away with everything. I think I've got Eustace Pilbrow. We certainly ought to ask him along. He's never been specially interested in these things, and he's not enormously enthusiastic, but I think I've got him. Put it another way: if Jago were a bit of a crank politically – saving your presence, Eliot – I believe Eustace would support him up to the hilt. As it is, I'm quite optimistic.'

'That only leaves young Luke,' said Chrystal. 'Everyone else has tabs on them. So I reckon at present.'

'Obviously we invite the other three, Pilbrow, Nightingale and Roy Calvert,' said Brown. 'The question is, Eliot, whether we invite young Luke. I must say that I'm rather against it.'

'He only needs a bit a persuasion,' Chrystal said sharply. 'Either side could get him for the asking. He's a child.'

In the months since Luke became a fellow, I had not come to know him, except as an observant, intelligent, and sanguine face at hall and college meetings. Once I had walked round the garden with him for half an hour.

'I wonder whether you're right,' I said to Chrystal. 'It may not be as easy as you think.'

'Dead easy for us. Dead easy for Winslow,' said Chrystal.

'I agree,' said Brown. 'I believe the Dean's right.

'That's why,' he went on, 'I'm against inviting him.' His face was flushed, but stubborn and resolute. 'I want to say where I stand on this. I won't be a party to over-persuading Luke. He's a young man, he's not a permanency here yet, he's got his way to make, and it would be a damned shame to hamper him. At the very best it won't be easy for the college to keep him when his six years are up: we've got one physicist in Getliffe, and it will be hard to make a case for another as a fixture.' (Roy Calvert and Luke were research fellows appointed for six years: when that period ended, the college could keep them or let them go. It was already taken for granted that a special place must be found for Roy.) 'It stands to reason that Luke has got to look to Crawford and Getliffe. They're the scientists, they're the people who can help him, they're the people who'll have to make a case if the college is ever going to keep him. You can't blame him if he doesn't want to offend them. If I'd started as the son of a dockyard hand, as that boy did, though no one would ever think it, I shouldn't feel like taking the slightest risk. I'm certainly not going to persuade him to take it. Whichever side he comes down on, I say that it isn't for us to interfere.'

'Look,' I said, 'Francis Getliffe is a very fairminded man—'

'I give you that,' said Brown. 'I'm not saying that voting for Jago would necessarily make a scrap of difference to Luke's future. But he may feel that it would. If he does, I for one wouldn't feel easy about talking him round.'

'You've got a point there,' said Chrystal.

'The furthest I feel inclined to go,' said Brown, 'is to send him a note saying that some of us have now decided to support Jago. I'll tell him we're meeting on Sunday to discuss ways and means, but we're not inviting people who still want time to make up their minds.'

'I'm sorry to say,' said Chrystal, 'that I think you're right.'

There we left it for the evening. It was easier to understand their hold on the college, I thought, when one saw their considerate good-nature, right in the middle of their politics. No one could run such a society for long without a degree of trust. That trust most of the college had come to place in them. They were politicians, they loved power, at many points they played the game only just within the rules. But they set themselves limits and did not cross them. They kept their word. And in human things, particularly with the young, they were uneasy unless they behaved in a fashion that was scrupulous and just. People were ready to believe this of Brown, but found it harder to be convinced that it was also true of his friend. They saw clearly enough that Chrystal was the more ruthless: they did not see that he was the more tender-hearted.

In this particular instance, as it happened, they did not evoke the response that they deserved. Luke sat next to me in hall that night. For a couple of nights past he had been less sanguine and bright-eyed than usual: I asked about his work.

'It seems to be describing a sine curve,' he said. I had to recollect that a sine curve went up and down.

He went on: 'Sometimes I think it's all set. Sometimes I think it's as useless as the Great Pyramid. I'm in the second phase just now. I'm beginning to wonder if I shall ever get the wretched thing out.'

He was depressed and irritable, and just then happened to hear Brown quietly inviting Roy Calvert to lunch in order 'to give Jago's campaign a proper start'.

'What is all this?' Luke asked me. 'Is this the reply to Winslow's meeting?'

'Roughly,' I said.

'Am I being asked?'

'I think,' I said, 'that Brown felt you hadn't yet made up your mind.'

'He hasn't taken much trouble to find out,' said Luke. 'I'll have it out with him afterwards.'

Passing round the wine in the combination room, he was quiet and deferential to the old men, as he always was. I was beginning to realise the check he imposed on his temper. An hour later, as Brown and I left the room and went into the court, Luke came rapidly behind us.

'Brown, why haven't I been invited to this bloody caucus?'

'It isn't quite a caucus, Luke. I was just going to write to explain—'

'It's a meeting of Jago's supporters, isn't it?'

'One or two of us,' said Brown, 'have come to the conclusion that he's the right man. And—'

'So have I. Why hasn't someone spoken to me about it? Why haven't I been told?'

It was raining, and we had hurried through the court into the gateway, for Brown was on his way home. We stood under the great lantern.

'Why, to tell you the truth, Luke, we thought you might naturally want to vote for Crawford. And we didn't want to put any pressure on you.'

'I'm buggered if I vote for Crawford,' cried Luke. 'You might have given me credit for more sense. Jago would make one of the best Masters the college has ever had.'

So Luke appeared for the Sunday lunch in Brown's rooms, once more effacing himself into discretion again, dressed with a subfusc taste more cultivated than that of anyone there except Roy Calvert. Unobtrusively he got in a preliminary taste of his glass of Montrachet.

Brown had placed Chrystal at one end of the table, and took the other himself. After we had sipped the wine, Brown said with satisfaction:

'I'm glad most of you seem to like it. I though it was rather suitable. After all, we don't meet for this purpose very frequently.'

Brown's parties were always modest. One had a couple of glasses of a classical wine, and that was all – except once a year, when his friends who had a taste in wine were gathered together for an evening. This Sunday there was nothing with lunch but the Montrachet, but afterwards he circulated a bottle of claret. 'I thought we needed something rather fortifying,' said Brown, 'before we started our little discussion.'

We were content after our lunch. Pilbrow was a gourmet, young Luke had the sensuous gusto to become one; Chrystal and Roy Calvert and I enjoyed our food and drink. Pilbrow was chuckling to himself.

'Much better than the poor old Achæans—' I distinguished among the chuckles. We asked what it was all about, and Pilbrow became lucid:

'I was reading the *Iliad* – Book XI – again in bed – Pramnian wine sprinkled with grated goat's cheese – Pramnian wine sprinkled with grated goat's cheese – Oh, can anyone imagine how *horrible* that must have been?'

Six of us went on enjoying our wine. Meanwhile Nightingale sat over a cup of coffee, envying us for our pleasure, trying to be polite and join in the party.

In time Brown asked Chrystal whether we ought not to make a start with the discussion. There was the customary exchange of compliments between them: Chrystal wondered why he should act as chairman, when Brown himself was there: Brown felt the sense of the meeting required the Dean. At last, the courtesies over, Chrystal turned sharply to business. He wished us each to define our attitude to the Mastership, in order of seniority; he would wind up himself. So, sitting round the littered table after lunch, we each made a speech.

Pilbrow opened, as usual over-rapidly. But his intention was clear and simple. He was sorry that Jago had some reactionary opinions: but he was friendly, he took great trouble about human beings, and Pilbrow would vote for him against Crawford. It was a notable speech for a man of seventy-four; listening with concentration, I was surprised how little he was attended to. Chrystal was spinning the stem of a glass between his fingers; even Brown was not peering with acute interest.

Brown was listened to by everyone. For the first time, he spoke his whole mind about Jago, and he spoke it with an authority, a conviction, a round integrity, that drew us all together. Jago would make an outstandingly good Master, and his election would be a fine day's work for the college. Put it another way: if the college was misguided enough to elect Crawford, we should be down twice: once by getting a bad Master, once by losing a first-class one. And the second point was the one for us to give our minds to.

Nightingale made a circuitous attack on Crawford, in the course of which he threw doubts, the first time I had heard him or anyone else suggest them, on Crawford's real distinction as a scientist. 'His work may be discredited in ten years, any work of his sort may be, and then the college would be in an awkward situation.' The others round the table became puzzled and hushed, while Nightingale smiled.

I developed Pilbrow's point, and asked them what human qualities they thought they wanted in a Master. For myself, I answered: a disinterested interest in other people: magnanimity: a dash of romantic imagination. No one could doubt Jago had his share of the last, I said, and got a laugh. I said that in my view he was more magnanimous than most men, and more interested in others.

Roy Calvert took the same line, at greater length, more fancifully. He finished with a sparkle of mischief: 'Lewis Eliot and I are trying to say that Jago is distinguished as a man. If anyone asks us to prove it, there's only one answer – just spend an hour with him. If that isn't convincing it isn't our fault – or Jago's.'

Luke said no more than he was sure Jago would be a splendid Master, and that he would vote for him in any circumstances.

Chrystal had made a note on the back of an envelope after each speech. Now he summed up, brusque, giving his usual hint of impatience or ill-temper, competent and powerful. He had wanted to be certain how far the party were prepared to commit themselves. Unless he had misunderstood the statements, Brown, Nightingale and Luke were prepared to vote for Jago without qualification; Eliot and Calvert would support him against any candidate so far mentioned; Pilbrow promised to support him against Crawford. 'Have I got anyone wrong?' he asked sharply.

Brown and I were each watching Nightingale. No one spoke. One by one, we nodded.

'That's very satisfactory as far as it goes,' said Chrystal. 'I'm not going to waste your time with a speech. I can go at least as far as Pilbrow, and I think I find myself with Eliot and Calvert. I'm for Jago against Crawford and any other names I've heard. I'm not prepared to go the whole way with Brown just yet. I don't think Jago is an ideal candidate. He's not well enough known outside. But he'll do.'

He looked across the table at Brown.

'There's a majority for Jago in this room,' he said. 'I don't think there's anything more to do this afternoon.'

We were all stimulated, there was a glow of success and conspirators' excitement round the table. Brown and Chrystal told of the moves which had gone on before the present Master was elected. I learned for the first time that Jago had tried, in that election, to get together a party for Winslow. I asked whether they were remembering right. 'Oh yes,' said Brown, 'they hadn't got across each other so badly then. I shouldn't have said they were ever specially friendly, though, should you?' he asked Chrystal.

The talk kept to elections of past Masters. Pilbrow began to laugh.

'I've just thought –' then he added with complete clarity: 'In my almost infinite period as a fellow, I've never even been mentioned as a possible candidate. And I've never taken the slightest useful part in getting one elected. That's a long-distance record no one can ever beat.' He went on laughing. He did not care. He was known, admired, loved all over Europe; he had great influence in letters: but nothing could make him effective at a college meeting. It was strange – and I thought again of Roy Calvert at the last meeting – that those two, both very natural men, should not be able to project themselves into a committee. Perhaps they were too natural. Perhaps, for influence in the affairs of solid men, one had to be able to send, as the Master said, the 'old familiar phrases reverberating round'. Neither Pilbrow nor Roy Calvert could do that without laughing. To be an influence in any society, in fact, one can be a little different, but only a little; a little above one's neighbours, but not too much. Pilbrow did much good, Roy Calvert was often selfless; but neither of them was humble enough to learn the language of more ordinary men.

But, even if they had tried to learn it, neither of them could ever have been the power that Brown or Chrystal was. Groups of men, even small groups, act strangely differently from individuals. They have less humour and simpler humour, are more easy to frighten, more difficult to charm, distrust the mysterious more, and enjoy firm, flat, competent expositions which a man by himself would find inexcusably dull. Perhaps no group would ever let itself be guided by Roy Calvert.

In the same way, the seven of us sitting at the table through the winter afternoon became more enthusiastic for Jago than any of us taken alone: our pleasure was simple, our exhilaration intense. Even Nightingale caught it. We were together, and for an hour everyone surrendered to the excitement; Jago would win, we wanted Jago, and all seemed bright.

The kitchen porters brought in tea at four o'clock. The excitement broke; we split into twos and threes; muffin in hand, Chrystal talked quietly to me about Sir Horace's visit a month hence. Then, as had been arranged, Jago came into the room.

'Good afternoon, Dean. Good afternoon, Brown. You mustn't let me interrupt. I expect you haven't finished your business. I should be so sorry to interrupt.'

He was restless with anxiety, and at his worst. Chrystal stood up, stiff and dominating. If Jago was to be Master, Chrystal wanted it clear between them that he had brought it about. His expression was hard, almost threatening.

'We've finished, Jago,' he said. 'I can tell you that we've had a satisfactory meeting.'

'Just so,' said Roy Calvert, trying to soothe Jago's nerves.

'I mustn't ask about your secrets,' said Jago. His smile was vivid but uneasy. There was a lull, and then Pilbrow asked about some old member in the Foreign Office. Would he help about a refugee? Was he approachable? What was he like?

'You'll find his general attitude utterly unsatisfactory according to your views,' said Jago. 'He's what the Dean and Brown and I would consider sound.'

'Sound,' Pilbrow said. 'You'll lose the bloody empire and everything else, between you. Sound.'

'I was going to say, however much we're on different sides, we're none of us above doing a job for a friend. I should be very much upset if—'

He promised to write that night about Pilbrow's refugee, and Pilbrow, mollified, asked about others at the Foreign Office. Jago was still on edge, eager to say yes, eager to keep the conversation alive. Did he know H——? A little. Sir P—— J——? Reluctantly, Jago said no. Did he know P——?

'Do I know P——?' cried Jago. 'Do I know P——, my dear Eustace? I should think I do. The first time I met him, he asked my advice about a minister's private life!'

He stayed in that vein, at his most flamboyant, until the party broke up. Roy Calvert and Brown knew the reason, and Roy, as though in fun, actually in kindness, laughed at him as if it were a casual tea-party and gave Jago the chance to score off him in reply. Jago took it, and amused us, especially Nightingale, with his jokes at Roy's expense. But the anxiety returned, and with it his flow of extravagance. Chrystal did not respond much, and went away early; then Pilbrow and Luke. Nightingale seemed to be enjoying himself, and I began to listen to the quarters, each time they chimed outside. So long as he stayed, Jago could not ask.

At last Nightingale went. The door closed behind him, and Jago turned to Arthur Brown with a ravaged look. 'Well?'

'Well,' said Brown comfortably, 'if the election had been this afternoon, you would have got in nicely.'

'Did everyone here—'

'Everyone you've seen said that, as things stood at present, they were ready to vote for you.'

'That's wonderful.' Jago's face lit up the room. 'That's wonderful.'

His smile was still radiant, but became gentler as he added:

'I'm touched to think of dear old Eustace Pilbrow throwing away his prejudices and being ready to support me. I don't suppose we've agreed on a single public issue since I became a fellow. We've disagreed on everything two men could disagree on. Yet he is willing to do this for me.'

'You ought to be touched about young Luke,' said Brown. 'He's the most enthusiastic supporter you've got. And he's acting against his own interests.'

'Ah, I think I'm better with young men than with people my own age.' He added, with a flash of extraordinary directness and simplicity: 'I don't have to show off to them, you see.'

Roy caught my eye. His smile was sharp.

Then Brown spoke:

'I don't want to be a skeleton at the feast, because I've been feeling very gratified myself, but I think it would be remiss not to remind you that the thing's still open.' Brown settled himself to give a caution. 'You oughtn't to let yourself think that we're completely home. If the election had come off today, as I told you, you would be Master. But you realise that these people can't give a formal pledge, and one or two actually made qualifications. I don't think they were important qualifications, but you mustn't think it's absolutely cut-and-dried. The picture might just conceivably alter – I don't think it's at all likely, but it might – before things happen to the present Master as they must.'

'But you're satisfied?' said Jago. 'Are you satisfied? Will you tell me that?'

Brown paused, and said deliberately:

'Assuming that the college was bound to be rather split, I consider things couldn't look much healthier than they do today.'

'That's quite good enough for me.' Jago sighed in peace, and stretched his arms like a man yawning. He smiled at the three of us. 'I'm very grateful. I needn't tell my friends that, I think.'

He left us, and we stood up and walked towards the window. It was a clear winter evening, the sky still bright in the west. The lamps of the court were already lit, but they seemed dim in that lucid twilight. The light in the Master's bedroom was already shining.

'I hope I didn't say too much,' said Brown to Roy Calvert and me. 'I think it's all right. But I'm not prepared to cheer until I hear the votes in the chapel. Some of us know,' he said to me, 'that you're very good at using your judgment of men. But, if you'll believe anyone like me, there are things you can only learn through having actually been through them. I've seen elections look more certain than this one does today, and then come unstuck.'

I was beginning to watch Jago walk slowly round the court.

'You see,' said Brown, 'we haven't much weight in our party. Pilbrow doesn't count for very much, and you're too young, Roy, and Eliot hasn't been here long enough. I suppose Chrystal and I are all right, but we could do with a bit more solid weight. Put it another way: suppose another candidate crops up. Someone who was acceptable to the influential people on the other side. I think it's just imaginable that Chrystal would feel we hadn't enough weight to stand out against that. He might feel obliged to transfer. You noticed that he covered himself in case that might happen. I don't say it's likely, but it's just as well to keep an eye open for the worst.'

Jago was walking very slowly round the court, past the door of the Lodge, past the combination room window, past the hall, back under Brown's window. He walked slowly, luxuriously, with no sign of his usual active, jerky step. He began to walk round again, and as he turned we saw his face. It was brilliant with joy. He looked at the grass as though he were feeling: '*my* grass'. He trod on the path, and then strayed, for the love of it, on to the cobbles; '*my* path, *my* cobbles'. He stood for a long moment in the middle of the court, and gazed round him in exaltation: '*my* college'.

He glanced at the lighted window in the Lodge, and quickly turned his head away.

'He looks happy, doesn't he?' said Arthur Brown, in a steady, affectionate, protective tone. 'He takes everything so much to heart. I only hope we manage to get him in.'

PART TWO

WAITING

CHAPTER XIII

PROGRESS OF AN ILLNESS

THE light in the Master's bedroom shone over the court each night; the weeks passed, and we still had to pay our visits, talking of next year's fellowships and how soon it would be before he could come into hall. Chrystal could not bear it, and made some ill-tempered excuse for not going into the Lodge. Hearing the excuse and taking it at its face value, Lady Muriel was contemptuous: 'I always knew he was common,' Roy Calvert reported her as saying.

Roy had become Lady Muriel's mainstay. He was the only man from whom she would ask for help. It fell to him to spend hours at the Master's bedside, keeping up the deception – and afterwards to sit with Lady Muriel in the great drawing-room, listening to doubts and sorrows that she could never manage to articulate.

Roy loved them both, and did it for love, but he was being worn down. For any of us, this service would have been nerve-racking; for Roy, with melancholia never far away, it was dangerous. But it was he who had to watch the Master's astonishment as, after weeks of pseudo-recovery, he found himself getting thinner and more exhausted.

We all knew that soon Lady Muriel would have to tell him the truth. Many of us wanted her to do it, just to be saved the pretence at the bed-side. Men as kind as Brown and Pilbrow could not help thinking of themselves, and wanted to be saved embarrassment even at the cost of agony for the Master and his wife. Theirs was the healthy selfishness which one needs for self-protection in the face of death. If one sees an-other's death with clear eyes, one suffers as Roy Calvert was suffering. Most of us see it through a veil of our own concerns: even Brown wanted Lady Muriel to tell the Master, so that Brown himself need no longer screw up his self-control before he went into the Lodge. Even Brown wanted her to tell him – but not before the feast, with everything arranged to receive Sir Horace Timberlake. As Brown said, with his usual lack of humbug: 'It can't make things worse for the Master if we have the feast. And we may not find another chance of getting Sir Horace down. So I hope Lady Muriel doesn't have to break the news till afterwards.'

As the day of the feast came near, that hope became strong all over the college. Some of us were ashamed of it; one's petty selfishnesses are sometimes harder to face than major sins. Yet we did not want to have to cancel the feast. As though by common consent, although we did not discuss it, not a hint was dropped in the Lodge. They were not likely to have remembered the date, or to have heard of Sir Horace's visit. We were too much ashamed to mention it. Lady Muriel must be left, we thought, to choose her own time.

The feast was fixed for Shrove Tuesday, and on the Sunday before I met Joan Royce in the court, both of us on our way to the Jagos for tea. She made a pretext for bringing in Roy's name with the first words she spoke: and I thought how we had all done the same, in love.

The Jagos kept open house for fellows at Sunday teatime, but when we arrived they were still alone; Mrs Jago welcomed us with a greater assumption of state than ever: she had been telling herself that no one wished to see her, that Jago's house was deserted because of her. In return, she mounted to great heights of patronage towards Joan and me.

Jago was patiently chaffing her – he was too patient, I thought – as he handed us our cups. The tea, like all the amenities which Mrs Jago chose, was the best in college; her taste was as fine as Brown's, though not as rich. Joan, who was not domesticated but enjoyed her food, asked her about some shortbread. Mrs Jago was feeling too umbraged to take the question as a compliment. But then, by luck, Joan admired the china.

'Ah, that was one of our wedding-presents,' said Mrs Jago.

'I suppose,' said Joan thoughtfully, 'there are some arguments in favour of a formal wedding.'

Mrs Jago forgot her complaint, and said with businesslike vigour:

'Of course there are. You must never think of anything else.'

'She means,' said Jago, 'that you'll miss the presents.'

Mrs Jago laughed out loud, quite happily:

'Well, they were very useful to us, and you can't deny it.'

'To tell you the truth,' said Joan, 'I was thinking the same myself.'

Jago's eyes were glinting with sadistic relish.

'You two!' he said. 'You pretend to like books. But you can't get away from your sex, neither of you. How dreadfully realistic women are.'

They both liked it. They liked being bracketed together, the ageing malcontent and the direct fierce girl. They were both melted by him;

his wife, for all her shrewishness, still could not resist him, and Joan smiled as she did for Roy.

Then the two women gazed at each other with a curious tenderness, and Mrs Jago asked gently and naturally about the Master's state.

'Is he in any pain?'

'No, none at all. Nothing more than discomfort sometimes.'

'I'm relieved to hear that,' said Mrs Jago.

Joan said:

'He's losing weight each day. And he's getting a little weaker. My mother knows that the truth oughtn't to be kept from him any longer.'

'When will she tell him?'

'Almost at once.'

Jago and I exchanged a glance. We did not know, could not ask, whether that meant before Tuesday.

'It must be a terrible thing to do,' said Mrs Jago.

'It's worse for them both now,' said Joan, 'than if she had told him that first night. I'm sure she should have done. I'm sure one should not hold back anything vital – we're not wise enough to know.'

'That's a curious remark,' said Jago, 'for a girl your age. When I was twenty, I was certain I knew everything—'

'You're a man,' said Joan, hitting back after his gibe. 'Men grow up very late.'

'Very late,' said Jago. He smiled at her. 'But I've grown up enough now to know how completely right you are about – your mother's mistake. She should have told him then.'

'I hope I shouldn't have shirked telling you, Paul,' said Mrs Jago, 'if it had happened to you.'

'I should be surer of your courage,' said Jago, 'than I should of my own.'

She smiled, simply and winningly. 'I hope I should be all right,' she said.

Perhaps she would always rise, I wondered, to the great crises of their life. I wondered it still, after Joan left suddenly to go to a party and Mrs Jago was once more affronted. When Joan had gone out, Jago said:

'There's fine stuff in that young woman. I wish she didn't look so sulky. But there's wonderfully fine stuff in her.'

'I dare say there is,' said Mrs Jago. 'But she must learn not to show that she's so bored with her entertainment.'

'It's ten to one that she's going to this party on the off-chance that Roy Calvert will be there,' I said.

'I hope she gets him,' said Jago. 'She would supply everything he lacks.'

'No woman ought to get him,' cried Mrs Jago. 'He's too attractive to be tamed.'

Jago frowned, and for a second she was pleased. Then she began to nag. She had been cherishing snubs all afternoon, and now she let them out. Lady Muriel, cried Mrs Jago, was too much a snob, was too much above the wives of the fellows, for anyone like herself to know the inside of the Lodge.

She could not very well ask Joan: but how did Jago expect her to make plans for furnishing it ready for them to move in?

It was then I wondered again how she would rise to the great moments.

'I can't think, Paul,' she was saying, 'how you can expect me to have the Lodge fit to live in for six months after we move. I shall be a burden on you in the Lodge anyway, but I want a fair chance to get the place in order. That's the least I can do for you.'

It would be awkward if she spoke in that strain to others, I thought, as I walked back to my rooms. Nothing would give more offence, nothing was more against the rules of that society: I decided Brown, as manager of Jago's caucus, must know at once. As I was telling him, he flushed. 'That woman's a confounded nuisance,' he said. For once he showed real irritation. Jago would have to be warned, but of all subjects it was the one where Jago was least approachable. 'I'm extremely vexed,' said Brown.

His composure had returned when he and Chrystal called on me after hall.

'It's nothing to do with the Mastership,' Brown said affably. 'We just want to make sure that we've got everything comfortable for Sir Horace.'

'Can you give us a line on his tastes?' said Chrystal.

'We noticed last time that he took an intelligent interest in his dinner,' said Brown. 'We thought you might have picked up some points that we missed.'

They were competent and thorough. They took as much trouble over putting up Sir Horace as over the campaign for the Mastership. No detail was too trivial for them to attend to. I could not help at all: anything I could have told them they had docketed and acted on already. Chrystal asked me to have Sir Horace to breakfast on the Wednesday morning.

'He'll have got tired of our faces by then,' he said. 'I want him to feel he's moving about without us following him.' He gave his tough smile. 'But I don't intend him to get into the wrong hands.'

'Winslow was asking,' said Brown, 'whether Sir Horace was down for any particular purpose. And if not why we should upset the seating arrangements for the feast. He wondered whether we had mistaken Sir Horace for a person of distinction.'

'Winslow is *amusing*,' said Chrystal. He made the word sound sinister. 'Anyway,' he added, 'things are pretty well tied up for Sir Horace now.'

'If we get him down, that is,' said Brown. 'There are forty-eight hours before Tuesday, and the last I heard from the Lodge wasn't very reassuring.'

I told them what Joan had said that afternoon.

'I'm not ready to say we've got Sir Horace down here,' said Brown, 'until I see the feast begin and him sitting at table.'

'It's lamentable,' said Chrystal.

There was a rap on the door. With surprise I saw Nightingale come in. He was looking harassed, pale and intent. In a strained effort to keep the proprieties, he said goodnight to me, and asked if I minded him intruding. Then he addressed himself to Brown.

'I looked in your rooms last night and tonight. You weren't there, so I had to try your friends.'

'Ah well,' said Brown, 'you've found us now.'

'Is it anything private?' I said. 'We can easily leave you together.'

'It may be private,' said Nightingale. 'But it's nothing that Chrystal and you won't know.'

He had sat down, and leant over the arm of his chair towards Brown and Chrystal.

'I want to find out,' he said, 'how the offices will go round, once Jago is Master.'

Chrystal looked at him, and then at Brown. There was a pause.

'Well, Nightingale,' said Chrystal, 'you know as much as we do.'

'No, not quite,' said Nightingale.

'You know as much as we do, Nightingale,' Chrystal repeated. 'The only office that can possibly be affected is a tutorship. You know as well as we do that tutors are appointed by the Master.'

'You're only telling me pieces out of the statutes,' said Nightingale. 'I can read them for myself.'

'I'm telling you the position.'

'I know all about that. Now I want to know how everything has been arranged behind the scenes.' Nightingale smiled, with the dreadful suspiciousness of the unworldly: it is the unworldly who see neat, black, conscious designs hidden under all actions.

'I take you up on that, Nightingale,' said Chrystal, but Brown interrupted him.

'If Jago becomes Master, as we hope, you'll find that he'll have a completely open mind about the appointment. Not a word has been said – either by him or anyone else.'

'That's the fact,' said Chrystal. 'The normal practice is for the Master to ask for advice—'

'I know all about that,' said Nightingale again.

'But he needn't follow it.' Chrystal's temper was very near breaking. 'I've known cases where it wasn't followed. If you're asking me what Jago will do, I can only tell you what I think. It won't take you very far. I assume he will make Brown Senior Tutor. That doesn't need saying. For the other tutor he'll have to look round.'

'No, it doesn't need saying,' said Nightingale, looking at Brown.

'It would be an outrage if it did need saying. Anyone in his senses would offer Brown that job if he had the chance,' I burst out angrily.

For a moment Nightingale was quiet. Then he said:

'I'll take your word for it that the other tutorship isn't earmarked yet. I want you to know that I expect to be considered for it myself.'

We looked at him. He went on:

'I'm a long way senior of all the people without offices in this college. Except for Crawford, who doesn't need them. I've been done out of every office since I was elected. I want to prevent it happening again.'

Brown said, knowing that he had to be soothed:

'I'm sure you can be absolutely certain that Jago will consider you very seriously. Put it another way: your standing in the college means that you're bound to be the first person considered. So now I shouldn't worry if I were you, until the vacancy has really happened.'

'I've been fobbed off like that before,' said Nightingale. 'It's too vague by half.'

'No one can be any more definite,' said Chrystal.

'Is that as much as you can tell me?' Nightingale asked, half-threatening, half-pleading.

'It is,' said Chrystal.

'I don't think anyone could possibly go any further,' said Brown, anxious to conciliate him. 'We couldn't conceivably commit Jago in any shape or form. You must see that that is quite unreasonable. If, when he had to make the appointment, he happened to ask our advice (as I dare say he might feel inclined to do), you can rest assured that we are the last persons to overlook your claim. We can guarantee that you'll receive an absolutely fair hearing.'

'It's not good enough,' said Nightingale.

'I'm sorry,' said Chrystal.

'I'm very sorry indeed,' said Brown. 'We're really going to the extreme limit, you know. I don't quite see what more we can possibly do.'

'I see what I can do.'

'What's that?'

'I shall go and tackle Jago myself,' said Nightingale.

It was late, too late for him to go round that night, I thought with relief, but he left at once.

CHAPTER XIV

COMMEMORATION OF BENEFACTORS

I woke early next morning, and lay listening to the series of quarter chimes, thinking of the alignment in the college. The parties had stayed constant since the two caucus meetings: no one had changed sides, although Francis Getliffe and Winslow had made an attempt to seduce Eustace Pilbrow. That was the only open attempt at persuasion so far made. Roy Calvert and I had wanted to have a go at old Gay, but Brown said wait. Both sides, in fact, were holding back; it was taken for granted that one or two in each caucus were waverers, but it was not yet time to attack them. In secret, Brown felt content because Pilbrow had been approached too early.

But, from the beginning, Nightingale had been our weakest spot. Waiting for Bidwell to announce nine o'clock that morning. I doubted whether we should hold him. How could one handle him in his present state? Last night he had wanted a promise. He would not be satisfied with less.

Looking down into the court after breakfast, I saw Jago walking through. I thought he should be warned at once, and so went down to meet him. I asked if he had seen Nightingale recently. He said no, and asked me why.

'He's coming to see you,' I said.

'What for?'

'He wants you to promise that, when you become Master, you'll offer him the tutorship.'

Jago's face was shadowed with anger: but, before he had done more than curse, we heard a tapping from one of the ground-floor windows. It was Brown beckoning us in.

He was standing in the bedroom of the set which the college used for guests. There was a fire burning in the grate, and he had put some books on the bedside table. One of them was a large history of the college, and another a volume of reminiscences of Cambridge in the eighteenth century.

'What ever are you doing, Brown?' said Jago.

'I'm just seeing that things are ready for Sir Horace tomorrow night.' Jago exclaimed.

'I think it's a mistake to have it too luxurious,' Brown explained. 'People like Sir Horace might get a wrong idea. They might think we weren't completely poverty stricken. So one's got to be careful. But I think there's no harm in seeing that the room is reasonably decent.'

'You oughtn't to be doing it,' said Jago. Angry at the news of Nightingale, his hurt pride broke out here. 'The college oughtn't to be an antiquarian hotel for wealthy men. And I don't like seeing them waited on by their betters.'

'For God's sake don't tell Chrystal that,' Brown said quickly, looking flushed and troubled. 'I don't mind. I'm always ready to accept things. But some people aren't. I don't mind what you think of Sir Horace, though, mark you, I'm quite convinced you're wrong. But, even if you were right, I should be prepared to use the instruments that providence puts in our hands.' He smiled at Jago with concern. 'Oh, by the way, I was going to talk to you this morning about another of those instruments – actually our friend Nightingale.'

'I've just mentioned it,' I said.

'I've never heard of such insolence,' Jago said.

'You must be statesmanlike,' said Brown.

'He's the last person I should think of making tutor.'

'I hope you won't consider it necessary to tell him so,' said Brown.

'I should dearly like to.'

'No. You can be perfectly correct – without giving him the impression that the door is absolutely closed. Remember, indignation is a luxury which we can't afford just at present.'

'We're not all as sensible as you, my dear friend.' But Jago's temper was simmering down, and shortly after he asked us who should be tutor.

'If I am lucky enough to be elected,' he said, 'I think I shall feel obliged to offer it to Getliffe.' Brown did not believe Francis would look at it (Brown was always inclined to see reasons why it was difficult for men to take jobs): he had only taken the stewardship under protest, he was 'snowed under' with his two kinds of research.

'Then it looks,' said Jago, 'as if I should have to come to you, Eliot.'

'I couldn't do it without giving up my work in London,' I said. 'And I can't afford that yet.'

'It's going to be difficult,' said Jago.

'Don't meet trouble half-way,' said Brown, settling down to give a caution. 'We can cross that bridge when we come to it. And I know you won't take it amiss if I say something that's been rather on my mind. It would be quite fatal to give people the impression that the Mastership was a foregone conclusion.'

'I'm sorry. I'll be very careful,' said Jago with an easy, repentant smile.

'And you won't mind my saying one more thing. Will you make sure that everyone connected with you is careful too?'

Jago's smile left him on the instant. He stiffened, and replied with a dignity that was unfriendly, lofty and remote:

'I am already sure of that.'

Soon he went away and Brown gave me a rueful look.

'Confound the woman. We can only hope that he'll talk to her in private. People do make things difficult for themselves. When I talk about the instruments of providence, and then think of Nightingale and that woman, I must say that I sometimes feel we might have had better luck. It's not going to be an easy row to hoe, is it?' He looked round the room again, and marshalled the books in a neat line.

'Ah well,' he said, 'I think I've got things shipshape for Sir Horace. I fancied it might encourage him if he read a bit about the history of the college. Always provided that we get him here. I suppose there's no fresh news from the Lodge this morning?'

There was, in fact, no fresh news that day. On the morning of Tuesday, the day of the feast, we learned that the Master had still not been told. Sir Horace had arrived by car at teatime, Brown told me in the evening, just as I was beginning to dress. 'I think it's all right,' said Brown. 'I think it's reasonably certain now that we shall get safely through the feast.'

He added that Jago had so far contrived to evade Nightingale.

The chapel bell began to peal at a quarter past six. From my window I saw the light over the chapel door bright against the February dusk.

Some of the fellows were already on their way to the service. This was the commemoration of benefactors, and in the thirties the only service in the year to which most of the fellows went.

That change, like many others in the college, had been sharp and yet not paraded. In Gay's young days, the fellows were clergymen who went to chapel as a matter of course; chapel was part of the routine of their lives, very much like hall. Sixty years after, most of the fellows were agnostics of one kind or another. Despard-Smith officiated at the ordinary services in chapel, the Master went regularly, Brown and Chrystal at times. Many of us attended only commemoration. I put a gown over my tail-coat, and went myself that night.

Everyone was there except the doctrinaire unbelievers, Winslow and Francis Getliffe. By Roy Calvert's side stood Luke, who would have liked to keep away and was there simply not to offend. Crawford came in with poised steps, a C.B.E. cross glinting under his white tie. On the coats of several men, when they pulled their gowns aside, glittered medals of the 1914–18 war. It struck me how inexplicable a thing was bravery. Nightingale was wearing a D.S.O. and an M.C. and bar, Pilbrow rows of medals of miscellaneous Balkan wars. They were both brave men, by any human standard. Who would have picked them out for courage, if he did not know the facts?

Brown and Chrystal entered, with Sir Horace Timberlake between them. They had decided it would be pleasant for Sir Horace to hear benefactors commemorated. He was the only man in chapel without a gown; one noticed his well-kept, well-washed, well-fed figure in his evening suit; his face was smooth, fresh, open and he had large blue eyes, which often looked ingenuous; he was older than Chrystal or Jago, but the only line in his face was a crease of fixed attention between his eyes. The chapel was full. Rain pattered against the stained-glass windows, but no radiance came through them at night, they were opaque and closed us in like the panelled walls. On this winter night, as the chapel filled with fellows, scholars and the choir, it contracted into a room small, protecting and confined.

We sang a psalm and a hymn. Gay's sonorous voice range out jubilantly from the backmost stall. Despard-Smith, aged and solemn in his surplice, intoned some prayers in a gloomy voice: and, in a prose version of the same voice, he read the list of benefactors. It was a strange jumble of gifts, going back to the foundation, arranged not in value but in order of receipt. A bequest from the sixth Master to provide five shillings for each fellow at the audit feast was read out at inexorable length, sand-

wiched between a great estate and the patronage of the college's most
valuable living. It was strange to hear those names and to know that some
of the benefactors had listened to the beginning of the higgledy-piggledy
list and had wished their own names to follow. I thought how the sound of
'Next, ——, twelfth Master, who left to the college five hundred pounds,
together with his collection of plate' would affect Jago that night – Jago,
who was sitting there with the threat of Nightingale still on his
mind.

But the only response I actually heard was from Gay, who at the end,
as we went into the ante-chapel, said resoundingly:

'Ah. I congratulate you, Despard. A splendid service, splendid. I
particularly liked that lesson "Let us now praise famous men". Perhaps
we hear slightly too much nowadays about praising the obscure. Often
very fine people in their way, no doubt, but they shouldn't get all the
praise.'

In little groups we hurried through the rain to the combination room.
Some of our guests were already waiting there, and they asked about the
Master, for that news was all round Cambridge. In the gossipy closeness
of the university, other high tables kept hearing on and off about the
progress of the illness and the choice of his successor.

'No change,' said Chrystal sharply to the room. 'They've not told him
yet. They can't avoid it soon.'

The combination room was becoming crowded, and men were pushing
past us, sherry glass in hand, to get a sight of the order of seating. I had
already seen it; it was unfamiliar, simply because Chrystal had insisted
that Sir Horace must sit at the principal table. Winslow had already seen
it also; but he came in late that evening, and studied it again with a sour
face.

Chrystal plucked him by the gown.

'Winslow, may I introduce Sir Horace Timberlake?'

'If you please. If you please.'

Winslow greeted Sir Horace with his usual sarcastic courtesy. The conversation spurted and floundered. Sir Horace turned uneasily to the
chapel service.

'I was very much impressed by your service, Mr Winslow. There was
nothing showy about it, you know what I mean?'

'Indeed?' said Winslow.

'I thought the chapel was very fine,' Sir Horace persisted. 'It's a very
good bit of eighteenth-century panelling you've got – I suppose it must be
eighteenth-century, mustn't it?'

'I'm sure you're right, Sir Horace,' said Winslow. 'But you're bound to be a far better authority than I am. I've only been inside the chapel to elect masters.'

Immediately after, Winslow asked Sir Horace to excuse him, so that he could join his guest, who had just arrived, together with Pilbrow and his French writer. Sir Horace looked downcast.

Jago did not enter the combination room until just on eight o'clock. Although he had a guest with him, the Master of another college, Nightingale approached him at once. I heard him say: 'I should like a word with you tonight, Jago.' Jago replied, his tone over-friendly, upset, over-considerate:

'I'm extremely sorry. I'm up to the ears with work. I'm completely booked for tonight.' He paused, and I heard him go on unwillingly: 'Perhaps we could fix something for tomorrow?'

CHAPTER XV

NEGOTIATIONS AFTER A FEAST

THE wall lights in the hall were turned off for the feast, and the tables were lit by candles. The candlelight shone on silver salts, candlesticks, great ornamental tankards, and on gold cups and plates, all arranged down the middle of the tables. Silver and gold shone under the flickering light; as one looked above the candlesticks, the linen fold was half in darkness and the roof was lost.

In order to seat Sir Horace as Chrystal insisted, Winslow had been brought down from the high table, and so had Pilbrow and Pilbrow's French writer. I sat opposite Winslow and started to talk across the table to the Frenchman. He was, as it turned out, very disappointing.

I recalled the excitement with which I heard Pilbrow was bringing him, and the cultural snobbery with which we had piqued Chrystal and dismissed Sir Horace. How wrong we were. An evening by Sir Horace's side would have been far more rewarding.

The Frenchman sat stolidly while Pilbrow had a conversational fling. 'Pornograms,' Pilbrow burst out. 'An absolutely essential word – Two meanings. Something written, as in telegram. Something drawn, as in diagram.' The Frenchman was not amused, and went on talking like a passage from one of his own books.

But, if he did not enjoy himself, others made up for it. All through the feast we heard a commentary from Gay, who sat at the end of the high table, not far away from us.

'Oysters? Excellent. You never did relish oysters, did you, Despard? Waiter, bring me Mr Despard-Smith's oysters. Capital, I remember having some particularly succulent oysters in Oxford one night when they happened to be giving me an honorary degree. Do you know, those oysters slipped down just as though they were taking part in the celebration.'

He did not follow our modern fashion in wines. Champagne was served at feasts, but it had become the habit to pass it by and drink the hocks and moselles instead. Not so Gay. 'There's nothing like a glass of champagne on a cold winter night. I've always felt better for a glass of champagne. Ah. Let me see, I've been coming to these feasts now for getting on for sixty years. I'm happy to say I've never missed a feast through illness, and I've always enjoyed my glass of champagne.'

He kept having his glass filled, and addressed not only the end of his own table, but also ours.

'My saga-men never had a meal like this. Grand old Njal never had such a meal. My saga-men never had a glass of champagne. It was a very hard, dark, strenuous life those men lived, and they weren't afraid to meet their fates. Grand chaps they were. I'm glad I've been responsible for making thousands of people realise what grand chaps they were. Why, when I came on the scene, they were almost unknown in this country. And now, if a cultivated man does not know as much about them as he knows about the heroes of the Iliad, he's an ignoramus. You hear that, Despard? You hear that, Eustace? I repeat, he's an ignoramus.'

We sat a long time over the port and claret, the fruit and coffee and cigars. There were no speeches at all. At last – it was nearly half past ten – we moved into the combination room again. Roy Calvert was starting some concealed badinage at the expense of Crawford and Despard-Smith. Like everyone else, he was rosy, bright-eyed and full of well-being. Like everyone except Nightingale, that is: Nightingale had brought no guest, was indifferent to food, and always hated drinking or seeing others drink. He stood in the crush of the combination room, looking strained in the midst of the elation. Winslow came up to Gay, who was making his way slowly – the press of men parted in front of him – to his special chair.

'Ah, Winslow. What a magnificent feast this has been!'

'Are you going to congratulate me on it?' asked Winslow.

'Certainly not,' said Gay. 'You gave up being Steward a great number of years ago. I shall congratulate the man responsible for this excellent feast. Getliffe is our present steward. That's the man. Where is Getliffe? I congratulate him. Splendid work these young scientists do, splendid.'

Chrystal and Brown did not mean to stay long in the combination room: it was time to get down to business. They caught Jago's eye and mine. We said goodbye to our guests, and followed the others and Sir Horace up to Brown's rooms.

'I wonder,' said Brown, after he had established Sir Horace in a chair by the fire, 'if anyone would like a little brandy? I always find it rather settling after a feast.'

When each of us had accepted our drink, Sir Horace began to talk: but he was a long time, a deliberately long time, in getting to the point. First of all, he discussed his 'nephew', as he called young Timberlake, who was actually his second cousin.

'I want to thank all you gentlemen, and particularly Mr Brown, for what you've done for the boy. I'm very grateful for all your care. I know he's not first class academically, and there was a time when it worried me, but now I've realised that he's got other qualities, you know what I mean?'

'I don't think you need worry about him,' said Brown.

'He's an extremely good lad,' said Jago, overdoing it a little. 'Everyone likes him. It's a miracle that he's not hopelessly spoiled.'

'I'm interested to hear you say that,' said Sir Horace. 'I haven't the slightest worry on that account. I've always been certain about his character. I saw that his mother took all the trouble she could about his education in that respect.'

'I'm sure that we all regard him as doing you the greatest credit,' said Brown.

'And speaking with due respect as a stupid sort of person in front of first-class minds, character does count, don't you agree with me?'

'There are times, Sir Horace,' Jago broke out, 'when I think young men like your nephew are our most valuable products. The first-class man can look after himself. But the man of personality who isn't much interested in learning – believe me, they're often the salt of the earth.'

'I'm glad to hear you say that, Dr Jago.'

So it went on. Sir Horace pursued the subjects of his nephew, education, character versus intelligence, the advantages of the late developer, the necessity of a good home background, enthusiastically and exhaustively. Jago was his chief conversational partner, though Brown now and then put in a bland, emollient word. Chrystal tried once or twice to make the conversation more practical.

'I must apologise for the old chap I introduced to you.' said Chrystal.

'Mr Winslow?' said Sir Horace, who did not forget names.

'Yes. He's one of our liabilities. He's impossible. By the way, he's the Bursar, and if he weren't so impossible we should have asked him to meet you. In case we had a chance of continuing where we left off last time.'

'Every organisation has its difficult men, you know,' Sir Horace replied. 'It's just the same in my own organisation. And that's why' – he turned to Jago – 'I do attach the greatest importance to these universities turning out—' Indefatigably he continued to exhaust the subject of education. I wanted to see Brown and Chrystal successful, I wanted to go to bed, but I was also amused. Sir Horace was showing no effects of wine; he was tireless and oblivious of time. He was as much a master of tactics as Brown and Chrystal, and he was used to men trying to pump him for money. It was like him to cloud his manœuvres behind a smoke screen of words, and when he was using this technique he did not much mind what he said. He called it 'thinking aloud'. Often, as was the case that night, he talked a lot of humbug. He was genuinely fond of his nephew, and was himself diffident in societies like the college which he did not know. But his own sons had real ability, and that was what Sir Horace valued. The idea that he had a veneration for stupid men of high character, or thought himself to be anything but intelligent, was absurd – and alone, in cold blood, he knew it was absurd.

Even Jago's vitality was flagging. Brown's eyes were not as bright as usual, Chrystal had fallen silent. The midnight chimes had sounded some time before. In the short lulls between Sir Horace's disquisitions, one heard the rain tapping on the windows. Sir Horace had worn us all down, and went on uninterrupted. Suddenly he asked, quite casually:

'Have you thought any more of expanding your activities?'

'Certainly we have,' said Chrystal, coming alertly to life.

'I think someone suggested – correct me if I'm wrong – that for certain lines of development you might need a little help. I think you suggested that, Mr Chrystal.'

'I did.'

'We can't do anything substantial, placed as we are,' said Brown. 'We can only keep going quietly on.'

'I see that,' Sir Horace reflected. 'If your college is going to make a bigger contribution, it will need some financial help.'

'Exactly,' said Chrystal.

'I think you said, Mr Chrystal, that you needed financial help with no conditions attached to it. So that you could develop along your own lines. Well, I've been turning that over in my mind. I dare say you've thought about it more deeply than I have, but I can't help feeling that some people wouldn't be prepared to exert themselves for you on those terms. You know what I mean? Some people might be inclined to see if financial help could be forthcoming, but would be put off at just making it over to you for general purposes. Do you agree with me? or don't you?'

Brown got in first:

'I'm sure I should be speaking for the college in saying that it would be foolish – it would be worse than that, it would be presumptuous – only to accept money for general purposes. But you see, Sir Horace, we have suffered quite an amount from benefactions which are tied down so much that we can't really use them. We've got the income on £20,000 for scholarships for the sons of Protestant clergymen in Galway. And that's really rather tantalising, you know.'

'I see that,' said Sir Horace again. 'But let me put a point of view some people might take. Some people – and I think I include myself among them – might fancy that institutions like this are always tempted to put too much capital into bricks and mortar, do you know what I mean? We might feel that you didn't need to put up a new building, for instance.'

'It's the go-ahead colleges who are building,' said Chrystal. 'Take some examples. There are two colleges whose reputation is going up while we stay flat—'

Chrystal showed great deference to Sir Horace, a genuine humble deference, but he argued crisply. Just as Sir Horace's tactics formed behind a cloud of vague words, Chrystal's and Brown's were hidden in detail. Sharp, precise, confusing details were their chosen weapon. Complete confidence in the value of the college: their ability to treat Sir Horace as a far more gifted man, but at the same time to rely on the absolute self-confidence of the college as a society: their practice at handling detail so that any course but their own became impossible: those were the means they opposed to Sir Horace's obstinate imagination.

The argument became lively, and we all took a hand. Sir Horace shook his head:

'I'm sorry, Mr Chrystal. For once I don't agree with you.'

'I'm sorry too,' said Chrystal, with a tough, pleasant, almost filial smile.

Sir Horace had guessed completely right. If the college secured a benefaction, Chrystal and Brown were eager to put up a building: they were eager to see the college of their time – *their* college – leave its irremovable mark.

At the beginning Brown had, as he used to say, 'flown a kite' for compromise, and now Chrystal joined him. Clearly, any college would welcome thankfully a benefaction for a special purpose – provided it could be fitted into the general frame. Sir Horace was assenting cordially, his eyes at their most open and naïf. All of a sudden, he looked at Chrystal, and his eyes were not in the least naïf. 'I also shouldn't be very happy about thinking of financial help which might be used to release your ordinary funds for building,' he said in his indefatigable, sustained, rich-sounding, affable voice. 'I can imagine other people taking the same line. They might be able to think out ways of preventing it, don't you agree with me? If people of my way of thinking got together some financial help, I'm inclined to believe it would be for men. This country is short of first-class men.'

'What had you in mind?' asked Brown.

'I'm only thinking aloud, you know what I mean. But it seems to an outsider that you haven't anything like your proper number of fellowships. Particularly on what I might call the side of the future. You haven't anything like enough fellowships for scientists and engineers. And this country is dead unless your kind of institution can bring out the first-rate men. I should like to see you have many more young scientific fellows. I don't mind much what happens to them, so long as they have their chance. They can stay at the university, or we shall be glad to take them in industry. But they are the people you want – I hope you agree with me.'

'That's most interesting,' said Jago.

'I'm afraid you're doubtful, Dr Jago.'

'I'm a little uncertain how much you want to alter us.' Jago was becoming more reserved. 'If you swamped us with scientific fellows – you see, Sir Horace, I'm at a disadvantage, I haven't the faintest idea of the scale of benefaction you think we need.'

'I was only thinking aloud,' said Sir Horace. In all his negotiations, as Chrystal and Brown perfectly understood, an exact figure was the last thing to be mentioned. Sums of money were, so to speak, hidden away behind the talk: partly as though they were improper, partly as though they were magic. 'Imagine though,' Sir Horace went on, 'people of my way of thinking were trying to help the college with – a fairly considerable sum. Do you see what I mean?'

'A fellowship,' said Chrystal briskly, 'costs £20,000.'

'What was that, Mr Chrystal?'

'It needs a capital endowment of £20,000 to pay for a fellowship. If you add on all the perquisites.'

'I fancied that must be about the figure,' said Sir Horace vaguely. 'Imagine that a few people could see their way to providing a few of those units—' His voice trailed off. There was a pause.

'If they were giving them for fellowships in general,' said Chrystal at last, 'it would be perfect. There are no two ways about that. If the fellowships were restricted to science—'

'I am interested to hear what you think, Mr Chrystal.'

'If they were, it might raise difficulties.'

'I don't quite see them.'

'Put it another way,' said Brown. 'On the books, today, Sir Horace, we've got four scientific fellows out of thirteen. I wouldn't maintain that was the right proportion, we should all agree it wasn't enough. But if we changed it drastically at a single stroke, it would alter the place overnight. I should be surprised if you regarded that as statesmanlike.'

'Even the possibility of a benefaction is exciting,' said Jago. 'But I do agree with my colleagues. If the fellowships were limited to one subject, it would change the character of our society.'

'You will have to change the character of your society in twenty years,' said Sir Horace, with a sudden dart of energy and fire. 'History will make you. Life will make you. You won't be able to stop it, Dr Jago, you know what I mean?'

He had heard from the others that Jago was likely to be the next Master, and all the evening had treated him with respect. Sir Horace was charmed, Jago had for him the fascination of the unfamiliar, he wanted to be sure of Jago's unqualified approval. Brown and Chrystal he was more used to, he got on well with them, but they were not foreign, exciting, 'up in the air'.

All of us were waiting for a concrete bargain. Sir Horace, however, was willing to let a talk like this fade inconclusively away. He said:

'Well, I can't tell you how valuable I've found it to have all your opinions. It's most stimulating, I hope you agree with me? It gives us all plenty to think about.'

He relished the power of giving or withholding money. It was always a wrench for him to relinquish it. He liked men waiting on him for a decision. There was sometimes a hidden chuckle beneath the anti-climax. Like Chrystal, he loved the feel of power.

It was after two o'clock, but he returned happily to the talk on education. He had great stamina and no sense of time, and another hour passed before he thought of bed.

CHAPTER XVI

AN HOUR OF PRIDE

When I went into my sitting-room next morning, half-an-hour before my usual time, there was Sir Horace, bright and trim and ready for his breakfast. He had had less than five hours' sleep, but he was as conversational as ever. He referred to our common acquaintances, such as Francis Getliffe's brother; he asked questions about the men he had met the night before. He was much taken with Jago. 'There's an unusual man,' said Sir Horace. 'Anyone could see that in five minutes. Remarkable head he's got. Will he be your next Master?'

'I hope so.'

'Brown and Chrystal want him, don't they?'

I said yes.

'Good chaps, those,' Sir Horace paused. 'If they were in industry, they'd drive a hard bargain.'

I put in the thin edge of a question. But, though he had begun the day so talkative and affable, Sir Horace was no more communicative than the night before. His intention became masked at once in a loquacious stream about how much his nephew owed to Brown's tutoring. 'I want him to get an honours degree. I don't believe these places ought to be open to the comfortably off, unless the comfortably off can profit by them,' said Sir Horace, surprisingly unless one knew his streak of unorganised radicalism. 'I hope you agree with me? If this boy doesn't get his honours degree, I shall cross off the experiment as a failure. But he'd never have touched it if it hadn't been for Brown. I'll tell you frankly, Mr Eliot, there have been times when I wished the boy didn't require so much help on the examination side.'

We had not long finished breakfast when Roy Calvert came in. They had met for a moment after the feast. Sir Horace was automatically cordial. Then he went to the window, and looked out at the court, lit by the mild sunshine of a February morning.

'How peaceful it all is,' Sir Horace observed. 'You don't realise what a temptation it would be to quit the rough-and-tumble and settle down here in peace.'

He smiled with his puzzled, lost, friendly look, and Roy smiled back, his eyes glinting with fun.

'I don't think we do,' said Roy. 'I'll change with you, Sir Horace.'

'You wouldn't get such peace.'

'I don't know. Are some of your colleagues on speaking terms? Ours just manage it. Should you call that specially peaceful?'

Sir Horace laughed uneasily: he was not used to affectionate malice from young men half his age. But he had an eye for quality. Up to that moment he had placed Roy as an ornament and a *flâneur*; now he captured his interest, just as Jago had done. He began asking Roy about his work. He was mystified by most of Roy's explanation, but he felt something here that he had not met. I saw him studying Roy's face when it was not smiling.

Soon he was asking if he could be shown Roy's manuscripts. They went off together, and I did not see them until midday. Then Roy ran up the stairs to say that the 'old boy' was going; he fetched Brown and Chrystal and we all met at the side door of the college, where the car was garaged. The chauffeur had just arrived, and Sir Horace was standing by the car in a tremendous fur coat, looking like a Russian general.

'I'm sorry I've not seen anything of you this morning, Mr Chrystal,' said Sir Horace. 'I've had a very interesting time looking at Mr Calvert's wonderful things. There were several points last night I should like to explore with you again, you know what I mean? I very much hope we shall have the opportunity some time.'

The car drove off, Sir Horace giving cordial waves. As it turned out of sight, Roy Calvert asked:

'Is he going to unbelt?'

'Don't ask me,' said Chrystal. He added loyally: 'Of course, men in his position have to make a hundred decisions a day. I expect he looks on this as very small beer – and just puts it off until he's got important things finished. It's unfortunate for us.'

'I'm not giving up hope yet,' said Brown, robust against disappointment. 'I can't believe he'd lead us up the garden path.'

'It would be funny if he did,' said Roy. 'And took a series of dinners off us. Never getting to the point.'

'I don't call that funny, Calvert,' Chrystal said.

'I believe it may come right,' said Brown. He added, in a hurry: 'Mind you, I shan't feel inclined to celebrate until I see a cheque arrive on the bursary table.' He said aside to Chrystal: 'We've just got to think of ways and means again. I should be in favour of letting him lie fallow for a month or two. In the meantime, we shall have time to consider methods of giving him a gentle prod.'

The sky was cloudless and china-blue, there was scarcely a breath of wind. The sun was just perceptibly warm on the skin, and we thought of taking a turn round the garden before lunch. Roy Calvert and Chrystal went in front. They were talking about investments. Since Roy was the only child of a rich man, Chrystal liked talking to him about money. Brown and I followed on behind. Our way to the garden was overlooked by the windows of the tutor's house, and as we walked I heard my name called in Jago's voice.

I stayed on the path, Brown strolled slowly on. Jago came out from his house – and with him was Nightingale.

'Can you spare us a moment, Eliot?' Jago cried. His tone was apologetic, almost hostile.

'Of course.'

'Nightingale and I have been discussing the future of the college. Naturally, we all think the future of the college depends on the men we attract to college offices.' Jago's words were elaborate, his mouth drawn down, his eyes restless. 'So that we've been speculating a little on which of our colleagues might consider taking various college offices.'

'These things have a way of being settled in advance,' said Nightingale.

'I hope it doesn't embarrass you to mention your own future,' Jago had to go on.

'Not in the slightest,' I said.

'I know it's difficult. No one can pledge themselves too far ahead. But I've just been telling Nightingale that, so far as I know, you wouldn't feel free to think of a college office in the next few years.'

'I shouldn't. I can be ruled out,' I said.

'Why? Why can we rule you out?' Nightingale broke out in suspicion.

I had to give a reason for Jago's sake.

'Because I don't want to break my London connection. I can't spend three days a week in London and hold an office here.'

'Your three days must be exceptionally well paid.' Nightingale smiled.

'It's valuable for the college,' said Jago with an effort to sound undisturbed, 'to have its young lawyers taught by a man with practical experience.'

'It seems to be rather valuable for Eliot.' Nightingale smiled again. But his suspicions had temporarily abated, and he parted from us.

'Good God,' muttered Jago, as Nightingale disappeared at the bottom of his staircase.

'I hope you contained yourself,' said Brown, who had been waiting for us to join him. We all three walked towards the garden.

'I was very tactful,' said Jago. 'I was *despicably* tactful, Brown. Do you know that he doubted my word when I said that Eliot here couldn't take a tutorship if it was offered him? He said he might believe it if he heard it from Eliot himself. I ought to have kicked the man out of my study. Instead of that, I inflicted him on Eliot, so that he could have the satisfaction of hearing it. I am so sorry, Eliot.'

'You had to do it,' I said.

'I call it statesmanlike,' said Brown.

'I call it despicable,' said Jago.

The garden was quiet with winter, the grass shone emerald in the sunlight, the branches of the trees had not yet begun to thicken. In the wash of greens and sepias and browns stood one blaze of gold from a forsythia bush. Roy and Chrystal were standing under a great beech, just where the garden curved away to hide the inner 'wilderness'.

'God forgive me,' said Jago bitterly, as we stepped on to the soft lawn. 'I've never prevaricated so shamefully. The man asked me outright what my intentions were. I replied – yes, I'll tell you what I replied – I told him that it might put us both in a false position if I gave a definite answer. But I said that none of those I knew best in the college could possibly take a tutorship. That's where your name came in, Eliot. He insisted on discussing you all one by one.'

'I hope you let him,' said Brown.

'I let him.'

'I hope you didn't give him the impression that you'd never offer him the job,' said Brown.

'I should be less ashamed,' said Jago, 'if I could think I had.'

Jago was angry and anxious. He was angry at what he had been forced to do: anxious that it might not be enough. But, most of all that morning in the sunny garden, he was angry, bitterly angry, at the insult to his pride. He had lowered himself, he had thrown his pride in front of his own eyes and this other man's, and now, ten minutes later, it had arisen and was dominating him. He was furious at the humiliation which policy imposed: was this where ambition had pushed him? was this the result of his passion? was this the degradation which he had to take?

Brown would not have minded. A less proud man would have accepted it as part of the game: knowing it, Jago looked at his supporter's kind, shrewd and worldly face, and felt alone. The shame was his alone, the wound was his alone. When he next spoke, he was drawn into himself, he was speaking from a height.

'I assure you, Brown, I don't think you need fear a defection,' he said, with a mixture of anxiety, self-contempt, and scorn. 'I handled him pretty well. I was as tactful as a man could be.'

CHAPTER XVII

'WE'RE ALL ALONE'

AFTER lunch that day Roy Calvert stopped me in the court. His lips twitched in a smile.

'Everyone was worried whether we should have the feast, weren't they?' he said.

'Yes.'

'Just so. Well, I heard a minute ago that it wasn't necessary. Joan and her mother never intended to tell him before the feast. They'd marked down the date weeks ago. They knew the old boy was coming down to unbelt – which he didn't – and they decided that we mustn't be disturbed. Isn't that just like the appalling sense of women?'

I could not help laughing.

'We've been sold,' said Roy. 'Not only you and me – but all those sensible blokes. We've been absolutely and completely and magnificently sold.'

But, though he was smiling, he was already sad, for he had guessed what was to happen that day. I did not see him again all afternoon and evening. His name was on the dining list for hall, but he did not come. Late at night, he entered my room and told me that he had been with Lady Muriel for hours. She had broken the news to the Master early in the afternoon.

I was distressed not only on their account, but on Roy's. He was beginning to have the look and manner which came upon him during a wave of depression. And I was not reassured when, instead of telling me anything that had been said in the Lodge, he insisted on going to a party. For, as he and I knew too well, the manic-depressive moods sent out their signals. I was more afraid for him in a state of false hilarity than in sadness.

However, he was genial at the party, although he did not speak of the Master until we had returned to college and were standing in sight of the Lodge windows. It was well into the small hours, but one light was still shining.

'I wonder,' Roy said, 'if he can sleep tonight.'

We stood looking at the window. The court was quiet beneath the stars.

Roy said:

'I've never seen such human misery and loneliness as I did today.'

Beside the fire in his sitting-room, he went on telling of the Master and Lady Muriel, and he spoke with the special insight of grief. Theirs had not been a joyous marriage. The Master might have brought happiness to many women, Roy said, but somehow he had never set her free. As for her, there was a terrible story that, when the Master was engaged to her, an aunt of hers said to him: 'I warn you, she has no tenderness.' That showed what her façade was like, and yet, Roy had told me and I believed him, it was the opposite of the truth. Perhaps few husbands could have called her tenderness to the surface, and that the Master had never done. She had given him children, they had struggled on for twenty-five years. 'She's never had any idea what he's really like,' said Roy. 'Poor dear, she's always been puzzled by his jokes.'

Yet they had trusted each other; and so, that afternoon, it was her task to tell him that he was going to die. Roy was certain that she had screwed herself up and gone straight to the point. 'She's always known that she's failed him. Now she felt she was failing him worst of all. Because anyone else would have known what to say, and she's never been able to put one word in front of another.'

Occasionally we had imagined that the Master saw through the deception, but it was not true. The news came as a total shock. He did not reproach her. She could not remember what he said, but it was very little.

'It's hard to think without a future.' That was one of the only remarks she could recall.

But the hardest blow for her was that, in looking towards his death, he seemed to have forgotten her. 'I was less use than ever,' Lady Muriel had cried to Roy.

It was that cry which had seared Roy with the spectacle of human egotism and loneliness. They had lived their lives together. She had to tell him this news. She saw him thinking only of his death – and she could not reach him. It did not matter whether she was there or not.

After she had gone out, and Joan had visited him for a few minutes, he had asked to be left to himself.

Roy said:

'We're all alone, aren't we? Each one of us. Quite alone.'

Later, he asked:

'If she was miserable and lonely today, what was it like to be him? Can anyone imagine what it's like to know your death is *fixed*?'

CHAPTER XVIII

RESULT OF AN ANXIETY

AFTER his demand on Jago, Nightingale seemed to be satisfied or to have lost interest. Brown's explanation was that he was enough open to reason to realise that he could go no further; for his own practical ends, it was sensible to stop. Brown did not let us forget Nightingale's practical ends: 'He may be unbalanced,' said Brown, 'he may be driven by impulses which I am sure you understand better than I do, but somehow he manages to give them a direction. And that concerns me most. He wants some very practical things, and he's going to be a confounded nuisance.'

That was entirely true. I learned a lot about men in action, I learned something of when to control a psychological imagination, from Arthur Brown. But it was also true that Nightingale was right in the middle of one of those states of anxiety which is like a vacuum in the mind: it fills itself with one worry, such as the tutorship; that is worried round, examined, explored, acted upon, for the time being satisfied: the vacuum is left, and fills immediately with a new worry. In this case it was the March recommendations of the council of the Royal Society: would he get in at last? would his deepest hope come off?

This anxiety came to Nightingale each spring. It was the most painful of all. And it seemed sharper because, unlike his worry over the tutorship, there was nothing he could do to satisfy himself. He could only wait.

Crawford had just been put on the council of the Royal Society for the second time, owing to someone dying. Crawford told us this news himself, with his usual imperturbability. Nightingale heard him with his forehead corrugated, but he could not resist asking:

'Do you know when the results will be out?'

Crawford looked at his pocket-book.

'The council will make its recommendations on Thursday March——'. He told Nightingale the date. 'Of course, they're not public for a couple of months after. Is there anyone you're interested in?'

'Yes.'

The intense answer got through even to Crawford.

'You're not up yourself, are you?'

'Yes.'

'I'm afraid I didn't realise it,' said Crawford, making an unconcerned apology. 'Of course your subject is a long way from mine. I don't think I've heard anything about the chemists' list. If I did, I'm afraid I paid no attention. If I knew anything definite, I should be tempted to tell you. I'm not a believer in unnecessary secrecy.'

Francis Getliffe had been listening to the conversation, and we went out of the room together. As the door closed behind us, he said:

'I wish someone would put Nightingale out of his misery.'

'Do you know the result?'

'I've heard the lists. He's not in, of course. But the point is, he's never even thought of. He never will get in,' said Francis.

'I doubt if anyone could tell him,' I said.

'No,' said Francis.

'When are you going to get in yourself, by the way?' I asked, forgetting our opposition, as though our ease had returned.

'I shan't let myself be put up until I stand a good chance. I mean, until I'm certain they'll take me within three or four years. I'm not inclined to go up on the off-chance.'

'Does that mean the first shot next year?'

'I'd hoped so. I'd hoped that, if I was put up next year, I was bound to be elected by 1942. But things haven't gone as fast as they should,' he said with painful honesty.

'You've been unlucky, haven't you?'

'A bit,' said Francis. 'I might have had a shade more notice. But that isn't the whole truth. I haven't done as much as I ought.'

'There's plenty of time,' I said.

'There's got to be time,' said Francis.

None of us, I thought, was as just as he was, or made such demands on his will.

About three weeks later, as I went into the porter's lodge one day after lunch, I heard Nightingale giving instructions. A special note in his tone caught my attention: it occurred to me that it must be the day of the

Royal results. 'If a telegram comes for me this afternoon,' he repeated, 'I want the boy sent to my rooms without a minute's delay. I shall be in till hall. Have you got that? I don't want a minute's delay.'

The afternoon was harshly cold; the false spring of February had disappeared, and before teatime it was dark, the sky overhung with inky clouds. I stayed by my fire reading, and then sent for tea before a pupil arrived. As I waited for the kitchen porter, I stood looking out of the window into the court. A few flakes of snow were falling. Some undergraduates came clanking through in football boots, their knees a livid purple, their breath steaming in the bitter air. Then I saw Nightingale walking towards the porter's lodge. The young men were shouting heartily: Nightingale went past them as though they did not exist.

In a moment, he was on his way back. He had found no telegram. He was walking quite slowly: the cold did not touch him.

In hall that night his face was dead white and so strained that the lines seemed rigid, part of the structure of his brow. Every few seconds he put a hand to the back of his head, and the tic began to fascinate Luke, who was sitting next to him. Several times Luke looked at the pale, grim, harassed face, started to speak, and then thought better of it. At last his curiosity was too strong, and he said:

'Are you all right, Nightingale?'

'What do you mean, all right?' Nightingale replied. 'Of course I'm all right. What do you think you're talking about?'

Luke blushed, but would not be shouted down.

'I thought you might have been overworking. You were looking pretty tired—'

'Overworking,' Nightingale said. 'I suppose you think that's the worst thing that can happen.'

Luke shrugged his shoulders, muttered a curse under his breath and caught my eye. He had a rueful, self-mocking sense of humour; his work was in a hopeful phase, and he lived at the laboratory from nine in the morning until it closed at night. It was hard to have his head bitten off for laziness.

We were already through the soup and fish when Crawford came into hall. He slipped into the seat next mine, but before he sat down called up the table to Winslow:

'My apologies for being late. I've had to attend the council of the Royal. And this weather wasn't very good for the train.'

He ate his way methodically through the first courses and had caught us up at the sweet. All the time Nightingale's eyes were fixed on him with a last desperate question of anxiety. But Crawford was untroubled and, having levelled up in eating, talked reflectively to me. It was like him that his conversation did not alter with the person he was addressing; if there was anything he wanted to deliver, I served to receive it as well as Francis Getliffe.

'Selecting people for honorific purposes is a very interesting job. But it's not as easy as you might suppose. As a matter of fact, I was thinking of the choice of Fellows of the Royal – which I happen just to have been concerned with. Speaking as a man of science, I should be happier if there were sharper criteria to help us make the choice. I'm not meaning the choice is made unfairly: no, I should say that on the conscious level they're as fair as human choices can be. But the criteria are not sharp, and it's no use pretending they can be. "Original work of distinction" – how can you compare one man with a new theory on the interior of the stars with someone else who has painstakingly measured the movements of a fish?'

The rest had finished the meal, Winslow was waiting to say grace, but Crawford finished saying what he had to say. On our way into the combination room, he suddenly noticed Nightingale, and called out:

'Oh, Nightingale. Just a minute.'

We passed on, leaving the two of them together. But we heard Crawford's audible, impersonally friendly voice saying:

'No luck for you this time.'

They followed us at once. Most of those dining went away without sitting down to wine, but Crawford said that he had had a busy day and needed a glass of port. So Winslow and I shared a bottle with him, and listened to his views on the organisation of science, the place of the Royal Society, the revolution in scientific technology. Nightingale attended to every word.

Crawford enjoyed talking; some were put off by his manner and could not bear to listen, but they lost something. He had not the acute penetrating intellect of Roy Calvert; in an intelligence test he would not have come out as high as, say, the Master or Winslow; and he had no human insight at all. But he had a broad, strong, powerful ,mind, not specially apt for entertaining but made to wear.

Nightingale sat outside the little circle of three round which the bottle passed. Since he learned the news, his expression was still taut with strain, but his eyes had become bright and fierce. There was nothing crushed about him; his whole manner was active, harsh, and determined as he listened to Crawford. He listened without speaking. He did not once give his envious smile. But, once as I watched him, his eyes left Crawford for an instant and stared inimically at mine. They were fever-ishly bright.

When I went away, the three of them were still at the table, and Craw-ford and Winslow were emptying the bottle.

The next evening, half an hour before dinner, I heard Francis Getliffe's firm, plunging, heavy step on the stairs. He used to call in often on his way to hall, but he had not done so since our quarrel.

'Busy?' he said.

'No.'

'Good work.' He sat in the armchair across the fire, took a cigarette, cleared his throat. He was uncomfortable and constrained, but he was looking at me with mastery.

'Look, Lewis, I think it's better for me to tell you,' he said. 'Your majority for Jago has been broken.'

He was triumphant, he enjoyed telling me – yet he felt a streak of friendly pity.

'Who's gone over?' I said, but I did not need to ask.

'Nightingale. He told Crawford himself last night. Winslow was there too.'

I blamed myself for having left them together, with Nightingale in that condition. Then I thought that was not realistic: it could have made no difference. And I did not want to show concern in front of Francis.

'If it weren't for the vote, which is a nuisance,' I said, 'I should wish you joy of him.'

Francis gave a grim smile.

'That makes it 6–5. Neither side has a clear majority. I hadn't reckoned on that. I don't know whether you had.'

CHAPTER XIX

'A NICE LITTLE PARTY'

As soon as Francis left me, I rang up Brown. He said that he was kept by a pupil, but would get rid of him and come. The moment he entered, I told him the news.

'So that's it,' said Brown. He accepted it at once.

'Things happen as they must,' he added in a round, matter-of-fact tone. 'They've gone pretty smoothly for us so far. We've got to be ready for our setbacks. I don't say this isn't a confounded nuisance, because it obviously is. Still, repining won't get us anywhere, and there's plenty to do if we're going to retrieve the position.'

'I shall be astonished,' I said, 'if Nightingale changes sides again.'

'I expect you're right,' said Brown. 'But we have other people to look after too, you know. Mind you,' he went on, with a trace of irritation, 'I always thought we handled Nightingale badly. We ought to have taken him round to Jago's that first afternoon. It would have been well worth waiting for him. I was wrong not to stick in my heels.'

But Brown did not spend much time blaming Chrystal or himself. He was thinking realistically of what it meant. 6–5 now. For Crawford – Winslow, Despard-Smith, Getliffe, Gay and Nightingale. For Jago – Brown, Chrystal, Calvert, Eliot, Pilbrow and Luke. 'It's bad to lose a clear majority. It affects your own party,' Brown reflected. 'Just at the moment, I should guess they're more confident than we are. We must take care that a rot doesn't set in.'

'Shall you do anything tonight?'

'No,' said Brown. 'We've got to wait. We needn't tell Jago yet. There's no point in worrying him unnecessarily. You see, we've only learned this from the other side. It explains a dig Winslow gave Chrystal today, by the way. But we shall be well advised not to take any action until we hear from Nightingale himself. Remember, he's always tried to do the proper thing, and he's bound to let Jago know. A decent man couldn't just cross over without sending some sort of explanation. And there's always the bare chance that he may think better of it.'

For once, Brown's patience guided him wrong. Gossip was going round the college that night and next morning; apparently Nightingale had already spoken with venom against Jago and 'his clique'. Jago had heard nothing of it, but I received accounts from several sources, differing a good deal from one another. Brown spoke to Chrystal, went back on his tactics laid down the previous night, and decided it was time to 'have it out'. They were planning to get Nightingale alone after hall, as though by chance. As it happened, Saturday, that very night, was made for their purpose. The number of men dining varied regularly with the days of the week; Sunday was always a full night – 'married men escaping the cold supper at home', old Despard-Smith used to complain. Saturday, on the other hand, was a sparse one, usually only attended by bachelors living in college. That particular Saturday happened to be specially sparse, for Despard-Smith had a cold, and there was a concert in the town which removed Pilbrow and also Roy Calvert, who was escorting Mrs Jago. Chrystal and Brown put their names down to dine that night, and there arrived in hall only the three of us, Nightingale and Luke.

Nightingale was silent during dinner. Brown kept up a stream of comfortable, unexacting conversation, but all the time, through the amiable remarks on college games, his glance was constantly coming back to Nightingale's defensive mask.

'How long is it since you saw the Lent races, Nightingale?' Chrystal asked.

'I haven't time for anything like that,' said Nightingale. They were his first words since we sat down.

'You'll make yourself ill,' said Chrystal, with genuine sympathy. 'Come on the towpath with me next week. It will do you good.'

'I can look after myself,' said Nightingale. Up to that night, he had held on to his politeness, but now it slipped away.

'I've heard that before,' said Chrystal. 'Listen to me for once.'

Nightingale's eyes were blank, as he sat there, exposed to Chrystal's crisp voice and Brown's rich, placid one: he knew what to expect.

Luke left immediately after hall. His work was occupying him more than ever, and he said that he had to work out some results. Whether or not it was because of his cautious tact I did not know. Brown said:

'Well, that does make us a nice little party.'

He ordered a bottle of claret and took his place at the head of the table. Nightingale was still standing up. He started to move towards the door. He was leaving, without saying goodnight. We were exchanging glances: suddenly he looked back at us. He turned round, retraced his steps, sat down defiantly at Brown's right hand. There was something formidable about him at that moment.

The decanter went round, and Brown warmed his glass in his hands.

'Has Jago been dining recently? I haven't seen him all the week,' Brown asked casually.

'He's not been here any of the nights I have,' I said.

'I've only dined once this week,' said Chrystal. 'He wasn't here.'

Nightingale stirred his coffee, and did not reply.

'Has he coincided with you, Nightingale?' Brown asked.

'No.'

'That reminds, me,' said Brown in the same conversational tone. 'I've been meaning to ask you for some time. How are you feeling about the Mastership now?'

'How are you?' Nightingale retorted.

'I'm still exactly where I was,' said Brown. 'I'm quite happy to go on supporting Jago.'

'Are you?' Nightingale asked.

'Why,' said Brown, 'I hope you haven't had any second thoughts. At least, not enough to upset your commitments—'

'Commitments!' Nightingale broke out. 'I'm not going to be bound because I made a fool of myself. I can tell you, here and now, I've thought better of it.'

'I'm very sorry to hear it,' said Brown. 'But perhaps we—'

'And I can tell you I've good reasons to think better of it. I'm glad I had my eyes opened before I'd done the damage. Do you think I'm going to vote for a man who's taking it for granted that he's been elected and is behaving like the Master before the present one is dead? And whose wife is putting on airs about it already?' He stopped, and asked more virulently: 'Do you think I'm going to put up with a Master who's backed by people who are getting the college a bad name—?'

'Who do you mean?' I was infuriated.

'I mean your friend Calvert, for one.'

'Anything you say about him is worthless,' I said.

'There are one or two others,' said Nightingale, 'who live apart from their wives. It's not for me to say whether they want to keep their liberty of action—'

'Stop that,' said Chrystal, before I could reply. 'You're going too far. I won't have any more of it, do you hear?'

Nightingale sank back, white-faced. 'I'm glad I've explained to you my reasons for changing,' he said.

What were his true motives, I thought, as I stared at him through my own anger. He was possessed by envy and frustration. Crawford talking unconcernedly of the 'Royal', making it sound like a club to which one belonged as a matter of course, turned the knife in the wound as if Nightingale were jealous in love and had just heard his rival's name. So did Chrystal and Brown, looking happy and prosperous in their jobs, going about to run the college. So did the sound of Mrs Jago's voice, asking the number of bedrooms in the Lodge or the kind of entertainment that undergraduates preferred. So did the sight of Roy Calvert with a girl. And Nightingale suffered. He did not suffer with nobility, he did not accept it in the grand manner, which, though it does not soften suffering, helps to make the thought of it endurable when the victim is having a respite from pain. Nightingale suffered meanly, determined to wound as well as be wounded. There was no detachment from his pain, not a glimmer of irony. He bared his teeth, and felt release through planning a revenge against someone who 'persecuted' him. He never felt for a day together serene, free and confident.

I could understand his suffering. One could not miss it, for it was written in his face. I was not moved by it, for I was cut off by dislike. But I could understand how he struggled with all his force, and went into action, as he was doing now, with the intensity of a single-minded drive. He had the canalised strength of the obsessed.

I could not begin to know why his envy had driven him first away from Crawford, now back to him. Had he, that night of the Royal results, found in Crawford's assurance some sort of rest? Did he feel that, by propinquity, some share of it might get transferred to him?

I could not see so far. But I was sure that, as Arthur Brown would remind me, there was a kind of practical veneer on his actions now. When he thought of what he was doing, he gave practical self-seeking reasons to himself. He probably imagined that Crawford would help get him into the Royal next year. He had certainly decided that Jago would not give him the tutorship, would do nothing for him. His calculation about Crawford was, of course, quite ridiculous. Crawford, impersonal even to his friends, would be the last man to think of helping, even if help were possible. Nevertheless, Nightingale was certain that he was being shrewd.

Chrystal was saying:

'You ought to have told us you were going over.'

'Ought I?'

'You owed it to us to tell us first,' said Chrystal.

'I don't see why.'

'I take you up on that, Nightingale. You can't pledge yourself to one candidate and then promise to vote for another. It's not the way things are done.'

'If I stick to the etiquette, no one else does. I'm not going to penalise myself any more,' said Nightingale.

'It's not the way to do business.'

'I leave business to your clique,' Nightingale replied. He rose and, without saying goodnight, went towards the door. This time he did not turn back.

'That's that,' said Chrystal. 'I don't know what's happening to Nightingale.'

'Well, there it is,' said Brown.

'Shall we get him back?' Chrystal asked.

'Not a hope in hell,' I said.

'Why are you so sure?'

'I must say,' said Brown, 'that I'm inclined to take Eliot's view. It's much safer to regard the worst as inevitable, because then it won't do us any harm if we turn out to be wrong. But that apart, I confess I shall be surprised if we see Nightingale back again.'

'You may be right,' said Chrystal.

'I haven't a doubt,' I said.

'Have you summed him up right?' asked Chrystal, still wanting to disbelieve.

'I'm ready to rely on Eliot's judgment,' said Brown.

'In that case,' said Chrystal, changing round briskly, 'we ought to see Jago at once.'

'Do you want to?' For once Brown shrank from a task.

'No. But we can't leave him in the dark.'

'I suppose it would be rather tempting providence—'

'If we don't tell him tonight,' said Chrystal, 'some kind friend will do him the service tomorrow or next day. It's lamentable, but it will come better from us.'

'I must say that it's going to be abominably unpleasant.'

'I'll go by myself,' said Chrystal. 'If you prefer that.'

'Thank you,' Brown hesitated. 'No, it will be better for him if we all go. It will let him realise that he's still got most of his party intact.'

Brown and I wanted an excuse for delaying, even if only for ten more minutes, in the combination room. It was Chrystal, buoyed up by action, never despondent when he could get on the move, who forced us out.

CHAPTER XX

THE DEPTH OF AMBITION

As we already knew, Jago was alone. We found him in his study reading. His eyes flashed as soon as he saw us; every nerve was alert; he welcomed us with over-abundant warmth. Chrystal cut him short by saying:

'We've got some bad news for you.'

His face was open in front of us.

'You must be prepared for changes to happen both ways,' said Brown, trying to cushion the blow. 'This isn't the last disturbance we shall get.'

'What is it? Jago cried. 'What is it?'

'Nightingale has gone over,' said Chrystal.

'I see.'

'You mustn't let it depress you too much,' Brown said. 'It was always a surprise to me that you ever attracted Nightingale at all. Put it another way: you can regard Nightingale as being in his natural place now, and you can think of the sides being linked up very much as we might have expected beforehand.'

Jago did not seem to hear the attempt to comfort him.

'I suppose he's done it because I didn't promise him the tutorship. I couldn't. It was a wretched position to be flung into. It was utterly impossible. I suppose it's too late to mend matters now. It's difficult to make a move—'

Brown was looking at him with an anxious glance.

'Forget Nightingale,' Brown broke in very quickly. 'Count him out.'

'If I'd offered him the tutorship it would have held him.' There was a passionate appeal in Jago's voice.

'I doubt it very much,' I said.

'If I could only have made something like a promise.'

'Jago,' said Chrystal, 'if you had promised that man the tutorship, you might have gained one vote – but you would have lost six others. So you can rest easy.'

'Are we letting him go without an effort?' cried Jago. 'Is it utterly impossible to persuade him back?'

'We think so,' said Chrystal.

Jago's whole expression was racked.

'*Shall I see him?*' he said.

'No,' said Chrystal.

'I don't think it would help much.' Brown's tone was as firm as Chrystal's, though he went on with a friendly explanation: 'He's an obstinate man. It might only carry things from bad to worse. There's no one so bitter as a turncoat, you know. I think it's very much safer to regard him as an enemy from now on.'

'If you don't,' said Chrystal, 'I can't answer for the consequences.'

He and Brown looked solid, earthy men of flesh and bone against Jago at that moment. Jago's face seemed only a film in front of the tortured nerves. They were telling him, as each of us in the room perfectly understood without a definite word being spoken, that he must make no attempt – by any suggestion of a promise – to bring Nightingale back.

He had wanted us to encourage him by a hint: he had been appealing for a piece of machiavellian advice 'you oughtn't to make Nightingale a promise: but there's no harm in his thinking you have done so: he'll be disappointed later, that's all'. If we had given him the most concealed of hints, he would have rushed to Nightingale, used every charm of which he was capable, safeguarded himself verbally perhaps but in no other way. If he could have made a bargain with Nightingale, whatever it meant letting Nightingale think he had been promised, he would have made it that night. It needed Chrystal's threat to stop him at last.

Just as he had been more angry than the others at Nightingale's first approach, now he was tempted to stoop lower than they would ever do. In the garden, on the February morning when Nightingale asked for the tutorship, he thought with disgusted pride – was this how ambition soils one? But that was when his ambition seemed still in his hands.

He heard Chrystal's threat. He looked at the firm, uncompromising face. Then at mine. Then, for a longer time, at Arthur Brown's, distressed, kindly, but unwavering.

Suddenly Jago's own face changed. He was thinking of himself without mercy. He was sickened by the temptation.

'Shall I withdraw from the election?' he asked with a kind of broken dignity.

Brown smiled in affectionate relief, and showed the depth of his relief by an outburst of scolding.

'You mustn't swing from one extreme to the other. We've still got an excellent chance. We've lost your most unreliable supporter, that's all. You're still in the lead. You must keep a sense of proportion.'

'I agree with Brown,' said Chrystal. His tone was not so warm as Brown's, but toughly reassuring. Jago smiled at us, a smile without defence.

'We shall have to reconsider some of our dispositions,' said Brown. 'You needn't worry, you can leave the staff work to us. The other side have got weak spots too, Eliot and Calvert have wanted to tap them, but I think Eliot agrees that it's still premature. The great thing at present is to take good care not to have any more confounded defections. I don't know whether you others agree with me, but I should say there was just one more vulnerable spot in our party.'

'I take it you mean old Eustace Pilbrow,' said Jago.

'He's a danger,' said Chrystal. 'He's always being got at by some crank or other.'

'He turned Winslow and Getliffe down when they spread themselves to persuade him,' Brown said. 'I believe we can keep him steady. He's very fond of you, providentially.'

'I can never quite believe it,' Jago replied. 'But—'

Chrystal broke in:

'When I look round, he seems to me the only weak spot. The rest are safe.'

Jago said:

'I believe you three are safe because you know the worst about me. If any of you left me now, I shouldn't only lose the Mastership. I should lose the confidence you've given me.'

Chrystal repeated: 'The rest are safe. There's no other weak spot. They'll never break five of your votes. You can bank on them.'

Jago smiled.

'Well,' said Brown, 'the essential thing for the present is to make sure of Pilbrow. If we hold him, we can't lose. Six votes for you means that they can't get a majority, since Crawford is fortunately debarred from voting for himself. Though I confess I feel uncharitable enough to think that he would consider it a reasonable action. And that reminds me that you and Crawford will soon have to settle how you're going to dispose of your own votes. They may be significant.'

'They're certain to be, now,' said Chrystal.

'Crawford sent a note this very day suggesting a talk. I was mystified—'

'The other side have got on to it too. They must have realised how much his vote and yours mean' – Brown was bright-eyed with vigilance – 'as soon as this confounded man told them he was ratting.'

'I'm compelled to discuss it if he wishes to,' said Jago. 'I can't decently do less than that.'

'But go carefully whatever you do. Examine any proposal he puts forward. It may seem harmless, but it's wiser not to commit yourself at once. Whatever you do, don't say yes on the spot.' Brown was settling down to an exhaustive, enjoyable warning: then his expression became more brooding.

'There's something else you ought to guard against.' He hesitated, Jago did not speak, and sat with his head averted. Brown went on, speaking slowly and with difficulty:

'We shouldn't be reliable supporters or friends unless we asked you to guard against something which might damage your prospects irretrievably. Put it another way: it has helped to lose us Nightingale, and unless you stop it, it might do you more harm than that.'

Jago still did not speak.

Brown continued:

'I know we didn't manage Nightingale very cleverly, any of us. We've made him angry between us. And one mistake we fell into that infuriated him was – I gave you a hint before – he thought some of us were acting as though you had the Mastership in your pocket. That's bound to be dangerous. I don't like doing it, but I'm compelled to warn you again.' He hesitated for some moments, then said: 'There seem to have been some women talking over the teacups.'

Brown was embarrassed but determined and intent. He looked at Jago, whose head had stayed bent down. Brown remembered that morning when, at a hint far slighter than this, Jago had drawn himself aloof and answered with a hostile snub. It had taken all Brown's stubborn affection to try again – and to try after what had already happened on this night.

'I am grateful for your friendship,' said Jago without looking up. 'I will accept your advice so far as I can.'

Suddenly he glanced at Brown, his eyes lit up.

'I want to ask one thing of my friends,' he said quietly. 'I trust you to take care that not a sign of these strictures reaches my wife. She would be more distressed than I could bear.'

'Will you have a word with her yourself?' Brown persisted.

I thought Jago was not going to reply. At last he said:

'If I can do it without hurting her.'

We were all quiet. None of us, not even Brown, dared to say more. Not even Brown could speak to him in this way again.

Soon afterwards, Mrs Jago came in from the concert, with Roy Calvert attending her. She was happier than I had ever seen her. She had been exalted by the music, she had been mixing with fashionable Cambridge and people had talked to her kindly, she had been seen in the company of one of the most sought-after young men in the town.

She flirted with Roy, looking up at him as he stood by her chair with his heels on the fender.

'Think of all the young women you might have taken out tonight.'

'Women are boring when they're too young,' said Roy.

'We should all like to believe that was true,' she said.

'You all know it's true,' he said. 'Confess.'

His tone was playful, half-kind, half-gallant, and, just for a moment, she was basking in confidence. She neither asserted herself nor shrieked out apologies. A quality, vivacious, naïve, delicate, scintillated in her, as though it were there by nature. Perhaps it was the quality which Jago saw when she was a girl.

It was a strange spectacle, her sitting happily near to Roy. Her black evening dress made her look no slighter, and her solid back loomed out of her chair: while Roy stood beside her, his shoulders pressed against the mantelpiece, his toes on the carpet, his figure cleanly arched.

She smiled at her husband.

'I'm positive you haven't had such a perfect evening,' she said.

'Not quite,' said Jago, smiling fondly back.

CHAPTER XXI

PROPAGANDA

SINCE Lady Muriel broke the news, the Master had wished to see none of his friends, except Roy. But towards the end of term, he began to ask us one by one to visit him. The curious thing was, he was asking us to visit him not for his own sake, but for ours. 'I don't think,' Roy said sadly, 'he wants to see anyone at all. He's just asking out of consideration for our feelings. He's becoming very kind.' He knew that we should be hurt if he seemed indifferent to our company. So he put up with it. It was a sign of the supreme consideration which filled him as his life was ending.

It was strange to go into his bedroom, and meet the selflessness of this dying man. It was stranger still to leave him, and return into the rancour of the college.

For Nightingale had already become a focus of hate, and had started a campaign against Jago. It was a campaign of propaganda, concentrated with all his animosity and force. He was devoting himself to finding usable facts; and each night, unless one of Jago's active friends was near, he would grind them out.

The sneers did not aim at Jago himself, but at those around him. First his wife. Nightingale brought out, night after night, stories of her assuming that the Lodge was already hers: how she had inquired after eighteenth-century furniture, to suit the drawing-room: how she had called for pity because she did not know where they were going to find more servants. He jeered at her accent and her social origin: 'the suburbs of Birmingham will be a comedown after Lady Muriel'.

That particular gibe made Brown very angry, but probably, both he and I agreed, did little harm.

Others were more insidious. Nightingale harped away about her absurd flirtations. It was true. They had been common in the past. They were the flirtations of a woman with not a shred of confidence in her attractions, trying to prove them – so much more innocent, yet sometimes more unbalanced, than the flirtations which spring up through desire.

After Mrs Jago, Nightingale's next point of attack was Jago's supporters and friends, and most of all Roy Calvert. I came in for a share of obloquy, but the resentment he felt for me seemed to become transferred to Roy. Roy's love affairs – for the first time they were discussed across the combination room table. Joan's name was mentioned. Someone said she would soon be engaged to Roy. Engaged? Nightingale smiled.

This gossip went seething round. Despard-Smith said one night in my hearing:

'Extraordinary young man Calvert is. I'm worried about him. I saw him in the court this afternoon and, after what I've heard recently, I asked if he was thinking of marriage. He made a most extraordinary reply. He said: "The Calverts are not the marrying kind. My father was, of course, but he was an exception". I'm worried about the young man. I'm beginning to be afraid he has no sense of humour.' Despard-Smith frowned. 'And I'm beginning to wonder whether, in his own best interests, he oughtn't to be advised to apply for a post in the British Museum.'

The propaganda began to endow Jago's side with a colour of raffishness. It was a curious result, when one thought of Brown and Chrystal, the leaders of the party and the solidest people in the college. Nevertheless, that was the result, and we in Jago's party were ourselves affected by it. In a short time, Nightingale had driven the two sides further apart. By the end of term, high table was often uncomfortable to dine at. Men formed the habit of looking at the names of those down for dinner, and crossing off their own if there were too many opponents present. It became less a custom to stay for wine after hall.

Among the gossip and faction, there was one man who stayed impervious. Crawford was not sensitive to atmosphere. He sat down self-assuredly to dinner with a party consisting entirely of Jago's supporters; he talked to me with sober, complacent sense about the state of Europe: he offered Roy Calvert a glass of sherry in the combination room, and gave his opinions of Germany. Either Crawford did not hear Nightingale's slanders or he took no notice of them. Once I heard Nightingale speak to him in a low voice in hall.

'I'm afraid,' said Crawford, cordially, loudly, but without interest, 'that I'm very stupid when it comes to personalia.'

After the last college meeting of the term, which had been dull but cantankerous, Crawford said, as we were stirring to go:

'Mr Deputy, may I be allowed to make an unusual suggestion?'

'Dr Crawford.'

'I should like your permission to retire with the Senior Tutor for five minutes. We shall then possibly be in a position to make a joint statement.'

Jago and Crawford left the room, and the rest of us talked, smoked, or doodled. On my right hand Nightingale turned ostentatiously away, and I chatted to Luke about his research. He had been chasing a red herring, he said: the last month's work was useless; it was like a 'blasted game of snakes and ladders'; he had just struck a gigantic snake. Then Jago and Crawford returned. They were talking as they entered, Jago excited, his eyes smiling, Crawford self-contained, his expression quite unmoved. None of us, after the Saturday night at Jago's, had heard whether Crawford's invitation had come to anything. Chrystal was annoyed, Brown concerned that Jago might commit a tactical mistake.

Crawford slid into his seat.

'Mr Deputy.'

'Dr Crawford.'

'Speaking as a fellow, I assume that I'm out of order in referring to the impending vacancy,' said Crawford. 'But if we dissolve ourselves into an informal committee, I suggest that difficulty can be overcome. Perhaps I can take the transformation as completed.' He gave a broad smile, enjoying the forms of business, as he always did. 'Speaking then as a member of this informal committee, I can go on to suggest that it may be useful if the Senior Tutor and I make a statement of intention.'

He stared impassively at Despard-Smith.

'I take it,' Crawford went on, 'that we are not going beyond reasonable common knowledge in regarding ourselves as candidates when the vacancy in the Mastership occurs. Further, I take it, from such expressions of current feeling as reach me, that we are justified in regarding ourselves as the most likely candidates. Finally, I take it that it is also reasonable common knowledge that a clear majority has not yet found itself to express the will of the college. In the circumstances, the votes which the Senior Tutor and I dispose, by virtue of being fellows, may be relevant. We have discussed whether we can reach agreement between ourselves on the use we make of them. The greatest measure of agreement we can reach is this: we do not feel it incumbent upon us to intervene in the college's choice. We do not consider ourselves justified in voting for one another. As matters stand at present, we shall abstain from voting.'

There was a silence.

'Ah. Indeed,' said Gay. 'Very well spoken, Crawford. I congratulate you.'

Jago said:

'I should like to add a word to my colleague's admirable précis. I am sure we should both choose to be frank with the society.'

Crawford gave a cordial assent.

'We both feel uncomfortably certain,' said Jago, 'that the other would not be our natural first choice. I know my colleague will correct me if I am misrepresenting him. We don't feel that it's reasonable for us to give our votes to each other, against our own natural judgment, just because we appear to be the only candidates.'

'Exactly,' said Crawford.

They were drawn close in their rivalry. Even as they said they would not vote for the other, they felt an inexplicable intimacy. They found real elation in making a statement together; they enjoyed setting themselves apart from the rest of us. It was not the first time I had noticed the electric attraction of rivalry: rivals, whether competing for a job, opposing each other in politics, struggling for the same woman, are for mysterious moments closer than any friends.

As we left the meeting, Chrystal and Brown drew me aside.

'Jago is *amusing*,' said Chrystal angrily. 'How can he expect us to get him in if he plays this sort of game without warning?'

'I don't suppose he had any option,' said Brown in a soothing tone. 'It looks pretty certain on the face of it that Crawford just sat smugly down and said nothing on earth would make him vote for Jago. I'm satisfied Jago did the best thing in the circumstances by giving no change himself.'

'We ought to have been told. It's lamentable,' said Chrystal. 'It looks as though we shall never get a majority for either. They've just presented us with a stalemate. There are times when I feel inclined to wash my hands of the whole business.'

'I can't follow you there.' Brown was for once short with his friend. 'This looks like a tight thing, I give you that. But there's one advantage. I don't see how Crawford can possibly get a majority now.'

'What use is that? If we can't get a majority ourselves.'

'If we're certain of avoiding the worst, I shall be happier. And we haven't started serious persuasion yet,' said Brown. 'The first thing is to close our own ranks.'

Chrystal agreed, a little shamefacedly, but left it to Brown to spend an hour with Pilbrow that night. For a fortnight, ever since Nightingale's defection, Brown had been trying to arrange a talk with Pilbrow. But Pilbrow's round of concerts and parties did not allow him much free time; and he was bored with college politics, and was not above dissimulating to avoid them. This day, at the college meeting, Brown had pinned him down.

I rather wished I had accompanied Brown myself, for I was Pilbrow's favourite among the younger fellows. He was attracted by Roy Calvert, but could not understand his political ambivalence; he could not understand how anyone so good-hearted could have friends of influence in the Third Reich. Whereas the old man knew that I was on the left of centre, and stayed there.

I wished decidedly that I had gone, when Brown told me what Pilbrow had said. I knew at once that Brown was not at ease.

'I think he'll come up to scratch,' Brown said. 'But I must say he's getting crankier as he grows older. Would you believe it, but he wanted me to sign a letter about the confounded Spanish war? I know you support that gang of cut-throats too, Eliot. I've never been able to understand why you lose your judgment when it comes to politics.'

'Well,' he went on. 'I hope he didn't take it amiss when I turned him down. I've never known Eustace Pilbrow to bear a grudge. And he made just the same kind of promise as he made at our caucus. He's still for Jago, just because he's rather fond of him.' He told me, word for word, what Pilbrow had said. It was, as Brown admitted, 'on the target' for an old man. He had replied in the same terms to the other side, telling them that he preferred Jago for personal reasons. It seemed satisfactory.

Yet Brown was wearing a stubborn frown. 'He's further away from this election than any of us,' he said. 'I wish we could bring him more into the swim of things.'

He added:

'Still, I don't see how he can help coming up to scratch.' He reflected. 'One thing I'm sure of. The other side aren't going to humbug the old man against his will. I've never realised before how obstinate he is. And that takes a load off my mind.'

CHAPTER XXII

THE SCENT OF ACACIA

THEN something happened which none of us had reckoned on. The course of the Master's disease seemed to have slowed down. Just after the Easter vacation, we began to suspect that the election might not be held that summer. Sitting in the combination room, the smell of wistaria drifting through the open window, we heard Crawford expound: in his judgment, the Master would not die until the early autumn. He had been just as positive in forecasting a quick end, I remembered, but he commented on the new situation without hypocrisy. 'Speaking as a friend of Royce's, I take it one should be glad. He's only in discomfort, he's not in pain, and I get the impression that he's still interested in living. I expect he'd prefer to go on even as he is than have anyone accelerate the process. Speaking as a fellow, it upsets our arrangements, which is a nuisance and I'm not going to pretend otherwise,' said Crawford. 'I had hoped we should have made all our dispositions by next academic year, and it doesn't look like that now.'

Imperturbably, Crawford gave us a physiological explanation of the slowing-down of the disease.

After that news, the air was laden with emotion. Each time I passed the wistaria in the court, I thought of the Master, who, Roy said, was amused at his reprieve: that odour was reaching him for the last time in his life. The college smelt of flowers all through the early summer: I thought of Joan, eating her heart out with love, and Roy, so saddened that I was constantly afraid.

As the news went round that the Master would live months longer, the college became more tense. Some people, such as Chrystal, were glad to forget the election altogether. Chrystal's interest passed entirely to the negotiations with Sir Horace, which had not gone much further since the night of the feast; Sir Horace wrote frequently to Brown, but the letters were filled with questions about his nephew's chances in the Tripos; occasionally he asked for a piece of information about the college, but Brown saw no hope of 'bringing him to the boil' until the boy's examination was over. Brown himself was coaching him several hours a week during that term. 'I don't know,' he said, 'whether Sir Horace is ever going to turn up trumps. But I do know that our prospects vanish, presuming they exist at all, if our young friend has to go down without a degree.'

But Chrystal, along with Pilbrow, was an exception in shelving the Mastership. With most men, the antagonism became sharper just because of the delay. Nerves were on edge, there was no release in any kind of action, there seemed no end to this waiting. Nightingale's gossip about Roy went inexorably on. It infected even Winslow, who normally showed a liking for Roy. Winslow was heard to say, 'I used to think that my colleagues were more distinguished for character than for the more superficial gifts of intelligence. The Senior Tutor appears to have chosen supporters who seem determined to remove part of that impression.'

The gossip came round to Roy, though we tried to shield him. His spirits had been darker since the day he comforted Lady Muriel, and now, as he heard how he was being traduced, there were nights when he sank into despondency. Usually he would have cared less than most men what others said, but just then the sky had gone black for him. His was a despondency which others either did not notice or passed over; it would have struck no one as specially frightening, except him and me. Often we walked round the streets at night. The whole town smelt of wallflower and lilac. The skies were luminous, windows were thrown open in the hot May evenings. I tried to lift Roy from sadness, if only for a minute: almost imperceptibly, he shook his head.

Nightingale was making other attacks, not only those on Roy. One night towards the end of May, Luke asked if he could talk to me. I took him up to my room, and he burst out: 'I've had about as much as I can stand of this man Nightingale. I'm beginning to think I've been quiet in this college for almost long enough. One of these days I shall do the talking, and by God they'll get a surprise.'

'What's Nightingale done now?'

'He's as good as told me that unless I switch over to Crawford they'll see that I'm not made a permanency.'

'I shouldn't pay too much attention—'

'Do you think I should pay attention? I told him as politely as I could – and I wished I hadn't got to be so blasted polite – that I'd see him damned first. Do they think I'm the sort of lad they can bully into going through any bloody hoop?'

'They probably do.' I was growing very fond of him. When he was angry, he was angry from head to toe, angry in every inch of his tough, square, powerful body. It was the same with every mood – his hopes or disappointments about his work, even his attempts at discretion. He threw the whole of his nature into each of them. On this night he was angry as one whole human integer of flesh and bone. 'They probably do. They're wrong.'

'They'll be surprised how wrong they are,' Luke fumed. 'I should like to be kept in this college, it's much nicer than the old dockyard, but do they think they've only got to whistle and I'm theirs? They can do their damnedest, and I shan't starve. A decent scientist will get some sort of job. They're just trying to blackmail me because I'm afraid to lose my comforts.'

I told him that 'they' could only be Nightingale himself. I could not believe that Francis Getliffe knew anything of this move, and I said that I would confront him with it. Luke, still enraged, went off to his laboratory in the summer evening.

I should have spoken to Francis the following night, but I found that he had left Cambridge (the examinations had begun, and lectures were over for the year) for some Air Ministry experiments. He was not expected back for a fortnight, and so I told Brown about Luke.

'Confound those people,' he said. 'I'm a mild man, but they're going too far. I'm not prepared to tolerate many more of these outrages. I don't know about you, but it makes me more determined to stick in my heels against Crawford. I'm damned if I'll see them get away with it.'

We each found ourselves holding the other side *collectively* responsible for Nightingale's doings. Just as young Luke stormed about what 'they' had threatened, so did Arthur Brown: and I felt the same. There were times when we all saw the other side through a film of enmity. We forgot who they were and what they were truly like. We were becoming victims of something like war hysteria. And that happened to Brown, who was as sensible, tolerant and level-headed as a man can be: it happened to me, who was not a partisan by nature.

At the same time we were a little ashamed of ourselves, and I thought, when I next saw Brown, that he was going a roundabout way to atone. 'I'm wondering about enlarging the claret party this year.' Brown's claret party took place each year at the beginning of June. 'I'm inclined to think it would be rather statesmanlike. After all, we've got to live with the present society even if we slide Jago in. Mind you, I'm all against trying to make arrangements with the other side over the election. But I should regard it as reasonable to remind them that we're still capable of enjoying their company. It would be a decent gesture to invite some of them to the party.'

And so the claret party consisted of Winslow, Crawford, Pilbrow, Roy Calvert, me and Brown himself. Like so much of that summer, it tantalised me. The night was tranquil, the college had never looked more beautiful. I should be lucky if I had the chance to drink wine so good again. But Roy's melancholy had got worse, and all the time I was fearing one of his outbursts. Most of that night, I could think of nothing else.

Twice I managed to signal to Roy that he must keep quiet. He was enough in control of himself to do so, though he was affected by the sight of another unhappy man. For Winslow was worried by his son's examination, which had just finished. As soon as the party began, Brown asked him how the boy had got on, and Winslow snubbed him:

'My dear Tutor, I cannot answer for the prospects of the semi-illiterate. I hope the wretched youth managed to read the questions.'

Roy heard the sadness in that answer, and it nearly touched the trigger of his own. But, to my momentary relief, we settled down to wine. It was ten o'clock, but the sun had only just set, and over the roof opposite Brown's window there was a brilliant afterglow. From one of the May week balls, we could just hear the throbbing of a band. There was the slightest of breezes stirring, and on it came the scent of acacia from the court beneath.

Pilbrow took charge of the party. He was an authority on wine, and had been Brown's master. His bald head gleamed in the fading light, shone when, towards midnight, Brown switched on the lamps; the ruddy cheeks flushed, but otherwise Pilbrow did not change at all as one decanter after another was left empty. He fixed one of us with a lively brown eye and asked what we noticed at each sip – at the beginning, middle and end of each sip. The old man rang all the changes possible with ten bottles of claret. When we were half-way through, he said with extreme firmness:

'I don't think any of you would ever be quite first-class. I give our host the benefit of the doubt—'

'I don't claim it,' said Brown. 'I shall never be anything like as good as you.'

Meanwhile, Roy had been drinking faster than the rest of us. The dangerous glint had come into his eyes. He began to talk to Winslow – and it was then I had to signal. Roy's smile was pathetic as he fell into silence.

Winslow was speaking again about his son, this time in a different tone.

'I shall be relieved,' he said with humility, 'if the examiners let him through.'

'Oh, they'll let him through,' said Brown.

'I don't know what will happen to him if they don't,' said Winslow. 'He's a stupid child. But I believe there's something in him. He's a very nice person. If they gave him a chance now, I honestly believe he may surprise you all in ten years' time.'

No one there had heard Winslow speak so openly. It was some moments before he regained his sardonic tone. Then he made himself say to Brown:

'My dear Tutor, you've had the singular misfortune to teach the foolish creature. I drink to you in commiseration.'

Brown insisted on drinking to young Winslow's success.

'Let me fill your glass. Which shall it be? You've gone a bit light on the Latour '24.'

We each had ten glasses in front of us, labelled to match the decanters. Brown selected the right one from Winslow's set.

'That will do very nicely. If you please. If you please.'

Crawford surveyed the glasses, the decanters, the gleam of crystal and silver, the faces all flushed, the scene of luxury and ease. Out of the window there was still a faint glow in the west. Girls' laughter came up from the court, as a party moved out of college to a ball.

'It's very hard to realise what the world is really like tonight – when one's enjoying your hospitality, Brown,' he announced. 'Speaking as a scientific observer, I should have to say that the world tonight is more unstable than it's ever been in human experience. But it's impossible to believe that, sitting with the present spectacle in front of us.'

'That's always so,' said Pilbrow unexpectedly. 'I've been caught in two revolutions, or not exactly caught, but . . . . One sees a woman in the garden by the railway line, just digging on a sunny morning. One can't believe that it's actually *begun*.'

'One can't believe tonight,' said Crawford, 'that one ought to be fighting against this mess Brown's political friends are plunging us into. I expect I shall remember very vividly tomorrow morning.'

'Yes! Yes!' cried Pilbrow, his eyes gleaming like buttons. He joined in Crawford's reflections, as the decanters were put away one by one. He talked about the 'mess'; he was off to the Balkans in three weeks to see for himself. At the age of seventy-four, he was as excited as a boy about his expedition. Brown had had a moment's anxiety when he saw how Pilbrow was vigorously applauding Crawford. But now the old man was safely talking of his travels and Brown was rubicund; though Roy was silent, Winslow subdued, Brown felt that this party had been a success.

After the party, Roy and I walked in the garden. The breeze had dropped, and on the great beeches no leaf stirred. The full moon hung like a lantern, and the scent of acacia pierced the air. Roy was very quiet, and we walked round in silence. Then he said, as though it were a consolation: 'I shall sleep tonight.'

When he was in a phase of depression, I had known him insomniac for four or five nights together. He would lie open-eyed through the minutes of a night, and then another, having to face his own thoughts. Until, his control broken, he would come to my room and wake me up: should we drive over to George Passant and make a night of it? Or to our friends in London? Or should we go for a walk all night?

The melancholy, the melancholy shot through with sinister gaiety, had been creeping upon him during the past few weeks. He could not throw it off, any more than a disease. When it seized him, he felt that it would never go.

We walked round, not talking, in a night so warm that the air seemed palpable. I thought that we had been lucky to escape that party scot free. I did not know how to stop him damaging himself.

I thought that, so long as I lived, I should be mocked by the scents of that summer. They might have come along with peace of mind, the wistaria, the wallflower, the lilac, the acacia.

CHAPTER XXIII

AFFLICTION

I HAD expected an outbreak from Roy at the claret party, but, when it did come, I was not prepared.

It was a fortnight later, a Saturday morning, and I woke early. There was a college meeting that day to consider examination results. Some were already published, sent round to tutors, stuck in the tailors' windows; most did not come out till this Saturday.

I knew that the envelopes reached the porters' lodge by a quarter to nine, so I did not wait for Bidwell's ritual awakening. I walked through the court in the cloudless morning, and found a large packet addressed to me. I was opening it when Brown entered the lodge, panting a little, still wearing trouser clips after cycling in from his house.

'I hope we haven't had too many disasters,' he said. He opened his own envelope, spread the sheets on the counter.

'Thank God for that!' he exclaimed in a moment. 'Thank God for that!'
'What's happened?'

'Young Timberlake's got through. They've given him a third. Which, between you and me, is probably slightly more than abstract justice required. Still, I think Sir Horace will be satisfied. If the young man had crashed, it might have been the most expensive failure in the history of the college. I'm breathing a great deal more freely, I can tell you.'

His cleverest pupil had been given a starred first. 'I always said he was our next real flier,' said Brown triumphantly.

He turned back, pencil in hand, to tick off the names on the history sheet. In a moment he gave a shrill whistle.

'I can't find Dick Winslow's name. He seems to have failed altogether. They don't seem even to have allowed him the ordinary degree. They don't seem to have made him any allowance at all. It's scarcely credible. I think I'd better ring up the examiners straight away. I did once find a name left off a list by mistake.'

He put through his call, and came back shaking his head.

'Absolutely hopeless,' he said. 'They say they just couldn't find any signs of intelligence at all. Well, I knew he was dense, but I shouldn't have believed that he was as dense as that.'

The meeting was called for half-past eleven. As the room filled up, one kept hearing whispers about young Winslow. In the midst of the bustle, men asked each other if they had heard. Some were speaking in malice, some in good nature, some in a mixture of the two. At last Winslow himself entered, heavy-footed, carrying his cap but not swinging it in his normal fashion. He was looking down, and went straight to his place.

'Ah, good morning, Winslow,' cried Gay, who had not grasped the news.

'Good morning to you,' said Winslow. His voice was deadened.

Despard-Smith was just opening the meeting when Gay said:

'I have a small presentation to make, before we begin our discussion on these excellent agenda. I wish to present to the society, for inclusion in the library, this copy of my latest publication. I hope and expect that most fellows have already bought it. I hope you've bought yours, Brown? I hope you have, Crawford?'

He rose precariously to his feet, and laid a copy in front of Despard-Smith.

'As a matter of fact, I haven't yet,' said Crawford. 'I've noticed one or two reviews.'

'Ah. Reviews,' said Gay. 'Those first reviews have a lukewarm tendency that I don't like to see.'

Suddenly, distracted from Winslow, I saw how nervous the old man was about his book's reception. Gay, the least diffident of men, had never lost that nervousness. It did not die with age: perhaps it became sharper.

The meeting began at last. There was only two minutes' business over livings, but under finance there were several items down. Despard-Smith asked the Bursar if he would 'take us through' his business.

Winslow's head was sunk down.

'I don't think it's necessary,' he muttered. He did not raise his eyes. Everyone was looking at him.

Then it came to Jago to describe the examination results. He passed from subject to subject in the traditional Cambridge order, mathematics, classics, natural sciences. . . . Most people at the meeting knew only a handful of the young men he was talking about; but his interest in each was so sharp that he kept a hold upon the meeting. He came to history. The table was very quiet. 'One brilliant and altogether deserved success,' he said in his thick voice. 'Some of us know the struggle that young man had to come here at all. I'm prepared to bet, Mr Deputy, that he's going to write his name in the story of this college.' Then with a grin, he said how much the society ought to congratulate Brown on squeezing Timberlake through. Jago then studied his papers, and paused. 'I think there's nothing else to report about the historians.' Very quickly, he turned to the next subject.

It was intended as chivalry, perhaps as more. I could not tell how Winslow received it. He still sat with his head sunk down. There was no sign that he had heard anything of the meeting. He did not speak himself: even for a formal vote, he had to be asked.

We broke off at one o'clock for a cold lunch, and most people ate with zest. Winslow stood apart, with his back to the room. I saw Roy's eyes upon him, glinting with wild pity. Since the party, his depression had grown heavier still, and he had kept himself alone. I was at once anxious as I saw him watching Winslow, but then someone offered him a decanter of wine and he refused. I thought that he was taking care, and I had no sense of danger.

When we resumed the meeting, Jago dealt with the results of the preliminary examinations. There were inquiries, one or two rotund criticisms, some congratulations.

'Of course,' said Despard-Smith, summing up, 'for a scholar of the college only to get a third class in a university examination is nothing short of s-scandalous. But I think the general feeling of the college is that, taking the rough with the smooth, we can be reasonably satisfied with the achievements of the men. I gather that is your opinion, Senior Tutor?'

'I should go further. We ought to be proud of them.'

'You don't dissent, Tutor?' Despard-Smith asked Brown.

'I agree with my senior colleague,' said Brown. 'And I should like to draw the college's attention to the remarkable results that the Dean has once more secured.'

Before the meeting ended, which was not long after, I was set thinking of Despard-Smith's use of the phrase 'the men'. That habit went back to the '90s: most of us at this table would say 'the young men' or 'the undergraduates'. But at this time, the late 1930s, the undergraduates themselves would usually say 'the boys'. It was interesting to hear so many strata of speech round one table. Old Gay, for example, used 'absolutely', not only in places where the younger of us might quite easily still, but also in the sense of 'actually' or even 'naturally' – exactly as though he was speaking in the 1870's. Pilbrow, always up to the times, used an idiom entirely modern, but Despard-Smith still brought out slang that was fresh at the end of the century – 'crab', and 'josser', and 'by Jove'. Crawford said 'man of science', keeping to the Edwardian usage which we had abandoned. So, with more patience it would have been possible to construct a whole geological record of idioms, simply by listening word by word to a series of college meetings.

This one closed. The fellows filed out, and I waited for Roy. Winslow was still sitting at the table, with the order-book and files in front of him; he seemed not to have the spirit to move. The three of us were left alone in the room. Roy did not glance at me or say a word: he went straight to Winslow, and sat down by his side.

'I am dreadfully sorry about Dick,' he said.

'That's nice of you.'

'And I am dreadfully sorry you've had to sit here today. When one's unhappy, it's intolerable to have people talking about one. It's intolerable to be watched.'

His tone was full of pain, and Winslow looked up from the table.

'You don't care what they say,' Roy cried, 'but you want them to leave you alone. But none of us are capable of that much decency. I haven't much use for human beings. Have you, Winslow, have you? You know what people are feeling now, don't you? They're feeling that you've been taken down a peg or two. They're thinking of the times you've snubbed them. They're saying how arrogant and rude you've been. But they don't matter. None of us matter.'

His voice was very clear, throbbing with a manic elation. Winslow stared at him.

'There is something in what they say, young man,' he said.

'Of course there is. There's something in most things that they say about anyone.' Roy laughed.

I went round the table to stop him. Roy was talking about the slanders on himself. I had him by the shoulder, but he shook me off. He told Winslow there was something in what Nightingale said.

'Would you like to know how much there is in it?' he cried. 'We're both miserable. It may relieve you just a bit.'

Winslow raised his voice:

'Don't trouble yourself, Calvert. It's no concern of mine.'

'That's why I shall do it.' There was a sheet of blank paper in front of Winslow. Roy seized it, and began to write quickly. I took hold of his arm, and jogged his pen. He cursed. 'Go away, Lewis.' He wrote on, talking as he did so. 'I'm giving Winslow a little evidence.' His face was wild with pure elation. 'This is only for Winslow and me.' He wrote more, then signed the page. He gave it to Winslow with a smile.

'This has been a frightful day for you,' Roy cried. 'Keep this to remind you that people don't matter.'

He said good afternoon, and went out of the room.

'This is distressing,' said Winslow.

'He'll calm down soon.'

'I never had any idea that Calvert was capable of making an exhibition of himself. Is this the first time it has happened?'

I had two tasks. I had to safeguard Roy as much as I could. And I had to think of politics. I told some of the truth, and some lies. I had never seen Roy lose control until this afternoon, I said. It was a shock to me. Roy was upset over the Master: it had worn his nerves to breaking-point to see such suffering.

'He's a considerable scholar, from all they say,' said Winslow. 'I had my doubts about him once, but I've always found him an engaging young man.'

'There's nothing whatever to worry about.'

'You know him well,' said Winslow. 'I expect you're right. I think you should persuade him to take a good long holiday.'

Winslow was studying the sheet of paper. At last he said:

'So there is something in the stories that have been going round?'

'I don't know what he has written there,' I said. 'I've no doubt that the stories are more highly painted than the facts. Remember they've been told you by people who envy him.'

'Maybe,' said Winslow. 'Maybe. If those people have this ammunition, I don't see how Master Calvert is going to continue in this college. The place will be too hot to hold him.'

'Do you want to see that happen?'

'I'm comparatively indifferent about the young man. He can be amusing, and he's a scholar, which is more than can be said for several of our colleagues.' Winslow stared at me. 'I'm comparatively indifferent, as I say. But I'm not indifferent about the possibility of your candidate becoming Master.'

'You mean,' I said, 'that if you let other people see Calvert's note, you could make a difference to Jago's chances?'

'I did mean that,' said Winslow.

'You can't do it,' I said.

'Why not?'

'You can't do it. You know some of the reasons that brought Calvert to the state he was in this afternoon. They're enough to stop you absolutely, by themselves.'

'If you'd bring it to a point—'

'I'll bring to a point. We both know that Calvert has lost control of himself. He got into a state pretty near despair. And he wouldn't have got into that state unless he'd seen that you were unhappy and others were pleased at your expense. Who else had any feeling for you?'

'It doesn't matter to me one way or the other,' said Winslow.

Then I asked:

'Who else had any feeling for your son Dick? You knew that Calvert was upset about him. Who else had any feeling for your son?'

I was taking advantage of his misery. Winslow looked as though he had no strength left. He stared down at the table, and was silent for a long time. At last, in a flat, exhausted mutter, he said:

'What shall I do with this?' He pointed to the sheet of paper.

'I don't mind,' I said.

'Perhaps you'd better have it.'

Winslow did not so much as look when I burnt the paper in the grate.

CHAPTER XXIV

ARGUMENT IN THE SUMMER TWILIGHT

I WENT straight from Winslow to Roy's room. Roy was lying on his sofa, peaceful and relaxed.

'Have I dished everything?' he asked.

He was *happy*. I had seen the course of his affliction often enough to know it by heart. It was, in fact, curiously mechanical. There was first the phase of darkness, the monotonous depression which might last for weeks or months: then that phase passed into another, where the darkness was lit up by flashes of 'gaiety' – gaiety which nearly overcame him at Brown's party, and which we both dreaded so much. The phase of gaiety never lasted very long, and nearly always broke into one frantic act, such as he had just committed. Then he felt a complete release.

For months, perhaps for longer, he knew that he was safe.

I was tired and weighed down. Sometimes I felt that the burden on me was unfair, that I got the worst of it. I told him that I should not always be there to pick up the pieces.

He was anxious to make amends. Soon he asked:

'I haven't dished Jago, have I?'

'I don't think so.'

'How did you work it? You're pretty competent, aren't you?'

I shook my head.

'It didn't need much working,' I said. 'Winslow may like to think of himself as stark, but he isn't.'

'Just so,' said Roy.

'I had to hit below the belt, and it wasn't pretty,' I said. 'He hates Jago. But it isn't the sort of hate that takes up much of one's life. All his real emotions go into his son.'

'Just so,' said Roy again. 'I think I'm lucky.'

'You are.'

'I couldn't have borne putting paid to Jago's chances,' said Roy. 'I'll do what I can to make up for it, old boy. I shall be all right now.'

That evening in hall Roy presented a bottle in order to drink Jago's health. When he was asked the occasion, so that Luke could enter it in the wine book, Roy smiled and said precisely:

'In order to atone for nearly doing him a disservice.'

'My dear Roy,' cried Jago, 'you couldn't possibly do me a disservice.

You've always been too kind to me. It even makes me forgive you your imitations.'

It was not only at the claret party that Roy mimicked Jago; he could not resist the sound of that muffled, sententious, emphatic voice; most of those round the table that night had heard him, and even Despard-Smith grinned.

As we went out that night, Arthur Brown reflected:

'You heard the reason Roy Calvert gave for presenting a bottle? Now I wonder exactly what he meant by it. Put it another way: a few years ago, whenever he said anything that wasn't straightforward, I used to expect one of his queer tricks. But I don't worry much about him now. He's become very much more stable. I really believe that he's settling down.'

I did not disagree. It was better for Brown to speculate amiably, just as fellows in the future, studying the wine book, might wonder what that singular entry could mean.

I told Brown that I was taking action to protect Luke. Francis Getliffe had returned for the meeting that morning, and his wife Katherine had asked me to dinner the following week, for the first time since our quarrel in January. I intended to use the opportunity: it would be easy to let drop the story of Nightingale's threat, and it was too good a chance to miss.

When I arrived for dinner at the Getliffes' house they welcomed me as in the old days. As Francis poured out sherry and took his wife a glass, he seemed less fine-drawn than in college. He looked at her with love, and his restlessness, his striving, his strenuous ambition, all died away; his nerves were steadied, he was content to the marrow of his bones. And she was happy through and through, with a happiness more continuous than a man could know.

The children were in bed. She talked of them with delight, with a pretence of not wanting to bore me. As she indulged her need to linger over them, she sat with matronly comfort in her chair; it seemed a far cry from the excited, apprehensive, girl of eighteen whom I met in her father's house at Bryanston Square nearly ten years before.

She talked of the past and her family, as we sat at dinner. Had I seen her brother recently? Then with great gusto, the nostalgia of a happy woman, she recalled days at her father's country house when Francis and I had both been staying there.

After dinner we moved into the garden at the back of the house. There we sat in the last of the light, as the western sky turned from flaming yellow to a lambent apple-green. The air caressed our faces. And languorous and heavy in the warm night wafted the scent of syringa, which brought back the end of other summer terms.

Drowsy in the scented air, I was just going to drop a hint about Luke when, to my astonishment, Katherine got in before me.

'I have been wanting a word with you, Lewis.'

'Have you?'

'You do agree that Francis is right about the Mastership, don't you? It is essential for us to have a liberal-minded Master, don't you agree?'

So they had invited me to play the same game. I was curiously saddened, as one is saddened when the gulf of marriage divides one from a friend. Once Katherine had listened to each word that her brother and I spoke, she had been friend and disciple, she saw things with our eyes. Now she was happy with her husband, and everyone else's words were alien.

'I think Francis is quite wrong,' I said.

'If we get saddled with a reactionary Master,' said Francis, 'Lewis will be responsible.'

'That's unfair.'

'Be honest, man,' said Francis. 'If you did what we should have expected you to do, Crawford would walk in. Several people would come over with you.'

'I must say,' Katherine broke in, 'it does seem rather gross, Lewis. This is important, don't you admit that it is important? And we've got a right to expect you not to desert our side. It's no use pretending, it does seem pretty monstrous to me.'

I knew they felt that I was being ungrateful. When I was in distress, so that I wanted a refuge to hide in, Francis had set to work to bring me to the college. He had done it with great delicacy; for four years they had felt possessively pleased whenever I dined at their house – and now, at the first major conflict, I betrayed him. I thought how much one expects from those to whom one does a good turn; it takes a long while to learn that, by the laws of human nature, one does not often get it.

'Look,' I said to Katherine, 'your brother Charles has got as much insight as anyone I've ever known. When you let yourself go, you're nearly as good. You know something of Crawford and Jago. Tell me, which is the more remarkable man?'

There was a pause.

'Jago,' she said reluctantly. Then she recovered herself, and asked: 'But do you want a remarkable man as Master, don't you admit that other things come first?'

'Good work,' said Francis. 'Lewis likes human frailty for its own sake.'

'No,' I said. 'I like imagination rather than ordinariness.'

'I'm afraid at times,' said Francis, 'that you forget about the solid virtues.'

'If you prefer it,' I spoke with anger, 'I like self-torment rather than conceit.'

They were profoundly out of sympathy with me, and I with them. We knew each other well enough to know there was no give on the other side. They became more obdurate in resisting any claim I made for Jago: my tongue got harsher when I replied about Crawford.

'Anyway,' said Katherine at last, '*she* is appalling.'

'She's pathetic,' I said. 'There's much humanity in her.'

'That's monstrously far-fetched, don't you admit it?'

'If you'd watched Jago take care of her, you might understand what I've been telling you about him,' I said.

'She'd be an intolerable nuisance in the Lodge,' said Katherine.

'We're not electing her,' I said. 'We're electing her husband.'

'You can't get out of it as though she didn't exist,' said Francis.

For a moment we broke off the argument. Without our having noticed the light go, the garden now lay in deep twilight; the apple-green sky had changed to an illuminated, cerulean blue; the first stars had come out.

It was then that I spoke of Luke – not, as I had planned, in the way of friendly talk, but at the moment when we had got tired of our barbed voices.

'I resent some of the comments that your side have made about her,' I said. 'But I don't want to talk about that now. There's something more important. It's another piece of tactics by one of your side. Did you know that Nightingale has been trying to coerce young Luke?'

'What do you mean?' said Francis.

I gave them the story.

'Is this true?' cried Francis. 'Are those the facts?'

'I've told you exactly what Luke told me,' I said. 'Would you believe him?'

'Yes,' said Francis, with no warmth towards me, angry with me for intruding this complaint, and yet disturbed by it.

'If you believe him,' I said, 'then it's quite true.'

'It's nasty,' Francis broke out. I could see him only dimly in the crepuscular light, but I was sure that his face had flushed and that the vein in his forehead was showing. 'I don't like it. These things can't be allowed to happen.' He went on: 'I needn't tell you that nothing of this kind will affect Luke's future. I ought to say that his chances of being kept by the college can't be very strong, so long as I stay. But that has nothing to do with this business. It's shameful. Luke's very good. He ought to be kept in Cambridge somehow.'

'He's a very nice boy,' said Katherine. She was not four years older, but she spoke like a mature woman of a child.

'By the way, it won't make the slightest difference to the election,' I said. 'Luke may be young, but he's not the first person one would try to cow. But I wanted to make sure you knew. I wasn't ready to sit by and see him threatened.'

'I'll stop it,' said Francis with angry dignity. 'I'll stop it,' he repeated. Yet his tone to me was not softened, but harder than it had been that night. His whole code of behaviour, his self-respect, his uprightness and sense of justice, made him promise what he had done; and I was certain, as certain as I should be of any man, that he would carry it out. But he did not embrace me for making him do so. I had caused him to feel responsible for a piece of crooked dealing; it would not have mattered so much if I had still been an ally, but now it stiffened him against me. 'You ought to remember,' he said, 'that some of your side are none too scrupulous. I'm not convinced that you've been too scrupulous yourself. Didn't you offer Nightingale that you wouldn't be a candidate for the tutorship, if only he'd vote for Jago? While you know as well as I do that Nightingale stands as much chance of becoming tutor as I do of becoming a bishop.'

Soon after I thanked them for dinner and walked back into the town through the midsummer night. We had parted without the glow and ease of friendship. I shouldn't have anticipated, just then, how much I should rely on Francis in the future, and how his character not only wore better than more labile ones, but came to interest me more.

Walking back under the stars, at the mercy of the last scents of early summer, I remembered a May week five years before, on just such a night as this. Those two and I had danced in the same party; we had loved our partners, and there had been delight to spare for our friends. Yet, a few minutes past, I had said goodnight to Francis and Katherine with no intimacy at all. Was it only this conflict between us? Or was it a sign of something inevitable, like the passing of time itself? The memory of anyone one had truly loved stayed distinct always and with a special fragrance, quite unaffected by the years. And the memory of one's deepest friendships had a touch of the same magic. But nothing less was invulnerable to time, or chance, or one's private trouble. Lesser friendships needed more care than the deepest ones; they needed attention and manners – and there were times, in the midst of private trouble, when those one could not give. Was it my fault that I could not meet Francis and Katherine as I once did?

CHAPTER XXV

AN OBSERVER'S SMILE

THROUGHOUT the long vacation most of the fellows did not go far away. We all knew that, as soon as the Master died, there would be a last series of talks, confidences, negotiations, until the day of the election, and we wanted to be at hand. Only two went out of England. Roy Calvert was giving a course of lectures in Berlin, and had to leave by the end of July; he went in cheerful spirits, promising to fly back at a day's notice if I sent for him. Pilbrow had departed for the Balkans shortly after Brown's claret party, and no one had heard a word from him since. He had guaranteed to return in time for the election, but when I last saw him he had no thoughts to spare for college conflicts.

During the summer no one changed his party. The bricks in Roy Calvert's room did not require moving; the score was still 6–5 for Jago, but not a clear majority of the whole 13 electors. Brown kept on persuading us to wait before we tried an attempt on Gay, or any other move. Chrystal, however, did make the first signs of an approach about Jago, one night when the old man was dining; he found him aware of the position but stubborn, and so went no further. In fact Chrystal was frustrated for lack of action, and his temper became shorter; they had heard nothing fresh from Sir Horace, apart from a long, effusive letter thanking Brown for his nephew's success. In that letter, for the first time, there appeared no encouraging hints about the college's future at all, and Chrystal and Brown were at a loss.

At the end of August the Master sent for me. He had a special message he wanted to give me, and he told me, almost as soon as I arrived, that I was to remind him of it if he rambled. He wanted to give me the message before I left.

His face was now an old man's. The flesh was dried and had a waxy sheen. His eyes were sunken. Yet his voice was a good imitation of its old self, and, with his heightened insight, he knew the tone which would distress me least. And he spoke, with his old sarcastic humour, of his reasons for changing the position of his bed. It stood by the window now.

'I prefer to lie here,' said the Master, 'because I got tired of the remarkable decoration' – he meant the painted college arms – 'which we owe to the misguided enthusiasm of one of my predecessors who had somewhat grandiloquent tastes. And, between you and me, I also like to look out of the window and see our colleagues walking about in twos and threes.' He smiled without sadness and with an extraordinary detachment. 'It makes me wonder how they are grouping themselves about the coming vacancy.'

I looked into the emaciated, wasted, peaceful face. 'It is surprisingly easy to face that kind of fact,' he said. 'It seems quite natural, I assure you. So you can tell me the truth. How much has been done about choosing my successor? I have only heard that Jago might be in the running – which, between ourselves, I could have guessed for myself. Will he get it?'

'Either he or Crawford.'

'Crawford. Scientists are too bumptious.' It was strange to hear him. even when so many of the vanities of self had gone, clinging to the prejudice of a lifetime.

I described the present position of the parties. It kept his attention and amused him. As I spoke, I did not feel anything macabre about his interest; it was more as though an observer from another world was watching the human comedy.

'I hope you get Jago in,' he said. 'He'll never become wise, of course. He'll always be a bit of an ass. Forget that, and get him in.'

Then he asked:

'I expect there's a good deal of feeling?'

'Yes,' I said.

'It's remarkable. People always believe that, if only they support the successful candidate, they've got his backing for ever. It's an illusion, Eliot, it's an illusion. I assure you, one feels a certain faint irritation at the faces of one's loyal supporters. They catch one's eye and smirk.'

A recollection of the Getliffes' garden came to me, and I said:

'Gratitude plays some queer tricks.'

'Gratitude isn't an emotion,' he said, watching the human comedy. 'But the expectation of gratitude is a very lively one.'

His mind was very active, but began to leap from point to point.

'Tell me,' he said. 'Did they think I was doing to die before this?'

'Yes.'

'They expected to get the election over before next academic year?'

'Yes.'

He *smiled*.

Soon after his mind began to wander, and I had to remind him about his message. Setting his will, his thoughts drifting, he forced himself to remember. At last it came back. He talked of Roy Calvert, his protégé and pupil, who had already outstripped him. He praised Roy's work. He wanted me to promise to look after him.

CHAPTER XXVI

STALEMATE

AT the beginning of October, the great red leaves of Virginia creeper flamed on the walls and blew opulently about the court. In the garden the leaves blazed on the trees. The mornings were misty, the days bright in a golden haze; in the evenings, the lights in the streets and the college were aureoled in the autumnal mists. In the evenings, a light still shone from the great bedroom of the Lodge.

The fellows came back from their September holidays: the freshmen waited in queues on Brown's staircase and walked round the courts in search of Jago's house. The college became noisy, the streets trilled with cycle bells as young men rode off to games in the afternoon. High table filled up: Brown presented a bottle to greet the new academic year: the whole society had returned to residence, except for Pilbrow and Roy Calvert.

It was only a few days later that Roy came back. He ran up my staircase one afternoon, looking very well. He had been free of depression since June, often he had managed to forget it. I had never seen him so settled. He was anxious to amuse me, concerned to help Brown and his other friends, eager to intrigue for Jago.

Tension in the college soon mounted again. Winslow had recovered some of his bite, and Nightingale ground away at his attacks with the stamina of a passion. Whispers, rumours, scandals, came to us at second or third hand. Roy Calvert figured in them less than in the summer; his actual presence as he was that autumn, equable, full of high spirits, prepared to devote himself to the shyest diner at high table, seemed to take away their sting – though once or twice I saw Winslow regarding him with a curious glance. But the slanders were fuller than ever of 'that impossible woman'. Nightingale had the intuitive sense of propaganda that one sometimes finds in obsessed men; he knew how to reiterate that phrase, smiling it out when anyone else would have grown tired; gradually all his outcries gathered round her. Even the sober members of his side, like Winslow and Francis Getliffe, were heard to say 'it's unthinkable to have that woman in the Lodge', and Brown and Chrystal were perturbed in private and did not know how to reply.

Brown, Roy and I considered how to stop every hole by which these slanders might get through to Jago. We were as thorough as we knew how to be; but there were nights when Jago sat silently in hall, his face white, ravaged. The long anxiety had worn him down, his outbursts of nervous emotion were more unpredictable. But it was the sight of him, his face engraved with his own thoughts, intolerably vulnerable, that distressed us most.

Did he know what was being said? Neither Roy nor I had any doubt.

The Master was spending more time asleep now; one still saw his room lit up when one came back to college on those hazy October nights under the serene and brilliant moon. An Indian summer had visited the town, and the buildings rested in the warmth. It made Jago's pallor more visible, as he walked through an evening so tranquil that the lines of the palladian building seemed to quiver in the haze.

It was strange to leave the combination room, and walk into such an evening. But the strain was growing more acute. There had been only one action which took away from it in the slightest; Francis had been as good as his word, and, by what means I did not know, had stopped the threats to Luke.

One night when Brown and I were both dining, Chrystal sharply asked if we could spare half-an-hour after hall. Brown and I each looked at him; we knew from his expression that he had something active to propose. I thought Brown even at that moment was a shade uneasy; but he took us to his rooms, and opened a bottle of hock, saying: 'I've a feeling it will be rather refreshing in this weather.'

He went on to talk of Sir Horace. At the end of the long vacation, they had persevered with schemes to get in touch with him again; finally they settled that Brown should write a letter, telling Sir Horace that they had been discussing his nephew's future and wondered whether it would not be wise for him to have a fourth year – 'not necessarily reading for a Tripos' – Brown said he could not endure that risk again. This letter had been sent and evoked several telephone calls from Sir Horace. For once they had got him undecided. He nearly sent the young man back, and then thought again; in the end he decided against, but there was a long telephone conversation, thanks of unprecedented cordiality, and a half-promise to visit the college during the winter.

Brown was willing to speculate on that visit, but for the first time Chrystal brushed all talk of Sir Horace aside.

'We've shot our bolt there. It's up to him now,' he said. 'I want to hear your views about this mess we're in.'

'You mean we haven't succeeded in making things safe for Jago?'

'It's not our fault. I don't accept any blame,' said Chrystal. 'But we're in a mess.'

'Well,' said Brown. 'We still have a lead of one. It's 6–5, providing Pilbrow troubles to come back. There's always a chance we might win someone over at the last minute. I've always thought there might be a chance with Gay.'

'I didn't get any change from him. I regard him as fixed,' said Chrystal.

'Well then, it's 6–5.'

'And 6–5 is stalemate. It's lamentable'

'I'm certain our wisest course,' said Brown firmly, determined to get in first, 'is to sit tight and see how things pan out. Funny things may happen before we actually get into the chapel. I know it's a confounded nuisance, but we've got to sit tight and have some patience. We're not in such a bad position.'

'I don't agree,' said Chrystal. 'The place is more like a beargarden than ever. And it's stalemate. I don't see how you can hope to make any progress.'

'It's worth trying Gay again,' I said.

'You'll be wasting your time. I rule him out,' said Chrystal.

'At the very last,' I said, 'we ought to try old Despard. We haven't shown our hand completely.'

'You can try,' said Chrystal with scorn.

He went on:

'I see it like this. The present position is the best we can hope for. We may lose a vote. We shan't gain one. Do you take me up on that? We can't expect anything better than the present voting.'

'I don't admit that it's certain,' said Brown, 'but I should regard it as a probability.'

I agreed.

'I'm glad you see it the same way,' said Chrystal. 'Where does it get us?'

'If the voting does stay in the present position,' Brown replied, 'and I admit we haven't any right to expect better, then the decision goes to the Visitor, of course.'

By statute, if the fellows could not find a clear majority of their number for one candidate, it was left for the Visitor to appoint. The Visitor had always been, right back to the foundation, the bishop of a northern diocese. I was sure, by the way, that Brown and Chrystal must have thought of this possibility as soon as Jago's majority was broken. I had myself at moments, though it took time for any of us to believe that a stalemate was the likely end.

'What happens then?' said Chrystal, pressing his point.

'I shouldn't like to guess,' said Brown. 'I suppose the greatest danger is that he would prefer the one who is more distinguished outside the college.'

'He couldn't appoint Jago,' said Chrystal. 'He's not a churchman, and he hasn't got any reputation for his work.'

'Surely Crawford's politics would be against him,' I remarked.

'I wish I were absolutely certain of that,' said Brown. 'Isn't the Bishop a bit of a crank himself? Isn't he one of those confounded Churchill men who want to make trouble? I've heard that he's not sound. We can't rely on him to do the statesmanlike thing.'

'He'll never give it to Crawford,' Chrystal announced. 'Everyone knows that he's an unbeliever too. He's never kept it dark. I can't credit that he'd give it to Crawford. You can rule that out.'

'I very much hope you're right. It's extremely reassuring to hear,' said Brown, smiling but with his watchful eyes on his friend. 'I'm becoming quite reconciled to the idea of the Visitor.'

'I don't intend you to be. In my view, he's certain to bring in an outsider.'

Chrystal spoke with assurance, almost as though he had inside knowledge. In fact, I suspected later that he had actually heard something from the other side.

It puzzled me, and it also puzzled me that he had asked me to join him and Brown that evening. Normally he would have had a discussion in secret with Brown, and they would have decided their policy before any of the party, or anyone else in the college, had a chance to know their minds. It puzzled me: I could see that it disconcerted Brown. But soon I felt that Chrystal knew, right from the beginning, that he and Brown were bound to disagree. In his curiously soft-hearted way, Chrystal fought shy of a scene; he did not want to quarrel; he was afraid of the claims of friendship.

So he had asked me to be present. He had avoided an intimate scene. He could not have borne to be prevented. He had seen a chance to act, and all his instincts drove him on.

He said: 'He's certain to bring in an outsider. That would be the biggest disaster.'

'I don't agree with you there,' said Brown. 'I could tolerate most outsiders in front of Crawford.'

'I'm sorry,' said Chrystal. 'I like to know whom we're getting. If it came to the worst, I should prefer the devil we know. With Crawford, we should be certain where we were from the start. No. I don't want an outsider. I don't want it to go to the Visitor.'

'Nor do I,' I said. I turned to Brown. 'It would mean that we had lost it for Jago.'

'I see that,' said Brown reluctantly.

'It's just conceivable the Visitor might put Crawford in,' I said. 'But he'd never give us Jago over Crawford's head. Jago's junior and less distinguished. If it goes to the Visitor, it will either be Crawford or a third person.'

'I don't see any way out of that,' said Brown.

'There isn't,' said Chrystal. 'But there's one thing we've never tackled. There are the two candidates themselves. I come back to them. We've got to force them to vote for each other.'

'Well,' said Brown, 'I don't for the life of me see how you're going to do that. You can't expect Crawford to make a present of the Mastership to Jago. That's all you're asking him to do. I don't see Crawford suddenly becoming a public benefactor.'

'Wait a minute,' said Chrystal. 'Suppose he's convinced that a stalemate means that he's out. He knows there's only one vote in it. As you said, funny things happen in elections. Don't you think he might gamble? It's the only chance he's got. It only means he has to win another vote. He may.' Chrystal looked with his full commanding eyes at Brown, and repeated: 'He may. Someone may cross over. Are you dead certain of Pilbrow?'

'No. But I shall be disappointed if we can't hold him.'

'I repeat,' said Chrystal, 'Crawford knows it's pretty even. He knows this way is his only chance. Why shouldn't he chance it?'

'What about Jago?'

'If we brought it off, we should be presenting him with a decent chance of victory on a plate,' said Chrystal fiercely. 'I shouldn't have much use for Jago if he raised difficulties.'

'That's all very well,' Brown was frowning, 'but they're both strong men in their different fashions. And they've gone out of their way to tell us definitely that they refuse to vote for each other.'

'We'll threaten them with a third candidate.'

Chrystal's plan was simple. The college was divided between two men, and did not wish for an outsider. It had a right to ask those two to save them from an outsider. Just one step was needed – for the 'solid people' on both sides to get together and threaten to switch to a third candidate if the other two refused. Chrystal had already heard something from Getliffe and Despard-Smith; they were no happier about the Visitor than he was; he was convinced that they would take part in his plan.

'I don't like it,' said Brown.

'What's the matter?' Chrystal challenged him.

'I like being as friendly with the other side as I can. But I don't like arrangements with them. You never know where they lead.'

They were speaking with all the difference of which they were capable. Brown, the genial, the peace-maker, became more uncompromising the more deeply he was probed. Both his rock-like stubbornness and his wary caution held him firm. While Chrystal, behind his domineering beak, was far more volatile, more led by his moods, more adventurous and willing to take a risk. The long stagnation had bored him; he was, unlike Brown, not fitted by nature for a conflict of attrition. Now all his interest was alive again. He was stimulated by the prospect of new talks, moves, combinations and coalitions. He was eager to use his nerve and will.

'It's worth trying,' said Chrystal. 'If we want to win, we've got no option.'

'I'm convinced we ought to wait.'

'It ought to be done tomorrow.'

'I shall always feel that if we hadn't rushed things about seeing Jago, we might have Nightingale in our pocket to this day,' said Brown.

It was the first time I had heard him reproach his friend.

'I don't accept that. I don't think it's a fair criticism. Nothing would have kept Nightingale sweet. Don't you think so, Eliot?'

'Yes,' I said.

Chrystal asked me another question:

'Do you agree that we ought to have a discussion with some of the other side?'

'Can you bring it off?' I replied. 'If not, I should have thought it was better not to try. We shall have exposed ourselves.'

'I'll bring it off,' said Chrystal, and his voice rang with zest.

'Then it might win the Mastership for Jago,' I said.

'It's worth trying,' said Chrystal. 'It must be tried.'

Brown had been watching me as I answered. Then he watched Chrystal, and sank into silence, his chin set so that one noticed the heavy, powerful jowl. He thought for some time before he spoke.

'I'll join a discussion if you arrange one. I don't like it, but I'll join in.' He had weighed it up. He saw that, with skill and luck, it might turn out well for Jago. He saw the danger more clearly than anyone there. But he was apprehensive that, if he did not join, Chrystal might make an overture on his own account.

He added:

'I shan't feel free to express myself enthusiastically if we do meet the other side. Unless they put it all plain and above board. And I shall not want to bring any pressure on the two candidates.'

'So much the better. If you and I disagree, they'll feel there isn't a catch in it,' said Chrystal, with a tough, active, friendly smile.

CHAPTER XXVII

CONFERENCE OF SIX

NEXT morning Chrystal was busy paying visits to some of the other side He saw Brown and me before lunch, and announced that he had arranged a conference for the coming Sunday night. There was a crowd dining that Sunday, and I heard Despard-Smith's usual grating protest – 'all avoiding the cold supper at home'; the number of diners that night helped to disguise the gap when six of us left after hall, but even so I wondered whether any suspicious eyes had noticed us.

We walked through the second court to Chrystal's rooms. It was an autumn night of placid loveliness; an unlighted window threw back a reflection of the hunter's moon; our shadows were black before us.

It was warm, but Chrystal had a bright fire burning. His sitting-room was comfortable, rather in the fashion of a club; on a small table, a pile of periodicals was stacked with Chrystal's unexpected, old-maidish tidiness; upon the walls stood out several cases with stuffed birds inside, which he had shot himself.

'Do you want to bring chairs by the fire?' said Chrystal. 'Or shall we get round the table?'

'I suggest round the table, if you please,' said Winslow. 'Your fire is so remarkably hospitable, my dear Dean. Almost excessively hospitable for this particular night, perhaps.'

Chrystal did not reply. He seemed resolved from the beginning not to be drawn by Winslow. With a plan in his mind, his temper had become much more level. So we sat round the table away from the fire – Despard-Smith, Winslow and Francis Getliffe on one side, Brown and I on the other. Before Chrystal took the chair at the head, he said he could not offer us Brown's variety of drinks, and filled for each of us a stiffish tumbler of whisky.

We all drank, no one had begun to talk, while Chrystal packed and lit his pipe. Suddenly he said:

'We've reached a stalemate over this election. Do you agree?'

'It looks like it,' said Francis.

'How do you all regard it?' said Chrystal.

'I regard it as disastrous,' Despard-Smith replied. His expression was lugubrious, his voice solemn; but he had already nearly finished his glass, and he was watching each word and movement on our side of the table.

'It makes me think slightly less warmly than usual,' said Winslow, 'of the mental equipment of some of my colleagues.'

'That is *amusing*,' said Chrystal, but he did not pronounce the word with his customary venom. 'But it doesn't get us anywhere, Winslow. We shan't get far if we start scoring points off one another.'

'I associate myself with you, Dean,' said Despard-Smith, with bleak authority.

'I am still unenlightened as to where we are trying to get,' said Winslow. 'Perhaps others know the purpose of this meeting better than I do.'

'It's simple.' Chrystal looked at the three of them. 'This election may go to the Visitor. Are you content?'

'The possibility hadn't escaped us,' said Winslow.

'I expect that most of us have thought of it occasionally,' said Brown. 'But somehow we haven't really believed that it would happen.'

'I have found it only too easy to believe,' said Despard-Smith.

'Are you content?' asked Chrystal.

'To be honest,' said Winslow. 'I could only answer that – if I knew the mysterious ways in which the Bishop's mind would work.'

'I should consider it a c-catastrophe,' said Despard-Smith. 'If we can't settle our own business without letting the Bishop take a hand, I look upon it as a scandalous state of affairs.'

'I'm glad to hear you say that,' said Chrystal. 'Now I'm going to put our cards on the table. If this election does go to the Visitor, I've got a view as to what will happen. It won't mean your candidate getting in. It won't mean ours. It will mean a third party foisted on us.'

'What do you think?' Francis asked Despard-Smith.

'I'm reluctantly bound to say that the Dean is right,' said Despard-Smith. He spoke, like Chrystal a few days before, as though he had the certainty of inside knowledge. I wondered if he had discovered anything through his clerical acquaintances. I wondered also if it was from him that Chrystal had picked up the hint. They were supporting each other at this table. And Despard-Smith's support was still, at the age of seventy, worth having. He was completely certain of his judgment. He poured himself another large whisky, and delivered an unshakeable opinion. 'I deeply regret to say it,' said the old clergyman, 'but the Dean is right. The way the Bench is appointed nowadays is of course disastrous. The average is wretchedly low. Even judged by that low average, this man doesn't carry a level dish. He can be relied upon to inflict some unsuitable person upon us.'

'Do you want that?' said Chrystal vigorously.

'I don't,' said Francis.

'I don't myself,' said Chrystal.

'It doesn't sound specially inviting,' I said.

Winslow gave a sarcastic smile.

'It somewhat depends,' he said, 'whether one would prefer either of our candidates to an unknown. I dare say some of you might. It may not be a completely universal view.'

'You mean there may be people who won't mind it going to the Visitor, Winslow,' said Chrystal. 'If they're determined to keep one of the candidates out at any costs.'

'Precisely, my dear Dean,' said Winslow.

Brown looked from Winslow to Chrystal: his eyes were sharp but troubled as they moved from his opponent to his ally.

'I think the time has almost come to explain where we stand,' he said. 'My own position hasn't altered since last January. I'm convinced that Jago is the right man for us, and so I've never thought any further. I think I can say that Crawford wouldn't be my second choice, if I'm forced to speak off-hand.'

'Mr dear Brown,' said Winslow, 'Jago wouldn't be my third choice. I don't find it easy to decide what number of choice he actually would be.'

'That being my position,' said Brown, 'I shouldn't be averse to passing the decision to the Visitor, if we couldn't scrape up a majority for Jago.'

'My reason is the exact opposite,' said Winslow. 'But I find myself surprisingly in agreement with the Tutor. I shan't worry if the Bishop has to use his wisdom.'

'I shall,' I said. 'For once I disagree with Brown. I'd rather have either of those two than anyone in the field. I'd certainly rather have either than anyone the Bishop is likely to choose.'

'Good work,' said Francis, in a quick, comradely manner, as in the days when we were always on the same side. 'I'm with Eliot there. I'm not in favour of Jago, but I'd rather put up with him than the Bishop's nominee.'

We all turned to Despard-Smith. He took a long sip from his glass, and said with deep solemnity: 'I too find myself among the Laodiceans.' He added, so gravely that no one took account of the anti-climax: 'I've never been ready to buy a p-pig in a poke.'

'Yes,' said Chrystal. 'Well, none of you will be surprised to hear how I feel.' He was addressing himself to Brown. 'I'm not voting for Jago to keep Crawford out. I'm voting for him because I think he's the better man. But either will do.' He went on: 'So that's four of us flat against letting it go to the Visitor. I regard that as enough reason to explore a bit further.'

Brown was looking flushed and concerned, but he said:

'I have made my reservations, but I am sure we should all like to hear what the Dean has in mind. We all know that it's bound to be valuable.' He was uneasy, I knew, but his affability covered him. I wondered whether it was friendship for Chrystal or party loyalty which had caused him to give help at this point. Almost certainly both – it was like him to mix policy and warmheartedness without thinking, it was just that mixture which made him so astute.

'Would you like to stay and hear it, Winslow?' said Despard-Smith.

'If you please,' Winslow said indifferently. 'If you please.'

'Right,' said Chrystal. 'First of all I want to count heads. I regard Jago as having five votes certain as far as votes can be certain in a college – I mean three of us here and our two young men, Calvert and Luke. Pilbrow has promised to vote several times – but I'm not going to mince matters either way. He may even not come back, he's not specially interested in this election.'

'That's fair enough,' said Francis Getliffe with a sudden creased smile.

Chrystal went on:

'I regard your side as having four votes certain. Yourselves and Nightingale. Nightingale can't cross over again, or he'll find that none of us can stand him. You're also counting on Gay, but I set him off against Pilbrow. He may have forgotten the name of your candidate before the election. He may vote for himself.'

'I have no doubt,' said Despard-Smith, 'that Gay will weigh his vote.'

'No, we've got to be fair,' said Francis. 'We can't rely on him. Chrystal has been quite objective.'

'Remarkably so,' Winslow added. 'But what does it all lead to? Bring it to a point, my dear Dean.'

'I shall get there in one minute,' said Chrystal. 'But I didn't want to hide the facts. Jago is in the stronger position. There are no two ways about it. I don't want to hide it: if I did, you would have a right to think I was going in for sharp practice. What I'm going to suggest may put Jago in. It will almost certainly put one of the two in. It will save us from the Visitor.' He paused and then said with extreme crispness:

'I suggest that we make ourselves clear to the two candidates. We tell them that four of us – or five or six if Brown or Winslow like to come in – will not tolerate this matter going to the Visitor. We tell them that they must vote for each other. It's the only way to bring a majority within reach. If they refuse, we say that we'll form a majority for another person. This will be someone *we* decide on. Not an outsider fobbed off on us by the Bishop. If we're forced to have a third candidate, we'll choose him ourselves.' Chrystal broke into a smile. 'But it will never come to that.'

'I must say that it's a beautiful thought,' said Winslow.

'It doesn't look unreasonable,' said Francis.

'I take it that it hasn't escaped you, Dean,' said Winslow, 'that your candidate commands a probable six votes – and Crawford's will neatly get him home?'

'I went out of my way to explain that,' said Chrystal. 'I said perfectly clearly that it might happen. I repeat: this is a way to escape the Visitor. So far as I can see, it's the only way.'

'That may very well be true,' said Francis.

'I cannot remember any step of this kind during my association with the college. It is a grave step even to consider. It is absolutely unprecedented,' said Despard-Smith. 'But I feel we owe it to the college to consider the suggestion with the utmost seriousness. To let the Visitor s-saddle us with some incubus of his own would in my judgment be an unmitigated disaster.'

From those first moments it was certain that Despard-Smith and Francis would support Chrystal's move in the long run. Their first response was 'yes!', however much they wrapped it round later. They seemed to be saying yes spontaneously even though it looked like giving Jago the game. They seemed to have lost their heads. Yet they were each of them strong-willed and hard-headed men.

I had no illusion that they were not calculating the chances. They thought, rightly or wrongly, that this was the best move for Crawford, although I could not imagine how they arrived at it.

I felt more than ever certain that they must have learned at least some piece of gossip about the Bishop's intention. They must have become quite certain that, if the Bishop had the power, Crawford would stand no chance. For an instant, I suspected also that they had some information, unknown to us, about one of Jago's side. But later I doubted it. It did not seem that they had any well-backed hope. It seemed most likely that in secret they were sure of Gay, and had a vague hope of Pilbrow and even (so I gathered with incredulity from a chance remark) of Roy Calvert, some of whose comments Despard-Smith took literally and misunderstood. So far as I could detect, they knew nothing definite that we did not know.

Those seemed their motives on the plane of reason. But they were also moved by some of the inexplicable currents that sweep through any intricate politics. Despard-Smith and Francis, just like Chrystal and I myself, suddenly panicked at the idea of an outsider for Master. It was as though our privacy were threatened: magic was being taken from us: this intimate world would not be so much in our power. It was nonsense when we thought of it in cold blood, but we shied violently from the mere idea. And also we enjoyed – there was no escaping the satisfaction – the chance of asserting ourselves against our candidate. There are some hidden streaks in any politics, which only flash to the surface in an intense election such as this. Suddenly they leap out: one finds to one's astonishment that there are moments when one loves one's rival – despises one's supporters – hates one's candidate. Usually these streaks do not make any difference in action, but in a crisis it is prudent to watch them.

Despard-Smith let fall some solemn misgivings and qualifications; Francis was guarded, though anxious to seem open to argument; but Chrystal knew he had won them over. He took it as a triumph of his own. And in fact it had been an impressive display. For the first time in this election, he had thrown his whole will into the struggle. He had something definite to achieve; and, even against men as tough as his opponents, his will told.

The talk went on. Winslow said:

'Even the idyllic spectacle of the lion lying down with the lamb does not entirely reconcile me to the Dean's ingenious idea.'

Later, Brown finished up for the night:

'In any case, before I come to any conclusion, I shall certainly want to sleep on it.'

'That goes without saying,' said Despard-Smith. 'It would be nothing less than s-scandalous for any of us to commit ourselves tonight.'

I was surprised to hear a couple of days later that Winslow had decided to join. He had talked to his party: what had been said, I did not know: I was uneasy, but I noticed that so was Francis. I was surprised that Winslow had not pushed his dislike of Jago to the limit. Was there a shade of affection, underneath the contempt? Once Jago had supported him: was there some faint feeling of obligation? Or was it simply that, despite his exterior, despite all his attempts to seem it, Winslow was really not a ruthless man?

Winslow's decision made it hard for Brown to stay outside. He felt his hand was forced, and he acquiesced with a good grace. But he was too cautious, too shrewd, too suspicious and too stubborn a man to be pleased about it. 'I still don't like it,' he confided to me in private. 'I know it improves Jago's chances, but I can't come round to liking it. I'd rather it had come later after we'd had one stalemate vote in the chapel. I'd rather Chrystal was thinking more about getting Jago in and less about shutting the Visitor out. I wish he were a bit stronger against Crawford.'

'Nevertheless,' Brown added, 'I admit it gives Jago a great chance. It ought to establish him in as strong a position as we've reached so far. It gives him a wonderful chance.'

The six of us met again, and drafted a note to the two candidates. Despard-Smith did most of the writing, but Brown, for all his reluctance to join the 'memorialists' (as Despard-Smith kept calling us), could not resist turning a sentence or two. After a long period of writing, rewriting, editing and patching up, we agreed on a final draft:

'In the view of those signing this note, it is most undesirable that the forthcoming election to the Mastership should be decided by the Visitor. So far as the present intentions of fellows are known to us, it seems that neither of the candidates whose names we have heard mentioned is supported by a clear majority of the college. We accordingly feel that, in conformity with the spirit of college elections and the desire of the college that this forthcoming election shall be decided internally, it would assist our common purpose if each candidate voted for the other. If they can see their way to take this step, it is possible that a clear majority may be found to declare itself for one or other candidate. If, on the other hand, they find themselves unable to cast their votes in this manner, the signatories are so convinced of the necessity of an internal decision that they will feel compelled to examine the possibility of whether a third candidate can be found who might command a clear majority of the college.

> A T D-S
> G H W
> A B
> C P C
> F E G
> L S E
> 29 Oct. 1937'

'In other words,' said Chrystal, 'there'll be the hell of a row.' He winked. There was often something of the gamin about him.

CHAPTER XXVIII

CLOWNING AND PRIDE

THE note was sent to all fellows. It caused great stir at once, and within a few hours we learned that Jago and Crawford wished to meet the six. Roy Calvert said: 'I must say it's a coup for Chrystal.' Jago had said nothing to Brown or me, not a telephone message, not a note. Later that day, Roy brought news that Jago was brooding over the ultimatum. He was half-delighted, so Roy said, because of his chances – and also so much outraged that he intended to speak out.

The two candidates arranged to meet us after hall, at half-past eight. Both came in to dinner, and Jago's face was so white with feeling that I expected an outburst straightaway. But in fact he began by *clowning*. It was disconcerting, but I had seen him do it before when he was strung up and about to take the centre of the stage. He pretended – I did not know whether it was a turn or a true story – that some undergraduate had that afternoon mistaken him for an assistant in a bookshop. 'Do I look like a shop assistant? I'm rather glad that I'm not completely branded as a don.'

'You're not quite smart enough,' said Roy, and in fact Jago was usually dressed in an old suit.

Jago went on with his turn. No one noticed a change in him when we were sitting in the combination room.

Word had gone round that the 'memorialists' were to confer with Crawford and Jago, and so by half-past eight the room was left to us. The claret was finished, and Crawford lit a cigar.

'I think we can now proceed to business, Mr Deputy,' he said.

'Certainly,' said Despard-Smith.

'Our answer is a tale that's soon told.' Crawford leaned back, and the end of his cigar glowed. 'The Senior Tutor and I have had a word together about your ultimatum. We haven't any option but to accept it.'

'I'm very glad to hear it,' said Chrystal.

'If there are no other candidates, we shall vote for each other,' said Crawford imperturbably. 'Speaking as a private person, I don't think one can take much exception to what you want us to do. I think I do take a mild exception to the way you've done it, but not so strongly as my colleague. However, that's past history, and it's neither here nor there.' He smiled.

Jago leaned forward in his chair, and slight as the movement was, we all looked at him. 'For my part, I wish to say something more,' he said.

'I should leave it alone,' said Crawford. 'What's done can't be undone. You'll only take it out of yourself.'

In fact, Jago was looking tired to breaking-point. His face had no colour left, and the lines were deep – with sombre anger, with humiliation, with the elation that he might be safe again.

'It's good of you,' said Jago to Crawford, 'but I should be less than honest if I didn't speak. I take the strongest exception to the way this has been done. It was unnecessary to expose us to this kind of compulsion. Apparently you' – his eyes went round the table – 'consider that one of the two of us is fit to be your Master: I should have hoped that you might in the meantime treat us like responsible persons. I should have hoped that was not asking too much. Why couldn't this have been settled decently amongst us?'

'We don't all share your optimism, my dear Senior Tutor,' said Winslow.

'We were anxious to get everything in order,' said Brown, eager to smooth things down. 'We didn't want to leave any loose ends, because none of us knows how much time we've got left.'

'That's no reason for treating Crawford and me like college servants,' said Jago.

'Since when have college servants been required to vote for each other?' Winslow asked.

Jago looked at him. His anger appeared to quieten. His white and furrowed face became still.

'You are taking advantage of my position as a candidate,' he said. 'A candidate is fair play for any kind of gibe. You know that he's not at liberty to speak his mind. No doubt he deserves any gibes you care to offer him. Anyone who is fool enough to stand for office deserves anything that comes his way.'

Winslow did not reply, and no one spoke, Crawford smoked impassively on, but all our attention was on Jago. He dominated the room.

'You have taught me that lesson,' he said. 'I shall vote for Crawford at the election.'

As we were leaving, Jago spoke in a low voice to Chrystal:

'I should like to say something to you and Brown and Eliot.'

'We can go back,' said Chrystal. So, standing in the combination room, Jago faced three of his supporters.

'I should have been told about this.' His voice was quiet, but his anger had caught fire again.

'I passed the word along as soon as we had decided to push forward,' said Brown.

'I should have been told. I should have been told at the first mention of this piece of – persuasion.'

'I don't see why,' said Chrystal.

'When I find my party is negotiating behind my back—'

'This isn't a party matter, Jago,' Chrystal broke in. 'It's a college matter.'

'I'm sorry,' said Jago, in a tone as brusque as Chrystal's, 'but I'm not used to having my actions dictated. Before my friends arrange to do so, I expect them to tell me first.'

'Perhaps the circumstances are a little unfortunate,' said Brown, 'but I'm inclined to suggest that we're all losing our sense of proportion. I think you're forgetting that something very notable has been achieved. I'm not saying that it's all over bar the counting of the votes, but I do put it to you that things look brighter than they have done since Nightingale split off. You're standing with a clear majority again, and the sensible course for us all is to keep it intact until we walk into the chapel.'

He went on:

'I expect you know that you owe it entirely to the Dean. Put it another way: the Dean is the only man who could have forced a vote out of the other side. It was a wonderful night's work.'

Beneath the round, measured, encouraging words there was strength and warning. Jago knew they were intended for him. He gazed into Brown's eyes; there was a pause, in which I thought I saw a quiver pass through his body; then he said:

'Your heads are cooler than mine. You must make allowances, as I know you're only too willing to do. I know Chrystal appreciates that I admire everything he does. This was an astonishing manœuvre, I know. I'm very grateful, Chrystal.'

'I'm glad it came off,' Chrystal replied.

I walked back with Jago to his house to fetch a book. He scarcely spoke a word. He was at the same time elated, anxious, and bitterly ashamed.

I was thinking of him and Crawford. That night, Crawford had been sensible, had even been kind to his rival. I could understand the feeling that he was the more dependable. It was true. Yet, of the two, which was born to live in men's eyes?

And Jago knew it. He knew his powers, and how they were never used. The thought wounded him – and also made him naked to life. He had been through heartbreak because of his own frailty. He had seen his frailty without excuses or pity. I felt it was that – not his glamour, not his sympathy, not his bouts of generous passion – it was that nakedness to life which made me certain we must have him instead of Crawford. He was vulnerable in his own eyes.

Why had he never used his powers? Why had he done nothing? Sometimes I thought he was too proud to compete – and also too diffident. Perhaps at the deepest level – as I had seen in Sheila's father – pride and diffidence became the same. Jago could not risk a failure. He was born to be admired from below, but he could not bear the rough-and-tumble, the shame, the breath of the critics. His pride was mountainous, his diffidence intense. Even that night he had been forced to clown before he scarified his enemies. He despised what others said of him, and yet could not endure it.

There was one other thing. Through pride, through diffidence, he had spent his life among men whose attention he captured without an effort, with whom he did not have to compete. But it was the final humiliation if they would not recognise him. That was why the Mastership lived in his mind like an obsession. He ought to have been engaged in a struggle for great power; he blamed himself that he was not, but it sharpened every desire of his for this miniature power. He ought to have been just Paul Jago, known to all the world, with no title needed to describe him, his name more glowing than any title. But his nature had forced him to live all his life in the college: at least, at least, he must be Master of it.

CHAPTER XXIX

'A VACANCY IN THE OFFICE OF MASTER'

In November we heard that the Master was near his death.

On the second of December, Joan told Roy Calvert: 'The doctor has just told us that he's got pneumonia. This is the end.' As we were going into hall on 4 December, the news was brought that the Master had just died. Despard-Smith made an announcement to the undergraduates, and there was a hush throughout the meal. In the combination room afterwards coffee was served at once, and we listened to a simple and surprising eulogy from old Despard-Smith.

'I shall miss him,' he said. 'He was a very human man.'

Soon, however, he and Winslow and Brown were occupied with procedure.

'I am no longer Deputy,' said Despard-Smith. 'I ceased to be Deputy the moment the Master died. The statutes are explicit on this point. The responsibility for announcing the vacancy passes to the senior fellow. I must say I view with apprehension having to rely on Gay to steer us through this business. It places us in a very serious position.'

They studied the statutes again, but they had done so frequently in the past weeks, and there was no way out. The governing statute was the one which Despard-Smith had read out at the first meeting of the Lent term.

'There's no escape,' said Brown. 'We can only hope that he'll get through it all right. Perhaps he'll feel the responsibility is too much for him and ask to be excused. If so, as Pilbrow isn't here, it will devolve on you, Despard, and everything will be safe. But we shouldn't be in order in passing over Gay. The only thing remaining is to let him know at once.'

Despard-Smith at once wrote a note to Gay, telling him the Master had died at 7.20 that night, explaining that it was Gay's duty to call a meeting the following day, telling him that the business was purely formal and that a meeting at the usual time need take only ten minutes.

'If you feel it is too dangerous to come down to college in this weather,' Despard-Smith added, 'send me a note in reply to this and we will see the necessary steps are taken.'

The head porter was called into the combination room, and asked to take the letter to Gay's house. He was told to see that it reached Gay's hands at once, whether he was in bed or not, and to bring back a reply.

I went off to see Roy Calvert: the others stayed in the combination room, waiting for Gay's reply.

The night was starless and a cold rain was spattering down. As I looked round the court, I felt one corner was strangely dark. No light shone from the bedroom window of the Lodge.

I found Roy alone, sitting at his table with one of the last pages of the proofs.

'You know, of course?' I asked.

'Yes,' said Roy. 'I can't be sorry for him. He must have gone out without knowing it. But it's the others who have to face what death means now, haven't they?'

Soon Joan came into the room, and he had to devote himself to her and her mother.

I had to telephone to the Chelsea house, to explain that I should stay in college until the election. Then I returned to the combination room, where Brown, Winslow and Despard-Smith were still waiting.

'It is nothing less than a disaster,' Despard-Smith was saying, 'that our statutes entrust these duties to the senior fellow.' He proceeded to expound the advantages of a permanent vice-master, such as some colleges had; from Winslow's expression, I guessed this ground had been covered several times already.

Before long the head porter arrived, his top hat tarnished from the rain. He handed Despard-Smith a large envelope, which bore on the back a large red blob of sealing-wax.

'Did you find Professor Gay up?' asked Brown.

'Certainly, sir.'

I wondered if there was the faintest subterranean flicker behind that disciplined face.

Despard-Smith read the reply with a bleak frown. 'This confirms me in my view,' he said, and passed the letter to us. It was written in a good strong nineteenth-century hand, and read:

Dear Despard,

Your news was not unexpected, but nevertheless I grieve for poor

Royce and his family. He is the fifth Master who has been taken from us since I became a fellow.

I am, of course, absolutely capable of fulfilling the duties prescribed to me by statute, and I cannot even consider asking the college to exempt me from them. It was not necessary for you to remind me of the statute, my dear chap, nor to send me a copy of the statutes: during the last weeks I have regularly refreshed my memory of them, and am now confident of being able to master my duties.

I do not share your opinion that tomorrow's proceedings are purely formal. I think that such a meeting would not show sufficient respect for our late Master. However, I concur that the meeting need not detain us overlong, and I therefore request that it be called for 4.45 p.m. I have never seen the virtue of our present hour of 4.30 p.m. I request also that tea be served as usual at 4.0 p.m.

Yours ever,

M. H. L. Gay.

'The old man is asserting himself,' said Brown. 'Well, there's nothing for it but to obey orders.'

Next afternoon most of the society, apart from Gay, arrived later than usual for tea in the combination room. They ate less and talked more quietly. Yet most of them were quiet through decorum, not through grief. The night before, there had been a pang of feeling through many there; but grief for an acquaintance cannot last long, the egotisms of healthy men revive so quickly that they can never admit it, and so put on decorum together with their black ties and act gravely in front of each other. All the fellows were present but Pilbrow; but only three bore the marks of strain that afternoon. There was Chrystal, brusque and harsh so that people avoided his company; Roy Calvert, who had dark pouches under his eyes after a night in the Lodge; Jago, whose face looked at its most ravaged.

Even of those, I thought, Jago was tormented by anxiety and hope. Perhaps only two mourned Royce enough to forget the excitement round them.

At half-past four many of us began to sit down in our places, but Gay finished his tea at leisure, talking loudly to anyone near. The clock struck the quarter before he said:

'Ah. The time I fixed for our meeting. Let us make a start. Yes, this is the time.'

He took the chair, and looked round at us. The hum died away. Then slowly and with difficulty Gay rose unstably to his feet, and supported himself by gripping the table with his hands.

'Remain seated, gentlemen,' he said. 'But I should like to stand, while I speak of what I have summoned you to hear today.' He looked handsome and impressive; his beard was freshly trimmed, it took years from his age to be presiding there that day. 'I have grievous news. Indeed I have grievous news. Yesterday evening our late Master passed away. In accordance with the statute I have requested you to meet on this the following day. First I wish to say a few words in honour of his memory.' Gay went on to make a speech lasting over half an hour. His voice rang out resonantly; he did not seem in the least tired. Actually, it was a good speech. Once or twice his memory failed him and he attributed to Royce qualities and incidents which belonged to earlier Masters. But that happened seldom; his powers had revived that afternoon; he was an eloquent man who enjoyed speaking, and he remembered much about Royce which was fresh to many of us. The uncomfortable feature of the speech was that he made it with such tremendous gusto; he was enjoying himself too much.

'And so,' he finished, 'he was stricken with the disease, which, as my old saga men would say, was his bane. Ah indeed, it was his bane. He bore it as valiantly as they would have borne it. He had also one consolation not granted to many of them. He died in the certainty of our Christian faith, and his life was so blessed that he did not need to fear his judgment in the hereafter.'

They Gay let himself back into his chair. There was whispering round the table, and he banged energetically with his fist.

'Now, gentlemen,' he said briskly and chidingly, 'we must set ourselves to our task. We cannot look back always. We must look forward. Forward! That's the place to look. It is part of my duties to make arrangements for the election of a new Master. I will read the statutes.'

He did read the statutes, not only that on the election of the Master, which he kept till last, but also those on the authority, qualifications, residence and emoluments. He read audibly and well, and a good many more minutes passed. At last he came to the statute on the election. He read very slowly and with enormous emphasis ' "When the fellows are duly assembled the fellow first in order of precedence attending shall announce to them the vacancy . . ." ' He looked up from his book, and paused.

'I hereby announce to you,' said Gay resoundingly, 'a vacancy in the office of Master.'

He went back to his reading.

' ". . . and shall before midnight on the same day authorise a notice of the vacancy and of the time hereby regulated for the election of the new Master, and cause this notice to be placed in full sight on the chapel door."

'Cause to be placed! Cause to be placed!' cried Gay. 'I shall fix it myself. I shall certainly fix it myself. Shall I write the notice?'

'I've got one here,' said Winslow. 'I had it typed ready in the Bursary this morning.'

'Ah. I congratulate you. Let me read it. I can't get out of the responsibility for any slips, you know. "Owing to the death of Mr Vernon Royce, there is a vacancy in the office of Master of this college. The fellows will meet in the chapel to elect a Master, according to statutes D–F, at ten o'clock in the morning of December the twentieth, 1937."

'That seems fair enough,' Gay went on, as though unwilling to pass it. 'December the twentieth? No one's made a slip there, I suppose?'

'The vacancy occurred in term,' said Winslow impatiently. 'It is fifteen days from today.'

'Indeed. Indeed. Well, it seems fair enough. Does everyone understand? Shall I sign it?'

'Is that necessary?' said Despard-Smith. 'It's not in the statutes.'

'It's fitting that I should sign it,' said Gay. 'When people see my signature at the bottom, they won't doubt that everything is in order. I shall certainly sign it.'

He wrote his great bold signature, and said with satisfaction:

'Ah. That's a fine notice. Now I must fix it.' Chrystal and Roy Calvert helped him with his overcoat, and as they did so he heard the clock strike. It was six o'clock. He chuckled:

'Do you know, our old friend Despard wrote to me last night and said this would be a purely formal meeting. And it's lasted an hour and a quarter. Not bad for a purely formal meeting, Despard, old chap! An hour and a quarter. What do you think of that, Winslow? What do you think of that, Jago?'

It was raining hard outside, and we put on overcoats to follow him. Roy slipped Gay's arms through the sleeves of his gown again. We followed him out into the court, and Chrystal opened an umbrella and held it over the old man as he shuffled along. The rest of us halted our steps to keep behind him, in the slow procession across the first court to the chapel. The procession moved slowly through the cold December evening.

When we arrived at the chapel door, it was found there were no drawing pins. Chrystal swore, and, while Luke ran to find some, tried to persuade Gay that it was too chilly for him to stay there in the open.

'Not a bit of it, my dear chap,' said Gay. 'Not a bit of it. There's life in the old dog yet.' Luke came back panting with the pins, and Gay firmly pushed in eight of them, one at each corner of the sheet and one in the middle of each side.

Then he stood back and admired the notice.

'Ah. Excellent. Excellent,' he said. 'That's well done. Anyone can see there's a vacancy with half an eye.'

PART THREE

NOTICE OF A VACANCY

CHAPTER XXX

JAGO THINKS OF HIMSELF AS A YOUNG MAN

THE funeral was arranged for 8 December, and in the days before a sombre truce came over the college. Full term ended on the seventh, and the undergraduates climbed Brown's stairs to fetch their exeats, walked through the courts to Jago's house, more quietly than usual; even the scholarship candidates, who came up that day, were greeted by the hush as soon as they asked a question at the porters' lodge. On the nights of the fifth and sixth, the two nights which followed Gay's meeting, I did not hear a word spoken about the Mastership. Chrystal was busy arranging for a fellows' wreath, to add to those we were each sending as individuals; Despard-Smith was talking solemnly about the form of service; there was no wine drunk. Roy Calvert did not dine either night; he was looking after Lady Muriel, and she liked having him eat and sleep in the Lodge.

On the afternoon of the seventh, I wanted to escape from the college for a time and went for a walk alone. It was a dark and lowering day, very warm for December; lights were coming on in the shop windows, a slight rain was blown on the gusty wind, the wind blew down the streets as though they were organ-pipes, umbrellas were bent to meet it.

I walked over Coe Fen to the Grantchester meadows, and on by the bank of the river. There was no one about, the afternoon was turning darker; a single swan moved on the water, and the flat fields were desolate. I was glad to return to the lighted streets and the gas flares in Peas Hill, all spurting furiously in the wind.

While I was looking at the stalls under the gas flares, I heard a voice behind me say: 'Good Lord, it's you. What are you doing out on this filthy day?'

Jago was smiling, but his face was so drawn that one forgot the heavy flesh. 'I've been for a walk,' I said.

'So have I,' said Jago. 'I've been trying to think straight.'

We walked together towards the college. After a moment's silence, Jago broke out:

'Would it be a nuisance if I begged a cup of tea in your rooms?'

'Of course not.'

'I've been trying to collect my thoughts,' he smiled, 'and it's not a specially pleasant process. It hurts my wife to see me, very naturally. If I inflict myself on you, you won't mind too much, will you?'

'Come for as long as you like,' I said.

In the first court, Brown's windows gleamed out of the dusk, but on the other side of the court the Lodge was dark behind drawn blinds.

'It is very hard to accept that he is dead,' said Jago.

We went up to my sitting-room, I ordered tea. And then I asked, feeling it kindest to be direct:

'You must be worrying about the election now?'

'Intolerably,' said Jago.

'You couldn't help it,' I said.

'I should be on better terms with myself if I could.'

'You wouldn't be human,' I said.

'I haven't been able to forget it for an instant this afternoon. I went out to clear my head. I couldn't put it aside for an instant, Eliot. So I've been trying to think it out.'

'What have you been trying to think out?'

'How much it means to me.'

He burst out:

'And I'm quite lost, Eliot, I don't know where I am.' He looked at me in a manner naïve, piercing and confiding. 'I can tell you what I shouldn't like to tell Chrystal and good old Arthur Brown. There are times when it seems absolutely meaningless. I'm disgusted with myself for getting so excited about something that doesn't matter in the slightest. There are times when I'd give anything to run away from it altogether.'

'And those times are when—'

Jago smiled painfully.

'When it seems quite certain I shall get it,' he said. 'Often I feel quite certain. Sometimes I think it will be taken from me at the last. Whenever I think that,' he added, 'I want it more than anything in the world. You see, I've no use for myself at all.'

'I should be the same,' I said.

'Should you? Do you really know what it is to have no use for yourself?'

'Oh yes,' I said.

'You seem more sensible than I am,' said Jago. 'Perhaps you wouldn't want so badly to run away from it altogether.'

'Perhaps not,' I said.

'Chrystal ought to be standing himself. He would have enjoyed it,' said Jago with a tired and contemptuous shrug.

I was thinking: it was the core of diffidence and pride flaming out again. He would have liked, even now, to escape from the content. He told himself 'it did not matter in the slightest'. He assured himself of that, because he could not bear to fail. Then again he revolted from the humiliations he had consented to, in order to gain an end that was beneath him. He had been civil to Nightingale, for months he had submitted himself to Chrystal's lead. He had just revealed something I had already guessed, something I believed that had worried Arthur Brown all along. Jago had always been far away from Chrystal. In the course of nature, as Chrystal ran the campaign, Jago liked him less. He came to think that Chrystal was a soulless power-crazed businessman, and it irked him to submit: his temper over the candidates' vote had been an outburst of defiance. Yet even that night he had been forced to retract, he could not bear to ruin his chances, he needed this place more even than he needed his pride.

'We must get it for you,' I said, with a feeling I had never had for him before. There was a pause. Jago said:

'I think I want it more than anything in the world.'

'It's strange,' he added in a moment. 'It's extremely strange. When I was a young man, Eliot, I was ambitious. I wanted everything that a man can want. I wanted honour, riches and the love of women. Yes, I was ambitious. I've suffered through it. And now this is what I have come to want. It can't be long now—'

He passed on to talk, with a curious content, of some appointments he would make as Master. He was enjoying in advance the pleasure of patronage: in his imagination the future was golden: for a moment he pictured the college in years to come looking back upon his reign – 'the greatest of our Masters'. Then that vision left him. He glanced at me almost fiercely and said:

'You'll be surprised how splendid my wife will turn out in the Lodge. She always rises to the occasion. I couldn't bear to lose it now, on her account. She's looking forward to it so much.'

I felt he wanted to say more about her, but he could not manage it. It had been a relief to talk of his ambition: perhaps it would have been a greater relief to let someone see into his marriage. But it was impossible. Certainly with me, a friendly acquaintance, a supporter, a much younger man. I believed that it would have been impossible with anyone. I believed he had never laid bare his heart about her. He had many friendly acquaintances, but, despite his warmth and candour, he seemed to have no intimate friends. I had the impression that he had not spoken even of his ambition so nakedly before.

Over tea, though he could not confide about his own marriage, he talked of one that would never happen. He had seen that Joan Royce longed to marry Roy. Jago switched from that one challenging remark about his wife to talk of them. She ought to have been right for Roy, said Jago. Jago had once hoped that she would be. But she simply was not. And so it would be madness for Roy to marry her. No one outside can tell who is right for one. There are no rules. One knows it without help. Sometimes the rest of the world thinks one is wrong, but they cannot know.

Then his thoughts came back to himself. 20 December.

'It can't be long now,' he said.

'Thirteen days.'

'Each day is a long time,' said Jago.

Next afternoon, the bell tolled and the chapel filled up for the funeral. Lady Muriel and Joan sat in the front rows with their backs like pokers, not a tear on their faces, true to their Spartan training: they would not show a sign of grief in public and it was only with Roy that they broke down. All the fellows attended but Pilbrow, from whom there was still no news; even Winslow came into the chapel, for the first time since Royce's election. Many of the heads of other colleges were there, all the professors of divinity, most of the orientalists and theologians in the university; and also a few men who went by habit from college to college for each funeral.

The wind had dropped, but the skies were low outside and a steady rain fell all day. Every light in the chapel was burning, and as they entered people blinked their eyes after the sombre daylight. The flowers on the coffin smelt sweet and sickly. There was a heavy quiet, even when the chapel was packed.

Despard-Smith recited the service, and Gay, less dispirited than anyone there, chanted his responses with lusty vigour. 'Lord, have mercy upon us,' cried Despard-Smith: and I could distinguish Roy Calvert's voice, light, reedy and abnormally clear, as he said Amen.

Despard-Smith put into the service a eulogy of Royce. On the night the news of the death came to the combination room, Despard-Smith had spoken simply and without thinking: 'he was a very human man'. But by now he had had time to think, and he pronounced the same praise as he had done so often. 'Our first thoughts must go to his family in their affliction. . . . Greater as their loss must be, we his colleagues know ours to be so catastrophic that only our faith can give us hope of building up this society again. We chiefly mourn this day, not the Master whom we all venerated, not the leader in scholarship who devoted all his life to searching for truth, but the kind and faithful friend. Many of us have had the blessing of his friendship for a lifetime. We know that no one ever turned to him for help in vain; no one ever found him to hold malice in his heart or any kind of uncharitableness; no one ever believed he was capable of entertaining an unkind thought, or heard him utter an unkind word.'

I glanced at Roy. He had loved Royce: his eyes lost their sadness for a second as he heard that last singular piece of praise; there was the faint twitch of a smile on his lips.

In the even and unfaltering rain, a cavalcade of taxis rolled out to a cemetery in the suburbs, rolled past the lodging-houses of Maid's Causeway, the blank street fronts of the Newmarket Road. The fellows were allotted to taxis in order of seniority: Francis Getliffe, Roy Calvert, Luke and I shared the last. None of us spoke much, the heaviness rested on us, we gazed out of the streaming windows.

At the cemetery, we stood under umbrellas round the grave. Despard-Smith spoke the last words, and the earth rattled on the coffin.

We drove back, more quickly now, in the same group. The rain still pelted down without a break, but we all felt an inexplicably strong relief. We chatted with comfort, sometimes with animation: Francis and Roy, who rarely had much to say to each other, exchanged a joke about Katherine's father. There were wild spirits latent in each of us just then, if our conventions had given us any excuse. As it was, when the taxis drew up at the college, knots of fellows stood in the shelter of the great gate. The same pulse of energy was passing round. I expected one result to be that the truce would be broken by dinner time that night.

CHAPTER XXXI

'A GOOD DAY FOR THE COLLEGE'

ACTUALLY, it took twenty-four hours for the truce to break in earnest. Then a rumour went round that Nightingale had threatened to 'speak out'. It was certainly true that Francis Getliffe spent the afternoon arguing with Luke; I heard of the conversation from Luke himself, who could not bear to be separated for an hour from his work just then. His fresh skin had lost most of its colour, there were rings under his eyes, and he said angrily: 'You'd have thought Getliffe was the last man in the bloody place to keep anyone away from the lab. – just when the whole box of tricks may be tumbling out.'

'You look tired,' I said.

'I'm not too tired to work,' he retorted.

'What did you tell Getliffe?'

'Everyone else in this blasted college may change their minds twice a week,' said young Luke, who was frantic with hope, who had anyway given up being tactful with me. 'But *I* bloody well don't.'

Francis's attempt was fair enough, and so was another by Winslow to persuade me. Neither caused any comment, in contrast to a 'flysheet' which Nightingale circulated to each fellow on 10 December. In the flysheet Nightingale put down a list of Crawford's claims to the Mastership, and ended with the sentence: 'Mrs Crawford appears to many members of the college to be well fitted for the position of Master's wife. This is not necessarily true of a candidate's wife, and they attach great weight to this consideration.'

He said no more, but I was stopped in the court several times between lunch and dinner: was this Nightingale's final shot? was he going further? I was ready for an open scene in hall that night. Roy and I were the only members of Jago's party dining, and Nightingale, Winslow and Despard-Smith were sitting together. I had braced myself to take the offensive – when Jago, who had not come into hall since the Master's death, walked in after the grace. Nightingale seemed to be waiting for a burst of fury, but there was none. Jago sat through the dinner talking quietly to me and Roy. Occasionally he spoke a civil word to Despard-Smith and Winslow. Nightingale he had come there to ignore, and not a word was spoken about the Mastership, either in hall or in the combination room.

As I was having breakfast next morning, 11 December, Brown came in, pink and businesslike.

'I've been wondering whether to answer Nightingale's latest effort,' he said, sitting in the window-seat. 'But I'm rather inclined to leave it alone. Any reply is only likely to make bad worse. And I've got a sneaking hope that, now he's started putting things on paper, he may possibly give us something to take hold of. I did sketch out a letter, but I had last-minute qualms. I don't like it, but it's wise to leave things as they are.'

'How are they?' I asked.

'I won't pretend to you that I'm entirely comfortable,' said Brown. 'Though mind you it's necessary for both of us to pretend to the other side. And perhaps' – he looked at me – 'it's even more necessary to pretend to our own. But, between ourselves, things aren't panning out as they should. I haven't had a reply from Eustace Pilbrow. I sent off cables to every possible address within an hour after poor Royce died. And I sent off another batch yesterday. I shall believe Pilbrow is coming back to vote when I see him walking through the gate.'

He went on:

'I had another disappointment last night. I went round with Chrystal to make another try to lobby old Gay. Well, we didn't get any distance at all. The old boy is perfectly well up to it, but he won't talk about anything except his responsibility for presiding over the college during the present period. He read the statutes to us again. But we didn't begin to get anywhere.'

'I wish you'd taken me,' I said sharply.

'I very much wanted to take Chrystal,' said Brown. He saw that I was annoyed (for I did not believe they had ever been good at flattering Gay), and he spoke more frankly about his friend than at any time before. 'I feel it's a good idea to – keep up his interest in our campaign. He's never been quite as enthusiastic as I should like. I have had to take it into account that he's inclined to be temperamental.'

The telephone bell rang. Was Mr Brown with me? Mr Chrystal was trying to trace him urgently. Brown offered to go to Chrystal's rooms; no, the Dean was already on his way up to mine.

Chrystal entered, his eyes alight with purpose and the sense of action. 'It's a good day for the college,' he said at once.

'What's happened?' asked Brown, quick and suspicious.

'I don't think I'm entitled to say much more till this afternoon,' said Chrystal. He was revelling in this secret. 'But I can tell you that Despard-Smith received a letter from Sir Horace by the first post today. It's very satisfactory, and that's putting it mildly. There's one thing that's a bit cranky, but you'll hear for yourselves soon enough. I'd like to tell you the whole story, but Despard showed me the letter in confidence.'

'It sounds perfectly splendid,' said Brown.

'Despard didn't see how we could do anything about it until we'd elected a Master. But I insisted that it would be lamentable to hold back the news of something as big as this,' Chrystal said. 'I had to tell Despard straight out that I wasn't prepared to let that happen. If he wouldn't summon an informal meeting himself, I would do it off my own bat.'

Brown smiled affably at his friend's brisk triumphant air.

'Wonderful,' he said again.

'That's how we left it. I've got the college office running round to get hold of people for this afternoon. It shocked old Despard too much to think of having an informal meeting in the combination room.' Chrystal gave a tough grin. 'So it will be in my rooms. I've called it for 2.30. I tell you, Arthur, we've done something between us. It's a good day for the college.'

When I arrived in Chrystal's sitting-room that afternoon, it was already arranged to seat the fellows, with a dozen chairs round the dining table. Ten men turned up by half-past two; Luke had gone early to the laboratory and did not return for lunch, so no message had reached him; Gay was not there, and I suspected that Chrystal had taken care that that invitation had miscarried. We sat down round the table, all except Chrystal, who stood watching us, like a commanding officer.

'It's time we began,' he said. 'I move Mr Despard-Smith take the chair.'

Brown seconded, and there was a murmur, but Despard-Smith said: 'I ought to say that I consider this meeting is definitely irregular. I find myself in a dilemma. It would be scandalous not to let the college know as soon as I properly can of a communication which I received this morning. On the other hand I cannot conceal from myself that the communication was sent to me under the misunderstanding that I still had the status of Deputy for the Master. I do not see the way clear for the college to receive any official communication during the *dies non* while there is a vacancy in the office of Master. I see grave difficulties whatever view we decide upon.'

At last Despard-Smith was persuaded to take the chair (which, as Roy whispered, he had been determined to do all the time). He began:

'The least irregular course open to us in my judgment is for me to disclose to you in confidence the contents of the communication I received this morning. I am p-positive that we cannot reply except to explain that I am no longer Deputy but that the letter will be laid before the new Master as soon as he is elected. Very well. The communication is from Sir Horace Timberlake, who I believe is a relative of one of our recent men. It will ultimately call for some very difficult decisions by the college, but perhaps I had better read it.'

"Dear Mr Deputy,

During the past year I have had many interesting talks upon the future of the college. I have had the privilege in particular of hearing the views of Dr Jago—" ' (I wondered for a second if Sir Horace had timed his letter to assist Jago in the election: he was quite capable of it) ' "and frequently those of Mr Brown and Mr Chrystal. I should like to add my own small share to helping the college, feeling as I do its invaluable benefits to my nephew and the great part I can see it playing in the world. I am clear that the most useful assistance anyone can give the college at the present time is the endowment of fellowships, and I am clear that a substantial proportion should be restricted to scientific and engineering subjects. I wish to lay the minimum conditions upon the college, but I should not be living up to my own ideas of the future if I did not ask you to accept this stipulation. If the college can see its way to agree, I should be honoured to transfer to you a capital sum of £120,000—" ' (there was a whistle from someone at the table) ' "which I take to be equivalent to the endowment of six fellowships. This capital sum will be made over in seven equal yearly instalments, until the entire endowment is in your hands by 1944. Four of these six fellowships are to be limited to scientific and engineering subjects and one is to be held in any subject that the college thinks fit. You will appreciate that this letter is not a formal offer and I shall crystallise my ideas further if I learn that the general scheme is acceptable to the college. I shall also be able to crystallise my ideas about the one remaining fellowship which I hope to designate for a special purpose." ' I saw puzzled frowns and could not imagine what was coming. ' "The best way to make a contribution to my purpose has not yet presented itself to me, but I am desirous of using this fellowship to help in the wonderful work of—" ' – Despard-Smith read solemnly – ' "Mr Roy Calvert, by which I was so tremendously impressed. Possibly his work could be aided by a fellowship on special terms, but no doubt we can pursue these possibilities together. I am not sufficiently conversant with your customs to know whether you attach distinguishing titles to your endowments, and I should not wish in any case even to express a view on such a delicate topic." '

Someone whistled again, as Despard-Smith finished. There were glances at Roy, who was looking serious. A rustle went round the table. The only person who stayed quite still was Winslow; he had been gazing down in front of him throughout the reading of the letter, and now he did not move.

'This is the largest benefaction the college has ever had,' said Chrystal, who could not contain himself no longer. 'I call this a day.'

'I foresee grave difficulties,' said Despard-Smith. 'I am positive that it will need the most serious consideration before the college could possibly decide to accept.'

'Somehow, though, I rather think we shall,' said Crawford, with the only trace of irony I had ever seen him show. 'I must say this is a fine achievement, Chrystal. I suppose we owe this to you, and you deserve a very hearty vote of thanks. Speaking as a man of science, I can see this college taking the biggest jump forward it's ever made.'

'Good work, Chrystal,' said Francis Getliffe. 'It's going to make a terrific difference. Good work.'

'I can't accept all these congratulations for myself,' said Chrystal, curt but delighted. 'There's one man who's been more responsible than I have. That's Brown. He nursed young Timberlake. He looked after Sir Horace. It's Brown you ought to thank. Without him, we shouldn't have come within shouting distance.'

'I'm afraid that I'm compelled to disagree,' said Brown, settling himself comfortably to enjoy passing a good round compliment to Chrystal. 'The sense of the college is absolutely right in thinking that we owe this magnificent endowment to the Dean, as no one is in a better position to appreciate than I am. If other fellows had been able to witness the time and trouble, the boundless time and trouble, that the Dean has bestowed upon securing this benefaction, I can assure the college that its sense of indebtedness to him would be even more overwhelming than it is. For his untiring devotion and unparalleled skill, I believe we ought to rank the Dean himself among the great benefactors of this society.'

'I associate myself wholeheartedly with those remarks,' said Crawford. Francis and others said hear, hear.

'I feel we also owe the deepest gratitude to our other colleague Brown,' said Jago. I joined in the applause, even Nightingale said an amiable word. Roy grinned.

'The old boy has unbelted to some purpose,' he said. 'I wonder how many free meals he could have taken off us before we gave him up.'

'You're not in a position to complain,' said Chrystal severely, provoked because Roy did not seem weighed down by his obligation.

'Certainly not.' Roy was still grinning. 'But it would have been very beautiful if the old boy's patience hadn't given out.'

'It will make your subject, young man,' Crawford reproved him.

'Just so. We'll polish it off,' said Roy.

Winslow had not yet spoken. Words went to and fro across the table, expressing gratification, mild misgivings, disapproval from some that

Roy Calvert had been singled out, triumphant emphasis from Brown, Jago and myself. In all of these exchanges Winslow took no part, but went on sitting with his head bent down – until at last, when the table happened to fall silent, he looked up from under his lids.

'I confess that I am not particularly confident of disentangling the sense of this remarkable letter,' he said. 'The style of our worthy friend is not apparently designed to reveal his meaning. But correct me if I am wrong – I gather some members of the college have been discussing this benefaction with Sir Horace?'

'In the vaguest terms you can possibly imagine,' said Brown, prompt and emollient. 'Put it another way: Sir Horace asked me among others one or two questions, and it wouldn't have been ordinary decent manners not to reply. I imagine the Dean was placed in the same rather embarrassing position.'

'It must have been most embarrassing,' said Winslow. 'I take it, my dear Tutor, you were forced most unwillingly to discuss the finances of the college?'

Roy was scribbling on a piece of paper. He passed it to me along the table: it read *Winslow will never recover from this*.

'Naturally we shouldn't consider ourselves competent,' said Brown. 'No one's got a greater respect for the Dean's financial acumen than I have – but, if either of us had had the remotest idea that Sir Horace was going to make a definite proposition without giving us time to look round our first thought would have been to go straight to the Bursar.'

'That doesn't need saying,' Chrystal joined in.

'I recall very vividly,' said Brown, 'one evening when the Dean asked me what I thought was the point of Sir Horace's questions. "I suppose it can't mean money," he said. "If I had the slightest hope it might" – I think I'm remembering him properly – "our first step would be to bring the Bursar in".'

'I'm very much affected by that reminiscence,' said Winslow. 'I'm also very much affected by the thought of the Dean expending "boundless time and trouble" without dreaming for a moment that there would be any question of money.'

'I'm sure I'm speaking for the Dean as well as myself,' said Brown, 'when I say that nothing would distress us more than that the Bursar should feel in the slightest degree left out. It's only the peculiar circumstances—'

'I've never had much opinion of myself as Bursar,' said Winslow. 'It's interesting to find others taking the same view. It looks at any rate as though my judgment remains unimpaired. Which will be a slight consolation to me in my retirement.'

Despard-Smith said: 'I hope you're not suggesting—'

'I'm not suggesting, I'm resigning,' said Winslow. 'I'm obviously useless when the college goes in for money seriously. It's time the college had someone who can cope with these problems. I should have a great deal more faith in the Dean or Mr Brown as Bursar than they can reasonably have in me.'

'I couldn't consider it,' said Chrystal, and Brown murmured in support.

'This is disastrous,' said Despard-Smith.

There were the usual exclamations of regret, incredulity, desire that Winslow should think again, that followed any resignation in the college. They were a shade more hurried than usual, they were more obviously mingled with relief. Despard-Smith remembered that no resignation could be offered or accepted while the college was without a Master. 'In that case,' said Winslow, 'the new Master will have a pleasant duty for his first.' His grim sarcasm was more repelling than ever now, and there was no warmth in the attempts to persuade him back. No one dared to be sorry for him. Then suddenly Jago burst out:

'This is a wretched exchange.'

'I don't follow you,' said Crawford.

'I mean,' Jago cried, 'that we're exchanging a fine Bursar for a rich man's charity. And I don't like it.'

'It's not our fault,' said Chrystal sharply.

'That doesn't make it any more palatable.' Jago turned to his old enemy and his eyes were blazing. 'Winslow, I want you to believe that we're more distressed than we can say. If this choice had lain with us, you mustn't be in any doubt what we should have chosen. Sir Horace would have had to find another use for his money. We can't forget what you've done for us. In one office or another, you've guided this college all your life. And in your ten years as Bursar the college has never been so rich.'

Winslow's astringent smile had left him, and he looked abashed and downcast.

'That's no thanks to me,' he said.

'Won't you reconsider it?' cried Jago.

Winslow shook his head.

The meeting broke up soon after, and Roy Calvert and I went for a stroll in the garden. A thick mist was gathering in the early evening, and the trees stood out as though in a Japanese print. We talked over the afternoon. Roy had enough trace of malice to feel triumphant; he imitated the look on some of their faces, as they heard of the bequest to him. 'Sir Timberlake's a bit of a humorist,' he said. 'Oh dear, I shall have to become respectable and stuffed. They've got me at last.'

We walked into the 'wilderness', and I mentioned Winslow. Roy frowned. We were both uncomfortable: we shared a perverse affection for him, we had not liked to watch his fall, we had admired Jago's piece of bravura at the end. But we were uneasy. Somehow we felt that he had been reckless and indiscreet; we wished he would be quiet until the election. Roy showed an unusual irritation. 'He will overdo things,' he said. 'He never will learn sense. All this enthusiasm about Winslow's work as Bursar. Absurd. Winslow's been dim as a Bursar. Chrystal would be much better. I should be an extremely good Bursar myself. They'd never let me be. They wouldn't think I was sound.'

It seemed odd, but all he said was true.

Then we saw Winslow himself walking through the mist, his long heavy-footed stride noiseless on the sodden grass.

'Hullo, Winslow,' said Roy. 'We were talking about you.'

'Were you?' said Winslow. 'Is there much to say?'

'Quite a lot,' said Roy.

'What shall you do, now you'll get some leisure?' I asked.

'Nothing. I can't start anything new.'

'There's plenty of time,' I said.

'I've never lacked for time,' he said. 'Somehow, I've never had the gift of bringing things off. I don't know why. I used to think I wasn't a fool. Sometimes, by the side of our colleagues, I thought I was a remarkably intelligent man. But everything I've touched has come to nothing.'

Roy and I looked at each other, and knew it was worse to speak than to stay silent. It would not have consoled him if we spoke. It was better to watch him, stoically facing the truth.

Together the three of us walked in silence through the foggy twilight. Bushes and trees loomed at us, as we took another turn at the bottom of the garden. We had covered the whole length twice before Roy spoke again, to ask a question about Dick Winslow. He had just got engaged, said Winslow. 'We scarcely know the girl,' he added. 'I only hope it's all right.'

His tone was warm and unguarded. His son had been the bitterest of his disappointments, but his love glowed on. And that afternoon the thought of the marriage refreshed him and gave him pleasure.

CHAPTER XXXII

THE VIRTUES OF THE OTHER SIDE

WHILE we were walking round the garden, Roy asked Winslow to go with him to the pictures. Winslow was puzzled by the invitation, grumbled that he had not been for years, and yet was touched. In the end, they went off together and I was left to go in search of Brown.

I wanted to talk to him alone, for I still thought it might be worth while for me to go round to Gay's. But, when I arrived, Chrystal was just sitting down. He was smoking a pipe, and his expression was not as elated as it had been that morning. Even when Brown produced a bottle of madeira – 'it needs something rather out of the ordinary to drink Sir Horace's health' – Chrystal responded with a smile that was a little twisted, a little wan. He was dispirited because his triumph, like all triumphs, had not been as intoxicating as he had imagined it.

He emptied his glass absently, and smoked away. He interrupted us with a sharp question:

'What was your impression of this afternoon?'

'My impression was,' said Brown, knowing that his friend needed heartening, 'that everyone realises you've done the best day's work for the college that anyone has ever done.'

'Not they. They just take it for granted,' said Chrystal.

'Everyone was full of it,' said Brown.

'I believe they think we've treated Winslow badly. That's the thought they've gone away with.' Chrystal added, with hurt and angry force: 'Jago is *amusing*.'

'He wanted to soften the blow,' said Brown.

'There may have been a bit of policy in it,' I suggested. 'He may have wanted to make a gesture. He's bound to be thinking of the election.'

'Certainly. I was glad to see him showing some political sense at last,' said Brown. He had followed my lead with his unceasing vigilance: he knew it was untrue, as well as I did: we were trying to take Chrystal's attention away.

'I don't believe it, Eliot,' retorted Chrystal.

'He's not a simple character,' I went on.

'I give you that,' Chrystal said. 'By God, I give you that. And there's something I wouldn't confess outside this room.' He paused and looked at us. 'There are times,' he said slowly, 'when I see the other side's case against Jago. He's too much up and down. He's all over you one minute.

Then he discovers some reason for getting under one's skin as he did this afternoon. I say, I wouldn't confess it outside this room, but there are times when I have my doubts. Don't you? Either of you?'

'No,' said Brown with absolute firmness.

'Some of what you say is true,' I said. 'But I thought it over when I decided on Jago. I didn't believe it mattered enough to count against him. I still don't.'

'Not more than you did?'

'No, less,' I said.

'I hope you're right,' said Chrystal.

Then Chrystal said, with a pretence of off-handedness:

'Anyway, it doesn't look as though we're going to get him in.'

'I don't quite follow you,' said Brown, but his eyes were piercing.

'Has Pilbrow cabled back to you yet?'

'Not yet.'

'There you are. I shall expect him when I see him. Sometime next year.'

'I've never known you rush to conclusions so fast,' Brown said, 'as you have done over this election.' A deep frown had settled on his face.

'I knew we shouldn't get over it,' said Chrystal, 'the day I heard about Royce's cancer. People still don't know what we've lost.'

'I can't regard that as a reason,' Brown said, 'for not settling down to play our hand.'

Chrystal said: 'You haven't denied the facts. You can't deny them.'

'What do you mean?'

'I mean, you've had no reply from Pilbrow. It's a bad sign. And the votes are 6–6.'

'There's nothing at all sensible to be done.'

'Nothing at all,' I added.

'Is that absolutely true?' Chrystal was talking to Brown in a tone of great reason and friendliness. 'Look, I'll put up a case for you to knock down. We threatened those two prima donnas that if they didn't play we'd settle on a third candidate. The other side were only too anxious to come in. Men like old Despard and Getliffe didn't like this lamentable position any more than we did. And I don't believe Crawford did. I've got some respect for their judgment. Did you notice that they were very forthcoming this afternoon? More than some of our own side. Well, I should like to know their line of thought tonight. What do they expect? They know it's 6–6 as well as we do. Do you think they've heard about Pilbrow?'

'I should consider that it's extraordinarily unlikely.'

'I should like to know,' said Chrystal, 'whether their thoughts have turned to a third candidate again.'

Brown was flushed.

'It's possible they may have,' he said, 'but it wouldn't be a very profitable speculation. It couldn't get anywhere unless we were foolish enough to meet them half-way.'

'I shouldn't like to dismiss it,' said Chrystal.

'I'm sorry to hear you say so,' said Brown.

'We should have to feel our way. We shouldn't have to give away a point. But I should like a chance to explore it.'

'Have they made any approaches?' I asked.

'Not to me,' said Chrystal.

'Do *you* intend to?'

He looked truculent.

'Only if I see an opening,' he said.

'I very much hope you won't,' said Brown sternly and with great weight.

'It's only as a last resort. If we can't get our man in.' All the time Chrystal was trying to placate Brown, trying to persuade him all was well: he was working to get rid of the heavy, anxious, formidable frown that had stayed on Brown's face. 'After all,' said Chrystal, with his trace of the gamin, 'you didn't like our last effort. But it came off.'

'We were luckier than we deserved.'

'We need a bit of luck.'

'Nothing will reconcile me,' said Brown, 'to any more approaches from our side. They can only give the others one impression. And that is, without putting too fine a point on it, that we've lost faith in our man.'

He looked at Chrystal.

'I realise you've always had your misgivings,' he went on. 'But that's all the more reason why you shouldn't have any dealings with the other side. This isn't the time to give them any inkling that you're not a wholehogger. The only safe course is to leave them in their ignorance.'

'If they make a move?'

'We ought to cross that bridge when we come to it.' Then Brown relaxed. 'I'm sorry Jago let his tongue run away with him this afternoon.'

'That didn't affect me one way or the other,' Chrystal said curtly. 'It doesn't alter the situation.'

'We'd better all sleep on it,' said Brown. 'I expect you'll agree tomorrow that we've got to sit tight. It's the only statesmanlike thing to do.'

'I should let you know,' said Chrystal, 'before I spoke to anyone.'

CHAPTER XXXIII

THAT WHICH DIES LAST

THE next day, 12 December, began for me with a letter which took my mind right away from the college. When I dined in hall that night, my private preoccupation had so affected me that I felt I was a visitor from outside. The college was full of rumours, hushed conversation, *tête-à-têtes*; in the combination room Francis Getliffe and Winslow spent several minutes talking in a corner. The chief rumours that night were that an informal meeting of the whole college was to be held to discuss the deadlock: and that Nightingale was just on the point of sending round another flysheet.

I had three impressions of extreme sharpness. The first was that Brown was deeply troubled, even more than he had been during the talk with Chrystal the previous night. Chrystal was not dining, and Brown slipped away by himself immediately after hall. I did not get the chance of a word with him. My second impression was that Nightingale behaved as though he was hiding his intention and at the same time pleased with it. And the third, and much the strongest, was that Jago felt that night assured that he was in.

Perhaps, I thought, it was one of those intermissions that come in any period of anxiety: one is waiting for an answer, one goes to bed anxious, wakes up for no reason suffused with hope, suffused with hope so strong that it seems the answer has already come.

Anyway, Jago was quite relaxed, his voice easy; he did not have to clown; he did not make a remark which drew attention to himself. He spoke to Crawford with such friendliness, such quiet warmth, such subdued but natural confidence, that Crawford seemed out of his depth. He had never seen his rival like this before, he had never felt the less comfortable of the two.

I walked away from the combination room with Jago. He had promised to show me a small comet which had become visible a night or two before, and we climbed to the top of a staircase in the second court. There, looking over the garden to the east, he made me see a blur of light close to the faintest star of the Great Bear. He had been an amateur astronomer since childhood, and from the stars he gained, despite his unbelief, something close to a religious emotion.

The silence of the infinite spaces did not terrify him. He felt at one with the heavens; it was through them that he knew a sense of the unseen.

But he only spoke of what he could observe. That night, he told me where the comet would have reached by the same time next day: how fast it was travelling: the size of its orbit: how long it would be before men saw it again.

Coming down the stairs, he was full of happiness. He was not even much excited when he saw Pilbrow's door open and his servant lighting a fire. I went in and asked the reason, and was told that Pilbrow had sent a telegram from London, saying that he was returning by the last train.

Jago heard the servant's answers from the landing, and I did not need to tell him that Pilbrow was coming back. 'He's a wonderful old boy,' said Jago. He did not say it with emphasis; for him, the news just completed the well-being of an evening. He said a contented good-night, and walked at a leisurely pace along the path to his house. I had not seen him walk so slowly since that afternoon of our first party meeting, when he felt the Mastership lay in his hands.

Once at least he lifted his eyes to the stars.

It was well past one o'clock next morning, and I was writing by my fire, when I heard the clang of the great gate's bell: gently once or twice, then a long impatient ring, then another. At last the porter must have woken up. I heard the opening of a door, and finally the rattle and clash as the gate was unlocked.

There were steps through the court. I wondered who had come in late, and turned back to my writing. A few minutes later, steps sounded on my own staircase. It was Pilbrow.

'I saw your light on my way past. I had to tidy up after the trip. I specially wanted to see you before you went to bed.'

He had burst in, looking ten years younger than his age. He was ruddily sunburned, and there were one or two patches on the top of his bald head from which the skin had peeled.

'I had lunch in Split thirty-six hours ago. Split! Split! I like the Slavs – Absurd names. Much more absurd than the Italian names.' He pronounced the name several times aloud, chuckling to himself. 'Astonishing number of beautiful people. You sit in the market-place and watch them. . . . Also extremely prudish. Why do people get steadily more beautiful as you go south-east from the Brenner? The Tyrolese are lovely. The Dalmatians are better still. They also get more prudish as they get more beautiful. The Tyrolese are moderately prudish. The Dalmatians extremely. . . . I suppose it's a law of nature. A very stupid one too.'

I could scarcely get in a word. He had been flown most of the way home. He had been travelling for two days: his cheeks shone, he did not seem in the least tired.

Soon he said, earnestly and without any introduction:

'Eliot, things are worse in Europe than they have been in my time.'

'You mean politically?'

'All our friends are in danger. Everything you and I believe in is going. . . . Our people are just sitting by and watching. And dining in the best houses. Bloody fools. Snobs. Snobbery will make this country commit suicide. These bloody snobs can't see who their enemies are. Or who are their friends. When a country is blinding itself to that, it's in a bad way.'

He told me of some of his doings. He had somehow managed to visit friends just out of a concentration camp. He was a very brave old man. He was also an acute one, underneath the champagne-like gaiety.

'I came to tell you', he said suddenly. 'That's why I was glad to see your light. I wanted to tell you before anyone else. I can't vote for Jago. I can't vote for someone who won't throw his weight in on our side. It's your side as well as mine. That's why I came to tell you first. . . .'

I was taken aback. I should not have been so surprised at the outset. I knew it had worried him, but I thought he had come to terms and satisfied himself. It would not have astonished me if he had found some reasonable excuse and stayed away. But I was not prepared for his journey home, his ebullient entry, and then this. I had not recovered myself when I asked flatly:

'What are you going to do?'

'Vote for the other man,' said Pilbrow without a pause. 'He's on the right side. He's always been on the right side. We can trust him in that way.'

I tried to shake off the shock, and do my best. I retraced the arguments I had had with Francis Getliffe. I searched for anything that might influence him: I told him that the three youngest fellows in the college were all supporting Jago – it was not like Pilbrow, I reproached him, to leave the side of youth. But he was obdurate – sometimes a little flustered in speech, but quite unshaken.

I tried once more.

'You know I feel about the world as strongly as you,' I said. 'If that's possible.'

Pilbrown smiled, pleased by the remark.

'You do know, don't you?'

'Of course,' Pilbrow replied. 'Of course. More than any of those. . . .'

'No,' I said. 'Not more than Getliffe or young Luke. But as much. Anyway, I take an even blacker view than you. I'm beginning to feel it like a personal sorrow.'

'Yes! Yes!' cried Pilbrow. 'Things outside have got to be very bad before they make one feel like that. But they are—'

'Even so,' I said, 'I can't believe that it ought to affect us here. We're choosing from two human beings.' I waited, in the hope it would sink in. 'You've always liked Jago, haven't you?'

'Yes,' said Pilbrow at once. 'He's warm. He's got a great gift of warmth.'

'You don't care for Crawford?'

'I'm neutral to him,' said Pilbrow.

'He's on the right side in politics,' I said, 'but you know very well that most of your kind of civilisation he doesn't begin to touch. If the books you've devoted your life to disappeared tomorrow, he wouldn't notice the difference.'

'No. But—' Pilbrow's bright brown eyes were troubled.

'You've always set a value on human beings. Surely you're not going to pass over the difference between those two? You're saying that you'll just vote for a programme. Are you really ready to forget what human beings mean?'

'We have got to sacrifice something.' Pilbrow had found his tongue, and spoke with vigour. 'If we don't sacrifice something, there'll be nothing left at all.'

I made a last attempt.

'You know what it means for Jago,' I said.

'Disappointing. . . .'

'You know it will be far worse than that.'

'Yes.'

'For you it wouldn't have mattered much – at any time. Would it? You're not such a diffident man as Paul Jago, you know. You'd never have thought of pinning your self-esteem on to a job. You've never given a damn whether people elected you to masterships or presidencies of buffaloes' clubs. It's not people like you who are ambitious for positions, Eustace. It is people like Jago – who need some support from outside. And he needs it *intolerably*. If he doesn't get the Mastership, it will hurt him more than anyone imagines. It won't be just disappointing. It will break his heart.'

I added:

'Don't you agree?'

'I'm afraid so.'

'Doesn't it affect you?'

'It's a pity,' said Pilbrow. 'He'll recover in time. They always. . . .'

He broke off. His tone was almost light-hearted, and I knew it was no good. Then he said, with extraordinary vigour, his eyes shining like brown beads, his whole body clenched with energy:

'I can't bear to have anyone say that I helped the wrong side. I can't do as much as I should like, but I shall throw in my weight wherever I can. I hope I have a few years left to do it.'

I knew it was no good. There was nothing to be done. No one could move Pilbrow now. He would vote for Crawford to the end.

And I felt something else. His vigour was marvellous and enviable: I wished I could imagine being so radiant at seventy-four: and yet, for the first time, I saw him overtaken by age.

A few years before he would not have said of Jago, as though human feelings were tiresome, 'he'll recover in time'. But in fact he had come to the point where human feelings *were* tiresome – no, not tiresome, so much as remote, trivial, a little comic. That was the sign of age. Pilbrow had been a man of strong affections. But those affections died off, except the strongest of all; as he became old, he could only feel moved by the great themes of his life; all else cooled down, although he struck no one as old, certainly not himself. And where he did not feel himself, he lost his sympathy for others' feelings. They did not seem important. Very little seemed important. Just as a mature man dismisses calf love with a smile, because he can no longer feel it (though it may once have caused him the sharpest pain), so Pilbrow, that vigorous old man, smiled indifferently at the triumphs and sufferings of the middle-aged. Suddenly one encountered blankness at a point where one expected sympathy and response. He looked just as he had looked ten years before; he could still feel passionately about his deepest concerns; but those concerns were narrowing, and one knew at last that he was growing old.

At times he knew it. At times he could not help but know it. So he clung more ardently to that which moved him still. It was that which died last. For Pilbrow, who had befriended so many, who had spent a lifetime in good causes, who had fought with body and mind, it was the picture of himself still 'throwing in his weight' on the side of light. That rang out of his last words. In them one heard the essence of the man: he was stripped by age of all that did not matter: and age revealed his vital core. In a sense, he was self-centred – more so than many men whose lives were selfish by the side of his. He was sweet-dispositioned, he was the most generous of men, but nothing could make him forget his picture of himself. That night I was too much upset to care, but later on it made me feel more brother-like towards him. I did not see in him the goodness that some did; but I felt the comradeship of common flesh, as well as great tenderness, for the gallant, lubricious, indomitable and generous old man, with the sturdy self-regard that nothing on earth could move.

He did not realise that I was deeply upset by his news. He went on talking about a Croatian writer, and it was getting on for four when he said that he was looking forward to a good long night.

I was too much disturbed to go to bed myself. I decided to wake Roy Calvert; it was a strange reversal of rôles, when I recalled the nights of melancholy in which he had wakened me. In his sitting-room the embers were still glowing. He must have had a large fire and sat up late. Proofs of the new book lay stacked on his lowest table, and I notice the dedicatory page IN MEMORY OF VERNON ROYCE.

He was peacefully asleep. He had not known insomnia since the summer, and always when he slept it was as quietly as a child. It took some time to wake him.

'Are you part of a dream?' he asked. They were his first coherent words. 'No.'

'Let me go to sleep. Rescue my books yourself. Is it a fire? I need to go to sleep.'

He looked tousled and flushed, and, though his hair was already thinning, very young.

'I'm very worried,' I said, and he shook himself into consciousness.

He jumped out of bed, and put on a dressing-gown while I told him of Pilbrow.

'Bad. Bad,' said Roy.

He was still sleepy, but we moved into the sitting-room, and he warmed himself over the remnants of the fire.

'What is our move, old boy?'

'We may be losing. I'm afraid for Jago now.'

'Just so. That gets us nowhere. What is our move?'

He took out his box of bricks and arranged the sides again. '7–6 for Crawford. That's the worst it's been.'

'We've got nothing to lose if we tackle any of them. I wish we had before. We certainly ought to try everything we know on old Gay,' I said.

'Just so. I like the sound of that. Ah. Indeed,' said Roy. He smiled at me. 'Don't be too worried.'

'We'll try everything, but the chances are against us.'

'I'm sorry for poor old Jago. You're frightfully sorry, aren't you? He's got hold of your imagination. Never mind. We'll do our damnedest.' Roy was enjoying the prospect of action. Then he smiled at me again. 'It's extremely funny for me to be consoling you.'

CHAPTER XXXIV

OBLIGATIONS OF LOVE

ALTHOUGH I had had only a few hours' sleep, I was lying wakeful when Bidwell called me. He drew the blind and let in the grey half-light of the December morning: I turned away, longing for sleep again, I wanted to shirk the day.

Bidwell had not lit the fire in my sitting-room early enough; there were only spurts of flame among the great lumps of coal. Smoke blew out of the grate, and it struck cold and raw in the lofty room. I sat down heavy-heartedly to my breakfast. With an effort, I roused myself to call down the stairs for Bidwell. He entered with his usual smile, intimate, defer-ential and sly. I sent him to find whether Pilbrow was up yet, and he returned with news that Pilbrow had pinned a note on his door saying he proposed to sleep until midday and was not to be disturbed.

I knew that, as soon as he was about, he would be punctilious in warning his former side of his change of vote. His views were eccentric for an old man, but his manners had stayed gentle and nineteenth-century; the only grumble I had ever heard him make about his young friends of the left was that, though he was sure there was some good reason for it, he could not for the life of him understand why they found it necessary to be so rude.

It was certain that Jago, Brown and Chrystal would receive his note of apology by the end of the day. I did not want to break more bad news to Brown; over breakfast, I decided to leave it, we would find out from Pilbrow's note soon enough. Then I thought I had better face the trouble, and sent out Bidwell with another message, asking Brown to visit me as soon as he came into college.

He was busy with the scholarship examination, and it was not until eleven o'clock that he arrived.

'Is it anything serious? Have you heard about a meeting?' he asked at once.

I told him of Pilbrow's visit. His face flushed an angry purple, and he

189

cursed with a virulence I had not heard from him before. He ended up:

'It's all his confounded politics. I always thought that he'd never grow up. It's bad enough having people with cranky opinions in the college, saving your presence, Eliot, but it's a damned scandal when they interfere with serious things. It's a damned scandal. I shall never think the same of Pilbrow.'

It was the first time in the whole year that he had lost his balance. At last he said, with regretful bitterness: 'I suppose we may as well tell Chrystal. I should have hoped at one time that he would take it as much amiss as I do.'

Chrystal listened to the news with attention, and received it quite differently from Brown.

'Well. That's that,' he said. 'I can't say I'm much surprised.'

His response was mixed from the first moment – mixed, with his soft-hearted concern for his friend's misery, his guilt at his friend's anger, his delight at a hidden plan, his strong but obscure gratification.

'It's just as well I established contact yesterday,' he said. 'We hadn't told you, Eliot. Brown was not happy about going on. But some people on the other side would welcome a meeting. Of everyone who wants to come. Throwing everything into the melting pot. I told Brown yesterday it was out best way out. Now I'm sure of it.'

'The position was different yesterday.'

'I took it for granted there were floating votes.'

'I don't want a way out from Jago, and I never should,' said Brown. I asked if the meeting had been decided on.

'I don't think they'll back out,' Chrystal replied. 'I'm not sure if they want to.'

'Not even,' I said, 'now that they can see a majority for Crawford? When they hear about Pilbrow, they'll feel they're winning for the first time. Why should they want a meeting?'

'They would be very foolish to contemplate such a thing,' said Brown heavily to Chrystal. 'Yesterday was a different situation. They stood to gain by saying yes to any approach you made. It was only decent common sense for them to draw you on. I shouldn't think much of their judgment if they hadn't welcomed any discussion you liked to suggest. They knew that we were showing our weakness.'

'It's turned out right. It may save us,' said Chrystal.

'I'll believe that when I see the slightest sign that they're willing to compromise – now they're sitting with the majority.'

'I'll see there's a meeting,' said Chrystal. 'It can be done. They'll be willing to compromise.'

After lunch, Roy and I were sitting in my rooms. We intended to walk out to Gay's house in time for tea; it was no use leaving the college until three, for the old man took his afternoon sleep according to the timetable which regulated all his actions and which had not varied for forty years.

I had deliberately kept back from Brown and Chrystal that we were making an attempt on Gay. Chrystal was now set on a compromise, and I did not think it safe to tell him. Unless Jago's chances were revived, there was nothing Chrystal would do to help: he was more likely to hinder.

'Just so,' said Roy. 'He's an interesting man. If he'd been as single-minded over poor Jago as he was about making Sir Timberlake unbelt, we should have raced home.'

We talked about personal politics, of which, not only in the college, we had now seen a good deal. One point had struck us both: will, sheer stubborn will, was more effective than cunning or finesse or subtlety. Those could be a help; but the more one saw, the more one was forced to the banal conclusion that the man you wanted on your side was the man who believed without a shade of doubt that you were right. Arthur Brown was cunning and resourceful; but he had been the mainstay of Jago's cause because, more powerfully than any of us, without any qualifications at all, he was determined to get Jago in. And Crawford's side, which had so long been numerically weaker, began with Despard-Smith, Winslow and Getliffe, not one of whom ever felt a doubt between Crawford and Jago. In that they were luckier than we had been; for Chrystal, whose will could be as strong as any of theirs, had had it split throughout the entire struggle.

As we were talking, there was a tap on the door and Mrs Jago came in. She said: 'I've been up to Roy's rooms. I had to find someone—' and burst out crying. I led her to a chair by the fireplace, tears streaming down her face: there she cried aloud, noisily, with abject and abandoned misery: she laid her head on the arm of the chair, but did not try to hide her face: her heavy body shook with the sobs.

Roy and I met each other's glance. Without speaking, we agreed to let her alone. When the weeping became quieter, when the convulsions no longer tore her, it was I who stroked her hand.

'Tell us,' I said.

She tried to summon up her dignity. 'Mr Eliot, I must apologise for this exhibition,' she said, with her imitation of Lady Muriel – then she began to cry again.

'What is the matter?' I said.

She tried again to be grand, and then broke down.

'They're all saying – they're all saying that I'm not fit to go into the Lodge.'

'Alice, what do you mean?' said Roy.

'They all hate me. Everyone here hates me. Even you' – she straightened herself in the chair, her cheeks glistening with tears, and looked at Roy – 'hate me sometimes.'

'Don't be foolish.'

'I'm not always as foolish as you think' She put a hand to the breast of her frock, and drew out a note. I looked at it and so did Roy over my shoulder. It was Nightingale's flysheet.

'What else does it mean?' she cried. 'I know I'm an ugly hysterical woman. I know I'm no use to anyone. But I'm not as foolish as you think. Tell me the truth. If you don't hate me, tell me the truth.'

'We don't hate you,' said Roy. 'We're very fond of you. So will you stop hurting yourself? Then I'll tell you the truth.'

His tone was affectionate, scolding, intimate. She dried her eyes and sat quiet.

'That paper means what you think,' said Roy. 'One or two men mean to keep Paul out at any cost. They're aiming at him through you. They've done the same through me.'

She stared at him, and he added gently:

'You're not to worry.'

'How can I help worrying?' she said. The cry was full of pain, but there was nothing hysterical in it.

'I should like to know how you saw this paper,' I said. 'Did Paul leave it about?'

'He'd never be careless about anything that might upset me – don't you realise he's always taken too much care of me?' she said. 'No, this one was sent so that I could see it for myself.'

'Poor thing,' said Roy.

'That must be Nightingale himself,' I said. 'What in God's name does he hope for?'

'He hopes,' said Alice Jago, with a flash of shrewdness, 'that it will make me do something silly.'

'It might be just malice,' said Roy.

'No, it's their one chance to keep Paul out. I'm his only weakness, you know I am,' she said. 'I suppose they know Paul is bound to be elected unless they shout the place down.' (Neither Roy nor I realised till then that she was still ignorant of the latest news.) 'I'm their best chance, aren't I? I've heard another whisper – I expect I was meant to hear it – that they're not going to leave me alone. They think I'm a coward. They're saying that this note is only a beginning. They believe that I shall want Paul to withdraw.'

'You couldn't help being frightened,' said Roy.

'I could hear them all talking about me,' she cried. 'I was hysterical. I didn't know what to do. I ran out of the house, I don't know why I came to you—'

I could not be certain what had happened. She had received the fly-sheet: but had it actually been sent by Nightingale? I could not think of any other explanation. Had there really been other rumours? Was she imagining it all? Now she was speaking, quietly, unhappily, and with simple feeling.

'I'm so frightened, Roy. I'm terribly frightened still,' she said. 'I've not been a good wife to Paul. I've been a drag on him all these years. I've tried sometimes, but I've never been any good. I know I'm horrible, but I can't prevent myself getting worse. But I've never done him so much harm as this. I never thought they'd use me to prevent him being Master. How can I stand it, how can I stay here if they do?'

'Think of Paul,' said Roy.

'I can't help thinking of myself too,' she cried. 'How can I stand seeing someone else moving into the drawing-room? And I know you think I oughtn't to worry about myself, but how can I stand the things they'll say about me?'

'It may not happen,' I said.

'It *will* happen.'

'If it does, you'll have to harden yourself.'

'Do *you* know what they'll say?' she asked me wildly. 'They'll say I wasn't good enough for Paul. And instead of doing my best for him, I couldn't resist making a fool of myself with other men. It's perfectly true. Though none of them wanted anyone like me.' She gave a smile, wan, innocent, and flirtatious. 'Roy, you know that I could have made a fool of myself with you.'

'You've always tried to make Paul love you more,' said Roy. 'You've never believed that he really loves you, have you? Yet he does.'

'How can he?'

Roy said: 'And you love him very much.'

'I've never been good enough for him,' she cried.

She was wretched beyond anything we could say to her: disappointment pierced her, then shame, then self-disgust. She had looked forward so naïvely, so snobbishly to the Lodge; she had boasted of it, she had planned her parties, she had written to her family. Could it still be taken away? We guessed that Jago had shielded her from all the doubts so far. Could it be taken away through her follies? She was sickened by shame; she had 'made a fool of herself' and now they might bring it against her. She did not feel guilty remorse, she was too deeply innocent at heart for that. She felt instead shame and self-hatred, because men spoke ill of her. She had never believed that she could be loved – that was the pain which twisted her nature. Now she felt persecuted, unloved, lost, alone. Had Paul always pretended to love her out of pity? She believed even that – despite the devotion, despite the proofs.

No one could love her, she knew ever since she was a girl, she never had the faintest confidence of being loved. If she could have had a little confidence, she thought, she might have given Paul more comfort; she would not have been driven to inflict on him the woes of a hypochondriac, the venom of a shrew, the faithlessness of one who had to find attention. He would never know how abjectly she worshipped him. All she had done was damage him (she saw the letter in her hand) so much that she could never make it up.

It was long past the time when Roy and I had planned to start for Gay's, and we had to give up our project for the day. Nothing we said was any help, but it was unthinkable to leave her. At last she invited us back to her house for tea. She walked between us through the courts. On our way, we were confronted by Nightingale, walking out of college. His hand moved up to his hat, but she looked away, with a fixed stare. We heard his footsteps dying away. She said almost triumphantly:

'They've cut me often enough.'

In their drawing-room Jago was standing, and the moment we entered he put his arm round her shoulders.

'I've been looking everywhere for you,' he said. 'Why didn't you leave word where you'd gone? You mustn't disappear without a trace. What is the trouble?'

'What is the trouble with you?' she cried. He had been standing in the twilight, but she had switched on the light as we went in. His face was haggard, his eyes sunken; even his lips were pallid.

'You two know by now?' said Jago. We nodded. He turned to his wife, his arm resting on her.

'Dearest, I'm afraid that I'm going to make you unhappy. It seems that I shall be rejected by the college.'

'Is this my fault?'

'How could it be your fault?' Jago replied, but her question, which pierced one like a scream, was not addressed to him. I answered:

'It's nothing to do with what we've been talking about. It's quite different. Old Eustace Pilbrow has crossed over – for political reasons. He can't even have read the flysheet when he decided, and he'd be the last man to take any notice—'

'Thank God,' she said, laying her head on Jago's shoulder. 'If they don't give it to you after all, Paul, I couldn't bear it to be because of me.'

'Does it concern us,' asked Jago bitterly, 'the precise reason why I'm thrown aside?'

'Yes! Yes!' she said. She rounded on me. 'Why didn't you tell me?' I said:

'I couldn't – until I was sure Paul knew.'

'Do you realise what it means? Do you realise that they're hoping to humiliate me now?' Jago cried.

'They couldn't,' she said. 'Nothing could. Nothing could touch you. You're big enough to laugh at anything they do. They know you're bigger than they are. That's why they fear you so.'

Jago smiled – was it to relieve her, as a parent pretends to an anxious child? Or had she brought him comfort?

He kissed her, and then said to Roy and me:

'I am sorry to receive you like this. But the news has knocked me out more than I expected.'

'We're not giving up,' I said.

'I'm not sure,' said Jago, 'that I shouldn't ask you to.'

He seemed suddenly tired, passive, and resigned. He sat down in his armchair as though the suffering had lost its edge but had worn him out. He enquired after tea, and Alice rang for it. Suddenly he said to her:

'Why did you ask whether it was your fault? What do you know about the flysheet?'

She began to speak, then said: 'No, Paul, I can't—' and turned to us for aid. I told Jago that someone, presumably Nightingale, had made sure that she should see the flysheet: she was afraid there might be more attacks upon her: she thought they wanted her to persuade Jago to withdraw; she had been in anguish for Jago's sake.

Very softly, Jago exclaimed.

Then he spoke to her in a quiet, familiar tone.

'I expect to be rejected now. Would you like me to withdraw?'

Tears had come to her eyes, but she did not cry. She could hardly speak. At last she managed to say:

'No. You must go on.'

'You knew what you had to say.' Jago gave her a smile of love.

When that smile faded, his expression was still sad and exhausted: but in his eyes, as he spoke again, this time to Roy and me, there was a flash of energy, a glitter of satanic pride.

'I've cursed the day that I ever exposed myself to these humiliations,' he said. 'I knew you and my other friends meant well, but you were not doing me a kindness when you persuaded me to stand. Whether the college rejects me or takes me, I am certain that I will not stand for another office so long as I live.' He paused. 'But I am equally certain that if those people hope to get me to withdraw through doing harm to my wife, I will stay in this election while I've got one single man to vote for me.'

He added:

'And I shall leave nothing to chance. I shall tell my rival so.'

CHAPTER XXXV

CRAWFORD BEHAVES SENSIBLY

AFTER Jago cried out that he 'would tell his rival so', he asked Roy to find from the kitchens whether Crawford was dining that night. The answer was yes. 'That is convenient,' said Jago.

Crawford arrived in the combination room at the same time as I did, and several of his party were already there. They were drinking their sherry in front of the fire, and there was an air of well-being, of triumph, of satisfied gloating. Crawford greeted them with his impersonal cordiality, and me as well. He seemed more than ever secure, not in the least surprised by what had happened; he took it for granted that it was right.

'Eliot,' Nightingale addressed me. He had not spoken to me directly for months.

'Yes?'

'I suppose you've heard about Pilbrow.'

'Of course.'

'I had a note from him this afternoon,' Crawford announced.

'Good work,' said Francis Getliffe.

'It's very civil of him to have written,' said Crawford, and went on to talk without hurry of a new theory of electrical impulses in nerves. Francis was making a suggestion for an experiment. Nightingale was listening with the strained attention that nowadays came over him in Crawford's presence, when Jago threw open the door and said:

'Crawford. I should like you to spare me a minute.'

Everyone looked up at Jago. He did not say good-evening, his eyes did not leave Crawford.

'Very well,' said Crawford, not quite at ease. 'Can we talk here, or would you prefer to go outside?'

'Nothing I have to say is secret,' Jago replied. 'I'm obliged to say it to you, because I'm not certain to whom it should be said by right.'

Crawford rose and said 'Very well' again. By the fire Despard-Smith and Francis made a pretence at conversation, but none of us could shut our ears to Jago's words.

'I do not hold you responsible for the outrages of your supporters, but I hope that you cannot be utterly indifferent to them.'

'You're going too fast for me,' said Crawford. 'I don't begin to know what you're referring to.'

'I shall explain myself.'

'I should much prefer it,' said Crawford, looking up into Jago's eyes, 'if we could keep this business on a friendly basis.'

'When you hear what I have to say,' said Jago, 'you will realise that is no longer easy.'

Jago's temper smouldered and suddenly flared out and smouldered again. It was different from one of his outbursts of indignation; no one in that room had seen this consuming rage. As they faced it, most men would have been uneasy; Crawford may have been, but his voice was steady and sensible. Angrily, I had to confess that he was holding his own.

'If that turns out to be true, I shall be very sorry for it, Jago,' he remarked.

'If you are elected, none of my friends would suggest that your wife was not entirely fit to adorn the Lodge,' Jago said.

'I should be very much surprised to hear it.'

'I was a little surprised to hear that my wife had received a copy of the flysheet by your supporter Nightingale.'

Jago's words were not loud, but Crawford stood silent in front of him.

'You have seen the flysheet I mean?'

'I am afraid that I have,' said Crawford.

'Can you faintly imagine what it would mean to a woman?'

Crawford stirred.

'Jago, I very much regret that this should have happened. I shall write to your wife personally, and tell her so.'

'That is not enough.'

'It is all I can do, unfortunately.'

'No,' said Jago. 'You can discover through what source the flysheet reached her. I may tell you that it was deliberately sent.'

Jago was at the limit of his anger. Crawford shook his head.

'No,' he said. 'I can understand your feelings, but you exaggerate my responsibility. I am sincerely sorry that your wife should suffer through any circumstances in which I am even remotely concerned. I consider it my duty to tell her so. But I don't consider it my duty to become a private detective. I have consented to be a candidate at this election, but I have taken no part whatever in any of the personal complications which have taken place, and I might take this opportunity of saying that I deprecate them.'

Jago was quietened for an instant by the solidity of that reply. Then he said:

'This attack on my wife is intended to make we withdraw.'

'I can't express any view on intentions in which I am not interested,' said Crawford.

'If you are not interested, your supporters may be,' said Jago. 'I shall protect my wife in all ways open to reason but also, while any of my colleagues are prepared to give me their votes, I shall remain a candidate for the Mastership.'

There was no reply from Crawford, and the whole room was silent, for the conversation round the fire had died right away.

The bell began to peal for dinner, and Crawford said, as though anxious for a cordial commonplace:

'Are you coming into hall, Jago?'

'No,' said Jago. 'I shall dine with my wife.'

There was a constrained hush as he walked out. Crawford was frowning, the smooth composed impassive look had gone. He sat next to me in hall, did not speak until the fish, and then complained:

'Speaking as a reasonably even-tempered person, I have the strongest possible objection to being forced to listen to those who insist on flying off the handle.'

'I'm glad he spoke to you,' I said.

'It's no concern of mine. He ought to know that I have never lent an ear to local tittle-tattle. I'm not prepared to begin now, and I shall wash my hands of the whole stupid business.'

But Crawford was in his fashion a man of justice and fair dealing, and he was shaken. He took the chair in the combination room with a preoccupied expression, when Despard-Smith left after hall. None of us asked for wine that night, and Crawford lit his pipe over the coffee.

'It does look,' he said, 'as though somehow Mrs Jago has come into possession of that circular of yours, Nightingale. I must say that it is an unfortunate business.'

'Very unfortunate.' Nightingale smiled.

'Naturally,' said Crawford, 'it can't have been sent to her by anyone connected with the college. Every one of us would take a grave view of an action of that kind.'

His tone was uncomfortable, and no one replied for some moments. Then Nightingale smiled again.

'Is there anything to show,' he asked, 'that she wasn't looking through her husband's letters on the quiet, and found one that wasn't meant for her?'

I stared at him.

'I believe she did not read your note by accident,' I said.

'How did you form that opinion?' he said.

'I spent the afternoon with her just after she'd read it.'

'That's as may be. What does it prove?'

'She was so miserable that I believe what she said,' I replied.

'Do you really expect us to be impressed by that?'

'I expect you to know that it was the truth.'

His eyes stared past mine, he did not move or blench. Nothing touched him except his own conflict. Find the key to that, and one could tear him open with a word. Touch his envy, remind him of the Royal Society, his other failures, and he was stabbed by suffering. But to everything else he was invulnerable. He did not see any of his actions as 'bad'. So long as he did not feel 'put upon' or weak, he did not worry about his actions. He regarded his attempts to blacken Jago's circle as a matter of course. He was not at peace enough to go in for the luxuries of conscience.

'I can't say your claim is completely convincing, Eliot,' said Crawford. 'She may have enemies, nothing to do with the college, who wanted to play an unpleasant practical joke.'

'Is that how you see it?' I said.

'Perhaps it is a storm in a teacup,' said Crawford. 'After all, she is just going through an awkward time of life. And Jago has always been over-emotional. Still, we must try and calm things down. I have occasionally felt that this election has generated more heat than light. We've got to see that people know where to stop.'

Then he laid down his pipe, and went on:

'I always think that the danger with any group of men like a college is that we tend to get on each other's nerves. I believe that everyone, particularly the unmarried fellows, ought to be compelled by statute to spend three months abroad each year. And also – and this I do suggest to you all as a practicable proposition – I think we ought to set for ourselves an almost artificially high standard of manners and behaviour. I suggest to you that, in any intimate body of men, it is important to have the rules laid down.'

I noticed that as Crawford delivered his steady impersonal reproof, Nightingale was watching him with anxious attention and nodding his head. It was more than attention, it was devoted deference.

As Crawford rose to go, he said:

'Nightingale, are you busy? You might walk part of the way home with me.'

The instant he heard the invitation, Nightingale's harsh strained face broke into a smile that held charm, pleasure and a youthful desire to please.

I was to blame, I told myself, for not having seen it before. No doubt he still craved Crawford's support for getting into the Royal Society, but somehow that longing for a favour had become transmuted into a genuine human feeling. He would do anything for Crawford now.

'I hope,' said Francis, when we were left alone, 'that Crawford tells him to shut up.'

I could not resist saying satirically:

'I thought that Crawford was remarkably judicious.'

'I thought he was pretty good. If he always handles situations as well as that, I shan't complain,' said Francis, with irritation.

'Some people would have gone further.'

'No responsible person could have gone further, on that evidence,' said Francis. 'Damn it, man, she's an unbalanced woman. Do you expect Crawford to take as absolute fact every word she says?'

'I think you do,' I said.

He hesitated.

'It's more likely true than not,' he said.

'You're finding yourself in curious company,' I said.

'There looks like being enough of it to win,' said Francis.

We could not get on terms of ease. I asked after his work; he replied impatiently that he was held up. I invited him to my rooms, but he made an excuse for going home.

CHAPTER XXXVI

VISIT TO AN AUTHORITY

THE next morning, 14 December, neither Brown nor Chrystal came into college, and it was from a few minutes' talk with Winslow in the court that I heard there might be a meeting. 'Not that any of my way of thinking were much impressed by that remarkable suggestion,' he said. 'We're comparatively satisfied with things as they are. But if it pleases you, it doesn't hurt us.'

His grin was still sardonic, but more friendly and acquiescent than it used to be. He was on his way to the bursary to clear up his work, so that he could resign as soon as the Master was elected. Nothing, he said with a trace of sadness, would make him stay a day longer.

That afternoon Roy and I were not baulked before we set out for Gay's. We walked through the Backs, going under the mourning sky, under the bare trees; Roy was in the best of spirits. It was with a solemn expression that he rang the bell of Gay's house, which stood just opposite the observatory. 'This is an occasion,' he whispered.

Gay was sitting in his drawing-room with a paper in his hands.

'Ah. Splendid,' he said. 'You've come to see my exhibits, I'll guarantee. I'm glad to see you, Calvert. I'm glad to see you, Nightingale.'

I avoided Roy's glance.

'Not Nightingale,' I said.

'No. Indeed. Tell me your name, will you?'

'I'm Eliot.' It was difficult to conduct this conversation without feeling uncomfortable.

'I absolutely remember. And what is your subject?'

'Law.'

'I congratulate you,' said Gay with splendid finality.

Although both Roy and I had been to the house several times before, he insisted on our looking round the room and out into the garden. It was all that befitted a middle-class donnish home in Cambridge – the furniture heavier and more old-fashioned than at the Getliffes', but nothing except the difference of years to pick it out from theirs. Gay, however, regarded it with singular satisfaction.

'I always say that I built this house out of my masterpiece. Three thousand pounds I made out of that work, and I put every penny of it into bricks and mortar. Ah, that was a book and a half. I haven't any patience with these smart alecks who tell us that one can't get fine scholarship home to the reading public. Why, I shouldn't have this fine house if they didn't lap it up. Lap it up, they did, Calvert. What do you think of that?'

'Wonderful,' said Roy.

He glanced at us affably and stroked his beard.

'I will give you young men a piece of advice. Satisfy the scholars first. Show them that you're better than any of them, that's the thing to do. But when you've become an authority, don't neglect your public. Why, I should welcome my books being presented by the films. I don't despise these modern methods. Fine films my sagas would make too. Nothing namby-pamby about them.'

Roy then produced greetings from a letter – I did not know whether it was invented – from one of the linguistic scholars in Berlin. Gay beamed. He seized the chance to tell us again of his honorary degree at Berlin – 'the great authority on the sagas'.

I made an attempt to get down to business.

'We very much wanted your advice,' I said. 'Now you've got this responsibility for presiding over the college till the election –'

'Ah. Indeed.'

'We should value your guidance over the Mastership. It's been on our minds a good deal. Are you satisfied with the way things are shaping?'

'December the twentieth,' said Gay resonantly. 'That's the great day. Six days from this morning. Splendid. I have everything in hand. I read the statutes each night before I go off to sleep. It's all in safe hands. You can be sure of that. Now you'll have been getting impatient to see my exhibits. That's something more interesting for you.'

We had seen the 'exhibits' each time we had gone to the house, but it was impossible not to see them again. Gay's wife, tiny and bird-like, as old as he but very active, came and wrapped his muffler round his neck and helped him into his overcoat. Then he led us at his shuffling pace to the bottom of the garden. All the 'exhibits' were connected with his life's researches on the sagas, and this first one was an enormous relief model of

Iceland, at least a hundred feet long – so long, in fact, that on it he was able to make visible each farmstead mentioned in the whole of the saga literature.

'No towns my saga-men had,' said Gay proudly. 'Just healthy farms and the wild seas. They knew what to do with towns. Just burn the houses and put the townsmen to the sword. That was the way to deal with towns.'

He remembered each farm as though he had lived among them as a child. And when we went back into the house, and his wife, coming in almost at the run, had taken off his coat again, he showed us models of Icelandic halls, longships, pictures drawn by himself of what, from the curt descriptions, he imagined the saga heroes to have looked like. His interest was as fervent, as vivid and factual, as it must have been when he was a young man. Some of the sketches had the talent of a portrait-painter: there was one of Gudrun that had struck me on my last visit, and another of Skarphedinn, pale, fierce, scornful, teeth projecting, carrying his great axe over his shoulder.

'Ah. That was a terrible weapon,' said Gay. 'That was an axe and a half.'

He loved each detail. And that was, I thought, part of the explanation of his fabulous success. He was not a clever man in the sense that Winslow was, who had done nothing at all. He was simple, exuberantly vain, as pleased with himself as a schoolboy who has just received a prize. But he had enormous zest and gusto, unbounded delight in his work. He had enjoyed every minute of his researches. Somehow all his vitality, mental and physical, had poured into them without constraint or inhibition or self-criticism. He did not trouble himself, he had not the equipment to begin, with the profound whys of existence – but in his line he had a strong simple unresting imagination. And he had the kind of realism which exactly fitted in. He could see the houses of his saga men, their few bits of furniture, their meagre food and stark struggle for a livelihood: he could see them simply as they were, often as men puzzled, ill-adjusted, frail, trained to a code of almost Japanese courage; and at the same time he could see them as a good deal larger than life. He had thrown every scrap of himself into their existence, and won – and no one could say it was unjust – success on a scale denied to more gifted men.

He talked about each model until a maid brought in a very large teatray.

'Ah ha. Tea,' said Gay, with a different but equal enthusiasm. 'That's a splendid sight.'

He appeared to eat as his daily tea a meal not much less copious than the one he put away before college meetings. He did not talk, except to ask us to pass plates, until he was well through. Then I decided to come back to our attempt.

'You're occupying an exceptional position in this election,' I said.

'Ah. Indeed,' said Gay, munching a slice of black fruit cake.

'You're the great scholar of the college.'

'The greatest Northern scholar of the age, my Berlin friends used to say,' Roy put in.

'Did they now, Calvert? Splendid.'

'You're also responsible as senior fellow for seeing that this election is properly carried out,' I went on. 'And we've noticed that you don't interpret that in a purely legalistic sense. You're not concerned simply with the ceremony. We know that you want to see the proper choice properly made.'

'Just so,' said Roy.

'I shall never want to escape my duty,' said Gay.

'Isn't that your duty?'

'I agree with you,' said Gay, cutting another piece of cake.

'We need a lead. Which only you can give. We're extremely worried,' said Roy.

'Ah. Indeed.'

'We want you to advise us on the two candidates,' I said. 'Crawford and Jago. We want you to show us how to form a judgment.'

'Crawford and Jago,' said Gay. 'Yes, I think I know both of them. Let me see, isn't Jago our present Bursar?'

This was baffling. We could not predict how his memory would work. Everything about the world of scholarship was clear before his eyes: but he would suddenly enquire the name of Despard-Smith, whom he had known for fifty years.

'I thought,' said Roy, 'that you had promised to support Crawford?'

'Perhaps I have, perhaps I have.' Suddenly he seemed to remember quite well, and he nodded his head backwards and forwards. 'Yes, I recollect indicating support for Crawford,' he said. Then, with a kind of simple, cheerful cunning, he looked at us:

'And you two young men want me to change my mind?' He guffawed: it seemed to him the best of jokes.

For a second, Roy blushed. I thought it was best to brazen it out.

'Well,' I said, 'you're not far off the mark.'

'You see,' said Gay, 'you can't pull the wool over my eyes.'

'Yes,' said Roy, 'we want you to think again about those two. You do remember them, don't you?'

'Of course I remember them,' said Gay. 'Just as I remember your address in Berlin last summer, young man. Jago – that's our Senior Tutor. He's not taken quite enough care of himself these last few years, he's lost a lot of hair and he's put on too much weight. And Crawford. A very sound man. I hear he's well spoken of as a man of science.'

'Do you want a scientist as Master? Crawford's field is a long way from yours,' I said.

'I should never give a second's thought to such a question,' Gay rebuked me. 'I have never attached any importance to boundary-lines between branches of learning. A man can do distinguished work in any, and we ought to have outgrown these arts-and-science controversies before we leave the school debating scoiety. Indeed we ought.'

I had been snubbed, and very reasonably snubbed. The only comfort was, the old man had his mind and memory working, and we were not fighting in a fog.

'What's your opinion of Jago?' asked Roy.

'Jago's a very sound man too. I have nothing but good to say for Jago,' Gay replied.

I tried another lead. 'At present you're in a unique position. There are six votes for each man without you. If it's understood that you vote for Crawford, the whole thing is cut and dried and the chapel election is just a formality.'

'Cut and dried,' Gay repeated. 'I don't like the sound of that.'

'It means,' said Roy, extremely quick, 'that the whole thing is settled from today. It's all over bar the empty form.'

Gay's faded blue eyes were screwed up in a frown.

'I certainly indicated support for Crawford. He's a very sound man. Jago is a very sound man too, of course.'

'Need that be final?' I asked. 'In those days it didn't look such a near thing. But you've had the opportunity, which none of the rest of us have, of surveying the whole position from on high.'

'Ah. Those old gods looked down from Odin's hall.'

'I should have thought,' I said, 'you might now consider it best to remove yourself from the contest altogether. Mightn't it be best to stand aloof – and then in your own good time decide the election one way or the other?'

'It would make every one realise how grave a choice it was,' said Roy.

Gay had finished his last cup of tea. He smiled at Roy. In looks he might have been Roy's grandfather. But I thought at that moment how young he was at heart.

'You two are still trying to bamboozle me into voting for Jago,' he said. This time Roy did not blush.

'Of course we are,' he said. 'I very much hope you will.'

'Tell me,' said Gay, 'why do you prefer him so much?' He was asking the question in earnest: he wanted to know.

'Because we like him better,' said Roy.

'That's spoken like an honest man,' Gay said. 'I congratulate you, Calvert. You're much closer to these two men than I am. I may survey the position from on high' – he was actually teasing us – 'but I'm too far away. And I've always had great faith in the contribution of youth. I respect your judgment in this matter, indeed I do.'

'Will you vote for Jago?' asked Roy.

'I won't give you an undertaking today. But I am inclined to reserve my vote.' Then he went on: 'The election mustn't be taken for granted. Our founders in their wisdom did not lay it down for us to meet in chapel just to take an election for granted. Why, we might just as well send our votes by post.'

'You will think of Jago, will you?' I persisted.

'I shall certainly think of Jago. I respect your judgment, both of you, and I shall take that very considerably into account.'

As we got up to go at last, Gay said:

'I congratulate you both on presenting me with the situation in this splendid way.'

'We're the ones who've learned something,' I said.

'I will write to Despard telling him I propose to reserve my vote. Casting vote, that's the line for me. Thank you for pointing it out. Thank you, Calvert. Thank you. Old heads on young shoulders, that's what you've got.'

In the dark, Roy and I walked down the Madingley Road. He was singing quietly in his light, clear, tuneful voice. Under the first lamp he glanced at me. His eyes were guiltless and sparkling.

'Well done,' he said.

'He didn't do so badly, either.'

'Shall we get him?'

'I shall be surprised if we don't,' I said.

'Just so. Just so.'

CHAPTER XXXVII

'SIX NIGHTS TO GO'

I LEFT Roy at the great gate, and walked round to Jago's house. Mrs Jago received me with a hostile, angry explanation that she had not been feeling well yesterday. Perhaps she could make amends by offering me some 'refreshment'? She was so self-conscious that it was painful to be near, jarringly apologetic, more resentful of me with each apology she made.

'I badly want to see Paul this evening,' I said.

'I can perfectly well understand that,' she replied. 'You naturally don't want to take the risk of me making an exhibition of myself again.'

'You don't think I mind, do you? It would have done you more harm to stay by yourself.'

'I know some people are willing to bear with me out of charity – but I won't accept it.'

'You've not been offered it,' I said. Perversely, I was coming to have more fellow-feeling for her. 'Is Paul free? I've got something to tell him that's fairly important.'

'He's very busy,' she said obstinately. 'I don't think he can be disturbed.'

'Look,' I said, 'I want to tell him that this election is not lost.'

'Has anything happened, has anything really happened?'

'Yes. Don't hope too much. But it's not lost.'

Her face exploded into a smile. She looked like a child, suddenly made happy. She ran out into the passage. 'Paul! Paul! You must come and see Mr Eliot at once! He's got something to tell you.'

Jago walked into the drawing-room, tense to his fingertips.

'It's extremely good of you to take this trouble, Eliot. Is it something – worse?'

'No,' I said. 'It's not impossible that Gay may finish on your side. He may not – but it's worth holding on for.'

'Old Gay?'

I nodded.

Suddenly Jago broke into roars of laughter.

'Gay! He's the vainest old boy I've ever met in my life.'

He went on laughing. 'The vain old boy!' It was an odd response, I thought later: yet on the spot it seemed completely natural.

Then he wiped his eyes and settled down: his tension returned in a different mode.

'I'm most grateful to you, Eliot,' he said. 'I don't know what I should have done without you right through this wretched business. This news changes everything. I think I was just teaching myself to face the humiliation. But this changes everything.'

I warned him, but it had no effect. He was always capable of being possessed by a rush of hope. Now there was no room for anything else. It all lay in his hands, the college, his whole desire. He looked at his wife with love and triumph. When I had gone, they would get busy on their plans again. He was alive with hope.

I tried once again to make him more moderate. In some ways it would have been kinder not to tell him about Gay at all.

'There is one thing you needn't warn me of, Eliot,' he said with a smile. 'There are still six nights to go. We've still six nights to get through.'

'You've got to rest,' she said.

'In a week's time,' said Jago, 'it will all be over.'

I went from his house straight to Brown's rooms, and found Brown and Chrystal talking of the meeting. It was as good as arranged for the following night, 15 December. To Brown's amazement, the other side had not backed out (were they so confident that they did not care? or did Despard-Smith like the last ounce of grave discussion?). They were talking of what line to begin on.

'Is that the meeting?' I asked.

'Certainly,' said Chrystal.

'It may not be necessary,' I said.

'What do you mean?' asked Brown very quickly.

'I think there's a good chance of Gay coming over.'

'Have you seen him? I didn't know you were thinking of seeing him—'

'No, I wasn't,' I said. 'Roy Calvert and I happened to drop in for tea.'

Brown cross-questioned me with the inquisitiveness he showed at any piece of news, but with an extra excitement and vigilance. His curiosity was always insistent; there were moments, as those sharp eyes watched one, when his company ceased to be bland and peaceful; now it was like being in the dock. Deliberately I played down the part Roy and I had taken – I was feeling Chrystal's silence on the other side of the fire. Roy had asked the old man a question or two, I said: and I gave word for word his last replies.

In the end Brown was satisfied.

'It's absolutely wonderful!' he cried. Then he turned, heavily but quickly, on his friend. 'Don't you think it's wonderful?' he said.

Chrystal did not look at him, but stared challengingly at me.

'Are you sure of this, Eliot?' he asked.

'I'm sure of what I've told you.'

'That doesn't get us very far. He didn't even say he might vote for Jago.'

'Not in so many words.'

'It's not good enough, Eliot. You're being led away by your optimism. Wishful thinking,' said Chrystal. 'Remember, I've had a shot at him myself. I know Gay.'

'I trust Eliot's judgment,' said Brown. His voice was comfortable and rich, as always – but I heard a stern, angry note.

'It's not good enough,' said Chrystal. 'I dare say the old man will withhold his vote. Just to have a bit of fun. What's to stop him coming down for Crawford at the end?'

'I trust Eliot's judgment,' said Brown. The stern note was clearer now.

'I can't be sure,' I said. 'No one can be sure. But I don't think so for a minute. Neither does Calvert.'

'I don't give twopence for Calvert's opinion. He's not lived long enough. He hasn't seen anything yet,' Chrystal replied.

'I should bet at least 4–1,' I said, 'that when we go into chapel Gay will write down Jago's name.'

'I accept that absolutely,' said Brown, still watching his friend.

'Well, we disagree,' said Chrystal. 'This is all *amusing* about Gay. But I don't see that it can alter our plans.'

'We may have this election in our hands,' said Brown.

'We may not.'

'I believe we have. Have you stopped listening to reason?' Brown's friendly blandness had broken at last, he spoke with a mixture of menace and appeal.

'I'm afraid we disagree, Arthur.'

'You can't disagree that the sensible course is to get out of this meeting,' said Brown. 'Anything else is ridiculous.'

'I wish I didn't disagree. I'm afraid I do.'

'I want an explanation,' said Brown.

'Yes. Well, I don't believe that Gay will come over. I expect Eliot has got everything he said right. But I've seen Gay myself.'

'A lot of water has flowed under the bridges since then,' cried Brown. 'These two may have been better at handling the old man than we were.'

'They wouldn't claim that themselves,' said Chrystal. 'I'm sorry to seem ungrateful for Eliot's efforts, but I don't believe in Gay. Even if I did, there's another point. I think we're bound to keep our understanding with the other side. They were willing to hold this meeting. They didn't try to back out when they seemed to be sitting pretty.'

'Did they ever mean business?' asked Brown, his voice no longer comfortable at all, but full of scorn.

'I think they did.'

'I think you deceived yourself. I think you've deceived yourself over many things you've done in this election. I know you've always wanted to find a way out from Crawford. I've never doubted that. But you've also been glad of a chance to find a way out from Jago. That's why you're giving me reasons that aren't anything like reasons, they're ridiculous after everything we've brought off together. You said yesterday that you'd stay with Jago if I could get him in. Now you're finding an excuse for spoiling it, just when we've got our last chance.'

'It won't spoil it, Arthur. If he does stand a chance,' said Chrystal. 'Very likely nothing will come out of this meeting. Then if old Gay remembers we might still be all right.'

'I keep thinking of the things we've brought off together. We shouldn't have managed them alone. We couldn't even have begun getting that benefaction alone. And that's been true for a good many years. It's a pity to find us divided now.'

'Do you think I don't feel that?' said Chrystal brusquely. He had been buoyed up, exhilarated, master of his plans, conscious that others were waiting for him, pleased perhaps to escape from Brown's steady imperceptible guidance. Yet he was moved by the reminder of their comradeship, by the call on his affection. His manner, which had been conciliatory, became at once tough and aggressive. He was angry to be so moved.

Brown, too, was moved. His composure was riven, he had spoken more jaggedly than I had known him. Through the rifts one saw the formidable core of the man. He had great feeling for his friend, he was warm and expansive – but that did not matter to him now. He was moved by the thought of defeat, by losing the struggle for Jago, by the sheer blank fury of losing. I was sure that he had called deliberately on their friendship, knowing that it would affect Chrystal far more than himself.

'Aren't you prepared to stop this meeting?' asked Brown.

'I don't see how I can,' said Chrystal.

'I regard it as a major disaster,' said Brown.

CHAPTER XXXVIII

A CAVE IS FORMED

THERE was a large gathering in hall on the night of 15 December: and afterwards, without waiting for wine, we moved off by twos and threes to Chrystal's rooms. As we turned under the light at the bottom of the staircase, I noticed Chrystal walking with Despard-Smith and Getliffe. Jago and Crawford appeared out of the darkness together: then Brown alone.

Everyone was there but Gay. Luke, who had not been dining but hurried in after, was apologising to Despard-Smith for not being able to stay. He made the same apology to Brown, in his youthful, deferential way. I was sitting near the door, and he had a word with me on his way out. 'I've got an experiment to finish,' he said in a whisper, forgetting all about tact, 'and I'm going to finish it if I sit up the whole blasted night. I've told these uncles that I'm going to vote for Jago. I've been bloody well telling them that ever since I can remember.'

Despard-Smith showed his usual hesitation before taking the chair ('Some day,' said Roy half-audibly, 'we'll take him at his word. Then he'll be dished.'). He explained solemnly that some fellows were 'increasingly exercised about the serious position' in which the college found itself over the election. He thought he could, without breach of confidence, mention that within the last twenty-four hours he had received two letters from Professor Gay. One he was not at liberty to disclose, since it was addressed to him as having presided over the caucus for one of the candidates, 'but I think I may say, in fact I think I must say, that our senior colleague in that letter expresses his intention to reserve his vote. The other letter refers to this meeting, and I propose to read it.' As always when reading, Despard-Smith passed into his chapel voice.

' "Dear Despard,

' "I learn with interest of your intention to have an informal pow wow" ' – Despard-Smith repeated the word with extraordinary and depressed gravity – ' "pow wow before the great day of our election. I thoroughly approve of this little venture, and you may go ahead with my blessing. Did not my saga men discuss cases in their booths before they came to the great debates in the Thing? I congratulate you on this attempt to clear your heads. Clear heads, those are what you most require. I do not, however, consider that it fits my present position of responsibility to take a hand in your little pow wow. You appear to suggest that I may not want to stay out at night because I am not so young as I was. Pray do not worry on that account. I can outlast some of you younger men yet. If I absent myself, it is on completely different grounds. I am entrusted with the grave responsibility of being at the helm while the college plunges through this stormy crossing. And I should further say that some of our colleagues have represented to me that I have an added trust because of such little distinction as I may have been fortunate enough to attain.

' "Weighing these responsibilities in my mind, I have reached the conclusion that I must stand aloof from any discussions among yourselves up to the great day of the election. I shall then cast my vote as my conscience guides me, and I hope to lead you all on that same course, so that we may make a worthy choice.

' "Good luck to your little pow wow.

' "Ever sincerely yours,
' "M. H. L. GAY." '

'This does *not* make our task lighter,' said Despard-Smith, looking up from the letter. 'So far as I am entitled to judge the intentions of the fellows, we have not yet attained a firm majority for either of our candidates. Some of us think this may lead us into a position which is nothing short of disastrous. I have never known anything comparable during my long association with the college. By this stage we have always been certain before who was going to win our suffrages. We were certain' – he said with one of his funereal anti-climaxes – 'who was going to draw the lucky n-number. But this time we have not been so wise. I should like us to hear the Dean's views on this most unfortunate dilemma.'

'It's lamentable,' Chrystal began, and went on to make a sharp, reasonable, friendly statement. It had been bad for the college to go through this prolonged suspense. He disliked being separated from his friends on the other side, and he hoped they disliked it too. Either of the candidates would be an excellent Master whom the college would be lucky to get. It was a sign of something wrong that the college should become unfit to live in just because they could not choose between two excellent men. But apparently they could not choose. 'I'm just pointing out the snags,' said Chrystal. 'It's lamentable. I don't pretend to see the solution. But I want to ask one question: has the time come to forget our disagreement? Has the time come to find a way out?'

From that moment the room was electric with attention. This was not just a talk: something was in the air. Even those who had not followed Chrystal's progress knew something hung on these minutes. Brown's face was lowering: Jago sat as though he did not hear.

We looked at each other, waiting for someone to begin. At last Crawford spoke. He was even more deliberate than his habit, not so impregnably assured: he was searching for his words.

'I wish this was such a pleasant occasion as the last time we met in this room. I should much prefer to hear the Dean explain again how he and our friend Brown had brought off their great coup for the college. The more I reflect, the more chances I think that coup of theirs opens up in front of us. As for the present position, I agree with a good deal of what the Dean says. But I don't consider this is the right time to act. I know this long wait hasn't improved some of our tempers. But it won't be much longer. Speaking as a fellow, I don't see any alternative to waiting. I didn't quite understand the Dean's suggestion. I do not know whether he thinks that other names ought to be canvassed now. Speaking as a candidate, I can't be expected to accept the view that other names should be considered at this late stage. I hope that the Senior Tutor agrees with me.'

'Utterly.'

'My advice is,' said Crawford, 'leave it until the day. One of us will be elected unless someone decides to throw away his vote. If neither of us is elected, then it will be time for us to have a talk.'

Jago had only spoken that one word since he entered the room. Now he roused himself. He had been keeping unnaturally still. By this night, even Crawford's expression bore a trace of worry: but it was nothing to Jago's. Yet he spoke with dignity.

'If the college votes in chapel and cannot reach a majority for either my colleague or myself, it will be necessary for us all to meet together,' he said. 'It is not fitting either for me or my colleague to say more now. If the need should arise, we shall give what help we can to find a solution for the college. It would be our plain duty to do so.'

His eyes had rested in turn on Chrystal, Despard-Smith and Brown. Now he looked at Crawford.

'If the others wish to continue with their discussion,' he said, 'I think we must remove ourselves. There is nothing left for us to add.'

'I agree,' said Crawford, and they left the room.

We listened to their footsteps down the stairs. Chrystal said curtly to Despard-Smith: 'I should like to hear what other people think.'

There was a pause. Pilbrow burst out that he was solid for Crawford, despite the lateness of his change, for reasons some of us knew. Another pause. Nightingale said with a smile that he would never vote for anyone but Crawford. Then Brown spoke, and during his whole speech his gaze did not leave Chrystal.

'I'm glad to have this opportunity of explaining to most of the college,' he said, 'that I think we're in danger of making a terrible mistake. Some people already know the strength of my views, but perhaps those of our number who support Crawford have not heard them. I should like to assure them that I believe Jago will be the best possible Master for the college, and I believe it with more absolute certainty than I have ever felt on such an occasion. Any departure from Jago would be a loss that the college might not be able to recover from for many years. During the rest of my time here, I should not be able to forget it.'

Everyone was looking at him and Chrystal. Many were puzzled, they did not know what was going on. Some saw the struggle clear. Yet everyone was looking at those two faces, the benign one, now flushed with anger, and the domineering.

No one spoke. Chrystal was regarding Brown as though there were a question to ask: there came an almost pathetic smile on Chrystal's firm mouth.

Suddenly Chrystal looked away.

'We're not getting far,' he said with a harsh bravado. 'I believe several of us are not satisfied with either candidate. Some of us never have been. I can speak out now they've gone. There's something to be said for Jago: I've been resigned to voting for him, as you all know. There's something to be said for Crawford: I've seen things in him lately that I like, and I understand his supporters' point of view. But we're not tied to either of them. I believe that's the way out.'

'What are you proposing?' said Despard-Smith.

'I want to bring it to a head,' said Chrystal. 'I'm ready to form a cave. Will any of you join me? I should like to find another man altogether.'

PART FOUR

MORNING IN THE CHAPEL

CHAPTER XXXIX

A GROUP TALKS TILL THE MORNING

'I WANT to bring it to a head,' Chrystal said again. 'I should like to find another man altogether. This is the time. We might get somewhere tonight.'

He leaned forward over the table, with an eager, alert, dominating smile.

There was a shuffle of feet, a cough, the squeak of someone's finger on the table top. Some moments passed, and then Pilbrow got to his feet.

'I don't think it's any good my staying, Despard,' he said. 'If you're going to find another man, which I suppose you are. I don't want to run away, but . . . I know I've wobbled disgracefully, but I don't feel like changing again. I'm content as I am.'

He had not left the room when Nightingale began talking. He was so excited that he had no politeness left.

'I always said it would happen. I always knew that that precious clique wouldn't let well alone. They were bound to put up one of themselves in the long run.'

'Are you going to stay, Nightingale?' said Despard-Smith bleakly. 'If you stay, you will hear what names are being discussed.'

'Stay!' Nightingale smiled. 'Do you think I want to hear the names? I could tell you them now.'

As he closed the door, Roy commented:

'I'll bet anyone that he rings up Crawford within five minutes.'

Solidly, heavily, Brown stood by the table, looking down on those of us still there.

'I can't see my way to remaining in this discussion,' he said to Despard-Smith. 'I've gone as far as I can to turn you all from it. In my judgment, it is completely ill-considered, and I should have nothing useful to add if I stayed with you.'

He gave Chrystal one glance, angry, troubled, yet steady and still intimate: he walked out, and we heard his deliberate tread down the stairs.

Chrystal was frowning – but he shrugged his shoulders and said, with confidence and zest:

'It's time to get down to it.'

There were only six of us now sitting round the table, Chrystal himself, Despard-Smith, Winslow, Francis Getliffe, Roy Calvert and I. It was not a good beginning for Chrystal: even if he could persuade us all, he still needed another for a majority. But his confidence was extreme, his energy flowed out just as when he had made us coerce the candidates in October. When someone mentioned that we were not much of a cave, Chrystal said:

'I don't mind that. We can bring others in. There's Luke. There's even Crawford. And the others – they may not want to stay out in the cold.'

Promptly he brought out his first candidate,

'I'm not going to be coy,' he said. 'I have someone in mind. In my view the time has come to look outside the college. I want you to think of Lyon.'

Most of us knew Lyon; he was a Reader, a fellow of another college, a man of good academic standing and a bit of a university politician. In a few minutes it was apparent that he would get no support. We all gave reasons for half-heartedness – but the reasons were a matter of courtesy, a way of saying we were not disposed to fall in.

Chrystal, still undeterred, canvassed another name, also from outside the college, and then another. Different reasons were brought against them, but there was never a chance that either would be looked at: at the sound of each name, everyone there was saying no. It was not that we had anything special against them; simply, we did not want to find them suitable. By now I was sure that Chrystal would get nowhere. I had seen him in October carry us, by sheer force of will, into dragooning the candidates to vote for each other. But then we had all been ready to be convinced, and now the reverse was true. He was exuding just as much will, and few men had more than Chrystal. But this time we were not persuadable; and in all the moves of politics, dexterity is meaningless, even will itself does not avail, unless there is some spot in one's opponent ready to be convinced. 'Most reluctantly,' said Despard-Smith, after we had discussed the third name, 'I am coming to the conclusion, Dean, that it is too late in the day to look outside the college.'

'I accept that for the moment, Despard,' said Chrystal, still brisk and good-tempered. 'But we've not finished. In that case we must look inside.'

It was late at night, the room was hot, smoke was spinning slowly under the light: the older men were sleepy, and once Winslow's eyes had closed. But, at the sound of that last remark, they were awake, vigilant, ready once more for the long cautious guarded talk. Winslow lit his pipe again; as the match flared, a trick of the shadows smoothed out the nutcracker lines of nose and chin, and his eyes gleamed, deep, bright – and anxious. Yes, anxious. Was there still a remnant of hope? 'We must look inside,' said Chrystal.

'Of course,' said Despard-Smith, 'all of us gave serious thought to the possibilities when we heard the disastrous news last spring. Or if we didn't we were very seriously negligent.'

'Never mind,' said Chrystal. 'I want to go over them once more. We shan't get the chance again. It's no use having second thoughts after Thursday.'

'Some of us,' said Despard-Smith, 'are always coming to bolt the stable door after the horse has f-flown.'

'They won't this time,' said Chrystal. He stared round at us all. 'Well, we've got to look inside. I'm going down the fellows in order of seniority. Gay. Pilbrow. You, Despard. The statutes won't let us have you.'

'I supported the new statute about the retiring age,' said Despard-Smith sombrely. 'I've often asked myself whether I did right. Some men of seventy are still competent to hold any position of responsibility—'

'You would be,' interrupted Chrystal. In his brusque way he was placating the old man. And he was looking two moves ahead: I thought I guessed his intention now. 'You would be. No one doubts it. But it can't happen.' He paused. 'Going on down the list.' He added in a tone which he kept casual and matter of fact: 'Winslow. Winslow, you're the next.'

'Curiously enough,' said Winslow, also trying to be casual, 'I was aware of that.'

'Do you think,' said Despard-Smith in a hurry, 'that you'd feel satisfied to take on such an office for a very short time? I doubt whether it is fair to ask a man to take an office with only five years to run.'

'I should actually have seven years. I was sixty-three in October,' said Winslow.

'You'd just learn the job. Then you'd have to go. I agree with Despard,' said Chrystal, looking at Winslow with a bold, embarrassed smile.

'I seriously doubt,' said Despard-Smith, 'whether it would be *fair* to ask you.'

'When is it fair to ask anyone?' said Roy Calvert. His eyes were glinting with mockery: he was moved for Winslow.

Before he could say more, Francis Getliffe put in:

'On general principles, there is something to be said for a younger man. We ought to have someone with at least ten years to go. I know you'd take that view yourself, wouldn't you?' He spoke to Winslow directly.

Francis had got on better with Winslow than most of the college, and the question was kind. But it did not soften the fact. Winslow's eyelids had drooped, he was staring at the table.

He said at last:

'No doubt you're right.'

'I was certain you'd see it that way, Winslow,' said Chrystal, with relief, with excessive heartiness. I was watching Roy, half-expecting him to say more: but he gave a twitch of a smile, and let it slide. It was too forlorn a hope even for him.

Chrystal proceeded down the list.

'Crawford. Jago. Already dealt with. Brown. The next senior is Brown,' he said. 'Brown. I'm asking you to think carefully about him. Isn't he the man for a compromise candidate?'

Winslow looked up for a second.

'That's a very remarkable suggestion, Dean,' he said with savage sarcasm, with a flicker of his old spirit.

'Isn't he much too young? I don't see how the college could possibly consider anyone so junior,' said Despard-Smith.

'He's forty-six,' said Chrystal.

'It's dangerous to have young men in these positions,' said Despard-Smith. 'One never knows how they'll turn out.'

'Brown won't alter till he dies,' I said. It seemed strange that anyone, even Despard-Smith, should think of Brown as young.

'I don't think his age is a reason against him,' said Francis. 'But—'

'I know everything you're going to say,' said Chrystal. 'I know all about Brown. I know him better than any of you. He's been my best friend since we were up together. He's not brilliant. He'll never set the Thames on fire. People would think it was a dim election. But there are things in Brown that you don't see until you've known him for years. He'd pull the place together.'

'My dear Dean,' said Winslow, 'it would mean twenty years of stodge.'

'I should have considered,' said Despard-Smith, 'that if we were to take the serious step of looking at such junior fellows, we should want to consider you yourself long before Brown.'

'I couldn't look at it,' said Chrystal. 'I'm not up to it. I know my limitations. I'm not fit to be Master. Brown is. I'd serve under him and think myself lucky.'

He spoke with absolute humility and honesty. It was not put on, there was none of the stately mannered mock-modesty of college proceedings. This was the humility and honesty of his heart. It was so patent that no one challenged it.

He pressed on about Brown. I said that I would prefer him to any other compromise candidate. Less warmly, Roy said that, if the first vote in chapel did not give Jago a majority, he would not mind transferring to Brown on the second turn. Francis Getliffe said that, if the first vote were a stalemate, he would consider doing the same as Roy. With that kind of backing, such as it was, Chrystal argued with the other two into the early morning: he was not touchy, he did not give way to pique, he just sat there and argued as the quarters went on chiming away the night; he sat there, strong in his physical prepotence, persuading, browbeating, exclaiming with violence, wooing and bursting into temper.

Everyone in the room but himself knew that he must fail. Winslow was mostly silent, but every word he spoke was edged with unhappy contempt. Despard-Smith was solemnly obstinate. Everyone knew but Chrystal that neither would ever consent to vote for Brown. The last hope of compromise had gone. Yet Chrystal seemed undiscouraged. By midnight the rest of us would have given it up as useless, but he kept us there till after two o'clock.

At the last he won one concession through the others' sheer fatigue. He got them to admit that Brown was the only possible third candidate.

'It's obvious,' he said. 'Several of us here have said they might come round to him. Do you quarrel with that, Despard?'

Despard-Smith wearily shook his head.

'That's good enough for me,' said Chrystal. 'It means that Brown must be asked whether he'll stand. It may come to it. We can't leave it in the air. I'll speak to him in the morning.'

His face was fresh, he was smiling, he was obscurely satisfied. He looked at his clock on the mantelpiece.

'I shan't have to wait long,' he said. 'It is the morning already.'

CHAPTER XL

'I'VE HAD A DISAPPOINTING LIFE'

CHRYSTAL had kept us up so late that I slept until the middle of the morning. It was 17 December, a dark and stormy day: the wind was howling again, for the westerly gales had returned; it was not cold, but the heavy clouds hung over the roofs, and in the afternoon Roy and I built up the fire in my sitting-room for the sake of the blaze. We compared impressions of Chrystal's tactics and manner on the night before. Why had he persisted against all rational sense? Why had he gone away so pleased? Was it because he wanted to prove to Brown that, whatever he did in this election, he was still completely affectionate and loyal? That was part of it, we felt sure: but we did not believe it was the end.

As we were talking across the fire, a double and deliberate knock sounded on the door. 'Uncle Arthur in person,' said Roy, and we both smiled as Brown came in. But Brown's smile in return was only formal.

He sat down, looked into the fire, and said in a constrained tone:

'I wanted to see you both. I am told that, without my consent, I was mentioned as a candidate last night. Did you have anything to do with this?'

He was grimly indignant. We told him what we had each promised.

'I was glad to do it,' I said. 'I should enjoy voting for you. It would be admirable to see you in the Lodge.'

He did not respond. After a time he said:

'I suppose you all intended it kindly.'

'I don't know about kindly,' I said. 'It was intended to show what we feel about you.'

'I hope you all intended it kindly,' said Brown.

'Chrystal wanted the chance to say you ought to be Master,' said Roy. 'So he told me.'

'It's quite true.'

'It should have been obvious to him that I could not conceivably be a candidate in these circumstances,' said Brown. 'The only result of my name being mentioned is to stand in Jago's light. It can only mean dissensions in Jago's party and no responsible man can see it otherwise. I am very sorry that Chrystal should have seen fit to use my name for that purpose. And I am obliged to tell you that I am sorry you two associated yourselves with it.'

'You ought to believe that we mean what we say,' I replied.

'I realise you didn't mind paying me a compliment,' said Brown, as though making an effort to be fair. 'What I can't make out is how anyone as astute as you can have lost your head and behaved in this irresponsible fashion. Surely you can see that nothing is gained by paying useless compliments when things are as delicate as they are now, three days away from the event. It is nothing more nor less than playing into the hands of the other side. It looks as though I was being made a tool of.'

'Have you told Chrystal?'

'I have. I'm not prepared to have people think that I'm being made a tool of.'

I had never seen him so completely shaken out of reason and tolerance and charity – not even when Pilbrow defected. His whole picture of 'decent behaviour' had been thrown aside. He liked to think of himself as the manager of the college, the power behind the meetings; but, as I had often noticed, as for instance in the first approach to Luke, he was always scrupulous in keeping within the rules; he was not easy unless he was well-thought-of and in good repute. It upset him to imagine that people were now thinking that he had planned an intrigue with his friend, so as to get in as a last-minute compromise. It upset him equally if they thought he was just a catspaw. In the end, he had an overwhelmingly strong sense of his own proper dignity and of the behaviour he wanted the world to see.

He was also, of course, the most realistic of men: he saw the position with clear eyes, and it made him angrier still with Chrystal. He knew very well that he was not being offered even a remote chance: he felt he was just being asked to salve Chrystal's conscience. And that was the most maddening of his thoughts: that was the one which made him come and reproach Roy and me as though he could not forgive us. For Brown could see – no one more sharply – the conflict, vacillation, temptation and gathering purpose of his friend. He could not control him now; for the first time in twenty years he found his own will being crossed by Chrystal. Chrystal might do more yet: in moments of foresight Brown could see the worst of ends. When Chrystal came to him with this gesture, Brown felt that he had lost.

He went away without any softening towards Roy or me, telling us that he must write round to each fellow, in order to say that in no circumstances would he let his name be considered. I suspected that he had shown his anger more nakedly to us than to Chrystal. He had controlled himself with Chrystal – then had to come and take it out of us.

As soon as he had gone, Roy looked at me.

'Old boy,' he said, 'I fancy Jago's dished.'

'Yes.'

'We need to do what we can. If we can entice someone over, we might save it.'

We decided to try Despard-Smith and Pilbrow that same day, and went together to Pilbrow's rooms after tea. We had no success at all. Roy used all his blandishments, the blandishments which came to him by nature, but which he could also use by art. He was as lively and varied as he was to women, in turns teasing, serious, attentive, flattering, mocking. He invited Pilbrow to visit him in Berlin in the spring. Pilbrow enjoyed the performance, he liked handsome young men, but he did not so much as flicker: it seemed to him impossible now to vote for anyone but Crawford. I took up the political argument, Roy lapped the old man with all his tricks of charm. But we got nowhere, except that he pressed us both to dine with an exiled writer in London, the night after the election.

We walked through the court. Roy was grinning at his own expense.

'I've lost face,' he said.

'You're getting old,' I said.

'You'd better try Despard by yourself,' said Roy. 'If I can't get off with old Eustace, I'm damned if I can with Despard.'

It was a fact that Despard-Smith still looked on him with mystified suspicion, and so after hall I went alone. Despard-Smith's rooms were in the third court, on the next staircase to Nightingale's and near Jago's house. He had not been to hall that night, and on the chest outside the door lay the dishes of a meal sent up from the kitchen. His outer door was not closed, but there was no one in his main room, and the fire had gone out. I tapped on the inside door: there was a gruff shout 'who's there?' When I answered, no reply came for some while: then there were movements inside, and a key turned in the lock. Despard-Smith looked out at me with bloodshot, angry eyes.

'I'm very busy. I'm very busy, Eliot.'

'I shan't keep you a moment.'

'You don't realise how busy I am. People here have never shown me the slightest consideration.'

His breath smelt of liquor; instead of being solemn, grave, minatory, he was just angry.

'I should like a word about the election,' I said. He glared at me.

'You'd better come in for two minutes.' he said in a grating tone.

His inner room was dark, over-furnished by the standards of the twentieth century, packed with cupboards, tables, glass-fronted cases full of collections of pottery. Photographs, many of them of the under-graduates of his youth, in boaters and wearing large moustaches, hung all over the walls. By his old armchair, which had projecting head-rests, stood a table covered with green baize, and on the table were a book and an empty tumbler. Bleakly he said: 'Can I offer you a n-nightcap?' and opened a cupboard by the fireplace. I had a glimpse of a great array of empty whisky bottles; he brought out one half-full and another glass.

He poured me a small whisky and himself a very large one, and he took a long gulp while we were still standing up.

He was not drunk but he was inflamed by drink. There had been rumours for years that he drank heavily in private, but he had no friends in college, his life was lonely, no one knew for certain how he lived it. Gossip had a knack of not touching him closely; perhaps he was too spare and harsh a figure to be talked about much. His natural authority seemed to protect him, even in his absence.

'I wondered if you were happy about the election,' I said.

'Certainly not,' said Despard-Smith. 'I taken an extremely grave view of the future of this college.'

'It isn't too late—' I began.

'It has been too late for many years,' said Despard-Smith ominously.

I said something about Crawford and Jago, and for a moment my hopes sprang up at his reply.

'Jago has sacrificed himself for the college, Eliot. Just as every college officer has to. Whereas Crawford has not sacrificed himself, he has become a distinguished man of science. On academic grounds his election will do us good in the outside world. I needn't say that I've always been seriously disturbed at the prospect of electing a bolshevik.'

I had not time to be amused by that term for Crawford, the sturdy middle-class scientific liberal: I had seized on the gleam of hope, was forcing the comparison between the two, when Despard-Smith brushed my question aside, and stared at me with fierce bloodshot eyes.

'The college has brought it upon itself,' he said. 'They've chosen not to pay attention to my warnings, and they can only expect disastrous con-sequences. They did it with their eyes open when they chose Royce. That was the f-first step down the slippery slope.' He put a finger inside his dogcollar and then took it out with a click. He said in a grating, accus-ing tone: 'They ought to have asked me to take on the burden. They said I wasn't known outside the college. That was the thanks I got for sacrificing myself for thirty years.'

I said a word or two, but he emptied his glass and faced me with greater anger still.

'I've had a disappointing life, Eliot,' he said. 'It's not been a happy life. I've not been given the recognition I had a right to expect. It's a scandalous story. It would not be to the credit of this college if I let everyone know how I'd been treated. I'm looking back on my life now, and I tell you that it's been one long disappointment. And I lay it all to the blame of the people here.'

From another man, the cry might have been softened by pathos. But there was nothing soft about Despard-Smith at seventy, drinking in secret, attacking me with his disappointment. 'I've had a disappointing life': he did not say it with the sad warmth of self-pity, but aggressively, certain that he was in the right.

'You're going to let them elect Crawford now?' I said.

'They ought to have asked me to take on the burden ten years ago. I tell you, this college would have been a different place.'

'Wouldn't Jago be more likely to take your line?'

'He's done better as Tutor than I bargained for,' said Despard-Smith. 'But he's got no head for affairs.'

'That needn't rule him out—'

'Royce had no head for affairs, and they chose him,' said Despard-Smith.

'I'm still surprised you should vote for Crawford.'

'He's made a name for himself. That's good enough for a Master. They wouldn't choose me because I wasn't known outside the college. Crawford will do. No one can deny that he will do. And if people don't like him when they've got him,' he said, 'well, they'll have to l-lump it for the next fifteen years.'

He fetched out the bottle again and poured himself another drink. This time he did not offer me any. 'I don't mind telling you, Eliot, that I've got a soft spot for Jago. If I were just voting on personal grounds, I would choose him before the other man. But the other man has made his name. And Jago hasn't. He's sacrificed himself for the college. If a man takes a college office, he makes a disastrous choice. He can't expect people to recognise him. Jago ought to be prepared to face the consequences of his sacrifice. He ought to know what happened to me.'

My hope had faded. At last I understood something of why he had stuck to Crawford from the beginning – Crawford, the 'bolshevik'. Despard-Smith had loved power so much in his austere fashion: it thickened the blood in his veins. He had loved his years as bursar, he had done what pleased him most, even though he believed that he was 'sacrificing himself'. But it rankled still that they had not made him Master. It seemed to have struck him as a surprise, as a physical shock. I wondered whether it was from those days, ten years ago, that he started his solitary evenings with the whisky bottle.

Unluckily for Jago, the old man saw in him his own misfortune re-created. He did like Jago: he was starved of affection, he was not without the power to enjoy friendship, though he could not take the first steps himself. But seeing that Jago might retrace his old distress, Despard-Smith wished simply and starkly that it should happen so. He wished it more because he liked the man. It was right that Jago too should sacrifice himself. He thought of his own 'disappointing life'. He thought of Jago, treated as he had been. And he felt a tinge of sadic warmth.

CHAPTER XLI

TWO CIGARS IN THE COMBINATION ROOM

THERE was nothing to do but wait. Both Roy and I had a sense of the end now, but we were tantalised by a fluctuating hope. On paper (if Gay did not fail us) we could still count a majority for Jago. If it were to be broken, we must get news soon. It could not be long. What was Chrystal doing, now that even he had to abandon the notion of a third candidate? He had to face the struggle of Jago and Crawford again. No news seemed good news. Throughout the morning of 18 December, forty-eight hours from the election, throughout that whole day, we heard nothing. I did not see either Chrystal or Brown, although Brown's letter arrived. It was much more mellifluous and stately than his outburst in the flesh, and said that 'though any member of the college ought to be honoured even to have his name mentioned as a possible candidate for the Mastership, I must after prolonged consideration and with many expressions of thanks ask my friends and colleagues to permit me to withdraw.'

That was all the news that day. It seemed that bargainings and confidential talks had ceased.

In the evening Jago came to my room.

'Have you heard anything fresh?' His tone was jaunty, but under his eyes the skin was stained and dry.

'Nothing at all.'

'I want you to tell me anything you know. The very moment it happens,' he said, menacing me with the force of his anxiety. 'This is a bad enough business without having to wonder whether one's friends are keeping anything back.'

'I'll keep nothing back,' I promised.

'I must be an unendurable nuisance to you.' He smiled. 'So there really isn't any news? When I lay awake last night, I thought of all the absolutely inexplicable things I had watched the college do—'

'Can't you sleep?'

'Never mind,' said Jago. 'I shall sleep in a couple of nights. So good old Arthur Brown wasn't prepared to be made a convenience of. That takes us back where we started. They really are obliged to make the bizarre choice between me and my opponent. And nothing has happened to upset the balance, so far as you know?'

His moods were not stable, he was strained and expectant, fervent and hostile, at odd moments sarcastically detached, all in the same excitement of the nerves. Above all, his optimism had not left him. To his wife I was certain he maintained that he would get in. Some men would have defended themselves by saying that they expected the worst. Jago in his proud and reckless spirit was not able to protect himself by such a dodge. There was something defenceless about his optimism. He seemed quite without the armour, the thickening of the skin, that most men take on insensibly as the years pass.

I wanted to guard him, but he resisted the slightest word of doubt. He listened and thanked me, but his eyes were flashing with an excitement that I could not touch. He knew very little of what had happened at the meeting in Chrystal's room, and even less about the cumulative disagreement between Brown and Chrystal. He did not want to know of it. That evening he still had hope, and as he lay sleepless through the long night to come it would steady his heart.

We went into the combination room together before hall; there were several men already waiting, but no one spoke. The constraint took hold of us like a field of force. Despard-Smith was there, Francis Getliffe, Nightingale, Roy Calvert. It was not that they had been talking of Jago, and were embarrassed to see him. It was not the constraint of a conversation left in the air – but simply the weight that comes upon men as a struggle is ending. Even Roy's sparkle was borne down under it. When we took our places in hall, there was still almost no word spoken. Despard-Smith sat at our head, solemnly asking for toast, muted and grave by contrast to the inflamed old man of the night before.

Then Luke bustled in late. He hurled himself into the seat next

Roy Calvert's, and swallowed a plate of soup at an enormous pace. He looked up and smiled round at us indiscriminately – at me, at Francis, at Nightingale. I had never seen a face more radiant with joy. One did not notice the pleasant youthful features: all one saw was this absolute, certain and effulgent happiness.

'Well?' I could not resist smiling broadly back.

'I've got it out! I know for sure I've got it out!'

'Which part of it?' said Francis.

'The whole damned caboodle. The whole bloody beautiful bag of tricks. I've got the answer to the slow neutron business, Getliffe. It's all just come tumbling out.'

'Are you certain?' asked Francis, unwilling to believe it.

'Of course I'm certain. Do you think I'd stick my neck out like this if I weren't certain? It's as plain as the palm of my hand.'

Francis cross-questioned him, and for minutes the technical words rapped across the table – 'neutrons', 'collision', 'stopping power', 'alphas'. Francis was frowning, envious despite himself, more eager to find a hole than to be convinced that Luke was right. But Luke was unperturbed, all faces were friendly on this day of certain joy; he gave his explanations at a great speed, fired in his homely figures of speech, was too exalted to keep back his cheerful swearwords; yet even a layman came to feel how clear and masterful he was in everything he said. Gradually, as though reluctantly, Francis's frown left his face, and there came instead his deep, creased smile. He was seeing something that compelled his admiration. His own talent was strong enough to make him respond; this was a major work, and for a moment he was disinterested, keen with admiration, smiling an experienced and applauding smile.

'Good work!' he cried. 'Lord, it's nice work. It's one of the most beautiful things I've heard for a long time.'

'It's pretty good,' said Luke, unashamed, with no pretence of modesty though his cheeks were flushing scarlet.

'I believe it's wonderful,' said Jago, who had been listening with intense interest, as though he could drown his anxieties in this young man's joy. 'Not that I understand most of your detestable words. But you do tell us that he has done something remarkable, don't you, Getliffe?'

'It's beautiful work,' said Francis with great authority.

'I'm more glad than I can say,' said Jago to Luke. Nightingale had turned his head away and was looking down the hall.

'When did you know you'd made a discovery?' cried Jago.

'I thought a week ago the wretched thing was coming out,' said Luke, who used a different set of terms. 'But I've thought so before a dozen bloody times. This time, though, I had a hunch that it was different. I've been pretty well living and feeding at the lab. ever since. That was why I didn't come to the meeting on Monday,' he added affably to Despard-Smith, who gave a bleak nod.

'The little pow wow,' Roy said to Despard-Smith, by way of explanation.

'I could almost have sworn it was right that night. But I've been bitten by false bloody dawns too many times. I've not been to bed since. I wasn't going to leave off until I knew the answer one way or the other.

'It's wonderful,' he burst out in a voice that carried up and down the table, 'when you've got a problem that is really coming out. It's like making love – suddenly your unconscious takes control. And nothing can stop you. You know that you're making old Mother Nature sit up and beg. And you say to her "I've got you, you old bitch". You've got her just where you want her. Then, to show there's no ill-feeling, you give : an affectionate pinch on the bottom.'

He leaned back, exhausted, resplendent, cheerful beyond all expression. Francis grinned at him with friendly understanding, Jago laughed aloud, Roy gave me half a wink (for young Luke's discretion had vanished in one colossal sweep) and took it upon himself to divert Despard-Smith's attention.

In the combination room, Jago presented a bottle to mark 'a notable discovery completed this day by the junior fellow', as he announced for the formal toast. Hearing what was to happen, Nightingale rushed away before the health was drunk. Despard-Smith, who had his own kind of formal courtesy, congratulated Luke and then settled down to the port. Luke took one of the largest cigars and smoked it over his glass, drowsy at last, his head humming with whirling blessedness. And Jago, with a gentle and paternal smile, did what I had never seen him do, and took a cigar himself. The two sat together, the square ruddy boy, happy as he might never be again, and the man whose face bore so much suffering. As each listened to the other, the tip of his cigar glowed. They were talking about the stars. It was thirty-six hours before the election.

Francis and I left them together, and walked to the gate. I hesitated about asking him up to my rooms, and then did not.

'That's very pretty work of young Luke's,' he said.

'I gathered as much from what you said.'

'I doubt if you know how good it is,' he said. He paused. 'It's better than anything I've done yet. Much better.'

He was so quixotic, so upright, so passionately ambitious: all I could do was to pretend to be ironic.

'It's time we two had a bit of luck,' I said. 'These boys are running off with all the prizes. Look at Roy Calvert's work by the side of mine. I may catch up if I outlive him twenty years.'

Francis smiled absently, and we stopped under the lantern.

'I ought to say something else, Lewis.'

'What's that?'

'I thought Jago showed up very well tonight. There's more in him than I allowed for.'

'It isn't too late,' I said very quickly. 'If you vote for him—'

Francis shook his head.

'No, I shouldn't begin to think of altering my vote,' he said. 'I know I'm right.'

CHAPTER XLII

THE LAST NIGHT

THE day before the election, 19 December, passed with dragging slowness. Throughout the morning there was no news: only Roy visited me, as we chatted we were waiting for the next chime of the clock: time stretched itself silently out between the quarters. It was not raining, but the clouds were a level dun. Before lunch we walked through the streets and Roy bought some more presents; afterwards he left me alone in my room.

There Brown joined me in the middle of the afternoon. It was a relief to see him, rather than go on trying to read. But there was something ominous in his first deliberate question.

'I was wondering,' he said, 'whether you had Chrystal with you.'

'I've not seen him since the meeting,' I said.

'I've not seen him,' said Brown, 'since he approached me afterwards in the sense that I've already given you my opinion of. But I thought it might not be unwise if I got into touch with him today. I've called round at his house, but they said that they thought he'd gone for a walk early this morning.'

I looked at the darkening window, against which the rain had begun to lash.

'It seems an odd day to choose,' I said.

'I've tried his rooms,' said Brown. 'But it looks as though they had been empty all day.'

'What is he doing?'

Brown shook his head.

'I'm afraid that he's in great distress of mind,' he said.

It was for one reason alone that he was searching for Chrystal: he might still be able to influence him: using all the pressure of their friendship, he might still be able to keep him to Jago. On that last day, Brown had no room for other thoughts. He knew as well as I did where Chrystal had been tending. But Brown was enough of a politician never to lose all hope until the end, even though it was forlorn. One could not be a politician without that kind of resilient hope. When Chrystal asked him to be a candidate, Brown had felt for a time it was all lost. But now he had got back into action again. Chrystal was undecided, Chrystal was walking about in 'distress of mind' – Brown was ready to call on all his years of understanding of his friend, there was still a chance of forcing him to vote for Jago next morning.

'I am rather anxious to see him before tonight,' said Brown, looking at me with his acute peering glance.

'If I see him,' I said, 'I'll let you know.'

'I should be very much obliged if you would,' said Brown. 'Of course, I can always catch him at his house late tonight.'

His manner was deliberately prosaic and comfortable. He was showing less outward sign of strain than any of us; when he was frayed inside, he slowed down his always measured speech, brought out the stead commonplaces, reduced all he could to the matter-of-fact.

'Well,' he said, 'I think I'd better be off to my rooms soon. I've still got some letters to write about the scholarships. Oh, there's just one thing. I suppose you don't happen to have talked to Jago today?'

I said that I had seen Jago in hall the night before.

'How did you think he was?'

'Hopeful. So hopeful that it frightened me.'

'I know what you mean. I had an hour with him this morning. He was just the same. I tried to give him a little warning, but I couldn't make any impression at all.'

'If he doesn't get in?—' I said.

'If he doesn't get in,' said Brown steadily, 'I don't believe he'll ever be the same man again.'

He frowned and said:

'It's annoying to think that, if we were certain Chrystal was going to be sensible, we should have a decent prospect of tomorrow turning out all right. It's a tantalising thought.'

Then he left me, and I went to have tea with Roy. I returned to my rooms through rain which had set in for the night, and I settled by the fire, not wanting to move until dinner time. But I had not been there half an hour when the door opened.

'Good evening, Eliot,' said Chrystal in his sharpest parade-ground voice. He was wearing a mackintosh, but it was only slightly damp at the shoulders, and his shoes were clean. He had not been walking much that day.

'I want a word with you.'

I asked him to sit down, but he would not even take off his coat.

'I'm busy. I've got to have a word with Brown.' He was brusquer than I had ever heard him.

'He's in his rooms,' I said.

'I'll go in three minutes. I shan't take long with either of you. I shan't stay long with Brown.'

He stared at me with bold, assertive, defiant eyes. 'I've decided to vote for Crawford,' he said. 'He's the better man.'

Like all news that one has feared hearing, it sounded flat.

'It has been a lamentable exhibition,' said Chrystal. 'I tell you, Eliot, we've only just missed making a serious mistake. I saw it in time. We nearly passed Crawford over. I never liked it. He's the right man.'

I began to argue, but Chrystal cut me short:

'I haven't time to discuss it. I'm satisfied with Crawford. I went round to see him this morning. I've been with him all day. I've heard his views on the college. I like them. It's been a satisfactory day.'

'I remember you saying—'

'I'm sorry, Eliot. I haven't time to discuss it. I've never been happy about this election. It's been lamentable. I oughtn't to have left it so late.'

'It's very hard to leave our party at this notice,' I said angrily.

'I joined it against my better judgment,' he snapped.

'That doesn't affect it. You're contracted to Jago. Have you told Brown?'

'I didn't want to write to Jago until I'd told Brown. I owe Brown an explanation. We've never had to explain anything to each other before. I'm sorry about that. It can't be helped.' He looked at me. 'You don't think I mind sending a note to Jago, do you? He would never have done.

Not in a hundred years. I'm saving us all from a calamity. You don't see it now, but you'll thank me later on.'

He kept his coat on, he would not sit down, but he stood talking for some time. He did not wish to face Brown, he longed for the next hour to be past, he was putting off the struggle: not through direct fear, the fear that some men are seized with when they cross their wills against a stronger one, but because he was too soft-hearted to carry bad news, too uncertain of his own part to display if before intimate eyes.

He did not like the part he had insensibly slipped into. Just as Jago hated the path of ambition which, once he had begun it, led him from step to step, each one springing naturally from the last, until he was tempted to humiliate himself in front of Nightingale – in the same way Chrystal hated the path of compromise, which, step by step, each one plausible, enjoyable, almost inevitable, had brought him now to quarrel with his friend and break his contract. It was all so natural. Angrily he justified himself to me, said 'you'll all thank me later on'. He had been torn one way and the other, he had drifted into the compromise. He had never been master of the events round him. It was that which he could not forgive.

He had never been fond of Jago, had never liked to think of him as Master, had only joined in to please Arthur Brown. Then, liking the feel of power, he had tried to find ways out. He had revelled in making the candidates vote for each other. Yet even so he had not struggled free from his indecisions. Was he too much under Brown's influence? His affection was hearty and simple; but his longing to be masterful was intense. Was he right in sacrificing his judgment, just to please Brown? Even here, where he felt each day that Brown had made a mistake?

For Chrystal had come to feel that electing Jago would be worse than a mistake; it would hinder all that Chrystal wanted, for himself and for the college. With Jago, there would be no chance of the college gaining in riches and reputation among solid men.

As the months went on, Chrystal found he could endure the thought of Jago less and less. He felt free in the conferences with the other side: in the pacts with them, the search for a third candidate, he could assert himself. Every time he was with the other side he felt that the whole election lay in his control. In those meetings, in the hours at night with Jago's opponents, he came into his own again.

And how much, I wondered, was due to hurt vanity – urgent in all men, and as much so in Chrystal as in most? He had been piqued so intolerably when Jago defended Winslow and laughed at Sir Horace and the benefaction – had he been piqued so intolerably that it turned the balance? Envy and pique and vanity, all the passions of self-regard: you could not live long in a society of men and not see them often weigh down the rest. How much of my own objection to Crawford was because he once spoke of me as a barrister *manqué*?

I did not know, perhaps I never should know, on what day Chrystal faced himself and saw that he would not vote for Jago. Certainly not in the first steps which, without his realising, had started him towards this afternoon. When he began the move to make the candidates vote for each other, his first move to a coalition with the other side, he could still have said to himself, and believed it, that he was pledged to Jago. He did not make any pretence of enthusiasm to Brown or me, and to himself his reluctance, his sheer distaste, kept coming into mind. Yet he would have said to himself that he was going to vote for Jago. He would still have said it when in search of a third candidate – he was going to vote for Jago unless we found another man. On 17 December, when he approached Brown, he would have gone on saying it to himself. He would have said it to himself: but I thought that there are things one says to oneself in all sincerity, statements of intention, which one knows without admitting it that one will never do. I believed it had been like that with Chrystal since the funeral. He believed he would vote for Jago, unless he brought off a coup: in some hidden and inadmissible way, he knew he never would.

Yet it was probably less than forty-eight hours before this afternoon when at last he saw with explicit certainty that he would not vote for Jago. He had tried Brown as a third candidate, to give himself an excuse for throwing away his vote. Brown had turned him down. There would be no third candidate. It must be Jago against Crawford to the end. Chrystal was caught. There was nothing for it now. So, within the last forty-eight hours, it had come to him. Everything became clear at one flash. With relief, with release, with extreme satisfaction, he knew that he would vote for Crawford. It was what he had wanted to do for months.

It was astonishingly like some of the moves in high politics, I thought afterwards when I had a chance of watching personal struggles upon a grander scale. I saw men as tough and dominating as Chrystal, entangled in compromise and in time hypnotised by their own technique: believing that they were being sensible and realistic, taking their steps for coherent practical reasons, while in fact they were moved by vacillations which they did not begin to understand. I saw men enjoying forming coalitions, just as Chrystal did, and revelling in the contact with their opponents. I saw the same impulse to change sides, to resent one's leader and become fascinated by one's chief opponent. The more certain men are that they are chasing their own concrete and 'realistic' ends, so it often seemed to me, the more nakedly do you see all the strands they could never give a reason for.

Such natures as Chrystal's are more mixed in action than the man himself would ever admit – more mixed, I sometimes thought, than those of stranger men such as Jago and Roy Calvert. Chrystal thought he was realistic in all he did: you had only to watch him, to hear his curt inarticulate outbursts as he delayed breaking the news to Brown, to know how many other motives were at work: yet it was naïve to think he was not being realistic at the same time.

In a sense, he was being just as realistic as he thought. He had his own sensible policy for the college: that was safer with Crawford than with Jago. He wanted to keep his own busy humble power, he wanted his share in running the place. For months, every sign had told Chrystal that with Jago it would not be so easy. His temper and pride over Nightingale, his fury at having his hand forced over his vote, the moods in which he despised riches and rich men – Chrystal had noticed them all. He noticed them more acutely because of his other motives for rejecting Jago: but he also saw them as a politician. He had come to think that, if Jago became Master, his own policy and power would dwindle to nothing within the next five years. And he was absolutely right.

He still stood in his mackintosh in front of my fire. He could not force himself to go out.

'You'd better come with me, Eliot,' he broke out. 'Brown's got to be told. He'll want to talk to you.'

I refused.

'There's nothing for me to say,' I told him. I was too downcast: why should I help spare his feelings?

'Brown's got to be told. I shan't take long about it,' said Chrystal, standing still.

'It's late already – to tell him what you're going to.'

'I accept that,' said Chrystal. 'Well, I'll do it. You'd better join us in a few minutes, Eliot. You see eye to eye with Brown on this. He'd like to have you there. I shall have to go. As soon as I've told him. I've got plenty to do tonight.'

As he spoke he stared out of the room. Half-an-hour later I followed him. Brown was sitting deep in his habitual armchair; his face was sombre. Chrystal, his mackintosh unbuttoned, stood with his back to the fire, and his mouth was drawn down into lines unhappy and ill-treated. When

I entered, it seemed as though neither had spoken for minutes past; and it was a time before Brown spoke.

'I gather that you have an inkling of this change in the situation,' he said to me.

I said yes.

A moment later, there were light very rapid footsteps on the stairs. In burst Jago, his eyes alight.

'I'm extremely sorry,' he said to Brown. His tone was wild, and he turned on Chrystal with a naked intensity. His skin was grey, and yet the grimace of his lips was for all the world as though he smiled. 'It was you I wanted to find,' he said. 'It is necessary for me to see you. This note you've been good enough to send me – I should like to be quite certain what you mean.'

'I hadn't realised,' said Brown in a quiet, measured voice, 'that you had informed Jago already. I rather got the impression that you were speaking to me first.'

Chrystal's chin was sunk into his chest.

'I wrote before I came,' he said.

CHAPTER XLIII

EACH IS ALONE

FOR an instant – was it an illusion? – they seemed quite motionless. In that tableau, Brown was sitting with his fingers interlaced on his waistcoat, his eyes fixedly watching the other two: Chrystal's head was bent, he was staring at the carpet, his forehead shone under the light, his chin rested on his chest: Jago stood a yard away, and there was still a grimace on his lips that looked like a smile.

'I must have got hold of the wrong impression,' said Brown.

'Many of us,' Jago flared out, 'have got hold of wrong impressions. It would have been extraordinary if we hadn't. I've seen some remarkable behaviour from time to time—'

Chrystal raised his head and faced Jago with an assertive gaze. What had passed between him and Brown I did not know; but I felt that he had said little, he had not tried to explain himself, he had stood there in silence.

'I'm not taking those strictures from you, Jago,' he said.

'At last I can say what I think,' said Jago.

'We can all say what we think,' said Chrystal.

'This isn't very profitable,' said Brown.

At the sound of that steady, minatory voice, Jago frowned. Then quite suddenly he began to talk to Chrystal in an urgent, reasonable-seeming, almost friendly manner.

'I think we've always understood each other,' Jago said to Chrystal. 'You've never made any pretence that you wanted me as Master on my own merits, such as they are. You were presented with two distinctly unpleasing candidates, and you decided that I was slightly the less unpleasing of the two. You mustn't think it was a specially grateful position for me to be placed in – but at any rate there was no pretence about it. We both knew where we stood and made the best of it. Isn't that true?'

'There's something in it,' said Chrystal. 'But—'

'There's everything in it,' cried Jago. 'We've had a working understanding that wasn't very flattering to me. We both of us knew that we had very little in common. But we managed to adjust ourselves to this practical arrangement. You disliked the idea of my opponent more than you did me – and we took that as our common ground. It's lasted us all these months until tonight. And it seems to me sheer abject folly that it shouldn't last us a few hours longer.'

'What do you mean?'

'This will all be over tomorrow morning. Why have you suddenly let your impatience get the better of you? I know only too clearly that you're not very pleased at the idea of me as Master. We've both known that all along. Chrystal, I know we don't get on. I'm not going to pretend: I know we never shall. But we've made shift for long enough now. It's too serious for us to indulge our likes and dislikes at the last minute. I'm ready now to talk over all the practical arrangements that we can conceivably make for the future. I'm asking you to think again.'

'There's no point in that.'

'I'm asking you to think again,' said Jago, with feverish energy. 'We can make a working plan. I'm prepared to leave certain things in the college to you. It won't remove the misunderstanding between us – but it will save us from the things we want most of all to avoid.'

'What do I want most of all to avoid?' asked Chrystal.

'Having my opponent inflicted on you.'

'You're wrong, Jago.' Chrystal shook his head.

'How am I wrong?'

'I don't mind Crawford being Master. I did once. It was my mistake. He'll make a good Master.'

Jago heard but seemed not to understand. His expression remained strained to the limit of the nerves, angry and yet lit by his nervous hope. It remained so, just as when one reads a letter and the words spell out bad news, one's smile takes some time to go. Jago had not yet realised in clear consciousness what Chrystal had said.

'You know as well as I do,' said Jago, 'that seeing him elected is the last thing any of us want.'

'I take you up on that.'

'Do you seriously deny it?'

'I do,' said Chrystal.

'I'm very much afraid that you're—'

'I'm sorry, Jago,' said Chrystal. 'I'd better make it clear. Crawford will be a good Master. You've got the advantage over him in some respects. I've always said that, and I stick to it.'

He paused. He kept his gaze on Jago: it was firm, satisfied and curiously kindly.

'That's not the whole story,' he went on. 'I don't like saying this, Jago, but I've got to. You've got the advantage over him in some respects – but by and large he will make a better Master than you would have done.'

Jago gasped. It seemed that that was the moment when he began to know and suffer.

'Don't worry too much,' said Chrystal, with his genuine, almost physical concern. 'It isn't everyone who's suitable to be a Master. It isn't always the best—'

'Now you want to patronise me,' said Jago, very quietly.

A faint flush tinged the thin-skinned pallor of Chrystal's cheeks. It was only then, when Jago was defeated, beginning to feel the first empty pang, knowing that the shame and suffering would grow, that he succeeded in touching Chrystal.

'You never give anyone credit for decent intentions,' snapped Chrystal. 'If you had done, you might have more support.'

'I regard it as useless,' Brown intervened, 'for either of you to say more.'

The two confronted each other. For an instant it felt as though they would clash with accusations of all they found alien in each other.

But those words were not spoken. Perhaps Brown had just managed to stop them. They confronted each other: Chrystal's face was fierce and sullen, Jago's ravaged by the encroaching pain: it was Chrystal who turned away.

'I'm going into hall,' he said.

'I rather think they're expecting me at home,' said Brown.

'I shall see you in chapel then. Tomorrow morning,' said Chrystal. Brown inclined his head. Chrystal gave a short good-night, and went out.

Jago threw himself, as though both restless and exhausted on to the sofa.

'So this is the end,' he said.

'I'm afraid it is, Paul,' said Brown steadily. 'Unless something very unexpected turns up to help us – and I couldn't let you hope anything from that.'

'I've got no hope left,' said Jago.

'I'm afraid we must resign ourselves,' said Brown. 'I don't need to tell you what your friends are feeling.'

'It's bitter,' I said.

'Thank you both,' said Jago, but his tone was far away. Suddenly he cried, as from a new depth of pain: 'How can I inflict this on my wife? How can I face seeing her?'

Neither Brown nor I replied. Jago twisted on the sofa, drew up his knees and turned again. The bell began to ring for hall.

'I can't dine with them,' said Jago. 'It would be intolerable to let them see me.'

'I know,' said Brown.

'I do not see,' said Jago quietly, 'how I am going to stay here. I shall be reminded of this for the rest of my life.'

'It sounds trite,' said Brown. 'but these wounds heal in time.'

'I've got no money,' said Jago. 'I am too old to move. Every time they see me, I shall be ashamed.'

He added:

'I shall have to watch another man in the place I should have filled. I shall have to call him Master.'

It was not a conversation. For minutes together he lay silent: then came a broken outburst. It was painful to hear the spurs of defeat wound him in one place, then another. Will the other side know tonight? Are they celebrating in hall at this very moment? When will the news go round the university? Has it got outside the college yet? Who would be the first of his enemies to laugh? Why had he allowed himself to be a candidate?

His grief became so wild that he rounded on Brown.

'Why did you expose me to this danger? No one has ever done me so much harm before.'

'I misjudged the situation,' said Brown. 'I regard myself as very much to blame for lack of judgment.'

'You oughtn't to take risks with your friends' happiness.'

'I shall always be sorry, Paul,' said Brown with affectionate remorse, showing no sign that he resented being blamed.

After an interval of quiet Jago suddenly sat up and faced us.

'I want to ask you something. Is it quite certain that this man will get a majority tomorrow?'

'I'm afraid it is. So far as it's given to us to be certain.'

'Is it?' cried Jago. 'Why should I vote for him? Why should I make up his majority? I was coerced into it by Chrystal. Why should I do it now?'

'I think you're bound by your promise,' said Brown. 'I never liked it, but I think you're bound.'

'That is for me to say,' said Jago.

'Yes, it is for you to say,' said Brown in the same even tone. 'But there is another reason why I hope you won't break your promise. If you do, people will say that Crawford would never have done so in similar circumstances. And that this was the best proof that they had been right all the time.'

'Do you think now that they have been right all the time?'

'I am as sure they are wrong as I've ever been.'

'Even though I've shown you that I'm prepared to break my promise?'

'I know,' said Brown, 'that you feel temptations that I'm lucky enough to escape. But I also know that you don't give way to them.'

'You're a good friend, Arthur,' said Jago. It was his first familiar touch that night.

He stared at us with his eyes distraught, and said:

'So I'm asked to sign my own rejection tomorrow morning. That's something else I have to thank Chrystal for – I know he's been your friend. But he's more detestable than any of the others.'

'It's natural for you to say so,' said Brown. 'But it isn't true.'

'Are you going to trust him again?'

Brown gave a sad, ironic, firm-hearted smile: I thought it meant that he would trust Chrystal as much or as little as he had trusted him before. For Brown loved his friends, and knew they were only men. Since they were only men, they could be treacherous – and then next time loyal. One took them as they were. That gave Brown his unfailing strength, and also a tinge, deep under the comfortable flesh, of ironic sadness.

'How are *you* going to live in this college?' said Jago.

'Paul,' said Arthur Brown. 'I've failed in the thing I've most wanted to bring off here. You're right to blame me, but perhaps you will remember that it isn't going to be pleasant even for me yet awhile. I don't welcome this difference with Chrystal. And I abominate the thought of Crawford as Master more than anyone in the college. After you, I believe I'm more affected than any of our friends.'

'I'm sure that's true,' I said.

'Still,' said Brown, 'I'm not prepared to become a hermit because we've lost. We've shown some bad management and we've had some bad luck, and I don't forgive myself for what it's going to mean to you. But it has happened, and we have to make the best of it. We're not children, and we must go on living decently in this place.

'For myself,' he added, 'I propose to try and make the college as friendly as possible. We ought to be able to heal some of these rifts. I admit that it will take time. It will be a few years before we stop being more divided than I should like.'

Jago looked at the most devoted of his supporters. Each of them took calamity according to his nature. To Jago, those last words were meaningless, were nothing but a noise that sounded outside his distress. He felt inescapably alone.

Brown saw Jago look more than ever harrowed, and yet could not begin to console him again. He had done all he could. He said to me: 'I always insisted that it wasn't a foregone conclusion. I expect you remember me giving you occasional warnings. I'm afraid they've turned out more than justified.'

He was moved for Jago to the bottom of his nature; he was defeated on his own account; and yet, I was all but sure, there came a spark of comfort as he thought how far-sighted he had been.

The telephone rang. It was Brown's wife, asking why he was half an hour late for dinner. Brown said that he did not like to leave us, but I offered to take Jago into my rooms and find him food.

CHAPTER XLIV

DEEPER THAN SHAME

JAGO sat down by my fire. The flames, flaring and falling, illumined his face, left it in shadow, at times smoothed out the lines of pain. He gazed into the fire, taking no notice of me. I smoked a cigarette, and then another. At last I went quietly, as though he were asleep, to see what I could give him to eat.

There was not much in my gyproom. Bidwell had seen to that. But there was a loaf of bread, cheese and butter, and, very surprisingly, a little jar of caviare (a present from a pupil), which Bidwell happened not to like. I put them on the little table between us, in front of the fire. I went out again to fetch some whisky and glasses. When I returned, Jago had already begun to eat.

He ate with extreme hunger, with the same concentration that a man shows when he has been starved for days. He did not talk, except to thank me when I filled his glass or passed a knife. He finished half the loaf and a great wedge of cheese. At the end he gave a smile, a youthful and innocent smile.

'I was glad of that,' he said.

He smiled again.

'Until tonight,' he said, 'I intended to give a celebration for my friends. Of course it would have been necessary to keep it secret from the rest. They mustn't – it would have been fatal to let them feel there were still two parties in the college. But we should have had a celebration to ourselves.'

He spoke very simply and freshly, as though he had put the suffering on one side and was able to rest. I was certain that he was still *hoping*. In his heart, this celebration was still going to take place. I knew well enough how slow the heart is to catch up with the brute facts. There was, somewhere within me, the memory of a certain Christmas Eve. One looks forward to a joy: it is snatched away at the last minute: and, hours later, there are darts of illusory delight when one still feels that it is to come. Such moments cheat one and pass sickeningly away. So, a little later, the innocence ebbed from Jago's face. 'There will be no celebration for my friends,' he said. 'I shall not even know how to meet them. I don't know who they are.'

It was worse for him than for a humbler man, I thought. A humbler man could have cursed and moaned among his friends and thrown himself without thinking upon their love. Jago could not lower himself, could not give himself away, could not take pity and affection such as soften fate for more pedestrian men. It was the fault of his pride, of course – and yet, one can be held back by one's nature and at the same time long passionately for what one cannot take. Jago could bring sympathy to young Luke or me or Joan Royce or twenty others; but he could not accept it himself. With him, intimacy could only flow one way. When he revealed himself, it was in the theatre of this world, not by the fireside to a friend and equal. He was so made that he could not bear the equality of give-and-take. People blamed him for it; I wondered if they thought it enviable to be born with such pride?

'Do you think for a moment,' I said, 'that it will make a difference to any of us?'

'Thank you for saying that,' said Jago, but none of us was close enough. We were allies, young men to be helped, protégés whom it was a pleasure to struggle for: we could not come closer. That was true of us all. Brown had a strong, protective affection for Jago – but I had just seen how Jago could not receive it. To him, Brown was another ally, the most useful and dependable of all. He was never easy with Brown. So far as he found ease with men at all, it was with his protégés.

'Do you think,' I persisted, 'we value men according to their office? Do you think it matters a damn to Roy Calvert or me whether you're called Master or not?'

'I wanted to hear it,' said Jago. His imagination turned a knife in his bowels. He could not keep it from running after all the humiliations to come. They passed before his eyes with the sharpness of a film. He could not shut away the shames of his disgrace. He was drawn towards them by a morbid attraction. He had to imagine Crawford in *his* place.

His place: he had counted on it with such defenceless hope. He had heard himself being called Master: now he would hear us all call Crawford so. Among the wounds, that rankled and returned. He saw – as clearly as though it were before his eyes – Crawford presiding in hall, taking the chair at a college meeting. He could not stand it. He could not go to dinner, with that reproach before him in the flesh.

He thought of meeting his acquaintances in the streets. The news would rush round Cambridge in a week: people would say to him, with kindness, with a cruel twinkle: 'I was surprised. I'd always hoped you'd be elected yourself.' Others would see the announcement in *The Times*. Had he kept his hope strictly to himself? He had dropped words here and there. The stories would go round; and they would gain colour as time passed, they would not be accurate, but they would keep the frailty and the bite of human life. Crawford's election – that was the time when Jago thought he had it in his pocket, he had actually ordered the furniture for the Lodge – Chrystal changed his mind on the way to the chapel, and said it was the wisest decision he ever made in his life.

They were the ways in which Jago would be remembered. Perhaps the only ways, for there would be nothing that did not die with the flesh; he would never get high place now, there was no memorial in words, there was no child.

The evening went on, as Jago sat by my fire: the chimes clanged out, quarter by quarter, hour by hour; the shames bit into him. They pierced him like the shames of youth, before one's skin has thickened. Jago's skin had never thickened, and he was at their mercy.

Shames are more acute than sorrows, I thought as I sat by him, unable even to soften that intolerable night. The wounds of self-consciousness touch one's nerves more poignantly than the deepest agonies of feeling. But it is the deep agonies that cut at the roots of one's nature. It is there that one suffers, when vanity and self-consciousness have gone. And Jago suffered there.

It was not only that he winced at the thought of seeing his acquaintances in the streets. That wound would mend, as Arthur Brown told him it was trite to say, in time. He had also lost something in himself, and I did not see how he could get it back. He was a man diffident among his fellows in the ordinary rub-and-wear of life; it was hard for him to be a man among ordinary men; he was profoundly diffident about his power among men. That diffidence came no one knew from where, had governed so many of his actions, had prevented him from reaching the fame and glory which he believed was his by right. Very slowly he had built up a little store of confidence. Somehow men had come to respect him – he nearly believed it at the age of fifty. This Mastership was a sign for him. That explained, as I had already thought, the obsessive strength of his ambition. The Mastership meant that men esteemed him; they thought of him as one of themselves, as better than themselves. Listening to Brown and Chrystal when they asked him to stand, Jago had felt that he could have had any kind of success, he felt infused by confidence such as he had never known. It was one of the triumphant moments of his life.

He had become obsessed by the ambition; he had hated the path along which it had led him; the disappointments, the anxieties, the inhibitions, the humiliations – they corroded him because they brought back his diffidence again. But always he was buoyed up when he thought of his party and the place they would win for him. Above all, he was buoyed up by the support of Brown and Chrystal. He did not like Chrystal; they were as different as men could be; but that antipathy made Chrystal's support more precious. He resented Chrystal's management, he thought Chrystal was a coarse-minded party boss – but even when he wanted to quarrel, he thought with wonder and delight 'this man believes in me! this man is competent, down-to-earth – and he's ready to make me Master! If such a man believes in me, I can believe in myself!'

That night Chrystal had drained away the little store of confidence. Would it ever be refilled? It would be harder now than when Jago first became ambitious, first wished to prove himself among men.

It was eleven o'clock, the clock was just striking, when he began to speak about his wife. She had been his first thought in Brown's room. He had not brought himself to mention her since.

'She will be waiting up for me,' he said. 'I shall hurt her beyond bearing when I see her. I've tried hard all my life not to hurt her. Now I can't see a way out.'

'Won't she guess there's something wrong?'

'That won't make it easier – when she hears it's true.'

'She'll bear it,' I said, 'because it comes from you.'

'That makes it a hundred times worse.'

'For you. But not for her.'

'If I brought bad news from outside,' said Jago, 'I should not be afraid for a single instant. She is very brave in every way in which a human being can be brave. If this place shut down and we'd lost every penny, I'd tell her the news and she'd start getting ready to work the next minute. But this is horribly different.'

I did not question him.

'Don't you see,' he cried, 'that she will accuse herself?'

He added quietly:

'She will be certain to think it is her fault.'

'We must tell her it isn't,' I said. 'Roy and I must explain exactly what has happened.'

'She will never believe you. She'll never believe any of you.' He paused. 'I'm very much afraid that she will not believe me.'

'Is it no use our trying?'

'I'm afraid that nothing will reassure her,' said Jago. 'I think she trusts me – yet she can't believe me when it concerns herself. I've not brought her peace of mind. If she'd married another man, she might

244

have found it. I don't know. I hoped I could make her happy, and I haven't done.'

'I know what you feel,' I said.

'So you do,' said Jago – a smile, evanescent but brotherly, shone for an instant through his pain.

'I don't believe anyone else could have made her as happy.'

'I've seen her in the worst hours,' said Jago. He went on in despair: 'Yet I've never done anything to hurt her until now. If I'd been the cruellest of men, I couldn't have found a way to hurt as much as this. I can't bear to see her face when I tell her. She will be utterly beside herself – and I shall be no good to her.'

With his chin in his hands, he looked into the fire. For many minutes he was silent. At last he spoke as though there had been no pause.

'I think I could endure it all,' he said, 'if it were not for her.'

CHAPTER XLV

THE ELECTION

ON the morning of the election, I woke while it was still dark. There were knocks at the great gate, the rattle of the door opening, the clink of keys, voices in the court; it was six o'clock, and the servants were coming in to work. Although I had been late to bed, telling Roy the final news, I could not get to sleep again. The court quietened, and the first light of the winter dawn crept round the edges of the blind. As the grey morning twilight became visible in the dark room, I lay awake as I had done in other troubles and heard the chimes ring out over the town with indifferent cheerfulness. I was full of worry, though there was nothing left to worry about.

The light increased; there were footsteps, not only servants', passing through the court; I recognised Chrystal's quick and athletic tread. Why was he in college so early? It was a solace when Bidwell tiptoed in. After his morning greeting, he said:

'So the great old day has arrived at last, sir.'

'Yes,' I said.

He stood beside the bed with his deferential roguish smile.

'I know it's wrong of us to talk among ourselves, sir, but we've had a good many words about who is to be the next Master.'

'Have you?'

'They're two very nice gentlemen,' said Bidwell. 'A very popular gentleman Dr Jago is. I shouldn't say there was a servant in the college who had ever heard a word against him.' He was watching me with sharp eyes out of his composed, deliberately bland and guileless face.

'Of course,' he said when I did not reply, 'Dr Crawford is a very popular gentleman too.' He hurried a little, determined not to be on the wrong side. 'Between ourselves, sir, I should say they were equally popular. We shall drink their healths all right, whoever you put in.'

I got up and shaved and put on my darkest suit. It was curious, I thought, how strongly ritual held one, even though one was not given to it. Out of the window, the court looked sombre in the bleak morning, and one of the last leaves of autumn had drifted on to the sill. Bidwell had switched on the light in my sitting-room, and for once the fire was blazing strongly in time for breakfast, though the air still struck cold.

I ate some breakfast without much appetite and read the morning paper: the news from the Spanish war seemed a little better. Roy ran up the stairs and walked about the room for a few moments.

'Hurry up, old boy,' he said. 'You mustn't miss the show.'

He was dressed with more than his usual elegance, and was wearing a black silk tie. When I asked him why, he said it was a sign of loss. He was less disturbed, more excited and far gayer than I was. He told me that he had met Chrystal in the court, and commiserated with him for being cursed with this temperamental indecision.

' "It must be a grave handicap," I said.' Roy's face became impassive. ' "It must make active life an impossible strain," I said.'

I grinned. 'How did he take it?'

'He looked rather puzzled.'

'It wasn't very wise.'

'Just so,' said Roy. 'But it was remarkably pleasing.'

He left to send a telegram before he went into chapel: he was off to Italy next day.

I stood by the window, and set my watch by the clock across the court. It was just ten minutes to ten. The chapel door stood open, and the head porter, his top hat gleaming in the grey morning, was waiting to give the signal for the bell to peal. But he had not done so when, through the great gate, appeared old Gay. He was wearing mortar board and gown, as he always did when he came to college; he was wrapped up in a new, heavy coat and padded thick with scarves; his beard looked as though it had been cut that morning. Step by step, foot and a half by foot and a half, he progressed towards the chapel. Two under-porters walked behind him; I thought he must have commanded them, for they seemed mystified and had nothing to do. Before he was half-way round the court, the bell began to ring. At the first sound, Gay looked up at the tower and gave an approving and olympian nod.

As the old man drew near, Brown emerged from the chapel door. His face glowed pink, and I guessed that he had been bustling about seeing that all was in order. Gay beckoned him, and he went along the path. Before they met Gay called out a resounding good-morning that I could hear even across the court and through my windows; when they came close enough, Gay enthusiastically shook hands.

At that moment, Chrystal and Despard-Smith were approaching from the second court, and Winslow came through the gate. The bell rang out insistently. It was time for me to go.

When I went into the chapel there was complete silence, though most of the college were already sitting there. A long table had been placed in the nave; it was covered with a thick rich crimson tablecloth I had never seen before; and there, with Gay at the head, Pilbrow on his right hand, Despard-Smith on his left, the others in order down its length, the fellows sat. The bell clanged outside: in each pause between the peals, there was complete silence. The chapel was solemn to some by faith; but others, who did not believe, who knew what the result of this morning must be, to whom it was just a form, were nevertheless gripped by the ritual magic.

The lights shone down on the red cloth. In the silence, once noticed more than ever the smell of the chapel – earthy, odorous from wood, wax, fusty books. Along with that smell, which never varied, came a new concomitant, a faint but persistent tincture of pomade. It must have been due, I thought, to old Gay's barber.

The bell still clanged. Ten o'clock had not yet struck. There were three empty places at the table. One was on my left, where Luke had not yet come. There was another between Despard-Smith and Brown, and a third between Winslow and Chrystal. Then Jago walked in, slowly, not looking at any of us. He stared at the table, took in the empty places. He saw where his must be. He took the chair between Winslow and Chrystal. No word was spoken, he made no indication of a greeting: but Brown, opposite to him gave a slight kind smile.

Luke came to his place, and we were still quiet. The bell gave its last peal: the chimes of ten were quivering above the chapel: Crawford moved, swiftly but without heat or fuss, to the last seat.

'I apologise if I'm late, Senior Fellow,' he said equably. They were the first words spoken since I went in.

The last stroke of ten had sounded, and there was no whisper in the chapel. Gay sat upright, looking down the table: Pilbrow and Despard-Smith faced each other: Winslow and Crawford: Jago and Brown: Chrystal and Nightingale: Getliffe and me: Roy Calvert and Luke. In front of each of us, on the crimson cloth, was a copy of the statutes, a slip of paper, and a pen. Down the middle of the table ran a series of four silver inkstands – one for Gay alone, one for each group of four.

Gay climbed to his feet.

'Ah,' he said. 'I propose to carry out the duties conferred on me by our statutes.' He began at once to read from his leather-covered copy. ' "At ten o'clock in the morning of the appointed day the Fellows shall assemble in the chapel, and of the fellows then present that one who is first in order of precedence shall preside. He shall first read aloud—" ' Gay looked up from the book. 'This is the appointed day, there's no doubt about that. And I am the fellow first in order of precedence. Now is the time to do my duty.'

In his strong and sonorous voice he read on. The words echoed in the chapel; everyone sat still while the seconds ticked past; I kept my eyes from Jago's face. The quarter struck, and Gay was still reading.

At last he finished.

'Ah,' he said, 'that's well done. Now I call upon you to stand and make your declarations.'

Gay vigorously recited: 'I, Maurice Harvey Laurence Gay, do hereby declare that I have full knowledge of the statutes just read and will solemnly observe them. I do also hereby declare that without thought of gain or loss or worldly considerations whatsoever I shall now choose as Master that man who in my belief will best maintain and increase the well-being and glory of the college. I vow this in sincerity and truth.'

In the ordinary elections, of a scholar or a fellow, it was the practice for each of us to repeat in turn the seven words of the promise. But now we heard Eustace Pilbrow go through the whole declaration, and Despard-Smith after him.

Despard-Smith's voice died away.

Winslow thrust out his underlip, and said:

'I vow this in sincerity and truth.'

Despard-Smith immediately whispered in Gay's ear. Gay said:

'The senior fellows consider that everyone should read the whole declaration.'

'Am I bound by the decision of the senior fellows?' said Winslow.

'We mustn't leave anything to doubt. No indeed,' said Gay. 'I have to ask you to comply. Then everyone else, right down the line. That's the proper way.'

'I do it under protest, Senior Fellow,' said Winslow sullenly, and read the declaration in a fast monotone.

When it came to Jago's turn, I felt the strain tighten among us as we stood. His voice was muffled but controlled. When he ended his promise, he threw back his head. His shoulder was almost touching Chrystal's.

The declarations passed across the table, came to the young men. At last Luke had completed his: we all stayed on our feet.

'Is that everyone?' said Gay. 'I want to be assured that everyone has made his declaration according to the statutes. That's well done again. Now we may sit down and write our votes.'

For some minutes – perhaps it was not so long – there was only the sound of the scratch of pens on paper. I noticed Chrystal, who was using his fountain pen, push towards Jago the inkstand that stood for them both to use. Someone higher up the table was crossing out a word. I finished and looked at Francis Getliffe, directly opposite: he gave me a grim smile. Several people were still staring down at the slips. Gay was writing away.

He was the last to look up. 'Ah. All ready? Pray read over your votes,' he said.

Then he called out:

'I will now request the junior fellow to collect your votes and deliver them to me. I shall then read them aloud, as prescribed in the statutes. I request the two next senior fellows to make a record of the votes as I announce them. Yes, that's the work for them to do.'

Pilbrow and Despard-Smith sat with paper in front of them. Young Luke walked down the nave, arranging the votes in order, so that they could be read from the juniors upwards.

'Well done,' said Gay, when Luke placed the little pile in his hands. 'Well done.'

He waited until Luke was once more in his seat.

'Now is the time to read the votes,' Gay announced. Once more he clutched the table and got to his feet. He held the slips at arm's length, in order to focus his faded, long-sighted eyes. He recited, in the clearest and most robust of tones:

'Here they are.

' "I, Walter John Luke, vote for Dr Paul Jago."

' "I, Roy Clement Edward Calvert, elect Paul Jago." '

My vote for Jago. There was no fixed form of voting, though Roy's was supposed to be the most correct. It struck me irrelevantly how one heard Christian names that one had scarcely known.

' "I, Francis Ernest Getliffe, elect Redvers Thomas Arbuthnot Crawford."

' "Ronald Edmund Alexander Nightingale votes for Dr Crawford."

' "Charles Percy Chrystal elects Dr Thomas Crawford." '

As Gay's voice rang out with Chrystal's vote, there was a quiver at the table. There may have been some, I thought, to whom it was a shock. Had the news reached everyone by ten o'clock?

' "I, Arthur Brown, elect Paul Jago." '

I waited anxiously for the next.

' "I, Paul Jago, elect Thomas Crawford."

' "Redvers Thomas Arbuthnot Crawford chooses Paul Jago."

' "Mr Winslow elects Dr Crawford, and signs his name as Godfrey Harold Winslow."

' "Albert Theophilus Despard-Smith elects Redvers Thomas Arbuthnot Crawford."

' "I, Eustace Pilbrow, elect Redvers Thomas Arbuthnot Crawford." '

Someone said: 'That's a majority.'

There was still Gay's own vote to come.

Gay read with doubled richness:

' "I, Maurice Harvey Laurence Gay, Senior Fellow of the college and emeritus professor in the university, after having performed my duties as Senior Fellow in accordance with the statutes and heard the declarations of the fellows duly assembled in chapel, do hereby cast my vote for Paul Jago as Master of the college." '

There was a movement, either of relaxation or surprise. I caught Roy Calvert's eye.

'There we are,' said Gay. 'There are the votes. Have you counted them?'

'Yes,' said Despard-Smith.

'Mind you count them carefully,' said Gay. 'We mustn't make a mistake at the last.'

'Seven votes for Dr Crawford,' said Despard-Smith. 'Six for Dr Jago. Seven votes make a clear majority of the college, and Dr Crawford is elected.'

'Ah. Indeed. Remarkable. Dr Crawford. I understood – You're certain of your records, my dear chap?'

'Certainly.' Despard-Smith was frowning.

'I think I must scrutinise them. I ought to make sure.' Still standing, the old man held the list of votes two feet from his eyes, and checked each one beside the written slips.

'I agree with you,' he said genially to Despard-Smith. 'Well done. Seven votes for Dr Crawford. I must declare him elected.'

For the last time, a hush fell in the chapel. Gay stood alone, smiling, serene and handsome.

'Dr Redvers Thomas Arbuthnot Crawford,' he called. Crawford rose. 'Senior Fellow,' he said.

'I declare you elected this day Master of the college,' said Gay.

He added, with a superb and natural air:

'And now I give the college into your charge.'

'I thank you, Senior Fellow,' said Crawford imperturbably. 'I thank the college.'

Without a word, Jago leaned across the table, shook Crawford's hand, and walked out of the chapel. Everyone watched him go. It was not until the outer door swung to that chairs were pushed back and men surrounded Crawford. We all congratulated him. Nightingale smiled at him, admiringly. Chrystal said: 'I'm very glad, Crawford.' Brown shook him by the hand with a polite, formal smile. Crawford was good-humoured and self-assured as ever while people talked to him. It was strange to hear him for the first time called Master.

CHAPTER XLVI

THE MASTER PRESIDES

I WENT away from the chapel with Roy Calvert, and we stood in the great gate, watching women bustle by to their morning shopping: the streets were full, the buses gleamed a brilliant red under the slaty sky.

'Dished,' said Roy. 'Old boy, one never feels the worst until it happens. I'm deflated.'

'Yes.'

'Why does one mind so much about things which don't matter? This doesn't matter to us.'

'It matters to Jago,' I said.

'Ought we to see him? I should be frightened to, you know. Did you see how he looked?'

'I did.'

'I should be frightened while he's so wretched. It's more in your line, Lewis.' He smiled, mocking both me and himself.

Soon he left me to get some money for his journey, and I turned back into the court. There was a knot of people at the chapel door, and I went towards them. Gay, Brown, Despard-Smith and Winslow were standing together, with the head porter a yard away: I saw that they had been pinning a notice to the door.

'What do you think of that, Nightingale?' Gay greeted me.

'Not Nightingale,' said Brown.

'What do you think of that?' said Gay. 'There's a notice and a half for you. There's no doubt about that. If they want to see who's been elected, they've only got to come and read. And they can see my signature at the bottom. I like a good bold signature. I like a man who's not ashamed of the sight of his own name. Well, my friends, it's all gone like clockwork. You couldn't have a better election than that. I congratulate you.'

'I've taken part in four elections,' said Despard-Smith. 'I don't expect to see another.'

'Come, come,' said Gay. 'Why, there is plenty of time for one or two more for all of us. I hope to do my duty at another one or two myself.'

He waved a jocular finger at Winslow.

'And there'll be no slackness, Winslow, my dear chap. Declarations in full, mind. I can see I shall have to keep you up to the mark.'

Winslow smiled sardonically.

'I still maintain I was right,' he said. 'I want it discussed. I've never believed in multiplying mummery—'

He flanked Gay on one side, Despard-Smith on the other, and they kept pace with his shuffle as they moved off arguing. 'Good-morning to you,' said Winslow to Brown and me. 'Good-morning, my dear chaps,' Gay shouted to us behind him.

I remained with Brown, and asked him what Roy had asked me: ought one of us to look after Jago? Would he go round himself? 'I should be useless to him,' said Arthur Brown. 'I'm very much afraid that I shouldn't be acceptable. I must reconcile myself to the fact that my company will distress him for a long time to come. He won't want to be reminded of our disaster.'

Brown spoke evenly, with resignation but with deep feeling. His concern would not flag, would not be snubbed away: his was not a nature to forget. Yet it was like him to have stayed behind with Gay to make sure that the formalities were properly complied with. No one else of

Jago's party would have cared whether or not the notice was affixed: Brown could not help scrutinising the ceremony to the end: even though Crawford was elected, the ceremonies must be performed, the college must be carried on. And now, standing by the chapel door, he said:

'I suppose everyone will want to drink some healths tonight. I'd better see that they're not forgetting to have a few bottles ready.'

For the rest of the day, until dinner, I heard only one more comment. It was from Chrystal, whom I met as he was walking out of college after lunch.

He looked at me with bold eyes, and gave his brisk good-afternoon.

'I tell you what, Eliot,' he said sharply, 'I didn't like Jago's behaviour this morning. He oughtn't to have gone off like that.'

'He's had something to put up with.'

'I know what he feels. I shouldn't like it myself. But one's got to put a face on things.'

It was true, I thought: he did know what it was like to be wounded.

'It makes me feel justified in the line I took,' said Chrystal. 'I know you disagree with me. I wasn't happy about it myself. But he's not dependable enough. He's a likeable man. But he wouldn't have done.'

I did not want to carry on the argument.

Before we parted, he said:

'You'll come and thank me in time, Eliot. I shouldn't be surprised if he doesn't turn up tonight. That won't be so good.'

By custom, all fellows came in to drink the new Master's health on the night of his election; it was to provide for this occasion that Brown had gone to the cellars.

Roy was busy packing and getting ready his notebooks for the Vatican library, so I spent the afternoon alone. I went out for tea in the town, and on my way ran straight into Mrs Jago. I began to tell her how distressed I was. She cut me dead.

In my rooms that evening, I kept thinking of that incident. It was easy to see it as a joke – but I had come to feel fond of her, and it was no joke at all. What state must she be in? How completely was she possessed? I tried to write her a note, but thought of the meanings she would read behind each word. I was more upset than I should have confessed even to Roy.

I went into the combination room some time before dinner, and found Crawford, Getliffe and Nightingale already there. Nightingale had accepted a glass of sherry from Crawford, and was as coy with it as a girl over her first drink. He had not touched a drop, he was saying, since Flanders. Crawford asked me to have a drink with impartial cordiality, and spoke to us all.

'Speaking now as Master,' he said, 'I expect one will have to exercise considerable selection over the meetings one addresses. I don't want to parade opinions which part of the college vehemently objects to but, speaking as a responsible citizen, I can't remain entirely quiescent in times like these.'

The room was filling rapidly. Despard-Smith, Chrystal, Brown and Winslow joined the group round Crawford. Francis Getliffe took me aside.

'Well, it's over,' he said.

'It's over.'

'I'm sorry if you're too disappointed.'

'I don't pretend to be overjoyed,' I said.

'It will shake down.' He smiled. 'Look, I need your advice. Come out and see us tomorrow night.'

I said yes as spontaneously as I could.

'Good work,' said Francis.

Nearly all the fellows had arrived. Each time the door opened, we looked for Jago. But first it was Pilbrow, sparkling with delight because he had received an invitation to go to Prague in the spring – then Gay, although he was breaking the routine of his nights. 'Ah, Crawford, my dear chap,' he said. 'I thought you would feel the gilt was off the ginger-bread unless I put in an appearance. Master I must call you now. I congratulate you.'

We were still waiting for Jago when the butler announced to Crawford that dinner was served.

'Well,' said Crawford, 'this seems to be the whole party. Gay, will you take my right hand? Eustace, will you come in on my left?'

He sat at the head of the table in hall, looking slightly magnified, as men do when placed in the chief seat. His face was smooth and buddha-like as he listened to old Gay through dinner. Down the table, I caught some whispers about Jago, and a triumphant smile from Nightingale. None of Jago's friends referred to him. We could not explain why he had not come. We said nothing: Luke looked at me and Brown, hurt that no one could put up a defence.

When we returned to the combination room, there were several decan-ters on the table, the glass glittering, the silver shining. Near them stood a pile of peaches in a great silver dish. Gay's eyes glistened at the sight. As he was congratulating the Steward, Crawford started to arrange us in our seats.

'I think we must have a change,' said Crawford. 'Gay, you must take my right hand again. That goes without saying. Chrystal, I should like you up here.'

Just as we were seated and Crawford had filled Gay's glass and his own and was pushing the first decanter on, the door opened and Jago came into the room. He was pale as though with an illness. All eyes were on him. The room was quiet.

'Jago,' said Crawford. 'Come and sit by me.'

Chrystal moved down one, we re-arranged ourselves, and Jago walked to the place on Crawford's left.

'I am so very sorry,' he said, 'to have missed your first dinner in hall. I had something to discuss with my wife. I thought I might still be in time to drink your health.'

The decanter was still going round. As glasses were being filled, Jago said, in a voice to which all listened:

'I think I can claim one privilege. That is what my wife and I have been discussing. We feel you should be our guest before you go to anyone else. Will you dine with us tomorrow' – Jago paused, and then brought out the word – 'Master?'

He had got through it. He scarcely listened to Crawford's reply. He raised his glass as Gay proposed the health of 'our new Master'. Jago did not speak again. He went out early, and I followed him, but he did not wish to say a word or hear one. He did not even wish for silent company along the path. In the blustering night, under the college lamps, he walked away. I watched him walk alone, back to his house.

REFLECTIONS ON THE COLLEGE PAST

OFTEN, during that year of the Mastership election, I thought how much the shape of our proceedings was determined by the past. Coming back from that first college meeting in January, I began thinking about the agenda, and wondered how long that rigid order had stayed unchanged. The minutes were, of course, a recent innovation; within living memory there had been no record of any decisions except for the most formal acts, such as elections and the sale of land. It had been left to the recollection of the senior fellows – which suggested some not uncolourful scenes. But first the livings, second money: it seemed our predecessors had kept that order for at least two hundred years.

Many forms had stayed unchanged in this place for much longer still. Fellows had elected their Master, as we had to do that year, by a practice that scarcely varied back to the foundation. The statute Despard-Smith had recited at that January meeting was dated 1926, but the provisions were the same as those of Elizabeth. And the period of thirty days after the death, if the vacancy happened out of term, was a safeguard to prevent a snap election without giving men time to ride across country to Cambridge.

The forms had stayed so much unchanged that it was sometimes hard to keep one's head and see the profound differences between us and our predecessors. It was very hard in a college like this, where so much of the setting remained physically unchanged. True, the college antiquaries told us that the windows had been altered in the seventeenth century, that the outer walls all over the college had been at least twice refaced, that the disarray of the garden was an eighteenth-century invention, that no one could trace the internal arrangement of the rooms. But those were small things; a sixteenth-century member of the college, dropped in the first court in the 1930s, would be instantaneously at home. And we felt it. However impervious one might be to the feeling of past time, there were moments when one was drugged by it. It was a haze which overcame one as one walked on the stones of the first court, touched the panelling in a room such as mine, looked over the roofs to King's: all these had been so long the same.

One felt it even in the streets of Cambridge. Walking as Roy and I had done on a rainy night, we passed through streets whose shape would have been comfortably familiar to our predecessors. The houses, the buildings, except for the colleges and churches, had all gone; but the colleges and churches defined the streets, and it was hard not to think of other men walking as we did, of the chain of lives going back so long a time, of others walking those same narrow streets in the rain.

As I said, this physical contact with past time made it hard to keep one's head. It was so easy to imagine our predecessors as they walked through the same court, dined in the same hall, drank their wine in the same combination room, elected a Master according to the same forms. It was easy to go a step further and think the election of a Master two or three hundred years ago was almost indistinguishable from ours now: it was easy to think that our predecessors and ourselves could be exchanged with no one noticing. One lost one's sense of fact. Of course, there would be resemblances between any elections to the Mastership; take a dozen men, ask them to elect their own head, and they will go through the same manœuvres as we went through that year; put an ambitious man like Jago in the college three hundred years ago, and he would have wanted the Mastership – put Brown there too, and he would have tried to work it for him.

But there would have been one deep difference between then and our own time. The dozen fellows would have been mostly youths in their early twenties. The core of solid, middle-aged, successful married men who in 1937 gave the college its strong and adult character – of these there could be no trace. The Winslows, Browns, Chrystals, Jagos, Gays, Getliffes, Crawfords could have no counterparts at all. One might expect to find in a seventeenth- or eighteenth-century college one or two old bachelors like Despard-Smith and Pilbrow – and apart from them only the very young. The average age of the fellows in 1937 was over fifty. In 1870 it was twenty-six. In 1800 it was twenty-seven. In 1700 it was twenty-five. For 1600 the figures are not so certain, but the average age seemed to have been even less.

This juvenile nature of the society meant incidentally that the Master had a predominance quite unlike our time. He was often elected as a young man (Francis Getliffe or I would have been a reasonable age for a seventeenth-century Master), but his dividends were much greater than the fellows', he did most of the administration of the college, including the work of the modern bursar, he remained in the post for life and could be married. It was not an accident that the Lodge had its stately bedroom, while fellows' sets, even those as handsome as mine, contained as sleeping places only their monastic cells. The Masters down to 1880 lived a normal prosperous adult life in the midst of celibates, young and old:

and they inclined in fact to form a separate aristocratic class in Cambridge society.

After the 1914-18 war that segregation had disappeared. The Mastership which Jago longed for would not make him rich among the fellows: as Brown calculated, he would lose a little money on it: in the modestly prosperous middle-class Cambridge of the thirties, most dons drew in between £1000 and £2000, Masters as well as the rest. The old predominance and powers had gone. The position still had glamour, repute, a good deal of personal power. It carried a certain amount of patronage. But its duties had faded away. Anyone who filled it had to create for himself the work to do.

This was one of the signs which showed how the college itself was changing. The forms remained, but the college was changing now, as it had changed in essence before in its six hundred years.

Few human institutions had a history so continuous, so personal, so day-to-day, I thought one night, listening to the rain on the windows. The cathedral schools of Milan and the like have histories of a kind which take one back to the Roman Empire; but they are not histories like the college's, of which one could trace each step in the fabric, in the muniment-room, in the library, in the wine books, in the names scratched on the windows and cut into the walls. Over the fireplace, a couple of yards from my chair, there were four names cut in the stone: in the sixteenth century they had shared this room, and slept in bunks against the panelling: those four all became (it is strange that they came together as boys) leaders of the Puritan movement: they preached at Leyden, wrote propaganda for the Plymouth plantation, advised Winthrop before he went to Boston. Two of them died, old men, in America.

It was astonishing how much stood there to be known of all those lives. The bottles of wine drunk by each fellow were on record, back almost for two hundred years.

I looked at the names carved into the fireplace, and I reverted to my thought of a few moments before. All this physical intimacy with the past could fill one's imagination as one sat before the fire; but there were times when it intoxicated one too much to see what the past was like. It was hard to remember, within these unchanging, yard-thick walls, how much and how often the college had changed, in all it stood for and intended to do.

It had begun as nothing very lofty. It had begun, in fact, as a kind of boarding-house. It was a boarding-house such as grew up round all the medieval universities; the universities drew students to the town, and there, as quite humble adjuncts, were houses for students to lodge – sometimes paid for by their clubbing together, sometimes maintained by an older man who paid the rent and then charged his lodgers.

The medieval universities came to full existence very quickly. They happened, it seems, because the closed, settled, stagnant world of the dark ages was at last breaking up; the towns, which had become small and insignificant in the seventh and eighth centuries, were growing again as – for some reason still not clear – trade began to flow once more over Europe, though still nothing like so freely as under the Antonines. By the twelfth and thirteenth centuries, the exchange of trade was becoming lively; and there was a need for an educated professional class to cope with affairs that were daily growing more complex, in particular with the ramifications of Canon Law. This seems to have been the reason why western Europe suddenly broke out in universities – Bologna, Salerno, Padua, Paris. In England Oxford became in the thirteenth century a university of European reputation; Cambridge, which originated by the simple process of a few masters leaving Oxford, setting up in the little fen market-town, and starting to teach, was not a rival in the same class for a long time.

In these universities, students attended to hear the teachers lecturing in the schools. The lectures began early in the morning, finished at dusk, in the cold, comfortless, straw-strewn rooms. The stuff of the lectures, the Quadrivium and the Trivium, seems to us arid, valueless, just word-chopping; but out of it the students may have gained plenty of zest and facility in argument. The course was a very long one, and many did not stay it. At the end there was a sort of examination; as with a modern Ph.D., everyone who stayed the course seems to have passed.

But this somewhat unattractive prospect did not put students off. They scraped money to come to Cambridge, some of them lived in bitter poverty and half starved. They were all destined to be clerics. There was one main motive; if they could get their degree, jobs lay ahead. Jobs in the royal administration, the courts, the church; jobs teaching in the schools – the fees were not light, and the teachers made a good living. The training was in fact vocational, and jobs lay at the end.

And the students liked the life. It was wild, free, and entirely uncontrolled. Some came as men, some as boys of fifteen or sixteen, some as children of twelve. They looked after themselves, and did as they wanted. The university offered them nothing but lectures, to which they went if they pleased. They found their own lodging, often in the garrets of the little town. Their time was their own, to talk, gamble, drink, fornicate.

They seem to have been unusually active with their knives. They must have felt the wild hopes of youth, reeling hilariously through the squalid streets. Some of them wrote poems in silver Latin, full or ardour, passion, humour and despair.

The students liked their life, but no one else did. Certainly not the townspeople; nor the students' parents; nor the teachers; nor possibly the more bookish and domesticated of the students themselves. So, almost from the origin of the university, there were attempts to get them out of their lonely lodgings into boarding-houses. Boarding-houses were cheaper, they could live four or five to a room and have meals in common – the salt meat, salt fish, beer and bread of a medieval Cambridge winter. It was possible to get a university teacher to live in the same house and keep an eye on them.

These boarding-houses had nothing to do with teaching: the students just lodged there, and went off in the morning to the schools. They were simply a sensible means of keeping those youths from the wilder excesses. Some of them were given money, rules, and became known as colleges, but their purpose remained the same.

They were a mixed crowd of people who endowed the first colleges – ecclesiastical politicians and administrators, country clergymen, noble ladies, local guilds, kings and lords. Behind the kings and noble ladies one can usually find the hand of some priestly adviser who had himself attended in the schools; those who knew the needs for direct experience set about getting money, and went as high as their influence could take them. And those who were persuaded, and provided a little money and the rents of a bit of land (for the gifts were small): what moved them? Possibly the sensible recognition of a need: not a specially important need, but one on which their confessor seemed to lay some stress. Possibly a spark of imagination. Certainly the desire to allay anxiety by having a few young clerks obliged to say each day in perpetuity a mass for the founder's soul. Certainly the desire to have their names remembered on earth: no one likes to leave this mortal company without something to mark his place. They were the same motives, rationalised into different words, as might now have moved Sir Horace Timberlake.

The endowments were small (no founder spent anything like the equivalent in medieval money of what Sir Horace ultimately provided). These glorified boarding-houses were not ambitious affairs. They were called colleges, for that was the jargon of the day for any collection of men – there were colleges of fishmongers, cardinals and undertakers. A large proportion of the endowments went into buildings, as is the usual wish of benefactors, since buildings are easy to see and give a satisfactory impression of permanence. They were good stout simple buildings, though not as a matter of fact as stout as they looked; for the money was never enough, there was a good deal of jerry-building, and the yard-thick walls of my rooms, for instance, contained two feet of rubble. In these buildings there were just the bare necessities of a medieval community: a kitchen; a large room to eat in; stark unheated rooms where the young men could live in twos and threes and fours; a set of rooms for the university teacher who was paid to look after the college and was called the Master (he was, of course, an unmarried priest till Elizabeth's time, and the Master's quarters in the early colleges were nothing like the great Lodges of later years). The only luxury was the chapel, which was larger than such a small community required; it was built unnecessarily large to the glory of God, and in it masses were celebrated for the founder's soul.

The community was usually a very small one. This college of ours was founded, by taking over a simple boarding-house, towards the end of the fourteenth century. It was given rents of a few manors in order to maintain a Master (usually a youngish teacher, a master of arts who lectured in the schools), eight fellow-scholars, who had passed their first degree and were studying for higher ones (they were normally youths of about twenty) and thirty-six scholars, who were boys coming up for the courses in the schools. These were the college; and it was in that sense that we still used the arrogant phrase 'the college', meaning the Master and fellows. 'The governing body' was a modern and self-conscious term, which betrayed a recognition of hundreds of young men, who liked to think that they too were the college. The eight fellow-scholars elected their own Master; the number stayed eight until the college received a large benefaction in the 1640s.

This was the college when it began. It was poor, unpretentious, attempted little save to keep its scholars out of mischief, counted for very little. It had the same first court as now, a Master, some of the same titles. In everything else it was unrecognisably different.

Then three things happened, as in all Oxford and Cambridge colleges of that time. Two were obvious and in the nature of things. The third, and the most important, is mysterious to this day. The first thing was that the Master and the young fellow-scholars took to looking over the young boys' studies. They heard their exercises, heard them speak Latin, coached them in disputing. Instead of staying a simple boarding-house, the college became a coaching establishment also. Before long, the college teaching was as important as the lectures in the schools. The university still consisted of those who lectured in the schools, conducted examinations, gave degrees; but, apart from the formal examination, the colleges took over much that the university used to do.

That was bound to happen. It happened in much the same fashion in the great mother university of Paris, the university of the Archpoet, Gerson, William of Ockham, and Villon, and in St Andrews, Prague, Cracow, the universities all over Europe.

It was also natural that the colleges should begin to admit not only scholars to whom grants were paid, but also boys and young men who paid their own way – the 'pensioners'. These young men were allowed into the colleges on sufferance, but soon swamped the rest in numbers. They added to the power and influence of the colleges, and considerably to their income – though the endowments were always enough, from the foundation down to the time of Brown and Chrystal, for the fellows to survive without any undergraduates at all.

That raises the question of the third process which gave Oxford and Cambridge their strange character and which is, as I said, still unexplained. For some reason or by some chance, the colleges flourished from the beginning. They attracted considerable benefactions in their first hundred years; this college of ours, which started smaller than the average, was enriched under the Tudors and drew in two very large benefactions in the seventeenth century (it then became a moderately prosperous college of almost exactly the middle size). The colleges became well-to-do as early as the Elizabethan period; old members gave their farms and manors, complete outsiders threw in a lease of land or a piece of plate. Astonishingly quickly for such a process, the colleges became wealthy, comfortable, in effect autonomous, far more important than the university. And the process once properly started, it went on accruing; the colleges could attract the university teachers to be Masters or fellows, because they could pay them more. The university was poor; no one left it money, it was too impersonal for that, men kept their affection and loyalty and nostalgia for the house where they had lived in their young manhood; the university had just enough to pay its few professorships, to keep up the buildings of the schools, where the relics of the old lectures still went on: the university still had the right to examine and confer degrees. Everything else had passed to the colleges. Quite early, before the end of the sixteenth century, they did all the serious teaching; they had the popular teachers, the power, the prestige, the glamour, and the riches. As the years passed, they got steadily richer.

And so there developed the peculiar dualism of Oxford and Cambridge. Nowhere else was there this odd relation between the university and the colleges – a relation so odd and intricate, so knotted with historical accidents, that it has always seemed incomprehensible to anyone outside.

It remains a mystery why this relation grew up only in England. Why was it only at the two English universities – quite independently – that the colleges became rich, powerful, self-sufficient, indestructible? At Paris, Bologna and all the medieval universities, boarding-houses were transformed into colleges, just as in England; at Paris, for example, they were endowed, given much the same start in property, and almost exactly the same statutes and constitution. Yet by 1550, when the Cambridge colleges were already dwarfing the university, those in Paris were dead.

At any rate, I thought, this college was, except in detail, typical of all the middle-sized English ones, and had gone through all their changes. By the sixteenth century it had long ceased to be a boarding-house, and become instead a cross between a public school and a small self-contained university. The boys up to seventeen and eighteen were birched in the college hall (which would have been unthinkable in less organised, less prosperous, freer days). The young men went out, some to country livings, some to the new service of administrative jobs required by Tudor England (though not many university graduates filled the high places). The Masters were usually married even now, the Lodge was enlarged, the great bedroom came into use; the fellows were predominantly, as they remained till 1880, unmarried young clerics, who took livings as their turn came round. Their interests were, however, very close to the social conflicts of the day: the active and unrebellious, men like Jago and Chrystal and Brown, were drawn into the Elizabethan bureaucracy; the discussions at high table, though put into religious words, must often have been on topics we should call 'political', and many of the idealistic young threw themselves into calvinism, were deprived of their fellowships by the government, and in exile led their congregations to wonder about the wilderness across the North Atlantic.

The seventeenth century saw, really for the first time, some fellows busy with scholarship and research. The times were restless and dangerous: trade was on the move, organised science took its place in the world. A few gifted men stayed all their lives in the college, and did solid work in botany and chemistry. Some of my contemporaries, I sometimes thought, would have fitted into the college then, more easily than into any time before our own.

The country quietened into the eighteenth-century peace, there was a lull before the technological revolution. For the first time since its foundation, the college, like all others, declined. In 1540 the college had been admitting 30 undergraduates a year, in 1640 the number had gone up to 50 (larger than at any time until after the 1914–18 war). In 1740 the number was down to 8. No one seemed very much to mind. The dividends stayed unaffected (about £100 a year for the ordinary fellow), the college livings did pretty well out of their tithes; it just remained for one of them to come along. The college had for the time being contrived to get cut off from the world: from the rough-and-ready experiments of the agricultural revolution, from any part in politics except to beg patronage from the great oligarchs. The college had stopped being a boarding-house, a school; had almost stopped being in any sense a place of education, though they took the tripos – or a mathematical examination – with some seriousness; it became instead a sort of club. Most people think affectionately now of an eighteenth-century Cambridge college; it was a very unexacting place. Most people have a picture of it – of middle-aged or elderly men, trained exclusively in the classics, stupefying themselves on port. The picture is wrong only in that the men in fact were not middle-aged or elderly, but very young: they were trained first and foremost, not in classics, but in mathematics; and they drank no more than most of their successors. Roy Calvert would have joined one of their harder sessions, and gone off without blinking to give a lecture in German on early Soghdian. But they had the custom of drinking their port twice a day – once after dinner, which began about two o'clock, and again after supper at seven. They must have been sleepy and bored, sitting for a couple of hours on a damp, hot Cambridge afternoon, drinking their wine very slowly, making bets on how soon a living would fall vacant, and how long before the last lucky man to take a living got married or had a child.

By the nineteenth century, the deep revolution (threatened faintly by seventeenth-century science: acted on, in the nineteenth-century factories) was visible everywhere. There had never been such a change so quickly as between the England of 1770 and the England of 1850: and the college felt it too. Something was happening: men wanted to know more. The country needed scientists. It needed every kind of expert knowledge. It needed somewhere to educate the commercial and industrial middle class that had suddenly grown up. Between 1830 and 1880 the college, like all Cambridge, modernised itself as fast as Japan later in the century. In 1830 the young clergymen still sat over their port each afternoon; in the 80s the college had taken on its present shape. Nine English traditions out of ten, old Eustace Pilbrow used to say, date from the latter half of the nineteenth century.

The university courses were revolutionised. The old rigid training, which made each honours student begin with a degree in mathematics, was thrown away. It became possible for a man, if he were so adventurous, to start his course in classics. In 1860 it even became possible to study natural science; and the Cavendish, the most famous of scientific laboratories, was built in 1874. Experimental science was taught; and the new university laboratories drew students as the old schools had drawn them in the middle ages; here no college could compete, and university teaching, after hundreds of years, was coming back to preeminence again.

The college kept up with the transformation. It made some changes itself, in others had to follow the Royal Commissions. Fellows need not be in orders; were allowed to marry; were no longer elected for life. At a step the college became a secular, adult, settled society. For five hundred years it had been a place which fellows went from when they could: at a stroke, it became a place they stayed in. By 1890 the combination room was inhabited by bearded fathers of families. The average age of the fellows mounted. Their subjects were diverse: there were scientists, oriental linguists, historians – and M. H. L. Gay, one of the younger fellows, had already published two books on the historical basis of the Icelandic sagas. The scholarly work of the college became greater out of all knowledge.

The college suddenly became a place of mature men. They were as frail as other men, but they won respect because of their job, and they had great self-respect. They were men of the same make as Winslow, Brown, Chrystal, Crawford, Jago and Francis Getliffe; and Gay and Pilbrow had lived through from those days to ours. From those days on, the college had been truly the same place.

Gay and Pilbrow, as young fellows, had seen the college, the whole of Cambridge, settle into the form which, to Luke for example, seemed eternal. Organised games, bumping races, matches with Oxford, college clubs, May week, competitive scholarships, club blazers and ties, the Council of the Senate, most Cambridge slang, were all nineteenth-century inventions. Gay had been elected at a time when some of his colleagues were chafing for the 1880 statutes to become law, so that they could marry. He had been through five elections to the Mastership. They were all elections dominated by the middle-aged, like this one in 1937. He had seen the college move to the height of its prosperity and self-confidence.

There was one irony about it all. Just as the college reached its full mature prosperity, it seemed that the causes which brought it there would in the end change it again, and this time diminish it. For the nineteenth-century revolution caused both the teaching of experimental science and the college as we knew it, rich, proud, full of successful middle-aged men, so comfortably off that the Master no longer lived in a separate society. The teaching of experimental science had meant the revival of the powers and influence of the university; for no college, however rich, not even Trinity, could finance physics and engineering laboratories on a modern scale. To cope with this need, the university had to receive contributions from the colleges and also a grant from the state. This meant as profound a change as that by which the colleges cut out the university as the prime source of teaching. It meant inevitably that the reverse must now happen. The university's income began to climb into millions a year: it needed that to provide for twentieth-century teaching and research: no college's endowment brought in more than a tenth the sum. By the 1920s the university was in charge of all laboratories, and all formal teaching: it was left to colleges only to supplement this by coaching, as they had done in their less exalted days. There were, by the way, great conveniences for the fellows in this resurrection of the university; nearly all of them had university posts as well as college ones, and so were paid twice. It was this double source of pay that made the income of Jago, Chrystal, Brown and the others so large; everyone between thirty and seventy in the college, except for Nightingale, was earning over £1000 a year, a good professional income in the 1930s. But it meant beyond any doubt whatever that the colleges, having just known their mature and comfortable greatness, would be struggling now to keep their place. It sometimes seemed that the time must come when they became boarding-houses again, though most superior ones.

I regretted it. I regretted it, in part against my intellectual judgment. They had their faults, but they had also great humanity.

However, the change was in the future. It did not trouble the fellows as I knew them. Of all men, they had the least doubts about their social value. They could be as fond of good works as Pilbrow, as modest as Brown, but still they were kept buoyed up by the greatest confidence and self-respect in their job. By the thirties, the conscience of the comfortable classes was sick: the sensitive rich, among my friends, asked themselves what use they were: but that was not a question one would have heard in the college. For everyone, inside and out, took it for granted that the academic life was a valuable one to live; scientists such as Crawford, Francis Getliffe, and Luke had become admired like no other professional men, and the rest of us, with a shade of envy, took a little admiration for ourselves.

In England, the country with the subtlest social divisions (Pilbrow said the most snobbish of countries), Oxford and Cambridge had had an unchallenged social *cachet* for a long time; even Lady Muriel, though she did not feel her husband's colleagues were her equals, did not consider them untouchable; and so a man like Francis Getliffe, when asked what was his job, answered with a double confidence, knowing that it was valued by serious people and also had its own curious place among the smart. Many able men entered the academic life in those years because, with a maximum of comfort, it settled their consciences and let them feel that their lives were not utterly without a use.

The New Men

The New Men

1939–47

CONTENTS

Contents

PART ONE

A QUESTION OF POSSIBILITY

CHAPTER I

ARGUMENT WITH A BROTHER

I HEARD the first rumour in the middle of an argument with my brother when I was trying to persuade him not to marry, but it did not seem much more than a distraction.

He had brought Irene to lunch with me on a wet, windy morning in late February. The year was 1939, and I was, for three or four days each week, still living in college. As we sat at table in my dining-room the rain slashed against the windows, and once or twice smoke from the open sixteenth-century grate blew across the room. It was so dark outside that I had turned all the sconce lights on, warm against the panelling; in that comfortable light, while the wind thudded against the window-panes, Irene set to work to get me on her side.

I had not met her before, but Martin had mentioned her name enough to make me guess about her. He had first picked her up in London, at one of his richer friend's, and I gathered that she had no money but plenty of invitations. This seemed to amuse Martin, but to me she sounded too much like a shabby-smart girl, who thought her best chance was to find an able husband.

The more I heard of her, the more anxious I was for Martin – as a father might be for a son, for there were nine years between us. He was only twenty-five, and while other people saw him as stable and detached, the last man to commit a piece of foolishness, abnormally capable of looking after himself, I could not stop myself worrying.

The day before this luncheon, Martin had asked, without seeming over-eager, whether I would like to meet Irene. Yet I knew, and she knew, that it was a visit of inspection.

She called me by my Christian name in her first greeting: and, as I poured her out a glass of sherry, was saying:

'I always imagined you as darker than Martin. You should be dark!'

'You should drink sherry,' I said. She had the kind of impudence which provoked me and which had its attraction.

'Is it always sherry before meals?'

'What else?' I said.

'Fixed tastes!' she cried. 'Now *that* I did expect.'

As we began to eat, she went on teasing. It was the teasing, at once spontaneous and practised, of a young woman who has enjoyed playing for the attention of older men. She had the manner of a mischievous daughter, her laughter high-pitched, disrespectful, sharp with a kind of constrained glee – and underneath just enough ultimate deference to please.

Yet, despite that manner, she looked older than her age, which was the same as Martin's. She was a tall woman, full-breasted, with a stoop that made one feel that she was self-conscious about her figure; often when she laughed she made a bow which reduced her height still more, which made her seem to be acting like a little girl. The skin of her cheeks looked already worn and high-coloured underneath the make-up.

Her features were not pretty, but one noticed her eyes, narrow, treacle-brown, glinting under the heavy upper lids. For me; in that first meeting, she had some physical charm.

Apart from that, I thought that she was reckless and honest in her own fashion. I could not satisfy myself about what she felt for Martin. She was fond of him, but I did not believe that she loved him; yet she longed to marry him. That was the first thing I was looking for, and within a few minutes I had no doubt. I still wanted to know why she longed for it so much.

She spoke like an adventuress, but this was a curious piece of adventuress-ship. That day she asked us, frankly, inquisitively, about our early life at home. She knew that we had come from the lower-middle-class back streets of a provincial town. Following after me, Martin had won a scholarship in natural science at the college, and I had been able to help pay his way. For nearly four years he had been doing research at the Cavendish.

As we talked, I realised that to Irene it seemed as strange, as exciting, as *different*, a slice of existence as Martin had found hers.

She had drunk more than her share of wine. She broke out:

'Of course, you two had a better time than I had.'

'It had its disadvantages,' said Martin.

'You hadn't got everyone sitting on your head. Whenever I did anything I wanted to, my poor old father used to say: "Irene, remember you're a Brunskill." Well, that would have been pretty destroying even if the Brunskills had been specially grand. I thought it was too grim altogether when they sent me to school, and the only girl who'd heard the wonderful name thought we were Norwegians.'

I told her of my acquaintance, Lord Boscastle, whose formula of social dismissal was 'Who *is* he? I'm afraid I don't *know* the fellow.' She gave her yelp of laughter.

'That's what I should get,' she said. 'And it's much more dismaying if you've been taught that you may be poverty-stricken but that you are slightly superior.'

In fact, as I discovered later, she was overdoing it, partly because she had a vein of inverted snobbery and was exaggerating her misfortunes in front of us. Her father was living on his pension from the Indian Army, but some of the Brunskills could have been called county. In secret, Irene kept her interest in the gradations of smartness among her smart friends.

She went on drinking, but, as we sat round the fire for our coffee, she took hold of herself and began questioning me about my plans. Was I going abroad that Easter vacation? When could she and Martin see me again? Wouldn't I meet them in London? Wouldn't I join them for a May Week ball?

'I'm afraid I can't,' I said.

'Do come. Wouldn't you like being seen with me?'

'My wife isn't fit to dance just now,' I said.

'Bring someone else.'

It was obvious that Martin had not told her of my wife's condition. She lived alone in London, and saw no one except me; increasingly those visits were hard to bear.

'I'm sorry,' I said.

'You don't want to dance with me. You're quite right, I'm not much good.'

'It must be seven or eight years since I went to a ball,' I reflected. 'Good Lord, time goes too fast.'

I had said it casually, platitudinously, but a line came between Irene's brows and her voice sharpened.

'That's near the bone,' she said.

'What's the matter?'

'I hate the thought of time.'

Quickly Martin smiled at her and was changing the subject, but she insisted.

'Time's wingèd chariot,' she said and looked at me. 'Do *you* like the thought of it?'

Soon she cheered up, and decided it was time to leave Martin and me together. She made some excuse; she might as well have invited us to discuss her.

I said goodbye to her in the little passage outside my gyp-cupboard, between the room-door and the oak.

'I'm afraid I've been horribly boring and talked too much,' she said, as she pressed my hand.

I passed it off.

'I always talk too much when I'm nervous.' She opened the outer door. Still she could not leave it alone; she glanced back over her shoulder, and called to me:

'I'm very nervous today, Lewis. Believe me, I am.'

She was begging me not to speak against her. As I turned back into the room a gust of wind crashed the door shut behind me. The smoke had cleared from the fireplace, the coal was cherry-red in the iron wicker of the grate. Across the hearth Martin's face was swept smooth in the unfluctuating glow.

He gave me a smile with his mouth tight and pulled down at one corner; it was a cagey, observant smile that he often wore, and which, together with his open expression and acute eyes, made his mood difficult to read.

His face was a young man's, but one that would not alter much until he was old; the skin would not take lines easily, except round the eyes; he was fair, and the hair curled, crisp and thick, close to his skull. He was shorter than I was, and not more than an inch or two taller than Irene, but his shoulders, neck and wrists were strong.

Without speaking, I sat down opposite to him. Then I said:

'Well?'

'Well?' he replied.

His smile had not changed. His tone was easy. It would have been hard to tell how painfully he cared that I should approve of her; but I knew it.

Our sympathy had always been close, and was growing closer as we grew older. Between us there was a bond of trust. But much of our communication was unspoken, and it was rare for us to be direct with each other, especially about our deeper feelings.

It was partly that, like many men who appear spontaneous at a first meeting, we each had layers of reserve. I sometimes broke loose from mine, but Martin's seemed to be part of his nature, as though he would never cease making elaborate plans to hide his secrets, to over-insure against the chances of life. I was watching him develop into a cautious, subtle and far-sighted man.

It was partly that reserve which kept us from being direct with each other; but much more it was the special restraint and delicacy which is often found in brothers' love.

'I think she's attractive,' I said, 'and distinctly good company.'

'Yes, isn't she?' said Martin.

Already we were fencing.

'Does she have a job of some kind?'

'I believe she's been someone's secretary.'

'Does that give her enough to live on, in London?'

'I've got an idea,' said Martin, with an appearance of elaborate reflection, 'that she shares a flat with another young woman.'

'She must find it pretty hard to keep going,' I said.

Martin agreed. 'I suppose it's genuinely difficult for them to make a living, isn't it?'

He was capable of stonewalling indefinitely. Trying another line, I asked whether he had decided anything about his own future. His research grant ran out by the summer, and, if there were no war (our habitual phrase that year), he would have to find a job. He would get a decent one, but, we both knew by this time, there were three or four contemporaries ahead of him, who would take the plums. His research was sound, so Walter Luke said, who supervised him: but Luke added that, judged by high standards, he was turning out good but not quite good enough.

I was more disappointed than I wanted Martin to see, for I had invested much hope in him, including hopes of my own that had up to now been frustrated. His own expectations, however, seemed to be humbler than those I dreamed up for him. He was ready to come to terms with his talents, to be sorry they were not greater, but to make the best of them. If he believed that he might surprise us all, he hid it. He accepted Luke's opinion as just. That afternoon he thought the likelihood was that he would get a post in a provincial university.

'If you thought of marrying,' I said, 'you couldn't very well manage on that.'

'I suppose it has been done,' he replied.

Then I asked:

'As a matter of fact, are you intending to marry her?'

There was a pause.

'It's not completely out of the question,' he said.

His tone stayed even, but just for an instant his open, attentive expression broke, and I saw his eyes flash. They were dark blue, hard, transparently bright, of a kind common in our family. As they met mine, I knew in my heart that his resolve was formed. Yet I could not help arguing against it. My temper was fraying; as I tried not to sound clucking and protective, I could hear with dislike the edge in my own voice.

'I must say,' I broke out, 'that I think it would be very unwise.'

'I wondered if you would feel that,' said Martin.

'She'd be a load on you.'

'Why do you think that, particularly?'

He had the interested air of a man discussing the love-affairs of an acquaintance, well liked, but for whom he had no intimate concern. It was assumed partly to vex me a little; but in part it was a protection against me.

'Do you think that she'd be much good as a professional man's wife?'

'I can see that she would have her disadvantages,' he said reasonably.

'You need someone who'll let you work in peace and for that you couldn't find anyone worse.'

'I think I could get my own way there,' said Martin.

'No, you couldn't. Not if you care for her at all, which I presume you do, otherwise you wouldn't be contemplating this piece of suicide.'

'Yes, I do care for her,' he said.

The coals fell suddenly, leaving a bright and fragile hollow in which the sparks stood still as fireflies. He leaned across to throw on coal. When he had sat back again I said:

'Then imagine what it would be like. She's rackety and you're prudent. She'd have all the time in the world on her hands, and do you think she's the woman to stay still? What do you think you'd find when you got home?'

'It's just possible that I might be able to settle her down.'

I was handling it badly, I knew. I said:

'You know, I'm not a great expert on happy marriages. But on unhappy ones I do know as much as most men.'

Martin gave a friendly, sarcastic smile. He might have guessed, when I asked what he would find on getting home, that I was speaking of myself. In fact, what I had said was more involuntary than that and held another irony which he could not know. I went on. He met each point on the plane of reason. He had reckoned them out himself; no one insured more carefully against the future. I was telling him nothing he did not know. I became angry again.

'She's pretty shallow, you know. I expect her loves are too.'

Martin did not reply.

'She's bright, but she's not very clever.'

'That doesn't matter to me,' he said.

'You'd find her boring in time.'

'I couldn't have done less so up to now,' said Martin.

'Just imagine her being bright – for – ten years. In ten years you'd be sick and tired of her.'

'*Ten years*,' said Martin. He added: 'If that's the worst that happens!'

'She'd be driving you off your head.'

'If this fission affair works,' said Martin, 'we shall be lucky if we have any heads.'

That was the actual moment at which I first heard the rumour. There was a touch of irritation in Martin's voice, because over his marriage I had pressed him too far.

He was putting me off. He had not spoken with any special weight, for he was thinking about Irene and my opposition; yet something in his tone compelled me, and I had to enquire:

'Is this anything new?'

'Very new,' said Martin. He was still trying to lead my attention away, but also he was half-caught up, as he said: 'It's very new, but I don't know how everyone missed it. I might have seen it myself!' He told me that, within the past fortnight, letters had been published in scientific journals in several countries, and that the Cavendish people and physicists everywhere were talking of nothing else. That I could understand. He then gave me an explanation which I could not understand, although I had heard plenty of the jargon of nuclear physics from him and Luke. 'Fission.' 'Neutrons.' 'Chain reaction.' I could not follow. But I could gather that as last the sources of nuclear energy were in principle open to be set loose; and that it might be possible to make an explosive such as no one had realistically imagined.

'Scientists always exaggerate,' I said.

'This isn't exaggerated,' said Martin. 'If it happens, one of these bombs would blow up Cambridge. I mean, there'd be *nothing* left.'

'Will it happen?'

'It seems to be about an even chance.'

I had stood up, as I attempted to follow his explanation. Then I walked across the room and looked out of the window into the court, where the rain was blowing before the wind, forming great driven puddles along the verges of the grass; in a moment I returned to where Martin was still sitting by the fire. We were both sobered, but to me this piece of news, though it hung over us as we faced each other, seemed nothing but a diversion or a diplomatic escape.

I came back, more gently now, to the prospect of his marriage. Had he really thought what, in terms of day-to-day living, it might mean? He was once more polite, sensible, brotherly. He would admit the force of any one of my doubts: he would say yes to each criticism. Although underneath I could feel his intention, embedded right in the core of his will, nevertheless he was ready to make any other concession to my worry.

Nothing said in anger would be remembered, he was as good as saying, with his good-natured, sarcastic smile. In fact, even in the bitterest moment of the quarrel, I had taken that for granted. It did not enter my mind that anything could touch the confidence between us.

CHAPTER II

A CODE NAME

MARTIN married Irene that autumn, but I could not visit them for some time afterwards. For the war had started: he was working at Rosyth in one of the first degaussing parties, and, as for me, I was already a temporary civil servant in London.

As the early months of war went by, I heard nothing, and thought little, about my brother's marriage; but the piece of scientific news which, when I was trying to turn him against Irene, he had used as a false trail, came several times into my office-work.

It happened so through some personal coincidences. It was because the Minister knew me that I went into his department, and it was because of his own singular position that we saw the minutes of the scientific committees. His name was Thomas Bevill, and he was a second cousin of Lord Boscastle. He had been a professional politician all his life without making much of a mark in public; in private, in any government milieu he was one of the most trusted of men. He had the unusual gift of being both familiar and discreet; forty years before, when he began his career, he had set himself never to give away a secret, and never to allow himself the bright remark that makes a needless enemy. So by 1939 he had become such a link as all governments needed, particularly at the beginning of a war, before the forms of administration had settled down: they needed a man like Thomas Bevill as the chairman of confidential committees, the man to be kept informed of what was going on, the supreme post-office.

Just before war began, he asked me to join him as one of his personal assistants. He had met me two or three times with the Boscastles, which was a virtue in his eyes, and I had been trained as a lawyer, which was another. He thought I was suitable raw material to learn discretion. Gradually, in the first autumn of the war, he let me item by item into his confidential files. That was why, one autumn afternoon, he sent word that he would like a 'little talk' with Hector Rose and me.

The Minister's room was only two doors from mine, and both, relics of the eighteenth-century Treasury, looked out over Whitehall itself, brilliant that afternoon with autumn sun that blazed from the windows opposite ours. The Minister was not in the room, but Sir Hector Rose was already sitting by the side of the coal fire. He was a man in the early forties, stocky, powerful, and youthful-looking, his official black coat and striped trousers cut to conceal his heavy muscles. The flesh of his cheeks shone as though untouched, and his face, hair and eyes had the same lightness. He greeted me with his usual excessive politeness. Then he said:

'I suppose you have no idea what our master is going to occupy us with?'

I said no, and it was clear that he had none.

'Has anyone else been summoned, do you know, Eliot?'

I did not think so. Rose said: 'That makes us a very cosy little party.'

He spoke with a flick of the tongue, but he did not mean that it was strange for him, the Permanent Secretary, to be invited along with some-one many rungs lower (I had started as what the Civil Service called a principal). Rose was too confident a man to bother about trivialities like that; he was himself formal, but he objected to informality in others only when it interfered with his administrative power.

The Minister came in, carrying a coal-scuttle, on his hand a grimy cloth glove. He knelt by the grate, picked out lumps of coal and built up the fire. He was naturally familiar and unobtrusive in manner, but sometimes I thought he had developed it into an act. When people called on him in Whitehall, he would take their hats and coats and stow them punctiliously away in his cupboard. Kneeling by the fire, he looked thin-shouldered, wispy, like an elderly clerk.

'I just wanted to have a word with you two,' he said, still bending down.

'An old boy came in to see me a day or two ago,' he went on, as he pulled up a chair between us, round the fire. The 'old boy' was an eminent physicist, not more than sixty, that is, ten years Bevill's junior. And the visit had taken place a week before: Bevill had been thinking things out.

'I think I ought to put you two in the swim,' he said. 'Though, as you may have gathered, I'm a great believer in no one knowing more than he's got to know to do his job. And I don't mind telling you that I've wondered whether either of you has got to know this time. But Eliot must, if he's going to be much use to me, and there may be some action for you, Rose, not now, perhaps in a year or so's time.'

'If you think it wiser that *I* shouldn't know till then, Minister,' said Rose. Underneath the courtesy, he was irked by Bevill's talent for using two words where one would do. I thought that he under-rated the old man, particularly when, as now, he settled down comfortably to another Polonius-like discourse on security. The first thing, said the Minister, was to forget all about the official hierarchy, the next was to forget that you had any relatives. If you possess a secret, he said, your secretary may have to know: but not your second-in-command: and not your wife.

'If you decide to leave me out at this stage, I shall perfectly well understand,' said Rose, getting back to relevance.

'No, my dear chap. It wouldn't be practical,' said the Minister. 'I shouldn't be able to pull the wool over your ears.'

The Minister sometimes got his idioms mixed up. Rose went on watching him with pale, heavy-lidded eyes, which met the old man's frank, ingenuous, blue ones. With the same simple frank expression, Bevill said:

'As a matter of fact, some of these scientists believe they can present us with a great big bang. Like thousands of tons of T.N.T. *That* would be futurist war, *if* you like. That old boy the other day said we ought to be ready to put some money on it.'

It sounded like the gossip I had heard in Cambridge, and I said so.

'Ought you to have heard?' said Bevill, who thought of science in nothing but military terms. 'These chaps will talk. Whatever you do, you can't stop them talking. But they're pushing on with it. I've collected three appreciations already. Forget all I tell you until you have to remember – that's what I do. But the stuff to watch is what they call a uranium isotope.'

He said the words slowly as though separating the syllables for children to spell. 'U. 235,' he added, as though domesticating a foreign name. To each of the three of us, the words and symbols might as well have been in Hittite, though Rose and I would have been regarded as highly educated men.

The Minister went on to say that, though the scientists 'as usual' were disagreeing among themselves, some of them believed that making a 'superbomb' was now only a matter of a series of techniques. They also believed that whichever side got the weapon first would win the war.

'These people always think that it's easier to win wars than I do,' he added imperturbably.

'How soon before it's a feasible proposition?' Rose asked him.

'Not tomorrow,' said Bevill. 'Anything up to ten years.'

'That's a very long-term prospect,' said Rose.

'I'm not an optimist,' the Minister replied. 'It may be a very long-term war. But I agree with you, my dear chap, it doesn't sound like business for us this time. Still it won't do any harm to watch out and keep our powder dry.'

'Many thanks for giving me the warning, Minister,' said Rose, deciding there was nothing more of use to be learned that afternoon. 'Many, many thanks.'

But before Rose could get away, Bevill showed us his private dossier of the uranium project. We must not refer to it again by that name, he said: as with all other projects of high secrecy, he copied out the 'appreciations' in his own hand, keeping no copies: the documents were then mounted in a loose-leaf cover, on which he printed a pet name.

'I'm going to show you my name for this new stunt,' he said, with a smile that was frank, shy and eager. And into that smile there crept the almost salacious pleasure that many men show as they talk of secrets.

He turned over the cover, and we saw, painted in bold capitals, the words:

MR TOAD

'That's what we'll call it here, if you don't mind,' he added.

CHAPTER III

WHAT MIGHT HAVE BEEN FORESIGHT

IT still did not seem significant. That winter, one or two of us who were in the secret discussed it, but, although we looked round the room before we spoke, it did not catch hold of us as something real.

Once Francis Getliffe, whom I had known longer than the other scientists, said to me:

'I hope it's *never* possible.'

But even he, though he did not want any men anywhere to possess this power, spoke without heaviness, as if it were a danger of the future, a piece of science-fiction, like the earth running into a comet's path.

All the arrangements of those first months of Mr Toad were on the pettiest scale – a handful of scientists, nearly all of them working part-time, scattered round three or four university laboratories: a professor wondering whether he might spend three hundred and fifty pounds for some extra help: an improvised committee, meeting once a month, sending its minutes to the Minister in longhand.

In the summer of 1940, on one of those mornings of steady, indifferent sunshine that left upon some of us, for years afterwards, an inescapable memory, I was walking down Piccadilly and noticed half-a-dozen men coming out of the Royal Society's door in Burlington House. I knew most of them by sight. They were scientists, nearly all youngish men; one or two were carrying Continental brief-cases; they might have been coming from an examiners' meeting. In fact, they were the committee, and the sight of them brought back the Minister's pet name, which, with the war news dragging like an illness, did not seem much of a joke.

Soon afterwards, in the Minister's office, we received intelligence that the Germans were working on the bomb. Although we had all assumed it, the news was sharp: it added another fear. Also it roughened the tongues of those who were crusading for the project. Step by step they won for it a little more attention. By the spring of 1941 they obtained sanction for a research establishment – not a grand establishment like those working on radio and the immediate weapons of war, but one with perhaps a hundred scientists to their thousands. For a site, they picked on a place called Barford – which I had not heard of, but found to be a village in Warwickshire, a few miles from Stratford on Avon.

It became one of my duties to help them collect staff. I could hardly have had a more niggling job, for almost all scientists were by this time caught up in the war. Even for projects of high priority it was difficult enough to extract them, and so far as priority was concerned, the Barford project still had none at all. The only good scientists not yet employed were refugees, and it was clear that they would have to form the nucleus of Barford.

Accepting those facts, the Barford superintendent and his backers still made a claim, a modest claim, for at least one or two of the better young Englishmen. It was thus that I was asked to sound Walter Luke; if we could get him released from his radio work, would he be willing to move to Barford?

Then I wondered about Martin. I had heard little from him. I should have heard, if things had been going well, if, like a good many scientists of his age, he had begun to make a name. For eighteen months he had been doing a piece of technical routine. He seemed to be doing it just as competently, neither less nor more, than a hundred other young men in the naval ports. From a distance I had been watching, without being able to help.

I could not say much about Barford; in any case I knew that in this matter his temperament would work like mine; we said yes, but we did not like to be managed. Nevertheless, I could drop a hint. He could see for himself that it might give him a chance.

Later, my memory tended to cheat; it made me look as though I had the gift of foresight. That was quite untrue. In the spring of 1941, there were several other projects on Bevill's files which seemed to me of a different order of importance from Mr Toad. As for Barford, I did not believe that anything would come of it, and my chief interest was that it might give Martin a better chance.

CHAPTER IV

RESULT OF A MANŒUVRE

It was some weeks before either Luke or Martin could get to London, but then I arranged to see them both on the same afternoon in May.

Martin was the first to arrive. It was over a year since we had met, and, as we enquired about each other, there was the sense of well-being, the wiping-away of anxiety's fret, that one gets only with those who have become part of the deep habit of one's life.

Soon I asked:

'How is Irene?'

'Very well,' said Martin, looking straight into my eyes, giving nothing away.

He walked round my office, admiring the Regency mantelpiece and the view over Whitehall. He was rejoicing that I was having something of a success – for, entirely through the Minister's backing, I had just been promoted. In a section of the war, I now had my bit of subfusc power. I was for shrugging it off; but Martin, however, set more store by official honours than I did.

'Are you sure you're making the most of it?' he said, with a proprietorial, insistent air.

He was delighted, and in his delight there was no envy. Yet suddenly he was sounding knowledgeable and worldly; it was strange, out of the haze of family memories, to see him standing there, a calculating man. If he had a success himself, I thought, he would have all the tricks ready to exploit it.

Actually, he had nothing to exploit. I listened to him saying that, as far as his job went, there was still nothing whatever to report. No change. I was full of irritation, for, when you hope for someone as I did for him, you blame them for their own misfortunes.

'So far as there's been any luck in the family,' I said, 'I've had it.'

'I don't believe in luck to that extent,' said Martin, without complaint.

'You've had none,' I said.

Then Martin smiled, and brought out a phrase which would have been meaningless to any but us two. 'You've got someone to live up to.' It was a phrase of our mother's, holding me up before him as an example, for I had been her favourite son. I recalled her as she lay dying, instructing me sternly not to think too little of Martin. No injunction could ever have been less called for; but later I believed that she was making amends to herself for not having loved him more.

Martin was talking of her when, an hour before I expected him, Walter Luke came in. Ever since I had known him as a younger man – he was still not thirty – he had thrown the whole of his nature into everything he felt. I had seen him triumphant with every cell of his body, as a human integer of flesh and bone: and I had seen him angry. That afternoon he was ashamed of himself, and it was not possible for a man to throw more of his force into being ashamed.

'Hello, Lewis. Hallo, Martin,' he said. 'I've just been ticked off. I deserved it, and I got it, and I'm beginning to wonder when I shall manage to grow up.'

He slumped on to a chair, immersed in his dejection. His backbone, usually so straight in his thick energetic frame, curved disconsolately against the leather; yet he exuded vigour, and both Martin and I were smiling at him. His cheeks were not as ruddy as when I first saw him at high table, five years before. In the last two years he had carried responsibility, and even on his physique the strain had told. Now he looked his age; there were grey hairs at his temples; but his voice remained eager, rich and youthful, still bearing a rumble from the Plymouth dockyard where he was brought up.

He had just come from one of the radio committees, where he had been arguing with someone he called a 'stuffed shirt' (and who was highly placed). The stuffed shirt had been canvassing his favourite idea, 'and I tell you,' said Luke, 'if I'd been asked to think of something bloody silly, I couldn't have thought up anything so fantastically bloody silly as that.' Luke had apparently proceeded to say so, using his peculiar resources of eloquence. The chairman, who was even more highly placed than the stuffed shirt, had told him this was not the right spirit: he was thinking of his own ideas, and didn't want the other's to work.

'The old bleeder was perfectly right,' said Luke with simplicity. He went on:

'I never know whether I've got cross because some imbecile is talking balderdash or whether my own precious ego is getting trampled on. I wish one of you shrewd chaps would teach me.'

Walter Luke was neither pretending nor laughing at himself; he was contrite. Then, with the same freshness and resilience, he had finished with his contrition. He sat up straight in his chair, and asked what I wanted to see him about.

I said we had better have a word alone. Luke said:

'Why have we got to turf Martin out?'

'Lewis is right,' said Martin, getting ready to go.

'It depends which surprise-packet he's going to pull out of the bag,' said Luke, with a broad, fresh grin. He looked at me: 'Barford?'

I was taken off guard.

'Teach your grandmother to suck eggs,' said Luke. 'We know all about *that*.'

Martin was smiling, as Luke began to talk to him. It was clear that Martin, though he was discreet, knew enough to horrify the Minister; as for Luke, he knew as much as anyone I had heard.

For anyone used to Bevill's precautions, this was startling to listen to. In terms of sense, it should not have been such a surprise. Word was going round among nuclear physicists, and Luke, young as he was, was one of the best of them. He had already been consulted on a scientific point; he could guess the test.

I had to accept it. There was also an advantage in speaking in front of Martin; it might be the most natural way to draw him in.

At that moment, he was listening to Luke with a tucked-in, sarcastic smile, as though he were half-admiring Luke's gifts, half-amused by him as a man.

'Well,' I said to Luke, 'as you know so much, you probably know what I've been told to ask.'

'I hadn't heard anything,' he replied, 'but they must be after me.'

'Would you be ready to go?'

Luke did not answer, but said: 'Who else have they got?'

For the first time that afternoon, I was able to tell him something. The Superintendent, Drawbell, the engineering heads—

'Good God alive,' Luke interrupted, 'Lewis, *who are these uncles?*'

A list of names of refugees – and then I mentioned Arthur Mounteney.

'I'm glad they've got hold of one scientist, anyway,' said Luke. 'He did some nice work once. He's just about finished, of course.'

'Do you feel like going in?' I asked.

Luke would not reply.

'Why don't they get hold of Martin?' he said. 'He's wasted where he is.'

'They're not likely to ask for me,' said Martin.

'Your name keeps cropping up,' I said to Luke.

Usually, when I had seen men offered jobs, they had decided within three minutes, even though they concealed it from themselves, even though they managed to prolong the pleasure of deciding. Just for once, it was not so.

'It's all very well,' said Luke. 'I just don't know where I can be most use.' He was not used to hesitating; he did not like it; he tried to explain himself. If he stayed where he was, he could promise us a 'bit of hardware' in eighteen months. Whereas, if he joined this 'new party' there was no guarantee that anything would happen for years.

There was nothing exaggerated in Luke's tone just then. I was used to the rowdiness with which he judged his colleagues, especially his seniors; it was the same with most of the rising scientists; they had none of the convention of politeness that bureaucrats like Sir Hector Rose were trained to, and often Rose and his friends disliked them accordingly. Listening to Luke that afternoon, no one would have thought, for instance, that the poor old derelict Mounteney was in fact a Nobel prizewinner aged about forty. But on his own value Luke was neither boastful nor modest. He was a good scientist; good scientists counted in the war, and he was not going to see himself wasted. He had lost that tincture of the absurd which had made Martin smile. He spoke without nonsense, with the directness of a man who knows what he can and cannot do.

'I wish some of you wise old men would settle it for me,' he said to me.

I shook my head. I had put Bevill's request, but that was as far as I felt justified in going. For what my judgment of the war was worth, I thought on balance that Luke should stay where he was.

He could not make up his mind. As the three of us walked across the park towards my flat in Dolphin Square, he fell first into a spell of abstraction and then broke out suddenly into a kind of argument with himself, telling us of a new device in what we then called R.D.F., and were later to call Radar. The evening was bright. A cool wind blew from the east, bringing the rubble dust to our nostrils, although it was some days since the last raid. Under our feet the grass was dust-greyed and dry. I was worried about the war that evening; I could see no end to it; it was a comfort to be with those two, in their different fashions steady-hearted and robust.

On the way home, and all the evening, Martin kept putting questions to Luke, steering him back to nuclear fission. I could feel, though, that he was waiting for Luke to leave. He had something to say to me in private.

At last we took Luke to the bus stop, and Martin and I turned back towards St George's Square. The full moon shone down on the lightless blind-faced streets, and the shadows were dark indigo. Flecks of cloud, as though scanning the short syllables in a line of verse, stood against the impenetrable sky. Under the moon, the roofs of Pimlico shone blue as steel. The wind had fallen. It was a silent beautiful wartime night.

'By the way—' said Martin, with constraint in his voice.

'Yes?'

'I'd be grateful if you could get me into this project somehow.'

I had never known him ask a favour of this kind before. He had not once come to me for official help, either at Cambridge or since. Now he was driven – scruple, pride, made his voice stiff, but he was driven.

'I was going to suggest it,' I said. 'Of course, I'll—'

'I really would be grateful.'

My manœuvre had come off, but as he spoke I felt no pleasure. I had taken it on myself to interfere; from now on I should have some responsibility for what happened to him.

Now the trigger had been touched, he was intent on going: why it meant so much, I could not tell. His career? – something of that, perhaps, but he was not reckoning the chances that night. Concern about his wife? – he would not volunteer anything. No: simple though the explanation might seem for a man like Martin, it was the science itself that drew him. Though he might have no great talent, nuclear physics had obsessed him since he was a boy. He did not know, that night, what he could add at Barford; he only knew that he wanted to be there.

He admitted as much: but he had more practical matters to deal with. Having swallowed his pride, he did not intend to prostrate himself for nothing.

'You're sure that you can get me in? I should have thought the first move was to persuade someone else to suggest me. Walter Luke would do. . . .' Could I write to Luke that night? Could I, as an insurance, remind Mounteney that Martin and I were brothers?

It was late before we went to bed; by that time Martin had written out an *aide-mémoire* of the people I was to see, write to, and telephone next day.

CHAPTER V

ADVICE FROM A MAN IN TROUBLE

MARTIN'S transfer went through smoothly, and he had begun work at Barford by June. With Luke, it took months longer.

In November I paid them an official visit. The Superintendent was still demanding men, and some of his sponsors in Whitehall had become more active; they even began to say that one of the schemes at Barford might give results within two years.

Francis Getliffe and the other scientific statesmen were sceptical. They were so discouraging that the Minister did not feel it worth while to inspect Barford himself; but, with his usual desire to keep all doors open, he sent me down instead.

I spent a morning and afternoon walking round laboratories listening to explanations I only one-tenth comprehended, listening also to the clicking, like one-fingered typewriting, of Geiger counters. But I comprehended one thing clearly. There were four or five main lines at Barford – one of them Luke had set up on his own, with a few assistants, and another was led by a man called Rudd. Rudd was the second-in-command of the establishment; his line was, in principle, to separate the isotope, and they were attempting several methods; it was one of these, on which Martin and a team of scientists were working, which Rudd was trying to sell. As an official, I had been exposed to a good deal of salesmanship, but this, for unremitting obsessive concentration, was in a class by itself.

It was having an effect on me. Next morning I was due for a conference with the Superintendent, and I needed to clear my head. So, as an excuse, I went off by myself to call on Luke.

It meant a walk through a country lane leading from the mansion, which had been turned into the administrative headquarters, to the air-field. The hedges were brittle and dark with the coming winter, the only touch of brightness was the green of the ivy flowers. At the top of the rise the mist was shredding away, and suddenly, on the plateau, the huts, hangars, half-built brick ranges, stood out in the light of the cold and silvery sun.

Inside Luke's hangar, the vista was desolate. A quarter of the roof was open to the sky, and a piece of canvas was hanging down like a velarium. The only construction in sight was a cube of concrete, about six feet high, with a small door in it standing slightly ajar, through which a beam of light escaped. The afternoon had turned cold, and in the half-light, lit only by that beam on the wet floor and a naked bulb on the side of the hangar, the chill struck like the breath of a cave. No place looked less like an engine-room of the scientific future; it might have been the relic of a civilisation far gone in decay.

There was not a person in sight. In a moment, as though he had heard me, Luke came out of the cube-door, muttering to someone within. He was wearing a windjacket, which made him seem more than ever square, like an Eskimo, like a Polar explorer. He beat his arms across his chest and blew on his fingers.

'Hello, Lewis,' he said. 'It's bloody cold, and this blasted experiment won't go, and I want to run away and cry.'

I was interrupting him, he was fretting to get back to work; a voice from inside the cube asked about the next move. For minutes together, Luke gave orders for a new start the following day. 'What shall we do tonight?' came the voice.

Luke considered. For once he did not find the words. At last he said: '*We'll just go home.*'

I walked back with him, for he and his wife had invited some of my old acquaintances to meet me at their house that evening. He was so dejected that I did not like to press him, and yet I had to confirm what everyone was telling me – that he was getting nowhere. Even so, my own question sounded flat in the bitter air.

'How is it going, Walter?'

Luke swore. 'How do *you* think it's going?'

'Is it going to come out?'

'Does it look like it?' he replied.

I told him that I should be talking next morning to Drawbell, that nothing I could say would signify much, but it all helped to form opinion.

'You didn't do much good bringing me here, did you?'

Then he corrected himself, though his tone was still dejected. 'That's not fair,' he said.

I asked more about his method (which aimed at plutonium, not the isotope).

'I'm not promising anything,' said Luke.

'Will it work in time?'

'I can't see the way tonight,' he said, with another curse.

'Shall you?'

He said, half depressed, half boastful:

'What do you think I'm here for?'

But that was his only burst of arrogance, and in the party at his house he sat preoccupied. So did Martin, for a different reason: for Irene had arranged to meet him there, and, when everyone else had arrived, still did not come.

Each time the door opened Martin looked round, only to see the Mounteneys enter, then the Puchweins. And yet, though he was saying little and Luke brooded as he went round filling glasses from a jug of beer, the evening was a comforting one. Out of doors, the countryside was freezing. It was a winter night, the fields stretching in frosted silence. Outside was the war, but within our voices and the light of the fire. It was a night on which one felt lapped in safeness to the finger-tips.

Ideas, hopes, floated in the domestic air. For the first time at Barford, I heard an argument about something other than the project. After science, in those wartime nights, men like Puchwein and Mounteney had a second favourite subject. They argued as naturally as most of us drink, I was thinking, feeling an obscure fondness for them as I listened to them getting down to their second subject, which was politics.

For Puchwein, in fact, I had the peculiar fondness one bears someone to whom one has done a good turn. Roy Calvert had taken risks to smuggle Puchwein out of Berlin in 1938, and several of us had helped support him. But Puchwein was not in the least got down by having to accept charity. His manner remained patriarchal, he received aid with the equanimity of one bestowing it. He had a reputation as a chemist. He was a very big man, bald and grey, though still under forty. When he took off his spectacles his eyes slanted downward, so that he always seemed about to weep. Actually, he was cheerful, kind, and so uxorious that his wife was showing lines of temper. But he forgot her, he was immersed, as he and she and Mounteney, and sometimes Nora Luke and I, threw the political phrases to and fro in front of the fire.

Some of those phrases, as used by both Puchweins and Mounteney but by no one else in the room, would have given me a clue if I had not known already. 'The party' for the Communist Party, 'Soviet' as an adjective for Russian, 'Fascists' as a collective term to include National-Socialists, 'The Daily' for the *Daily Worker*, 'social democrats' to describe members of the Labour Party such as Luke, or even unorthodox liberals such as Martin and me – all those were shibboleths, and meant, if one had ever listened to the dialect of intellectual communism, that those who used them were not far from the party line.

Neither Puchwein nor Mounteney concealed it. Throughout the thirties it had been nothing to conceal. They did not hold party cards, so far as anyone knew; but they were in sympathy, Mounteney in slightly irregular sympathy. None of us was surprised or concerned that it should be so, certainly not in that November of 1941, when not only to the Puchweins but to conservative-minded Englishmen, it seemed self-evident that the war was being won or lost on Russian land.

Just then Luke went round with the beer again, the argument suddenly quietened, and I heard Emma Mounteney whispering to Hanna Puchwein with a glance in Martin's direction:

'Where is our wandering girl tonight?'

Hanna looked away, but Emma was hard to stop.

'I wonder,' she whispered, 'if T——' (a man I scarcely knew) 'is on his lonesome.'

Martin was on the other side of the fire. I thought that he could not have heard. Nevertheless, before Puchwein began again, Martin apologised for Irene. She was finishing some work, he said; it must have taken longer than she reckoned, and it looked as though she might not get there at all. His composure was complete. I had once known a similar situation, but I had not summoned up half his self-command. Yet, as the talk clattered on, his eyes often gazed into the fire, and he was still listening for a ring at the door.

Martin had not spoken since his apology, and I wanted to shield him from going home with the Mounteneys, whose house (at Barford the scientists and their families were crammed on top of each other, as in a frontier town) he shared. So I invented a pretext for us to walk home together.

In the village street, all was quiet. A pencil of light edged the top of a blacked-out window-frame. Otherwise the village was sleeping as it might have done on a Jacobean night, when some of these houses were built. Martin's footsteps, slower and heavier than mine although he was the lighter man, seemed loud on the frosty road. I left him to break the silence. Our steps remained the only noise, until he remarked, as though casually:

'Walter Luke didn't say much tonight, did he?'

I agreed.

'He must have had something in his mind. His experiment, I suppose.' And that was all he said.

Martin was doing what we have all done, refer to ourselves, half apologise, half confide, by pretending an interest in another. If I had been an intimate friend but not a brother, perhaps even if I had been a stranger, I thought that just at that moment he would have unburdened himself. Often it is the reserved who, when a pain, or even more, a humiliation, has lived inside them too long, suddenly break out into a confidence to someone they scarcely know. But I was the last person to whom he could let go.

As we both showed when we first talked of his engagement, there was a delicacy in our kind of brothers' love; and the closer we came to our sexual lives, the more that delicacy made us speak in terms of generalisation and sarcasm. We knew each other very well by instinct. We could guess which women would attract the other, and often it was an attraction that we shared. Yet I had never told him any detail either of my married life or of a love affair. I should have felt it, not so much embarrassing to speak, though that would also have been true, but worse than embarrassing to force him to listen. It was the same from him to me. He could not tell me whom he suspected she went to bed with; he could not tell me what she was like in his own bed; and so it was no relief to speak at all.

At the crossroads he asked if I minded walking a few yards to the bridge; it was as though he wanted an excuse for not returning home (or was it superstition, as though, if he did not hurry back, all would be well?). It was a moonless night, and the stars were faint, but there was a glimmer on the river. All of a sudden a November meteorite scorched its way across the sky, and then another.

'More energy there than *we* shall make,' said Martin, nodding in the direction of the establishment.

Now that my eyes were accustomed to the light I could make out the expression on his face. It was set and sad – and yet he was controlling his voice, he was beginning to speak seriously about the project.

'By the way,' he said, 'I suppose the people here are putting some pressure on you?'

I said yes.

'They want you to invest in this place in a big way?'

Again I said yes.

'As long as you all realise that *nothing* here is within years of being tested—' He broke off, and then said:

'It would be very nice for me if Rudd's show came off. I should get some reflected glory, which I could do with.'

For a moment his voice was chilled, as though his secret thoughts were too strong: but I understood.

'You don't think it *will* come off?'

He paused.

'I haven't got the grasp some of these people have, you know, and most of them believe in it.' Then he added: 'But I shouldn't like you to plump for it too far.'

'What's the matter with it?'

'I think your own reputation will look nicer,' he said, 'if you go fairly slow this time.'

It was not until we were walking towards his house that he said:

'I can't explain why I'm not convinced. I wish I were better at this game, then perhaps I could.'

When we had mounted to his landing above the Mounteneys, there was no light under the door. As soon as we were inside the room Martin said, and for an instant his voice had become unrecognisable:

'I detest living in other people's houses.'

In that instant his face was white with temper. Was he thinking that Emma Mounteney would know the exact time that Irene climbed up the stairs? Then he spoke, once more calmly:

'I think I'd better wait up for her. I don't think she's taken a key.'

CHAPTER VI

MORNING BEFORE THE OFFICE

NEXT morning I woke out of heavy sleep, and was dragged at by a memory of muttering (it might have been a dream, or else something heard in the distance) from the bedroom next door. When I got up and went into breakfast, Irene told me that Martin had already left for the laboratory. She was wearing a dressing-gown, her voice was quiet but tight; without her make-up, she looked both drabber and younger.

In silence I ate the toast and jam of a wartime breakfast. Looking down from the window into the sunny morning, I could see the river flash through the elm-branches. I was aware that her gaze was fixed on me.

Suddenly she cried out:

'Why do you dislike me so?'

'I don't,' I said.

'I can't bear not be liked.'

Very quickly, almost as though she had been rehearsing it, she told me a story of how, when she was twelve, she went to stay with a 'glamorous' schoolfriend, and how the other girl had been asked by an aunt: 'Who is your best friend? Is Irene your best friend?' And the answer had come, polite and putting-off, 'Oh, Irene has so many friends.'

'I couldn't face her again,' said Irene, and then: 'I wish *you* would like me.'

'It doesn't matter to either of us.'

'I want you to.' Her tone was at the same time penitent, shameless, provocative; it was easy to imagine how she spoke to her husband. I had to rouse myself.

'You want it both ways, you know,' I said.

'What have I done against you?' she burst out defiantly.

'Nothing.'

'Then why can't we get on?'

'You know as well as I do. Do you expect me to approve of you as my brother's wife?'

'So that's it,' she said.

'Don't pretend that's news,' I said. 'Why have you started this – *this morning*?'

She had crossed over to the window-seat, and was watching me with sharp eyes, which were beginning to fill with tears.

'You've taken against me, just because I couldn't stand the very thought of those people last night.'

'You know perfectly well that that's not all.'

'Would you like me to tell you what I was really doing?'

I shook my head. 'You're not a fool. You must realise that you're damaging him—'

'I suppose my *dear* friends were wondering who I'd taken to bed, weren't they?'

'Of course.'

'Who did they think?'

I would not reply.

'Whose name did you hear?' she cried.

Impatiently I repeated Emma's question about T——. She gave a yelp of laughter. She was for an instant in high spirits, nothing but amused.

'They *can't* think that!'

She stared at me: the tears had gone.

'You won't believe me, but they're wrong. It wasn't him, it wasn't anyone. I just couldn't stand their faces any more, I had to get out on my own. They're hopelessly wrong. Please believe me!'

I said:

'Whether they're right or wrong – in a place like this you mustn't give anyone an excuse to gossip, it doesn't matter whether it's justified or not.'

'How often I've heard that,' she said with a glint in her eyes.

'When?'

'All night long. Do you think you're the *first* to scold me?' She looked at me, and went on: 'He was specially angry because *you* were here to see.'

After a moment, I said: 'That's neither here nor there.'

'Isn't it?' said Irene.

'The only thing I've got a right to talk about,' I said, 'are the practical consequences. Unless you want to damage his career, the least you can do for Martin is behave yourself on the outside.'

'I promised him that this morning,' she said in a thin voice.

'Can you keep your promise?'

'You needn't worry.' Her voice was thinner still.

Then she stood up, shook herself, went to the looking-glass and remained there, studying her reflection.

'We ought to be moving soon,' she said, her voice full again, brisk and matter-of-fact. 'These people aren't altogether wrong about me. I may as well tell you that, though I expect you know.'

I was getting up, but she said no, and sat down opposite me.

'They've got the idea right, but it's my past coming back on me.' She added, without emotion: 'I've been a bad girl. I've had some men.'

Yes, she would have liked to be an adventuress: but somehow she hadn't managed it. 'Perhaps you've got to be cooler than I am to bring it off,' she said, half-mystified.

It was she who had been used, not her lovers; and there was one who, when she thought of him, still had power over her.

'Martin knew about him before we married,' she said. 'Have you heard of Edgar Hankins?'

I had not only heard of him, but ten years before had known him fairly well.

'I loved him very much,' she said. She went on: 'I ought to have made him marry me.'

'Was it a matter of will?' I said, feeling more tender to her.

'No,' said Irene, 'I've got the will, but I can't trust my nerves.'

Then I asked why she had married Martin. She began not by answering the question, but by saying: 'You shouldn't worry too much about Martin.'

'Why not?'

'I fancy he's a harder man than you are.'

She said it as though she were praising him. Reverting to her business-like manner, she went on about her reasons for the marriage. She had found some of her friends competing for him, she said; and that provoked her. But most of all she wanted safety.

'I was getting notorious,' she said. 'When people heard my name, they were beginning to say "Oh, her".'

Curiously, by this time she and I were on easy terms. Nevertheless, I did not know how much to believe. She was anxious not to give herself the benefit of the doubt, she was putting herself in the coldest light. Nearly always, I thought, there was something men or women were protecting, when deliberately, and with pride, almost with conceit, they showed you their most callous side.

All of a sudden she looked at me with her eyes narrowed and frightened.

'Why did you ask me – about marrying him?'

I tried to put her off.

'Do you want him to leave me?'

'That's not my business,' I said.

'Are you trying to take him away?' Her tone had been brittle, the tears had been near again, and she sighed.

Then she threw her head back, and put on her matey, hard-baked smile. 'You can try anything you like,' she said. 'Nothing will have any effect on him, you ought to know that by now.'

Within ten minutes we were walking along the footpath to the laboratories, Irene's face groomed as though nothing were more impossible than tears or anger, both of us talking as though there had been no scene between us. Just once, she referred back to it, when she commented without explanation, as though out of free air:

'Mornings before the office.'

It was her phrase for any kind of morning drama: it was a phrase that only had meaning if your working life was disciplined, as all of ours had by this time become. Whatever was left behind at home, the files were waiting. As we walked along the country footpath, I was myself sorting out my official thoughts, collecting what I could safely say to Drawbell.

Before I called on Drawbell, I said goodbye to Martin. He was standing in his laboratory, looking at one of the counters: tiny neon lamps, the size of buttons, flickered in and out, the noise tapped on: on the indicator the figures moved like a taxi register.

'Any progress?' I asked.

'Nothing new,' said Martin patiently. He and others had already explained to me that what was true of pure scientific research was truer still of this: that the days of crisis were few: that it was only after long periods of preparation, measured in months, not days, that they came to a 'result' – one day of excitement, and afterwards another period of building, routine, long-drawn-out suspense.

In the office where Drawbell's secretaries worked, I was kept waiting among the typing stools and dictaphones before I could see him. I suspected that he was doing it on purpose, as I went on chatting to Hanna Puchwein and her assistant, Mary Pearson, the wife of one of the chief engineers, a young woman who at that first impression seemed just spectacled and flushing. At last the bell trilled on Hanna's desk, and she took me in.

Drawbell's office had in the past been the main drawing-room of the Barford house. On the high walls, where the white paint was chipping from the panels, were pinned charts, tables of organisation, graphs, diagrams. The room was so long that there was time to notice my footsteps on the parquet as I went towards Drawbell's desk. He sat, steadily regarding me, watching me come towards him without changing his expression or making a sound.

All this was put on. I had met him several times, in that office as well as in London. He was not an academic, and Luke and the others said, with their usual boisterous lack of respect, that he was not a scientist at all. In peacetime he had been head of another government station. Though I knew that he was not unformidable, I knew also that he was a bit of a humbug and a bit of a clown.

He remained silent. I sat down in an armchair by his desk. He went on gazing at me, with an unwinking inflexible stare from his right eye; the other had little vision and turned blankly off at forty-five degrees. He was bald: square-jowled: podgy-nosed: wide-mouthed, with upturning melon-lips. I studied him, also without speaking.

'Eliot,' he said at last, 'I'm not satisfied with the support that we're receiving.'

I said that this was what I had come to talk about.

'Now you've had an opportunity to see what we're doing.'

I said yes.

'I hope you've made the most of it. I hope you are beginning to realise that this place may be – I don't say that it is, I say *may be* – the most important institution in the entire world. And I'm going to ask you straight out: what help am I to expect from headquarters?'

I hesitated.

'Naturally, I expect some positive results from you,' said Drawbell.

I was the wrong man for this opening, but I had to be patient. I had two problems on my mind. What was going to happen? I had not much doubt of the answer – but how frankly should I tell it to Drawbell?'

I knew in cold blood what was bound to happen. Even if Rudd's scheme worked (perhaps Martin was under-estimating its chances), it would take years. All the scientists they wanted were working elsewhere, most of them on R.D.F., on work that would (as the Minister said) pay dividends in one year or two, not in the remote future: no one in authority could take the risk of moving them; even if the Barford result was certain, instead of uncertain, no one at that stage of the war could do much more.

If I were to be any use as an administrator to Barford, I had to get them to trust me: so I decided to be open with Drawbell. I said that no one could spend any time with his scientists without becoming infected with their faith. He nodded his head. I should report that to Hector Rose and the Minister, for what it was worth: but Drawbell must not expect too much.

'Why not?'

I told him what I had been thinking to myself. He was up against the facts of war. Whatever I reported to the Minister, or the Minister represented to his committees, or the committees recommended on their own, would make little difference. Barford would get buildings and equipment without any serious trouble, but could only hope for a few extra scientists. However much faith anyone had, the men just did not exist.

'Strip the country,' said Drawbell.

I told him any set of responsible persons would have to say no. We couldn't weaken ourselves in 1943 or 1944 for the sake of a gigantic gamble.

'I won't tolerate the word gamble,' said Drawbell, in a loud monotonous voice, speaking like a man trying to hold back his anger.

I had expected him to be reasonable; I had misjudged him.

He would not listen to my case. He shouted me down. He tried cajoling me, saying that I was the only man in the Minister's entourage with any imagination. He tried threatening me, asking how I should feel when the Germans dropped the first uranium bomb on London.

I was used, like any official who has had to carry bad news, to being blamed for it, but it was an effort to keep my temper.

'Quite frankly,' said Drawbell, meaning by that phrase that something unpleasant was coming, 'I hoped that you were going to be less obstructive.'

He went on:

'Of course, I shan't be able to hide it from your *superiors* that we've been disappointed by your visit.'

I said that was up to him.

'If your superiors take the same hopeless attitude as you do, Eliot, it will be a black day for this country.'

'You must tell them so.'

Suddenly Drawbell gave a surprisingly sweet smile. 'I've told them already, Eliot, and I shall go on telling them.'

He behaved as though it were no use abusing me further, and began to talk in a realistic manner.

'Well,' he said, 'assuming that you're right to be hopeless – how many scientists shall I get?'

I had not replied before Drawbell put on a grin, half coaxing, half jeering:

'Come on. Just between you and me.'

So all that display of indignation had been an act; he was ready to use his own moods, my comfort, anything or anyone else, for the sake of Barford.

This time I was cautious. I said that another establishment, doing work of the highest war priority, had just been allowed to search for thirty scientists of reputation. If the Minister and the committees made out the strongest case for Barford, they might get ten to twenty.

'Well, if it's only ten,' said Drawbell, surprisingly reasonable, 'that's better than a slap in the belly with a wet fish.'

He regarded me with good nature, as though I had, through no special fault of my own but for a higher purpose, been roughly handled. It was amiably that he enquired:

'Would you like to know what I shall do with them?'

I expected him to say – they will go to Rudd.

Drawbell made a theatrical pause, and said: '*I shall put them where they are most needed.*'

I asked, impatient at this new turn, where that would be.

'Rudd thinks he will get them all,' said Drawbell.

'Will he?'

'Not on your life. It's not good for anyone to think they're the only runners in the field.'

He gave a cheerful, malevolent chuckle. One could tell how he enjoyed using his power, keeping his assistants down to their proper level, dividing and ruling.

To complete the surprise, he was proposing to reinforce Luke, whom he disliked, whom he had heard disparaged for weeks.

'It doesn't matter who brings it off,' he said, 'so long as someone does.'

He nodded, for once quite natural: 'I don't know whether you pray much, Eliot, but I pray God that my people here will get it first. Pray God we get it.'

CHAPTER VII

VOICE FROM A BATH

LOOKING back, I re-examined all I could remember of those early conversations at Barford, searching for any sign of troubled consciences. I was tempted to ante-date the conflict which later caused some of them suffering. But it would have been quite untrue.

There was a simple reason why it should be so. All of them knew that the enemy was trying to make a fission bomb. For those who had a qualm of doubt, that was a complete ethical solvent. I had not yet heard from any of the scientists, nor from my friends in government, a single speculation as to whether the bomb should be used. It was just necessary to possess it.

When Drawbell prayed that the Barford project might succeed, he was not speaking lightly; he happened to have kept intact his religious faith. In different words, Puchwein and the fellow-travellers, for just then there was no political divide, would have uttered the same prayer, and so should I.

When I first heard the fission bomb discussed in the Minister's room, my response had been the same as Francis Getliffe's, that is, to hope it would prove physically impossible to make. But in the middle of events, close to Martin and Luke and the others, I could not keep that up. Imperceptibly my hopes had become the same as theirs, that we should get it, that we should get it first. To myself I added a personal hope: that Martin would play a part in the success.

During my November visit to Barford my emotions about the project were as simple as that, and they remained so for a long time.

Yet, soon after that visit, I was further from expecting a result even than I had been before. Within quite a short time, a few weeks, the wave of optimism, which had been stirred up by Drawbell, died away; others began to accept what Martin had warned me of by the Barford bridge. It was nothing so dramatic as a failure or even a mistake; it was simply that men realised they had under-estimated the number of men, the amount of chemical plant, the new kinds of engineering, the number of years, before any of the methods under Rudd could produce an ounce of the isotope.

Then America came into the war, and within a few weeks had assigned several thousand scientists to the job. The Barford people learned of it with relief, but also with envy and a touch of resentment. There seemed nothing left for them to do. A good many of them were sent across to join the American projects. The Minister, whose own post had become shaky, was being pushed into letting others go.

By the early summer of 1942, the argument had begun as to whether or not Barford should be disbanded.

Just as that rumour was starting, we heard the first rumours of Luke's idea. Could the Canadians be persuaded to set up a heavy-water plant? the Minister was asked. If so, Luke saw his way through the rest.

No one believed it. The estimates came in, both of money and men. They were modest. No one thought they were realistic. Nearly all the senior scientists, though not Francis Getliffe, thought the idea 'long-haired'.

Following suit, Hector Rose was coming down against it, and deciding that the sensible thing was to send the Barford scientists to America. High officials like Rose had been forced to learn how much their country's power (by the side of America's) had shrunk; Rose was a proud man, and the lesson bit into his pride, but he was too cool-minded not to act on it.

I did not believe that Luke's idea would come to anything. I did not know whether anything could be saved of Barford. As for Martin, I was angry with him again because his luck was so bad.

I was wondering if I could help find him another job, when in July I received a message that he urgently wished to talk to me and would be waiting at my flat.

It was a hot afternoon, and the Minister kept me late. When I arrived at Dolphin Square, I could see no sign of Martin, except his case: tired, out of temper, I began to read the evening paper, comfortless with the grey war news. While I was reading, I heard a splash of water from the bath, and I realised that Martin must be there. I did not call out. There would be time enough for the bleak conversation in front of us.

Then I heard another sound, inexplicable, like a series of metallic taps, not rhythmical but nearly so, as though someone with no sense of time were beating out a very slow tattoo on the bathroom wall. Inexorably it went on, until I cried out, mystified, irritated:

'What *are* you doing?'

'Trying to lodge the pumice-stone on the top of the shaving-cupboard.'

It was one of the more unexpected replies. From his tone, I knew at once that he was lit up with happiness. And I knew just was he was doing. He kept his happiness private, as he did his miseries; and in secret he had his own celebrations. I had watched him, after a success at Cambridge, stand for many minutes throwing an indiarubber up to the cornice, seeing if he could make it perch.

'What have you been up to?' My own tone had quite changed.

'I moved into Luke's outfit a few weeks ago.'

'What?'

'I've got in on the ground floor.'

It was quite out of character – but I did not care about that, I had ceased to respond to his joy, I was anxious for him again, cross that I had not been consulted.

'Was that wise?' I called.

'I should think so.'

'It must have meant quarrelling with your boss' (I meant Rudd).

'I'm sorry about that.'

'What about Drawbell? Have you got across him?'

'I thought it out' – he seemed amused that I should be accusing him of rashness – 'before I moved.'

'I doubt if Luke's scheme will ever see the light of day,' I cried.

'It must.'

'How many people believe in it?'

'*It's the way to do it.*'

There was a pause. Once more, there came a tinkle on the bathroom floor, meaning that he had missed his aim again.

'Do you really think that?' I said.

'I'm sure.'

'How long have you been sure?'

'I was more sure when I got into this bath than I've ever been.'

'What do you mean?'

'It came to me. *It was all right.*'

Without altering his tone, still relaxed and joyful, he announced that he was going to leave off his efforts with the pumice; he would get out and join me soon. As I waited, although I was trying to think out ways-and-means, although I had a professional's anxiety (how could we manœuvre Luke's scheme through?), although I could not keep my protectiveness down, yet I was infused with hope. Already I was expecting more for him than he did himself.

I passed as a realistic man. In some senses it was true. But down at the springs of my life I hoped too easily and too much. As an official I could control it; but not always as I imagined my own future, even though by now I knew what had happened to me, I knew where I was weak. Least of all could I control it when I thought of Martin: with myself, I could not help remembering my weaknesses, but (exactly like Mr March regarding his son) I could forget his. So, given the least excuse, as after listening to his voice from the bath, I imagined more glittering triumphs for him than ever, even fifteen years before, I had imagined for myself.

He came in wearing a dressing-gown of mine, and at once I was given enough excuse to hope as much as I could manage. As with most guarded faces, his did not lose its guard in moments of elation – that is, the lines of the mouth, the controlled expression, stayed the same; but his whole face, almost like one of the turnip masks that we used to make as children, seemed to be illuminated from within by a lamp of joy.

We did not begin at once to discuss tactics, for which he had come to London. Sometime that night we should have to; but just for this brief space we put the tactics out of our minds, we gave ourselves the satisfaction of letting it ride.

Martin had been visited by an experience which might not come to him again. So far as I could distinguish, there were two kinds of scientific experience, and a scientist was lucky if he was blessed by a visitation of either just once in his working life. The kind which most of them, certainly Martin, would have judged the higher was not the one he had just known: instead, the higher kind was more like (it was in my view the same as) the experience that the mystics had described so often, the sense of communion with all-being. Martin's was quite different, not so free from self, more active: as though, instead of being one with the world, he held the world in the palm of his hand; as though he had, in his moment of insight, seen the trick by which he could toss it about. It did not matter that the trick had been invented by another; this was a pure experience (just as pure as its mirror image, when one is descended on by a catastrophe), without self-regard, so pure that it brought to Martin's smile, as well as joy, a trace of sarcastic surprise – 'Why has this happened to *me*?'

He told me as much, for that evening there was complete confidence between us. Suddenly, he began to laugh outright.

I asked what was the matter.

'I just thought what an absurdly suitable place it was, to feel like this.'

I was at a loss.

'What was?'

'Your bath.'

Then I remembered the legend of Archimedes.

'*He* must have had the feeling often enough,' said Martin.

With a smile, sharp-edged, still elated, now eager for the point of action, he added:

'The trouble is, the old man was a better scientist than I am.'

PART TWO

THE EXPERIMENT

CHAPTER VIII

GAMBLING BY A CAUTIOUS MAN

SOON after Martin's visit, people in the secret began to become partisans about Luke's scheme, either for or against. A decision could not be stalled off for long. Luke had managed to arouse passionate opposition; most of the senior scientists, as well as Hector Rose and his colleagues, wanted to kill the idea and despatch Luke and the others to America. But Francis Getliffe and a few other scientists were being passionate on the other side. And I also was totally committed, and, while they argued for Luke in the committee rooms, did what little I could elsewhere.

I made Hector Rose listen to the whole Luke case. Although we were not easy with each other – I was coming to feel for him not precisely dislike, but something nearer antagonism – he gave me a full hearing, but I did not shift him.

I did better with the Minister, who had in any case felt a sneaking sympathy with the scheme all the time. The difficulty was that he was losing his influence, and was above all concerned for his own job. While I was trying to persuade him to pay a visit to Barford, he was on edge for a telephone call from Downing Street, which, if it came, meant the end.

However, he agreed to pay the visit.

'If I can see those prima donnas together, I might get some sense out of them,' he said to Rose.

Rose politely agreed – but he was speculating on how many more weeks Bevill would stay in office. Rose had seen ministers come and go before, and he wanted all tidy in case there was a change.

Lesser functionaries than the Minister would have travelled down to Barford by government car; Hector Rose, who himself had no taste for show, would at least have reserved a compartment for the party, so that he could talk and work. Bevill did neither. He sat in a crowded train, reading a set of papers of no importance, exactly like a conscientious clerk on the way to Birmingham.

The train trickled on in the sunshine; troops yobbed out on to the little platforms, and once or twice a station flower garden which had been left intact gave out the hot mid-summer scents. There was no dining car on the train; after several hours of travelling the Minister pulled out a bag, and with his sly, gratified smile offered it first to Rose and then to me. It contained grey oatmeal cakes.

'Bikkies,' explained the Minister.

When Drawbell received us in his office, he did not spend any time on me, and not much (in which he was dead wrong) on Hector Rose. Drawbell had no illusions about the dangers to Barford. His single purpose was to get the Minister on his side; but his manner did not overdo it. It was firm, at times bantering and only obscurely deferential.

'I've done one thing you could never do,' he said to the Minister.

The Minister looked mild and surprised.

'Just before the war,' Drawbell went on, 'I saw *you* on *my* television set.'

The Minister gave a happy innocent smile. He knew precisely what was going on, and what Drawbell wanted; he was used to flattery in its most bizarre forms, and, incidentally, always enjoyed it.

But Bevill knew exactly what he intended to do that afternoon. Drawbell's plans for him he side-stepped; he did not want Rose or me; he had come down for a series of private talks with the scientists, and he was determined to have them.

It was not until half-past five that Martin came out of the meeting, and then he had Mounteney with him, so that we could not exchange a private word. Old Bevill was still there talking to Rudd, and Mounteney was irritated.

'This is sheer waste of time,' he said to me as we began to walk towards their house, as though his disapproval of old Bevill included me. Although at Cambridge we had been somewhere between acquaintances and friends, he did at that moment disapprove of me.

He was tall and very thin, with a long face and cavernous eye-sockets. It was a kind of face and body one often sees in those with a gift for conceptual thought; and Mounteney's gift was a major one. He was a man of intense purity of feeling, a man quite unpadded either physically or mentally; and he had an almost total inability to say a softening word.

'It would have been more honest if you had all come here in uniform,' he said to me.

He meant that the government was favouring the forces at the expense of science, in particular at the expense of Barford. It seemed to him obvious – and obvious to anyone whose intelligence was higher than an ape's – that government policy was wrong. He was holding me responsible for it. All other facts were irrelevant, including the fact that he knew me moderately well. It was shiningly clear to him that government policy was moronic, and probably ill-disposed. Here was I: the first thing was to tell me so.

I gathered that the Minister had talked to them both privately and in a group. Luke had been eloquent: his opponents had attacked him: Martin had spoken his mind. The discussion had been rambling, outspoken and inconclusive. Mounteney, although in theory above the battle, was not pleased.

'Luke *is* quite bright,' he said in a tone of surprise and injury, as though it was unreasonable to force him to give praise.

He then returned to denouncing me by proxy. Bevill had said what wonderful work they had done at Barford. Actually, said Mounteney, they had done nothing: the old man knew it; they knew it; they knew he knew it.

'Why *will* you people say these things?' asked Mounteney.

Irene was sitting in a deckchair in what had once been the garden behind their house, though by this time it was running wild. The bindweed was strangling the last of the phlox, the last ragged pansies; the paths were overgrown with weed. When Mounteney went in to his children, Martin and I sat beside her, on the parched grass, which was hot against the hand. At last Martin was free to give a grim smile.

'Well,' he said to me, 'you'd better see that Luke's scheme goes through.'

'What have you been doing?' she asked.

Martin was still smiling. 'Not only for patriotic reasons,' he went on.

'What *have* you been doing?' She sounded, for the moment, as she might have done if accusing him of some amatory adventure, her voice touched with mock reprobation and a secret pride.

'Something that may not do us any good,' he said, and let us hear the story. He had told Bevill, in front of Drawbell and Rudd, that he and the other young scientists were agreed: either they ought to concentrate on Luke's scheme, or else shut Barford down.

'If I had to do it, it was no use doing it half-heartedly,' he said.

'*I'm glad you did it*,' she said, excited by the risk. The teasing air had faded; there was a high flush under her eyes.

'Wait until we see whether it was worth while,' said Martin.

'Never mind that,' she said, and turned to me: 'Aren't you glad he did it?'

Before I answered Martin looked at her and said:

'We may not get our way, you know.'

'I don't care.'

'It would be an odd time to move.'

They were glancing at each other with eyes half challenging, half salacious.

'Why would it be so odd?' I asked, but did not need an answer.

'You can tell Lewis,' said Martin.

'I am going to have a child, dear,' she said.

For the first time since their marriage, I felt nothing but warmth towards her, as I went to her chair and kissed her. Martin's face was softened with delight. If he had not been my brother I should have envied him, for my marriage had been childless, and there were times, increasing as the years passed, when the deprivation nagged at me. And, buried deep within Martin, and to an extent in me, there was a strong family sense, so that it was natural for him to say:

'I'm glad there'll be another generation.'

As he went indoors to fetch something to drink in celebration, Irene said to me:

'If it's a boy we'll call it after you, Lewis dear. Even though you don't approve of its mother.'

She added: 'He is pleased, isn't he? I did want to do something for him.'

'It's very good news,' I said, as she got up from her chair in the low sunlight, and began to walk about the patch of derelict garden. The evening scents were growing stronger, mint and wormwood mingled in the scorched aromatic tang of the August night. Irene came to a clearing in the long grass, where a group of autumn crocuses shone out, amethyst and solitary, flowers that in my childhood I had heard called 'naked ladies'. Irene bent and picked one, and then stood erect, as though she were no longer concealing the curve of her breast.

'When I was a little girl,' she said, 'I always thought I should have a brood of children.'

'Should you like them?' I asked.

'Time is going on,' she said: but, in the smoothing amber light, she looked younger than I had seen her.

After Martin returned, and we sat there in the dipping sun, the three of us were at peace together as we had not been before. Our content was so strong that Martin did not disturb it when he began speculating again about transferring to Luke, and speaking out that afternoon; he did not disturb it in us, least of all in himself.

'I don't see what else I could have done,' he said.

Martin went on with his thoughts. It was going to be a near thing whether Luke got his head: wasn't that true? So if one could do anything to bring it about, one had to.

'I should have been more sorry if I hadn't spoken.'

If the luck went wrong, it meant a dim job for the rest of the war and probably after. If the luck went right, no one could tell – Martin smiled, his eyes glinted, and he said:

'I'm not sorry that I've gone in with Luke.'

We all took it for granted that he was the most prudent of men, always reckoning out the future, not willing to allow himself a rash word, let alone a rash action. Even I assumed that as part of his flesh and bone. In a sense it was true. And yet none of us had made a wilder marriage, and now, over Barford and his career, he was gambling again.

CHAPTER IX

VIEW OF A TRUE MARRIAGE

FROM Martin's I went off to an evening party at Drawbell's. Mrs Drawbell had set herself to catch old Bevill for a social engagement; he had refused tea or dinner, and insisted on returning to London that night, but he had not been able to elude this last invitation, a 'little party' before we caught the train.

Most of the senior Barford staff were already there, and I found my way to a corner next to Walter Luke. From near the window we looked into the centre of the room, where upon the hearthrug Mrs Drawbell, a heavy woman, massive as a monument upon the rug, waited for the Minister.

'Where is this uncle?' said Luke.

'He'll come,' I said. The Minister has not been known to break a social engagement.

Luke's thoughts became canalised once more.

'Does he believe in Jojo?' (Luke's proposal already had a name.)

He corrected himself.

'I don't care whether he believes in it or not. The point is, will he do anything useful about it?'

I said that I thought he was well disposed, but would not find it easy to put through.

'There are times,' said Luke, 'when I get sick and tired of you wise old men.'

Whole hearted and surgent, he said:

'Well, I suppose I'd better mobilise some of the chaps who really know against all you stuffed shirts.'

I was warning him to go carefully (he would still listen to me, even when he was regarding me as a 'wise old man') when the Minister entered. With his unobtrusive trip Bevill went towards Mrs Drawbell.

'I am sorry I haven't been able to get out of the clutches of these fellows,' he said, smiling innocently.

'I am glad you were able to come to my party, Mr Bevill,' she replied. Her voice was deep, her expression dense, gratified, and confident. She had looked forward to having him there; he had come. And now – she had nothing to say.

The Minister said, what a nice room. She agreed. He said, how refreshing to have a drink after a hot, tiring day. She was glad he liked it. He said, it was hard work, walking round the laboratories, especially hard work if you weren't a scientist and didn't understand much. She smiled, heavily, without comment. She had nothing to say to him.

It did not seem to depress her. She had him in her house, the grandson of the last Lord Boscastle but one (his being in the Cabinet had its own virtue, but did not give her the same collector's joy). To her this visit was a prize which she would hoard.

She kept him to herself, standing together on the rug. It was not until she was forced to greet a new arrival that her eyes were distracted, and the Minister could slip away towards the window. He beckoned to us, so that we could make a circle round him, Luke, me, a couple of young scientists whom I did not know by name, Mary Pearson. He caught sight of Mary Pearson's husband, and beckoned also to him.

I had had business talks with Pearson before, for he was one of the top men at Barford and was said to be their best electrical engineer. In those talks I had found him too pleased with himself to give more than a minimum reply. He was a man in the early thirties with a cowlick over his forehead and a wide lazy-looking mouth.

As Bevill crooked his finger, Pearson gave a relaxed smile and came unconcernedly into the ring.

'Now, my friends, we can talk seriously, can't we?' said the Minister.

He basked in the company of the young, and felt quite natural with them. But, as often when he was natural, he was also mildly eccentric; with the intellectual young, he felt most completely at ease, and satisfied with himself, in discussing what he called 'philosophy'. He took it for granted that this was their conception of serious conversation, too; and so the old man, so shrewd and cunning in practice, dug out his relics of idealist speculation, garbled from the philosophers of his youth, F. H. Bradley, and MacTaggart, and talked proudly on, forcing the young men to attend – while all they wanted, that night of nights, was to cut the cackle and hear his intentions about Barford and Luke's scheme.

'I don't know about you chaps' – the Minister, who had been rambling on for some time, looked out of the window towards the west – 'but whenever I see a beautiful sunset, I wonder whether there isn't an Ideal Sunset outside Space and Time.'

His audience were getting impatient. But he thought they were taking a point.

'Perhaps you'll say, the Phenomenon is enough. Is the Phenomenon enough? I know it sometimes seems so, to all of us, doesn't it? – when you see a beloved woman and see from her smile that she loves you back. I know it seems enough,' said Bevill earnestly and cheerfully.

All of a sudden, only half listening, for I had heard the Minister showing off his philosophy before, I saw the flush on Mary Pearson's face, I saw the smile on Pearson's as he glanced at her. I had not often seen a man so changed. When I met him, he had filled me with antipathy; it came as a shock to see his face radiant. Somehow Bevill's bumbling words had touched a trigger. The conceit had vanished, the indifference about whether he pleased: it was just a face lit up by a mutual love. And so was hers. Her skin was flushed down to the neck of her dress, behind her spectacles her eyes were moist with joy.

Anyone watching as I was would have had no doubt: those two must be sharing erotic bliss. You can share erotic bliss with someone and still not be suffused by love as those two were, but the converse does not hold, and no husband and wife could be so melted by each other's smile without the memory of bliss, and the certainty that it would soon be theirs again. I guessed that their physical happiness was out of the common run. It had been worth listening to the Minister's philosophising to see it shine.

I was not the only one who saw it shine, for, a few minutes afterwards,

as the Minister was saying his goodbyes before we left for the railway
station, Luke and I strolled in the lane outside and he said:

'Funny what people see in each other.'

'Is it?'

'It's lucky those two think each other wonderful, because I'm damned
if anyone else would.'

He added, with a thoughtful, truculent grin:

'Of course, they might say the same of me and Nora.'

As he walked beside me his whole bearing was jaunty, and many
women, at a glance, would have judged him virile. Yet he was sexually a
genuinely humble man. He did not believe that women noticed him, it
would not have occurred to him to believe it.

'I envy you, you know!' he broke out.

'Whatever for?'

'You know that I'm an innocent sort of chap. Why are you making me
talk?'

For once, he had forgotten about the project. Like me, he had been
stirred by the Pearsons' smile. With his usual immoderation, he was
bursting to confide. Confide he did, insisting often that I was pumping
him.

'I've kept myself out of things when I ought to have rushed in. I
thought I couldn't spare the time from science. It wasn't ambition, I
just felt I had to get on. And I didn't know what I was missing. So now
I'm batting about trying to make up my mind on problems which you
must have coped with when you were twenty. I'm frightened of them, and
I don't like being frightened.'

I said that he had not done badly: he had made a happier marriage than
most, while mine had been miserable. He knew that my wife was dead:
but that was all he knew, and I did not tell him any more.

'But you know your way about. So does your brother Martin. Neither
of you feel like some little brat with his nose up against the shop window
and wondering what he has got to do to get inside.'

Totally immersed, he went on:

'I can't bear being left out of things. There are times when I want to
to see all the places and read all the books and fornicate with all the women.
Now you're certain where you stand about all that, you've had your share.
What I want to know is, how do I get mine without hurting anyone
else?'

I thought, in a way he was right about himself: how young he was. But
it was more than calendar youth (at that time he was thirty-one), it was

more than a life blinkered and concentrated by his vocation. Perhaps he would never lose his sense of being deprived, of being left out of the party – of being outside in the road, of seeing the lights of houses, homes of voluptuous delight denied to him. Yet I had felt that so often myself, not being such an outsider as Luke, but more so that he would have believed.

'I suppose I shall get my share in the long run,' said Luke. 'Somehow I must manage it. I'm damned well not going to die feeling I was too frightened to discover what it was all about.' He was looking towards the establishment, and the energy seemed to be pulsing within him, so that in the softening light his sanguine colour became deeper, even his hair seemed to have more sheen.

'Wait till I've got this scheme to go. There's a time for everything,' he said, 'when we've tied this up!'

CHAPTER X

A NIGHT AT PRATT'S

BACK in Whitehall, the Minister plumped in on Luke's side. It was gallant for a man whose job was tottering, for it meant opposing those in power. It meant acting against Bevill's own maxims – if those above had it in for you, never make a nuisance of yourself and never go away. For once in his life he disregarded them.

No one could understand why. With Bevill, everyone looked for some cunning political motive. I believed that, just this once, there was none. Underneath the politics, the old man had a vein of narrow, rigid, aristocratic patriotism. He had been convinced that Luke's scheme might be good for the country; that may have been a reason why Bevill made enemies in order to give Luke his head.

A minister likely to be out of office next month had, however, not many cards to play. Probably his single effort in self-sacrifice did not count much either way; what was more decisive was Francis Getliffe's conversation with Hector Rose. I was not present, but within a short time of that conversation, Rose, against his preconceived opinion, against most of his prejudices, changed his mind. He had concluded that the other side's case, in particular Getliffe's case, was stronger than his own. I wondered with some shame – for I could not like him – whether in his place I should have been so fair.

So the despatch boxes went round, Rose lunched with his colleagues at the Athenæum, the committees sat: on a night early in November, the Minister went off to a meeting. It was not a cabinet, but a sub-committee of ministers; he believed that, one way or the other, this would settle it. I remained in my office, waiting for him to return.

It was half past eight; in the pool of light from the reading lamp, the foolscap on my desk shone with a blue luminescence; I was too restless to work. I went across the passage to the little room where my new personal assistant was sitting. I had told her to go hours before, but she was over-conscientious; she was a young widow called Vera Allen, comely but reserved, too diffident to chat, stiff at being alone in the building with a man.

I heard the Minister scamper up the stairs, with the light trotting steps that sounded so youthful. I returned to my room. He put his head in, without taking off his bowler hat.

'Still at it?' he said.

He went on:

'I think it's all right, Eliot.'

I exclaimed with relief.

Bevill was flushed, looking curiously boyish in his triumph. He tipped his hat back on his thin grey hair.

'We mustn't count our eggs before they're hatched, but I think it's in the bag,' he said.

In jubilation, he asked if I had eaten and took me off to Pratt's.

He had taken me there before, when he was pleased. He only did it because he had a soft spot for me. For business, for talks with Rose, he went elsewhere; Pratt's was reserved for friends, it was his fortress, his favourite club.

When he first took me inside, I had thought – it seemed strange – of my mother. She had been brought up in a gamekeeper's cottage on a Lincolnshire estate; she was dead years since, she had not seen what happened to me – but just the sight of me with Thomas Bevill, in his most jealously guarded club, eating with men whose names she had read in the papers, would have made her rejoice that her life was not in vain.

Yet if she could have seen me there, she would have been a little puzzled to observe that we were sitting with some discomfort in rooms remarkably like the cottage where she was born. A basement: a living room with a common table and a check cloth: a smoking kitchen with an open hearth: in fact, a landowner's idea of his own gamekeeper's quarters.

That was the place to which Thomas Bevill went whenever he wanted to be sure of meeting no one but his aristocratic friends.

Looking at him after our meal, as he sat by the kitchen hearth, drinking a glass of port, I thought that unless one had the chance to see him so, one might be quite misled. People called him unassuming, unsnobbish, realistic, gentle. Unassuming: yes, that was genuine. Realistic: that was genuine too; unlike his cousin, Lord Boscastle, he did not take refuge, as society evened itself out, in a fantastic and comic snobbery; yet in secret, he did take refuge with his friends here, in a cave-of-the-past, in a feeling, blended of fear, foresight and contempt, that he could preserve bits of his past and make them last his time. Gentle, a bit of an old woman: that was not genuine in the slightest; he was kind to his friends, but the deeper you dug into him the tougher and more impervious he became.

'Well, if they're going to sack me, Eliot,' he said, 'I've left them a nice kettle of fish.' He was simmering in his triumph over Barford. He ordered more glasses of port.

'One of these days,' he said, 'those chaps will blow us all up, and that will be the end of the story.'

The firelight winked in his glass; he held it up to admire the effect, brought it down carefully and looked into it from above.

'It's funny about those chaps,' he reflected, 'I used to think scientists were supermen. But they're not supermen, are they? Some of them are brilliant, I grant you that. But between you and me, Eliot, a good many of them are like garage hands. Those are the chaps who are going to blow us all up.'

I said, for I was not speaking like a subordinate, that a good many of them had more imagination than his colleagues.

Bevill agreed, with cheerful indifference.

'Our fellows can't make much difference to the world, and those chaps can. Do you think it will be a better world, when they've finished with it?'

I thought it might. Not for him, probably not for me and my kind: but for ninety per cent of the human race.

'I don't trust them,' said Thomas Bevill.

Then he said:

'By the by, I like the look of your brother, Eliot.'

It was partly his good manners, having caught himself in a sweeping statement. But he said it as though he meant it.

'He put the cat among the pigeons, you know, that afternoon down there. It's just as well he did, or Master Drawbell mightn't have seen the red light in time, and if they'd all gone on crabbing Luke I couldn't have saved the situation.'

He began laughing, his curious, internal, happy laugh, as though he were smothering a dirty joke.

'Those Drawbells! Between them they'd do anything to get a K, wouldn't they?'

He meant a knighthood. He was constantly amused at the manœuvres men engaged in to win titles, and no one understood them better.

'Never mind, Eliot,' he said. 'We saved the situation, and now it's up to those chaps not to let us down.'

It was his own uniquely flat expression of delight: but his face was rosy, he did not look like a man of seventy-three, he was revelling in his victory, the hot room, the mildly drunken night.

'If this country gets a super bomb,' he said cheerfully, 'no one will remember me.'

He swung his legs under his chair.

'It's funny about the bomb,' he said. 'If we manage to get it, what do we do with it then?'

This was not the first time that I heard the question: once or twice recently people at Barford had raised it. It was too far away for the scientists to speculate much, even the controversialists like Mounteney, but several of them agreed that we should simply notify the enemy that we possessed the bomb, and give some evidence: that would be enough to end the war. I repeated this view to Bevill.

'I wonder,' he said.

'I wonder,' he repeated. 'Has there ever been a weapon that someone did not want to let off?'

I said, though the issue seemed remote, that this was different in kind. We had both seen the current estimate, that one fission bomb would kill three hundred thousand people at a go.

'Oh, I don't know,' said Bevill. 'Think of what we're trying to do with bombing. We're trying to kill men, women and children. It's worse than anything Genghiz Khan ever did.'

He said it without relish, without blame, with neutrality.

Soon the room grew warmer, the port went round again, as men came in from a late night meeting. A couple of them were Ministers, and Bevill looked towards them with a politician's insatiable hope. Had they any news for him? He could not help hoping. He was old, he had made such reputation as he could, if he stayed in office he would not add a syllable to it; he knew how irretrievably he was out of favour, and he did not expect to last three months; yet still, on that happy night, he wondered if he might not hear of a reprieve, if he might not hear that he was being kept on, perhaps in an obscurer post.

I saw that his flicker of hope did not last long. From their manner he knew they had nothing to tell him. It did not weigh him down, he was pleased with himself that night. And they brought other news: the invasion fleet was safely out of Gibraltar, and all looked well for the North African landing.

A little later, Bevill and I went out into St James's Street. He twirled his umbrella, a slight little figure in a bowler hat, under the full moon; an old man, slightly drunk, expecting the sack, and full of well-being. He said to me with an extra sweep of his umbrella:

'Isn't it nice to be winning?'

I was not sure whether he was talking about Barford, or the war.

He repeated it, resoundingly, to the empty street:

'Isn't it nice to be winning?'

CHAPTER XI

TWO KINDS OF DANGER

AFTER the Minister's night of victory, there was for months nothing I could do for Luke and Martin. I had to set myself to wait, picking up any rumour from Barford, or anything I heard in Whitehall. Because I could do nothing, the suspense nagged at me more.

That was the reason I started into anxiety, the instant Hanna Puchwein enquired about Martin's fate.

I was having dinner with the Puchweins at the Connaught, at the farewell party they gave me before Kurt Puchwein left for Chicago. They were standing me a lavish treat; as I sat by Hanna's side, with her husband opposite, in the corner near the door, lights flashed on glass and sank warmly into the rosewood, and I was reflecting, if you were used to English fellow-travellers, how incongruous Hanna Puchwein seemed. There was nothing of the self-abnegation of the English radical about her, none of the attempts, so common among other acquaintances of mine, to imitate the manners of the working class. Hanna's glossy head gleamed trimly in our corner, and she was the best-groomed woman in the room. She was in her early thirties. She had a small head, narrowing catlike to a pointed chin. Her forehead was white, bland, unlined; but her eyes flashed as she talked, and she had an air that was, I thought, at the same time cultivated and *farouche*.

Meanwhile Kurt was presenting me with gifts: he was a man who found it delectable to give, even more than to receive. He liked doing good turns and letting one know it; but that had always seemed to me more amiable than not liking to do good turns at all. He gave me wine. He gave me his opinion that, out of Luke's project, he and Martin would 'do themselves good in the long run'.

Yet, although he was expanding himself to make me cheerful, his own mood was overcast. He and Hanna spoke little to each other; and it occurred to me that probably in an unexacting friendliness, such as he felt for me, one saw the best of him. In a closer relation, he could be violent, spoiled, bad tempered.

That night he went to bed early, leaving me and Hanna together, on the excuse that he had some last letters to write. He spun out his goodbye to me, pressing my hand.

'It may be a long time before we meet again, my friend,' he said. He was flying the Atlantic within forty-eight hours. I looked at him – his great prow of a nose, his mouth pinched in, as though with press studs, that night.

'Ah, well,' he said. 'We shall meet once again in the world.'

As soon as he had gone, I spoke to Hanna. Once or twice before I had talked to her intimately, as I had never done with Kurt. I asked, outright:

'Why is Kurt so anxious to go to America?'

He could have stayed at Barford. Apart from Luke's project, some others, including Rudd's, had been left in being. Nothing official ever got closed down flat, old Bevill used to say.

Hanna stared at me, first with a blank, washed, open look (her temper was as formidable as his), then with an expression I could not read.

'Why ask me?' she said. Then quickly:

'Why don't you persuade your brother to go also?'

It was then I started. She went on:

'Wouldn't it have been better for him?'

I said, at once hyper-sensitive, on the defensive:

'It depends whether Luke's scheme comes off – but a good many of them believe in it. You heard what Kurt said.'

Hanna said:

'Oh that! You are a most single-minded man.'

Her smile had an edge.

'I didn't mean that at all,' she said.

'What did you mean?'

'If he went to America,' she said, 'he might be able to escape from that woman.'

'I don't know whether he wants to escape,' I said.

'I know that he ought to,' said Hanna.

She reminded me that geographical distance, like time, helped one to recover from unhappy love. Three thousand miles could be as good as the passage of six months. Hanna's eyes were flashing with impatience, in which there was, however, a trace of the pleasure with which a man and a woman, not attached but not totally unaware of each other, spread out before them the platitudes and generalisations of love.

I said that I hoped the child might heal their marriage.

'Have you never known women have a child and leave their husbands flat?'

She went on:

'With women like her, children break marriages more often than they save them.'

'Well,' I said, 'if she did leave him, you wouldn't break your heart.'

'Unless he's got free of her first,' she said, 'he might break his.'

I was frowning, and she said:

'I suppose you know that he's been passionately in love with her? And may be still?'

'I think I did know that,' I said.

'She is quite useless to him,' she said. 'If he isn't lucky and doesn't get away, she will destroy a great part of his life.'

I was thinking: when I worried about the danger of Martin's marriage, it had been for cruder reasons than these, it had been because Irene might do him 'practical' harm in terms of money and worldly standing and jobs. I had almost deliberately shut my eyes to what he felt for her: and it was left for Hanna, herself someone whom I had always thought a selfish woman, to show the consideration, the imaginative sympathy, in which I had failed.

It was partly that our loves are entirely serious only to ourselves; years of my own life had been corroded by a passion more wretched than Martin's, and yet, as a spectator of his, I felt as my friends used to feel about mine. We would 'get over it', it was irritating to watch a man dulled by his own infatuation, it seemed, certainly not tragic, scarcely even pathetic, almost his own fault. In fact, all loves but one's own have an element of the tiresome: and from the way I behaved about Martin's until that evening when Hanna forced me to face it, I came to think that was even more true of a brother's unhappy love than of a friend's.

'She gives him nothing he couldn't get from any woman he picked up,' she said. 'And in self-defence he has learned to give nothing back.'

'I think he can bear it,' I said.

'Of course he can bear it. But sometimes it is a greater danger to bear it than not to bear it.'

She went on:

'One can stand so much that one gets frightened of anything better. Isn't that true of you?'

'There's something in that,' I said.

'It isn't noble,' Hanna said. 'It is just that one has become too frightened to choose, and then one goes on standing it. Well, I want to see Martin stop suffering patiently. I want to see him take himself in hand and make his choice.'

As I listened to her, speaking with the bite that sounded at the same time intimate and cross, I felt a touch of concern – for her. It was disturbing to hear her talk so intently of another – not through tenderness for Martin, though she had a little, not even because she was putting me off from talking of her husband, though that was also true. It was disturbing because she was really talking of herself. She was behaving like Martin that night when he and I walked towards his empty house, she was unable to say outright that she too was coming near a choice. About her there clung the desperation, the fragility, of a woman who still looks young but no longer feels it to herself – or rather who, still feeling young, becomes self-conscious that others are marking off the years – and who has become obsessed that she has only one choice to make, one, no more, before she is old.

CHAPTER XII

A ROUTINE INTERVIEW

THOSE in the secret did not talk easily with each other, and as the months passed and Luke's 'pile' went up, it was hard to judge how many believed in him. In committee heads were shaken, not much was said, yet feelings ran high. Luke was one of those figures who have the knack, often surprising to themselves, of stirring up controversy; people who did not know him, who had no conception of his surgent, exuberant, often simple-hearted character, grew excited about him, as someone who would benefit the country or as a scandalous trifler with public money, almost as a crook.

Of his supporters, the most highly placed of all was lost in the April of 1943, when Bevill was at last told that his job was wanted for another.

Now that his suspense had ended, I was astonished by the old man's resilience. He moved his papers from Whitehall the same day. Briskly he said goodbye to his staff and made a speech with a remarkable, indeed an excessive, lack of sentimentality. He was not thinking of his years in the old office; he was thinking of nothing but the future. Without any procrastination at all he refused a peerage. If he accepted it, he was accepting the fact that he was out of politics for good: at the age of seventy-four, he was, with the occupational hope of politicians, as difficult to kill as the hope of a consumptive, reckoning his chances of getting back again.

As soon as he left, my own personal influence diminished; I could intervene no more than other civil servants of my rank (in his last month of office, Bevill had got me promoted again, which Rose thought excessive). All I did had to go through Rose, and we were more than ever uncomfortable with each other.

Nevertheless, Rose intended not to waste my inside knowledge of Barford. He merely requested as a favour that I should report to him any 'point of interest' I picked up on my visits there.

Each of us was being punctilious. When I next went down to Barford, a month or two after Bevill's dismissal, for the christening of Martin's son, I set out to obey Rose to the letter. I held back one incident only and I did so because neither of us would have thought it worth our while.

It was a morning late in May, the sky bright and pale, with an east wind that took the scent out of the wistaria, when I went into the hangar with Martin, in order to see the pile going up before we went to church. The tarpaulins in the roof, still not repaired, flapped in the wind. In the hangar it was cold; I had not known it anything else; but, instead of the dripping floor of winter, it had suddenly gone dusty, and grit blew about in the spring air. Labourers, wearing jerseys, were working in the bleak half-light; they were laying bricks for an outer wall, while further away one could see a kind of box, about eight feet each way; outside was another wall, the first part of the concrete case. Further down still, Luke's experimental structure lay deserted. Between stood some tables, one or two screened off, packed with radio valves and circuits; on others, as though abandoned, were strewn metal tubing and tea cups. There was no sign of busyness. Labourers padded on, muttering among themselves. The foreman had his hand on the concrete shield, and was listening to Luke.

The paradox was that, as they worked against time, as they studied the German intelligence reports or heard gossip from America (news had come through that the Chicago pile had already run, in the previous December), Luke had nothing like enough to do.

Once he had had his idea, there was no more room for flair or scientific imagination for months, perhaps years to come: the rest was a matter of getting the machine built. It was a matter of organisation, extreme attention to detail, knowing when a contractor could not work faster and when he could be pressed. It was a matter of organisation that differed only in scale and in what depended on it, but not at all in kind, from being the Clerk of Works to some new public baths. Any competent man could do it, and Martin was there to do it as efficiently as Luke and with less fuss. Luke, who was as lavish with praise as abuse, admitted this. But he could not keep his hands off. Engineers, going as fast as men could within the human limits, heard his swearwords over the telephone. They did no great harm. It meant an expense of temper. It meant that, for the most critical months of Luke's working life, he still had nothing to do.

When he came across to speak to me, I noticed that the colour of his face had gone more sallow and that, although the skin under his eyes was fresh and full, without the roughness of true anxiety, it had taken on a bruised, a faint purple tint. He was restless on the balls of his feet. He did not offer to come to church. When he left us, I asked Martin what Luke was going off to do. Martin gave an amused, half-indulgent smile.

'He's going to play the piano,' he said.

'What?'

'Just now,' said Martin, 'he plays the piano all day. Five or six hours a day, at least, except when he's having a row.'

'Does he play well?'

'Oh no,' Martin replied. 'He never learned after he was ten. He plays his old Associated Board pieces.'

In church, with a beam of early afternoon sun falling across the font, a beam in which the motes spun and jiggled and in which Martin's hair was turned to silver gilt, I thought he was standing the strain better than Luke. He smiled at the child with a love more open than he ever showed for his wife.

Just for a moment, though, Martin's smile altered. The parson and Irene and the baby had already left the church, and Martin and I were following, when an old woman entered with a busy air. Martin asked what she was doing, and she replied, full of well-being:

'There's a corpse coming in here soon, sir, and I just wanted to see that everything was nice for him.'

Martin smiled at me, and we followed the others into the sunlight. He did not need to explain; we both had a superstitious sense. He smiled at the thought of the old woman, and did not like it.

It was in the afternoon that I attended to the piece of business which seemed just routine, not interesting enough to discuss with Rose. Drawbell had invited me to what they called an 'allocation meeting' at which they interviewed some of that year's intake of young men. His motive was to demonstrate how few and poor they were, but that worn-out argument could get no further. He sat behind a table with his heads of sections on each side; Rudd was there, Mounteney, a couple of Jewish refugees and Martin, deputising for Luke. Increasingly Luke left the chores to Martin. I could understand it. I could remember being underworked and over-anxious, doing so little that one needed to do less.

As the interviews went on, the only flicker of interest for me was that one of the young men came from the same town as Martin and myself and had attended the same grammar school. His family had lived not far from ours in the red-brick streets, and Martin could recall him as a small boy. His name, which was Eric Sawbridge, had a flat, unmemorable Midland note.

As he answered questions, he spoke with the faintly aggressive, reproving tone that one often heard at interviews. He was twenty-four, large, heavy, mature, with a single thick line across his forehead; he was a lighter blond than Martin, and might have been a Scandinavian sailor. He had got his First three years before, and had gone on to research. His answers sounded competent, not over-gracious; Martin made a reference to schooldays and Sawbridge's expression was, for a second, less suspicious. Then Drawbell took the general questioning out of Martin's hands.

'Have you any outside interests?'

'I don't know what you mean.'

'Did you belong to any societies at the university?'

'One or two.' He mentioned a film society in wartime Oxford.

'Do you play any games?'

'I *prefer* the cycle.'

'Do you read anything?'

'I haven't had much time.'

The scientists smiled. These non-technical questions and answers were perfunctory on both sides of the table. Anything outside science was a frippery. That was all. As soon as Sawbridge went out of the room, he was being competed for. Perhaps he was the ablest on view: but Rudd wanted him because he was English, after a Pole, two German Jews, an Irishman. An argument blew up, Rudd suddenly violent. Rudd wanted him: Mounteney wanted him: but Martin got him.

It was a piece of domestic routine, and I felt I could have spent the three hours better. I should have been astonished to know that, two years later, I was forcing my memory to recall that interview with Sawbridge. While it actually happened, I wrote it off. On the other hand, I could not dismiss the conversation I had with Mounteney and Martin late that night.

CHAPTER XIII

BESIDE THE SMOOTH WATER

AFTER the interviews, Mounteney had come away intransigent. He was irritated because he had lost over Sawbridge, and could not understand just where Martin had been more adroit. He also could not understand why Martin, like himself an unbeliever, had allowed his son to be baptised.

'Rain making!' said Mounteney. He went on denouncing Martin: if traditions led to decent men telling lies ('what else have you been doing except tell lies?') then they made us all mentally corrupt.

His affection for Martin did not soften Mounteney's remarks, nor, when we returned to the house, did his wife's gaze, at once cocky and longing for a transformation, as though she expected him to give up controversy and say that he had come home in search of her. In fact, he and Martin and I drove in by ourselves to Stratford, where, since there was no room for me in Martin's house, I was staying the night. There all of a sudden Mounteney became gentler.

The three of us had had dinner, and walked down past the theatre to the river's edge. There was little in the sky, and over towards Clopton Bridge the dim shapes of swans moved upon the dark water. Under the willows, the river smell brought back a night, not here, but in Cambridge: I had been thinking of Cambridge all through dinner, after Martin had mentioned the name of Roy Calvert, who had been killed that spring.

On our way past the dark theatre, I heard Mounteney whisper to

Martin: to my astonishment he seemed to be asking what was the matter with me. At any rate, as we stood by the river, he tried, with a curious brusque delicacy, to distract me: that was how the conversation began.

So awkwardly that he did not sound kind, Mounteney asked me if I were satisfied with the way I had spent my life – and at once started off saying that recently he had been examining his own. What had made him a scientist? How would he justify it? Ought his son and Martin's to be scientists too?

Soon we were talking intimately. Science, said Mounteney, had been the one permanent source of happiness in his life; and really the happiness was a private, if you like a selfish, one. It was just the happiness he derived from seeing how nature worked; it would not have lost its strength if nothing he had done added sixpence to practical human betterment. Martin agreed. That was the obscure link between them, who seemed as different as men could be. Deep down, they were contemplatives, utterly unlike Luke, who was as fine a scientist as Mounteney and right out of Martin's reach. For Luke, contemplation was a means, not a joy in itself; *his* happiness was to 'make Mother Nature sit up and beg'. He wanted power over nature so that human beings had a better time.

Both Mounteney and Martin wished that they shared Luke's pleasure. For by this time, their own was beginning to seem too private, not enough justification for a life. Mounteney would have liked to say, as he might have done in less austere times, that science was good in itself; he felt it so; but in the long run he had to fall back on the justification for himself and other scientists, that their work and science in general did practical good to human lives.

'I suppose it *has* done more practical good than harm to human lives?' I said.

Mounteney's dialectic was not scathing that night. Everyone asked these questions in wartime, he said, but whatever the appearance there was no doubt about the answer. It was true that science was responsible for killing a certain number in war – Mounteney broke off and apologised: 'I am sorry to bring this up.'

Roy Calvert had been killed flying.

'Go on,' I said.

We got the numbers out of proportion, he said. Science killed a certain number: it kept alive a much larger number, something of a quite different order. Taking into account war-danger, now and in the future, this child of Martin's had an actuarial expectation of life of at least seventy years. In the eighteenth century, before organised science got going, it would have been about twenty-five. That was the major practical effect of science.

'It's such a big thing,' said Mounteney, 'that it makes minor grumbles insignificant. It will go on *whatever happens.*'

It was then that I mentioned the fission bomb.

'If you people bring that off—'

'I've done nothing useful towards it,' said Mounteney counter-suggestibly.

'If someone possesses the bomb,' I said, 'mightn't *that* make a difference?'

There was a pause.

'It could,' said Mounteney.

'Yes it could,' said Martin, looking up from the water.

The river-smell was astringent in the darkened air. Somewhere down the stream, a swan unfolded its wings and flapped noisily for a moment before settling again and sailing away.

'If those bombs were used in war,' said Mounteney, 'they might be as lethal as an epidemic.' He added: 'But that won't happen.'

'It mustn't happen,' said Martin.

I told them how, in my conversation with old Bevill at Pratt's, he did not think it incredible that the bomb would be used.

'What else do you expect,' said Mounteney, 'of a broken-down reactionary politician?'

'He wasn't approving,' I said. 'He was just saying what might happen.'

'Do you believe it could?'

I was thinking of what the Third Reich had done, and said so.

'That's why we're fighting them,' said Mounteney.

Mounteney had brought some buns for his family. Martin begged one and scattered crumbs on the water, so that swans sailed towards him out of the dark, from the bridge, from down the Avon where it was too dark to make out the church; they moved with a lapping sound, the bow waves catching glimmers of light like scratches on a mirror.

Did I believe it would be used?

'Do you believe it?' Mounteney returned to the question.

'Assuming that it's our side which gets it—'

'Of course,' said Mounteney.

'If anyone gets it,' said Martin, touching wood. It was his turn to ask me:

'You don't believe that we could use it?'

I took some time to answer.

'I find it almost incredible,' I said.

'I'm glad to hear it,' said Mounteney. 'Particularly as you're a pessimistic man.'

'I think it is incredible,' said Martin.

His voice was harsh. He was more moved than Mounteney who, despite his cantankerousness, was a gentle man, to whom any kind of cruelty seemed like a visitation from another planet. Mounteney had never had to struggle with a sadic strain in his own nature. It is men who have had to struggle so who hate cruelty most. Suddenly, listening to the revulsion in Martin's voice, I knew he was one of them.

Sternly, he went on speaking:

'But we ought to take a few sensible steps, just to make sure. I suppose they can be taught to realise what dropping one bomb means.'

We all knew the estimates of deaths the bomb would cause: we knew also the manner of those deaths.

'We can teach them,' said Mounteney. 'We'd better see that the scientists are ready to assert themselves in case there is any whisper of nonsense.'

I said: 'Why scientists specially?'

Mounteney answered: 'Because no one could do it if they could imagine the consequences. The scientists can imagine the consequences.' He gave an ironic smile, unfamiliar on him. 'After all, scientists are no worse than other men.'

Martin smiled. It all seemed far in the future, the shadow of horror passed away.

Suddenly Martin exclaimed. 'It's a mistake to be absentminded,' he said. We asked him what the matter was.

The swan was stretching his neck, asking for more. 'I've just given him a piece from the palm of my hand,' Martin remarked. 'I'm glad he left my fingers on.'

He threw the last piece of bun into the water, then stood up.

'It wouldn't do any harm,' he said, returning to the discussion, but only out of his habit of precaution, 'to drop a word in high places if we get a chance.'

CHAPTER XIV

UNEXPECTED ENCOURAGEMENT

I DECIDED to report that conversation about the use of the bomb to Hector Rose. To him it seemed almost unbelievably academic.

'I fancy our masters will cross that bridge when they come to it,' he said. He was as impatient as he ever allowed himself to be. Scientists talked too much; here they were, speculating about ethical dilemmas which might never arise, as though they were back in their student days. 'But I'm grateful to you for keeping me in the picture, my dear Eliot, many, many thanks.'

To Rose, Barford did not present any problems for decision, either then or for months to come. The pile was going up, the first instalment of heavy water had arrived; so far, so good. He was immune to the excitement that had infected me, and, as 1943 went on, I had nothing new to tell him. On my visits, I could see no change. Luke paid a visit to Canada, but otherwise was still fretting his nerves away, unoccupied, playing his piano. Martin spent much time on the hangar floor, watching the builders putting up the frame inch by inch, correct to a thousandth, making a progress perceptible to them and himself, but not to me.

By this time he was showing the strain – though in a fashion opposite to Luke's. Instead of blowing and cursing, Martin sank into a kind of frozen quietness. He was more capable of pretending than Luke, and was still reasonable company. He and Irene seemed friendly when I saw them together; she was a better mother than many people were willing to believe, and the scandal about her had died down. At Barford her name was mentioned without malicious gossip, and in consequence with disappointment, lack of tone and interest.

Often, alone with Martin, I wondered how much in those months of waiting and semi-idleness, he harassed himself about her. How right was Hanna? Was he living with that suspense, as well as the public one?

Even the public one he kept clamped down, but occasionally he was remote, as though thinking of nothing but the day when they would test the pile.

I was beginning to feel confident for him, even confident enough to ask Pearson's opinion, the most certain of all to be discouraging, when he called at my flat one evening that autumn.

He was just leaving for Los Alamos, and had come to fetch some papers. I had not been into the office that day, because of an attack of lumbago:

Pearson had no more taste for conversation than usual, and intended to take the documents and depart without the unnecessary intermediate stage of sitting down. But, as he was glancing the papers over, the sirens blew, and we heard gunfire in the distance: it sounded like the start of one of the short, sharp air raids that were becoming common that November.

'I think you'd better stay a little while,' I said.

'I might as well,' said Pearson.

He sat down, without having taken off his mackintosh. He sat as though he were quite comfortable; he did not speak until we heard the crunch of bombs, probably some way the other side of the river. Pearson looked at me through glasses which magnified his calm eyes.

'How old is this house?'

That summer I had moved from the Dolphin block into the square close by. As I told Pearson, the houses must be about a hundred years old, run up when Pimlico was a new residential district, now left with the stucco peeling off the porticos.

'A bit too old to stand up well,' said Pearson.

We heard the whine of a bomb, then the jar and rumble. The light bulbs swung, and flecks of plaster fell on to the carpet.

'About a quarter of a mile away,' said Pearson, after a second's consideration. He picked a spicule of plaster off his lapel.

I said I often wished that I had not moved from the steel and concrete of Dolphin Square.

Twice we heard the whine of bombs.

'What floor was yours?' asked Pearson, with impassive interest.

'The fourth.'

'The factor of safety was about eight times what you've got here.'

I was frightened, as I was whenever bombs fell; I could not get used to it. I disliked being frightened in the presence of Pearson, who happened to be brave.

Four bombs: one, Pearson guessed, nearer than a quarter of a mile: then the gunfire slackened overhead and we could hear it tailing away down the estuary.

'If I were you,' he remarked, 'and they began to drop them near this house, I should get a bit nervous.'

Soon he got up.

'That's all for tonight,' he said.

But even Pearson felt a touch of the elation which came to one after an air raid. He was not quite unaffected; because bombs had been dropping

near us, he was a little warmer to me. When I suggested that I should walk
part of the way to Victoria, he said, more considerately than I had heard
him speak:

'Of course, if you feel up to it.'

In the square the night was misty, but illuminated across the river
by a pillar of fire, rose and lilac round an inner tongue of gold, peacefully
beautiful. It seemed to be near Nine Elms, but might have been a little
further off, perhaps at Battersea.

'It's silly, trying to knock towns out by high explosive,' said Pearson,
as we turned our backs to the blaze and walked towards Belgrave Road.
'It just can't be done,' he said.

I had never known him so communicative, and I took advantage of
it.

'What about the other bomb?'

He turned his face towards me, and in the light of another, smaller
fire, I saw his eyes, lazy, half suspicious.

'What about it?' he said.

'What's going to happen?'

After a pause, he did not mind answering:

'We're going to get it.'

'Who is?'

'Who do you think?' He meant, of course, the American party he was
working in. As with most of the scientists nationalism in its restricted
sense touched him very little – when he said 'we', he thought of nothing
but his own group.

'You're sure?' I asked, but he was always sure.

'It stands to reason.'

Then I asked, expecting a flat answer:

'So you don't think anything will come of Luke's affair?' I was prepared
for the flat answer; what I actually heard sounded too good to be true.

'I shouldn't like to go as far as that,' he replied, looking in front of him
indifferently.

'You believe it might work?' I said.

'When he started talking about it, I thought he'd do himself a bit of
no good.' He gave a contented, contemptuous grin. 'But it doesn't seem
to have been all hot air.'

'You really think they'll pull it off?'

'I'm not a prophet.'

I asked him again.

'Oh, well,' said Pearson, 'in time Master Luke might show a bit of return for his money. Though' – he gave the same contemptuous grin again – 'he won't do it as soon as he thinks he will.'

I did not receive any greater assurance until the spring, when, in March, I received a note from Luke himself. It said:

> 'The balloon is due to go up on the 22nd. The machine ought to work some time that afternoon, though I can't tell you correct to the nearest hour. We want you to come and see the exhibition. . . .'

I had no doubt that Martin did not know of the letter; it would have seemed to him tempting fate. For myself, I felt the same kind of superstition, even a misgiving about going down to watch. If I were not there, all would happen according to plan, Luke triumph, Martin get some fame. If I sat by and watched – yet, of course, I should have to go.

CHAPTER XV

SISTER-IN-LAW

THE twenty-second was only a week away when, one evening just as I was leaving the office, Martin rang me up. He was at Barford; he sounded elaborate, roundabout, as though he had something to ask.

'I suppose you don't happen to be free tonight?'

But I could not help interrupting:

'Nothing wrong with the pile?'

(Although, over the telephone, I used a code word.)

'Not that I know of.'

'Everything fixed for next week?'

'I hope so.'

For the first time, I was letting myself wonder what Martin would do with his success.

'Shall you be in your flat tonight?' He had come round to his question.

'I could be,' I said.

'I wish you'd look after Irene a bit, if she comes in.'

'Why should she?'

'I think she will.' He went on: 'She's in rather a state.'

I said I would do anything I could. I asked: 'Is it serious?'

'I'd rather you formed your own opinion.'

I had heard little emotion in his voice – maybe he was past it, I thought. But he apologised for inflicting this on me, and he was relieved to have someone to look after her.

Later that night, I was reading in my sitting-room when the bell rang. I went to open the door, and out of the darkness, into the blue-lit hall, came Irene.

'I'm not popular, am I?' she said, but her laugh was put on.

Without speaking, I led her in.

'This room makes an enemy of me,' she said, still trying to brazen it out. Then she said, not with her childish make-believe but without any pretence:

'I couldn't come to anyone but you. Martin knows about it.'

For a few moments I thought she had left him; as she went on speaking I realised it was not so simple. First she asked, as though the prosaic question drove out all others:

'Have you got a telephone?'

She looked round the room, her pupils dilated, her eyes taking in nothing but the telephone she could not see.

'Yes,' I said, trying to soothe her. It stood in the passage.

'Can I use it?'

I said of course.

Immediately, her eyes still blind, she went out, leaving the door open. I heard her dial, slowly because in the wartime glimmer she could hardly make out the figures. Then her voice: 'Mrs Whelan, it's me again. Is Mr Hankins back yet?'

A mutter from the instrument.

'Not yet?' Irene's voice was high.

Another mutter.

'Listen,' said Irene, 'I've got a telephone number where he can get me now.'

I heard her strike a match and give the Victoria number on my telephone.

Another mutter.

'I'll be here a couple of hours at least,' replied Irene into the telephone. 'Even if he's late, tell him I'll be here till one.'

She came back into my room.

'Is that all right?' she asked, her eyes brighter now, focused on me.

I said yes.

'It's for him,' she said. 'It's not for me. He wants to speak to me urgently, and there's nowhere else I can safely wait.'

She stared at me.

'I think he wants me back.'

I tried to steady her: 'What can you tell him?'

'What can I tell him?' she cried, and added, half crying, half hysterical: 'Can I tell him *I'm defeated*?'

The phrase sounded strange, I was mystified: and yet it was at this point I knew that she was not leaving Martin out of hand.

On the other hand, I knew also that she was reading in Hankins's intentions just what she wanted to read. Did he truly want her back? Above all, she would like to believe that.

Perhaps it was commonplace. Did she, like so many other unfaithful wives, want the supreme satisfaction of coming to the crisis and then staying with her husband and turning her lover down?

For all her faults, I did not think she was as commonplace as that. Looking at her, as she sat on my sofa, breathing shortly and shallowly as she listened for the telephone, I did not feel that she was just enjoying the game of love. She was febrile: that proved nothing, she could have been febrile in a flirtation. Her heart was pounding with emotion; I had seen other women so, taking a last fervent goodbye of a lover, on their way back to the marriage bed. But she was also genuinely, wildly unhappy, unhappy because her life was being driven by forces she could not govern or even understand, and unhappy also for the most primal of reasons, because the telephone did not ring and she could not hear his voice.

I tried to comfort her. I spoke of the time, ten years before, when I knew Hankins. It was strange that he, I was thinking, should have been her grand passion, her infatuation, her romantic love – people gave it different names, according to how they judged her. Why should he be the one to get under the skin of this fickle, reckless woman?

No, that did not soothe her. I made a better shot when I talked of her and Martin. I assumed there was something left for both of them, which was what she wanted to hear. We talked of the child, whom she fiercely loved.

I recalled the reason she had given, at her breakfast table, for marrying him. 'Tell me,' I said, 'why did *he* marry *you*?'

'Oh, that's simple,' said Irene, 'he just liked the look of me.'

For once that night she spoke with zest, something like triumph.

Soon her anxiety came back. She asked: Should we hear the telephone bell through the wall? Several times she started up, thinking it was beginning to ring. Twice it did ring, and twice she went to the receiver. One call was for me, one a wrong number. The minutes passed, the half hours. Midnight came, one o'clock. She had ceased trying to keep up any conversation long since.

It was not in me to condemn her. I scarcely thought of her as my brother's wife. Faced with the sight of her nervous expectant face, pinched to the point where anxiety is turning into the dread of deprivation, I felt for her just the animal comradeship of those who have been driven to wait for news by telephone, to wait in fear of the post because there may not be a letter, to walk the streets at night waiting for a bedroom light to go out before they can go to sleep. To have lived, even for a time, helpless in the undertow of passionate love – at moments one thought that one must come home to it, even if it was a dreadful home, and anyone moving to that same home, as Irene was, seemed at such moments a sister among the others, among all the untroubled strangers going to their neater homes.

At half past two I persuaded her to go to bed. The next morning there was still no message; she wanted to ring up again, but some relic of pride, perhaps my presence and what she had said to me, prevented her. She put on her smart, brazen air to keep her courage up, and with a quip about having spent the night alone with me in my flat, took a taxi to Paddington and the next train back to Barford, waving with spirit till she was out of sight up Lupus Street.

Neither that morning, nor the previous night, had I wished, as I had often wished in the past, that Martin was rid of her.

CHAPTER XVI

POINTS ON A GRAPH

MOST people I met, even on the technical committees, were still ignorant about the whole uranium project. But some could not resist letting one know that they were in the secret too. In the lavatory of the Athenæum a bald bland head turned to me from the adjacent stall.

'*22 March*,' came the whisper and a finger rose to the lips.

On the evening of the twenty-first, just as I was leaving to catch the last train to Barford, Hector Rose gave his ceremonious knock and came into my office.

'Very best wishes, Eliot,' he said. He was awkward; he was for once excited, and tried to hide it.

'This may be a mildly historic occasion,' he said. 'We may all qualify for a footnote to history, which would be somewhat peculiar, don't you think?'

Next morning, sitting opposite to Mrs Drawbell at the breakfast table, I thought there was one person at least immune from the excitement. Drawbell had left for the laboratory, so full of animation that he let the *diablerie* show through: 'If I were giving honours, Eliot, I shouldn't give them to the prima donnas – no, just to the people who do the good, hard, slogging work.' He gave his melon-lipped grin; he was thinking of his own rewards to come; more than ever, he felt the resentment of a middle man for those who make his fortune. When he went out, the psychological temperature fell.

Mrs Drawbell watched me, heavy and confident in her silence. She said: 'I hope you are enjoying your kipper,' and returned to impassivity again. I said:

'Everyone will be glad when today is over, won't they?'

The women at Barford had had to be told that an experiment was taking place that day; Mrs Drawbell did not know what it was, but she knew this was a crisis. Nevertheless, mine seemed a new idea.

'Perhaps they will,' said Mrs Drawbell.

'It's going to be a strain,' I said.

She gave an opaque smile.

'It's a strain on your husband,' I said.

'He's used to it,' said Mrs Drawbell.

Had she any feeling for him, I wondered? She was his ally; in her immobile fashion, she tried to help him on: it was she who, finding that Martin and Irene had no room to spare, had invited me to stay. Yet she spoke of him with less tenderness than many women speak of their doctors.

Then she talked of Mary Pearson's children; Mrs Drawbell was looking after them for the day. She was confident that their mother's treatment was wrong and her own right. Densely, confidently, with a curious air of being about to offer affection, she pressed her case upon me and was demanding my moral support. I could not help remembering her on my way to the hangar, irritated as I was in any period of suspense that other lives should be going on, with their own egotisms, claiming one's attention, intruding their desires.

I felt my suspense about that day's experiment increase, having been forced to think of something else. When I saw Mary Pearson, sitting at a bench close to the pile, I was short to her; her skin flushed, her eyes clouded behind her spectacles. I made some sort of apology. I could not explain that I felt more keyed up because her name had distracted me.

The hangar was noisy that morning, like a cathedral echoing a party of soldiers. Workmen, mechanics, young scientists, went in and out through the door in the pile's outer wall; Luke was shouting to someone on top of the pile; Martin and a couple of assistants were disentangling the wire from an electrical apparatus on the floor. There were at least twenty men in the hangar, and Mary Pearson was the only woman. And in the middle, white-walled, about three times the height of a man, stood – catching our eyes as though it were a sacred stone – the pile.

Luke greeted me. He was wearing a windjacket tucked into his grey flannel trousers.

'Well, Lewis,' he shouted, 'we're in the hell of a mess.'

'It will be all right on the night,' said someone. There was a burst of laughter, laughter noisy, exultant, with just a prickle of nerves.

The 'pipery' (Luke meant the pipes, but his scientific idiom was getting richer as he grew more triumphant) had 'stood up to' all tests. The uranium slugs were in place. In the past week, Martin had put in a dribble of heavy water, and a test sample had picked up no impurities. But there was one 'bloody last-minute snag' like finding just at the critical moment that you have forgotten – Luke produced a bedroom simile. Most of the 'circuitry', like the pipery, was in order: there was trouble with one switch of the control rods.

'We can't start without them,' said Luke. Martin joined us: I did not wish to ask questions, any question seemed to delay the issue, but they told me how the control rods worked. 'If the pile gets too hot, then they automatically shut the whole thing off,' said Luke.

'Otherwise,' said Martin, 'there is a finite danger that the reaction would be uncontrollable.'

That meant – I knew enough to follow – the pile might turn into something like a nuclear bomb.

Both Luke and Martin were themselves working on the circuits. A couple of radio engineers wanted Luke to let them improvise a switch.

'Think again,' said Luke. 'That cut-off is going to work as we intended it to work, if it means plugging away at the circuits until this time tomorrow.'

Someone went on arguing.

'Curtains,' said Luke.

As Martin returned to the labyrinth of wires, both he and Luke ready to finger valves for hours to come, I wished I had stayed away or that they had a job for me. All I could do was drag up a chair to Mary Pearson's bench. She was self-conscious, perhaps because I had been brusque, perhaps because, with her husband away, she was uncomfortable in the presence of men. Already that morning I had seen some of the youths, gauche but virile, eyeing her. When I sat beside her, though she was not comfortable herself, it was in her nature to try to make me so.

In front of her were instruments which she had been taught to read; she was a competent girl, I thought, she would have made an admirable nurse. There was one of the counters whose ticking I had come to expect in any Barford laboratory; there was a logarithmic amplifier, a D.C. amplifier, with faces like speedometers, which would give a measure – she had picked up some of the jargon – of the 'neutron flux'.

On the bench was pinned a sheet of graph paper and it was there that she was to plot the course of the experiment. As the heavy water was poured in, the neutron flux would rise: the points on the graph would lead down to a spot where the pile had started to run, where the chain reaction had begun.

'That's going to be the great moment,' said Mary.

The tap and rattle, the curses and argument, the flashes of light, went on round us, I continued to talk to Mary, lowering my voice – though there was no need, for the scientists were shouting. Once or twice she contradicted me, her kind mouth showed a touch of sexual obstinacy. Like many happy, passionate, good-natured women, she had just a trace more than her fair share of self-regard. The morning ticked on, mid-day, the early afternoon, none of us had spoken of eating. It must have been after two o'clock when one of the refugees discovered the fault.

At once a conference sprang up, between Mary Pearson's bench and the pile. If they wanted a 'permanent solution', so that they need not worry about the control rods for the next year, it would take twenty-four hours: on the other hand it would be very little risk to patch up a circuit for a trial run, and that could be ready by evening.

Luke stood by himself, square, toeing the floor, his lips chewed in.

'No,' he said loudly, 'there are some risks you have to take and there are some you haven't. A week might possibly matter, but a day damned well can't. We'll get it right before we start.'

A voice complained: 'We said we should be running on the twenty-second.'

Luke said: 'Well, we now say that we shall be running on the twenty-third.'

He was right. They all knew it. It was only Martin, who, as he and Luke came out of the scrimmage towards me, said, in a tone that the others could not hear:

'It's a pity for the sake of public relations.'

'You'd better look after them,' said Luke. For a moment, his energy had left him. Everyone who was working there trusted him, because they felt (as his seniors did not) that underneath his brashness there was a bedrock of sense. But for Luke himself, it took an effort for the sense to win.

'Tell them we've called it a day,' said Luke with fatigue. 'They can see the fireworks about teatime tomorrow.'

'Not earlier than eight tomorrow night,' said Martin.

For an hour, Martin went off to play politics: explaining to the senior men at Barford, Drawbell, Mounteney and the rest, who were expected to come to the 'opening' that night, the reason for the delay: telephoning Rose and others in London. I offered to get the news through to Rose myself, but Martin chose to do it all.

Mary Pearson left to fetch sandwiches, voices blew about the hangar, Luke and his team were stripping a lead on top of the pile, and I was able to slip away.

Out of duty, I visited Irene and the child, who was just a year old. Irene said nothing of our last meeting, but as I was playing with the baby she remarked, all of a sudden:

'Lewis, you'd rather be alone, wouldn't you?'

I asked what she meant.

'You and Martin are very much alike, you know. You'd like to hide until this thing is settled, wouldn't you?'

With her eyes fixed on me, I admitted it.

'So would he,' said Irene.

With the half-malicious understanding that was springing up between us, she sent me off on my own. I did not want to speak to anyone I knew at Barford, not Mounteney, not Luke, Martin least of all. I made an excuse to Mrs Drawbell that some old acquaintance had asked me out to dinner, but in fact I took the bus to Warwick and spent the evening in a public house.

There I saw only one person from Barford – young Sawbridge, whom we had interviewed twelve months before. Somehow I was driven to be friendly, to get some response of goodwill out of him, as though he were a mascot for the following night.

I stood him a drink, and said something about our native town.

'I've not got much use for it,' said Sawbridge.

It would have soothed me to be sentimental that night. I mentioned some of my friends of the twenties – George Passant – no, Sawbridge had never heard of him.

I kept affectionate memories of the town then, and said so.

'You just lump it down anywhere in America,' said Sawbridge with anger, 'and no one could tell the difference.'

I gave it up, and asked him to have another drink.

'I don't mind if I do,' said Sawbridge.

The next day I got through the hours in the same fashion, sitting in the library, walking by the riverside. The afternoon was quiet, there was no wind; it would have been pleasant to be strolling so, waiting for nothing, with that night's result behind me. The elm twigs were thickening, the twigs in the hedges were dense and black, but there were no leaves anywhere. All was dusky, just before the break of the leaf – except for a patch where the blackthorn shone white, solid, and bare, standing out before the sullen promise of the hedgerow.

I went straight from the blackthorn blossom and the leafless hedge back to the hangar, where the shadow of the pile lay black on the geometrically levelled floor. Martin and Luke were drinking tea on a littered bench close to Mary's and someone was calling instructions by numbers.

They told me that all was ready 'bar the juice'. The juice was heavy water, and it took the next hour to carry it into the hangar. I went with some of the scientists in the first carrying party; they walked among the huts in the spring evening laughing like students on their way back from the laboratory. The heavy water depot stood on the edge of the airfield, a red-brick cube with two sentries at the door; there was a hiatus, then, because the young men had no sense of form but the storekeeper had. He was an old warrant officer with protruding eyes; his instructions said that he could not deliver heavy water except on certain signatures. Against curses, against the rational, nagging, contentious, scientific argument, he just pointed to his rubric, and Martin had to be fetched. He was polite with the storekeeper; to me, he smiled, the only smile of detachment on his face in those two days. The scientists followed into the depot one by one, and came out with what looked like enormous thermos flasks, which were the containers of heavy water.

Casually the young men joggled back, the silver flasks flashing in the cold green twilight. About it all there was an overwhelming air of jauntiness and youth; it might have been a party of hikers carrying bottles of beer. It was a scene that, even as it took place, I felt obliged to remember

– the file in sweaters and grey flannel trousers, swinging the silver flasks, the faces young, thin, disrespectful, masculine.

'Each of those flasks cost God knows what,' said Martin as we watched. He did some mental arithmetic. 'About two thousand pounds.'

By seven o'clock some hundreds of flasks were standing behind the pile. When I discovered that the heavy water from those flasks was going to be poured in by hand, it did not strike me as foreign. It was like much that I had picked up in the air at Cambridge and which Luke and Mounteney and Martin had carried with them. The pile, engineered to a thousandth of an inch; the metals, analytically pure as metals had not been pure before; the whole structure, the most perfect example of the quantitative accuracy of the age; and then Martin and his men were going to slop in the heavy water as though filling up a bath with buckets. They did not mind being slapdash when it did not matter; they took a certain pride in it, like the older generation of Cambridge scientists; the next pile they made, they conceded, they would have the 'juice' syphoned in.

'All set, I think,' said Martin to Luke. Mary Pearson was sitting at her bench, an assistant watching another instrument at her side. Martin's team formed a knot by the pile door. The wall close by was filling with the rest of Luke's staff, for word had gone round that the experiment was due to begin. Drawbell was also there and – it seemed a gallant gesture – Rudd. Mounteney had sent a message that he would come 'as soon as things got significant' (all knew that, for an hour or so, till the pile was half full of heavy water, no one could tell whether it was about to 'run').

Drawbell and the security officers had thought it unrealistic to keep the experiment secret within the establishment. Anyone was allowed in the hangar who would normally have been let in there in the course of business – so that several of the wives, employed in the Barford offices, came in.

The women in the hangar were wearing jerseys and overcoats to guard against the sharp night. Among the blur of faces I saw Hanna Puchwein's glossy head close to young Sawbridge's. Nora Luke, her hair piled up in a bun, had gone pallid with the months of tension which had not lined, but puffed out, her face.

At half past seven there were about seventy people in the hangar, perhaps a third of them spectators. They occupied a crescent that left the pile and the instrument tables free, encroached nowhere near the ranks of heavy water flasks and the filling station, and which marked out a kind of quarter deck where Luke could walk to and fro, from the pile to Mary Pearson's graph.

He was there alone, now that Martin had gone to the filling place. Luke had slept three hours the night before, he was still wearing the windjacket and crumpled trousers, but he made the quick exercising movements of a man about to start a long-distance race.

'Anything stopping you?' he called to Martin.

'Nothing at all,' said Martin.

'Then let her go.'

For an hour it was anti-climax. We could not see much of it, just the scurry of Martin and the others behind the pile, pouring in flask after flask. 'A quarter full,' Martin said at eight o'clock.

Mary Pearson read the flux and made a point on the graph. Luke and Martin nodded; all was as it should be. Martin said: 'My turn to do some more pouring.'

'Glug glug,' said Luke.

As the level of heavy water rose, they poured more slowly. At last: 'Half full.' Mary scrutinised the indicator and inked in another point. Did she know, I was thinking, exactly where those points should fall to mean success? Luke looked over her shoulder.

'There or thereabouts,' he said quietly to Mounteney, who had come in a quarter of an hour before.

Although he had spoken in a low tone, somehow the crowd picked up the first intimation of good news. The excitement was sharper, they were quiet, they were on edge for something to cheer. Once more Martin came round and also studied the graph. 'Not so bad,' he whispered to Luke, raising an eyebrow, and then called out to the man at the filling place: 'Slowly now. Only when I say.'

Flask by flask, the level went up from halfway. Mary was reading the flux each minute now. To the first points after halfway, neither Luke nor Martin paid much attention. Then, as the minutes went on, they both stood by her watching each point. No one else went near the instrument. The excitement stayed, they were ready for Luke to say – 'In —— minutes from now the chain reaction will begin.'

Luke and Martin were staring down at the graph. I could not see their faces. I had almost no fears left. Certainly I did not watch Mary's hand as the level went up to 0.55, inserting a point as though her fingers were weighed down. As her pen stopped above the next point, Luke and Martin straightened themselves and looked at each other. Still the mood round me, the expectancy and elation, had not changed. Luke's glance at Martin might have told me nothing; but Martin's at Luke in one instant let me know the worst.

CHAPTER XVII

QUARREL AT FIRST LIGHT

As Martin and Luke looked at each other, no one round realised what the graph had told them. Someone threw in a scientific gibe about 'cooking' and Luke replied. He said to the men at the filling place: 'Hold it for a minute.' Even then, no one, not even Mounteney, suspected.

Luke left Mary's bench, pushed through the crowd, and, his stiff strong back straight, walked rapidly to his little office at the hangar side. That was nothing startling; he had done so three times since the experiment began. Martin remained on the 'quarter deck' space, strolled over to the pile and back to Mary's instrument bench, then, with an air of casualness, as it were absentmindedly, followed Luke. The scientists were chattering round me, relaxed until Luke came back; I did not attract attention, when in a moment I also followed.

In the office Martin was sitting on a chair, his arms rigid by his sides, while Luke paced from the window to the door, three stamping steps, turned, three steps to the window, like a wild dog in the zoo.

As I went in, Martin did not move, greeted me only with his eyes.

'Hallo,' he said.

'If only I'd made the whole thing bigger!' Luke was saying, in a grinding voice.

'In fact we didn't,' said Martin.

'How bad is it?' I had to ask.

'It's pretty bad,' said Martin.

Luke cried:

'If only I'd made the thing fifty per cent bigger. Then whatever's gone wrong, it would still have worked!'

'I can't blame ourselves for *that*,' said Martin. His tone was bitter.

'What do you blame us for?' Luke stopped and rounded on him.

'We spoke too soon,' said Martin.

'You mean,' said Luke, 'that I never know when to keep my mouth shut.'

'It doesn't matter what caused it,' said Martin, and his temper for once was ready to match Luke's. 'We've got to take the consequences.'

'Yes,' Luke broke out, 'you're going to look a fool because of me.'

They each felt the fury of collaborators. The fabric of businesslike affection opened, and one saw – Martin's anger at having been led astray, his dislike of trusting his leader too far, perhaps his dislike of having a leader at all, perhaps a flicker of the obscure, destructive satisfaction that comes to a junior partner in a failure for which he is not to blame. One saw Luke's resentment at the partner to whom he had done harm, the ferocious resentment of the leader to someone he has led into failure. Luke was a responsible, confident man, he knew Martin had served him with complete loyalty: in disaster he was choked with anger at the sight of Martin's face.

But those feelings were not their deepest. Each was face to face with his own disaster. Each was taking it in his own fashion. I did not know which was being hurt more.

Martin said: 'It will give some simple pleasure in various quarters.'

He had tried to teach himself not to be proud, he had set out to be sensible, calculating, prepared to risk snubs, but there was a nerve of pride hidden beneath. Now he was preparing himself for a humiliation. He had tried to be content with little, but this time he had believed that what he wanted was in his hands; he was composing himself again to expect nothing.

To Luke, even to me, his stoicism seemed enviable. To himself, it was like an invalid pretending to feel better for the benefit of his visitors and then sinking down when they had gone.

Luke made no attempt at stoicism, less than most men. He assumed that he was the more wretched.

'Why are the wise old jaw-bacons always right?' he cried, repeating criticisms that had been made of him, dwelling on them, sometimes agreeing with them. 'When shall I blasted well learn not to make a mess of things? If ever the jaw-bacons had a good idea, they would handle it without any of this nonsense. How can I go and tell them that their damn silly short-sighted fatuous bloody ignorant criticism has just turned out right all the time?'

Yet, though he might feel more ashamed than Martin, though he would have no guard at all when he heard what Mounteney and the others had to say, he would recover sooner. Even in his wretchedness, his powers were beginning to reassert themselves. It was frustration to him to feel those powers deprived, to know that through his own fault he had not fulfilled them; until the pile was running, he would know self-reproach like a hunger of the flesh; but underneath the misery and self-accusation his resolve was taking shape.

'It was just on the edge of being right,' he said. 'Why in God's name didn't I get it quite right?

'What is stopping them [the neutrons]?

347

'Brother Rudd will have a nice sleep tonight. Well, I can't grudge him that.

'The heavy water is all right.

'The electronics are all right.

'The engineering is all right.

'I only hope the Germans are capable of making bloody fools of themselves like this. Or anyone else who gets as far. I tell you we've got as near as kiss your hand.

'*The engineering is all right.*

'*The heavy water is all right.*

'*The uranium is all right.*

'*The uranium is all right.*

'No, it blasted well can't be.

'*That must be it.* It must be the uranium – there's something left there stopping the neuts.'

Martin, who had been sitting so still that he might not have heard Luke's outburst, suddenly broke in. From the beginning they had known that the uranium had to be pure to a degree that made them need a new metallurgy. After all, that still might not be pure enough. Was there an impurity, present in minute quantities, which happened to have great stopping power? I heard names strange to me. One Luke kept repeating (it was gadolinium, though on the spot my ear did not pick it up). 'That's it,' he cried.

'There might be others,' said Martin.

'No,' said Luke. '*That's it.*'

'I'm not convinced,' said Martin.

But he was. Even that night, Luke's authority had surged up again.

Later, other scientists said there was nothing wonderful about Luke's diagnosis; anyone would have reached it, given a cool head and a little time. What some of them did praise (even those who only passed compliments on those securely dead) was his recuperative power.

They did not see him just a moment after his flare of certainty. He knew what was wrong, he could stiffen himself to months' more work: but there was something to do first.

He stopped his pacing, put a hand on the desk and spoke to Martin. 'Do you think they rumbled?'

(He meant the other scientists waiting by the pile.)

'I doubt it,' said Martin.

'I should have thought they must. They must be thinking that I've given then the laugh of a lifetime.'

'I don't think so,' said Martin.

'They've got to be told.'

Martin nodded. His own face pale, he was watching Luke's. Luke broke out:

'I can't do it.' His bounce had quitted him; his active nature had gone dead.

Martin pressed in his lips.

'I'll do it,' he said.

Then Luke took hold of the desk and shook himself, shook his heavy shoulders like a dog on the beach.

'No, I must do it,' he said. 'You've got more nerve than I have, but you'd be too diplomatic. It's a mistake to be diplomatic about a bloody fiasco.'

'You're right,' said Martin. For the first time since I came into that office, there was a comradely glance between them.

Luke went straight to the door.

'Here we go,' he said.

But, as they stood in the open hangar, with the crowd between them and the pile, Luke muttered:

'I'm going to try another reading, just on the off chance.'

Even now he was hoping for a miracle to save him. He walked, arms swinging, to the instrument bench, and once more studied the graph. He called out:

'Take her up to o.6.' Martin stood by his side. They had been gone less than twenty minutes. There was a stir in the spectators round me, but I did not hear any word of doubt. Mary Pearson's hair was close to the table as she read the indicator. With a slow sweep, like the movement of someone drugged, retarded but not jerky, her hand moved over the graph paper. The instant her pen point came to rest, Luke snatched the sheet from her. He glanced – showed it to Martin – threw it on to the bench – more quickly than a man could light a cigarette. He took a step forward, and in a loud, slow, inflexible voice said:

'It's a flop. That's all for tonight. We'll get it right, but it's going to take some time.'

A hush. A hysterical laugh. A gasp. Men talking at once. Pushing up her glasses, Mary Pearson began to sob, tears rolling down her face. I caught sight of young Sawbridge, his mouth open with pain like a Marathon runner's: for once I saw emotion on his face, he too was nearly crying.

Drawbell, Rudd and Mounteney pushed towards the graph.

'What is all this?' Mounteney was asking irritably. 'What has the k got up to?'

Rudd said to Martin: 'Never mind, old chap. It might happen to anyone.'

'Not quite like this,' said Martin, looking straight into Rudd's eyes, in search of the gloating that he expected in all eyes just then.

In the hubbub, the high questions, the hot wash of feeling more alive that men get from any catastrophe not their own, Drawbell took command. Mounting on Mary Pearson's chair he shouted for attention; and as they huddled round him, as round an orator in Hyde Park, he stood quite still with an expression steady, friendly, undisturbed.

When they were looking up at him, he spoke, with the same steadiness:

'Now I'm going to send you home. We'll begin the inquest tomorrow, and I shall give you a statement all in good time. But I don't want you to go home tonight in the wrong frame of mind. It's true that the experiment hasn't worked according to plan, and Luke was right to tell us so. I'm not going to raise false hopes, so I shan't say any more about that. But I do tell you something else: that even if the worst comes to the worst, this experiment had taught us more about our job than any establishment in the world, except our friends across the Atlantic. We shall finish up better because we've had our setbacks. This isn't the end, this is the beginning.'

Without a flash of his own disappointments, free from the thought of honours receding from him that night, without a tremor of *schadenfreude* at Luke's fall, Drawbell stood there, happier with a crowd than ever with a single person, engrossed in infecting them with his own curious courage, delighted (as the complex sometimes are) because he was behaving well. It was he who cleared the hangar, to allow Luke and Martin to get back to their office undisturbed. Outside on the floor round the pile, there was soon no one left, except Nora Luke; we looked at each other without a word, unable to go away.

'We'd better ask,' she said at last, as we stood helplessly there, 'whether we can be any use.'

In the office, Luke and Martin were both sitting down. As Nora saw her husband she said, awkwardly, wishing from the bottom of her heart that she could let herself go:

'Bad luck.'

It was Martin who replied, picking up Drawbell's speech with harsh irony:

'We shall finish up better because we've had our setbacks.'

To his wife, Luke said,
'Let's have some tea.'

That was the first pot of tea. Nora made five others before the night ended. Like other men of action, Luke talked more as he grew more tired. What to do? – decisions of his kind were not made in monosyllables, they were made in repetitive soliloquies, often in speeches that got nowhere, that were more like singing than the ordinary give and take of talk. Yet out of that welter sprang, several times that night, a new resolve, one more point ticked off.

Meanwhile, Nora sat by, calculating for him how many (if his assumption were right) uranium slugs would have to be replaced, before the pile would run. It was a long calculation; she carried it out like the professional mathematician that she was; sometimes she glanced at Luke, distrusting herself, thinking that another woman might have given him rest. But she was wrong. His bad time was behind him, of us all he was the least broken.

As Luke talked more, Martin became more silent. He took in each new plan, he answered questions; but through the small hours he sat volunteering no words of his own, giving his opinion when Luke asked for it, like a sensible second-in-command – and yet each time I heard that controlled voice I knew that he was eating himself up with hopes in retrospect, with that singular kind of might-have-been (such as I had known myself often enough and last seen in Jago when he lost the Mastership) that twists one's bowels because it still grips one like a hope.

As I looked at Martin, my disappointment for him, which had started anew, the instant I caught the glance between him and Luke over the graph, was growing so that it drained me of all other feelings, of patience, of sympathy, of affection. This might have been the night of his success. Now it came to the test, that was my only hunger. I had none to spare for the project; on the other hand, I did not give a thought for our forebodings with Mounteney by the river. I had none of the frustration that Luke felt and perhaps Martin also, because they were being kept at arm's length from a piece of scientific truth. For me, this ought to have been the night of Martin's success. I was bitter with him because it had gone wrong.

At last Luke said, his voice still resonant, that we had done enough for one night, and Martin and I walked together out of the hangar door. The sky was dark, without any stars, but in the east there was a pallor that seemed less comforting.

'First light,' said Martin.

I could not help myself. I broke out of control:

'Is this ever going to come off?'

'Is what ever going to come off?'

It was one of his stoical tricks, to pretend not to understand.

'You know what I mean.'

Martin paused.

'I should think your guess is about as good as mine,' he said.

I tried, but I could not keep quiet:

'Perhaps it's a pity that you burned your boats.'

'That's possible,' said Martin.

'Perhaps it wasn't sensible to invest all your future in one man.'

'I've thought of that,' said Martin.

'Luke's enemies have always said that he'd make one big mistake,' I said. I could hear in my own voice, and could not hold it down, the special cruelty that can break out of any 'unselfish' love, of a father's or a brother's, with anyone who is asking nothing for himself – except that the other person should fulfil one's dreams, often one's self-identificatory dreams. If you see yourself in another, you see all you would like to be: so you can be more self-sacrificing than in any other human relation, because it does not seem like sacrifice: for the same reason you can be more cruel. Would Martin have liked to be told that he would go through an unselfish love like that – when his son grew up?

'I've thought of that also.'

'Is this going to be his big mistake?' I asked.

For the first time, Martin turned against me; his voice was quieter but as bitter as mine.

'You're not making it any easier,' he said.

Ashamed, suddenly stricken by his misery, I said that I was sorry, and we walked in silence, making our way towards the Drawbells' house. We had quarrelled only once before, when I interfered over his marriage, and that had been just skin deep. Finding I could not put the words together to comfort him or tell him my regret for the past minutes, I muttered that I would see him home.

'Do,' said Martin.

Neither of us said much, as we walked along the footpath in the cold, slow dawn. What we had said could not be taken back; yet it seemed to have passed. Once Martin made a formal attempt to console me. He said:

'Don't worry too much: it may turn out all right.'

A little later, he said:

'If I had the choice about Luke to make all over again, I should do exactly the same as before.'

The hedges smelt wet, the blackthorn blossom was ectoplasmic on the morning dark. We came to the little road that led to Martin's. In front of us, stretching from the path to a cottage roof, was the dim shape of a ladder. As I went under, I could feel Martin hesitate and then take three quick steps round. He said, with a sarcastic smile: 'I need all the luck I can get.'

Making out his face in the twilight, I was wondering whether he, too, in that moment of superstition, had thought of our mother: who also had been superstitious: who, with her toes pointed out, would go round any ladder: who possessed just his kind of stoicism, invented to conceal an insatiable romantic hope: and who in his place, this morning after the fiasco, would be cherishing the first new pictures of wonderful triumphs to come.

It was strange to think that the same might be true of him.

PART THREE

A RESULT IN PUBLIC

CHAPTER XVIII

REQUEST FOR AN OFFICIAL OPINION

As soon as I woke, the night's fiasco clinched itself out of the morning light. It was mid-day, not many hours since I left Martin outside his house.

Unable to keep myself away, hurrying to the laboratories to hear remarks that I did not want to hear, I found Luke and Martin already there. They might have been following old Bevill's first rule for any kind of politics: if there is a crisis, if anyone can do you harm *or* good, he used to say, looking simple, never mind your dignity, never mind your nerves, but *always be present in the flesh*.

Even that morning, Martin might have had the self-control to act on such advice: but it was more likely, in Luke's case certain, that they had come in order to argue a way through the criticisms and get to work the same day.

There were many criticisms. There was – to my ears, used to a different climate, less bracing and perhaps more hypocritical – astonishingly little sympathy. Most people had no thought to spare for Luke's or Martin's feelings; they were concerned with why the pile had not run last night, whether Luke's diagnosis was correct, how long the 'mods' (modifications) would take.

There were scientists' jokes. Was this, Mounteney asked, the most expensive negative result in scientific history? It was their own kind of jibing, abstract, not specially ill-natured. I should have preferred to go on listening, rather than return to London and make my report to Hector Rose.

Arriving in the office late that afternoon I found a message waiting for me: Sir Hector's compliments, and, when I could spare the time, would I make an opportunity to call on him?

I went at once to get the interview over. Rose's room looked over the trees of St James's Park, stirring that evening in the wind, bright in the cold sunshine. Rose was standing up, bowing from the waist, greeting me with his elaborate courtesy.

'It's very, very good of you to spare me a minute, my dear Eliot.' He put me in the armchair near his desk, from which I could smell the hyacinths on the little table by the window: even in wartime, he replaced his flowers each day. Then he offered me his cigarette case. It was like him to carry cigarettes for his visitors, though he did not smoke himself. Had my journey that afternoon been excessively uncomfortable, he asked, had I been able to get a reasonable luncheon?

Then he looked at me, his face still unnaturally youthful, expressionless, his eyes light.

'I gather that everything did not go precisely according to expectation?' I said that I was afraid not.

'You will appreciate, my dear Eliot, that it is rather unfortunate. There has been slightly too much criticism of this project to be comfortable, all along.'

I was well aware of it.

'It may have been a mistake,' said Rose, 'not to take the course of least resistance, and pack them all off to America.'

'It may have been,' I said. 'If so, I helped to make it.'

'I'm afraid you did,' said Rose, with his usual cool justice. With the same justice, he added: 'So did I.'

'It may have been a mistake,' he went on smoothly, 'but it was Dr Luke and his comrades who led us up the garden path.'

Suddenly the smooth masterful official tone crackled: he had a blaze of ordinary human irritation.

'Good Lord,' he snapped, 'they talk too much and do too little!'

But Rose had the gift of being able to switch off his disappointment. Sometimes I thought it the most useful gift a man of affairs could possess, sometimes the most chilling.

'However,' said Rose, 'all that can wait. Now I should like to benefit by your advice, my dear Eliot. What do you suggest as the next step?'

I had been waiting for it.

I said, as honestly as I could, that there seemed to me two possible courses: one, to cut our losses, break up Barford, and distribute the scientists among the American projects (for Luke and Martin, that would be open failure): two, to reinvest in Luke.

'What is your personal opinion?'

'I'm not entirely impartial, you know,' I said.

'I'm perfectly sure that you can see the problem with your admirable detachment,' said Rose. The remark had the sarcastic flick of his tongue: but it was not meant as a sarcasm. For Rose it was easy to eliminate a personal consideration, and he would have despised me if I could not do the same.

I tried to. I said, as was true, that most people at Barford believed the pile would ultimately work; it might take months, it might (if Luke's diagnosis were wrong) take several years. There was a chance, how good I could not guess, that the pile would still work quickly; it meant giving Luke even more money, even more men.

'If you're not prepared for that,' I said, hearing my voice sound remote. 'I should be against any compromise. You've either got to show some faith now – or give the whole thing up in this country.'

'Double or quits,' said Rose, 'if I haven't misunderstood you, my dear chap?'

I nodded my head.

'And again, if I haven't misunderstood you, you'd have a shade of preference, but not a very decided shade, for doubling?'

I nodded my head once more.

Rose considered, assembling the threads of the problem, the scientific forecasts, the struggles on his committees, the Ministerial views.

'This is rather an awkward one,' he said. He stood up and gave his polite youthful bow.

'Well,' he said, 'I'm most indebted to you and I'm sorry to have taken so much of your valuable time. I must think this one out, but I'm extremely grateful for your suggestions.'

CHAPTER XIX

A NEW WHISPER

THOUGH Hector Rose had left me in suspense about his intention, I did not worry much. Despite our mutual unease I trusted his mind, and for a strong mind there was only one way open.

Thus Luke, in the midst of disapproval, got all he asked for, and went back to playing his piano. There were months to get through before the pile was refitted. He and Martin had to set themselves for another wait.

It was during that wait that I had my first intimation of a different kind of secret. One of the security branches had begun asking questions. They had some evidence (so it seemed, through the muffled hints) that there might have been a leakage.

As men spoke of it, their voices took on that hushed staccato in which all of us, even on the right side of the law, seemed like conspirators. None of us knew what the evidence was, and the only hints we received were not dramatic, merely that a Barford paper had 'got loose'. We were not told where and the paper itself was unimportant. It was nothing but a 1943 estimate of the destructive power of the nuclear bomb. I looked it up in our secret files; it was signed by a refugee called Pavia, by Nora Luke and other mathematicians, and was called *Appreciation of the Effects of Fission Weapons*.

The typescript was faded, in the margin were some corrections in a high, thin, Italian hand. Much of the argument was in mathematical symbols, but, after twenty pages of calculation, some conclusions were set out in double spacing, in the military jargon of the day, with phrases like 'casualisation', 'ground zero', 'severe destruction'.

These conclusions meant that, in one explosion over the centre of a town, about 300,000 people would be killed instantly, and a similar number would later die of injuries. This was the standard Barford calculation at that time, and it was the figure that we had in mind when Mounteney, Martin and I talked by the river at Stratford.

Anyone who worked on the inside of scientific war saw such documents. And most men took it as part of the day-by-day routine, without emotion; it had to be done, if you were living in society, if you were one ant in the anthill. In fact most men did not need to justify themselves, but just performed their duty to society, made the calculations they were asked to make, and passed the paper on.

Once, alone in my office in the middle of the war, it occurred to me: there must exist *memoranda* about concentration camps: people must be writing their views on the effects of a reduction in rations, comparing the death rate this year with last.

I heard of the leakage, I re-read the appreciation, I heard the name of Captain Smith. He was high up, as I already knew, in one of the intelligence services. I also knew that he was a naval officer on the retired list, several times decorated in the first war, the son of a bishop. But when he came to visit me, I did not know what to expect.

He was a man in the fifties, with fairish hair and a lean, athletic figure. His face was stiff and strained, both in the cheeks and mouth. His eyes seemed to protrude, but more exactly had a fixed, light-irised stare. He was dressed with the elegance of an actor. His whole bearing was stiff, and soon after he came in, when a flying bomb grunted and vibrated outside, cut off, and then jarred the floor beneath us (it was by now the July of 1944), all the notice he took was a slight stiff inclination sideways, arms straight by his side.

That impression might have been both putting-off and appropriate when one knew in advance his berserk record; but it did not last. It was destroyed, very oddly, by a smile which was so sudden, so artificial, that it might have been switched on. I had never seen a smile so false, and yet somehow it sweetened him.

He had come, he said, for a 'little confab' about some of our 'mutual friends' at Barford.

'I've been told,' I said, 'that you've been having a bit of trouble.'

'We don't want to blot our copy book,' said Captain Smith mysteriously, in a creaking and yet ingratiating voice.

'Nothing very serious has got out, has it?'

'I wish I knew: do you?' he said with his formidable stare, then switched on his smile.

'If one thing gets out, another can. That's why we get all hot and bothered,' he added.

Suddenly he asked:

'Know anything of a young man called Sawbridge?'

I had imagined that he might bring out other names. I felt relief because this one meant little to me. I explained that I had been present at Sawbridge's interview, and since then had talked to him alone just once at Warwick, the night before the failure of the pile.

'I didn't get much out of him,' I said.

'I just thought you might have known him at home,' said Smith.

He had found out – it was one up to his method – that Sawbridge's family had lived close to mine. I said that, when I left the town for London in 1927, he could only have been eight or nine. My brother Martin was more likely to know him.

'I haven't forgotten M. F. Eliot,' said Smith, with his false, endearing smile.

I had spent enough time with security officers to leave the talking to him: but he was too shrewd to do what some did, and bank on the mystery of his job. He stared at me.

'I suspect you're wondering what all this is in aid of,' he said.

I said yes.

'There are one or two straws in the wind, and we've got an idea that the young man may not have been altogether wise.'

He gave me two facts, maybe in order to conceal others. Sawbridge had attended anti-war meetings, organised by the Communist Party, in 1940–1: at the University he had been a member of a pro-Communist group.

'He's certainly gone off the rails a bit,' said Smith.

At Barford they thought that Smith was a fool. They were quite wrong; he was highly intelligent, and very far, much further than many of the scientists, from being a commonplace man. The trouble was, he did not speak their language.

His axioms of behaviour were simple, though his character was not. Duty: obedience: if you were told to make a weapon you did so, and kept it secret. There was nothing more to it than that.

To him, the race in nuclear bombs was as natural as a race in building battleships. Your enemies were in it: so were you, so was Russia. You told no one anything, certainly not the Russians. Good fighters, yes, but almost a different species.

Intellectually, he knew something of communism; but he could no more imagine becoming a communist himself, or his friends or relations doing so, than I could imagine becoming a professional burglar.

He had not lived among scientists, their habits of feeling were foreign to him and his to them. As for his axioms of behaviour, most of the scientists, even those not far to the left, could not feel them so; what to him was instinct, to them meant a moral uneasiness at each single point.

Some days after Smith's call, I talked to Martin. It was our first serious talk since the fiasco; his tone sounded unwilling and hard, though that could have been the effect of long-drawn-out suspense. For the first time, his face was pallid and carried anxious lines. He was waiting for the last batch of purified uranium, with unfillable time on his hands.

I asked him if Captain Smith had interviewed him.

Martin nodded.

'I think we ought to have a word,' I said.

He would have liked to put me off. Without showing his usual even temper, he went with me into the park; at times we felt a neurosis of security, and only talked freely in an open space.

The park was empty. It was a windy afternoon with black and ragged clouds; in the distance we heard, as we took two chairs on to the patch of grass nearest the Mall, the cranking of a flying bomb. I said:

'I suppose Smith told you about Sawbridge?'

'Yes.'

'How much is there in it?'

'If you mean,' said Martin, 'that Smith has cleverly found out that Sawbridge is left-wing, that's not exactly news.' He went on: 'If Smith and his friends are going to eliminate all the left-wing people working on fission here and in America, there won't be enough of us left to finish off the job.'

'Do you think Sawbridge has parted with any information?'

'I haven't the slightest idea.'

'Would you say it was impossible?'

Martin said, 'You know him nearly as well as I do.'

I said, 'Do you like him any better?'

Martin shook his head.

'He's a bit of a clod.'

That was my impression. Heavy: opaque: ungracious. I asked if Martin could imagine him fanatical enough to give secrets away.

Martin said: 'In some circumstances, I can imagine better men giving them away – can't you?'

Just for an instant he was speaking without constraint. At that time, his politics were like mine, liberal, considerably to the right of Mounteney, a little to the left of Luke. He had more patience than either with the practical running of the state machine, he was less likely to dismiss Smith out of hand.

Nevertheless, as he heard Smith's enquiries, he felt, almost as sharply as Mounteney, that his scientific code was being treated with contempt.

Martin was a secretive man; but keeping scientific secrets, which to Smith seemed so natural, was to him a piece of evil, even if a necessary evil. In war you had to do it, but you could not pretend to like it. Science was done in the open, that was a reason why it had conquered; if it dwindled away into little secret groups hoarding their results away from each other, it would become no better than a set of recipes, and within a generation would have lost all its ideals and half its efficacy.

Martin, who was out of comparison more realistic than Mounteney or even Luke, knew as well as I did that a good many scientists congratulated themselves on their professional ethic and acted otherwise: in the twenties and thirties, the great days of free science, there had been plenty of men jealous of priority, a few falsifying their results, some pinching their pupils'.

But it had been free science, without secrets, without much national feeling. Men like Mounteney hankered after it as in a murky northern winter one longs for the south Mediterranean. In the twenties and thirties, Mounteney had felt more at home with foreigners working in his own subject than he ever could with Captain Smith or Rose or Bevill.

Some of that spirit had come down to the younger men. Pure science was not national; the truth was the truth, and, in a sensible world, should not be withheld; science belonged to mankind. A good many scientists were as unselfconscious as Victorians in speaking of their ideals as though they were due to their own personal excellence. But the ideals existed. *That* used to be science; if you were ashamed of a sense of super-national dedication, men like Mounteney had no use for you; in the future, *that* must be science again.

Meanwhile, the war had forced their hands; but they often felt, even the most realistic of them, that they were mucking away in the dark. Though they saw no option but to continue, there were times, at this talk of secrets, leakages, espionage, when they turned their minds away.

It was startling to hear Martin break out, because of a violated ideal. In most respects, I thought of him as more earthbound than I was myself. But he would not take part in any more discussion about Sawbridge.

Soon he fell silent, the thoughts of pure science drained away, and he was brooding over the next test of the pile. His nerves had stayed steady throughout the fiasco, but now, within months or weeks of the second chance, they were fraying at last. In the windy August afternoon, the low black clouds drove on.

'If it doesn't go this time,' he said to me, more angrily than he had spoken after the failure, as though holding me to blame, 'you needn't reckon on my future any more.'

CHAPTER XX

THE TASTE OF TRIUMPH

NIGHT after night that September I stayed by my sitting-room window with the curtains open, watching the swathe of light glisten on the dusty bushes in the square. The flying bombs had ceased, and it should have been easy to sleep; often I was wondering when I should get a message from Barford, giving the date of the second attempt to start the pile.

I decided that this time I would not go – but was the date already fixed? From Martin's state I felt it could not be far off.

Sitting by the open window, tasting the autumn nights for the first time since 1939, I thought with regret of my own past troubles – with regret, not because I had undergone them, but because I was living through a quiet, lonely patch. Occasionally I thought of Martin: how many months in his adult life had been free from some ordeal approaching? Was this new one the biggest? Sometimes, from my quiet, I wished I were in his place.

One night at the end of the month, the telephone slowly woke me out of a deep sleep. Faintly it burred, in the hall, as though far away. When at last I understood the noise, I went towards it with dread.

The blue paint had not been taken from the hall bulb. In the crepuscular, livid light, I found the receiver: I heard Martin's voice, active, repeating 'Hallo, hallo, hallo.' Up to that moment I had not thought of him, just of the pounce of bad news, any bad news.

As I muttered his voice came:

'Is that you?'

'Yes.'

'*It's all right.*'

I was stupefied, half awake, half comprehending:

'What's all right?'

I heard:

'The pile began to run an hour ago. 3.5 a.m., the night of 27–8 September – just for purposes of reference.'

The words had been steady, but the flourish gave his joy away.

'Why didn't you tell me you were starting?' I answered with exultation, yet heard my temper rise.

'I thought it was better like this.'

Then I congratulated him.

'Yes, it's something. They can't take this from us.'

In his voice I could hear pure triumph, the words came out with the attack of triumph. If I had heard a friend speak so, even a most intimate friend, I should have known a splinter of rancour – the jag of the question, the egocentric, the irresistible: 'Why hasn't this happened to me?'

Listening to a brother in the pride of triumph, you could not feel even that splinter. It had been the same when I heard the news of his child. Just as in 'unselfish' love you can be crueller (as I was in Martin's failure, which we had neither of us forgotten), so for the same reason you can be less envious. The more unassailable they are in success, the more total your rejoicing: for it is your own.

He could not resist telling me some details, there and then, in the middle of the night. It had been his idea to hold a 'dress rehearsal'. During the summer, they had built a syphoning plant for the heavy water, so they had not required many hands: even of those present, few realised that this was the 'real thing'. They had begun just after midnight, and the filling was still going on. For ten minutes, at the halfway stage, the graph points seemed to be going wrong again. 'That was pretty hard to take,' said Martin. Then the points began to come out according to calculation. In fact, they were coming out slightly better than calculation. Martin for once forgot his listener, and broke into technical language: 'The k is 1.2 already, it's too hot to put in more than three-quarters of the heavy water.

'It's embarrassing that it's gone too well,' he added. 'Still, it's quite a tolerable way to be embarrassed.'

The following afternoon, when he met me at the station, he was just as happy. It was no longer self-discipline that kept his expression firm; one could see the happiness beneath the skin; he was not a man to lose appetite for triumph the moment he had it.

We shook hands, which we did not often do.

'The pile, I think,' said Martin, without asking me where we should go first. He said, as we walked along:

'When it looked as though we were due for another fiasco last night – that was getting near the bone.'

Contentedly browsing over past dramas, Martin led me into a hangar. It was empty, not a single human being in sight; it was noiseless, the pile standing silent in the airy space.

'There she goes,' said Martin. But he did not see the curious sinister emptiness of the place. He was thinking not of the silent, blank-faced pile but of the reaction going on within. He took me to the control room, a cubbyhole full of shining valves with one kitchen chair placed, domestic and incongruous, in front of a panel of indicators. Sitting there was the only other man I had seen that afternoon.

'All well?' asked Martin.

'All well, Dr Eliot,' said the duty officer.

'I still can't quite believe it,' Martin said to me.

As we went out, there was a hallooing from close by, and Luke, who had just tramped in, called us into his office.

'Well, Lewis,' he said, 'this is a bit better.'

'To say the least of it,' I said.

'They ought to have known it was the neatest way to do it.'

'They' were Luke's collection of enemies and detractors, and without malice, or even much interest, he dismissed them. He was sitting on his desk, and suddenly his whole face and body became vigorous.

'There's only one thing that matters now, as I've been saying to Martin this morning,' he said, 'and that is, how soon can we finish it off?'

Martin smiled. For himself, he would have been glad of a breathing space, to luxuriate in the success; to him, it was real success, the first he had had. But then Martin, less humble than Luke as a man, was far more so as a scientist. Luke knew his powers; he knew that this project had not stretched them; it had tested his character, but in terms of scientific imagination, it had needed little. He did not take much pride in the achievement; this was no place to rest; with all his energies, he wanted to push on.

'We've got to make the bloody bomb while we're about it,' said Luke. 'Until we've got the plutonium out, I shan't be able to put my In-tray on top of my Out-tray and go back to something worth doing.'

As I already knew, making the pile work was only the first stage, though the most important, in producing a bomb; second by second, the pile was now changing minute amounts of uranium into plutonium. In a hundred and fifty to two hundred days, they calculated, the transformation would have gone far enough: the slugs could then be taken out to cool: in another ninety days Luke and Martin could begin extracting the plutonium. Luke said they might cut a little off those periods, but not much.

'Perhaps we can begin extracting in March,' he said. 'Which leaves one question sticking out, when is the war going to end?'

This was late September 1944: we all agreed that there was no chance of an end that year. The intelligence teams in Germany were reporting that the Germans had got nowhere with their pile – but Luke and others at Barford found it hard to credit.

'What we can do, so can they,' said Luke. 'Which is one reason why I want to whip that plutonium out. It would be too damn silly if they lifted this one out of the bag before us.'

'What are the other reasons?'

Luke said quietly:

'To tell you the truth, Lewis, I'd rather we got it first – so that we should have some influence in case any maniac wants to use the damned thing.'

It was the first time I had heard Luke talk about anyone using the bomb.

'That is a point,' said Martin.

'But it isn't the real point,' said Luke, his face open and truculent once more. 'Let's come clean with you, Lewis. That's a very good reason, but it isn't the real reason, and you both know that as well as I do. The real reason is just that I can't bear not to come in first.'

They could not touch the rods before 1 March; what was the earliest possible date to possess the plutonium?

Martin said: 'The operative word is "possible".'

Luke said: 'I'll get that stuff out in six weeks from 1 March if it's the last thing I do.'

Martin said: 'It may be.'

'What is the matter?' I said.

Luke and Martin looked at each other.

'There are some hazards,' said Luke.

That was the term they used for physical danger. Luke went on being frank. The 'hazards' might be formidable. No one knew much about handling plutonium; it might well have toxic properties. There would not be time to test each step for safety, they might expose themselves to illness: conceivably grave illness, or worse.

'Is that fair?' Luke said to Martin, when he had finished.

'Quite fair,' said Martin.

There was a silence, which Martin broke:

'I agree with you,' he said, speaking straight to Luke. 'There are good reasons for pushing ahead.'

'I'm glad you admit it at last, anyway,' said Luke.

'I also agree that we've got to accept certain hazards,' said Martin. 'I'm not happy about it, but I'm prepared to take a few modest risks. I don't think, though, that I'm prepared to take the risks you are. I don't believe the reasons justify them.'

'They're ninety per cent conclusive,' said Luke.

'I don't think so,' said Martin.

'I haven't thought it out yet,' said Luke. 'I must get it clear with myself where I stand about the risks. But I think I shall take them.'

'You're not the only person involved,' said Martin.

'Look here,' Luke said, 'this is going to be like walking blindfold, and I'm not beginning to answer for anyone but myself.'

Some of this repartee sounded as though they were repeating the morning's argument, but, for a few moments past, they had seemed surprised by each other. Martin's voice was sharp:

'What do you mean?'

'I mean that I can't ask any of our chaps to put their hands inside the blasted stew,' Luke replied. 'If anyone is going to dabble in chemistry with the lid off, it's me.'

'Just before Lewis arrived,' said Martin, on his side producing something new, 'someone was wanting to volunteer.'

'Who?'

'Sawbridge.'

'Good for him,' said Luke, 'but I can't let him.'

'Yes, I'm quite sure,' said Martin slowly, 'we can't ask any of the others, or even let them volunteer.'

Luke's face was flushed; his tone was quiet and sincere. 'I'm not even asking you,' he said.

Martin considered, rubbing the back of his forefinger across his lip. He was steady with the well-being of success; but he was also resentful, pinched with shame, as a prudent man is on being rushed by a leader much braver than himself.

'I wish I could let you risk it by yourself,' said Martin. 'If I thought it was quite unjustified, I think I might.'

'I'd rather do it myself,' said Luke.

'It may not be possible to let you.'

Suddenly Luke jumped down from the desk.

'Well,' he said, 'there's no need to make the decision yet awhile. It's something that we should be bloody fools to settle until we've had a good cool look at it.'

'If you ask me,' said Martin, rubbing his forefinger across his lip again, 'I'm afraid the decision is already made.'

CHAPTER XXI

BEAM OF LIGHT OVER THE SNOW

THE decision was, in fact, already made. There were months in which to draw back, but no one suggested that Luke could or would. Even to those who disliked and envied him, he gave an impression of simple physical courage; it was the one virtue which, like any other group of men, the Barford scientists uncritically admired.

In those months, he received more respect than ever before.

'Perhaps we ought to be *doing* something for Luke,' I heard a rotund voice say in the Athenæum. That meant, give him a decoration: he was passing into the ranks of solid, respectable men.

Just about the same time, people at Barford noticed that Drawbell, whose Christian name no one had been known to utter, whose friends called him 'C.F.', had begun to sign himself with a large, plain, mesomorphic 'Cyril Drawbell.'

'A bad case of knight starvation,' said someone. It was the kind of joke the scientists did not get tired of.

It was true that Drawbell spent many days in London, calling on Rose and the new Minister; no longer noncommittal, but instead proclaiming 'the success of our Barford policy'. With urgency he told Rose one day that the 'team' deserved some public credit. Rose, who had decided not to meet him halfway, responded with even more than his usual civility.

Drawbell tried his set of personal arts against Rose's politeness, but could not get the response he was playing for. Yes, it was wonderfully exciting, yes, the Minister was well informed of the history of the project, Rose went on mellifluously, but gave no outright official praise to Drawbell, who, with the meeting inconclusive, returned with me to my room.

For once he looked dejected and tired, as though his vitality had sunk low. Suddenly he asked:

'Eliot, do you hate this life?'

He meant the life of officials.

'Sometimes I hate it,' said Drawbell.

He stared at me.

'If anyone asked my reason for existence, what should I tell them?'

I tried to cheer him up, but he interrupted me:

'I'm just a pedlar of *other men's* dreams.'

Like many tricky men, he was wishing his character were simpler. He wished he were not self-seeking. But he did not exude the pathos one often finds in tricky men; his nature was harder than most of theirs. He was angry with himself, still more angry with Rose, and he took it out of me as Rose's proxy.

At Barford he made one intervention, after trying to persuade Luke and Martin to go slow until the health risks were worked out. The only thing he had a right to insist on, he said, was this: they must not both expose themselves to danger at the same time. If one should happen to be laid out, the other must be left intact. It was reasonable, and the two of of them promised it.

All that winter they were experimenting with protective clothing, with various kinds of divers' suit in order to do chemistry-at-a-distance. Sawbridge, who was still asserting his claim to take part, had developed a set of instruments for manipulating the rods out of sight.

Martin spent many of his evenings reading case histories of radiation illness. It seemed probable, he decided, that they would find, as well as the radiation hazards, that plutonium was also a chemical poison.

Luke scoffed at what he called Martin's 'visits to the morgue'. To him, if you could do nothing about a danger, it was best to forget it. But Martin's attitude was the exact opposite; if he were going to face a danger, he wanted to live with it beforehand. If he could become familiar in advance with the radioactive pathologies, he could more easily bear the moment of test. His clinical researches, which seemed to the others morbid, stiffened his resolve. With nothing like Luke's or Sawbridge's bravery of the fibres, Martin was training himself to face the March experiments with resignation.

Meanwhile, he continued to enjoy his taste of success. He was getting rather more than the credit due to Luke's right-hand man; scientific elder statesmen, civil servants like Rose, found him comfortable to talk to, after Luke; he was cagey in speech, he showed respect for etiquette, he had good manners; they were glad when he attended London committees instead of his chief, and on those visits he was taken to the Athenæum more frequently than Luke had ever been.

He liked it. He seemed to view this official life with detachment, but really he saw it through a magnifying glass. I thought to myself that those like Martin, who were born worldly, were always half taken in by the world. Later, I also thought to myself – if you're not half taken in by the world, you won't do anything in it. Including any good you might like to do.

Even with 1 March coming on him, he still kept his satisfaction at having, in a modest sense, 'arrived'. In January, he and Irene, when they came to London for a week's leave, stood me a celebratory dinner. They had borrowed a flat in the first stretch of the Bayswater Road, just opposite the Albion Gate; it was still a luxury to let light stream out across the pavements, striking blue that night from the unswept snow. As we looked out, the middle of the road was dark, for the street lamps had not yet been lit.

We were saying (it was the kind of commonplace that we did not want to escape, since we were so content) how time had slipped by unnoticed, how the street lamps had now been dark for five and a half years. It was six years since Irene and I first met in my old rooms in Cambridge.

'Too long for you, dear?' said Irene to me, mechanically asking for approval.

'You won't go back there, will you?' said Martin to me.

I shook my head: we were each talking at random, the past and future both seemed close.

'You'll have to make your plans, this can't last much longer,' said Martin. We all knew that the war must soon end; as he spoke, Irene started to reply, but stopped herself, her eyes restive.

Martin asked her to bring in the child to say good-night. As she carried him in he stayed quiet, and Martin took him in his arms. Their glances met, the child's a model of the man's, fixed, hard, transparently bright; then with a grave expression, the child turned into his father's shoulder.

Martin's glance did not move from the child's head.

'We must make some plans for you too,' he said. 'I've told you, we've made one or two plans for you already.'

It was after dinner that Martin spoke with an openness that came without any warning, that I had not heard more than twice in his life. He was smoking a cigar, emblem of the celebration that night, but he had drunk little and was cold sober. He had just been mentioning Hector Rose, for whom perversely he had taken a liking – and I teased him about his friends at court.

Martin smiled and without any preliminary said:

'It's nice to have a little confidence.'

He said it simply, naturally, and with gratification.

'I never had enough,' he said to me.

Perhaps it was true, I was thinking: in his struggle to be a scientist, to live in the same air as Mounteney or Luke, he had never believed in himself.

He was still speaking to me:

'I got a bad start.'

'We both did,' I said.

'Mine was worse.'

'How?'

He said:

'You always overshadowed me, you know.'

It was so unexpected that I could not have left it there, but he went on:

'This has done me good.'

I was just beginning to speak when Irene, who had been biting back a worry all the evening, could keep quiet no longer. She cried:

'Then why don't you sit tight when you've got it?'

'That's not so easy,' said Martin.

'Just when we're getting everything we wanted, you're ready to throw it away.'

He said to her:

'We've talked this out, haven't we?'

'I can't let you go on with this madness. Do you expect me just to sit quiet and wait for the end of the war to stop you? I suppose if the war does end you will have a glimmer of sense?'

'If the war ended there wouldn't be any necessity to go so fast,' he said, curiously stiff. His smile had an edge to it. 'I shouldn't be sorry if the necessity didn't arise.'

'You know you're frightened.'

'I am extremely frightened,' said Martin.

'Then why don't you think of yourself?'

'I've told you.'

What had he told her? Probably the coldest motive – that, if he did not follow Luke's lead, he would lose the ground he had won.

'Why don't you think of me?'

'I've told you that, too.'

Her face puckered, she said:

'All you've done is to think of Lewis [the baby]. And I don't know whether you believe it's enough just to insure yourself for him. Do you believe it really matters whether he goes to the sort of school that you two didn't go to?'

For the first time, Martin's tone showed pain. He said:

'I wish I could do more for him.'

Suddenly she switched off – to begin with it was so jarring that one's flesh crept – into a wail for her life in London before her marriage. Though she was wailing for past love affairs, her manner was fervid, almost jaunty; she was talking of a taxi drive in the snow. I had a vivid picture of a girl going hot-faced on a night like this across the park to a man's flat. I believed, though she was just delicate enough not to mention the name, that she was describing her first meeting with Hankins, and that she was using private words so that Martin should know it. Bitterly she was provoking his jealousy. To an extent she succeeded, for neither then nor later was he unmoved by the sound of Hankins's name.

As I listened, I thought I must do like other friends of his, and finish with her. Then I saw the look in her eyes – it was not lust, it was not malice, it was a plea. She had no self-control, she would always be strident – but this was the only way she knew to beg him to be as he used to be.

All of a sudden, I understood a little. I could hear her 'I am defeated' in my flat that night last year which, if it had led one to think that she was leaving Martin, was totally misleading. It was he before whom she felt defeat. I could hear the tone in which, this evening, she had pressed him about the child. Their marriage was changing, in the sense that marriages which start with their disparities often do; the balance of power was altering; their marriage was changing, and she was beating about, lost, bewildered, frightened, trying to keep it in its old state, which to her was precious.

Perhaps it was that the birth of the child had, as Hanna Puchwein had foreseen, disturbed the bond between them. But if so, it had disturbed it in the diametrically opposite direction from that which Hanna had so shrewdly prophesied. It was Martin who was the freer, not Irene.

It seemed possible that the birth of the child had removed or weakened one strand in his love for her. He still had love for her, but the protective part, so powerful in him, so much a part of his whole acceptance of her antics, had been diverted to another. Hearing him speak to his son that evening, or even hearing him speak to her about his son, I felt – and now I knew she felt it also – that all his protective love had gone in love for the child. He would be too anxious about his son, I thought, he would care too much, live too much in him – just as I had at times lived too much in Martin.

So, although he had much feeling left for Irene, he no longer felt driven to look after her. All that was gone; he wanted her to be happy; in his meticulous fashion he had made arrangements for her future in case, in the March experiments, he should be incapacitated or killed; but when he thought of the danger, both of what he might lose and those who might miss him, his only fear that counted alongside his own animal fear was for the child.

While Irene, who when he loved her passionately and protectively had wanted to get away from the protective clutch, now wished it back. She wished him to think first of her, she was anxious about him with all the hungers of vanity, self-esteem, habit, anything that makes us want someone who has drawn into himself.

With another switch, she began asking, with a nagging insistence, about the programme for March.

'This is supposed to be a celebration,' said Martin.

She nagged on. As both she and I knew, the date for the first dissolving of the rods had been put back from 1 March to 10 March.

'That's all right,' she said, 'but which of you is going to make a fool of himself first?'

'Unless anyone insists, which won't be me, I suppose we might have to toss up for it.'

'Have you settled that?' she cried.

He shook his head. 'I haven't spoken to Walter Luke about it recently.' It was the flat truth.

Wildly she turned to me. I was her last hope. Could not I make him behave decently?

I knew that it was no use. Both he and I were behaving with consideration for each other, but any authority I had had was worn away. For me to interfere in his life again would be too much of a risk. I knew it, and so did he. I had to accept that it was not only marriage relations which changed.

CHAPTER XXII

SWEARING IN A HOSPITAL WARD

ALTHOUGH none of us knew it at the time, Luke and Martin did not toss up. Even they themselves had not settled, until March was on them, which should 'go first': and how they settled it, they kept secret. It was long afterwards when I found out what had happened.

Martin had been as good as his word, no better, no worse. With his feeling for precision and formality, he had actually written Luke a note a week before the experiment, suggesting that they tossed up, defining what the toss should mean – heads Martin went first, tails Luke. Luke would not have it. Swearing at getting a letter from Martin whom he saw every day, he said that the extraction was his idea, his 'bit of nonsense', and the least he could do was have the 'first sniff'.

Luke got his way. Martin did not pretend to himself that he was sorry to be overruled.

The results of his being overruled came so fast that even at Barford, much more so in London, they were hard to follow. First Luke decided that he could not begin the experiment without another pair of hands; after his and Martin's arrangement with the Superintendent, which meant that Martin was excluded, they had to give Sawbridge his wish.

During the last waiting period, Luke had had a 'hot' laboratory built, rather like a giant caricature of a school laboratory, in which, instead of dissolving bits of iron in beakers under their noses, they had a stainless steel pot surrounded by walls of concrete into which they dropped rods of metal that they never dared to see. In each section of the hot laboratory were bell pushes, as though it were a bath arranged for a paralysed invalid who for safety was in need of a bell within inches of his head.

Luke and Sawbridge went alone into the hot laboratory on a morning in March. The next that Martin heard, just three hours later, was the sound of the bell. That same evening I received news that Luke and Sawbridge were both seriously ill, Luke much the worse. The doctors would have said not fatally, if they had known more of the pathology of radiation illness. So far, they looked like cases of severe sunstroke. It might be wise for their friends to be within reach.

Sawbridge had carried Luke away from the rods, and it was Sawbridge who had pushed the bell. The irony was, they had been knocked out by a sheer accident. They had got safely through the opening of the aluminium cans, in which the rods were taken from the pile; the cans had been stripped off under ten feet of water. Then something 'silly' happened, as Sawbridge said, which no one could have provided against. A container cracked, Luke went down, and Sawbridge a matter of minutes afterwards.

The next day's news was hopeful. Sawbridge seemed scarcely ill, and was a bad patient; Luke was able to talk about the changes they could make in the hot laboratory, before he or Martin had 'another go'.

They went on like this for several days, without anything the doctors could call a sign. Several times Luke wanted them to let him out of bed. Eight days after the stroke, he broke out: *'What is the matter with me?'* Though he could not explain how, he felt physically uneasy; soon he was said to be low-spirited, a description which shocked anyone who knew him. He was restlessly tired, even as he lay in bed.

Within three more days he was ill, though no one had seen the disease before. His temperature went up; he was vomiting, he had diarrhoea, blood spots were forming under his skin; the count of his white blood cells had gone steeply down. In two more days, he was bleeding inside the mouth.

Sawbridge escaped some of the malaise, and the blood spots had not formed. Otherwise his condition seemed a milder variant of the same disease. I was ready to go to Barford at short notice to visit Luke, but during those days he was so depressed that he wanted only to be alone. Once a day he saw his wife; he sent for Martin but spoke very little when he came; he tried to give some instructions, but they were not intelligible. His chief comfort seemed to be in following the scientific observations of his illness. He and Sawbridge had been moved into a special ward at the establishment hospital; not only the Barford doctors, but others studying the clinical effects of radiation, watched each measurement. There was a mutter from Luke's sick-bed which spread round Barford: 'The one thing they [the doctors] still don't know is whether to label mine a lethal dose or only near lethal.'

Mounteney told me that much, one afternoon in my office. More physically imaginative than most men, Mounteney was enraged at the thought of Luke's illness. His eyes burnt more deeply in their sockets, his face looked more than ever Savanarola-like.

'It oughtn't to have been let happen, Eliot,' he said. 'It oughtn't to have happened to anyone, let alone a man we can't spare. Some of you people ought to have realised that *he's* one of the men we can't spare.'

Although his distress was genuine, it was like him to turn it into an attack. Somehow he implied that, instead of Luke being ill, Whitehall officials ought to be. But, as the afternoon went on, he became gentler though more harassed.

'I should like anyone who's ever talked about using the nuclear bomb to have a look at Luke now,' he said.

I was thinking of that night in Stratford, which now seemed far away and tranquil, when Martin fed the swans.

'It would teach them what it means. If ever a nuclear bomb went off, this is exactly what would happen to the people it didn't kill straight off.' He added:

'There are enough diseases in the world, Eliot. It's no business of science to produce a new one.'

That visit from Mounteney took place three weeks after Luke and Sawbridge were pulled out of the hot laboratory. In another few days – actually E+29, as the scientists called it in the jargon of the day, meaning twenty-nine days after the exposure – Luke was said to be brighter, the bleeding had lessened. It might only be an intermission, but at least he was glad of people at his bedside.

Although I arrived in Barford the day I got that message, I was not allowed in the ward until the following morning. And, just as I was going inside, Mrs Drawbell, watching from the nurses' ante-room, intercepted me. Her husband detested Luke; when he was healthy she herself had never shown any interest in him; but now – now there was a chance to nurse. Triumphantly she had argued with Nora Luke. Nora had a piece of mathematical work to finish: anyone could do part-time nursing, only Nora could complete that paper. The wives who had no careers of their own criticised Nora, but it was Mrs Drawbell who became installed as nurse.

'You mustn't tire him, Mr Eliot,' she said accusingly. *She* (Nora Luke) was already in the ward, Mrs Drawbell said. She went on, stern and obscurely contented: 'They used to be such fine strong men!'

I had not heard her so articulate. She said: 'It's a case of the wheel of fortune.'

The first time I heard Luke's voice, it sounded husky but loud and defiant. I was only just inside the door; the ward was small, with a screen between the two beds, Sawbridge's in the shade and further from the window. The light spring sunshine fell across Nora sitting by the other bed, but I could not see Luke's face.

'I've got a bone to pick with you, Lewis,' he said.

It was the kind of greeting that I used to expect from him. He went on:

'We must have more bods.'

'Bods' meant bodies, people, any kind of staff: scientists were bods, so were floor cleaners, but as a rule Luke used the words in demanding more scientists.

I felt better, hearing him so truculent – until I noticed Nora's expression. At a first glance, she had looked, not cheerful, certainly, but settled; it was the set tender expression not unexpected at a husband's sick-bed, but that some would have been surprised to see in Nora. But, as Luke shouted at me, pretending to be his old rude resilient self, that expression changed on the instant to nothing but pain.

As I moved out of the sunlight I saw Luke. For a moment I remembered him as I had first met him, in the combination room of our college, when he was being inspected as a fellowship candidate ten years before. Then he had been ruddy, well fleshed, muscular, brimming with a young man's vigour – and (it seemed strange to remember now) passionately self-effacing in his desire to get on. Now he was pale, not with an ordinary pallor but as though drained of blood; he was emaciated, so that his cheeks fell in and his neck was like an old man's; there were two ulcers by the left-hand corner of his mouth; bald patches shone through the hair on the top of his head, as in an attack of alopecia.

But these changes were nothing beside the others. I said, answering his attempt to talk business:

'We'll go into that any time you like. You'll get all the people you want.'

Luke stared at me, trying to concentrate.

'I can't think what we want,' he said.

He added, in a sad, exhausted tone:

'You'd better settle it all with Martin. I'm a bit out of touch.'

He could not get used to the depression. Into his sanguine nature it seemed to grow, as though it was seeping his spirits away; he had never had to struggle against a mood before, much less to feel that he was losing the struggle.

Propped up by his pillows, his back had gone limp. His eyes did not focus on Nora nor me nor on the trees in the hospital garden.

I said, hearing my voice over-hearty as though he were deaf:

'You'll soon get in touch again. It won't take you a week, when you get out of here.' Luke replied:

'I may not be good for much when I get out of here.'

'Nonsense,' I said.

'Are you thinking of *that* again?' said Nora.

'What is it?' I said.

'He's worried that he might be sterile,' said Nora.

Luke did not deny it.

'Are you having that old jag again?' said his wife.

'The dose must have been just about big enough,' he said blankly, as though he had nothing new to say.

'I've told you,' said Nora, 'as soon as the doctors say yes we'll make them have a look. And it'll be all right.'

With the obstinacy of the miserable, Luke shook his head.

'I told you that if by any miracle there is anything wrong, which I don't credit for a minute, well, it doesn't matter very much,' said Nora. 'We've got our two. We never wanted any more.'

She sounded tough, robust, maternal.

Luke lay quiet, his face so drawn with illness that one could not read it.

I tried to change the subject, but Nora knew him better and had watched beside him longer.

She said suddenly:

'You're thinking something worse, aren't you?'

Very slightly, he inclined his head.

'Which one is it?'

'Does it matter?'

'You'd better say,' she said.

'There must be a chance,' he said, 'that some of this stuff will settle in the bone.'

There was a silence. Nora said:

'I wish I could tell you there wasn't a chance. But no one knows one way or the other. No one can possibly know.'

Luke said:

'If I get through this bout, I shall have that hanging over me.'

He lay there, imagining the disease that might lie ahead of him. Nora sat beside him, settled and patient, without speaking. Sawbridge coughed, over by the wall, and then the room stayed so quiet that I could hear a match struck outside. We were still silent when Mrs Drawbell entered. Martin had come to visit Dr Luke; only two people were allowed in the ward at a time; when one of us left, Martin could take his place. Quickly Nora got up. She would be back tomorrow, whereas this was my only time with Luke. I thought that she was, like anyone watching another's irremovable sadness, glad to go.

With a glance towards Sawbridge, Martin walked across the floor towards Luke's bed. As he came, it struck me – it was strange to notice such a thing for the first time – that his feet turned out, more than one would expect in a good player of games. He looked young, erect, and well. With bright, hard eyes he scrutinised Luke. but his voice was gentle as he asked:

'How are you?'

'Not so good,' replied Luke from a long way off.

'You seem a bit better than when I saw you last.'

'I wish I believed it,' said Luke.

Martin went on to enquire about the symptoms – the hair falling out, the ulcers, the bleeding.

'That [the bleeding] may have dropped off a bit,' said Luke.

'That's very important,' Martin said. 'Don't you see how important it is?' He was easier with illness than I was, ready to scold as well as to be gentle. But after he had learned about the symptoms – he was so thorough that I longed for him to stop – he could not persuade Luke to talk any more than Nora or I could. Luke lay still and we could not reach the thoughts behind his eyes.

Martin gave me a glance, for once tentative and lost. He said quietly to Luke: 'We're tiring you a bit. We'll have a word with Sawbridge over there.'

Luke did not reply, as Martin, with me following, tiptoed over to the other bed.

'I'm not asleep,' said Sawbridge, in a scornful and unwelcoming tone. We stood by the bed and looked down on him; his skin in health had its thick nordic pallor, and the transformation was not as shocking as in Luke; but the bald patches of scalp shone through, his eyes were filmed over, half opaque. When Martin enquired about him, he said:

'I'm all right.'

Martin was reading the charts – white blood counts, red blood counts, temperature – over the bedhead.

'Never mind that,' said Sawbridge. 'I tell you, I'm all right.'

'The figures look encouraging,' said Martin.

'I've never been as bad as he was—' Sawbridge inclined a heavy eye towards Luke's bed.

'We've been worried about you, all the same.'

'There was no need.' Sawbridge said it with anger – and suddenly, under the shroud of illness, under the familiar loutishness, I felt his bitter pride. He did not want to admit that he was ill or afraid; he had heard the fears that Luke let fall, he could not help but share them; but neither to the doctors nor his relatives, certainly not to his fellow sufferer or to us, would he give a sign.

It was a kind of masculine pride that did not make him more endearing, I was thinking; in fact it made him more raw and forbidding; it had no style. Until this accident I had heard little of him from Martin. No one had mentioned the security enquiries, which I assumed had come to nothing; the little that Martin said had not been friendly, and at the bedside he was still put off. But he managed to keep, what Sawbridge could not have borne, all pity out of his voice.

Of the three in the ward, the two invalids and Martin, Luke and Sawbridge were beyond comparison the braver men. Like many brave men, they did not bear a grudge against the timid. But, like many ill men, they resented the well. Sawbridge was angry with Martin, and with me also, for being able to walk upright in the sun.

Martin could feel it, but he would not let silence fall. Both he and Sawbridge cultivated an amateur interest in botany, and he mentioned flowers that he had seen on his way to the hospital.

'There's a saxifrage in the bottom hedge,' he said.

'Is there?'

'It seems early, but there's one spire out on the flowering chestnut.'

Then Sawbridge broke out, slowly, methodically, not hysterically but with a curious impersonal anger, swearing at the flowering chestnut. The swearwords of the midland streets ground into the room, each word followed by the innocent tree, '—the flowering chestnut.' The swearing went on and on. Strangely, it did not sound as though Sawbridge were losing his head. It did not even sound as though he were trying to keep his courage up. Somehow it came, certainly to me, as the voice of a man cursing his fate, dislikeable but quite undefeated.

It must have come to Luke so, for during a break in Sawbridge's machine-like swearing, there sounded a husky whisper from the other bed.

'Bugger the flowering chestnut,' whispered Luke. Somehow the younger man's brand of courage had tightened his.

We all listened to him, and soon Sawbridge's voice stopped, while Martin stood between the beds. Luke's face had changed from blankness to pain, but there was sight in his eyes. He spoke fast and rationally, lying there supine, calling on his fibres for an effort they could scarcely make, calling on the will behind his fibres.

'How fast are you getting on with the new bay?' he croaked to Martin.

After a moment's stupefaction, Martin replied as coolly as though they were in the hangar.

'How long are you going to take about it?' said Luke. 'Good Christ, how long?'

'The new hot laboratory,' said Martin, 'should be ready by June.'

'It's too long.'

There was a voice from Sawbridge's bed. 'Essential' – a curse, another curse – 'not to let the others get years ahead.'

Luke strained himself to the effort. He and Martin, with one or two interruptions from Sawbridge, talked sharp and quick, words coming out like 'hazard points', 'extracts', 'cupferron'.

'By the end of June at the outside, we must start again,' said Luke. Hoarsely he went on:

'I expect it will have to be you this time.'

'Yes,' said Martin. He had been studying Luke and Sawbridge with a clinical curiosity that unnerved me, because he wanted to know what might happen to himself. But, as Luke made his effort, as he called on an ultimate reserve of hope when his body had none, for an end which to them all seemed at that moment as simple as getting first to the top of a mountain, Martin lost the last peg of his detachment.

It was not that he felt fonder of Luke or overwhelmed with sorrow for him; just then none of these three men was interested in another; there was something to do, that was all; in this they were one.

Luke was tired out, but as we stood over the bed, he still kept up a harsh whisper.

'We must have more bods. Tell them we must have more bods.'

CHAPTER XXIII

'EVENTS TOO BIG FOR MEN'

I WAS in suspense during the last days of the German war. The scientific teams in Germany had reported, months before, that the Germans had got nowhere with their pile; but now, when one could count days to the surrender, I kept thinking – could there have been one hidden? In terms of reason, I told myself, it was impossible, it was superstitious nonsense – but during those last few days I became nervous when I heard an aircraft.

It was not until the formal end that I could go to my flat and sleep twelve hours in anti-climax and relief. It was because the anti-climax stayed with me, because I did not want to share the sadness of the first weeks of peace, that I saw nothing of my Barford friends that May. Later I wished that I had heard them talk, immediately the German war finished. All I heard in fact was that the new laboratories were being built ready for the second attempt in June; that Sawbridge was a good deal better, and that Luke was now definitely expected to live.

Then came the morning of Pearson's news.

The rain had just stopped; through the windows of Rose's room drifted the smell of wet leaves from the park. It was right at the end of May, and the kind of dark warm morning which brought back days of childhood, waiting at the county ground for the umpires to come out again. Instead, Rose was meeting his five senior colleagues on a problem of reconstruction – 'an untidy one', he said. We were getting towards the end of the morning, when his personal assistant brought in a note for Rose. He read it, and passed it to me. It said:

'Dr Pearson has just arrived back from Los Alamos, and says he wants to see the Secretary at once. He says it can't want.'

Rose glanced at me under his lids. Himself the most ceremonious of men in dealing with others' dignity, he never stood on his own. He said:

'I really am most apologetic, but this is something I probably ought to attend to, and perhaps we've got nearly as far as we can go today. I do apologise.' He asked me to stay, and, when the others had left, Rose and I sat looking out over the rainwashed trees. Just once Rose, who did not spare time for useless speculation, remarked:

'I wonder if there really is anything in the wind, or whether this man has just dropped in to pass the time of day.'

As soon as the girl brought Pearson in, Rose was on his feet, bowing, showing Pearson the armchair opposite mine, hoping that he had had a pleasant journey.

'As pleasant as flying the Atlantic in bumpy weather can be,' said Pearson.

'When did you actually arrive?'

'I wanted to get rid of this commission' ('commission' was one of their formal words, and simply meant that he had been asked to give news by word of mouth), 'so I came straight here.'

'That was very, very good of you, Dr Pearson, and I can't tell you how extremely grateful I am. I do hope you're not too tired?'

'As tired as I want to be, thanks. I shan't be sorry to sleep in my own bed tonight.'

Rose, unwearying in politeness, said:

'We are grateful to you for many other reasons, of course, Dr Pearson. We have heard the most glowing accounts of you from the American authorities. They told us that you've been of inestimable value, and it's very nice to have you and some of our friends putting up our stock over there. I do congratulate you and thank you.'

It was all true. Pearson had been a great success in America, working on the actual firing mechanism of the bomb.

'Oh, I don't know about that,' he said, with a diffidence that was awkward and genuine, but lay on top of his lazy invulnerable confidence.

'You may not know, but we do,' said Hector Rose. Then lightly: 'You said you had a little business for us, did you?'

Pearson did not reply at once but glanced edgewise through his spectacles at me. He said to Rose:

'I've got a piece of information that I am to give you.'

'Yes, Dr Pearson,' said Rose.

'I've no authority to give it to anyone else,' said Pearson.

Rose was considering.

'I take it,' he said, 'this information is to go to the committee?'

'The sooner the better,' said Pearson.

'Then I can authorise you to speak in front of Eliot, with many thanks for your precautions. Because you see, Dr Pearson, Eliot is part of the secretariat of the committee, and in any case I should have to pass him this information at once.'

Pearson tilted back his head. He did not care for me, but that was not moving him; he was a rigid, literal, security-minded man. On the other hand, he was a practical one.

'If Eliot's got to channel it through the committee, he might as well know now as after lunch, I suppose,' he said.

'That would be my view,' said Hector Rose.

'As long as it's understood that this is a time when there mustn't be one word out of school. I'm not authorised to speak to anyone at Barford, and neither are you. This is for the committee and no one else in this country.'

'We take that point, Dr Pearson.' Rose inclined his head.

'Oh well then,' said Pearson, in a flat casual tone, 'we've got a bomb.'

He announced it as though it were an off-hand matter of fact, as though he were informing two people, neither of whom he thought much of, that he had bought a new house.

Rose's first reply was just as flat.

'Have you indeed?' he said. Then he recovered himself:

'I really must congratulate you and our American colleagues. Most warmly.'

'We're just putting the final touches to the hardware,' said Pearson. 'It's nearly ready for delivery.'

Rose looked from Pearson's face, pale from travel but relaxed, out to the soft, dank, muggy morning. Under the low sky the grass shone with a brilliant, an almost artificial sheen.

'It really is a remarkable thought,' said Rose.

'I always expected we should get it,' said Pearson.

I broke in: 'What happens now?'

'Oh, before we make many more, there are lots of loose ends to tie up,' said Pearson.

I said:

'I didn't mean that. I suppose you'll soon have two or three, won't you? What happens to them?'

Pearson pushed up his spectacles.

'They're going to explode one in the desert soon,' he said, 'just to see if it goes off all right.'

'And the others?'

'I didn't have much to do with the military,' he said, in the same off-hand tone, 'but there's some talk they'll try one on the Japs.'

I said:

'How do the scientists over there take that?'

'Some of them are getting a bit restive.' He might not have heard the feeling in my question, but he was not a fool, he knew what lay behind it. 'Some of the people at Barford will get restive too,' he said. 'That's why they mustn't hear until there's proper authority.'

It was no use arguing just then. Instead, I asked about friends of mine working on the American projects, O——, S——, Kurt Puchwein.

'Puchwein moved from Chicago to Berkeley,' said Pearson. 'He's said to have done a good job.'

He yawned, stretched his legs, and announced.

'Oh well, I think that's all. I may as well be going.'

'Thank you very, very much for coming here so promptly this morning,' said Rose. 'I'm immensely grateful to you, many, many, many thanks.'

When Pearson had shut the door, we heard his slow steps lolloping down the corridor. Rose was sitting with his arms folded on his chest, his glance meeting mine; we were each thinking out consequences, and some of our thoughts were the same.

'I must say I'm sorry we didn't get in first,' he said.

'Yes.'

'It's clear to me that the Pearson man is right. This information is restricted to us and the committee, and that there's nothing that we can usefully do at the present juncture.'

'When can we do anything?'

'I think I know what's on your mind,' he said.

'What do you mean?'

Rose said:

'Now that the American party has produced this bomb, you're thinking it's obviously unreasonable for our people to break their necks trying to save a couple of months. I need hardly say that I agree with you. I propose to take it upon myself to prevent it happening.' He added in a polite, harsh, uneasy tone: 'Please don't think I'm taking care of this arrangement for the sake of your brother. We simply want to avoid unnecessary waste, that's all.'

I thanked him, uneasy in my turn. Even that morning, we could not be natural to each other. Curiously, although Rose had picked out and settled what was most likely to be worrying me, at that moment it happened to be taking second place.

'It's important,' I broke out, 'that the Barford people should know what we've just heard.'

'Why is it important, Eliot?' asked Rose in his coolest voice.

Watching me as I remained silent, he went on, sounding as competent as ever:

'I think I can go some of the way with you. If there is any temptation to make a practical demonstration of this weapon – on the whole I shall believe that when I see it – then the scientists are likely to have their own views. In fact, they might have more influence with the soldiers and politicians than any of us would have. In that case, I suggest to you that two points arise: first, the scientists concerned won't be listened to if they get the information through a security leakage; second, that there is every conceivable advantage in the scientists acting entirely by themselves. I put it to you that, even if you and I were free agents, which we're very far from being, the balance of sense would be in favour of leaving it strictly to the scientists.'

I was looking at him, without being ready to say yes or no.

'Mind you,' said Rose, 'I can appreciate the argument that it's totally unreasonable for scientists to make a fuss at this stage. A good many people hold the perfectly tenable view that all weapons are scientific nowadays and you can't draw a division between those we've already used and this new one. It's arguable that any scientific hullabaloo on this affair would be a classical case of straining at the gnat and swallowing the camel.'

'I can't see it as quite so simple,' I said.

I was thinking, this was what official people might come to. Rose was often one jump ahead of official opinion; that was why they called him a man of judgment. His judgment was never too far-sighted for solid men, it led them by a little but not too much, it never differed in kind from theirs.

Yet, as we sat together beside his desk, he gave me a heavy glance.

'There are times, it seems to me,' he said, 'when events get too big for men.'

He said it awkwardly, almost stuttering, in nothing like his usual brisk tone; if I had taken the cue, we might have spoken off guard for once. Almost immediately he went on:

'That may conceivably be the trouble with us all. If so, the only course that I can see is to play one's particular game according to the rules.'

It was one of his rare moments of self-doubt, the sharpest I had seen in him. Neither then nor later did I know whether that morning he had any sense of the future.

He got up from his chair and looked out at the sky, so dark and even that one could not see the rim of any cloud.

'At any rate,' he said, 'our first job is to call the committee at once. Perhaps you will be good enough to look after that?'

I said that I would do it first thing in the afternoon.

'Many, many thanks.' He put on his neat raincoat, his black trilby hat.

'I suppose I can't have the pleasure of giving you luncheon at the Athenæum?'

It was not just his formal cordiality; the news had been a shock, and he wanted a companion – while I, after the same shock, wanted first of all to be alone.

CHAPTER XXIV

'WHAT IS IMPORTANT?'

THE news rippled out. More scientists followed Pearson across. By the end of June, not only the Whitehall committee, but the top men at Barford all knew that completed bombs were in existence: that the trial was fixed for the end of July: that there was a proposal, if the trial went according to plan, to use a second bomb on a Japanese town. Of my acquaintances, perhaps thirty were in possession of those facts.

Among those I was closest to, the first responses were variegated. Several men of good will felt above all excitement and wonder. In the committees there was a whiff almost of intoxication; the other conquests of nature were small beside this one; we were within listening distance of the biggest material thing that human beings had done. Among people who had been flying throughout the war between America and England, who had been giving a hand on both sides and who had, like so many scientists, little national feeling, there was a flash of – later I did not wish to over-state it, but I thought the emotion was awe; a not unpleasurable, a self-congratulatory awe.

In the first days of the news reaching London, I did not catch much political prevision. But I did hear someone say: 'This will crack Russia wide open.'

At Barford, the response was, from the moment the news arrived, more complex. For Luke and Martin, it was a time of desolating disappointment, so that they had hours of that dull weight of rancour, of mindless, frustrating loss, that Scott and his party felt as, only a few miles away, they saw the ski marks of Amundsen's party and then the black dot of the tent at the South Pole.

To Luke it seemed that he had wasted years of his life, and perhaps his health for good, just to have all snatched away within sight of the end.

On the other hand, Martin found considerable comfort for himself. There were great consolations, he remarked, in reverting to being as timid as he chose.

But Martin, like the others at Barford, showed one radical difference from those I met round committee tables, waiting for the news from America. They all heard the bomb might 'conceivably' or 'according to military requirements' be used on Japan. It was mentioned only as a possibility, and most people reacted much like Hector Rose; they did not believe it, or alternatively felt there was nothing they could do. 'War is war,' someone said.

The Barford scientists were nothing like so resigned. Rumours of the bomb coming into action reached them late in June, and there was some sort of confirmation on 3 July. From that day they took it seriously; like their elders on the committees, some believed that it could not happen, that the report was misjudged: but none of them was for sitting still. Some of the engineers, such as Pearson and Rudd, held off, but the leading scientists were unanimous. Drawbell tried to cajole them – it was not their business, he cried, it would do Barford harm – but they threw him over.

On 4 July they held a meeting in Luke's hospital ward. How long had they got? The trial would not take place before 20 July, and American scientists had sent messages about a joint deputation. Was there a better way to stop it? How could they make themselves heard?

No one in London knew what they intended – and only those they trusted, such as Francis Getliffe and I, knew that they intended anything. All through that July, my information lagged days behind the events.

On 5 July I received a telephone call from my office: it was Emma Mounteney, whom I had known at Cambridge, but had scarcely had a word with since: she wanted to see me urgently, and had a confidential note for me. I was surprised that they should use her as a messenger, but asked her to come round at once. She entered, wearing her youthful, worn, cheeky smile, dressed in a summer frock and a pre-war picture hat. She slid a letter on to my blotting pad, and said:

'*Billet-doux* for you.'

I was cross with her. I was even more cross when I saw that the envelope was addressed in Irene's handwriting. As soon as I opened it, I saw that it had no connection with the scientists' plans – it just said (so I gathered at the first glance) that she could not worry Martin when he was worried enough, that Hankins was still at her to pick up where they left off, would I explain as much to him as I safely could?

Unless I had seen Irene, that evening of our celebration in the Albion Gate flat, I should have wondered why she was brandishing bad behaviour to prove that she could be temporarily decent. There was no need for it; she could have turned Hankins down by letter (even if her story were true); she could have avoided this rackety fuss. The answer was that, once she felt part of Martin's love had slipped away, she was losing her confidence: once you lost your confidence in a love relation, you made by instinct, not the right move, but the one furthest from being right.

She was trying to prove to Martin, through me, that she was thinking of his well-being. She was trying, in case the day came when she was going to be judged, to accumulate a little evidence to speak for her.

A few days later, as a result of Irene's letter, I was giving dinner to Edgar Hankins. It was years since we had met, and at once he was exuding his own brand of interest, his bubbling malicious fun. He was getting fat now (he was five years older than I was), his fair hair had gone pepper-and-salt; as in the past, so that night, as soon as he came to my table in the restaurant, we enjoyed each other's company. It was only when we parted that neither of us felt like meeting again.

Hearing him flatter me, recognising that more than most men he raised the temperature of life, I had to remind myself that his literary personality contained little but seedy, dispirited, homesick despair. He was a literary journalist of the kind not uncommon in those years, who earned a professional income not so much by writing as through broadcasting, giving official lectures, advising publishers, being, as it were, high up in the civil service of literature.

We had a good many friends in common, and, sitting in a corner at the White Tower, we began to exchange gossip. Very soon we were talking intimately; I realised, finally, that part of Irene's stories was true. There was no doubt about it; he could not get her out of his imagination, he was, despite his hesitations and comings-and-goings, in love with her.

'It was only after she married that I realised her husband was your brother,' he said.

'That doesn't make it easier to say what I've got to say,' I said.

'I don't think it should make it any harder,' said Hankins. He was apprehensive, but stayed considerate.

'I'd rather you told me,' he said. Then, with the defiance of a man who is keeping his courage up:

'But don't if it's embarrassing. If you don't, I shall have to make her see me.'

I looked at him.

'That is the trouble,' I said.

'Isn't she going to see me?'

'I've got to tell you that she can't see you: that she asks you not to write: that she wants to stop communication between you, but can't tell you why.'

'Can *you* tell me why?'

For a moment he had the excitement, the excitement that is almost pleasure, of someone in touch with the person he loves, even if he is going to hear bad news. I thought how the phenomena of love did not lose their edge as one got older. Here was this middle-aged, experienced man feeling as he had felt at twenty. Perhaps there seemed less time, that was all.

'I can tell you the reason she gave me,' I said. 'My brother is in the middle of a piece of scientific politics. She says she's not prepared to do anything that might put him off his stroke.'

Hankins's face went heavy.

'That's not the real reason,' he said. After a moment, he said: 'There aren't many reasons for not seeing someone you want to. What does it sound like to you?'

I shook my head.

He was too subtle a man to bluff.

'All I can say is that she is speaking the truth—'

'What on?'

'There is a scientific struggle going on, and my brother is mixed up in it. I can't tell you anything about it, except to say that she isn't exaggerating.'

'How do you know?' He was the most inquisitive of men; even at that moment he could not resist the smell of a secret. I put him off, and he asked:

'Is it important?'

'Yes.'

Hankins's interest faded, his head sank down, the flesh bulged under his chin.

'It was futile, asking you whether it was important. What is important? If you were lying ill, and expected to die, what use is it if one of your scientific friends comes bounding up and says, "Old chap, I've got wonderful news! I've found a way – which won't come into effect for a few years as a matter of fact – of prolonging the life of the human race." '

A smile, malicious, fanciful, twisted his lips.

'What is important? Is your brother's piece of politics important? Is it important to know whether Irene is shouting goodbye or whether she's just expecting me to press her?' He continued to smile at me. 'Would you consider that an important question, Lewis, or is it the most trivial one you've ever heard?'

CHAPTER XXV

STANDARD ROSES IN THE SUNSHINE

For a fortnight after my dinner with Hankins there was no firm news from America. One rumour was that the decision about using the bomb had been postponed. Among the people that I met, no one knew the truth, not ministers nor Hector Rose nor any of the scientists.

Late in July – from a record I could later place it as the morning of 27 July – Francis Getliffe entered my office.

As he entered he gave a creased smile, but his face, as a young man's high-strung and quixotic, had grown more closed. In recent years, he had carried much responsibility, and I some; in public and in private we had each had to hide a good deal; we were becoming middle-aged.

Before he said anything to the point, he walked with his plunging stride across my room, from door to window, back again, back to the window. He made some small talk, staring down Whitehall, so that I could see his knave-of-diamonds profile. Then he turned full on me.

'Look, Lewis,' he said, 'it might be useful if you came down to Barford with me. Can you make it?'

'When?'

'At once.'

I looked at my In-tray, then shook myself out of the neurosis of routine; Francis was not the man to invite one for a jaunt.

I nodded. 'Yes, that's all right.'

'Good work,' said Francis.

I asked: 'Is anything new happening?'

'Slightly,' said Francis. He added:

'We've just had a signal from New Mexico.'

That meant the trial.

'It went off?'

'Oh yes, it went off.'

Neither of us spoke, then I said:

'What happens now?'

'I wish I knew.'

He had telephoned the Barford scientists (who heard this kind of official news later than we did in the London offices) and they asked him to go down. As we were driven out of London, in Francis's departmental car, along the Bayswater Road, I asked:

'Why do they want me too?'

'I don't know that they do,' Francis said. 'But I thought you might help.'

'Why?'

'In case they try to do something silly. I don't mind them doing something silly if it achieves the object – but I'm afraid they might do it just because there's nothing else to do.'

The shabby streets, the peeling house fronts, shrank under the steady sun. In that wet and windy summer, it was one of the few halcyon days – out in the country the hedges were as still as though they were painted, over the river meadows the air quivered like a watermark.

Suddenly, after neither of us had spoken for some miles, Francis said:

'They can't be such fools.'

For an instant, I imagined he was still thinking of the Barford scientists, but he went on:

'You can't expect decency from any collection of people with power in their hands, but surely you can expect a modicum of sense.'

'Have we seen much of that?' I asked.

'They can't drop the bomb.'

The car drove on, past the unshaded fields. Francis went on to say that, even if we left moral judgments out, even then it was unthinkable for a sensible man to drop the bomb. Non-scientists never understood, he said, for how short a time you could keep a technical lead. Within five years any major country could make these bombs for itself. If we dropped them first—

At the establishment, which lay well ordered in the sunlight, by this time as neat, as hard, as a factory in a garden suburb, Francis left me in the room where the meeting was to happen. It was a room in a red-brick range, a single storey high; between the ranges were lawns, lush after the weeks of rain, with standard roses each few yards looking like presentation bouquets wired by an unimaginative florist. I remained alone in the room, which was trim, hygienic, as the rest of the establishment had become, with a blackboard on the wall in a pitch-pine frame. From the windows one saw the roses, the lawns, the next red-brick range, the roof of the new hot laboratory, all domesticated, all resting in the sun.

Martin was the first to join me; but before we had done more than greet each other, Hanna Puchwein followed him in. She came so quickly after him that she might have been keeping watch – and almost at once there was another constraint in the room.

'Where have you been these days?' she said to Martin. 'You knew I wanted to see you.'

As she spoke, she realised that I was also there. She gave a smile, curiously tomboyish for anyone so careful of herself. I found Martin guiding the conversation, leading me so as not to mention her husband's name. I could not tell whether he just guessed that she and Puchwein had finally parted.

Then I found him guiding the conversation in another sense.

'What brings you down here, Lewis?' she asked in a light tone.

Quickly, but as though indifferently, Martin replied for me:

'Oh, just an ordinary visit from headquarters.'

'I didn't know we had much to visit, till you and Walter had got going again,' she said. She said it with a toss of her head that made her seem both bad-tempered and young. In fact, she was standing the years better than any of us, with her small strong bones, her graceful hamitic head.

'I don't think there is much to visit,' said Martin, telling her it was no good going on.

'Why are you wasting your time?' she turned on me. But, as I was replying, she flashed out at Martin: 'Do you really believe that no one has any idea what's in the wind?'

'No, I don't believe that,' he said, and in the same breath began to talk of what we should do the following day.

Hanna's eyes filled with what seemed like tears of anger. Just for a second, as Mounteney and others entered the room and she left us, Martin glanced at me. He was frowning. Even when he had been snubbing her, he had sounded as though they had once been in each other's confidence, to an extent which came as a surprise.

The room was noisy, as the scientists sat themselves at the desks, one or two banging the lids, like a rowdy class at school. Most of them wore open-necked shirts, one or two were in shorts.

It struck me that all the top scientists at Barford were present, but none of the engineers. As an outsider, it had taken me years to understand this rift in technical society. To begin with, I had expected scientists and engineers to share the same response to life. In fact, the difference in the response between the physicists and engineers often seemed sharper than the difference between the engineers and such men as Hector Rose.

The engineers, the Rudds and Pearsons, the people who made the hardware, who used existing knowledge to make something go, were, in nine cases out of ten, conservative in politics, acceptant of any regime in which they found themselves, interested in making their machines work, indifferent to long-term social guesses.

Whereas the physicists, whose whole intellectual life was spent in seeking new truths, found it uncongenial to stop seeking when they had a look at society. They were rebellious, questioning, protestant, curious for the future and unable to resist shaping it. The engineers buckled to their jobs and gave no trouble, in America, in Russia, in Germany; it was not from them, but from the scientists, that came heretics, forerunners, martyrs, traitors.

Luke was the last to arrive, a stick supporting him on one side and his wife on the other. If one had seen him near his worse, one no longer thought of him as ill, though the improvement made him look grotesque, for his hair had begun to grow again in tufts, shades fairer than the wings over his ears. With an attempt at jauntiness, he raised his stick before he sat down, while men asked him if he had heard details of the New Mexico explosion.

Luke shook his head.

'All I know is that the bloody balloon went up all right.'

Someone said, with more personal sympathy than the rest:

'It's a pity it wasn't yours.'

'Ours ought to go a bit higher when it does go,' replied Luke.

Francis sat on a desk, looked down the small room, began to talk about reports from America – the argument was still going on, some scientists there were pressing the case against using the bomb, the military for; and all the statements for and against most of us knew by heart.

Then there was an interruption.

Mounteney leaned back, protruded his lean prow of a chin, and said, with unexpected formality:

'Before we go on, I should like to know who invited L. S. Eliot to this meeting.'

'I did,' said Francis. 'I take it no one objects.'

'I do,' said Mounteney.

For a second, I thought it was a scientist's joke, but Mounteney was continuing: 'I understood that this was a meeting of scientists to find ways of stopping a misuse of science. We've got to stop the people who don't understand science from making nonsense of everything we've said, and performing the greatest perversion of science that we've ever been threatened with. It's the general class of people like Eliot who are trying to use the subject for a purpose none of us can tolerate, and I don't see the point in having one of them join in this discussion. Not that I mean anything against L. S. Eliot, of course. I don't suppose he personally would actually authorise using the fission bomb.'

It was only later that I remembered that he liked me, and that this was a triumph of impersonality.

Francis raised his voice. 'We all know that Eliot thinks as we do. He also knows a great deal more than any of us about the government machines. That's why he can be useful this afternoon.'

'I don't want anyone who knows anything about government machines,' said Mounteney. 'People who know about government machines all end up by doing what the machine wants, and that is the trouble we have got ourselves in today.'

Luke and Martin were exchanging glances, and Luke spoke.

'We want Lewis Eliot in on this,' he said.

'Why?' asked Mounteney.

'Because you're a wild man, Arthur, and he's a cunning old dog.'

'If you really do want him,' said Mounteney, 'I suppose I'm prepared to stay.'

'I should think you are.'

'But I still object in principle.'

Later, a good many scientists, not so wild as Mounteney, would have considered that in principle he was right.

Francis returned to the arguments in America. For weeks everyone in that room had thrashed them out.

Some of them gave an absolute no to the use of the bomb for reasons which were too instinctive to express. For any cause on earth, they could not bear to destroy hundreds of thousands of people at a go.

Many of them gave something near to an absolute no for reasons which, at root, were much the same; the fission bomb was the final product of scientific civilisation; if it were used at once for indiscriminate destruction, neither science, nor the civilisation of which science was bone and fibre, would be free from guilt again.

Many, probably the majority, gave a conditional no with much the same feeling behind it: but if there had been *no other way* of saving the war against Hitler, they would have been prepared to drop the bomb.

I believed that that was the position of Francis Getliffe; it was certainly Luke's.

None of those attitudes were stated at this meeting. They had been agreed on long before, and they gave us much common ground. But those who answered with a conditional no could not dismiss the military counter argument out of hand. In America, so Francis said, those in favour of the bomb were saying: Our troops have to invade Japan, this bomb will save men's lives; a soldier must do anything, however atrocious, if by doing so he could save one single life under his command.

As Francis said, that was a case which one had to respect. And it was the only case one could respect. Using the bomb to forestall the Russians or for any kind of diplomatic motive – that was beneath the human level.

Yet, if the dropping of a bomb could make the Japanese surrender, the knowledge that we possessed it might do the same?

'Several of us,' said Francis Getliffe, 'had made a scheme, in case we had it before the end of the German war. Step one. Inform the enemy that the bomb was made, and give them enough proof. Step two. Drop one bomb where it will not kill people. Step three. If the enemy government will not budge, then' – Francis had faced his own thoughts – 'drop the next on a town.'

By this time, the meeting was in a state of deep emotion. 'If there is any sense or feeling left,' said Francis (it was only afterwards that I recalled that 'sense and feeling' was the one emotional phrase in his speech), 'don't begin by using this bomb on human beings.'

That was the case which scientists were putting up in Washington.

'How are they taking it?' asked a refugee.

'Some are listening,' said Francis.

'Is that going to be good enough?' said someone.

'No one knows yet,' said Francis. He added:

'We've had one optimistic message.'

'Who from?'

Francis gave the name.

Luke shook his head.

'He'd believe anything that a blooming general told him. I must say, it doesn't sound safe enough to leave.'

'I agree,' said Francis.

'What more can we do?' came a voice.

'There's plenty we can do,' said Luke.

'There's plenty we can do,' said Mounteney, speaking into space, 'but there's only one way we can make it impossible for them.'

'What's that?' said Francis.

'Issue a statement saying what has happened about the bomb and what is proposed. That will settle it in one.'

'Who is to issue the statement?' said Nora Luke.

'We are.'

'Breaking the law?' said Francis.

'I know that,' said Mounteney.

'Breaking our oaths?' said Francis.

Mounteney hesitated for some moments.

'I detest that. But there's no other way.'

'We're still at war,' said Luke. 'We shall never get the statement out.'

'I think we should,' said Mounteney.

'It'd all be hushed up. A few of us would be in jug, and the whole bloody game would be discredited.'

'We might be unlucky,' said Mounteney. 'In that case a few scientists would be discredited. If we do nothing, then all scientists will be discredited. I can understand some of you fighting shy of signing the statement. I shan't mind putting it out by myself.'

That was a false note. He was a daring man, but so were others there. He was a man of absolute integrity, but most of them did not trust his judgment. Just at that turning point, they were undecided.

Francis had expected some such suggestion all along; for himself, he was too disciplined to act on it. So was Luke. But it was Martin who spoke.

'No, Arthur,' he said, smiling to Mounteney. 'That's not fair. What's more important, it isn't realistic, you know. We couldn't let you do it unless (*a*) it was certain to work, (*b*) there was no alternative. It just wouldn't work. The only result would be that a Nobel prize-winner would be locked up for trying to break the Official Secrets Act, and the rest of us wouldn't be able to open our mouths. Don't you see that, if you try something illegal and it doesn't come off – then we've completely shot our bolt? Whatever governments decided to do with the bombs, we should have lost any influence we might have had.'

There was a murmur in the room. If you were used to meetings, then you knew that they were on Martin's side. I was astonished at the authority he carried with them.

It happened to be one of those occasions when it was easier to make a prudent case than a wild one. Nearly everyone there was uneasy about

395

breaking an oath – uneasy both out of fear and out of conscience. They were not men to whom gesture-making came lightly: they could not believe, that sunny afternoon, that it was demanded of them. So they took Martin as their spokesman.

But also, I thought, he was speaking with an inner authority of his own; his bit of success had been good for him; he carried the weight of one who is, for the first time, all of a piece.

'I don't see any other way,' said Mounteney.

'We do,' said Martin.

Mounteney, as well as being cantankerous, was the most obstinate of men. We were ready for him to argue for hours. Yet without explanation he gave way. I did not even wonder how mysterious his surrender was; we were too much in the middle of events to care.

Immediately, Martin brought out his proposal: that two or three English scientists should be flown over to America to say again what they had said that afternoon. It was known that a number of the scientists working on the American project had signed a protest: the English emissaries would take over a corresponding list of names. Those names were already known – of the scientists at Barford, everyone was willing to sign except Drawbell himself and two obscure chemists. There would also be some signatures, but a much smaller proportion, from the engineers and technicians.

Everyone in the room agreed; they were active men, and they were soothed by action for its own sake. Francis could arrange for an official aircraft within twenty-four hours. Who should go? There was a proposal, backed by Mounteney, that it should be Luke and Martin, the people who had done the work.

Luke was willing to agree, but Martin would not have it. Neither of them was known in America, said Martin: it was no use sending local reputations. Whereas Mounteney had his Nobel prize and Francis Getliffe a great name in Washington for his war work: they were the two who might count.

It was agreed. They would be in America by 29 July. Francis said that they would hope to send us news before the middle of August.

CHAPTER XXVI

NEED FOR A BROTHER

On those first days of August, I had little to do in the office except wait for news. The 'leave season' had set in, as it had not done for six years; rooms round me were empty; the files ended 'cd we discuss on my return?'

When I arrived in the morning, I looked for a despatch from America: but none came. I got through my work in an hour. Then I rang up Martin at Barford, hoping that Francis might have signalled to them and not to London: no news. There was nothing to do. Often, in the afternoons, I went off by myself to Lords.

It was the week before Bank Holiday. The days were like the other days: a sharp cool wind was blowing, more like April than full summer, the clouds streamed across the sky, at the cricket ground one watched for the blue fringe behind them.

On the Friday, I had still had no word from America; when I telephoned Martin (it was becoming a routine), nor had he. 'We're bound to hear before long,' he said.

Saturday was the same. On the Sunday I stayed in my flat all day, half expecting that Martin was right, that a message was on its way.

Next morning I was restless; once more I went off (half thinking, as when one waits for a letter in a love affair, that if I were out of the way, a message was more likely to arrive) to St John's Wood, and sat there watching the game.

The ground was shabby that summer. The pavilion was unpainted; like the high Victorian afternoon of which it might have been the symbol, it had sunk into decay. Yet the smell of the grass was a comfort; it helped me to tell myself that though I had cares on my mind, they were not the deepest. Like the scientists, more often than not I felt this trouble about the bomb could be resolved. And in myself I was lonely rather than unhappy; nearly forty, I had not reshaped my life. Perhaps that was why I took to heart this trouble at one remove. So I sat, watching those hours of cricket in the flashing rainsharp sunshine, taken over by well-being, thoughtless and secure.

It must have been about a quarter to six when I left Lord's. I walked in a meaningless reverie down to Baker Street and then along the Marylebone Road; the light was brilliant after rain, and in it the faces of passers-by stood out sharp-edged. At last I went at random into a pub off Portland

Place. I heard my name. There, standing at the bar beside a man in a polo sweater, was Hankins.

I began by saying something banal, about not meeting for years and then twice in a month, but he cried loudly:

'This is my producer. I've just been giving a talk on Current Shakespeareana.'

He said that he had had only one drink, but his bright, heavy face was glistening, he was talking as if he were half drunk.

'And all the time I was thinking of my words going out to the villages and the country towns and clever young women saying "That was a good point!" or "I should like to take that up with him". And then I came out of the studio and met the man who had been reading the six o'clock news just before I went on.'

'Is there any news?' I asked.

'There is,' said Hankins.

I knew.

'So they've dropped it, have they?' I asked dully. I felt blank, tired out.

'Were you expecting something then?' said Hankins. But his inquisitiveness for once was swamped: yes, the six o'clock news had contained the announcement about the bomb and he, in innocence, had broadcast just after.

'I wonder how many people listened to my immortal prose!' cried Hankins. 'Current Shakespeareana. I wish it had been something slightly more obscure. The influence of the Duino Elegies on the later work of C. P. Cavafy – that's how I should like to have added the only comment literary culture was entitled to make on this promising new age.'

He was upset and hilarious, he wanted an audience, human bodies round him, drink.

'The chief virtue of this promising new age, and perhaps the only one so far as I can tell, is that from here on we needn't pretend to be any better than anyone else. For hundreds of years we've told ourselves in the west, with that particular brand of severity which ends up in paying yourself a handsome compliment, that of course we cannot live up to our moral pretensions, that of course we've established ethical standards which are too high for men. We've always assumed, all the people of whom you,' he grinned at the producer and me, 'and I are the ragtag and bobtail, all the camp followers of western civilisation, we have taken it for granted that, even if we did not live up to those exalted ethical standards, we did a great deal better than anyone else. Well, anyone who says that today isn't a fool, because no one could be so foolish. He isn't a liar, because no one could tell such lies. He's just a singer of comic songs.'

The producer said that next day he had a programme on the care of backward children. 'One can't help thinking,' he said, 'whether there'll be any children left to care for.'

Hankins suddenly clapped a hand to his head.

'I suppose this wasn't the piece of scientific policy we were interested in, you and I, Lewis, last time we met?'

'It was.'

'You said it was important,' he said, as though in reproof. I nodded.

'Well, perhaps I could concede it a degree of importance. What is important, after all?' He had a writer's memory for the words we had each spoken. 'Did Irene know about this?' he flashed out.

'No.'

'Did your brother and the rest of them?'

'None of them knew that this bomb was going to be dropped.'

'But they'd been working heroically on it, I suppose,' said Hankins. 'And now they're getting the reward for their labours. It must be strange to be in their shoes tonight.'

It was also strange to hear him speak with such kindness, with his own curious inquisitive imagination.

We went on drinking, as Hankins talked.

'The party's nearly over,' he said. 'The party for our kind of people, for dear old western man – it's been a good party, but the host's getting impatient and it's nearly time to go. And there are lots of people waiting for our blood in the square outside. Particularly as we've kept up the maddening habit of making improving speeches from the window. It may be a long time before anyone has such a good party again.'

If I had stayed I should have got drunk, but I wanted to escape. I went out into the streets, on which the anonymous crowds were jostling in the summer evening. For a while I lost myself among them, without a name among many who had no name, a unit among the numbers, listening but hearing no comment on the news. In the crowd I walked down Oxford Street, was carried by the stream along Charing Cross Road: lights shone in the theatre foyers, the plays had all begun, in the wind relics of newsprint scuffled among our feet.

Near Leicester Square I drifted out of the crowd, into another pub. There some had heard the news, and as they talked I could pick out the common denominator of fear, sheer simple fear, which, whatever else we thought, was present in us all, Hankins and his producer, the seedy travellers, agents, homosexuals in the Leicester Square bar. Hankins's rhetoric that night: Francis Getliffe's bare words on the way down to Barford: they were different men, but just for once their feelings coincided, they meant the same things.

But in the pub there were also some indifferent. They had heard, and thrown it off already.

One, an elderly man with a fine ascetic face, sat with strained eyes focused on the doors. From a passing remark, I gathered that he was waiting for a young man, who had been due at six.

I walked across Piccadilly Circus, up Vigo Street and then west of Bond Street, through the deserted fringes of Mayfair, towards my club. As soon as I entered, acquaintances spoke to me with interest, with resignation, with the same damped-down fear. Had I known? Was there a chance that we could make ourselves safe again? What would happen to this country in another war? To this town? There was one interruption, as I stood in a party of four or five, standing round the empty grate. A young member, elected that year, asked if he could have a word with me. He had been invalided out of the Navy, his face was sallow, he had a high-strung, delicate, humorous look. But he spoke with urgency:

'Is this bomb all they say?'

I answered yes, so far as I knew.

'Do you think it will finish the Japanese? Do you think the war's going to stop?'

'I should have thought so,' I replied.

'I don't believe it. Bombs don't end wars.'

I was puzzled, but the explanation was straightforward. He was arguing against his own hopes. He had an elder brother, who was booked to fight in the invasion of Malaya. He could not let himself believe that the war would end in time.

When I left the club, I began to walk across London, trying to tire myself. But soon the energy of distress left me, almost between one step and another: although it was not yet eleven I found myself tired out. I took a taxi back to Pimlico, where from the houses in the square the lights were shining, as serene as on any other night of peace, as enticing to a lonely man outside.

I went straight off to sleep, woke before four, and did not get to sleep again. It was not a bad test of how public and private worries compare in depth, I thought, when I remembered the nights I had lain awake because of private trouble. Public trouble – how many such nights of insomnia had *that* given me? The answer was, just one. On the night after Munich, I had lain sleepless – and perhaps, as I went through the early hours of 7 August, I could fairly count another half.

As I lay there, I wished that I were able to speak to someone I was close to. The thoughts, the calculations of the future, pressed on me out of the morning dusk; it might have taken the edge off them if I could have confided to Martin. Soon after breakfast, I rang him up.

'So this is it,' I said.

'Yes, this is it,' came his voice, without any stress.

For some instants neither of us spoke, and I went on:

'I think I should like to come down. Can you put up with me?'

A pause.

'It might be better if I came to London,' he replied. 'Will that do?'

'I can come down straightaway,' I said.

'The other might be better. Is it all right for you?'

I said it was, but I was restless all morning, wondering why he had put me off. It was just after one when he came into my room.

As soon as I saw him, I felt, as often when we met, the familiar momentary wiping-away of fret. I had felt the same, over five years before, when he visited me in that office, and we talked of the bomb, and I induced him to work on it.

'Well, it's happened,' I said.

'I'm afraid so,' said Martin.

It was a curious phrase, inadequate and polite.

'I don't find it easy to take,' I said.

'It's not pretty,' said Martin.

I looked at him. His eyes were hard, bright and steady, the corners of his mouth tucked in. I felt a jolt of disappointment; I was repelled by his stoicism. I had turned to him for support, and we had nothing to say to each other.

Without pretending to be lighthearted, Martin kept up the same level, disciplined manner. He made some comments about his journey; then he asked where we should eat.

'Where you like,' I said.

His eyes searched mine.

'Would you rather wait a bit?'

'I don't care,' I said.

'I mean,' said Martin, his eyes harder, 'would you rather wait and talk? Because if so it may take some time.'

'It depends what we talk about—'

'What do you think I'm going to talk about?'

His voice was not raised – but suddenly I realised it was unsteady with anger.

'I thought you felt it wasn't any use—'

'It may be a great deal of use,' said Martin. His voice was still quiet, his temper utterly let go.

'What do you mean?'

'You don't expect me to sit by and hear about this performance, and not say that I should like my dissent recorded in the minutes?'

'I've felt the same,' I said.

'I know you have,' said Martin. 'But the question is: what is a man to do?'

'I doubt if you can do anything,' I said.

Martin said: 'I think I can.'

'It's happened now,' I said. 'There's nothing to do.'

'I disagree.'

At that moment, each of us, staring into the other's eyes, shared the other's feeling, and knew that our wills must cross.

PART FOUR

A RESULT IN PRIVATE

CHAPTER XXVII

AN UNEFFACEABLE AFTERNOON

BIG Ben had just struck, it must have been the half-hour, when Martin said:
'I disagree.'

He continued to look at me.

'I oughtn't to have stopped Arthur Mounteney sending his letter,' said Martin. Just then, that was the focus of his remorse.

'It wouldn't have done any good,' I said.

'It would have done the trick,' said Martin.

I shook my head. He said:

'So now I shall have to send a letter myself.'

He added, in a tone that was casual, cold, almost hostile:

'Perhaps you'd better have a look at it.'

He opened his wallet, and with his neat deliberate fingers unfolded a sheet of office paper. He leant across and put it on my blotter. The words were written in his own handwriting. There were no corrections, and the letter looked like a fair copy. It read:

'To the Editor of *The Times*' (which failing, *Daily Telegraph*, *Manchester Guardian*). Sir, as a scientist who has been employed for four years on the fisson bomb, I find it necessary to make two comments on the use of such a bomb on Hiroshima. First, it appears not to have been relevant to the war : informed persons are aware that, for some weeks past, the Japanese have been attempting to put forward proposals for surrender. Second, if this had not been so, or if the proposals came to nothing, a minimum respect for humanity required that a demonstration of the weapon should be given, e.g. by delivering a bomb on unpopulated territory, before one was used on an assembly of men, women and children. The actual use of the bomb in cold blood on Hiroshima is the most horrible single act so far performed. States like Hitler's Germany have done much wickedness over many years, but no State has ever before had both the power and the will to destroy so many lives in a few seconds. In this respect our scientists and our government have been so closely interwoven with those of the U.S.A. that we have formed part of that power and that will. . . .'

'You've not sent this?' I said, before I had finished reading.

'Not yet.'

'How many people know you've written it?'

'Only Irene.'

That was the reason, I thought, why he had not wished me to go to Barford.

If this letter were published, it meant the end of his career. I had to get him out of it. From the moment he said that he was proposing to act, I had known that I must prevent him.

Even though I agreed with almost all he said.

As I began to make the first opposing moves, which he was already expecting, I was thinking, his was a letter which an able man only writes when he is near breaking-point. Only his mask was stoical, as he sat there, his fingers spread like a starfish on the arms of his chair. In his letter – whatever he had written I should be trying to suppress it – he had not made the best of his case.[1] Yet I agreed with him in all that mattered. Looking back, years later, I still agreed with him.

I felt it so, that afternoon, when I set myself to make Martin keep quiet. I shut away the sense of outrage, my own sense of outrage as well as his, and brought out the worldly wise, official's arguments, such as we had displayed at Barford in July, such as he had used himself. It was not worth while making gestures for no result. One such gesture was all you were allowed; you ought to choose a time when it could do good. We had found ourselves in responsible positions; we could not give them up overnight; for everyone's sake we had to get through the next few years without a war; then one could make gestures.

There was something in what I said, but they were not the reasons, they were nowhere near the reasons, why I was calling on each ounce of nature that I possessed to force him to conform. It was, in fact, incomparably more simple. For a brother as for a son, one's concern is, in the long run, prosaic and crude. One is anxious about their making a living; one longs for their success, but one wants it to be success as the world knows it. For myself, my own 'respectable' ambitions had damped down by now, I should perhaps have been able, if the choice was sharp enough, to throw them away and face a scandal. For myself; but not for him.

[1] The passage about diplomatic overtures, for example, only complicated the argument.

I had seen friends throw away what most men clung to, respectability, money, fame. Roy Calvert: Charles March: in a more perverted sense, George Passant. I understood why they had done it, I should have been the last to dissuade them. But they were friends, and Martin was a brother. The last thing you want with a brother is that he should fulfil a poetic destiny.

Martin met my argument point by point; we were getting nowhere. All of a sudden he began looking down beside his chair, under the desk, by the hatstand.

'Did I bring in a briefcase?' he said.

I said that I had not noticed, and he went on searching.

'Does it matter?' I was put out.

He said that it contained notes of the new method for extracting plutonium: it was top secret. He must trace it. He thought he remembered leaving it in his car: would I mind walking to the garage with him? Irritated at the interruption, I followed beside him, down Whitehall, across Victoria Street: Martin, his forehead lined with anxiety, was walking faster than usual, and we were both silent. The offices, the red-brick houses of Great Smith Street, glowed shabby in the sunshine. Just as on the night before, I felt a tenderness for the dirty, unfriendly, ugly streets such as I had never felt before. I even felt something like remorse, because what had happened to another town might happen here.

The briefcase was not in the car. Martin said nothing, except that he must ring up Barford from my office. Back there, he sat leaning forward, as though by concentrating he could make the call come through. It was minutes before the telephone whirred. Martin was talking to his secretary, his words fast but even then polite. 'Would you mind looking . . . ?' He waited, then cried out:

'Thank God for that!' With elaborate thanks he put the receiver down, and gave me a sharp, deprecating grin.

'I never brought it. It's sitting there in its proper place.'

'It seemed a curious thing to worry about,' I said.

For an instant he looked blank. Then his face broke into a laugh, the kind of noiseless laugh with which as children we used to receive family jokes. But soon his expression hardened. He asked, had I anything more to say before he sent the letter?

'A good deal more,' I said.

'I wish you'd say it.'

His tone was so inflexible that I became more brutal.

'How are you going to live?' I said.

'A decent scientist can make some sort of a living,' he said.

'Whatever trouble you get into?'

'It wouldn't be a good living, but I can make do.'

'What does your wife think of that?'

There came a surprise. Martin smiled, not affectionately, but as though he held a trump which I had miscounted. He said:

'As a matter of fact, she wants me to do it.'

He spoke with absolute confidence. I had made a mistake. I should have remembered the way she welcomed his first risk. I tried another tack.

'Have you thought of your son?'

'Yes, I've thought of him,' said Martin. He added:

'I've also thought of you. I'm sorry if it harms you, and I know that it must.' He said it formally.

I cast round again. He and I took too much responsibility on ourselves, I said. That was true in our human relations.

He stared at me, and for an instant I was silent.

I went on with the argument. We might be better men if we took less upon our shoulders. And scientists as a class had the same presumption. They thought too much of their responsibility. Martin that day had no more guilt to carry than any other man.

'Again I disagree,' said Martin. After a silence, he went on:

'In any case, I can make a more effective noise.'

'Yes,' I said, feeling another spot to probe – he and Luke and the others would be listened to. But if he were patient, some day he would be listened to in a way that did effective good. Not now. It would be a nine-days wonder, he would be ruined and powerless. But wait. In the next few years, if he and Luke brought their process to success, they would have more influence than most people. That was the only way in which Martin could gain authority: and *then*, if a protest had to be made, if a martyr were needed, *then* he could speak out without it being just a pathetic piece of defiance, a lonely voice in Hyde Park.

A girl brought us cups of tea. The argument went on, flashes crossed the wall from bus roofs reflected in the sun. Neither then nor afterwards did I detect the instant at which the hinge turned. Perhaps there was no such instant. Perhaps it was more like a turn of the tide. Towards the end of the afternoon, Martin knew, and I knew, that I had made him give up.

I did not, even then, believe that any reasons of mine had convinced him. Some had been sound: some were fabricated: some contradicted others. So far as reasons went, his were as good as mine. The only advantage I had was that, in resolving to stop him acting, I had nothing to dilute my purpose. Whereas he intended to act, but deep down had his doubts. Some of these doubts I had brought into the open: the doubts that fed on responsibility, on caution, on self-interest, on a mixture of fears, including the fear of being disloyal.

As the afternoon sun made blazons out of the windows across the street, Martin said:

'Very well, I shall just do nothing.'

He spoke sadly, admitting what, for some time past, we had each known.

I asked him to have dinner with me, and stay in my flat. For a second his face had the look of refusal, but then his politeness came back. We were both constrained as we walked across the parks to Hyde Park Corner. In Green Park we stood for a while watching some boys of eight or nine play, in a clearing by the bandstand, a primitive game of cricket. The trees' shadows stretched across the lumpy grass, and we saw something that had the convincing improbability of a dream; at three successive balls the batsman made a scooping shot, and gave a catch which went in a gentle curve, very softly, to point; the first catch was seriously and solemnly missed. So was the second. So was the third.

'We shall never see that again,' I said to Martin.

Usually he would have been amused, but now he only gave a token smile.

We walked along the path.

'By the way,' said Martin, in a tone dry and without feeling, 'I heard one story about tactics that might interest you.'

He had heard it from someone present after the bomb was made.

'There was a good deal of discussion,' he said, 'about how to drop it with maximum results. One ingenious idea was to start a really spectacularly pretty flare a few seconds before the bomb went off.'

'Why?'

'To make sure that everyone in the town was looking up.'

'Why?'

'To make sure they were all blinded.'

I cried out.

'That's where we've come to in the end,' he said. He added: 'But I agree with you, now I've got to let it go.'

We walked on, set apart and sad.

CHAPTER XXVIII

'WHAT DO YOU EXPECT FROM HIM NOW?'

Two days later, as we drove down to Barford in the afternoon, Martin and I talked civilly of cricket and acquaintances, with no sign on the surface of our clash of wills.

In Banbury I bought an evening paper. I saw that another bomb had been dropped. Without speaking I passed the paper to Martin, sitting at the wheel, the car drawn up in the market place beside the kerb. He read the paragraph under the headline.

'This is getting monotonous,' he said.

His expression had not changed. We both took it for granted that the argument was not to be reopened. He was too stable a character to go back on his word. Instead, he commented, as we drove into Warwickshire, that this Nagasaki bomb must have been a plutonium one.

'The only point of dropping the second,' said Martin, his tone neutral, the last edge of feeling dried right out, 'must have been for purposes of comparison.'

As soon as we went inside the canteen at Barford he made a similar remark, and was immediately denounced by Luke as a cold fish. Martin caught my eye; just for an instant, his irony returned.

Inside that room, four floors up in the administration building, so that one looked out over the red-brick ranges towards the dipping sun and then back to the teacups and the white linoleum on the tables, the voices were loud and harsh.

There were a dozen people there, Mary Pearson, Nora Luke, Luke himself, erect and stiff-backed as he had not been for a year; I had never seen them so angry.

The news of Hiroshima had sickened them; that afternoon had left them without consolation. Luke said: 'If anyone had tried to defend the first bomb, then I might just have listened to him. But if anyone dares try to defend the second, then I'll see him in hell before I listen to a single word.'

They all assumed, as Martin had done, that the plutonium bomb was dropped as an experiment, to measure its 'effectiveness' against the other.

'It had to be dropped in a hurry,' said someone, 'because the war will be over and there won't be another chance.'

'Not just yet,' said Luke.

I had known them rancorous before, morally indignant, bitter: but it was something new to hear them cynical – to hear that last remark of Luke's, the least cynical of men.

Eric Pearson came in, smiled at his wife, nodded to others, threw back his quiff of hair. He sat down at a table, while most of us were standing. Suddenly I thought I should like to question him. Of them all, he was the only one who had worked directly on the actual bombs, that is, he had had a small part, a fractional part, in what they would call 'the hardware', the concrete objects that had been dropped on those towns. Even if it was only a thousandth part, I was thinking, that meant a good many lives.

'How do you feel about it?' I asked.

'Nothing special,' said Pearson.

As usual he irritated me with his off-hand manner, his diffidence, his superlative inner confidence.

'I should have thought,' I said, 'you might wish it hadn't happened?'

'Oh,' he said, 'I haven't lost any sleep about it.'

Suddenly his wife broke out, her face flaming, tears starting from her eyes:

'Then you damned well ought to have!'

'I'm sorry.' His manner changed, he was no longer jaunty. 'I only meant that it wasn't my business.'

She brushed away the tears with the back of her hand, stared at him – and then went out of the room. Soon Pearson followed her. The others dismissed him as soon as he had gone, while I wondered how long that breach would last. Pitilessly they forgot him, and Luke was shouting to me:

'Lewis, you may have to get me out of clink.'

He stood between the tables.

'It's no use bellyaching any more,' he cried. 'We've got to get something done.'

'What is to be done?' said a voice.

'It stands out a mile what is to be done,' said Luke. 'We've got to make a few of these damned things ourselves, we've got to finish the job. Then if there's going to be any more talking, we might have our share.'

In the midst of their indignation, the proposal did not startle them. Luke was a man of action, so were many of them. Political protests, associations of scientists – in their state of moral giddiness, they were looking for anything to clutch on to. For some, Luke was giving them another hold. He had always been the most nationalistic of them. Just as old Bevill kept the narrow patriotism of the officer élite, so Luke never quite forgot that he had been brought up in a naval dockyard, and kept the similar patriotism of the petty officer.

That afternoon the scientists responded to it.

'Why is it going to lead you in clink?' I cut across the argument.

'Because if we don't get the money to go ahead, I don't mean next month, I don't mean tomorrow, I mean now, I'm going to stump the country telling them just what they're in for. Unless you old men' – he was speaking to me – 'get it into your heads that this is a new phase, and that if we don't get in on the ground floor there are just two things that can happen to this country – the best is that we can fade out and become a slightly superior Spain, the worst is that we get wiped out like a mob of Zulus.'

Nora said:

'When you see what the world is like, would that matter so much?'

'It would matter to me,' said Luke. Suddenly he gave up being a roughneck. 'I know it seems as though any chance of a little decency in the world has been wiped out for good. All I can say is that, if we're going to get any decency back, then first this country must have a bit of power.'

Someone asked how much time he needed.

'It depends on the obstacles they put in our way,' said Luke. He said to Martin: 'What do you say, how long do we need?'

Since we entered the canteen Martin had been standing by the window, just outside the group, and as I turned my eyes with Luke's question, I saw him, face half averted, as though he were watching the western sky, the blocks of buildings beneath, rectangular, parallel, like the divisions in a battle map. It was many minutes since he had spoken.

He gazed at Luke with a blank face. Then, businesslike, as in a routine discussion, he replied:

'Given the personnel we've got now?'

'Double it,' said Luke.

'Two years, at the best,' said Martin. (By this time, even Luke admitted that his early estimates had not been realistic.) 'About three, allowing for an average instalment of bad luck.'

All he had promised me was to keep quiet. Now he was going further. He was taking the line I had most urged him to take. They began arguing about the programmes: and I left them to it.

As I walked along the path to Martin's flat, where Irene had been told to expect me, the evening was serene; it should have been the end of a calm and nameless day. The sky was so clear that, as the first stars came out, I could distinguish one that did not twinkle, and I was wondering which planet it was, as I made my way upstairs to Irene.

When I got inside their sitting-room, I found that she had just begun to wash her hair.

She asked, without leaving the bathroom, whether I would not go into the village and have a meal alone. No, I said, I was tired; any kind of snack, and I would rather stay. Still through the open door, she told me where to find bread and butter and tinned meat. Then she ignored me.

Sitting on the drawing-room sofa, I could see her across the passage, her hair, straight and fine, hanging down over the basin. Later, hooded in a towel, she was regarding herself in the looking-glass. Her face had thinned down and aged, the flesh had fallen away below the cheekbones, while on her body she had put on weight; some men would find excitement in the contrast, always latent in her, but now in her thirties established, between the body, heavy, fleshly and strong, and the nervous, over-exhausted face.

In towel and dressing-gown she surveyed herself sternly, as though, after trying to improve her looks for years, she was still dissatisfied.

She had finished washing, there was no reason to prevent her chatting with me, but still she sat there, evaluating her features, not paying any attention that I had come. I had no doubt that it was deliberate; she must have decided on this toilet as soon as she heard that I was on the way. It was quite unlike her, whose first instinct was to be ready to get a smile out of me or any other man.

I could not resist calling out:

'Aren't you going to talk to me tonight?'

Her reply took me aback. Her profile still towards me, and gazing at her reflection, she said:

'It could only make things worse.'

'What is all this?' I said roughly, as though she were sulky and needed shaking. But she answered without the least glint of sex:

'It will be better if we don't talk until Martin comes back.'

It sounded like melodrama, of which she had her share: but also, like much melodrama, it was meant. I went into the bathroom and she turned to confront me, the towel making her face open and bald. She looked nervous, frowning – and contemptuous.

'This isn't going to clear up without speaking,' I said.

She said:

'You've done him harm, haven't you?'

I was lost. For a second, I even thought she was speaking of Hankins, not Martin. She added:

'He's going to toe the line, isn't he? And that can only be your doing.'

Then, in the scent of powder and bath salts, a remark swung back from the previous afternoon and I said:

'You'd rather he ruined himself, would you?'

'If that's what you call it,' said Irene.

Like the scientists in the canteen I was morally giddy that day.

'He makes up his own mind,' I said.

'Except for you,' she cried. She burst out, her eyes bright with resentment, with an obscure triumph:

'Oh, I haven't fooled myself – and I should think you must have a glimmering by now – I'm perfectly well aware I haven't any influence on him that's worth a row of beans. Of course, he's easygoing, he's always good natured when it doesn't cost him anything. If I want to go out for a drink, he never grumbles, he just puts down whatever he's doing: but do you think, on anything that he cares about, I could ever make him budge an inch?'

It was no use contradicting.

'You can,' she cried. 'You've done it.'

She added:

'I hope you'll be satisfied with what happens to him.'

I said:

'We'd better wait till we've got over this shock—'

'Oh, never mind that,' she said. 'I wash my hands of that. It's him I'm thinking of.'

She looked at me with eyes narrowed.

'Do you know,' she said, 'I'm beginning to wonder whether you understand him at all?'

She broke off. 'Don't you like extravagant people?' she asked.

'Yes,' I said.

'Unless it comes too near home.' She went on: 'He's one at heart, have you never seen that?'

She stared at her reflection again.

'That's why he gets on with me,' she said, as though touching wood.

'That might be true,' I said.

'He's capable of being really extravagant,' she broke out. 'Why did you stop him this time? He's capable of throwing the chains right off.'

She stared at me and said:

'I suppose you were capable of it, once.'

It was said cruelly, and was intended to be cruel. For the first time in our relation she held the initiative. Through her envy of my intimacy with Martin, through her desire to be thought well of, through the attraction that smoulders often between in-laws, she could nevertheless feel that she was thinking only of him.

When I replied, I meant to tell her my real motive for influencing him, but I was inhibited.

Instead, I told her that he was not alone, he was not living in a vacuum, nor was I. What he did affected many others. Neither he nor I could live as though we were alone.

She said:

'He could have done.'

I said:

'Not this time.'

'It would have been a glorious thing to do,' she cried.

She rounded on me:

'I've got one last word for you,' she said. 'You've stopped him doing what he wanted to. I won't answer for the consequences. I should like to know what you expect from him now.'

CHAPTER XXIX

HUSHED VOICES UNDER THE BEAMS

ONE night soon after, coming out of the theatre at Stratford, I was forced to remember how – the evening the news of Hiroshima came through – I had walked through the West End streets in something like wretchedness. Now I was leaving the play, the sense of outrage had left me alone for days, I was one among a crowd, lively and content in the riverside lights. Around me was a knot of elderly women whom I had noticed in the theatre, who looked like schoolteachers and to whom, by some standards, life had not given much; yet their faces were kind, shining with a girlish, earnest happiness, they were making haste to their boarding house to look up the text.

It was there by the river, which was why I was forced to remember, why I became uncomfortable at being content under the lamplit trees, that Martin and Mounteney and I, on the dark wartime night, so tunnel-like by the side of this, agreed that there was no serious chance that the bomb could be used.

Yet I was lighthearted under the belts of stars.

How long can you sustain grief, guilt, remorse, for a horror far away?

If it were otherwise, if we could feel public miseries as we do private ones, our existences in those years would have been hard to endure. For anyone within the circle of misery, it is a blessing that one's public memory is so short; it is not such a blessing for those outside.

Should we be left with only one reminder, that for thoughtful men there would stay, almost like a taste on the tongue, the grit of fear?

In the following days at Stratford, where I was taking my first leave that year, all I heard from the establishment was that Luke was driving his team as though in his full vigour, and that Martin was back in place as second-in-command. Martin had not spoken to me alone.

For most of that August there was no other news from Barford except that Mounteney had made his last appearance in the place, taken down the nameplate from his door, emptied his In-tray on top of his Out-tray, as he and Luke had once promised, and gone straight back to his university chair.

A few days later, without any warning, Drawbell came into Stratford to see me with a rumour so ominous that he spoke in whispers in the empty street. The rumour was that there had been at least one 'leakage', perhaps more: that is, data about the American experiments, and probably the Barford ones also, had been got through to Russia.

Within a few hours of that rumour – it was the end of August, and my last week in Stratford – I received a telephone call at my hotel. It was from Luke: Martin and he had a point to raise with me. I said I could come over at any time, but Luke stopped me. 'I don't like the cloak-and-dagger stuff,' he said, 'but it might be better just this once if we happen to run across you.'

They drove into Stratford that evening, and we met at the play. In the intervals, there were people round us; even outside on the terrace in the cool night, we could not begin to talk. Afterwards, with the wind blowing like winter, we went to the hotel sitting-room, but there for a long time, while Luke breathed hard with impatience, a couple of families were eating sandwiches after the theatre. The wind moaned outside, we drank beer, the beams of the low room pressed down on us as we waited; it was a night on which one was oppressed by a sense of the past.

At last we had the room to ourselves. Luke gave an irritable sigh, but when he spoke his voice, usually brazen, was as quiet as Martin's.

'This is Martin's show,' he said.

'I don't think so,' said Martin.

'Damn it,' said Luke, and it was curious to hear him angry in an undertone, as we sat with heads bent forward over the gate-legged table, 'we can't pass the buck as though we were bloody well persuading each other to sing.'

'No,' said Martin, 'I'd speak first if I had the responsibility.'

Luke glowered at him. Martin looked blank-faced.

'The problem,' said Luke brusquely, 'is security. Or at least you' – he thrust his lip towards Martin – 'are making it a problem.'

'I'm not making it,' said Martin. 'The world's doing that.'

'Blast the world,' said Luke. Luke was frowning: he uttered 'security' like a swearword, but he could not shrug it off: in the fortnight since the dropping of the bombs, it had fallen upon them more pervasively than ever in the war. Now they knew, as I did, that the rumour of the leakages was more than a rumour. So far as one could trust the intelligence sources, it was true.

Already that day, Luke had been forced to concede one of Martin's points. Kurt Puchwein, who had been working at Berkeley, had recently arrived back in England, and wanted to return to Barford as Luke's chief chemist. Luke had admitted that it was too dangerous to take him. None of us believed that Puchwein had been spying, but he was a platform figure of the left; if the leakages became public, Martin had made Luke agree, they could not stand the criticism of having re-engaged him at Barford. So Puchwein had arrived home, found that Hanna was finally leaving him and that he had no job. As for the latter, Luke said that he was 'taking care' of that; there were a couple of universities who would be glad to find a research readership for Puchwein; it would happen without commotion, one of those English tricks that Puchwein, for all his intellect and father-in-Israel shrewdness, could never completely understand.

That point was settled, but there was another.

'Martin is suggesting,' said Luke, 'that I ought to victimise someone.'

Our heads were close together, over the table; but Martin looked at neither of us, he seemed to be set within his carapace, guarded, official, decided.

'I think that's fair comment,' he said.

'You want to dismiss someone?' I asked.

'Yes,' said Martin.

'On suspicion,' said Luke.

'It may save trouble,' said Martin.

They were speaking of Sawbridge. I had heard nothing of Captain Smith's investigations for over a year. I had no idea whether Sawbridge was still suspected.

'Do you know anything I don't?' I said to Martin.

For once he replied directly to me, his eyes hard and with no give in them at all.

'Nothing,' he said.

All they knew was that, in the last few months, since his recovery, Sawbridge had spoken like a milk-and-water member of the Labour Party.

'What does that prove?' said Martin.

'All right, what does it prove?' said Luke. 'He might have gone underground. How do you know that I haven't, as far as that goes? How do I know that you haven't been for years – both of you? I expect we were all tempted, ten years ago.'

'This isn't getting us very far,' said Martin.

'Do you think you're getting us very far? You want me to get rid of my best radio-chemist—' Luke said it with anger (his professional feeling had risen up, he was thinking of the project, of the delay that losing Sawbridge might mean), and then lowered his voice again. 'I don't pretend that as a chap he's much my cup of tea, but he's been in this thing with us, he's entitled to his rights.'

Luke was not a sentimental man. He did not mention that Sawbridge had taken his share of the risks, and had suffered for it.

'We've got to balance his rights against the danger,' said Martin without expression.

'You've not given one single piece of evidence that he's got anything to do with the leakage,' said Luke.

'I don't intend to. That's not the point.'

'What is the point?'

'I've made it clear enough before. I'm not prepared to say whether he is or is not connected with the leakage, or whether there's any danger that he ever will be. I'm saying something quite different and much simpler. For the purpose of anyone running Barford, the world has divided itself into two halves. Sawbridge belongs to the other. If we keep him at Barford, it is likely to do the place finite harm. And it may not be nice for you and me.'

'I've told you before, and I will tell you again,' said Luke, 'you're asking me to throw Sawbridge out because a lot of old women may see bogies. Well, I'm not prepared to do it, unless someone can give me a better reason than that. There's only one reason that I should be ready to listen to. That is, is he going to give anything away?'

We all knew that Martin was right in his analysis. The world had split in two, and men like us, who kept any loyalty to their past or their hopes, did not like it. Years before, people such as Luke or Francis Getliffe or I had sometimes faced the alternative – if you had to choose between a Hitler world or a communist world, which was it to be? We had had no doubt of the answer. It had seemed to us that the communists had done ill that good might come. We could not change all the shadows of those thoughts in an afternoon.

It had been different, of course, with men like Thomas Bevill and his friends, or many of my old colleagues at Cambridge and the Bar. Most of them, in their hearts, would have given the opposite answer: communism was the enemy absolute: incidentally, it said something for the patriotism of their class that, full of doubts about the German war, knowing what it meant for them, win or lose, they nevertheless fought it.

Now it was men like Luke and Francis and me who felt the doubts, the scientists most of all. Often they were sick at heart, although despair was unnatural to them and they believed that the split in the world – the split which seemed to them the anti-hope – would not last for ever.

Martin said:

'I've explained to you, that doesn't begin to be the point.'

'For me,' Luke's voice became loud, 'it's the beginning and the end. Here's someone who, as far as you know, will never be any closer to a leakage than you or me. And you're saying we ought to find a bogus reason for putting him in the street – just because some old women might natter. I'm simply not playing that game. Nor would Lewis. If we have to start insuring ourselves like that, we might as well pack up.'

As he knew, my sympathies were on his side. It was he, not Martin, who had insisted on seeing me that night – because he wanted my support. But also he had asked for my advice as an official, and I had to give it. No prudent man could ignore Martin's case. True, the responsibility for security rested with Captain Smith and his service: true, also, that Martin's proposal to get rid of the man out of hand was indefensible. But the risks were as great as Martin said.

As I was advising Luke (I wanted him at the least to talk to the new chairman), I watched them both and thought – yes, Martin's case was clear, he was showing his usual foresight, and yet there was another motive behind it. Luke was frowning, his head bent over the table;

Martin was sitting slightly back, his forehead unlined, more controlled, more like an official, than the other two of us that night. He seemed remote from any sign or memory of the conflict in my office, only three weeks before. But, though he was remote, I believed I could see his motive.

As the hushed voices, his and Luke's and mine, whispered and hissed under the beams, I saw him for a moment with the insight of kinship: I thought I knew what he was aiming at. If I were right, I did not like it.

We had talked for a long time, when Luke pushed the table away. He had just repeated that he would not budge unless someone gave him new evidence; this was the finish.

'I'm damned if I get rid of Sawbridge,' he said, and his force was formidable.

Martin replied, unmoved:

'In that case I shall send you my views on paper.'

'Damn it, man,' for the third time Luke forgot to be quiet, 'we've talked it out, I don't want any bumf.'

Martin said:

'I'm sorry, but I want to have it on the record.'

CHAPTER XXX

A JOYOUS MOMENT IN THE FOG

THAT autumn it was strange to hear the scientists alone, trying to examine their consciences, and then round a committee table. Outsiders thought them complacent, opaque: of those that I knew best, it was not true.

'There aren't any easy solutions,' said Luke. 'Otherwise we should all take them.'

He was speaking first of scientists, but also of all others in a time of violence; for the only root-and-branch 'solutions' which could give a man absolute reason for not working at Barford on the bomb, were not open to many. Unqualified pacificism or communism – if you believed either, your course was clear. But no other faith touched the problem. Among the new recruits to Barford, there were a number who were religious, but none of the churches gave them a direction.

Either/or, said Luke. Either you retired and helped to leave your country defenceless. Or you made a weapon which might burn men, women and children in tens of thousands. What was a man to do?

'I don't think we have any option,' said Francis to me in the Athenæum, one night after his return from America. 'Luke's right, the Barford boys are right, we've got to make the infernal thing.'

After these conversations, I saw the same men in their places on the committees, experienced in business after six years of war, many of them, including Francis himself and Martin, having become skilful at the committee arts, disposing of great budgets, all caught up, without so much as a stumble of reservation, on getting the plutonium made at Barford. No body of men could have sounded less introspective; as their new chairman said, with the jubilation of a housemaster who sees the second eleven at the nets, they were the *keenest* committee he had ever had.

The new chairman was – to the irritation of his own friends and the Government backbenchers – old Thomas Bevill. In those first months of office, the Government had a habit of resurrecting figures from early in the war. Bevill was an ex-Minister, a Tory, but atomic energy had started under him; now it was in the limelight, he might soften criticism; so he was brought out of retirement like an old man of the tribe. On his side, he havered about taking a job under a Labour administration, but he was by this time seventy-six, they would be in for five years, he might never get another job and he just could not resist it.

At his first committee he slipped unobtrusively, happily into the chair, as though in literal truth, not in his own inexorable cliché, he was 'glad to be back in the saddle'. He gazed round the table and greeted each man by name. No one was less effusive by nature, but he always felt that effusiveness was called for on such occasions, and so he called out 'Dr Getliffe! old friend!' and so on clockwise round the table. 'Mr Drawbell! old friend!' 'Dr Luke! old friend!' and finally round to me, at his right hand: 'Our secretary, Mr Eliot! old friend!'

Mounteney, sitting near me, was disgusted. One might have asked why he was there at all, after his disappearance from Barford, never to return. Actually, Mounteney's self-exile from atomic energy had lasted exactly two months. He remained in his professorship, but accepted a seat on the committee. He was so austere that no one dared to ask why. Duty? Yes. The desire that real scientists should have a voice? No doubt. But for myself, I believed that his chief motive was the same as Bevill's, whom he so much despised – that he could not bear to be out of things.

So, in the autumn of 1945, Bevill was listening to the scientists, hearing Mounteney's minority opinion, trotting round the corner to the Treasury with Rose. It was on one of his committee afternoons, the technical sub-committee which I did not attend, that Irene came up with Martin for the day. On this committee Martin had a place as well as Luke, and as I took Irene out through the park, in the foggy afternoon, to tea, I pointed up to a window whose lights streamed out into the whirling white.

'There they are,' I said.

'Busy as beavers,' said Irene.

She was smiling with a tenderness unusual in her. Perhaps she felt the safety we all snuggle in, when someone about whom we worry is for a couple of hours securely locked away. Certainly she was gratified that he was up there, in the lighted room, among the powerful. Had her prediction – 'I should like to know what you expect from him now' – been nothing more than hitting out at random? She had not seen him that night at Stratford; she showed no concern for what he might be planning.

Although she had been behind him in his outburst, had quarrelled with me so bitterly that we had not been reconciled till that afternoon, she nevertheless, with a superb inconsistency, had blotted all that out and now simmered with content because he was 'getting on'.

But her smile, tender, coming from within, held more than that.

'I love the fog, don't you?' she said. She said a little more: and I realised that this scene of subfusc grandeur, the back of Whitehall with window lights tumbling out in the fog of St James's Park, at first lay heavy on her mind, as though there were a name she had forgotten and yet was lurking near her tongue, and then suddenly lifted, to let rise a memory not so grand but full of mellowing joy: another foggy afternoon years before, a street in Bayswater, the high shabby-genteel houses, the joy of childhood autumn.

Under a lamp in the Mall, I looked at her, and thought I had never seen her face so happy. Her youth was going, she still had her dash, she still looked a strapping, reckless woman – and on her mouth was a tender, expectant, astonished smile. I wondered if she had smiled so before she begun her adventures. I wondered if she had come to the end of them, if she were what she called 'settled down'?

How would she take it, when that end came? I had not yet seen a woman, or a man either, who had lived a life of sexual adventure, give it up without a bitter pang that the last door had clanged to. Nevertheless, I had a suspicion that she might struggle less than most. I did not believe that she was, in the elemental sense, passionate. There were many reasons which sent people off on their sexual travels, and sheer passion was one of the less common. If you were searching for a woman moved by passion, you would be more likely to find her in someone like Mary Pearson, who had not been to bed with a man except her husband. Of those two, it was not Mary Pearson, it was Irene, who had racketed so long, it was she who would in the long run, and not unwillingly, give way to age and put her feet up with a sigh.

If that day came, I wondered – walking through the fog, taking her to tea as a sign that there was peace between us – whether she and I would at last cease to grate on each other? Was that walk through the park a foretaste? I had not noticed her restlessness, she spoke as though she trusted me, remembering in the sight of the lighted window a spate of joy which seemed, as such joys of memory seem to us all, like the intimation of a better life from which we have been inexplicably cut off.

CHAPTER XXXI

SITUATION DESIGNED FOR A CLEAR HEAD

ON New Year's Eve, just as the Whitehall lamps were coming out, Bevill sent for me. The room which had been found for him as chairman was at the end of the passage, and even more unpretentious than his room as Minister; Bevill did not grumble, he had never in his life grumbled at a minor slight, he settled there and called it his 'hutch'. But that afternoon, as soon as I entered, I saw his face heavily flushed, with an angry blood-pressure flush that one did not often see in so spare a man, the relics of grey hair twisted over his head so that he looked like a ferocious cockatoo.

Rose was sitting with him, arms folded, unaffected except that the pouches under his eyes seemed darker.

'This is a nasty one,' Rose was saying. 'Yes, it is a distinctly nasty one.'

'The swine,' said Thomas Bevill.

'Well, sir,' said Rose, 'it means some publicity that we could do without, but we can cope with that.'

'It knocks the feet from under you, that's what it does,' said Bevill.

In the war, whatever the news was like, he had been eupeptic, sturdily hopeful – not once rattled as he was that afternoon.

He turned to me, his eyes fierce, bewildered.

'Captain Hook's just been in,' he said.

'Captain Hook' was his name – partly one of his nursery jokes, partly for secrecy's sake – for Smith, the retired naval captain, the chief of the security branch. 'One of your scientists has been giving us away to the

Russians. A chap who's just come back from Canada. They're going to put him inside soon, but it's locking the stable door after the horse is lost.'

I asked who it was.

'I didn't get the name. One of your Cambridge men.' Bevill said it accusingly, as though I were responsible for them all.

Rose told me that it was a man who had at no time been employed at Barford.

'That isn't the half of it,' said Bevill. 'There's another of them at least who they're waiting for. *They oughtn't to have to wait*,' he burst out. 'We're too soft, any other country in the world would have risked a bit of injustice! Sometimes I think we shall go under just because we put too high a price on justice. I tell you that, Rose, though I don't want it to go outside this room.' He said to me: 'This chap's still knocking about at Barford now. He's a young chap called Sawbridge. Do you know him?'

'A little,' I said.

'Is he English?' said Bevill.

'As English as I am,' I said.

The blood was still heavy in Bevill's temples, as he shook his head.

'I can't understand it.'

He shook his head again. 'I don't want to set up as better than anyone else, and I can understand most things at a pinch. I expect we've all thought of murder, haven't we?' said the old man, who as a rule looked so mild. He went on, forgetting his nursery prattle, and speaking like a Hanoverian. 'As for rape and' – he listed the vices of the flesh – 'anyone could do them.'

Hector Rose said, surprisingly: 'We're none of us spotless.'

'But as for giving away your country, I can't understand it,' said Bevill. 'I could have done the other things, but I couldn't have done that.

'I don't want to put the clock back,' he said. 'But if it were in my hands, I should hang them. I should hang them in Trafalgar Square.'

At Barford next day, Bevill himself sat in with Captain Smith as he broke the news to the leading scientists one by one. He interviewed them, not in Drawbell's office, but his secretary's, both Bevill and Smith sitting on typing stools among the hooded typewriters and dictaphones; sometimes I was called in to hear the same half-explanations, the same half-questions.

It was only Drawbell, alone with me during the morning, who let out a spontaneous cry. This was the first day of 1946, which in Drawbell's private calendar marked the last stage of the plutonium process, with luck the last year of plain Mr Drawbell. He had to complain to somebody, and he cried out:

'This isn't the kind of New Year's gift I bargained for!'

And then again:

'This isn't the time to drop bricks. They couldn't have picked a worse time to drop bricks!'

When I heard Smith talking to scientist after scientist, the monotony, the strain, seemed to resonate with each other, so that the light in the little room became dazzling on the eyes.

To the seniors, Smith had to tell more than he liked. In his creaking, faded, vicarage voice, he said that his 'people' knew that Sawbridge had passed information on.

'How do you know?' said one of them.

'Steady on, old son,' said Captain Smith. He would not explain, but said that beyond doubt they knew.

They also knew which information had 'gone over'.

Another of the scientists speculated on how much time that data would save the Russians. Not long, he thought; a few months at the most.

Bevill could not contain himself. He burst out:

'If our people are killed by their bomb, it will be this man's doing.'

The scientist contradicted him, astonished that laymen should not realise how little scientific secrets were worth. He and Bevill could not understand each other.

Bevill did not have to put on his indignation; it was not just the kind of politician's horror which sounded as though it had been learnt by heart. He was speaking as he had done yesterday, and as I was to hear others speak, not only among the old ruling classes, but among the humble and obscure for years to come. Bevill had not been shocked by the dropping of the bomb; but this was a blow to the viscera.

Whereas, as they heard the first news of the spies, the scientists were unhappy, but unhappy in a different tone from Bevill's. They had been appalled by Hiroshima, still more by Nagasaki, and, sitting in that typists' office, I thought that some at least had got beyond being appalled any more. They were shocked; confused; angry that this news would put them all back in the dark. They felt trapped.

To two of them, Smith, for reasons I did not know, said that one arrest, of the man who had been working in Canada, would happen within days. There had been at least three scientific spies, whom most of the men Smith had interviewed that day had known as friendly acquaintances.

For once even Luke was at a loss. Smith seemed to be wasting his time. He had come for two purposes, first to satisfy himself about some of the scientists whom we knew least, and second, to get help in proving his case against Sawbridge. But all he discovered were men shocked, bewildered, sullen.

There was one man, however, who was not shocked nor bewildered nor sullen. It was Martin. His mind was cool, he heard the news as though he had foreseen it and made his calculations. I did not need to look at him, as Smith brought out his elaborate piece of partial explanation. I had expected Martin to see it as his time to act.

Smith asked to have a 'confab' with him and Luke together, since Sawbridge was working directly under them. As they sat on the secretary's desk, he told them, speaking frankly but as though giving an impersonation of frankness, that Sawbridge's was the most thorough piece of spying so far. The difficulty was, to bring it out against him. Smith's conclusive evidence could not be produced. The only way was to break him down.

'You've tried?' said Luke.

'Well, we've just been exploring the ground,' said Smith, with his false smile.

'Without any result?'

'He's a tough one,' said Smith.

'What does he say?'

'He knows when to keep mum,' said Smith.

Bevill's voice and Luke's sounded soggy with exasperation, but not Martin's, as he asked:

'How long can he keep that up?'

His eyes met Smith's, but Luke disturbed them.

'Anyway,' Luke was saying, 'the first thing is to get this chap out of the laboratory before we shut up shop tonight.'

'I don't think that's right,' said Martin.

'What are you getting at, Eliot?' asked Bevill.

'I suggest that the sensible thing, sir,' said Martin speaking both modestly and certainly, 'is to leave him exactly where he is.'

'With great respect,' Smith said to Luke, after a pause, 'I wonder if that isn't the wisest course?'

'I won't have him in my lab a day longer,' said Luke.

'He might get away with your latest stuff,' cried old Bevill.

Martin answered him quietly:

'That can be taken care of, sir.'

'If we move him,' Smith appeared to be thinking aloud, 'we've got to make some excuse, and if he isn't rattled he might require a very good excuse.'

'How in God's name can you expect us to work,' Luke shouted, 'with a man we can't talk in front of?'

'If we leave him where he is,' said Martin, without a sign of excitement, 'he would be under my eyes.'

He added:

'I should very much prefer it that way.'

In the middle of the argument, the telephone rang on the far table. It was from Drawbell's personal assistant, the only person who could get through to us; she was asking to speak to me urgently. In a whisper, only four feet from old Bevill, I took the call.

'I'm sorry, Mr Eliot,' she said, 'but Hanna Puchwein is pressing me, she says that she must speak to you and your brother this afternoon. I said that I mightn't be able to find you.'

'That's right,' I said.

'I suppose you can't speak to her?'

'No,' I said, with routine prudence.

'She said, if I couldn't get you, that I was to leave a message. She's most anxious. She told me to say it was urgent for her – for you and Dr Eliot [Martin] to see her before dinner tonight.'

I went back to my place, wrote down the message, put it in an envelope (it was curious how the fug of secrecy wrapped round one, how easy it was to feel like a criminal) and had it passed across the room to Martin. I watched him staring at the note, with his pen raised. Without his face changing, he wrote: 'No, not until we have discussed it with Smith.'

Uncertain of himself as I had not seen him, Luke soon gave way. Sawbridge was to stay under observation, and we left Smith alone with Luke and Martin, making arrangements about how Sawbridge must be watched.

Although Martin and I had not once talked without reserve since the August afternoon, I was staying, as usual, in his house. So I waited for him in his laboratory, while he finished the interview with Captain Smith.

As I waited there alone, I could not help trying to catch a glimpse of Sawbridge. His state of jeopardy, of being in danger of hearing a captor's summons (next week? next month?), drew me with a degrading fascination of which I was ashamed.

It was the same with others, even with Smith, who should have been used to it. The sullen, pale face had only to come within sight – and it was hard to force one's glance away. It might have been a school through which there moved, catching eyes afraid, ashamed, desiring, a boy of superlative attraction. On the plane of reason I detested our secret; yet I found myself scratching at it, coming back to it.

Waiting for Martin, I manufactured an excuse to pass through Sawbridge's laboratory, so that I could study him.

He knew his danger. Just like us who were watching him, he was apprehending when the time – the precise instant of time – would come. It seemed that at moments he was holding his breath, and he found himself taking care of ordinary involuntary physical acts. Instead of walking about the laboratory with his heavy, confident clatter, he went lightly and jaggedly, sometimes on tiptoe, like a man in trepidation by a sick bed. He had grown a moustache, fair against the large-pored skin. He was working on, taking his measurements, writing results in his stationery office notebook. He knew that we were watching. He knew all we knew. He was a brave man, and his opaque, sky-blue eyes looked back with contempt.

Martin, sooner than I counted on, found me there. He called Sawbridge: 'How is it coming out?'

'Eighty per cent reliable.'

'Pretty,' said Martin.

They looked at each other, and as Martin took me out he called good-night.

CHAPTER XXXII

DISTRESS OUT OF PROPORTION

As soon as we reached Martin's laboratory, he switched on the light behind an opalescent screen. He apologised for keeping me, said that he wanted to have a look at a spectroscopic plate; he stood there, fixing the negative on to the bright screen, peering down at the regiments of lines.

I believed this work was an excuse. He did not intend to talk about his action that day. I was out of proportion distressed.

Though nothing had been admitted, we both took it for granted that there was a break between us; but it was not that in itself which weighed on me. Reserve, separation, the withdrawal of intimacy – the relation of brothers, which is at the same time tough and not overblown, can stand them all. And yet, as he stood over the luminous screen and we did not speak, I was heavy-hearted. The reason did not seem sufficient; I disliked what he planned to do about Sawbridge; but I could not have explained why I minded so much.

I had had no doubt what he intended, from that night at Stratford, when he put forward his case in front of Luke. He had foreseen the danger about Sawbridge: he had also foreseen how to turn it to his own use. It was clear to him, as in his place it might have been clear to me, that he could gain much from joining in the hunt.

It was cynical, but I could not lay that against him. It might be the cynicism of the rebound, for which I was at least in part responsible. His suggestion at Stratford had been unscrupulous, but it would have saved trouble now. And I could not lay it against him that now he wanted to put Sawbridge away. We had never talked of it, but we both had the patriotism, slightly shamefaced, more inhibited then Bevill's, of our kind and age.

We took it out in tart, tough-sounding sentiments, that as we had to live in this country, we might as well make it as safe as could be. In fact, when we heard of the spies, we were more shaken than we showed.

Concealing our sense of outrage, men like Martin and Francis Getliffe and I said to each other, in the dry, analytic language of the day – none of us liked the situation in which we found ourselves, but in that situation all societies had their secrets – any society which permitted its secrets to be stolen was obsolescent – we could not let it happen.

But accepting that necessity was one thing, making a career of it another.

Yet was that enough to make me, watching him, so wretched?

Was it even enough that he was throwing other scruples away, of the kind that my friends and I valued more? Among ourselves, we tried to be kind and loyal. Whereas I had no doubt that Martin was planning to climb at Luke's expense, making the most out of the contrast between Luke's mistake of judgment over Sawbridge and Martin's own foresight. That day he had taken advantage of Luke's confusion, in front of Bevill. And Martin had a card or two still to play.

Was that enough reason for my distress?

Carefully Martin packed the photographic plate in the box, made a note on the outside, and turned to me. He apologised again for keeping me waiting; he was expecting a result from another laboratory in ten minutes, and then he would be ready to go.

We made some conversation with our thoughts elsewhere. Then, without a preliminary and also without awkwardness, he said:

'I'm sorry we had to brush Hanna off.'

I said yes.

'I'm sure it was wise,' said Martin.

'Is there any end to this business?'

'Not yet.'

He went on: 'Hanna will understand. She's a match for most of us.'

I glanced at him, his face lit from below by the shining screen. He was wearing a reflective, sarcastic smile. He said:

'Why don't you and I marry women like that?'

I caught his tone. He knew what my marriage had been like, and he had guessed that I might soon make another.

'Because we want a quiet life,' I said. It was the kind of irony that we could still share.

'Exactly,' said Martin.

We seemed close enough to speak. It was for me to take the first step if we were to be reconciled. I said:

'We look like being in an unpleasant position soon.'

Martin said:

'Which one?'

I said:

'About Sawbridge.'

'Maybe,' said Martin.

I said:

'It would be a help to me if I knew what you were thinking.'

'How, quite?'

'These are times when one needs some help. So far as I'm concerned I need it very much.'

After a pause, Martin said:

'The trouble is, we're not likely to agree.'

Without roughness, he turned the appeal away. He began asking questions about the new flat into which I was just arranging to move.

CHAPTER XXXIII

WIFE AND HUSBAND

THE spring came, and Sawbridge remained at liberty. But the scientist about whom the warning came through on New Year's Eve had been arrested, had come up at the Old Bailey, pleaded guilty and been given ten years. His name, which Bevill had forgotten that day, made headlines in the newspapers.

Later, I realised that most of us on the inside hid from ourselves how loud the public clamour was. We knew that people were talking nonsense, were exaggerating out of all meaning the practical results; and so, just like other officials in the middle of a scandal, we shut our ears off from any remark we heard about it, in the train, at the club bar, in the theatre-foyer, as though we were deaf men who had conveniently switched off our hearing aids.

Myself, I went into court for the trial. Little was said there; for many people it was enough, as it had been for Bevill, to add to the gritty taste of fear.

Always quick off the mark, Hankins, in his profession the most businesslike of men, got in with the first article, which he called The Final Treason. It was a moving and eloquent piece, the voice of those who felt left over from their liberal youth, to whom the sweetness of life had ceased with the twenties, and now seemed to themselves to be existing in No-Man's Land. For me, it had a feature of special interest. That was a single line in which he wrote, like many writers before him, a private message. He was signalling to Irene, reminding her that she had not always lived among 'the new foreigners' – that is, the English scientists. For Hankins had come to think of them as a different race.

Soon after came news, drifting up from Barford to the committees, that Luke was ill. 'Poorly' was the first description I heard. No one seemed to know what the matter was – though some guessed it might be an after-effect of his 'dose'. It did not sound serious; it did not immediately strike me that this put Martin in effective charge.

I thought so little of it that I did not write to enquire, until towards the end of March I was told by Francis Getliffe that Luke was on the 'certain' list for that year's elections to the Royal Society. I asked if I could congratulate him. Yes, said Francis, if it were kept between us. Luke himself already knew. So I sent a note, but for some days received no reply. At last a letter came, but it was written by Nora Luke. She said that Walter was not well, and not up to writing his thanks himself; if I could spare the time to come down some day, he would like to talk to me. If I did this, wrote Nora in a strong inflexible handwriting, she asked me to be sure to see her first. Then she could give me 'all the information'.

I went to Barford next morning, and found Nora in her laboratory office. On the door was a card on which the Indian ink gleamed jet bright: N. Luke, and underneath P.S.O., for Nora had, not long before, been promoted and was at that time the only woman at Barford of her rank.

As soon as I saw her, I said:

'This is serious, isn't it?'

'It may be,' said Nora Luke.

She added:

'He asked me to tell you. He knows what the doctors think.'

'What do they think?'

Sitting at her desk, with her hair in a bun, wearing rimless spectacles, her fawn sweater, her notebook in front of her, she looked as she must have done when she was a student, and she and Luke first met. Steadily she answered:

'The worst possibility is cancer of the bone.'

It was what he had feared, in his first attack.

'That may not happen,' Nora went on in a reasonable tone. 'It seems to depend on whether this flare-up is caused by the gamma rays or whether it's traces of plutonium that have stayed inside him and gone for the bone.'

'When will you know?'

'No one can give him any idea. They haven't any experience to go on. If this bout passes off, he won't have any guarantee that it's not going to return.'

I muttered something: then I enquired how many people knew.

'Most people here, I suppose,' said Nora. Suddenly she was curious: 'Why do you ask that?'

In my middle twenties, I also had been threatened with grave illness. I had tried to conceal it, because it might do me professional harm. Instead of telling Nora that, I just said how often I had seen people hide even the mention of cancer.

'He wouldn't have any patience with that,' said Nora. 'Nor should I. Even if the worst came to the worst' – she stared straight at me – 'the sooner everyone here knows the dangers the more they can save themselves.'

How open she was, just as Luke was himself! Sometimes their openness made the ruses, the secretiveness, of such as I seem shabby. Yet, in my own illness, it would have been feeble not to be secretive. They were able to be open as, fifteen years before, I couldn't be. Even so, learning from Nora about her husband's illness, I felt that she was too open, I was more embarrassed than if she could not get a word out, and so I was less use to her.

I asked where Luke was, and who was nursing him. In the establishment hospital as before, said Nora; Mrs Drawbell, also as before.

'She's better at it than I am,' said Nora.

She added, her light eyes right in the middle of her lenses, her glance not leaving mine:

'If he's knocked out for years, I suppose I shall have some practice.'

She went on: 'As a matter of fact, if I've got him lying on his back for keeps, I shall be grateful, as long as I've got him at all.'

She said it without a tear. She said it without varying her flat, sensible, methodical voice. Nevertheless, it made me realise how, even five minutes before, and always in the past, I had grossly misunderstood her. The last time Luke was ill, and she had left the ward, I had thought to myself that she was glad to escape, that like me she could not stand the sight of suffering. Nonsense: it was a carelessness I should not have committed about a wilder woman such as Irene; at forty I had fallen into the adolescent error of being deceived by the prosaic.

Actually Nora would have stayed chained to her husband's bedside, had it kept the breath of life in him a second longer. She had the total devotion – which did not need to be passionate, or even emotional – of one who began with no confidence in her charms, who scarcely dared think of her charms at all. Her self-esteem she invested in her mind which in fact she thought, quite mistakenly, was in her husband's class. But, in her heart, she was always incredulous that she had found a man for life. Rather than have him taken away she would accept any terms.

Illness, decay, breakdown – if only he suffered them in her care, then she was spared the intolerable deprivation of losing him. It was those total devotions which sprang from total diffidence that were the most possessive of all. Between having him as an abject invalid, and having him in his full manhood but apart from her, there would not have been the most infinitesimal flicker of a choice for Nora.

When I entered Luke's ward, the room was dark, rain was seeping down outside, he seemed asleep. As I crossed the floor, there was a rustle in the bed; he switched on the reading lamp and looked at me with a flushed, tousled face. The last patch of alopecia had gone, his hair was as thick as it used to be, the flush mimicked his old colour, but had a dead pallor behind it.

'I've heard the doctors' opinions,' I said, searching for some way of bringing out regret. To my amazement, Luke said:

'They don't know much. If only there hadn't been more interesting things to do, Lewis, I'd have liked to have a shot at medicine. I might have put some science into it.'

I could not tell whether he was braving it out – even when he went on:

'I shall be surprised if they're going to finish me off this time. I don't put the carcinoma theory higher than a twenty per cent chance.'

If that was his spirit, I could only play up. So I congratulated him again on the Royal Society election.

'Now that's the only bloody thing that really frightens me,' said Luke, with a grim, jaunty laugh. 'When the old men give you your ticket a year or two early, it makes you wonder whether they're hurrying to get in before the funeral.'

'I haven't heard any whispers of that,' I said.

'Are you lying?'

'No.' He had been elected on his second time up, while not yet thirty-five.

'That's a relief,' said Luke, 'I tell you, I shall believe that I'm done for when I see it.'

I thought, how easy he was to reassure.

'One thing about people trying to dispose of you like this,' said Luke, 'it gives you time to think.'

Half-heartedly (I did not feel much like an argument) I asked what he had been thinking about.

'Oh, the way I've spent my life so far,' said Luke. 'And what I ought to do with the rest of it.'

He was not speaking with his old truculence.

'I couldn't help being a scientist, could I? It was what I was made for. If I had my time over again, I should do the same. But none of us are really going to be easy about that blasted bomb. It's the penalty for being born when we were – but whenever we have to look into the bloody mirror to shave, we shan't be a hundred per cent pleased with what we see there.'

He added:

'But what else could we do? You know the whole story, what else could chaps like me do?'

I mentioned that I had once heard Hector Rose say – Hector Rose, who stood for so much that Luke detested – that 'events may get too big for men.'

'Did he? Perhaps he's not such a stuffed shirt after all. Of course we've all thought events may be too big for us.'

He fell silent. Then he said:

432

'It may be so. But we've got to act as though they're not.'

He knew that I agreed.

'It's a bit of a nonsense,' said Luke, 'but it isn't so easy to lose hope for the world – if there's a chance that you're going to die pretty soon. The moment you feel these things aren't going to be your concern much longer, then you think how you could have made a difference.'

He said:

'When I get over this, I shall make a difference. And if I don't, I don't know who can.'

He was so natural that I teased him. I inserted the name of the younger Pitt, but Luke knew no history.

He went on:

'I've been lowering my sights, Lewis. I want to get us through the next twenty years without any of us dropping the bomb on each other. I think if we struggle on, day by day, centimetre by centimetre, we can just about do that. I've got to get the bomb produced, I've got to make the military understand what they can do with it and what they can't. I shall have some fights on my hands, inside this place as well as outside, but I believe I can get away with it. Twenty years of peace would give us all a chance.'

He sat up against his pillows with a grin.

'It won't be good for my soul, will it?'

'Why not?'

It was nerve-racking that he thought so much of the future.

'I like power too much, I'm just discovering that. I shall like it more, when I've got my way for the next few years.'

He broke off:

'No, it won't be good for my soul, but if I do something useful, if I can win us a breathing space, what the hell does it matter about my soul?'

He had not once enquired about Martin or referred to him, except perhaps (I was not sure) when he spoke of internal enemies.

He made an attempt to ask about my affairs, but, with the compulsion of illness, came back to himself. He said, in a quiet, curiously wistful voice:

'I once told you I had never had time for much fun. I wonder when I shall.'

A memory, not sharp, came back to me. Luke, younger than now, in the jauntiness of his health, grumbling outside a Barford window.

From his bed he frowned at me.

433

'When these people told me I might die,' he said, 'I cursed because I was thinking of all the things I hadn't done. If they happen to be right, which I don't believe, I tell you, I shall go out thinking of all the fun I've wasted. That's the one thought I can't bear.'

Just for an instant his courage left him. Once again, just as outside Drawbell's gate (the memory was sharper now) he was thinking of women, of how he was still longing to possess them, of how he felt cheated because his marriage had hemmed him in. His marriage had been a good one, he loved his children, he was getting not too far from middle age; yet now he was craving for a woman, as though he were a virgin dying with the intolerable thought that he had missed the supreme joy, the joy greater in imagination than any realised love could ever be, as though he were Keats cursing fate because he had not had Fanny Brawne.

In those whom I had seen die, the bitterest thought was what they had left undone.

And, as a matter of truth, though it was not always an easy truth to take, I had observed what others had observed before – I could not recall of those who had known more than their share of the erotic life, one who, when the end came, did not think that his time had been tolerably well spent.

CHAPTER XXXIV

DEMONSTRATION WITHOUT RISK

MARTIN was the last man to move too quickly. The summer came, Sawbridge was still working in the plutonium laboratory, there was nothing new from Captain Smith. From Luke's ward there came ambiguous, and sometimes contradictory reports; some doctors thought that it was a false alarm. Whoever was right, Martin could count on months in control. The press kept up articles on traitors and espionage, but Barford was having a respite out of the news.

In July, Martin let us know that the first laboratory extraction of plutonium metal was ready for test. Drawbell issued invitations to the committee, as though he were trying to imitate each detail of the fiasco with the pile. The day was fixed for 16 July, and Bevill was looking forward to it like a child.

'I believe tomorrow is going to be what I should call a Red Letter Day,' he said earnestly, as soon as he met the scientists at Barford, as though he had invented the phrase. At dinner that night, where there came Drawbell,

Martin, Francis Getliffe, Mounteney, Hector Rose, Nora Luke, ten more Barford scientists and committee members, he made a long speech retracing the history of the project from what he called the 'good old days', a speech sentimental, nostalgic, full of nursery images, in which with the utmost sincerity he paid tribute to everyone's good intentions, including those people whom he regarded as twisters and blackguards.

As we were standing about after dinner, Martin touched my arm. He took me to the edge of the crowd and whispered:

'There's no need to worry about tomorrow.'

Looking at him, I saw his mouth correct, his eyes secretive and merry. I did not need an explanation. In estrangement, it was still possible to read each other's feelings; he had just considered mine with a kind of formal courtesy, as he would not have needed to consider a friend's.

I was not staying with him that night, but he asked me to escape from the party for a quarter of an hour. We went inside the establishment wire, and walked quickly along the sludgy paths.

In an empty room of the hot laboratory, he found me a set of rubber clothes, cloak, cowl, gloves, and goloshes, and put on his own. He took me down a passage marked DANGER. 'Never mind that,' said Martin. He unlocked a steel door which gave into a slit of a room, empty except for what looked like a meat-safe, with a small window. Gazing through it, I saw a small floppy yellowish bag. There hovered over the bag the kind of artificial hand I had seen before at Barford. Martin showed me how to work it from outside, so the fingers descended and pushed the bag an inch or two.

'Now you can say you've touched plutonium,' he said.

'How much?'

'Not much. I suppose it's worth a few hundred thousand pounds.' He looked through the window with a possessive and almost sensual glance. I had seen collectors look like that.

For once, Martin was taken unawares. He was disconcerted to see me lost in an absent-minded content.

'Are you all right?' he asked.

'Quite,' I said.

Next day, the demonstration was conducted as though Martin and his staff did not know whether it would work.

At the end, however, Martin would not accept the congratulations, insisting that they were due to Luke, and he took Bevill and the others to Luke's bedside.

Hector Rose and I followed behind.

'Are you going with them, Eliot?' said Rose.

I was surprised by the constraint in his voice.

'I think we'd better,' I said.

'As a matter of fact, I think I'll just take a stroll round the place,' he said.

It was so impolite, so unlike him that I did not begin to understand. Although I accompanied him, I could get no hint of the reason. Later I picked it up, and it turned out to be simple, though to me unexpected. Hector Rose happened to feel a morbid horror of cancer; he tried to avoid so much as hearing the name of the disease.

By ourselves, in Drawbell's office, Rose was for him relaxed, having extricated himself from an ordeal; he let fall what Bevill would have called one or two straws in the wind, about the future management at Barford. He and Bevill wanted to get it on a business footing: Drawbell was dead out of favour. If they made a change of superintendent, and if Luke were well, it would be difficult to sidetrack him – but none of the officials, and few of the elderly scientists, relished the idea. He had made mistakes: he talked too loud and too much: he was not their man.

Already they trusted Martin more. He was younger, he was not in the Royal Society, to give him the full job was not practical politics; but, if Luke's health stayed uncertain, was there any device by which they could give Martin an acting command of Barford?

The luck was playing into Martin's hand. I knew that he was ready, just as he had been ready since that night in the Stratford pub, to make the most of it. Even when he paid his tribute to Luke he had a double motive, he had one eye on his own future.

It was true that he was fair-minded, more so than most men. He would not receive more credit than he had earned. Better than anyone, he could estimate Luke's share in the project, and he chose to make it clear.

But although what he said of Luke was truthful, he also knew that men required it. Men liked fairness: it was part of the amenities, if in Bevill's and Rose's world you wanted your own way.

Now Martin was coming to his last move but one.

To Drawbell's room, Bevill and Martin and Drawbell himself returned from the sickbed. Mounteney and Francis accompanied them. Martin wanted those two on his side as well as the officials. If the opportunity did not arrive without forcing it, he was ready to wait. In fact, it came when Bevill asked about Luke's health.

'Is that poor chap,' said Bevill, 'going to get back into harness?'

'I hope so,' said Martin. 'The doctors seem to think so.'

'We just don't know,' said Drawbell.

'He may never come back, you mean?' said Bevill.

'I believe he will,' said Martin, once more speaking out deliberately on Luke's behalf.

'Well,' said Bevill to Drawbell, 'I suppose Eliot will carry on?'

'He's been doing it for months,' said Drawbell. 'I always tell my team no one is indispensable. If any of you go there's always a better man behind you!'

'I suppose you *can* carry on, Eliot, my lad?' said Bevill to Martin in a jollying tone.

At last Martin saw his opening.

Instead of giving a junior's yes, he stared down at his fingers, and then, after a pause, suddenly looked straight at Bevill with sharp, frowning eyes.

'There is a difficulty,' he said. 'I don't know whether this is the time to raise it.'

Drawbell bobbed and smiled. Now that the young men had grown up, he was having to struggle for his say.

'I don't see the difficulty,' said Bevill. 'You've been doing splendidly, why, you've been delivering the goods.'

'It would ease my mind,' said Martin, 'if I could explain a little what I mean.'

Bevill said, 'That's what we're here for.'

Martin said: 'Well, sir, anyone who is asked to take responsibility for this project is taking responsibility for a good deal more. I think it may be unreasonable to ask him, if he can't persuade his colleagues that we're shutting our eyes to trouble.'

Bevill said: 'The water is getting a bit deep for me.'

Martin asked a question:

'Does anyone believe we can leave the Sawbridge business where it is?'

'I see,' said Bevill.

In fact, the old man had seen minutes before. He was playing stupid to help Martin on.

'I am sorry to press this,' said Martin, 'but I couldn't let myself be responsible for another Sawbridge.'

'God forbid,' said Bevill.

'Is there any evidence of another?' said Francis Getliffe.

'None that I know of,' said Martin. He was speaking as though determined not to overstate his case. 'But if we can't touch this man, it seems

437

to me not impossible that we should have someone follow suit before we're through.'

'It's not impossible.' Francis had to give him the point.

'It's not exactly our fault that we haven't touched your present colleague,' said Rose.

'I have a view on that,' said Martin quietly.

'We want to hear,' said Bevill, still keeping all clear for Martin.

'Everything I say here is privileged?'

'Within these four walls,' the old man replied.

'I think there's a chance that Sawbridge can be broken down,' said Martin.

'Captain Hook has tried long enough.'

'That's true,' said Martin, 'but I think there's a chance.'

'How do you see it happening?'

'It could only be done by someone who knows him.'

'Who?'

'I'm ready to try,' said Martin.

Martin, in the same tone, went on to state his terms. If Sawbridge stayed at large in the project, it was not reasonable to ask Martin, feeling as he did, to take the responsibility. If he were to take it, he needed sanction to join Captain Smith and try to settle 'the Sawbridge business' for good and all.

Bevill was enthusiastically in favour; Rose thought it a fair proposal.

'We want two things,' said Rose. 'The first is safety, and the second is as little publicity as we can humanly manage. We should be eternally grateful, my dear Eliot' (he was speaking to Martin), 'if only you could keep us out of the papers.'

'That won't be possible,' said Martin.

'You mean, there'll be another trial?' said Francis.

'It's necessary,' said Martin.

Martin had counted on support from Bevill and Rose; he had also set himself to get acquiescence from the scientists. Suddenly he got more than acquiescence, he got wholehearted support where one would have looked for it last. It came from Mounteney. It happened that Mounteney possessed, as well as his scientific ideals, a passionate sense of a man's pledged word. He forgot about national secrecy (which he loathed) and communism (which in principle he approved of) in his horror that a man like Sawbridge could sign the undertaking of secrecy and then break it. In his pure unpadded integrity Mounteney saw nothing but the monstrosity of breaking one's oath, and, like Thomas Bevill, whom he resembled in no other conceivable fashion, he cried out: 'I should shoot them! The sooner we shoot them the better!'

In that instant I understood at last the mystery of Mounteney's surrender before the bomb was dropped, the reason his protest fizzled out.

It was Francis Getliffe who took longest to come round.

'I should have thought it was enough,' he said, 'for you to give Smith all the information you can. I don't see why you should get involved further than that.'

'I'm afraid that I must,' said Martin patiently.

'There are a great many disadvantages, and no advantages to put against them, in scientists becoming mixed up in police work, even now.'

'From a long-term view, I think that's right,' said Martin.

'Good,' said Francis.

'But,' said Martin, 'there are times when one can't think of the long-term, and I suggest this is one.'

'Why?'

'Because otherwise no one will make this man confess.'

'It isn't proved that you can make the difference.'

'No,' Martin replied. 'I may fail. But I suggest that is not a reason for stopping me.'

At last Francis shook his head, unwillingly assenting, and said:

'We've gone so far, someone was bound to go the whole distance.'

He, who carried so much authority, sounded for once indecisive: as though the things he and others had been forced to do had prepared the way for younger, harder men.

Then Martin put in his last word that afternoon:

'I think, before we settle it, that I ought to mention that Luke and I have not been in complete agreement on this problem.'

'That's appreciated,' said Hector Rose.

Martin spoke as fairly, as firmly, as when he had been giving the credit to Luke.

'I proposed easing Sawbridge out last summer,' he remarked. 'I felt sufficiently strongly about it to put it on the file.'

'I take it,' asked Rose, 'that Luke resisted?'

'It's no use crying over spilt milk,' said Bevill. 'Now you put us straight.'

CHAPTER XXXV

THE BRILLIANCE OF SUSPICION

THE day after Martin's piece of persuasion I did what, at any previous time, I should not have thought twice about. Now I did it deliberately. It was a little thing: I invited Kurt Puchwein to dinner.

As a result, I was snubbed. I received by return a letter in Puchwein's flowing Teutonic script:

'My friend, that is what I should have called you when Roy Calvert brought us together ten years ago. I realise that in volunteering to be seen with me again you are taking a risk: I am unwilling to be the source of risk to anyone while there is a shred of friendship left. In the life that you and your colleagues are now leading, it is too dangerous to have friends.'

The letter ended:

'You can do one last thing for me which I hope is neither dangerous for yourself, nor, like your invitation, misplaced charity. Please, if you should see Hanna, put in a word for me. The divorce is going through, but there is still time for her to come back.'

Within a few hours Hanna herself rang up, as though by a complete coincidence, for so far as I knew she had not been near her husband for months. It was the same message as at Barford on New Year's Day – could she speak to me urgently? I hesitated; caution, suspiciousness, nagged at me – and resentment of my brother. I had to tell myself that, if I could not afford to behave openly, few men could.

In my new flat Hanna sat on the sofa, the sun, on the summer evening still high over Hyde Park, falling across her but leaving her from the shoulders up in shadow. Dazzled, I could still see her eyes snapping, as angrily she asked me:

'Won't you stop Martin doing this beastly job?'

I would not begin on those terms.

'It's shabby! It's rotten!' Her face was crumbled with rage.

'Look, Hanna,' I said, 'you'd better tell me how it affects you.'

'You ought to stop him out of decency.'

Without replying, I asked about a rumour which I had picked up at Barford: for years Hanna's name had been linked with that of Rudd, Martin's first chief. Martin, who knew him well, was sure that she had picked wrong. She was looking for someone to master her; she thought she had found it in Rudd, who to his subordinates was a bully; yet with a woman he would be dependent. I asked, did she intend to marry him?

'Yes,' said Hanna.

'I was afraid so,' I said.

'You have never liked him.'

'That isn't true.'

'Martin has never forgiven him.'

'I wouldn't mind about that,' I said, 'if he were right for you.'

'Why isn't he right for me?'

'You still think you'd like some support?'

'Oh God, yes!'

'You had to bolster up Kurt for years, and now you're going to do the same again.'

'Somehow I can make it work,' she said, with an obstinate toss of her head.

She was set on it: it was useless, and unkind, to say more.

'That is,' she said, 'if Martin will let me marry him without doing him harm.'

'What do you mean?'

'I mean that it may be fatal to anyone at Barford to have a wife with my particular record.'

She seemed to be trying to say: 'I want this man. It's my last chance. Let me have him.' But she was extraordinarily inhibited about speaking from the heart. Both she and Irene, whom the wives at Barford envied for their sophistication, could have taken lessons from a good many of those wives in the direct emotional appeal. Anger, Hanna could express without self-consciousness, but not much else.

I asked if Rudd knew of her political past. Yes, she said. I told her (it was the only reassurance I could give her) that I had not heard her name in any discussion about Barford.

'Whose names have you heard?'

I told her no more than she already knew.

'Why don't you drag Martin out of the whole wretched business?'

I did not reply.

'I suppose he has decided that persecution is a paying line.'

Again I did not reply.

'If you will forgive a Jew for saying so,' she said with a bitter grin, 'it seems rather like St Paul going in the opposite direction.'

She went on:

'Does Martin know that he has been converted the wrong way round?'

Just then the rays of the sun, which had declined to the tops of the trees, began streaming into her eyes, and I drew the curtains across the furthest window. As I glanced at her, her face was open and bleached, as many faces are in anger, grief, pain.

She cried:

'Is there no way of shifting him?'

Then she said:

'Do you know, Lewis, I could have had him once.'

It might be true, I was thinking. When he had been at his unhappiest over Irene, in the first year at Barford – then perhaps Hanna could have taken him away. She threw back her neat small head, with a look that seemed most of all *surprised*. She said something more; she had considered him for herself, but turned him down because she had not thought him strong enough. Intelligent but lacking insight, with a strong will that had so long searched for a stronger, she had never been able to help underrating the men she met, especially those of whom she got fond. It came to her with consternation, almost with shame, that, now her will had come up in earnest against Martin's, she, who in the past had thought him pliable, did not stand a chance. She was outraged by his behaviour, and yet in her anger and surprise she wished that when they first met she had seen him with these fresh eyes.

She made another attack on me.

'He cannot like what he is doing,' she said. 'It cannot be good for him.'

She turned full on me, when I was sitting near the window with my back to the sunlight.

'I always thought you were more heavyweight than he was – but that he was the finer man.'

Making her last attempt, she was using that oblique form of flattery, which delights a father by telling him how stupid he is compared to his son. But for once it had no effect. I had no room for any thoughts but two.

The first was, the time would have to come when Martin and I faced each other.

The second – it was so sharp that it dulled even the prospect of a final quarrel – was nothing but suspicion, the sharp-edged, pieces-fitting-together, unreal suspicion of one plumped in the room where a crime had taken place. How did Hanna know so much of Martin's actions? What was she after? How close was she really to Puchwein nowadays? Was their separation a blind?

In that brilliance of suspicion, one lost one's judgment altogether. Everything seemed as probable, as improbable, as anything else. It seemed conceivable, that afternoon, that Hanna had lived years of her life in a moment-by-moment masquerade, more complete than any I had heard of. If one had to live close to official secrets (or, what sounded different but produced the same effect, to a crime of violence) one knew what it must be like to be a paranoiac. The beautiful detective-story spider-web of suspicion, the facts of every day clearer-edged than they have ever been, no glue of sense to stick them in their place.

That evening, each action of Puchwein's and Hanna's, for years past, stood out with a double interpretation – on one hand, the plunging about of wilful human beings, on the other, the master cover of spies. The residue of sense pulled me down to earth, and yet, the suspicions rearranged themselves – silly, ingenious, unrealistic, exciting, feelingless.

CHAPTER XXXVI

A CARTOON-LIKE RESEMBLANCE

THE same evening that Hanna visited me, Martin was talking to Captain Smith. Sawbridge was called by telephone some hours later, and 'invited to a conference', which was Smith's expression, on the following day. Smith rang me up also; he wanted me there for the first morning (he assumed that the interrogation would go on for days) in order to retrace once more the facts of how Sawbridge first entered Barford.

In past interrogations Smith had questioned Sawbridge time and again about his movements, for those days and hours when Smith was certain (though he could not prove it in a court) that Sawbridge had walked down a street in Birmingham, watched for a man carrying two evening papers, exchanged a word, given over his information; and this, or something close to it, had happened not once but three times, and possibly four.

In the morning we waited for him. Smith had borrowed a room in an annexe outside New Scotland Yard, behind Whitehall on the side opposite my office. The room smelt of paint, and contained a table, half a dozen shiny pitch-pine chairs, a small desk where a shorthand writer could sit; the walls were bare, except for a band of hat pegs and a map of Italy. I did not know why, but it brought back the vestry of the church where my mother used to go, holding her own through the bankruptcy, still attending parish meetings and committees for sales-of-work.

Smith walked about the room, with his actor's stride; he was wearing

a new elegant suit. Most of the conversation, as we waited, was made by
an old acquaintance of mine, a man called Maxwell, whom I had known
when I practised at the Common Law Bar. He had just become a detective
inspector in the special branch. He was both fat and muscular, beautifully
poised on small, strong, high-arched feet. His eyes, which were hot and
inquisitive, looked from Martin to me. We were both quiet, and apart
from a good-morning had not spoken to each other.

To Smith, Martin talked in a matter-of-fact tone, as though this were
just another morning. His face was composed, but I thought I noted,
running up from eyebrow to temple, a line which had not fixed itself
before.

Sawbridge was brought in. He had expected to see Smith but not the
rest of us; he stared at Martin; he did not show any fear, but a touch of
perplexity, as though this was a social occasion, and he did not know the
etiquette.

The smell of paint seemed stronger. I felt the nerves plucking in my
elbows.

'Hallo, old son,' said Smith in his creaking voice.

'Are you all right?' Sawbridge responded. It was the greeting that
Martin and I used to hear on midland cricket grounds.

'Let's get round the table, shall we?' said Smith.

We sat down, Smith between Sawbridge and Martin. He shot from one
to the other his switched-on, transfiguring smile.

'You two knew each other before ever you went to the varsity, didn't
you?'

Sharply Martin said:

'Oh yes, we peed up against the same wall.'

It might have been another man speaking. I had not heard him false-
hearty before; and, as a rule, no one knew better how to wait. Just then,
I knew for certain the effort he was making.

In fact, the phrase was intended to recall our old headmaster, who used
it as his ultimate statement of social equality. Sawbridge took it at its
face value, and grinned.

'I thought,' said Captain Smith, 'that it mightn't be a bad idea to have
another yarn.'

'What's the point of it?'

'Perhaps we shall see the point of it, shan't we?'

Sawbridge scarcely moved, but Martin held his eye, and began:

'You knew about how the Canadian stuff was given away?'

'No more than you do.'

'We're interested in one or two details.'

'I've got nothing to say about that.'

'You knew —— ' (the man convicted that spring), 'didn't you?'

'No more than you did.'

'Your ring was independent of that one, was it?'

I could hear that Martin's opening had been worked out. He was master of himself again, at the same time acute and ready to sit talking for days. To my surprise Sawbridge was willing, though he made his flat denials, to go on answering back. If I had been advising him (I thought, as though I were a professional lawyer again), I should have said: At all costs, keep your mouth shut. But Sawbridge did not mind telling his story.

On the other side there was no pretence that anyone thought him innocent. As in most investigations, Smith kept on assuming that Sawbridge had done it, that it was only necessary for him to admit the facts that Smith produced.

Smith talked to him like an old friend going over anecdotes familiar to them both and well liked ' 'hat was the time you took the drawings...' '... but you had met – before, hadn't you?' ... Smith, trying to understand his opponent, had come to have a liking for him – the only one of us to do so.

Even that morning, Smith was fascinated by the discovery he kept making afresh – that, at the identical time when (as Smith repeated, without getting tired of it) Sawbridge was carrying secrets of the Barford project to a contact man, he was nevertheless deeply concerned for its success. He had worked night and day for it; few scientists had been more devoted and wholehearted in their science; such scientific ability as he had, he had put into the common task.

I remembered the night of Luke's fiasco; it did not matter personally to Sawbridge, and he was not a man who displayed much emotion; but it was he who had been crying.

Smith shook his head, half gratified, as when one sees a friend repeat an inexplicable oddity; but to Martin it did not seem an oddity at all. Science had its own imperatives; if you were working on a problem, you could not help but crave for it to 'come out'. If you could be of use yourself, it was unnatural not to. It was not Sawbridge alone, but most of the scientific spies who had their own share, sometimes a modestly distinguished share, in producing results which soon after (like Sawbridge, walking to a commonplace street corner, looking for a man with an evening paper) they, as spies, stole away.

All this Martin understood much better than I did. Watching him and

Sawbridge facing each other across the table, I could hear them speaking the same language. The two young men stared at each other without expression, with the faces of men who had learned, more deeply than their seniors, to give nothing away. They did not even show dislike. At that moment, there was a cartoon-like resemblance between them, both fair, both blue-eyed: but Sawbridge's face was heavier than Martin's and his eyes glaucous instead of bright. Of the two, though at twenty-nine he was three years younger, he looked – although for the first time his expression was bitten into with anxiety – the more unalterable.

Martin's eyes did not leave him. He could understand much that to me was alien; to do so, one had to be both a scientist and young. Even a man like Francis Getliffe was set back by the hopes of his youth – whereas Martin by an effort seemed able to throw those hopes away, and accept secrets, spying, the persistence of the scientific drive, the closed mind, the two world-sides, persecution, as facts of life. How long had it been since he made such an effort? I thought, watching him without sympathy, though once or twice with a pulse of kinship. Was it his hardest?

CHAPTER XXXVII

<h2 style="text-align:center">THE LONELY MEN</h2>

I LEFT the room at mid-day, and saw no more of him for several days, although I knew that he was going on with the interrogation. Irene did not know even that, nor why he was staying so long in London. One afternoon, while Martin was sitting with Captain Smith and Sawbridge in the paint-smelling room, she had tea with me and asked about him, but casually, without anxiety.

In fact, she showed both enjoyment at his rise to fame, and also that sparkle of ridicule and incredulity which lurks in some high-spirited wives when their men come off. It was much the same incredulity as when she told me that 'E.H.' (Hankins) was at last on the edge of getting married.

'Caught!' she said. 'Of course the old boy can still slip out of it. But he's getting on, perhaps he's giving up the unequal struggle.'

Her unrest was past and buried, she was saying – but even so she was not as amused as she sounded. I was thinking that she, to whom marriage had sometimes not seemed so much of a confining bond, regarded it in her old lover with the same finality as her mother might have done. Like most of us, she was more voracious than she admitted to herself; even if he had been a trivial capture, the news of his marriage would have cost her a wrench. As for Hankins – though I listened to the squeal of glee with which she laughed at him, within weeks of being domesticated at last – I felt that she was half thinking – 'If I wanted, I should still have time to break it up!'

Although she did not know it, I read that night, as on each night for a week past, what her husband was doing. Evening by evening Captain Smith walked along from the room to my office with the verbatim report of what he called 'the day's proceedings'. Those reports had the curious sodden flatness which I had come to recognise years ago at the Bar in conversation taken down word by word. Most of the speeches were repetitive, bumbling, broken-backed. The edge was taken off Martin's tongue, and the others sounded maundering. There was also, as in all investigations I had been anywhere near, very little in the way of intellectual interchange. Martin and Sawbridge were men trained in abstract thought, and Martin could use the dialectic as well as Sawbridge; but in practice neither of them found this the time to do so.

Over ninety per cent of all those words, day by day for more than a week already, were matter-of-fact. Captain Smith's organisation was certain, from the sources they could not reveal, that Sawbridge had walked down a named street on a named day, and passed over papers. Ninety per cent, probably ninety-five per cent, of the records consisted of questions and answers upon actions as prosaic as that.

Out of the first days' transcript I read nothing but details. 'You were in Birmingham, at the corner of Corporation Street and New Street, on 17 October 1943?' (that was only a few months after Sawbridge arrived at Barford). Flat negatives – but one or two were broken down by ordinary police facts. Who could remember the events of an afternoon three years ago, anyway? Why not be vague?

Sawbridge denied being in Birmingham on any day that month: then he fumbled: Maxwell produced a carbon copy of a receipt (dated not 17 October but 22 October) given him by a Birmingham bookshop.

The next impression, of the later days of the first week, was that Martin was taking more and more of the examination. It looked as though Smith and the Special Branch between them had run out of facts, certainly of producible facts. Was Sawbridge experienced enough to guess it? Or did he expect there was evidence to come?

From the first, Martin's questions were more intimate than the others. He took it for granted that, as soon as Sawbridge knew that Barford was

447

trying to make the fission bomb, he did not feel much doubt about how to act.

E. (Martin) Did you in fact know what Barford was set up for before you arrived?

SA. (in the record, this symbol was used throughout to distinguish Sawbridge from Smith). No.

E. Hadn't you thought about it? (i.e. the bomb).

SA. I read the papers, but I thought it was too far off.

E. When did you change your mind?

SA. As soon as I was appointed there and heard about the background.

E. Then you believed it would happen?

SA. Of course I did, just like you all did.

E. That is, you believed this country or America would have the bomb within 3-4 years?

SA. We all did.

E. And you thought of the effect on politics?

SA. I'm not sure what you mean by politics.

E. You thought of the possibility that the West would have the bomb, and the Soviet Union wouldn't?

(Despite Sawbridge's last remark, Martin was using 'politics' in a communist sense, just as he steadily referred to the Soviet Union, as though out of politeness to the other man.)

SA. I thought if we'd seen that the thing might work then the Soviet physicists must have done the same.

E. But you didn't know?

SA. What do you take them for? Do you think you're all that better than they are?

E. No, but there are more of us. Anyway, you'd have felt safer if they knew what we were doing?

SA. I thought it was wrong to keep secrets from allies, if that's what you mean.

E. The Soviet Union wouldn't be safe until someone told them?

SA. I didn't say that.

E. But you thought it might be your duty to make certain?

SA. I thought it was the Government's duty.

E. You knew that wouldn't happen. You knew that the Soviet Union might be more at a disadvantage than they've been since the civil war?

SA. I didn't think they'd be far behind.

E. But they would be behind. They had to be kept up to date – even if
none of them was able to extend to us a similar courtesy?

(That was the only sarcasm of Martin's that came through the record.)

SA. They weren't in the same position.

E. You were thinking all this within a month of getting to Barford,
weren't you? Or it didn't take as long as a month?

SA. There wasn't much difficulty about the analysis.

E. You talked to a contact straightaway, then?

SA. No.

All through that exchange, Martin assumed that in origin Sawbridge's
choice had been simple. To introduce national terms, or words like
treachery, was making things difficult for yourself, not for Sawbridge. He
did not think of the Soviet Union as a nation, opposed to other nations;
his duty to it over-rode all others, or rather included all others. It was by
doing his duty to the Soviet Union that he would, in the long run, be
doing his duty to the people round him. There was no conflict there; and
those who, preoccupied with their own conflicts, transposed them to
Sawbridge, could not make sense of the labyrinths they themselves invented in him. It was Martin's strength that he invented none: from the
start, he treated Sawbridge as a man simple and tough, someone quite
unlike a figure out of Amiel or Kierkegaard, much more like Thomas
Bevill in reverse.

In fact, Martin assumed Sawbridge did not think twice about his duty
until he acted on it. Then he felt, not doubt, but the strain of any man
alone with his danger – walking the streets of Birmingham under the
autumn sun, the red brick gleaming, the Victorian gothic, the shop
fronts – so similar to the streets of the town twenty miles away, where both
he and Martin had waited at other street corners. The homely, commonplace, ugly street – the faces indifferent, the busy footsteps – no one
isolated or in any danger, except one man alone, looking out for an
evening paper, the homely evening paper which, not many years ago, he
would have bought for the football results. That was the loneliness of
action, the extreme loneliness of a man who was cutting himself off from
his kind.

From Martin's questions, he understood that too, as pitilessly he kept
on, waiting for an admission.

What had sent Sawbridge on those walks, cut off from the others safe
on the busy street? I could not find a satisfactory answer. Nearly everyone
found him dislikeable, but in a dull, unspecific fashion. His virtues were

the more unglamorous ones – reliability, abstinence, honesty in private relations. In some respects he resembled my *bête noire*, Pearson, and like Pearson he was a man of unusual courage. He possessed also a capacity for faith and at the same instant for rancour.

No doubt it was the rancour which made him a dynamist. Compare him, for example, with Puchwein, whose communism sprang from a magnanimous root – who was vain, impatient, wanted to be benevolent in a hurry. And, just as with many Romans who turned to Christianity in the fourth century, Puchwein wanted to be on the side of history. He had no question intellectually that, in the long run, the communists must win. But those motives were not so compelling as to drive him into danger; to go into action as Sawbridge did, benevolence was not enough.

Then what was? The hidden wound, people said: the wound from which he never took the bandages and which gave him his sullen temper, his rancour. None of us knew him well enough to reach it.

Did Martin see the wound clearer than I did? Did he feel any resemblance to himself?

If so, he shut it away. Behaviour matters, not motive – doing what he was doing, he could have no other thought.

The visits to Birmingham, the autumn transaction (giving the news that the pile was being built), the three visits in the spring, one just before Sawbridge had accompanied Luke into the hot laboratory: on each visit, what data had he given over?

Denial, denial again.

Martin increased the strain.

He knew, via Captain Smith, the information that had passed. He knew, which no one else but Luke could, that one piece of that information was false; while waiting for the rods to cool, they had decided on which solvent to use for the plutonium – and then, a good deal later, had changed their minds. It was the first method which had been reported to the agent; only Luke, Sawbridge and Martin could know the exact circumstances in which it had been decided on, and also given up.

Martin asked Sawbridge about those decisions. For the first and only time in the investigation, Martin gained an advantage through being on the inside. So far as I could judge, he used his technical familiarity with his usual deliberate nerve; but that was not the major weight with which he was wearing Sawbridge down.

The major weight came from his use of Sawbridge's loneliness, and his sense of how it was growing as the days dripped by. Against it Martin brought down, not only his bits of technical knowledge, not only the facts of the meetings at the Corporation Street corner – but also all the opinions of Barford, every sign that men working there were willing to dismiss Sawbridge from their minds, so that he should feel separate even from those among whom he had been most at home.

No one knew better than Martin how even the hardest suffer the agoraphobia of being finally alone.

On the seventh day, the record ran:

E. I suppose you have got your notebooks about the work at Barford?
SA. Yes.
E. We shall want them.
SA. I shall want them if I go back.
E. Do you think you will go back?
SA. I hope you realise what it will mean to Barford if I do not.
E. You might have thought of that before.
SA. I thought of it more than you have given me credit for.
E. After you made the first contact with ——.
SA. I have not admitted that.
E. After you made the first contact, or before?
SA. I thought of it all along.

For those seven nights running Captain Smith brought the record into my office. He made excuses to stay with me as I read; it looked like a refinement of security, but afterwards he liked to go out with me for a drink, taking his time about it. I discovered that he had a valetudinarian wife, for whom, without letting out a complaint, he had sacrificed his pleasure ever since he was a young man; but even he was not above stealing a pretext for half an hour away from her.

On the eighth night, which was Thursday, 23 September, he came into my office hand on hip, and, as he gave me the typescript, said:

'Now we shan't be long.'

'What?'

'Our friend is beginning to crack.'

'Is it definite?'

'Once they begin to crack, they never take hold of themselves again.'

He said it in his parsonical tone, without any trace of elation.

I felt – visceral pity; a complex of satisfactions: anxiety that the time was near (I neither wanted to nor could have done it while the issue was not settled) when I must speak to Martin.

'How long will he get?' I asked.

'About the same as the other one.'

He stared at me.

'Ten years, there or thereabouts,' he went on. 'It's a long time for a young man.'

I nodded.

'We've got to do it,' he said, in exactly the same neutral, creaking tone. He had not spoken of Sawbridge's sentence with sentimentality, but as a matter of fact; but also I had not heard him condemn Sawbridge. Smith had more moral taste than most persons connected with crime and punishment; the country had a right to guard itself, to make sure that men like Sawbridge were caught; but, in his view, it had no right to insult them.

The next night, the Friday, Smith was late arriving at my office. When he did so, fingering the rolled-up record as though it were a flute, he said:

'Our friend is going to make a complete statement on Monday morning.'

CHAPTER XXXVIII

WORDS IN THE OPEN

SMITH decided that we ought to take the news at once to Bevill and Rose. I followed him down the corridor to Rose's room, where, as Smith began a preamble about having a 'confab', I glanced out of the window into the dark muggy twilight, with the lights already shining (although it was only half-past six on a September evening) from windows in Birdcage Walk.

Bland behind his desk, Rose was bringing Smith to the point, but, as he did so, there was a familiar step outside, a step brisk and active, which did not sound like an old man pretending to be young – and Bevill came in, with a flushed happy look. He left the door open, and in a moment Martin entered.

'This is good news for us all,' said Bevill.

With one question, aside to me, Rose grasped what news they brought.

'It's jolly good work,' said Bevill.

'I suppose, in the circumstances, it is the best solution,' said Rose, and added, with his customary coolness: 'Of course, it will mean a good many awkward questions.'

'I hope this will encourage the others,' said Bevill.

'There mustn't be any more,' said Martin, speaking for the first time since he came in.

Bevill, who had been congratulating Smith, turned to Martin.

'You needn't think we don't know how much we've got to thank you for.' The old man beamed at him.

Martin shook his head.

Rose said: 'It's been a real contribution, and we're very grateful. Many, many congratulations.'

'What I like,' said Bevill, 'is that you've done it without any fuss. Some of your chaps make such a fuss whatever they do, and that's just what we wanted to avoid. I call you a public benefactor.' Bevill was rosy with content.

The party broke up, Smith leaving first. As Martin and I walked away down the corridor, not speaking, I heard the brisk trip behind us.

'Just a word,' said Bevill, but waited until we reached my room. 'This is a clever brother you've got, Lewis,' said the old man paternally. 'Look, I want to stand you both a dinner. Let's go to my little club. I didn't ask friend Rose up the passage, because I knew he wouldn't want to come.'

It was completely untrue, and Bevill knew it; Rose would have loved to be taken to Pratt's. But Bevill still refused to introduce his Whitehall acquaintances there. In his heart, though he could get on with all men, he did not like them, especially Rose. It was a fluke that he happened to like me, and now Martin.

The evening was sultry, and it was like a greenhouse in the club kitchen, where the fire blazed in the open grate. The little parlour was empty, when we had dinner at the common table off the check tablecloth, but one or two men were drinking in the kitchen.

That night, as on other occasions when I had watched him there, Bevill was unbuttoned; he stopped being an unobtrusive democrat the instant he passed the porter in the hall. His well-being was so bubbling that I could not resist it, though I had resolved to speak to Martin before the end of the night. Nevertheless, that seemed far away.

Bevill shouted to his friends through the parlour door. He was too natural to assume that Martin would know them by their Christian names, or alternatively would not be curious about the company he was in. Accordingly, Bevill enunciated a couple of the famous English titles: Martin attended to him. Looking at them, sharing some of the old man's euphoria (the evening was still early), I thought of the young Proust.

Unlike the young Proust, Martin was drinking pints of bitter. He appeared to be enjoying himself without reserve, without any sign of the journey that had brought him there.

Bevill, who still had a taste for a night's drinking, was having our tankards filled before we went on to port. For a time, while we sat alone round the table, he became elated with drink and could not resist a bit of philosophy.

'What do all our concerns matter, you two, when you put them in their proper place? They're just phenomena, taking place in time – what I like to call false time – and everything essential exists in a different and more wonderful world, doesn't it, right outside of space and time? That's what you ought to think of, Martin, when you're worried about fellows like Sawbridge, or your project. All our real lives happen out of time.

'That isn't to say,' he said, temporarily giving up speculative thought, 'that it won't be nice when you people at Barford give us a good big bang.

'Fine words butter no parsnips,' went on Bevill gravely, waving a finger at Martin, who in fact had not spoken. 'You chaps have got to deliver the goods.'

'That's bound to happen. It's cut and dried, and nothing can stop it now,' said Martin.

'I'm glad to hear you say so.' Bevill looked from Martin to me. 'You know, you chaps have got something on your hands.'

'What do you mean?' I said.

'It's not so easy pulling this old country through as it was when I was your age. If chaps like you don't take over pretty soon, it's not a very bright look-out.'

Martin and I both replied to him direct, not talking across to each other. But we agreed. Obviously the major power, which he had known, had gone: the country would have to live by its wits: it could be done: better men had known worse fates.

Bevill gave a cherubic, approving nod.

'You two ought to know, I shouldn't call myself a socialist,' he said, as though making an astonishing but necessary revelation, 'but I don't care all that much what these fellows [the government] do, as long as we keep going.'

It was spoken in drink, but it happened to be true. Half drunk myself, I loved him for it.

Cheerful, naïf (one could forget that he was a cunning old intriguer), he rambled on, 'philosophising' again to his heart's content, until in the kitchen, with sweat pouring down his face and mine, and beads at the roots of Martin's hair, he said:

'I want to say something, Martin, before I get beyond it.'

He said it in a different tone, sharp and businesslike.

Perhaps Martin did not know what I did – that when it came to action, it did not matter what state Bevill was in, or what nonsense he had been talking. On serious matters, like jobs or promises, he would not say a word out of turn or one he did not mean.

Martin listened as though he knew it too.

'You're sitting pretty at Barford, young man,' said Bevill.

'I suppose I am,' said Martin.

'I'm telling you, you are. We shan't forget what you've done for us, and it's time we did something for you.'

Bevill went on:

'There are different views on how to run the place – and who's to do it, I needn't tell you that. But I can tell you that whatever arrangement we make, it won't be to your disadvantage. You can just sit back and wait and see.'

'I didn't expect this,' said Martin.

'Didn't you? You must have been working things out,' said Bevill. I thought once more, that in such matters he was no man's fool. He continued: 'Now you can forget everything that I've told you. But a nod's as good as a wink to a blind horse.'

Few men who have longed for success can have known the exact instant when it came; but Martin must have known it, sitting at the side of the baking hearth at Pratt's, with the old man lifting his glass of port, and someone from the foot of the staircase calling out 'Tommy', so that Bevill, flushed, still businesslike, said to Martin, 'That's tipped you the wink,' and turned his head and began talking loudly to his acquaintance at the door.

I looked at Martin, leaning back while Bevill talked across him. One side of his face was tinged by the fire: his mouth was tucked in, in a sarcastic smile: his eyes were lit up.

I wished that the party would stretch on. Anyway, why should I ask him anything? It was not like me, or him either, to speak for the sake of speaking; as soon as one admitted out loud a break in a human relation, one made it wider.

I went on drinking, joining in Bevill's reminiscences of how he saved Barford years before. I told a story of my own which exaggerated Martin's influence and judgment at that time, giving him credit for remarks which Francis Getliffe made, or that I had made myself.

At last the old man said:

'Time for bye-byes!' We helped him up the stairs, found him a taxi, received triumphant good-byes, and watched as the rear lamp climbed the slope of St James's Street up to Piccadilly. Martin and I exchanged a smile, and I said something to the effect that the old man's ancestors must have gone up this street many times, often drunker than that.

'Occasionally soberer,' said Martin.

We looked across the road, where the lights of Boodle's shone on to the moist pavement. After the room we had left, the humid night was sweet. We stood together, and I thought for an instant that Martin expected me to speak.

'Well then, good-night,' he said, and began walking down the street towards the palace. He was staying in Chelsea; I hesitated, before turning in the opposite direction, on my way north of the park.

Martin had gone ten paces along the pavement. I called out:

'No, I want a word with you.'

He turned, not jerkily, and walked with slow steps back. He did not pretend to be puzzled, but said, with an expression open, concerned, as intimate as in the past:

'Don't you think it would be better not to?'

'It's too late for that.'

'I am sure that we shall both regret it.'

Mechanically, for no reason, we dawdled side by side along the pavement, while I waited to reply. We had gone past Brooks's before I said: 'I can't help it.'

It was true, though neither of us at that moment could have defined what drove us on. Yes, I was half sad because of what he had done; but there was hypocrisy in the sadness. In warm blood, listening to Bevill, I should not have repined because a brother had stamped down his finer feelings and done himself well out of it. Success did not come often enough to those one was fond of that one's responses could be so delicate.

It would have been pleasant to have been walking that night as allies, with his name made.

We were further from allies than we had ever been. I was bitter, the bitterness was too strong for me. As we walked by the club windows I could think of nothing else.

Nevertheless, the habits of the human bond stayed deeper than the words one spoke. I was not attempting – as I had attempted on New Year's

Day – to end the difference between us. Yet the habit endured, and as I said 'I can't help it' under the St James's Street lights, I had a flash of realisation that I was still longing for his success *even then*. And, looking into his face, less closed than it had been for months, I realised with the same certainty that he was still longing for my approval *even then*.

'I think you ought to leave it alone, now,' I said.

'How?'

'You ought to have nothing more to do with the Sawbridge business.'

'I can't do that,' said Martin.

'It's given you all you expected from it.'

'What did I expect from it?'

'Credit,' I said.

'You think that's all?'

'You would never have done it if you hadn't seen your chance.'

'That may be true.' He was trying to be reasonable, to postpone the quarrel. 'But I think I should also say that I can see the logic of the situation, which others won't recognise. Including you.'

'I distrust seeing the logic of the situation,' I said, 'when it's very much to your own advantage.'

'Are you in a position to speak?'

'I've done bad things,' I said, 'but I don't think I could have done some of the things you've done.'

We were still talking reasonably. I accepted the 'logic of the situation' about Sawbridge, I said. I asked a question to which I knew the answer: 'I take it the damage he's done is smaller than outsiders will believe?'

'Much smaller,' said Martin.

Led on by his moderation, I repeated:

'I think you should leave it alone now.'

'I don't agree,' said Martin.

'It can only do you harm.'

'What kind of harm?'

'You can't harden yourself by an act of will, and you'll suffer for it.'

On the instant, Martin's control broke down. He cried out: '*You* say that to me?'

Not even in childhood, perhaps because I was so much the older, had we let our tempers loose at each other. They were of the same kind, submerged, suppressed; we could not quarrel pleasurably with anyone, let alone with one another. In the disagreement which had cut us apart, we had not said a hard word. For us both, we knew what a quarrel cost. Now we were in it.

I brought out my sharpest accusation. Climbing on the Sawbridge case was bad enough – but climbing at Luke's expense, foreseeing the mistake that Luke's generous impulse led him into, taking tactical advantage both of that mistake and his illness – I might have done the rest, but if I had done that I could not have lived with myself.

'I never had much feeling for Luke,' he said.

'Then you're colder even than I thought you were.'

'I had an example to warn me off the opposite,' he said.

'You didn't need any warning.'

'I admit that you're a man of strong feeling,' he said. 'Of strong feeling for people, that is. I've had the example of how much harm that's done.'

We were standing still, facing each other, at the corner where the street ran into Piccadilly; for a second an association struck me, it brought back the corner of that other street to which Sawbridge walked in a provincial town. Our voices rose and fell; sometimes the bitterest remark was a whisper, often I heard his voice and mine echo back across the wide road. We shouted in the pain, in the special outrage of a family quarrel, so much an outrage because one is naked to oneself.

Instead of the stretch of Piccadilly, empty except for the last taxis, the traffic lights blinking as we shouted, I might have been plunged back into the pain of some forgotten disaster in the dark little 'front room' of our childhood, with the dying laburnum outside the windows. Pain, outrage, the special insight of those who wish to hurt and who know the nerve to touch. In the accusations we made against each other, there was the outrage of those bitter reproaches which, when we were at our darkest, we made against ourselves.

He said that I had forgotten how to act. He said that I understood the people round me, and in the process let them carry me along. I had wasted my promise. I had been too self-indulgent – friends, personal relations, I had spent myself over them and now it was all no use.

I said that he was so self-centred that no human being mattered to him – not a friend, not his wife, not even his son. He would sacrifice any one of them for his next move. He had been a failure so long that he had not a glimmer of warmth left.

There were lulls, when our voices fell quiet or silent, even one lull where for a moment we exchanged a commonplace remark. Without noticing it we made our way down the street again, near the corner where (less than half an hour before) Martin had said good-night, in sight of the door out of which we had flanked old Thomas Bevill.

I said: What could he do with his job, after the means by which he had won it? Was he just going to look on human existence as a problem in logistics? He didn't have friends, but he had colleagues; was that going to be true of them all?

I said: In the long run he had no loyalty. In the long run he would turn on anyone above him. As I said those words, I knew they could not be revoked. For, in the flickering light of the quarrel, they exposed me as well as him. With a more painful anger than any I had heard that night, he asked me:

'Who have you expected me to be loyal to?'

I did not answer.

He cried: 'To you?'

I did not answer.

He said: 'You made it too difficult.'

He went on: I appeared to be unselfish, but what I wanted from anyone I was fond of was, in the last resort, my own self-glorification.

'Whether that's true or not,' I cried, 'I shouldn't have chosen for you the way you seemed so pleased with.'

'You never cared for a single moment whether I was pleased or not.'

'I have wanted a good deal for you,' I said.

'No,' he said. 'You have wanted a good deal for yourself.'

PART FIVE

TWO BROTHERS

CHAPTER XXXIX

TECHNIQUE BEHIND A HIGH REWARD

I DID not attend Sawbridge's trial. Like the others of the series, it was cut as short as English law permitted; Sawbridge said the single word 'Guilty', and the only person who expressed emotion was the judge, in giving him two years longer than Smith had forecast.

The papers were full of it. Hankins wrote two more articles. Bevill said: 'Now we can get back to the grindstone.' I had not spoken to Martin since the night in St James's Street, although I knew that several times he had walked down the corridor, on his way to private talks with Bevill.

It was the middle of October, and I had to arrange a programme of committees on the future of Barford. Outside the windows, after the wet summer, the leaves were turning late. Rarely, a plane leaf floated down, in an autumnal air that was at the same time exhilarating and sad.

One morning, as I was consulting Rose, he said:

'Your brother has been colloguing with Bevill a little.'

'Yes,' I said.

'I wondered if you happened to know.' Rose was looking at me with what for him was a quizzical and mischievous glance.

'Know what?'

'My dear chap, it's all perfectly proper, nothing could possibly have been done more according to the rules. I rather reproach myself I hadn't started the ball rolling, but of course there was no conceivable chance of our forgetting you—'

'Forgetting me?' I said.

'I shouldn't have allowed that to happen, believe me, my dear Eliot.'

I said: 'I know nothing about this, whatever it is.'

'On these occasions,' Rose was almost coy, the first time I had seen him so, 'it's always better not to know too much.'

I had to persuade him that I knew nothing at all. For some while he was unusually obtuse, preferring to put it down to discretion or delicacy on my part. At last he half believed me. He said:

'Well, it's a matter of reckoning your deserts, my dear Eliot. The old gentleman is insisting – and I don't think there will be anyone to gainsay him – that it's high time you had a decoration.'

He paused, with a punctilious smile. 'The only real question is exactly what decoration we should go for.'

This was what Martin had been prompting the old man about. I was not touched.

It might have appeared a piece of kindness. But he was being kind to himself, not to me. It was the sort of kindness which, when there is a gash in a close relationship, one performs to ease one's conscience, to push any intimate responsibility away.

Meanwhile Martin's own reward was coming near. The committee sat in Rose's room, and on those autumn mornings of sun-through-mist, I went through the minuets that by this time I knew by heart. These men were fairer, and most of them a great deal abler, than the average: but you heard the same ripples below the words, as when any group of men chose anyone for any job. Put your ear to those meetings and you heard the intricate, labyrinthine and unassuageable rapacity, even in the best of men, of the love of power. I had heard this in Arthur Brown and others years before. If you have heard it once – say, in electing the chairman of a tiny dramatic society, it does not matter where – you have heard it in colleges, in bishoprics, in ministeries, in cabinets: men do not alter because the issues they decide are bigger scale.

The issues before Bevill and his committee were large enough, by the standards of this world. Barford: the production plant: a new whisper of what Bevill called the super bomb: many millions of pounds. 'The people who run this place are going to have plenty on their plate,' said Bevill. 'Sometimes I can't help wondering – is one Top Man enough? I'm not sure we ought to put it all under one hat.' Then they (Bevill, Rose, Getliffe, Mounteney and three other scientists) got down to it. Drawbell must go.

'That can be done,' said Hector Rose, meaning that Drawbell would be slid into another job.

Next there was a proposal which Mounteney and another scientist did not like, but which would have gone straight through: it was that Francis Getliffe should go to Barford and also become what Bevill kept calling Top Man of atomic energy. It would have been a good appointment, but Francis did not want it; he hesitated; the more he dickered, the more desirable to the others the appointment seemed, but in the end he said no.

That left two possibilities: one, that Luke, who appeared to have partially recovered, though the doctors would not make a certain prognosis either way, should be given Barford, which he was known to want.

The other possibility had been privately 'ventilated' by Bevill and Rose ever since Rose mentioned it to me in the summer: assuming that there was a doubt about Luke, couldn't one set up a supervisory committee and then put M. F. Eliot in as acting superintendent?

They were too capable to have brought up this scheme in the committee room unless they had found support outside. But Rose mentioned it – 'I'm just thinking aloud,' he said – on a shining autumn morning.

For once Francis spoke too soon.

'I'm not happy about that idea,' he said immediately.

'This is just what we want to hear,' said Bevill.

'I know Luke has his faults,' said Francis, 'but he's a splendid scientist.'

Mounteney put in:

'Even if you're right about Luke—'

'You know I'm right,' said Francis, forgetting to be judicious, a vein swelling angrily in his forehead.

'He's *pretty* good,' said Mounteney, in the tone of one who is prepared to concede that Sir Isaac Newton had a modest talent, 'but there's no more real scientific thinking to be done at Barford now, it's just a question of making it run smooth.'

'That's a dangerous argument. It's always dangerous to be frightened of the first-rate.'

I had seldom seen Francis so angry. He was putting the others off, and he tried to collect himself. 'I'm saying nothing against M. F. Eliot. He's a very shrewd and able man, and if you want a competent administrator I expect he's as good as they come.'

'Administrators, of course, being a very lowly form of life,' said Rose politely.

Francis flushed: somehow he, as a rule so effective in committee, could not put a foot right.

There was some technical argument among the scientists, taking up Mounteney's point: weren't the problems of Barford, from this time on, just engineering and administrative ones? Someone said that Martin, despite his calendar youth, was mentally the older of the two.

When we broke off for lunch, Francis and I walked across the park together. For a time he strode on, in embarrassed silence, and then said:

'Lewis, I'm very sorry I had to come out against Martin.'

'Never mind,' I said.

'I couldn't have done anything else,' he said.

'I know that,' I said.

'Do you agree with me?'

By good luck, what I thought did not count. I said:

'He'd do better than you give him credit for.'

'But between him and Luke?'

'Luke,' I said.

Nevertheless, Francis had mishandled his case, and that afternoon and at the next meeting, it was Luke against whom opinion began to swell. Against Luke rather than for Martin, but in such a choice it was likely to be the antis who prevailed. They had, of course, a practical doubt, in Luke's state of health. I was thinking, if you wanted a job, don't be ill: for it had an almost superstitious effect, even on men as hard-headed as these; somehow, if you were ill, your *mana* was reduced.

'Is it in Luke's own best interests to ask him to take a strain like this?' someone said.

It was not a close thing. Francis, who was a stubborn man, kept the committee arguing through several meetings, but in truth they had made up their minds long before. He twisted some concessions out of them: yes, Luke was to become a chief adviser, with a seat on the supervisory committee: yes, Luke would get 'suitable recognition' when his turn came round (Sir Walter Luke: Sir Francis Getliffe: Sir Arthur Mounteney: in five years' time, those would be the styles). But the others would not give way any further. It was time a new arrangement was drawn up, and Bevill and Rose undertook, as a matter of form, to get Martin's views.

On an afternoon in November, Martin came into Rose's room. Bevill did not waste any words on flummery.

'We've got a big job for you, young man,' he burst out.

Martin sat still, his glance not deflecting for an instant towards me, as Bevill explained the scheme.

'It's an honour,' said Martin. Neither his eyes nor mouth were smiling. He said: 'May I have a few days to think it over?'

'What do you want to think over?' said Bevill. But he and Rose were both used to men pulling every string to get a job and then deliberating whether they could take it.

'We should all be very, very delighted to see you installed there,' said Rose. Martin thanked him, and said:

'If I could give an answer next week?'

CHAPTER XL

VISIT TO A PRISONER

THE day after Bevill offered Martin the appointment, Captain Smith came into my office and unravelled one of his Henry James-like invitations, which turned out to be, would I go with him to Wandsworth Gaol and have a chat to Sawbridge? I tried to get out of it, but Smith was persistent. He was sensitive enough to feel that I did not like it; but after all, I was an official, I had to live with official duty, just as he did himself.

In the taxi, he told me that he was clearing up a point about the Puchweins. It was worth 'having another try' at Sawbridge, who occasionally talked, not giving anything away, more for the sake of company than because he was softening. As we drove through the south London streets in the November sunshine, he told me more of Sawbridge. He had not recanted; others of the scientific spies gave up their communism in prison, but not Sawbridge. For a few days, sitting opposite to Martin, he had been 'rattled'. During that time he made his confession. He had blamed himself ever since.

'He's quite a lad, is our friend. He doesn't make any bones about it,' said Smith with proprietorial pride, stiff on his seat while we rocked over the tram-lines, through the down-at-heel streets scurfy in the sun.

At the prison, Smith took me to an assistant-governor's room, which in his view gave a 'better atmosphere' for his talks with Sawbridge. For myself, I should have preferred the dark and the wire screen. This room was bright, like a housemaster's study, with a fire in the grate, photographs of children on the desk, and on the walls Medici prints. The smell of tobacco rested in the bright air. Outside the grated window, the morning was brighter still.

When a warder brought Sawbridge in, he gave a smile as he saw Smith and me standing by the window, a smile not specially truculent but knowing, assertive, and at the same time candid. Above his prison suit his face looked no paler than in the past, and he seemed to have put on a little weight.

Smith had arranged for the warder to leave us alone. We heard him

464

close the door, but there were no steps down the passage. Sawbridge, who was listening, cocked his thumb, as though at the warder waiting behind the door, and repeated his smile.

Smith smiled back. With me, with his colleagues, he was never quite at ease; but he was far less put off inside that room than I was.

'Here we are again,' he said.

'Yes,' said Sawbridge.

Smith made him take the easy chair by the fire, while Smith sat at the desk and I brought up a hard-backed chair.

'Have a gasper?' said Smith.

'I still don't smoke,' Sawbridge replied, with his curious rude substitute for humour.

Smith began enquiring into his welfare. Was he getting enough reading material? Would he like Smith to enquire if he could be allowed more?

'I don't mind if you do,' said Sawbridge.

Was he getting any scientific books?'

'I could do with some. Thanks,' said Sawbridge.

Smith made a note; for once, Sawbridge was allowing himself to let slip a request.

Then Smith remarked that we had come down for a 'spot of talk'.

'What are you after?'

'We should like to have a spot of talk about Puchwein,' said Smith, surprisingly direct.

'I've not got anything to say about him.'

'You knew him and his wife, didn't you?'

'I knew them at Barford, like everybody else. I've not got anything to say.'

'Never mind about that, old man,' said Smith. 'Let's just talk round things a bit.'

As Smith foretold, Sawbridge was willing, and even mildly pleased, to chat. He had no objection to going over his story for yet another time. It occurred to me that he was simply lonely. He missed the company of his intellectual equals, and even talking to us was better than nothing. Methodically he went over the dates of his spying. As in each statement he had made, he would mention no name but his own: he had inculpated no one, and maintained all along that he was alone.

'People remember seeing you at Mrs Puchwein's,' said Smith.

'I shouldn't be surprised,' said Sawbridge.

'Don't you think you ought to be surprised?'

'I don't see why.'

'I can't think of anything obvious you have in common.'

'Why should we have anything obvious in common?'

'Why were you there?'

'Social reasons.'

'Did you ever pay any other social calls of any kind?' Smith asked.

'Not that you'd know of.'

'Why were you there?'

'As far as that goes,' said Sawbridge, turning on me with his kind of stolid insolence, 'why were *you*?'

Smith gave a hearty, creaking laugh. He went on questioning Sawbridge about Puchwein – where had he met him first?

'You soon found out that he was left-wing?' said Smith.

'I tell you, I haven't anything to say about him.'

Smith persisted.

'When did you first hear that he was left-wing?'

All of a sudden, Sawbridge broke into sullen anger.

'I shouldn't call him left-wing.'

'What would you call him?' I said.

'He's no better,' said Sawbridge, 'than you are.'

His voice was louder, at the same time impersonal and rancorous, as he let fly at Francis Getliffe, Luke, me, all liberal-minded men. People who had sold out to the enemy: people who would topple over at the first whistle of danger, that was what he thought of liberal men.

'That chap Puchwein isn't any better than your brother,' said Sawbridge. Impersonally, he lumped Martin in with the rest of us, only different in that he was more effective. 'I'm not sure he isn't worse. All Puchwein knows is when it's time to sit on the fence.'

'I thought you'd nothing to tell us about him,' said Smith.

'Well, I've told you something, haven't I?' said Sawbridge. 'We've got no use for chaps like that.'

Back in a café in Westminster, Smith, sipping China tea with his masquerade of preciousness, went over Sawbridge's replies.

'We didn't get over much change out of our young friend,' he said.

'Very little,' I replied.

'No, I wouldn't say that, old son,' said Smith. But, as he argued, I was thinking of Sawbridge – and it was a proof of his spirit that, neither in his presence nor out of it, did I think of him with pity. Faith, hope and hate: that was the troika which rushed him on: it was uncomfortable to remember that, for the point of action, hate was a virtue – but so also, which many of us were forgetting in those years, was hope.

Could one confront the Sawbridges without the same three forces? He was a man of almost flawless courage, moral and physical. Not many men would have bent as little. Then, against my will, for I was suppressing any comparison with Martin, I was teased by a thought in my brother's favour, the first for long enough. It was difficult to imagine him taking Sawbridge's risk; but, if he had had to pay Sawbridge's penalty, his courage would have been as stoical and his will as hard to break.

CHAPTER XLI

LIGHTS TWINKLING IN THE COLD

Two nights later (it was Sunday) I was walking up Wigmore Street towards Portman Square, hurrying because of the extreme cold. The weather had hardened, the lights twinkled frigidly across the square, I was paying attention to nothing except the minutes before I could get back to a warm room. There were few people in the square, and I did not notice the faces as I hurried past.

I did not notice the couple standing near the corner, in the half-shadow. Without knowing why, I looked over my shoulder. They were standing oblivious of the cold, the man's overcoat drooping open, flapping round his knees. They were Irene and Hankins.

At once I turned my head and started down the side-street, out of sight. A voice followed me, Irene's -- 'What are you running away for?'

I had to go back. As they came towards me under the lamp, they both looked pinched, tired, smiling.

'Why haven't I seen you all these months?' said Hankins. We went into a hotel close by and sat drinking in the lounge, among the palms and the sucking noise from the revolving door.

Hankins was quieter than usual, and when he spoke the words seemed dredged up through other thoughts. We asked about each other's careers. He had just got a good job; he had made a reputation before, but now, for the first time in his life, he was free from worry about his next year's rent. I congratulated him, but his thoughts absented themselves again.

Soon he looked at Irene with an odd expression. His face, like that of many with a quickly changing inner life, was emotional but hard to read. 'I think I must be going now,' he said. Her eyes sharpened.

'Goodbye,' said Hankins, and the revolving door sucked round behind

him, sucking empty air. (Yes, I had seen someone else leave like that:
now the thought did not trouble me, I could afford to let it in.)

He had gone so quickly that they might have arranged to meet again,
when I was disposed of.

Irene stared at me with full eyes.

'I had to see him,' she said. 'I couldn't sit down under things any
longer.'

'What are you going to do?'

She did not reply, but continued to stare at me as though I knew. Just
for a second, on her mouth there appeared a tart smile. She settled herself
against the arm of her chair, and I noticed that her shoulders were getting
rounder. In the last year she had thickened both in the midriff and the
upper arm.

'Fancy the old thing pulling in a regular salary at last,' she said.

'Both of them have done pretty well for themselves,' I replied.

She looked puzzled. I had to explain that 'both of them' meant Hankins
and Martin, the two men who had meant most to her. They were coming
to the top of their professions at the same time.

'The top?' she said.

'The head of Barford,' I replied.

'Oh.' She fixed me with a glance which seemed malicious, regretful,
sympathetic.

'And as for Hankins,' I said, 'so far as there is anything left of literary
London, this job will put him in the middle of it.'

'He'll dote on that!' she cried. Quietly she added:

'And so should I.'

She spoke straight out:

'It would suit me better than anything I have ever had with Martin,
or anything that I could ever have.'

Once more she gave me a glance edged with fellow-feeling. Without
explanation, with her expression malicious and ominous, she went on:

'I'm not cut out for it. I can see Martin going on patiently and getting
a bit drier every year. What sort of life do you think that means for me?'

We looked at each other, without speaking for some moments. I said:
'But you're going to live it, aren't you?'

'You don't think I'm going off with E.H.?'

'No,' I said.

'I could stop his marriage. I could have everything I wanted ten years
ago. Why shouldn't I now?'

'You won't,' I said.

'You're positive?' Suddenly she slumped down, her hand fell on her breast, her tone no longer brittle, but flat, lazily flat, as she said:

'You're right.'

She went on:

'I never knew where I was with E.H. I never even knew if he needed me. While Martin doesn't need me – he could get on without me or anyone else, but he wants me! He always has! I never had much faith that anyone would, until he came along.'

So at last, under the palm trees of that aseptic lounge, preoccupied by the suspicion, which she had provoked, of a crucial turn in Martin's life, I was given a glimpse of what bound Irene to him. In the past I had speculated often. Why should she, in the ultimate run, be anchored to Martin instead of Hankins? I had looked for qualities in Martin which could make some women love him, rather than another man. They were present, but they did not count.

It was true that Martin was the stronger: it was true also that Martin was, if these cant terms mean anything, the more masculine. Hankins was one of those men, and they are not uncommon, who invest much emotion in the pursuit of women without having the nature for it; he thought he was searching for the body's rapture, but his profoundest need was something less direct, the ambience of love, its meshes of unhappiness, its unfulfilled dreams, its tears for the past and its images of desire. Many women found it too delicate, but not Irene.

With her, there was a hypnotic charm about his capacity for feeling; he could feel as she did, he had the power to enter into, as all important, each emotion of love. It was that which she first loved in him, and which held her fascinated for years, her whom other women obtusely thought was searching only for a partner in bed. Against that emotional versatility Martin could not compete. Yet never once, if she had been faced with the choice, would she have left Martin.

The real reason which delivered her to Martin lay not in him, but in herself.

She had just told it to me, so simply that it was difficult to believe. In fact, Irene had suffered all her life from a diffidence which seemed, at a first glance, the last one would expect in her. In her childhood, even more totally than with other girls, love and marriage filled her day-dreams; those daydreams had not left her alone all her life; yet they had never been accompanied by the certainty of the fibres, that she had it in her to draw the love she coveted. More than most she studied herself in the looking-glass, but not with narcissistic pleasure; only with a mixture of contemptuous liking and nervousness that such a face, such a body, might never bring what she craved.

In the hotel lounge, hearing the revolving doors swing round, I thought of another woman so different from Irene that any resemblance seemed like a joke. Nora Luke, dowdy, professionally striving, in the home a scolding faithful housewife – Irene, once notorious for her love affairs, the most reckless of women – yet in secret they had found life difficult in the same manner. At the root of their nature they were sisters.

Irene had spoken simply, and maybe it was as simple as she said. Hankins, so tentative and undecided himself, she had never had the confidence to reach for; while Martin, all else forgotten, was the one man who wanted her enough to stay with her at any cost, to give her the assurance, so far as she was capable of accepting it, that he would stay steady, that he would be there to make her feel that she was as lovable as, her nerves twitching under the adventuress's skin, she had never since she was a child been able to believe.

That night, she had sent Hankins away. It was only after he had gone that I realised this was the end between them, that under the lamps of Portman Square they had spoken the last words. Hankins pushing round the door might have been leaving her for half an hour; in fact, they would not meet again: it was curious that he, at any other time so eloquent, had gone in silence.

Irene smiled at me, as though, sitting before her looking-glass, she was putting on her dashing face.

'He will have me on his hands,' she said. She was speaking of Martin. She added:

'I shall be a drag on him in this new game.'

She was keeping me in the dark, she was obscurely triumphant.

'What are you telling me?' I asked.

'You knew, of course you knew, about this offer that Martin had last week?'

I said yes.

'You knew he expected it before it came?'

'He must have expected it for weeks.'

'I guessed as much.'

She went on, not knowing the break between Martin and me, but knowing something I did not. For days (it must have been during the first sittings of the committee, and he might have had inside information, probably from Mounteney) he was excited that the job was coming his way. She said that he was lively, active, restless with high spirits; she remembered how he had talked to his son one evening, talked to the three-year-old boy as though they were both adults and he was letting himself boast.

'Well, Lewis,' Martin had said to the child, 'now I'm going further than anyone in the family's ever gone. It will give you a good start. You'll be able to build on it, won't you?'

In the next few days Irene felt a change. She could not ask him; with her, in his own home, he let his moods run more than I had seen him, but she dared not to try to penetrate them. It was still several days before the offer was made. For the only time she could remember, Martin stayed away from the laboratory without a reason. The weather had turned foggy; he sat silent by the fire. He did not ask her advice, but occasionally spoke of the advantages of being the Barford superintendent, of the entertaining she could do there. Occasionally also he spoke of some disadvantages, as though laughing them off.

'He wouldn't talk about them,' Irene flared out. 'But I didn't need him to. I hadn't forgotten the letter he didn't send.'

One foggy afternoon, he suddenly said:

'The head of Barford is just as much part of the machine as any of the others.'

He went on:

'If I take the job, I shan't have the trouble of thinking for myself again.'

Irene said to me, simply and quietly:

'Then I knew that he would never take it.'

That had happened the previous Saturday, three days before the offer came. I asked how he had behaved when he actually had the offer in his hand.

'He was shaken,' said Irene. 'He was terribly shaken.'

With the fog outside the windows, he had sat by the fire so absent that he let it go out. Then she made it up, and I imagined the firelight reflected into the room from the fog-backed window. Martin only roused himself from that paralysis of the nerves to play again with the little boy – the two of them under the window, young Lewis shouting, Martin patiently rolling a ball, and still silent.

Both Irene and I, through our different kinds of knowledge of him, took it for granted that he would not alter his resolve.

'I don't pretend to understand it,' she said to me. 'Do you?'

I shook my head, and, as lost and open as she was, I asked:

'What do you think he intends to do?'

'I don't think, I know,' she replied.

During the past weeks, so as to be ready, he had been making enquiries, unknown to me, of our college. If he decided to give up his work at Barford and return to pure science, could they find a niche for him?

'It'll be funny for him, not having any power,' she said.

She added:

'He's going into dimness, isn't he? He won't make much of a go of it?'

She went on asking, what were his chances in pure science? Would he do enough to console himself?

'They all say he hasn't got quite the talent,' I replied. He would publish a few respectable papers, he would not get into the Royal Society. For a man as realistic as Martin, it would be failure.

'He's got a real talent for his present job,' I said.

'It'll be difficult for him to lead a dim life,' she said, 'having had a taste of something different.'

She said it in a matter-of-fact tone, without any sign of tenderness. I broke out:

'And I suppose you're glad about it?'

'What do you mean?'

'You wanted him to make his protest. I suppose this is the next best thing?'

Irene was flushing down the neckline of her dress. With difficult honesty she turned her eyes away, and said:

'No. I'm not cut out for this.'

'Why aren't you?'

'I'm a sprinter. I could have stood a major row, it would have been something to live through. I should have been more use to him than any of you.'

I said: 'I believe you would.'

She flashed out:

'It isn't often you pay me a compliment.'

'It was meant,' I said.

'But you mustn't give me too much credit. I'm not high-minded. I shouldn't have worried if Martin had become the boss at Barford. I should have enjoyed the flah-flah.'

Then she asked:

'Why ever is he doing it? I wish you'd tell me that.'

I was confused.

'Do you think,' she said, 'he's just trying to be a good man?'

'I should like to believe it,' I said.

'You think he's got another motive, do you?'

'We usually have.'

To my astonishment, she burst out laughing, with her high-pitched yelps of glee.

'I believe you think,' she cried, 'that he's doing it to take it out of me. Just to show me that things have changed since he married me, and that he holds the whip hand now.'

It had not even crossed my mind.

'You're wrong!' she shouted. 'If he's reacting against anyone, it isn't me!'

Her eyes glinted triumphant, good-natured, malicious at my expense. She said: 'You won't be able to influence him now, will you?'

CHAPTER XLII

A PLACE TO STAND?

MARTIN did not give his answer to Bevill until the last day of his period of grace. He called in my office first, just as he used to – but we were each constrained. On the window the frost, coming early that winter, masked the buses in Whitehall. Martin swept a pane with his sleeve, saying that after he had had the interview with Bevill and Rose, he would like to talk to me.

He assumed that I knew what his answer was going to be. When he actually delivered it, he spent (so I learned later) much skill in saving his supporters' credit. He did not once suggest a moral choice; he just used the pretext that, unless he did some real science soon, he never would; in which case his usefulness would be finished in ten years.

The scientists took the explanation at its face value. It was only Bevill who smelt that there was something wrong. In his experience men did not turn down a good job unless by doing so they got a better. So he fell back on what was always his last resource, and put the blame on to Martin's wife.

Bevill and Rose had been too long at their craft not to recognise the inevitable; that morning, while Martin was on his way back to my office, they had already decided that now, well or ill, wild man or not, it had to be Luke. Rose's sense of justice made him insist that they could not even attempt to put Luke in leading strings, as they had Martin. Thus it was to be Luke in full power.

Meanwhile Martin had returned to my room. His gestures were relaxed, as though to light a cigarette were a pleasure to be taken slowly; yet we could not speak to each other with ease. With anyone else, I felt, he would be smiling with jubilation, with a trace of sadness too.

With me, he could not be so natural

'That's settled,' he said.

He asked if he could waste the rest of the afternoon for me, and I said:

'Of course.' I added, meaninglessly: 'Can you spare the time?'

'Very soon,' said Martin, with a sarcastic grin, 'I shall have plenty of time.'

For many minutes we sat there, looking down over Whitehall, saying nothing to the point, often falling into silence. It was not until we took a walk in the icy park that Martin made his first effort.

'I'm happy about this,' he said, as we trod along the path where, on the verges, each blade of grass stood out separated by the frost.

He added:

'It's a change from the last time.'

He meant the last time we had walked there, the day after the bomb had dropped. It had been sixteen months before. The leaves had been thick then; now we looked past the bare trees, into the mist fuming above the leaden water.

'Since then,' said Martin, 'I haven't found a place to stand.'

He spoke slowly, as though with the phrase he recalled that afternoon when, in the Dolphin Square bathroom, he saw the scientific way ahead.

He went on: 'Up till now.'

In return I made my effort.

'I hope,' I said, 'that I haven't made it harder for you to find it.'

There seemed a long interval before Martin replied. Our steps rang in the frost. As a habit, each of us had the trick of using irony to cheat out of its importance the moment in which we breathed: each of us that afternoon had set ourselves to speak without easing the moment away. That was why we stumbled so.

'You can see too much in personal causes,' he said.

'They exist,' I said.

'Without them,' said Martin, 'I think I should have done the same.'

'I should like to be sure,' I said.

'Motives aren't as important to me as they are to you,' he said. 'I'm more concerned with what one does.'

'You have done some contradictory things,' I said.

'I can tell you this. That night we went to Pratt's – it hasn't affected me one way or the other. As far as I can answer for myself at all, I tell you that.'

He groped less when he spoke of his Sawbridge policy. He did not have to stumble; there we understood each other. We both knew the temptations of action, and how even clear-sighted men did not enquire what their left hand was doing. It was nonsense to think that Martin had been dissimulating all the time and that he had always intended to retire. Men were not clever enough to dissimulate for long.

He had, of course, been after the top job. Until quite recently he consciously intended to take it. For months he had been acting, as many men were acting on both sides of the great divide, out of the cynicism of self-preservation. Many men, delicate in their personal relations, had come to behave, and even to think, with that kind of cynicism, even though we concealed it from ourselves.

'Some of us have been too delicate about personal relations,' said Martin, back in my office, sitting by the window in the murky afternoon. 'People matter; relations between them don't matter much.'

I stood looking out of the window, where the lights scintillated under a sky ochreous and full of snow.

'Lewis!' His voice was quiet; it was rare, when we were alone, for either of us to use the other's name.

'That night after old Bevill left you said some true things,' he said.

'You also,' I said.

'I am colder-hearted than you are. I care much less for the people round me.'

'Why are you saying this?'

'If it weren't so, I couldn't have made this choice.'

For any of us who had been concerned with the bomb, he repeated Luke's earlier comment, there was no clear-cut way out. Unless you were a Sawbridge. For the rest of us, said Martin, there were just two conceivable ways. One was the way he had just taken: the other, to struggle on, as Luke was doing, and take our share of what had been done and what might still be done, and hope that we might come out at the end of the tunnel. Being well-meaning all the time, and thinking of nothing worse than our own safety.

'For a warm-hearted man who's affected by the people round him,' said Martin, 'perhaps it's the only way. It's the way you're going, though you're more far-sighted than they are.'

'It wouldn't be easy for me,' I said after a pause, 'to break right away.'

'If you do choose their way,' he said with sudden energy, 'I've shown you how to do it.'

He meant that you could not compromise. If you accepted the bomb, the burnings alive, the secrets, the fighting point of power, you must take the consequences. You must face Sawbridge with an equal will. You were living in a power equilibrium, and you must not pretend; the relics of liberal humanism had no place there.

'I completely disagree,' I said.

'You can't find a compromise. But your personal ties keep you making them,' said Martin. 'That's why you leave it to worse men to take the other way.' He went on:

'Sometimes it's only the cold who can be useful.'

It had taken him a long time to be positive about what he must do: but now he spoke as though he had it in the palm of his hand. Previously he had wondered about leaving science altogether. He had contemplated 'doing a Charles March' – but Martin decided that for him it was too 'artificial', too much out of his line. For him, there was only one course, to go back to pure science.

Most unusually for him, he showed a flicker of bravado.

'I shall be just a little better than those pundits say,' he said.

He had not many illusions, though perhaps, just as he contrived to see Irene both with realistic observation and also surrounded with a romantic aura, he could still feel, in his secret self, a tremor of the magic that science had once evoked there.

He told me in so many words that he had not lost faith that science – though maybe not in his lifetime – would turn out for good. From some, after his history, it would have sounded a piece of facile scientists' optimism. From him it had a different note. For to Martin it was jet-clear that, despite its emollients and its joys, individual life was tragic: a man was ineluctably alone, and it was a short way to the grave. But, believing that with stoical acceptance, Martin saw no reason why social life should also be tragic: social life lay within one's power, as human loneliness and death did not, and it was the most contemptible of the false-profound to confuse the two.

'As long as the worst things don't happen' – said Martin. 'That's why some of us must get clear of office and friends and anything that ties our hands.'

'Is that what you thought of most?'

'I hope they'll leave me alone,' he said. 'But there may come a time when people like me have to make a nuisance of themselves.'

He went on:

'I'm the last man for the job. It may be dangerous and I'm not cut out for that.'

It might not be necessary, I said. In my view, the danger was over-rated and the betting was against it.

'All the better,' said Martin. 'All the more reason for having a few sensible men who aren't committed.'

He meant, good could happen as well as evil; men might run into a little luck; if we were too much hypnotised by the violence we had lived through, if each man of good will was mobilised, paid and silenced, we might let the luck slip.

'That may be the best reason of all for getting outside the machine,' said Martin. 'If a few of us are waiting for the chance, we might do a little good.'

He turned in his chair. In the tenebrous afternoon, the room had gone dark outside the zone of the desk light; and past the window, flakes of snow were dawdling down on to the Whitehall pavement. He was looking at me. Suddenly, with no explanation necessary between us, he said:

'You know, I shall never have the success you wanted me to have.'

Again we were speaking without ease, as though each word had to be searched for.

'If I had not wanted it for you, would you have liked it more?'

'I said before, you can see too much in personal causes.'

'Have they made it harder for you?'

'That doesn't matter,' he replied. 'In the end, I should have done what I am doing now.'

Our intimacy had not returned, but we were speaking of ourselves more deeply than we had done before.

That afternoon, at last, Martin was answerable to no one. Speaking of his future, he had lost the final residue of a younger brother's tone, and took on that of equal to equal, contemporary to contemporary, self-made to self-made.

CHAPTER XLIII

A NEW EMPIRE

MARTIN left Barford at the end of the year: Luke became Chief Superintendent the following May. A few weeks later, I went down to do some business with him on my way to Cambridge, where Martin had invited me to a college feast.

The Drawbells had not yet finished moving house, although Drawbell's own new appointment had been announced. It was a come-down. Perhaps that was why, more bullying even than in the past, he insisted that I should stay my night at Barford with them, not with the Lukes. I could not say no: in his decline he was hard to resist, partly because his personality was one of those that swell, become more menacing, the more he saw his expectations fade away.

He and his wife had waited for each post the preceding November, looking for a letter about the New Year's honours list; and they were doing it again before the birthday list. There was nothing for them. They still pretended to expect it. At breakfast, in a room with covers on some of the chairs, ready to move that week, Drawbell made believe to threaten me, fixing me with his sound eye.

'My patience is exhausted,' he said, as though making a public speech – but it was the kind of joke which is not a joke. 'It's high time the Government did its duty.'

He may have suspected that I knew his chances. I did. But, for the last time with Drawbell, I had to follow his lead, do my best to be hearty and say nothing.

For his chances were nil. I had heard Hector Rose rule him out. It was the only time I had known Rose be, by his own standards, less than just. By Rose's standards, Drawbell had done enough for a knighthood: Barford had 'made its contribution', as Rose said, and Drawbell had been in charge for five years. According to the rules, the top man got the top decoration; but for once Rose would not have it so. He asked cold questions about who had done the work; with the methodicalness of a recording angel, he put down to Drawbell's credit the occasions when he had scored a plus – and then turned to the other side of the sheet. The final account, in Rose's mind, did not add up to a knighthood.

At the breakfast table, Drawbell, still ignorant of that decision, hoping against hope, put on his jocular act and threatened me. His wife regarded me, monumental, impassive; she was looking forward to getting Mr

Thomas Bevill down to the new establishment. Between her and her husband, I had never seen any real affection, only that thread of that friendliness-cum-dislike which comes in lifelong marriages that are wrong at the core: yet she remained his loyal and heavy-footed ally. She was no more defeated than he was. And when finally his last hope wilted, they would, without knowing it, be supports to each other.

That morning, Drawbell gave just one open sign of recognition that he was on the way down. He refused to come with me to his old office, which Luke was already occupying. He could not face the sight of someone who had passed him, who had – in Drawbell's eyes and the world's – arrived.

Yet Luke himself would have had his doubts, I thought, sitting beside his desk, behind which, in his shirt-sleeves, he tilted back in his chair – in that room where he had made his first proposal about the pile. He would have had his doubts about his arrival, if ever he had spared time to consider it, which – as he remained a humble and an immediate man – he was most unlikely to.

He knew that he would not now leave much of a scientific memorial behind him. You could not do real scientific work and become a 'stuffed shirt', as he used to argue rudely in the past. Ironically, he, so richly endowed for the pure scientific life, had, unlike Martin, put it behind him. There were times when he felt his greatest gift was rusting. His corpus of work would not stand a chance of competing with Mounteney's.

Nevertheless, Luke was enjoying himself. His chair tilted back against the wall, he gave the answer I had come for. Gave it with the crispness of one who, in reveries, had imagined himself as a tycoon. Once or twice he shot a response out of the side of his mouth.

'Curtains,' he said once, indicating that the discussion was at an end.

'Come off it, Walter,' I said.

Luke looked startled. As always, he had got into the skin of his part. Then he gave a huge cracked grin.

I had come to clear up one or two administrative tangles, which in Martin's time would have been dealt with at Barford, and we were talking of getting Luke a second-in-command to tidy up after him. Luke was determined to appoint Rudd, who had, as soon as Drawbell was superseded, transferred his devotion to the new boss.

'He's a snurge,' said Luke. 'But he can be a very useful snurge.'

Was he the man that Luke wanted? In my view, Luke needed someone to stand up to him.

'No,' said Luke. 'I can make something of him. I can make a difference to that chap.'

Already, I thought, Luke was showing just a trace of how power corrodes. As we walked round the establishment, in the drizzling rain, I teased him, bringing up against him his old ribald curses at 'stuffed shirts'.

'If ever you think I'm becoming one, Lewis,' said Luke, 'you come and kick my behind.'

He was limping as he walked. His knee was still giving him pain, and at the back of his mind there was the ache of not knowing whether he had recovered. Nevertheless, limping, grey at the temples, not disguising his fear of whether his life was going to be cut short, he seemed physically to expand as he took me into bay after bay of the new buildings. By this time they stretched for many acres on both sides of the river: in and out of the rain we dodged, as he took me to see the new piles being built, where the floors were busy with scientists and artisans. Then he took me to the two piles already working, working in the humanless space. The building looked less crude now; above was a large chimney, and there hummed the faint noise of fans. This had become Luke's empire.

Like any sentient man, he had had his hesitations about this project (for my benefit, he was reckoning up, as we stood beside the working pile, just how many such machines existed in the world). He had given his reasons why he went on with it, and why he believed all might turn out well. But now he had shut both doubts and justifications within him. He was not one of those who can work and at the same time remain detached about whether or not they are doing good. This was Luke's empire, and as he looked over it he thought of nothing but how best to make it run.

CHAPTER XLIV

TWO BROTHERS

THAT evening, in Martin's rooms in Cambridge, which by a touch of college sentiment were those I had lived in before the war, I described that talk with Luke. Martin and I were alone, and there was an hour before dinner; only the first fringe of rain had reached Cambridge, and the sun was shining, after a shower which filled the room with a smell of wistaria from the court beneath.

There, in the high room, which the sunlight did not reach, Martin questioned me about Luke: how was his regime turning out? How were the latest plans working? For Martin, although he had changed his life, did not pretend that he could will away his interest, and liked to talk of the place where he had had an influence which would not come to him again.

He disagreed with one of Luke's arrangements and gave his reason, which sounded sensible.

'Why doesn't someone tell him so?' he said.

'Some people are going to get more than they bargained for,' I said.

'It's not necessary.' Martin was not displeased to find fault. I said that, though Luke's methods might be rough and ready, under him Barford would be a success.

'Poor old Walter!' Martin said, with a smile, with an edge of envy.

Martin had not gone back on his choice, although by this time he knew, what one can never imagine until one lives it, the wear and tear, hour by hour and day by day, as one tries to reshape a life. In that way, imagination was enviously weak: as old Arthur Brown had impressed on me, in this same college, though on a lesser occasion. Martin now knew precisely what it was like to work in the same laboratory as his juniors, and realise that they were outclassing him. He came to them as a man with a big outside reputation, and felt a nobody. At colloquia and laboratory teas he became nervous in front of young men whose confidence, unlike his own, was absolute.

He believed now that his critics were right: from every practical point of view, his choice had been stupid: he would stay there, doing his college teaching, without a realistic chance of achievement for the rest of his life.

He had always been quiet, but in the days of his power it had been the quietness, trained and confident, of a high functionary, the quietness of Hector Rose. Now it had changed; it had the special quality that you see in one who has learned something from life and who has lost his high spirits during the lesson. His interest had become passive. Sitting in the darkness of his room, looking out of the window at the court brilliant in the rain-clear sunlight, he had none of the authority of action that men like Luke carried on their brow.

But he was happy. It was a curious kind of happiness that had come upon him almost without his knowing it. It occurred to me that I had seen others make renunciations similar in kind to his: in each case they gained happiness. It might have been otherwise, it might have been one of the ironies of the human condition that, when you throw away the game with a chance of winning it, you regret it ever after: but, in the cases I had seen, it proved the contrary.

I was glad that he should be happy. Suddenly I thought that, hoping so much for him, with the fraternal concern that identified myself in him, I had worried little about his happiness. Even now – in the room where he had first mentioned the proof of fission, which had led us both to the fringe of such events as had darkened our consciences and given him the chance of secret power – he could not, now that he had resigned the power and found his inner happiness, share any part of it with me.

My concern for him had, in the midst of those convulsions, shown the flaw which exists in any of its kind, which, if we had been luckier, might not have come out so clear.

If we had been luckier, if events had not taken hold of us, there might have been no occasion for him to tell me, as he had done in St James's Street, when I said that I had wanted much for him:

'No. You have wanted a good deal for yourself.'

It was the truth; it was the reason why the most sacrificial of human affections twist into the most self-seeking of all. It can cripple those who receive it, and those who give can never find anything of what they seek.

I had looked to him to go the way I chose for him. In the Sawbridge case, he had done the opposite, and, whichever of us was right in the abstract, that was why I had felt it like a betrayal. It was clear now. As men went, we were sensible and did not expect over much from human beings: but events had taken hold of us, and had shown up the nature of my concern.

As Irene perceived, with the insight of jealousy, the time came when he had to cut himself quite free.

If you identify yourself in another, however tough the tie between you, he cannot feel as you do, and then you go through (you who have been living your life in another) a state for which the old Japanese found a name, which they used to describe the sadness of a parent's love: a darkness of the heart.

I had seen that in Mr March's feeling for his son Charles. I ought to have known it at first hand, for my mother had tried to relive her life in me; and I had not been able to return that kind of love. I too had been compelled to cut myself quite free.

It was a little thing, the human price that Martin and I had paid, as a result of those events which Hector Rose called 'too big for men' – and yet that was what I thought of, sitting in that dark room, the sky brilliant over the roofs opposite, waiting for the college bell. Through being forced together in our corner of those events, I had out of the nature of my affection done him harm. I had brought some sadness on myself. We were both too realistic to expect that our intimacy would soon be complete again.

The dinner bell began to toll. Martin gave an indrawn, sarcastic smile. As we stood up I was thinking that, though we had paid our modest price, we had regained most of the ease of old habit in each other's company. We were on our way to repairing something of what had happened between us. Of the human relations I had so far known, I had found, despite our mistakes, none more steady and comforting than that with my brother; I hoped that in time he would feel the same.

September
25, 1986

Homecomings

Homecomings

1938–51

CONTENTS

PART ONE. HOMECOMING

PART TWO. THE SELF-DEFEATED

Contents

PART THREE. CONDITION OF A SPECTATOR

PART FOUR. THE UNDETACHED

Contents

PART FIVE. ANOTHER HOMECOMING

PART ONE

HOMECOMING

CHAPTER I

LIGHTED WINDOW SEEN FROM THE STREET

It was a February afternoon of smoky sunshine, as I walked home along the Embankment to my wife. The river ran white in the sun, the plume from a tug's funnel came out blue as cigarette-smoke; on the far bank the reflections from windows shone through haze, and down towards Chelsea where I was walking the smoke was so thick that the skyline, the high chimneys, had smudged themselves into it.

The day was a Tuesday, the year 1938; I had not been home since the Thursday before, which was my usual routine, as I had to spend half my week in Cambridge. I felt an edge of anxiety, a tightness of the nerves, as I always did going home after an absence, even an absence as short as this. Ever since I could remember, seeking deep into my childhood, I had felt this dread on the way home, this dread of what might be waiting for me.

It was nothing serious, it was just one of the reasonless anxieties one had to live with, it was no worse than that. Even now, when sometimes it turned out not so reasonless, I had got used to it. On those Tuesday evenings, walking home from Millbank to Chelsea along the river, I was anxious as I always had been, returning home, but I had put out of mind the special reason why.

Yet that day, as soon as I reached Cheyne Walk, my eyes were straining before I was in sight of our house. When I did see it, the picture might to a stranger have looked serene and enviable. The drawing-room lights were already on, first of the houses along that reach; the curtains had not been drawn, and from the road, up the strip of garden, one could see the walls, high with white-painted panels. If I had been a stranger, looking up the garden from Cheyne Walk, that glimpse of a lighted room would have had for me the charm of domestic mystery and peace.

As I walked up the path, I did not know how she would be.

The hall was brilliantly lit, pernicketily tidy, the hall of a childless couple. No voice greeted me. I went quickly inside the drawing-room.

Here also the lights attacked me, as in the dazzle I saw my wife. Saw her quiet, composed, preoccupied. For she was sitting at a small table, away from the fireplace, looking down at a chessboard. On the board were only a few pieces, each of them much bigger than an ordinary chessman, part of an Indian set which, out of some whim, Sheila had bought herself the year before. So far as I could see, she was not playing a game, but working out a problem. She looked up.

'Hallo, you're in, are you?' she said. 'You'd better help me with this.'

I was flooded with relief, relief so complete as to be happiness, just as I always was when I found her free from strain. Whatever I had expected, it was not this. I drew up a chair opposite her, and, as she bent her head and glanced at the board, I looked through the tall pieces at her forehead, the lines of which were tightened, not as so often with her own inner care, but with simple calculation.

'I don't see it,' she said, and smiled at me with great light-filled grey eyes.

At this time she was thirty-two, the same age within months as I was myself. But she looked much older than her age. When I first fell in love with her, as long ago as thirteen years before, men had thought her beautiful. Since then her face had changed, though I, who had watched it as no one else had, would have been the last to recognise how much.

The lines, which when she was a girl had been visible on her forehead and under her eyes, were now deep; her fine, strong nose had sharpened; her expression had become both harder and more still, drawn and fixed with unhappiness. Only her eyes were untouched, and they, so large that they might have been mournful as a lemur's, had not shared in the sadness of her face. Even at her worst, they could still look lively, penetrating, not-taken-in; just as her body, beneath the lined, overwrought face, was strong, almost heavy, the body of a woman powerful, healthy and still young.

Seeing her through the chess pieces, I noticed none of these changes, for I was only concerned with her state from day to day. I knew the slightest change in her expression, but I could not see what would be obvious to others. Trying to keep her steady, over the hours, the days, the years, I had lost my judgment about whether she was getting better or worse. All I knew was that tonight she was gay, anxiety-free, and that for this night, which was as far as I could see ahead, there was nothing to worry about.

I had loved her all through my young manhood, and, although my love had changed because of what had happened to us, I loved her still. When

I first met her, I thought that the luck was on her side; she was beautiful, she was intelligent, she was comfortably off, above all she did not love me when I passionately loved her. That meant that she had power over me, and I none over her; it meant that she could tantalise me for years, she could show me the cruelty of one who feels nothing. It meant also, but I did not realise it then, that she was the more to be pitied. For it turned out that it was not only me she could not love, but anyone. She craved to; she tried to find someone to love; she tried to find psychiatrists and doctors who would tell her why she could not. Then, all else failing, she fell back on me, who still loved her, and let me marry her.

It could not have gone well. It might have gone a little better, I sometimes thought, if we had had children, which each of us longed for. But we were left with nothing but ourselves.

'I must get it out,' she said, staring long-sightedly at the board. With two fingers she touched a piece shaped like a howdahed elephant, which in a European set would have been a castle. Out of anxious habit, my glance fixed, not on the strong broad-tipped fingers, but on the nails. Once again that night I was relieved. Though they were not painted, they were clean and trimmed. There had been times when her sense of deprivation froze her into stupor, when she no longer took care of herself. That frightened me, but it had not happened for some years. Usually she dressed well enough, and as she walked by the Embankment pubs or along the King's Road, people saw a woman with her head high, a muscular stride, a face handsome and boldly made up.

'You'd better start again systematically,' I said.

'Teach me,' said Sheila.

It was like her to be willing to take a lesson in the theory of chess problems. It was like her also not to have asked a single question about what I had been doing, although she had not seen me for four days. Cambridge, my London job, they did not exist for her. From before our marriage, from the time when she no longer hoped that all would come well for her, she had become more shut up within herself. In fact, trying to look after her, I had broken my career.

When I married, I thought I knew what it would be like. I should have to watch over her dreads; I had seen something of the schizoid chill; I could imagine how tasks trivial to the rest of us were ordeals to her, how any arrangement in the future, even the prospect of going to a dinner party, could crack her nerves. But I had been borne along by passionate love for her, physical passion pent up for years, and perhaps more than that. So I went into it, and, like others before me, like my brother Martin later on, soon knew that no imaginative forecast of what a life will be is anything like that life lived from day to day.

I did my best for her. It scarcely helped her at all. But it left me without much energy free. When we married, I had just got a foot in at the Bar; I was being thought of as a rising junior. Unless I parted from Sheila, I could not keep up that struggle. And so I found less strenuous jobs, a consulting one with Paul Lufkin's firm and a law fellowship at Cambridge, the latter taking me away from the Chelsea house three or four nights a week. When she was at her most indrawn, sitting by her gramophone for hours on end, I was glad, although it was a cowardly relief, to get away.

That February evening, as we sat opposite each other at the chess table in the bright room, I thought of none of these things. It was quite enough that she seemed content. It gave me – what sometimes can exist in the unhappiest of marriages, although an outsider does not realise its power – a kind of moral calm. Habit was so strong that it could wipe away ambitions put aside, crises of choice, a near-parting, all that had gone on in my secret life with her: habit was sitting near her, watching her nails, watching for the tic, the pseudo-smile, that came when strain was mastering her.

'I saw R.S.R. today,' she said without any lead-in.

'Did you?'

'I've got an idea he was looking for me.'

'I shouldn't be surprised,' I said.

'We had a drink. He was in good form.'

Once that would have been a way to provoke my jealousy. Not now. I welcomed anything that would give her interest or hope. She still had bursts of activity in which she lost herself – once or twice, for those were the thirties, in politics, but usually in trying to help some lame dog whom she had met by chance. A little backstreet café where she went by herself – I found that she had lent the proprietor money to keep on the lease. A derelict curate, terrified that he was going to be prosecuted – she was on call for him at any time he wanted. Utterly uninterested in my goings-on, her family's, her old friends', she could still become absorbed in those of someone new. With them she was selfless, they gave her a flash of hope, she became like the young woman I had first known.

'He began to talk very airily about getting himself financed again,' said Sheila.

'He's not losing any time, is he?'

'I wonder if I could do anything for him,' she said.

'Plenty of people have tried, you know,' I said.

It was true. I had met R. S. Robinson only once; he was a man of sixty, who before 1914 had made a reputation as the editor of an *avant-garde* monthly. Since then, he had been a hanger-on of letters, ghosting for agents, bringing out uncommercial magazines, losing money, making enemies, always ready with a new project. It was not long since he had manœuvred an introduction to Sheila; the manœuvres had been elaborate, he might as well have shouted out loud that he had heard she was well off.

'Yes, plenty have tried,' she said. 'So much the worse for them.'

She gave me a realistic jeering smile. She always met her down-and-outs with her eyes open. She added: 'But that isn't much comfort for him, is it?'

'But if other people have got involved,' I said, some second-hand rumour running through my mind, 'it isn't encouraging for you.'

'You've heard things against him?'

'Of course.'

'I expect,' said Sheila, 'he's heard things against me.'

She gave a curious mocking laugh, almost brazen-sounding, a sign that her hopes were high. It was a long time since I had seen them so.

'Perhaps even against you,' she said.

I smiled back, I could not depress her; at moments like this her spirits could still make mine spring from the earth. But I said:

'I tell you, he's run through plenty of well-wishers. There must be something the matter.'

'Of course there's something the matter. If not,' she said, 'he wouldn't have any use for me.' Again she smiled: 'Look, it's those with something the matter who need someone. I should have thought even you might have grasped that by now.'

She stood up, went over to the fireplace, grasped the mantelpiece and arched her back.

'We're all right for money, aren't we?' she asked. Just for once, she, who usually spoke so nakedly, was being disingenuous. She knew our financial state as well as I did. She would not have been her father's daughter otherwise. Actually, prepared to throw money away as she was, she had a shrewd business head. She knew exactly to what extent money need not trouble us. With my earnings and her income, we drew in more than two thousand a year, and lived well within it, even though we kept up this comfortable home and had a housekeeper to look after us.

I nodded yes, we were all right.

'That's one thing settled then.'

'As long,' I said, 'as you're not going to be too disappointed —'

'I don't expect too much.'

'You mustn't expect anything,' I said.

'But he is a gifted man, isn't he?' cried Sheila, her face softer and less worn.

'I think he is,' I said.

'I might be able to get him going again,' she said.

She went on, wistfully and yet with something like bravado:

'That would be *something*. If I haven't done anything else, that would be something, wouldn't it?'

CHAPTER II

TWO KINDS OF BUSINESS METHOD

ON the track of someone she might serve, Sheila worked as fast as a confidence trickster. It must have been that same week, probably the very next day, that R. S. Robinson came to dine. Certainly I arrived straight from Lufkin's office; for long afterwards the juxtaposition struck me as ironic.

I had spent all day in Lufkin's suite. To begin with, he had asked me to be available in the early morning and had then kept me waiting, which was not unusual, for a couple of hours. Outside his office, in an ante-room so thickly carpeted that men walked through it with no noise at all, I passed the time with the member of Lufkin's entourage whom I knew best, a man of my own age called Gilbert Cooke. He was a kind of personal assistant to Lufkin, in theory giving advice on export problems, just as in theory I gave advice on legal ones; but in practice Lufkin used us both as utility men. The company was one of the smaller oil-businesses, but the smallness was relative, and in 1938, the fourth year of Lufkin's chairmanship, he had already a turnover of thirty million pounds. He had also his own legal staff, and when he offered me a consultant's job he did not want another lawyer; but it suited him to pick up young men like me and Cooke, keep them on call, and sometimes listen to them.

In the ante-room, Gilbert Cooke pointed to the office door.

'He's running behind time,' he said, as though Lufkin were a train. Cooke was fleshy, powerfully muscled, with a high-coloured Corinthian face and hot brown eyes; he gave at once an impression of intimacy, kindness and considerable weight of nature. In fact, he spoke as though we were more intimate than we actually were.

'How is Sheila just now?' he asked me while he waited, as though he knew the whole history.

I said she was well, but he was not put off.

'Are you absolutely sure she's been to the right doctor?' he said.

I said she had not been near one for some time.

'Who did she go to?'

He was intrusive, pressing, but kind: it was hard to remember that he had been inside our house just twice. He had taken me often enough to his clubs, we had talked politics and games and Lufkin's business, but I had not given him a confidence.

At last we were shown into Lufkin's office: in that suite, as one moved from room to room, the air wafted against the skin like warm breath.

Lufkin sat up straight in a hard chair. He scarcely greeted us: he was inconsiderate, but also informal and without pomp. He was off-hand in personal relations because he was so bad at them, and yet, perversely, they gave him pleasure.

'You know the point?' he said.

Yes, we had both been briefed.

'What do I do?'

It sounded as though we should have finished in ten minutes. In actuality, it took all day, and nothing we said mattered much. Lufkin sat there, indifferent to time, straight, bony, skull-faced. He was only ten years older than Cooke or me; his skin was dark, and his business enemies put it about that he looked Jewish and that his name was Jewish, while as a matter of fact his father was a nonconformist parson in East Anglia.

The point before us was simple enough. He had been asked whether he wanted to buy another distributing business; should he? From the beginning of the talk, throughout the long, smoky, central-heated, unromantic hours, two things stood out. First, this was a point on which neither Cooke's judgment nor mine was worth much – certainly no more than that of any moderately intelligent man round the office. Second, I was sure that, whatever we or anyone else argued, Lufkin had already made up his mind to buy.

Yet all day Cooke behaved like a professional no-man. He became argumentative and rude, oddly so for a middle-rank employee in the presence of a tycoon. The tone of the discussion was harsh and on the whole impersonal; the arguments were prosaic. Cooke was loquacious, much more than Lufkin or me: he went on pestering, not flattering: as I listened, I knew that he was closer to Lufkin than most people in the firm, and wondered why.

Many of the men Lufkin bought had a bit of professional success behind them; but Cooke had nothing to show but social connections, except for his own curious kind of personal force.

Once, in the middle of the afternoon, after we had lunched on sandwiches and coffee, Cooke switched from his factual line. Suddenly, staring at Lufkin with his full eyes, he said:

'I'm afraid you're liable to overstretch yourself.'

'Maybe.' Lufkin seemed willing to consider the idea.

'I mean, with any empire *like yours*' – their eyes met, and Lufkin smiled bleakly – 'there comes a time when you've got to draw in your horns, or else—'

'What do you say to that, Eliot?'

I said that the firm was short of men, and that the able ones were spread thin. He ought to acquire a dozen future managers before he bought much more.

'I agree that,' he said. For half-an-hour he got down to detail, and then asked:

'That make you feel any better, Cooke?'

'No, it seems easy to you, but it's not easy.'

'What seems easy?'

'Biting off more than *anyone* can chew.'

Underneath his remote, off-hand manner, Lufkin was obscurely gratified. But he had a knack of pushing away his own gratification, and we returned to figures again.

The sky outside the office windows darkened, the air seemed more than ever hot. Nothing was settled. There had scarcely been a flight of fancy all day. No one would have guessed, though it was the truth, that Lufkin was a man of remarkable imagination; nor that this marathon talk was his technique of coming to the point of action; nor that Gilbert Cooke was swelling with pride, ardent but humble, at being in on anything so big.

When at last we parted, it was nearly seven and still nothing was settled. The whole range of facts about the new business had been re-sorted, except the purchase price, which Lufkin had only mentioned once, and then obliquely. 'There's always money for a good business,' he had added indifferently, and passed on. And yet that purchase price gave a tang to the repetitive, headachey hours, the only tang I was left with on the way to Chelsea in the cold taxi, for it could not have been less than a good many million pounds.

When I reached home, I met a different kind of business method. R. S.

Robinson was already there in the drawing-room; he was standing plumply by the fire, soft silver-shining hair venerable above smooth baby skin. He looked comfortable, he looked sedate; behind his spectacles, his eyes glinted from Sheila to me, sharp with merriness and suspicion. He made no secret that he wanted Sheila's backing for a sum as great as he could persuade out of her, as great as a thousand pounds.

'I've not come here just for the sake of your intelligent conversation,' he told her. His voice was fluent, modulated, flattering, high-spirited.

'I mustn't come on false pretences, must I?' he said. 'I warn you, I'm a dangerous man to let into your house.'

A thousand was the maximum which he let himself imagine; he did not hope to get away with so much, although he was not too delicate to mention it. He set himself to persuade her, and incidentally me as a possible influence, with all the art of which he was so proud.

Strange, I was thinking as we tasted our drinks, that fifteen, sixteen years before, he had been part of our youth. For he had done, on his own account, a little coterie publishing in the days of the *English Review*, the Imagists, the rebels of the first war. It had been R. S. Robinson who had published a translation of Leopardi's poems under the inept title of *Lonely Beneath the Moon*. Both Sheila and I had read it just before we met, when we were at the age for romantic pessimism, and to us it had been magical.

Since then everything he had touched failed. He was trying to raise money from Sheila for another publising firm, but himself was not able to put down five pounds. And yet we could not forget the past, and he did not want to, so that, as he stood between us on our own hearthrug, it was not Sheila, it was not I, it was he who dispensed the patronage.

'I was telling Mrs Eliot that she must write a book,' he told me soon after I joined them.

Sheila shook her head.

'I'm sure you could,' he said to her. He turned on me: 'I've just noticed that you, sir, you have artists' hands.' He had lost no time getting out his trowel; but Sheila, who shrank with self-consciousness at any praise, could take it from him. Unlike Chelsea acquaintances of our own generation, he had not begun by using our christian names, but instead went on calling me 'sir', and Sheila 'Mrs Eliot', even when he was speaking with insidious intimacy face to face.

Standing between us, he dispensed the patronage; he had dignity and presence, although he was inches shorter than Sheila, who was tall for a woman, and did not come up to my shoulder. Round-shouldered and plump, he stroked down a crest of his silver hair.

He had come to the house in a dinner-jacket, which had once been smart and was now musty, while neither Sheila nor I had dressed; and it was Robinson who set to work to remove embarrassment.

'Always do it,' he advised us, as we went into the dining-room. I asked him what.

'Always put people at a disadvantage. When they tell you not to dress take no notice of them. It gives you the moral initiative.'

'You see,' he whispered to Sheila, sitting at her right hand, 'I have the moral initiative tonight.'

In the dining-room he congratulated Sheila on the fact that, since the food came up by the serving hatch, we were alone.

'So I needn't pretend, need I?' he said, and, tucking into his dinner, told stories of other meals back in the legendary past, at which he had tried to raise money to publish books – books, he did not let us forget, that we had all heard of since.

'I expect you've been told that I was better off then?' He looked up from his plate to Sheila, with a merry, malicious chuckle.

'Don't you believe it. People always get everything wrong.' Stories of multiple manœuvres, getting promises from A on the strength of B and C, from B on the strength of A and C. . . . 'The point is, one's got to refuse to play the game according to the rules,' he advised Sheila. Stories of personal negotiations of such subtlety and invention as to make my business colleagues of the afternoon seem like modest subordinates.

All the time, listening to him, I had spent most of my attention, as throughout our marriage, watching how Sheila was. She had turned towards him, the firm line of her nose and lip clear against the wall; her face had lost the strained and over-vivid fixity, there was no sign of the tic. Perhaps she did not show the quiet familiar ease which sometimes visited her in the company of her protégés; but she had never had a protégé as invincible as this. It took me all my time to remember that, on his own admission, Robinson was destitute, keeping an invalid wife and himself on £150 a year. More than anything, Sheila looked – and it was rare for her – plain mystified.

Just for an instant, out of dead habit, I wondered if he had any attraction for her. Maybe, those who are locked in their own coldness, as she was, mind less than the rest of us about the object of attraction, about whether it is unsuitable or grotesque in others' eyes. Doing a good turn for this man of sixty, whom others thought repellent, Sheila might have known a blessed tinge of sexual warmth. At any rate, her colour was high, and for an hour I could feel responsibility lifted from me; she had managed to forget herself.

Robinson, as natural about eating as about his manœuvres, asked her for a second helping of meat, and went on describing his recent attempts at money raising. Some prosperous author, who had known him in his famous days, had given him an introduction to an insurance company. Robinson digressed, his elephant eyes glinting, to tell us a scandalous anecdote about the prosperous author, a young actor, and an ageing woman; as he told it, Robinson was studying Sheila, probing into her life with me.

Pressing the story on her, but drawing no response, he got going about the insurance company. They had made him go into the City, they had given him coffee and wholemeal biscuits, and then they had talked of the millions they invested in industrial concerns.

'They talked to me of *millions*,' he cried.

'They didn't mean anything,' I said.

'They should be more sensitive,' said Robinson. 'They talked to me of millions when all I wanted was nine hundred pounds.'

I was almost sure he had dropped the figure from a thousand for the sake of the sound, just as, in the shops where my mother used to buy our clothes, they did not speak of five shillings, but always four and eleven three.

'What's more,' said Robinson, 'they didn't intend to give me that. They went on talking about millions here and millions there, and when I got down to brass tacks they looked vague.'

'Did they offer anything?' said Sheila.

'Always know when to cut your losses,' Robinson said in his firm, advising tone. It occurred to me that, in a couple of hours, he had produced more generalisations on how to run a business than I had heard from Paul Lufkin in four years.

'I just told them, "You're treating me very badly. Don't talk of millions to people who need the money," and I left them high and dry.'

He sighed. 'Nine hundred pounds.'

At the thought of humiliation turned upside down, Sheila had laughed out loud, for the first time for months. But now she began asking questions. Nine hundred pounds: that would go nowhere. True, he had kept his old imprint all those years, he could publish a book or two and get someone else to distribute them – but what good was that? Surely if he did that, and it went off half-cock, he had dissipated his credit, and had finished himself for good?

Robinson was not used to being taken by surprise. He flushed: the flush rose up his cheeks, up to the forehead under the white hair. Like many ingenious men, he constantly underrated everyone round him. He had made his judgment of this beautiful hag-ridden woman; he thought she would be the softest of touches. He had marked her down as a neurotic. He was astonished she should show acumen. He was upset that she should see through him.

For, of course, he contrived to be at the same time embarrassingly open and dangerously secretive. Was he even truthful about his own penury? He had been trying on Sheila an alternative version of his technique of multiple approach. This time he was working on several people simultaneously, telling none of them about the others.

'Always keep things simple,' he said, trying to wave his panache.

'Not so simple that they don't make sense,' said Sheila, smiling but not yielding.

Soon she got some reason out of him. If he could collect it, he wanted several thousand; at that period, such a sum would let him publish modestly but professionally, for a couple of years. That failing, however, he still wanted his nine hundred. Even if he could only bring out three books under the old imprint, the name of R. S. Robinson would go round again.

'You never know what might happen,' he said, and blew out wonderful prospects like so many balloons. With three books they would remember him again, he said, and he gave up balloon blowing and spoke of the books he would bring out. He stopped flattering Sheila or using the other dodges which he believed infallible, and all of a sudden one saw that his taste had stayed uncorrupt. It was a hard, austere, anti-romantic taste, similar to Sheila's own.

'I could do for them,' he said, 'what I did before.'

'You want some money,' said Sheila.

'I only want enough to put someone on the map,' he cried.

She asked: 'Is money all you need?'

'No. I want someone like you to keep people from getting the wrong impression. You see, they sometimes think I'm a bit of an ass.'

He was not putting on one of his acts. He had said it angrily, hotly, out of resentment, not trying to get round her. But soon he was master of himself again, enough to calculate that he might extract an answer that night. He must have calculated also that she was on his side and would not shift – for he made an excuse to go to the lavatory, so as to leave the two of us alone.

As soon as I returned without him to the dining-table, where we were still sitting, Sheila said the one word:

'Well?'

We had been drinking brandy, and with a stiff mass-production gesture, she kept pushing the decanter with the side of her little finger.

'Well?' she said again.

I believed, then and afterwards, that if I had intervened I could have stopped her. She still trusted me, and no one else. However much she was set on helping him, she would have listened if I had warned her again. But I had already decided not to. She had found an interest, it would do more good than harm, I thought.

'If you want to risk it,' I said, 'I don't see why you shouldn't.'

'Do you think any better of him?'

I was thinking, he had raised the temperature of living for her. Then I realised that he had done the same for me. If she was taken in, so was I.

I grinned and said:

'I must say I've rather enjoyed myself.'

She nodded, and then said after a pause:

'He wouldn't be grateful, would he?'

'Not particularly.'

'Don't soften it.' Her great eyes swung round on me like searchlights. 'No one's grateful for being looked after. He'd be less grateful than most.'

It was the kind of bitter truth that she never spared herself or others, the only kind of truth that she thought worth facing. Who else, I wondered, would have faced it at that moment, just as she was committing herself? Other people could do what she was doing, but not many with that foresight of what lay ahead.

We sat silent, her eyes still levelled at mine, but gradually becoming unfocused, as though looking past me, looking a great distance away.

'If I don't do it,' she said, 'someone else will. Oh well, I suppose it's more important to me than it is to him.'

Soon afterwards Robinson came back. As he opened the door, we were quiet, and he thought it was because of him. His manner was jaunty, but even his optimistic nerve was strained, and as he sat down he played, too insidiously, too uneasily, his opening trick.

'Mrs Eliot, I've been thinking, you really ought to write a book yourself.'

'Never mind about that,' she said in a cold brittle tone.

'I mean it very much.'

'Never mind.'

The words were final, and Robinson looked down at the table.

She remarked, as though it were obvious:

'I may as well tell you straight away, I will do what I can to help.'

For a second time that night, Robinson flushed to the temples. In a mutter absent-minded, bewildered, he thanked her without raising his eyes, and then took out a handkerchief and wiped it hard across his forehead.

'Perhaps you wouldn't mind, sir, if I have another little drink?' he said to me, forcing his jollity. 'After all, we've got something to celebrate.' He was becoming himself again. 'After all, this is an historic occasion.'

✳

CHAPTER III

THE POINT OF A CIRCUITOUS APPROACH

AFTER that February evening, Sheila told me little of her dealings with Robinson, but I knew they preoccupied her. When, in the early summer, she heard that her parents wished to spend a night in our house, she spoke as though it were an intolerable interruption.

'I can't waste the time,' she said to me, her mouth working.

I said that we could hardly put them off again; this time Mr Knight was visiting a specialist.

'Why can't I put them off? No one will enjoy it.'

'It will give more pain not to have them.'

'They've given enough pain in their time. Anyway,' she said, 'just for once I have something better to do.'

She wrote back, refusing to have them. Her concentration on Robinson's scheme seemed to have become obsessive, so that it was excruciating for her to be distracted even by a letter. But Mrs Knight was not a sensitive woman. She replied by return, morally indignant because Sheila had made an excuse not to go home to the vicarage last Christmas, so that we had not seen them for eighteen months; Sheila's father, for all Mrs Knight's care and his own gallantness, would not always be there for his daughter to see; she was showing no sense of duty.

Even on Sheila, who dreaded their company and who blamed her torments of self-consciousness upon them, the family authority still had its hold. No one else could have overruled her, but her mother did.

So, on a morning in May, a taxi stopped at the garden gate, and, as I watched from an upstairs window, Mr and Mrs Knight were making their way very slowly up the path. Very slowly, because Mr Knight was taking tiny steps and pausing between them, leaning all the time upon his wife. She was a big woman, as strong as Sheila, but Mr Knight tottered above her, his hand on her heavy shoulder, his stomach swelling out from the middle chest, not far below the dog collar; he was teetering along like a massive walking casualty, helped out of battle by an orderly.

I went out on to the path to greet them, whilst Sheila stayed at the door.

'Good morning, Lewis,' said Mr Knight very faintly.

'No talking till we get him in,' Mrs Knight announced.

'I'm sorry to lay my bones among you,' whispered Mr Knight.

'Don't strain yourself talking, dear,' said Mrs Knight.

At last the progress ended in an armchair in the drawing-room, where Mr Knight closed his eyes. It was a warm morning, and through a half-open window blew a zephyr breath.

'Is that too much for you, dear?' said Mrs Knight, looking accusingly at me.

'Perhaps a little,' came a whisper from the armchair. 'Perhaps a little.'

At once Mrs Knight rammed the window up. She acted as though she had one thought alone, which was to keep her husband alive.

'How are you?' I asked, standing by the chair.

'As you see,' came the answer, almost inaudible.

'What do the doctors say?'

'They know very little, Lewis, they know very little.'

'So long as we can keep him free from strain,' said Mrs Knight implacably.

'I sleep night and day,' breathed Mr Knight. '*Night and day.*'

Once more he composed his clever, drooping, petulant face. Then he whispered, 'Sheila! Sheila, I haven't seen my daughter!' As she came near, he turned his head, as though by a herculean effort, through a few degrees, in order to present her his cheek to be kissed. Sheila stood over him, strained, white-faced. For an instant it looked to me as though she could not force herself. Then she bent down, gave him a token kiss, and retreated out of our circle into the window seat.

To her mother, it seemed unnatural; but in fact Sheila believed he was making a fool of himself, and hated it. Valetudinarian: self-dramatising: he had been so since her childhood, though not on such a grandiose scale as now, and she did not credit that there was anything wrong with him. In her heart she wanted to respect him, she thought he had wasted his ability because he was so proud and vain. All he had done was marry money: for it was not the pug-faced, coarse-fibred Mrs Knight who had

507

climbed through marriage, but her husband, the self-indulgent and hyper-acute. Sheila could not throw off the last shreds of her respect for him, and at the sight of his performances her insight, her realism, even her humour failed her.

When we were sitting round the dining-room table, she could not make much pretence of conversation. I was on edge because of her, and Mr Knight, with eyes astute and sly, was surreptitiously inspecting us both. He had time to do so, for Mrs Knight would not let him eat more than a slice of cold ham. It was an effort for him to obey, for he was greedy about his food. But there was something genuine in his hypochondria: he would give up even food, if it lessened his fear of death. Disconsolately, he ate his scrap of ham, his eyes under their heavy lids lurking towards his daughter or me, whenever he thought he was unobserved.

Of the four of us, the only person who came carefree from the meal was Mrs Knight. We rested in the drawing-room, looking down the garden towards the river, and Mrs Knight was satisfied. She was displeased with her daughter's mood, not upset by it, and she was used to being displeased and could ignore it. For the rest she was happy because her husband had revived. She had put away a good meal; she was satisfied at least with her daughter's kitchen and the bright smart house. In fact, she was jollying me by being prepared to concede that Sheila might have made a worse marriage.

'I always knew you'd have a success,' said Mrs Knight. Her memory could not have been more fallacious. When as a poor young man I was first taken by Sheila to the vicarage, Mrs Knight had thought me undesirable in the highest degree, but in our drawing-room she was certain that she was speaking the truth.

Complacently, Mrs Knight called over the names of other men Sheila might have married, none of whom, in her mother's view, had gone as far as I had. For an instant I looked at Sheila, who recognised my glance but did not smile. Then came Mr Knight's modulated voice:

'Is he, is our friend Lewis, content with how far he's gone?'

'I should think so,' said Mrs Knight sturdily.

'Is he? I never have been, but of course I've done nothing that the world can see. I know our friend Lewis has been out there in the arena, but I should like to be certain that he is content?'

What was he getting at? No one had a sharper appraisal of worldly success than Mr Knight.

'Of course I'm not,' I said.

'I rather fancied you might feel that.' Circuitous, not looking at me, he went on: 'Correct me if I'm wrong, I am a child in these matters, but I vaguely imagined that between the two activities you've chosen, you don't expect the highest position in either? I suppose there couldn't be anything in that impression?'

'It is absolutely true,' I said.

'Of course,' Mr Knight reflected, 'if one were of that unfortunate temperament, which some of us are spared, that doesn't feel on terms with life unless it collects the highest prizes, your present course would mean a certain deprivation.'

'Yes, it would,' I said.

He was talking to me, painfully near the nerve. He knew it: so did Sheila, so did I. But not so Mrs Knight.

'Most men would be glad to change with Lewis, I know that,' she said. She called out to Sheila, who was sitting on a pouf in the shadow:

'Isn't that true, Sheila?'

'You've just said it.'

'It's your fault if it's not true, you know.'

Mrs Knight gave a loud laugh. But she could see Sheila's face, pale with the mechanical smile, fixed in the shadow; and Mrs Knight was irritated that she did not look more hearty. Healthy and happy herself, Mrs Knight could see no reason why everyone round her should not be the same.

'It's time you two counted your blessings,' she said.

Mr Knight, uneasy, was rousing himself, but she continued:

'I'm speaking to you, Sheila. You're luckier than most women, and I hope you realise it.'

Sheila did not move.

'You've got a husband who's well thought of,' said Mrs Knight, undeterred, 'you've got a fine house because your parents were able to make a contribution, you've got enough money for anything in reason. What I can't understand is—'

Mr Knight tried to divert her, but for once she was not attending to him.

'What I can't understand is,' said Mrs Knight, 'why you don't set to work and have a child.'

As I listened, the words first of all meant nothing, just badinage, uncomprehending, said in good nature. Then they went in. They were hard enough for me to take; but my wound was nothing to Sheila's wound. I gazed at her, appalled, searching for an excuse to take her out and be with her alone.

Her father was gazing at her too, glossing it over, beginning some preamble.

To our astonishment Sheila began to laugh. Not hysterically, but matily, almost coarsely. That classical piece of tactlessness had, for the moment, pleased her. Just for an instant, she could feel ordinary among the ordinary. To be thought a woman who, because she wished to be free to travel or because she did not like to count the pounds, had refused to have a child – that made her feel at one with her mother, as hearty, as matter-of-fact.

Meanwhile Mrs Knight had noticed nothing out of the common, and went on about the dangers of leaving it too late. Sheila's laugh had dried; and yet she seemed ready to talk back to her mother, and to agree to go out with her for an afternoon's shopping.

As they walked down the path in the sunshine, Sheila's stride flowing beneath a light green dress, our eyes followed them, and then, in the warm room, all windows still closed to guard Mr Knight's health, he turned his glance slowly upon me.

'There they go,' he said. His eyes were self-indulgent, shrewd and sad: when I offered him a cigarette, he closed them in reproof.

'I dare not. I dare not.'

As though in slow motion, his lids raised themselves, and, not looking at me, he scrutinised the garden outside the window. His interest seemed irrelevant, so did his first remark, and yet I was waiting, as in so many of his circumlocutions, for the thrust to come. He began:

'I suppose that, if this international situation develops as between ourselves I believe it must, we shall all have too much on our minds. . . . Even those of us who are compelled to be spectators. It is a curious fate, my dear Lewis, for one to sit by in one's retreat and watch happen a good deal that one has, without any special prescience, miserably foretold.'

He continued, weaving his thoughts in and out, staying off the point but nevertheless leaving me in apprehension of the point to come. In his fashion, he was speaking with a kind of intimacy, an intimacy expressed in code. As he described his labyrinthine patterns he inserted some good sense about the world politics of that year, and what we had to look forward to; he always had a streak of cool detachment, startling in a selfish timid man. With no emphasis he said:

'I suppose that, if things come to the worst, and it's a morbid consolation for a backwoodsman like myself to find that someone like you, right in the middle of things, agree that it is only the worst they can come to – I suppose that to some it may take their minds, though it seems a frivolous way of putting delicate matters, it may take their minds off their own distress.'

This was the beginning.

'It may,' I said.

'Will that be so with her?' he asked, still with no emphasis.

'I do not know.'

'Nor do I.' He started off circuitously again. 'Which ever of us can claim to know a single thought of another human being? Which ever of us can claim that? Even a man like you, Lewis, who has, if I may say so, more than his share of the gift of understanding. And perhaps one might assume that one was not, in comparison with those one meets, utterly deficient oneself. And yet one would not dare to think, and I believe you wouldn't, that one could share another's unhappiness, even if one happened to see it under one's eyes.'

His glance, sly and sad, was on me, and once more he shied off.

'Perhaps one feels it most,' he said, 'when one has the responsibility for a child. One has the illusion that one could know' – just for a moment the modulated voice hesitated – 'him or her as one does oneself. Flesh of one's flesh, bone of one's bone. Then one is faced by another human being, and what is wrong one can never know, and it is more grievous because sometimes there is the resemblance to one's own nerves. If ever you are granted a child, Lewis, and you have any cause for anxiety, and you should have to watch a suffering for which you feel responsible, then I think you will grant the accuracy of what I have tried, of course in-adequately, to explain.'

'I think I can imagine it.'

As he heard my sarcasm, his eyelids dropped. Quietly he said:

'Tell me, what is her life like?'

'It hasn't changed much,' I said.

He considered. 'How does she spend her time in this house?'

I said that she had recently found another occupation, she was trying to help a man who had fallen on bad days.

'She was always good with the unfortunate.'

His mouth had taken on a pursed, almost petulant smile: was he being detached enough to reflect how different she was from himself, with his passionate interest in success, his zest in finding out, each time he met one, exactly what price, on the stock exchange of reputations, one's own reputation fetched that day?

He began on another circuit, how it might be a danger to become sentimental about failure: but he cut off short, and, his gaze on the middle distance, said:

'Of course it is not my responsibility any longer, for that has passed to you, which is better for us all, since I haven't the strength to bear responsibility any longer, and in fact the strain of talking to you confidentially like this means that I am likely to pay the price in my regrettable health. Of course it is your responsibility now, and I know you take it more willingly than most men would. And of course I know my daughter has never been at her best in the presence of my wife. It has been a grief to me, but for the present we must discount that. But even if today has given me a wrong impression, I must not leave undone those things I ought to have done. Because you see, allowing for everything, including the possibility that I may be totally mistaken, there is something which I should feel culpable if I did not say.'

'What is it?' I cried out.

'You told me a few minutes ago that you thought she was much as usual.'

'Don't you?'

He said:

'I'm afraid, I can only hope I'm wrong and I may well be, but I'm afraid that she has gone a little further from the rest of us than she ever was before.'

He shut his eyes, and as I started speaking shook his head.

'I can only leave her with you. That's all I can say,' he whispered. 'This room is just a little stuffy, my dear Lewis. Do you think it would be safe to open a window, just the smallest chink?'

CHAPTER IV

HANDCLASP ON A HOT NIGHT

ONE evening, soon after the Knights' visit, I broke my walk home from Millbank at an Embankment pub, and there, sitting between the pin-tables and the looking-glass on the back wall, was a group of my acquaintances. As I went up to them, it seemed their talk damped down; it seemed also that I caught a glance, acute, uneasy, from the one I knew best, a young woman called Betty Vane. Within moments, though, we were all, not arguing, but joining a chorus of politics, the simple, passionate politics of that year, and it was some time before Betty and I left the pub together.

She was a smallish, sharp-featured woman of thirty, with a prow of a nose and fine open eyes. She was not pretty, but she was so warm and active that her face often took on a glow of charm. She did not expect to be admired by men; her marriage had failed, she was so unsure of herself that it prevented her finding anyone to love her.

I had met her first in circumstances very different, at the country house of the Boscastles, to whom she was related. But that whole family-group was savagely split by the political divide, and she was not on speaking terms with half her relations. She had become friendly with me because we were on the same side; she had gone out to find like-minded persons such as the group in the pub. Sometimes it seemed strange to me to meet her in a society which, to Lord Boscastle, would have seemed as incomprehensible as that of the Trobriand Islanders.

Upon the two of us, as we walked by the river, each with private worries, the public ones weighed down too; and yet, I was thinking, in other times Betty would have been as little political as Mrs Knight. She had dropped into her long, jostling stride that was almost mannish; yet there was no woman less mannish than she. It was her immediate self-protective manner, drawn out of the fear that I or any man might think her ready to make advances. It was only as the evening went on that her gait and her speech became relaxed, and she was warmed by the feeling that she had behaved serenely.

We had fallen into silence when I asked: 'Were you talking about me when I came in just now?'

She had dropped out of step with me: she gave a skip to right herself. 'Not exactly,' she said. She looked down. I saw her lips tighten.

'What about, then?' As she did not at once reply I repeated: 'What about?'

It was an effort for her to look up at me, but when she did so her glance was honest, troubled, steady.

'You must know.'

'Sheila?'

She nodded. I knew she did not like Sheila: but I asked what was being said.

'Nothing. Only nonsense. You know what people are.'

I was silent.

She burst out, in a curiously strident, social voice, as if rallying a stranger at a party: 'I don't in the least want to tell you!'

'That makes it harder for me.'

Betty stopped walking, put her hand on the Embankment wall, and faced me. 'If I do tell you I shan't be able to wrap it up.' She knew I should be angry, she knew I had a right to hear. She was unwilling to spoil the evening for herself and could not keep out of her voice resentment that I should make her do it.

I told her to go on.

'Well, then' – she reverted to her social tone – 'as a matter of fact, they say she's as good as left you.'

I had not expected that, and I laughed and said, 'Nonsense.'

'Is it nonsense?'

'Whom is she supposed to be leaving me for?'

She replied, still in the same social, defensive voice: 'They say she prefers women.'

There was not a word of truth in it, and I told Betty so.

She was puzzled, cross because I was speaking so harshly, though it was only what she had foreseen.

I cross-questioned her. 'Where did this start?'

'Everyone says so.'

'Who does? Where do they get it from?'

'I'm not making it up,' she said. It was a plea for herself, but I did not think of her then.

I made her search her memory for the first rumour.

The effort of searching calmed her: in a moment her face lightened a little. 'I'm sure it came,' she said, 'from someone who knew her. Isn't she working with someone? Hasn't she something to do with that man who looks like a frog? The second-hand bookseller?'

Robinson had had a shop once, but had given it up years before: I could scarcely believe what I seemed to be hearing, but I exclaimed:

'Robinson? Do you mean him?'

'Robinson? He's got beautiful white hair, parted in the middle? He knows her, doesn't he?'

'Yes,' I said.

'Well, he started the word round that she's mad about women.'

I parted from Betty at the corner of Tite Street without taking her to her flat, blaming her because she had brought bad news. The falser the gossip, it sometimes seemed, the more it seared. On my way home, I continued angry with Betty: I should have liked to believe that she had garbled it, she who was both truthful and loyal.

But Robinson? It made no sense: he could not have done it, for reasons of self-interest alone. No one had more to risk from upsetting her.

I wondered whether I should tell Sheila the rumour, and decided not to. Maybe in itself it would not disturb her much; I was not sure: we had both lived in a segment of society which set out to tolerate all kinds of sex. And yet gossip, this gossip that pawed, had something degrading about it, especially for one like Sheila. The story that it originated in Robinson, credible or incredible, had been shameful for me to hear, let alone Sheila; if I could, I wanted to spare her that.

Instead of telling her the gossip that night, I listened to her invoking my help for Robinson. He planned to start with three books in the following spring. 'That may be all he ever does,' said Sheila, with her business feet on the ground, 'but if they are all right—' She meant, though she did not finish, for the phrase was too highfalutin for her, that she would have achieved a purpose: she thought she would have saved his self-respect.

The trouble was, of the foreign books he had counted on, he had acquired the rights of only one. The balloons he had blown up at our dinner-table had most of them exploded, she admitted that; he had believed in his own fancies, he always did, he had only to wish for a property hard enough to feel that he possessed it. Yet, in another sense, he kept his judgment. Nothing would make him substitute bad, or even mediocre, books for those he had fancied were in the bag: either something good, or nothing.

Could I help him find an author? There must be one or two pioneer works going begging, and she knew that I had friends among writers. In fact, although she neither had, nor pretended to have, even a remote acquaintance with my official life, she assumed that it was to writing I should devote myself in the end. Mysteriously, the thought gave her some pleasure.

Could I help Robinson?

I wrote several letters on his behalf, because Sheila had asked me; one reply was encouraging enough for her to act on. Then, a fortnight later, I had other news of him.

I was working in the Lufkin suite, when a telephone call came through. Betty Vane was speaking in a sharp, agitated, seemingly angry voice: could she see me soon? That same afternoon she sat in an armchair by my desk, telling me that she was unlucky. More gossip had reached her, and in decency she could not keep it from me. She did not say it, but she knew my temperament, she had watched me last time: I should not be pleased with her for bringing such news. Still, there seemed to her no choice.

By now the rumours were proliferating. Sheila was not only eccentric but unbalanced, the gossip was going round. She had spent periods in the hands of mental specialists; she had been in homes. This explained the anomalies in our married life, why we had given up entertaining, why she was not seen outside the house for weeks at a time, why we had not dared to have a family.

Some of the rumours referred to me, such as that I had married her, knowing her condition, only because her parents had bribed me with a settlement. Mainly they aimed at her, and the most cruel was that, if we had been poor and without influence, she would have been certified.

Nearly all this gossip was elaborate, circumstantial, spun out with rococo inventiveness, at one or two points just off-true; much of it an outsider could believe without bearing her any ill will, once he had observed that she was strange. One or two of the accretions, notably the more clinical, seemed to have been added as the rumours spread from the point of origin. But the original rumours, wonderfully and zestfully constructed, with a curious fluid imagination infusing them, were unlike any I had heard.

This time I could not pretend doubt to myself, not for an instant; there was only one man who could have begun to talk in such a style. I knew it, and Betty knew I knew it.

She said that she had denied the stories where she could.

'But who believes you when you deny a good story?' she asked, realistic, obscurely aggrieved.

Walking along the river that evening, the summer air touching the nostrils with pollen, with the rotting sweet-water smell, I found my steps heavy. That morning, I had left Sheila composed, but now I had to warn her; I could see no way out. It had become too dangerous to leave her ignorant. I did not know how to handle the news, or her.

I went upstairs to our bedroom, where she was lying on her bed, reading. Although it was rarely that I had her – (as our marriage went on, it was false to speak of making love, for about it there was, though she did not often refuse me, the one-sidedness of rape) – nevertheless she was easier if I slept in the same room. That evening, sitting on my own bed, I watched her holding her book under the reading lamp, although the sunlight was beginning to edge into the room. The windows were wide open, and through them came the smell of lime and petrol; it was a hot still night.

It was the heat, I took it for granted, that had sent Sheila to lie down. She was wearing a dressing-gown, smoking a cigarette, with a film of sweat on her forehead. She looked middle-aged and plain. Suddenly, I felt close to her, close with the years of knowledge and the nights I had seen her so, and my heart and body yearned for her.

'Hot,' she said.

I lay back, longing not to break the peace of the moment.

In the room, the only sound was Sheila's turning a page: outside, the skirl of the Embankment traffic. On her bed, which was the further from the window, Sheila's back was half turned to me, so as to catch the lamp-light on the book.

In time – perhaps I put off speaking for half-an-hour – I called her name.

'Hallo,' she said, without stirring.

'We ought to talk a bit.'

'What about?' She still spoke lazily, she had caught nothing ominous yet.

'Robinson.'

All of a sudden she turned on her back, with her eyes staring at the ceiling.

'What about him?'

I had been thinking out the words to use, and I answered:

'If I were you, I should be careful how much you confide in him.'

There was a long silence. Sheila's face did not move, she gave no sign that she had heard.

At last she said, in a high cold voice:

'You're telling me nothing that I don't know.'

'Do you know what he's actually said?'

'What does it matter?' she cried.

'He's been spreading slander—'

'I don't want to hear.' Her voice rose, but she remained still.

After a pause, she said, into the silent room:

'I told you that he wouldn't be grateful.'

'Yes.'

'I was right.'

Her laugh was splintered. I thought how those like her, who insist on baring the harsher facts of the human condition, are those whom the same facts ravish most.

She sat up, her back against the bed-head, her eyes full on me.

'Why should he be grateful?'

'He's tried to do you harm.'

'Why should he be grateful?' Her glacial anger was rising: it was long since I had seen it. 'Why should he or anyone else be grateful just because someone interferes with his life? Interferes, I tell you, for reasons of their own. I wasn't trying to do anything for R.S.R.'s sake, I just wanted to keep myself from the edge, and well you know it. Why shouldn't he say anything he wants? I don't deserve anything else.'

'You do,' I said.

Her eyes had not left me; her face had gone harsh and cruel.

'Listen,' she said. 'You've given years of your life to taking care of me, haven't you?'

'I shouldn't call it that.'

'What else would you call it? You've been taking care of someone who's useless by herself. Much good has it done you.' In a cold, sadic tone, she added: 'Or me either.'

'I know that well enough.'

'Well, you've sacrificed things you value, haven't you? You used to mind about your career. And you've sacrificed things most men want. You'd have liked children and a satisfactory bed. You've done that for me? – Why?'

'You know the reason.'

'I never have known, but it must be a reason of your own.' Her face looked ravaged, vivid, exhausted, as she cried out:

'And do you think I'm grateful?'

After that fierce and contemptuous cry, she sat quite still. I saw her eyes, which did not fall before mine, slowly redden, and tears dropped on to her cheeks. It was not often that she cried, but always in states like this. It frightened me that night—even though I had watched it before – that she did not raise a hand but sat unmoving, the tears running down her cheeks as down a window pane, wetting the neck of her dressing-gown.

At the end of such an outburst, as I knew by heart, there was nothing for me to do. Neither tenderness nor roughness helped her; it was no use speaking until the stillness broke, and she was reaching for a handkerchief and a cigarette.

We were due at a Soho restaurant at half past eight, to meet my brother. When I reminded her, she shook her head.

'It's no use. You'll have to go by yourself.'

I said that I could put him off without any harm done.

'You go,' she said. 'You're better out of this.'

I was uneasy about leaving her alone in that state, and she knew it.

'I shall be all right,' she said.

'You're sure?'

'I shall be all right.'

So with the familiar sense of escape, guilty escape, I left her: three hours later, with the familiar anxiety, I returned.

She was sitting in almost the same position as when I went away. For an instant I thought she had stayed immobile, but then, with relief, I noticed that she had fetched in her gramophone; there was a pile of records on the floor.

'Had a good time?' she asked.

She inquired about my brother, as though in a clumsy, inarticulate attempt to make amends. In the same constrained but friendly fashion, she asked:

'What am I to do about R.S.R.?'

She had been saving up the question.

'Are you ready to drop him?'

'I leave it to you.'

Then I knew she was not ready. It was still important for her, keeping him afloat; and I must not make it more difficult than need be.

'Well,' I said, 'you knew what he was like all along, and perhaps it doesn't alter the position, when he's behaving like himself—'

She smiled, lighter-hearted because I had understood.

Then I told her that one of us must let Robinson know, as explicitly as we could speak, that we had heard of his slanders and did not propose to stand them. I should be glad, and more than glad, to talk to him; but it would probably do more good if she took it on herself. 'That goes without saying,' she said.

She got up from her bed, and walked round to the stool in front of her looking-glass. From there she held out a hand and took mine, not as a caress, but as though she was clinching a bargain. She said in an uninflected tone:

'I hate this life. If it weren't for you, I don't think I should stay in it.'

It was unlike her to go in for rhetoric, but I was so relieved that she was stable again, so touched by the strained and surreptitious apology, that I scarcely listened to her, and instead just put my other hand over hers.

CHAPTER V

INADMISSIBLE HOPE

WHEN Sheila taxed Robinson with spreading slander he was not embarrassed; he just said blandly that his enemies were making mischief.

When I accompanied her to his office a few days later, he received us with this twinkling old-fashioned politeness, quite unabashed, as though her accusations were a breach of taste which he was ready to forget.

He had taken two garret rooms in Maiden Lane. 'Always have the kind of address that people expect from you,' he said, showing me writing paper headed R. S. Robinson Ltd, 16 Maiden Lane, London, W.C.2. 'It sounds like a big firm, doesn't it? How is anyone to know anything different?' he said, with his gusto in his own subtlety, his happy faith that all men were easy to bamboozle.

He was dead sober, but his spirits were so roaringly high that he seemed drunk. As he spoke of his dodges, he hiccupped with laughter – pretending to be a non-existent partner, speaking over the telephone as the firm's chief reader, getting his secretary to introduce him by a variety of aliases. He called to her: she was typing away in the little room beyond his, the only other room he rented, just as she was the only other member of his staff. She was a soft-faced girl of twenty, straight from a smart secretarial college – as I later discovered, the daughter of a headmaster, blooming with sophistication at being in her first London job, and confident that Robinson's was a normal way for literary business to be done.

'We impressed him, didn't we, Miss Smith?' he said, speaking of a recent visitor, and asking Miss Smith's opinion with much deference.

'I think we did,' she said.

'You're sure we did, aren't you? It's very important, and I thought you were sure.'

'Well, we can't tell till we get his letter,' she said, with a redeeming touch of realism.

'Don't you think he must have been impressed?' Robinson beamed and gleamed. 'We were part of the editorial department, you see,' he explained to Sheila and me, 'just part of it, in temporary quarters, naturally—'

He broke off, and with a sparkle in his eye, an edge to his voice, said:

'I've got an idea that Sheila doesn't altogether approve of these bits of improvisation.'

'It's waste of time,' she said. 'It gets you nowhere.'

'You know nothing at all about it,' he said, in a bantering tone, but rude under the banter.

'I know enough for that.' Sheila spoke uncomfortably and seriously.

'You'll learn better. Three or four good books *and* a bit of mystification, and people will take some notice. Putting a cat among the pigeons – I'm a great believer in that, because conventional people can't begin to cope.

You're an example, Sheila, the minute you hear of something unorthodox you're helpless, you can't begin to cope. Always do what conventional people wouldn't do. It's the only way.'

'Others manage without it,' said Sheila.

'They haven't got along on negative resources for forty years, have they? Do you think you could have done?' He maintained his bantering tone.

Often, when boasting of his deceits, he sounded childlike and innocent. He had a child's face: also, like many of the uninhibited, he had a child's lack of feeling. Much of his *diablerie* he performed as though he did not feel at all: and somehow one accepted it so.

But that was not all. There was a fibre in him which had brought him through a lifetime of begging, cajoling, using his arts on those he believed his inferiors. This fibre made him savage anyone who had been of use to him. It filled him with rancour that *anyone* should have power and money, when he had none. That afternoon he had been charming to Miss Smith, as though he considered her opinion as valuable as any of ours, or more so: he propitiated me because I had done nothing for him, and might even be an enemy: but to Sheila, who through the injustice of life had the power and will to befriend him, he could not help showing his hate.

I was in a delicate position that afternoon. I should have liked to be brutal; but all I could safely do was to demonstrate that he ought to bear me in mind. For Sheila was not ready to draw out. It was not a matter of the money, which was trivial, nor of any feeling for him, which had not decided her in the first place and had turned to repulsion now. But her will had always been strong, and she had set it to do something for this man. He had turned out more monstrous than she reckoned on, but that was neither here nor there; her will would not let her go.

All I could do was listen while Robinson and Sheila discussed a manuscript, which he admired and she thought nothing of. He said goodbye to us at the top of the stairs, gleaming and deprecatory, like a host after a grand party. I was sure that, the instant the door closed behind him, he grinned at Miss Smith, congratulating himself on how he had ridden off the afternoon.

That summer, while I was reading the papers with an anxiety which grew tighter each month, Sheila paid less and less attention to the news. Her politics had once been like mine, she had hoped for and feared much the same things. But in the August and September of '38, when for the first time I began listening to the wireless bulletins, she sat by as though uninterested, or went out to continue reading a manuscript for Robinson.

On the day of Munich she disappeared without explanation in the morning, leaving me alone. I could not go out myself, beause for some days I had been seized with lumbago, which had become a chronic complaint of mine, and which gave me nights so painful that I had to move out of our room during an attack. All that day of Munich, I was lying on a divan in what, when we first bought the house, had been Sheila's sitting-room; but since it was there that I had once told her I could stand it no longer, a decision I went back on within an hour, she no longer used it, showing a vein of superstition that I had not seen in her before.

Like those of our bedroom, the windows looked over the garden, the trees on the Embankment road, the river beyond; from the divan, as the hours passed that day, I could see the tops of the plane trees against the blue indifferent sky.

The only person I spoke to from morning to late evening was our housekeeper, Mrs Wilson, who brought me lemonade and food which I could not eat. She was a woman of sixty, whose face bore the oddity that a mild, seeping, lifelong discontent had not aged, but had·rather made it younger; the corners of her mouth and eyes ran down, her mouth was pinched, and yet she looked like a woman in early middle age whose husband was neglecting her.

Just after she had come up with tea, I heard her step on the stairs again, quick instead of, as usual, reproachfully laborious. When she entered her cheeks were flushed, her expression was humorous and attractive, and she said:

'They say there isn't going to be a war.' She went on, repeating the word which was going through the streets, that the Prime Minister was off to Munich. I asked her to fetch me an evening paper. There it was, as she said, in the stop press news. I lay there, looking at the trees, which were now gilded by the declining sun, the pain lancinating my back, forgetting Sheila, lost in the fear of what would come, as lost as though it were a private misery.

About seven o'clock, when through the window the sky was incandescent in the sunset, Sheila's key turned in the lock downstairs. Quickly I took three aspirins, so as to be free from pain for half-an-hour. When she came she said, bringing a chair to the side of the divan:

'How have you been?'

I said, not comfortable. I asked how her day had gone. Not bad, she said. She volunteered the information (in my jealous days, I had learned how she detested being asked) that during the afternoon she had called at Maiden Lane. He still insisted that he would bring out a book in the spring. She did not guarantee it, she said, with a jab of her old realism.

I was impatient, not able to attend. I said: 'Have you heard the news?'

'Yes.'

'It's as bad as it can be.'

Since tea-time I had wanted to talk to a friend who thought as I did. Now I was speaking to Sheila as I should have spoken years before, when she still had part of her mind free. It would have been a little surcease, to speak out about my fears.

'It's as bad as it can be,' I repeated.

She shrugged her shoulders.

'Don't you think it is?' I was appealing to her.

'I suppose so.'

'If you can have much hope for the future—'

'It depends how much the future interests you,' said Sheila.

Her tone chilled me; but I was so desolate that I went on.

'One can't live like that,' I cried.

Sheila replied:

'You say so.'

As she stared down at me, with the sunset at her back, I could not make out her expression. But her voice held a brittle pity, as she said:

'Try and rest. Anyway, this will give us a bit of time.'

'Do you want a bit of time on those terms?'

She said:

'It might give us time to get R.S.R. a book out.'

It sounded like a frivolity, a Marie-Antoinettish joke in bad taste: but that would have been preferable. For she had spoken out of all that was left of her to feel, out of dread, obsessive will, the inner cold.

I shouted:

'Is that all you're thinking of, tonight of all nights?' She did not speak again. She filled my glass with lemonade, and inspected the aspirin bottle to see that I had enough. For a time she sat silently beside me, in the room now taken over by the darkness. At last she said:

'Is there anything else I can do for you?'

I said no, and in poised, quiet steps she left me.

It was hot that night, and I did not sleep more than an hour or two. The attacks of pain kept mounting, so that I writhed on the bed and the sweat dripped off me; in the periods of respite, I lay with thoughts running through my mind, dark and lucid after the day's news, lucid until the next bout of pain. For a long time I did not think of Sheila. I was working out repetitively, uselessly, how much time there was, when the next Munich night would follow, what the choice would be. As the hours passed, I began to ask myself, nearer the frontier of sleep, how much chance there was that we should be left – no, not we, I alone – with a personal life? More and more as the morning came, the question took on dream-shapes but stayed there: if this happened or that, *what should I do with Sheila*?

I took it for granted that I was tied to her. In the past years when I faced, not just the living habit of marriage, but the thought of it, I knew that other men would have found it intolerable: that did not support me, for it made me recognise something harsher, that this was what my nature had sought out. Not because I took responsibility and looked after others: that was true but superficial, it hid the root from which the amiable and deceptive parts of my character grew.

The root was not so pretty. It was a flaw or set of flaws, which both for good and ill, shaped much of how I affected others and the way my life had gone. In some ways I cared less for myself than most men. Not only to my wife, but to my brother, to Roy Calvert, to others, I devoted myself with a lack of self-regard that was, so far as it went, quite genuine. But deeper down the flaw took another shape. Had Sheila been thinking of it when, in our bedroom, she broke out about people helping others *for reasons of their own*?

At the springs of my nature I had some kind of pride or vanity which not only made me careless of myself but also prevented me going into the deepest human relation on equal terms. I could devote myself; that was all right; so long as I was not in turn understood, looked after, made to take the shames as well as the blessedness of an equal heart.

Thus, so far as I could see within, I had been in search of such a marriage as I found with Sheila – where I was protecting her, watching her face from day to day, and getting back no more interest, often indeed far less, than she would spend on her housekeeper or an acquaintance in a Chelsea pub. It was a marriage in which I was strained as far as I could bear it, constantly apprehensive, often dismally unhappy; and yet it left me with a reserve and strength of spirit, it was a kind of home.

There was a lot of chance, I knew, in human relations; one cannot have seen much unless one believed in chance; I might have been luckier and got into a relation less extreme; but on the whole, I had to say of myself what I should have said of others – in your deepest relations, there is only one test of what you profoundly want: it consists of what happens to you.

And yet, no one can believe himself utterly foredoomed. I was not ready to accept that I was my own prisoner. In the early morning, after the night of Munich, I recognised the question, which now formed itself quite clear: *what shall I do with Sheila?* interspersed among the shapes of the future. Once I had tried to leave her; I could not do so again. Often, though, I had let myself imagine a time in which I might be set free.

Now, in that desolate night, among the thoughts of danger, there entered the inadmissible hope, that somehow I should get relief from the strain of watching over her. In the darkness of the months to come, I might at least (I did not will it, but the hope was there) be freed from the sight of her neurosis. It could happen that I need be responsible no more. As the pain abated and the sky lightened I lay on the threshold of sleep, with the dream-thought that, throwing responsibility away, I should then find something better.

CHAPTER VI

FROWN UNDER THE BEDSIDE LAMP

FEW of my acquaintances liked Sheila. Many men had been attracted to her and several had loved her, but she had always been too odd, too self-centred and ungiving, to evoke ordinary affection. As she grew older and the bones of her character showed through, that was more than ever true. Some of the helpless whom she was kind to idolised her, and so did those who worked for her, including Mrs Wilson, who was the last person to express unconsidered enthusiasm. Apart from them, I had no one to talk to about her when the rumours began to spread; no one I knew in the Chelsea bars and parties would defend her, except one or two, like Betty Vane, who would do so for my sake.

That autumn, I could not discover how much the rumours were alive. I had the impression that after Sheila had confronted Robinson there had been a lull. But Robinson – it was only now that I realised it clearly – became so merry with gossip that he never let it rest for long; exaggerating, transmogrifying, inventing, he presented the story, too luscious to keep, to anyone who met him; everything became a bit larger than life, and I heard, through a chain of word-of-mouth which led back to him, that Sheila's private income was £4000 a year, when in fact it was £700.

Thus I thought it likely that Sheila was still being traduced; watching her, I was convinced that she knew it, and that none of her attempts to forget herself had exposed her so. Sometimes, towards the end of the year, I fancied that she was getting tired of it. Even obsessions wear themselves out, I was thinking, just as, in the unhappiest love affair, there comes eventually a point where the forces urging one to escape unhappiness become infinitesimally stronger than those which immerse one in it.

In fact, Sheila's behaviour was becoming more than ever strange. She went out less, but she was not playing her records hour after hour, which was her final refuge. She seemed to have a new preoccupation. Twice, returning home earlier than usual from Millbank, I heard her footsteps running over the bedroom floor and the sounds of drawers shutting, as though she had been disturbed by my arrival and was hiding something.

It was not safe to ask, and yet I had to know. Mrs Wilson let fall that Sheila had taken to going, each morning, into the room we used as a study; and one day, after starting for the office, I came back as though by accident. Mrs Wilson said that, following her new routine, Sheila was upstairs in the study. It was a room at the back of the house, and I went along the landing and looked in. Beside the window, which looked over the Chelsea roofs, Sheila was sitting at the desk. In front of her was an exercise book, an ordinary school exercise book ruled with blue lines; her head thrown back because of her long sight, she was looking at the words she had just written, her pen balanced over the page. So far as I could see from across the room, it was not continuous prose she was writing, nor was it verse: it looked more like a piece of conversation.

Suddenly she realised that the door was open, that I was there. At once she slammed the exercise book shut and pressed her hand on it.

'It's not fair,' she cried, like an adolescent girl caught in a secret.

I asked her something neutral, such as whether I could change my mind and dine at home that night. 'It's not fair,' Sheila repeated, clutching her book. I said nothing. Without explanation she went across into the bedroom, and there was a noise of a drawer being unlocked and locked again.

But it did not need explanation. She was trying both to write and to keep it secret: was she thinking of Emily Brontë and Emily Dickinson? Had she a sisterly feeling for women as indrawn as herself? Usually, when we had spoken of them, she had – it was cool, I thought, coming from her – shown no patience with them, and felt that if they had got down to earth they might have done better.

Anyway, neither she nor I referred to her writing, until the night of the

Barbican dinner. The Barbican dinner was one of the festivals I had to attend, because of my connection with Paul Lufkin. The Barbican was an organisation consisting largely of members of banks, investment trusts and insurance companies, which set out to make propaganda for English trade overseas. To this January dinner Lufkin was invited, as were all his senior executives and advisers, and those of his bigger competitors.

I would have got out of it if I could; for the political divide was by this time such that even people like me, inured by habit to holding their tongues, found it a strain to spend a social evening with the other side. And this was the other side. Among my brother and his fellow scientists, in the Chelsea pubs, in the provincial back streets where my oldest friends lived – there we were all on one side. At Cambridge, or even among Betty Vane's aristocratic relatives, there were plenty who, to the test questions of those years, the Spanish Civil War, Munich, Nazism, gave the same answers as I did myself. Here there was almost none.

I could hear my old master in chambers, Herbert Getliffe, the rising silk, wise with the times as usual: he was singing in unison, as it were, and so were the active, vigorous, virile men round him: yes, Churchill was a menace and a warmonger and must be kept out at all costs: yes, war was getting less likely every day: yes, everything had been handled as well as it possibly could be handled, everyone knew we were ready to play ball.

I was frightened just as I had been on the night of Munich. I knew some of these men well: though they were less articulate than my friends, though they were trained to conform rather than not to conform, they were mostly able; they were tougher and more courageous than most of us: yet I believed that, as a class, they were self-deceived or worse.

Of all those I knew, there was only one exception. It was Paul Lufkin himself. He had taken his time, had tried to stay laodicean, but at last he had come down coldly among the dissidents. No one could guess whether it was a business calculation or a human one or both. There he sat, neat-headed, up at the benefactors' table, listening to the other bosses, impassively aware that they sneered about how he was trying to suck up to the Opposition, indifferent to their opinion or any other.

But he was alone, up among the tycoons: so was I, three or four grades down. So I felt a gulp of pleasure when I heard Gilbert Cooke trumpeting brusquely, on the opposite side of the table not far from me, telling his neighbours to make the most of the drink, since there would not be a Barbican dinner next year.

'Why not?'

'We shall be fighting,' said Gilbert.

'Let's hope it won't come to that,' said someone.

'Let's hope it will,' said Cooke, his face imperative and flushed. Men were demurring, when he brought his hand down on the table.

'If it doesn't come to that,' he said, 'we're sunk.'

He gazed round with hot eyes: 'Are you ready to see us being sunk?'

He was the son of a regular soldier, he went about in what one might still call society, he was less used to being over-awed than the people round him. Somehow they listened, though he badgered and hectored them, though he was younger than they were.

He saw me approving of him, and gave a great impudent wink. My spirits rose, buoyed up by this carelessness, this comradeship.

It was not his fault that recently I had seen little of him. He had often invited me and Sheila out, and it was only for her sake that I refused. Now he was signalling comradeship. He called out across the table, did I know the Davidsons? Austin Davidson?

It was a curious symbol of alliance tossed over the heads of those respectable businessmen. Davidson was an art connoisseur, a member of one of the academic dynasties, linked in his youth with high Bloomsbury. No, I called out, I knew his work, of course, but not him. I was recalling to myself the kind of gibes we used to make a few years before about those families and that group: how they carried fine feelings so far as to be vulgar: how they objected with refined agony to ambition in others, and slipped as of right into the vacant places themselves. Those were young men's gibes, gibes from outside a charmed circle. Now they did not matter: Davidson would have been an ally at that dinner; so was Gilbert, brandishing his name.

When Gilbert drove me home I had drunk enough to be talkative and my spirits were still high. We had each been angry at the dinner and now we spoke out, Gilbert not so anxious as I about the future but more enraged; his fighting spirit heartened me, and it was a long time since I had become so buoyant and reassured.

In that mood I entered the bedroom, where Sheila was lying reading, her book near the bedside lamp, as it had been the evening we quarrelled over Robinson: but now the rest of the room was in darkness, and all I could see was the lamp, the side of her face, her arm coming from the shoulder of her nightdress.

I sat on my bed, starting to tell her of the purgatorial dinner – and then I became full of desire.

She heard it in my voice, for she turned on her elbow and stared straight at me.

'So that's it, is it?' she said, cold but not unfriendly, trying to be kind.

On her bed, just as I was taking her, too late to consider her, I saw her face under mine, a line between her eyes carved in the lamplight, her expression worn and sad.

Then I lay beside her, on us both the heaviness we had known often, I the more guilty because I was relaxed, because, despite the memory of her frown, I was basking in the animal comfort of the nerves.

In time I asked:

'Anything special the matter?'

'Nothing much,' she said.

'There is something?'

For an instant I was pleased. It was some sadness of her own, different from that which had fallen on us so many nights, lying like this.

Then I would rather have had the sadness we both knew – for she turned her head into my shoulder, so that I could not watch her face, and her body pulsed with sobbing.

'What is the matter?' I said, holding her to me.

She just shook her head.

'Anything to do with me?'

Another shake.

'What then?'

In a desperate and rancorous tone, she said:

'I've been weak-minded.'

'What have you done?'

'You knew that I'd been playing with some writing. I didn't show it to you, because it wasn't for you.'

The words were glacial, but I held her and said, 'Never mind.'

'I've been a fool. I've let R.S.R. know.'

'Does that matter much?'

'It's worse than that, I've let him get it out of me.'

I told her that it was nothing to worry about, that she must harden herself against a bit of malice, which was the worst that could happen. All the time I could feel her anxiety like a growth inside her, meaningless, causeless, unreachable. She scarcely spoke again, she could not explain what she feared, and yet it was exhausting her so much that, as I had known happen to her before in the bitterness of dread, she went to sleep in my arms.

CHAPTER VII

TRIUMPH OF R. S. ROBINSON

WHEN Sheila asked Robinson for her manuscript back, he spent himself on praise. Why had she not written before? This was short, but she must continue with it. He had always suspected she had a talent. Now she had discovered it, she must be ready to make sacrifices.

Reporting this to me, she was as embarrassed and vulnerable as when she confessed that she had let him blandish the manuscript out of her. She had never learned to accept praise, except about her looks. Hearing it from Robinson she felt half-elated, she was vain enough for that, and half-degraded.

Nevertheless, he had not been ambivalent; he had praised with a persistence he had not shown since he extracted her promise of help. There was no sign of the claw beneath. It made nonsense of her premonition, that night in my arms.

Within a fortnight, there was a change. A new rumour was going round, more detailed and factual than any of the earlier ones. It was that Sheila had put money into Robinson's firm (one version which reached me multiplied the amount by three) but not really to help the arts or out of benevolence. In fact, she was just a dilettante who was supporting him because she wrote amateur stuff herself and could not find an easier way to get it published.

That was pure Robinson, I thought, as I heard the story – too clever by half, too neat by half, triumphant because he could expose the 'lie in life'. To some women, I thought also, it would have seemed the most innocuous of rumours. To Sheila – I was determined she should not have to make the comparison. I telephoned Robinson at once, heard from his wife that he was out for the evening, and made an appointment for first thing next day. This time I meant to use threats.

But I was too late. Sitting in the drawing-room when I got home, Sheila was doing nothing at all. No book, no chessmen, not even her gramophone records – she was sitting as though she had been there for hours, staring out of the lighted room into the January night.

After I had greeted her and settled down by the side of the fire, she said:

'Have you heard his latest?'

She spoke in an even tone. It was no use my pretending.

I said yes.

'I'm handing in my resignation,' she said.

'I'm glad of that,' I replied.

'I've tried as much as I can,' she said, without any tone.

In the same flat, impassive voice, she asked me to handle the business for her. She did not wish to see Robinson. She did not care what happened to him. Her will was broken. If I could manage it, I might as well get her money back. She was not much interested.

As she spoke, discussing the end of the relation with no more emotion than last week's accounts, she pointed to the grate, where there lay a pile of ash and some twisted, calcined corners of paper.

'I've been getting rid of things,' she said.

'You shouldn't have done,' I cried.

'I should never have started,' she said.

She had burned all, her own holograph and two typescripts. But, against the curious farcical intransigence of brute creation, she had not found it so easy as she expected. The debris in the grate represented a long time of sitting before the fire, feeding in papers. In the end, she had had to drop most of the paper into the boiler downstairs. Even that night, she thought it faintly funny.

However, she had destroyed each trace, so completely that I never read a sentence of hers, nor grasped for certain what kind of book it was. Years later, I met the woman who had once been Miss Smith and Robinson's secretary, and she mentioned that she had glanced through it. According to her, it had consisted mostly of aphorisms, with a few insets like 'little plays'. She had thought it was 'unusual', but had found it difficult to read.

The morning after Sheila burned her manuscript, I kept my appointment with Robinson. In the Maiden Lane attic, the sky outside pressed down against the window; as I entered, Robinson switched on a single light in the middle of the ceiling.

'How are you, sir?' he said. 'I'm glad you've conquered that fibrositis, it must have made life miserable.'

Courteous and also cordial, he insisted on putting me in the comfortable chair and fitting a cushion to ease the backache of six months before. His eyes were suspicious, but struck me as gay rather than nervous.

I began:

'I was coming to see you on my own account—'

'Any time you have nothing better to do,' said Robinson.

'But in fact I've come on my wife's.'

'I haven't seen her for two or three weeks; how is she?'

'She wants,' I said, 'to finish any connection with you or what you call your firm or anything to do with you.'

Robinson blushed, as he had done at our dinner party. That was the one chink in his blandness. Confidentially, almost cheerfully, he asked:

'Shouldn't you say that was an impulsive decision?'

He might have been a friend for years, so intimate that he knew what my life had been, enduring an unbalanced wife.

'I should have advised her to take it.'

'Well,' said Robinson, 'I don't want to touch on painful topics, but I think perhaps you'll agree that it's not unreasonable for me to ask for an explanation.'

'Do you think you deserve it?'

'Sir,' he flared up, like a man in a righteous temper, 'I don't see that anything in our respective positions in the intellectual world entitles you to talk to me like that.'

'You know very well why my wife is quitting,' I said. 'You've made too much mischief. She isn't ready to stand any more.'

He smiled at me sympathetically, putting his temper aside as though it were a mackintosh.

'Mischief?' he said.

'*Mischief*,' he repeated, reflectively, like one earnestly weighing up the truth. 'It would help me if you could just give me an example of what sort of mischief I'm supposed to be guilty of, just as a rough guide.'

I said that he had spread slander about her.

'Remember,' he said, in a friendly merry manner, 'remember you're a lawyer, so you oughtn't to use those words.'

I said that his slander about the book had sickened her.

'Do you really think,' he said, 'that a sane man would be as foolish as you make me out to be? Do you think I could possibly go round black-guarding anyone who was supporting me? And blackguarding her very stupidly, according to your account, because for the sum she lent me she could have published her book several times over. I'm afraid, I don't like to say it, but I'm afraid you've let Sheila's difficulties infect you.'

For a second his bland reasonableness, his trick of making his own actions sound like a neurotic's invention, his sheer euphoria, kept me silent.

'Yes,' he said. 'I'm afraid you've let poor Sheila's state infect you. I suppose it *is* the beginning of schizophrenia, isn't it?'

'I am not going to discuss my wife,' I said. 'And I don't think it profitable to discuss your motives—'

'As for her book,' he said, 'I assure you, it has real merit. Mind you, I don't think she'll ever become a professional writer, but she can say original things, perhaps because she's a little different from most of us, don't you know?'

'I've got nothing to say to you,' I said. 'Except to arrange how you can pay my wife's money back.'

'I was afraid she might feel like that—'

'This is final,' I said.

'Of course it is,' said Robinson with his gay, wholehearted laugh. 'Why, I knew you were going to say that the very moment you came into the room!'

I had been strung up for a quarrel. It was a frustration to hear my words bounce back. If he had been a younger man, I might have hit him. As it was, he regarded me with sympathy, with humour in his small, elephantine eyes, the middle parting geometrically precise in his grandfatherly hair.

'You've done her harm,' I said in extreme bitterness, and regretted the words as soon as they were out.

'*Harm?*' he enquired. 'Because of her association with me? What kind of harm?'

He spread out his hands.

'But, as you said, this isn't the time or place to consider the troubles of poor Sheila. You came here to take her money out, didn't you? Always recognise the inevitable, I'm a great believer in that. Don't you think it's time we got down to business?'

I had run into another surprise. As I sat beside his desk, listening to Robinson's summary of his agreement with Sheila and his present sitution, I realised he was a man of unusual financial precision and, so far as I could judge, of honesty. It was true that, cherishing his own secretiveness, he concealed from me, just as he had originally concealed from Sheila, some of his sources of income and his expectations of money to come. Somehow he had enough money to continue in his office and to pay Miss Smith; meanwhile, he was postponing his first 'list' until the autumn; it struck me, was he glad of the excuse? Day-dreaming, planning, word-spinning about the revival of past glories, that was one thing. Putting it to the test was another. Maybe he would like that date deferred.

No one could have procrastinated less, however, about repaying Sheila: he offered to write her a cheque for £300 that day, and to follow it with two equal instalments on 1 June and 1 September.

'Interest?' he asked, beaming.

'She wouldn't take it.'

'I suppose she wouldn't,' said Robinson with curiosity.

At once he proposed that we should go round to his solicitor's. 'I never believe in delay,' said Robinson, putting on a wide-brimmed hat, an old overcoat trimmed with fur at the collar and sleeves. Proud of his incisiveness, behaving like his idea of a businessman (although it was no more like Paul Lufkin's behaviour than a Zulu medicine man's), he walked by my side through Covent Garden, the dignified little figure not up to my shoulder. Twice he was recognised by men who worked in the publishers' or agents' offices round about. Robinson swept off his grand hat.

'Good morning to you, sir,' he cried affably, with a trace of patronage, just as R. S. Robinson, the coterie publisher, might have greeted them in 1913.

His face gleamed rosy in the drab morning. He looked happy. It might have seemed bizarre to anyone but him that he should have spent all his cunning on acquiring a benefactor, and then used equal ingenuity in driving the benefactor away. Yet I believed he had done it before, it was one of the patterns of his career. To him it was worth it. The pleasures of malice, the pleasures of revenge against one who had the unbearable impertinence to lean down to him – they were worth a bigger price than he had ever had to pay.

And more than that, I thought, as we sniffed the smell of fruit and straw in the raw air, Robinson walking with the assurance of one going to a reputable business rendezvous, it was not only the pleasure of revenge against a benefactor. There was something more mysterious which sustained him. It was a revenge, not against Sheila, not against a single benefactor, but against life.

When I reached home that afternoon, I heard the gramophone playing. That worried me; it worried me more when I found her not in the drawing-room, not in our bedroom, but in the sitting-room where I had spent the night of Munich and which to her was a place of bad luck. In front of her, the ash-tray must have held thirty stubs.

I began to say that I had settled with Robinson. 'I don't want to hear anything about it,' she said, in a harsh flat tone.

I tried to amuse her, but she said:

'I don't want to hear anything about it.'

She put on another record, shutting out, not only the history of Robinson, but me too.

CHAPTER VIII

'YOU'VE DONE ALL YOU COULD'

IN the summer, I no longer spent half my time away from Sheila. We were waiting for the war to begin; I slept each night in our bedroom, saw her waking and sleeping, without break, as I had not done for years. As soon as war came, I assumed that I should go on living beside her in the Chelsea house, as long as one could foresee.

Those September nights, we were as serene, as near happy, as ever in our marriage. I used to walk, not from Millbank now but Whitehall, for I had already taken up my government job, all along the Embankment, often at eight o'clock and after; the air was still warm, the sky glowed like a cyclorama; Sheila seemed glad to see me. She was even interested in the work I was doing.

We sat in the garden, the night sounding more peaceful than any peacetime night, and she asked about the department, how much the Minister did, to what extent he was in the pocket of his civil servants, just where I – as one of his personal assistants – came in. I told her more of my own concerns than I had for a long while. She laughed at me for what she often called my 'automatic competence', meaning that I did not have to screw myself up to find my way about the world.

I was too much immersed in my new job to notice just when and how that mood broke up. Certainly I had no idea until weeks later that to herself she thought of a moment of collapse as sharp as the crack of a broken leg – and she thought also of as sharp a cause. All I knew was that, in the well-being of September, she had, unknown to me, arranged to join someone's staff on the first of January. It was work that needed good French, which she had, and seemed more than usually suitable. She described it to me with pleasure, almost with excitement. She said:

'I expect it will turn out to be R.S.R. all over again,' but she spoke without shadow. It was a gibe she could only have made in confidence and optimism.

Soon afterwards, not more than a fortnight later, I came home night following night to what seemed to me signs of the familiar strain, no different from what we each knew. I was disappointed the first time I came home to it; I was irritated, because I wanted my mind undistracted; I set myself to go through the routine of caring for her. Persuading her to leave her records and come to bed: talking to her in the darkness, telling her that, just as worse bouts had passed, so would this: discussing other people whose lives were riven by *angst* – it domesticated her wretchedness a little to have that label to pin on. It was all repetitive, it was the routine of consolation that I knew by heart, and so did she. Sometimes I thought you had to live by the side of one like Sheila to understand how repetitive suffering is.

All the time I was looking after her, absentmindedly, out of habit; it seemed like all the other times; it did not occur to me to see a deterioration in her, or how far it had gone. Not even when she tried to tell me.

One night, early in November, I came out of my first sleep, aware that she was not in her bed. I listened to her outside the door, heard a match strike. None of this was novel, for when she could not sleep she walked about the house smoking, considerate of me because I disliked the smell of tobacco smoke at night. The click of the bedroom door, the rasp of a match, the pad of feet in the corridor – many nights they had quietly wakened me, and I did not get to sleep again until she was back in bed. This time it was no different, and according to habit I waited for her. The click of the door again: the slither of bedclothes, the spring of the bed. At last, I thought, I can go back to sleep: and contentedly, out of habit, called out – 'All right?'

For an instant she did not answer; then her voice came:

'I suppose so.'

I was jerked back into consciousness, and again I asked:

'*Are* you all right?'

There was a long pause, in the dark. At last a voice:

'Lewis.'

It was very rare for her to address me by my name.

I said, already trying to soothe her:

'What is it?'

Her reply sounded thin but steady:

'I'm in a pretty bad way.'

At once I switched on my bedside lamp, and went across to her. In the shadow, for my body came between the light and her face, I could see her, pale and still; I put my arm round her, and asked what was the matter.

All of a sudden her pride and courage both collapsed. Tears burst from her eyes and, in the transformation of moments, her face seemed decaying, degenerate, almost as though it were dissolving.

'What is the matter?'

'I'm worried about January 1st.'

She meant the job she had to take up that day.

'Oh, that!' I said, unable to keep down an edge of anti-climax, of sheer boredom.

I ought to have known that anything could be a trigger for her anxiety: but nothing, I knew also, was more boring than an anxiety one did not share.

'You must understand,' she cried, for once making an appeal.

I tried to speak in the tone that she would trust. Soon – in those states she was easy to persuade – she trusted me as she had done before.

'You do see, don't you?' she cried, the tears stopping as she broke into speech that was incoherent, excited, little like her own. 'The other day, three weeks ago next Monday, it was in the afternoon just after the post came, I realised that on January 1st I was going to get into the same state as I did over R.S.R. It is bound to happen, you do see that, don't you? There will be just the same kind of trouble, and it will all gather round me day after day.'

'Look,' I said, reasoning with her carefully, for long ago I had found the way that reassured her most, 'I dare say there'll be trouble, but it won't be the same kind. There's only one R.S.R., you know.'

'There's only one me,' she said, with a splinter of detachment. 'I suppose I was really responsible for the fiasco.'

'Truly I don't think so,' I said. 'Robinson would have behaved the same to me.'

'I doubt it,' she said. 'I've never done any good.'

Her face was excited and pressing. 'You must understand, as soon as I get among new people, I shall be caught in the same trap again.'

I was shaking my head, but she broke out, very high:

'I tell you, I realised it that afternoon just after the post came. And I tell you, in the same second I felt something go in my brain.'

She was trembling, although she was not crying any more. I asked her, with the sympathy of one who has heard it before and so is not frightened, about her physical symptoms. Often, in a state of anxiety, she had complained of hard bands constricting her head. Now she said that there had been continual pressure ever since that afternoon, but she would not describe the physical sensation that began it. I thought she was shy, because she had been exaggerating. I did not realise that she was living with a delusion, in the clinical sense. I had no idea, coaxing her, even teasing her, how much of her judgment had gone.

I reminded her how many of her fears had turned out nonsense. I made some plans for us both after the war. Her body was not trembling

537

by this time, and I gave her a tablet of her drug and stayed by her until she went off to sleep.

Next morning, although she was not anxiety-free, she discussed her state equably (using her domesticating formula – 'about twenty per cent *angst* today') and seemed a good deal restored. That evening she was strained, but she had a good night, and it was not for several days that she broke down again. Each night now, I had to be prepared to steady myself. Sometimes there were interludes, for as long as a week together, when she was in comfortable spirits, but I was tensed for the next sign of strain.

My work at the office was becoming more exacting; the Minister was using me for some talks face-to-face where one needed nothing else to think about and no tugs at the nerves; when I left Sheila in the morning, I wished that I were made so that I could forget her all through the day – but at some time, in the careful official conversation, a thought of her would swim between me and the man I was trying to persuade.

More than once, I found myself bitter with resentment against her. When we first married she had drained me of energy and nerve, and had spoiled my chance. Now, when I could least afford it, she was doing so again. That resentment seemed to exist simultaneously, almost to blend, with pity and protective love.

The first week in December, I was in the middle of a piece of business. One afternoon, about half past five, when I was counting on working for an hour or two more, the telephone rang. I heard Sheila's voice, brittle and remote.

'I've got a cold,' she said.

She went on:

'I suppose you couldn't come home a bit early ? I'll make you some tea.'

It was abnormal for her to telephone me at all, much less ask me to see her. She was so unused to asking that she had to make those attempts at the commonplace.

I took it for granted that something more was wrong, abandoned my work, and took a taxi to Chelsea. There I found that, although she was wretched and her tic did not leave her mouth, she had nothing new to say. She had fetched me home just to work over the moving belt of anxiety – the bits and pieces came round and round before us – Robinson, 1 January, her 'crack-up'. My impatience not quite suppressed, dully I said:

'We've been over all this before.'

'I know it,' she said.

'I've told you,' I said mechanically, 'worse things have passed, and so will this.'

'Will it?' She gave a smile, half-trusting, half-contemptuous, then broke out:

'I've got no purpose. You've got a purpose. You can't pretend you haven't.' She cried out: 'I've said before, I've handed in my resignation.'

I was tired of it, unable to make the effort of reassurance, irked that she had dragged me from the work I wanted to do. With the self-absorption that had now become complete, she dismissed all my life except the fraction of it I spent supporting her. We were sitting by the fire in the drawing room. I heard myself using words that, years before, I had used in her old sitting room. For there, in my one attempt to part from her, I had said that our life together was becoming difficult for me. Now I was near repeating myself.

'This is difficult for me,' I said, 'as well as for you.'

She stared at me. Whether or not the echo struck her, I did not know. Perhaps she was too drawn into herself to attend. Or perhaps she was certain that, after all that had happened, all that had changed, I could no longer even contemplate leaving her.

'It is difficult for me,' I said.

'I suppose it is,' she replied.

On that earlier occasion, I had been able to say that for my own sake I must go. But now, as we both knew, I could not. While she was there, I had to be there too. All I could say was:

'Make it as easy for me as you can.'

She did not reply. For a long time she gazed at me with an expression I could not read. She said, in a hard and final tone:

'You've done all you could.'

CHAPTER IX

A GOODBYE IN THE MORNING

Up to 20 December there was no change that I noticed. As I lived through those days they seemed no more significant than others. Later, when I tried to remember each word she and I said, I remembered also the signs of distress she showed about 1 January, and the new job. She was still too proud to ask outright, but she was begging me to find an excuse to get her out of it.

Otherwise she had fits of activity, as capricious as they used to be. She put on a mackintosh, in weather that was already turning into bitter winter, walked all day along the river, down to the docks, past Greenwich, along the mudflats. When she got home, flushed with the cold, she looked as she must have done as a girl, after a day's hunting. She was cheerful that night, full of the enjoyment of her muscles; she shared a bottle of wine with me and fell asleep after dinner, a little drunk and happily tired. I did not believe in those flashes of cheerfulness, but also I did not totally believe in her distress. It did not seem, as I watched her, to have the full weight of her nature behind it.

Her moods fluctuated, not as Roy Calvert's did in cycles of depression, but in splinters from hour to hour; more exactly, her moods could change within a single moment, they were not integral; sometimes she spoke unlike an integral person. But that had always been so, though it was sharper now. She still made her gibes, and, the instant she did so, I felt the burden of worry evanesce. This phase was nothing out of the ordinary, I thought, and we should both come through it, much as we had done for the past years.

In fact, I behaved as I had seen others do in crises, acting as though the present state of things would endure for ever, and occasionally, as it were with my left hand and without recognising it, showing a sense of danger.

One day I got away from my meetings and confided in Charles March, who at this time a doctor in Pimlico. I told him, in sharper tones than I used to myself, that Sheila was in a state of acute anxiety, and I described it: was it any use bringing in another psychiatrist? The trouble was, as he knew, she had consulted one before, and given him up with ridicule. Charles promised to find someone, who would have to be as clever and as strongwilled as she was herself, whom she might just conceivably trust. But he shook his head. 'I doubt if he'll be able to do much for her. All he might do is take some of the responsibility off you.'

It was on 20 December that Charles rang me up at the office and gave me a doctor's name and address. It happened to be the day I was bringing my first substantial piece of departmental business – the business from which Sheila had called me away a fortnight before – to an issue. In the morning I had three interviews, in the afternoon a committee. I got my way, I was elated, I wrote a minute to my superior. Then I telephoned the doctor whom Charles had recommended; he was not at his surgery and would not be available for a fortnight, but he could see my wife in the first week in January, 4 January. That I arranged, and, with a throb of premonition, my own work shelved for a day or two, free to attend to her, I telephoned home.

I felt an irrational relief when she answered. I asked:

'How are you?'

'Much the same.'

'Nothing's happened?' I asked.

'What could have happened?'

Her voice sharpened:

'I should like to see you. When shall you be here?'

'Nothing wrong since this morning?'

'No, but I should like to see you.'

I knew her tone, I knew she was at her worst. I tried to coax her, as sometimes one does in the face of wretchedness, into saying that she was not so bad.

Flatly the words came to my ear:

'I'm not too bad to cope.'

She added:

'I want to see you. Shall you be long?'

When I went into the hall, she was waiting there for me. She began to speak before I had taken my coat off, and I had to put my arm round her shoulders and lead her into the drawing-room. She was not crying, but I could feel beneath my hand the quiver of her muscles, the physical sign that frightened me most.

'It's been a bad day,' she was saying. 'I don't know whether I can go on. It's no use going on if it's too hard.'

'It won't be too hard,' I said.

'Are you sure?'

I was ready with the automatic consolation.

'Have I got to go on? Can I tell them I shan't be able to come on January 1st?'

That was what she meant, I had assumed, by 'going on'; she spoke like that, whenever she winced away from this ordeal to come, so trivial to anyone else.

'I don't think you ought,' I said.

'It wouldn't matter much to them.' It was as near pleading as she had come.

'Look,' I said, 'if you get out of this, you'll get out of everything else in the future, except just curling up into yourself, now won't you? It's better for you to come through this, even if it means a certain amount of hell. When you put it behind you, all will be fine. But this time you mustn't give up.'

I was speaking sternly. I believed what I said; if she surrendered over this test, she would relapse for good and all into her neurosis; I was hoping, by making my sympathy hard, to keep her out of it. But also I spoke so for a selfish reason. I wanted her to take this job so that she would be occupied and so at least partially off my hands. In secret, I looked forward to January as a period of emancipation.

I thought of mentioning the doctor whom Charles March had recommended, and the appointment that I had made. Then I decided against.

'You ought to go through with it,' I said.

'I knew you'd say that.' She gave me a smile, not bitter, not mechanical, quite transformed; for a second her face looked youthful, open, spiritual.

'I'm sorry for giving you so much trouble,' she said, with a curious simplicity. 'I should have been luckier if I could have cracked up altogether, shouldn't I?' Her imagination had been caught by an acquaintance who had solved her problems by what they called a 'nervous breakdown', and now seemed happy and at peace. 'I couldn't pull that off somehow. But I ought to have been able to manage by myself without wearing you out so much.'

As I listened I was moved, but, still trying to stiffen her nerve, I did not smile or show her much affection.

That night we played a couple of games of chess, and were in bed early. She slept quietly and next morning got up to have breakfast with me, which was unusual. Across the table her face looked more ravaged and yet more youthful without its make-up. She did not refer to what had been said the evening before; instead, she was talking, with amusement that seemed light and genuine, about my arrangements for the coming night. Gilbert Cooke had invited me to dinner at his club; getting back to Chelsea I said, in the blackout, having had a fair amount of drink, was not agreeable. Perhaps it would be better if I slept at my own club. How much should I have had to drink? Sheila wanted to know – with a spark of the inquisitiveness about male goings-on, the impudence that one saw sometimes in much younger women, high-spirited, not demure, but brought up in households without brothers.

On those light, teasing terms, we said goodbye. I kissed her and, in her dressing-gown, she came to the door as I went down the path. At the gate I waved, and standing with her arms by her sides, poised, erect and strong, she smiled. It was a dark morning, and I could not see her clearly but I thought her expression was both friendly and gibing.

CHAPTER X

NO LETTER IN THE ROOM

AT White's that night, Gilbert Cooke and I had a convivial dinner. He had invited me for a specific reason and yet, despite his unselfconscious raids into other people's business, he could not confess this bit of his own until I helped him out. Then he was loose and easy, a man with an embarrassing task behind him; he ordered another bottle of wine and began to talk more confidentially and imperiously.

The favour he asked would not have weighed so heavy on most men. It appeared that he had been trying all ways to get into uniform, but he kept being turned down because he had once had an operation for mastoid. Gilbert was ashamed and sorry. He wanted to fight, with a lack of pretence that men of our age had felt twenty-five years before; in 1939 the climate, the social pressures, had changed; most other men I met in Gilbert's situation blessed their luck, but he felt deprived.

However, by this time, he had accepted his loss; since he could not fight, he wished to do something in the war. Stay with Paul Lufkin?

'Why does he want me to?' Gilbert Cooke enquired, with his suspicious, knowing, hot-eyed glance.

'Because you're useful to him, of course.'

'No, he's thinking out something deeper than that. I'd give fifty quid to know just what.'

'Why in God's name should he not want you to stay?'

'Haven't you realised he thinks about all of us five moves ahead?'

Gilbert's face was shining, as he filled his glass and pushed the bottle across. I did not realise what he wanted me to (which seemed to me conspiratorial nonsense), but instead I did realise another thing. Which was, that Gilbert, despite his independent no-man air in Paul Lufkin's company, was at heart more than normally impressionable: he gave Lufkin brusque advice, but in private thought he was a great man: so that Lufkin received the pleasures of not being flattered, and of being deeply flattered, at one and the same time.

But Gilbert, as well as being susceptible to personality, was a sincere and patriotic man. The country was at war, and with Lufkin, although Gilbert was hypnotised by the human drama, he was not doing anything useful. So this lavish bachelor dinner, this elaborate wind-up, led to nothing but a humble question, at which he was too diffident to do more than hint.

'You mean,' I said, 'that you'd like a job in a government department?'

'If they'd possibly have me.'

'Why shouldn't they?'

'Oh, I was never up to their class as a brain, I don't see why they should.'

In fact, able active men of thirty-five, with decent academic careers, permanently exempt from call-up, were bound soon to be at a premium. I told him so.

'I'll believe that when it see it,' said Cooke.

'They'd take you as a principal tomorrow.'

'How could they think I was any use to them?'

A little drunk, half-irritated that he would not trust my judgment, half-touched by his modesty, I said:

'Look here. Would you like to work in my place?'

'You don't mean there would be a chance?'

'I can take the first step tomorrow.'

Gilbert regarded me with bold eyes, determined to see the catch in it, diffident about thanking me. From that instant he just wanted a comradely evening. Brandy by the fire: half-confidences: the stories, gilded at the edges, of youngish men on a happy alcoholic night. One thing struck me about Gilbert's stories. He was an adventurous, versatile man, always on the move: but he was meticulously pure in speech, and, although he spoke of women with liking, he did not talk openly of sex.

Next morning, in the breakfast room of my club, the coal fire crackled and spurted: the unfolded newspapers glinted on the table under the light: in the street outside the pavement looked dark with cold. Although I had a headache, it was not enough to put me off my breakfast, and food was still good, so early in the war. I ate the kidneys and bacon, and, indulging my thirst, went on drinking tea; the firelight was reflected back from the grey morning mist outside the windows. Acquaintances came to the tables, opening their *Times*. It was all warm and cared-for, and I enjoyed stretching out the minutes before I rang up Sheila. At a quarter-past nine, I thought, she would be getting up. In comfort, I drank another cup of tea.

When I got through to our house, the telephone burred out perhaps twenty times, but I was not anxious, thinking that Sheila must still be asleep. Then I heard Mrs Wilson's voice.

'Who is it?'

I asked, was Sheila up..

'Oh, Mr Eliot,' came the thin, complaining voice.

'What's the matter?'

'Something's happened. I think you ought to come back straightaway, I think you must.'

I knew.

'Is she all right physically?'

'No.'

'Is she dead?'

'Yes.'

'She's killed herself?'

'Yes.'

I was sick with shock, with the first numbness; I heard myself asking: 'How did she do it?'

'It must have been her sleeping tablets, there's the empty bottle lying by the side of her.'

'Have you called a doctor?'

'I'm afraid she's been dead for hours, Mr Eliot. I only found her ten minutes ago, and I didn't know what to do.'

I said that I would arrange everything, and be with her in half an hour.

'I'm very sorry about it myself. I was very fond of her, poor soul. It was a great shock for me, finding her,' came Mrs Wilson's voice, in a tone of surprise, aggrievement, injury. 'It was a great shock for me.'

At once I rang up Charles March. I must have a doctor whom I could trust, I thought. As I waited, it occurred to me that neither Sheila nor I had used a regular doctor in London. Apart from my lumbago, we had been physically healthy people.

Charles was out at a patient's. I left a message, saying that I needed him with extreme urgency. Then I went into the street and took a taxi home. In the freezing morning the desolate park skimmed by, Exhibition Road, the knot of shop-lights by South Kensington station. Twice the smell of the taxi's leather made me retch. I seemed at a distance from my own pain: somehow, dimly, numbly, I knew that grief and remorse were gnawing inside me, twisting my bowels with animal deprivation, with the sensual misery of loss. And also I felt the edge of a selfish and entirely ignoble fear. I was afraid that her suicide might do me harm; I shied from thinking of what kind of harm, but the superstitious reproach hung upon me, mingled with remorse. The fear was sharp, practical and selfish.

In the hall, Mrs Wilson's eyes were bloodshot, and she squeezed her handkerchief and pressed it into the corner of one eye and then the other: but her manner had the eagerness, the zest, of one living close to bad news.

'She's not in the bedroom, Mr Eliot,' she whispered. 'She did it in her old sitting-room.'

I wondered whether it was a chance, or whether she had chosen it.

'Did she leave any letters?' I asked, and I also was near whispering.

'I couldn't see anything. I looked round, of course, but I couldn't see a piece of paper in the room. I went up with her tea, Mr Eliot, and I knocked on the bedroom door, and no one answered, and I went in and there was no one there—'

Although Mrs Wilson wished to follow me, I went upstairs alone. The sitting-room curtains were drawn, though I did not know by whom, it might have been by Mrs Wilson a few minutes before. In the half-light I was struck by the dread that came on me as a child when I went into the room where my grandfather's body was stretched out. Before looking at her, I pulled the curtains open; the room stood bare to the leaden light. At last I forced my eyes towards the divan.

She was lying on her back, dressed in a blouse and skirt such as she wore in the house on an ordinary afternoon, her head a quarter turned towards the window. Her left hand was by her side and her right fell across her breast, the thumb wide apart from the fingers. The lines of her face were so softened by death that they had become only grazes, as though her living face had been photographed through muslin; her cheeks, which had never hollowed, now were as full as when she was a girl. Her eyes were shut, her mouth half open. From one angle her mouth ceased to be a dark hole and looked as though fixed in a defensive, deprecatory, astonished grin, exactly the grin she wore when she was taken at a loss and exclaimed, 'Well, I'm damned'.

There was, just visible because of the tablets she had taken, a dried trickle of saliva down the side of her chin, as though she had dribbled in her sleep.

I stared for a long time, gazing down at her. However one read her expression, the moment of death seemed not to have been tragic or unhappy. I did not touch her; perhaps, if she had looked sadder, I should have done.

By the divan stood the bedside table, just as on the night of Munich, when she had placed my bottle of aspirin there for me. Now another bottle rested on the cherry wood, but empty and without its stopper, which she must have dropped on to the floor. Beside the bottle was a tumbler, containing about three fingers' depth of water, stale with the night's bubbles. There was nothing else at all. Into that room she brought nothing but her bottle and the glass of water.

I searched for a note as though I were a detective. In that room – in the bedroom – in my study – I studied the envelopes in the wastepaper baskets, looking for any line to her parents or me. In her handbag I found her pen unfilled. On her writing desk the paper was blank. She had gone without a word.

Suddenly I was angry with her. I was angry, as I looked down at her. I had loved her all my adult life; I had spent the years of my manhood upon her; with all the possessive love that I had once felt for her, I was seared because she had not left me a goodbye.

Waiting for Charles March, I was not mourning Sheila. I had room for nothing but that petty wound, because I had been forgotten; the petty wound, and also the petty fear of the days ahead. As I waited there, I was afraid of much, meeting the Knights, going to the office, even being seen by my friends.

CHAPTER XI

CLAUSTROPHOBIA IN AN EMPTY HOUSE

WHILE Charles March was examining her I went into the bedroom, where I gazed out of the window, aware of nothing but fears and precautions. The only recognition that I gave to Sheila was that my eyes kept themselves away from any glance at her bed, at the undisturbed immaculate bed.

There I stayed until Charles's step outside warned me. I met the concerned glance from his sharp, searching eyes, and we walked together to the study.

'This is bound to be a horror for you,' he said. 'And nothing that I or anyone else can say is going to alter that, is it?'

Nowadays Charles and I did not see each other often. Since the days when he had befriended me, he had changed his way of life, and as a hard-working doctor did not move at all in his former circles. When we did meet the old intuitive sympathy sparked between us. But that morning he did not realise how little I was feeling, or what that little was.

'There is no doubt, I suppose?' I asked.

'You don't think so yourself?' he answered.

I shook my head, and he said:

'No, there's no doubt. None at all.'

He added, with astringent pity:

'She did it very competently. She had a very strong will.'

'When did she do it?' I had gone on speaking with neutrality. He was studying me protectively, as though he were making a prognosis.

'Some time last night, I think.'

'Yes,' I said. 'I was out for the evening. I was having a cheerful time at a club, as a matter of fact.'

'I shouldn't take that to heart, if I were you.'

He leaned forward in his chair, his eyes brilliant in the dark room, and went on:

'You know, Lewis, it wasn't such an intolerable wrench for her to die as it would be for you or me. She wasn't so tied to life as we are. People are as different in the ways they die as in the ways they live. Some go out as though they were shrugging their shoulders. I imagine that she did. I think she just slipped out of life. I don't think she suffered much.'

He had never liked her, he had thought her bad for me, but he was speaking of her with kindness. He went on: 'You're going to suffer a lot more, you know.'

He added:

'The danger is, you'll feel a failure.'

I did not respond.

'Whatever you'd done or been, it wouldn't have helped her,' he said, with energy and insistence.

'Anyway,' I said, 'that doesn't matter.'

'It matters, if you're going to feel you've failed. And no one but yourself can be any good to you there.'

Again I did not respond.

He gazed at me sternly: he knew that my emotions were as strong as his: he had not seen them dead before. He was using his imagination to help me, he did not speak for some time, his glance stayed hard and appraising as he reached a settlement in his own mind.

'The only thing I can do for you now is superficial, but it might help a little,' he said, after a silence.

'What do you mean?'

'Does anyone else know about her?'

'Only Mrs Wilson,' I said.

'Would she keep quiet?'

'It's possible,' I replied.

'If necessary, could you guarantee it?'

I did not reply at once. Then I said:

'If necessary, I think I could.'

Charles nodded. He said:

'I expect it will make you just a little worse to have other people knowing about her death, I know it would me. You'll feel that your whole life with her is open to them, and that they're blaming you. You're going to take too much responsibility on yourself whatever happens, but this will make it worse.'

'Maybe,' I said.

'Well, I can save you that,' he broke out.

He went on:

'It won't help much, but it will a little. I'm willing to sign a certificate that she died a natural death.'

Charles was a bold man, who lived in close touch with moral experience. Perhaps he had that special boldness, that ability to act in isolation, that one found most commonly in men born rich. Between perjuring himself, which he would dislike more than most, and leaving me exposed he had made his choice.

I was not altogether surprised: in fact, in sending for him rather than for any of the doctors near, I had some such hope half-concealed.

I was tempted. Quickly I was running through the practical entanglements: if there was any risk to him professionally I could not let him run it. We had each been thinking of that, while he questioned me. Could I answer absolutely for Mrs Wilson? Who else need know the truth? The Knights must, as soon as they arrived. But they would keep the secret for their own sakes.

I thought it over. As I did so, I had little insight into my own motives. It was not entirely, or even mainly, because of practical reasons or scruples about Charles's risk that I answered:

'It's not worth it.'

'Are you sure?'

'Quite sure.'

Charles went on persuading me until he was convinced that my mind was made up. Then he said that he was relieved. He left to enquire about the inquest, while I telephoned the Knights': I told Mrs Knight the bare news and asked them to come that afternoon. She sounded reliable and active in the face of shock, but she cried: 'I don't know how he'll get through it.'

That same afternoon I had to go to a committee, among civil, sensible strangers.

Back in the house, blacked-out early on the December night, I could not stay still until the Knights came. Mrs Wilson had gone out to shop, getting a meal ready for them, and I was alone in the empty house. Yet no house seemed empty while someone lay dead: the reverse was true, there was a claustrophobic pressure, although I had not visited the sitting-room again.

In my restlessness I turned over Sheila's books once more, re-read the letters in her desk, in the silly hope that I might find news of her. By a fluke, I did find just a little, not among her books or papers, but in her bag. Expecting nothing, I picked out her engagement diary and riffled through it; most of the pages shone bare, since the appointments with Robinson in January and February: since then, she had seen almost no one. But in the autumn pages I caught sight of a few written words – no, not just words, whole sentences.

It was an ordinary small pocket book, three inches by two, and she had scaled down her writing, which as a rule was elegant but had a long-sighted tallness. There were only seven entries, beginning in October, a week after the afternoon which she referred to as her 'crack-up'. As I read, I knew that she had written for herself alone. Some of the entries were mere repetitions.

4 November: Ten days since the sensation in my head. No good. No one believes me.

12 November: 1 January bad enough anyway. Seems hopeless after something snapped in head.

28 November: Told I must go on. Why should I? That's the one comfort, I needn't go on.

5 December: Bit better. Perhaps I can go on. It's easier, when I know I needn't.

Nothing more than that – but for the first time I knew how fixed her delusion was. I knew also that she had contemplated suicide for weeks past, had had it in her mind when I tried to hearten her.

Perhaps even when she first said she was handing in her resignation, that was a hint, as much as eight months ago. Had she intended me to understand her? But she was not certain, she had done no more than hint, even to herself. Had she been certain two nights before, when I told her again she must go on? Had she been certain next morning at break-fast, the last time I saw her alive, when she was making fun of me?

I heard Mrs Wilson's step downstairs. I did not look at Sheila's writing any more: it was not to think, it was because of the claustrophobic pressure upon me in the house, that I went out of the front door and walked along the Embankment in a night as calm as the last night, as calm as when, quite untroubled, I had walked up St James's Street with Gilbert Cooke. The sky was dark, so was the river, so were the houses.

CHAPTER XII

THE SMELL OF HERB TOBACCO

WHEN I got back to the house there was a sliver of light between the black-out curtains of the drawing-room; as soon as I stood inside the hall I heard a woman's voice, Mrs Knight's, raised, sustained, unrelenting. The instant I entered the room, she stopped: there was a silence: she had been talking about me.

Mr Knight was sitting in an armchair by the fire, and she had drawn up the sofa so as to be beside him. Her eyes fixed on mine and did not budge, but his gazed into the fire. It was he who spoke.

'Excuse me if I don't get up, Lewis,' he said, still without looking at me, and the polite whisper fell ominously into the silent room. Still politely, he said that they had caught an earlier train and I could not have expected them at this time. His eyes had stayed hidden, but his expression was pouched and sad. He said:

'Your housekeeper has shown us—'

'Yes.'

The intimations of pain and sorrow, so weak all day, quite left me. I felt nothing but guilt, and irrational fear.

'She left no word for anyone?'

'No.'

'Not for you *or* us?'

I shook my head.

'I don't understand that. I don't understand *that*.'

I wondered if he believed me, if he suspected that I had destroyed a note. Certainly Mrs Knight, suddenly set loose, suspected it.

'Where were you last night?'

I replied that I was dining out – the jolly carefree evening came back to me.

'Why did you leave her? Hadn't you any consideration for her?'

I could not answer.

Why hadn't I looked after her? Mrs Knight asked, angry and denouncing. All through our marriage, why had I left her to herself? Why hadn't I carried out what I promised? Why hadn't I taken the trouble to realise that she wanted looking after? Couldn't I have given her even a modicum of care?

'Oh no, he's done that,' whispered Mr Knight, with his eyes closed.

'You've left her alone in this empty house,' Mrs Knight went on.

'He's done as much as anyone could have.' Mr Knight spoke up, a little louder, defending me. She looked baffled, even frustrated, and began another attack.

'*Please*, my dearest,' he ordered her in a loud voice, and she gave way. Then with the gentleness he always showed to her, he said, as though explaining:

'It is his affliction as well as ours.'

Out of the corner of his eye he glanced at me, and murmured: 'The last time I saw her,' – he meant the visit eighteen months before – 'I couldn't help thinking she was in a bad state. I believe I mentioned it, didn't I, Lewis, or did I just think it to myself? The last time I saw her. I wish that I had been wrong.'

And yet, the fact that he had been perceptive, more perceptive than I or anyone else had been, gave him a vestigial comfort; even that night his vanity glowed for an instant.

'She shouldn't have done it,' cried Mrs Knight, in anger but with the only tears I had seen in her eyes.

'I have no comfort to give you, dearest,' he said. 'Or you either.' Once more he was gazing into the fire, the corner of his eyes sidling towards me. In my hearing he had not once spoken of the consolations of his religion. The room was quiet, all we heard was the ticking of the clock. Somehow we had passed into a patch of those doldrums which often lurk in the path, not only of a quarrel, but of any scene of violent feeling.

Breaking the quiet, Mrs Knight asked whether there would have to be an inquest. I said yes. When? I told her that it was already arranged, for the following afternoon. Mr Knight half-raised his lids with a speculative expression, looked as though he had something to say but had thought better of it. Then he mentioned casually: 'Tomorrow afternoon? Not that I want anyone to give it a thought except my doctor, but it will presumably be a considerable strain on me.'

'You've stood it well so far,' said Mrs Knight.

'If Ross [his doctor] were here, he would tell us it was dangerous,' Mr Knight continued. 'I'm morally certain he would forbid it. But he won't have to know until he has to patch me up afterwards.'

In a new kind of numbness I exclaimed:

'Never mind, don't take any risks. I can get through it by myself.'

Mrs Knight cried:

'No, we can't think of leaving you.'

Mr Knight muttered:

'I wouldn't willingly think of leaving you, it would throw all of it on to your shoulders—'

Mrs Knight broke in: 'We can't do it.'

Mr Knight went on: 'One doesn't like to think of it, but Lewis, in case, in the remote case, that my wretched heart was getting beyond its degree of tolerance tomorrow afternoon, are you sure that you could if need be manage by yourself?'

So Mr Knight, whose empathy was such that he knew more than most men both what my life with Sheila had been and what my condition was that night, was only anxious to escape and leave me to it: while Mrs Knight, who blamed me for her daughter's unhappiness and death, felt that they ought to stand by me in the end, give their physical presence if they could give nothing else. She felt it so primally that for once she gave up thinking of her husband's health.

There were those, among whom I had sometimes been one, who believed that, if she had not pampered his hypochondria, he would have forgotten his ailments half the time and lived something near a normal life. We were wrong. She had a rough, simple nature, full of animal force: but, despite her aggressiveness, she had always been, and was now as much as ever, under his domination. It was he who felt his own pulse, who gave the cry of alarm, and she who in duty and reverence echoed it. Even that night he could not subdue it, and for a few moments she was impatient with him.

In the end, of course, he got his way. She soon realised that the inquest would tax his heart more than she could allow; she became convinced that it was he who out of duty insisted on attending, and she who was obliged to stop him; she would have to forbid his doing anything so quixotic, even if I was prostrate without them.

As it was, I said that I would settle it alone, and they arranged to return home next morning. I did not mention Charles March's offer to give a false certificate, so that we could have avoided the inquest. I wondered how Mr Knight would have reconciled his conscience, in order to be able to accept that offer.

In his labyrinthine fashion, Mr Knight asked how much publicity we had to be prepared for. I shrugged it off.

'No,' said Mr Knight, 'it will hurt you as much and more than us, isn't that true?'

It was, but I did not wish to admit it, I did not like the times that day when the thought of it drove out others.

Perhaps the war news would be a blessing to us, Mr Knight was considering. I said I would do my best with my press acquaintances. The Knights could go home next morning: I would do what could be done.

Relieved, half-resentful, half-protective, Mr Knight began inquiring where I should sleep tomorrow night, whether I could take a holiday and get some rest. I did not want, I could not bear, to talk of myself, so I made an excuse and left them alone.

At dinner none of us spoke much, and soon afterwards, it must have been as early as nine o'clock, Mrs Knight announced that she was tired and must go straight to bed. Of all women, she was the least well designed for subterfuges; she proclaimed her piece of acting like a blunt, embarrassed, unhappy schoolgirl. But I had no attention to spare for her; Mr Knight was determined to speak to me in intimacy, and I was on guard.

We sat in the drawing-room, one each side of the fireplace, Mr Knight smoking a pipe of the herb tobacco which out of valetudinarian caution he had taken to years before. The smell invaded me and I felt a tension nearly intolerable, as though this moment of sense, the smell of herb tobacco, was not to be endured, as though I could not wait to hear a word. But when he did speak, beginning with one of his circuitous wind-ups, he astonished me: the subject he wanted to get clear before they left next day was no more intimate than the lease of the house.

When I married Sheila, I had had no capital, and Mr Knight had lent us the money to buy a fourteen-years lease, which had been in Sheila's name. This lease still had seven years to run, and Mr Knight was concerned about the most business-like course of action. Presumably, after all that had happened, and regardless of the fact that the house was too large for a man alone, I should not wish to go on living there? If it were his place to advise me, he would advise against. In that case, we ought to take steps about disposing of the lease. Since the loan had been for Sheila's sake as well as mine, he would consider it wiped off, but perhaps I would think it not unreasonable, as he did himself, particularly as Sheila's own money would come to me under her will, that any proceeds we now derived from the lease should go to him?

Above all, said Mr Knight, there was a need for speed. It might be possible to sell a house before the war developed: looking a few months ahead, none of us could guess the future, and any property in London might be a drug on the market. I had always found him one of the most puzzling and ungraspable of men, but never more so than now, when he took that opportunity to show his practical acumen. I promised to put the house in the agents' hands within a few days.

'I'm sorry to lay this on your shoulders too,' he said, 'but your shoulders are broad – in some ways—'

His voice trailed away, as though in the qualification he might be either envying me or pitying me. I was staring into the fire, not looking at him, but I felt his glance upon me. In a quiet tone he said:

'She always took her own way.'

I did not speak.

'She suffered too much.'

I cried out: 'Could any man have made her happy?'

'Who can say?' replied Mr Knight.

He was trying to comfort me, but I was bitter because that one cry had escaped against my will.

'May she find peace,' he said. For once his heavy lids were raised, he was looking directly at me with sad and acute eyes.

'Let me say something to you,' he remarked, his words coming out more quickly than usual, 'because I suspect you are one of those who take it on themselves to carry burdens. Perhaps one is the same oneself, perhaps one realises the danger of those who won't let themselves forget.'

For an instance his tone was soft, indulgent with self-regard. Then he spoke sharply: 'I beg you, don't let this burden cripple you.'

I neither would nor could confide. I met his glance as though I did not understand.

'I mean the burden of my daughter's death. Don't let it lie upon you always.'

I muttered. He made another effort: 'If I may speak as a man thirty years older, there is this to remember – time heals most wounds, except the passing of time. But only if you can drop the burdens of the past, only if you make yourself believe that you have a life to live.'

I was gazing, without recognition, into the fire; the smell of herb tobacco wafted across. Mr Knight had fallen silent. I reckoned that he would leave me alone now.

I said something about letting the house. Mr Knight's interest in money did not revive; he had tried for once to be direct, an ordeal for so oblique a man, and had got nowhere.

For minutes, ticked off by the clock, again the only sound in the room, we stayed there; when I looked at him his face was sagging with misery. At last he said, after neither of us had spoken for a long while, that we

555

might as well go to bed. As we went out to the foot of the stairs, he whispered: 'If one doesn't take them slowly, they are a strain on one's heart.'

I made him rest his hand on my shoulder, and cautiously, with trepidation, he got himself from tread to tread. On the landing he averted his eyes from the door of the room in which her body lay.

Again he whispered:

'Good night. Let us try to sleep.'

CHAPTER XIII

A SMOOTH BEDCOVER

It was three nights later when, blank to all feeling, I went into the bedroom and switched on the light. Blankly, I pulled off the cover from my own bed; then I glanced across at hers, smooth, apple-green under the light, undisturbed since it was made four days before. All of a sudden, sorrow, loss, tore at me like a spasm of the body. I went to the bed and drew my hands along the cover, tears that I could not shed pressing behind my eyes, convulsed in the ravening of grief. At last it had seized me. The bed was smooth under the light. I knelt beside it, and wave after wave of a passion of the senses possessed me, made me grip the stuff and twist it, scratch it, anything to break the surface, shining quietly under the light.

Once, in an exhausted respite, I had a curious relief. The week to come, some friends had invited us to dinner. If she had been alive, she would have been anxious about going, she would have wanted me to make excuses and lie her out of the evening, as I had done so many times.

Then the grief flooded through me again. In the derangement of my senses, there was no time to come: all time was here, in this moment, now, beside this bed.

I learned then, in that devastation, that one could not know such loss without craving for an after life. My reason would not give me the illusion, not the fractional hope of it – and yet I longed to pray to her.

PART TWO

THE SELF-DEFEATED

CHAPTER XIV

LOAN OF A BOOK

OUTSIDE the window, in the September sunshine, a couple of elderly men were sitting in deckchairs drinking tea. From my bed, which was on the ground floor of a London clinic, I could just see past them to a bed of chrysanthemums smouldering in the shadow. The afternoon was placid, the two old men drank with the peace of cared-for invalids; for me it was peaceful to lie there watching them, free from pain. True, Gilbert Cooke would be bringing me work, I should have to be on my feet by Thursday; but there was nothing the matter with me, I could lie idle for another twenty-four hours.

The day was Tuesday, and I had only entered the clinic on the previous Saturday afternoon. Since Sheila's death nearly two years before (this was September of 1941) I had been more on the move than ever in my life, and the pain in my back had not been giving me much rest. It was faintly ludicrous: but, in the months ahead, I was going to be still more occupied, and it was not such a joke to think of dragging myself through meetings as I had been doing, or, on the bad days, holding them round my office sofa. It was not such a joke, and also it watered one's influence down: in any kind of politics, men listened to you less if you were ill. So I had set aside three days, and a surgeon had tried manipulating me under an anaesthetic. Although I was incredulous, it seemed to have worked. Waiting for Cooke that afternoon, I was touching wood in case the pain returned.

When Gilbert Cooke came in, he had a young woman with him whose name, when he made an imperious gobbled introduction, I did not catch. In fact, taking from him at once some papers marked urgent, I realised some moments afterwards, absent in my reading, that I had not heard her name. Then I asked for it only with routine politeness. Margaret Davidson. He had mentioned her occasionally, I recalled; she was the daughter of the Davidson whom he had talked of at the Barbican dinner and whom I had been surprised to hear that Gilbert knew.

I glanced up at her, but she had withdrawn to near the window, getting out of our way.

Meanwhile Gilbert stood by my bed, a batch of papers in his hand, haranguing me with questions.

'What have they been doing to you?

'Are you fit for decent company at last?

'You realise you must stay here until you're well enough not to embarrass everyone?'

I said I would take the committee on Thursday. He replied that it was out of the question. When I told him how I should handle that day's business he said that, even if I were fool enough to attend, I could not use those methods.

'You can't get away with it every time,' he said, jabbing his thumb at me in warning. He stood there, his massive shoulders humped, his plethoric face frowning at me. After the fussy, almost maternal concern with which he looked after my health, as he had done since he came into my office, he turned brusquer still. He was talking to me like a professional no-man, just as he used to talk to Paul Lufkin. He did so for the same reason – because he regarded me as a success.

Working under me for nearly two years of war, Gilbert had seen me promoted; he had his ear close to the official gossip. He magnified both what I had done and what was thought of it, but it was true enough that I had made, in those powerful anonymous *couloirs*, some sort of reputation. Partly I had been lucky, for anyone as close to the Minister as I was could not help but attract attention: partly, I had immersed myself in the job, my life simplified for the first time since I was a boy, with no one to watch over, no secret home to distract me.

To Gilbert, who had joined my branch soon after Sheila died, I now seemed an important man. As a consequence, he was loyal and predatory about my interests when I was not present, but face to face insisted on backchat.

On the coming Thursday we should have to struggle with a problem of security. Some people in one of the 'private armies' of the time were busy with a project that none of us believed in; but they had contrived so to enmesh themselves in security that we could not control them. I knew about their project: they knew that I knew: but they would not talk to me about it. I told Gilbert that their self-esteem might be satisfied if we went through a solemn minuet: they must be asked to explain themselves to the Minister, which they could not refuse to do: he would then repeat the explanation to me: then on Thursday both they and I could hint obliquely at the mystery.

It was the kind of silly tactic that any official was used to. I made some remark that it was dangerous to give secrets to anyone with exaggerated self-esteem: it was bad for business, and worse for his character.

I heard a stirring by the window. I looked at the young woman, who had been sitting quietly there without a word, and to my astonishment saw her face transfigured by such a smile that I felt an instant of ease, almost of expectancy and happiness. Never mind that my piece of sarcasm had been mechanical: her smile lit up her eyes, flushed her skin, was kind, astringent, lively, content.

Until that moment I had scarcely seen her, or seen her through gauze as one sees a stranger one does not expect to meet again. Perhaps I should have noticed that her features were fine-cut. Now I looked at her. When she was not smiling her face might have been austere, except for the accident that her upper lip was short, so that I could not help watching the delicate lines of her nostril and the peak of her lip. As she smiled her mouth seemed large, her face lost its fine moulding: it became relaxed with good nature and also with an appetite for happiness.

Looking at her, I saw how fine her skin was. She had used very little make-up, even on the lips. She was wearing a cheap plain frock – so cheap and plain that it seemed she had not just picked up the first in sight, but deliberately chosen this one.

As she sat by the window, her amusement drying up, she had a curious awkwardness, like an actor who does not know what to do with his hands. This posture, at the same time careless and shy, made her look both younger and frailer than she was in fact. The little I knew of her was collecting in my mind. She must be about twenty-four, I thought, twelve years younger than Gilbert or me. When she laughed again, and her head was thrown back, she did not look frail at all.

I smiled at her. I began to talk to her and for her. I was beating round for something to link us. She was working in the Treasury – no, she was not easy about the people or her job.

Acquaintances in Cambridge – we exchanged names, but no more.

How should I occupy myself tomorrow, I asked, staying here in this room?

'You oughtn't to do anything,' she said.

'I'm not good at that,' I replied.

'You ought to do as Gilbert tells you.' She had taken care to bring him in, she broke the duologue, she smiled at him. But she spoke to me again: she was positive.

'You ought to rest all the week.'

I shook my head; yet a spark had flashed between us.

No, I said, I should just have tomorrow to bask in and read – I was short of books, what would be best for the day in bed?

'You want something peaceful,' she said.

Not a serious novel, we agreed – not fiction at all, maybe – journals that one could dip into, something with facts in them. Which were the most suitable journals, Bennett's, Gide's, Amiel's?

'What about the Goncourts?' she asked.

'Just what I feel like,' I said.

I asked, how could I possibly lay my hand on the books by tomorrow?

'I've got them at home,' she said.

Suddenly the air held promise, danger, strain. I had not enough confidence to go ahead; I needed her to make the running, to give me the sign I longed for; I was waiting for her to say that she would bring a book, or send it to me. Yet I could feel, as she folded her fingers in her lap, that she was diffident too.

If it had been Sheila when I first knew her – some half-memory made me more constrained – she would not have given a thought that Gilbert had brought her into the room: she would have announced, in ruthlessness and innocence, that she would deliver the book next morning. But Margaret would not treat Gilbert badly, even though their relation appeared to be quite slight. She was too good-mannered to give me the lead I sought. But, even if Gilbert had not been present, could she have done so? She was not only too gentle, but perhaps also she was too proud.

Looking at her, her head no longer thrown back, her eyes studying me, I felt that she had a strong will, but no more confidence that moment than I had myself.

It was Gilbert who snapped the tension off. He would arrange, he said, brusque and cheerful, to get the books round to the clinic first thing next morning. Soon afterwards they left, Margaret saying goodbye from the door: as soon as I heard their steps in the corridor, I was suffused with happiness.

In a beam of evening sun which just missed my bed, the motes were spinning. Outside it, in the twilight, I cherished my happiness, as though by doing so I could stretch it out, as though, by letting myself live in the moment of recognition between this young woman and me half an hour before, I could stay happy.

Several times since Sheila's death, my eyes had lit up at the sight of a woman, but I had not been able to free myself enough, it had come to nothing. The qualms were not buried; this could come to nothing too. But, just as the old do not always or even most of the time feel old, so someone whose nerve is broken can forget past disasters and cherish the illusions of free will. I felt as free to think of this young woman as if I had not met Sheila, as if I were beginning.

It occurred to me that I had never been able to remember my first meeting with Sheila. It was the second time I could remember, her face already lined, handsome and painted, at nineteen looking older than Margaret in the middle twenties. Yes, I was comparing Margaret with her, as I did when letting my imagination dwell on any woman; it appeared that I had to make sure there was no resemblance, to be convinced that anyone I so much as thought of was totally unlike what I had known.

There was the same comparison in my mind as I thought of Margaret's nature. She had enough spirit to be exciting – but she seemed tender, equable, easy-going. An hour after she had left, I was making daydreams of her so.

That evening, lying in bed outside the beam of sunlight, I basked in a kind of uncommitted hope; sometimes homesick images of the past filtered in, as well as the real past that I feared. But I was happy with the illusion of free will, as though this girl who had just left me was mine if I chose it.

Nevertheless I need do nothing; I had admitted nothing to myself beyond recall; I could refrain from seeing her again without more than a spasm of regret and reproach for my own cowardice.

For that night, I could rest in an island of peace, hoarding my chance of bliss as I used to hoard sweets as a child, docketing them away in a bookshelf corner so that they were ready when I felt inclined.

CHAPTER XV

CONFIDENTIAL OFFER

STILL acting as though uncommitted, I invited Margaret and Gilbert together, three times that autumn. For me, there was about those evenings the suspense, the inadmissible charm, that abides in a period of waiting for climactic news, as it were an examination result, from which one is safe until the period is up. The meeting in a pub, where Gilbert and I went together from the office and found her waiting: the communiqués in the evening papers: the wartime streets at night: the half-empty restaurants, for London was not crowded that year: the times at dinner when we spoke of ourselves, the questions unspoken: the return alone to Pimlico in the free black night.

One evening in late November Gilbert had accompanied me out of the office for a drink in my club, as he often did. That day, as on most others, we went on discussing our work, for we were engrossed in it. Much of the time since Sheila's death, I had thought of little else: nor had Gilbert, intensely patriotic, caught up in the war. He had by now picked up some of the skills and language of the professional civil servants we were working with: our discussion that evening, just as usual, was much like the discussions of two professionals. I valued his advice: he was both tough and shrewd, and tactically his judgment was better than mine.

There was just one point, however, at which our discussion was not simply business-like. Gilbert had developed Napoleonic ambitions, not for himself, but for me: he saw me rising to power, with himself as second-in-command: he credited me with the unsleeping cunning he had once seen in Paul Lufkin, and read hidden meanings in moves that were quite innocent. Either as result or cause, his curiosity about my behaviour was proliferating so that I often felt spied upon. He was observant quite out of the ordinary run. He would not ask a disloyal question, but he had a gossip-writer's nose for information. I was fond of him, I had got used to his inquisitiveness, but lately it had seemed to be swelling into a mania.

We could be talking frankly about policy, with no secrets between us, when I happened to mention a business conversation with the Minister. A look, knowing and inflamed, came into Gilbert's eyes: he was wondering how he could track down what we had said. He was even more zestful about my relations with the Permanent Secretary, Sir Hector Rose. Gilbert knew that the Minister wished me well; he was not so sure how I proposed to get on terms with Rose. About any official scheme, Gilbert asked me my intentions straight out, but in pursuit of a personal one he became oblique. He just exhibited his startling memory by quoting a casual remark I had made months before about Hector Rose, looked at me with bold, hinting eyes, and left it there.

So that I was taken unawares that night when, after we had settled a piece of work, he darted a glance round the bar, making certain no one had come in, and said:

'How much are you interested in Margaret?'

I should have been careful with anyone, with him more than most.

'She's very nice,' I said.

'Yes?'

'She's distinctly intelligent.'

Gilbert put down his tankard and stared at me.

'What else?'

'Some women would give a lot for her skin and features, don't you think?' I added: 'I suppose some of them would say she didn't make the best of herself, wouldn't they?'

'That's not the point. Are you fond of her?'

'Yes. Aren't you?'

His face overcast and set so that one could see the double chins, Gilbert stared at the little round table on which our tankards stood. He said:

'I'm not asking you just for the fun of it.'

With angry energy he was twisting into the carpet the heel of one foot, a foot strong but very small for so massive a man.

'I'm sorry,' I said and meant it, but I could go no further. Ill-temperedly he said:

'Look here, I'm afraid you might be holding off her because of me. I don't want you to.'

I was saying something neutral, when he went on:

'I'm telling you not to worry. She'd make someone a wonderful wife, but it won't be me. I should slip away, whether you want to do anything about it or not.'

He faced me with a fierce opaque gaze of one about to insist on giving a confidence.

'You're wondering why she wouldn't be the wife for me?'

He answered the question:

'I should be too frightened of her.'

He had started the conversation intending to be kind, not only to me, but to Margaret. For he did not like the spectacle of lonely people: he could not help stirring himself and being a matchmaker. Yet, getting on towards forty, he was still a bachelor himself. People saw this self-indulgent, heavy-fleshed, muscular man, taking women out, dropping them, returning to his food and drink and clubs: and some, the half-sophisticated, wrote him down as a homosexual. They were crass. The singular thing was that Gilbert was better understood by less sophisticated persons; Victorian aunts who had scarcely heard of the aberrations of the flesh would have understood him better than his knowledgeable acquaintances.

In fact, if one forgot his inquisitiveness, he was much like some of his military Victorian forebears. He was as brave as those Mutiny soldiers, and like them good-natured, more than that, sentimental with his friends: and he could have been as ferocious as they were. His emotional impulses were strong beyond the normal, his erotic ones on the weak side. It was that disparity which gave him his edge, made him formidable and also unusually kind, and which, of course, kept him timorous with women.

He wanted to explain, he went on to tell me so over the little table in the bar, that he was frighened of Margaret because she was so young. She would expect too much: she had never had to compromise with her integrity: she had not seen her hopes fail, her spirits were still overflowing.

But, if she had been older and twice married, he would have been even more frightened of her – and would have given another reason just as eloquent and good.

CHAPTER XVI

FOG ABOVE THE RIVER

In the week after that talk with Gilbert, I wrote twice to Margaret, asking her to come out with me, and tore the letters up. Then, one afternoon at the end of December, I could hold back no longer, but, as though to discount the significance of what I was doing, asked my secretary to ring up Margaret's office. 'It doesn't matter if you don't find her,' I said. 'If she's not in, don't leave a message. It doesn't matter in the least.' As I waited for the telephone to ring, I was wishing to hear her voice, wishing that she should not be there.

When she spoke, I said:

'I don't suppose you happen to be free tonight, do you?'

There was a pause. 'Yes, I am.'

'Come and see me then. We'll go out somewhere.'

'Lovely.'

It sounded so easy, and yet, waiting for her that night in my flat in Dolphin Square, where I had moved after Sheila's death, I was nervous of what I did not know. It was not the nervousness that I should have felt as a younger man. I longed for an unexacting evening: I hoped that I could keep it light, with no deep investment for either of us. I wished that I knew more of her past, that the preliminaries were over, with no harm done.

Restlessly I walked about the room, imagining conversations, as it might have been in a day-dream, which led just where I wanted. The reading lamp shone on the backs of my books, on the white shelves; the room was snug and confined, the double curtains drawn.

It was seven by my watch, and on the instant the door-bell buzzed. I let her in, and with her the close smell of the corridor. She went in front of me into the sitting-room, and, her cheeks pink from the winter night, cried: 'Nice and warm.'

When she had thrown off her coat and was sitting on the sofa, we had less to say to each other than on the nights we had dined with Gilbert. Except for a few minutes in restaurants, this was the first time we had been alone, and the words stuck. The news, the bits of government gossip, rang like lead; the conversations I had imagined dropped flat or took a wrong turn; I felt she also had been inventing what she wanted us each to say.

She asked about Gilbert, and the question had a monotonous sound as though it had been rehearsed in her mind. When those fits and starts of talk, as jerky as an incompetent interview, seemed to have been going on for a long time, I glanced at my watch, hoping it might be time for dinner. She had been with me less than half an hour.

Soon after, I got up and went towards the bookshelves, but on my way turned to her and took her in my arms. She clung to me; she muttered and forced her mouth against mine. She opened her eyes with a smile: I saw the clear and beautiful shape of her lips. We smiled at each other with pleasure but much more with an overmastering, a sedative relief.

Although the lids looked heavier, her eyes were bright; flushing, hair over her forehead, she began to laugh and chatter. Enraptured, I put my hands on her shoulders.

Then, as if she were making a painful effort, her face became sharp and serious, her glance investigatory. She looked at me, not pleading, but screwing herself up to speak. She said:

'I want to ask you something. It's important.'

Since I touched her, I had thought all was going as I imagined it. She was pliant, my reverie was coming true at last. I was totally unprepared to see her face me, a person I did not know.

My face showed my surprise, my letdown, for she cried:

'You don't think I want to upset you, do you, now of all times?'

'I don't see why you should,' I said.

'I've got to ask – before it's too late.'

'What is it?'

'When you were with Sheila' – I had not talked much of her, but

Margaret spoke as though she knew her – 'you cared for her, I mean you were protecting her all the while. There wasn't any more to it, was there?'

After a pause, I said:

'Not much.'

'Not many people could have done it,' she said. 'But it frightens me.'

Again I did not want to speak: the pause was longer, before I said:

'Why should it?'

'You must know that,' she said.

Her tone was certain, not gentle – my experience and hers might have been open before us.

'It wasn't a relationship,' she went on. 'You were standing outside all the time. Are you looking for the same thing again?' Before I had replied, she said: 'If so—' Tears had come to her eyes. 'It's horrible to say it, but it's no good to me.'

Still crying, she said:

'Tell me. Are you looking for the same thing again?'

In my own time, in my own fashion, I was ready to search down into my motives. With pain, certainly with resentment, I knew I had to search in front of her, for her. This answer came slower even than my others, as though it had been dragged out. I said:

'I hope not.' After a silence, I added:

'I don't think so.'

Her face lightened, colour came back to her cheeks, although the tears still marked them. She did not ask me to repeat or explain: she took the words as though they were a contract. Her spirits bubbled up, she looked very young again, brilliant-eyed, delighted with the moment in which we both stood.

In a sharp, sarcastic, delighted voice, she said:

'No wonder they all say how articulate you are.'

She watched me and said:

'You're not to think I'm rushing you. I don't want you bound to anything – except just that one thing. I think I could stand any tangle we get into, whatever we do – but if you had just needed someone to let you alone, just a waif for you to be kind to, then I should have had to duck from under before we start.'

She was smiling and crying. 'You see, I shouldn't have had a chance. I should have lost already, and I couldn't bear it.'

She stroked my hand, and I could feel her shaking. She would have let me make love to her, but she had called on her nerves so hard that what she wanted most, for the rest of the night, was a breathing space.

Going out of the flat to dinner, we walked, saying little, as it were absently, along the Embankment. It was foggy, and in the blackout, the writhing fog, our arms were round each other; her coat was rough under my hand, as she leant over the parapet, gazing into the high, dark water.

CHAPTER XVII

BUSINESS ON NEW YEAR'S DAY

ON the morning of New Year's Day, when I entered the Minister's office, he was writing letters. The office was not very grand; it was a cubbyhole with a coal fire, the windows looking out over Whitehall. The Minister was not, at a first glance, very grand either. Elderly, slight, he made a profession of being unassuming. When he left the office he passed more unnoticed even than his civil servants, except in a few places: but the few places happened to be the only ones where he wanted notice, and included the Carlton Club and the rooms of the party managers.

His name was Thomas Bevill, and he was a cunning, tenacious, happy old man; but mixed with his cunning was a streak of simplicity that puzzled one more the closer one came. That morning of 1 January 1942, for instance, he was writing in his own round schoolboyish hand to everyone he knew whose name was in the honours list.

No one was more hard-baked about honours that Bevill, and no one was more skilled in obtaining them for recipients convenient to himself. 'Old Herbert had better have something, it'll keep him quiet.' But when on New Year's Day the names came out, Bevill read them with innocent pleasure, and all the prizewinners, including those he had so candidly intrigued for, went up a step in his estimation. 'Fifty-seven letters to write, Eliot,' he said with euphoria, as though knowing that number in the honours list reflected much credit both on them and him.

A little later his secretary came in with a message: 'Mr Paul Lufkin would be grateful if the Minister could spare time to see him, as soon as possible.'

'What does this fellow want?' Bevill asked me.

'One thing is certain,' I said. 'He doesn't want to see you just to pass the time of day.'

At that piece of facetiousness, Bevill gave a simple worldly chuckle.

'I expect he wants to know why his name isn't in the list this morning.' His mind wandered back. 'I expect he wants to be in next time.'

To me, that did not sound in the least like Lufkin's style. He was after bigger prizes altogether; he was not so much indifferent to the minor rewards as certain they must come.

I had no doubt that he meant business; and I was anxious that we should find out what the business was, before the Minister received him. Make an excuse for today and prepare the ground, I said.

I did not want the Minister to get across Lufkin: even less did I want him to waffle. I had good reasons: Lufkin was rising to power, his opinion was one men listened to, and on the other hand Bevill's position was nothing like invulnerable. There were those who wanted him out of office. I had many reasons, both selfish and unselfish, for not giving them unnecessary openings.

However, the old man was obstinate. He had made such a technique of unpretentiousness that he liked being available to visitors at an hour's notice: he was free that morning, why shouldn't he see 'this fellow'? On the other hand, he was still suspicious about a personal approach on the honours list and he did not want a *tête-à-tête*, so he asked me to be at hand, and, when Lufkin was shown in, remarked lightly:

'I think you know Eliot, don't you?'

'Considering that you stole him from me,' Lufkin replied, with that off-hand edginess which upset many, but which bounced off the Minister.

'My dear chap,' said Bevill, 'we must try to make up for that. What can I do for you now?'

He settled Lufkin in the armchair by the fire, put on a grimy glove and threw on some coal, sat himself on a high chair and got ready to listen.

To begin with there was not much to listen to. To my surprise, Lufkin, who was usually as relevant as a high civil servant, seemed to have come with a complaint in itself trivial and which in any case was outside the Minister's domain. Some of his key men were being called up: not technicians, whom the Minister could have interfered about, but managers and accountants. Take away a certain number, said Lufkin, and in a highly articulated industry you came to a critical point – efficiency dropped away in an exponential curve.

Bevill had no idea what an exponential curve was, but he nodded wisely.

'If you expect us to keep going, it doesn't make sense,' said Lufkin.

'We don't just expect you to keep going, we rely on you,' said Bevill.

'Well then.'

'I don't mind telling you one thing,' said Bevill. 'That is, we mustn't kill the goose that lays the golden eggs.'

He added:

'I can't promise anything, my dear chap, but I'll put in a word in the right quarter.'

Uneasily I felt that they were underrating each other. Bevill was an aristocrat; he had an impersonal regard for big business, but in his heart rarely liked the company of a businessman. In Lufkin's presence, as in the presence of most others of the human race, Bevill could sound matey; he was not feeling so, he wanted to keep on amiable terms because that was the general principle of his life, but in fact he longed to bolt off to his club. While Lufkin, who had made his way by scholarships and joined his firm at seventeen, felt for politicians like Bevill something between envy and contempt, softened only by a successful man's respect for others' success.

Nevertheless, although he made Bevill uncomfortable, as he did most people, he was not uncomfortable himself. He had come for a purpose and he was moving in to it.

He said:

'There is one other point, Minister.'

'My dear chap?'

'You don't bring us into your projects soon enough.'

'You're preaching to the converted, you know. I've sown seeds in that direction ever since the war started – and I've still got hope that one or two of them may come home to roost.'

The old man's quiff of hair was standing up, cockatoo-like; Lufkin gazed at him, and said:

'I'm glad to hear you say that, Minister.' He went on, and suddenly he had brought all his weight and will into the words:

'I'm not supposed to know what you're doing at Barford. I don't know, and I don't want to know until it's time for me to do so. But I do know this – if you're going to get any results in time for this war, you ought to bring us in the instant you believe you can produce anything. Your people can't do big-scale chemical engineering. We can. We should have gone out of business if we couldn't.'

'Well, *that's* a prospect that's never cost any of us an hour's sleep,' said Bevill, gaining time to think, smiling with open blue eyes. In fact, the old man was worried, almost shocked. For Lufkin was speaking as though he knew more than he should. Barford was the name of the establishment where the first experiments on atomic fission had been started, nine months before; apart from the scientists on the spot, only a handful of people were supposed to have a glimmer of the secret, a few Ministers, civil servants, academic scientists, less than fifty in all. To Bevill, the most discreet of men, it was horrifying that even the rumour of a rumour should have reached Lufkin. Bevill never quite understood the kind of informal intelligence service that radiated from an industrialist of Lufkin's power; and he did not begin to understand that it was one of Lufkin's gifts, perhaps his most valuable one, to pick up hints that were floating through the technical air. For recognising others' feelings Lufkin had no antennae; but he had an extra set, more highly sensitised than those of anyone round him, for catching the first wave of a new idea.

That morning Bevill was determined to play for time, hiding behind his smoke-screen of platitudes like an amiable old man already a bit ga-ga. Even if the Barford project came off, even if they had to invoke the big firms, he was not sure whether he would include Lufkin. For the present he was not prepared to trust him, or anyone outside the secret, with so much as a speculation about Barford.

'My dear chap,' he said, more innocent than a child, 'I'm not feeling so inclined to count my chickens yet awhile, and believe me, if we don't mention any of these little games to our colleagues in industry, *or want anyone else to breathe a word about them*' (that was Bevill's way of telling a tycoon to keep his mouth shut), 'it's because it is all Lombard Street to a china orange that they'll turn out to be nothing but hot air.'

'I suggest that it's a mistake,' said Lufkin, 'to act on the basis that you're going to fail.'

'No, but we think too much of you to waste your time—'

'Don't you think we're capable of judging that?'

'Your great company,' said the Minister, 'is doing so much for us already.'

'That isn't a reason,' replied Lufkin, deliberately losing his temper, 'why you should leave us out of what may be the most important business you'll ever be responsible for.'

The tempers of men of action, even the hard contrived temper of Lufkin, had no effect on Bevill, except to make him seem slightly more woolly. But he was now realising – it was my only reassurance that morning – that Lufkin was a formidable man, and that he would not be able to evade him for ever. Expert in judging just how much protests were going to matter, Bevill knew that, if he consulted other firms before Lufkin's, there was certain to be trouble, and probably trouble of a kind that no politician of sense would walk into.

He knew that Lufkin was set in his purpose. It was not simply that, if the Barford project turned into hardware, there would be, not in a year, not during the war, but perhaps in twenty years, millions of pounds in it for firms like Lufkin's. It was not simply that – though Lufkin calculated it and wanted more than his share. It was also that, with complete confidence, he believed he was the man to carry it out. His self-interest did not make him hesitate, nothing would have seemed to him more palsied. On the contrary his self-interest and his sense of his own powers fused, and gave him a kind of opaque moral authority.

Throughout that interview with the Minister, despite the old man's wiliness, flattery and distrust, it was Lufkin who held (I had to remember R. S. Robinson's phrase) the moral initiative.

CHAPTER XVIII

THE SWEETNESS OF LIFE

On the ceiling, the wash of firelight brightened; a shadow quivered and bent among the benign and rosy light; there was the noise of a piece of coal falling, the ceiling flickered, faded, and then glowed. It might have been a holiday long forgotten or an illness in childhood, as I lay there in a content so absolute that it was itself a joy, not just a successor of joy, gazing up at the ceiling. In the crook of my arm Margaret's neck was resting; she too was gazing up.

Despite the blaze the air in the room was cold, for Margaret had to eke out her ration of coal, and the fire had not been lit until we arrived. Under the bedclothes our skins touched each other. It was nine o'clock, and we had come to her room two hours before, as we had done often on those winter evenings. The room was on the ground floor of a street just off Lancaster Gate, and in the distance, through the cold wartime night, came the sound of traffic, washing and falling like the tide over a pebbly beach.

She was speaking, in spasms of talk that trailed luxuriously away, of her family, and how blissful and intimate they had been. Her hair on my shoulder, her hip against mine, that other bliss was close too; she had slipped into talking of it, once I had given her a cue. For I had mentioned, grumbling lazily in bed, that soon I should have some quite unnecessary exertion, since the Chelsea house I used to live in had been damaged in a raid the year before and its effective owner had begun pestering me with another list of suggestions.

'That's Sheila's father?' Margaret had said.

571

I said yes, for an instant disturbed because I had let the name creep in. Without any constraint, she asked:

'How did they get on?'

'Not well.'

'No, I shouldn't have thought they would,' she said.

Running through my mind were letters from the vicarage, business-like, ingenious, self-pitying, assuming that my time was at Mr Knight's disposal. Reflectively, Margaret was saying:

'It was different with me.' She had always loved her father – and her sister also. She spoke of them, both delicately and naturally; she was not inhibited by the comparison with Sheila; she had brought it to the front herself.

Yet she too had rebelled, I knew by now – rebelled against her father's disbeliefs. It was not as easy as it sounded, when she told me their family life used to be intense and happy, and that anyone who had not known it so could not imagine what they had missed.

It was nine o'clock, and there was another hour before I need go out into the cold. By half past ten I had to be back in my flat in case the Minister, who was attending a cabinet committee after dinner, wanted me. I had another hour's grace in which I could hide in this voluptuous safety, untraceable, unknown. Though it was not only to be safe and secret that we came to her room rather than mine, but also because she took pleasure in it, because she seized the chance, for two or three hours among the subterranean airless working days, of looking after me.

I gazed at her face, her cheekbones sharp in the uneven light; she was relaxed because I was happy, just as I had seen her abandoned because she was giving me pleasure. Used as I was to search another's face for signs of sadness, I had often searched hers, unable to break from the habit, the obsession, sensitive beyond control that she might be miserable.

One night, not long before, this obsession had provoked a quarrel, our first. All that evening she had been subdued, although she smiled to reassure me; as we whispered in each other's arms, her replies came from a distance. At last she got up to dress, and I lay in bed watching her. Sitting naked in front of the looking-glass, with her back to me, her body fuller and less girlish than it appeared in clothes, she was brushing her hair. As she sat there, I could feel, with the twist of tenderness, how her careless-ness about dress was a fraud. She made up little, but that was her special vanity; she had that curious kind of showing-off, which wraps itself in the unadorned, even the shabby, but still gleams through. It was a kind of showing-off that to me contained within it some of the allure and mystery of sensual life.

In the looking-glass I saw the reflection of her face. Her smile had left her, the sweet and pleasure-giving smile was wiped away, and she was brooding, a line tightened between her eyebrows. I cried out:

'What's the matter?'

She muttered an endearment, tried to smooth her forehead, and said: 'Nothing.'

'What have I done?'

I expected her moods to be more even than mine. I was not ready for the temper which broke through her.

She turned on me, the blood pouring up into her throat and cheeks, her eyes snapping.

'You've done nothing,' she said.

'I asked you what was the matter.'

'It's nothing to do with us. But it soon will be if you assume that you are to blame every time I'm worried. That's the way you can ruin it all, and I won't have it.'

Shaken by her temper, I nevertheless pressed her to tell me what was on her mind. She would not be forced. Her wiry will stood against mine. At last, however, seeing that I was still anxious, with resentment she told me; it was ludicrously hard for me to believe. The next day, she was due to go to a committee as the representative of her branch, and she was nervous. Not that she had ambition in her job, but she felt humiliated if she could not perform creditably. She detested 'not being equal to things'. She was, as the civil servants said, 'good on paper', but when it came to speaking in committee, which men like me had forgotten could ever be a strain, she was so apprehensive that she spent sleepless hours the night before.

It occurred to me, thinking her so utterly unlike Sheila as to be a diametrical opposite, that I had for once caught her behaving precisely as Sheila would have done.

After she had confided, she was still angry: angry that I was so nervous about causing her unhappiness. It was not a show of temper just for a bit of byplay; it had an edge and foreboding that seemed to me, feeling ill-used, altogether out of proportion.

This night, as we lay together watching the luminescence on the ceiling, the quarrel was buried. When I looked at her face, the habit of anxiety became only a tic, for in her eyes and on her mouth I saw my own serenity. She was lazier than usual; as a rule when I had to make my way back to my telephone at Dolphin Square, she accompanied me so as to make the evening longer, though it might mean walking miles in the cold and dark; that night, stretching herself with self-indulgence, she stayed in bed. As I said goodnight I pulled the blankets round her, and, looking down at her with peace, saw the hollow of her collar-bone shadowed in the firelight.

CHAPTER XIX

TWO SISTERS

IT was not until a Saturday afternoon in May that Margaret could arrange for me to meet her elder sister. At first we were going for a walk in the country, but a despatch-box came in, and I had to visit the Permanent Secretary's office after lunch. As I sat there answering Hector Rose's questions, I could see the tops of the trees in St James's Park, where I knew the young women were waiting for me. It was one of the first warm days of the year and the windows were flung open, so that, after the winter silence in that office, one seemed to hear the sounds of spring.

Before Rose could write his minute to the Minister, he had to ring up another department. There was a delay, and as we sat listening for the telephone Rose recognised the beauty of the afternoon.

'I'm sorry to bring you back here, my dear Eliot,' he said. 'We ought to be out in the fresh air.' Disciplined, powerful, polite, he did not really mind; but he was too efficient a man to stay there working for the sake of it, or to keep me. He worked fourteen hours a day in wartime, but there was nothing obsessive about it; he just did it because it was his job and the decisions must be made. The only thing obsessive about him was his superlative politeness. That afternoon, with Margaret and her sister outside in the park, Rose many times expressed his sorrow and desolation at taking up my time.

'I really am most exceedingly sorry,' he was saying.

The words sounded effusive and silly: in fact he was the least effusive and silly of men, and, of those I knew, he was with Lufkin the one with most aptitude for power. Since the war began he had been totally immersed in it, carrying responsibility without a blink. It was a lesson to me, I sometimes thought, about how wrong one can be. For, in the great political divide before the war, it was not only Lufkin's business associates who were on the opposite side to me. Bevill, the old aristocratic handyman of a politician, had been a Municheer: so had Rose and other up-and-coming civil servants. I had not known Rose then: if I had done, I should have distrusted him when it came to a crisis. I should have been dead wrong. Actually, when war came, Bevill and Rose were as wholehearted as men could be. Compared with my friends on the irregular left, their nerves were stronger.

Rose continued to apologise until the call came through. Then, with remarkable speed, he asked me for one fact and wrote his comment to the Minister. He wrote it in the form of a question: but it was a question to which only a very brash minister could have given the wrong answer.

'Ah well,' said Rose, 'that seems to conclude your share in the proceedings, my dear Eliot. Many many many thanks. Now I hope you'll go and find some diversions for a nice Saturday afternoon.'

His politeness often ended with a malicious flick: but this was just politeness for its own sake. He was not interested in my life. If he had known, he would not have minded: he was not straitlaced, but he had other things to speculate about.

Released into the park, I was looking for Margaret – among the uniforms and summer frocks lying on the grass, I saw her, crowded out some yards away from our rendezvous. She was stretched on her face in the sunshine, her head turned to her sister's, both of them engrossed. Watching the two faces together, I felt a kind of intimacy with Helen, although I had not spoken to her. Some of her expressions I already knew, having seen them in her sister. But there was one thing about her for which Margaret had not prepared me at all.

Sitting erect, her back straight, her legs crossed at the ankles, she looked smart: unreasonably, almost tastelessly smart in that wartime summer, as if she were a detached observer from some neutral country. The black dress, the large black hat, clashed against that background of litter, the scorched grass, the dusty trees.

She was twenty-nine that year, four years older than Margaret, and she seemed at the same time more poised and more delicate. In both faces one could see the same shapely bones, but whereas in Margaret's the flesh was firm with a young woman's health, in her sister's there were the first signs of tightness – the kind of tightness that I had seen a generation before among some of my aunts, who stayed cared-for too long as daughters and settled down at Helen's age to an early spinsterhood. Yet Helen had married at twenty-one, and Margaret had told me that the marriage was a happy one.

They were so engrossed that Margaret did not notice me on the path. She was talking urgently, her face both alive and anxious. Helen's face looked heavy, she was replying in a mutter. Their profiles, where the resemblance was clearest, were determined and sharp. I called out, and Margaret started, saying: 'This is Lewis.'

At once Helen smiled at me; yet I saw that it was an effort for her to clear her mind of what had gone before. She spoke one or two words of formal greeting. Her voice was lighter than Margaret's, her speech more clipped; but she intimated by the energy with which she spoke a friendliness she was too shy, too distracted, to utter.

As I sat down – 'Be careful,' she said, 'it's so grimy, you have to take care where you sit.'

Margaret glanced at her, and laughed. She said to me: 'We were clearing off some family business.'

'Dull for other people,' said Helen. Then, afraid I should think she was shutting me out, she said quickly, 'Dull for us, too, this time.'

She smiled, and made some contented-seeming remark about the summer weather. Only a trace of shadow remained in her face; she did not want me to see it, she wanted this meeting to be a successful one.

Yet each of the three of us was tongue-tied, or rather there were patches of silence, then we spoke easily, then silence again. Helen might have been worrying over her sister and me, but in fact it was Margaret who showed the more concern. Often she looked at Helen with the clucking, scolding vigilance that an elder sister might show to a beloved younger one, in particular to one without experience and unable to cope for herself.

As we sat together in the sunshine, the dawdling feet of soldiers and their girls scrabbling the path a few yards away, Helen kept being drawn back into her thoughts; then she would force herself to attend to Margaret and me, almost as though the sight of us together was a consolation. Indeed, far from worrying over her sister, she seemed happiest that afternoon when she found out something about us. Where had we met, she had never heard? When exactly had it been?

Shy as she was, she was direct with her questions, just as I had noticed in other women from families like theirs. Some of the concealments which a man of my kind had learned would have seemed to Helen, and to Margaret also, as something like a denial of integrity. Helen was diffident and not specially worldly: but, if Margaret had hidden from her that we were living together, she would have been not only hurt but shocked.

For minutes together, it pulled up her spirits, took her thoughts out of herself, to ask questions of Margaret and me: I believed that she was making pictures of our future. But she could not sustain it. The air was hot, the light brilliant; she sat there in a brooding reverie.

CHAPTER XX

A DARKENING WINDOW

HOPING that Helen might talk to her sister if they were alone, I left them together in the park, and did not see Margaret again until the following Monday evening. She had already told me over the telephone that she would have to dine with Helen that night: and when we met in a Tothill Street pub Margaret said straight away:

'I'm sorry you had to see her like this.'

'I like her very much,' I said.

'I hoped you would.' She had been looking forward for weeks to my meeting with Helen: she wanted me to admire her sister as she did herself. She told me again, anxious for me to believe her, that Helen was no more melancholy than she was, and far less self-centred.

'No one with any eyes would think she was self-centred.'

'It's such an awful pity!' she cried.

I asked her what it was.

'She thought she was going to have a child at last. Then on Saturday she knew she wasn't.'

'It's as important as that, is it?' I said. But she had told me already how her sister longed for children.

'You saw for yourself, didn't you?'

'How much,' I asked, 'is it damaging her marriage?'

'It's not. It's a good marriage,' she said. 'But still, I can't help remembering her when she was quite young, even when she was away at school, she used to talk to me about how she'd bring up her family.'

She was just on the point of going away to meet Helen when Betty Vane came in.

As I introduced them, Betty was saying that she had telephoned the office, got Gilbert Cooke and been told this was one of my favourite pubs – meanwhile she was scrutinising Margaret, her ears sharp for the tone in which she spoke. Actually Margaret said little: she kept glancing at the clock above the bar: very soon she apologised and left. It looked rude, or else that she was deliberately leaving us together: it meant only that, if she had had to seem off-hand to anyone, she would make sure it was not to her sister.

'Well,' said Betty.

For an instant I was put out by the gust of misunderstanding. I made an explanation, but she was not accepting it. She said, her eyes friendly and appraising:

'You're looking much better, though.'

I had not seen her for some time, though now I was glad to. When Sheila died, it had been Betty who had taken charge of me. She had found me my flat, moved me out of the Chelsea house; and then, all the practical help given and disposed of, she got out of my way; she assumed I did not want to see her or anyone who reminded me of my marriage. Since then I had met her once or twice, received a couple of letters, and that was all.

Unlike most of our circle, she was not working in London, but in a factory office in a Midland town. The reason for this was singular: she, by a long way the most loftily born of my close friends, was the worst educated; in the schoolroom at home she had scarcely been taught formally at all; clever as she was, she did not possess the humblest of educational qualifications, and would have been hard pushed to acquire any.

Here she was in the middle thirties, opposite me across the little table in the pub, her nose a bit more peaked, her beautiful eyes acute. She had always liked her drink and now she was putting down bitter pint for pint with me: she did not mention Sheila's name or any trouble she had seen me through, but she enjoyed talking of the days past; she had a streak of sentiment, not about any special joy, but just about our youth.

There was a haze of homesickness over us, shimmering with pleasure, and it stayed as we went out to eat. Out to eat better than I had eaten all that year, for Betty, even though she was not living in London, kept an eye on up-and-coming restaurants; she took as much care about it, I thought, as a lonely, active and self-indulgent man. Thus, at a corner table in Percy Street, we questioned each other with the content, regard, melancholy and comfort of old friends – edged by the feeling, shimmering in the homesick haze, that with different luck we might have been closer.

I enquired about the people she was meeting and what friends she had made, in reality enquiring whether she had found a lover or a future husband. It sounded absurd of me to be euphemistic and semi-arch, as circuitous as Mr Knight, to this woman whom I knew so well and whose own tongue was often coarse. But Betty was coarse about the body – and about her emotions as inhibited as a schoolgirl. She just could not utter, I knew from long ago, anything that she felt about a man. Even now, she sounded like a girl determined not to let herself be teased. Yes, she had seen a lot of people at the factory: 'Some of them are interesting,' she said.

'Who are they?'

'Oh, managers and characters like that.'

'Anyone specially interesting?' I was sure she wanted to talk.

'As a matter of fact,' she blurted out, 'there's someone I rather like.'

I asked about him – a widower, a good deal older than she was, moderately successful.

'Of course,' I said, 'you've never met people of that kind before.'

'He's a nice man.'

'It sounds all right,' I said affectionately.

'It might be all right,' she said with a touch of the hope she never quite lost, with absolute lack of confidence.

'My dear, I beg you,' I broke out, 'don't think so little of yourself.'

She smiled with embarrassment. 'I don't know about that—'

'Why in God's name shouldn't it be all right?'

'Oh well,' she said, 'I'm not everyone's cup of tea.'

She spoke out firmly. She was relieved to have confessed a little, even in such a strangulated form. She shut up, as though abashed at her own outpouringness. Sharply, she began to talk about me. In a moment she was saying:

'What about the girl who rushed out of the pub?'

'I met her last autumn,' I replied.

'Is it serious?'

'Yes, it is.'

Betty nodded.

She said, in a companionable, almost disapproving tone:

'You have had such a rotten time. This isn't another of them, is it?'

'Far from it.'

She stared at me.

'It would be nice,' she said, her voice going suddenly soft, 'if you could be happy.'

She added: 'There's no one who deserves it more.'

In the restaurant corner, the air was warm with a sentimental glow. Betty was a realistic woman: about herself, realistic to an extent that crippled her: to most people she did not give the benefit of the doubt. But about me her realism had often been blurred, and she thought me a better man than I was.

How much better than I was – I could not avoid a glint of recognition an hour after. I had gone expectantly from the restaurant to Margaret's room, where she was talking to Helen. When I arrived they were happy. Helen's spirits had revived; like Margaret, she did not give up easily. I gathered she had been to a doctor; and then she refused to talk further that evening of her own worry. When I came in, it was clear that they had been talking instead – with pleasure and amusement – about Margaret and me.

In the midsummer evening, the folding door between Margaret's bedroom and sitting-room was thrown open; their chairs were opposite each other round the empty grate in the sitting-room, which in the winter we had never used. Outside in the street, still light although it was getting on for ten, children were playing, and just across the area, close to the window and on a level with our chairs, passed the heads and shoulders of people walking along the pavement. It might have been the 'front room' of my childhood.

In it, Helen, dressed with the same exaggerated smartness as in St James's Park, looked more than ever out of place. I thought for an instant how different they were. Despite her marriage, despite her chic, something of my first impression of her lingered, the touch of the clever, delicate, and spinsterish. And yet they had each the same independence, the same certainty that they were their own judges, bred in through the family from which Margaret, more than her sister, had rebelled, bred in each one just as much as the mole over the hip which she had told me was a family mark. About Helen there was nothing of Margaret's careless-ness; and yet in other ways so unlike her sister, Margaret, who rejoiced in giving me pleasure, who had the deep and guiltless sensuality of those women to whom giving pleasure is major one, answered just as deliberately for herself.

'You oughtn't to live like this, you know,' Helen said, glancing about the room, 'it is really rather messy. Miles says you'd do far better—'

'Oh, Miles,' Margaret said. 'He would.' They were speaking of Helen's husband, whom they both appeared to regard with a kind of loving depreciation, as though they were in some way leagued in a pact to save him from himself. Yet from what I had heard he was an effective man, amiable, self-sufficient, regarding responsibility as a kind of privilege. 'It's lucky he chose the right one of us.'

'Very lucky,' said Helen, 'you would have made him quite miserable.' When she spoke of him her face grew tender, content. It was a maternal contentment: like a warm-hearted and dutiful child, he gave her almost all she desired.

Margaret smiled back at her, and for a second I thought I saw in her face a longing for just such a contentment, just such a home; ordered, settled, the waiting fire, the curtains drawn against the night.

'It wouldn't have been my sort of thing,' she said.

It was at this moment that I felt my talk with Betty, which had left me in such a glow, had suddenly touched a trigger and released a surge of sadness and self-destruction.

It seemed like another night, drinking with Betty, going home to Sheila – not a special night, more like many nights fused together, with nothing waiting for me but Sheila's presence.

That night lay upon this. I was listening to Margaret and Helen, my limbs were heavy, for an instant I felt in one of those dreams where one is a spectator but cannot move.

When Margaret had talked, earlier that evening, of the children her sister wanted, she was repeating what she had told me before; and, just as before, she was holding something back.

I had thought, when I saw them together in that room half an hour before, that, unlike in so much, they were alike in taking their own way. But they were alike at one other point. It was not only Helen who longed for children; Margaret was the same. Once we had spoken of it, and from then on, just as tonight, she held back. She did not wish me to see how much she looked forward to her children. If she did let me see it, it would lay more responsibility upon me.

Listening to them, I felt at a loss with Helen because she was confident I should make her sister happy.

When she got up to go, I said how much I had enjoyed the evening. But Margaret had been watching me: after seeing her sister to the door, she returned to the empty sitting-room and looked at me with concern.

'What is the matter?' she said.

I was standing up. I took her in my arms and kissed her. Over her head, past the folding doors, I could see the bed and the windows beyond, lit up by the afterglow in the west. With an effort, disproportionately great, I tried to throw off the heaviness, and said:

'Isn't it time we talked too?'

'What about?'

'We ought to talk about us.'

She stood back, out of my arms, and looked at me. Her eyes were bright but she hesitated. She said:

'You don't want to yet.'

I went on:

'We can't leave it too long.'

For an instant her voice went high.

'Are you sure you're ready?'

'We ought to talk about getting married.'

It was some instants before she spoke, though her eyes did not leave me. Then her expression, which had been grave, sharp with insight, suddenly changed: her face took on a look of daring, which in another woman might have meant the beginning of a risky love affair.

'No,' she said. 'I want you. But I want you in our freedom.'

That phrase, which we had just picked up, she used to make all seem more casual to us both. But she was telling me how much she knew. She knew that, going about in high spirits, I still was not safe from remorse, or perhaps something which did not deserve that name and which was more like fear, about Sheila. That misery had made me morbidly afraid of another; Margaret had more than once turned her face away to conceal the tears squeezing beneath her eyelids, because she knew that at the sight of unhappiness I nowadays lost confidence altogether.

She accepted that, just as she accepted something else, though it was harder. It was that sometimes I did not have fear return to me with the thought of Sheila, but joy. Cheated by memory, I was transported to those times – which had in historical fact been negligible in the length of our marriage – when Sheila, less earthbound than I was, had lifted me off the earth. Cheated by memory, I had sometimes had that mirage-joy, that false past, shine above a happy time with Margaret, so that the happiness turned heavy.

She knew all that; but what she did not know was whether I was getting free. Was I capable of a new start, of entering the life she wanted? Or was I a man who, in the recess of his nature, manufactured his own defeat? Searching for that answer, she looked at me with love, with tenderness, and without mercy for either of us.

'Don't worry,' she said, putting her arms round me, 'there's plenty of time.'

She muttered, her head against my chest:

'I'm not very patient, you know that now, don't you? But I will be.'

Below my eyes her hair was smooth; the window had darkened quickly in the past minutes; I was grateful to her.

CHAPTER XXI

THE ACQUIESCENT VERSUS THE OPAQUE

THROUGH the spring and summer, the Minister had been able to go on stalling with Paul Lufkin. The Barford project had run into trouble, it looked likely that there would be no development in England, and nothing for the industrialists to do. All of which was true and reasonable, and Lufkin could only accept it; but he was alert when, in the autumn, a new rumour went round. It was that a fresh idea had sprung up at Barford, which some people, including Bevill himself, wanted to invest in.

As usual, Lufkin's information was something near accurate. None of us was cetain whether Barford would be saved or the scientists sent to America, but in October the struggle was going on; and while we were immersed in it, Lufkin did not visit the Minister again but without any excuse or pretext invited me to dinner.

When I received that note, which arrived a week before the decision over Barford was to be made, I thought it would be common prudence to have a word with Hector Rose. So, on an October morning, I sat in the chair by his desk. Outside the window, against a windy sky, the autumn leaves were turning. Even by his own standards Hector Rose looked spruce and young that day – perhaps because the war news was good, just as in the summer there had been days when, tough as he was, he had sat there with his lips pale and his nostrils pinched. The flower bowl was always full, whatever the news was like; that morning he had treated himself to a mass of chrysanthemums.

'Well, my dear Eliot,' he was saying, 'it's very agreeable to have you here. I don't think I've got anything special, but perhaps you have? I'm very glad indeed to have the chance of a word.' I mentioned Lufkin's invitation. In a second the flah-flah dropped away – and he was listening with his machine-like concentration. I did not need to remind him that I had, not so long ago, been a consultant for Lufkin, nor that Gilbert Cooke had been a full-time employee. Those facts were part of the situation; he was considering them almost before I had started, just as he was considering Lufkin's approaches to the Minister.

'If our masters decide to persevere with Barford' – Rose spoke as though some people, utterly unconnected with him, were choosing between blue or brown suits: while he was totally committed on Barford's side, and if the project survived he would be more responsible, after the scientists, than any single man – 'if they decide to persevere with it, we shall have to plan the first contact straightaway, that goes without saying.

'We shall have to decide,' added Rose coldly, 'whether it is sensible to bring Lufkin in.'

He asked:

'What's your view, Eliot? Would it be sensible?'

'So far as I can judge, it's rather awkward,' I said. 'His isn't obviously the right firm — but it's not out of the question.'

'Exactly,' said Rose. 'This isn't going to be an easy one.'

'I think most people would agree that his firm hasn't got the technical resources of the other two—' I named them.

'What has Lufkin got?'

'I'm afraid the answer to that is, Lufkin himself. He's much the strongest figure in the whole game.'

'He's a *good chap*,' said Hector Rose incongruously. He was not speaking of Lufkin's moral nature, nor his merits as a companion: Rose meant that Lufkin was a pantocrator not dissimilar from himself.

He stared at me.

'My dear Eliot,' he said, 'I'm sure it's unnecessary for me to advise you, but if you do decide that he is the right man for us, then of course you're not to feel the least embarrassment or be too nice about it. The coincidence that you know something about him – the only significance of that is, that it makes your judgment more valuable to us. It's very important for us not to fall over backwards and, for quite inadequate reasons, shirk giving the job to the right man, that is, if we finally decide that he does turn out to be the right man.'

I was a little surprised. No one could have doubted that Hector Rose's integrity was absolute. It would have been high farce to try to bribe him; he assumed the same of me. Nevertheless, I expected him to be more finicky about the procedure, to talk about the necessity of justice not only being done, but being seen to be done. In fact, as the war went on and the state became more interleaved with business, civil servants like Rose had made themselves tougher-minded; nothing would be accomplished, if they thought first how to look immaculate.

In the same manner, when I asked whether I might as well let Lufkin entertain me, Rose replied: 'The rule is very simple, my dear Eliot, and it remains for each of us to apply it to himself. That is, when some interested party suddenly becomes passionately desirous of one's company. The rule is, do exactly as you would if the possibility of interest did not exist. If you wouldn't normally accept an invitation from our excellent friend, don't go. If you would normally accept, then do go, if you can bear it. I can't say that I envy you the temptation,' said Rose, whose concept of an evening out was a table for two and a bottle of claret at the Athenæum.

When I came to spend the evening at Lufkin's, I would have compounded for a table for two myself. As in the past when I was one of his entourage, I found his disregard of time, which in anyone else he would have bleakly dismissed as 'oriental', fretting me. In his flat at St James's Court, his guests were collected at eight o'clock, which was the time of the invitation, standing about in the sitting-room drinking, nine of us, all men. Lufkin himself was there, standing up, not saying much, not drinking much, standing up as though prepared to do so for hours, glad to be surrounded by men catching his eye. Then one of his staff entered with a piece of business to discuss: and Lufkin discussed it there on the spot, in front of his guests. That finished, he asked the man to stay, and beckoned the butler, standing by the dinner table in the inner room, to lay another place. Next, with the absence of fuss and hurry of one in the middle of a marathon, which he showed in all his dealings, he decided to telephone: still standing up, he talked for fifteen minutes to one of his plants.

Meanwhile the guests, most of whom were colleagues and subordinates, stood up, went on drinking and exchanged greetings to each others' wives. 'Give my regards to Lucille.' 'How is Brenda?' 'Don't forget to give my love to Jacqueline.' It went on, just as it used when I attended those dinners, and men heartily enquired after Sheila and sent messages to her: not that they knew her, for, since she never went to a party, they could only have met her for a few minutes, and by accident. But, according to their etiquette, they docketed her name away and afterwards punctiliously enquired about her, as regularly as they said good evening. No doubt most of those husband-to-husband questions that night, so hearty, so insistent, were being asked about women the speakers scarcely knew.

It was nearly half past nine when Lufkin said: 'Does anyone feel like eating? I think we might as well go in.'

At the crowded table Lufkin sat, not at the head, but in the middle of one side, not troubling to talk, apparently scornful of the noise, and yet feeling that, as was only right, the party was a success. There was more food and drink than at most wartime dinners: I thought among the noise, the hard male laughter, how little any of these men were giving themselves away. Orthodox opinions, collective gibes, a bit of ribbing – that was enough to keep them zestful, and I had hardly heard a personal remark all night. It made me restless, it made me anxious to slither away, not only to avoid conversation with Lufkin, but also just to be free.

The walls pressed in, the chorus roared round me: and, in that claustrophobia, I thought longingly of being alone with Margaret in her room. In a kind of rapturous daydream, I was looking forward to marrying her. In the midst of this male hullabaloo my confidence came back. I was telling myself, almost as one confides, brazenly, confidently and untruthfully to an acquaintance on board ship, that it was natural I should trust myself so little about another marriage after the horror of the first.

Listening to someone else's history, I should not have been so trustful about the chances of life. Thinking of my own, I was as credulous as any man. Sitting at that table, responding mechanically and politely to a stranger's monologue, I felt that my diffidence about Margaret was gone.

When one of Lufkin's guests said the first goodnight, I tried to go out with him. But Lufkin said: 'I've hardly had a minute with you, Eliot. You needn't go just yet.'

That company was good at recognising the royal command. Within a quarter of an hour, among thanks and more salutations to wives, the flat was empty, and we were left alone. Lufkin, who had not stirred from his chair as he received the goodbyes, said:

'Help yourself to another drink and come and sit by me.'

I had drunk enough, I said. As for him, he always drank carefully, though his head was hard for so spare and unpadded a man. I sat in the chair on his right, and he turned towards me with a creaking smile. We had never been intimate, but there was a sort of liking between us. As usual, he had no small talk whatsoever; I made one or two remarks, about the war, about the firm, to which he said yes and no. He started off:

'Quite frankly, I still don't like the way Barford is being handled.'

He said it quietly and dryly, with a note of confident blame that was second nature to him, or even first.

'I'm sorry about that,' I said.

'It's no use being sorry,' he replied. 'The thing is, we've got to get it right.'

'I'm at a bit of a disadvantage,' I said, 'not being able to say much about it.'

'You can say quite enough for the purpose.'

I asked straight out:

'How much do you know?'

'I hear,' Lufkin replied, in his bluntest and most off-hand tone, 'that you people are wasting your own time and everyone else's debating whether to shut the place up or not.'

'I hope they'll come down in favour,' I said, feeling my way. 'But I'm by no means sure.'

'In that case you're losing your grip,' Lufkin gave a cold, jeering smile. 'Of *course* they'll keep it going.'

'Why do you say that?'

For a second I did not put it past him to have inside knowledge, but he answered:

'No one ever closes a place down. Governments can't do it; that's one of the things that's wrong with them.'

Old Bevill, not the man he admired most, would have agreed with him, I thought.

He went on:

'No, you'd better assume that they'll keep it ticking over. But not putting enough behind it, blowing hot and cold the whole wretched time. That's what I call making the worst of both worlds.'

'You may be right,' I said.

'I've been right before now,' he said. 'So it won't be much satisfaction.'

In his negotiations Lufkin made much use of the charged silence, and we fell into one now. But it was not my tactic that night to break it; I was ready to sit mute as long as he cared. In time he said: 'We can assume they're going to hopelessly underestimate their commitment, and unless someone steps in they'll make a mess of it. The thing is, we've got to save them from themselves.'

Suddenly his eyes, so sad and remote in his hard, neat, skull-like head, were staring into mine, and I felt his will, intense because it was canalised into this one object, because his nature was undivided, all of a piece.

'I want you to help,' he said.

Again I did not reply.

He went on: 'I take it the decisions about how this job is done, and who makes the hardware, are going to be bandied about at several levels.'

Lufkin, with his usual precision and realism, had made it his business to understand how government worked; it was no use, he had learned years before, to have the entrée to cabinet ministers unless you were also trusted by the Hector Roses and their juniors.

'I'm not prepared to let it go by default. It's not my own interests I'm thinking of. It's a fourth-class risk anyway, and, as far as the firm goes, it's neither here nor there. As far as it matters to me, no one's ever going to make a fortune again, so it's pointless one way or the other. But I've got to be in on it, because this is the place where I can make a contribution. That's why I want your help.'

It sounded hypocritical: but Lufkin behaved just as he had to Bevill the previous New Year's Day, not altering by a single inflection as he talked to a different man, just as stable and certain of his own motives. It sounded hypocritical, but Lufkin believed each word of it, and that was one of his strengths.

For myself, I could feel a part of me, a spontaneous part left over from youth, which sympathised with him and wanted to say yes. Even now the temptation was there – one that Lufkin had never felt. But, since I was a young man, I had had to learn how, in situations such as this, to harden myself. Just because I had to watch my response, which was actually too anxious to please, which wanted to say yes instead of no, I had become practised at not giving a point away: in a fashion different from Lufkin's, and for the opposite reasons, I was nearly as effective at it as he was himself.

That night, I still had not decided whether I ought to throw in my influence, such as it was, for him or against him.

'I can't do much just yet,' I said. 'And if I tried it would certainly not be wise.'

'I'm not sure I understand you.'

'I've been associated with you,' I told him, 'and some people will remember that at the most inconvenient time. You can guess the repercussions if I overplayed my hand—'

'What would you say, if I told you that was cowardly?'

'I don't think it is,' I said.

For his own purposes, he was a good judge of men, and a better one of situations. He accepted that he would not get further just then and, with no more ill grace than usual, began to talk at large.

'What shall I do when I retire?' he said. He was not inviting my opinion; his plans were as precise as those he sent to his sales managers, although he was only forty-eight; they were the plans such as active men make, when occasionally they feel that all their activity has done for them is carve out a prison. In reality Lufkin was happy in his activity; he never really expected that those plans would come about – and yet, through making them, he felt that the door was open.

As I heard what they were, I thought again that he was odder than men imagined; he did not once refer to his family or wife; although I had never heard scandal, although he went down to his country house each weekend, his plans had been drawn up as though she were dead.

'I shall take a flat in Monaco,' he announced briskly. 'I don't mean just anywhere in the principality, I mean the old town. It isn't easy to get a place there for a foreigner, but I've put out some feelers.'

It was curious to hear, in the middle of the war.

'What ever shall you do?' I said, falling into the spirit of it.

'I shall walk down to the sea and up to the casino each day, there and back,' he said. 'That will give me three miles walking every day, which will do for my exercise. No man of fifty or over needs more.'

'That won't occupy you.'

'I shall play for five hours a day, or until I've won my daily stipple, which ever time is the shorter.'

'Shan't you get tired of that?'

'Never,' said Lufkin.

He went on, bleak and inarticulate:

'It's a nice place. I shan't want to move, I might as well die there. Then they can put me in the Protestant cemetery. It would be a nice place to have a grave.' Suddenly he gave a smile that was sheepish and romantic. In a curt tone, as though angry with me, he returned to business.

'I'm sorry,' he put in as though it were an aside, 'that you're getting too cautious about the Barford project. Cold feet. I didn't expect yours to be so cold.'

I had set myself neither to be drawn nor provoked. Instead I told him what he knew already, that at most points of decision Hector Rose was likely to be the most influential man – and after him some of the Barford technicians. If any firm, if Lufkin's firm, were brought in, its technicians would have to be approved by the Barford ones. Lufkin nodded: the point was obvious but worth attending to. Then he said, in a cold but thoughtful tone:

'What about your own future?'

I replied that I simply did not know.

'I hear that you've been a success at this job – but you're not thinking of staying in it, there'd be no sense in that.'

He was not asking a question: as such, he knew he was right.

I repeated that it was too early to make up my mind.

'Of course,' said Lufkin, 'I have some reason to expect you to come back to me.'

'I haven't forgotten that,' I said.

'I don't understand all you want for yourself,' said Lufkin. 'But I can give you some of it.'

Looking at him, I did not know whether it was his harsh kindness, or a piece of miscalculation.

CHAPTER XXII

MENTION OF A MAN'S NAME

WAKING, I blinked my eyes against the light, although it was the dun light of a winter afternoon. By the bedside Margaret, smiling, looked down on me like a mother.

'Go to sleep again,' she said.

It was Saturday afternoon, the end of a busy week; the day before, Barford's future had been settled, and, as Lufkin had forecast, we had got our way. Soon, I was thinking, lying there half-asleep in Margaret's bed, we should have to meet Lufkin officially—

'Go to sleep again,' she said.

I said that I ought to get up.

'No need.' She had drawn an armchair up to the bed, and was sitting there in her dressing-gown. She stroked my forehead, as she said:

'It's not a sensible way to live, is it?'

She was not reproaching me, although I was worn out that afternoon, after the week's meetings and late nights, dinner with Lufkin, dinner with the Minister. She pretended to scold me, but her smile was self-indulgent. It was pleasure to her to look after anyone; she was almost ashamed, so strong was that pleasure, she tried to disparage it and called it a lust. So, when I was tired and down-and-out, any struggle of wills was put aside, she cherished me; often to me, who had evaded my own mother's protective love, who had never been cared for in that sense in my life, it was startling to find her doing so.

Yet that afternoon, watching her with eyes whose lids still wanted to close, letting her pull the quilt round my shoulders, I was happy, so happy that I thought of her as I had at Lufkin's, in her absence. For an interval, rare in me, the imagination and the present flesh were one. It must go on always, I thought, perhaps this was the time to persuade her to marry me.

She was gazing down at me, and she looked loving, sarcastic, in charge.

No, I thought, I would not break this paradisal state; let us have it for a little longer; it did not matter if I procrastinated until later that night, or next week, so long as I was certain we should be happy.

Thus I did not ask her. Instead, in the thickness of near-sleep, in the luxury of fatigue, I began gossiping about people we knew. Her fingers touching my cheeks, she joined in one of those conspiracies of kindness that we entered into when we were at peace, as though out of gratitude for our own condition we had to scheme to bring the same to others. Was there anything we could do for Helen? And couldn't we find someone for Gilbert Cooke? We were retracing old arguments, about what kind of woman could cope with him, when, suddenly recalling another aspect of my last talk with Lufkin, I broke out that Gilbert might soon have a different kind of problem on his hands.

I explained that, like me, he would be engaged in the negotiations over which firm to give the contract to – which, now that the decision had gone in favour of the project, was not just a remote debating point but something we should have to deal with inside a month. Just as Lufkin was too competent not to know my part in the negotiations, so he would know Gilbert's; it might be small, but it would not be negligible. And Gilbert, after the war, would certainly wish to return to Lufkin's firm; would he be welcome, if he acted against Lufkin now?

I told Margaret of how, right at the end of our *tête-à-tête*, when we were both tired and half-drunk, Lufkin had let fly his question about my future, and I still could not be sure whether it was a threat. Gilbert might easily feel inclined to be cautious.

Margaret smiled, but a little absently, a little uncomfortably, and for once brushed the subject aside, beginning to talk of a man she had just met, whose name I had not heard. He was a children's doctor, she said, and I did not need telling how much she would have preferred me to live such a life. The official world, the corridors of power, the dilemmas of conscience and egotism – she disliked them all. Quite indifferent to whether I thought her priggish, she was convinced that I should be a better and happier man without them. So, with a touch of insistence, she mentioned this new acquaintance's work in his hospital. His name was Geoffrey Hollis; perhaps it was odd, she admitted, that so young a man should devote himself to children. He was as much unlike Gilbert as a man could be, except that he also was a bachelor and shy.

'He's another candidate for a good woman,' she said.

'What is he like?'

'Not much your sort,' she replied, smiling at me.

Years before, each time Sheila had thrown the name of a man between us, I had been pierced with jealousy. What had passed between us then had frightened me of being jealous, and with Margaret, though sometimes I had watched for it, I had been almost immune.

Nevertheless, the grooves of habit were worn deep. Hearing of Hollis, even though her face was holding nothing back, I wished that I had asked her to marry me half an hour before, when there was not this vestigial cramp keeping me still, when I had not this temptation, growing out of former misery and out of a weakness that I was born with, to retreat into passiveness and irony.

I was gazing at her, sitting by the bedside in the cold and browning light. Slowly, as her eyes studied mine, her mouth narrowed and from it edged away the smile of a loving girl, the smile of a mother. Upon us seeped – an instant suddenly enlarged in the rest and happiness of the afternoon – the sense of misunderstanding, injustice, illimitable distance, loss.

In time she said, still grave:

'It's all right.'

'Yes,' I answered.

She began to smile again and asked, putting Gilbert's dilemma aside, what I was going to do about Lufkin and how much I minded. She had never pressed me before about what I should choose to do when the war ended. I could break with the past now, there were different ways of earning a living ahead of me, she had been content to leave it so; but now in the half-light, her hands pressing mine, she wanted me to talk about it.

CHAPTER XXIII

GIGANTESQUE

THE Minister tended to get irritated with me when there was an issue which he had to settle but wished to go on pretending did not exist. His manner remained matey and unpretentious but, when I had to remind him that the Barford contract must be placed within a fortnight, that two major firms as well as Lufkin's were pressing for an answer, Bevill looked at me as though I had made a remark in bad taste.

'First things first,' he said mysteriously, as though drawing on fifty years of political wisdom, the more mysteriously since in the coming fortnight he had nothing else to do.

In fact, he strenuously resented having to disappoint two or three influential men. Even those like me who were fond of the old man did not claim that political courage was his cardinal virtue. To most people's astonishment, he had shown some of it in the struggle over Barford; he had actually challenged opinion in the Cabinet and had both prevailed and kept his job; now that was over, he felt it unjust to be pushed into more controversy, to be forced to make more enemies. Enemies – old Bevill hated even the word. He wished he could give the contract to every-one who wanted it.

Meanwhile, Sir Hector Rose was making up his own mind. The secret Barford file came down to me, with a request from Rose for my views on the contract.

It did not take me much time to think over. I talked to Gilbert, who knew the inside of Lufkin's firm more recently than I did. He was more emphatic than I was, but on the same side. It was an occasion, I decided without worry, to play safe both for my own sake and the job's.

So at last I did not hedge, but wrote that we ought not to take risks; this job did not need the special executive flair that Lufkin would give it, but hundreds of competent chemical engineers, where the big chemical firms could outclass him; at this stage he should be ruled out.

I suspected that Rose had already come to the same opinion. All he committed himself to, however, were profuse thanks on the telephone and an invitation to come myself, and bring Cooke, to what he called 'a parley with Lufkin and his merry men'.

The 'parley' took place on a bitter December morning in one of the large rooms at the back of our office, with windows looking out over the Horse Guards towards the Admiralty: but at this date most of the glass had been blown in, the windows were covered with plasterboard, so that little light entered but only the freezing air. The chandeliers shone on to the dusty chairs: through the one sound window the sky was glacial blue: the room was so cold that Gilbert Cooke, not over-awed enough to ignore his comfort, went back for his overcoat.

Lufkin had brought a retinue of six, most of them his chief technicians; Rose had only five, of whom a Deputy Secretary, myself and Cooke came from the department and two scientists from Barford. The Minister sat between the two parties, his legs twisted round each other, his toes not touching the ground; turning to his right, where Lufkin was sitting, he began a speech of complicated cordiality. 'It's always a pleasure, indeed it's sometimes the only pleasure of what they choose to call office,' he said, 'to be able to sit down round a table with our colleagues in industry. You're the chaps who deliver the goods and we know a willing horse when we see one and we all know what to do with willing horses.' The Minister continued happily, if a trifle obscurely; he had never been a speaker, his skill was the skill of private talks, but he enjoyed his own speech and did not care whether he sounded as though his head were immersed in cotton-wool. He made a tangential reference to a "certain project about which the less said the better', but he admitted that there was an engineering job to be done. He thought, and he hoped Mr Lufkin would agree, that nothing but good could accrue if they all got together round the table and threw their ideas into the pool.

Then he said blandly, with his innocent old man's smile, 'But now I've got to say something which upsets me, though I don't expect it will worry anyone else.'

'Minister?' said Lufkin.

'*I'm afraid I must slip away,*' said Bevill. 'We all have our masters, you know.' He spoke at large to Lufkin's staff. 'You have my friend Lufkin, and I'm sure he is an inspiring one. I have mine and he wants me just on the one morning when I was looking forward to a really friendly useful talk.' He was on his feet, shaking hands with Lufkin, saying that they would never miss him with his friend and colleague, Hector Rose, to look after them, speaking with simple, sincere regret at having to go, but determined not to stay in that room five minutes longer. Spry and active, he shook hands all the way round and departed down the cold corridor, his voice echoing briskly back, 'Goodbye all, goodbye all!'

Rose moved into the chair. 'I think the ceremonies can be regarded as having been properly performed,' he said. 'Perhaps it would set us going if I try to clear the air.' For once he was not at his most elaborately polite. I felt certain it was only just before the meeting that he had heard of the Minister's intention to flit. But his statement was as lucid and fair as usual, and no one there could have guessed whether he was coming down for or against Lufkin. There was just one single job to be performed, he said; not much could be said, but, to make possible some kind of rational exchange, he took it on his own responsibility to tell Lufkin's technicians a bare minimum. There was no money in it; the Government would pay as for a development contract. Further, the best expert opinion did not think this method economically viable in peacetime.

'So that, whoever we ask to take this job on, we are not exactly conferring a benefit on them.'

'It is a matter of duty,' said Lufkin, sounding hypocritical and yet believing every word. 'That's why I'm prepared to undertake it.'

'You could do it, with your existing resources?'

Lufkin replied: 'I could do it.'

When he spoke like that, offhandedly but with confidence and weight, men could not help but feel his power, not just the power of position, but of his nature.

For some time the parties exchanged questions, most of them technical: how long to build a plant in Canada, how pure must the heavy water be, what was the maximum output. Listening, I thought there was an odd difference between the civil servants and the businessmen. Lufkin's staff treated him with extreme, almost feudal deference, did not put questions on their own account, but made their comments to him. Whereas the civil servants, flat opposite to the others' stereotype of them, spoke with the democratic air of everyone having his say, and as though each man's opinion was as worth having at Sir Hector Rose's.

This was even true of John Jones. Jones was over fifty, had just become a Deputy Secretary, and would not go further. The wonder to me was that he had gone so far. He had a pleasant rosy-skinned face, an air of one about to throw away all constraint and pretence and speak from the bottom of his heart. But when he did speak, it was usually in praise of some superior.

Yet even he kept at least a tone of independence and like many in the department called Rose, the least hearty of men, by his Christian name, which would have been not so much improper as unthinkable from Lufkin's subordinates towards the boss.

Sitting by me, sprawled back in his chair but with his chins thrust into his chest, Gilbert Cooke had been making a noise as though half sniffing, half grunting to himself. As the discussion went on, he sniffed more impatiently, ceased to sprawl back as though in the bar at White's, and hunched himself over the committee table, a great stretch of back filling out the vicuna coat.

'I don't understand something you said,' he suddenly shot out across the table to Lufkin.

'Don't you?' Lufkin twitched his eyebrows.

'You said you can do it with your existing resources.'

'I did.'

'You can't, you know, if by resources you include men, which you've got to.'

'Nonsense.' Lufkin shrugged it off and was speaking to Rose, but Gilbert interrupted.

'Oh no. For the serious part of this job you've only got three groups of men you can possibly use, the ——'s and ——' Rapidly, inquisitively, Gilbert was mentioning names, meaningless to most people there. He said:

'You've got no option, if you're not going to make a hash of this job, you've got to transfer eighty per cent of them. That means taking them off your highest-priority jobs, which other departments won't bless any of us for, and you'll come rushing to us demanding replacements which we shall have to extract from other firms. It is bound to make too much havoc whatever we do, and I don't see rhyme or reason in it.'

Lufkin looked at the younger man with a sarcastic, contemptuous rictus. They knew each other well: often in the past it had surprised me that they were so intimate. Within a few moments both had become very angry, Lufkin in cold temper, Gilbert in hot.

'You are talking of things you know nothing about,' said Lufkin. Furiously Gilbert said:

'I know as much as you do.'

Then, his temper boiling over, he made a tactical mistake; and to prove that he remembered what he had known about the business four years before, he insisted on producing more strings of names.

Recovering himself, sounding irritated but self-contained, Lufkin said to Rose: 'I don't see that these details are likely to help us much.'

'Perhaps we can leave it there, can we, Cooke?' Rose said, polite, vexed, final.

Lufkin remarked, as though brushing the incident aside: 'I take it, all you want from me about personnel is an assurance that I've got enough to do the job. I can give you that assurance.'

Rose smoothly asked:

'Without making any demands on us for men, either now or later?'

Lufkin's face showed no expression. He replied: 'Within reason, no.'

'What is reason?' Rose's voice was for an instant as sharp as the other's.

'I can't commit myself indefinitely,' said Lufkin calmly and heavily, 'and nor can any other man in my position.'

'That is completely understood, and I am very very grateful to you for the statement,' said Rose, returning to his courtesy. With the same courtesy, Rose led the discussion away. The morning went on, the room became colder, several times men stamped their numbing feet. Rose would not leave an argument unheard, even if his mind was made up at the start. It was well after one o'clock when he turned to Lufkin.

'I don't know how you feel, but it seems to me just possible that this is about as far as we can go today.'

'I must say, I think we've covered some ground,' said John Jones.

'When do we meet again?' said Lufkin.

'I shall, of course, report this morning's proceedings to my master.'

Rose said the word with his customary ironic flick; but he was not the man to scurry to shelter. Unlike the Minister, he did not mind breaking bad news. Indeed, under cover of the ritual minuet, he did it with a certain edge. 'I'm sure he will want to go into it further with you. Perhaps you and he, and I think I might as well be there, could meet before the end of the week? I can't anticipate what we shall arrive at as the best course for all of us, but it seems to me just possible – of course I am only thinking aloud – that we might conceivably feel that we are making such demands on you already that we should not consider it was fair to you to stretch you in a rather difficult and unprofitable direction, just for the present at least. We might just conceivably suggest that your remarkable services ought to be kept in reserve, so that we could invoke them at a slightly later stage.'

I wondered if Lufkin recognised that this was the end. At times his realism was absolute: but, like other men of action, he seemed to have the gift of switching it off and on at will. Thus he could go on, hoping and struggling, long after an issue was settled; and then stupefy one by remarking that he had written the business off days before. At that moment he was speaking to Rose with the confidence and authority of one who, at a break in a negotiation, assumed that he will with good management get his way.

The same evening Gilbert came into my office. It was about the time I was leafing through my in-tray, packing up for the night; it was about the time, that, the year before, when he and I and Margaret used to go out together, he habitually called in and sat waiting for me.

For months past he had not done so. Often, when I lunched with him or when we walked in the park afterwards, he jabbed in a question about me and Margaret, led up to traps where I had to lie or confide; he knew her, he knew her family and acquaintances, it could not be a secret that she and I spent many evenings together, but, taking that for granted, I responded to him as though there were nothing else of interest to tell.

Seeing him loom there, outside the cone of light from the desk lamp, I felt very warm to him.

'Well,' I said, 'we shouldn't have won without you.'

'I don't believe anyone was listening to my piece,' Gilbert replied. It rang mock-shy, like someone wanting praise for a short article on modern verse. In fact, it was genuine. Gilbert found it hard to credit that men paid attention to him.

Then he gave the hoarse high laugh one often hears from very strong, fleshy, active men.

'Damn it, I enjoyed it,' he cried.

'What exactly?'

'I enjoyed throwing a spanner into the works!'

'You did it all,' I told him.

'No, I just supplied the comic act.'

He had no idea that his courage was a support to more cautious people. I wanted to reassure him, to tell him how much I admired it. So I said that I happened to be going out that night with Margaret: would he care to come too?

'I'd love it,' said Gilbert.

Without concealment, he did love it, sitting between us at the restaurant. Although he was so large a man he seemed to be burrowing between us, his sharp full eyes sensitive for any glance we exchanged. He enjoyed his food so much that he automatically raised his standard of living, for men obscurely felt that they owed him luxury they would never aspire to themselves; even that night, right in the middle of the war, I managed to stand him a good bottle of wine. It was freezing outside, but the nights had been raidless for a long time; in London it was a lull in the war, the restaurant was crowded and hot, we sat in a corner seat and Gilbert was happy. He infected me, he infected Margaret, and we basked in his well-being.

Suddenly, towards the end of the meal, with eyes glistening he said to me:

'I've stolen a march on you.'

'What have you been up to?'

'I've been inside a house you might be interested in.'

I shook my head.

'The house of a family that means something to you,' said Gilbert, knowing, hot-eyed, imperious. Then he said, gazing straight at Margaret: '*Nothing to do with you.*'

For an instant, I wondered whether he had met the Knights.

'Who is it?' I asked.

'Put him out of his misery,' said Margaret.

'He ought to be able to guess,' said Gilbert, disappointed, as though his game were not quite a success.

'No,' I said.

'Well, then,' Gilbert spoke to Margaret. 'He's got a new secretary. I've found out about her young man and his family. I've had tea with them.'

It was such an anti-climax that I laughed out loud. Even so, the whole performance seemed gigantesque. It was true that I had a new secretary, a young widow called Vera Allen: I did not know anything about her life. Gilbert told us that she was in love with a young man in the office, whose family he had tracked down.

When Gilbert described the visit, which he had planned like a military operation, his curiosity – for that alone had driven him on – made him appear more gigantesque, at times a little mad. Telling us with glee of how he had traced their address, made an excuse for an official visit to Kilburn, called at the house, found they were out, traced them to a pub and persuaded them to take him home for a pot of tea, he was not in the slightest gratifying a desire to go slumming. He would have gone off on the same chase if the young man's father had been a papal count.

Gilbert's inquisitiveness was so ravening that he was as happy, as unceremonious, wherever it led him, provided he picked up a scrap of human news. Having an evening pot of tea with this young man's parents, he felt nothing but brotherliness, except for the same hot-eyed zest with which he collected gossip about them, Helen, her marriage, perhaps at fourth-hand about Margaret and me.

'You are a menace,' said Margaret, but with indulgence and a shade of envy for anyone who could let himself rip so far.

When we went out from the restaurant into the bitter throat-catching air, we were still happy, all three of us. Gilbert continued to talk triumphantly of his findings and, walking between us, Margaret took his arm as well as mine.

CHAPTER XXIV

MILD WIND AFTER A QUARREL

ROSE worked fast after the meeting, and within a fortnight the contract was given to one of Lufkin's rivals. During that fortnight, several of the Minister's colleagues were rumoured to have gone to dinner at St James's Court; the Minister's own position was getting weaker and some of those colleagues did not wish him well. But, once the contract was signed, I thought it unlikely that Lufkin would waste any more time intriguing against the old man. Lufkin was much too practical a person to fritter himself away in revenge. For myself, I expected to be dropped for good, but no worse than that. Lufkin cut his losses, psychological as well as financial, with a drastic simplicity that was a taunt to more contemplative men.

With that business settled and my mind at ease, I walked early one Saturday afternoon along the Bayswater Road to Margaret's flat. It was mid-December, a mild wet day with a south-west wind; the street, the park, lay under a lid of cloud; the soft wind blew in my face, brought a smell from the park both springlike and rich with autumnal decay. It was a day on which the nerves were quite relaxed, and the mild air lulled one with reveries of pleasures to come.

For a couple of days I had not seen Margaret; that morning she had not telephoned me as she usually did on Saturday, but the afternoon arrangement was a standing one, and relaxed, comfortable with expectancy I got out the latchkey and let myself into her room. She was sitting on the stool in front of her looking-glass: she did not get up or look round: the instant I saw her reflection, strained and stern, I cried:

'What is the matter?'

'I have something to ask you.'

'What is it?'

Without turning round, her voice toneless, she said:

'Is it true that Sheila killed herself?'

'What do you mean?'

Suddenly she faced me, her eyes dense with anger.

'I heard it last night. *I heard it for the first time.* Is it true?'

Deep in resentment, I stood there without speaking. At last I said:

'Yes. It is true.'

Few people knew it; as Mr Knight had suggested that night we talked while Sheila's body lay upstairs, the newspapers had had little space for an obscure inquest; I had told no one.

'It's incredible that you should have kept it from me,' she cried.

'I didn't want it to hang over you—'

'What kind of life are we supposed to be living? Do you think I couldn't accept anything that has happened to you? What I can't bear is that you should try to censor something important. I can't stand it if you insist on living as though you were alone. You make me feel that these last twelve months I have been wasting my time.'

'How did you hear?' I broke out.

'We've been pretending—'

'How did you hear?'

'I heard from Helen.'

'She can't have known,' I cried out.

'She took it for granted that I did. When she saw I didn't, what do you think it was like for both of us?'

'Did she say how she'd heard?'

'How could you let it happen?'

Our voices were raised, our words clashed together.

'Did she say how she'd heard?' I shouted again.

'Gilbert told her the other day.'

She was choked both with rage and distress. And I felt the same sense of outrage; though I had brought the scene upon myself, I felt wronged.

Suddenly that desolation, that dull fury, which I wanted to visit on her, was twisted on to another.

'I won't tolerate it,' I shouted. Over her shoulder I saw my face in her looking-glass, whitened with anger while hers had gone dark.

'I'll get rid of him. I won't have him near me.'

'He's fond of you—'

'He won't do this again.'

'He's amused you often enough before now, gossiping about someone else.'

'This wasn't a thing to gossip about.'

'It's done now,' she said.

'I'll get rid of him. I won't have him near me.'

I said it so bitterly that she flinched. For the first time, she averted her glance: in the silence she backed away, rested an arm on the window sill, with her body limp. As I looked at her, unseeing, my feelings clashed and blared – protests, antagonism, the undercurrent of desire. Other feelings swept over those – the thought of Gilbert Cooke spying after Sheila's death, searching the local paper, tracking down police reports, filled my mind like the image of a monster. Then a wound re-opened, and I said quietly:

'There was someone else who went in for malice.'

'What are you talking about?'

In jerky words, I told her of R. S. Robinson.

'Poor Sheila,' Margaret muttered, and then asked, more gently than she had spoken that afternoon: 'Did it make much difference to her?'

'I've never known,' I said. I added:

'Perhaps not. Probably not.'

Margaret was staring at me with pity, with something like fright; her eyes were filling with tears; in that moment we could have come into each other's arms.

I said:

'I won't have such people near me. That is why I shall get rid of Gilbert Cooke.'

Margaret still stared at me, but I saw her face harden, as though, by a resolution as deliberate as that on the first evening we met alone but more painful now, she was drawing on her will. She answered:

'You said nothing to me about Robinson either, or what you went through then.'

I did not reply. She called out an endearment, in astonishment, in acknowledgment of danger.

'We must have it out,' she said.

'Let it go.'

After a pause she said, her voice thickening:

'That's too easy. I can't live like that.'

'Let it go, I tell you.'

'No.'

As a rule people thought her younger than she was, but now she looked much older. She said:

'You can't get rid of Gilbert.'

'I don't think that anything can stop me.'

'Except that it would be an unfair thing to do. And you are not really so unfair.'

'I told you my reason,' I cried.

'That's not your reason. You're lying to yourself.'

My temper was rising again. I said:

'I'm getting tired of this.'

'You're pretending that Gilbert was acting out of malice, and you know it isn't true.'

'I know more of men like Gilbert than you ever will. And I know much more of malice.'

'He's been perfectly loyal to you in every way that matters,' she said, conceding nothing. 'There's no excuse on earth for trying to shift him out of your office. I couldn't let you do it.'

'It is not for you to say.'

'It is. All Gilbert has done is just to treat you as he treats everyone else. Of course he's inquisitive. It's all right when he's being inquisitive about anyone else, but when he touches you – you can't bear it. You want to be private, you don't want to give and take like an ordinary man.' She went on: 'That's what has maddened you about Gilbert. You issue bulletins about yourself, you don't want anyone else to find you out.' She added: 'You are the same with me.'

Harshly I tried to stop her, but her temper was matching mine, her tongue was cooler. She went on: 'What else were you doing, hiding the way she died from me?'

I had got to the pitch of sullen anger when I did not speak, just stood choked up, listening to her accusations.

'With those who don't want much of you, you're unselfish, I grant you that,' she was saying. 'With anyone who wants you altogether, you're cruel. Because one never knows when you're going to be secretive, when you're going to withdraw. With most people you're good,' she was saying, 'but in the end you'll break the heart of anyone who loves you.

'I might be able to stand it,' she was saying, 'I might not mind so much, if you weren't doing yourself such harm.'

Listening to her, I was beyond knowing where her insight was true or false. All she said, her violence and her love, broke upon me like demands which pent me in, which took me to a breaking point of pride and anger. I felt as I had done as a boy when my mother invaded me with love, and at any price I had, the more angry with her because of the behaviour she caused in me, to shut her out.

'That's enough,' I said, hearing my own voice thin but husky in the confining room, as without looking at her I walked to the door.

In the street the afternoon light was still soft, and the mild air blew upon my face.

CHAPTER XXV

CATCH OF BREATH IN THE DARKNESS

Soon I went back to her, and when we took Helen out to dinner in January, we believed that we were putting a face on it, that we were behaving exactly as in the days of our first happiness. But, just as subtle bamboozlers like R. S. Robinson waft about in the illusion that their manœuvres are impenetrable, whereas in fact they are seen through in one by the simplest of men – so the controlled, when they set out to hide their moods, take in no one but themselves.

Within a few weeks, Helen rang me up at the office saying that she was in London for the day, and anxious to talk to me. My first impulse was to put her off. It was uneasily that I invited her to meet me at a restaurant.

I had named the Connaught, knowing that of all her family she was the only one who liked the atmosphere of the opulent and the smart. When I arrived there, finding her waiting in the hall, I saw she was on edge. She was made up more than usual, and her dress had a rigid air of stylishness. She might like the atmosphere, but she could not help the feeling that she had been brought up to despise it; perhaps the slight edge of apprehension, of unfamiliarity, with which, even after all these years, she was troubled whenever she entered a world which was not plain living and high thinking, was one of its charms for her. She did not, as Betty Vane did, take it for granted; for her it had not lost its savour. But added to this temperamental unease, was uneasiness at what she had to say to me.

Sheltered in a corner in the inner dining-room, she did not speak much. Once, as though apologising for her shyness, she gave me a smile like her sister's, at the same time kind and sensuous. She made some remark about the people round us, commented admiringly on a woman's clothes, then fell into silence, looking down at her hands, fiddling with her wedding-ring.

I asked her about her husband. She replied as directly as usual, looking a little beyond my face as if seeing him there, seeing him with a kind of habitual, ironic affection. I believed that she had known little of physical joy.

Suddenly she raised her eyes, which searched mine as Margaret's did. She said:

'You'd like it better if I didn't speak.'

'Perhaps,' I said.

'If I thought I could make things worse, I wouldn't come near either of you – but they're as bad as they can be, aren't they?

'Are they?'

'Could things be worse, tell me?'

'I don't think it's as bad as that.'

To Margaret and me, holding to each other with the tenacity that we each possessed, truly it did not seem so bad: but Helen was watching me, knowing that words said could not be taken back, that there are crystallisations out of love, as well as into it. She knew of my deception over Sheila's suicide: did she think that that had caused such a crystallisation? That as a result Margaret could not regain her trust?

'You know, Lewis, I mind about you both.'

'Yes, I know that.'

It was easy, it was a relief, to reply with her own simplicity.

'When I first saw you together,' she said, 'I was so happy about it.'

'So was I.' I added: 'I think she was too.'

'I know she was.'

'I thought you had been lucky to find each other, both of you,' she was saying. 'I thought you had both chosen very wisely.'

She leant towards me.

'What I'm afraid of,' she broke out, quietly and clearly, 'is that you are driving her away.'

I knew it, and did not know it. Margaret was as tenacious as I was; but she was also more self-willed, and far less resigned. In a human relation she was given to action, action came as naturally and was as much a release as in a more public setting it came to Paul Lufkin or Hector Rose. Sometimes I felt that, although her will was all set to save us, she was telling herself that soon she must force the issue. Once or twice I thought I had detected in her what I had heard called 'the secret planner', who exists in all of us often unrecognised by ourselves and who, in the prospect of disaster, even more so in the prospect of continuing misery, is working out alternative routes which may give us a chance of self-preservation, a chance of health.

'There's still time,' said Helen, and now she was nerving herself even harder, since there was a silence to break, 'to stop driving her away.' She pulled on her left glove and smoothed it up to the elbow, concentrating upon it as if its elegance gave her confidence, made her the kind of woman with a right to say what she chose.

'I hope there is.'

'Of course there is,' she said. 'Neither of you will ever find the same again, and you mustn't let it go.'

'That is true for me. I am not sure it's true for her.'

'You must believe it is.'

She was frowning, speaking as though I were obtuse.

'Look, Lewis,' she said, 'I love her, and of course I'm not satisfied about her, because what you are giving each other isn't enough for her, you know that, don't you? I love her, but I don't think I idealise her. She tries to be good, but I don't think she was given the sort of goodness that's easy and no trouble. She can't forget herself enough for that, perhaps she wants too many different things, perhaps she is too passionate.'

She was not using the word in a physical sense.

'And you – you wouldn't do for everyone, would you, but you can match her all along the line, you're the one person she needn't limit herself with, and I believe that's why it was so wonderful for her. She'd be lucky to have a second chance.

'I don't think that she'd even look for one,' Helen went on. 'But I wasn't thinking mainly of her.'

Helen's tone was for a second impatient and tart, she was in control of herself: and I was taken aback. All along I had assumed that she had forced herself to tax me for Margaret's sake. 'I think it's you who stand to lose,' she said. 'You see, she wouldn't expect so much again, and so long as she found someone to look after, she could make do with that.'

I thought of the men Margaret liked, the doctor Geoffrey Hollis, other friends.

'Could you make do?' Helen asked insistently.

'I doubt it.'

After Helen's intervention I tried to hearten both Margaret and myself. Sometimes I was hopeful, I could show high spirits in front of her; but my spirits were by nature high, despite my fears. I had lost my judgment: sometimes I remembered how Sheila had lost hers, I remembered the others I had seen at a final loss, the unavailing and the breakdowns: now I knew what it was like.

I tried to bring her back, and she tried with me. When I was with her, she made believe that she was happy, so as to fight the dread of another sadness, the menace of a recurrent situation. I wanted to believe in her gaiety, sometimes I did so: even when I knew she was putting it on for my sake.

One evening I went to her, the taxi jangling in the cold March light. As soon as I saw her, she was smiling, and on the instant the burden fell away. After we had made love, I lay there in the dark, in the quiet, comforted by a pleasure as absolute as any I had known. Drowsily I could shake off the state in which, somewhere deep among my fears, she took the place of Sheila. At first I had seemed to pick her out because she was so unlike; yet of late there had been times in which I saw Sheila in my dreams and knew that it was Margaret. I had even, not dreaming but in cold blood, discovered points of identity between them; I had gone so far as to see resemblances in Margaret's face.

I was incredulous that I could have thought so, feared so, as I lay there with her warm against my arms.

In the extreme quiet I heard a catch of her breath, and another. At once I shifted my hand and drew it lightly over her cheek: it was wet and slippery with tears.

The last hour was shattered. I looked down at her, but we had no fire that night, the room was so dark that I could scarcely see her face, even for the instant before she turned it further from me.

'You know how easily I cry,' she muttered. I tried to soothe her; she tried to soothe me.

'This is a pity,' she said in anger: then she cried again.

'It doesn't matter,' I said mechanically. 'It doesn't matter.'

I could not find the loving kindness to know that for her physical delight was a mockery, when there was this distance between us.

I had no self-knowledge left. I felt only uselessness and what seemed like self-contempt. Walking with her in the park later than night, I could not speak.

CHAPTER XXVI

FROM THE LAST LIGHT TO THE FIRST

WHEN she walked with me across the park that night, and on other nights in the weeks that followed, the cold spring air taunted us; often we hoped that all would come well, that we should have confidence in each other again.

Then, one morning in April, I heard of Roy Calvert's death. In the past two years I had seen him little, for he was flying in the Air Force, and, though Margaret and he knew what the other meant to me, they had never met. Yet it was true that each had disliked the sound of the other's name. Roy was not fond of women of character, much less if they had insight too; if I were to marry again, he would have chosen for me someone altogether more careless and easy-going.

In return she suspected him of being a *poseur*, a romantic fake without much fibre, whose profundity of experience she mostly discounted and for the rest did not value. In her heart, she thought he encouraged in me much that she struggled with.

At the news of his death she gave no sign, so far as I could see through the smear of grief, of her dislike, and just wanted to take care of me. I could not respond. I was enough of an official machine – as I had been in the weeks after Sheila's death – to be civil and efficient and make sharp remarks at meetings: as soon as I was out of the office I wanted no one near me, not even her. I recalled Helen's warning; I wanted to pretend, but I could not.

It did not take her long to see.

'You want to be alone, don't you?' she said. It was no use denying it, though it was that which hurt her most. 'I'm less than no help to you. You'd better be by yourself.'

I spent evenings in my own room, doing nothing, not reading, limp in my chair. In Margaret's presence I was often silent, as I had not been with her before. I saw her looking at me, wondering how she could reach me, clutching at any sign that I could give her – and wondering also whether all had gone wrong, and if I were exaggerating my misery in order to make a last escape.

On a close night, near mid-summer, the sky not quite dark, we walked purposelessly round the Bayswater streets and then crossed over to Hyde Park and found an empty bench. Looking down the hollow towards the Bayswater Road we could see the scurf of newspapers, the white of shirts and dresses in couples lying together, shining out from the grass in the last of the light. The litter of the night, the thundery closeness: we sat without looking at each other: each of us was alone, with that special loneliness, containing both guilt and deprivation, containing also dislike and a kind of sullen hate, which comes to those who have known extreme intimacy, and who are seeing it drift away. In that loneliness we held each other's hand, as though we could not bear the last token of separation.

She said quietly, in a tone of casual gossip. 'How is your friend Lufkin?'

We knew each other's memories so well. She was asking me to recall that once, months before, when we were untroubled, we had met him by chance, not here, but on the path nearer the Albert Gate.

'I haven't seen him.'

'Does he still feel misunderstood?'

Again she was making me recall. She had taught me so much, I told her once. She had said: 'So have you taught me.' Most of the men I talked to her about had not come near her father's world: she had not realised before what they were like.

'I'm sure he does.'

'*Snakes-in-the-grass*.' It was one of Lufkin's favourite exclamations, confronted by yet another example, perpetually astonishing to him, of others' duplicity, self-seeking, and ambition. Margaret could not believe that men so able could live cut off from their own experience. It had delighted her, and, searching that night for something for us to remember, she refound the phrase and laughed out loud.

For a while we talked, glad to be talking, of some of the characters I had amused her with. It was a strange use for those figures, so grand in their offices, so firm in their personae, I thought later, to be smiled over by the two of us, clutching on to the strand of a love affair, late at night out in the park.

We could not spin it out, we fell back into silence. I had no idea of how the time was passing, now that the night had come down. I could feel her fingers in mine, and at last she called my name, but mechanically, as though she were intending an endearment but was remote. She said:

'A lot has happened to you.'

She did not mean my public life, she meant the deaths of Sheila and Roy Calvert.

'I suppose so.'

'It was bound to affect you, I know that.'

'I wish,' I said, 'that I had met you before any of it happened.'

Suddenly she was angry.

'No, I won't listen. We met when we did, and this is the only time together we shall ever have.'

'I might have been more—'

'No. You're always trying to slip out of the present moment, and I won't take it any more.'

I answered sullenly. The present moment, the existent moment – as we sat there, in the sultry darkness, we could neither deal with it nor let it be. We could not show each other the kindness we should have shown strangers: far less could we allow those words to come out which, with the knowledge and touch of intimacy, we were certain could give the other a night's peace. If she could have said to me, it doesn't matter, leave it, some day you'll be better and we'll start again – If I could have said to her, I will try to give you all you want, marry me and somehow we shall come through – But we could not speak so, it was as though our throats were sewn up.

We stayed, our hands touching, not tired so much as stupefied while the time passed: time not racing hallucinatorily by, as when one is drunk, but just pressing on us with something like the headaching pressure of the thundery air in which we sat. Sometimes we talked, almost with interest, almost as though we were going out for the first time, for the first meal together, about a play that ought to be seen or a book she had just read. After another bout of silence, she said in a different tone:

'Before we started, I asked what you wanted from me.'

I said yes.

'You said, you didn't want anything one-sided, you didn't want the past all over again.'

I replied: 'Yes, I said that.'

'I believed you,' she said.

Over Park Lane the sky was not so densely black, there was a leaden light just visible over the roofs. The sight struck more chilly than the dark had been. The midsummer night was nearly over. She asked:

'It looks as though we have come to a dead end?'

Even then, we wanted to hear in each other the sound of hope.

CHAPTER XXVII

VIEW OF A SWINGING DOOR

WITHOUT seeing Margaret again I went off travelling on duty, and it was a fortnight before I returned to London. The day I got back, I found a note on my desk. Margaret had telephoned, would I meet her that evening in the foyer of the Café Royal? At once I was startled. We had never gone there before, it was a place without associations.

Waiting, a quarter of an hour before the time she fixed, I stared at the swinging door and through the glass at the glare outside. The flash of buses, the dazzle of cars' bonnets, the waft of the door as someone entered but not she – I was at the stretch of waiting. When at last the door swung past and showed her, minutes early, I saw her face flushed and set; but her step, as she came across the floor, was quick, light and full of energy.

As she greeted me her eyes were intent on mine; they had no light in them, and the orbits had gone deeper and more hollow.

'Why here?' I broke out.

'You must know. I hope you know.'

She sat down: I had a drink ready, but she did not touch it.

'I hope you know,' she said.

'Tell me then.'

She was speaking, so was I, quite unlike the choked hours in the park: we were speaking at our closest.

'I am going to get married.'

'Who to?'

'Geoffrey.'

'I knew it.'

Her face at the table came at me in the brilliant precision of a high temperature, sharp-edged, so vivid that sight itself was deafening.

'It is settled, you know,' she said. 'Neither of us could bear it if it wasn't, could we?'

She was speaking still with complete understanding, as though her concern for me was at its most piercing, and mine for her; she was speaking also as one buoyed up by action, who had cut her way out of a conflict and by the fact of acting was released.

I asked:

'Why didn't you write and tell me?'

'Don't you know it would have been easier to write?'

'Why didn't you?'

'I couldn't let you get news like that over your breakfast and by yourself.'

I looked at her. Somehow, as at a long distance, the words made me listen to what I was losing – it was like her, maternal, irrationally practical, principled, a little vain. I looked at her not yet in loss, so much as in recognition.

She said: 'You know you've done everything for me, don't you?'

I shook my head.

'You've given me confidence I should never have had,' she went on. 'You've taken so many of the fears away.'

Knowing me, she knew what might soften the parting.

Suddenly she said:

'I wish, I wish that you could say the same.'

She had set herself to be handsome and protective to the end, but she could not sustain it. Her tears had sprung out. With a quick, impatient, resolved gesture, she was on her feet.

'I hope all goes well with you.'

The words, doubtful and angry in their tone, heavy with her concern, were muffled in my ears. They were muffled, like a sad forecast, as I watched her leave me and walk to the door with a firm step. Not looking back, she pushed the door round, so hard that, after I had lost sight of her, the empty segments sucked round before my eyes, sweeping time away, leaving me with nothing there to see.

PART THREE

CONDITION OF A SPECTATOR

CHAPTER XXVIII

A CHANGE OF TASTE

AFTER Margaret gave me up, I used to go home alone when I left the office on a summer evening. But I had plenty of visitors to my new flat, people I cared for just enough to be interested to see, friendly acquaintances, one or two protégés. For me they were casual evenings, making no more calls on me than a night's reading.

Sometimes, in the midst of a long official gathering, I thought, not without a certain enjoyment, of how baffled these people would be if they saw the acquaintances with whom I proposed to spend that night. For now I had been long enough in the office to be taken for granted: since the Minister lost his job, I did not possess as much invisible influence as when I was more junior, but in official eyes I had gone up, and the days were stable, full of the steady, confident voices of power. Then I went home from one of Hector Rose's committees, back to the dingy flat.

Just after Margaret said goodbye, I had to move out of the Dolphin block and, not in a state to trouble, I took the first rooms I heard of, in the square close by. They took up the ground floor of one of the porticoed Pimlico houses; the smell of dust was as constant as a hospital smell; in the sitting-room the sunlight did not enter, even in high summer, until five o'clock. In that room I listened to the acquaintances who came to see me; it was there that Vera Allen, my secretary, suddenly broke out of her reserve and told me of the young man whom Gilbert had identified. He seemed to love her, Vera cried, but he would neither marry nor make love to her.

Of my old friends, the only one I saw much of was Betty Vane, who came in to make the flat more liveable, just as she had busied herself for me after Sheila's death. She knew that I had lost Margaret: about herself she volunteered nothing, except that she had left her job and found another in London, leaving me to assume that she and I were in the same state.

Irritable, undemanding, she used to clean up the room and then go with me round the corner to the pub on the Embankment. Through the open door the starlings clamoured: we looked at each other with scrutiny, affection, blame. We had been friends on and off for so long, and now we met again it was to find that the other had got nowhere.

When she or any other visitor let herself out last thing at night, there was likely to be a pad and scuffle outside my door and a soft, patient, insidious knock. Then round the door would insinuate a podgy shapeless face, a great slack heavy body wrapped in a pink satin dressing-gown. It was Mrs Beauchamp, my landlady, who lived on the floor above mine and who spent her days spying from her room above the portico and her nights listening to steps on the stairs and sounds from her tenants' rooms.

One night, just after Betty had left, she went through her routine:

'I was just wondering, Mr Eliot, I knew you won't mind me asking, but I was just wondering if you had a drop of milk?'

The question was a matter of form. With each new tenant, she cherished a hope of heart speaking unto heart, and, as the latest arrival, I was going through the honeymoon period. As a matter of form, I asked her if she could manage without the milk for that night's supper.

'Ah, Mr Eliot,' she breathed, a trifle ominously, 'I'll do what I can.'

Then she got down to business.

'That was a very nice young lady, if you don't mind me saying so, Mr Eliot, that seemed to be coming to see you when I happened to be looking down the street tonight, or at least, not exactly young as some people call young, but I always say that none of us are as young as we should like to be.'

I told her Betty was younger than I was: but as she thought me ten years older than my real age, Mrs Beauchamp was encouraged.

'I always say that people who aren't exactly young have feelings just the same as anyone else, and sometimes their feelings give them a lot to think about, if you don't mind me saying so, Mr Eliot,' she said, with an expression that combined salacity with extreme moral disapproval. But she was not yet satisfied.

'I shouldn't be surprised,' she said, 'if you told me that that nice young lady had come of a very good family.'

'Shouldn't you?'

'Now, Mr Eliot, she does or she doesn't, I'm sorry if I'm asking things I shouldn't, but I like to feel that when anyone does the same to me I don't send them away feeling that they have made a *faux pas*.'

'As a matter of fact she does.'

'Breeding will out,' Mrs Beauchamp exhaled.

The curious thing was, she was an abnormally accurate judge of social origin. The derelicts who visited me she put down to my eccentricity: the respectable clerks from the lower middle classes, like Vera Allen and her Norman, Mrs Beauchamp spotted at once, and indicated that I was wasting my time. Of my Bohemian friends, she detected precisely who was smart and who was not.

She went on to tell me the glories of her own upbringing, the convent school – 'those dear good nuns' – and of Beauchamp, who was, according to her, entitled to wear *seventeen distinguished ties*. Improbable as Mrs Beauchamp's autobiography sounded when one saw her stand oozily in the doorway, I was coming to believe it was not totally untrue.

Whenever I answered the telephone in the hall, I heard a door click open on the next floor and the scuffle of Mrs Beauchamp's slippers. But I could put up with her detective work, much as I used, before he touched a nerve, to put up with Gilbert Cooke's.

All this time, since the day when he told Margaret's sister of the suicide, I had been meeting Gilbert in the office; I talked business with him, even gossiped, but I had not once let fall a word to him about my own concerns. He was the first to notice signs of anyone withdrawing, but this time I was not sure that he knew the reason. I was quite sure, however, that he had discovered the break with Margaret, and that he was expending some effort to observe how I was living now.

Coming into my office one evening in the autumn, he said imperiously and shyly:

'Doing anything tonight?'

I said no.

'Let me give you dinner.'

I could not refuse and did not want to, for there was no pretence about the kindness that brimmed from him. As well as being kind, he was also, I recognised once more, sensitive: he did not take me to White's, since he must have imagined – the last thing I should have mentioned to anyone, to him above all – how I linked our dinner there with the night of Sheila's death. Instead, he found a restaurant in Soho where he could order me one or two of my favourite dishes, the names of which he had stored away in that monstrous memory. He proceeded to bully me kindly about my new flat.

'It's near the Dolphin, isn't it?' (He knew the address.) 'It's one of those 1840ish houses, I suppose. Not much good in air raids, you must move out if they start again,' he said, jabbing his thumb at me. 'We can't let you take unnecessary risks.'

'What about you?' I said. His own flat was at the top of a ramshackle Knightsbridge house.

'It doesn't matter about me.'

Brushing my interruption aside, he got back to the subject, more interesting to him, of my living arrangements.

'Have you got a housekeeper?'

I said I supposed that one could call Mrs Beauchamp that.

'Doesn't she make you comfortable?'

'Certainly not.'

'I don't know,' he cried impatiently, 'why you don't do something about it!'

'Don't worry yourself,' I said, 'I genuinely don't mind.'

'What is she like?'

I wanted to warn him off, so I smiled at him, and said:

'To put it mildly, she's just a bit inquisitive.'

When I had spoken I was sorry, since it suddenly struck me as not impossible that Gilbert would find occasion to have a confidential talk with Mrs Beauchamp. For the moment, however, he laughed, high-voiced, irritated with me.

The meal went on agreeably enough. We talked official shop and about the past. I thought again, everything Gilbert said was his own, in his fashion he was a creative man. He was being lavish with the drink, and now there was half-a-bottle of brandy standing before us on the table. It was a long time since I had drunk so much. I was cheerful, I was content for the evening to stretch out. As I was finishing some inconsequential remark I saw Gilbert leaning over the table towards me, his big shoulders hunched. His eyes hot and obsessive, he said:

'I can tell you something you've been waiting to know.'

'Never mind,' I replied, but I was taken off guard.

'Have you seen Margaret since she got married?'

'No.'

'I suppose you wouldn't!' He laughed, satisfied, on top. 'Well, you needn't get too bothered about her. I think she'll be all right.'

I wanted to cry out, 'I don't intend to listen', just as I had avoided going near anyone who knew her or even hearing the date of her wedding. The only news I had not been able to escape was that she was married. I wanted to shout in front of Gilbert's inflamed eyes – 'I can stand it, if I don't hear'. But he went on: Geoffrey Hollis had taken a job at a children's hospital, they were living at Aylesbury.

'I think she'll be all right,' said Gilbert.

'Good.'

'He's head over heels in love with her, of course.'

'Good,' I said again.

'There is one other thing.'

'Is there?' I heard my own voice dull, mechanical, protecting me by thrusting news away.

'She's going to have a child.'

As I did not reply, he continued:

'That will mean a lot to her, won't it?'

'Yes.'

'Of course,' said Gilbert, 'she can't have started it more than a month or two—'

While he was talking on, I got up and said that I must have an early night. There were no taxis outside, and together we walked up Oxford Street: I was replying to his chat affably if absently: I did not feel inimical; I already knew what I was going to do.

The next morning I sat in my office thinking of how I was going to say it, before I asked Vera Allen to fetch Gilbert in. He slumped down in the easy chair beside my desk, relaxed and companionable.

'Look,' I said, 'I want you to transfer to another branch.'

On the instant he was braced, his feet springy on the floor, like a man ready to fight.

'Why?'

'Will it do any good to either of us to answer that?'

'You just mean, that you want to get rid of me, after four years, without any reason, and without any fuss?'

'Yes,' I said. 'I mean that.'

'I won't accept it.'

'You must.'

'You can't force me.'

'I can,' I replied. I added: 'If necessary, I shall.' I was speaking so that he would believe me. Then I added in a different tone:

'But I shan't have to.'

'Why do you think you can get away with it?'

'Because I need you to go to make things easier for me.'

'Good God,' cried Gilbert, his eyes angry and puzzled, 'I don't think I deserve that.'

'I've got great affection for you, you know that,' I said. 'You've been very good to me in all kinds of ways, and I shan't forget it. But just now there are parts of my life I don't want to be reminded of—

'Well?'

'While you're about, you can't help reminding me of them.'

'How do you mean, I can't help it?'

'You can see.'

Hotly, angrily, without self-pity or excuse, Gilbert said:

'It's my nature. You know how it is.'

I knew better than he thought; for in my youth I had been as tempted as most men by the petty treachery, the piece of malice warm on the tongue at a friend's expense, the kind of personal imperialism, such as he had shown the night before, in which one imposes oneself upon another. Even more I had been fascinated by the same quicksands in other men. As to many of us when young, the labile, the shifting, the ambivalent, the Lebedevs and the Fyodor Karamazovs, had given me an intimation of the depth and wonder of life. But as I grew up I began to find it not only unmagical, but also something like boring, both in others and myself. At the age when I got rid of Gilbert Cooke I found it hard to imagine the excitement and attention with which, in my young manhood, I had explored the transformation-scene temperaments of Jack Cotery or Herbert Getliffe or others like them. As I got near forty, my tastes in character had changed, I could not give that attention again. If I had still been able to, I could have taken Gilbert as an intimate friend.

CHAPTER XXIX

FIRST INTERVIEW OF GEORGE PASSANT

WHEN I told Rose that I wished to transfer Gilbert Cooke, I had an awkward time.

'Of course, I have only a nodding acquaintance with your dashing activities, my dear Lewis,' said Rose, meaning that he read each paper word by word, 'but I should have thought the present arrangement was working reasonably well.'

I said that I could see certain advantages in a change.

'I must say,' replied Rose, 'that I should like to be assured of that.'

'It would do Cooke good to get a wider experience—'

'We can't afford to regard ourselves as a training establishment just at present. My humble interest is to see that your singular and admirable activities don't suffer.' He gave his polite, confident smile. 'And forgive me if I'm wrong, but I have a feeling that they will suffer if you let Mas..r Cooke go.'

'In many ways that's true,' I had to say in fairness.

'I shouldn't like us to forget that he showed a certain amount of moral courage, possibly a slightly embarrassing moral courage, over that Lufkin complication last year. I scored a point to his credit over that. And I have an impression that he's been improving. He's certainly been improving appreciably on paper, and I've come to respect his minutes.'

As usual, Hector Rose was just. He was also irritated that I would not let him persuade me. He was even more irritated when he learned how I proposed to fill Gilbert's place. For, finding me obstinate, and cutting the argument short, he admitted that they could probably give me an 'adequate replacement'; it was the end of 1943, there were plenty of youngish officers invalided out, or a few capable young women 'coming loose'.

No, I said, I would not take a chance with anyone I did not know through and through; the job was going to get more tangled, and parts of it were secret; I wanted someone near me whom I could trust as I did myself.

'I take it that this specification is not completely in the air, and you have some valuable suggestion up your sleeve?'

I gave the name: George Passant. I did not tell Rose that he had been the first person to help me in my youth. I had to reveal, however, that he had been working as a solicitor's managing clerk in a provincial town for twenty years. The only point in his favour in Rose's eyes was that his examination record was of the highest class.

Further, I had to tell Rose that George had once got into legal trouble, but he had been found innocent.

'In that case we can't count it against him.' Rose was showing his most frigid fairness, as well as irritation. He dismissed that subject, it was not to be raised again. But sharply he asked me what proofs 'this man' had given of high ability. His lids heavy, his face expressionless, Rose listened.

'It isn't an entirely convincing case, my dear Lewis, don't you feel that? It would be much easier for me if you would reconsider the whole idea. Will you think it over and give me the benefit of another word tomorrow?'

'I have thought it over for a long time,' I replied. 'If this job' – I meant, as Rose understood, the projects such as the headquarters administration of Barford, which came in my domain – 'is done as it needs to be done. I can't think of anyone else who'd bring as much to it.'

'Very well, let me see this man as soon as you can.'

Just for that instant, Hector Rose was as near being rude as I had heard him, but when, three days later, we were waiting to interview George Passant, he had recovered himself and, the moment George was brought in, Rose reached heights of politeness exalted even for him.

'My dear Mr Passant, it is really extremely good of you, putting yourself to this inconvenience just to give us the pleasure of a talk. I have heard a little about you from my colleague Eliot, whom I'm sure you remember, but it is a real privilege to have the opportunity of meeting you in person.'

To my surprise George, who had entered sheepishly, his head thrust forward, concealing the power of his chest and shoulders, gave a smile of delight at Rose's welcome, immediately reassured by a display of warmth about as heartfelt as a bus conductor's thanks.

'I don't get to London very often,' said George, 'but it's always a treat.'

It was a curious start. His voice, which still retained the Suffolk undertone, rolled out, and, as he sat down, he smiled shyly at Rose but also man-to-man. They were both fair, they were both of middle height, strongly built, with massive heads; yet, inside that kind of structural resemblance, it would have been hard to find two men more different.

Even spruced up for the interview, George looked not so much untidy as dowdy, in a blue suit with the trouser legs too tight. His shoes, his tie, separated him from Rose as much as his accent did, and there was not only class, there was success dividing them. George, never at his ease except with protégés or women, was more than ever fiddling for the right etiquette in front of his smooth youngish man, more successful than anyone he had met.

Sitting down, he smiled shyly at Rose, and of all the contrasts between them that in their faces was the sharpest. At forty-six Rose's was blankly youthful, the untouched front of a single-minded man, with eyes heavy and hard. George, three years younger, looked no more than his age; he was going neither grey nor bald; but there were written on him the signs of one who has found his temperament often too much to manage; his forehead was bland and noble, his nose and mouth and whole expression had a cheerful sensual liveliness – except for his eyes, which, light blue in their deep orbits, were abstracted, often lost and occasionally sad.

With the practised and temperate flow of a civil service interview, Rose questioned him.

'I wonder if you would mind, Mr Passant, just helping us by taking us through your career?'

George did so. He might be shy, but he was lucid as always. His school career: his articles with a Woodbridge solicitor –

'Forgive me interrupting, Mr Passant, but with a school record like yours I'm puzzled why you didn't try for a university scholarship?'

'If I'd known what they were like I might have got one,' said George robustly.

'Leaving most of us at the post,' said Rose with a polite bow.

'I think I should have got one,' said George, and then suddenly one of his fits of abject diffidence took him over, the diffidence of class. 'But of *course* I had no one to advise me, starting where I did.'

'I should hope that we're not wasting material like you nowadays, if you will let me say so.'

'More than you think.' George was comfortable again. He went on about his articles: the Law Society examinations: the prizes; the job at Eden & Martineau's, a firm of solicitors in a midland town, as a qualified clerk.

'Where you've been ever since. That is, since October 1921,' put in Rose smoothly.

'I'm afraid so,' said George.

'Why haven't you moved?'

'You ought to be told,' said George, without any embarrassment, 'that I had an unpleasant piece of difficulty ten years ago.'

'I have been told,' said Rose, also without fuss. 'I can perfectly well understand that trouble getting in your way since – but what about the years before?'

George answered: 'I've often asked myself. Of course I didn't have any influence behind me.'

Rose regarded him as though he wanted to examine this lack of initiative. But he thought better of it, and dexterously switched him on to legal points. Like many high-class civil servants, Rose had a competent amateur knowledge of law; I sat by, without any need to intervene, while George replied with his old confidence.

Then Rose said: most countries recruit their bureaucracy almost exclusively from lawyers: our bureaucracy is not fond of them: who is right? It was a topic which Rose knew backwards, but George, quite undeterred, argued as though he had been in Permanent Secretaries' offices for years: I found myself listening, not to the interview, but to the argument for its own sake: I found also that Rose, who usually timed interviews to the nearest two minutes, was letting this over-run by nearly ten. At last he said, bowing from the waist, as ceremonious as though he were saying goodbye to Lufkin or an even greater boss:

'I think perhaps we might leave it for the moment, don't you agree, Mr Passant? It has been a most delightful occasion and I shall see that we let you know whether we can possibly justify ourselves in temporarily up-rooting you—'

With a smile George backed out, the door closed, Rose looked not at me but out of the window. His arms were folded on his chest, and it was some moments before he spoke.

'Well,' he said.

I waited.

'Well,' he said, 'he's obviously a man of very high intelligence.'

In that respect, Rose in half an hour could appreciate George's quality more than his employer in the solicitors' firm, who had known him half a lifetime. He went on:

'He's got a very strong and precise mind, and it's distinctly impressive. If we took him as a replacement for Cooke, on the intellectual side we should gain by the transaction.'

Rose paused. His summing-up was not coming as fluently as usual.

He added: 'But I must say, there seems to be altogether too much on the negative side.'

I stiffened, ready to sit it out.

'What exactly?'

'Not to put too fine a point on it, a man of his ability who just rests content in a fourth-rate job must have something wrong with him.'

A stranger, listening to the altercation which went on for many minutes, would have thought it business-like, rational, articulate. He might not have noticed, so cool was Rose's temper, so long had I had to learn to subdue mine, that we were each of us very angry. I knew that I had only to be obstinate to get my way. I could rely on Rose's fairness. If George had been an impossible candidate, he would have vetoed him. But, although Rose felt him unsuitable and even more alien, he was too fair to rule him out at sight.

That being so, I should get George if I stuck to it; for this was the middle of the war, and I was doing a difficult job. In peacetime, I should have had to take anyone I was given. Rose had been trained not to expect to make a personal choice of a subordinate, any more than of an office chair: it offended him more, because mine was nothing but a personal choice. It was wartime, however; my job was regarded as exacting and in part it was abnormally secret. In the long run I had to be given my head. But I knew that I should have to pay a price.

'Well, my dear Lewis, I am still distinctly uneasy about this suggestion. If I may say so, I am slightly surprised that you should press it, in view of what I have tried, no doubt inadequately, to explain.'

'I wouldn't do so for a minute,' I replied, 'if I weren't unusually certain.'

'Yes, that's the impression you have managed to give.' For once Rose was letting his bitter temper show. 'I repeat, I am surprised that you should press the suggestion.'

'I'm sure of the result.'

'Right.' Rose snapped off the argument, like a man turning a switch. 'I'll put the nomination through the proper channels. You'll be able to get this man started within a fortnight.'

He glanced at me, his face smoothed over.

'Well, I'm most grateful to you for spending so much time this afternoon. But I should be less than honest with you, my dear Lewis, if I didn't say that I still have a fear this may prove one of your few errors of judgment.'

That was the price I paid. For Rose, who in disapproval invariably said less than he meant, was telling me, not that I might turn out to have made an error of judgment, but that I had already done so. That is, I had set my opinion against official opinion beyond the point where I should have backed down. If I had been a real professional, with a professional's ambitions, I could not have afforded to. For it did not take many 'errors of judgment' – the most minatory phrase Rose could use to a colleague – docketed in that judicious mind, to keep one from the top jobs. If I became a professional, I should have the future, common enough if one looked round the Pall Mall clubs, of men of parts, often brighter than their bosses, who had inexplicably missed the top two rungs.

I did not mind. When I was a young man, too poor to give much thought to anything but getting out of poverty, I had dreamed of great success at the Bar; since then I had kept an interest in success and power which was, to many of my friends, forbiddingly intense. And, of course, they were not wrong: if a man spends half of his time discussing basketball, thinking of basketball, examining with passionate curiosity the intricacies of basketball, it is not unreasonable to suspect him of a somewhat excessive interest in the subject.

Yet, over the last years, almost without my noticing it, for such a change does not happen in a morning, I was growing tired of it: or perhaps not so much tired, as finding myself slide from a participant into a spectator. It was partly that now I knew I could earn a living in two or three different ways. It was partly that, of the two I had loved most, Sheila had ignored my preoccupation with power, while Margaret actively detested it. But although I believed that Margaret's influence might have quickened the change within me, I also believed it would have happened anyway.

Now that I felt a theme in my life closing, I thought it likely that I had started off with an interest in power greater than that of most reflective men, but not a tenth of Lufkin's or Rose's, nothing like enough to last me for a lifetime. I expected that I should keep an eye open for the manœuvres of others: who will get the job? and why? and how? I expected also that sometimes, as I watched others installed in jobs I might once have liked, I should feel regret. That did not matter much. Beneath it all, a preoccupation was over.

As it vanished step by step, so another had filled its place. But this other was genuine; I had been clear about it, although I had had to push it out of sight, even when I was a child. I had known that sooner or later I should have some books to write; I did not worry about it; I was learning what I had to say. In trouble, that knowledge had often steadied me, and had given me a comfort greater than any other. Even after Margaret left me, in the middle of the war, when I was too busy to write anything sustained, nevertheless I could, last thing at night, read over my note-books and add an item or two. It gave me a kind of serenity; it was like going into a safe and quiet room.

Some of this, Sheila had known and liked. And that was true years before, of an elderly confidante of mine, Lady Boscastle, who was a chilly woman but who had wished me well. Margaret knew it all. The working patterns of a literary life don't have much meaning except for fellow professionals, and I shall not spend time describing mine. But it had a result without which the rest of my life cannot be properly under-stood. For a long time, I was living a double existence, one side of it in action. In that side, however, though it taught me much, I was to an extent different from those with whom I worked, psychologically in-dependent, and, fairly soon, practically independent also.

After the cold parting with Rose I went to my own office, where George was sitting by the window smoking a pipe.

'That will be all right, barring accidents,' I told him at once.

'He was extraordinarily nice to me,' said George enthusiastically, as though the manner of his reception by Rose was much more important than the prosaic matter of the verdict.

'You'd expect him to be civil, wouldn't you?'

'He was extraordinarily nice to me, right from the minute I went in,' said George, as though he had anticipated being tripped up inside the door.

I realised that George had not speculated on why Rose and I had been discussing him for so long. He was not given to meeting danger halfway; he had been happy, sitting by my window, looking down into Whitehall, waiting for me to bring the news. He was happy also, later that evening, as we walked through the streets under a frigid moon, though not in the way I was. I was happy that night because it took me back through the years to the time when he and I walked the harsher streets of the provincial town, George making grandiose plans for me, his brightest protégé – to the time which seemed innocent now, before I met Sheila, to those years in the early twenties when the world outside us seemed innocent too.

It was unlikely that George gave a thought to that past, for he was not in the least a sentimental man. No, he was happy because he enjoyed my company, my company as a middle-aged man in the here and now: because he had been received politely by an important person: because he was obscurely scoring against all the people who had kept him dim and unrecognised so long: and because, in the moonlit night, he saw soldiers and women pairing off in the London streets. For George, even in his forties, was one of those men who can find romantic magnificence in sex without trappings; the sight of the slit of light around the night-club door, and he was absentminded with happiness; his feet stumped more firmly on the pavement, and he cheerfully twirled his stick.

CHAPTER XXX

SPECTATOR'S PARADISE

WE were busy that winter sketching out a new project, and on many nights George Passant and my secretary worked later than I did at the office and then went on to my flat to get a draft finished. At the flat they met some of my acquaintances; George, whose eyes brightened at the sight of Vera Allen, did not know what had happened to me, nor speculate much about it.

It would not have occurred to him that I was getting consolation from being a looker-on. It would have occurred to him even less that, just occasionally, when I was listening, trying to give sensible advice, there came thoughts which I had to use my whole will to shut out. In that rational, looking-on, and on the whole well-intended existence, I would suddenly have my attention drained away, by something more actual than a dream, in which a letter was on the way from Margaret, asking me to join her.

George would have believed none of that. To him I appeared quieter and more sober than I used to be, but still capable of high spirits. He assumed that I must have some secret source of satisfaction, and often, if we were left alone in the flat, he would say with an air of complacence, correct and smug:

'Well, I won't intrude on your private life.'

Then he would walk happily off up the square, twiddling his stick and whistling.

On the nights she came home with us, Vera Allen used to leave when she thought George was still occupied, so that he would not have an excuse to walk with her to the bus. He remained good-humoured and aware of her until one evening, when they arrived at the flat half an hour before me, there was a constraint between them so glaring that it was almost tactless not to refer to it. That evening it was George who left first.

When I heard his steps clumping defiantly along the pavement, I gazed with amusement at Vera. She was standing up ready to hand me papers, not showing any tiredness after the night's work, her figure neat and strong as a dancer's. It was that figure which made her seem so comely, for her face, with the features flattened and open, was not beautiful, was scarcely even pretty; yet behind the openness of her expression, there was some hint – often I had thought it illusory, but that did not matter – of hidden hopes which tempted men, which made a good many speculate on how surprising she might be in one's arms. But most men, unlike George, knew it was futile.

She was a simple, direct and modest young woman. Although she was only twenty-seven, her husband had been killed four years before. Now she was in love again, with an absolute blinkered concentration of love, so that she seemed to breathe and eat only as means to the end of having Norman to herself. They were not lovers, but she had not a second's recognition of the flesh to spare for any other man. She was – as far as I could guess about her – both passionate and chaste.

I smiled at her. She trusted me now. I asked:

'What's the matter with Mr Passant?'

Vera's eyes, clear and unblinking, met mine: there might have been a tinge of colour on her cheeks and neck, as she considered.

'I should have thought he was a little highly strung, Mr Eliot.'

She paused, like a politician issuing a statement, and added:

'Yes, he is *on the highly strung side*. I don't think I can put it better than that.'

I nearly told her I did not think she could have put it worse. Vera, although not sophisticated, was also not coy: but she had a knack of finding insipid words which satisfied herself though no one else, and then of gripping on to them as though they were so many umbrellas. Highly strung. From now on she would firmly produce that egregious phrase whenever George was mentioned. What did it mean? Amorising, importunate, randy, gallant? Something like that: I doubted if she had made a distinction, or could recognise at sight the difference between a violently sensual man like George and some of her flirtatious hangers-on. She just put them impartially aside. For a woman of her age, she was curiously innocent.

But there was one authority who did not regard her so. Soon after I had asked her about George – she would not give away any more – I let her out, and, as I was returning along the hall-passage to my room, heard an excited, insinuating voice from the next landing.

'Mr Eliot! Mr Eliot!'

'Yes, Mrs Beauchamp?' I called out irritably. I could not see her, this was early in 1944, the black-out was still on, and the only light was from the blue-painted bulb in the hall.

'I must have, that is if you can spare the time of course, I must have a little private word *entre nous*.'

I went up the stairs and made her out, in the spectral light, standing outside her own closed door.

'I think I must tell you, Mr Eliot, I'm sure I shouldn't be doing my duty if I didn't.'

'Don't worry too much.'

'But I do worry when it's my duty, Mr Eliot, I'm the biggest worrier I've ever met.'

It was clear that I had not yet found a technique for dealing with Mrs Beauchamp.

'You see, Mr Eliot,' she whispered triumphantly, 'before you came in this evening the door of your room just happened to be open and I just happened to be going upstairs, actually I had just been doing a bit of shopping, not that I should ever think of looking in your room if I didn't hear a noise, but I thought, I know Mr Eliot would want me to pay attention to that, I know you would, Mr Eliot, if you'd seen what I'd seen.'

'What did you see?'

'Always respect another person's privacy, Major Beauchamp used to say,' she replied. 'I've always done my best to live up to that, Mr Eliot and I know you have,' she added puzzlingly as though I, too, had sat under Major Beauchamp's moral guidance.

'What did you see?'

'*Écrasez l'infâme*,' said Mrs Beauchamp.

In a whisper, fat-voiced and throbbing, she broke out:

'Oh, I'm sorry for that poor friend of yours, poor Mr Passant!'

This seemed to me an absurd letdown; to imagine that George, having been turned down, was going out heartbroken into the night, was too much even for Mrs Beauchamp.

'He'll get over it,' I said.

'I'm sure I don't quite follow you,' she replied virtuously.

'I mean, Mr Passant won't worry long because a young woman doesn't feel free to have dinner with him.'

Speaking to Mrs Beauchamp I often found myself, as if hypnotised by her example, becoming more and more genteel.

'If it were only that!'

Dimly, I could perceive her hands clasped over her vast unconfined bust.

'Oh, if only it were that!' She echoed herself.

'What else could it be?'

'Mr Eliot, I've always been afraid you think too well of women. A gentleman like you is always apt to, I know you do if you don't mind my saying so, you put them on a pedestal and you don't see their feet of clay. So did Major Beauchamp and I always prayed he'd never have reason to think different, because it would have killed him if he had and I hope it never will you, Mr Eliot. That secretary of yours, I don't like to speak against someone who you are so good to, but I'm afraid I have had my eyes on her from the start.'

That did not differentiate Vera sharply from any other woman who came to the house, I thought.

'Looking as though butter wouldn't melt in ner mouth,' said Mrs Beauchamp with a crescendo of indignation. She added: '*Cherchez la femme!*'

'She's a friend of mine, and I know her very well.'

'It takes a woman to know another woman, Mr Eliot. When I looked into the room tonight, with the door happening to be open and hearing that poor man cry out, I saw what I expected to see.'

'What in God's name was that?'

'I saw that young woman, who's so nice and quiet when she wants to be with gentlemen like you, like a ravening beast seeking for whom she may devour.'

'What are you wanting to tell me?' I said. 'Do you mean that Mr Passant was trying to seduce her, or that she was encouraging him, or what?'

'Nice people talk about men seducing women,' Mrs Beauchamp remarked in an oozing, saccharine whisper. 'Nice people like you, Mr Eliot, can't believe that it's the other way round, it's not even six of one and half a dozen of the other; you should have seen what I saw when I was going up those stairs!'

'Perhaps I should.'

'No, you shouldn't, I should have kept your eyes away from that open door.'

'Now what was it?'

'It's only that I don't like to tell you, Mr Eliot.'

But Mrs Beauchamp could not hold back any longer.

'Because I saw that young woman, at least I suppose she'd call herself a young woman, and even from where I was I could see that she was crammed with the lust of the eye and the pride of life, I saw her standing up with her arms above her head, and offering herself with the light full on, ready to gobble up that poor man, and he was cowering away from her, and I could see he was shocked, he was shocked to the soul. If that door hadn't been open, Mr Eliot, I don't like to imagine what she would have been doing. As it was, it was a terrible thing for me to have to see.'

I supposed she must have seen something: what the scene had actually been, I could not even guess. Just for an instant, such was the mesmerism of her gothic imagination, I found myself wondering whether she was right – which, the next day in cold blood, I knew to be about as probable as that I myself should make proposals to Mrs Beauchamp on the landing outside her door. I could make no sense of it. It was conceivable that Vera had been slapping George's face, but though George was awkward he was not brash, he was slow moving until he was certain a woman wanted him. Anyway, they had somehow planted themselves in a moment of farce; and when I saw them in the office, Vera tweeded and discreet,

George bowing his great head over the papers, I should have liked to know the answer.

Constraint or no constraint, they had to work at close quarters, for we were occupied more intensely and secretly than before on a new project. It was in fact not so much a new project, as an administrator's forecast of what was to be done if the Barford experiment succeeded. It happened to be the kind of forecast for which the collaboration of George and me might have been designed. George was still out of comparison better than I was at ordering brute facts: within weeks, he had comprehended the industrial structures on which we had to calculate with an accuracy and speed that only two men I knew could have competed with, one of those two being Hector Rose. On the other hand, George lacked what I was strong in, a sense of the possible, the nose for what not to waste time thinking about. It was I who had to pick my way through conferences with Lufkin and other firms' equivalents of Lufkin.

When I had to negotiate with Lufkin, he was as reasonable as though our previous collision had never occurred. For my part I realised that I had been quite wrong in keeping him out: we should have gained three months if the first contract had gone to him. No one held it against me: it had been one of those decisions, correct on the surface, for which one gathered approval instead of blame. Yet I had not made a worse official mistake. It was clear enough now that, if the Barford project came off, we should be fools to keep Lufkin out again.

When, in the late spring, I delivered my report to Rose, he first expressed his usual mechanical enthusiasm:

'I must thank you and congratulate you, if you will allow me, my dear Lewis. I do thank you most warmly for doing this job for us.'

I was so used to his flourishes, taking the meaning out of words, that I was surprised when he said, in his rarer and drier tone:

'This looks about the best piece of work you've done here.'

'I think it may be,' I said.

'It really does suggest that we can see our way through the next three years without looking unnecessarily imbecile. It really does look as though we might possibly do ourselves some good.'

He was meaning high praise, the plan seemed to him realistic; and that was praise from a master.

Very pleased, I replied: 'I don't deserve much of the credit.'

'May I enquire who does?'

'Passant has done at least sixty per cent of the job and probably nearer seventy per cent.'

'My dear Lewis, that's very handsome of you, but I don't think you need indulge in quite such excessive magnanimity.'

He was smiling, polite, rigid, closed.

'It's perfectly true,' I said, and described what George had done. Patient as always, Rose heard me out.

'I am very much obliged to you for that interesting example of job analysis. And now, my dear man, you must allow others the pleasure of deciding just how much credit is due to you and how much to your no doubt valuable acquisition.'

Meanwhile George walked about with a chuff smile, complacent because he knew the merit of his work, complacent because he was certain it was recognised. For years he had endured being underestimated and, now that at last he was among his intellectual equals, he felt certain that he would get his due. At one time that impervious optimism had annoyed me, but now I found it touching, and I was determined to make Rose admit how good he was. For Rose, however antagonistic to George, would think it his duty to give him a fair deal.

Oblivious of all this, George went happily about, although, after his first weeks in London, he did not accompany me on reflective bachelor strolls at night. An absentminded, unfocused look would come into his eyes as we took our after-office drink and, like a sleep-walker, he would go out of the pub, leaving me to walk back to Pimlico alone.

Curiously enough, it was from Vera, wrapped in her own emotions, neither observant nor gossipy, that I received a hint. One evening in May, as she came in for the last letters of the day, she stared out of the window with what – it was quite untypical of her – looked like a simper.

'We don't seem to be seeing so much of Mr Passant, do we?' she said.

'Haven't you?'

'Of course not.' She flushed. She went on:

'Actually, there's a story going about that he has found someone who's keeping him busy.'

When she told me, it sounded both true and the last thing one would have expected. For the girl who was taking up George's time was a typist in another department, virginal, obstinate, and half his age; their exchanges seemed to consist of a prolonged argument, suitable for the question-and-answers of an old-fashioned women's magazine, about whether or not he was too old for her. Even to Vera, it seemed funny that George should be so reduced; but, so the story ran, he was captivated, he was behaving as though he were the girl's age instead of his own. No one would have thought he was a sensualist; he was only eager to persuade her to marry him. I remembered how he had tried to get married once before; I did not know for certain, but I believed that it was he, not the girl, who got frightened off.

'Isn't it amusing?' said Vera, with fellow-feeling, with a lick of malice. 'I say good luck to him!'

I was thinking, with a spectator's impatience, that she and George would have been well matched. She might be dense, or humourless, or self-deceiving, but George would have minded less than most men, and underneath it she was as strong as he was. Instead, she had found someone who it seemed could give her nothing, which was a singular triumph for the biological instinct. Now, to cap it all, George was doing the same. Yet she was totally committed, and so perhaps was he. Speculating about them both, I felt extreme curiosity, irritation, and a touch of envy.

CHAPTER XXXI

ANNOUNCEMENT IN A NEWSPAPER

INTO my dusty bedroom, where the morning light was reflected on the back wall, Mrs Beauchamp entered with the breakfast tray at times which tended to get later. Breakfast itself had reached an irreducible minimum, a small pot of tea and a biscuit.

'I do what I can, Mr Eliot,' said Mrs Beauchamp, not apologetically but with soft and soothing pride.

While she stood there, as though expecting congratulations, and then paddled about on the chance of more exposures of human wickedness, I picked up the newspaper. Each morning, gripped by an addiction I could not control, like one compelled to touch every pillarbox in the street, I had to run my eye down the column of Births, searching for the name of Hollis. After Gilbert's final piece of gossip, this habit had taken hold of me long before Margaret's child could possibly be born: and, each morning I did not find the name, I felt a superstitious relief and was ready to pander to Mrs Beauchamp.

One morning in May – we were waiting for the invasion, there was a headline on the outside of *The Times* – I was giving way to the addiction, the routine tic, scanning through the 'H's' before I opened the paper.

The name stood there. It stood there unfamiliar, as it might be in an alphabet like Russian, which I did not easily read and had to spell out. Margaret. A son.

'Anything interesting, Mr Eliot?' came Mrs Beauchamp's unctuous voice, as from the end of an immense room.

'Nothing special.'

'There never is, is there?'

'And old friend of mine has just had a child, that's all.'

'There was a time when I should have liked a little one, Mr Eliot, if I may put it like that. But then when I saw what they grew up into, I must say I thought I'd had a blessing in disguise.'

When I got rid of her, I read the notice meaninglessly time and time again, the paper still unopened. Despite my resolutions, I could not drive the thought down, the thought of seeing her. I wrote a note, in words that were no different from when I used to write to her, to say I had read the news.

I knew the wisdom of those who cut their losses: how often had I advised others so? Don't meet, don't write, don't so much as hear the name: come to terms, give your imagination to others, dismiss the one who has gone. That was what I had set myself, mainly for my own sake, perhaps with a relic of responsibility for her. It was not much help to remember it now; then at last I managed to tear the letter up.

Walking along the square, I was trying to domesticate the news. She would be very happy: even if she had not been happy without qualification before, which I did not wish to think of, this would make up for it. Maybe her children would become more important than her husband. That might have been so with me. Then as I thought of her, with detachment and almost with pleasure, the possessive anger broke through, as though my stomach had turned over and my throat stopped up. This child ought to have been mine.

I was trying to domesticate the news, to think of her gently as though we had known each other a long time before; she would be an over-careful mother, each mistake she made with the child she would take to heart; she did not believe so much in original endowment as I did, she believed that children were a bit more of a blank sheet; the responsibilities would weigh on her, would probably age her – but, with children, she would not think that her life was wasted.

As I thought of her gently, the anger stayed underneath.

With an attention more deliberate than before, I set myself to squeeze interest out of the people round me. It was then I really got to know the predicament of Vera and Norman. Towards the end of the summer, when the flying bombs stopped and we could talk in peace, they visited me together several times: and then Norman took to coming alone.

When I first saw them together, I thought that beside her he was insignificant. He was small, with a sallow, delicate face; he had been unfit for the Army and had stayed in his civil service job which, like Vera, he had entered at sixteen. He seemed to have nothing to say, although his expression was sensitive and fine; when I tried to lead him on, throwing out casts about books or films, I found he was as uncultivated as she. They went to dances, listened to a little music, walked in the country at weekends; they were each earning about £400 a year, which to them meant comfort, and their lives were oddly free from outside pressure. To me, remembering the friends in my young manhood, whose origins were similar to theirs, Vera's and Norman's whole existence, interests and hopes seemed out of comparison more tame.

Even Vera, who was brimful of more emotion than she seemed to understand, was chiefly preoccupied in Norman's company that night with the unrewarding problems of my domestic arrangements. Why should I live in such discomfort?

'It's not logical,' she said.

I told her that it would not make much difference to me.

'I'm not convinced about that,' she said.

I told her that it was sometimes a psychological help not to give a thought about how one lived.

Vera shook her head.

'You'd be just as independent in a proper service flat,' she said.

She had missed the point, but I saw Norman looking at me.

'You want someone to run the place for you,' said Vera. She added:

'Please don't think I'm saying anything against Mrs Beauchamp. She's as kind as anyone you'll ever get, I knew that the first time I saw her. Of course, she's the motherly type.'

I was thinking, Vera was as unperceptive about people as anyone I knew, when suddenly I was distracted by a smile from Norman, a smile which, loving and clear-eyed, reflected precisely the same thought. It was a smile of insight. Suddenly I took to him. I felt a sharper sympathy with him than I could with her.

I encouraged him to come and see me, although I soon knew what I was letting myself in for; most of the time it was hard work.

As I knew him better, I discovered that my impressions had been right, it was true that he had a natural understanding of others: more than that, he often made me feel that he was genuinely good. But that understanding and goodness seemed to be linked in him, as I had known them once or twice before, with a crippling infirmity. He was a neurotic; he was beset by anxiety, so that he could barely cope with his life.

The better I knew him, the more I liked him and the less I thought of his chances. By the end of the year, when he was repeating to me the stories that I knew by heart, I was coming to believe that he was too far gone.

One night in December, not long after Norman had left me, Mrs Beauchamp's head came ectoplasmically round the door. She had not made the instantaneous appearance with which she greeted the departure of a woman visitor; it must have been ten minutes since the door clicked to, but I was still sitting in my chair.

'You're looking tired, if you don't mind my saying so,' she whispered.

I felt it: to be any support to Norman, one needed to have one's patience completely under control, to show no nerves at all.

'I'll tell you what I'm going to do,' she said. 'I'm going to find you just a little something to eat, which I'd invite you to have upstairs, if I had got my place quite shipshape, which I haven't been able to.'

Although I was hungry, I regarded Mrs Beauchamp with qualified enthusiasm. These fits of good nature were spontaneous enough, and had no motive except to cheer one up – but in restrospect she admired them, realised how she had performed services right outside the contract, and so felt justified in lying in bed an hour later.

Mrs Beauchamp returned into my room with a tin of salmon, a loaf of bread, two plates, one fork and one knife.

'If you don't mind me cleaning the cutlery after you've had a little snack,' she said. 'Somehow I haven't been able to manage all the washing-up.'

Thus I got through my salmon, and then sat by while Mrs Beauchamp munched hers. Despite the shiny look of enjoyment on her face she felt obliged to remark:

'Of course, it isn't the same as fresh.'

Suddenly I was reminded of my mother, to whom fresh salmon was one of the emblems of the higher life for which she had so proudly longed.

'But I like to think of you having something tasty last thing at night. I hope you don't mind my saying so, but I do my best, Mr Eliot.'

She looked at me with an expression at the same time invulnerable, confident and ingratiating.

'Some do their best and *some don't*, Mr Eliot,' she whispered. 'That's why it's so unfair on people like you and me, if I may say so of both of us, who really set themselves out to do their best. Do you think anyone appreciates us? Do you think so?'

Mrs Beauchamp was becoming more excited: as she did so her expression stayed firm and impassive, but her eyes popped, and her cheeks became more shiny: her voice sank into a more insidious whisper.

I shook my head.

'When I think of the help that you try to give people – and so do I, if you don't mind me saying so, in my own way, without pushing myself forward – when I think of the help we give, and then what certain persons *do*! Sometimes I wonder if you ever let yourself realise what those people *do*, Mr Eliot.'

She went on whispering:

'I scarcely dare think of it.'

Her voice became still more hushed:

'If we looked out of that window, Mr Eliot, we could see the windows on the other side of the square. Have you ever thought what we should see *if we pulled the blinds*? It's terrible to think of. Sometimes I fancy what it would be like if I became invisible, like the man in the film, and had to go and stand in all the rooms in the square, one after another, so that I should be there in the corner and couldn't help seeing what people do.'

Mrs Beauchamp, day-dreaming of a voyeuse's paradise, seeping herself into invisibility, sat enormous in her pink satin, cheeks flaming and eyes dense.

'If I had to watch all that, Mr Eliot,' she said, 'I doubt if I should ever be the same again.'

I said that I was sure she would not be.

'Rather than do what some people do,' she said, 'I'd stay as I am for ever with my own little place upstairs, looking after myself as well as I can, and doing my best for my tenants and friends, if you don't mind me calling you that, Mr Eliot. People may laugh at me for doing my best, but they needn't think I mind. Some of them don't like me, you don't have to pretend, Mr Eliot, I'm not such a softy as I look and I tell you they don't like me. And I don't mind that either. If a person does her best it doesn't matter what people think of her. I expect they believe I'm lonely. But I am happier than they are, Mr Eliot, and they know it. No one's ever said – there's poor old Mrs Beauchamp, she wants someone to look after her, she's not fit to live by herself.'

It was quite true. No one had thought of her so.

'I shouldn't be very pleased if anyone did say that,' Mrs Beauchamp remarked in a whisper, but with ferocity.

Then affable, glutinous again, she said:

'What I say is, the important thing is to grow old with dignity. I know you will agree with me, Mr Eliot. Of course, when I come to the evening of my life, and I don't regard myself as quite there yet, if some decent good man had the idea that he and I might possibly join forces, then I don't say I should turn down the proposition without thinking it over very, very seriously.'

CHAPTER XXXII

OUTSIDE THE HOUSE

ON an evening in May, just after the German war had ended, Betty Vane called on me. I had seen little of her during the spring: once or twice she had rung up, but I had been busy with Vera or Norman or some other acquaintance; Betty, always ready to believe she was not wanted, had been put off. Yet she was one of the people I liked best and trusted most, and that evening when she came in, bustling and quick-footed, I told her that I had missed her.

'You've got enough on your hands without me,' she said.

It sounded ungracious. She had never been able to produce the easy word. She was looking at me, her eyes uncomfortable in her beaky face. She said curtly:

'Can you lend me fifty pounds?'

I was surprised, for a moment – because previously when she was hard-up I had pressed money on her and she would not take it. She was extravagant, whenever she had money she splashed it round: she was constantly harassed about it, she lived in a clutter of card debts, bills, pawnshops, bailiffs. Hers was, however, the poverty of someone used to being dunned for a hundred pounds when behind her there were trusts of thousands. She had invariably refused to borrow from me, or from anyone who had to earn his money. Why was she doing so now? Suddenly I realised. Bad at easy words, bad at taking favours, she was trying to repay what I had just told her: this was her way of saying that she in turn trusted me.

As she put my cheque into her bag, she said in the same curt, forbidding tone:

'Now you can give me some advice.'

'What is it?'

'It involves someone else.'

'You ought to know by now that I can keep quiet,' I said.

'Yes, I know that.'

She went on awkwardly:

'Well, a man seems to be getting fond of me.'

'Who is he?'

'I can't tell you.' She would say nothing about him, except that he was about my own age. Her explanation became so constrained as to be almost unintelligible – but now she was speaking of this man 'liking her', of how he wanted to 'settle down' with her. Every time she had confided in me before, it had been the other way round.

'What shall I do?' she asked me.

'Do I know him?'

'I can't tell you anything about him,' she replied.

'You're not giving me much to go on,' I told her.

'I'd like to tell you the whole story, but I can't,' she said, with the air of a little girl put on her honour.

I was thinking, a good many men were frightened of her, she was so sharp-eyed and suspicious, her self-distrust making her seem distrustful of others. But when she let herself depend on anyone her faith was blind.

'Do you love him?' I asked her.

Without hesitation, straight and confiding, she replied:

'No.'

'Do you respect him?' For her, no relation would be tolerable without it. This time she hesitated. At last she said:

'I think so.'

She added:

'He's a curious man.'

I looked at her. She smiled back, a little resentfully.

'On the face of it,' I said, 'I can't possibly say go ahead, can I? But you know more than I do.'

'I've not been exactly successful so far.'

'I just don't see what the advantages are. For you, I mean.'

For the first time that evening she gazed at me with affection.

'We're all getting on, you know. You're nearly forty, and don't you forget it. I was thirty-seven this March.'

'I don't think that's a good reason.'

'We haven't all got your patience.'

'I still don't think it's a good reason for you.'

She gave a cracking curse.

'I haven't got all that to look forward to,' she said.

She was so unsure of herself that she had to break in, before I could reply:

'Let's skip it. Let's go to a party.'

A common acquaintance had invited her, she wanted to take me. In the taxi, on the way to Chelsea, she was smiling with affection, the awkwardness had gone, the resented confidence; we might have just met, I might have been giving her a lift to a party, each of us pleasurably wondering whether anything would come of it. After all the years she had gone to parties, she still had the flush, the bright eye, the excited hope that something, someone, might turn up.

As soon as we arrived at the studio, I saw a man I knew; pushing into the corner of the room, he and I stood outside the crowd and he told me about a new book. While I was listening, I caught a voice from the window seat behind us. From the first words, I recognised it. It was R. S. Robinson's.

He was sitting with his back to me, his beautiful hair shining silver, his neck red. Listening to him was a woman of perhaps thirty, who looked intelligent, amiable and plain. It was soon clear that she had recently published a novel.

'I have to go back a long way to find a writer who opens the window of experience to me as you do,' he was saying. 'Not that you do it all the time. Sometimes you're rather tantalising, I must tell you. Sometimes you give me the sensation that you are opening a window but not running up the blinds. But at your best, in those first thirty pages – I have to go back a long way. Who do you think I have to go back to?'

'You're making too much of it,' came the woman's voice, abashed, well-bred.

'I have to go back a long way.' Robinson was speaking with his old authority, with the slightly hectoring note of one whose flattery is rejected and who has to double it: 'Beyond my dear Joyce – I'm not telling you that your achievement is equal to his, but I do say your vision is nearer to the springs of life. I have to go back beyond him. And beyond poor old Henry James. Certainly beyond George Eliot. They can say what they like, but she was heavy as porridge most of the time, and porridgy writers have to be much greater than she was. Those first pages of yours aren't porridgy at all, they're like one's first taste of first-class *pâté*. I have to go back a bit beyond her, why I don't mind going back to – you won't guess who—'

'Do tell me.'

'Mrs Henry Wood.'

Even then, flattering her for his own purposes, he could not resist that piece of *diablerie*, that elaborate let-down. She sounded a modest woman, but there was disappointment and mild protest in her voice: 'But she was nothing like so good as George Eliot.'

Robinson rapidly recovered himself.

'George Eliot had all the talent in the world, and not a particle of genius. Mrs Henry Wood had very little talent and just a tiny vestige of the real blessed thing. That's what people ought to have said about you, and believe me it's the most important thing that can be said about any writer. I should like to have the responsibility of making them say it about you. Does anyone realise it?'

'No one's ever told me.'

'I always say it takes an *entrepreneur* with a bit of his own genius to recognise a writer who has it too. That's why it's a providential occasion, you and I meeting here tonight. I should like to put over another piece of the real thing before I die. I'm absolutely sure I could do it for you.'

'What firm is yours, Mr Robinson?'

Robinson laughed.

'At present I can't be said to have a firm. I shall have to revive the one I used to have. Haven't you heard of R. S. Robinson?'

She looked embarrassed.

'Oh dear,' he said, with one of his bursts of hilarious honesty, 'if you'd been at a party like this twenty-five years ago and hadn't heard of me, I should have left you and gone to find someone interesting. But you will hear of R. S. Robinson's again. We're going to do things together, you and I. I assure you, we're bound to put each other on the map.'

Then I tapped him on the arm. He looked up to see who I was. With complete good humour he cried:

'Why, it's Lewis Eliot! Good evening to you, sir!'

I smiled at the young woman, but Robinson, sparkling with cunning, did not intend me to talk to her. Instead, he faced into the room, and said, either full of hilarity or putting on a splendid show of it:

'Is this a fair sample of the post-war spirit, should you say?'

I broke in:

'It's a long time since I met you last.'

Robinson was certain that I was threatening his latest plan, but he was not out-faced. He had not altered since the morning I recovered Sheila's money; his suit was shabby and frayed at the cuffs, but so were many prosperous men's after six years of war. He said to the young woman, with candour, with indomitable dignity:

'Mr Eliot was interested in my publishing scheme a few years ago. I'm sorry to say that nothing came of it then.'

'What have you been doing since?' I asked.

'Nothing much, sir, nothing very much.'

'What did you do in the war?'

'*Nothing at all.*' He was gleeful. He added:

'You're thinking that I was too old for them to get me. Of course I was, they couldn't have touched me. But I decided to offer my services, so I got a job in – (he gave me the name of an aircraft firm) – and they subsidised me for four years and *I did nothing at all.*'

The young woman was laughing: he took so much delight in having no conscience that she also felt delight. Just as Sheila used to.

'How did you spend your time?' she asked.

'I discovered how to be a *slow clerk.* Believe me, no one's applied real intelligence to the problem before. By the time I left, I could spin a reasonable hour's work out into at least two days. And that gave me time for serious things, that is, thinking out the programme you and I were talking about before Mr Eliot joined us.'

He grinned at me with malicious high spirits, superiority and contempt.

'I suppose you've been doing your best for your country, sir?' Just as I remembered him, he felt a match for any man alive.

I enquired:

'Have you got a job now?'

'Certainly not,' said Robinson.

I wondered if, with his bizarre frugality, he had saved money out of his wages at the factory. Then I spoke across him to his companion:

'I don't think we've been introduced, have we?'

Soon after I heard her name I left them, to Robinson's surprise and relief. I left them with Robinson's triumphant 'Good evening to you, sir' fluting across the room, and muttered to Betty that I was slipping away. Alone in that room, she knew that something had gone wrong for me; disappointed after the promise of the early evening, she could read in my face some inexplicable distress.

'I'm sorry,' she whispered.

She was right. I had been upset by the sound of the young woman's name. As soon as I heard it, I knew she was a cousin of Charles March's. She was likely, therefore, to be a woman of means, and in fact Robinson would not be pouring flattery over her if she were not. But that did not matter; it would be easy to pass word to Charles about Robinson; it was not for her sake that I left the party, went out into Glebe Place, turned down towards the Embankment, and, without realising it, towards the house I had lived in years before. I was not driven so because of anything that happened at that party; no, it was because, for the first time for years, my grief over Sheila had come back, as grinding as when, after her death, I went into our empty room.

At the first murmur of Robinson's voice, I had felt a presentiment; listening to what otherwise might have amused me, I had been rigid, nails against my palms, but still impervious, until, when I asked the young woman her name, the reply set loose a flood of the past. Yet I had only heard that name before in circumstances entirely undramatic, having nothing to do with Sheila or her death: perhaps Charles March had mentioned it in the days we saw each other most often, before either of us had married, walking about in London or at his father's country-house. That was all; but the flood that name set loose drove me down the dark turning of Cheyne Row towards the river.

Down Cheyne Row the windows were shining, from the pub at the Embankment corner voices hallooed; I was beset as though I were still married and was going through the back streets on my way home.

I was not seeing, nor even remembering: it was not her death that was possessing me: it was just that, walking quickly beside the bright houses, their windows open to the hot evening breeze, I had nothing but a sense of failure, loss, misery. The year before, when I received bad news, fresher and more sharply wounding, the news of Margaret's child, I could put a face on it, and make myself shove the sadness away. Now this older sadness overcame me; my stoicism would not answer. I felt as I had not done since I was eight years old, tears on my cheeks.

Soon I was standing outside the house, which, since I left it in the spring after Sheila died, I had not been near, which I had made détours not to see. Yet the sight dulled my pain, instead of sharpening it. One outer wall had been blasted down, so that, where Mrs Wilson used to have her sitting-room, willowherb was growing, and on the first floor a bath jutted nakedly against the cloud-dark sky. The light from an Embankment lamp fell on the garden-path, where grass had burst between the flags.

Gazing up at the house, I saw the windows boarded up. Among them I could pick out those of our bedroom and the room next door. In that room Sheila's body had lain. The thought scarcely touched me, I just looked up at the boards, without much feeling, sad but with a kind of hypnotised relief.

I did not stay there long. Slowly, under the plane trees, past the unpainted and sunblistered houses, I walked along the Embankment to my flat. The botanical gardens were odorous in the humid wind, and on the bridge the collar of lights was shivering. Once the thought struck me: had I come home? Was it the same home, from which I had not been able to escape? The lonely flat – how different was it from the house I had just stood outside?

CHAPTER XXXIII

PATHOLOGY OF SPECTATORS

During the rest of that year, I was on the edge of two dramas. The first was secret, known only by a handful of us, and was going to overshadow much of our lives; it was the result of those meetings of old Bevill's early in the war, of the intrigues of Lufkin and the science of men like my brother; it was the making of the atomic bomb. The second was public, open for three mornings to anyone who read newspapers, and important to not more than half a dozen people of whom, although I did not fully realise it till later, I was one.

Innocent, tossed about by blind chance, Norman Lacey, and through him Vera, lost their privacy that autumn – for Norman's father was tried at the Old Bailey. If he was guilty, the crime was a squalid one; but the after-effects of the trial ravaged those two, so that for a time I thought that Norman at least would not recover. In the end, she was strong enough to carry them both – for me the lesson was how poorly I myself behaved.

Norman and Vera asked help from me, help which would be embarrassing, and possibly a little damaging, for me to give. They looked to me to go into court with a piece of evidence which could do neither them, nor Norman's father, any practical good, and might do me some practical harm. It was evidence so trivial that no lawyer would have subpœnaed me to give it. All it did in effect was to show that I knew them well; clutching at any hope, they had a sort of faith that my name might protect them.

It was the kind of demand which, had it come from an acquaintance, I should have evaded with a clear conscience. I had taken some responsibility for these two; they thought I had given them intimacy, could I just shut it off when otherwise I had to accept the consequences?

As soon as I had smelt the danger ahead of them, I had wanted excuses to absent myself. It was a dilemma I did not like, any more than I liked my own feelings. I did what I had not done for years, and asked advice. I did not want worldly advice; I longed for Margaret's; indeed, one night I read through the Hollises in the London directory, wondering whether they might have returned to the town, knowing that I had a true reason for writing to her, knowing also that it was a pretext. At last I went with my trouble to George Passant.

A few months past, the young woman he had been pursuing with such adolescent ardour had closed their years of argument and gone back home. She had refused to marry him; she had refused to sleep with him; and George, comically frustrated for a man of passion, seemed to an observer to have got nothing out of it. But that was not what he thought. 'It's been a magnificent affair!' he cried, as though his gusto had mysteriously slipped into the wrong groove. As he grew older, he seemed to luxuriate more and more in his own oddity.

Nevertheless when on an autumn night we went into the Tothill Street pub and I confessed the story, he was surprisingly prosaic.

'It would be absolutely ridiculous for you to take the slightest risk,' he said.

I had told him my relations with Vera and Norman as accurately as I could. I also told him what I suspected Norman's father had been up to: it looked as though he had been blackmailing homosexuals. With George, however uproarious his own life was being, any secret was safe.

As he listened to me, he looked concerned. It occurred to me that he took pride in my public reputation. He did not like to see me rushing into self-injury as he might have done himself: he had always had a streak of unpredictable prudence: that evening, he was speaking as sensibly as Hector Rose.

'If you could make any effective difference to the old man's [Lacey's] chance of getting off, then we might have to think again,' said George, 'though I warn you I should be prepared to make a case against that too. But that question doesn't arise, and there is obviously only one reasonable course of action.'

George ordered pints of beer, facing me with his aggressive optimism, as though the sane must triumph.

'I'm not so sure,' I said.

'Then you're even more incapable of reason that I ever suspected.'

'They'll feel deserted,' I said. 'Especially the young man. It may do him a certain amount of harm.'

'I'm afraid,' said George, 'I can't take into account every personal consequence of every action. Particularly as the poor chap's going to have such harm done him anyway that I can't believe your demonstrating a little common sense would matter a button in the general catastrophe.'

'There's something in that,' I replied.

'I'm glad you're showing signs of recognition.'

'But I took them both up,' I said. 'It's not so good to amuse myself with them when they're not asking anything – and then not to stand by them now.'

'I can't admit that they've got the slightest claim on you.' George's voice rose to an angry shout. He pulled down his waistcoat and, his tone still simmering, addressed me with a curious formality.

'It's some considerable time since I have spoken to you on these matters. I should like to make it clear that everyone who has had your friendship has had the best of the bargain. I am restricting myself to talking of your friendships, I had better emphasise that. With some of your women, I couldn't give you such a testimonial. So far as I can make out, you treated Margaret Davidson badly and stupidly. I shouldn't be surprised if the same weren't true of Betty Vane and others. I expect you ought to reproach yourself over some of those.'

I was thinking, George was not so inattentive as he seemed.

'But I don't admit that anyone alive has any right to reproach you about your friendships. I should like to see anyone contradict me on that point,' said George, still sounding angry, as though he were making a furious debating speech. But his face was open and heavy with affection. 'I can work it out, I might remind you that I can work it out as well as anyone in London, exactly what you've given to those two. You've been available to them whenever they've wanted you, haven't you?'

'Yes.'

'You've never protected yourself, have you? You've let them come to you when you've been tired and ill?'

'Sometimes.'

'You've let them take precedence over things you enjoy. You've kept away from smart parties because of them, I should be surprised very much if you haven't.'

I smiled to myself. Even now, George kept a glittering image of 'smart parties' and of the allure they must have for me. Yet he was exerting his whole force, he was speaking with a thumping sweetness.

'I know what you've given them. A good many of us can tell from personal experience, and don't forget my experience of you goes back further than the others. Sometimes I've thought that you haven't the faintest idea of how people appreciate what you've done for them. I should like to inform you that you are known to be a preposterously unselfish friend. I have the best of reasons for knowing it.'

George was a human brother. He fought with his brother men, he never wanted to be above the battle. He did not understand the temptation, so insidious, often so satisfying to men like me, of playing God: of giving so much and no more: of being considerate, sometimes kind, but making that considerateness into a curtain with which to shut off the secret self I could not bear to give away. Some of what he said was true: but that was because, in most of the outward shows of temperament, what one loses on the swings one gains on the roundabouts. Because I had been so tempted to make myself into a looker-on, I asked little of those I was with. I was good-natured, sometimes at a cost to myself, though not at a fundamental cost. I had become unusually patient. I was fairly tolerant by temperament, and the curve of my own experience made me more so. Judged by the ordinary human standards, I was interested and reliable. All that, I had gained – it was what George saw, and it was not quite negligible – by non-participation. But what George did not see was that I was being left with a vacuum inside me instead of a brother's heart.

In the end, I gave the evidence. I tried to accept my responsibility to Vera and Norman as though I felt it. So far as the gossip reached me, I did not lose much; although I did not recognise it for months to come, I gained something.

That winter, sitting alone in my room, I thought often of myself as I had done on the night of Munich; but I had learned more of myself now, and disliked it more. I could not help seeing what had gone wrong with me and Margaret, and where the profound fault lay. It could have seemed the legacy that Sheila had left me: that was an excuse; the truth was meaner, deeper, and without any gloss at all. It was the truth that showed itself in my escape into looking-on. I knew now how much there was wrong with those who became spectators. Mr Knight was a spectator of the world of affairs, because he was too proud and diffident to match himself against other men: and I could see how his pride-and-diffidence was as petty as vanity, he would not match himself because they might see him fail. Superficially, unlike Mr Knight, I was not vain: but in my deepest relations, it was the same with me.

There was another comparison distinctly less congenial. There was someone else who looked on, and felt lifted above ordinary mortals as she did so. Mrs Beauchamp – yes, we had something in common. Yes, Mr Knight and she and I were members of the same family.

Lonely in that first winter of peace, I thought of how joyful Margaret and I had been at first, and how towards the end I had gone to her, the taxi racketing in the steely light, guilt beating on me like rain upon the window. I could understand more of it now. First I had tried to make her into a dream image, a kind of anti-Sheila: then I had transformed her into Sheila come again: I had been afraid to see her as she was, just herself, someone whose spirit was as strong as mine.

Although I did not know it, I was gaining something.

Just as, when Margaret at last admitted defeat about our relation, I had seen in her a secret planner devising (almost unknown to herself) a way out – so now, myself defeated, disliking what I had come to, the secret planner began to work in me.

Often, when a branch of one's life has withered, it is others who first see the sap rise again. One is unconscious of a new start until it is already made: or sometimes, in the same instant, one knows and does not know. Perhaps when, believing myself preoccupied over Vera and Norman, I furled through the telephone directory for Margaret's address, I was already committing myself to a plan which might re-shape my life; perhaps, months earlier, when I stood outside the house of my first marriage and thought I had no hope of any other home, hope was being born.

Perhaps I knew and did not know. But, in fact, the first signs of the secret planner which I observed, as though I were watching an intruder and a somewhat tiresome one, were a little absurd. For all of a sudden I became discontented with my flat at Mrs Beauchamp's. Instead of being able to put up with anything, I could scarcely wait to make a change. Restlessly, quite unlike myself, I called on agents, inspected half a dozen flats in an afternoon, and took one before night. It was on the north side of Hyde Park, opposite the Albion Gate, and too large for me, with three bedrooms and two sitting-rooms, but I told myself that I liked the view over the seething trees, over the Bayswater Road, along which I used to walk on my way to Margaret.

That night, for the first time, I was in search of Mrs Beauchamp and not she of me. I rapped on her door, rattled the letter-box, called her name, but, although I did not believe that she was out, got no reply. So I left a note and, feeling that her technique was well proved and that I might pay her a last compliment by copying it, sat with the door open listening for her steps. Even then I did not hear her until the scuffle of her slippers was just outside my door.

'Mr Eliot, I found your little letter saying that you wanted to speak to me,' she whispered.

I asked if she had been out, knowing for certain that she could not have been.

'As a matter of fact, I haven't, Mr Eliot,' she said. 'To tell you the honest truth, I've been getting so worried about the catering that I just can't sleep until daylight, and so I have been allowing myself a little doze before I have to set about my bit of an evening meal.'

Whatever she had been doing, I believed it was not that. Her expression was confident, impenetrable, wide-awake. 'Catering' meant getting my morning tea, and her remark was a first move towards stopping it.

'I'm sorry to drag you down,' I said.

'It's part of my duty,' she replied.

'I thought I ought to tell you at once,' I said, 'that I shall have to leave you soon.'

'I'm very sorry to hear you say that, Mr Eliot.' She gazed at me with a firm glance, disapproving, almost inimical, but also a little pitying.

'I shall be sorry to go.'

I said it as a civility: oddly, Mrs Beauchamp compelled civility, it was impossible to suggest to her what I thought of her and her house.

'I shall be sorry to go,' I repeated. Then I felt a pang of genuine, ridiculous, irrational regret.

'No one has to live where they don't want to, Mr Eliot.'

Her expression showed no diminution of confidence. If I felt a pang of sadness, she had never appeared less sad. Others might find any parting a little death, but not Mrs Beauchamp.

'If you don't mind me asking, after the little talks we've had when you've been lonely and I was trying to cheer you up,' her tone was soft as ever, perhaps a shade less smooth, 'but if you don't mind me asking, I was wondering if you intended to get married again?'

'I haven't been thinking of it.'

'Well, then, that's something, and, without pushing in where I'm not welcome, that's the wisest thing you've said tonight or for many a long night, Mr Eliot. And I hope you'll remember me if any woman ever gets you in her clutches and you can't see a glimpse of the open door. *Never notice their tears*, Mr Eliot.'

After that exhortation, Mrs Beauchamp said briskly: 'Perhaps we ought to have a little chat about the catering, Mr Eliot, because you'll be here another two or three weeks, I suppose.'

Most people, on being given notice, served their time out with a good grace, I was thinking: in fact, they were more obliging in that last fortnight than ever before. But Mrs Beauchamp's was a tough nature. She had decided that making my morning tea was too much for her; the fact that I was leaving soon did not weaken her. In a good-natured whisper she told me that I should get a nice breakfast, much nicer than she had been able to do for me, over in Dolphin Square. She looked at me with a sly, unctuous smile.

'Well, Mr Eliot, I'm sure you'll live at better addresses than this, if I may say so. But, though I suppose I'm not the right person to tell you and it doesn't come too well from me, I just can't help putting it to you, that a lot of water will have to flow under the bridges, before you find a place where you'll be as much at home.'

CHAPTER XXXIV

CONFIDENTIAL OFFER IN REVERSE

WHEN I decided to take up again with Gilbert Cooke, I knew what I was doing. Or at least I thought I did. I had left open no other line of communication with Margaret; he would have news of her; I had to hear it. Beyond that, my foresight was cut off.

So I telephoned to his new office late on a May afternoon. Was he free that night? His voice was stiff. No, he was not certain. Yes, he could find time for a quick meal. Soon we were walking together across St James's Park; under the petrol-smell of a London summer there was another, mixed from the grass and the wallflowers, sharpened by the rain. It brought back walking in London as a student, the smell of the park promising and denying, taunting to a young man still chaste.

Massive beside me, his light feet scuffing the ground, Gilbert was saying little: unless I asked a question, his lips were squashed together under the beaky nose. I had forgotten that he was proud. He was not prepared to be dropped and then welcomed back. I had forgotten also that he was subtle and suspicious.

He did not believe that I suddenly wanted him for his own sake. He guessed that I was after something, perhaps he had an inkling of what it was. He was determined not to let me have it.

Yet he could not resist letting me know that he still had his ear to the ground. As we climbed the Duke of York's Steps, he said, out of the air:

'How's the new flat?'

648

I said – irked that he could still surprise me – all right.

'Is it going to work?'

'I think so.'

'It'll be all right if the old lady gets better or worse. Because if she gets worse the agents will have to put someone else in. But it's going to be fatal if she stays moderately ill.'

His information was accurate. Mine was one of four service flats, looked after by a manageress; within the last fortnight, she had gone to bed with a heart-attack.

'It's pretty adequate,' I said, as though apologising for myself.

'I don't know about that,' said Gilbert.

Like other apolaustic men, he had the knack of making one's living arrangements sound pitiful. I felt obliged to defend mine.

'It's better anyway,' Gilbert conceded. 'I grant you that, it's better.'

Although he had dropped into speaking of my physical comforts with his old concern, he would not volunteer a word about my common friends, anyone I might be interested in, let alone Margaret. The May night, the petrol-smell, the aphrodisiac smell: as we walked he talked more, but it was putting-off, impersonal talk, deliberately opaque.

As I watched him, stretched out in a leather armchair at my club, just as he had been the night he offered to stand down over Margaret, his body was relaxed but his eyes shone, unsoftened, revengeful. There was nothing for me but to be patient. I set myself to speak as easily as when he was working for me. How was he? What was happening to him? What was he planning for his future? He did not mind answering. It gave him a pleasure edged with malice to go on elaborating about his future, knowing that I was getting nowhere near my object. But also, I thought, he was in a difficulty and glad of an opinion. Now that the war was over, he could not settle what to do. Perhaps the civil service would keep him; but, if he had the choice, he would prefer to return to Lufkin.

'The trouble is,' said Gilbert, 'I don't believe for a second he'll have me.'

'Why shouldn't he?'

'What about the bit of fun-and-games when I slipped one under his ribs?'

'It was fair enough.'

'Paul Lufkin has his own idea on what's fair. Opposing him isn't included.'

'I got in his way as much as you did,' I said, 'and I'm on definitely good terms with him now.'

'What's that in aid of?' said Gilbert. He added:

'The old thug will never have me back. I wish to God he would.'

'Why do you want to go back so much?'

He said something about money, he said that he might be marrying at last. At that moment he was speaking cordially, even intimately, his face flushed in the clubroom half-light; I believed that the mention of marriage was not a blind, I even wondered (he kept all clues from me) who the woman might be.

I said: 'As I told you a minute ago, I get on well with Paul Lufkin nowadays. Better than I used to, if it comes to that. Will you let me feel out the ground about you?'

'Why should you?' His glance was suspicious, and at the same time hopeful.

'Why not?'

He cupped his hands round the tankard on the table.

'Well,' he said, with a hesitating, unwilling pleasure, 'if it's not too much of an infliction, I should be damned relieved if you would.'

The room, not yet lit up, was cool as a church in the summer evening, but Gilbert glowed in his chair: other men had gone up to dinner and we were left alone. He glowed, he swallowed another pint of beer, in the chilly room he seemed to be exuding warmth; but that was all he gave out. Although he had accepted my offer, he was returning nothing.

I was thinking: I should have to play his game, and bring in her name myself. It meant a bit of humiliation, but that did not matter; what did matter was that he would see too much. It was a risk I ought not to take. As I bought myself a drink, I asked:

'By the way, have you seen Margaret lately?'

'Now and again.'

'How is she?'

'Is there anything wrong with her?' His eyes were sparkling.

'How should I know?' I replied evenly.

'Isn't she much as you'd expect?'

'I've quite lost touch.'

'Oh.' He was briskly conversational. 'Of course, I've kept my eye on all of them, I suppose I see them once every two months, or something like that.' He was spinning it out. He told me, what I knew from the newspapers, that Margaret's mother had died a year before. He went on to say, with an air of enthusiasm and good-fellowship:

'Of course, I've seen quite a lot of Helen and her husband. You did meet him, didn't you? He's a decent bird—'

'Yes, I met him,' I said. 'When did you see Margaret last?'

'It can't have been very long ago.'

'How was she?'

'I didn't notice much change.'

'Was the child all right?'

'I think so.'

I broke out:

'Is she happy?'

'Why shouldn't she be?' Gilbert asked affably. 'I should have thought she had done as well as most of us. Of course you can't tell, can you, unless you've known someone better than I ever did Margaret?'

He knew, of course, how my question had been wrung out of me. He had been waiting for something like it: I might as well have confided straight out that I still loved her. But he was refusing to help. His mouth was smiling obstinately and his eyes, merry and malicious, taunted me.

CHAPTER XXXV

SIMPLE QUESTION ON TOP OF A BUS

I HAD to honour my offer to Gilbert, and I arranged to call on Paul Lufkin. When I arrived at the Millbank office, where in the past he had kept me waiting so many stretches of hours and from which I used to walk home to Sheila, he was hearty. He was so hearty that I felt the curious embarrassment which comes from the spectacle of an austere man behaving out of character.

Some of his retinue were waiting in the ante-room but I was swept in out of turn, and Lufkin actually slapped me on the back (he disliked physical contact with other males) and pushed out the distinguished visitors' chair. Now that I was, in his eyes, an independent success, a power in my own right though still minor compared to him, he gave me the appropriate treatment. The interesting thing was, he also truly liked me more. He knew that I was staying in Rose's department, not as a full-time established civil servant, but on my own terms. Perversely, the independence which writing had begun to win for me made Rose and his colleagues eager to give me jobs and even honours. Or perhaps that thought was not as fair as Rose himself was being: he had scored up mistakes (such as George Passant) against me: he still did not really like me, but he had decided both that I was useful and that I ought to have what to him seemed proper rewards.

Lufkin said: 'Well, old chap, sit down and make yourself comfortable.'

He was sitting at his own desk, showing less effects of the last years than any of us, his handsome skull face unravaged, his figure still as bony as an adolescent's.

'Believe it or not,' he went on, 'I was thinking of asking you to come to one of my little dinner parties.

'We must fix it,' he said, still acting his impersonation of heartiness. 'We've had some pretty jolly parties in our time, haven't we?'

I responded.

'There's a secret I was going to tell you. But now you've given me the pleasure of a visit' – said Lufkin with an entirely unfamiliar politeness – 'I needn't wait, I may as well tell you now.'

I realised that he was delighted to have me sitting there. He wanted someone to talk to.

'As a matter of fact,' he said, 'these people want to send me to the Lords.'

'These people' were the first post-war Labour government, and at first hearing it sounded odd that they should want to give Lufkin a peerage. But although he was one of the most eminent industrialists of his day, he had, with his usual long-sightedness, kept a foot in the other camp. He had never been inside the orthodox Conservative party: he had deliberately put some bets on the other side, and since 1940 that policy had been paying off.

In private his politics were the collectivist politics of a supreme manager, superimposed on – and to everyone but himself irreconcilable with – a basis of old-fashioned liberalism.

'Shall you go?'

'I don't see any good reason for turning them down. To tell you the honest truth, I think I should rather like it.'

'Your colleagues won't.'

I meant what he must have thought of, that his fellow-bosses would regard him as a traitor for taking titles from the enemy.

'Oh, that will be a nine-days wonder. If I'm any use to them, they'll still want me. And the minute I'm not any use they'll kick me, whether I've got a coronet or not.'

He gave a savage, creaking chuckle.

'Most of them would give their eyes for one, anyway. The main advantage about these tinpot honours – which I still think it's time we got rid of –' he put in, getting it both ways, as so often, 'isn't the pleasure they cause to the chaps who get them: it's the pain they cause to the chaps who don't.'

He was very happy, and I congratulated him. I was pleased: he was as able in his own line as anyone I knew, in the world's eye he had gone the furthest, and I had an inexplicable liking for him.

I enquired what title he would choose.

'Yes, that's the rub,' said Lufkin.

'Haven't you settled it?'

'I suppose it will have to be the Baron Lufkin of somewhere or other. Lord Lufkin. It's a damned awful name, but I don't see how I can hide it. It might be different if I believed in all this flummery. It would have been rather fun to have a decent-sounding name.'

'Now's your chance,' I teased him, but he snapped:

'No. We're too late for that. It's no use rich merchants putting on fancy dress. It's damned well got to be Lord Lufkin.'

He had the shamefaced, almost lubricious, grin of a man caught in a bout of day-dreaming. He had been writing down names on his blotter: Bury St Edmunds was his birthplace, how would Lord St Edmunds look? Thurlow, Belchamp, Lavenham, Cavendish, Clare, the villages he knew as a boy: with his submerged romanticism, he wanted to take a title from them. He read them out to me.

'Pretty names,' he said, inarticulate as ever. That was all the indication he could emit that they were his Tansonville, his Méséglise, his Combray.

'Why not have one?' Just for once I wanted him to indulge himself.

'It's out of the question,' he said bleakly.

I thought he was in a good mood for my mission. I said I had a favour to ask him.

'Go ahead.'

'I should like to talk to you about Gilbert Cooke.'

'I shouldn't.' Instantaneously the gracious manner – finger-tips together, Lufkin obliging a friend – had broken up. All at once he was gritty with anger.

As though not noticing him, I tried to put my case: Cooke had done well in the civil service, he was highly thought of by Hector Rose and the rest—

'I don't think we need waste much time on this,' Lufkin interrupted. 'You mean, you're asking me to give Cooke his job back?'

'I wanted you to hear—'

'That's what it boils down to, isn't it?'

I nodded.

'Well, my answer is short and simple. I wouldn't pay Cooke in washers.'

It was no use. Implacable, tied up in his anger, as rude as I had seen him, he cut me short.

When I reported the answer to Gilbert, he said:

'That's burnt it.' His face flushed, he went on:

'I never ought to have let him get the smallest blasted bleat from my direction, I never ought to have let you go near the man. There it is!

'Well,' he said defiantly, 'I'd better make sure that the chaps here want me. I've always said that in business you've either got to be a tycoon or a born slave, and damn it, I'm not either. I once told P.L. that.'

'What did he say?'

'Offered me a three-year contract.'

On his disappointment Gilbert put a dashing face; when he turned it towards me it was still pursed with comradely malignance. I fancied that, whether I brought him good news or bad from Lufkin, he would not have relented. He had so often relished letting slip a piece of gossip, but he was relishing even more holding on to one.

Before I could search for another link with Margaret there happened what at the time seemed a wild coincidence, a thousands-to-one-against chance. One Saturday morning, thinking nothing of it, I was rung up by old Bevill, who, after a period of what he himself described as 'the wilderness', had returned to Whitehall as chairman of the atomic energy project. He was just off to the country for the weekend, he said: he had a 'little job' he wanted to 'unload' on to me: would I mind going with him as far as Charing Cross?

In the circumstances, I thought he might have risen to a taxi: but no, Bevill stood at the bus stop, briefcase in hand, bowler hat on head, getting a modest pleasure out of his unpretentiousness. At last we mounted a bus, the top deck of which was empty, so that Bevill, instead of waiting until the platform at Charing Cross, was able to confide.

'I'm being chased, Lewis,' he said, looking over his shoulder to make sure no one was coming up, and somehow giving the impression that he was really on the run.

'Who by?'

'People who always know better than anyone else,' the old man replied. 'I don't know about you, Lewis, but I don't like people who're always positive you're wrong and they're right. Particularly intellectuals, as I believe they're called nowadays, or else have the impertinence to call themselves. The nigger in the woodpile is, they can make a hell of a lot of noise.'

'What do they want?'

'Do you remember that fellow Sawbridge?' The question was rhetorical; old Bevill, my brother and the Barford scientists, Hector Rose and I were not likely to forget Sawbridge, who had not long since been sent to jail for espionage.

The bus in front of us disappeared out of Whitehall with a swishing scarlet flash: we were stopped at the traffic lights, and Bevill stared up at Nelson's statue.

'Now that chap up there, he was a different kettle of fish from Sawbridge. You can't make me believe he would have betrayed his country.' In action, the old man could be as capable and cynical as most men: in speech he could be just as banal.

'You can't make me believe he would have had any use for intellectuals,' Bevill went on darkly. 'Kicked them in the pants, that's what he would have done.'

As we curved round Trafalgar Square, Bevill told me that some people unspecified were asking 'silly questions' about the trials of the atomic spies: why had they all pleaded guilty, why were the prison terms so long?

'Long,' said Bevill. 'If you ask me, they were lucky to get away with their necks.

'But I tell you, Lewis,' he went on, more like his patient political self, 'some people are asking questions, all in the name of civil liberties, if you please, and we don't want any more questions than we can help because of the effect on our friends over the other side. And so it may be a case where a bit of private conversation can save a lot of public fuss, even if it does seem like eating humble-pie.'

He gave a furtive grin, and said:

'That's where you come in, my lad.'

'You want me to talk to them?'

'No, Lewis, I want you to listen to them. Listening never did any of us any harm, and talking usually does,' said Bevill, in one of his Polonian asides. 'Someone's got to listen to one of those fellows, and you're the man for the job.

'You see,' said Bevill, staring uncomplainingly down at a traffic block, 'they might trust you, which they'd never begin to do with Rose or me. They'd never get it out of their heads that I was an old diehard who didn't understand what they were talking about and didn't care a kipper for what was bothering them. And I'm not sure,' said Bevill, with his customary realism and humility, 'I'm not sure that they'd be far wrong.'

'Who is it,' I asked, marking down a tiresome, tricky, but not important date for the following week, 'that you want me to see?'

'One of those fellows who write about pictures,' Bevill replied, pointing intelligently at the National Gallery. 'His name is Austin Davidson. I expect you've heard of him.'

'Yes, I have.'

'Somehow he gave the impression, or someone else did, that he knew you. Do you know the fellow, Lewis?'

'I've never met him.'

'I suppose he's one of those chaps who makes a painter's reputation and then gets his share of the takings when the prices go up,' said Bevill, with a simple contempt that he would not have thought of applying to a politician or even a businessman. But I was not paying attention to that accusation, which was about the last that, from Davidson's eminence, he could ever have imagined being uttered against himself, casually but in cold blood. Instead, staring down at the pavement artist in front of the Gallery, hearing old Bevill bring out the name of Margaret's father, I was full of an instantaneous warmth, as though I were completely relaxed and could count, so delectably sharp were they, the leaves of grass on the verges down below.

'Are you positive you haven't met the chap?' Bevill was enquiring.

'Quite.'

'Well, I got the impression, if I'm not muddling things, that he gave me to understand, or he may have said so to Rose, that you'd be very acceptable as someone to talk to. And that suggests to me that you'd be able to keep those fellows from making any more fuss.'

The bus started, and Bevill was peering through the window, trying to see the clock on Charing Cross.

'I needn't tell you,' he said cheerfully, 'not to tell them anything they oughtn't to know.'

CHAPTER XXXVI

READING-LAMP ALIGHT IN A PEACEFUL ROOM

HEARING that Davidson was to be given a private explanation, George Passant stormed with fury.

'If one of my relations,' he cursed, 'had been uncomfortable about the Sawbridge case or any other blasted case, are you going to tell me that

that old sunket Bevill would have detailed a high civil servant to give them an interview? But this country doesn't use the same rules if you come from where I did instead of bloody Bloomsbury.'.

It was a long time since I had heard George explode with the radical fervour of his youth.

'I suppose,' he said, 'you don't feel inclined to tell this man there's no reason on God's earth why he should get special treatment.'

I said no.

'Your proper answer to these people,' George cried, 'when they come begging favours, is Doctor Johnson's to Lord Chesterfield.'

I was not sure what obscure grievance George was hugging on my behalf.

'Bloody Bloomsbury': George's swearwords crackled out with 'Bloomsbury' after each one. George's political passions were still rooted in the East Anglican earth, where his cousins were farm labourers: like most rooted radicals, he distrusted upper-class ones, he felt they were less solid men than reactionaries such as old Bevill.

Then he simmered down and said, with a bashful friendliness: 'Well, there's one thing, I'm glad this didn't happen when you were still thinking about Margaret. It would have been a bit embarrassing.' He added comfortably: 'That's all over and done with, at any rate.'

Two days later, not waiting for his name to be called out, Davidson walked, head bent, across the floor of my office. He was not looking at me or Vera Allen or anyone or anything: he was so shy that he would not glance up, or go through any formula of introduction.

As he sat in the armchair I could see his grey hair, of which a quiff fell over his forehead, but not his face. He was wearing an old brown suit, and his shirt-sleeves were so long that they covered half his hands; but, among that untidiness, I noticed that the shirt was silk. He said, without any preamble at all, self-conscious and brusque:

'You used to be a lawyer, didn't you?'

I said yes.

'How good were you?'

'I should never,' I replied, 'have been anything like first-class.'

'Why not?'

Despite his awkwardness, he was a man to whom one did not want to give a modest, padded, hypocritical answer.

'It's the sort of career,' I said, 'where you've got to think of nothing else, and I couldn't manage it.'

He nodded, and then, for an instant looked up. My first impression of his face was how young it was. At that time he was in his middle fifties, but his skin, under layers of sunburn, was scarcely lined – except that his neck had the roughness of an ageing man's. My second impression was of a curious kind of beauty. Each of his daughters had inherited his fine bones; but Davidson's face, at the same time delicate and sculptured, had an abstract beauty which theirs missed. His eyes, quite unlike Margaret's, which were transparent and light, shone heavily – pigmented, deep sepia brown, opaque as a bird's.

As he looked up, his face broke into a grin.

'That's not entirely to your discredit,' he said. Soon he was looking at his knees, again, and saying: 'You're said to know about this Sawbridge business, is that true?'

'Yes.'

'You really do know about it, you haven't just seen the papers?'

I began: 'I was present when he was first appointed—' and again Davidson gave an evanescent grin.

'That sounds good enough. No wonder you've got your reputation as a picker. It would be simplest if you told me about it from there.'

So I told the story, from the time Sawbridge entered Barford after three years' research in an Oxford laboratory: the first suspicion that he was passing information to a Russian agent, as far back as 1944: the thicker suspicion, a year later: the interrogation, in which my brother, who had been his scientific leader, took a part: his confession, arrest and trial.

All the time I was speaking Davidson did not stir. His head was bent down, I was addressing myself to his grey hair, he moved so little that he might not have heard at all, and when I finished he remained immobile.

At last he said: 'As an expositor, with Maynard Keynes marked at 100, your score is about 75. No, considering the toughness of the material, I put you up to 79.' After that surprising evaluation he went on:

'But none of what you tell me is satisfactory – is it? – unless I can get answers to three questions.'

'What are they?'

'To begin with, is this young man really guilty? I don't mean anything fancy, I just mean, did he perform the actions he was charged with?'

'I have no doubt about that.'

'Why haven't you any doubt? I know he confessed, but I should have thought the one thing we've learned in the last ten years is that in suitable circumstances almost anyone can confess to almost anything.'

'I hadn't any doubt long before he confessed.'

'You had some other evidence?'

He looked up, his face troubled, stern, and suspicious.

'Yes.'

'What was it?'

'It was intelligence information. I'm not free to tell you more than that.'

'That doesn't sound specially reassuring.'

'Look—' I started, stumbled over his name and finally said uneasily 'Mr Davidson', as though I were going to my first dinner party and was not sure which fork to use. It was not that he was older; it was not that he was a man of liberal principle, disapproving of me; it was simply that I had loved his daughter, and some odd atavistic sense would not let me address him unceremoniously by his name.

When I had got over my stuttering I told him that most intelligence secrets were nonsense, but that some weren't: some ways of collecting information any government had to keep tight, so long as we had governments at all: this was a case in point.

'Isn't that extremely convenient?' said Davidson.

'It must seem so,' I said. 'Nevertheless it's true.'

'You're certain of that?'

'Yes,' I said.

Again he looked at me. As though satisfied, he said:

'Accepting that, then, I come straight on to the next question. Why did he plead guilty? If he hadn't, from what you've just said he'd have had you all in difficulties—'

I agreed.

'Then why did he?'

'I've often wondered,' I said, 'and I've got no explanation at all.'

'What I want to be convinced of,' said Austin Davidson, 'is that there were no unfair threats – or unfair inducements as far as that goes – before he was tried.'

Once more I did not resent the words, they were too impersonal for that. Instead of replying with official palaver, I was searching for the literal truth. I said that, after Sawbridge was arrested, my firsthand knowledge ended but I thought it very unlikely that anything unfair had been done.

'Why do you think that?'

'I've seen him since, in prison. And if there had been anything of the sort, I can't imagine why he shouldn't complain. It isn't as though he's been converted. He's still a communist. If he had anything to complain of, I don't think he'd be excessively considerate about our feelings.'

'That's a genuine point,' said Davidson. I could feel he was believing me, as he continued:

'Well, I've only one more question. Fourteen years seemed to most of us a savage sentence. Was there any influence from government or your official people to suggest that he ought to be made an example of?'

'On that,' I replied, 'I know no more than you do.'

'I should like to know what you think.'

'I should be astonished if there were anything said directly,' I said. 'The most that can have happened is that judges, like all the people round them, are affected by a climate of thought.'

Staying very still, Davidson did not speak for some time, until, throwing back his forelock like a boy, he said: 'Well, I don't think there's any more you can tell me, and I'm glad to have found someone who could speak straight.'

He continued: 'So on the whole you are happy about the Sawbridge business, are you?'

He might have meant it as a formal ending, but I was suddenly provoked. I had not enjoyed defending authority: but I was also irked by the arrogance of men of decent feeling like Davidson, who had had the means to cultivate their decent feelings without the social interest or realism to imagine where they led. I spoke sharply, not like an official. I finished up:

'You ought not to think that I like what we've done. Or a good many other things we're having to do. People of my sort have only two choices in this situation, one is to keep outside and let others do the dirty work, the other is to stay inside and try to keep off the worst horrors and know all the time that we shan't come out with clean hands. Neither way is very good for one, and if I had a son I should advise him to do what you did, and choose a luckier time and place to be born.'

It was a long time since I heard my own temper running loose. Davidson was looking at me with a friendly and companionable frown.

'Yes,' he remarked, 'my daughter said you must be feeling something like that.

'I asked her about you,' he went on casually, and added, with a simplicity that was at the same time arrogant and pure: 'I've never fancied myself at judging people when I first meet them. So I have to find out about them in my own fashion.'

For a fortnight I was immersed in that kind of comfort which is like a luxurious cocoon as one delays before a longed-for and imminent fate, which I had also known after my first meeting with Margaret. I was still not calculating; I, who had calculated so much, went about as though the machine had been switched off; now that I had a card of re-entry into the Davidson family, I still felt the future free.

I still felt so, when I wrote a note to Davidson, telling him I had a little more information about the Sawbridge case, if he chose to call. He did call: he seemed satisfied: afterwards we walked together down Victoria Street. It was a blazing hot day, people were walking in the shade, but Davidson insisted on keeping to the other side.

'We mustn't miss a second of this sun,' he said, as though it were a moral axiom.

He walked with long strides, his head down, his feet clumpingly heavy on the pavement for so spare a man. His shirt sleeves hung beneath his cuffs, over-long and unbuttoned. Shabby as he was, passers-by noticed him; he was the most striking and handsome figure in the street. I thought how like that shabby carelessness was to Margaret's.

Suddenly he said:

'I'm giving a show at my house next week.' A private view, he explained, for two young painters. 'Would that interest you?'

'Very much,' I said. I said it eagerly, without any guard.

Not looking at me, Davidson lolloped along.

'Wait a minute,' he said. 'Do you know anything about pictures? It's a waste of your time and mine if you don't, don't you know.'

'I know a little.'

'You're not bluffing, are you?'

'I don't think so.'

'I'd better ask you a few questions.'

There and then, in Victoria Street in the sweating sunshine, as we passed offices of consultant engineers, Davidson gave me a brisk viva. Embarrassed, anxious to pass, doing my best, I nevertheless felt a twinge of amusement, as a comparison struck me. To Davidson, whose taste had no use for concealments, this was a matter to be cleared up in the open; it was just a question of whether I was equipped to look at pictures or not; there were no overtones, no other motives, on his side or mine.

It did not occur to him that I was snatching at the chance to meet his daughter again. Yet he was a man who, so I had heard and I had no reason to doubt it, had once been well known for his love affairs. Sheila's father, the Reverend Laurence Knight, had been a faithful husband, living obscurely all his life in a country vicarage: yet, in Davidson's place, he would have known precisely what I was after, not now, when it was easy to see, but within minutes of our first meeting. Mr Knight, incidentally, would have tantalised me and then found some excuse for holding back the invitation.

Davidson did not go in for any flourishes: he just formed his opinion, and announced:

'You'd never have made a living at it, don't you know.'

I was in suspense; I agreed.

'It might just be worth your while to come along,' he said, staring at the pavement in front of him. 'But only just.'

Waiting in my flat on the evening of the private view I saw the sky over Hyde Park turn dark, sodden with rain to come. Standing by the window I kept glancing at my watch, although it was still not time to leave, and then gazed out again over the trees into the leaden murk. Then I looked back into the room. On the little table by the sofa the reading-lamp was gleaming, and a book which I had left open shone under the light.

It was peaceful, it had never seemed so peaceful. For an instant I wanted to stay there, and not go out. It would be easy to stay; I need only telephone and make an apology, in that party I should not be missed, the significance I was giving it was my own invention, and besides myself no living person knew. I looked at the lamp and the sofa, with a stab almost of envy.

Then I turned back to the window, reading my watch, impatient that it was still not time to go.

PART FOUR

THE UNDETACHED

CHAPTER XXXVII

SMELL OF LEAVES IN THE RAIN

In the hall of Davidson's house the brightness, clashing with the noise of the party within, took me aback; it was Davidson himself who came to greet me.

'You decided it was worth while, did you?' he asked.

As I was putting my coat down, he said:

'I met someone who knew you this morning.' He gave the name of an elderly acquaintance. 'She was anxious to get in touch with you. I'd better hand this over before I forget.' It was a card with an address and telephone number.

I asked if it could wait, but Davidson had discharged his commission and was not interested any more.

'If you *fancy yourself* at the telephone, there's one under the stairs,' he said. He spoke in a severe minatory voice, as though telephony were a difficult art, and it was presumptuous on my part to pretend to have mastered it. In fact Davidson, who was so often the spokesman of the modern, whose walls were hung with the newest art, had never come to terms with mechanical civilisation. Not only did he go deaf if he put a receiver to his ear: even fountain pens and cigarette lighters were white-man's magic which he would have no dealings with.

While I was making my call, which turned out to be of no possible importance, I was by myself listening to the continuum of noise from the unknown rooms. I felt a prickle of nervousness not, it seemed, because Margaret might be there, but just as though I had ceased to be a man of forty, experienced at going about amongst strangers: I felt as I might have done when I was very young.

When at last I went in I stayed on the outskirts of the room, trying to put myself at ease. I looked away from the pictures, from the unknown people, out through the window to a night so dark, although it was only nine o'clock in July, that the terrace was invisible: in the middle distance twinkled the lamps along Regent's Park. Down below the window lights, the pavement was bone-white, the rain had still not fallen.

Then I walked round the room, or rather the two rooms which, for the show, had had their dividing doors folded. There must have been sixty or seventy people there, but apart from Davidson, alert and unpompous among a knot of young men, I did not see a face I knew. Along one long wall were hung a set of non-representational paintings, in which geometrical forms were set in a Turnerian sheen. Along the other were some thickly painted portraits, not quite naturalistic but nearly so. Trying to clamp myself down to study them, I could not settle to it.

I found myself falling back into the refuge I had used at twenty. I used to save my self-respect by the revenges of my observation, and I did so now. Yes, most of the people in these rooms were different animals from those one saw at Lufkin's dinners or round the committee tables with Hector Rose: different animals in an exact, technical sense: lighter-boned, thinner, less heavily muscled, their nerves nearer the surface, their voices more pent-in: less exulting in their bodies' strength than so many of Lufkin's colleagues – and yet, I was prepared to bet, in many cases more erotic. That was one of the paradoxes which separated these persons from the men of action; I thought of acquaintances of mine in Lufkin's entourage who walked with the physical confidence, the unselfconscious swagger, of *condottieri*; but it was not they who were driven, driven to obsession by the erotic life, but men as it might be one or two I saw round me that night, whose cheeks were sunken and limbs shambling, who looked, instead of bold and authoritative like Lufkin's colleagues, much younger than their years.

Soon someone recognised me, and, opposite one of the non-representational patterns, I was caught up in an argument. In a group of five or six I was the oldest man, and they treated me with respect, one even called me 'sir'. It was an argument such as we knew by heart in those years, about the future of abstract art. I was talking with the fluency of having been through those tricks before, talking with the middle-aged voice, the practised party voice. They called me 'sir', they thought me heterodox, they were not as accustomed to debating or so ready for shock tactics. None of them knew that, five minutes before, I had been nervous and lost.

All the time I was arguing, I was staring over them and past them, just as though I were a young man on the make, looking out at a party for someone more useful than his present company. I had seen no sign of her, and, as the minutes seeped on, I could not keep my glance still.

At last I saw her. She came out of the crowd by the wall opposite ours and further down the room; she was speaking to a woman, and she spread out her hands in a gesture I had often seen, which suddenly released her animation and gaiety. As she talked my glance was fixed on her: it was many instants before her eyes came my way.

She hesitated in front of a neglected picture and stood there by herself. A young man at my side was speaking insistently, heckling me with polite questions. She was walking towards us. As she came inside our group, the young man halted his speech.

'Go on,' said Margaret.

Someone began to introduce me to her.

'We've known each other for years,' she said, protectively and gently. 'Go on, I don't want to interrupt.'

As she stood, her head bent down and receptive, I saw her for a moment as though it were first sight. Excitement, a mixture of impatience and content, had poured into my nerves – but that seemed disconnected from, utterly uncaused by, this face which might have been another stranger's. Pale, fine rather than pretty, just missing beauty, lips and nostrils clean-cut, not tender until she smiled – it was an interesting face, but not such a face as in imagination I admired most, not even one that, away from her, I endowed her with.

Then the first sight shattered, as I thought she had changed. Five years before, when I had first met her, she could have passed for a girl: but now, at thirty, she looked her full age. Under the light, among the dark hair glinted a line of silver; her skin which, with her blend of negligence and subfusc vanity she used to leave untouched, was made up now, but there were creases round her mouth and eyes. Suddenly I remembered that when I knew her there were some broken veins just behind her cheekbones, odd for so young and fine-skinned a woman; but now under the powder they were hidden.

Standing in the middle of this group she was not embarrassed, as she would have been once. She rested there, not speaking much nor assertively, but a woman among a crowd of younger men: now there was no disguising her energy, her natural force.

The light seemed brighter on the eyes, the pictures further away, the crowd in the room noisier, voices were high around me, questions came at me, but I had dropped out of the argument. Once, glancing at Margaret, I met her eyes: I had not spoken to her alone. At last the group moved on, and we were left just for an instant isolated, no one listening to us. But now the chance had come, I could not speak: the questions I wanted to ask, after three years of silence, would not come to the tongue, I was like a stutterer needing to bring out his dreaded consonant. We gazed at each other, but I could not utter. The silence tightened between us.

Foolishly I creaked out some remark about the pictures, asking how she liked them, as banal a question as though she was a boring acquaintance with whom I had to make my ration of conversation. In the midst of that nonsense my voice broke away from me, and I heard it sound intense, intimate and harsh.

'How are you?'

Her tone was kinder, but just as edged: 'No, how are you?'

Her eyes would not leave mine. Each willed the other to answer first; I gave way.

'I haven't much to tell you,' I said.

'Tell me what there is.'

'It could be worse.'

'You've always been ready to bear it, haven't you?'

'No, my life isn't intolerable,' I said, trying to tell her the precise truth.

'But what?'

'There's not much in it,' I replied.

'Yes, I was afraid so.'

'Were you?'

'People often talk about you, you know.'

The crowd pressed upon us, they parted me from her, although before we had to talk at large, she was muttering about something she wished for me. She had begun to say it with an impatient, eager smile.

As I was speaking to the newcomers, I noticed a tall youngish man detach himself from another group and whisper to Margaret, who was glancing in my direction.

She looked tired, she seemed to be wanting to go home, but soon she beckoned to me.

'You haven't met Geoffrey, have you?' she said to me.

He was a couple of inches taller than my six feet, very thin, long-handed and long-footed; he was thirty-five, goodlooking in a lantern-jawed fashion, with handsome eyes and deep folds in his cheeks. The poise of his head was arrogant, other men would judge him pleased with his looks; but there was nothing arrogant about him as we shook hands, he was as short of conversation as I had been with Margaret a few minutes before, and just as I had opened imbecilely about the pictures, so did he. He had known about me and Margaret long before he married her; now his manner was apologetic, quite unlike his normal, so I fancied, as he asked my opinion of the pictures, in which his interest was, if possible, less than mine.

Margaret said they must be going soon, Helen would be waiting up for them.

'That's my sister-in-law,' Geoffrey explained to me, still over-embarrassed, over-considerate. 'She's sitting in with the infant.'

'She still hasn't any of her own?' I asked Margaret. I recalled the time when, joyful ourselves, we had arranged her sister's well-being, the conspiracies of happiness. Margaret shook her head:

'No, poor dear, she's had no luck.'

Geoffrey caught her eye, and he said, in what I took to be his confident doctor's voice:

'It's a thousand pities she didn't get some sensible advice right at the beginning.'

'But yours is well?' I spoke to both of them, but once more I was asking Margaret.

It was Geoffrey who replied.

'He's all right,' he said. 'Of course, if you're not used to very young children, you might get him out of proportion. Actually, for general development, he'd certainly be in the top ten per cent of two-year-olds, but probably not in the top five.'

His tone was exaggeratedly dry and objective, but his expression was innocent with love. He went on, with the pretence of objectivity which professionals believe conceals their pride:

'Only yesterday, it's simply an example, he took a flashlamp to pieces and put it together again. Which I couldn't have done at the age of four.'

Conscious of Margaret's silence, I expressed surprise. Geoffrey's tone changed, and as he spoke to me again I thought I heard something hard, jaunty, almost vindictive:

'You'd better come and see him for yourself.'

'No, he wouldn't enjoy it,' said Margaret quickly.

'Why shouldn't he come for lunch, then he can inspect the boy?'

'It would be very inconvenient for you.' Margaret spoke straight to me.

I replied to Geoffrey:

'I'd like to come.'

Soon afterwards, sharply, Margaret said again that they must be going home. I walked with them out of the room, into the hall, where, through the open door, we could hear the rain pelting down. Geoffrey ran out to bring the car round, and Margaret and I stood side by side staring out into the dark terrace, seeing the rain shafts cut through the beam of light from the doorway. On the pavement the rain hissed and bounced; the night had gone cool; a clean smell came off the trees, making me feel for an instant calm when, knowing nothing else for certain, I knew I was not that.

Neither of us turned towards the other. The car came along the kerb, veils of rain shimmering across the headlights.

'I shall see you then,' she said, in a flat, low voice.

'Yes,' I said.

CHAPTER XXXVIII

SIGNIFICANCE OF A QUARREL

As I sat between Margaret and Geoffrey Hollis at their dining-table, I wanted to speak amiably to him.

Outside the sun was shining, it was a sleepy middle-of-the-day; no one was to be seen in the Sumner Place gardens; the only sound, through the open windows, was the soporific sweep of buses along the Fulham Road. I had only arrived a quarter of an hour before, and we spoke, all three of us, as though we were subdued by the heat. Geoffrey was sitting in a shirt open at the neck, and Margaret in a cotton frock; we ate boiled eggs and salad and drank nothing but iced water. In between times Geoffrey and I exchanged polite curiosity about our working days.

In the dining-room, which was like a pool of coolness after the streets, all we said sounded civil. I was hearing what it meant to be a children's doctor, the surgery hours, the hospital rounds, the proportion of nights on which he could expect a call. It was useful, it was devoted, it was no more self-indulgent than the meal he ate. Nor was the way he talked about it. He had admitted that in some respects he was lucky. 'Compared with other doctors anyway,' said Geoffrey. 'Any other sort of doctor is dealing with patients who by and large are going to get worse. With children most of them are going to get better. It gives it quite a different flavour, you see, and that's a compensation.'

He was provoking me: it was enviable, it was admirable: I wanted to prove it wasn't.

Suspicious of myself, I changed the subject. Just to keep the conversation easy, I asked him what he thought of some news from the morning's paper.

'Oh yes,' he said indifferently, 'a parent who came in mentioned it.'

'What do you think?'

'I haven't any idea.'

'It's pretty plain, isn't it?'

'Maybe,' he replied. 'But, you see, I haven't read a morning paper.'

'Are you as busy as all that?' I tried to be companionable.

'No,' he said, with pleasure, tilting his head back like someone who has brought off a finesse. 'It's a matter of general policy. Twelve months ago we decided not to take a daily paper. It seemed to me that, far more days than not, it was going to make me slightly miserable without any gain to anyone, and with just conceivably a fractional loss of efficiency to myself. In any case I don't believe in adding to the world's stock of misery, even if it's through my own. So we decided the sensible course was to stop the paper.'

'I couldn't do that,' I broke out.

'Quite seriously,' said Geoffrey, 'if a lot of us only bit off what we could chew, and simply concentrated on the things we can affect, there'd be less tension all round, and the forces of sweetness and light would stand more chance.'

'I believe you're wrong,' I said.

Again he was provoking me; the irritation, which would not leave me alone at that table, was jagging my voice; this time I felt I had an excuse. Partly it was that this kind of quietism was becoming common among those I knew, and I distrusted it. Partly Geoffrey himself seemed to me complacent, speaking from high above the battle; and, like many people who led useful and good lives, even like many who had a purity of nature, he seemed insulated by his self-regard.

Suddenly Margaret spoke to me.

'He's absolutely right,' she said.

She was smiling, she was trying to speak easily, as I tried to speak to Geoffrey, but she was worried and angry.

'Why do you say that?'

'We've got to deal with things that are close enough to handle,' she said.

'I don't believe,' I said, getting angrier, 'that you can cut yourself off from the common experience around you. And if you do, I am sure you lose by it.'

'Lose by it how?'

'Lose by it as a person. Just like very optimistic people who shut off anything that is painful to see. I should have thought you diminish yourself unless you suffer your sufferings as well as enjoy your joys.'

Margaret gave a smile half malicious, as though gratified that my temper had gone higher than hers.

'The trouble,' she said, 'with the very realistic men who live in this world, like you, is that they're so hopelessly unpractical when it comes to the point. You don't think Geoffrey's realistic, but he's so much more practical than you are that you don't begin to start. He likes dealing with children and he likes being happy. Hasn't it occurred to you that no one except you worries whether they're "diminishing themselves" or not?'

I was getting the worst of it; I could not overbear her – I was hurt because she had taken his side with such an edge.

In return, I found myself talking to hurt.

I reminded her that I had never been comfortable about recipes for the good life – like those of her father's friends twenty years before – which depended on one's being an abnormally privileged person.

'To be honest,' I looked at Geoffrey and then at her, 'yours doesn't seem to me a great improvement. Your whole attitude would be unthinkable unless you happened to have one of the very few jobs which is obviously benevolent, and unless both of you happened to come from families who were used to doing good rather than having good done to them.'

'Lewis,' she called out my name for the first time for three years, but furiously, 'that's quite unfair!'

'Is it?' I asked her, watching the flush mount from her neck.

'Well, I wouldn't deny,' said Geoffrey, with exasperating fairness and a contented, judicious smile, 'that there may be something in it.'

'Do you really say that I patronise anyone?' she cried.

'With individuals, no, I shouldn't say so. But when you think about social things, of course you do.'

Her eyes were dark and snapping; her cheeks were flushed; it was as I remembered her when angry, the adrenalin was pumping through her, all pallor had left her and she looked spectacularly well.

'I must say,' Geoffrey remarked pacifically, 'I'm inclined to think he's right.'

'I suppose you'll say I'm a snob next?' Her eyes, still snapping, were fixed on me.

'In a rarefied sense, yes.'

Geoffrey reminded her that it was half past one, time to give Maurice his meal. Without speaking, her shoulders set with energy, with anger against me, she took the tray and led us to the nursery.

'There he is,' said Geoffrey, as I got my first glance at the child.

His pen was just outside a strong diagonal of sunlight; sitting with his back to the bars, like an animal retreating at the zoo, he was slowly tearing a magazine to pieces. I had only my brother's boy to compare him with, and despite what I had heard of his manual precocity, I could not see it. I just saw him tearing up the paper with that solemn, concentrated inefficiency characteristic to infants, which made his hand and elbow movements look like those of a drunken man photographed in slow motion.

I did not go up to him, but went on watching as, after Margaret spoke to him, he continued obsessively with his task. He was, and the sight wounded me though I had prepared for it, a most beautiful child. The genes had played one of their tricks, and had collected together in him the best looks of parents and grandparents, so that already, under the indiarubber fat, one could pick out the fine cheekbones of his mother and the poise of his father's neck.

Margaret was telling him that his meal was ready, but he replied that he did not want it.

'What do you want?' she asked, with that matter-of-fact gentleness she showed to a lover.

The little boy was gripping a ping-pong ball, and, as soon as she lifted him from his pen, he began to lam it at a looking-glass over the mantelpiece, and then at a picture near the cot.

Geoffrey left, to fetch something missing from the tray, but the boy paid no notice, and went on throwing the ball. As he let fly, I was scrutinising the boneless movement of his shoulder, as fluid as though he were double-jointed. Margaret said to me:

'It's a nice way for him to be.'

'Isn't he rather strong?' I said.

She was smiling at me, the quarrel smoothed away by the animal presence of her son. As she stood with him thigh-high beside her, she could not conceal – what at her father's party she remained silent about, when Geoffrey was so voluble – her passion for the child. It softened and filled out her face, and made her body lax. Pained again as by the boy's good looks, I knew that I had not seen her look more tender.

'It's nice for him just to chuck himself about,' she said.

I caught her meaning. Like many of the sensitive, she had wished often, especially before she gained the confidence that she could make a man happy, that her own childhood had been less refined, had been coarser and nearer the earth.

I put in a remark, to let her know I understood. She smiled again: but

Maurice began shouting, violent because she was talking away from him.

While he had his meal I remained outside the circle of attention, which was lit by the beam of sun gilding the legs of the high chair. Geoffrey sat on one side, Margaret in front, the child facing her with unflickering eyes. After two or three spoonfuls he would not eat until she sang; as I listened, it occurred to me that, when I had known her, I had not once heard her singing voice. She sang, her voice unexpectedly loud and deep; the child did not take his eyes off her.

The robust sound filled the room: Geoffrey, smiling, was watching the boy: the beam of sunlight fell on their feet, as though they were at the centre of a stage, and the spotlight had gone slightly off the mark.

The meal was over, Geoffrey gave the child a sweet, for an instant the room went dead quiet. They were still sitting with the sunlight round their feet, as Margaret gazed at her son, either unselfconscious or thinking she was not observed. Then after a moment she raised her head, and I felt rather than saw, for I had looked away, that her glance had moved from the child to me. I turned towards her: her face went suddenly sad. It was only for an instant. She gazed again at the little boy, and took his hand.

It had only been for an instant, but I knew. I should have known before, when we parted after her father's party, certainly when she quarrelled with me in defence of Geoffrey at the dining-table, if I had not desired it too much: I knew now that she was not free of me, any more than I of her.

In the hot room, noisy now with the boy's demands, I felt, not premonition, not responsibility, not the guilt that would have seemed ineluctable if I had seen another in my place, but an absolute exaltation, as though, all in one move, I had joy in my hands and my life miraculously simple. I did not recognise any fear mixed with the joy, I just felt happy and at one.

CHAPTER XXXIX

ILLUSION OF INVISIBILITY

IT was a September afternoon when I was waiting, for the first time since her marriage, to meet Margaret alone. It was the day on which I had been helping to interview Gilbert Cooke. Half an hour before I was due at our rendezvous he entered, having already heard from Hector Rose that he was safe.

'So I diddled them, did I?' he said, not so much with pleasure as a kind of gloating triumph: which was the way in which he, who did not expect much success, greeted any that came to him. Actually, this was more than a success, for in fact, though not in form, it settled his career for life. Hector Rose was deciding his final judgment on each of the men in the department who wished to be established in the service; once a week, a committee of four of us sat and interviewed; George Passant's turn would arrive soon.

'It can't come unstuck now, can it?' Gilbert said, flushed, his eyes bloodshot. I told him that Rose's nomination would have to be accepted.

'Damn it,' cried Gilbert, 'I never reckoned on finishing up as a civil servant.'

'What did you reckon on?' I knew he would scarcely be able to answer: for in his career he had always been a curiously vague and unself-seeking man.

'Oh,' he said, looking badgered, 'there was a time when I thought I might make something of it as a soldier. That was before the doctors did me in the eye. And then I thought I might collect some cash with that old shark Lufkin. I don't know. But the last thing I should ever have dreamt of was finding myself here for good. To tell you the honest truth,' he burst out, 'I should never have credited that I was clever enough!'

Oddly, in a certain restricted sense, he was not: he had nothing of the legalistic accuracy and lucidity of the high-class civil servant: the deficiency would stop him going very far, as Rose and the others had agreed that day: he would most likely get one rung higher and stop there.

Nevertheless, he had put up a good performance before those men so different from himself. He was so little stiff that Rose felt his own stiffness soften, and enjoyed the sensation: sometimes his refusal to stay at a distance, his zest for breathing down one's neck, made him paradoxically welcome to correct and buttoned natures. Hector Rose and his colleagues did not over-value him much; they were too experienced, and their judgment too cool for that; they were probably right to keep him; but still, there was no doubt that, if the decision had been a closer thing, he had the advantage that respectable men liked him.

I wondered what they would have thought, if they had guessed at his wilder activities. For instance, it would have startled them to know that, sitting in my office that afternoon, I – after being a friend for a dozen years and his boss for several – was frightened of him. Frightened, that is, of his detective work. I did not dare let out a hint that I was slipping away for tea. Even then I was still nervous of his antennae, as though they might pick up the secret in the air.

Thus, sweating and fretted, I was late when at last I reached the café opposite St James's Park tube station. Margaret was sitting there, stubs of cigarettes in the ash-tray. She looked anxious, but unreproachful and glad.

'I'll tell you why I was late,' I said.

'It doesn't matter, you're here now.'

'No, I'd better tell you.' I could not have got away from Gilbert, I explained, without the danger of his finding out that I was meeting her.

'Oh well,' she said. She spoke as though she had not admitted to herself the thought of concealment. At the same moment, her face was flushed with happiness and a kind of defiant shame. Firmly, she began to ask me what I had been doing.

'I told you, nothing that matters.'

'No,' she said, still with energy and animation, 'I don't even know where you're living. You know much more about me than I do about you.'

I told her what I was writing. I said that I was not held any longer by the chessboard of power: I had gone as far as I intended in the official life.

'I thought so,' she said with pleasure.

'I'm not sure that it would have happened but for you.'

'It would,' she said. 'It would, for absolute certain.' The cups of tea steamed, a cigarette end smouldered against the metal ash-tray, the smell was acrid: I saw her as though the smoked glass of care had been snatched from in front of my eyes. Twenty minutes before I had been on edge lest anyone, as it might be Gilbert, should pass the window and see us sitting there. Now, although we were smiling at each other and our faces would have given us away to an acquaintance, I felt that secrets did not matter, or more exactly that no one could notice us; I had been taken by one of those states, born of complicity, desire and joy, in which we seem to ourselves anonymous and safe. It was a state which I had seen dangerous to discreet men going through an illicit love affair, when suddenly, in a fugue of astonished bliss, such a man can behave as if he believed himself invisible.

Her hand was on the table, and I touched her fingers. We had made love together many times, we had none of that surprise to come: but, at the touch, I shivered as though it were a complete embrace.

'Let me talk to you,' I said.

'Can't we leave it?' she cried.

'Can we?'

'It'd be better to leave it, just for a while.' She spoke in a tone I had not heard – it held both joy and fear, or something sharper than fear.

'I used to be pretty expert at leaving things just for a while,' I said, 'and it wasn't an unqualified success.'

'We're peaceful now,' she broke out.

She added:

'When a thing is said, we can't come back where we are.'

'I know it.' There was a hush. I found myself trying to frame the words, just as when she first forced me on that evening years before – with an inarticulateness more tormenting to one used to being articulate, with the dumbness I only knew when I was compelled to dredge my feelings. 'It is the same with me,' I said at length, 'as when I first met you.'

She did not move or utter.

'I hope,' I said, the words dragging out, 'it is the same with you.'

She said: 'You don't hope: you know.'

The room was dark; in the street the sun had gone out. She cried – her voice was transformed, it was light with trust, sharp with the curiosity of present joy:

'When were you certain it was the same with you?'

'Some time ago.'

'Was it that night at my father's?'

'If not before,' I answered. 'I've thought of you very much. But I was afraid my imagination might be cheating me.'

'What time that night?'

'I think when you were standing there, before we spoke.'

I asked: 'When were you certain?'

'Later.'

She added: 'But I wanted you to come that night.'

'If we hadn't met again there, we should have soon,' I said.

'I talked about you to my father. I lied to myself, but I was trying to improve the chances of meeting you—'

'You needn't worry, I should have seen to it that we did.'

'I'm not worrying,' she said. 'But I wanted to tell you that we're both to blame.'

To both of us, blame seemed remote or rather inconceivable; the state of happiness suffused us with its own virtue.

We said no more except chit-chat. Yes, when she could get Helen to look after the child again, she would let me know. It was time for her to go. We went out into the street, where the light had that particular density which gives both gentleness and clarity to the faces of passers-by. The faces moved past us, softly so it seemed, as I watched Margaret put her foot on the taxi-step and she pressed my hand.

CHAPTER XL

HAPPINESS AND MAKE-BELIEVE

IN the same café a week later Margaret sat opposite me, her face open and softened, as though breathing in the present moment. When I first met her I had been enraptured by her capacity for immediate joy, and so I was now. There had been none of the dead blanks of love between us, such as a man like me might have run into. Once there had been struggle, resentment and dislike, but not the dead blank.

In the aura from the table lamp, she was smiling. Outside the window the afternoon light was muted, so that on the pavement faces stood out with a special delicacy. She took the sight in, content and rapacious, determined to possess the moment.

'It's like last week,' she cried. 'But last week it was a few shades darker, wasn't it?'

We had not much time. She would have to be home by six, to let her sister go. With a mixture of triumph, humility and confusion she had told Helen that it was I she was meeting.

She was not used to lying, I thought. She had not before done anything unstraightforward or that caused her shame.

She was happy sitting there opposite me. But I knew that she was, to an extent and for the first time, making believe. What she had replied, when I had declared myself the week before, was true. As we talked, she felt a joy she could not restrain: together, we were having an intimation of a life more desirable than we had known. But I knew that for her, though not for me, it was not quite real. It was a wonderful illusion; but the reality was when she got back to her husband and the child.

In a marriage unhappier than hers, I could not forget how, returning to Sheila in the evening, I gained just one recompense, a feeling of what I used to think of as moral calm: and I was sure that in Margaret's own home, in a marriage which was arid but for the child, it was just that moral calm which she knew. It came upon her when she went home after our meeting, at the first sight of the child. It did not so much wipe away the thought of our meeting as make it seem still delectable but unreal.

It was that which I had to break. I did not want to: we were in a harmony that seemed outside of time: we could go on talking as though it were a conversation more serene than any the most perfect marriage could give, with no telephone bell, no child's voice, to interrupt. But my need was too great, I could not leave it there.

Once more I was dredging for what I had to say.

'When I told you,' I began, 'that it was the same with me, there is one difference.'

'Is there?' She said it with doubt and reluctance.

I went on:

'In our time together you were right and I was wrong.'

'That doesn't matter.'

'Yes, it does, because there is a difference now. I hope I've changed a little in myself, I know I've changed in what I want.'

Her eyes were as brilliant as when she was angry: she did not speak.

I said:

'I want for us exactly what you always did.'

'I never thought I should hear you say that!'

She had cried out with joy: then, in an instant, her tone was transformed.

'Other things have changed too,' she said.

She looked straight at me, and asked:

'Are you sure?'

In a time so short that I could not measure it, her mood had flickered as I had never seen in her, from triumphant joy to bitterness and shame, and then to concern for me.

'No,' she broke out, 'I take that back, I shouldn't have said it. Because you couldn't have done this unless you were sure.'

'I'm sure of what I want,' I repeated. 'As I say, I hope I've changed in myself, but of that I can't be sure, it's very hard to know what's happening in one's own life.'

'That's rather funny, from you.' Again her mood had switched, she was smiling with affectionate sarcasm. She meant that, herself used to being in touch with her own experience, she had discovered the same in me. On the surface so unlike, at that level we were identical. Perhaps it was there, and only there, that each of us met the other half of self.

'Once or twice,' I said, 'I've woken up and found my life taking a course I'd never bargained on. Once upon a time I thought I knew the forces behind me pretty well – but now it seems more mysterious than it used to, not less. Isn't that so with you?'

'It may be.'

She added:

'If it is, it's frightening.'

'For me, it's made me less willing to sit down to—'

I stumbled for a moment.

'Sit down to what?'

'To my own nature: or anyway the side of it which did us both such harm.'

'It wasn't all your doing,' she said.

I answered:

'No, not all. I agree, I won't take all the responsibility, not more than I have to.'

We fell into a silence, one of those doldrums that sometimes take over in a mutual revelation, just as in a scene of violence.

She began, in a manner gentle and apparently realistic: 'If it were possible for us to start again, you'd look very foolish, wouldn't you? Especially to those who know our story.'

I nodded.

'It would seem inconceivably foolish at the best,' she said.

'They'd have a certain justice,' I replied.

'You haven't had much practice at looking foolish, have you? Have you begun to imagine how humiliating it would be? Particularly when people think you're so wise and stable?'

'I can ride that,' I said.

'It might not be so nice.'

She went on:

'Those who love you would blame poor Sheila – and those who don't would say there'd always been something wrong with you and now you've come out into the open and shown it.'

'One's enemies are often righter than one's friends.'

'They're not. That's the sort of remark that sounds deep and is really very shoddy.' She said it with love.

The café was emptying, our time was running out. She said, in a sharp, grave tone:

'But what they would think of you, perhaps you're right, that's not the real point. The real point is, you've not had much practice at behaving badly, have you?'

I said:

'You're wrong. I've done bad things.'

'Not like what this would be.'

'The way I behaved to you before,' I said, 'was worse than anything I have to do now.'

'This way,' she said, 'you know what you would be asking me to do.' She meant – do harm to others, act against her nature and beliefs.

'Do you think I haven't faced that?'

She said:

'I was not absolutely sure.'

Yet, though she seemed to be speaking realistically, there was a haze of happiness round her, and me also. Incongruously I recalled the night when Lufkin, at the height of his power, indulged a romantic dream of retiring to Monaco. She too was speaking of a future that in her heart she did not expect to see. Usually her spirit was nakeder than mine: for once it was the other way about. Her face, her skin, her eyes were happy: yet she was levitated with something like the happiness of a dream.

I did not doubt that, in my absence, she would have to listen again to what I had said.

Once more she spoke gently, reasonably, intimately.

'If we could make a new start, I should be afraid for you.'

'I need it—'

'You know,' she said, 'you've just said you know, what it would mean for me to come to you. You'd be committed more than anyone ought to be. If things ever went wrong, and it might be harder for you day by day than you could possibly foresee, then I'm afraid you'd feel obliged to endure for ever.'

'You can't be much afraid,' I said.

'I should be, a little.'

She could keep her words honest, so could I – while, with the lamp on the table between us, our hopes were expanding, sweeping us with them into a gigantic space of well-being. Our hopes no longer had any connection with the honest, doubting words we said.

CHAPTER XLI

END OF AN EPOCH

AFTER that second meeting, and before we could contrive another, a chance to be unclandestine came along, for we were invited to the same wedding-party. In itself, the occasion would have been startling enough: when I saw the invitation I felt fooled. The party was to announce the marriage that had taken place, weeks before, in secret – the marriage of Gilbert Cooke and Betty Vane.

As I walked along the river to the house they had borrowed for the night, a house near Whistler's, which in those years had become just a place to be hired, I was both elated, because of Margaret, and faintly sad, self-indulgently in tune with the autumn night. It was drizzling and warm, the leaves slippery on the pavement, the smell of must all round: it was an autumn night which held more sensual promise than the spring.

I was not thinking much about Betty and Gilbert. When I first heard the news I had been piqued because she had not confided in me. Maybe she had, it occurred to me, a year or more ago: more likely than not, this was what she meant by her chance to settle down. Should I have told her that I did not believe the marriage could work? She was so shrewd, she would know what I felt without my saying it. I knew too well, however, that the shrewd and clear-sighted, if they are unhappy and unsettled and lonely enough, as she was, can delude themselves at least as much as, perhaps more than, less worldly people.

Yet, as I went towards the party, the lights from the windows shimmering out into the drizzle, I was aware of other thoughts drifting through my mind, as though this marriage were an oddly final thing. For me it seemed to call out time, it was the end of an epoch. I had known them each so long, Betty for nearly twenty years. We had seen in each other youth passing, causes dribbling out, hopes cutting themselves down to fit our fates: our lives had interleaved, we had seen each other in the resilience of youth's flesh, on and off for years we had, in the other's trouble, helped pick up the pieces. Now we saw each other when the covers and disguises were melting away, when the bones of our nature were at last showing through.

Our life of the thirties, our wartime life, was over now. Somehow the gong sounded, the door clanged to, more decisively through her marriage than through any fatality to those who touched me to the roots – through her, who was just a comrade, someone I had been fond of without fuss.

In the house, the first person I recognised was old Bevill, drinking a glass of champagne at the bottom of the stairs and talking to a pretty girl. The downstairs rooms were already full of people, and I had to push my way upstairs to reach the main origin of noise. As I passed him, Bevill told me that Gilbert and his wife were 'up above'. He said:

'I always wondered when our friend would succumb. Do you know, Lewis, I've been married forty-eight years. It makes you think.'

The old man was radiant with champagne and the company of the young. He began to tell us the story about Betty Vane's father – 'We were at school together, of course. We never thought he'd come into the title, because there was that cousin of his who went off his head and stayed off his head for thirty years. So it didn't look much of a cop for Percy Vane. We didn't call him Percy, though, we called him Chinaman Vane – though I haven't the faintest idea why; he didn't look like a Chinaman, whatever else they could say about him.'

This incongruity struck Bevill as remarkably funny, and his bald head flushed with his chortles: he was content to stand in the hall without inserting himself into the grander circles of the party. But there were others who were not: the main room upstairs was packed with immiscible groups, for Gilbert and Betty had invited guests from all the strata they had lived among. There was Lord Lufkin and some of his court, from Gilbert's business past: acquaintances from Chelsea before the war, the radicals, the ill-fitting, the *lumpen*-bourgeoisie.

There were a good many civil servants, among them Hector Rose, for once at a disadvantage, abnormally uncomfortable and effusively polite, detesting the sight of any society except in the office and the club. There was George Passant, moving about alone, with that expression unfocused, reverie-laden, absently smiling, which at this time more and more came over him in the proximity of women. There were Gilbert's relatives, many of them soldiers, small-headed, thin, gravel-voiced. There were Betty's, the younger women talking in the curious distorted Cockney of their generation of the upper class, huddled together like a knot of scientists at the British Association anxious not to be interrupted by camp-followers.

In all those faces there was only one I looked for. Soon I discovered her, listening but not participating at the edge of a large circle, her eyes restlessly looking out for me. As at her father's, we met alone in the crowd.

'That's better,' she said.

'I wish I could have brought you,' I said.

'I was touching wood, I didn't like to ask for you.'

She was excited; as she lit a cigarette, there was a tremor in her fingers.

'Who have you been talking to?'

'Oh, I haven't got as far as that.' She was laughing, not only with excitement, but at herself. Even now that she was grown-up, she was still shy. If this had been an ordinary party, not a cover for the two of us to meet, she would still have had to brace herself to cope; though,when once she had started, she revelled in it.

'We're here, anyway, and that's lucky,' I said.

'It is lucky,' she replied with an active, restless smile.

I was just telling her that soon we could slip away downstairs and talk, when Betty herself joined us.

'Lewis, my dear. Won't you wish me luck?'

She held out her arms, and I kissed her cheek. Then, bright-eyed, she glanced at Margaret.

'I don't think we've met, have we?' said Betty.

'You have,' I was putting in, when Betty went on:

'Anyway, I'm sorry, but will you tell me who you are?'

It sounded at best forgetful, it sounded also rude, for Betty's manner to a stranger was staccato and brusque. Yet she was the least arrogant of women, and I was at the same time astonished by her and upset to see Margaret wilt.

'My name,' she said, with her chin sunk down, 'is Margaret Hollis.'

'Oh, now I know,' cried Betty. 'You used to be Margaret Davidson, didn't you?'

Margaret nodded.

'I've heard my husband talk about you.'

With the same heartiness, the same apparent lack of perception, Betty went on with meaningless gossip, not caring that Margaret and I were looking strained. Yes, her husband Gilbert was a friend of Margaret's sister Helen, wasn't he? Yes, Gilbert had spoken about Helen's husband. At last Betty broke off, saying to Margaret:

'Look, there are some people here who I want you to meet. I'll take you along straightaway.'

Margaret was led off. I had to let her go, without protecting her. It was a bitterness, known only to those in illicit love, not to be able to be spontaneous. I was reckoning how much time I had to allow before I could take her away.

Meanwhile, myself at a loss, I looked round. Gilbert, high-coloured, was surveying his guests with bold, inquisitive eyes. They were the collection of acquaintances of half-a-lifetime; I expected his detective work was still churning on; but I was thinking again, as I had done walking to the house, how this was some sort of end. For Gilbert who, despite his faults, or more precisely because of them, cared as little for social differences as a man can do, had travelled a long way through society, just as I had myself, in the other direction.

So had Betty: the unlucky mattered, politics mattered, friends mattered and nothing else. When I had first met them both, it had seemed to us all self-evident that society was loosening and that soon most people would be indifferent to class. We had turned out wrong. In our forties we had to recognise – later in my life I thought that we had had the recognition more black-and-white than it really was – that English society had become more rigid, not less, since our youth. Its forms were crystallising under our eyes into an elaborate and codified Byzantinism, decent enough, tolerable to live in, but not blown through by the winds of scepticism or individual protest or sense of outrage which were our native air. And those forms were not only too cut-and-dried for us: they would have seemed altogether too rigid for nineteenth-century Englishmen. The evidence was all about us, even at that wedding-party: quite little things had, under our eyes, got fixed, and, except for catastrophes, fixed for good. The Hector Roses and their honours lists: it was a modern invention that the list should be systematised by civil service checks and balances: they had ceased to be corrupt and unpredictable, they were now as hierarchically impeccable as the award of coloured hats at the old Japanese Court. And I did not believe that I was seduced by literary resonances when I imagined that Betty Vane's and Thomas Bevill's relatives were behaving like Guermantes.

Just as the men of affairs had fractionated themselves into a group with its own rules and its own New Year's Day rewards, just as the arts were, without knowing it, drifting into invisible academies, so the aristocrats, as they lost their power and turned into ornaments, shut themselves up and exaggerated their distinguishing marks in a way that to old Bevill, who was grander than any of them, seemed rank bad manners, and what was worse, impolitic. But old Bevill belonged to a generation where the aristocracy still kept some function and so was un-selfconscious: in his time it was far more casual, for example, where you went to school; when he told his anecdote about Percy Vane, the school they were both attending was not Eton; yet it was to Eton, without one single exception in the families I knew, that they sent their sons, with the disciplined conformity of a defiant class. With the same conformity, those families were no longer throwing up the rebels that I had been friendly with as a young man; Betty Vane and Gilbert Cooke had no successors.

Looking round their wedding-party, I could not shake off a cliché of those years, this was the end of an epoch; I should have liked the company of those who could see one beginning.

A twitch at my arm, and Betty was glancing up at me.

'All right?' she said.

'Are you?' Angrily, I wanted to ask why she had been rude to Margaret: but once more I had to calculate.

'Yes, my dear.'

'I never thought of this happening to you.'

'I can manage it,' she said. It was not just her courage and high spirits: she meant it.

She broke off sharp: 'I'm sorry I had to cart her off. But people were watching you.'

'Does that matter?' I replied blank-faced.

'You ought to know.'

'What do you expect me to know?'

'So long as you realise that people were watching you.'

'I see.'

'That's all I can do for you now,' said Betty.

She was, of course, warning me about her husband. It removed my last doubt that she might not know him right through, and on her account I was relieved. She was too loyal to say more, perhaps this was the one crack in her loyalty I should ever see, and she only revealed it because she thought I was running into danger. She had done me so many good turns; I was touched by this last one.

And yet, I could not be sure why she had been so uncivil to Margaret. It had not been necessary, not even as a ruse. At their only other encounter, she had thought Margaret rude: was she getting her own back? Or had she genuinely forgotten Margaret's face? No one had indulged less in petty spite – just for a second, had she been doing so?

Just as I had got out of the room, on the balcony on my way downstairs to Margaret, someone intercepted me. For minutes I was pegged there, the glasses tinkling on the trays as they were carried past, the noise climbing in amplitude and pitch, Gilbert leaning from the door and taking note.

Over the banisters, when I broke away, I saw Margaret standing about down below.

'I feel a bit badgered,' I said as soon as I reached her, all tension leaving me.

'So do I.'

'Still, we're here, and it's worth it.'

She called out my name, quietly but with all her force, more of an endearment than any could be. Her expression was brilliant, and until she spoke again I totally misread it.

'Isn't it?' I cried.

In the same quiet and passionate tone, she said:

'We're deceiving ourselves, aren't we?'

'About what?'

'About us.'

'I've never been so sure,' I said.

'It's too late. Haven't we known all along it's too late?'

'I haven't.'

'I'm just not strong enough,' she said. I had never known her ask for pity before.

'You will be,' I said.

'No. It's too late. I knew it, tonight. I knew it,' she said.

'We can't decide anything now.' I wanted to soothe her.

'There's nothing to decide.' She used my name again, as though that was all she could tell me.

'There will be.'

'No, it's too hard for me.'

'Come out with me—'

'No. Please get me a taxi and let me go home.'

'We shall have to forget all this.'

For an instant I heard my voice hard.

'There's no future in it,' she cried, using the slang flatly instead of her own words. 'Let me go home.'

'I shall speak to you tomorrow.'

'It will be cruel if you do.'

Guests were passing us on their way out, and looking at her, knowing that she was near breaking-point, I could do nothing. I called out to the porter and asked him to find a cab. She thanked me, almost effusively, but I shook my head, my eyes still on her, trying to make my own choice, trying not to be crippled by the habits of defeat, the recurrent situations, the deepest traps within me.

CHAPTER XLII

APPARENT CHOICE

Listening the next afternoon to George Passant talking of his future, I said nothing of mine. For months, almost for years, since my resolve about Margaret began to form, I had not hinted even at a hope, except to her; but it was not only secretiveness that kept me reticent with George, it was something like superstition. For I had telephoned Margaret that morning, insisting that we should meet and talk it out, and she had given way.

685

'Assuming that I'm kept in this department, which I take it is reasonable, then I may as well plan on living in London for the rest of my life,' said George.

His interview was arranged for a fortnight hence; and George, with the optimism which he had preserved undented from his youth, through ill-luck and worse than ill-luck, took the result for granted.

'I haven't any idea,' I said – it was true, but I could not help being alarmed by George's hubris – 'what Rose intends to do about you.'

'Whatever we think of Rose,' George replied comfortably, 'we have to admit that he's a highly competent man.'

'His personal choices are sometimes odd.'

'I should have said,' George was unaffected, 'that he paid some attention to justice.'

'I don't deny that,' I said. 'But—'

'In that case we're reasonably entitled to consider that he's pretty well informed of what I've done here.'

'Within limits that's probably so.'

'You're not going to tell me,' George was getting argumentative, 'that a man as competent as Rose isn't going to see a certain slight difference in effectiveness between what I've done here and what some of those other nice young gentlemen from upper-class Bastilles [George meant public schools] have twittered about trying to do. Take old Gilbert. He's not a bad chap to have a drink with, he's always been exceedingly pleasant to me, but, God preserve my eternal soul, I can shift more in an afternoon than Gilbert can manage dimly to comprehend in three weeks' good hard slogging.'

'You're preaching to the converted,' I said.

'Well, if you're handsome enough to concede that simple point,' George replied, 'you can perhaps understand why I don't propose to indulge in unnecessary worry.'

Yet I, who was upset by George's kind of hope, lived with my own: I found it driving me almost as though I were obeying another person's instructions: I found it driving me, a little absurdly, to talk to a lawyer about divorce. Just as it was slipping out of control, I asserted some caution, even more absurdly: so that, setting out to talk to a lawyer, I did not go to one of the divorce experts whom I had known when I was practising at the Bar, but instead, as though avoiding going under a ladder at the last minute, just paid as it were a friendly call on my old master Herbert Getliffe.

The morning was dark: murk hung over the river, and in chambers the lights were on. It might have been one of the autumn mornings nearly twenty years before, when I sat there, looking out of the window, with nothing to do, avid for recognition, bitter because it would not come. But I felt no true memory of that past: somehow, although I had not revisited the place for years, no trigger released the forces of past emotion, my sense of faint regret was general and false. No trigger clicked, even when I read the list of names at the foot of the staircase, a list where my own name had stood as late as the end of the war: Mr Getliffe, Mr W. Allen . ... they had been there before my time. No trigger clicked, even when I went into Getliffe's room, smelt the tobacco once so familiar, and met the gaze of the bold, opaque and tricky eyes.

'Why, it's old L.S.,' said Herbert Getliffe, giving me his manly, forthright handshake. He was the only man alive who called me by my initials: he did it with an air both hearty and stern, as though he had just been deeply impressed by a code of gravitas. He was by this time getting on towards sixty, but he remained, despite his cunning, mercurial and also impressionable. When he was performing his most magisterial acts, his flat rubbery face grave, his red lips pressed together, there was still an imp not far from his eyes. Did he remember, I sometimes wondered, that, when I worked in his chambers, he had treated me with lavish unscrupulousness: since then we had kept an affection, desultory and suspicious, for each other. Even now, it surprised me that he was one of the more successful silks at the common law bar: but that was the fact.

I had seen him only once or twice since the night of the Barbican dinner before the war, when I went home to Sheila drunk and elated. I asked how he was getting on.

'It would be ungrateful to grumble,' he replied in a stately fashion. 'One manages to earn one's bread and butter' – as usual, he could not keep it up, and he winked – '*and* a little piece of cake.'

'What about you, L.S.?' He was genuinely curious about others, it was one of his strengths. 'Every time I hear about you, you seem to be flourishing.'

Yes, I said things had gone comparatively well.

'You go from power to power, don't you? Backstairs secrets and gentlemen like you in little rooms with XYZ after their names, all clamping collars round our necks,' he said, with a kind of free association. He broke out:

'There was a time when I used to think you'd become an ornament here.' He grinned: 'In that case, just about this year of grace we should have begun to cut each other's throats.'

'I'm sure we should,' I said.

Getliffe, his mood changing within the instant, looked at me in reproach.

'You mustn't say those things, L.S. You mustn't even think them. There's always room at the top and people like you and me ought to help each other.

'Do you know,' he added in a whisper, 'that just now one has to turn down cases one would like to take?'

'Too busy?'

'One's never too busy for a thousand smackers,' said Getliffe frowning: he was, unexpectedly so after the first impression he made, one of the most avaricious of men.

'Well then?'

'One comes to a stage when one doesn't want to drop any bricks.'

He was coy, he repeated his allusion (I must have heard that phrase three times already from men at crises in their careers), looked at me boldly like a child expecting to be caught out, but would not explain. Then I realised. There would be vacancies on the Bench soon, Getliffe was in the running, and throughout his whole career he would have sacrificed anything, even his great income, to become a judge. As he sat there that morning I thought I was seeing him almost on top of his world, Getliffe *in excelsis*, one of the few men I had seen in sight of all he wanted. It was to him at that moment that I had to let my secret out.

'Herbert,' I mentioned it casually, 'I may want, it isn't certain but I may, a bit of advice about a divorce case.'

'I thought your poor wife was dead,' Getliffe replied, and his next words overlay the first: 'I'm very sorry to hear it, L.S.'

'I may want some professional advice about how to get it through as painlessly as possible.'

'*I've* always been happily married,' Getliffe reproved me. 'I'm thankful to say that the thought of divorce has never come into either of our heads.'

'Anyone would like to be in your position,' I told him. 'But—'

'I always say,' Getliffe interrupted, 'that it takes a sense of humour to make a success of marriage. A sense of humour, and do-unto-others – especially one other – as-you-would-they-should-do-unto-you. That's what it takes.'

'Some of us aren't quite as lucky.'

'Anyway,' said Getliffe, suddenly curious, 'what position are you in?'

I knew that, although tricky, he was also discreet. I told him that I had known a woman, whose name did not matter at present, before her marriage: she had been married under four years and had a child not yet three: now she and I had met again, and wished to get married ourselves.

'Well, L.S., I've got to tell you what I think as man-to-man, and I've got to tell you that your decent course is to get out.'

'No, I shan't do that,' I said.

'I've thought of you as a fellow-sinner, but I've never thought of you as heartless, you know.'

He looked at me without expression, and for an instant his tricks, his moral indignation and boasting dropped away: 'Tell me, old chap, is this desperately important for you?'

I said the one word: 'Yes.'

'I see.' His tone was kind.

'Well,' he said, 'it's no use saying any more about what I think. I can tell you the best chap to go to, of course, but you probably know that yourself. But, if you must, I should go to —— Do you know that he's pulling in £20,000 a year these days? It's a very easy side of the profession, L.S., and sometimes one wishes that one hadn't started off with one's principles.'

'At this stage,' I said, 'I doubt if he could say anything that you and I don't know. You see, the woman I want to marry has nothing to complain of from her husband.'

'Will he play? Between you and me and these four walls, I shouldn't if I were in his shoes.'

'It wouldn't be reasonable to ask him, even if we felt able to,' I replied. 'He happens to be a doctor.'

Getliffe regarded me with a hot-eyed, flustered look:

'Tell me, L.S., are you cohabiting with her?'

'No.'

I was not sure that he believed me. He was, at one and the same time, deeply religious, prudish and sensual: and, as a kind of combined result, he was left with the illusion that the rest of mankind, particularly those not restrained by faith, spent their whole time in unregulated sexual activity.

Recovering from his excitement, he became practical about legal ways and means, which I was conversant with, which normally I should have found tiresome or grittily squalid, but which that morning gave me a glow of confidence. The smoke-dark sky, the reading-lamp on Getliffe's desk, the tobacco smell: the hotel evidence we should want: the delay between the suit being filed and the hearing: the time-lag before the decree absolute: as I discussed them, I had forgotten how much I had invited, talking to Getliffe. It sounded down-to-earth, but for me it was the opposite.

The next afternoon, the November cloudcap still lay low over the town, and looking out from my flat, past the reflection of the lamp in the window whose curtains were not drawn, I saw Hyde Park prematurely grey. Each instant I was listening for the lift outside, for Margaret for the first time had promised to come to me there. She was not yet due, it was only ten to four, but I had begun to listen for her early. With five minutes still to go, I heard the grinding and cranking of the antique machine, and went out on to the dark landing. The lights of the lift slowly moved up; there she was in the doorway, her cheeks pink from the cold air, hands tucked inside her fur coat, her eyes brilliant as though she were relaxed at being in the warm.

Straightaway she came into my arms, the fur comforting under my palms as I held her. After we had kissed, but while she was still close to me, she said: 'I've thought about being with you.'

She added:

'It's been a long time.'

As she took off her coat her movements were assured, flowing and without nerves: she was enjoying herself; she was so different from the woman who had left me at the party that I was both delighted and taken aback. Somehow I felt that, high as her spirits were, they were still deluding her.

Sitting on the sofa, she held out her feet to the electric fire, and I took my place beside her and put my arm round her. It was all as simple, as domestic, as though we had never parted.

'I'm sorry about that night,' she said.

'I was afraid.'

'You needn't have been.'

'I didn't believe it was the end.'

'It's not so easy to end as all that, is it?' she said, with a sarcastic smile but her eyes light.

'I hope it's not,' I said. 'I don't only hope it, but I think it.'

'Go on thinking it,' she cried, leaning back against my arm.

We were both looking across the room towards the windows, where, the sky having darkened and closed in, we saw nothing but the images of the room's lights. We were each in that state – and we knew it in the other – which was delectable and deceptive, lazy on the tide of unadmitted desire.

'I don't want to move,' she said.

It was some time, it might only have been seconds, before she made herself sit straight and look at me. She had the air of positive resolve which comes to one when cutting through a tangle. She had gone through nights, just as I had, when all seemed simple: then next morning the tangle was unresolvable again. That afternoon, she had come feeling all was clear.

'Whatever we do, it isn't going to be easy, is it?' she said.

'No.'

'I mean,' she went on, 'nothing can be easy when we have so many people to think of.'

I was not ready to reply, when she reiterated:

'It isn't only ourselves, there are two others I'm bound to care for.'

'You don't think I've forgotten about Geoffrey and the child, do you?'

'You can't ask me to hurt either of them. I'll do anything for you if I don't have to hurt them. I'm all yours.'

Her face was passionate and self-willed. She said:

'That's the proposition I've got to make. We have to hide it. I never thought I should want to hide anything, but I'll do it for you, I'll do it because I need you. It will take some hiding, I shall have to let Helen into it so that I can get away, I shan't be able to come to you more than once or twice a week, but that will make up for everything. It'll rescue us, we can go on for ever, and we're luckier than most people ever will be in their lives.'

The sight of the flush on her cheeks, usually so pale, excited me.

I went to the fireplace. As I looked down at her, I had never wanted her more. I was seized with memories of making love, the words we had muttered; I was shaken by one memory, a random one, not specially ecstatic, of lifting her naked in front of a looking-glass, which came from so deep as to be almost tactile.

I was thinking also how perfectly it would suit me to have her as my mistress, a relation which would give me the secretive joy I doted on, make no new claims on me, leave me not struggling any more to reshape my life.

It seemed as near a choice as I had had.

I heard my own voice, thick and rough:

'No.'

'Why not?'

'It must be all or nothing.'

'How can it be either?'

'It must be.'

'You're asking too much.'

'Have you begun to think,' I asked, 'what a secret affair would mean to you? It would have its charm to start with, of course it would, everyone who's lived an open life always hankers after concealments and risks. But you'd soon get over that, and then you'd find it meant lies upon lies. Corroding every other relation you had in order to sustain one that you began to dislike more and more. You haven't been used to playing confidence tricks. It would mean for you that you'd never behave again as you like to behave—'

'I dare say it would mean all that,' she said. 'But, if it avoids pain for others, do you think I should be put off?'

My hand gripping the mantelpiece, I said as simply as I could:

'It wouldn't avoid pain for me.'

'I was afraid of that.'

'I don't mean jealousy, I mean deprivation. If I took you on your terms, I should lose what I want most of all. I'm not thinking of you at all now, I'm just thinking of myself.'

'I'm glad,' she said.

'I want you to be with me all the time. I believe we shall be happy, but I can't promise it. You know it better than anyone will ever do, I'm not good at living face-to-face with another human being. Unless you're with me I shall never do it.'

As I spoke, she had bent her head into her hands, so that I could only see her hair.

'I can't be sad, I can't be,' she said at last. 'But I don't see that there is a way through.'

She looked up, her eyes lucid, and said:

'I can't get out of talking to you about Geoffrey, though you won't like it.'

'Go on,' I replied.

'I don't want to make it too dramatic. I'm fond of him, but I'm not driven to him as I am to you. I'm not even sure how much he depends on me—'

'Well then.'

'It may be a good deal. I must tell you this, I used to hope it was.'

She went on:

'I don't know him, I never have done, as well as I do you. I don't know how strong his feelings are. His senses are strong, he enjoys himself very easily, he's inclined to be impatient with people who don't find life as easy as he does.'

She wanted to believe that that was all. She was trying not to give herself the benefit of the doubt. The words she said – just as when we first met secretly in the café – were honest. But once again her hopes, and mine also, were stronger than the words. She wanted to believe that he did not need her much. I wanted to believe it too.

Then she burst out – 'He's never done a thing to me or said a thing to me that isn't as considerate as it could be. He's not given me a single bad hour to hold against him. How can I go to him and say, "Thank you, you've been good to me, now for no reason that I can possibly give you I intend to leave you cold."'

'I'm ready to speak to him,' I said.

'No,' she said violently. 'I won't be talked over.'

For an instant, temper, something deeper than temper, blazed from her eyes. She smiled at me:

'I'm sorry,' she said. 'I wish I could be angry with him, and it makes me angry with you instead.'

'As for talking me over,' she added, 'he might not mind, he might regard it as civilised. But you and I aren't civilised enough for that.'

'I'll do anything to bring him to the point,' I said.

'Not that.'

'Then will you?'

'After what I've said, you oughtn't to ask me.'

As I stood by the mantelpiece in the bright room, watching her on the sofa, the curtains still not drawn and the winter sky black above the park, the air was heavy between us, heavy in a way no tenderness could light.

'Do you think I like you having the harder part?' I said.

'I'll do anything but that.'

'It's our only hope.'

'I beg you,' she said, 'let's try my way.'

It was a long time before, in the heavy thudding air, I could reply.

'No,' I said.

CHAPTER XLIII

VISIT FROM A WELL-WISHER

ONE afternoon in the following week, when I was still in suspense, my secretary came into the office and said that Mr Davidson was asking to see me. Behind my papers, for I was busy that day, I welcomed him, apprehensive of the mention of Margaret's name which did not come.

I was incredulous that he had dropped in just because he was in tearing spirits and liked my company.

'Am I interrupting you?' he said, and chuckled.

'That's an unanswerable question,' he broke out. 'What does one say, when one's quite openly and patently in the middle of work, and some ass crassly asks whether he's interrupting you?'

'Anyway,' I said, 'this can all wait.'

'The country won't stop?' With a gesture as lively as an undergraduate's, he brushed the quiff of grey hair off his forehead. 'You see, I'm looking for someone to brag to. And there's no one else in this part of London whom I can decently brag to, at least for long enough to be satisfactory.'

He had just, calling at the Athenæum, received the offer of an honorary degree, not from his own university but from St Andrews. 'Which is entirely respectable,' said Davidson. 'Of course, it doesn't make the faintest difference to anything I've tried to do. If in twenty years five people read the compositions of an obsolete critic of the graphic arts, it won't be because some kind academic gentlemen gave him an LL.D. In fact, it's dubious whether critics ought to get any public recognition whatever. There's altogether too much criticism now, and it attracts altogether too much esteem. But still, if any criticism is going to attract esteem, I regard it as distinctly proper that mine should.'

I smiled. I had witnessed a good many solid men receive honours, men who would have dismissed Davidson as bohemian and cranky: solid men who, having devoted much attention to winning just such honours, then wondered whether they should accept them, deciding, after searching their souls, that they must for their wives' and colleagues' sakes. By their side, Austin Davidson was so pure.

'The really pressing problem is,' said Davidson, 'to make sure that all one's acquaintances have to realise the existence of this excellent award. They have a curious tendency not to notice anything agreeable which comes one's way. On the other hand, if someone points out in a very obscure periodical that Austin Davidson is the worst art critic since Vasari, it's quite remarkable how everyone I've ever spoken to has managed to fix his eyes on that.

'Of course,' Davidson reflected happily, 'I suppose one would only be kept completely cheerful if they had a formula to include one's name in most public announcements. Something like this. "Since the Provost and Fellows of Eton College have been unable to secure the services of Mr

Austin Davidson, they have appointed as Headmaster . . ." Or even "Since H.M. has not been successful in persuading Mr Austin Davidson of the truths of revealed religion, he has elevated to the See of Canterbury. . . ." ' He was so light-hearted, I did not want to see him go, the more so as I knew now he had detected nothing about Margaret and me. A few months before, I had been hyperæsthetised for the opposite reason, hoping to hear him bring out her name.

Enjoying himself, he also did not want to part. It was getting too late for tea in the cafés near Whitehall, and Davidson drank little: so I suggested a place in Pimlico, and, as Davidson had a passion for walking, we started off on foot. He lolloped along, his steps thudded on the dank pavement; his fancies kept flicking out. When we passed the dilapidated rooms-by-the-hour-or-night hotels of Wilton Road, he jerked with his thumb at one, a little less raffish, with its door shut and the name worse for wear over the fanlight.

'How much should I have to pay you to spend a night there?'

'You pay the bill too?'

'Certainly I pay the bill.'

'Well then, excluding the bill, three pounds.'

'Too much,' said Davidson severely, and clumped on.

I had wanted to escape that meeting, and it turned out a surprise: so did another which I did not want to escape – with his daughter Helen. When she telephoned and said, not urgently so far as I could hear, that she would like to see me, I was pleased: and I was pleased when I greeted her on the landing of my flat.

It was years since I had seen her; and, as soon as I could watch her face under my sitting-room light, I wondered if I should have guessed her age. She was by now in her late thirties, and her cheeks and neck were thinning; her features, which had always had the family distinction without her sister's bloom, had sharpened. Yet, in those ways passing or already passed into scraggy middle-age, she nevertheless had kept, more than any of us, the uncovered-up expression of her youth: she had taken on no pomp at all, not even the simple pomp of getting older: there was nothing deliberate about her, except for the rebellious concern about her clothes, which, I suspected, had by now become automatic, even less thought-about than Margaret's simplicity. Her glance and smile were as light as when she was a girl.

'Lewis,' she said at once, 'Margaret has told me about you two.'

'I'm glad of it.'

'Are you?' She knew enough about me to be surprised: she knew that, holding this secret, I would not have shared it with my own brother, intimate though we were.

'I'm glad that someone knows whom we can trust.'

Staring at me over the sofa-head, Helen realised that I meant it, and that this time, unlike all others, the secrecy was pressing me in. The corners of her eyes screwed up: her mouth was tart, almost angry, with the family sarcasm.

'That's not the most fortunate remark ever made,' she said.

'What do you mean?'

'I wasn't very anxious to come to see you today.'

'Have you brought a message from her?' I cried.

'Oh no.'

For an instant I was relieved; she was more tense than I was.

'Margaret knows that I was coming here,' she said. 'And I believe she knows what I was going to say.'

'What is it?'

She spoke fast, as though beset until she had it out:

'What you're planning with Margaret is wrong.'

I gazed at her without recognition and without speaking.

After a time, she said, quite gently, now she had put the worst job behind her:

'Lewis, I think you ought to answer for yourself.'

'Ought I?'

'I think so. You don't want to frighten me off, do you? You've done enough of that with other people, you know.'

I had always had respect for her. After a pause, I said:

'You make moral judgments more easily than I do.'

'I dare say I overdo it,' said Helen. 'But I think you go to the other extreme. And that has certain advantages to you when you're planning what you're planning now.'

'Do you think I'm specially pleased with myself about it?'

'Of course you're worried.' She studied me with her sharp bright eyes. 'But I don't know, I should have said you seemed much happier than you used to be.'

She went on:

'You know I wish you to be happy, don't you?'

'I know,' I said.

'And I wish it for her too,' said Helen.

Suddenly, across the grain of feeling, she smiled.

'When a woman comes to anyone in your predicament and says "Of course, I wish both of you well, I couldn't wish anyone in the world better, *but*—" it means she's trying to break it up. Quite true. But still I love her very much, and I was always fond of you.'

There was a silence.

She cried out, sharp, unforgiving:

'But the child's there. That's the end of it.'

'I've seen him—' I began.

'It didn't stop you?'

'No.'

'I can't understand you.' Then the edge of her voice turned away. 'I'm ready to believe that you and she could make something more valuable for each other than she and Geoffrey ever could. I always hoped that you'd get married in the first place.'

She said:

'But just because you're probably right for each other, just because you're capable of being good to and for each other, you can't go back to it now.'

For the first time I was irritated and confused, I stumbled to find an answer in her own terms.

'You can't,' she said, pushing my retort aside, 'take the slightest risk about the child. It's not only for his sake, it's for hers, because you know what it would mean for her, if anything went wrong with him.'

'I'm not afraid that anything would go wrong.'

'You can't take the risk.' She went on:

'If things didn't go right for the child, then it wouldn't matter if you felt it wasn't your fault and that he'd never have coped anyway. What do you think she would feel?'

She said:

'She must see this as well as I do. I can't understand her.'

I began to answer her. Whatever Margaret and I did, I said, there was no way of behaving as we wished to behave. Each of us knew the responsibilities, I said.

'If anything went wrong with him, she'd never forgive herself.'

'Whether she does—'

'It would be there, coming between you, for the rest of your lives,' Helen said.

'I've imagined even that,' I replied.

'You've no right to do it,' she burst out. I had been forcing down anger, but hers had broken loose.

'You must let us answer for ourselves,' I said.

'That's too easy,' she cried. She was gentler than her sister; I had not seen violent temper released in her before. 'I'd better tell you now, if you go ahead with this, I won't give either of you the slightest help, I won't make things easier for you by half an hour.'

'Do you hope that will change our minds?'

'I hope so very much,' she said. 'If I can stop her coming to you, I shall do it.'

I tried to control myself, and meet her case.

As I spoke, I was thinking that in Helen maternal love was stronger beyond comparison than any other. It was her unassuageable deprivation that she had not had children, and she still went from doctor to doctor. She had the maternal devotion of a temperament emotional but sexually cool; she could not but help feel that the love for a child was measured on the same plane as sexual love.

To Margaret that would have been meaningless. For her, those loves were different in kind. Almost as maternal as her sister, she had scarcely spoken to me about the boy, and yet all along she had been thinking what Helen had just threatened us with. Her feeling for the child was passionate. It had more ferocity than Helen's would have had, yet it could not cancel out that other feeling which pulled her as it were at right angles – that feeling which, unlike Helen's idea of it, was at root neither gentle nor friendly, that feeling which, although it contained an element of maternal love, was in totality nearer to that love than it was to self-destruction or self-display.

Helen's insight was acute, I was thinking; she had learnt more than most, and all she said about human actions you could trust – unless they were driven by sex. Then it was as though the drawing-pins had worked loose, the drawing-pins which fitted so accurately when she charted a description of a nephew sucking up to an aunt. Suddenly, if she had to describe sexual feeling, the paper was flapping, she was not hopelessly far away but the point never quite fitted. Somehow she sketched out friendships and trust and a bit of play and imagined that was sexual love. I remembered how many observers I had listened to and read, whose charts flapped loose exactly as hers did – observers wicked as well as high-minded, married as well as Jane Austens, men and women. Often their observations sounded neat when you were not in trouble, but when you were they might as well have been nonsense verse.

Yet I could not shrug off Helen's warning about the child. When I was younger, I might have thought that, by explaining to myself why she felt so deeply, I was explaining it away. Now I could not delude myself so conveniently.

I had to answer something to which there was no straight answer, telling her that for my part I would accept the penalties and guilt, and that I believed the tie between us would bear what the future laid upon it.

I had made up my mind, I told her: I did not know whether Margaret would come to me, but I was waiting for her.

CHAPTER XLIV

SECOND INTERVIEW OF GEORGE PASSANT

NEXT morning after breakfast – the sky over the park was so brilliant in November sunshine that I hushed the give-away words, the secret irked me more – I rang up Margaret: I had to tell her of my conversation with her sister, without softening any of her sister's case.

'I knew she was against us,' came Margaret's voice.

'She said nothing that we hadn't thought,' I said, reporting Helen's words about the child.

'Perhaps we should have told each other.'

'It has made no difference.'

'I never expected her to be so much against us.' There was a note of rancour in Margaret's tone, a note almost of persecution, very rare in her. Anxiously, I thought that the weeks of deception were wearing her down: they had begun to tell on me, who was better adapted for them: in so many ways she was tougher, and certainly braver, than I was, but not in this.

I said that we must meet. No, there was no one to look after the child. Tomorrow? Doubtful.

'We must settle it,' I said, for the first time forcing her.

'It will be easier next week.'

'That's too long.'

The receiver went dead, as though we had been cut off. Then she said a word and stopped. She, usually so active, could not act: she was in a state I also knew, when it was easier to think of disrupting one's life, so long as the decision were a week ahead, than to invent an excuse to go for a walk that afternoon.

At last: 'Lewis.' Her voice had the hardness, the hostility of resolve. When I replied, it came again: 'I'll go for tea to my father's on Friday, you can call and find me there.'

699

For the moment relieved, waiting for the Friday which was two days ahead, I arrived at Whitehall in the dazzling morning: odd, it struck me sometimes, to arrive there after such a scene (my brother's wife once talked of *mornings before the office*, referring to scenes of her own), to meet one's colleagues with their shut and public faces, and confront them with one's own.

That particular morning, as it happened, was not routine: I had to go straight to Rose's room, where I was required for two interviews, of which the second was to be George Passant's.

On Rose's desk chrysanthemums bulged from the vases, the burnt smell bit into the clean, hygienic air, along with Rose's enthusiastic thanks to me for sparing time that morning, which in any case I was officially obliged to do.

'Perhaps we might as well get round the table,' he said, as usual punctual, as usual unhurried. The two others took their places, so did I, and the first interview began. I knew already – I had heard Rose and Jones discuss the man – that the result was not in doubt. He was an ex-regular officer who had entered the department late in the war, and they agreed – his work had not come my way – that he was nowhere near the standard of the administrative class.

Polite, patient, judicious, Rose and the others questioned him, their expressions showing neither encouragement nor discouragement, neither excessive interest nor dismissal. They were all three sensible at judging men, or at least at judging men as creatures to do business with. They were on their own ground, selecting for the bureaucratic skills in which not only Rose, but also the youngest of the three, Osbaldiston, was expert.

The third was John Jones, who was now Sir John and a year off retirement: still looking handsome and high-coloured, and as though bursting with a heterodox opinion, a revelation straight from the heart, but after forty years of anxiety to please hypnotised by his own technique, unable to take his eye away from watching Rose's response. Rose found him agreeable: granted Jones's modest degree of talent, he had got on a good deal better as a snurge than he would have done as a malcontent, and it was romantic to think otherwise: but, when it came to serious business, his view did not count with Rose by the side of Osbaldiston's, who was twenty-five years younger.

Osbaldiston, a recent arrival, was an altogether more effective man. Unlike Rose or Jones, he had not started in a comfortable professional family, and socially he had travelled a long way, further than me or my friends: born in the East End, a scholarship, Oxford, the civil service examination. In the Treasury he had fitted so precisely that it seemed, though it was not, a feat of impersonation: Christian names, the absence of jargon, the touch of insouciant cultivation carried like a volume in the pocket – they all sounded like his native speech. Long, thin, unworn, he seemed to many above the battle and a bit of a dilettante. He was as much above the battle as a Tammany boss and as much a dilettante as Paul Lufkin. He was so clever that he did not need to strain, but he intended to have Rose's success and more than Rose's success. My private guess was that he was for once over-estimating himself: nothing could prevent him doing well, one could bet on his honours, one could bet that he would go as high as Jones – but perhaps not higher. It might be that, in the next ten years when he was competing with the ablest, he would just lack the weight, the sheer animal force, to win the highest jobs.

The first interview closed in courtesies from Rose to the candidate. As the door closed, Rose, without expression, looked round the table. Osbaldiston at once shook his head: I shook mine, then Jones shook his.

'I'm afraid the answer is no,' said Rose, and without any more talk began writing on the nomination form.

'He's a nice chap,' said Osbaldiston.

'Charming,' said Jones.

'He's been quite useful within his limits,' said Rose, still writing.

'He's got a service pension of seven hundred a year, as near as makes no matter,' said Osbaldiston. 'He's forty-six, and he's got three children, and it's a bit of a fluke whether he collects another job or not. What I can't see, Hector, is how on those terms we're going to recruit an officer corps at all.'

'It's not our immediate pigeon,' replied Rose from his paper, 'but we shall have to give it a bit of thought.'

The curious thing was, I knew that they would.

'Well,' said Rose, signing his name, 'I think we'll have Passant in now.'

When George entered, he wore a diffident, almost soapy smile, which suggested that, just as on his first appearance in the room, he expected to be tripped up inside the door. As he sat in the vacant chair, he was still tentatively smiling: it was not until he answered Rose's first question that his great head and shoulders seemed to loom over the table, and I could, with my uneasiness lulled, for an instant see him plain. His forehead carried lines by now, but not of anxiety so much as turbulence. Looking from Osbaldiston's face and Rose's to George's, one could see there the traces of experiences and passions they had not known – and yet also, by the side of those more disciplined men, his face, meeting the morning light, seemed mysteriously less mature.

Rose had begun by asking him what he considered his 'most useful contribution so far' to the work of the department.

'The A—— job I'm doing now is the neatest,' said George, as always relishing the present, 'but I suppose that we got further with the original scheme for Tube Alloys' (that is, the first administrative drafts about atomic energy).

'Would you mind running over the back history, just to get your part and the department's part in something like perspective?' Rose inquired with unblinking politeness. 'Perhaps you'd better assume that our colleague here' – he looked at Osbaldiston – 'is pretty uninformed about the early stages, as he wasn't in at the beginning.'

'Perhaps you'd better,' said Osbaldiston offhandedly. 'Though as a matter of fact I've done some of my homework since.'

Starting to enjoy himself, George gave the history of the atomic energy project from the time he entered the office. Even to me, his feat of memory was fantastic; my own memory was better than most, I had been closer to this stuff than he had, but I could not have touched that display of recapitulation. I could feel that, round the table, they were each impressed, and all took for granted that it was unthinkable for him to give a date or a paper fact wrong. But he was a shade too buoyant, and I was not quite easy. It was partly that, unlike Osbaldiston, he had not taken on a scrap of protective coloration; given the knowledge, he would have made his exposition in the identical manner, in the same hearty voice, when I first met him in a provincial street twenty-five years before. And also – this made me more uneasy – he had not put our part in the project in exact proportion: we had been modestly important, but not quite so important as he thought.

George was beaming and at ease. Jones, who I knew liked him, put in some questions about method which might have been designed to show George at his most competent. George's answer was lucidly sober. Just then it seemed to me unthinkable that any body of men, as fair-minded as these, could reject him.

Jones had lit a pipe, so that the chysanthemum smell no longer prevailed over the table; outside the windows at our back, the sun must have been brilliant to make the room so light. Rose continued with the interview: present work? how much could be dispensed with? One answer business-like, another again too buoyant and claiming too much, the third fair and good. At all interviews Rose was more than ever impassive, but he gave a slight acquiescent nod: so at once did Jones.

Then, as though lackadaisically, Osbaldiston spoke.

'Look here,' he said to George, 'there's something we are bound to have at the back of our minds, and it's far better to have it in the open, I should have thought. You're obviously an intelligent chap, if I may say so. But with due respect you don't seem to have done much with your life until you got dragged here by the war, and then you were forty-three already. It's bound to strike all of us as curious. Why was it? Can you give us some sort of lead?'

George stared at him.

'I'm afraid,' George said, with diffidence, 'that I didn't get much of a start.'

'Nor did a lot of us, you know.'

'I've got to make it clear that my family was very poor.'

'I bet it wasn't as poor as mine.' Osbaldiston made a point of not being snobbish about his origin. It was for that reason that he was more pressing about George's lack of ambition than Rose had been in the first interview three years ago.

'And of course,' said George, 'everyone at school thought that becoming a solicitor's clerk was a step up in the world for me, a bit above my station, as a matter of fact. No one ever pointed out, even if they knew, which I'm inclined to doubt, that there was anything else open to me.'

'I suppose schools were worse in your time,' said Osbaldiston. 'But afterwards you were with your firm, Eden & Martineau, for over twenty years and I take it the job is still open for you – I confess I'm still puzzled that you didn't see your way out.'

'Perhaps I didn't give it as much attention as others might have done, but at first there were things which interested me more. Somehow the right chance never seemed to present itself—'

'Bad luck,' said Osbaldiston casually, but they were looking at each other with incomprehension, the young man who, wherever you put him, knew how the successful world ticked, George who was always a stranger there.

Osbaldiston told Rose that he had no more questions: punctiliously Rose asked George if he had anything more he wished to tell us. No, said George, he thought he had been given a very full hearing. With a curious unobsequious and awkward grace, George added:

'I should like to say that I am grateful for your consideration.'

We listened to George's footsteps down the corridor. When they had died away, Rose, again without expression and in a tone utterly neutral, said:

'Well, what do you think of him?'

Quick off the mark and light-toned, Osbaldiston said:

'At any rate, he's not a nobody.'

'I thought he interviewed rather well,' said Jones.

'Yes. He had his ups and downs,' said Osbaldiston. 'On the whole he interviewed much as you'd expect. He showed what we knew already, that there's something in him.'

Rose said nothing, while Osbaldiston and Jones agreed that George's mind was better than the previous man's, that he would have done well in any academic course. If he had sat for the competitive examination as a young man at the regulation age, he would have got in comfortably, Osbaldiston reflected, and had an adequate career.

'What do you think, Hector?' Jones enquired.

Rose was still sitting silent, with his arms folded on his chest.

'Perhaps he would,' he said after a pause. 'But of course that isn't the point. He's not a young man now, he's a middle-aged one of forty-seven, and I think it's fair to say a distinctly unusual one.

'I'm inclined to think,' Rose added, his face blank, 'that the answer this time isn't immediately obvious.'

At once, I knew what I was in for. Indeed, I had known it while Rose sat, politely listening to the other's views, noncommittal in his quietness. For, in the long run, the decision was his: the rest of us could advise, argue, persuade: he would listen to the sense of opinion, but his was the clinching voice. Though it did not sound like it, though the manners were egalitarian and not court manners, this was as much a hierarchy as Lufkin's firm, and Rose's power that morning, concealed as it was, was as free as Lufkin's.

The only chance was for me to match will against will. He had opposed George's entry right at the beginning; Rose was not the man to forget his own judgments. In that one impartial comment of his, I could hear him believing inflexibly that he had been right.

Yet within the human limits he was a just man: and, screwing myself up for the argument, there were some fears which I could wipe away. I could rely on it that he would not mention George's prosecution fourteen years before: he had been acquitted, that was good enough. I could also rely on it that neither he nor the others would be much put off by rumours of George's womanising. Compared with those three round the table that morning, not many men, it struck me afterwards, would have been so correct, uninquisitive, unbiased.

'It might help us,' said Rose, 'if Lewis, who has seen more of Passant's work than any of us, would give us his views. I'm very anxious,' he said to me, 'that you should feel we've been seized of all the information we ought to have.'

Addressing myself to Rose, I made my case. Probably I should have made it more fluently for anyone but George. I was not relaxed, I had to force myself into the professional idiom.

I described his work, trying to apportion his responsibility, remembering that to Rose it would not seem right if I did not also demarcate my own. I said that he was a man of immense capacity. It was true – I was straining not to overstate my case – that his immediate judgment was not always first-class, he hadn't the intuitive feel for what could or could not be done. But he had two qualities not often combined – zest for detail and executive precision, together with a kind of long-term imagination, a forecaster's insight into policy. In the area between detail and the long term, he was not so good as our run-of-the-mill administrators: but nevertheless his two qualities were so rare that he was more valuable than any of them.

I had been talking on the plane of reason, but I heard my own voice harsh, emphatic without helping the sense.

'We're most grateful to you for that piece of exposition, my dear Lewis. We really are very, very much obliged to you.'

Jones sucked at his pipe: one could feel him sniffing dissension in the air: he said:

'I imagine that, if old Passant didn't get established, he'd just go straight back to those solicitors and it wouldn't be any terrific hardship for him.'

'He'd be about £200 a year better off with us,' said Osbaldiston, 'but you can knock some of that off for living in London.'

'I wonder whether it would be really a kindness to establish him?' Jones was meditating. 'Because he's obviously an unusual man, as Hector says, but with the best will in the world we can't do much for him. He'd have to begin as a principal and he's nearly fifty now, and at his age he couldn't possible go more than one step up. That's not much for someone who really is a bit of a fellow in his own way.'

'It may not be much, but he wants it,' I burst out.

'All that is off the point,' said Rose, with untypical irritation. 'We're not required to say what is good for him or what isn't, and we're not concerned with his motives. He's applied to be established, and he's got a right to apply, and our business starts there and ends there. The only conceivable point we have to decide is whether on his merits we ought to recommend him. I suggest,' he said, recapturing his politeness but with a flick in his tone, 'that we shall find the problem quite sufficiently intricate without introducing any psychological complications.'

'I'm not sure,' said Osbaldiston, 'that I can see a strong enough reason for not having him.'

'Do you see one, Hector?' asked Jones.

'Aren't you making very heavy weather of it?' I said, thinking the time for caution had gone. 'Here's a man everyone agrees to have some gifts. We're thinking of him for a not desperately exalted job. As a rule we can pass people, like Cooke for example, without half this trouble. Does anyone really consider the Cooke is a quarter as competent as Passant?'

'I didn't want to give my opinion,' said Rose smoothly and slowly to Jones, 'before I had some indication of what you others thought. I still don't want to rush things, but perhaps this is a reasonable time to sketch out the way my mind's been tending. As for your question, Lewis, I don't consider that we've been making unduly heavy weather of this business. We want to see that this man gets fair treatment: and we also don't want to take an unjustified risk for the department. It isn't entirely easy to reconcile those two objectives. I'm inclined to think that you slightly, not very greatly, but perceptibly, exaggerate Passant's mental qualities, but I won't quarrel with the view that he is a distinctly better mind than Cooke, for example, or, as far as that goes, than most of the ordinary principals in the department. I think I remember saying much the same thing when I first saw him. On the other hand, that doesn't entirely persuade me that keeping him wouldn't be a mildly regrettable risk where the department stands to lose slightly more than it stands to gain. After all, if we keep Passant, we gain a principal in some ways rather better than the average, in some ways, as you very properly pointed out, Lewis, rather worse. And at the same time we take on a definite hazard, not of course a serious one or one likely to materialise in fact, but the kind of hazard that you can't escape if you commit yourself to a man of, I don't want to do him an injustice but perhaps I can reasonably say, powerful, peculiar and perhaps faintly unstable personality. There's bound to be a finite chance that such a man wouldn't fit in for his remaining thirteen years or whatever it is. There's a finite chance that we should be making trouble for ourselves. There might just possibly be some row or commotion that wouldn't do us any good. I don't think that it is responsible to take those risks for the sake of an appointment at this level. I think I should conceivably have come down in Passant's favour if we were able to consider him for something more senior. He's the sort of man, in fact, who might have been far less trouble as a cabinet minister than he'd be in the slightly more pedestrian ranks of the administrative service.'

'Well,' said Jones, 'I don't think anyone could add much to a summing up like that.'

While there had seemed a doubt, Osbaldiston had been as painstaking as Rose himself. Now he tilted back his chair, and sounded more than ever offhand.

'Agreed,' he said, as if anxious not to waste any more time. 'Though perhaps it's a pity that we didn't catch the chap young.'

'In that case, with your approval,' Rose remarked, 'I propose to report on him to the Commission in terms something like this. I'll send you a draft. But I propose to say that he has filled a principal's place here quite up to standard form, and in one or two respects better than standard form. That we consider him intellectually well up to the level of the administrative class. But that at his age, bearing in mind certain features of his personality, we shouldn't feel entirely easy about fitting him into the department as an established man.'

'It might be a friendly thought,' said Jones, and he was speaking with good nature, 'to tell him to withdraw and not fag to go up to the Commission. Because there will be nothing they can do but say no.'

'I agree,' said Rose.

I began, keeping my voice down, still seeming reasonable, to open the argument again, but in a moment Osbaldiston broke in:

'It's no use going over old ground.'

'I really don't think it's very profitable,' said Rose.

Then I lost my temper. I said they were too fond of the second-rate. I said that any society which deliberately made safe appointments was on the way out.

'I'm sorry that we can't carry you with us, Lewis,' Rose's eyes were cold, but he was keeping his own temper.

'You don't realise your own prejudices,' I cried.

'No, this isn't at all profitable and we must agree to differ.' Rose spoke with exaggerated calm. 'You've had more experience in selecting men than any of your colleagues. As you know, I for one have often been guided by you. But you'd be the first to admit that no man can be infallible. And even very wise people sometimes seem no more infallible than the rest of us, the nearer they get towards home.'

He had permitted himself that last arctic flick. Then, leaning back in his chair, his face smooth, he said:

'Well, I think that is all for this morning. Thank you all very, very much for sparing your valuable time. Thank you, John. Thank you, Douglas. Thank you *very* much, Lewis.'

Back in my room, I stared out into the sun-bright Whitehall with the gauze of anger, of something like anxiety, of despondent restless bitterness in front of my eyes. It was the state that I used to know more often, that I had lived in during my worst times. It was a long while since I had been so wretched.

It had come pretty easy, it had not given me much regret, to slip out of the struggles of power – as a rule I did not mind seeing the top places filled by the Osbaldistons, those who wanted them more. But that morning, gazing blankly down at the sunny street, I was wretched because I was not occupying them myself. Then and only then I could have done something for George and those like him.

The men I sat with in their offices, with their moral certainties, their comfortable, conforming indignation which never made them put a foot out of step – they were the men who managed the world, they were the people who in any society came out on top. They had virtues denied the rest of us: I had to give them my respect. But that morning I was on the other side.

CHAPTER XLV

FRIGID DRAWING-ROOM

IN Whitehall the fog was dense: it was a little whiter, I could make out the lights in the shop-fronts, as the taxi nosed up Baker Street. By the time we reached Regent's Park, the pavements were clear to the view as far as the glowing ground-floor windows. Trying to damp down expectation, I was soothed by the fog shutting me in: instead of the joggle of the taxi, the reminder of adult expectations to which one did not know the end, I felt the easy snugness of a childhood's winter afternoon.

Whatever my expectations had been, I was surprised when I entered Davidson's study. For Margaret smiled at me, without much trace of trouble: Davidson did not look up: they were playing a game. In the fireplace stood a teapot, cups, a plate of crumpets, but on Davidson's side the tea had a skin on it. The crumpet's butter was solid. He was leaning, his face still distinguished even though his mouth was open with concentration, over the board. So far as I could pick up at a glance, the board was homemade, something like a chess board but not symmetrical and with at least three times the number of squares on the base line: at some points there appeared to be blanks and obstacles. They were using ordinary chessmen, but each had some extra pieces, together with small boxes whose function I did not begin to understand.

As I looked at Margaret's face, it seemed to me that I remembered returning to the house in Chelsea, finding Sheila staring with psychotic raptness at her chessmen: it was not a jab of pain, it was more like the pleasure (the exact converse of the Dantesque misery) with which, in the company of someone whom one safely loves, one looks in at a place where one has been miserable.

'She said that you might be coming,' said Davidson without preamble, gazing up under his eyebrows and then back at the board.

I said, 'Just for a few minutes,' but Davidson ignored me.

'You'll have to play, of course,' he said sternly. 'It's a much better game with three.'

It was, in fact, a war game which Davidson had perversely invented while he and his friends were pacifists in 1914–18. So far as I could judge, who envisaged the game stretching on, the three of us kept speechless there, it was elaborate but neat, crisp because he had a gift for concepts: Davidson wanted to explain it to me in all its beauties, irritated because I did not seem to be attending. I did not even pay enough attention, Davidson indicated, to the names of the two sides. They were Has-beens and Humbugs. The Has-beens were the side Davidson was commanding: their officers were chosen from his allies, associates and teachers, for Davidson, with his usual bleak honesty, knew critical fashion when he saw it. The other side was picked from Davidson's irremovable aversions, among them D. H. Lawrence, Jung, Kierkegaard; various Catholic intellectuals and communist art critics had places as brigadiers.

I did not know enough about the game to lose on purpose. All I knew was that Davidson would never be bored with it.

I could not even guess whether Margaret was willing to break the peace-of-the-moment.

Just then she was threatening one of her father's rooks, who stood for an academic philosopher known to all three of us.

'He oughtn't to be on your side anyway,' said Margaret.

Davidson studied the battle-plan.

'Why shouldn't he?' he said without attention.

'He's going to be the next convert, or so the Warden says.'

'The Warden,' Davidson remarked, still preoccupied with his move, 'is a good second-class liar.'

At last he guarded the rook, and was able to gather together the conversation – 'he [the philosopher] is about as likely to be converted as I am. He's a perfectly sensible man.'

'And you couldn't say fairer than that, could you?'

Davidson smiled: he liked being teased by his daughter: it was easy to feel how he had liked being teased, perhaps still did, by other women.

'He was always perfectly sensible,' he said.

'How ever did you know?'

'I don't remember him ever saying anything really crass,' said Davidson.

'But you all said the same things,' said Margaret. 'I always wondered how you could tell each other apart.'

It was the first time I had seen her alone with her father. I had heard her talk of him often, but never to him: and now I listened to her sounding gay and very much his daughter. Although I should have known better, I was surprised.

It was true that she felt something stronger than dislike for the beliefs of her father and his friends, and still more for their unbeliefs. She had been passionately convinced ever since she was a child that their view of life left out all that made men either horrible or splendid.

And yet, seeing her with her father, upset because I wanted nothing but to speak to her alone, I had to notice one thing – that she was proud of him. Her language was more like his than mine; in some ways her nerves were too.

I noticed something else, as I tried to calculate when the game might end – that she was disappointed by him. By the standards of his friends, he, who in his youth had been one of the most glittering of them, had not quite come off. He was no sort of creative person, he was not the critic that some of them had been. He had no illusion about it: at times, so Margaret divined, he had suffered because of it, and so did she. She could not help feeling that, if she had been a man, she would have been stronger than he had. That protest, born of their relation or edged by it, had been too deep for me to see, in our first time together. I imagined her as other people did: all they imagined was true, she was loving, she was happy to look after those she loved – it was all true: but it was also true (and the origin of much that she struggled with) that her spirit was as strong as her father's or mine, and in the last resort did not subdue itself before either of us.

The game continued. Repeatedly Margaret was glancing at me, until suddenly, as though screwing herself to the threshold edge, she said:

'I want to talk to Lewis for a minute.'

It was Davidson's move, and with a faint irritation he nodded. In an instant I followed Margaret into the hall; she led me into the drawing-room, which was dark except for a dim luminescence from the street lamp outside, bleared by the fog: the room struck chilly, but her cheek, as my fingers touched it, was hot, and I could feel my own skin flushed. She switched on a light: she looked up at me, and, although we were alone in the long room, although there was no one else in the house except Davidson, her voice was faint.

'Don't worry,' she said.

'That's easy to say.'

'No, it's not easy to say.' She had roused herself. Her face was wide open: it might have been smiling or in pain.

'I tell you,' she cried, 'there's no need to worry!'

I exclaimed.

'Do you believe me?' she cried.

'I want to believe you.'

'You can.' Then she added, in a matter-of-fact but exhausted tone:

'I'll do it.'

She went on:

'Yes, I'll tell him.'

We were standing in the corner of the frigid room. I felt for an instant the rip of triumph, then I shared her tiredness. It was the tiredness which comes after suspense, when the news may be good or bad: suddenly the good news comes, and in the midst of exaltation one is so light-headed with fatigue that one cannot read the letter through. I felt that happiness had sponged my face, taking away care like the smell of soap in the morning: I saw her face, also washed with happiness.

We stood quiet, our arms round each other: then I saw there was another purpose, a trouble, forming underneath the look of peace.

She said:

'I'll tell him. But you must wait a little.'

'I can't wait any longer.'

'You must be patient, just this once.'

'No, you must do it straightaway.'

'It's not possible,' she cried.

'It's got to be.'

I was gripping her shoulders.

'No,' she said, looking at me with knowledge of us both, 'I don't want you to, it would be bad. I promise you, it won't be long.'

'What are you waiting for?' To my bewilderment, she replied in a tone sounding like one of her aunts, astringent, cynical.

'How often have I told you,' she said, 'that if you're going to hurt anyone, it's no use being timidly considerate over the time you choose to do it?

'I always told you,' she could not leave it alone, 'that you did more harm by trying to be kind. Well, there's nothing like practising what one preaches.'

She was trapped, so that she could not bring herself to tell the truth to Geoffrey, or even mildly upset him. By a minor irony, the reason was as prosaic as some which had from time to time determined my own behaviour. It happened that Geoffrey was within a fortnight of sitting his examination for Membership, that is, his qualification as a specialist. It happened also that Geoffrey, so confident in general, was a bad and nervous examinee, who had failed his Membership several times already. She had at least to coax him through, take care of him for this last time: it meant dissimulating, which to her was an outrage, it meant not taking action, which was like an illness – and yet not to look after him, just then, when he was vulnerable, would mean a strain she could not bear.

'If you must,' I agreed at last.

She was relieved, she was abandoned to relief. Soon this would be behind us, she said. Then, as though at random, she cried:

'Now I want to do something.'

'What?'

'I want us to go and tell my father.'

Her cheeks and temples had coloured, her eyes were bright with energy, her shoulders were thrown back. She led me back through the house, her steps echoing excitedly in the empty hall, until we threw open the door of the study where her father, his beautiful head sunk on his chest, was staring with a mathematician's intensity at the board.

'I've got something to tell you,' she said.

He made a cordial but uninterested noise.

'You'll have to listen. Or have I got to write you a letter about it?'

Reluctantly he looked up, with intelligent, brilliant, opaque eyes. He said:

'If you're going to disturb the game, I hope it isn't something trivial.'

'Well. Lewis and I want to get married.'

Davidson looked blank-faced. He seemed to have had no intimation whatsoever of the news: she might have been telling him that she had just seen a brontosaurus.

'Do you, by God?' he said.

Then he became convulsed with laughter.

'Perhaps you were within your rights to disturb the game. No, I can't say that the news is entirely trivial.'

'I haven't told Geoffrey yet,' she said. 'I can't for a little while. I don't know whether he'll let me go.'

'He'll have to,' said Davidson.

'It may be difficult.'

'I should have thought he was a moderately civilised man,' he replied. 'In the long run, one has no choice in these things, don't you know?'

She would have preferred her father not to be quite so casual: but telling him had given her the pleasure of action. It was a joy to let us be seen in another's eyes.

For once her father's glance had not dropped; he looked at her with a sharp, critical, appreciative smile, and then at me.

'I'm quite glad,' he said.

I said:

'You ought to be prepared for some unpleasantness. We shall be giving anyone who wants plenty to get hold of.'

'Anyone who wants,' he replied indifferently, 'is welcome to it, I should have thought.'

I supposed he did not know our story, but went on: 'Even well-wishers are going to find it slightly bizarre.'

'All human relationships are slightly bizarre unless one is taking part,' said Davidson. 'I don't see why yours is any more so than anyone else's.'

He went on:

'I've never known a situation where it was worth listening to outsiders.'

He was the last man to talk for effect: he meant it. It was a kind of contempt which was much more truly aristocratic than that of Betty Vane's relatives: it was the contempt of an intellectual aristocracy, who never doubted their values, least of all in sexual matters: who listened to each other, but not at all to anyone outside. Sometimes – it had often alienated his daughter – his lack of regard for opinion implied that those outside the magic ring might as well belong to another species. But, in times of trouble, it made him inflexible, one to whom the temptations of disloyalty did not exist.

'As a general rule and nonsense apart,' he said, 'when people are in your position the only help of any conceivable good is practical.'

With a surprisingly brisk and executive air, he asked:

'Are you all right for money?'

It sounded more surprising, for Davidson, who had never got acclimatised to fountain-pens or radio sets, seemed the most unpractical of men. In fact, the concentration he applied to art-history or to home-made games went also into his investments and he had been consistently and abnormally successful with them. Playing the market was more than a hobby for him, something nearer an obsession.

I told him that money was not a problem. Still executive, he said:

'I've known it to be useful to have somewhere to live where people don't expect to find you. I could arrange to let you have this house for six months.'

Margaret said she might take him at his word. She would want somewhere to live with the child until we could be married.

Davidson was satisfied. He had no more to contribute. Once more he studied his daughter's face with pleasure, then his eyes dropped to their habitual level. Although he did not openly suggest that we should finish the game, his glance began to stray towards the board.

CHAPTER XLVI

LAST TRAIN TO A PROVINCIAL TOWN

EACH morning, as I telephoned Margaret, the winter sky heavy over the trees outside, I heard her forcing her voice to hearten me. At last, so near the time when I trusted her to come to me, I was jealous. I could not stand the thought of her life from day to day, I had to switch my imagination off. I could not stand the thought of her keeping his spirits up; I went through those prosaic miseries of the imagination in which one is tormented by the hearth-glow of another's home, even if it is an unhappy home.

I told myself her part was the harder, but I began to be frightened of the telephone, as though it did nothing but force me to think of her home, of the two of them together.

As we talked, I never inquired about the exact date of his Membership. It was partly that I was trying to keep my side of the bargain, she was to choose her time: but it was also that I did not want to know, either that or anything else about him.

Christmas passed. On a morning just as I was getting ready to ring her up, the telephone bell rang. I heard her voice, though it was distorted and forced.

'It will be all right.'

'You've told him?' I cried.

'Yes, I've told him.'

'Is all well?'

'All will be well.' She was crying.

'When?'

'Soon.'

'Very soon?' I burst out.

She said:

'For a long time he wouldn't believe it.'

'When shall I fetch you?'

'I had to make him believe me.'

'The sooner I'm with you—'

'He can't understand why this has happened to him.'

'Has he accepted it?'

'Yes, but he's bitter.'

She had deceived herself when we talked of him, she was saying. I replied, if that was true, I had deceived myself as much. Then crying, sometimes dragged back to the night just past (for they had talked right through it) she was asking, as she had not done before, for me to reassure her, to tell her what we should give each other.

When would she come to me? Not that day, she said, in a tone that made me feel there was one last way in which she was trying to look after him. Not that day, but the next.

'At last,' she said, in a tone neither sad nor young.

The same evening, I was having a drink with George Passant, who had served his final day at the office and was returning to the provincial town by the last train. We met in a public house, for George had not adapted himself to clubs: there he sat by the fire, enjoying himself as comfortably as in our youth. I told him again, as I had done many times, how angry I was with the department, and how I still uselessly thought of methods by which I might have presented the case better.

'It was a nuisance,' said George. 'But anyway I had three interesting years; I wouldn't have been without them for the world.'

Somehow he could still draw a line across the past, regard it with an invulnerable optimism as though it had happened to someone else.

'The more I think of it,' said George, with a complacent smile, 'the better it seems. I've had three remarkably interesting years and done some work which I know the value of better than anyone else. The value in question is incidentally considerable. In the process I've been able to estimate the ability of our hierarchical superiors and there's no danger that I shall be tempted to get them out of proportion. And also I've managed to seize the opportunity for a certain amount of private life. Which all constitutes a pretty fair return for a very minor bit of humiliation.'

When he first heard that he had been rejected, he had broken into a comminatory rage, cursing all who had ever been in authority over him, all officials, all members of the new orthodoxy, all who conspired to keep him in the cold. But very soon he had been exaggeratedly reasonable, pointing out 'Of course, I couldn't expect anything different . . .' and he would produce some ingenious, highly articulated and quite unrealistic interpretation of why Rose, Jones and Osbaldiston found it necessary to keep him out.

So now he sat comfortably by the fire, drinking his beer, proving to me that he was not damaged.

'All I hope is that you invite me up here pretty regularly,' said George. 'In future, an occasional visit to London will be essential to my well-being.'

It might have been some new night-spot he had discovered: it might have been the balm, mysterious to all but himself, of meeting what he regarded as 'respectable' acquaintances: probably it was both, but I did not attend, for I had meant to tell him my news and this was the opening.

'Of course,' I said.

I had listened while Margaret, rejoicing in candour, had broken our secret to her father. Myself, I had not said anything, open or implicit, even to my brother or to a friend as old as George – except when, to my own astonishment, I came out with it to Herbert Getliffe. Even with George that night I did not wish to talk: I still wanted to be timid with fate: I found myself speaking with an obliqueness I could not quite control.

'Next time you come,' I said, 'there's just a faint possibility that I may not be alone.'

'I'll give you plenty of notice,' said George obtusely.

'I mean, I may have someone in my flat.'

George chuckled.

'Oh well, she won't be there for ever.'

'As a matter of fact,' I said, 'it's not quite inconceivable, of course, it's too early to say—'

George was puzzled. He had not often heard me so incoherent; he had not heard me anything like so incoherent twenty years before, when my friends and I told glorious stories of fornications we had not yet in fact committed. At last I made it clear enough, and he was on his feet towards the bar, saying in a great voice: 'Well, this is a new start, and I'm damned if we don't have a celebration!'

Superstitiously I tried to stop him, but he turned on me:

'Is this a new start or isn't it?'

'I hope it is.'

'Don't sit on the blasted fence. Of course it is, and I'm not going to be done out of celebrating it.'

George continued in that state of noisy argumentative well-being until, when he had drunk more, he said:

'There's a certain beautiful symmetry in the way we stand tonight. You're just coming out of your old phase of existence – just at the precise moment that I am neatly returning to mine.'

He laughed out loud, not rancorously, not enviously, but with a curious pleasure, pleasure it seemed in the sheer pattern of events. He was a happy man: he always had been, but was growing even happier in middle age, when it seemed to all external eyes that he had totally failed. As he said, he was returning to his old existence, to the provincial town, to the firm of solicitors, where he would continue not as partner but as managing clerk: and there, one would have bet that night, George the first to do so, he would stay for the rest of his life. But he breathed in a happiness that begins to visit some in middle age: it was the happiness which comes to those who believe they have lived according to their nature. In George's own view he had been himself, he had lived as himself, more than anyone round him. He blamed his external calamities to that cause and still thought – partly as a consolation, partly because in the happiness of his senses it seemed true – that he had had the best of the bargain. He believed he had paid the price, and at that stage did not envisage that there could be more to pay.

With five minutes to go before the last train left, we arrived at St Pancras. I told George, as we walked down the platform in the cold, the red lights smeared out by an eruption of sulphurous smoke, that this was the identical train I used to catch, going home from London after eating dinners at the Inn. But George's capacity to respect the past, never large, was full up for one night. He merely said absently: 'I expect you did,' and instead gazed with absorption into a first-class carriage. There a fat, high-coloured, pursy man of about thirty, elegantly dressed, was waving a finger with stern, prissy disapproval at a companion, seedy, cheerful-looking and twenty years older. As we left them to it George, gazing out under the dome, into the smoky dark, yelled with laughter.

'It might have been me!' he shouted. 'It might have been me! That young chap is like A——'

Whistles were blowing, the train was ready to leave London, and he was thinking of nothing but his internal joke.

'Like A——,' he cried, looking down at me from the window. 'Like A—— expecting me to sympathise because he's hard pressed on three thousand a year. And immediately giving me advice on how much I ought to save out of eight hundred.'

CHAPTER XLVII

MIDDLE OF THE NIGHT

THE room was dark as I woke up: at the edge of the curtains lurked the fringes of luminescence which, with a kind of familiar comfort, told me that it was the middle of the night. I felt happy; at the same time I was taking ease and comfort, not only from the familiar fringe of light, but also from a scent in the bedroom which was strange there. Basking, I stretched and sat up, looking down at Margaret asleep. In the dimness I could just make out her face, turned into the pillow, one arm thrown above her head, the other trailing at her side. She was fast asleep, and, when I bent and put my mouth to her shoulder, the warm flesh did not move, her breathing did not so much as catch, went on slow and steady in the relaxed air.

Often in the past months I had woken up, seen the fringe of light round the window curtains, had become conscious of my worries about her and known that it would be a long time before I got off to sleep again. Now I was rested; I had only to turn over – it was odd to look into the darkness with nothing on my mind, to sleep as deeply as she was sleeping.

Just then it was a luxury to stay awake. I got out of bed and went towards the door, which we had left open so that we could hear a sound from the child's room: he, too, was peacefully asleep. Walking quietly through the dark rooms, I felt there was no resistance between me and the air, just as I had sometimes felt on warm evenings in the streets of towns. Yes, I could think of the problems ahead of us, many of them the same problems over which I had worried through the broken nights: but I thought of them without worry, almost without emotion, as though

718

they were there to be picked up. Perhaps that was a state, it seemed to me later, in which men like Lufkin or Rose lived much of their lives.

Standing by the sitting-room window I looked down at the road, where the lights of cars kept giving form to the bushes by the park edge. The cars and lorries went by below: above them, the lamps suspended over the middle of the road swung in the night wind: watching them, I was happy without resistance. I had woken into a luminous happiness, and it stayed with me.

PART FIVE

ANOTHER HOMECOMING

CHAPTER XLVIII

BIRTH OF A SON

WAITING in the dark bedroom I heard Margaret's steps as she returned to bed. I asked if anything was the matter, and in a matter-of-fact whisper she told me to cover my eyes, she was going to switch on the light.

Then she said:

'Well, it's no use saying that I hope I'm not going to disturb you.' Her tone was sarcastic and calm. For an instant, not calm myself, I nevertheless recalled her father laughing at me in the same tone, one afternoon when he interrupted my work at the office.

'I'm pretty certain,' she said, 'that it's coming early.'

She was a fortnight from her time, and I was startled.

'No,' she said, 'it's nothing to upset you. I'm quite glad.'

She sounded so happy, above all so calm, that I could not help respond. What could I do for her, I asked?

'I think it might be as well to ask Charles March to come round.'

Charles March, who had moved to a practice north of the park, had looked after her during her pregnancy: when we were waiting for him after I had telephoned, I told Margaret, trying to match her nerve, that I seemed only to meet him at the crises of my life.

'This isn't a bad one, though,' she said.

'I touch wood more than you do,' I replied.

'You are superstitious, aren't you?' she said. 'When I first noticed it, I couldn't believe it. And I daren't ask you, because I thought I must be wrong.'

I had drawn the curtains. Outside the window a red-brick parapet solidified the first morning sunshine: below and beyond were gardens misty, washed-out in the dawn, but the glaring bricks glowed near, a starling stood immobile on the wall, harshly outlined as if it were cardboard.

Margaret was sitting up in bed, pillows behind her, twitting me not only to give me reassurance, but also because she was steady-hearted and full of a joy I could not share. For her the child was living now, something to love.

As Charles March examined her, and I stood gazing down from the sitting-room into the park, I felt afraid for her because we were happy. I was afraid for the child because I wanted it. I had a special reason for fear, as Charles March had told me that we ought not to have another.

Down below, the first bus sped along in the milky light. Since she came to me, we had been happy. Beforehand, we had both taken it for granted that to reshape a life took effort, humility and luck; I did not know whether I could manage it. That we should stay together was certain: in the world's eyes we should bring it off, but we should judge ourselves by what we saw in each other's. Up to now we had been blessed.

Only in one aspect, I thought, had she found me absenting myself – and only she would have perceived it. She perceived it when she saw me with her boy, Maurice, Geoffrey's child; for with him I was not natural, I did not let myself go. I was well disposed to him through conscience, not through nature, and she knew it. I was as considerate as I could be, but that was my old escape, turning myself into a benevolent spectator.

It made us more than ever anxious for children of our own.

After we married, in the July of the year she came to me, which was 1947, four months passed before she conceived. She had watched me play with the little boy during those months: he liked me because I was patient and more even-tempered than she was. When she became pregnant she felt happiness for me first, and only later love for the coming child.

That summer dawn, listening to the rumble of Charles's voice through the walls, I left the sitting-room window and found myself restlessly dawdling into Maurice's nursery: his cot was empty and most of his toys had gone, for Helen had taken him for the next month. There I was glancing at one of his picture-books when Charles March found me.

He was not shaved, his eyes were sharp with a doctor's interest, with his own fellow-feeling: he would drive her to the clinic, he said, and, with a sarcastic flick not unlike hers, added that it was better to err on the safe side.

It was only lately, when he had been married for years, that he had had a family himself. There had been a time during my separation from Margaret when he and I had sympathised with each other, knowing that we both wanted children and might be deprived of them. As I looked at him I remembered that we had spoken without reserve.

Nevertheless, if he had just been a doctor and not an intimate friend, I should have asked more questions. As it was, I went into the bedroom, where Margaret had nearly finished packing her dressing-case. She was wearing a coat over her nightgown: as I held her in my arms, she said:

'You might as well go to that dinner tonight.'

Then she added:

'I'd rather be there than where I shall be. Yes, I'd even rather be at Lufkin's.'

It might have been intended as a gibe, but as I held her, it told me more. I did not need even to think or reply: this was the communication, deeper than emotion or sensuality, though there is sensuality in it, which two people close together cannot save each other from. I knew that her nerve for once had faltered: her imagination was showing her a lonely, hygienic room, the bedside light. Brave in so many ways, she had her phobias, she dreaded a lonely room: she even felt the sense of injustice that cropped up in her, in and out of place. Why did she have to go through with it, while others were enjoying themselves?

Enjoying themselves at Lufkin's – it was, however, not a reasonable description of people's behaviour there; it never had been, it still was not. I arrived ready to be elated, with the peculiar lightheadedness of an ordeal put off: for at breakfast time, a few hours after Margaret arrived at the clinic, they had told me that the child might be born within forty-eight hours, then at five o'clock had said that it was not likely for a week and that I could safely spend the night out.

Just as there used to be in Lufkin's suite, there was drink, there was noise; in my lightheadedness I could take the first and put up with the second, but as for elation, it did not bear up in many under Lufkin's inflexible gaze. The curious thing was that he believed it did. When the women left us, and Lufkin, as always indifferent to time, began a business talk that lasted an hour, he had a satisfied smile as though all his guests were feeling jolly.

Nearly all of them belonged to his own staff. Despite his own forecast, he had not been forgiven by his fellow-tycoons for taking an honour from their enemies and socially they cold-shouldered him. Not that he gave any sign of caring: he just went on inviting to dinner the younger bosses with whom by now he had filled the top places in his firm: men more educated, more articulate than the old ones, looking and speaking more like civil servants, and in his presence sounding less like a chorus of sycophantic cherubim. And yet, when he made a pronouncement which they believed to be nonsense and which everyone round the table knew they believed to be nonsense, none of them said so, though several of them had gone so far that Lufkin could do them neither harm nor good. His *mana* was as strong as ever.

I was glad to watch it all again. It gave me – I was relaxed, I should enjoy my sleep that night, the worry of the dawn, because it was put off, was washed away – the luxury of recalling a past less happy. Nights at that damped-down table before the war: other able men choosing their words: back to the Chelsea house. It seemed to me strange that I could have lived that life.

I had another reminder of it, before Lufkin let us go from the table. There had been talk of a legal case the firm was concerned with, and, among the names of the barristers, Herbert Getliffe's came up.

'You devilled for that chap once, Lewis, or am I wrong?' said Lufkin. On such points he was never wrong.

I asked whether he knew Getliffe. To nod to, said Lufkin.

I asked whether Getliffe would soon be going to the Bench.

'Not on your life,' said Lufkin.

He sounded positive, even for him.

'What's happened?' I enquired.

'Well, within these four walls, he's blotted his copybook. He's been doing some jiggery pokery with his income tax, and they've had to be persuaded not to prosecute him.' Lord Lufkin said it not so much with malice, as with the certainty and satisfaction of inside knowledge. 'I've got no pity for the damned fool. It not only does him harm, which I can bear reasonably philosophically, but it does harm to the rest of us. Anyway, he won't be able to live this one down.

'That chap's finished,' said Lufkin, declaring the conversation closed.

When, after midnight, the party broke up he drove me home himself, less offhanded with me than the others because I was no longer a member of his court. Sitting back as the car paced through the Mall, up St James's, past the club windows, I felt a moment's disquiet, mysterious and heavy, the first that night; and then once more the sense of privilege and power which I still was subject to in his company. The car, as opulent as he was austere, moved up Piccadilly, past the Ritz, the Green Park. There were not enough men for the top jobs, Lufkin was saying: the number of top jobs was going up as society became more complex, and the number of competent men had not gone up at all. True, the rewards weren't much these days: perhaps we should have to deal out a few perks. If we didn't find enough good men to run the show, Lufkin said, the country was sunk.

For once his tone had lost its neutrality and become enthusiastic; but when the car drew up in front of my flat, he spoke as bleakly as though I were a stranger. What he said was: 'Give my regards to your charming wife.'

As I thanked him for the dinner, he went on:

'She'll have received some flowers from me this evening.' He said it just as bleakly, as though his only gratification was that he had mastered the etiquette and had all the apparatus of politeness at his command.

Out of a deep sleep, into which I had fallen as soon as I left Lufkin and went straight to bed, I heard a distant burr, and my heart was thudding with dread before I was awake enough to be conscious that it was the telephone. As I stumbled across the room, across the hall, switched on and was dazzled by the light, my throat was sewn-up. The telephone burred loudly now, like all the bad news I had ever had to hear.

As I took up the receiver Charles March's voice came at once, unusually loud even for him, so that I had to hold the instrument inches away:

'Lewis? Is that you?'

'Yes?'

'You've got a son.'

'Are they safe?'

'I think they're pretty well.'

His voice came to me, still loud, but affectionate and warm:

'You've had good luck for once and I envy you.'

His own children were girls, he had wanted a son and had apologised for it as a piece of Jewish atavism: but he knew that I did too.

I could not see them until the morning, he said. He told me the time her labour started, and the time of the birth; he was full of happiness because he could give me some. 'It's not often we've had anything good to tell each other, don't you agree?' His voice spoke out of our long friendship. He said that I could do with some rest myself, and that I was to get back to bed now.

I neither could nor wanted to. I dressed and went down into the street, where the night air was thundery and close. Just as, when expecting a joy and suddenly dashed with disappointment (as had happened to me years before on a Christmas Eve that sometimes comes back to mind), one has moments when the joy is still expected – just so, the shadow of fear can survive the opposite shock, the shock of happiness. I was still shaken, out of comparison more so than I had been at Lufkin's table: for an instant, it reached me that this was a happy night, and then I reverted to feeling, with a hallucinatory sharpness, that it had not yet occurred.

As I walked across the park the thundery cloudcap was so low that it was hard to make out the interlocking couples on the grass; I passed close by, in the headaching and stale air, the seat where Margaret and I had sat in the desolating night when it seemed that we had worn each other out. Yet that was unrealistic too, as unrealisable as Charles March's news.

Retracing without intention the way Lufkin had driven me, I came to the mouth of St James's Street. It was empty now, and not one of the club windows was alight; all of a sudden I stopped repressing the disquiet that had seized me in Lufkin's car. For, looking into those windows from the car, I had not dared to think of another evening when I had dined out without my wife – when I had dined with Gilbert Cooke, and simultaneously Sheila was dying. Now I could let the past come back blank and harmless, so that, going slowly down the street, I did at last credit my reason for happiness.

It was not until I saw Margaret next morning, however, that I felt happy. Suddenly the sight of her in bed, her hair straight as a schoolgirl's, her collar-bone plain where the bedjacket and nightgown had fallen away, made the tear glands smart, and I cried out. I said that I had not seen her look like that; then when I let her go and gazed at her again, I had to ask:

'How are you?'

'What century do you think you're living in?'

She was tired, she spoke with the indulgence of not concentrating. She went on:

'I wish I could have another for you.'

I interrupted her, and then she said, inspecting me:

'What do you think you've been doing?'

'Walking about.'

'If you'd listened to me—' but she could not go on teasing me. When had I heard? What exactly had I been doing when I heard? Who told me? What did I say? She cried out:

'He's a dear little boy and I love him very much.'

Sitting up, she turned her head on the bank of pillows and looked out of the window into the clinic garden. The cloudcap was still dense, ominous over the trees. She said:

'The room where I first saw you – it must be somewhere in the wing over there.'

It was part of the same establishment; until that morning I had not been near it again.

'It must have been about four in the afternoon, but it was later in the year, wasn't it?" she said, exact in her memory because she was happy. She added:

'I liked you. But I don't believe I thought I should ever be your wife.'

She said, in a tone relaxed and both diffident and proud:

'At any rate, I've done something for you now.'

Soon afterwards she rang and asked the nurse to bring the baby in. When she did so, I stood up and, without finding anything to say, stared at him for what seemed a long time. The nurse – she had a smooth and comely Italianate face – was saying that he was not a whopper, but a fine boy, 'all complete and perfect, as they say': I scarcely listened, I was looking at the eyes unfocused, rolling and unstable, the hands waving slowly and aimlessly as anemones. I felt utterly alien from this being in her arms: and at the same time I was possessed by the insistence, in which there was nothing like tenderness, which was more savage and angry than tender, that he must live and that nothing bad should happen to him.

As the nurse gave him to Margaret his head inclined to her, and I saw his side-face, suddenly transfigured into a cartoon of an adult's, determined, apprehensive. Grasping him, Margaret looked at him with an expression that was no longer youthful, that held responsibility and care, as though the spontaneous joy with which she had spoken about him had been swallowed up in pity.

I stood and watched her holding the child. Partly I felt I could not get used to it, it was too much for me, it had been too quick, this was only a scene of which I was a spectator. Partly I felt a tug at the fibres, as though I were being called on in a way I did not understand; as though what had entered into me could not yet translate itself into an emotion, into terms of anything I could recognise and feel.

CHAPTER XLIX

A CHILD LOOKING AT THE MOON

WHEN, fifteen months after the child's birth, I received a letter from Mrs Knight saying that her husband had been very ill and wished to see me, I did not think twice before going. They were staying, so she told me in the letter, at Brown's Hotel – 'so as to get him to the seaside by easy stages. Of course, he has such a sense of duty, he says he must get back to his parish work. But I trust you not to encourage him in this. He is not to think of returning to the Vicarage until the summer.'

Apparently he was not to think of retiring either, it occurred to me, though by this time he was over seventy: they had never needed the stipend, it was negligible beside her income: but that did not prevent Mr Knight from clinging on to it. As for his cure of souls, for years he had found that his ill-health got worse when confronted with most of his daily tasks, except those, such as preaching and giving advice, which he happened to enjoy.

When I first caught sight of him in the hotel that afternoon he looked neither specially old nor ill, although he was lying stretched out on his bed and only whispered a greeting. Mrs Knight plunged straight into the drama of his illness. They were doing themselves well, I noticed: they had taken a suite, and I walked through a sitting-room lavish with flowers on the way to their bedroom. By Mr Knight's bed stood grapes, books, medicine bottles and tubes of drugs: by Mrs Knight's stood magazines, a box of chocolates, a bottle of whisky and a syphon of soda. It had an air of subfusc comfort, of indulgences no longer denied, that I had seen before in elderly couples travelling.

Mrs Knight sat on her bed, describing her husband's symptoms: in a dressing-gown, his coat and collar off, Mr Knight lay on his, his eyes closed, his clever petulant mouth pulled down; he lay on his back, his legs relaxed, like a figure on a tomb or one in a not disagreeable state of hebetude.

According to Mrs Knight's account, he had for a long time past been starting up in the middle of the night with his heart racing.

'I take his pulse, of course,' she said energetically to me. 'Ninety! A hundred! Sometimes more!'

'I decided,' she looked at me with her active innocent eyes, 'that I ought to keep a diary of his health. I thought it would help the doctors.'

She showed me a quarto day-book, two days to the page, and in it some of the entries in her large hand. . . .

'L. woke up as usual: pulse 104. Quietened down to 85 in twenty minutes. . . .' 'Better day. I got his heart steady for twenty-four hours. . . .'

It sounded to me like the physical condition of a highly strung and hyperæsthetic man, but it would not have been profitable to tell Mrs Knight so. Apart from 'good afternoon', she had said nothing to me since I arrived that did not concern her husband's health.

'It was always the same, though,' she cried. 'We couldn't stop it!

Him waking up in the middle of the night with his heart pounding away like this— '

Sitting on the bed she moved both her thick, muscular arms up and down, the palms of her hands facing the floor, at the rate of hundreds a minute. For the first time, the silent figure on the other bed joined in: Mr Knight used one arm, not two, and without opening his eyes flapped a hand to indicate the rapid heart-beats, but not so quickly as his wife, not in time.

'And I couldn't get him to be examined properly,' she said. 'He's always been frightened of his blood pressure, of course. He wouldn't let the doctors take it. Once I thought I had persuaded him to, but just as the doctor was putting the bandage round his arm he shouted "Take it away! Take it away!" '

Mr Knight lay absolutely still.

'Then one night last year, it was in September because he was just thinking about his harvest thanksgiving sermon, it was a nice warm night and he'd had a couple of glasses of wine with his dinner, I woke up and I didn't hear him at all, but I knew he was awake. As a rule, of course, he calls out to me, and I knew – it was just like second sight – I knew there was something wrong because he didn't call out. Then I heard him say, quite quietly, just as though he were asking me for a glass of water: "Darling, I think I'm going".'

A sigh came from the other bed.

'I didn't say "I think I'm *going*," ' came a whisper from Mr Knight. 'I said "Darling, I think I'm *dying*".'

Still good-tempered, still urgent, Mrs Knight accepted the correction: she told me of the visit of the doctor, of his opinions, encouragements and warnings, her own activity, Mr Knight's behaviour. Oddly enough, despite her hero-worship of her husband, her narrative was strictly factual, and pictured him as comporting himself with stoicism perceptibly less than average. After his one protest he did not object or open his eyes again, until at last he said, faintly but firmly:

'Darling, I should like to talk to Lewis just for a little while.'

'As long as it doesn't tire you.'

'I don't think it need tire me, if we're careful,' said Mr Knight – with a concern that equalled hers.

'Perhaps it won't be too much for you,' she said. 'Anyway I shan't be far away.'

With injunctions to me, she removed herself to the sitting-room: but she did not go out of sight, she left the door open and watched as though she were a policeman invigilating an interview in gaol. Very painstakingly Mr Knight hitched his head higher up on the pillow; his eyes were no longer shut, he appeared to be staring out of the window, but he gave me an oblique glance that was, just as I remembered it, shrewd, malicious, and sharp with concealed purpose.

'I don't receive much news nowadays, naturally, Lewis, but all I hear of you suggests that you're prospering.'

He began again, just as I remembered, some distance from the point: I was ready for him to weave deviously until his opening came. 'Should you say that, allowing for the uncertainties of life and not claiming too much, that that was true?'

'In many ways it is.'

'I'm glad for you, I'm glad.'

In part, I thought, he meant it; he had always had an affection for me. Then, probing again, he said:

'In *many* ways?'

'In more than I reckoned on.'

'There is bound to be much that you and I find difficulty in asking each other, for reasons that would distress us both to think of, and yet I should like to think that you perhaps have known what it is to have the gift of a happy marriage?'

I was sure that this was not the point he was winding towards. He asked it quite gently, and in the same tone I said yes, I was coming to know it.

'It is the only good fortune I've been given, but I've been given it more completely than most men,' said Mr Knight. 'And if you will let me tell you, Lewis, there is nothing to compare with it.'

He was whispering, his wife could not hear: but again, singular as it might have seemed to a spectator, he meant it. He went on:

'I seem to remember, forgive my meanderings if I am wrong, that I caught sight of the announcement of a birth in the *Times* – or the *Telegraph* was it? Or perhaps both? – that somehow I connected with your name. Could that possibly be so?'

I said yes.

'I seem to remember, though again you might forgive any mistakes I make, it was of the male sex?'

I said yes.

'It seemed to come back to me that you announced his names as Charles George Austin. Somehow, not knowing anything of your recent adventures, of course, I connected the name George with that eccentric figure Passant, whom I recalled as being an associate of yours in the days that I first heard about you.'

Yes, I said, we had called him after George Passant.

'Not bad,' Mr Knight gave a satisfied smile, 'for an old man in a country vicarage, long out of touch with all of you and the world.'

But he was still skirmishing, right away from his point of attack. He went on:

'I hope your boy gives you cause to be proud of him. You may be one of those parents whose children bring them happiness.'

Then he changed direction again. He said, in a light, reflective tone:

'Sometimes, when I've heard mention of an achievement of yours, I go back to those days when you first came into my house, should you say that's because I've had nothing to occupy me? Does it occur to you that it was a quarter of a century ago and more? And sometimes, with all respect to your achievements and acknowledgment of the position you've secured for yourself, I find myself wondering, Lewis, whether all that time ago you did not contemplate even more of the world's baubles than – well, than have actually accrued to you. Of course I know we all have to compound with our destinies. But still, I sometimes felt there might have been hours when you have looked at yourself and thought, well, it could have gone worse, but nevertheless it hasn't gone perfectly, there have been some disappointments one didn't expect.'

I was wondering: was this it? I replied:

'Yes. At that age I should have expected to cut more of a figure by now.'

'Of course,' Mr Knight was reflecting, 'you've carried a heavy private load so much of your life. And I suppose, if you'd been going to take a second wind and really go to the top, you wouldn't at your present age have readjusted yourself to a wife and child.'

Was this it? Had he got me there simply to remind me that my public career had not been wonderful?

If so, I could bear it, more easily than he imagined. But somehow I thought he was still fencing. It was just that at seventy, believing himself ill, taking such care of his life that he had no pleasure left, he nevertheless could not resist, any more than in the past, tapping the barometer of an acquaintance's worldly situation. And he was, also as in the past, just as good at it as Rose or Lufkin. He had never been outside his parish, he had been too proud and vain to compete, but at predicting careers he was as accurate as those two masters of the power-ladder.

Curiously, when any of the three of them made mistakes, it was the same type of mistake. They all tended to write men off too quickly: they said, with a knell not disagreeable to themselves, he's finished, and so far as his climbing the ladder in front of him went, they were nearly always right. But they forgot, or undervalued, how resilient human beings were. Herbert Getliffe would never be a judge: Gilbert Cooke would never be more than an assistant secretary: George Passant would stay as a managing clerk at eight or nine hundred a year until he retired: but each of them had reserves of energy left. They were capable of breaking out in a new place: it was not so certain as the prognosticians thought that we had heard the last of them.

'Should you say,' Mr Knight continued to delve, 'we are likely to hear more of you in high affairs?'

'Less rather than more,' I said.

'I suppose your books are a consolation?'

'Much more than that.'

'And yet, that is not quite the same, I should have thought, as being a leader in the great world.'

His lids drooped down, his expression had saddened. For once he had misjudged me.

'Perhaps,' he said, 'if it hadn't been for my daughter, you would have got a better start.'

'It would have made no difference in the end,' I replied.

'I can't help thinking how you must have been held back.'

'In the long run, I should have done much the same,' I said.

Just for an instant he turned his head and looked at me with eyes wide open.

'I think of her and ask myself about her,' he said. 'And I've wondered if you do also.'

At last. This was the point. Now he had led up to it, it turned out not to be a dig at me.

'I have done often,' I said.

'I know you ask yourself what you did wrong, and how you ought to have helped her.'

I nodded.

'But you're not to blame, I can't put the blame on you. Time after time I've gone over things she said to me, and how she looked when she was a girl. She had become strange before ever you met her or she brought you to my house.'

He was speaking more directly than I had heard him speak.

'I keep asking myself what I should have done for her. I suppose I

731

pretended to myself that she was not so very strange. But I don't know to this day what I should have done. As a very little girl she was remote from either of us. When I told her she was pretty, she shrank away from me. I remember her doing that when she was six or seven. I was very proud of her, and I used to enjoy saying she was beautiful. I can see her eyes on me now, praying that I should stop. I don't know what I should have done. I ought to have found some way to reach her, but I never could.'

He added:

'I ought to have helped her, but I never could. I believe now I did her more harm than good.'

He asked:

'What could I have done?'

Just then Mrs Knight came bustling out of the sitting-room, scolding him because he was tiring himself, indicating to me that it was time I left him to rest.

In an instant the veil of self-concern came over Mr Knight.

'Perhaps I have talked too much,' he said. 'Perhaps I have.'

On my way home across the edge of the park I was moved because I had seen Mr Knight, the most hypochondriacal and selfish of men, bare a sorrow. How genuine was it? In the past his behaviour had baffled me often, and it had that afternoon. Yet I thought his sorrow lived with him enough so that he had to summon me to listen to it. I found myself sorry for him. It was the heaviest feeling I took away with me, although, when his invitation came and I knew that I should be reminded of Sheila, I had not been certain how much it would disturb me.

It seemed that I might feel the same pain as that which seized me the night I caught sight of R. S. Robinson at the party. But in fact I had felt it not at all, or very little.

Talking to her father, I had thought of Sheila with pity and love: but the aura which had surrounded her in my imagination, which had survived her death and lasted into the first years with Margaret, had gone altogether now. Once her flesh had seemed unlike any other's, as though it had the magic of someone different in kind. Now I thought of her physically with pity and love, as though her body was alive but had aged as ours had aged, as though I wished she were comfortable but found that even my curiosity about her had quite gone.

When I arrived, Margaret was in the nursery playing with the children. I did not talk to her about the Knights at once, although she detected at a glance that I was content. We did not speak intimately in front of Maurice because anxiously, almost obsessively, she planned to keep him from jealousy. Her nerves were often on the stretch for him; she not only loved him, but could not shut out warning thoughts about him.

That afternoon, we both paid him attention before I spoke to Charles. Maurice was sitting at a little table with a set of bricks and steel rods. He was now five and had lost none of the beauty he showed when I first saw him. By what seemed an irony, he had shown no perceptible jealousy of his half-brother. His temper, which had been violent in infancy, had grown better. When he was placid a load lifted from Margaret's brow; that afternoon, he was building with a mechanic's interest, and in peace. We turned to Charles, lifted him from his pen and let him run between us.

Looking at him, I was suffused with pleasure, pleasure unqualified. In the days when Margaret and I first lay together watching the firelight on the ceiling, I thought that I had not known before the sweetness of life, and that here it was. Here it was also, as I looked at the little boy. He had learned to walk, but although he was laughing, he would not move until we were both in place; he beamed, he was jolly, but he was also sharp-eyed and cautious. Rotating an arm, head back, he ran, trusting us at last.

He had none of Maurice's infant beauty. His face was shield-shaped, plain and bright: he had eyes of the hard strong blue common in my family. A few minutes later, when Maurice had gone into another room, Margaret touched my arm and pointed – the child's eyes were concentrated and had gone darker, he was staring out of the window where the moon had come up among a lattice of trees. He kept reiterating a sound which meant 'light', he was concentrated to the depths of his being.

It was then, in happiness, that I reported to Margaret how Mr Knight had pointed out the extent to which I had failed to live up to my promise, and the number of disappointments I had known.

'He doesn't know much about you now,' she cried.

'He knows something,' I said.

'What did you say?'

'I said there was a good deal in it.'

She read my expression and smiled, happy herself.

I added:

'I didn't tell him what I might have done – that I think I could accept most miseries now, except—' I was watching the child – 'except anything going wrong with him.'

She began to speak and stopped. Her face was swept clean of happiness: she was regarding me protectively, but also with something that looked like fright.

COMPARISON OF MARRIAGES

WHEN I was alone, I thought sometimes of the warning Margaret had not spoken. But neither of us so much as hinted at it, until a night over a year later, a night still unshadowed, when we had Gilbert and Betty Cooke to dinner.

To my surprise – I had expected the worst, and got it wrong – that marriage was lasting. They often came to see us since – also to my surprise – Betty and Margaret had become reconciled. Thus, by the most unexpected of back-doors, Gilbert's inquisitiveness at last found our house wide open. That inquisitiveness, however, had lost its edge. We had looked for every reason for his wanting to marry Betty except the simple one; he was devoted to his wife, and humbly, energetically, gratefully, he was engrossed in making the marriage comfortable for her.

On the surface, it was a curious relation. They quarrelled and snacked. They had decided not to have children and spent much thought, disagreeing with each other, on food and drink and how to decorate their flat. With an income much less than ours, they had achieved twice the standard of luxury, and they went on adding to it, simultaneously attending to and criticising each other.

It was easy to imagine them at sixty, when Gilbert retired, knowing just the hotels to squeeze the last pound's worth out of his pension, badgering restaurant proprietors all over Europe, like the Knights without the hypochondria, a little cantankerous, a little scatty except about their comforts, carping at each other, but, to any remark by any intruder, presenting a united front. It might have seemed a come-down, compared with Betty in her twenties, so kind and slapdash, so malleable, anxious for a husband to give purpose to her existence: or compared with Gilbert at the same age who, enormities and all, was also a gallant and generous young man.

But they had done better than anyone saw. They were each of them unvain, almost morbidly so: the prickles and self-assertiveness which made them snack did not stop them depending on each other and coming close. They were already showing that special kind of mutual dependence which one occasionally sees in childless marriages, where neither the partners nor their relation ever seem to have quite grown up, but where, in compensation, they preserve for each other the interest, the absorption, the self-centredness, the cantankerous sweetness of young love.

Looking at them at our dinner table I saw Gilbert, in his middle forties, getting fatter and redder in the face; Betty, well over forty, her eyes still fine, but her nose dominating, more veins breaking through the skin, the flesh thickening on her shoulders. And yet Margaret, in years and looks so much the younger, was older in all else – so that, watching them, one had to keep two time-scales in one's head, one non-physiological; and on the latter, Betty, with her gestures as unsubdued as when she was young, allied with Gilbert in a conspiracy to secure life's minor treats, was standing delectably still.

That night they had come a little late, so as to avoid seeing the children; increasingly, like two self-indulgent bachelors, they were cutting out exercises which they found boring. But for politeness' sake Betty asked questions about the boys, in particular about mine: and Gilbert did his bit by examining and hectoring us about our plans for their education.

'There's nothing to hesitate about,' he said, bullying and good-natured. 'There's only one school you need think about,' he went on, referring to his own. 'You can afford it, I can't conceive what you're hesitating for.

'That is,' he said, his detective passion suddenly spurting out, gazing at Margaret with hot eyes, 'if you're not going to have a big family—'

'No, I can't have any more,' Margaret told him directly.

'Well, that's all right then,' cried Gilbert.

'No, it hangs over us a bit,' she said.

'Come on, two's enough for you,' he jollied her along.

'Only one is Lewis's,' she replied, far less tight-lipped, though still far shyer, than I was. 'It would be safer if he had more than one.'

'Anyway, what about this school?' said Betty briskly, a little uneasily, as though sheering away from trouble she did not wish to understand.

'It's perfectly obvious they can well afford it, there's only one school for them.' Gilbert was talking across the table to her, and across the table she replied.

'You're overdoing it,' she said.

'What am I overdoing?'

'You think it's all too wonderful. That's the whole trouble, none of you ever recover from the place.'

'I still insist,' Gilbert was drawing a curious triumph out of challenging her, he looked plethoric and defiant, 'that it's the best education in the country.'

'Who's to say so?' she said.

'Everyone says so,' he replied. 'The world says so. And over these things the world is usually right,' added Gilbert, that former rebel.

They went on arguing. Betty had preserved her scepticism more than he had; she recalled days when, among aristocrats of her own kind, intellectuals like the Davidsons, it was common form to dislike the class subtleties of English education; she had known friends of ours who had assumed that, when they had families, they would break away from it. She said to Gilbert:

'You're just telling them to play the same game with their children as everyone round them.'

'Why shouldn't they?'

Betty said:

'If anyone can afford not to play the same game, Lewis and Margaret can.'

Duty done, with relief they grumbled about their last weekend. But I was absent-minded, as I had been since Margaret spoke about the child. The talk went on, a dinner-party amiable, friendly, without strain, except that which gripped me.

'It would be safer—' She had meant something more difficult, I knew clearly, than that it would be a life-long risk, having an only son. That was obvious and harsh enough.

But it was not that alone of which Margaret was afraid. No, she was afraid of something which was not really a secret between us but which, for a curious reason, she would not tell me.

The reason was that she distrusted her motive. She knew that she expected perfection more than I did. She had sacrificed more than I had; it was she who had, in breaking her marriage, taken more responsibility and guilt; she watched herself lest in return she expected too much.

But in fact, though she distrusted herself, her fear was not that I should be compelled to lose myself in my son, but that, in a final sense, I should desire to. She knew me very well. She had recognised, before I did, how much suffering a nature can bring upon itself just to keep in the last resort untouched. She had seen that the deepest experiences of my early life, unrequited love, the care I spent on Roy Calvert or my brother, my satisfaction in being a spectator, had this much in common, that whatever pain I went through I need answer to myself alone.

If it had not been for Margaret, I might not have understood. It had taken a disproportionate effort – because under the furrows of such a nature as mine there is hidden an inadmissible self-love – to think that it was not good enough.

Without her I should not have managed it. But the grooves were cut deep: how easy it would be, how it would fit part of my nature like a skin, to find my own level again in the final one-sided devotion, the devotion to my son.

When Betty and Gilbert, each half-drunk and voluble, had at last left us, at the moment when, after drawing back the curtains, I should have started gossiping about them, the habit of marriage as soothing as the breath of the night air, I said instead:

'Yes, it is a pity that we've only the one.'

'You ought to have been a bit of a patriarch, oughtn't you?' she said. She was giving me the chance to pass it off, but I said:

'It needn't matter to him, though, need it?'

'He'll be all right.'

'I think I've learned enough not to get in his way.'

I added:

'And if I haven't learned by now, I never shall.'

She smiled, as though we were exchanging ironies: but she understood, the mistakes of the past were before us, she wished she could relieve me of them. And then I seemed to change the subject, for I said:

'Those two' – I waved the way Betty and Gilbert had gone '– they'll make a go of it now, of course.'

On the instant, she knew what I was doing, getting ready to talk, through the code of a discussion of another marriage, about our own. It was stuffy in the room, and we went down into the street, our arms round each other, refreshed: the night was close, cars were probing along the pavement, we struck in towards one of the Bayswater squares and then walked round, near to each other as we spoke of Betty and Gilbert.

Yes, she repeated, it was a triumph in its way. She thought that what had drawn them together was not desire, though they had enough to get some fun, was nothing more exalted than their dread of being lonely. Betty was far too honourable to like Gilbert's manoeuvres, but they were lonely and humble-spirited, they would fly at each other, but in the long run they would confide and she would want him there. If they had had children, or Betty had had a child by her first marriage, they might not have been so glued together, I said: I was trying to tell the truth, not to make things either too easy for myself or too hard: they were going to need each other more, at the price of being more selfish towards everyone else.

In the square, which had once been grand and had now become tenement flats, the last lights were going out. There was no breeze at all: we were holding hands, and talking of those two, we met each other, and spoke of our self-distrust.

CHAPTER LI

LISTENING TO THE NEXT ROOM

As we walked round the square that night, both children were well. A fortnight later we took them to visit their grandfather, and the only illness on our minds was his. In the past winter Davidson had had a coronary thrombosis: and, although he survived, it was saddening to be with him now. Not that he was not stoical: he was clear-sighted about what he could expect for the rest of his life: the trouble was, he did not like what his clear sight told him, his spirits had gone dark and he would have thought it unreasonable if they had not.

Up to that illness he had lived the life of a young man. His pleasures had been a young man's, even his minor ones, his games and his marathon walks. He looked more delicate than most men, but there was a pagan innocence about him, he had not been compelled to adjust himself to getting old. Then it had happened at a blow.

He was out of comparison more stoical than Mr Knight. Though Davidson believed that when he died he was going into oblivion, he feared death less than the old clergyman. He had found life physically delightful until near on sixty, while Mr Knight had immobilised himself in hypochondria more than twenty years before. But of the two it was Davidson who had no consolation in the face of a sick old age.

What he did was concentrate fanatically on any of his pastimes still within his power, games at the Stock Exchange. No one could strike another spark of interest out of him; that Saturday afternoon Margaret was screwing herself up to try.

As we entered his study with the children, he was playing the war game against Helen, the board spread out on a table so that he could be comfortable in an armchair. In the quiet both boys backed shyly to Margaret, and momentarily the only noise we heard was Davidson's breathing, a little shorter, a little more strenuous than a healthy man's, just audible on the close air.

The silence cracked as Maurice went straight to Helen, to whom he talked more fluently than any other adult, while the little boy advanced and stared from the board to Davidson. While Helen took Maurice away into the corner, Charles asked:

'What is Grandpa doing?'

'Nothing very dazzling, Carlo.'

Although Davidson's voice had none of the spring and tone it used to have, although the words were mysterious to him, the child burbled with laughter: being called 'Carlo' made him laugh as though he were being tickled. He cried out that his grandfather called him Carlo, he wanted the joke repeated. Then Davidson coughed and the child looked at him, transparent indigo irises turned upon opaque sepia ones, the old man's face sculptured, the child's immediate and aware.

'Are you better?' the child asked.

'Not really. Thank you,' Davidson replied.

'Not quite better?'

'No, not quite better.'

'A little better?'

For once not replying with the exact truth, Davidson said:

'Perhaps a little better.'

'Better soon,' said the child, and added, irrelevantly and cheerfully: 'Nanny is a little better.' It was true that the nurse who came in half the week had been ill with influenza.

'I'm very glad to hear that, Carlo.'

I wanted to distract the child from his grandfather. I could hear – beneath Davidson's tone, offhand rather than polite, which he used to the infant not yet three as to a Nobel Prize winner – I could hear a discomfort which by definition, as Davidson himself might say, was beyond help. So I asked the little boy to come and talk to me instead.

He replied that he would like to talk to his grandfather. I said that I would show him pictures. He smiled but said: 'Grandpa called me Carlo.'

He went round the board, nearer to Davidson, staring applaudingly into his face. Then Margaret spoke to Charles, explaining that he could come back later and that I had splendid new pictures for him.

'Go with daddy,' she told him.

The child gazed at me, his eyes darkened almost to black.

As a rule he was amenable, but he was enjoying the clash of wills. He was searching for words, there was a glint in his eye which in an adult one would have suspected as merry, obstinate, perceptibly sadic.

'Go with daddy,' Margaret said.

Clearly and thoughtfully he replied:

'I don't know who daddy is.'

Everyone laughed, me included: for the instant I was as hurt as I had been at eighteen, asking a girl to dance and being turned down. Then I was thinking how implacable one's egotism is, thinking from mine just wounded to this child's.

Gazing at him beside his grandfather's chessboard, I felt unusual confidence, without any premonition that, as he grew up, he would be good-natured: within the human limits, he would be amiable and think of others. But one had to learn one's affections: the amiability and gentleness one dressed up in, but the rapacious egotism had been there all the time beneath. It protruded again, naked as in infancy, as one got into old age. Looking from the smiling little boy to his grandfather, dispirited and indrawn, I thought that by a wretched irony we were seeing its re-emergence in that man, so stoical and high-principled, who only a year before had been scarcely middle-aged.

As we tried to persuade the child away from his grandfather's side, he was bad-tempered in a manner uncommon with him. He cried, he was fractious, he said he had a cough like grandpa, he practised it, while Margaret listened, not knowing how much was genuine, except that he had woken up with the faint signs of a cold that morning.

She put her hand to his forehead, and so did I. He seemed just warm with passion. Through anger, he kept telling us he would like to stay with grandpa: he repeated, as though it were a reason for staying, that he had a cough like grandpa, and produced it again.

'I think he's over-excited, I don't think it can be more than that,' said Margaret to me in an undertone, hesitating whether to look after him or her father, her forehead lined. Then she made up her mind; she had come to speak to her father, she could not shirk it and leave him with his spirits dead. She called to Helen, telling her that Charles was upset, would she take care of him for half an hour? Helen nodded, and got up. It was curious to see her, trim yet maternally accomplished as Margaret would never be, since Helen's instinct was so sure that it left her no room for wondering whether she might not be taking the wrong course, saying the wrong thing. As effortlessly as a hypnotist, she led him and Maurice out of the room, other attractions wiped out of Charles's mind as though his memory were cut off.

Left with her father, Margaret's first act was to take Helen's side of the war game, at which she was the only person who could give Davidson a run. In silence, they finished the game. Davidson's expression had lightened a little: partly it was that Margaret was his favourite daughter, partly the anodyne of the game – but also, where many men would have drawn comfort from their grandchildren, to him the sight of them seemed a reminder of mortality.

He and Margaret were staring down at the board: his profile confronted hers, each of them firm and beautiful in their ectomorphic lines, their diagonals the mirror-image of each other. He had a winning position, but she contrived to make the end respectable.

'For neatness,' said Davidson, his tone lively again, 'I give that finish 65 out of a 100.'

'Nothing like enough,' said Margaret. 'I want 75 at least.'

'I'm prepared to compromise on 69.'

He sounded revivified. He looked at the clock and said eagerly: 'If we're quick, there's time for another one.'

Reluctantly Margaret said no, they'd better leave it till next week, and his face went heavy, as though the skin were at last bagging out over the architecture of the bones. Afterwards, she had to ask him questions to keep him from sinking numb into his thoughts. His replies were uninterested and dull. Were there any pictures we ought to see? One exhibition, he said flatly, was possibly worth our time. When would he be able to go himself? Not yet. When? Margaret asked. They said – his reply was indifferent – that in a month or two he might be able to take a taxi and then walk through a couple of rooms. You must do that as soon as you can, she said. He hadn't the slightest inclination to, he said.

She understood that she was on the wrong tack. He had said all he had to say about pictures when he was well; he had written about them at the height of his powers; he could do so no more, and it was better to cut it out absolutely, not to taunt himself by seeing a picture again.

Casting about, she mentioned the general election of the past winter, and then the one she thought must soon follow.

'I should have thought,' said Davidson, 'that one had to be a morbidly good citizen to find the prospect beguiling.'

'I don't think anyone does,' said Margaret.

'I should have thought that it would lack picturesque features to a remarkable extent.' He was making an effort to keep up the conversation now.

'No,' he added, 'there would be one mildly picturesque feature as far as I'm concerned. That is, if I had the strength to get as far as voting, which I must say seems improbable. But if I did manage to vote, I should be voting conservative for the first time in my life.'

I was thinking how most of those I knew, certainly eight out of ten of my professional acquaintances, were moving to the right.

Margaret, taking advantage of the chance with Davidson, broke in.

'Going back to your voting,' she said, 'it would have seemed incredible thirty years ago, wouldn't it?'

'Quite incredible,' he replied.

'You and your friends didn't have much idea of the way things would actually go, did you?'

'By and large,' he said, 'they've gone worse than we could possibly have imagined.'

'Thirty years ago,' he added, 'it looked as though they would turn out sensibly.'

'If you had your time again,' she said, 'how would you change what you were all thinking?'

'In my present form,' he was not speaking dully now, she had stung him, 'the thought of having one's time over again is rather more than I can take.'

'I know it,' she said: her tone was as sharp. 'That's why you've got to tell us. That's why you've got to write it down.'

'I don't trust the views of a man who's effectively done for.'

'For some things,' she said, throwing all gentleness away, 'they're the only views one can trust.'

She went on:

'You know very well, I've never much liked what your friends stand for. I think on all major issues you've been wrong. But don't you see how valuable it would be to see what you think—'

'Since the future doesn't interest me any more.' They were each being stark; she was tired with the effort to reach him, she could not go much further, but his eyes were shining with interest, with a kind of fun.

'On most major issues,' he caught her phrase, 'we were pretty well right. He gazed at her. After a pause he said: 'It might be worth thinking about.'

Another pause, in which we could hear his breathing. His head was bent down, but in his familiar posture, not in dejection.

'It might give me something to think about,' he said.

With a sigh, she said that now she must go and find the children.

'I'll think about it,' said Davidson. 'Mind you, I can't promise. It'd be a bit of a tax physically and I don't suppose I'm up to it.'

He said goodbye to me, and then turned to Margaret.

'I'm always very glad to see you,' he said to her. It was a curious parting from his favourite daughter: it seemed possible that he was not thinking of her as his daughter, but as the only person who looked straight at him in his illness and was not frightened off.

We went into the drawing-room, where I had not been since the evening Margaret said she would come to me. In the summer afternoon, with Helen and the children playing on the floor, it seemed much smaller, as diminished as one of childhood's rooms revisited.

In the contracted room, Helen was saying that Charles did seem a little out of sorts: perhaps we ought to take him home soon. The child, picking up most of the conversation, cried because he did not want to go: he cried again, in inexplicable bursts, in the taxi; in the nursery his cheeks were flushed, he laughed with an hysterical echo, but was asking, with a customary reasonableness, where Auntie Helen was and when he would see her again. Then he said, with a puzzled and complaining expression:

'My feet hurt.'

There seemed nothing wrong with his feet, until Maurice said that he meant they were cold, and Margaret rubbed them between her hands.

'Clever boy,' Margaret said to Maurice.

'Shall we clap him?' said Charles, but his laughter again got out of control. He cried, became quiet, and then, with a return of the complaining expression, said: 'My head hurts.'

Under our eyes his cold was growing worse. His nose ran, he coughed, his temperature was a little up. Without speaking to each other, Margaret and I were thinking of his nurse's influenza. At once, no worry in her voice, Margaret was arranging for Maurice to sleep in the spare room: still not hurrying, as though she were ticking off her tasks, she had a word with me alone before she put Charles to bed.

'You're not to be too anxious,' she said.

Her face, like many whose nerves are near the surface, was always difficult to read, far more so than the poker faces of Rose or Lufkin, because it changed so quickly. Now it was as calm as when she spoke to the children. Yet, though she was steady, and I was letting my anxiety go, I suddenly knew that for no reason – not because of any of his symptoms, nor anything she knew or noticed which I had not – her anxiety was deeper.

'If he's not better tomorrow, we'll have Charles March in straight-away,' I said.

'Just to give you a decent night,' she said, 'perhaps we might as well have him now.'

Charles March had arrived and was in the nursery before Margaret had finished putting the child to bed. Standing in the drawing-room I listened to their voices, insistent, incomprehensible, more ominous than if I could have picked out the words, just as their voices had been when I listened in this same room, the morning before he was born. It seemed longer than on that morning before they came to join me, but at once Charles gave me a kind, protective smile.

'I don't think it's anything very terrible,' he said.

Just for an instant I felt total reassurance, like that of a jealous man who has had the moment's pretext for jealousy wiped away.

He sat down and, his eyes sharp and cautious, asked me about the nurse's 'flu'. What was it like? More catarrhal than usual? Had any of us had it? Yes, Margaret replied, she had, mildly: it had been going round the neighbourhood.

'Yes,' said Charles, 'several of my patients have had it.'

He was thinking out what he could safely say. It caught my eye that his suit was old and shabby, fading at the lapels: he was seedier to look at than when I first knew him as a smart young man: but the seediness did not matter and he was wearing well: his hair was still thick and fair, his eyes bright. This life he had chosen, which had once seemed to me quixotic and *voulu*, was suiting him.

'Well, obviously,' he said, 'it would be slightly far-fetched to look for anything else in the boy's case. I am a bit of an old woman with very small children. I can't help thinking of the rare things that might just possibly happen to them. But I can't see any justification for suspecting any of them here. No, we may as well call it "flu", this brand of "flu" that seems to be in the air.'

As he spoke, he was setting out to reassure me. But, as well as being a man of strong feeling, he had made himself a good doctor. He knew that he started by being both over-cautious and over-ingenious. With any child – more than ever with the child of a close friend – his temptation had been to spend time over remote dangers. It had meant alarm, it was bad medicine, it was a private irritation. For Charles was a devoted man, but he had an appetite, personal as well as professional, for being right.

When Charles March had gone, the child had a bout of crying, and Margaret went to sit beside him. Afterwards she read to Maurice until his bedtime, making it up to him for having been so long away. It was not until eight o'clock, having spent herself on each in turn, that she came to me.

We were listening for a cry in the next room. She had gone dead tired; she talked, not of the child, but of her father: had she done him any good? When she spoke as she had had to speak to him, she did not like herself much. Ought she just to have left him to himself? She was tired out, she was asking nothing deep or new, just a guilty question from a daughter who had broken loose. I was listening to the next room, but that worry was a little lulled, and she wanted me to strengthen her. To her, who took so much responsibility, to whom much of love meant that, it was a final release of love to shed it.

Listening to the next room, I could lull that worry enough to attend to Margaret. And yet, for both of us, it was only just lulled, so that by a consent unspoken we did not allow ourselves any of the ordinary evening's pleasure, as though even a glass of wine with our meal, or standing outside on the roof garden and smelling the flowers in the humid air, were a provocation to fate.

CHAPTER LII

PHOTOPHOBIA

THE child woke three times during the night, but he had no more than a sleep-flush when we went into him in the morning. He was lying on his back talking to himself, and when we looked down into the cot he smiled. I found myself asking him, as though he were an adult, how he was feeling: mechanically, imitating his nurse, he replied very well, thank you. I asked if his head were hurting: he looked surprised and then troubled, but at last said no.

When Margaret had taken his temperature, reading the thermometer by the window in the morning sunlight, she cried:

'It's gone down. It's only just over 99.'

Her joy filled the room. Delighted with her because she told good news, I thought how absolute was her capacity for joy. Many thought of her as gentle and responsible: some, who knew her better, saw the fibre of her will: but perhaps one had to love her to feel her capacity for joy. I loved it in her.

I asked, didn't he seem easier? The catarrh was less, the look of strain had gone. After the night before, no adult would have looked as bright. Yes, we weren't imagining it, he was far brighter, she said.

As we talked about him over his head, the child had been listening: he knew that we were pleased with him. With something like vanity or gratification, he said: 'Better now.'

Then he told us that grandpa was a little better, nanny was a little better. Amiably he asked:

'Are we a little better? Are we quite better?'

He did not object, however, when Margaret told him that he was to stay in his cot. He was content to lie there while we read to him and showed him his toys: as it was Sunday morning Maurice was at home, and so I stayed alone in the nursery, reading Charles's favourite books time after time, watching for any change in his cough, his hand moving to his head or ear, with an intensity of observation that co-existed with boredom, with an emotion so strong that it seemed incredible I could at one and the same time be bored.

About midday Charles March called. The temperature was still down, and he was satisfied. He was so satisfied that he spoke to us sternly, as though we were careless or indifferent parents, and ordered us to ring him up at once if there were any deterioration. My tongue lightened, I said it was the most unnecessary advice that even he had ever given me: and as Margaret and I laughed he was taken off guard, his professional authority departed, he blushed and then guffawed.

We were standing in the hall, and from the nursery came the child's voice, shouting for his mother and father. As Margaret opened the door, he called out: 'What were they laughing at?'

'Someone made a joke, that's all,' she said.

'They laughed.'

'Yes, we shouldn't have made such a noise,' she said.

The child produced an artificial 'ha-ha-ha' which led to a genuine one, not hysterical, but somehow real mirth self-induced.

All that afternoon and evening, there was no change that either she or I could be sure of. I felt in myself, I knew it in her, that state of physical constraint in which one is aware of one's own footsteps, even knows that one's own breath is catching. I had seen it before, in Sawbridge when he was waiting to be arrested. But in us it was a denial of the moment, the more we secretly thought that next day he might be well.

Most of the afternoon I played with Maurice, whilst she took her spell at the bedside. Among his birthday presents Maurice had been given a game similar to the halma I remembered in my own childhood: suddenly that sunny afternoon, refusing to walk with me to the Serpentine, he developed an obsession for it. For a long time I sat there with him – the air brilliant over the park, the sun streaming into the room, our corner shaded – not resenting the occupation, time dripping by that way as well as any other, letting him win. He mentioned the child only once, when without any explanation he referred to him by a pet name, and said:

'Will he have to stay in his cot tomorrow?'

'I expect so,' I said.

'And the day after that?'

'Perhaps.'

'And lots and lots of days?'

He did not seem to be speaking out of either malice or affection, but something more like scientific curiosity.

'Lewis,' he asked, his handsome face lit up with interest, 'has anyone had to stay in bed for a *thousand* days?'

'Yes,' I said.

'Has anyone I know?'

He pursued his researches. Had I ever had to? Or Margaret? Or his father? Or his grandfather? Raptly, he asked:

'Has anyone ever had to stay in bed for a *million* days?'

'People don't live as long as that.'

He thought again:

'If I had a space-ship, I could get to the moon in a thousand days.'

'Yes, you could.'

'No, I couldn't. You're wrong,' he cried with superiority and triumph. 'Of course, I could get further than the moon in a thousand days. I could get to Venus, you ought to know that. Anyone knows that.'

Charles did not go to sleep at his usual time, and cried for his mother to stay with him: he was restless and cried again before nine o'clock; but neither her eyes nor mine could find any change. We stayed up for some time, but there was no sound, and at last we went to bed. Waking out of my first sleep, I was listening at once, but there was still no sound: all was quiet, I did not hear Margaret breathing in her sleep.

Trying to rouse myself, I said:

'Are you awake?'

'Yes,' she replied.

'Haven't you been to sleep?'

'Not yet.'

'Is anything the matter with him?'

'No, I've been in to see him once, he's sleeping.' Her voice was clear, but also, now that I was awake myself, I could hear how wakeful it was, and tight with care.

'What are you thinking of?' I said.

After a pause she replied:

'Yes, there is something.'

'Tell me.'

'I think he's on the mend, and we probably shan't need it. Perhaps we needn't say anything. But I've been thinking, if he should have a set-back, I don't want you to mind, I want you to let me have Geoffrey in to see him.'

In the words, jagged with anxiety, I could hear the hours of her sleepless night: but now I was turned hard and angry.

'It seems strange,' I replied.

'I don't care what it seems, he's a first-class children's doctor.'

'There are other first-class children's doctors.'

'He's the best I've seen.'

'There are others as good and better.'

My anger was sullen, hers on the flash-point. But it was she, more violent than I was, who controlled herself first.

'This isn't a good time to quarrel,' she said in the darkness.

'We mustn't quarrel,' I said.

'Let me try and come out with it.'

But she could not make a clear explanation. She had been thinking, she said, just as I had been thinking, what it would be like if he got worse. And there was Maurice, she wanted to be sure that he was looked after. If Charles got worse, it would be too much to bear, unless she had complete confidence in a doctor. Her voice was shaking.

'Would it have to be Geoffrey?'

'I should know we'd done the best we could.'

For each of us, the choice was dense with the past. I was jealous of him, yes: jealous as one can be of someone one has misused. Even the mention of him reminded me of the time I had lost her. I had avoided seeing him since Margaret came to me. It was part of his bargain, in letting her keep Maurice, that he should visit him when he wanted. He made a regular visit each week, but on those days I had not once been there.

On her side, although she liked Charles March, she felt for him a fainter jealousy, the jealousy for parts of my youth that, except at second-hand, were for her unknown and irrecoverable.

There was something else. In a fashion that seemed right out of character, but one I had noticed in older women, she liked to hero-worship her doctor, make a cult of him; perhaps because of the past, she could not manage to do that with Charles March.

'All that matters,' I said, 'is that he is looked after. We can forget everything else.'

'Yes.'

'If you should need Geoffrey, then you'd better have him.'

Very soon, not more than five minutes after, she was sleeping for the first time that night, but it was a long time before I got to sleep again.

In the morning, when we went in together to see the child, that anxiety in the darkness seemed remote. He looked as he had done the day before, he greeted us, his temperature was the same. As soon as Maurice had gone to school, the two of us sat beside the cot all the morning, watching him.

His cough had slackened, but his nose was still running. Otherwise he did not grumble, he lay there being read to, at times apathetic. At other times he became impatient with reading, stopping us when we were halfway through a book, demanding that we start again. It was a trick, I insisted to myself, that he often did.

Just after midday, looking down at him, I could not keep back the question – was he more flushed than ten minutes before?

For an instant I glanced at Margaret; our eyes met, fell away, turned back to the cot; neither dared to speak. Twice I took my eyes away from the child, to the floor, anywhere, while I counted the instants, in the hope that when I looked again I should see it had been an illusion.

Since my first alarm – not more than a few minutes past – I had not looked at Margaret. She was gazing at him. She too had seen. When our eyes met this time, each saw nothing but fear. When we looked back at the child, his expression also seemed to be showing fear. His cheeks were flushed, and his pupils were dilating.

I said to Margaret:

'I'll ring up Charles March. If he's not already on the way, I'll tell him we want Geoffrey too.'

She muttered thanks. As soon as I had returned, she would get on to Geoffrey.

Charles was on his rounds, so his wife told me. He would be calling at his house before coming to us, so I could leave a message. As I was re-entering the nursery, the child was crying resentfully:

'His head hurts.'

'We know, dear,' said Margaret, with the steadiness in which no nerve showed.

'It hurts.'

'The doctors will help you. There will be two doctors soon.'

Suddenly he was interested:

'Who are two doctors?'

Then he began crying, hands over his eyes, holding his head. As Margaret went to the telephone, she whispered to me that his temperature was right up; for a second she gripped my hand, then left me with him.

Crying with his head turned to the pillow, he asked where she was, as though he had not seen her for a long time. I told him that she had gone to fetch another doctor, but he did not seem to understand.

Some minutes passed, while I heard the trill of telephone bells as Margaret made calls, and the child's whimpering. Whatever I said to him, he did not make clear replies. Then, all of a sudden, he was saying something feverish, urgent, which seemed to have meaning, but which I could not understand. Blinking his eyes, his hand over them, he was pointing to the window, demanding something, asking something. He was in pain, he could not grasp why I would not help him, his cries were angry and lost.

Myself, I felt lost too, lost, helpless and abject.

Once more he asked, imploring me in a jumble of words. This time he added 'Please, please', in anger and fever, utterly unlike a politeness; it was a reflex, produced because he had learned it made people do things for him.

I begged him to speak slowly. Somehow, half-lucid, he made an effort, his babble moderated. At last I had it.

'Light hurts.' He was still pointing to the window.

'Will you turn light off? Light hurts. Turn light off. Please. Please.'

As I heard, I drew the curtains. Without speaking, he laid his face away from me. I waited beside him in the tawny dark.

CHAPTER LIII

ACT OF COURAGE

SOON after Margaret returned, the child vomited. As she cleaned him, I saw that his neck was stiff, strained like a senile man eating. The flush was crimson, his fingers pushed into his eye sockets, then his temples.

'Head hurts,' he cried angrily.

He was crying with a violent rhythm that nothing she said to him interrupted. In the middle of it, a few minutes later, he broke into a new fierce complaint.

'My back hurts.'

In the same tone, he cried:

'Stop it hurting. It is hurting me.'

When either of us came close to him, he shouted in irritation and anger: 'What are they doing?'

The regular crying hooted up to us; neither she nor I could take our glance from him, his face fevered. We watched his hands pushing unavailingly to take away the pain. Without looking at Margaret I knew, as of something within one's field of vision, that her expression was smooth and young with anguish.

We were standing so, it was just on two o'clock, when Charles March came in. Impatiently he cut short what I was telling him; he glanced at the child, felt the stiff neck, then said to me, in a tone heavy, brotherly and harsh:

'It would be better if you weren't here, Lewis.'

As I left them, I heard him beginning to question Margaret: was there any rash? How long had his neck been rigid?

I was dazzled by the afternoon light in the drawing-room; I lit a cigarette, the smoke rose blue through a gleam of sun. The child's crying ululated; I thought I noticed that since I first entered the gleam of sun had moved just perceptibly along the wall. All of a sudden, the ululation broke, and there came, pressing like a shock-wave, a hideous, wailing scream.

I could not bear to be away, I was just on my way back to the child, when Charles March met me at the drawing-room door.

'What was that?' I cried.

The scream had died down now.

'Oh, that's nothing,' said Charles. 'I gave him penicillin, that's all.'

But there was nothing careless or even professional in his voice now, and his face was etched with sadness.

'If it could have waited I wouldn't have done it, I'd have left it for Hollis,' he said.

He added that I did not need telling that his diagnosis had been wrong. He did not explain that it was a reasonable mistake; he would not get over what he felt he had brought upon me. He said in a flat tone:

'I've done the only thing for him that we can do on the spot. Now I shall be glad to see Hollis arrive.'

'He's seriously ill, of course?'

'I'm afraid so.'

'Will he get over it?'

'He ought to stand a good chance – but I can't tell you much—'

He looked at me.

'No,' he said, 'if we've got it in time he ought to be all right.'

He said:

'I'm desperately sorry, Lewis. But what I'm feeling doesn't exist by the side of what you are.'

At any other time I should have known that, both because of his tenderheartedness and his pride, he was ravaged. But I had no attention to spare for him; I was interested only in what he had done for the child, whether he had taken away any of the suffering, whether he was being any use to us.

In the same animal fashion, when at that moment I heard Geoffrey Hollis arrive, I felt nothing like embarrassment or remorse, but just a kind of dull hope, that here might be someone bringing help.

As we all four of us gathered in the hall, it was Geoffrey alone who seemed uncomfortable, the others were too far gone. As he nodded to me his manner was offhand, but not as certain as usual; his fair head looked as unchangingly youthful, but his poise was not as jaunty. It was with something like relief that he listened to Margaret's first words, which were:

'It's worse than I told you.'

Once more I stood in the drawing-room, staring at the beam of sunlight along the wall. There was another scream, but this time it was minutes – I knew the exact time, it was five past three – before they joined me, Geoffrey speaking in an undertone to Charles March. The child's crying died down, the room was as quiet as when Charles had given us his opinion there less than forty-eight hours before. Through the open window came the smell of petrol, dust and summer lime.

'Shall I begin or will you?' said Geoffrey to Charles March, in a manner informal and friendly: there was no doubt of the answer. Geoffrey was speaking without pomposity, but also, even to Margaret, quite impersonally.

'The first thing is,' he said, 'that everything has been done and is being done that anyone possibly can. He'll have to be moved as soon as we have checked the diagnosis and my people have got ready for him in the isolation ward. You'll be able to drive round with the sample straight-away?' he said to Charles March.

Charles inclined his head. He was a man of natural authority and if they had met just as human beings he would have overweighted this younger man. But now Geoffrey had the authority of technique.

'I might as well say that the original diagnosis is one which we should all have made in the circumstances two days ago. The symptoms were masked to begin with and then they came on three or four hours ago, after that intermission yesterday, which is quite according to type, except that they came on with a rather unusual rush. If I had seen him on Saturday, I should never have thought this was a serious possibility my-self.'

Charles's face, drawn and pallid, did not move.

'And I shouldn't yesterday, and it's out of the question that anyone would. We ought to thank our lucky stars that Dr March got the penicillin into him when he did. We may be glad of that extra half-hour.'

It was, I remembered later, impersonally cordial, a little patronising, and scientifically true. But at the moment I actually heard it, I was distracted by this wind-up. I said:

'What has he got?'

'Oh, neither Dr March or I think there is much doubt about that. Don't you agree?' He turned to Charles March, who nodded again without his expression changing.

'It's a meningitis,' said Geoffrey Hollis. 'A straightforward one, we think.

'Mind you,' he said to me, not unkindly, with a curious antiseptic lightness, 'it's quite bad enough. If this had happened twenty years ago I should have had to warn you that a large percentage of these cases didn't recover. But nowadays, with a bit of good fortune, we reckon to cope.'

It was after Charles March had left, and Geoffrey had rung up the hospital, telling them to expect him and the case, that he said:

'That's all we can do just now. I've got to see another patient. I'll be back to take the boy along in a couple of hours.'

He spoke to Margaret.

'You must stop Maurice coming here until we've got things straight.'

'I was going to ask you,' she said.

He was businesslike, he said that he did not intend them to take even a negligible risk: Maurice had already been exposed to infection; she was to watch him for a vestige of a cold, take his temperature night and morning: at any sign, right or wrong, they would inject him.

As she listened, he could not have doubted that all he said would be carried out. He gave a smile of relief, and said that he must go.

I longed for him to stay. With him in the room, the edge of waiting was taken off. It did not matter that he was talking to her about their son. I said, hoping against hope that he would stay with us, that I had better go in and see the child.

'I'll do that myself on the way out,' he said, again not unkindly, 'but I don't see the point of it for you.'

He added:

'I shouldn't if I were you. You'll only distress yourself, and you can't do any good. It's not pretty to watch. Mind you, we don't know what they feel in these conditions, possibly nature is more merciful than it looks.'

In the hours when Margaret and I sat alone by the cot, the child did not cry so regularly: much of the time he lay on his side, moving little, muttering names of people, characters from his books, or bits of nursery verses. Frequently he complained that his head hurt, and three times that his back did. When either of us spoke to him his pupils, grossly dilated, confronted us as though he had not heard.

He seemed to be going deaf: I began to think that he no longer recognised us. Once he gave a drawn-out scream, so violent and rending that it seemed as though he were not only in agony, but horribly afraid. During the screams Margaret talked to him, tried piteously to reach him: so did I, my voice mounting until it was a shout. But he did not know us: when the scream was over, and he was babbling to himself again, his words were muddled, his mind had become confused.

When Geoffrey came back to us at a quarter to five, I felt an instant's dependence and overmastering relief. He glanced down at the child: his long, smooth, youthful face looked almost petulant, he clicked his teeth with something like disapproval.

'It's not working much yet,' he said.

He had a nurse waiting outside, he told us: they would take him at once: he looked again at the child with an expression not specially compassionate or grave, more like that of someone whose will was being crossed. He said that he would give him his second shot of penicillin as soon as they got him into his ward; it would be early, but worth trying. He added casually:

'The diagnosis is as I thought, by the way.'

'Yes,' said Margaret. Then she asked:

'Can we come with him now?'

Geoffrey looked at her deliberately, without involvement, without memory, competent with his answer as if she had been nothing but the mother of a patient.

'No,' he said. 'You'd only be slightly in the way. In any case, when we've got him settled, I couldn't let you see him.'

'You'll ring us up if there's any change,' she said steadily, 'for better or worse?'

For once his tone was personal. 'Of course I shall.'

He told us, once more antiseptic, that we could telephone the ward sister at any time, but there was no point in doing so before that night. If it was any relief to us, he himself would be glad to see us at the hospital the following morning.

After the ambulance drove away, my sense of time was deranged. Sitting in the early evening with Margaret and Maurice, I kept looking at my watch as though feeling my pulse in an illness; hoping for a quarter of an hour to have passed, I found it had only been minutes. Sometimes I was so much afraid that I wanted time to be static.

All the time I was watching Margaret look after her other boy. Before he came in, she was so sheet-pale that she had made up more than usual, not to alarm him. She had explained how Charles had been taken away with a bad cold, and how she would have to take his own temperature and fuss over him a bit. Then she sat with him, playing games, not showing him any anxiety, looking very pretty, the abnormal colour under her cheekbones becoming her; her voice was level, even full, and the only sign of suffering was the single furrow across her forehead.

She was thankful that Maurice's temperature was normal, that he seemed in the best of health.

Watching them, I resented it because she was so thankful. I took my turn playing with the boy: though I could not entertain him much, I could stick at the game and go through the motions: but I was resenting it also that he could sit there handsome and untouched, above all that he should be well. With a passion similar in kind to my mother's, who in an extreme moment of humiliation had once wanted a war to blot it out and destroy us all, so I wanted the danger to my son to hang over everyone round me: if he was not safe, then no one should be: if he should die, then so should the rest.

When she took Maurice to bed I sat in the drawing-room doing nothing, in that state of despondency and care combined which tied one's limbs and made one as motionless as a catatonic, reduced to a single sense, with which I listened to the telephone. Without either of us speaking, Margaret came and sat down opposite to me, on the other side of the fireplace; she was listening with an attention as searing as mine, she was looking at me with another care.

The telephone rang. She regarded me with a question on her face, then answered it. The instant she heard the voice on the wire, her expression changed to disappointment and relief: it was a woman acquaintance asking her to dinner the next week. Margaret explained that the little boy was ill, we couldn't go out anywhere because of the risk of letting our host down: she was as gentle and controlled as when she played with Maurice. When she returned to her chair, she mentioned the woman's name, who was a private joke between us, hoping to get a smile from me. All I could do was shake my head.

The vigil lasted. Towards nine o'clock she said, after calling out my name:

'Don't forget we should have heard if he were any worse.'

I had been telling myself so. But hearing it from her I believed her, I clutched at the comfort.

'I suppose so.'

'I know we should. Geoffrey promised—' she had reminded me of this already, with the repetitiveness with which, in the either-or of anxiety, one repeats the signs in favour as though they were incantations. 'He'd be utterly reliable about anything like this.'

'I think he would.' I had said it before: it heartened me to say it again.

'He would.'

She went on:

'This means he's got nothing to tell us yet.'

She said:

'Look, there can't be anything much to hear, but would you like to ring up the nurse and see what she says?'

I hesitated. I said:

'I daren't.'

Her face was strained and set. She asked:

'Shall I?'

I hesitated for a long time. At last I nodded. At once she went towards the telephone, dialled the number, asked for the ward. Her courage was without flaw: but I took in nothing, except what her expression and tone would in an instant mean.

She said she wanted to enquire about the child. There was a murmur in a woman's voice, which I could not catch.

For an instant Margaret's voice was hard.

'What does that mean?'

Another murmur.

'You can't tell me anything more?'

There was a longer reply.

'I see,' said Margaret. 'Yes, we'll ring up tomorrow morning.'

Simultaneously with the sound of the receiver going down, she told me:

'They said that he was holding his own.'

The phrase fell dank between us. She took a step towards me, wanting to comfort me: but I could not move, I was incapable of letting her.

CHAPTER LIV

'COME WITH ME'

IN the middle of the night, Margaret was at last asleep. We had both lain for a long time, not speaking; in the quiet I knew she was awake, just as I had listened and known years before, when Sheila was beside me in insomnia. But in those nights I had only her to look after, as soon as she was asleep my watch was over: that night, I lay wide awake, Margaret's breathing steady at last, in a claustrophobia of dread.

I dreaded any intimation of sound that might turn into the telephone ringing. I dreaded the morning coming.

I should have dreaded it less – the thoughts hemmed me in, as though I were in a fever or nightmare – if I had been alone.

It had been easier when I had just had to look after Sheila. Of the nights I had known in marriage, this was the most rending. Margaret had been listening too, lying awake, until she could be sure I was safe out of consciousness: it was only exhaustion that had taken her first: she wanted to look after me, she was thinking not only of the child but of me also.

She wanted to look after me but I could not let her. In this care and grief I had recessed, back to the time when I wanted to keep my inner self inviolate.

As a child I had not taken a sorrow to my mother, I had kept my sorrows from her, I had protected her from them. When I first loved I found, and it was not an accident, someone so self-bound that another's sorrows did not exist.

But with Margaret they existed, they were at the core of our marriage: if I kept them from her, if I did not need her, then we had failed.

In the darkness I could think of nothing but the child. The anxiety possessed me flesh and bone: I had no room for another feeling: it drove me from any other person, it drove me from her.

I thought of his death. In the claustrophobia of dread, it seemed that it would be an annihilation for me too. I should want to lose myself in sadness, have no one near me, I should not have the health to admit the claim of the living again. In sadness I should be alone: I should be finally and at last alone.

I thought of his death, as the light whitened round the curtains. The room pressed me in; I had a picture, sudden and sharp as an hallucination, it might have been a memory or a trick with time, of myself walking along a strip, not of sand but of pavement, by the sea. I did not know whether I was young or an old man: I was walking by myself on the road, with the sea, leaden but calm, on my right hand.

I slept a little, woke with an instant's light-heartedness, and then remembered. Margaret was already dressing. As she looked at me, and saw the realisation come into my face, hers went more grey. But she still had her courage: without asking me this time she said that she would ring the ward. Remaining in the bedroom I heard her voice speaking, the words indistinguishable, the cling of the bell as she rang off, the sound of her feet returning: they were not light, I dreaded to see her eyes. She told me:

'She said there's no change to speak of.'

All I could make myself reply was a question about our visiting Geoffrey at the hospital: when would she be ready to leave? I heard my voice deaden, I could see her regarding me with pity, with injury and rejection, with her own pain.

Whilst she gave Maurice breakfast I did not move from the bedroom. At last she returned to me there: I said that it was time we were setting out.

She looked at me with an expression I could not read. She said:

'I think perhaps it would be better if you went alone.'

All of a sudden I knew that she understood. The night's dreads – she had divined them. She had endured her own suffering about the child, and mine also. What could she do now either for the child or me? She could not bear, any more than I could, not to be with him; yet she was trying to tend me. Her tone was tight, she was admitting as much as she could bear.

It was a moment in which I could not pretend. To refuse her offer just because she craved I should – that was not in me. To refuse out of duty, or the ordinary kind surface of love – that was not in me either. There was only one force out of which I could refuse, and that was not love, but need.

All of a sudden, I knew that the fugue of the night was over. That part of me, which she understood even if it cost her her last hope, was not overmastering now.

Somehow the moment held not only the strains of our past, but something like a prophecy. I thought of the child's death, as I had in the night. If I lost him, I knew – it was the certainty of the fibres, not of thought – I should not be much good to her, but I should need her.

'No,' I said, 'come with me.'

CHAPTER LV

EFFECTS OF AN OBLIGATION

THROUGH the underground corridor of the hospital, which smelt of brick dust and disinfectant, Margaret and I were finding our way to Geoffrey's office. Along the passage, whose walls, as bare as those of a tube railway, carried uncovered water-pipes, went mothers with children. At a kind of junction or open space sat a group of women, their children in pushchairs, as though expecting nothing, waiting endlessly, just left there, children not specially ill, their fate not specially tragic, waiting with the resignation that made hospitals seem like forgotten railway stations littered with the poor and unlucky camping out for the weekly train. Nurses, their faces high-coloured and opaque, moved past them with strong, heavy-thighed steps as though they did not exist.

When at last we saw a notice, turned down a subsidiary passage and reached the office, which was still underground, Geoffrey's secretary told us that he was with the child, that he had been giving him his sixth injection. That, if we liked, we could wait in the doctor's room until he returned. Like the nurses in the corridor, she was a strong young woman, her face comely and composed with minor power. When she spoke to us it was in a tone which was brisk and well ordered, but which held an undertone of blame, as though we were obscurely responsible for our ill fortune. It was the tone which is not far distant from most of us, when we have to witness suffering and address it, as though when the veils of good nature were off we believed that the suffering were merely culpable, and that suffering was a sin.

In the office, so small that the walls pressed round us, the light was switched on although through a window one could look at the sky. The room glistened under the light, both naked and untidy – a glass-fronted bookcase full of textbooks and sets of journals, a couple of tubular chairs, a medical couch. We sat down, she put her hand on mine: there we stayed like those others in the corridor, waiting as they were, not expecting to be picked up, too abject to draw attention to ourselves.

I was aware of her palm touching the back of my hand: of my own breathing: of the sheets of typescript on the desk, which looked like a draft of a scientific paper, and the photograph of a woman, handsome, dashing, luxurious.

The telephone rang, the secretary swept in and answered it. It was the mother of a patient: there was a misunderstanding about an address and the secretary was confused. As it happened, I knew the answer: I could not get the words out. It was not malice, I wanted to help, I even wanted to propitiate her, but I was dumb.

When she went out, having at length solved the problem, I muttered to Margaret that I had known all along, but she did not understand. At last she had become no braver than I was, all she could do was press my hand. We had each got to the point of apprehensiveness which was as though we were not thinking any more, as though we were no longer waiting for release. This was all we knew, sitting there together; we were incapable of looking for an end to it.

There was a noise outside, and Geoffrey banged the door open. As soon as I saw his face, I realised. He was shining with a smile of triumph and elation, with a kind of repleteness such as one might see in a man who has just won a tennis match.

Margaret's fingers touched me. Suddenly our hands were slippery with sweat. Without a word said, we were certain.

In the same instant, Geoffrey cried:

'He'll be all right. He'll do.'

Margaret exclaimed, the tears spilled down her cheeks, but Geoffrey was oblivious of them.

'It's interesting,' he said, 'I've noticed it before, how the very instant the objective signs are beginning to go right, then the child seems to know it himself, one's only got to look at his face. It's interesting, one might have thought there'd be a time-lag. But the minute that the count in the lumbar fluid showed we had really got this one under control, then the boy was able to hear again and his mind began to clear.'

Suddenly he said, still wrapped up in his triumph:

'By the way, you needn't worry, there oughtn't to be any after-effects. He's a fine boy.'

It was not a compliment, it was just his statement of biological fact. He was brimming with his own victory at seeing the child recover: but also, uninterested in so many things which preoccupied the rest of us, not reading the news, contemptuous of politics, laughing off art as a play-thing, he nevertheless was on the side of the species. He drew his most unselfcentred happiness, with a kind of biological team spirit, from the prospect of a strong and clever child.

I was giddy with Margaret's joy, which resonated with mine, so that I could not have distinguished which was which. I wanted to abandon myself to praise of Geoffrey: I was in the sublime state in which all my extravagance, so long pent in, was pelting against the wall of tact, or even of ordinary human consideration. I wanted to patronise him and be humble; I wanted to ask him outright whether he intended to marry the woman in the photograph. I should have liked to ask him if I could be of any use to him.

But I was moved by a compulsion which came from something deeper among the three of us.

'He's a fine boy,' Geoffrey repeated. I was compelled to say:

'So is yours.'

For an instant he was surprised—

'Yes, I suppose he is.'

He added, with his head tossed back, with his student vanity: 'But then, I should have expected him to be.'

He was staring at Margaret. Her tears were not dry, her expression was brilliant with rapture and pain. She said:

'I'm watching for the first sign of anything wrong with him.'

'Yes,' said Geoffrey. 'If nothing happens within a fortnight from now, then he's clear.'

'I shall do anything you tell me,' she said.

He nodded.

'I'd better see him two or three times a week until the incubation period's over.'

She cried:

'We must save him from anything we can!'

She had known, when she came to me, the loads that she was taking: some could shrug them off, not she: even now, in the midst of rapture, they lay on her, lay on her more heavily, perhaps, because she was uplifted. Somehow the boy's chance of infection stood before her like an emblem. When she spoke of it, when she said we must save him from anything in our power, she was speaking, not only of the disease; but of the future.

I said:

'Yes, we must save him from everything we can.'

It was a signal of understanding between us. But Geoffrey, who had also heard her affirmation, appeared to have missed it. He replied, as though illness was the only point:

'Well, even if he does show any signs, which incidentally is much less likely than not, you needn't take it too tragically. We should be pretty incompetent if we didn't get it in time. And children are very tough animals, you ought to remember that.'

He said it with detached satisfaction. Then, in a totally different tone, he said:

'I'm glad I was able to do something for your child.'

In the constricted office, he was sitting on the desk, above us, and as he spoke he looked down first at her, then at me. In the same tone, which was sharp, insistent, not so much benevolent as condescending, he said:

'I'm glad I was able to do something for you.'

He was free with us now. Before, he had been constrained, because he was a man, light-natured but upright, who did not find forgiveness easy, who indeed felt not revengeful but inferior and ineffective in the presence of those whom he could not forgive. Now he had us under an obligation. He was ready to be fond of her again: he was even ready to like me. He felt happy, released, and good.

So, it might have seemed incongruous, did we. She, and I also, had previously felt for him that resentment which one bears towards someone to whom one has done harm – a resentment in which there lurks a kind of despising mockery, a dislike in which one makes him smaller than he is. Now he had been powerful when we were abject. We had been in his hands; and, for both of us, for her more violently, but for me also, the feeling swept hidden shame away.

He sat there, above us, his head near the light bulb. Margaret and I looked up at him; her face was blanched with sleeplessness and anxiety, her eyes were bloodshot; so must mine have been. He showed no sign of a broken night: as usual, vain about his appearance, he had his hair elegantly brushed and parted, he smelt of shaving lotion.

He was happy: we were sleepy with joy.

CHAPTER LVI

THE SHORT WALK HOME

JUST over a fortnight later, on a humid July afternoon, the clouds so dense that some windows were already lit at six o'clock, Margaret called at my office to take me home. She was wearing a summer frock, and in the heat she was relaxed with pleasure, with delectable fatigue, coming from the hospital, where she had been arranging for the child to return to us next day.

He was well and cheerful, she said. So was Maurice, who had escaped the infection altogether: there was no one in her charge to worry her now, she was lazy with pleasure, just as she had been when Gilbert first brought her into my sick room.

Just then there sounded Rose's punctilious tap at the door. As soon as he saw Margaret, whom as it happened he had not met, he broke into apologies so complex and profuse that even I began to feel embarrassed. He was so extremely sorry: he had looked forward all these years to the pleasure of meeting Lewis's wife: and now he had just butted in, he was making a nuisance of himself, he only wanted to distract her husband for a moment, but even that was an infliction. They had neither of them got better at casual introductions: Rose, inflexibly, wearing his black coat and striped trousers in the steaming heat, went on talking according to his idea of gallantry, his eyes strained; Margaret faced him as she might as a girl at one of her father's exhibitions, hating the social forms, doing her best to be easy with an awkward and aspiring clerk.

I saw that they mildly liked each other, but only as partners in distress. When Rose had finished his piece of business with me, which with his usual economy took five minutes, he made his protracted and obsequious goodbyes. After he had at last departed, I told her that he was one of the most formidable men I had known, in some ways the most formidable: she had heard it before, but now in the flesh she could not credit it. But she was too tired, too happy to argue; she did not want to disagree, even on the surface: she said, let us go home.

As soon as we had left the well-like corridors of the old building and went into the street, we pushed against the greenhouse air: sweat pricked at the temples: it was in such weather, I remembered, holding Margaret's arm, as when I first walked from Lufkin's office to the Chelsea house, getting on for twenty years before.

Now, in the same weather, we turned the other way, sauntered up Whitehall towards Trafalgar Square, and there got a bus. I told her how I had once sat on a bus alongside old Bevill, and he had mentioned her father's name, which gave me a card of re-entry into her life. As the bus spurted and braked up Regent Street, we talked about the child as we might have done in bed between waking and sleeping, the diary of his days, the conspiracy of hope which, during his illness, we had put away as though we had never played with it.

We talked of the children and then put them aside: along Oxford Street we were talking of ourselves. We talked at random, of the first nights we spent together, of what we had feared for each other in the last month, of thoughts of each other during the years we were separated.

As we got off at Marble Arch and walked along the pavement rustling with litter, under the trees, Margaret gave a smile of pretended sarcasm, and said:

'Yes, I suppose there are some who'd say we had come through.'

I put my arm round her and held her to me as we walked slowly, as slowly as though we planned to spin the evening's happiness out. The vestigial headache, seeping in with the saturated air, seemed like a sexual ache. There was a smell of hot grass and fumes, and, although the lime was almost over, just once I fancied that I caught the last of it.

Her smile sharp, she said:

'I suppose some would really say that we'd come through.'

She had more courage than I had. She was not anything like so given to insuring herself: her spirit was so strong that when she rejoiced, she rejoiced without qualification. To her, victories were absolute; at that moment, as we walked together, she had all of them she wanted: she wanted no more than this. And yet, by a perversity which she would not lose, she, whose bone and flesh spoke of complete happiness, could not use the words.

That evening she had to dissimulate her faith, put on a smile that tried to be ironic, and deny the moment in which we stood. Just as I had done so often: but now it was I, out of comparison more suspicious of fate than she was, who spoke without troubling to placate it.

We were in sight of home. A light was shining in one room: the others stood black, eyeless, in the leaden light. It was a homecoming such as, for years, I thought I was not to know. Often in my childhood, I had felt dread as I came near home. It had been worse when I went, as a young man, towards the Chelsea house. Now, walking with Margaret, that dread had gone. In sight of home my steps began to quicken, I should soon be there with her.

It was a homecoming such as I had imagined when I was lonely, but as one happening to others, not to me.

The Affair

The Affair

1953–54

CONTENTS

Contents

PART ONE

THE FIRST DISSENTIENT

CHAPTER I

AN UNSATISFACTORY EVENING

WHEN Tom Orbell invited me to dinner at his club, I imagined that we should be alone. As soon as I saw him, however – he was waiting by the porter's box, watching me climb up the steps from the street – he said, in a confidential, anxious whisper: 'As a matter of fact, I've asked someone to meet you. Is that all right?'

He was a large young man, cushioned with fat, but with heavy bones and muscles underneath. He was already going bald, although he was only in his late twenties. The skin of his face was fine-textured and pink, and his smile was affable, open, malicious, eager to please and smooth with soft soap. As he greeted me, his welcome was genuine, his expression warm: his big light-blue eyes stayed watchful and suspicious.

He was telling me about my fellow-guest.

'It's a young woman, as a matter of fact. Lewis, she is really rather beautiful.'

I had forgotten that this club, like a good many others in London in the fifties, had taken to letting women in to dine. While he was talking, I had no doubt at all that I was there to serve some purpose, though what it was I could not begin to guess.

'You're sure you don't mind?' Tom pressed me, as I was hanging up my coat. 'It is all right, isn't it?'

He led the way, heavy shoulders pushing forward, into the reading room. The room was so long, so deserted, that it seemed dank, though outside it was a warmish September night and in the grates coal fires were blazing. By one fire, at the far end of the room, a man and woman were sitting in silence reading glossy magazines. By the other stood a young woman in a red sweater and black skirt, with one hand on the mantelpiece. To her Tom Orbell cried out enthusiastically:

'Here we are!'

He introduced me to her. Her name was Laura Howard. She was, as he had promised, comely. She had a shield-shaped face and clear grey eyes, and she moved with energy and grace. Tom got us sitting in armchairs on opposite sides of the fire, ordered drinks, dumped himself on the sofa between us. 'Here we *are*,' he said, as though determined to have a cheerful drinking evening.

He proceeded to talk, flattering us both, using his wits and high spirits to get the party going.

I glanced across at Laura. One thing was clear, I thought. She had been as astonished as I was to find she was not dining alone with Tom Orbell: quite as astonished, and much more put out.

'When are you going to come and see us again?' Tom was addressing himself to me, tucking into a large whisky. 'We really do miss you, you know.'

By 'us', he meant the Cambridge college of which I had been a fellow before the war. I still had many friends there, including my brother Martin, who was himself a fellow, and went to see them two or three times a year. It was on one of those visits that I had first met Tom, just after he had taken his degree in history. He had made a reputation as a bright young man, and I had heard my old friends saying that they would have to elect him. That had duly happened – so far as I remembered, in 1949, four years before this dinner in his club.

'We really do miss him,' Tom was explaining confidentially to Laura. 'It's like everywhere in this country, the right people are never where you want them. Everything's got into the hands of those awful old men, and when anyone like Lewis comes along he goes and does something frightfully important and leaves the old men to sit on the heads of the rest of us. He's a very powerful and slightly sinister figure, is Lewis. Oh, yes, he is. But he's on the right side. I assure you he is. We miss him very much, do you believe me?'

'I'm sure you do,' she said, in a tone which could scarcely have been less interested.

Tom continued to talk – was he trying to distract her? – as though we were all in a sociological conspiracy. Generalisations poured out: the good young middle-aged, said Tom, flattering me, for I was forty-eight, had got caught up trying to keep the country afloat. The generation coming up, he said, flattering her, for she was about thirty, had got to fight some other battles, had got to smash the 'awful old men'.

'We are all in it together,' he said. He had had three stiff drinks, he sounded both hearty and angry. 'We're going to show them. I mean it very sincerely, both of you.'

Upstairs in the dining-room, with Laura sitting between us at a dark corner table, Tom went on with his patter. There were a couple of decanters waiting for us, shining comfortably under the three candles, and soon Tom had put down the best part of a bottle of wine. But, though he showed the effects of drink very quickly, he did not get any more drunk. He was spontaneous, as he usually seemed to be, but whatever his policy was for this evening he had not lost hold of it. He was spontaneous, at the same time he was wily: somehow he managed to use the spontaneity as part of his stock-in-trade.

Meanwhile he was enjoying his dinner with a mixture of appetite and discrimination, with a gusto so intense that he appeared to be blushing. After he had ordered our meal with analytical care, he suddenly had a second thought about his own. Beckoning the waitress, he whispered to her as confidentially as though they were having a love affair. She reappeared with some gulls' eggs while Laura and I forked away at the smoked salmon.

'Delicious, delicious,' said Tom Orbell, in a gourmet's transport.

It was when he repeated this performance over the savoury that Laura lost her patience. As he talked at large, she had been half-polite, half-sulking. Not that she was irritated because he was not paying attention to her as a woman. Actually, he was. He was a susceptible young man, he wanted to make a hit with her. To which she was totally indifferent; something was on her mind, but not that.

Tom had just had a new and delectable afterthought about the savoury. When our mushrooms on toast arrived, he had another piece of happy whispering with the waitress. 'Do you think I could possibly have . . . ?' Soon he was munching away at chicken livers and bacon, murmuring with content.

Then Laura said to him:

'I do want to get down to business, if you don't mind.'

Tom looked at her, his glance at the same time defensive and bold:

'Is there really anything we can do tonight?'

'When are any of you going to move?'

'It isn't any use me moving by myself, is it?'

'That's not the point.'

'But isn't it the point, my dear? Do you think that the blasted Court of Seniors is going to listen to a solitary junior fellow? Remember this is the last shot you've got, if you don't mind me speaking frankly. And I'm speaking with great affection for you, even more than for Donald, and that isn't a monstrous thing to say, is it?'

She was looking angry and determined, which made her seem more handsome, and he gazed at her admiringly. 'Forgive me,' he said, 'I'm afraid I'm slightly drunk.' He was not: he was trying to put up a smoke-screen.

'If you don't mind me speaking very frankly, you've got to be very, very careful about your tactics,' he went on. 'And so have I, because there might come a time when I could be a bit of use to you, in a minor way, and it would be a mistake to have shot my bolt before the right time came, wouldn't it?'

'Not so much a mistake as doing nothing at all.'

'Is there any reason why I shouldn't let Lewis into this?' he said, beating another retreat.

'Haven't you heard about it already?' Almost for the first time, she spoke to me directly.

In fact, as I had been listening to them, I knew something of the story. My brother was the most discreet of men: but he and Francis Getliffe had thought that, as an ex-fellow, I had a right to know. Even so, they had told me the bare minimum. The scandal had been kept so tightly within the college that I had not caught a whisper from anyone else. All I had picked up was that one of the younger fellows had been caught out in a piece of scientific fraud. Without any noise at all, he had been got rid of. It was a kind of dismissal that had only happened in the college once within living memory. It had been done, of course, after something like a judicial investigation. I assumed that it had been done with more obsessive care even than in a process at law. The final dismissal had happened six months before: and, as I had realised as soon as Laura set to work on Tom Orbell, the man concerned was her husband, Donald Howard.

I said that I knew what they were talking about.

'Have you heard that it's a piece of unforgivable injustice?' she demanded.

I shook my head.

'You've got to remember, just for the sake of getting your own tactics right,' said Tom, 'that no one in the college takes that view; haven't you got to remember that?'

'Have you heard that it's the result of sheer blind prejudice?'

I shook my head again, and Tom put in:

'With great respect, my dear Laura, that's just misleading you. Of course there's some strong feeling about it, it wouldn't be natural if there wasn't. Of course most of them don't agree with his opinions. I don't myself, as you know perfectly well. But then, I don't agree with

Lewis's opinions either, and I think Lewis would feel pretty safe in his job if I suddenly came into power. Speaking with great affection, you're really on the wrong track there.'

'I don't believe it for an instant.'

'Truly you're wrong—'

'I will believe it when you've done something to prove it.'

I watched them as she went on bullying him. Tom Orbell was as clever as they came; psychologically he was full of resource and beneath the anxiety to please there was a tough, wilful core. But his forehead was sweating, his voice was not so mellifluous or easy. He was frightened of her. While she sat there, pretty, set-faced, strong-necked, she had only one thought in her head. She had come to talk to him and make him act. Talking to Tom, who was so much cleverer, she had (to use a phrase which for me had worn a groove) the complete moral initiative.

She said: 'I'm not asking you anything difficult. All I want is to get this business re-opened.'

'How can you expect me to do that? I'm just one out of twenty, I'm a very junior person, I'm not a majority of the college. And I've tried to explain to you, but you won't realise it, that you're dealing with a society and a constitution, that you need a majority of the college before the thing can be so much as raised again.'

'You can't get a majority of the college unless you make a beginning now,' she said.

Tom Orbell looked at her with something like appeal. I thought she had got him down. Then I realised that I had underrated him, when he said:

'Now look, my dear. I've got a serious suggestion to make, and I want you to consider it very carefully. I don't believe that anyone as junior as I am is going to make any impact on this situation at all. What I suggest, and I mean it very deeply, is that you should try to persuade Lewis here to talk to some of his friends. I'm not saying that you could possibly want him to commit himself to an opinion one way or another, any more than I could commit myself, as far as that goes. But if you could get him so much as to raise the question with the people he knows – after all, he's become the nearest approach we have to an elder statesman, has Lewis. He can talk to them as I can't possibly and shan't be able to for twenty years. I do mean that, I assure you.'

So now I understood why he had enticed me there.

She looked at me with steady, bright, obstinate eyes.

'You don't see much of them there nowadays, do you?' she asked.

'Not very much,' I said.

'You can't possibly be really in touch, I should think, can you?'

I said no.

'I don't see what you could expect to do.'

She said it dismissively and with contempt. Contempt not for Tom Orbell, but for me. I felt a perceptible pique. It was not agreeable to be written off quite so far. But this young woman had decided that I was no good at all. She did not seem even to be considering whether I was well disposed or not. She just had no faith in me. It was Tom in whom she still had faith.

When we returned to the reading room, even she, however, was deterred from forcing him any more. Tom sat there, his face cherubic, sketching out visions of the future like roseate Tiepolo clouds, high-spirited visions that seemed to consist of unworthy persons being ejected from positions of eminence and in their places worthy persons, notably the present company and in particular Tom himself, installed. I thought Laura would start on him again as soon as she got him alone. But for that night, at any rate, he was secure. For he had revealed to us that he was staying in the club, and at last it became my duty to take Laura out into Pall Mall and find her a taxi.

She said a cold good-night. Well, I thought, as I went along the street, looking for a taxi for myself, it would not be easy to invent a more unsatisfactory evening. None of the three of us had got away with what he wanted. Laura had not cornered Tom Orbell. He had not managed to slide her off on to me. And I had not done any better. I was not much interested in this story of her husband: it did not even begin to strike me as plausible that there had been an injustice of that kind. No, I was not thinking of that at all, but I was faintly irked. No one likes to be treated as a vacuum inhabited solely by himself.

CHAPTER II

NO SENSE OF THE PAST

A FEW weeks after the evening in Tom Orbell's club, I was sitting in my brother's rooms in college. It was a routine visit: I had gone down, as I did most years, for the Michaelmas audit feast. It gave me a curious mixture of comfort and unfamiliarity to be sitting there as a guest; for I had once used that great Tudor room as my own dining-room, and had sat talking in it as I now sat talking to Francis Getliffe, on October nights like this one, with draughts running under the wainscot, the fire in the basket grate not quite hot enough to reach out to the window seats.

In the study next door, my brother was interviewing a pupil, and Francis Getliffe and I were alone. After knowing him for nearly thirty years, I didn't find it easy to recognise just where he had changed. He still looked quixotic and fine-featured; his sunburned flesh was dark over his collar and white tie. But success had pouched his cheeks a little and taken away the strain. In the past few years the success which he had wanted honourably but fiercely as he started his career, and which had not come quickly, had suddenly piled upon him. He was in the Royal Society and all over the world his reputation was as high as he had once longed for it to be. In addition, he had been one of the most effective scientists in the war. It was for that work, not his pure research, that he had been given the C.B.E. whose cross he wore on his shirtfront. For a combination of the two he had, two years before, been knighted.

He was chatting about some of our contemporaries who also had done well. He would always have been fair about them, because he had a strict code of fairness: but now, it occurred to me, he was sometimes sharp-tongued but perhaps just a shade more fair. He was showing that special affection which one who has in his own eyes come off feels towards others who have done the same.

Martin came in through the inside door. He had changed before his tutorial hour, and was already dressed for the feast. Straightaway he began to ask Francis's advice about the pupil he had just been seeing: was he, or was he not, right to change from physics to metallurgy? Martin worried away at the problem. He had recently become Junior Tutor, and he was doing the job with obsessive conscientiousness. He enjoyed doing it like that.

Unlike Francis, whose prestige had been rising for years past, Martin's had been standing still. A few years before, he had had the chance of becoming one of the atomic energy bosses. He had got the chance, not through being a scientist in Francis's class, which he never could be, but because people thought he was hard, responsible and shrewd. They were not far wrong: and yet, to everyone's surprise, he had thrown up the power and come back to the college.

He did not seem to mind having a future behind him. With the obsessive satisfaction with which he was now speaking of his pupil's course, he applied himself to his teaching, to the bread-and-butter work that came his way. He looked very well on it. He was getting on for forty, but he might have passed for younger. As he spoke to Francis, his eyes were acute, brilliant with a kind of sarcastic fun, although everything he said was serious and businesslike.

Then he mentioned another pupil called Howarth, and the name by chance plucked at something at the back of my mind to which, since the night in Tom Orbell's club, I had not given a thought.

'Howarth, not Howard?' I said.

'Howarth, not Howard,' said Martin.

'As a matter of fact,' I said, 'I heard something about your ex-colleague Howard. In September young Orbell introduced me to his wife.'

'Did he now?' said Martin, with a tight smile. 'She's a pretty girl, isn't she?'

'She was crying out loud that there had been a miscarriage of justice. I suppose that's all nonsense, isn't it?'

'Quite nonsense,' said Martin.

Francis said:

'There's nothing in that.'

'She seemed to think that he'd been turned out because of some sort of prejudice, which I never got quite clear—'

'That's simple,' said Francis. 'He was, and I suppose he still is, a moderately well-known fellow-traveller.'

'He wouldn't be the favourite character of some of our friends, then, would he?'

'If I'd thought that was deciding anything, I should have made a noise,' said Francis. 'I needn't tell you that, need I?'

He said it stiffly, but without being touchy. He took it for granted that no one who knew him, I least of all, would doubt his integrity. In fact, no one in his senses could have done so. In the thirties, Francis himself, like so many of his fellow scientists, had been far to the left. Now he was respectable, honoured, he had moved a little nearer to the centre, but not all that much. In politics both he and Martin remained liberals and speculative men, and so did I. It was a topic on which the three of us in that room were close together.

'I don't want to give you a false impression,' Francis said. 'This man was disliked inside the college, of course he was, and there's no getting away from it; with most of them his politics made them dislike him more. But that wasn't the reason why we had to throw him out. It was a reason, if you like, why we found it difficult to get him elected in the first place. We had to be pretty rough with them, and tell them that politics or no politics, they mustn't shut their eyes to an Alpha man.'

'In which,' said Martin, 'we don't seem to have done superlatively well.'
Francis gave a grim smile, unamused.

'No,' he said, 'it's a bad business. He just went in for a piece of simple
unadulterated fraud. That's all there is to it.'

So far as he could make it intelligible to a layman, Francis told me
about the fraud. A paper of Howard's, published in collaboration with
his professor, an eminent old scientist now dead, had been attacked by
American workers in the same field – and the attack had said that the
experimental results could not be repeated. Francis and some of his
Cavendish colleagues had had private warning that there was something
'fishy' about Howard's published photographs. Two of the scientists in
the college, Nightingale and Skeffington, had had a look at them. There
was no doubt about it: at least one photograph had been, as it were, forged.
That is, a photograph had been enlarged, what Francis called 'blown up',
to look like the result of a totally different experiment: and this photograph became the decisive experimental evidence in Howard's fellowship
thesis and later in his published paper.

The fraud could not be accidental, said Francis. Neither he nor Martin
had worked on Howard's subject, but they had looked at the photograph.
It was only too straightforward. The technical opinion that Nightingale
and Skeffington had given was the one that any other scientist would
have had to give, and it was on this technical opinion that the Court of
Seniors had acted. The Court of Seniors, so Francis and Martin told me,
had been the Master, Arthur Brown, old Winslow, and Nightingale, this
time in his capacity as Bursar. 'Of course,' said Francis, 'they had to go
on what the scientists told them. Nightingale's the only one of them
who'd have any idea what a diffraction photograph was.'

'Still,' he added, 'they went into it very thoroughly. If it hadn't been a
clear case, they would still have been at it.'

Somehow a question of mine set him reflecting on other cases of
scientific fraud. There hadn't been many, he said, less even than one
might expect. Considering the chances and the temptation, the number
was astonishingly low. In the last fifty years, he could tick off the notorious
ones on the fingers of two hands. He produced names at which Martin
nodded, but which, of course, meant nothing to me. Rupp, the J-
phenomenon ('but that, presumably, was an honest mistake'): Francis
spoke of them with the incredulous relish which professional scandals
often evoke in a hyper-scrupulous man. He was wondering about the
motives of those who perpetrated them, when the college bell started
clanging for the feast.

As we picked up our gowns and went downstairs ino the court, Francis was saying:

'But there's no mystery why Howard did it. He just wanted to make his marble good.'

Sitting in hall in the candlelight, I let the story drift unresistingly out of mind. It was over and tied up now, and the college was going on. I was enough of a stranger to draw an extra pleasure out of being there. I was also enough of a stranger to be put up on the dais among the old men. This was not such a privilege as it looked: for my next-door neighbour was so old that the places beside him were not competed for.

'Ah,' he said, gazing at me affably. 'Excuse me. Do you mind telling me your name?'

The colour in his irises had faded, and they were ringed with white. Otherwise he did not show the signs of extreme age: his cheeks were ruddy pink, his hair and beard silky but strong.

I said that I was Lewis Eliot. It was the second time since dinner began that he had asked the question.

'Indeed. Tell me, have you any connection with the college?'

It was too embarrassing to tell him that we had been fellows together for ten years. This was M. H. L. Gay, the Icelandic scholar. In his presence one felt as though confronted by one of those genealogical freaks, as I once felt when I met an old lady whose father, not as a boy but as a young man, had been in Paris during the French Revolution. For Gay had been elected a fellow over seventy years before. He had actually retired from his professorship before Tom Orbell and half a dozen of the present society were born. He was now ninety-four: and in a voice shaky, it is true, but still resonant, was loudly demanding a second glass of champagne.

'Capital. Ah. That's a drink and a half, if ever there was one. Let me persuade you, sir' – he was addressing me – 'to have a glass of this excellent wine.'

He began to speak, cordially and indiscriminately, to all around him:

'I don't know whether you realise it, but this is positively my last appearance before my annual hibernation. Indeed. Yes, that is a prudent measure of mine. Indeed it is. I adopted that prudent measure about ten years ago, when I had to realise that I was no longer as young as I used to be. So after this splendid audit feast of ours, I retire into hibernation and don't make the journey into college until we have the spring with us again. That means that I have to miss our fine feast for the Commemoration of Benefactors. I have suggested more than once to some of our colleagues that perhaps the summer might be a more opportune time for that fine feast. But so far they haven't taken the hint, I regret to say.'

For an instant his face looked childish. Then he cheered up:

'So I retire to my own ingle-nook for the winter, indeed I do. And I listen to the great gales roaring over the Fens, and I thank God for a good stout roof over my head. Not one of those flat roofs these modern architects try to foist off on us. A good stout pitched roof, that's what a man wants over his head. Why, one of those flat roofs, our Fenland gales would have it off before you could say Jack Robinson.'

A few places along the table, a distinguished Central European architect was listening. 'I do not quite understand, Professor Gay,' he said, with a serious, puzzled and humourless expression. 'Are you thinking of the turbulent flow round a rectangle? Or are you thinking of the sucking effect? I assure you—'

'I am thinking of the force of our Fenland gales, sir,' cried Gay triumphantly. 'Our ancestors in their wisdom and experience knew about those gales, and so they built us good, stout, pitched roofs. Ah, I often sit by my fire and listen, and I think, "That's a gale and a half. I'd rather be where I am than out at sea." '

Old Gay kept it up throughout the feast. Sitting by him, I found it impossible to feel any true sense of the past at all. The candles blew about, in the middle of the table the show-pieces of gold and silver gleamed; all, including Gay's conversation, was as it would have been at a feast twenty years earlier. The food was perhaps a little, though only a little, less elaborate, the wines were just as good. No, I got pleasure out of being there, but no sense of the past. True, I now knew half the fellows only slightly. True, some of those I had known, and the one I had known best, were dead. But, as I sat by Gay, none of that plucked a nerve, as a visitant from the true past did. I could even think of the Baron de Charlus's roll-call of his friends, and say to myself, 'Despard-Smith, *dead*, Eustace Pilbrow, *dead*, Chrystal, *dead*: Roy Calvert, *dead*.' Not even that last name touched me; it was all a rhetorical flourish, as though one were making a nostalgic speech after a good dinner. Now I came to think of it, wasn't Charlus's roll-call just a flourish too?

In the shadows on the linenfold, I noticed a picture which was new since my last visit. Above the candlelight it was too dark to make out much of the face, although it did not look any better done than most of the college portraits. On the frame I could, however, read the gold letters:

Doctor R. T. A. Crawford, F.R.S., Nobel Laureate, Forty-First
Master.

Master 1937–

My eyes went from the picture to the original, solid, Buddha-faced,
in the middle of the table. His reign, so they all said, had been pretty
equable. There did not seem to have been much to scar it. Now it was
nearly over. They had prolonged him for three years above the statutory
age of seventy, but he was to go in a year's time: he would preside at the
next Michaelmas audit feast, and that would be his last.

'Ah. Master,' Gay was calling out. 'I congratulate you on this splendid
evening. I congratulate you. Indeed I do.'

From his previous conversation, I thought he was not clear which, of
all the Masters he had known, this was. Masters came and Masters
went, and Gay, who was telling us that port did not agree with him,
applied himself to the nuts.

In the jostle of the combination room afterwards, I felt my arm being
squeezed. 'Nice to see you,' came a round, breathy, enthusiastic whisper.
'Slip out as soon as you decently can. We still finish up in my rooms, you
know.'

It was Arthur Brown, the Senior Tutor. Some time passed before I
could get free and when I entered Brown's sitting-room it was already full.
Brown gripped my hand.

'This is more like it,' he said. 'I've been telling them, people got into
the habit of dropping in here after feasts more years ago than I care to
remember. I take it amiss that you haven't been here since this time last
year. You mustn't forget us altogether, you know. Now I hope I can
tempt you to a drop of brandy? I always think it's rather soothing after
a long dinner.'

By this time he was sixty-three, but in his forties his flesh had been as
padded and his colour as high. The residual wings of hair were white
over his ears. He looked kind, he looked like someone who enjoyed
seeing others happy: and that was true. He looked a bit of a buffer – to
those who did not notice the eyes behind his spectacles, sparkling with
inquisitiveness, or how, under the paunchy flesh, he carried his
stomach high. In fact, when I had been a colleague of his in the college,
I thought that he was one of the shrewdest managers of people that I
had met. I still thought so, after meeting a good many more. He contrived
to be at the same time upright, obstinate and very cunning.

The room was cosier, the temperature higher, than in most college sets.
On the walls hung a collection of English water-colours, of which Brown

had come to be a connoisseur. There were so many men in the room that they had split up into groups: that would not have happened in the first after-feast parties which I had attended there. The college was larger now, the average age of the fellows lower, the behaviour just perceptibly less formal. Glass in hand, Francis Getliffe was talking to a knot of three young scientists; Martin and a handsome man whom I recognised as Skeffington were away in a corner with two arts fellows, Clark and Lester Ince, both elected since I left.

By the fire, Brown and I were sitting drinking our brandy when Tom Orbell came and joined us. His face was pink, flushed and cheerful, but in Brown's presence he was comporting himself with decorum, with a mixture of expansiveness and caution. What could be done about the chaplain? he was asking. Apparently there was a danger that he would be enticed away. He was intelligent, so Tom was saying, and it wasn't all that easy nowadays to find an intelligent man in orders.

'Of course,' he turned to me with a flush of defiance, 'that wouldn't matter to you, Lewis. You wouldn't mind if every clergyman in the country was mentally deficient. I expect you'd think it would make things easier if they were. But Arthur and I can't take that view, can we?'

'I should have thought it was slightly extreme,' said Brown.

But he was not prepared to let Tom flaunt his piety at my expense. Brown was a 'pillar of society', conservative and Anglican, but he went to church out of propriety more than belief, and he was not entirely easy when young men like Orbell began displaying their religion. So Brown told a story in my favour, designed to show how careful I was about others' faith.

'I'm sorry, Lewis,' said Tom, at his jolliest and most repentant, instantaneously quick to catch the feeling of someone like Brown, 'it was absolutely monstrous of me to accuse you of that. You're frightfully good, I know you are. And by the way, it was absolutely monstrous of me to inflict that evening on you with Laura Howard.'

'What's that?' said Brown, his eyes alert and peering. 'How did you come to be meeting Mrs Howard, Lewis?'

'I saddled him with it, I'm afraid,' Tom replied. 'You see, she was wanting me to raise Cain in the college about her husband – which, as I believe all those protests of hers are just sheer nonsense, I couldn't very well do, could I? Just sheer nonsense which she's managed to make herself believe because she loves him, God knows why. So I didn't want to make it easy for her to get to work on me, did I? Mind you, Arthur,' he said, 'if I thought there was the slightest bit of sense in her case or even the chance that there could be a bit of sense in it, I'd have come and told you straight out that I was going to bring it up. I do mean that. I think it's very important that people of my age should be ready to throw their weight about. I know you agree, Arthur, don't you?'

Soon afterwards, Tom attached himself to Martin's group. I was thinking that, as he explained himself to Brown, he had shown a delicate blend of the deferential and the man-to-man, beautiful to listen to. In private, out of hearing of persons in authority, few people rebelled as eloquently as Tom Orbell. In the hearing of persons in authority, the eloquence remained, but the rebellion not. In the company of Arthur Brown, Tom seemed above all desirous of growing into someone just like Arthur Brown – solid, rooted, statesmanlike, a man on top.

'So our young friend has been involving you with the Howards, has he?' asked Arthur Brown.

'You've been having more trouble than I thought, haven't you?' I said.

'I need hardly say,' said Brown, 'that none of this ought to be so much as mentioned outside the college. I don't have to tell you that, I know. Put it another way: I should have thought it was safer, if you only talked about it, even in this place, with Martin or the people you know well.'

'What's this man Howard like, Arthur?' I asked.

The colour, heavy puce, deepened in Brown's cheeks. He was frowning as though angry with me even for asking the question.

'He's an unmitigated swine,' he said.

For an instant I was astonished. I did not know many people more tolerant of others than Brown was. Also, he had spent so many years guarding his speech that it often seemed he couldn't speak any other way.

Even Brown himself seemed startled at hearing his own outburst. He said, once more judicious, weighing his words: 'No, I don't think I feel inclined to withdraw what I've just said. I never have been able to find anything to set down in his favour. He's a twister, but there are plenty of twisters that have some redeeming qualities, and I can't recall this chap showing a single one. He's graceless, he's never been able to get on with anyone, and I shouldn't be surprised if that's why he wants to pull the world down round our ears. But I might have been able even to put up with that, if he hadn't behaved so vilely to the people he owed everything to. When he started biting the hand that fed him, I decided I wasn't going to look for any more excuses or listen to anyone else making them. He's no good, Lewis. I don't mind telling you that I considered at the time, and I still do, that we ought to have gone the whole hog and struck his name off the books.'

Brown had been speaking in a reasonable, moderate tone, but heavily, almost as though he had been giving his judgment to the other seniors. He added:

'There's only one good thing to be said about this wretched business. The whole college was absolutely solid about it. I don't need to tell you that that's not exactly common form. But if the college hadn't been solid for once, it would have made things difficult. The place wouldn't have been any too comfortable to live in. And I don't want to exaggerate, but we might have walked straight into trouble outside. This is just the kind of thing that could have got us into the papers, and if that had happened, it would have done us more harm that I like to think about.'

Francis Getliffe had already gone, and the party was breaking up. Just as Martin said good-night to Brown, and waited to take me across the staircase to his rooms, I was remarking on the new picture of the Master in the hall. 'There's exactly room for one more beside it,' I said, as I stood up to go, 'and then you'll have to think again.'

I noticed Brown glancing sharply at me. Still sitting in his armchair, he tugged at my sleeve.

'Stay here a few minutes,' he said. He smiled at Martin: 'He can find his own way to your bedroom, can't he? After all, he's done it plenty of times, more than you have, I suppose. And I don't get many chances to talk to him these days.'

Martin said that it was time he went home to his wife. Like me, he suspected that Arthur Brown was not just idly keeping me back for the sake of company. When we were left alone, Brown made sure that I was settled in the chair opposite to him. He became more than ever hospitable and deliberate. 'More brandy?'

No, I wouldn't drink any more that night.

'Old chap,' he said, 'it's very nice to see you sitting there again.'

He had always been fond of me. At times he had defended and looked after me. Now he had the warm, sharp-edged, minatory affection that one feels for a protégé who has done pretty well. Was everything going all right? How was my wife? My son?

'So everything's reasonably smooth just now, is it? That's perfectly splendid. Do you know, Lewis, there was a time when I was afraid things weren't going to turn out smooth for you.'

He gave me a kind, satisfied smile. Then he said, quite casually: 'By the way, when you were talking about the Master's picture, it just crossed my mind that you might have heard something. I suppose you haven't, by any chance, have you?'

'No,' I said, surprised.

Brown said: 'No, of course, I thought you couldn't have.'

His expression was steady and unperturbed.

'Just for a moment, though on second thoughts I can see you couldn't have been, I fancied you might be casting a fly.'

I shook my head, but now I thought I was following him.

'Well, what's happening?' I said.

'The trouble is,' said Brown with satisfied gravity, 'I'm not quite sure how much I'm at liberty to tell you. The whole matter is very much at the stage where no one has wanted to come out in the open. In my judgment the longer they put it off the more chance we have of avoiding ructions and coming to a decent conclusion.'

'What's the point?' I asked again.

Brown pursed his lips. 'Well, within these four walls, I think I'm not breaking any obligations if I tell you this. When the present Master retires, which is at the end of next year, not the academic but the calendar year, some of the society have asked me whether I would consider offering myself as a candidate.'

Yes, I had got there five minutes before. But, until he began to talk, I had not been expecting it. I had taken it for granted that Francis Getliffe had the next Mastership in the bag. On and off over the last two years, I had heard it discussed. The only name that anyone mentioned seriously was that of Francis

'Who are your backers, Arthur?' I asked.

'No,' he said, 'without their permission I don't think that I ought to specify them at this stage, but I believe they'd let me say that there are enough of them to make the suggestion not entirely frivolous. And I think I might indicate that there were one or two of them recently present in this room.'

He was smiling blandly. He did not seem anxious, elated or depressed.

'If I were to ask for your advice whether to let my candidature go forward or not, Lewis, I wonder what you'd say?'

I hesitated. Both Francis and he were friends of mine, and I was glad that I should be out of it. But I was hesitating for a different reason. I was afraid, despite what Brown had just said, that he would get few votes – perhaps so few as to be humiliating. I did not like the thought of that. I could not see any college not preferring Francis when it came to the choice.

'I think I know what's in your mind,' Brown was saying. 'You're thinking that our friend Francis is out of comparison a more distinguished man than I am, and of course you're right. I've never made any secret of it, I should be satisfied to see Francis Getliffe as Master of this college. Between ourselves, there are only three distinguished men here, and he's one of them, the other two being the present Master and I suppose we've still got to say old Gay. I've never had delusions about myself, I think you'll grant me that, old chap. I've never been really first-rate at anything. It used to depress me slightly when I was a young man.'

He meant, I knew, precisely what he said. He was genuinely humble: he did not credit himself with any gifts at all.

I said: 'I was thinking something quite different.'

Brown went on: 'No, it's perfectly right that the college should consider whether they could put up with an undistinguished person like me, in comparison with a very distinguished one like Francis. But one or two members of the society have put an interesting point of view which has made me think twice before saying no once and for all. Their view is that we've just had a Master of great external distinction, even more so than Francis's. So one or two people have represented to me that the college can afford someone who wasn't much known outside but who would keep things going reasonably well among ourselves. And they paid me the compliment of suggesting that I might have my uses in that respect.'

'They are dead right,' I said.

'No,' he said, 'you've always thought too much of me. Anyway, some time within the next twelve months I shall have to decide whether to let my name go forward. Of course, it's my last chance and it isn't Francis's. Perhaps I should be justified in taking that into account. Well, I've got plenty of time to make up my mind. I don't know which way I shall come down.'

He had, of course, already 'come down'. He was thinking, I was sure – although he had no vanity, he was a master-politician – about how his supporters ought to be handling his campaign and about how much more capably he would do it in their place. He was thinking too, I guessed, that it had been useful to talk to me, apart from warmth, affection and reciprocal support. I believed that he was hoping I should mention this conversation to Martin.

CHAPTER III

A SEALING-DAY

ABOUT half past twelve the next morning, which was a Sunday, Martin and I were sitting in one of his window seats gazing out over the court. On the far wall, most of the leaves of creeper had fallen by now, but in the milky sunlight one or two gleamed, nearer scarlet than orange. Martin was just saying to me – did I notice one difference from before the war? There were no kitchen servants carrying trays round the paths, green baize over the trays. Martin was saying that for him green baize was what he first remembered about the college, when the telephone rang.

As he answered it, I heard him reply: 'Yes, I can come. Glad to.' Then he was listening to another question, and answered: 'I've got my brother Lewis here. He'll do for one, won't he?' Martin put the receiver down and said, 'The Bursar's polishing off some conveyances, and he wants us to go and sign our names.'

'Is he working on Sunday?'

'He enjoys himself so much,' said Martin with a sharp but not unfriendly grin.

As we climbed up the Bursary staircase, which was in the same court, Nightingale had thrown open the door and was waiting for us.

'I must say, it's good of you to come.' He shook hands with me. He greeted me with a kind of cagey official courtesy, as though anxious to seem polite. He was much better at it than he used to be, I thought. When we had both lived in the college, we had never got on. So far as I had had an enemy, it had been he. Now he was shaking hands, as though we had been, not friends exactly, but at any rate friendly acquaintances.

He was getting on for sixty, but he had kept his fair wavy hair, and he was well preserved. He did not look anything like so strained as he used to. Several times I had heard Martin and others saying that he was a man whose life had been saved by the war. When I knew him, he had been a scientist who had not come off, and at the same time an embittered bachelor. But he happened, so it seemed, to be one of those people who were made for the military life. He had had a hard war, spectacularly hard for a man of his age: he had been decorated, as he had been in 1917, and he finished up as a brigadier. On top of that, while in hospital, he had managed to get married to a nurse. When he returned, people in the college thought he was transformed. They were so impressed that they wanted to do something for him. As it happened, C. P. Chrystal, who was then Bursar, died suddenly: and almost unanimously, or so I gathered, they had given Nightingale the job. They all said that he loved it. No incumbent had ever spent so much time in the bursarial office. As he showed us in, his whole manner was active and proud.

'I'm sorry to drag you up here, Martin,' he said, 'but there's no point in letting things pile up.'

'That would be very serious, wouldn't it?' Martin was teasing him. I was surprised to see that the two of them were on such easy terms. Yet I ought to have known that when, as with Nightingale and me, two people dislike each other without reason, or more strongly than reason justifies, either of them often tends to make it up with some close attachment of the other.

The Bursary was like a lawyer's office, the walls piled with metal boxes painted black, letters standing out in white. From the window one could see the hall and lodge, newly washed Ketton stone, light gold in the autumn sun. The room was full of the smell of melted wax.

'I don't know whether you've ever taken part in a sealing, Martin,' Nightingale said with bustling officious pride. 'I'm afraid we shall have to leave you out of this one, Eliot,' he turned to me, with the same pleasure in performing the ceremonies, in getting the ritual right. 'Only present fellows are allowed to sign after the college seal. When I put the seal on, I am afraid that for our purpose ex-fellows don't exist.' He gave a trimphant smile.

In the mould, the wax shone crimson and he tested it with the tip of a finger. Steadily, with a scientist's precision, he laid the wafer-covered seal on top, closed the mould, and took it to an antiquated iron vice. He spun the arm of the vice round and back, putting pressure on the mould: then he brought it out, replaced it on the table, and undid it. 'If it hasn't taken,' he said, 'I shall just have to do it again, of course.'

Meticulously he studied the wax.

'No, it's all right,' he cried.

As a matter of fact, the result was not startling: for on each side of the impress was a wafer of paper, so that all one could see were indentations something like a faint brass rubbing.

'Now, Martin, if you don't mind,' said Nightingale, 'will you sign on this line here? I shall want another fellow's signature, of course. I've asked Skeffington to come along. To make it absolutely watertight he ought to have witnessed the sealing too, but I think I'm prepared to stretch a point.'

Within a few minutes, Skeffington had entered the office, while

Nightingale was cleaning the great seal. As Skeffington wrote his name on the line beneath Martin's, Nightingale with delicate, patient fingers extracted fragments of wax. Then reverently he laid the seal on the table in front of us.

'It is a beautiful thing, isn't it?' he said.

It was not really beautiful. It was a piece of fifteenth-century silver-work, heavy and over-elaborate. Nightingale looked at it as though there could not be a more delectable sight. To him it was lovely. He looked at it with piety for all it meant to him. He had had so many grudges, he had never trusted anyone; he had longed for the college to trust him, and had not expected them to. Now here he was in the Bursary. What to most men would already have become a habit, was to him a delight, a security, a joy.

'Well,' he said, 'now this is where Eliot comes in. If you don't mind filling in your present address and occupation, we want those too. You're not allowed to put "sometime fellow of the College", I'm afraid.'

His voice was gleeful. He liked reminding himself that others – particularly me, that morning – were outside the charmed circle, that they did not possess the *mana* of the college, the *mana* that he shared in and loved.

After we had signed, Nightingale brought out a bottle of sherry and three glasses. It was a surprise to me, for he had always been a teetotaller, the only one in the college in my time. He still was, so it appeared: but somehow, he was explaining, he always liked to let people celebrate a sealing.

As we were drinking the sherry and getting ready to go, Martin pointed to one of the black boxes on which was painted, in white letters, PROFESSOR C. J. B. PALAIRET, F.R.S.

'Howard's professor,' he remarked.

'What?' I said.

'The old man Howard worked with. Francis G. was telling you about him last night.'

Even now, I was slow to pick up the reference. In the Howard affair I was an outsider; it still meant nothing to me. Whereas they had been living within the situation. They had kept it to themselves; so all three in that room, together with Brown, Francis, Orbell and the others, had lived within the situation more completely even than a society as closed as theirs was used to doing. They all knew every move that had been made.

'The old man's left a nice bequest to the college, I'm glad to say,' said Nightingale. 'Which makes it all the worse.'

'It was a bad enough show anyway, God knows,' said Skeffington. 'But I agree, that last gambit – that's more than anyone can take.'

Just for a second, they were showing their anger. Then Nightingale said:

'Wait a minute. I suppose we oughtn't to discuss it while Eliot is with us, ought we?'

I was irritated. I said:

'I'm not quite a stranger here, you know.'

'I'm sorry,' said Nightingale. 'But I believe that no one outside the college ought to have heard a word.'

'Arthur Brown and Getliffe didn't take that view. They were talking to me about it last night.'

'I'm sorry. But I think they're wrong.'

'I also heard some of it from Howard's wife,' I said, 'and I can't for the life of me see how you're going to keep her quiet.'

'We shall keep it all quiet enough for our purposes,' said Nightingale.

When we had left Nightingale alone in the Bursary, and the three of us were walking through the court, Skeffington said: 'Bad mark from the Bursar. Loose talk.'

He was a very tall man, and he threw back his head. Just as I had been irritated, so was he. He was a man of means, he had been a regular officer in the Navy: he did not like being what he called 'ticked off'. He seemed arrogant and also vain: vain of his striking looks, among other things, I thought. He had strong features, a fleshy chin and handsome eyes; they were the kind of looks that seem to chime with riches, an influential family, an easy life. Nevertheless, he had not chosen such an easy life as he could have had. He was about Martin's age, just under forty: his career in the Navy had been going according to plan, when he decided that he wanted to make himself into a scientist. That had happened just after the war, and at thirty-two he had started as an undergraduate, taken his degree, and then gone on to research. It was only two years since the college had elected him a research fellow. Academically he was junior not only to Martin and his other contemporaries, but to young men like Tom Orbell. His fellowship was not yet a permanent one, and within the college he was on probation.

'The Bursar would have been right, if it had been anyone but you, don't you think?' Martin said to me. He was himself tight-mouthed as a clam.

'The trouble is,' I said, 'keeping it a secret as you have done – if ever the story breaks, you're in a worse mess than ever, aren't you?'

'There's something in that,' said Skeffington.

'There's something in it. But it's not the whole story,' said Martin. We had stopped at the foot of his staircase. 'We took the risk into account. You don't think we were all that careless, do you?'

'If I'd been you,' I replied, 'I'm sure I should have wanted the college to come right out with it as soon as you'd made up your minds.'

'And I'm moderately sure that you'd have been wrong. The point is,' said Martin, 'we've got enough against this man so that it's a fair bet he'll have to go on holding his tongue. Then if he doesn't hold his tongue, we have the option to bring it all into the open and explain in so many words why we've been keeping it dark—'

'Softlee softlee catchee monkey,' said Skeffington.

Quietly, his eyes sharp, Martin explained what they had done. I began to think I had been airy-fairy in my criticism. The more I heard of the story, the more I thought that they had been decent, cautious, hard-headed. When the two men who were asked to enquire into Howard's work – that is, Nightingale and Skeffington himself – reported to the Master and Seniors that at least one of Howard's photographs could not be explained in any way other than as a fraud, he had been asked for any defence he wanted to put up. He had been interviewed twice by the Court of Seniors, and each time he had said nothing to the point. Both the Master and Brown had written to him formally, telling him to put his case on paper. He had still produced nothing as a defence: until, quite suddenly, he asked to appear again before the Court. Then he announced that he had now decided there had been a fraud, but that the fraud was not his but old Palairet's.

'Which must have taken some cooking up,' said Skeffington.

At last I could understand some of the eddies of anger. Palairet had just died; as long as most of us could remember, he had been a college worthy. Not that he had visited the place much, even when he was younger. I recalled seeing him at a feast once or twice, twenty years before, when he must have been in his fifties. He had gone off when he was a young man to be a professor at a Scottish university and had stayed there till he died. He had had a long and eminent career, not quite as distinguished as the Master's, but about on the level of Francis Getliffe's.

Just then a couple of undergraduates passed by us on the path and Skeffington, his face flushed and authoritative, had to hold himself in. When he could speak, he had become more savage, not less so.

'It's a bad show,' he said. 'Only the worst sort of Red would have done anything like that.'

'Does that come in?' I asked. But my detachment, which usually had an effect on Skeffington, only vexed him more.

'If the man had had anything to keep him straight,' he said furiously, 'if he'd had a faith or even had the sort of code you two have, he might have done lots of bad things but he would never have done that.'

I said that the younger generation in the college were moving to the right so fast that survivals like myself would soon be left standing outside the gates. Skeffington was not amused. He was a devout Anglo-Catholic, more pious, so I thought, than Tom Orbell, though not so given to protesting his faith. He was also a Tory, as Tom Orbell claimed to be. In fact, my gibe was somewhere near the truth. Most of the young fellows were conservative, if they were political at all. At high table one heard a good deal of the reactionary apologists Tom and his friends had resurrected, such as De Maistre and Bonald. I did not mind that so much: but I did mind the tone in which Skeffington had just introduced Howard's politics.

Nevertheless, I thought, as Martin went on explaining, no body of men could have been much more thorough, when it came to investigating the fraud. When Howard made his accusation-cum-defence, the Seniors had insisted that, though it was the most improbable anyone could have invented, they must act as though it might be true. The old man's executors were asked to turn over his working notebooks to the college, which, since he had bequeathed them his entire estate, was within the rules. He had, incidentally, left thirty-five thousand, and Nightingale wanted to put the money into a building fund and call it after him.

'It was a slap in the eye for the family,' said Skeffington. Then I discovered, what was news to me, that his wife was Palairet's niece.

The notebooks, scientific papers, fragments of researches, had arrived in batches at the Bursary, and after Nightingale and Skeffington had inspected them, were filed in the college archives. If Howard's story had had any foundation, there would have been signs of faked evidence in some of the old man's recent notebooks: all the scientists were certain of that. There was no such sign. Not only Skeffington and Nightingale, but also Francis Getliffe and Martin, and those who worked in related subjects, had gone through the notebooks. Each one of the old man's diffraction photographs, taken either by himself or his collaborators, had been studied millimetre by millimetre.

'It was about as likely we should find anything wrong,' said Skeffington, 'as that any of us would be nabbed in the buttery lifting a case of whisky.'

To him there was no doubt. All that search had seemed disrespectful to the dead. It was to his credit, I thought, that he had worked as scrupulously as anyone. I also thought, once again, that no body of men I knew of would have been more punctilious and fair.

CHAPTER IV

TWO UNITED FRONTS

ONE night in December, not long before Christmas, when my wife and I were sitting in our drawing-room, the telephone rang. She answered it. As she listened, she sounded puzzled and obscurely amused.

'Won't I do?' I could hear her speaking in the hall. She went on: 'Yes, I can get him if it's really necessary. But he's very tired. Are you certain it can't wait?'

For some time the cross-talk went on, and I was inquisitive enough to stand close by. Then Margaret raised an eyebrow and held the receiver away from her. 'It's Mrs Howard,' she said. 'I'm afraid you'd better.'

Down the telephone came a strong, pleasant-toned, determined voice.

'This is Laura Howard. Do you remember that we met one night in Tom Orbell's club?'

I said yes.

'I'm really asking if you can spare me half an hour one day this week?'

I said that I was abnormally busy. It was true, but I should have said it anyway. Somewhere in her tone there was an insistent note.

'I shan't keep you more than half an hour, I promise you.'

I began reciting some of my engagements for the week, inventing others.

'I can manage any time that suits you,' her voice came back, agreeable, not at all put off.

I said that I might be freer after Christmas, but she replied that 'we' were only in London for a short time. She went on: 'You were in Cambridge a few weeks ago, weren't you? Yes, I heard about that. I do wish I'd had a chance to see you there.'

She must, I thought, have revised her first impression of me. Presumably she had made enquiries and people had told her that I might be useful. I had a feeling that she didn't in the least mind her judgment being wrong. She just wiped it off, and resolved to chase me down.

Margaret was smiling. She found it funny to see me overborne, cut off from all escape routes.

Aside, I said to her:

'What in God's name ought I to do?'

'You're under no obligation to spend five minutes on her, of course you're not,' said Margaret. Then her face looked for a second less decorous. 'But I don't know how you're going to avoid it, I'm damned if I do.'

'It's intolerable,' I said, cross with her for not keeping her sense of humour down.

'Look here,' said Margaret, 'you'd better ask her round here and get it over. Then you've done everything that she can possibly want you to.'

That was not quite so. Laura was also set on having me meet her husband. Since his dismissal, she told me over the telephone, he had been teaching in a school in Cambridge: that was the reason he could not often get to London. In the end, I had to invite them both to dinner later that same week.

When they arrived, and I looked at Howard for the first time – for now I realised that I had not once, visiting the college while he was still a fellow, so much as caught sight of him – I thought how curiously unprepossessing he was. The skin of his face was coarse and pale: he had a long nose and not much chin. His eyes were a washed-out blue. He had a long neck and champagne-bottle shoulders; it was a kind of physique that often went with unusual muscular strength, and also with virility. Somehow at first sight he would have struck most people as bleak, independent, masculine, even though his voice was high-pitched and uninflected. As he spoke to me, he seemed awkward, but not shy.

'I believe you know that chap Luke, don't you?' he said.

He meant Walter Luke, the head of the Barford atomic energy establishment. Yes, I said, Luke was an old friend of mine.

'He must be an extraordinary sort of chap,' said Howard.

'Just why?'

'Well, he's got a finger in this bomb nonsense, hasn't he? And I don't know how a scientist can bring himself to do it.'

I was annoyed, more annoyed that I was used to showing. I was fond of Walter Luke: and also I had seen how he and his colleagues had tried to settle it with their consciences about the bomb, Luke choosing one way, my brother Martin the other.

'He happens to think it's his duty,' I said.

'It's a curious sort of duty, it seems to me,' replied Howard.

Meanwhile Margaret and Laura had been talking. Glancing at them, vexed at having this man inflicted on me, I noticed how young and slight Margaret looked beside the other woman. Against Laura's, Margaret's skin, still youthful over her fine bones, seemed as though it would be delicate to the touch. Actually it was Margaret who was ten years the elder, who had had children; but she seemed like a student beside the other, dark, handsome, earnest.

I could not hear what they were saying. As we sat round the table in the dining-room, Howard mentioned one or two more acquaintances he and Margaret and I had in common. Listening to him, I had already picked up something that no one had told me. He was *farouche* and a roughneck, and some of his manners might – to anyone without an English ear – have seemed working-class. Actually he was no more working-class than Margaret, who had been born among the academic aristocracy. His parents and hers could easily have gone to the same schools, though his probably came from service families, not from those of officials or dons. It was his wife who had gone up in the world, Howard not at all.

Margaret, who was watching Laura's face, did not let the chit-chat dribble on.

'You've come to tell Lewis something, haven't you?' she said before we had finished the soup. She was kind: and she did not like being oblique. 'Wouldn't you rather do it straightaway?'

Laura smiled with relief. She looked across at her husband: 'Who's going to begin?'

'I don't mind,' he said, without any grace.

'We're not going to ask you very much,' said Laura to me, her brows furrowed. 'They're still shilly-shallying about opening the case again, and we want you to use your influence on them, that's all.'

Suddenly she said, in a formal, dinner-party manner, addressing Margaret in full style: 'I'm afraid this is boring for you. How much have you heard about this difficulty of ours?'

'I think about as much as Lewis has, by now,' said Margaret.

'Well, then, you can understand why we're absolutely sickened by the whole crowd of them,' cried Laura. Her total force – and she was a passionate woman, one could not help but know – was concentrated on Margaret. But Margaret was the last person to be overwhelmed. She looked fine-nerved, but she was passionate herself, she was tough, and her will was at least as strong as Laura's.

She was not going to be bulldozed into a conviction she did not feel, or even into more sympathy than she had started with.

'I think I can understand the kind of time you've had,' she said, gently but without yielding.

'Perhaps I ought to say,' I broke in, 'that I know a good deal more about this business now—'

'How do you know?' Laura cried.

'I heard a certain amount in college.'

'I hope you were pleased with everything you heard,' she said.

There had been a time when I should have found this kind of emotion harder to resist than my wife found it. Though it was difficult for people to realise, though Laura exerted her first effort on Margaret because she seemed the softer option, I was more suggestible than she was. I had had to train and discipline myself out of it. But actually I had no temptation to acquiesce too much that night. Laura had not got me on her side; I felt antipathy for Howard; I was ready to speak plainly.

'That's neither here nor there,' I said. I waited until the next course was in front of us, and then spoke to Laura again: 'You talked about people in the college shilly-shallying about opening your case again. That's nothing like the situation.'

'What do you mean?'

'I mean that, so far as I heard, and I think I should have heard if it was being talked about, no one there has the slightest intention of opening the case again.'

'Do you believe that?' said Laura to her husband.

'I shouldn't be surprised,' he said.

She stared at me steadily, with angry eyes. She came straight out: 'If you were still there, would you be content with that?'

For an instant I caught Margaret's eye, and then looked at Howard on her right. His head was lowered, as it were sullenly, and he did not show any sign of recognition at all. I turned back to his wife and said:

'I am afraid I haven't yet heard anything which would make me take any steps.'

I felt, rather than heard, that Howard had given something like a grin or snigger. Laura flushed to the temples and cried:

'What right have you got to say that?'

'Do you really want me to go on?'

'What else can you do?'

'Well, then,' I said, trying to sound impersonal, 'I couldn't take any other view, in the light of what the scientists report about the evidence. Remember, I'm totally unqualified to analyse the evidence myself, and so are most of the people in the college. That's one of the difficulties of the whole proceedings. If I were there, I should just have to believe what Francis Getliffe and the other scientists told me.'

'Oh, we know all about them—'

I stopped her. 'No, I can't listen to that,' I said. 'Francis Getliffe has been one of my closest friends since I was a very young man.'

'Well—'

'I trust him completely. So would anyone who knew him.'

'Getliffe,' Howard put in, in a tone both sneering and knowing, 'is a good example of a man who used to be a progressive and has thought better of it.'

'I shouldn't have thought that was true,' I replied. 'If it were true, it wouldn't make the faintest difference to his judgment.'

'Then I should like to know what would,' Howard went on in the same sneering tone.

'You must know what would.' I had nearly lost my temper. 'And that is what he thought, as a scientist, of the evidence under his eyes.'

'I suppose they weren't prejudiced when I gave them the explanation?'

'I've heard exactly what they did about it—'

'Who from?'

'Skeffington.'

Laura laughed harshly.

'Did you think *he* wasn't prejudiced?'

'I don't know him as I know Getliffe, but he strikes me as an honest man.'

'He's a religious maniac, he's the worst snob in the college—'

'I also heard from my brother.'

'Do you really think he worried?' Laura burst out. 'All he wants is to step into old Brown's shoes—'

I saw Margaret flinch, then look at me with something like apprehension, as if she felt responsible for her guest.

'I suppose you think,' said Howard, 'that the precious Court of Seniors weren't prejudiced either? I suppose they weren't anxious to believe what Skeffington and that crowd told them?'

I had got tired of this. I went on eating and, as I did so, organised a scheme of questions in my mind, just as I used to when, a long time before, I had practised at the Bar.

Everyone was quiet.

'I'd like to clear up two or three points, simply for my own satisfaction,' I said to Howard. 'May I?'

'I don't mind,' he said.

'Thank you. According to my information, you actually appeared before the Court of Seniors several times. Is that true?'

He nodded his head.

'How many times?'

'I suppose it must have been three.'

'That agrees with what I've been told. The first time you appeared there you were told the scientists had decided that one of the photographs in your paper was a fraud. Were you told that?'

'I suppose that is what it amounted to.'

'It must have been clear one way or the other, mustn't it? It's important. Were you told in so many words that the photograph was a fraud?'

'Yes, I suppose I was.'

His eyes had not dropped but risen. They were fixed on the picture-rail in the top left-hand corner of the room. It was a good many years since I had examined a witness, but I caught the feel of it again. I knew that he had gone on the defensive right away: he was hostile, slightly paranoiac, beating about to evade the questions. I asked:

'Was it, in fact, a fraud?'

He hesitated: 'I don't quite get you.'

'I mean just what I say. Was that photograph a fraud? That is, was it faked to prove something in your paper?'

He hesitated again: 'Yes, I suppose you could say that.'

'Is there any shade of doubt whatsoever?'

Just for a second, his upturned, averted eyes looked at me sidelong with enmity. He shook his head.

'Did you agree with the Court of Seniors, then, when they told you it was a fraud?'

'Yes, I told them so.'

'My information is that you denied it totally the first couple of times you appeared before them. Is that true?'

'I told them.'

'On your third appearance?'

'Yes.'

'Why did you deny it before?'

'Because I didn't believe it was true.'

'Yet every other competent scientist who saw the evidence didn't take long to be certain it was true?'

He broke out: 'They were glad of the chance to find something against me—'

'That won't get us anywhere. Why did you take so long to be certain?

Here was this photograph, you must have known it very well? But even when you'd been told about it, you still didn't admit that it was a fraud? Why not?'

He just shook his head. He would not answer: or rather, it seemed that he could not. He sat there as though in a state of catatonia. I pressed him, but he said nothing at all.

I took it up again:

'In the long run, you decided it really was a fraud?'

'I've told you so.'

'Then, when you decided it was a fraud, you were able to produce an explanation?'

'Yes, I was.'

'What was it?'

'You must have picked up that,' he said offensively, 'among the other information they've given you.'

'In fact, you blamed the fraud on to your collaborator?'

He inclined his head.

'Who'd just died, at the age of, what was it, seventy-five? Your explanation was that he had faked one of your own photographs in your own thesis?'

'Yes, it was.'

'Did that seem to you likely?'

'Of course it didn't,' Laura broke in, her expression fierce and protective. She spoke to her husband: 'You had a great respect for him, of course you had.'

'Did you have a great respect for him?' I asked.

'Not specially,' he answered.

'What reason did you think he could have, at that age and in his position, for this kind of fraud?'

'Oh, he must have gone gaga,' he answered.

'Were there any signs of that?'

'I never noticed.'

'One last question. When you decided that he had faked this photograph of yours, you also said that you'd seen similar photographs before – did you say that?'

'Yes.'

'Who had taken those photographs?'

'The old man, of course,' he said.

'How many had you seen?'

He looked confused. His reactions seemed very slow.

'I can't tell you,' he said at last.

'Many?'

'I shouldn't think so.'

'Only one?'

'I don't know.'

'You're sure you saw one? At least one more, besides yours?'

'I've told you I did.'

'Did you know there are no signs of any such photographs in the whole of his scientific notebooks?'

His face went vague and heavy. 'I suppose they told me that,' he said. Then he asked: 'What I want to know is, who looked?'

Then I stopped. 'I don't think it's any use going further,' I said.

Margaret tried to make some conversation, I joined in. Howard fell into silence, with an expression that looked both injured and apathetic. Even Laura had lost her nerve. She did not refer to the case again. The evening creaked slowly on, with gaps of strained silence as Margaret or I invented something to say. I offered them whisky within half an hour of the end of dinner: Laura took a stiff one, he would not drink at all. At last, it was only a few minutes after ten, she said that they must go. Margaret, usually gentle-mannered and polite, was out of her chair with alacrity.

As we stood by the door, waiting for Howard to come out of the lavatory, Laura suddenly looked up at me.

'Well? Will you talk to Getliffe or your brother?'

I was startled. Even now, she did not know when she was beaten.

'What do you think I could say?'

'Can't you just tell them that they've got to open this business all over again?'

Her eyes were wide open. She looked like a woman making love. She was so fervent that it was uncomfortable to be near her.

'I shall have to think whether there's anything I can do,' I said.

By then Howard was on his way towards us, and she did not speak any more.

As the door closed behind them, Margaret remarked, '*Of course* there isn't anything you can do.'

'Of course there isn't,' I said.

'He hasn't got a leg to stand on, has he?'

'Less than that, I should have thought.'

We sat down, neither of us in good spirits, and held hands.

'No one,' I said, 'could call that a particularly agreeable party.'

'Anyway,' said Margaret, 'you're not required to see them again.'

I said no.

Margaret was smiling.

'I must say, I thought you got pretty rough with him.'

'I couldn't think of anything else to do.'

'That's not quite all, is it?'

I smiled. We knew each other's intuitive likes and dislikes too well.

'I can't pretend,' I said, 'that he's exactly my cup of tea.'

'Whereas, if he hadn't done what he unfortunately has done, you wouldn't be surprised if I thought he'd got a sort of integrity, would you?'

We were laughing at each other. The fret of the evening was passing away. We were reminding each other in the shorthand of marriage that, when we made mistakes about people, they were liable to be a specific kind of mistake. As a young man, I had been fascinated by, and so had overvalued, the ambivalent, the tricky, the excessively fluid, and even now, though they no longer suggested to me the mystery of life as they once did, I had a weakness for them. I saw value in Tom Orbell, for instance, that others didn't. Certainly not Margaret, whose own weakness was the exact opposite. The moral roughneck, the *mauvais coucheur*, often seemed to her to have a dignity and elevation not granted to the rest of us. She was not taken in by the fluid, but on the other hand, just because a character was not fluid, was craggy in its egotism, she was likely to think it specially deserving of respect. If, as she said, grinning at her own expense, Howard had come to us with different credentials, I could easily have imagined her regarding him as a man of fine quality.

'I grant you that he's not two-faced,' I said. 'But what's the use of that, when the one face he has got is so peculiarly unpleasant?'

CHAPTER V

A PARTY FOR A PURPOSE

DURING our parting from Laura Howard, when she was demanding that I talk to my brother, we had not told her that we were spending Christmas in his house. In fact, we arrived there on Christmas Eve, and after dinner Martin's wife and I were for a few minutes alone in the drawing-room. Or alone, to be more exact, in a room of which the drawing-room was only half: for Irene had invited some of the fellows and their wives for wine and cheese at nine o'clock, and she had already furled back the bronze doors between drawing-room and dining-room. Yes, bronze doors: the house, before the college acquired it, had been a piece of luxurious modernist building of a generation before. Now it was divided into two sections, and let out to college officers. By the standards of the fifties, Martin's section, which was the larger one, was sizeable for a professional man's house.

The children were all in bed, their boy and girl, Margaret's son by her first marriage, and ours. Margaret was upstairs: Martin was uncorking bottles in the kitchen: Irene and I sat alone on opposite sides of the fire. She had been asking me about my work, and presumably I gave a heavy reply, for she broke out with a yelp of glee: 'The trouble is, Margaret doesn't make fun of you enough!'

If one had just heard her voice without seeing her, one would have guessed that she was a very young woman, mischievous, light, high-spirited. Actually, as I glanced across the fireplace, I saw a woman of forty, looking much more worn than her husband. She had always been tall and big-framed, but recently her shoulders had rounded and she had put on weight; not only had her bosom got full and shapeless, but she had thickened through the middle. By contrast to this body, comfortably slumped into middle-age, her face seemed thinner and fined-down; the skin of her cheeks had lost its bloom, and underneath the make-up there was a faint, purplish undertint. And yet, it was still a reckless face. Some men would still find her attractive. Underneath full lids, her eyes were narrow, treacle-brown, disrespectful and amused.

Nevertheless, when Martin came in with a complaint, she was not amused, but dead serious. Where was the specimen he had picked up yesterday on Wicken Fen? Who would have moved it? Martin was for once off-balance. There was a distraught, hare-like look in his eye. As a small boy he had been more of a collector than any of us. Now the addiction was coming back. Was it because he was reconciling himself to not making a go of academic physics? Was that why he concentrated so much on his pupils, and then in his spare time went off in search of botanical species? Anyway, he was methodically ticking off the English flora. That night he thought he had lost one: he was showing the signs of a phobia of loss.

Worried, active, Irene started from her chair and went out with him. Within three minutes she was back.

'That's all right,' she said, her expression relieved and earnest.

'The trouble is,' I said maliciously, 'you don't make fun of him enough.'

Irene giggled, but she did not really think that it was funny. She broke out: 'But how do you think he is?'

'Don't you know?'

'I think so,' she said honestly, 'but I'm never sure.'

I nodded. He was a secretive man: people, even those nearest to him, thought him cautious, calculating, and capable of being ruthless.

'I don't believe you need worry,' I said. 'I fancy he's pretty happy.'

'Do you?' She shone with pleasure.

'I should be surprised if he wasn't.'

'I must say,' she cried, 'I should like to bring off something for him.'

'What do you mean?'

'Wouldn't it be good if he could get something?'

For a second, I was surprised at her. She was no fool. She knew that, after throwing away the chance of power, even if he had thrown it away for a qualm or set of qualms that she did not share or understand, he must have times when he would like the chance back again. So, with the energy she had once scattered on her own adventures, she was now not only longing, but working, for him to get another kind of job. It was mildly ironic, when one thought how, as a young woman, she had shocked the bourgeois, to find her set on seeing him a steady, bourgeois success. She had closed her mind to what she used to think of as 'the big world': she wanted him to climb in the college's little one.

'That's what this is in aid of,' she said, pointing to the glasses in the dining-room.

She was doing it without hypocrisy. She did not possess in the slightest degree the gift, so desirable in the life of affairs, of being able to keep the right hand from knowing what the left is doing. Her right hand knew, all right. Shamelessly, innocently, she wanted to help push him up the college ladder and install them both in the Lodge before the end.

When I realised what she was up to, I thought she was pitching her hopes far too high. The Mastership, the Vice-Chancellorship – her fancy was making pictures of them, just as it used to make pictures of the dashing ideal lover when she was a girl. But Martin had no chance at all of ever becoming Master. She was not cut out for politics, she did not know when to hope and when not to hope. The most she could expect for Martin was that, if Arthur Brown were elected next year (which I still could not believe was on the cards), Martin might get the Senior Tutorship. That was his ceiling, so far as the college was concerned. Then I remembered Laura Howard's sneer, that Martin was planning to step into

Brown's shoes. Was that true, I wondered? I had seen my brother's command of tactics when he was spending his time in (I was thinking of a term he and I once exchanged) the corridors of power. Why should I think he was committed to Francis Getliffe? Why should not Martin be preparing to come in on Brown's side, incidentally freeing an agreeable niche for himself?

At any rate, I was prepared to bet that this was in Irene's mind. Soon the first guests were coming into the room, and I could not get more out of her. But I began to watch those whom she had invited. Was it just a coincidence that the Getliffes were not coming? Were the people here going to form the hard core of Brown's party?

Standing up, plate and glass in hand, overhearing a conversation about the English faculty, I found myself talking to G. S. Clark. Like the other fellows at that party, he had been elected since the war; but unlike Tom Orbell and Ince, and two or three of the others, he was not a young man. I did not know for certain, but I guessed that he was over forty. He had been paralysed by poliomyelitis as a child, and his face had the gentle, petulant, youthful and hopeful expression that one sometimes sees in cripples; his skin was pink and fresh. Although his left leg was in a metal brace, he would not sit down. He stood there obstinately and argued with me.

'No,' he said, 'with great respect, I don't agree.'

I teased him. I said I had only made the modest suggestion that the examination system as it existed in Cambridge that night, 24 December 1953, might just possibly not be perfect for all time. Was that so shocking? He smiled, a gentle, patient, invalid's smile.

'But I'm making the modest suggestion,' he said, 'that it's easy to tamper with things just now and make them worse.'

Whenever I met him, which was fairly often, since he occupied the other section of Martin's house, I liked his sweet and hopeful smile and then ran up against that kind of brick wall. But this was not the night for an argument: I asked him about his work. He was a don in Modern Languages, and he was writing a book about the German novelist Fontane. His accent became broader and flatter as he warmed up to the nineteenth-century romantic-realists: he came from Lancashire, his origins were true working-class. It was very rare, I had thought before, for anyone genuinely working-class to struggle through to the high table, though a sprinkling had come, as I did myself, from the class just above. In the whole history of the college, there could not have been more than three or four who started where he did.

Just then his wife's voice, just a shade off-English, the consonants a little too sharp for English, broke in.

'I'm going to take Lewis from you, G.S. Remember, I have known him longer than I have you.'

That was true. When she first knew me, she had been a refugee and the wife of another. Then she had been called Hanna Puchwein; she had been a pretty, elegant young woman with a neat, glossy, hamitic head, snapping black eyes, disconcerting in her integrity and bitter temper. She had got rid of Puchwein in what seemed a fit of pique; there were plenty of men round her, and she nearly married the most unsuitable. We had thought her then the worst of pickers: even so, I was astonished when I heard that she had suddenly married Clark. It was not only astonishing to hear, it was obscurely disagreeable.

That night, her face was still pretty, her forehead bland and intelligent in her pointed, cat-like face: but the black hair was going grey, and she was not bothering to do anything with it, even to keep it tidy. She used to be beautifully groomed, but she seemed to have given up.

She said that she had been talking to Margaret, she asked after our child, but with the touch of impatience of people who hadn't any. In turn I asked her how she liked Cambridge now.

'It is all right,' she said, with sharpness and pride.

Did she see much of the college, I asked her.

'As much as a woman can.'

'What are they thinking about just now?'

'Are they ever thinking about anything?' She said it just as contemptuously as she would have in the past. I was glad, it showed the old Adam was not dead. She corrected herself: 'No, that is not fair. Some of them are clever men, some of them do good work. But a lot of them are not precisely what I was brought up to think of as intellectuals. Even those who do good work are often not intellectuals. Perhaps that is one of the secrets of this country that a foreigner is not expected to understand.'

I asked her, were there any major rifts in the college at present?

'What is there for them to have rifts about?' she said.

I grinned to myself. She had always had a lucid grasp of theoretical politics: I imagined that, unlike her husband, she was passionately radical still. But, intelligent as she was, she had not much insight, less perhaps than anyone of her intelligence I had known.

'Lewis!' came an enthusiastic, modulated voice over my shoulder. 'Hanna, my dear Hanna!' Tom Orbell came between us, carrying not only a glass but a bottle, his cheeks gleaming pink almost as though they were a skin short, sweat on his forehead, his blue eyes cordial and bold. Punctiliously he gave me the bottle to hold, murmuring happily, 'I'm afraid I'm rather drunk,' seized Hanna's hand and bent down to kiss it.

'My dear and most admired Hanna!' he said.

'Have you finished that article?' Her tone was cross, but there was a dash of affection it.

'Of course I have,' said Tom, with the indignation of one who, for once, is in the right. As a matter of fact, I knew, and she ought to have known, that he was an industrious man

'I'm very glad to hear it,' said Hanna.

'Will you let me tell you about it? When will you let me give another little dinner-party for you?'

'Oh, in the New Year, ' she said. 'Now look, Tom, I don't often see Lewis—'

'Why have I got to leave you with him? He's a bit of a menace, is Lewis—'

Hannah frowned, and Tom, who had regripped the bottle, gave it to me again. Once more with great elaboration, and a bow that became something like a genuflexion, he kissed her hand.

When he had merged into the party, Hanna said,

'Why does that young man behave in the way he imagines Continentals to behave? I suppose he imagines that Continentals are polite to women. Why does he think so? Why does he think I should like it? Why do young Englishmen like that go in for hand-kissing? Is it only those like that young man who are sexually insecure?'

She still sounded ratty. Nevertheless, I thought she had a soft spot for him.

'Yes,' she was saying with asperity, 'I think it is because he is sexually insecure that he kisses hands. You cannot imagine Martin performing like that, can you?' I could not. 'Or that *lourdaud* Lester Ince?'

Irene split us up, and for a few moments I stood on the fringe of the party, watching Martin, as usual deliberate, easy-mannered, planted among this guests, while his wife moved avidly about.

As a young woman she would have been on the look-out for a man. She still moved about just as frenetically, just as darting-eyed. Yet that had gone, all gone. Not that she regretted it much, I thought. She was happy here, and across the room I could hear her squeals of glee.

I heard another sound of glee at my shoulder, and Tom, in a state of airborne hilarity, was whispering to me a story about Mrs Skeffington.

She had not long arrived, and within two minutes, Tom was telling me, had dropped her biggest 'clanger' yet. I did not know her, and across the room he pointed her out. She was very tall, almost as tall as her husband, but as plain as he was handsome. According to Tom she was something of what he called a high-born dame and, what made it worse, spoke like one. Apparently she had improved the occasion, soon after she got to the party, by announcing to Irene: 'I think it's so sensible of people to think out how to entertain, and strike out for themselves. If they *can't* give dinner-parties, why *shouldn't* they give bits and pieces afterwards?'

Tom rejoiced. Observant, labile, malicious, he was a very good mimic. Somehow he managed, not only to sound, but to look like Mrs Skeffington, county to the bone, raw-faced.

'It still goes on, my dear Lewis,' said Tom. '*It still goes on.*'

'At some levels,' I said, 'I think it's getting worse.'

'Give me your hand.' Tom, halfway between inflation and rage, insisted on gripping my hand in his, which was unexpectedly large and muscular for so fat a man. He wanted to go on denouncing exponents of English snobbery, radicals, complacent politicians, unbelievers, all the irreconcilable crowd of enemies that he managed to fuse into one at this time of night. He had not said a word about the Howards. They had not been so much as mentioned since I arrived at Martin's house.

'But what do you *want*, Tom?' I enquired, getting impatient.

'I want something for this college.'

'Do other people here –' I waved my hand at the party – 'want anything definite?'

He gazed at me with eyes wider open, but guarded. He was deciding not to let me in.

'I want something for this college, Lewis. I mean that very sincerely.'

Before long I was confronted by Skeffington, who called his wife and introduced me to her. I thought that, though his manner was as lofty as ever, he looked jaded and ill at ease. He did not say much, while his wife and I conscientiously made some Cambridge exchanges – new buildings, traffic, comparison of college gardens. Suddenly Skeffington interrupted us: 'What are your plans for tomorrow?' he said.

It seemed a curious question.

'Well,' I said, 'we've got four children in this house—'

'Yes, but when the fun and games are packed up and you've got them to bed?'

It still seemed an odd cross-examination. However, I said that, since we should have the big meal at mid-day ('quite right,' said Mrs Skeffington) Martin and I had thought of giving our wives a rest and dining in hall at night.

'I've never done it before on Christmas Day,' I said.

Skeffington was not interested in my experiences.

'That's cut and dried, is it? You're going to show up there?'

'Well, we've put our names down,' I said.

Skeffington nodded, as though for the time being placated.

He did not appear to resent it, when Lester Ince, who had broken away from his own group, put in:

'Well, I call that a nice Christmassy programme for old Lew.'

No one, either living or dead, had been known to call me Lew before. I was senior enough, however, to find it agreeable. It was not often that I met anyone as off-hand as this young man. He had a heavy, pasty, cheerful face. Although his stance was slack, he was thick-set and strong. He was not really a *lourdaud*, as Hanna thought. He had a sharp, precise mind which he was devoting – incongruously, so it seemed to most people – to a word-by-word examination of *Nostromo*. But though he was not really a *lourdaud*, he liked making himself a bit of a lout.

'Come to that,' he said to Skeffington, 'how do you propose to celebrate the Nativity?'

'Much as usual.'

'Midnight service with all the highest possible accompaniments?'

'Certainly,' Skeffington replied.

'Stone the crows,' said Lester Ince.

'It happens to be a religious festival. That's the way to do it, you know.' Skeffington looked down at Ince, who was not a short man, from the top of his height, not exactly snubbingly, but with condescension and a gleam of priggishness.

'I tell you what I'm going to do,' said Ince. 'I shall have to do my stuff with wife and kiddies, confound their demanding and insatiable little hearts. I shall then retire with said wife – who's doing herself remarkably well over there in the corner, by the way – I shall retire with her and three bottles of the cheapest red wine I've been able to buy, and the old gramophone. We shall then get gently sozzled and compare the later styles of the blessed Duke with such new developments as the trumpet of Miles Davis. You wouldn't know what that means, any of you. You two wouldn't know, it's since your time,' he said to Skeffington and his wife. 'As for old Lew, he's certainly non-hep. I sometimes have a suspicion that he's positively anti-hep.'

Soon after, just as the Skeffingtons were leaving, Tom Orbell wafted himself towards me again. 'I wish I could get Hanna to myself,' he confided, 'but she's holding a court and they won't leave her alone, not that I'm in a position to blame them.' He was the only person in the room who had been drinking heavily, and he had now got to the stage when, from instant to instant, he was switched from exhilaration to fury, and neither he nor I knew which way he was going to answer next. 'It is a great party, I hope you agree that it's a great party, Lewis?' I said yes, but he wanted more than acquiescence. 'I hope you agree that the people here ought to throw their weight about in the college. These are the people who ought to do it, if we're not going to let the place go dead under our feet.' He looked at me accusingly.

I said, 'You know the position, and I don't.'

'That's not good enough,' said Tom Orbell.

He seemed just then – did this happen often? – to have changed out of recognition from the smooth operator, the young man anxious to please and on the make. He nodded his head sullenly: 'If that's what you think, then that's all right.' He said it as though it were at the furthest extreme from being all right.

'What do you want me to say?'

'I've told you, I want something for this college. There are some people I'll choose for my government, and some people I'll see in hell first.'

He spoke of 'my government' as though he were a Prime Minister who had just returned from the Palace with the job. His own studies of history seemed to be taking possession of him. 'Some of these chaps I'll have in my government straightaway. There are some in the college we've got to keep out, Lewis, or else the place won't be fit to live in. I know he's supposed to be a friend of yours, but do you think I'm going to have *Sir Francis Getliffe* in my government?'

'What do you mean? Now then, what is all this about?' I spoke brusquely, to make him talk in the plane of reason.

Without paying attention he went on.

'There are one or two others who think as I do, *I* can tell you. I wish we knew what your brother Martin thought.'

He was still enough in command of himself to be trying to sound me. When he got no response, he gave his sullen nod.

'Martin's a dark horse. I should like to know what he wants for the college. I can tell you, Lewis, I want something for it.'

'So you should,' I said, trying to soothe him.

'Give me your hand,' he said. But he was still obscurely angry, with me, with Martin, with the party, with – I suddenly felt, though it seemed altogether overdone – his own fate.

Just then I noticed that Skeffington, though he was wearing his overcoat, had still not left the house. For once he looked dithering, as though he was not sure why he was hanging about. All he did was check with Martin, in the peremptory tone he had used to me, that we were likely to be dining in college the following night.

CHAPTER VI

COLLEGE DINNER ON CHRISTMAS DAY

THE Cambridge clocks were striking seven when, on Christmas Day, Martin and I walked through the Backs towards the college. It was a dark night, not cold, with low cloud cover. After the noisy children's day, we, who were both paternal men, breathed comfortably at being out in the free air.

As we made our way along the path to Garret Hostel Bridge, Martin said, out of the dark, in his soft, deep voice:

'Stinking ditches.'

We smiled. We had not been talking intimately: we had not done so for a long time: but we still remembered what we used to talk about. That was a phrase of a colleague of Martin's when he first started his researches, an Antipodean who had come to Cambridge determined not to be bowled over by the place.

'Wouldn't some of these boys like Master Ince think that was a reasonable description?'

'I must walk along the Backs with him and see,' said Martin. He sounded amused. I asked him more about the people I had been speaking to the night before. Yes, he found Ince's knockabout turn a bit of a bore: yes, he wished Ince had settled down rather less and Tom Orbell considerably more.

Of course, said Martin, G. S. Clark was the strongest character among them.

If so, I had quite misjudged him. It set me thinking, and I asked:

'What are they like inside the college?'

'Well, it's never been altogether an easy place, has it?'

Whether he had his mind on politics at all, I still did not know. If he had, he was not going to show it. Nevertheless we were both relaxed, as we went through the lane, all windows dark, to the back of the Old Schools and out into the market-place. There it was empty: no one was walking about on Christmas night, and the shop-windows were unlighted. It was the same down Petty Cury: and in the college itself, entering the first court in the mild blowy evening, we could see just one window shining. Everything else was dark under the heavy sky. The Lodge looked deserted, nothing but blank windows in the court: but between the masses of the Lodge and the hall there was a window glowing, dull red through the curtains, golden through a crack between them.

'Snug,' said Martin.

It was the combination room. Unlike most colleges of its size, ours kept up the tradition of serving dinner every night of the year; but in the depth of vacation, the fellows dined in the combination room, not in hall. When we entered, the table, which at this time on a normal night would be set out for the after-dinner wine, was laid for the meal. The napery gleamed under the lights; the side of the tablecloth nearest the fire had a rosy sheen. In the iron grate, the fire was high and radiant, altogether too much for so mild a night. Old Winslow, the only man to arrive before us, had pulled his chair back towards the curtains, out of the direct heat. He gave us a sarcastic smile, the lids hooded over his eyes.

'Escaping the cold supper at home, as a colleague of mine used to say?' he greeted us.

'Not entirely,' I said.

'We don't expect the singular pleasure of the company of married men on these occasions, my dear Eliot.'

'I'm afraid you're going to get it,' I said.

When I had lived in the college, I had got on better than most with Winslow. Many people had always been frightened of him. He was a savage, disappointed man who had never done more than serve his time in college administrative jobs. When he was Bursar, people had been more frightened of him than ever. After he retired, it seemed for a time that the old sting had left him. But now at eighty, with the curious second wind that I had seen before in very old men, he could produce it again, far more vigorously than ten years before. Why, no one could explain. His son, to whom he had been devoted, was living abroad and had not visited him for years: his wife had died, and in his late seventies he had come back to live in college. By all the rules he should have been left with nothing, for the bitter, rude old malcontent had had a marriage happier than most men's. But in fact, whenever I met him, he appeared to be in some subfusc fashion enjoying himself. He looked very old; his cheeks had sunk in; his long nose and jaw grew closer together. To anyone unused to old men, he might have seemed in the same stage of senescence as M. H. L. Gay. Yet, as one talked to him, one soon forgot to take any special care or make any allowances at all.

'My dear Tutor,' he was saying to Martin, 'I suppose we ought to consider ourselves indebted to you – for producing your brother to give us what I believe is known as "stimulus" from the great world outside?'

'Yes, I thought it was a good idea,' said Martin, in a polite but unyielding tone. Like me, he did not believe in letting Winslow get away with it. 'Perhaps I might present a bottle afterwards to drink his health?'

'Thank you, Tutor. Thank you.'

Tom Orbell came in, deferential and sober, and after him the chaplain, a middle-aged man who was not a fellow. Then two young scientists, Padgett and Blanchflower, whom I knew only by sight, and another of the young fellows whom I did not know at all. '*Doctor* Taylor,' Winslow introduced him, inflecting the 'doctor' just to make it clear that he, in the old Cambridge manner, disapproved of this invention of the Ph.D. 'Doctor Taylor is our Calvert Fellow. On the remarkable foundation of Sir Horace Timberlake.'

It did not strike strange, it sounded quite matter-of-fact, to hear of a fellowship named after a dead friend. Taylor was stocky, small and fair: like all the rest of us except one of the scientists, he was wearing a dinner-jacket, since that was the custom when the college dined in the combination room on Christmas Day. I was thinking that, since the college, which in my time had been thirteen, had expanded to twenty, some of the young men seemed much more like transients than they used to. Blanch-flower, for example, stood about like a distant acquaintance among a group of people who knew each other well.

I was thinking also that, if Martin and I had not dropped in by chance, no one present would have had a wife. One old man who had lost his: one bachelor clergyman: and the rest men who were still unmarried, one or two of whom would never marry. About them all there was that air, characteristic of bachelor societies, of colleges on days like this, of the permanent residents of clubs – an air at the same time timid, unburdened, sad and youthful. Somehow the air was youthful even when the men were old.

We took our places at table, Winslow at the head, me at his right hand. We were given turtle soup, and Tom Orbell at my side was muttering, 'Delicious, delicious.' But he was on his best behaviour. Champagne was free that night, as the result of a bequest by a nineteenth-century tutor:

Tom, shining at the thought of his own abstinence, took only a single glass.

Smoothly he asked Winslow if he had been to any Christmas parties.

'Certainly not, my dear Orbell.'

'Have you really neglected everyone?'

'I gave up going to my colleagues' wives' parties before you were born, my dear young man,' Winslow said.

He added: 'I have no small talk.'

He made the remark with complacency, as though he had an abnormal amount of great talk.

Just then I heard Taylor talking in a quiet voice to his neighbour. Taylor was off to Berlin, so he was saying, to see some of the Orientalists there: he produced a couple of names, then one that, nearly twenty years before, I had heard from Roy Calvert, Kohlhammer. The name meant nothing to me. I had never met the man. I did not know what his speciality was. Yet hearing that one word mumbled, in a pinched Midland accent, by Taylor, I was suddenly made to wince by the past. No, it was not the past, it was the sadness of the friend dead over ten years before, present as it used to be. That simple name gave me a stab of grief, sickening as a present grief – whereas the name of Roy Calvert himself I had heard without emotion. Often enough in the college, I had looked up at the window of his old sitting-room, or as at the feast made up my own Charlusian roll-call of the dead – all with as little homesickness as though I were being shown round a new library. But at the sound of that meaningless German name, I felt the present grief.

I could still hear Tom Orbell deferentially baiting Winslow.

'Have you been to any services today, Winslow?'

'My dear young man, you should know by now that I don't support these primitive survivals.'

'Not even for the sake of *gravitas*?'

'For the sake of what you're pleased to call *gravitas* – which incidentally historians of your persuasion usually misunderstand completely – I am prepared to make certain concessions. But I'm not in the least prepared to give tacit support to degrading superstitions.'

The chaplain made a protesting noise.

'Let me bring it to a point, my dear chaplain. I'm not in the least prepared to lend my presence to your remarkable rituals in the chapel.'

'But I've seen you set foot in the place, haven't I?' I said.

Winslow replied: 'I've now been a fellow of this college for slightly more than fifty-eight years. I was elected fifty-eight years ago last June, to be precise, which is no doubt not a date which many of my colleagues would feel inclined to celebrate. During that period I have attended exactly three obsequies, or whatever you prefer to call them, in the chapel. Each of those occasions I went against my better judgment, and if I had my time again I should not put in an appearance at any one of them. I believe you have never gone in for these curious superstitions, Eliot?'

'I'm not a believer,' I said.

'Nor you, Tutor?'

Winslow turned to Martin with a savage, cheerful grin.

'No.'

'Well, then, I hope you will keep my executors up to the mark. In my will, I have given strict instructions that when I die, which in the nature of things will be quite shortly, there is to be not the faintest manifestation of this mumbo-jumbo. I have endeavoured to make testamentary dispositions which penalise any of my misguided relatives who attempt to break away from these instructions. I should nevertheless be grateful to men of good sense if they keep an eye open for any infringement. Your co-believers, my dear chaplain, are remarkably unscrupulous and remarkably insensitive about those of us who have come perfectly respectably, and with at least as much conviction as any of you, to the opposite conclusion.'

Winslow was enjoying himself, so were some of the others. I thought the chaplain was not fair game, though Tom Orbell would have been, and so I said:

'You've been in chapel more than three times, you know.'

'My dear boy?'

'Electing Masters and so on.'

'I take the point,' said Winslow. 'Though I'm not sure that those occasions can fairly be counted against me. But yes, I grant you, I've been inside the building four times for magisterial elections. Three of which, it became fairly clear soon after the event, showed the college in its collective wisdom choosing the wrong candidate.' He added: 'Now I come to think of it, I suppose that by this time next year I shall have to go inside the building again for the same purpose. My dear Tutor, have you worked out when the election falls due?'

'December 20th,' said Martin without hesitation.

'Unless I die first,' said Winslow, 'I shall have to take part in that ceremony. But I'm happy to say that this time I can't see even this college being so imbecile as to make a wrong choice. Just for once, the possibility does not appear to be open.'

'You mean—'

'It's not necessary to ask, is it? Francis Getliffe will do it very well.'

No one contradicted the old man. I could not resist making things slightly more awkward for Tom Orbell.

'I seem to remember,' I said, 'having heard Brown's name mentioned.'

'My dear Eliot,' said Winslow, 'Brown's name was mentioned last time. I then said it would mean twenty years of stodge. I should now say, if anyone were crass enough to repeat the suggestion, that it would mean seven years of stodge. It is true, seven would be preferable to twenty, but fortunately it is impossible for my colleagues, even with their singular gift for choosing the lowest when they see it, to select stodge at all this term.'

'Getliffe is generally agreed on, is he?'

'I've scarcely thought the matter worth conversation,' said Winslow. 'The worthy Brown is not a serious starter by the side of Francis Getliffe. And that is the view of all the seniors in the college, who are showing surprising unanimity for once in a way. I had a word with the Bursar recently. We agreed that there would have to be a pre-election meeting, but we saw no reason why there should be more than one. Which, I may tell you young men' – Winslow looked round the table – 'is entirely unprecedented in the last sixty years in this college. I even find that our late Senior Tutor, the unfortunate Jago, is completely at one with the Bursar and myself. As I say, we all think Getliffe will do it very well.'

As my eyes met Tom Orbell's, his were bold, light, wide-open. For whatever reason, he was not going to argue. Was it deference, or was he just not ready to show his hand? While Martin, listening politely to Winslow, gave no sign whether he agreed or disagreed. In a moment he got the old man talking of past college follies: of how a 'predecessor of mine in the office of Bursar showed himself even more egregiously unfitted for it' by selling the great Lincolnshire estate. 'If it hadn't been for that remarkable decision, which shouldn't have been made by anyone with the intelligence of a college servant, this institution would be approximately half as rich again.'

Further inanities occurred to Winslow. As we stood up while the waiters cleared the table and arranged chairs in a crescent round the fire, he was reflecting on the number of fellows in his time who had been men of a 'total absence of distinction'.

'A total absence of distinction, my dear Tutor,' he said to Martin, with even greater cheerfulness.

'Wasn't there something to be said for old —— ?' said Martin, his own eyes bright.

'Nothing at all, my dear boy, nothing at all. He would have made a very fair small shopkeeper of mildly bookish tastes.'

He settled into the President's chair, which was the second, as one proceeded anti-clockwise, from the far side of the fireplace. In the middle of the room, the rosewood table shone polished and empty: when the college dined in the combination room, it was the habit to drink wine round the fire.

'It can't be too often said,' Winslow addressed himself to Taylor and the youngest of the others, both in their twenties, well over fifty years his juniors, 'that, with a modicum of exceptions, Cambridge dons are not distinguished men. They are just men who confer distinctions upon one another. I have often wondered who first uttered that simple but profound truth.'

The port glasses were filled as Winslow announced:

'I believe this bottle is being presented by Dr Eliot, for the purpose – correct me if I am wrong, my dear Tutor – of marking the appearance here of his brother. This is a remarkable display of fraternal good wishes.'

With sardonic gusto, Winslow proposed my health and then Martin's. We sipped the port. The fire was warm on our faces. Martin and I, not to be outfaced by Winslow, spoke of previous times when we had dined together in that room. The old man, satisfied with his performance, was becoming a little sleepy. The room was hot and comfortable. Some of the young men began to talk. Then the door clicked open: for a second I thought it was the waiter with the coffee, coming early because it was Christmas night: but it was Skeffington.

Winslow roused himself, his eyes red round the rims.

'My dear boy,' he said, 'this is a most unexpected pleasure. Pray take a glass of port.'

'I apologise, Mr President,' said Skeffington. I noticed that his first glance had been in the direction of Martin.

'Don't apologise, but sit down and fill your glass.'

It was unusual, but not startlingly so, for fellows who had missed dinner to drop in afterwards for wine. As a rule, one would have taken it without curiosity, as most of them were taking it that night. But I couldn't: nor, I felt sure, could Martin. Skeffington had sat down, and in silence watched his glass being filled. He was not dressed: for him, so formal and stiff with protocol, that was odd in itself. In a blue suit, his head thrown back, his cheeks high-coloured, he looked out of place in that circle.

The conversation went on, but Skeffington did not take part in it and Winslow was nearly asleep again. It was not long before Martin got to his feet. When we had said our good-nights, and were outside in the court, I was not surprised to hear Skeffington come up behind us.

'As a matter of fact,' he said to Martin, 'I should like a word with you.'

'Do you want me alone?' said Martin.

'I'd just as soon Lewis knew,' said Skeffington.

Martin said that we had better go up to his rooms. They struck dank and cold, even on that muggy night. He switched on the electric fire, standing incongruously in the big sixteenth-century hearth.

'Well, Julian?' said Martin.

'I didn't think I ought to keep it to myself any longer.'

'What is it?'

'The last few days I've been going more into the business of this chap Howard.'

'Yes?' Martin was still impassive, but bright-eyed.

'I can't see any way out of it. I believe that he's been telling the truth.'

CHAPTER VII

THE COMPONENT OF CONTEMPT

FOR an instant, none of us moved. It would have been hard to tell whether Martin had heard what Skeffington had just said. He was not looking at Skeffington. He gazed steadily at the hearth, in which the electric fire had one small incandescent star, much brighter than the glowing bars, where a contact had worked loose.

'What made you go into the business again?' he said at last, as though merely curious, as though that were the only question on his mind.

'I tell you,' said Skeffington, temper near the surface, 'that he's been telling the truth.'

'Can you prove it?' said Martin sharply.

'I can prove it enough to satisfy myself. Damn it, do you think I *want* to blackguard the old man?'

'That's fair comment,' said Martin. 'But have you got a hundred per cent proof that'll satisfy everybody else?'

'Have you?' I asked.

'What do you mean?'

'I don't know what you intend to do,' I said, 'but can you do anything without what a lawyer would think of as a proof? Have you got one?'

He looked flushed and haughty.

'In that sense,' he said, 'I'm not sure that I have. But it will be good enough for reasonable people.'

'Then what *do* you intend to do?' Martin took up my question.

'The first thing is to get this chap Howard a square deal. That goes without question.'

He said it simply, honourably, and with his habitual trace of admonition and priggishness.

'When did you decide that?'

'The moment I realised that there was only one answer to the whole business. That was yesterday afternoon, though for forty-eight hours I hadn't been able to see any other option.'

'I'm sorry,' said Martin, turning to him, 'but it's not so easy to accept that there can't be one.'

'Don't you think I've made sure that I've closed all the holes?'

'Don't you think you might be wrong? After all, you're saying you've been wrong once before, aren't you?'

'You'll see that I'm not wrong,' said Skeffington. 'And there's one point where I'd like your advice, both of you.'

He began answering the question Martin had asked first – what had made him 'go into the business again'? It happened that, though Skeffington's wife had not often seen her uncle Palairet while he was alive, she was on good terms with his solicitors. A partner in the firm had mentioned to the Skeffingtons that the last box of the old man's papers was being sent to the college. Skeffington had, of course, thought it his duty to go through them.

As he explained, I thought, as I had done before, that his voice did not live up to his looks. It was both monotonous and brittle. But his mind was more competent than I had given him credit for. It was precise, tough, not specially imaginative, but very lucid. People had given me the impression that he was an amateur, and lucky ever to have been elected. I began to doubt it.

I was interested in his attitude towards old Palairet. Obviously he had not known him well. Skeffington seemed to have had an impersonal respect for him as a scientist of reputation, such as Skeffington himself longed to be. For Skeffington felt a vocation for science. He might be rich, he might be smart: he was not at ease with the academics, he could not talk to them as he had been able to talk to his brother-officers: the reason why he could get on with Martin and me was that he had met us in the official world, and knew some of the people we knew. Yet for all that, though he could not in his private self accept most of 'those chaps' as social equals, he longed to win their recognition. He longed to do good work, as Palairet and Getliffe had done; he might have said this was setting his sights too high, but he was seeking exactly that kind of esteem.

'How did your wife get on with her uncle?' I asked, just as he was leading off into the scientific exposition.

'Oh,' said Skeffington, 'he never saw her jokes.'

For a second I caught a sparkle in Martin's eye. As I had heard him give both Skeffingtons maximum marks for humourlessness, I wondered what astonishing picture that reply conveyed.

As Skeffington went on, I found both him and Martin agreeing that whatever the old man was like, most of his scientific work was sound and safely established on the permanent record. His major set of researches were 'textbook stuff', Skeffington insisted.

'That's what I don't understand,' said Skeffington, simple, high-minded, incredulous. 'Because, assuming that he cooked this other business, it couldn't have done him tuppence-ha'penny worth of good. It just doesn't count beside the real good solid stuff he'd got behind him. Was he *crackers*, do you think?'

The old man had done first-class scientific research, they told me: his major work, on the diffraction of atomic particles, was 'quite water-tight': some of the photographs were reproduced in the standard books. Martin fetched down a couple of volumes, and showed me the photographs, rather like rifle targets with alternate rings of light and dark. Those results were beyond dispute: they had been repeated, time and time again, in laboratories all over the world.

It was also beyond dispute that Palairet had become interested in an extension of his technique – not an important extension, something which only counted 'marginally', by the side of his established work. He had expected to be able to apply his technique to a slightly different kind of particle-diffraction. 'For a rather highbrow reason, that no one could possibly have thought up a year ago, we now know it couldn't work,' said Skeffington. But the old man had expected it to work. So had Howard, doing his research under the old man's eye. The photograph in Howard's paper demonstrated that it *did* work, said Martin, with a bleak chuckle: demonstrated it by the unorthodox device of taking a genuine diffraction photograph and 'blowing it up', just like enlarging an ordinary photo-graph, so as to increase the distances between the light rings and the dark. It was from these distances that Howard in his paper had calculated the wavelengths of the particles. 'After blowing it up, someone got the results he expected,' said Skeffington.

For the first time I heard how the fraud had been detected. When the negative had been 'blown up', the hole left by a drawing-pin which had held it up to dry had been expanded too. As soon as the result had been proved to be theoretically impossible, the Americans had enquired why the white blob at the top centre of the photograph seemed so singularly large. It was just as simple as that.

According to Howard, when at last he gave the Court of Seniors his explanation, that photograph had not been the first the old man had shown him. He had told me the same.

To credit his story, one had to assume that he was absolutely trusting. If it were feasible at all, it meant that he had been indoctrinated before-hand. However uncritical he was, he must have been ready to believe in the evidence, he must have taken for granted that the technique was 'on', before he put that final photograph into his paper.

'Even so,' said Martin, 'he would have to be pretty wooden.'

'That's as may be,' said Skeffington, who had until a few days before thought the whole account so preposterous as to be an insult. It was only out of mechanical duty, automatic conscientiousness, that when he heard that more of the old man's manuscripts had reached the college, he went into the Bursary, borrowed the key of the Palairet box, and took them away.

'Had the Bursar told you they'd arrived?' asked Martin.

'The usual piece of formal bumf,' said Skeffington. As soon as any scientific document arrived from Palairet's executors, Nightingale sent a reference number to Skeffington, so I gathered.

Without interest Skeffington had sat in his rooms, reading through the last notebooks.

'Have we got them all now?' asked Martin.

'So far as they know, we've got them all.'

Without interest, Skeffington had read on. 'Old man's stuff, most of it,' he said. Jottings about researches which Palairet would never do: occasional sets of data, corrections of earlier papers. But at last, on the Saturday afternoon before Christmas, something had turned up. 'I don't mind telling you, I didn't take in what it meant. I was sitting in my rooms in the Fellows' Building, and I went out and walked in the garden, and I couldn't see anything that made sense. I don't mind telling you, I wasn't very bright about it.'

He looked at Martin. 'As a matter of fact, I've brought it along with me.'

'May I see it?' Even Martin's politeness was wearing sharp.

Skeffington opened a briefcase which he had brought with him into the room, and produced a thick exercise book, such as I remembered using in the Oxford Senior class at school. Sticking out of it was a bookmarker. 'Yes,' said Skeffington, 'I've kept the place.' It sounded so matter-of-fact as to be absurd. Just as it did when he assured us that he had signed a receipt for the exercise book with the Bursar's clerk.

'All right, Julian,' said Martin. Then Skeffington put his fingers, delicate, square-tipped, on the marker and said: 'Here we are.'

I had gone across to glance at the book over Martin's shoulder. My first impression was of an almost empty page. Then I read at the top, in a spiky, old-fashioned holograph, the date 20 July 1950. Underneath the date were several lines of handwriting, which began: *Tried diffraction experiments using neutron source A and crystal grating B, encouraging results.* Then a blank space in the middle of the page, with a rim of sticky paper, as though something had been removed. Underneath, at the bottom of the page, the handwriting went on: *Above print gives strong support for view that diffraction of neutrons at higher speeds, corresponding to wavelengths shown above, follows precisely the same pattern as at low speeds (see C.J.B.P., Proc. Roy. Soc. A ... 1942, 1947). Have always predicted this. Follow up.*

'The photograph's missing, is it?' said Martin.

'The point is,' Skeffington said loudly to me, 'that what he says at the bottom can't be true. This is where the Howard paper starts off.' He tapped the page. 'It can't be true.'

'If there ever was a print there,' Martin was reflecting, 'either it couldn't have shown anything at all—'

'Or else that had been blown up too.'

'Where is it?' said Martin.

Skeffington shrugged his shoulders.

'Something was there once, wasn't it?'

'The point is,' he went on loudly again, 'if Howard saw that print and that entry, then his story stands up as near as makes no matter. However you read that entry, the old man was fooling himself, if he wasn't fooling anybody else. I don't know what he was up to – he must have been crackers. But I do know that it goes with the Howard story, and I don't believe that there's any way out of it. *Can you see one?*'

'If the print were there,' said Martin in a soft, deliberate tone, 'then I don't think I could.'

'But still.'

Martin sat frowning. He asked me for a cigarette. After a time he said: 'I can't believe there isn't a way out of it.'

'Do you think *I* want to believe it?' Skeffington's tone, just as when he started to explain, was haughty and annoyed. 'It isn't exactly pleasant for me to stir up mud about the old man – and, if I had to stir up mud about someone connected with my family, I shouldn't choose to do it on behalf of anyone like Howard. We never ought to have let in a chap like that. But the point is, we did let him in, and I believe he's an innocent man—'

'Oh, yes, Julian,' Martin roused himself, and for once was speaking restlessly, sarcastically, and without civility. 'We know that you believe that. It's like G. H. Hardy's old crack: If the Archbishop of Canterbury says he believes in God, that's all in the way of business, but if he says he doesn't, one can take it he means what he says. We don't need persuading that you mean what you say. We know you believe it. But I don't see that recognising your conviction gets us very far.'

At Martin's tone, so untypically sharp, Skeffington showed no resentment. He just threw his head back and said:

'It might get us a bit further when I've settled what to do next.'

Martin was composed and cautious again. He said:

'I hope you won't do anything until we've all thought it over.'

'I can't wait long.'

'I'm not asking you to wait long.'

'I should like to see Nightingale tomorrow.'

'I hope you won't do anything,' said Martin, 'until we've thought it over.'

'I can't put it off. That isn't good enough—'

'No one's asking you to put it off. Look, it's Boxing Day tomorrow. I'd be grateful for another twenty-four hours after that. Then I'll be ready to talk.'

Reluctantly, Skeffington acquiesced. He went on:

'But there's something I want your advice on now. Lewis, you've heard the state of the game. I want to know, shall I write to this chap Howard tonight? I mean, I don't feel specially inclined to talk to him. But he hasn't had a square deal, and I think he's entitled to know that someone like me is going to make it his business to see that he gets one.'

'It would be a good thing to write to him, I should have thought,' I said. 'So long as you make it clear you're only speaking for yourself.'

I was thinking, Skeffington was a brave and honourable man. He had not had an instant's hesitation, once he believed that Howard was innocent. He was set on rushing in. Personal relations did not matter, his own convenience did not matter, nor how people thought of him. Both by nature and by training, he was single-minded: the man had his rights, one had to make sure that justice was done. Yet, inside that feeling, there was no kindness towards Howard. There was no trace of a brotherly emotion at all. The only residue of feeling he had for Howard was *contempt*. Contempt not because he and Skeffington had not an idea in common, but merely because he was an object of justice. I had seen the same in other upright men: one was grateful for their passion to be just, but its warmth was all inside themselves. They were not feeling as equals: it was *de haut en bas*: and, not only towards those who had perpetrated the injustice, but also, and often more coldly, towards the victim, there was directed this component of contempt.

'The chief thing is, isn't it,' I said, 'that you mustn't raise false hopes?'

'I think it would be much better,' said Martin, 'if you didn't write at all until we've talked it over. Won't that give you a clearer idea of just what you can and cannot say?'

PART TWO

WHY SHOULD ONE ACT?

CHAPTER VIII

AMBIGUOUSNESS AND TEMPER

THROUGH the wet and windy Boxing Day, Martin played in the big drawing-room with the children – played just as I remembered him in our own childhood, concentrated and anxious to win. Irene and Margaret were laughing at us when he and I had a game together. He had invented a kind of ping-pong, played sitting down with rulers at a low table, and complicated by a set of bisques.

Though our wives knew what was on Martin's mind, for we had told them last thing the night before, no one would have guessed it. He was out to win, within the rules, but just within the rules. His son, Lewis, watched with the same concentration as his father's: so did my son. When we had finished, Martin coached them both, patiently showing them how to cut the ball, repeating the stroke while the minutes passed, as though going through his head there was no thought of Skeffington's conversion, no thought of anything except the cut-stroke at ping-pong. Outside, through the long windows, one could see the trees lashing and the grass dazzling in the rain.

Just before tea, the children went off to put records on their gramophone. Martin said to me:

'I don't know. I don't know. Do you?'

For years we had talked like acquaintances. But we could still get on without explanation: we caught the tone of each other's voice.

I replied: 'I wish I understood the scientific evidence better. I suppose understanding that does make it a bit easier, doesn't it?'

'I suppose it might,' said Martin, with a tucked-in smile.

He did not say any more that day. At the same time the following afternoon, when again we were having a respite from the children, we were sitting with Irene and Margaret. The rain was slashing the windows and the room had turned dark except for a diffused gleam, reflected from the garden, of green and subaqueous light.

'This is a wretched business,' said Martin at large, not with worry so much as annoyance. Again I knew he had not been thinking of much else.

'Tomorrow morning I shall have to have this talk with Skeffington,' he said to me.

'Can't you put him off?' said Irene.

'What are you going to tell him?' I said.

He shook his head.

Margaret said: 'I can't help hoping you'll be able to agree with him.'

'Why do you hope that?' Irene broke out.

'If Skeffington's right, it must have been pretty shattering for Howard, mustn't it? And I should have thought it was even worse for her,' said Margaret.

'What are you going to say tomorrow?' I came back at Martin.

Margaret asked: 'Is Skeffington right?'

Martin looked straight at her. He had a respect for her. He knew that, of all of us, she would be the hardest to refuse an answer to.

He said: 'It makes some sort of sense.'

She said: 'Do you really think he could be right?' Her tone was even, almost casual: she did not seem to be pressing him. Yet she was.

'It seems to make more sense,' said Martin, 'than any other explanation. But still, it's very hard to take.'

'Do you believe he's right?'

Martin replied: 'Possibly.'

Unexpectedly, Margaret burst into laughter, laughter spontaneous and happy. 'Have you thought,' she cried, 'what awful fools we should all look?'

Martin said:

'Yes, I've thought of that.'

'All of us thinking how much we know about people!'

For once Irene did not see any sort of joke. Frowning, she said to Martin:

'Look here, have you got to get yourself involved too much with all this?'

'What do you mean?'

'Suppose Skeffington goes ahead. There's going to be a row, isn't there?'

Martin glanced at me. 'That's putting it mildly.'

'Well, have you got to get into it? I mean, have you got to start it? It isn't your business, is it?'

'Not specially, no.'

'Whose is it?' Margaret asked.

He told her that constitutionally it would be for the sub-committee –
Nightingale and Skeffington – to take the first steps.

'Well then,' said Irene, 'do you need to do much yourself?'

'No, I don't need to,' said Martin. He added: 'In fact, if I don't want
to quarrel with half the society, I can keep out of it more or less.'

'*Can* you?' said Margaret. She had flushed. She said passionately to
Irene, 'Do you really want him to sit by?'

Almost as though by reflection, Irene had flushed also. Surprisingly,
she and Margaret got on well. Neither then nor at any time could Irene
bear to have her sister-in-law disapprove of her, much less to think her
crude and selfish. For Irene, despite, or to some extent because of, her
worldliness, had both a humble and generous heart.

'Oh,' she said, 'someone will put it right if there's anything to put
right. If old Martin were the only chap who could, I suppose he'd have
to. But let Julian S. do the dirty work, that's what he's made for. Those
two won't mind getting in bad with everyone here. All I meant was,
we're settling down nicely now, we haven't got any enemies for the first
time in our lives.'

'Isn't there a danger – you're frightened that if Martin makes a fuss
over this – it might stand in his way?'

Irene replied, shamefaced with defiance: 'If you want the honest
truth, yes, I'm frightened of that too.'

Margaret shook her head. Even now, after marrying me, and meeting
my colleagues, and getting a spectator's view of the snakes-and-ladders
of power, she could not quite believe it. Her grandfather and great-uncle
had resigned fellowships over the Thirty-Nine Articles. I sometimes
teased her, did she realise how much difference it had meant to them and
even to her, that they had both been men of independent means? Yet she
stayed as pure as they had been. She did not think that Martin or I were
bad men: because she loved me, she thought that in some ways I was a
good one: but she could not sympathise with the shifts, the calculations,
the self-seekingness of men making their way.

'Do you think,' she said, apparently at random, 'that Laura ever had
any doubts about him?'

'No,' I said.

'She's totally wrapped up in him,' said Martin. 'I don't imagine she
ever had a second's doubt.'

'In that case, she must be the only person in the world who didn't. I
wonder what it's been like for her?'

Margaret, I knew, was deliberately playing on our human interest.

She, too, was subtle. She knew precisely what she wanted Martin – and, if I could take part, me also – to do.

But Irene sidetracked her by saying casually: 'Well, she'd never tell *me*. She just can't bear the sight of me.'

'Why ever not?' I asked.

'I just can't think.'

'I expect she fancies,' said Martin, 'that you've cast an eye at Donald.'

'Oh, she can't think that! She *can't*!' cried Irene, as usual hilarious (though she detested Howard and had been for years a faithful wife) at the bare prospect of adultery.

Then she said to Margaret: 'It isn't going to be fun, doing anything for them, don't you see that?'

'I tell you, that's putting it mildly,' said Martin.

'You won't stick your neck out if you don't need to? That's all I'm asking you. Will you?'

'Do you think I ever have done?' said Martin.

None of us was certain how he proposed to act, or whether he proposed to act at all. Even when he sounded for opinion that night at the Master's dinner table, he did it in the same ambiguous tone.

Until Martin began that sounding, the dinner had been a standard and stately specimen of the Crawford régime. It would not have happened if I had not been in Cambridge, for the Crawfords had returned to the Lodge only late on Boxing Day. But Crawford, who had never been a special friend of mine, acted upon his own impersonal protocol that ex-fellows who had achieved some sort of external recognition should not stay in Cambridge uninvited: so that night, in the great drawing-room at the Lodge, ten of us were drinking our sherry before dinner, the Nightingales, the Clarks, Martin and Irene, me and Margaret, and the Crawfords themselves, the men in white ties and tails, for Crawford, an old-fashioned Cambridge radical, had refused in matters of etiquette to make concessions to the young.

He stood, hands in pockets, coat-tails over arms, warming his back at his own fireplace, invincibly contented, so it seemed. He was a heavy, shortish, thickly made man who still, at the age of seventy-two, had a soft-footed, muscular walk. He looked nothing like seventy-two. His Buddha-like face, small-featured and round, had something of the unlined youthfulness, or rather agelessness, that one sees often in Asians, but very rarely in Europeans: his hair, glossy black, was smoothed down and did not show any grey at all.

He talked to each of us with impersonal cordiality. He said to me that he had 'heard talk' of me in the 'club' (the Athenæum) just before Christmas, to Nightingale that the college had done well to get into that last list of American equities, to Martin that a new American research student seemed to be highly thought of. When we had gone in to dinner and settled down to the meal, with the same cordiality he addressed us all. The subject that occurred to him, as we ate an excellent dinner, was privilege. He went on: 'Speaking as the oldest round this table by a good few years, I have seen the disappearance of a remarkable amount of privilege.'

Crawford continued to deliver himself. The one thing on which all serious people were agreed, all over the world, was that privilege must be done away with; the amount of it had been whittled away steadily ever since he was a young man. All the attempts to stop this process had failed, just as reaction in its full sense had always failed. All over the world people were no longer prepared to see others enjoying privilege because they had a different coloured skin, or spoke in a different tone, or were born into families that had done pretty well for themselves. 'The disappearance of privilege – if you want something that gives you the direction of time's arrow,' said Crawford, 'that's as good as anything I know.'

Hanna could not restrain herself. With a sharp smile, she said:

'It's still got some way to go, shouldn't you say?'

She looked round the table at the white ties, the evening dresses, the panelled walls beyond, the amplitude of the Lodge dining-room, the lighted pictures on the walls.

'Fair comment, Mrs Clark,' said Crawford, imperturbable, gallant. 'But we mustn't be misled by appearances. Speaking as the present incumbent, I assure you that I can't imagine how my successors in the next generation are going to manage to run this Lodge. Unless indeed a society which is doing away with privilege decides to reward a few citizens for achievement by housing them in picturesque surroundings that no one else is able to afford. It would be interesting if a certain number of men of science in the next generation were still enabled to live in Lodges like this or the Carlsberg mansion at Copenhagen.'

As the talk became chit-chat, I was paying attention to Mrs Nightingale, whom I had not met before. She was a plump woman in the late thirties, a good twenty years younger than he was. Her shoulders and upper arms were beginning to ham out with fat; her eyes were full, sleepy, exophthalmic. But that sleepy plumpness was deceptive. Underneath she seemed energetic and quick-moving. When I said to her, pompously, as we were considering whether to pour sauce on to the pudding: 'Now if we're wise—' she replied, dead-pan but instantaneous: '*Don't* let's be wise.' Between her and Nightingale there passed glances sparkling with both humour and trust. She referred to him as the Lord Mayor, a simple private joke which continued to delight him. They were happy, just as Martin and the others had told me. I was astonished that he had found such a nice woman.

I had been half-expecting Martin to lead in Howard's name. All through dinner he did not mention him; he was still playing his part in the chit-chat when the women left us. But in fact it would have been surprising if he had not waited until the men were alone. College manners were changing in some of the young men, but not in Martin. He would no more have thought of discussing college business in front of wives than Crawford would, or Brown, or old Winslow. Though Martin was used to the company of women like Margaret or Hanna, though he knew how they detested the Islamic separation, he would not have considered raising his question that night until they had gone.

When the door had closed behind them, Crawford called for us to sit nearer to him. 'Come up here, Nightingale! Come beside me, Eliot! Will you look after yourself, Martin?' It occurred to me, still thinking of Martin's manners, that while he kept some of old-style Cambridge, Crawford had, in just one respect, dropped his. Crawford called his contemporaries by their surnames, and that had been common form until the twenties. Even in my time, there were not many fellows who were generally called by their Christian names. But, since the young used nothing else, since Martin and Walter Luke and Julian Skeffington had never been known by anything but their Christian names to their own contemporaries, the old men also began to call them so. With the result that Crawford and Winslow, who after fifty years of friendship still used each other's surnames, seemed oddly familiar when they spoke to the younger fellows. As it happened, I came just at the turning-point, and to both Crawford and Winslow, though my brother was 'Martin', I remained 'Eliot'.

The five of us had been alone for some time, the decanter had gone round, before Martin spoke. He asked, in a casual, indifferent, almost bored manner:

'Master, I suppose you haven't thought any more about the Howard business?'

'Why should I? I don't see any reason why I should, do you?' said Crawford.

Martin replied:

'Why should you indeed?'

He said it dismissively, as though his original question had been silly. He was sitting back in his chair, solid and relaxed, with Clark between himself and Crawford. Though he looked relaxed, his eyes were vigilant, watching not only Crawford, but Nightingale and Clark. He said:

'As a matter of fact, I thought I heard that it was just possible some fresh evidence might still turn up.'

'I don't remember hearing the suggestion,' said Crawford. He spoke without worry. 'I must say, Martin, it sounds remarkably hypothetical.'

'I suppose,' said Martin, 'that if more evidence really did turn up, we might conceivably have to consider reopening the case, mightn't we?'

'Ah well,' said Crawford, 'we don't have to cross that bridge till we come to it. Speaking as a member of our small society, I've never been fond of hypothetical situations involving ourselves.'

It was a reproof, good-humoured, but still a reproof. Martin paused. Before he had replied, Nightingale gave him a friendly smile and said:

'There's a bit more to it than that, Master.'

'I'm getting slightly muddled,' said Crawford, not sounding so in the least. 'If there is any more to it, why haven't I been informed?'

'Because, though there is a bit more to it on paper,' Nightingale went on, 'it doesn't amount to anything. It certainly doesn't amount to enough to disturb you with at Christmas. I mean, Martin is perfectly right to say that a certain amount of fresh evidence has come in. It's not fair to accuse him of inventing hypothetical situations.'

Crawford laughed. 'Never mind about that. If he's not used to being misjudged at his age, he never will be.'

'No,' Nightingale persisted. 'I for one am grateful that he mentioned the matter.'

'Yes, Bursar?' said Crawford.

'It gives us the chance to settle it without any more commotion.'

Martin leaned forward and spoke to Nightingale:

'When did you hear about this?'

'Last night.'

'Who from?'

'Skeffington.'

Just for an instant, Martin's eyes flashed.

'It's all perfectly in order, Master,' Nightingale said to Crawford. 'You'll remember, Skeffington and I were the committee deputed to make a technical report to the Seniors in the first instance. Naturally we've assumed it was our duty to keep our eyes open for any development since. It happens that the last instalments of Professor Palairet's scientific papers have arrived at the Bursary since the Seniors made their decision. Both Skeffington and I have gone through them. I think it's only fair for me to say that he's made a more thorough job of it than I've been able to do. The only excuse I've got is that the Bursary manages to keep me pretty busy.'

'We all know that,' said Crawford.

'So these very last notebooks I hadn't been able to do more than skim through. It was those that Skeffington brought to my attention last night.'

'When did *you* hear?' Suddenly Clark spoke in a quiet voice to Martin, but Nightingale had gone on:

'I'm glad to say that I saw nothing which makes the faintest difference to my original opinion. If I were writing my report to the Seniors again today, I should do it in the same terms.'

'That's exactly what I should have expected.' Crawford said it with dignity and authority.

'I don't think I ought to conceal from you, in fact I'm sure I oughtn't,' said Nightingale, 'that in the heat of the moment Skeffington didn't take entirely the same view. He gave to one piece of evidence an importance that I couldn't begin to, and I think, if I have to take the words out of his mouth, that he would have felt obliged to include it, if he were re-writing his own report. Well, that's as may be. But even if that happened, I am quite sure that in the final result it wouldn't have had the remotest effect on the Seniors' findings.'

'Which means,' said Crawford, 'that we should have been bound to take the same action.'

'Inevitably it does,' said Nightingale.

'Of course,' said Clark.

Crawford had settled himself, his hands folded on his paunch, his eyes focused on the wainscot.

'Well, this is a complication we could reasonably have been spared,' he said. 'I am inclined to think the Bursar is right, Martin has done us a service by bringing up the subject. Speaking as Master for a moment, there is one thing I should like to impress upon you all. I should also like to impress it on Skeffington and our other colleagues. In my judgment, this college was remarkably lucky to avoid a serious scandal over this business. I never took the violent personal objection to Howard that some of you did, but a piece of scientific fraud is of course unforgivable. And any unnecessary publicity about it, even now, is as near unforgivable as makes no matter. We've come out of it internally with no friction that I know of. And externally, better than any of us could have hoped. I do impress on you, this is a time to count our blessings and not disturb the situation. In my view, anyone who resurrects the trouble is taking a grave responsibility upon himself. We did justice so far as we could, and as the Bursar says, we have every reason within the human limits to believe that our findings were the right ones. Anyone who tries to open it all over again is going to achieve nothing except a certain amount of harm for the college, and a risk of a good deal more.'

'I'd just like to ask again, as I've asked you all in private often enough,' said Nightingale, 'if this man felt he had been hard done by, why in Heaven's name didn't he bring an action for wrongful dismissal?'

'I agree with every word you've both said,' Clark broke in. He was hunched round to ease the weight on his leg. His smile was sweet, a little helpless, a little petulant. All of a sudden I realised that, just as Martin had said, he was a man of formidable moral force. 'Except, if I may say so, personally I think worse of the man responsible for it all. I always thought it was a mistake to elect him, and I was sorry that our scientific friends got their way. I know we all kept off the question of his politics. Politics is becoming a taboo word. I'm going to be quite frank. I should have to be convinced that, in present conditions, a man of Howard's politics can be a man of good character, as I understand the term. And I am not prepared to welcome such men in the name of tolerance, the tolerance that they themselves despise.'

'I wish I'd had the courage to say that earlier,' Nightingale broke out.

Martin had not spoken for a long time. In the same tone, neither edgy nor over-concerned, in which he had made his first approach, he said: 'But that isn't really the point, is it? The real point is what the Bursar said about the evidence.'

Clark replied:

'What the Bursar said settled that, didn't it?'

The curious thing was, I thought, that Nightingale, Clark, and Martin liked one another. When we went into the drawing-room there was no sign of argument on any of them. In fact, there had not been a word of disagreement spoken.

As the college clock struck the half-hour, it must have been half past eleven, Martin and Irene, Margaret and I, were walking up Petty Cury on the way home. In the empty street, Martin said softly:

'I got even less change than I reckoned on.'

He had spoken in a matter-of-fact tone, but when Margaret said:

'The Nightingales know all about it, don't they?' he turned on her:
'How did you hear that?'

'I wanted to see what she and Hanna were thinking—'

'You talked about the Howard business, did you?'

'Of course—'

'You told them that Skeffington was worried?'

'Naturally.'

'Can none of you be trusted?' Martin broke out.

'No, I won't take that—'

'Can none of you be trusted?' He had quite lost his temper, something so rare for him that Irene and I glanced at each other with discomfort, a discomfort different from just looking on at her husband and my wife snacking. As his voice sharpened, his face lost its colour: while Margaret, whose hot temper had risen to meet his cold one, was flushing, her eyes snapping, looking handsome and less delicate.

'Has everyone got to talk the minute you get hold of a piece of gossip? Has that fool Skeffington got to blurt out the whole story before any of us have had a chance to have a look at it? Has none of you any idea when it's useful to keep your mouths shut?'

'Don't you realise Connie Nightingale is a good sort? She and Hanna will have some influence—'

'They'll have that, without your talking to them before the proper time.'

'Why should you think no one else can judge the proper time?'

'Just from watching the mess you're all getting into.'

'I must say,' said Margaret violently, 'you seem to assume this is a private game of yours. I'm damned if that is good enough for me. You'd better face it, this isn't just your own private game.'

Speaking more quietly than she had done, but also more angrily, Martin said:

'It might be more convenient if it were.'

CHAPTER IX

TREAT FOR A WORLDLY MAN

THE next morning, the twenty-eighth, Martin was as controlled as usual. Without fuss, without making an explicit apology to Margaret, he did apologise to her, by asking if she could bear to sit round and join the 'conference' with Julian Skeffington. 'I remember that you've shown an interest in the matter,' Martin permitted himself to say, unsmiling but bright-eyed.

Skeffington was due at ten o'clock: Margaret and I had to go back to London that afternoon. It was a bright morning, the sunny interval in the warm cyclonic weather, and the children were playing in the garden. The air was so mild that we left the french windows open, and from the end of the long lawn we could hear them shouting, as they chased each other through the bushes. On the grass there shone a film of dew, gossamer white in the sunshine, with firm black trails of footsteps across it, like a diagram in a detective story.

When Skeffington came in, punctual to the first stroke of ten, he gazed round the room with what looked like distaste or pity for our sloppiness. Where we had had breakfast, in the garden end of the big double room, Irene had not yet cleared away; I was wearing a sweater instead of a jacket. Himself, he stood there beautifully groomed, blue tie pinned down, hair smooth, skin ruddy. Before we had moved from the table he was into his problem.

'I've got to admit it,' he told Martin, 'I can't come to terms with some of those chaps of ours.'

'Who in particular?'

'I was dining in the combination room last night, there were only one or two chaps there, I told them that Howard's case would have to be re-opened.'

'You did, did you?' said Martin.

'I didn't see any point in beating about the bush,' said Skeffington. 'Well, one of those chaps – they were both very junior – said that meant getting a majority of the college. Do you know what he said then?'

Martin shook his head.

'He had the brass to tell me that he didn't feel very much like helping to form that majority.'

'Who was this?'

'That man Orbell.'

Irene yelped with surprise, Margaret caught my eye. Martin was saying, at his most disciplined, without any sign of irritation: 'I can't help wishing you hadn't jumped the gun. You know, it might have been better to tackle Orbell later—'

'It couldn't have been worse,' said Skeffington. 'I'm sorry. False move.'

'By the way,' Martin went on, 'you spoke to Nightingale the night before, so I heard. I thought we were going to leave that until we'd thought it over?'

'Yes, I spoke to him. I'm not sorry about that. He's the other man on the committee. After I saw you, I decided I was under an obligation to tell him. It was the straightforward thing to do.'

'I suppose it was the straightforward thing to do.' Martin's voice was neutral. Just for an instant I saw in his face the temper of the night before. But he had realised that it was profitless to scold Skeffington. It was done now. Martin contented himself by saying: 'You're not making it any easier for yourself, you know.'

'That can't be helped.'

'You understand that it isn't going to be easy, don't you?'

'I hadn't thought much about it. But it's not going to be a pushover, I see that.'

'Doesn't Orbell's reaction show you something?'

'It was a bit of a facer, yes.' Skeffington threw back his head, and his expression was puzzled, irritated, sulky.

'It's a good deal more than that.' Martin leaned forward into the fireplace, picked up a spill from the holder, twisted it into a knot. Then he looked across at Skeffington and began to speak, naturally and in earnest. 'Look, this is what I wanted to talk to you about. I want you to be absolutely clear what the position is. I wouldn't like you to do any more, I really didn't want you to do anything at all, before you realise what you're running yourself in for.'

'I think I know the form,' said Skeffington.

'Do you?' Martin was watching him. 'I intend to make sure you do. That's the whole object of this exercise.'

Skeffington had begun to ask me a question but Martin interrupted:

'No, I really want to say this. There are just two courses you can take, it seems to me. Now this evidence has come along, and taking the view of it you do—'

'And you do too,' Margaret broke in.

'Taking that view of it, you're bound to do something. If you wrote a statement and sent it to the Master saying, for the sake of argument, that some new technical data made it seem to you extremely unlikely that Howard had been responsible for any fraud – that's all that reasonable men could expect you to do. I think you're obliged to do that. I'm the last man to run into unnecessary trouble, but if I were you I'm afraid I should have to do that.'

'I should think you damned well would,' said Skeffington.

'And I shouldn't expect it to have any effect,' said Martin with a grin that was calculating, caustic, and uncharacteristically kind. 'You see, the evidence isn't quite clinching enough to convince anyone who desperately doesn't want to be convinced. There are quite a number of our friends who desperately don't want to be convinced. I suppose you have realised that?'

'They've got to be, that's all,' said Skeffington.

'Well, that is the second course. Which means you set yourself, first, to get the case re-opened and then, which I might remind you isn't the same thing, make the Seniors go back on their decision about Howard. I don't say it's impossible—'

'That's something,' Skeffington said.

'—but it's going to be very difficult. Some of the steps you've taken already have made it slightly more difficult. It's going to need a certain number of qualities I am not sure you possess.'

Martin said it simply. Skeffington blushed. His haughtiness had left him for an instant: he wasn't used, as Martin and I and our friends were, to direct personal examination.

'Come clean. What does it need?'

'Obstinacy,' said Martin. 'We're all prepared to credit you with that.'

Irene laughed as though glad of the excuse, just to break the tension.

'Patience,' said Martin. 'How do you fancy yourself in that respect?'

Skeffington gave a sheepish smile.

'Persuasive power,' said Martin. 'There you might be better than you think. And, I'm afraid this is going to be necessary, considerable command of tactics. I mean, political tactics. I don't think you'll like it, I don't think Margaret will, but it's going to need a good deal of politics to put Howard in the clear.'

'Perhaps you know more about that than I do—'

'I do, Julian.'

Martin was still explaining carefully. 'This business is going to split the college from top to bottom. Anyone who's seen anything of this kind of society would know that. Lewis knows it as well as I do. It will make the place unlivable in and do some of us a certain amount of harm into the bargain. And this is the last thing I want to say to you. I wouldn't feel quite easy until I'd said it in so many words, before you plunge in. If you do plunge in, you'll have to be ready for certain consequences to yourself. You're bound to make yourself conspicuous. You're bound to say things which people don't want to hear. The odds are that it will damage your chances. Look, let me be brutal. I know you want your fellowship renewed when it runs out. I know you'd like to be a fixture. I'd like you to be, too. But if you make too much of a nuisance of yourself, there's going to be a cloud round the name of Skeffington. I don't mean that they'd do anything flagrantly unjust, or which they thought was unjust. If you were Rutherford or Blackett or Rabi or G. I. Taylor, they would keep you as a fellow even if you insulted the Master every night of your life. But most of us aren't all that good. With most of us there is a perfectly genuine area of doubt whether we're really any better than the next man. And *then*, if there's a cloud round your name, they're liable to think, and it's very hard to blame them, that perhaps they might let your fellowship run out, and give someone else a go. Just as they might think, perfectly reasonably, that half a dozen people would do the Senior Tutorship as well or better than I should. So, if they have anything against us, the net result is liable to be that Skeffington is out, and M. F. Eliot doesn't get promotion.'

'What does all that add up to?' said Skeffington.

'I just wanted you to know. If I'm going to take a risk myself, I like to reckon out the chances beforehand.'

'Do you seriously think any of that is going to keep me quiet?' Skeffington had flushed again, and he looked at Martin as though he despised him.

'No, I didn't think so.'

'So you are going in up to the neck, are you?' Irene asked Skeffington.

'What else do you expect me to do?'

Suddenly she turned to her husband, and said:

'What about you?'

Martin answered straightaway:

'Oh, there's nothing for it. I shall have to help him as much as I can.'

'I knew you would! I knew you would!' Irene cried out, half in reproach, half in pleasure, still youthful, that he should do something dashing.

Of us all, Skeffington was the only one totally surprised. He sat with his mouth slightly open; I wondered if Martin remembered that our mother used a word for just that expression – 'flabbergasted'. Just for an instant, Skeffington did not seem pleased to have a comrade; he had an expression of resentment, as if Martin had made a fool of him. He liked Martin, and he expected people he liked to behave like himself, simply and honourably. He had been led astray by Martin's deviousness, his habit, growing on him as he became older, of giving nothing away.

Myself, I believed that Martin had two motives. The nearer one was to him, the more often he seemed hard, selfish, cautious, calculating. With his wife, for instance, he was so inconsiderate that it could be harassing to be in their house. And he could not stop himself planning the next move ahead on the chessboard of power. I was pretty sure that the rumours about him were right, that he had not been able to resist working out the combinations for the next magisterial election. I was pretty sure that he had decided it was worth trying for Brown as Master, so that if it came off, he could walk into the Senior Tutorship himself.

That was all true. But it was not all. There was something else within him which made him a more interesting man. At its roots it might not be more amiable than those other roots which made him a hard self-seeker; but it certainly made him more surprising and more capable of good. It was something like a curious kind of self-regard. He knew as well as anyone else that he was hard, selfish, obsessively careful: but he knew, what no one else did, that he had sometimes wanted to be different from that. This self-regard, 'romantic' if you like, had twice in his life made him step right out of his ordinary casing. He had, as it were deliberately, made an imprudent marriage, not only by his own standards but by any-one else's. He had been more than imprudent when humanity got the better of him and, with real power waiting on his table, he had quit the atomic establishment and come back to hide himself within the college.

Now he was doing it again. Not out of patrician high principle edged with contempt, as in Skeffington. Martin, who was not such a lofty character, had no contempt for his brother men. No, out of that special kind of self-regard, tinged with and disentangleable from his feeling that he had to be responsible. He did not like being pushed so – out of the predictable, calculating life, with its pickings, small-scale but predictable for years ahead. That would be disturbed now. He did not like it: that was why he had been so bad-tempered the night before. But he was pushed, and he could not stop himself.

That was one motive. The other, it seemed to me, was much simpler. Martin was a natural politician. Inside the college, there was no one in his class, except Arthur Brown. Like anyone with a set of unusual skills, Martin enjoyed using them. This was a perfect opportunity. He felt like an opening bowler on a moist morning, his first two fingers itching for the ball. It looked to Martin a situation adapted to his talents. Skeffington would certainly mishandle it. If anyone could take it through to success, Martin could.

There was one other thing, I thought. Martin enjoyed using his political skills. As a rule, he had used them for his own purposes, some-times petty, often selfish. It was a treat for him – and I believed that unless one understood this, one didn't understand him or other worldly men – to think of using them for a purpose which he felt, without any subtlety or complexity at all, to be nothing but good.

CHAPTER X

PREOCCUPATION OF
A DISTINGUISHED SCIENTIST

As we sat in the sunny room after Irene had cried, 'I knew you would', Martin got down to tactics. He reiterated what he had already told Skeffington, that getting a majority to re-open the case was only the start. This wasn't the sort of argument that would be settled by 'counting heads'. The essential thing was to bring in men who would 'carry weight'. Could Skeffington, or Martin himself, persuade Nightingale to stay neutral? Even after the night before, Martin thought it worth trying. Above all, Francis Getliffe was a key man. Get him active, and all the scientists, the Master included, would have to listen.

Within half an hour, Martin had telephoned the Cavendish, and he and Skeffington and I were on our way there. At first I was surprised that Martin had not only asked if I would care to come with them, but pressed me to. Then I realised that he had a reason. He wanted Francis at his easiest. He knew that with me Francis still sometimes talked like a young man, like the young man I still – with the illusion that invests a friend one has known since twenty – half-thought him to be. But his juniors in the college, even Martin, did not think of him in the least like that. To them – it struck me with one of the shocks of middle age – he had become stiff and inaccessible.

Yet, when we had climbed up the steps of the old Cavendish, and walked down the dingy corridors to his room, we found him lit up with happiness. The room, which was not his laboratory but his office, was dark and shabby, a room that minor civil servants would have refused to live in. On the walls were graphs, scientific photographs, pictures of scientists, one of Rutherford. At one side stood two packing-cases covered with dust. On the desk, under two anglepoise lamps, were pinned down what looked like long stretches of photographic print, with up-and-down curves in white clear upon them.

'Have a look at this,' called Francis. No man could have been less stiff. 'Isn't it lovely?'

He explained to them, he explained to me as though I knew as much as they did, what he had found out. 'It's a new *kind* of source,' he was saying. 'I've been keeping my fingers crossed, but this is it.'

They were all three talking quickly, Martin and Skeffington asking questions which were incomprehensible to me. Out of it all I gathered that he was 'on to something', not as big as his major work, but scientifically unexpected and sharp-edged. He had made his name by research into the ionosphere, but since the war he had moved into radio-astronomy; he was over fifty, he was keeping on at creative work when most of his contemporaries had stopped. As I watched him, his long face warm with delight, I thought this discovery was giving him as much joy as those of twenty years before – perhaps a purer joy, because then he had not satisfied his ambitions. Now he was free to be enraptured with the thing itself.

'Really it is beautiful,' he said. He smiled at us all, shamefaced because he was so happy.

Then reluctantly, in a sharp brisk tone, he broke off: 'But I mustn't go on talking all morning. I think you had something to see me about, Martin?'

'I'd rather go on with this,' said Martin.

'Oh, this can wait – that is, if your job is important. Is it?'

'In a way, it might be. But we want your advice on that.'

'You'd better go ahead.'

With dexterous care, Francis was fitting a plastic cover over the print; he was still studying the trace, and his eyes did not leave it as Martin spoke.

'As a matter of fact, it's Julian's show more than mine.'

'Well then?'

Skeffington began to explain, much as he had done on the night of Christmas Day. The story was better organised than it had been then; he had had time to get it into proportion. The instant he said that they had been blaming the wrong man, Francis looked up from the print. He gazed at Skeffington without any interruption or gesture, except to draw at his pipe. As he gazed, his expression, which had been happy, receptive and welcoming when we first saw him, changed so much that one did not know what to expect.

When Skeffington paused, Francis said in a harsh voice:

'That all?'

'Yes, I think it puts you in the picture,' Skeffington replied.

'Is that what you call it?' Francis broke out. 'It's just about the most incredible picture I've ever heard of.' He was flushed with resentment. His courtesy, which was usually just a shade more formal than most of ours, had quite left him, and he was speaking to Skeffington with the special hostility kept for those who bring bad news. In fact, he spoke to Skeffington as though he, and only he, were the culprit and that it was his duty to obliterate the bad news and restore the peace of the morning.

'What do you mean, incredible?' said Martin, in a conversational tone. 'Do you mean it's incredible that we've all been such fools?'

'I should like to be told when we stop being fools,' Francis snapped. Then he tried to collect himself. In a level, reasonable voice, but his face still stern, he said to Skeffington:

'Don't you see that your explanation is very hard to credit?'

Skeffington had become angry too. He answered back:

'Then are you prepared to make a better one?'

'From what you've told me, I shouldn't have thought it was beyond the wit of man.'

'If we'd believed that,' said Skeffington, 'we shouldn't have come to waste your time.'

I said something, and Francis was sharp with me: 'Lewis, you're not a scientist, after all.'

'If you studied the evidence, what else do you think you could make of it?' said Skeffington. He had begun his exposition with much deference towards Francis, and now, though he looked angry and baited, the deference had not all gone.

Francis ignored the question and spoke coldly:

'Don't you want to realise how this is bound to strike anyone who isn't committed one way or the other?'

'We not only want to realise that, we've got to,' said Martin.

Was he as puzzled as I was by Francis's response? He did not know him so well: perhaps that made it less mystifying to Martin than to me. But he was certainly at a loss to know now to get on terms with Francis, and was feeling his way.

'Remind me,' Francis said to Skeffington, 'who acted as referees on Howard's work when we elected him?'

'There was one external – old Palairet, naturally. One internal – Nightingale. I was asked to write a note along with Nightingale's. Of course, I was still a new boy myself.'

'And you and Nightingale reported on his work when we dismissed him. That's fair enough. But you admit that it isn't precisely convincing when you suddenly tell us that you and Nightingale have ceased to agree?'

'He's not got a leg to stand on—'

'That won't do,' said Francis. 'He knew as much as you did about the whole background, didn't he?'

'Yes.'

'And you showed him the new data and told him your explanation, and he didn't think there was much in it?'

'He didn't think there was anything in it,' said Skeffington.

'Well, there it is,' said Francis. 'If you're going to attack the memory of a distinguished old man, you'll want something firmer than that.'

'The facts are firm,' Skeffington broke out.

Martin spoke quietly and fairly, still trying to persuade Francis to match his tone:

'At any rate, they're as firm as one could expect. If only that photograph weren't missing.'

'Presuming that there was ever a faked photograph there,' said Francis.

'Presuming that. Given that photograph, I should have thought there was enough evidence to satisfy a court of law. What do you think, Lewis?'

I also set out to be fair.

'It would be a terribly difficult case for an ordinary court, of course. Too much would depend on the technical witnesses. But I think I agree with Martin. I believe that if that photograph weren't missing a court would probably see that Howard was cleared. Without it – without it he wouldn't stand more than an even chance.'

Francis looked from Martin to me, but without any sign that he was willing to talk our language. He said to Skeffington:

'I take it Nightingale knows all the facts you know, by now?'

'He's seen everything.'

'And he still doesn't admit the facts are firm?'

'I told you right at the beginning. I didn't want to give you any false impression. Nightingale wouldn't admit to me – and I hear he said the same a good deal more strongly when these two were at the Lodge – he wouldn't admit that the facts add up to anything.'

For some instants Francis sat silent. Somewhere in the room a clock gave a lurching, clonking tick: I thought I had noticed it as we came in, tapping out the half-minutes, but I did not look round. I was watching Francis's expression. Despite his strong will, he hadn't any of the opacity that I was used to in men of affairs. By their side his nerves were too near the surface. When in the war he was successful among them, it had been through will and spirit, not through the weight of nature most of them had. As he sat at his desk, faced with a situation that colleagues of mine like Hector Rose would have taken in their stride without a blink, the shadows of his thoughts chased themselves over his face as theirs never would. His expression was upset and strained, out of proportion, much more than Skeffington's or Martin's had been at any time in the last few days. As he sat there, his eyes clouded, his lips pulled themselves in as though he had had a new thought more vexing than the rest.

At last he said, putting his hands on the table, making his voice hearty and valedictory:

'Well, that seems as far as we can go just now.' He continued, in the same dismissive tone, but deliberately, as though he had been working out the words:

'My advice to you' – he was speaking to Skeffington – 'is to keep on at Nightingale and see if you can't convince each other of the points that are still left in the air. By far the best thing would be for the two of you to produce a combined report. The essential thing is that the two of you ought to agree. Then I'm sure nearly all the rest of us would accept your recommendation, whether you wanted us to stay put or take some action. In fact, I'm sure that's the only satisfactory way out, either for you or the rest of us.'

'Do you think it's likely?' Martin asked sharply, pressing him for the first time.

'That I don't know.'

Francis's thoughts had turned into themselves again. Martin rose to go. He knew they were getting nowhere: it would be a mistake to test Francis any more that day. But Skeffington, although he got up too, was not acquiescing. In an impatient, aggrieved tone, he said to Francis:

'When you mentioned me changing my mind about the explanation, you don't seriously think that's on the cards, do you? You don't seriously think that now I've had this evidence through my hands, I could possibly change my mind, do you? If you still think I could, why don't you have a look at the evidence for yourself?'

'No,' said Francis. 'I've got enough to do without that.'

He had replied bleakly. When he was opening the door for us he said to Skeffington, as though intending to take the edge off the refusal: 'You see, these new results of mine are taking up all my time. But if you and Nightingale do a report, either alone or together, then I'll be glad to have a look at that.'

CHAPTER XI

LOOKING OUT INTO THE DARK

THAT night, when we were back in our flat in London and the children had gone to bed, Margaret told me that she would like to write to Laura Howard. Just as Skeffington felt on Christmas Day, she wanted them to be sure she was on their side.

'Do you mind?' she asked, her eyes steady and clear. She would take care not to harm me; but she was irking to act, springy on her feet with restlessness. She was more headstrong than the rest of us.

'I'm thinking of writing to her fairly soon,' said Margaret speculatively, as though it might be within the next month, while she was moving with the certainty of a sleep-walker towards her typewriter.

During the weeks which followed, she heard several times from Laura, and it was in that way that I kept an insight into the tactics. Nothing had come of Francis Getliffe's idea of a combined report. It became common knowledge that both Skeffington and Nightingale were writing to the Master on their own. Before either report was in, the sides were forming. They were still three or four votes short of a majority for re-opening the case. By the end of January Skeffington's report was known to be complete and in the Master's hands. It was said to go into minute detail and to run to a hundred pages of typescript. (I wondered how Martin had let that pass.) Nightingale's, which was delivered a little later, was much shorter. Within the college, these reports were not secret and any fellow could read them who chose. But it had been agreed, for security reasons, that there should only be three copies of each in existence.

Laura's letters were a curious mixture of businesslike information and paranoia. Margaret said:

'Has it ever struck you that when people get persecution mania, they usually have a good deal to feel persecuted about?'

It all seemed to be going slowly, but on the lines one could have forecast. It was clear that Martin could not risk putting forward a formal motion for re-opening until he had his majority secure.

One Friday evening in February, I arrived home later than usual, tired and jaded. It was raining hard, and I had had to walk from Marble Arch the quarter of a mile or so along the Bayswater Road. The warmth of the flat was comforting. From the nursery I could hear Margaret playing with the little boy. I went into the drawing-room looking forward to the quiet, and there, sitting under the standard lamp by the window, the light full on her face, was Laura Howard.

I saw her with surprise, and with something stronger than surprise, involuntary recoil. I had a phobia of entering a room expecting to be by myself, and finding someone there. For an instant I was inclined to gibber. Was Margaret looking after her? I asked, my tongue feeling too large for my mouth, resentfully wishing to push her out, knowing – what usually I did not know at all – exactly what it is to be pathologically shy. Of course Margaret was looking after her, said Laura, firm, composed, utterly unflirtatious. She added:

'We've been putting our heads together.'

'Have you?'

'I'm not satisfied with the way things are going. I don't want them to get stuck, and they will get stuck unless we're careful.'

I was recovering myself. She did not think of explaining what 'things' were. She was as single-minded as ever. I had not seen a woman of her age so inseparably fused into her husband's life. She sat there, pretty, healthy, and most men would have felt that beneath her skin there was the inner glow of a sensual, active, joyous woman. Most men would have also known that none of that inner glow was for them.

When Margaret came in, she heard Laura repeating that 'things were getting stuck'.

'Yes,' said Margaret, glancing at me guiltily, her colour high, 'Laura rang me up and so I thought it might be useful if she came along.'

'I see,' I said.

'Would you like to hear what she's been telling me?'

I could not refuse.

Succinctly, competently, Laura brought out something new. According to 'information from the other side', there had been a suggestion that, if the feeling became strong enough, the Seniors ought to offer to re-open the case before a majority asked for it. I nodded my head. That sounded reasonable, precisely the sort of step that experienced men would consider. Apparently the suggestion had been made by Crawford first, and 'the other side', or rather, the more influential members, Arthur Brown, Nightingale and Winslow, had spent some time discussing it. Now they had decided that it wasn't necessary: the feeling was not more than 'a storm in a teacup', it would soon blow over. All they had to do was 'dig in their heels'.

Even the phrases sounded right.

'Your intelligence service is pretty good, isn't it?' I said to Laura.

'I think it is.'

'Where does it come from?'

'I'm not at liberty to say,' she replied without a blench.

She was not worried. The situation was less promising than three weeks before – 'We've gone backwards,' she said. But, like so many active people, like Margaret herself, she was freed from worry just by taking action. Why had things deteriorated, I was trying to get her to explain. So far as I could gather, it must have been the effect of the reports. Nightingale's seemed to have been fair in tone, but uncompromising in its conclusion, and that had gone home.

What were Martin and Skeffington doing? I asked her. Martin was 'plugging on'. She did not complain of the way he was handling the tactics. To her, men were good or bad. Skeffington and Martin, who had been bad men the first time she came to our house, had now been transformed into good. When she trusted, she trusted absolutely. But she wanted 'to put on some more pressure'. One waverer had decided not to vote for re-opening: they were now four short of a majority. Who was against, of the people I knew, I asked? The old men and the reactionaries, she said with passion (whether she started with any politics I could not tell, but she had taken over her husband's), Arthur Brown, Winslow, Nightingale of course. One or two – such as Gay, because he was 'too old to understand', and Crawford from magisterial neutrality – would not vote either way, but that was equivalent to voting against. The 'reactionaries', like G. S. Clark and Lester Ince, were flat against. So was Tom Orbell. As she mentioned his name, Laura swore and Margaret joined in. Abusing him, they made a united front – 'Blast the fat snake,' said Margaret.

Francis Getliffe? I asked. Laura cursed again. 'He's still sitting on the fence.' She gave an account, second-hand from her husband, with the pained, knowing smile of the innocent being cynical, of how one can never trust people who pretend to be liberal. They were always the worst. It seemed hardly tactful of her, since she was disposing of Margaret, Martin, and, Skeffington apart, their entire side.

Meanwhile Margaret was frowning, not because Laura was being heavy-footed, but because Francis was a favourite of hers. Of my old friends, he was the one she respected most.

While Laura was with us, Margaret did not ask me anything direct. I could see that she was anxious for Laura to go. Once or twice Laura missed her cue. Then Margaret promised to ring her up during the week, and at last we were alone.

I had gone to the window, and was looking down on the road, over the centre of which the vapour lamps were swinging in the wind. A bare and lurid glimmer reached the trees opposite, but it was too dark to make out the fringes of the park. As I stood there, Margaret had put her arm round me.

'This isn't going too well, is it?' she said.

'Well, it looks as though it might take some time.'

'Is that fair?'

'I should have thought so.' I was being evasive, and we both knew it. She wanted us to be loving, but she was too much committed to stop.

'No,' she said. 'Doesn't it look as though it might go wrong?'

'Everything that can be done is being done, you needn't worry about that. Martin knows that place like the palm of his hand.'

'But it can go wrong, can't it?'

'However do I know?'

Just for an instant, she smiled at me, the smile of marriage, the smile of knowledge. Then, with all her ardour, she broke out:

'Do you feel like taking a hand yourself?'

She knew, just as well as I did, that I should be cross, should feel trapped. She had known that, when she let Laura stay there, so that I was plunged into the middle of it. She knew, better than I did because she had struggled with it, how I disliked a choice forced upon me, not approached by myself 'in my freedom'. Now she had done precisely that.

The choice was there. Left to myself I could have blurred it. I wasn't unused to living with situations which were morally ambiguous, or aspects of myself that I didn't specially like. I didn't have so much self-regard as Martin, and thus I hadn't so much compulsion to make a gesture. I had lived for a long time among high officials. It was a condition of living there that the gestures were not made. Most of my colleagues, the men who had the power, would not have considered interfering about Howard. They would have said it wasn't the business of anyone outside the college. They were not cynical, but they kept their eyes on the sheet of paper in front of them. They were not in the least cynical: they believed, quite humbly though comfortingly for themselves, that (as I had heard one of them say) the world was usually right.

I was too much of an odd man out to believe that. In fact, doing so seemed to me one of the less dramatic but most dangerous of all the temptations of power. Yet I had lived that disciplined life for fifteen years. Perhaps I was the last person to see the changes it made, just as one doesn't see the changes in one's own face, and then, in a photograph, notices an ageing man – can that be me?

I could fairly think to myself that I had no responsibility about Howard.

It just was not my business. If I did as Margaret was pressing me, some of my old friends would resent it, because I was being a busybody. They would resent it more, incidentally, because I was being a busybody on the opposition side. I was not likely to be in Arthur Brown's confidence again. That would be a sacrifice, nothing like so heavy a one as Skeffington risked in the line of duty, but still a sacrifice. Why should I make it, when I had lost any taste for exhibition that I ever had, when I plain disliked even the prospect of being thought officious?

If I had added up the arguments, there would scarcely have seemed any in favour. True, I was inquisitive, acutely so, and my inquisitiveness was not weakening: the only way I could satisfy it in this business was to get right inside. Also I knew, and I knew it with the wreckage and guilt of part of my life behind me, that there were always good, sound, human, sensitive reasons for contracting out. There is great dignity in being a spectator: and if you do it for long enough, you are dead inside. I knew that too well, because it was only by luck that I had escaped.

As I stood there, though, gazing down on the road, Margaret's arm round me, I was not searching down into my experience. I was merely aware of a kind of heavy vexation. I was thinking, I had met few people who, made aware beyond all self-deception of an inconvenient fact, were not at its mercy. Hypocrites who saw the naked truth and acted quite contrary – they were a romantic conception. Those whom we call hypocrites simply had a gift for denying to themselves what the truth was. On this occasion, that was a gift which I did not possess.

I said to Margaret, ungraciously, that I would think it over. She had heard me say, often enough, that choices never took as long to make as we pretend: the time was taken in finding the reasons to justify them. She was watching me, face averted, looking out into the dark. She knew precisely what was going on. She knew that I was fretted and sullen because she had not let me evade, or put off, the choice – and that I was not willing to admit to her that it was already made.

CHAPTER XII

THE STARE OF DELUSION

THERE was another result of the disciplined life, I thought when I was in a better mood, as well as its temptations. It was a week before I could manœuvre even a day or two free in Cambridge. So far as leisure went, I was living my life backwards: while Martin and the others in the college were no more tied than I had been as a young man.

On the Thursday afternoon following Laura's visit, Martin, to whom I had telephoned, had arranged for us both to meet Howard at his school. My train was late: the taxi slithered through the wet streets, the shop windows already spilling pools of light on to the pavement; through the streets of Romsey town, in which I could not recall, in my time at Cambridge, having been before, which seemed as remote from the collegiate Cambridge as the town where I was born. The school was right at the edge of the suburb: as the taxi drove up, there outside the gates, in the February murk, stood Martin.

He wanted a word about some questions we should ask Howard. While the rain drizzled on us, we agreed how to try it. Then we started to push our way through crowds of children, rushing and squealing into the corridor, just set free from the last lesson of the afternoon.

A boy took us into the physics classroom, where Howard was sitting on the lecture table. As we went in, he muttered some sort of greeting, but, if he looked at us, it was only out of the corner of his eye. To make conversation I said, glancing round the room, that it was an improvement on those I had been taught in as a boy.

'If they had some apparatus,' said Howard, 'you might begin to talk.'

'Still, it's better than nothing—'

'Not much,' he said.

That seemed the end of that. It was, in fact – I was gazing round for want of anything to say – a model of a room, new, bright, shining, with seats at a good rake and windows taking up the two side walls. On the blackboard behind the table Howard had been writing: the smell of chalk hung in the air. His writing was high, stiff, broken-backed. There were calculations I couldn't follow: this must have been a sixth-form lesson. One word stuck out – 'inductence'. Could that be right? It didn't seem possible, even in scientific English. Was he one of those people, without visual memory, who just couldn't spell?

'Can we talk here?' said Martin.

'I don't see why not.'

Martin settled himself against one of the desks in the front row.

'I don't think I've got any news for you yet awhile—' he began.

'Why did you want to see me, then?'

'There are one or two things we'd like to ask—'

'I'm sick and tired of going over stuff you know as well as I do,' said

Howard, not meeting Martin's eye, staring unfocused beyond the darkening windows.

'It's mainly for my benefit,' I said.

'I'm not clear where you come in.'

'Perhaps Lewis had better tell you,' said Martin, glancing at me.

'Yes,' I said. 'It's very simple. I should like to say that I believe you are in the right in this business. I'm sorry that I doubted you before. If I can be of any use at this stage, I should like to do what I can.'

For an instant, Howard's gaze flickered in my direction and then away again. He said:

'You don't expect me to be exactly overcome with gratitude, do you?'

As a rule I was not touchy, but Howard had a knack of his own. Martin intervened.

'Come off it, Donald.' His tone was hard but comradely. 'We've got enough to cope with, without you.'

Howard, whose head had been turned away, brought it round to face us: but it sank down on to his chest and he was staring, not at the window, but at his feet.

'Anyway,' he said, without a mollifying word, 'I don't see what you can do.'

He was speaking to me, and I replied: 'I've known some of these people a long time. I've arranged to see Francis Getliffe tomorrow morning, I thought it might be worth while.'

'A fat lot of good that will do.'

'I'm glad you're doing that—' Martin was saying, but Howard interrupted:

'I don't believe in seeing these people. The facts are on paper. They can read, can't they? Well, let them get on with it.'

The curious thing was that, though he spoke with such surliness, he was full of hope. It wasn't simply one of those flashes of random hope that come to anyone in trouble. This was a steady hope that he had kept from the beginning. At the same time he managed to be both suspicious and childishly hopeful.

Martin started to question him about the missing photograph. It seemed to be old ground for both of them, but new to me. Had Howard still no idea when old Palairet could have taken such a photograph? Had he never seen one which fitted the caption at the bottom? Couldn't he make his memory work and find anything that would help?

'I'm not a lawyer,' he said, gibing at me, 'it's no use asking me to cook up a nicer story.'

'That isn't specially valuable, even in the law,' I replied. Martin, who knew him better, was rougher with him.

'We're not asking you that. We're asking you to use what you're pleased to call your mind.'

For the first time that evening Howard grinned.

I went on to say that anything he could tell us about Palairet might be a point of argument. Even people whose minds were not closed couldn't be swung over until they had some idea what had happened. None of us seemed to have a completely clear idea: I certainly hadn't myself.

'Why should you think I have?' asked Howard. 'I didn't have anything to do with him apart from the work. He was always decent to me. I don't pay any attention to what other people say about a man. I take him as I find him, and by how he is to me.'

'And you're satisfied with the result?' I could not resist saying, but he did not see the point. He described how Palairet had given him the photograph which he had used in his thesis – the photograph with the dilated pin-marks. According to Howard, Palairet had said that it would 'help out' the experimental evidence. Howard had not wondered for an instant whether it was genuine or not. He had just taken it with gratitude. Even now, he could not imagine when Palairet had faked the photograph. He said, with a curiously flat obstinacy, that he was not certain it was a conscious fake at all.

'What else could it be?' said Martin sharply.

'Oh, just an old man being silly.'

'No,' said Martin.

I was thinking that Howard was one of the two or three worst witnesses I had listened to. So bad that it seemed he could not be so bad. Once or twice I found myself doubting my own judgment.

Howard said that he had seen another photograph of the same kind: he had repeated that often enough. But this photograph could not have been the one missing from the notebook. Whatever the photograph in the notebook had been, he had never seen it.

'You're positive about that?' I said.

'Of course I am.'

'It's a pity,' said Martin.

'Then it's got to be a pity,' said Howard.

Martin said, 'If that photograph was still in the notebook, there might have been a bit of resistance, but there's no doubt we should have got you home in the end.'

As Martin spoke, not with any special edge, saying something which we all knew, Howard's expression had undergone a change. His eyes had widened so that one could see rims of white under the irises; the sullen dead-pan, sniping obstinacy had all gone; instead his face seemed stretched open, tightly strained, so exposed that he had lost control over his eyes and voice. In a high, grating tone he said:

'Perhaps that's why it isn't there.'

'What do you mean?' Martin asked him.

'Perhaps the people who wanted to get at me found it convenient to get rid of that photograph. Perhaps it isn't an accident that it isn't there.'

I had heard someone, in a state of delusion, speak just like that. Martin and I glanced at each other. Martin nodded. We both knew what had to be said, and Martin began:

'You must never say anything like that again. That is, if you want to have a fighting chance. We can't do anything for you, we couldn't even take the responsibility of going on, if there's the slightest risk of your saying that again.'

'I don't see why not.'

'It's time you did,' said Martin. I broke in:

'Don't you see that it's a very serious accusation? Don't you see that, if it once got round the college, you'd have to answer for it—'

'So would the people who were standing up for you,' said Martin. 'Either you cut it out, or we shall have to wash our hands of the whole business.'

Without speaking, without any sign of acquiescence, Howard had lost the wild open look. He had slumped back again, looking at his feet, his head on his chest.

'All right?' said Martin.

Howard raised his eyes and Martin was satisfied. The classroom clock showed five to six, and he said that it was time to go out for a drink. As he led us out of the room, Martin said: 'All aboard,' like a cricket captain calling his men out to field, or like an old leader of mine before we went into court. He could put on that kind of heartiness very easily. That evening, it worked better with Howard than anything I could have done. In the pub, he was less suspicious than I had seen him. It was a new and shining pub, as bright, as freshly built as the school. Among the chromium plate and the pin-tables, Howard sank into a corner as though he were for the time being safe, and put down a pint of bitter. The second tankard was soon in front of him, and he was replying almost good-naturedly to Martin, who had abandoned his normal carefulness and was questioning him head on. Did he like teaching? Yes, said Howard surprisingly, he wouldn't have minded making his career at it. Why had he settled in a Cambridge school? Was it just to embarrass the college? Howard, who had previously shown no sense of humour, thought that was a good joke.

Martin, who had drunk a couple of pints himself, asked if he were deliberately following the good old college pattern. There had only been one other fellow in living memory who had ever been dismissed. Did Howard know the story? Howard, prepared to think Martin a remarkably good comedian, said no. Martin said that he was disappointed. He had hoped Howard was following suit. The story was that during the nineties, the college had elected someone from outside, actually from as far away as Oxford, as a fellow. He had turned out to be an alcoholic of a somewhat dramatic kind, and his pupils, attending for supervision at five o'clock, had found him not yet out of bed and with empty bottles on the floor. So the college had sacked him. He had promptly married a publican's daughter and set up in a fish-and-chip shop two hundred yards from the college's side gate. I remembered hearing the story used, forty years later, by one of the old men as an argument against electing a fellow from outside.

'Don't you admit the precedent is rather close?' Martin said to Howard. 'You must have decided that by staying in Cambridge you could make more of a nuisance of yourself. Now didn't you?'

'Oh, well,' said Howard, 'if I'd cleared out it would have made things easier for them. I was damned if I could see why I should.'

That reminded me of another question, which Nightingale had brought up at the Lodge.

'In that case,' I said, 'I wonder you didn't think of appealing to the Visitor, and then bringing an action for wrongful dismissal.'

'I did think of it.'

'Why didn't you bring it, then?'

'Should I have won it?'

'I don't think so. But it wouldn't have made things easier for them, would it?'

He hedged. He did not want to answer straight. I was nothing like so good with him as Martin was. He prevaricated, became embarrassed and wrapped up in his own thoughts. He said that he had preferred other methods. I did not begin to understand why he was suddenly so shy. I asked again:

'I should have thought, when nothing happened, you might have brought an action?'

'I wasn't keen on washing this kind of dirty linen in public.'

That was all I could get out of him. After we had all three taken a bus into the town, he left us in the Market Place. He offered to drop my bag in the college, where I was sleeping, since I wanted to go off with Martin to have supper at his house.

'Do you mind?' I said.

'Do I mind putting my head in the porter's lodge,' said Howard, prickly but not at his most offensive, 'is that what you mean? The answer is, I don't.'

As Martin and I were walking towards the Backs, Martin said:

'Not as useful as it might have been, was it?' He meant the last few hours.

'Have you ever got anything more out of him?'

'Nothing to speak of.' Martin went on: 'I suppose we might have found someone more difficult to work for, but offhand I can't think of one.'

Then he asked, how was I going to handle Francis Getliffe next day? He thought I ought to come right out in the open, and say that we should probably never be able to prove our case 'down to the last drawing-pin'. Without the second photograph we could not do it. With a man like Francis, it would be a mistake to minimise the difficulties or try to cover up where we were weak.

As we planned, each of us felt kinship and a curious kind of support. It was comforting – it was more than comforting, it was an active pleasure – to be at one, to be using our wits on the same side.

CHAPTER XIII

TURNS ACROSS THE LAWN

THE next morning, after breakfast I was looking out of the guest-room window into the Fellows' Garden when Francis arrived. The trees were bare, the branches were not stirring. Francis said that it was warm outside, we might as well walk in the garden, I should not need a coat.

The turf was soft with rain, still springy under our feet, brilliant as moss. In the flower-bed to our right I could not see a single flower, not even the last of the snowdrops. We were walking slowly, but Francis nevertheless moved with lunging strides, a foot longer than mine, although he was two or three inches the shorter man.

We had not gone far, we had not gone out of the formal garden into the 'wilderness', when Francis said:

'I think I know what you've come for.'

'Do you?'

'It doesn't really need an inspired guess, does it?' Then he said, stiffly and proudly, 'I'm going to save you a certain amount of trouble. I'd better say straight away that I regard myself as very much to blame. I'm sorry that I've delayed so long. There's no doubt about it, Martin and Skeffington have produced a case that no one has a serious answer to yet. I'm sorry that I didn't tell them so, when they first came to see me. The sooner this business is cleared up, the better.'

I felt a sense of anti-climax, a sense of absurd let-down, as though I had put my shoulder against a door which was on the latch. Also I felt embarrassed, because Francis was so ashamed of himself, stiff with me because he was ashamed.

'What are you going to do?' I asked.

'It's done.'

'What have you done?'

'I've just sent this out. It went off before I came to see you.'

'This' was a mimeographed note with '*Confidential: to all Fellows*' in the top left-hand corner. It read: 'I have now studied the new evidence relating to the thesis and publications of D. C. Howard and the notebooks of the late C. J. B. Palairet, F.R.S. In my view, Dr Skeffington is right in representing that there is a case to answer. I think it is urgent that the college should request the Court of Seniors to consider this case without delay. F.E.G. 19.2.54.'

This note, as I knew, would be taken round by the college messenger. It would reach most of the fellows by the lunchtime delivery, and all of them that day.

'I should have thought,' I said, 'that ought to collect a majority for re-opening the case, anyway.'

'I should hope so,' Francis said.

'I noticed you don't say that you're a hundred per cent convinced yourself?'

'That was as far as I felt inclined to go.'

In silence we walked through to the inner lawn, right at the bottom of the garden, close to the college wall. In the greenhouse in the corner great carnations shone into the water-washed morning, into the green and grey. Francis suddenly broke out, his voice tight with anger:

'This man Howard must be as stupid as they come.'

I asked what had gone wrong now. Francis paid no attention and went on:

'I want you to realise one thing. It's his fault we've got into this absurd position. I mean by that, if he had had the scientific judgment of a newt, he'd never have taken the old man's experiments on trust. It's almost unbelievable that anyone working in his field accepted them without having another look. If Howard's innocent, which I'm inclined to think he is, then he must break all records for stupidity. I must say, there are times when stupidity seems to me the greatest crime.'

We did another turn across the lawn. Francis broke out again:

'Of course, we never ought to have elected him in the first place.'

I told him, because I wanted to make him easier, that that reminded me of his father-in-law on an occasion we both knew, looking for a first cause. Francis gave a reluctant grin, but his voice did not soften.

'Now we've got to clear up this mess,' he said. 'All I hope is that it doesn't take too long.'

'Why is the time it takes worrying you so much?'

I asked him straight out, not knowing whether he wanted to reply. We had been friendly for more than twenty-five years, and I had not seen him at such a disadvantage before. I was bewildered to know why. True, he didn't like being wrong, even less than most of us. Like most men of his granite-like integrity, he had a streak of vanity inextricably fused within it. He did not like falling below the standard he set himself, either in his own eyes or anyone else's. He did not like my having to make this visit, to remind him of his duty. It was the first time it had happened, though several times in our friendship he had reminded me of mine. None of that seemed to explain a distress as strong as his, as we walked backwards and forwards across the lawn. We had walked like that before. The inner lawn was not overlooked by any window, and as young men we used to go there at night and talk out our plans or troubles undisturbed.

After a time, he said in a voice no longer angry but quiet and surprised:

'You're quite right. I didn't want any friction in this place just now.'

I did not say anything. On the next turn he went on: 'I'm afraid it's only too simple. When those two came to see me, I wasn't as completely impressed by their case as they were. That was genuine, and to a limited extent it still is. But if I'd been reasonably responsible, I should have got down to what they had to say. The fact was, Lewis, I didn't want to.'

He was speaking with the candour, the freshness, which sometimes comes to men not given to introspection when they talk about themselves.

'No, I didn't want to. I didn't want the risk of making myself unpleasant to everyone who counts for anything here. I just didn't want to blot my copybook. I needn't tell you why, need I?'

I did not say anything.

'You know, Winslow and Nightingale and those others, they're my backers. The election's coming on this autumn, and the fact of the matter is' – he hesitated – 'I should like it.'

As we turned, he went on:

'The curious thing is, I can't really tell why I should like it so much. I should make a pretty fair job of it, as good as anyone else they're likely to put in the Lodge, by and large. But that doesn't come into it. It's not really the sort of thing that matters to me, I should have said. All I seriously wanted was to do some adequate research and leave some sort of record behind me. Well, I haven't done as much as I should have liked, but I've done something. I believe I've got ten more years' work in me, and I shall do some more. The work's come off pretty well, all things considered. Looking back to the time we both started, I should have been moderately content with what I've been able to do. That's all that ought to matter. As for the rest, I've had more than my share of the honours going round. I didn't think I was specially greedy: and so why should I want the Mastership into the bargain? But I do, you know. Enough to make me put up a disgraceful exhibition about this wretched case.'

As we went on walking, in a silence more relaxed than before, I was thinking, I could have given him one reason why he wanted it. Francis, who had gone through so many struggles, in college, in government, even in public, was not a rebel by nature. His politics had come through duty and intellect, not through a passion of nonconformity, not even through that residue of identification with those outside, pushing their noses against the shop-window, that I, on the surface a more compromising man than Francis, and one who had lived closer to the established world, still preserved. In the long run Francis, who out of principle would stick out as one dissenting voice in the council of the Royal or any group of respectable bosses, wished to end his days with them. His intellect, his duty, would not let him alter his opinions, but in a curious sense he wanted to be 'respectable', and to be received by the respectable. He would be soothed, a final uneasiness assuaged, if the men he had argued with so long, the Winslows and Nightingales and Arthur Browns, made him Master. He still would not qualify anything he said: but he would have come home.

Suddenly I was reminded of another person who, comically different in temperament, also wished for what Francis did. It was Irene, who in her youth had been a reckless man-chaser and who now wanted nothing better than for her and her husband to end up staidly in the Lodge. The resemblance pleased me, but, as I walked with Francis in the quiet damp garden – his face lighter but surprised because he had made a confession, the first I had heard from him, his voice comradely and quite free from resentment, as though glad to have me there – I did not tell him so.

CHAPTER XIV

TWO VIEWS OF RETIREMENT

AFTER Francis, there was no one else I had arranged to see that Friday until I dined in hall. So in the afternoon, with nothing to do, I went on a round of bookshops. It was in the third of these, not Heffer's, not Bowes & Bowes, that, as I was glancing at the latest little magazine, I heard a voice I used to know well.

'I'm sure you're right. I'm sure you've laid your finger on it.'

The voice was plummy, thick and muffled, but it spoke warmly, with teasing affection. I was standing by the rack of periodicals near the door: as I looked up I saw in the inner room, just visible behind the main display shelf, Paul Jago talking to his wife.

As I looked up, so did he. I was certain that he had seen me. But he darted his eyes back to his wife, talked to her rapidly and intimately as though pretending that they were quite alone, as though hoping that I should not notice or disturb them.

Should I slip out, I thought? It would be easy to get into the street, so that he would not be embarrassed. Then I revolted. I had known him well once, and had been fond of him, in the days when he was Senior Tutor and had, in the 1937 election, just missed the Mastership. That had been a traumatic blow to him. He had gone on with his routine duties, but he had given up dining and – so I had heard – no one, not even his closest friends, had seen much of him.

I went into the inner room and said:

'Well. It's a long time since we met.'

Not for ten years, not since Roy Calvert's memorial service. Jago's appearance had altered since then, but in a way I could not define. He had always looked older than his age, but now his age was catching up with him; he was bald, the fringe of hair had gone quite white, but he was sixty-eight and looked no more. His cheeks and neck were fleshy, but the moods seemed close beneath the skin, so that his expressions were liquid, and even now one could not say that it was a sad face. Behind thick lenses his eyes were still brilliant.

'Why, it's you!' he cried. Even though he was prevaricating, even though he wanted to evade me, he could not help the warmth flowing out.

Then I thought I saw what had changed. He had become much fatter, but fatter in a way that did not suggest self-indulgence. As a younger man he had had a paunch, but moved lightly; now he showed that special kind of discouraged heaviness which sometimes seems linked with a life of dissatisfaction or strain.

'Darling,' he turned to his wife with an elaborate mixture of protectiveness, courtesy and love, 'I think you remember—' Formally he introduced me. 'I think you know him, don't you?'

Of course she knew me. I must have been inside her house twenty or thirty times. But she dropped her eyes, gave me a limp hand and what appeared to be her idea of a great lady being gracious to someone who might, in the multitude of her acquaintances, conceivably be one.

'Do you spend much time in Cambridge—?' and she addressed me in full style as though it were a condescension on her part.

'I think he's kept pretty busy in Whitehall,' said Jago. She knew it perfectly well.

'I wish we could offer you better weather,' said Alice Jago. 'Cambridge can look very attractive at this time of year.'

Now she was speaking as if I did not know the town. She too had grown fatter, but she was more strongly boned and muscled than her husband and could carry it better. She was a big woman with a plain, white, anxious face. She had a sensibility so tight-drawn that she could detect a snub if one said good-morning in the wrong tone; but it was the kind of sensibility which took it for granted that though her own psychological skin was so thin, everyone else walked about in armour. She was so insecure that the world seemed full of enemies. In fact, she had made many. She had done her husband much harm all through his career. But for her, he might have got the Mastership. They both knew it.

His manner to her, which had always been tender, had become more so. When he spoke, he was trying to make her happy, and even while he listened to her he seemed to be taking care of her.

'How are you?' I asked him.

'I've quite retired now, I'm thankful to say.'

'He has to spend all his time with me,' said Mrs Jago.

'We're reading all the books that we've always wanted to read,' said Jago. 'I've been looking forward to this for a long time.'

I asked: 'Do you see any of our old friends?'

'Oh, I run into them now and then,' said Jago. He said it as though he wished to drop the subject.

'Don't you think they miss him?' I let slip the remark to Alice Jago.

'If you think I try to prevent my husband going to the college, then you're very much mistaken.'

'No,' said Jago, 'I was glad when I'd shaken hands with my last pupil. The chains had been chafing for a long time, can you understand that? When I used to go into my study in the morning, for my first tutorial hour, I used to think, I shall only have to do this another thousand times. Then another hundred. Then another ten.'

I had seen many people get through years of routine, and come to their last day. Nearly all of them were sad. I asked, didn't he feel just a tinge of regret at the end?

'Not for a single instant,' said Jago with a flash of pride. 'No, I felt that for a good many years I had been wasting too much of my life. Now I was ceasing to. And I was also ceasing to be reminded of some associations that I was only too willing to forget.'

He looked at me. He was a man of quick human sympathy and recognised it in others. He knew that I had followed him.

'Mind you,' he went on, 'I'd taken care not to be reminded of them more than I could help. It was one thing to go on with my pupils and do my best for them. It was quite another to inflict myself on some of our colleagues. I hadn't seen some of them for years, apart from college meetings, which I couldn't cut until I gave up office—'

'And now you needn't go to any more of them,' cried Alice Jago triumphantly.

'I think I can bear that deprivation, don't you?' he said to me.

'I suppose, while you were still attending, you heard of this Howard business, didn't you?'

I hesitated about trying it. Mrs Jago looked blank and resentful, as though the name meant nothing and I was shutting her out.

'I couldn't very well help hearing, could I? I might have had to waste some time over it, because I was third Senior and was due to serve on the Court. But I thought that that was another deprivation I could bear, and so I begged leave to be excused.'

'I should think you did,' she said.

He seemed quite uninterested in the case. I wanted to find out if Francis Getliffe's circular had reached him: but apparently he did not open his college documents until days after they arrived.

He asked after my doings. He still couldn't keep back his interest and looked friendly when I spoke about my wife and son. But he brought out no kind of invitation. He did not suggest that I should see him again.

'Well,' he said, a little over-busily, 'we mustn't take up your time. We must be going ourselves.'

'I hope,' said Alice Jago graciously, 'that you enjoy the rest of your visit.' She added, 'And good luck in your career,' as though I were one of her husband's pupils and she was safely projecting me into the future.

Getting back to my rooms after tea, I found a letter on the table. It was addressed in an old man's hand that I had either forgotten or did not know. When I opened it and looked at the signature, I saw to my astonishment that it was M. H. L. Gay. The handwriting was bold in outline, only a little shaky, and the letter read:

'My dear Eliot,

I learn upon good authority that you are residing temporarily in the college. I must ask you most urgently to visit me tonight after my evening meal, which I take at six-thirty upon medical advice, and before eight, which is the time when I nowadays have to suspend my labours for the day. Pray regard this visit as having *first priority*. The question we have to discuss will brook no delay. You are essential to me because of your legal studies.

I shall await you at seven-fifteen or thereabouts.

Yours ever sincerely,
M. H. L. GAY.'

I was irritated even more than astonished. Perhaps it wasn't so odd that he should, out of the blue, remember who I was: even when he was less senile, his memory had come and gone. Why should he want me? I was irritated, because I had planned to see Arthur Brown in hall and on the side pick up such gossip as was going. I didn't fancy missing my dinner for the sake of conversation with someone who might not recognise me. Still, there seemed nothing for it. One could not refuse the very old. I had to telephone Brown, saying that instead of that night in hall it would have to be Sunday. I explained why, and Brown, who had guessed the reason for my visit and was at his most impenetrable, nevertheless gave a fat man's chuckle over the wire. 'You'll find him pretty exigent, old chap. He'll never let you get away at eight o'clock. If I were you, I should make sure that there are some sandwiches waiting for you in your rooms when you get back.'

The joke seemed even more against me as I walked up the Madingley Road. I had made a mistake in walking at all, because it had begun to rain, a steady seeping rain; the road was dark, Gay's house was nearly opposite to the observatory, and the lights of the observatory seemed a long way off. The rain was percolating inside the collar of my overcoat: I could feel the damp against my neck, and wet sleeves against my wrists.

In the hall of Gay's house, the pretty young housekeeper gazed at my clothes. In a foreign accent she asked if I wanted a towel.

From an open door, Gay's voice resounded:

'No, indeed, he doesn't want a towel! He wants to get down to business! You be sure he does.'

Her brow puzzled, she led me through the door into his study, where Gay, a scarf round his neck, was sitting in an armchair by an enormous fire. Fitting on the armchair was an invalid's tray, and he still had spoon in hand, working away at his meal.

'That's the man,' said Gay. He seemed to know my face. 'You're not wet, are you? You're not wet, I'll be bound.' He felt the shoulder and arm of my jacket. 'Ah, that's nothing,' said Gay, 'that's not what I call wet. You don't understand about our English climate yet, my dear,' he said to his housekeeper. 'A fine climate ours is, it's a climate and a half. It makes us the men we are, I've not a shadow of a doubt about that.' He gazed at me with faded eyes. 'Pray sit down, Eliot. Pray sit down and enjoy yourself.'

I was too much occupied with discomfort, crude physical discomfort, to be amused. As for his housekeeper, pretty as she was, she did not seemed to be amused in any circumstances. She kept her puzzled frown.

'Please to offer our guest some cocoa,' Gay said to her.

No, I put in rapidly, I didn't drink cocoa.

'Now that's an error on your part, my dear boy. A splendid drink, cocoa is. Why, I sometimes drink a dozen cups a day. Indeed I do.'

Did he mind if I smoked? I asked.

'Ah, now *that's* not good for you. It's not good for me either. I have to be careful with my bronchials at this time of year. I don't want bronchial trouble at my time of life. It could turn to pneumonia, the doctors say. Old man's friend, they used to call pneumonia, when I was born. Old man's friend – no, I don't like the sound of that. I'm not prepared to give up all that easily, I assure you I'm not.'

I sat in my armchair, not smoking, steam rising from my trouser-legs, while Gay finished his supper. He finished it in an unusual fashion. On one plate he had what appeared to be some sort of trifle, on another a piece of Cheshire cheese and two slices of bread. Methodically Gay cut the cheese into thin sections and put them in the trifle. Then he took a slice of bread and crumbled it over the mixture, which he stirred vigorously with his spoon and then swallowed in six hearty mouthfuls.

'It all goes the same way home,' he explained himself to me.

I had known some old men, but not anyone as old as this. Sitting there, watching him, I thought he was pretty far gone. Then all of a sudden he seemed at least as lucid as he would have been at eighty. He had rung a handbell to fetch his housekeeper back. She removed the tray and went out again, followed by cries of: 'Splendid! That was a splendid supper you gave me!'

I was studying the drawings on the walls, drawings of the saga heroes that he had made himself, some of which I remembered from my visits before the war, when he said:

'Ah, I thought today – it's very fortunate we have Eliot here. Eliot is a lawyer by training, he's the man to go to for legal guidance. Indeed he is.'

'How did you know I was here at all?'

'Ah ha! I have my spies. I have my spies.' (How in the world, I wondered, did the old man pick up jargon of the forties and fifties, like that phrase, or 'first priority'?)

He stroked his beard with self-satisfaction and asked:

'Do you know, Eliot, why I thought of you today? He's the man, I thought. No, you can't be expected to see the connection. Why, I've just received a remarkable communication from one of our fellows. If you go to that desk, my dear chap, you'll find this communication under the paperweight. Certainly you will. I don't mislay important communications, whatever certain people think.'

The 'communication' was Francis Getliffe's note. I handed it to Gay who, from the interstices of his chair, brought out a reading-glass.

'There it is. *To all Fellows*. No, I don't like that. I think a special copy should have been sent to me, what? Initialled at the bottom by "F.E.G." I have looked up our college list, and I find that must be young Getliffe. *To all Fellows*. These young men aren't careful enough. Indeed. But still, this isn't a time to think of our *amour propre*. These are important issues, Eliot, important issues.'

'Do you mean,' I said, 'that you're concerned about what Getliffe says?'

With cunning, with a certain grandeur, Gay replied:

'I'm concerned in a very special way about what Getliffe says.'

'You mean, you're interested in forming a majority?'

'Oh, no, my dear chap. I've seen too many flysheets in my time. What do you think of that? I must leave these minutiae to the younger men. They must make up their own majorities. I trust them to get on with their own little squabbles, and I expect they'll do very well. Fine young men we've got. Getliffe's a fine young men. Brown's a fine young man. Oh no, I'm not the one to take part in little differences within the college. They all come right in a few years. But no, my dear chap, *that isn't the point at all.*'

'What is the point?'

'I want to draw your attention to a very remarkable feature in this communication.'

'What is it?'

'Come and look here. Over my shoulder. You see those words – "The Court of Seniors"? You're sure you see them?'

I said yes.

After I had gone on saying yes, he let me go back to my chair.

'Well, now. What do those words suggest to you?'

I was at a loss, and shook my head.

'Come now. This isn't being on the spot. This isn't what I expect from a lawyer. Tell me, who is the Senior Fellow of this college?'

'You are, of course.'

'Indeed I am. Now that *is* the point, my dear chap. Does it surprise you to hear that when the Court of Seniors was meeting – over this little trouble of Getliffe's, I presume, but that's neither here nor there – when that Court was meeting I was not invited to take my rightful place?'

Gay threw back his noble head.

'I'd never thought—' I began.

'But you should have thought. Does it surprise you that I was not only not invited to take my rightful place, but absolutely discouraged? I had letters from the Master implying that it might be too much for me, if you please. Letters full of flattering sentiments, but fine words butter no parsnips, my dear chap. They even implied that I could not make the journey into college. Stuff and nonsense! Why, the Court could meet in the summer, couldn't it? Or if they were in a special hurry, what was to prevent them meeting here? If Mahomet can't go to the mountain! Yes, indeed. No, they are treating me as though I were not *compos mentis.* That's the long and the short of it. And I think it's time they were taught a lesson.'

I tried to soothe him, but Gay, his scarf slipping from his shoulder, was now in full voice.

'This is where you come in, Eliot,' he said in triumph. 'Tell me, am I or am I not entitled to sit on the Court of Seniors, unless I withdraw of my own free will?'

I said that I must re-read the statutes.

'Tell me, have they or have they not deprived me of my place without my consent?'

'So it seems.'

'Tell me, will or will not the fact that I have been deprived of my place be known to all the fellows of the college?'

'Certainly to some of them.'

'Tell me, will or will not that fact be taken to mean that in the opinion of the Master and his advisers I am no longer *compos mentis?*'

'Not necessarily—'

'That's what it will be taken to mean. I have been libelled, Eliot. That is why I am contemplating seeking legal redress from the college.'

I had been expecting various things, but not this. Trying to humour him, I said that it could not, in technical terms, be a libel. Gay was not to be humoured.

'I believe there must still be justice in England. You remember Frederick the Great – there are still judges in Berlin. A fine city, they gave me an honorary degree in that city. I am positive that damaging a man's reputation cannot be done with impunity. And that ought to be true of people who have achieved some little distinction, quite as much as of anyone else. Indeed it ought. Not letting a man take a place which is his of right – that is a comment on his fitness, my dear chap, and I am absolutely convinced people cannot make such comments with impunity.'

He was becoming more obstinate. Incredulously, I began to think that he might not forget this. How far, I was calculating, with a faint suppressed *schadenfreude* at Arthur Brown's expense, could he go before he was stopped?

'If I proceed against them,' said Gay, 'that will be an action and a half.'

I said the situation was complicated.

'You're too genteel, you young men.'

Gay was chuckling with gusto and malice. Oddly enough, it did not sound like senile malice. I was astonished at how much vigour he had summoned up. The prospect of litigation had made him younger by twenty years. 'You're too genteel. I'm absolutely positive that this action of mine would lie. Indeed it would. That would teach them a lesson. I don't believe in being too genteel, my dear chap. That's why I've attained a certain position in the world. It's a great mistake, when one has attained a certain position in the world, to be too genteel about teaching people a lesson.'

CHAPTER XV

'NEVER BE TOO PROUD TO BE PRESENT'

THE following afternoon, Saturday, Martin rang me up in college. Some progress, he said. No special thanks to us: after Francis's circular, we couldn't avoid it. Anyway, two people had come over – Taylor (the Calvert fellow) and another man I did not know. On paper the score was now ten to nine against. That is, nine men were pledged to sign the request for re-opening the case. 'I think we're pretty well bound to pick up another. Then the real fun begins,' came Martin's voice with a politician's mixture of optimism and warning.

For reasons of tactics – 'just to show we mean business' – Martin was anxious to get the majority decided soon. Would I have a go at Tom Orbell? Would I also dine in hall and see if there was anyone I could talk to? It would be better if he and I were acting separately. We could meet later that night at his house.

I obeyed, but I drew blank. In the mizzling afternoon, so dark that the lights were on all over the college, I walked through to the third court. For an instant I looked up at Tom Orbell's windows: I could have sworn that they were lighted too. But when I climbed the stairs his outer door was sported. I rattled the lock and called out that I was there. No response. I had a strong suspicion that Tom had seen me coming.

Frustrated, irritated, I gazed at the name above the door, 'Dr T. Orbell'. The letters gleamed fresh on the unlit landing. I remembered faded letters there, and the name of Despard-Smith, who had been a fellow for fifty years. He had been a sanctimonious old clergyman. At that moment I felt a mixture of rancour and disgust; it seemed that the rancour, long suppressed, was directed at that old man, dead years before, not at Tom Orbell who kept me waiting there.

However, I met Tom before the end of the afternoon. I had been invited to tea by Mrs Skeffington, to what, I discovered when I arrived, was something very much like an old-fashioned Cambridge tea-party. That was not the only odd thing about it. To begin with, the Skeffingtons were living in one of a row of two-storeyed houses just outside the college walls, which used to be let to college servants. Why they were doing it, I could not imagine. They were both well off: was this Skeffington's notion of how a research fellow ought to comport himself? If so, they were not making all that good a shot at it: for in the tiny parlour they had

brought in furniture which looked like family heirlooms, and which some
of the guests were cooing over. Sheraton? someone was asking, and Mrs
Skeffington was modestly admitting: 'Oh, one must have something to
sit on.'

Round the wall there were pictures that did not look at all like heirlooms, and I recalled someone telling me that Skeffington had taste in
visual things. There was a Sickert, a recent Passmore, a Kokoschka, a
Nolan.

So, in the parlour, smaller than those I remembered in the back streets
of my childhood, we sat on Sheraton chairs and drank China tea and ate
wafers of brown bread-and-butter. Another odd thing was Mrs Skeffington's choice of guests. I had imagined that Skeffington wanted to talk
over the case with me and that everyone there would be on his side. Far
from it – there was Tom Orbell, hot and paying liquid compliments, and
also, though without their husbands, Mrs Nightingale and Mrs Ince. To
balance them, Irene was there without Martin. Did Mrs Skeffington
think it was her duty to pull the college together? Quite possibly, I
thought. Not through policy. Certainly not through doubts of her
husband's case: she was as firm as he was. But quite possibly through
sheer flat-footed duty, as though to the tenantry.

The case was not referred to. What was referred to, was a string of
names, as though everyone were playing a specifically English kind of
Happy Families. Someone mentioned an acquaintance in the Brigade:
Mrs Skeffington trumped that by having known the last Colonel. County
names, titled names, token names, they all chanted them as though the
charmed circle were tiny and as though one kept within it by chanting in
unison. And yet those who were chanting the loudest needn't have done
so. There was nothing bogus about the Skeffingtons' social roots: Tom
was the son of a bishop, Irene the daughter of a soldier. I discovered that
Mrs Ince, whom I rather liked, had been to a smart school. That I
shouldn't have guessed. She wore spectacles, like her husband she had
adopted a mid-Atlantic accent, she was cheerful, ugly, frogfaced, and
looked as if she enjoyed a good time in bed.

The only person not chanting was Mrs Nightingale. With unfailing
accuracy Mrs Skeffington asked if she knew ——

'Oh, no,' said Mrs Nightingale, impassive, exophthalmic.

Had she known —— or ——?

'Of course not,' said Mrs Nightingale with complete good-temper.
'We were living in Clapham Junction at the time.'

'Were you, now?' Mrs Skeffington could not help speaking as though a junction were a place that one passed through. She brightened. 'Then you may have known the —s when they had one of those nice Georgian places over in the Old Town?'

'Oh no, my father could never have lived there. That was before the big money started to come in.'

Tom guffawed. Soon afterwards he slipped out. When he found that I had followed him and caught him up on the cobbles outside, he said, in a defiant tone:

'Hullo, Lewis, I didn't know you were coming.'

I had just been quick enough to prevent him letting himself into the college by a side gate, to which I did not have a key. Instead we walked round by the wall. Under a lamp, I caught sight of his eyes, blue, flat and mutinous. I said: 'What were you doing this afternoon?'

'What do you mean, what was I doing?'

'I came up to your rooms. I wanted to talk to you.'

'Oh, I was working very hard. I did some really good work. I was extremely pleased with it for once.'

'I'm glad of that—'

'Hanna's always bullying me to produce more, you know she is. But you know, Lewis, I'm really producing quite as much as anyone of my age—'

He was steering the conversation into a comparison of the academic output of young historians. I interrupted:

'You know what I wanted to talk about, don't you?'

'Don't you think I've had enough of that?'

'Who from?'

'Hanna, of course. She says that I'm behaving like a beast.'

I had not realised till then that she was taking such an open part. That remark was right in her style. I wondered, did she think he was weaker than he really was? He seemed – it might have crystallised by now – in love with her. It would be like Hanna to assume that he was easy to persuade. But in fact, though he was so labile, he was also intensely obstinate. When one dug deeper into him, he became both less amiable and less weak.

'I don't think you're behaving up to your usual standard.'

'I'm sorry to hear that.'

'I've always thought you tried to be detached, when it came to a personal issue,' I said.

'I'm sorry we don't agree on this. I mean that very sincerely.' He was speaking with hostility.

'Look here, won't you talk this over on the plane of reason? Preferably with Martin—?'

'I haven't the slightest desire to talk to Martin. I shall only hear what you've just said and what Hanna says, ten times worse.'

We had come round to the front of the college. Tom caught sight of a bus slowing down before the stop. 'As a matter of fact,' he said, moving towards it, 'I've got to go off to see a pupil. He's not well and I said I'd supervise him in his rooms. Perhaps I shall see you in hall. Is that all right?'

I did not expect to see Tom return from his putative visit, and I did not expect to see him in hall. In fact, there were only six names on the list when I arrived in the combination room, and one was that of an old member of the college up for the weekend. Of the four fellows dining, three were young men whom Martin had already made sure of. The other was old Winslow. He had a bout of sciatica and was in a temper that made ordinary civil conversation hard enough. The six of us sat chastened at the end of the high table; Winslow was scarcely speaking, the young men were overawed. As for the old member making a pious return to the college, it must have seemed a sombre Saturday night.

Down in the body of the hall the undergraduates were making a hubbub. Winslow roused himself.

'To what do we owe this curious display?' he asked.

Someone thought the college fifteen had won a cup-tie.

'I've never been able to see why we should encourage dolts. They would be far happier at some decent manual work.' Winslow regarded the old member. 'I apologise if you've ever been concerned with this pastime. Have you?'

The old member had to say yes. Winslow made no further comment.

Back in the combination room after dinner, Winslow announced that his complaint made wine seem like poison. '*Poison*,' he said. 'But don't let that deter the rest of you.'

It did. Lugubriously we sat, Winslow's chin sunk down as though he were studying the reflection of his coffee-cup in the rosewood, two of the young fellows talking in low voices.

Leaving the room in that devastated hush, I reached Martin's house so early that he thought I must have news. I said that I had never spent such a useless day. As I described it, Martin grinned with brotherly malice.

'Well,' he said, 'I've got one last treat for you. We're going next door to see G.S.'

I cursed, and asked to be let off.

'He says we can have some music.'

'That doesn't add to the attractions.'

Martin smiled. He knew that I was tone-deaf.

'No,' he said, 'we must go.'

He was too realistic to think there was a chance of winning Clark over. But he was acting on rule-of-thumb experience. In this kind of struggle – neither of us needed to tell the other, we had heard it often enough from the first Minister I served, old Bevill – the first maxim was: forget you're proud, forget you're tired. *Never be too proud to be present.*

Between their half of the house and the Clarks' they had kept a communicating door and Irene unlocked it and came with us. As soon as we crossed into the Clarks' it was like going from Italy into Switzerland. The Clarks' passage, even, was immaculate and bright: the drawing-room shone and glistened, with the spotlessness of a house without children. Clark struggled to his feet to greet us, but there was pain tucking up his mouth as he stood in his brace, and soon Hanna helped him back into his chair.

Coffee and Austrian cakes were waiting for us. When we all three refused drinks, it was a relief to them both. Clark was a hospitable man, he liked displaying the bottles on the sideboard, but he had never forsaken his Band of Hope piety. While as for Hanna, she could not, after twenty years in England, eradicate her belief in both Anglo-Saxon phlegm and Anglo-Saxon alcoholism.

'Delicious,' said Irene, munching a cake, glancing at Hanna. She sounded mischievous: was she deliberately mimicking Tom Orbell?

'Before we start to enjoy ourselves,' said Clark gently, 'I think we'd better put one thing behind us, hadn't we?'

He was looking at Martin, then at me, with his beautiful afflicted eyes.

'If you like,' said Martin.

'Well, I've thought over this *démarche* of Getliffe's. I don't think I ought to make any bones about it to you two. I'm very much afraid that my answer has to be no.'

'I'm sorry about that,' Martin replied, but easily and without indignation.

'I think I can understand the position you're all in. I mean, you two and Getliffe. I exclude Skeffington, because I don't pretend to know how his mind works. And I'm not convinced that he's a man of any judgment. But you others were in a genuinely difficult position, I can see that. You had to balance the possibility that there's been a certain amount of individual injustice – you've had to balance that against the certainty that, if you raise the point, you're going to do a much larger amount of damage to us all. I can see that you were in a difficult position. Granted all your preconceptions and back histories, I can understand what you chose to do. But, with great respect, I'd like to suggest that it was the wrong choice.'

'We're tied up with the word "possibility",' Martin said.

'You're not prepared to say "certainty",' said Clark.

'Can't I explain to you the nature of scientific evidence?' said Martin. But he was more respectful to Clark than to most men. There was no doubt that, in some fashion, Clark had the moral advantage over him.

'I must say,' I put in, 'your view seems to me almost unbelievably perverse.'

'We have got different values, haven't we?' he said, with sweetness and composure.

'I told him that I disagreed,' Hanna said to me.

'Of course you disagree, my dear. Of course these two do. As I say, with your preconceptions and back histories, it would be astonishing if you did anything else.'

'What do you mean?'

'I mean that you and the Eliot brothers and Getliffe have been what you'd call liberals all your lives. I haven't, and I don't pretend to be. That's why I can understand some of your attitudes, which you all think are detached and based on the personal conscience, but which really aren't quite as detached as you'd all like to think. In the long run, anyone who has been as tinged with liberal faiths as you have is bound to think that by and large the left is right, and the right is wrong. You're bound to think that. It's the whole cast of your minds. And it shows itself in quite small issues like this present one, which *sub specie aeternitatis* isn't quite as earth-shaking as we're making out. *Of course* you want to think that this man has been a victim. *Of course* all your prejudices, your life-histories, your *weltanschauung* are thrown in on his side. You must forgive some of us if we're not so easily convinced.'

'Do you really think a scientist of international reputation, like Francis Getliffe, is quite as capable of deceiving himself on a point like this?' I said.

'I've got to be persuaded that he isn't.'

'You would seriously take Nightingale's opinion rather than Getliffe's – that's what it amounts to, doesn't it, G.S.?'

Martin was talking to him better-temperedly than I could. It struck me that there was a protective tone in Martin's voice. I wondered – it was the kind of thing near the physical level, that one did not easily recognise in a brother – whether if, like many robust men, he wanted to turn his eyes from a cripple and so had to go out of his way to compensate.

'Yes, I think that's fair. It amounts to that.'

'Forgetting Skeffington,' said Hanna. 'Whom even you could not regard as a man of advanced opinions, I should think.'

'Forgetting Skeffington.' He brushed her aside more contentedly than anyone I had seen. 'You see, I can respect Getliffe's opinions and the Eliots', even when I disagree with them. But I'm not going to give equivalent weight to playboys.'

'That's special pleading,' I said.

'Take it as you like,' said Clark. 'In my view, and you're naturally at liberty to think it's wrong, the question is very much as Martin put it. If I've got to take a side, I've got to decide between Nightingale's opinion and Getliffe's. Now I'd be the last person to say that Getliffe wasn't by far the more distinguished scientist. People competent to judge have decided that for me, and of course there's no room for reasonable doubt. But, with respect, it seems to me that their scientific merits aren't under discussion. So far as I'm concerned, there is room for reasonable doubt about whose guidance I accept on a piece of scientific chicanery.'

'How well do you know Nightingale?' I was provoked enough to say it. As soon as I did, I knew it was a false step.

'I know them both well enough to form my own judgment. And that's something one must do for oneself, isn't it?' He looked around with his fresh smile, the smile edged with physical strain. 'Well, we shan't convince each other, shall we? I think this is the time to agree to differ, don't you?'

After Clark had said that he was going to play us some Berlioz, I was left out of the party. All of the others were musical, Clark passionately so: while as soon as he had put on the record, I drifted into the kind of woolgathering that music induced in me. On the bright wall opposite I caught sight of a couple of Piranesi prints. They set me speculating on what sort of inner life Clark had, Berlioz and Piranesi, the march to the scaffold, the prisons deep under the earth.

Why in the world had Hanna married him? There she sat, curled up on the sofa, in her mid-forties, her body lean, tense, still young, her face still young apart from the grey in her hair which, before she married Clark, when she was one of the most elegant of women, she would never have left there. Why had she married him? She was not happy here. It did not need her ambiguous relation to Tom Orbell to say she was unhappy. She had not taken Clark into her confidence, even at the start, so far as I could see. There had been a time when she was far more politically committed than he thought. When he spoke of her as in the same political grade as Francis Getliffe, he did not know what Martin and I knew.

Did he know that once she had been fond of Martin?

Yes, Martin had been fond of her in return. A good many men were roused by her sharp, shrewish charm and wanted to tame her. But though she liked such men, they were not the ones she disrupted her life for. Instead she seemed to be searching for someone to look after. It must have been that, it could only have been that, which led her to take on Clark.

As the music went on, I felt both indulgent to her and impatient. For, of course, the irony was that she could scarcely have picked worse. She was so brave, much more than most of us, she was intelligent, she had her sharp-edged attractions. But she had no insight. She was a good judge of men's intellects, but compared with a hundred stupid women she despised, she had no idea what men were like. Martin, I now admitted, had been dead right about Clark. It did not require clairvoyance to see that, though he might be crippled, he had a character like a rock. Not an amiable character; one fused out of bad luck and pain, not giving pity to others, and not wanting it himself. One might help him across a room, but he would not like one the better for that. As for offering him tenderness – one ought to know that gently, inexorably, he would throw it back in one's teeth.

Sitting there, daydreaming in the sound, I believed Hanna knew that now. She had no insight, but she learned. I was not specially sad for her. She was younger than most women of her age, she still had force and nerve and the hope of the fibres. She was capable of sacrificing herself and enduring more than others could take. In the past she had gone on with a sacrifice for years, and then come to a snapping-point. Then she had saved herself. Could she do so again?

CHAPTER XVI

THE GOVERNMENT

WHEN the butler came into the combination room on the Sunday night and ritually announced, 'Master, dinner is served,' Crawford told me that, since there were no visitors dining, I was to follow him in and sit at his right hand. As we stood in our places waiting for the grace to finish, I saw the heavy face of Arthur Brown, dead opposite to me.

It was a full Sunday night, and we had scarcely spoken in the combination room. Once we had sat down to our soup, he gave me a smile of recognition, and told me that he had already asked the Master's permission to present a bottle after dinner to drink my health. He knew why I was in the college, but he was at the same time too warm-hearted and too cunning to let that affect his welcome. Crawford nodded, with impregnable cordiality. He liked a glass of port, he didn't mind me, he wasn't what Gay would have called 'on the spot' as to what had been going on that week-end.

Brown gazed down the table. He noticed, just as I did, that neither Francis Getliffe nor Nightingale were dining. Martin was there, so were Tom Orbell and most of the younger fellows: there were also several members of the college present who were not fellows but had university jobs. Brown must have been calculating that, until and unless they dispersed, there was no chance of a showdown that night. Whether he found the thought satisfactory, I could not guess. As though it were the only trouble on his mind, he was informing the Master that Winslow's sciatica was worse.

'Ah, well,' said Crawford, who was inclined to take a biological, or alternatively a cosmic, view of human miseries, 'a man of eighty ought to expect that bits of the machine are beginning to run down.'

'I don't think he'd find that much consolation just at present,' said Brown.

'Speaking as one trained in medicine, I should have thought he'd been remarkably lucky with his physical constitution. And with his medical history, if it comes to that. I can't think of many men who've lived as long and had so little wrong with them.'

'The old chap seemed rather sorry for himself when I dropped in on him before hall,' Brown said.

'That was very considerate of you, Senior Tutor,' said Crawford. Without irony at his own expense, or anyone else's, he said: 'Do you think I ought to visit him?'

Brown considered: 'There's certainly no need to put yourself out. No, I'm inclined to think he's had enough visitors for twenty-four hours. But if you could send round a note? And perhaps a book? He complained of being short of reading matter.'

'That shall be done,' said Crawford. He kept his Buddha-like, contented smile. He was either oblivious that he was being told how to do his job, or else he accepted it. He was capable of thinking 'Brown is better at these *personalia* than I am,' and it would not disturb him in the least.

This was the way things worked, I thought. Since Chrystal's death, those two had been the government of the college. No doubt other people had been let in, sometimes and for some things – Nightingale now and then, after he became Bursar, and occasionally Francis Getliffe. But if I knew Brown, they would never have been let right in. Nor should I, though he liked me better, if I had stayed in the college.

The curious thing was, as men, Crawford and Brown had not much use for each other. Crawford was not one to whom friends mattered: he probably thought of Brown as a dullish colleague, a run-of-the-mill administrator, one of those humble persons who kept the wheels going round. While Brown had once had a positive dislike for Crawford. Deep down, I believed – Arthur Brown was loyal and tenacious in all things, including his antipathies – that it remained. He had opposed Crawford's election with every resource that he could pull out. When he lost, people thought that his days of influence in the college were over. They could not have been more wrong. Crawford was arrogant, not over-active, not interested in men's motives, but quite a fair judge of what they could do. He was also human enough to like the support of a man who had previously been all against him. Frequently it was not a friend to whom a normal man wanted to give the spoils of office, but an enemy who had just come over. So when Crawford saw Brown settling himself to help, the supreme college manager, he not only accepted, but welcomed him.

As for Brown, he loved managing so much, that, whoever had been Master, he could not have avoided waiting there at his side. For people like him, who lived in affairs, it was part of the rub of life to put loves and hates, particularly hates, out of sight, and almost out of mind. Brown's happened to be unusually strong, stronger than a politician's ought to be: even so, he could behave, not for days but for years, as though he had forgotten. With a practical purpose, like running the college, in front of him, he seemed able to conceal from himself an inconvenient personal dislike. I thought that if I reminded him what he really felt for Crawford, he would be shocked, he would take it as a blemish on good taste.

Through dinner, Crawford, in good world-historical form, was enquiring of me, of Brown, of anyone at large, how China could avoid becoming the dominant power on earth? Not in the vague future, but in finite time: perhaps not in our time, but in our sons'. It was not until we were sitting round the table in the combination room that Brown got in much of a word.

The company had dwindled. I watched Brown peer inquisitively as several of the younger fellows, not waiting for wine, said good-night and went out in a bunch. There was a party at Lester Ince's house, Martin told Brown. 'In my young days,' said Brown, 'our seniors would have looked down their noses if we hadn't stayed in the room on Sunday night. Still, it leaves a nice little party to drink Lewis's health.' In fact, it left him and the Master, Martin, Tom Orbell and me, and a couple of non-fellows. 'Which means one glass apiece,' said Brown. 'That's rather meagre for a beastly winter night and an old friend. I think I should like to ask permission, Master, to order another bottle.'

'Very generous of you, Senior Tutor, very generous indeed.'

I was now certain that Brown wanted to keep the non-fellows at the table and so avoid an argument. He did not manage it. They each of them drank their port but, quite early, before half past eight, they had got up and gone. The rest of us were alone, one of the bottles still half-full. I glanced at Martin, who gave the slightest of nods. I was just going to lead in, when Crawford himself addressed us round the table:

'I suppose you've all had the opportunity to read Getliffe's fly-sheet by now, haven't you? I seem to remember, Eliot –' he said, imperturbably gazing at me – 'that you're familiar with this unfortunate business.'

'I think we can take it,' said Arthur Brown, 'that Lewis is quite familiar with it. I fancy he was able to study Francis Getliffe's production at least as soon as any of us.'

He spoke with his usual lack of hurry, but he was irritated that the Master had opened the subject. Himself, he would have let others make the running.

'I know the situation pretty well,' I said to Crawford. 'I think I ought to say straightaway that I am *parti pris*.'

'What exactly do you mean, Eliot?'

'I mean, that if I were a fellow now, I should be in favour of re-opening this case, without any qualification at all.'

'I'm surprised to hear you say that,' Crawford said. 'You must forgive me, Eliot, but it does sound like a premature judgment.'

'I'm surprised to find that you feel in a position to make any judgment whatever,' said Brown sternly. 'Do you think that the people who decided this issue were altogether irresponsible? I think you might remember that we spent several months devoting as much care to our decision as I for one have ever devoted to anything.'

'It's not a decision which anyone in our position could have taken lightly,' said Crawford.

'Do you seriously think,' said Brown, 'that we were as irresponsible as what you've just said seems to indicate? I should like you to consider that question too, Martin.'

Martin met my eye. This was going to be rough. Tom Orbell, who had been quiet all the evening, was effacing himself and listening. I thought the only thing was to take the offensive.

'All you say is fair,' I replied. 'Of course you're not irresponsible men. I've never known people less so. But as far as that goes, do you think that Francis Getliffe is a man to go in for premature judgments? Do you think he would have written as he did, unless he were convinced of it?'

'To an extent, I think you have a point there,' said Crawford. 'Getliffe is a distinguished man of science—'

'I'm sorry, but I can't accept that as a reason for giving up our own responsibility.' Brown's voice was steady and full. 'I've known Francis a long time. Of course we all recognise how distinguished he is. But I have known him make mistakes in judgment. If you were a scientist, Lewis, and were giving your opinion on this case, I should be disposed to give more weight to it than I feel able to give to Francis's. Put it another way. There are two of you who are trying to make us take what to my mind would be a false step. Francis is a scientist and a master of technicalities, but gives me some reason to have reserves about his judgment. While I have respect for your judgment, Lewis, but I know you can't master the technicalities any more than I can.'

Conciliating, flattering, dividing and ruling, even when he was angry – he was very angry, but he had not lost his touch.

'Of course, I'm in general agreement with you, Senior Tutor,' said Crawford, 'but for the sake of fairness we ought perhaps to remember that this isn't simply a matter of one individual's judgment. I still consider we were right to resist them, but several men of science in the college, not only Getliffe, have suggested there was a case for enquiry. That's still your feeling, for instance, Martin, isn't it?'

'It is, Master.'

'I'm obliged to say,' Brown put in, 'that I'm not specially happy about the way all this is being done. I exempt you from that remark, Martin. I can't pretend I think you've been well advised' – he gave his jolly laugh, but his eyes were sharp – 'but I'm prepared to admit that any step you've taken has been correct. But I'm afraid I can't say as much for most of your associates. I'm very disappointed in Skeffington. I should have thought he'd have known the way to do things. When we elected him, I didn't imagine for a second that he'd turn out to be a trouble-maker. As for Francis Getliffe, he's done nothing more nor less than put a pistol to our heads.'

'The danger about pistols,' said Crawford, 'is that sometimes they go off.'

That was as near to a joke as I had heard him make. Tom Orbell gave a suppressed snort, and for an instant Crawford beamed, like a humorist who is appreciated at last. Brown was not beaming, and said:

'In a small society, I've always felt that it's a mistake to rush your colleagues as he's tried to do. Some of us are not all that fond of being threatened.'

'Agreed,' said Crawford.

'If he'd come to see you about his difficulty, Master,' Brown was now turning his full weight on to Crawford, 'I might feel differently about it. That would have been the proper thing to do. He ought to have spoken to you before he put a word on paper. Then perhaps we could have smoothed things down in a reasonable fashion. But the way he's gone about it, it's making the college into a bear-garden.'

(From the dead past, I recalled that singular phrase.)

'Again, I agree,' said Crawford. 'One would have thought that Getliffe wouldn't have wished to create unnecessary commotion. I'll try to have a word with him next Thursday at the Royal Society.'

'Meanwhile,' Brown was continuing to talk, not to the rest of us but to the Master, 'I've thought about the proper position to adopt, and I think I can say I've come down to this. If the college chooses to let itself be rushed, and there's a majority for asking the Seniors to re-open the case, then by the statutes the Seniors naturally have to do so. That's all cut and dried. But I don't see the college losing its head like that. I believe we're interpreting the wishes of the college if we go on resisting attempts to sweep us off our feet against our better judgment.'

'Are you sure you're interpreting the wishes of the college?' asked Martin.

'Yes.'

'I don't want to do too much counting heads,' Martin went on, speaking Brown's own language, 'but there are nine out of nineteen feeling the other way.'

'Is that a firm figure, Martin?' Crawford asked.

'There are nine fellows willing to vote for re-opening.'

'I confess I should be happier,' said Crawford, 'if there were a clearer weight of opinion one way or the other.'

'I accept Martin's figures,' said Brown. Well he might, I thought:

those two knew each other's measure and also the score, ball by ball. 'But I'm sure he'd agree with me when I say that the nine he's referred to don't include, apart from Getliffe and himself – well they're people who haven't taken much part in the college yet.'

'That's quite true,' said Martin. He was not going to overstate his case.

'Still,' said Crawford, 'it would be more satisfactory to all concerned if the numbers were wider spaced.'

Once again Martin and I glanced at each other and saw that we agreed. It was time to stop. Quickly I got in before Brown and said that they might be in for another kind of trouble. I explained that old Gay was asking advice about how to sue the college.

Crawford did not think that that was funny. He went to a cupboard and fetched a copy of the statutes. He showed us that, in order to disqualify Gay from the Court of Seniors, the college would have to pass a formal motion. That had never been done, so far as the college history had been traced. So they – not only the Master, but Brown and Winslow – had visited him, written him letters, assuming that he was withdrawing of his own free will. He had not made much protest, once or twice he had verbally acquiesced: but, with a kind of old man's cunning, more animal than senile, he had not acquiesced on paper.

I had a feeling that Brown felt the Master had not been resourceful or punctilious enough. When Crawford asked me what the legal position was, I said that they didn't have much to worry about. I could help them string the old man along for a time. If he went to his solicitors, they wouldn't let him bring such an action. It was just possible that, if he had enough stamina, he could get into touch with an unscrupulous firm – but I couldn't imagine a man of ninety-four keeping up a grudge long enough, not even Gay.

'I shan't believe we're out of that particular wood until we've attended his memorial service in the chapel,' said Arthur Brown. His previous annoyance made him less emollient than he would normally have been. Conscientiously he added, 'Not that he hasn't been a grand old boy in his way.'

CHAPTER XVII

CONTRACTING OUT

A FEW minutes later, Martin and I were in a taxi on our way to Lester Ince's house in Bateman Street. Martin was asking: didn't I think that, when the argument over the case got sharp, Brown had spent all his effort keeping the Master up to scratch? Yes, I said. It wouldn't take much, probably one conversation with Getliffe, for the Master to decide that the case ought to be re-heard.

'That means the majority is in the bag,' said Martin. He went on: 'But we don't want it to come like that, do we? They've made a mistake, not offering a re-hearing the minute three or four people wanted it. Just for once, Arthur hasn't played his hand right. It's a point to us if we can force this majority on them, so that they're up against it as soon as they start the case again. We don't want them to let us have it as a favour.'

On the pavement in Bateman Street we could hear the noise of the party three storeys above. After I rang the bell we could still hear the noise, but no footsteps on the stairs. It took minutes of ringing before Ince came down to let us in. Out of the hall, lights streamed into the dark and dripping street. 'Hallo, Lew,' said Lester Ince. There were two prams in the hall, and the smell, milky and faecal, of small children. As we climbed up the stairs of the old, high, narrow-fronted Victorian house, Martin and I were whispering. 'You needn't bother,' said Ince in his usual voice, 'it would take the crack of doom to wake them up.'

Bits of the wall were peeling, a banister leg was loose. The four children were sleeping, 'dotted about', said Ince, on the first two floors. He owned the whole of the shabby house, and let off the basement. When we got into the party, it seemed to me – I thought it must have seemed to Martin – like going back to parties we used to know when we were poor young men in the provincial town. Beer bottles on the table: the room, which in earlier days would have been a main bedroom, cleared for dancing: a gramophone in the corner: the floor full of couples. There were just two differences. Ince's gramophone was a handsome new record-player, and the couples were jiving.

Ince picked up a glass of beer from the table, drank it, grinned all over his robust, pasty face, and said: 'I'm not going to miss this.' He crooked his finger at a pretty young woman, and began swinging her round with vigour. His wife winked at him. About the whole party, certainly about Ince, there was a cheerful, connubial, sexy air.

Like his wife, I was thinking, even more than his wife, Ince was a bit of a social fraud. But a fraud in reverse, so to speak. Instead of wanting to be taken for something grander than he was in fact, he seemed to be aiming at the opposite. He was actually a doctor's son, born in the heart of the middle classes, educated like the quintessence of the professional bourgeoisie, middling prep-school, middling public school. He insisted on behaving, talking, and often feeling, as though he had come up from the ranks. Just as with the other kind of social mimic, one listened to his speech. Beneath the curious mixture of what he thought, often not quite accurately, to be lower-class English or happy-go-lucky American, one could hear the background of an accent as impeccably professional as Arthur Brown's.

One odd thing was, that while the Inces imitated those lower down the social ladder, they were not in the least political. I had been used, years before, to upper-class left-wingers, conscientiously calling each other Des, and Pat, and Bert, and on envelopes punctiliously leaving off the 'Esquire'. But this was nothing like the same thing. It was not a 'going to the people'. The Inces did not even trouble to vote. They weren't making an intellectual protest. They just felt freer if they cut the ties of class.

It seemed to suit them. If they weren't happy that night, they gave a remarkable impersonation of being so. Between each dance Lester Ince drank a bottle of beer: he had the sort of heavy, games-playing physique, not unlike Martin's, that could mop it up. He danced with his wife, as though he were uxorious and glad of it. Ugly, frog-like, fleshy, she had such appeal for him that she took on charm for us watching. The temperature of the room, thermometric and psychological, was rising. The young dons were getting off with the women. Married couples, research students with an eye for girls, intellectual-looking girls with an eye for the research students – I was speculating about the *idée reçue* dear to men of action, businessmen and people in the great world, that intellectual persons were less interested in sex than they were. So far as one could generalise at all, in my experience the opposite was true.

In the taxi, Martin had said that we should have to talk to Ince. It wasn't a good time, but in view of Crawford's 'wobbling' we mightn't have another. And so, after we had been there an hour, Martin caught him on the landing outside the room and beckoned to me.

'Christ,' Ince was saying, 'I'd a hell of a sight sooner go back to my wife.'

'Two minutes,' said Martin. Then he said straight out that Getliffe's note had 'put the cat among the pigeons', and he wanted just one more vote.

'You've got a one-track mind, Marty. Strike me pink you have.'

'I shouldn't have thought so,' said Martin, 'but still—'

Ince had drunk a lot of beer but he was not drunk, just cheerful with drink. Standing with heavy legs firmly planted, he considered and then said:

'It's no go. I'm not playing.'

'You can't dismiss it like that, you know.'

'Can't I hell?'

I did not know him well, but I felt that at heart he was decent, sound and healthy. It came as a shock to find his tone not only flippant, but callous. I said that I was surprised.

'It's good for you to be surprised, Lew. If it comes to that, why in Christ's name are you messing about here?'

I replied, just as rudely:

'Because people like you are behaving like fools or worse.'

'I won't take that from you or anyone else.'

'You've damned well got to take it,' said Martin.

Ince stared at us, legs immovable, with a matey smile. He was neither abashed nor at a loss.

'I'm just not playing, Marty,' he said.

'Why not?'

'I don't feel obliged to give a reason. I didn't know they'd made you a sort of confessor for anti-God men—'

For an instant I saw Martin's face go pale. He was more provoked than I was by the insolence of younger men. But though his temper had risen he did not let it go. He would not do that, except as a tactical weapon or at home.

'I think you are obliged to give a reason,' he said.

'Why?'

'If you want to be taken seriously. Which I hope you do.'

For the first time, Ince's expression was clouded. He was a strong character, but he gave me the impression that he had not often crossed wills with other strong characters: while for Martin, this was nothing new.

'I'm not interested,' he said.

'That's a meaningless thing to say,' Martin replied.

'So far as I'm concerned, this is a squabble among scientists. All I want is for you to go and sort it out among yourselves, and good luck to you and a nice long goodbye kiss.'

'It's not a squabble among scientists,' I said. 'That's just letting yourself out. We're telling you, you can't—'

'I'm telling you, can't I hell?'

'Look,' I said,' you must admit, there's a chance, we think it's a near certainty, that an innocent man has been victimised. Do you think that's so good?'

'Oh, if that sort of thing happens, it always comes out all right in the wash.'

'Good God above,' I said, 'that's about the most optimistic statement on human affairs that I've ever heard.'

'Oh, it's not true of your sort of affairs. Not the big stuff. Not on your life,' said Ince. 'How many people have you seen done down in your time?'

'Quite a lot,' I said, 'but not quite—'

'Then why the sweet hell don't you go and put that right?'

'I was going to say,' I replied, 'not quite in this way. And just because a lot of people are done down inevitably, that's no reason to add another.'

'If you really want to know, that's why I wash my hands of this schemozzle,' said Ince. 'There's too much Pecksniffery about it for me. Christ knows what you've seen, Lew, but then you come here and do a Pecksniff on me. And you're not the worst of them. There's too much Pecksniffery about your scientists, Marty. You think you can do anything you like with the rest of us, and switch on the moral uplift whenever you feel good. That's why I'm bleeding well not playing. You go and do good. I shan't get in your way. But I don't want to hear about it. I'm nice and happy as I am, thank you very much.'

CHAPTER XVIII

CONVERSION

NEXT day, when Martin came to my rooms to take me to lunch, neither of us had any more news. In hall, where half a dozen fellows were already sitting, no one spoke a word about the case, though there were some there, such as Nightingale and Tom Orbell, who must have known each move that had been made. Apart from an old man, not a fellow, a deaf clergyman from a village outside the town, who had come in to lunch each day since before my time, the rest of them had been lecturing or working in the laboratories. Lester Ince announced that he had been talking to a class about Beowulf. 'What have you been telling them?' asked Tom Orbell.

'That he was a God-awful bore,' said Ince.

Below the high table, relays of undergraduates came in and out. The doors flapped, the servants slapped down plates. It was a brisk, perfunctory meal, the noise level in the hall very high: afterwards only four of us,

Martin and I, Nightingale and Orbell, went into the combination room for coffee.

After the cosiness of the room at night, it looked bleak, with no fire to draw the eye, no glasses on the table to reflect the light. Through the windows one could see the head and shoulders of a young man running round the court; but the room seemed darker than at night, the beams of the ceiling nearer to one's head.

The four of us sat round the gaping fireplace, with the coffee jug on a low table close by.

'Shall I be mother?' said Nightingale, as though he were in the mess, putting on a cockney accent. As he poured out, he seemed in high spirits, quite unresentful of my presence, less worried by the situation than either Crawford or Brown had been the night before. He was not exactly indifferent to it, but full of a suppressed, almost mischievous satisfaction. He behaved like a man with inside knowledge concealed from us, which if it were disclosed would make us recognise that we did not stand a chance.

He was talking about his plans for a new building. He had an ambition, perhaps the last ambition he had left, to leave his mark upon the college. He wanted to put up a building with another eighty sets of rooms.

'If we're going to do it, we've got to do it properly,' said Nightingale, 'I intend to do the young gentlemen well.'

Of course, he said, in the minatory tone of someone talking about past waste of money, if the college had built in the thirties it would have cost only seventy thousand. 'That's what we ought to have done in your time, Eliot.' As it was, the building he was determined on would 'run us in' for a quarter of a million. 'But the college has to pay for its mistakes,' said Nightingale. 'I won't have bed-sitters. I mean to put up a building that we shall be proud of when we're all dead and gone.'

He explained his scheme for choosing an architect. He intended to select two 'orthodox' men and two 'modernists', and ask them to submit plans. 'Then it will be up to the college!' said Nightingale triumphantly.

'Do you know, Bursar,' I said, 'I'm prepared to have a modest bet in bottles that I've just the faintest sneaking suspicion which the college in its taste and wisdom will prefer?'

'Oh, I don't know about that, Eliot. I don't know about that.'

Brisk and busy, Nightingale stood up, said that he had a Bursars' meeting at two-thirty, and must spend half an hour in his rooms briefing himself beforehand. He glanced at Tom Orbell. Nightingale was a little chary of leaving him with Martin and me.

'Coming, Orbell?' he said affably.

'Not just yet, Bursar. Will you excuse me?' said Tom in his most honeyed tone. 'As a matter of fact, I've got a letter I ought to send off. Is that all right?'

I was puzzled that he was willing to face us. I was even more puzzled when, after we had heard Nightingale's steps down the passage, Tom said:

'Well now, how is the Affair going?'

'From whose point of view?' Martin was on his guard.

'It came over me, when we were here last night, that it is pure Dreyfus, you know. At least, there really is something similar between Dreyfus and poor old Howard. And Julian Skeffington would make a reasonably good Picquart, at a pinch. I can't cast you, Martin, you don't seem to fit in. And one's got to stretch a point to cast the others, I suppose. But still hasn't it ever struck you, either of you, that it is a bit like "*l'Affaire*"?'

Tom Orbell was flushed, excited, apparently with the sheer beauty of the historical analogy. Martin shook his head.

'No, it hadn't,' he said. 'Actually, things are going none too badly—'

'I'm very glad. I mean that, very sincerely.'

'How do you cast yourself?' I said.

'No, that isn't so easy either.'

'I shouldn't think so,' I was saying, when Tom gave me what seemed a defiant stare, and said:

'You haven't got your majority yet, have you?'

'Not yet,' said Martin, 'but we shall.'

'How are you going to do it?'

Tom knew too much of the detail for Martin to bluff.

'If the worst comes to the worst, the Master will have to make it up. Just to give us a hearing—'

'That's exactly the kind of thing he would do,' Tom burst out. He rushed on:

'Yes, that's what he was chewing over last night God rot those awful old men and their beastly, puritanical, unbelieving, Godless, so-called liberal souls. Well, I can save him the trouble, or alternatively we can stop him having the satisfaction. I'll come in with you, by God I will!'

'You're sure?'

'I mean it.'

'Do you need some time to change your mind?' said Martin deliberately.

'By God, I've got to come in with you. I can't stand awful old men. When I heard Crawford talking about "trouble-makers", that was the last straw. Trouble-makers! What else in the name of heaven and earth do they expect honourable men to be? Have they forgotten what it was like to think about one's honour? God knows I don't like Howard; but was one word said last night, was one word even thought, about the man himself? It was so de-humanised it made my blood boil. Have they forgotten what it's like to be human?'

'This business apart,' I said, 'Arthur Brown is a very human man.'

'I'm very glad to hear you say that,' said Tom, 'because it's only on this business that I've changed sides, remember. Mind you, I don't agree with either of you on many things. We think differently. Nothing's going to persuade me that Getliffe ought to be the next Master of this college. What I'm saying now isn't going to affect what I do this autumn. I'm not going along with you about him – that is, presuming you want him?'

Martin did not reply, and Tom stormed on:

'I'd sooner have Arthur Brown a hundred times. Even though some of your friends say he's a stick-in-the-mud. But as for the rest of the old guard, I just can't sit down under them. Trouble-makers. Judgment. Keeping us in our places till we're fifty! I can't abide it, and I won't. It's about time someone spoke up for honour. By God, this is the time to do it!'

With a smile both forced and curiously sweet he said:

'Anyway, it'll be nice being on the same side as you two again. We're all in the same lobby this time, aren't we?'

We had known, for minutes past, almost from his first question, that he was joining us. But his tone was not what one might have expected. He kept some of his desire to please; he was trying to sound warm, to feel what most of us feel when we are giving our support. He did not manage it. He had thrown away his prudence, his addiction to keeping in with the top; but he had not done it out of affection for us. Nor out of devotion to Hanna. Nor out of the honour that he was protesting about. Instead he seemed to be acting partly from direct feeling for a victim, partly from frustrated anger. One felt, under the good-living, self-indulgent, amiable surface, how violent he was to himself. He was a man who couldn't take authority just as it was; he surrounded it with an aura, he longed for it and loathed it. He couldn't listen to the Master as though he were just a brother human being speaking. In fact, he listened wrong. The phrase which had inflamed him – 'trouble-makers!' – he attributed to the Master, but it had actually been spoken, in the singular, by Arthur Brown.

'Good,' said Martin. But he was less at home with natures like Tom's than I was. Now that Tom had committed himself, my instinct would have been to trust him. Martin's wasn't. He was not as easy as usual, as he said:

'Look here, I'd like to get this cut and dried. It would be a good idea to tell Crawford tonight that we have a majority signed, sealed and delivered. I wonder if you'd mind writing me a note?'

Tom flushed. 'You'd like it on paper, would you?'

Martin said, 'Well, it would be a final piece of ammunition—'

'Very well,' said Tom. He went, shoulders pushing forward, eyes hot, to the writing-desk by the window. He wrote a few lines, signed his name, put the sheet of paper in an envelope. Then, with his back to us, he started laughing. It was a loud laugh, both harsh and hearty.

'I told Nightingale I was going to stay to write a letter, didn't I?'

PART THREE

THE OFFER

CHAPTER XIX

REMARK FROM AN OFFICIAL GUEST

THE Court of Seniors was taking its time, so Margaret and I heard in London. Weekly meetings, a summons to Howard to give written evidence, a summons to Francis Getliffe – it all looked, both inside the college and to us, as though they were being stately to save their faces. Laura told Margaret that, when Howard was reinstated, they proposed to stay a couple of years in Cambridge and then move. There seemed surprisingly little gossip about the affair within the college: certainly none reached us. Some of them were beginning to get busy about the autumn election, however, and there were reports that both Brown's 'caucus' and Getliffe's had already met.

For myself, I received one direct communication from the college. It came from old Gay. He reminded me that I had promised to 'take legal soundings' and finished up by a reference to 'certain infractions of privilege, of privilege won by a lifetime's devotion to scholarship, which, for the sake of others, are not lightly to be borne nor tamely to be brooked.'

In April I had to go to Cambridge on official business. On business which was, as it happened, at that time top secret: for Walter Luke, the head of the Atomic Energy Establishment at Barford, wanted to talk to the Cavendish about the controlled thermo-nuclear reaction. There was a slice of the work he planned to divert to Cambridge. It had to be done with what Luke called our 'masks and false noses' on, and when he went to negotiate I, as one of his bosses in the hierarchy, went too.

Outside the conference room windows it was a piercing blue April afternoon, a sunny afternoon with a wind so cold and pure that it made one catch one's breath. As we sat there in the Old Schools, I looked out at the bright light, resentful at being kept in, resentful without understanding why, as though the strings of memory were being plucked, as though once I had been out in the cold free air and known great happiness. And yet, my real memories of days like that in Cambridge were sad ones.

Shaking myself, I got back to the argument. Round the table were the Vice-Chancellor, Crawford as an ex-Vice-Chancellor, three scientists, one of them Francis Getliffe, Walter Luke and me. Negotiations were going slowly, and not well. They were not going well partly because Luke, as well as being a good deal the youngest man present, was also a good deal the most impatient. Incidentally he was – and that didn't make it easier either – potentially the most gifted. There was a fair amount of ability in the room, two Nobel Prize winners, five Fellows of the Royal Society. For imagination and sheer mental drive, I would have put Luke before any of them. But for persuasive power in a genuinely difficult situation, he wouldn't have been the first partner I should have chosen.

It was a genuinely difficult situation. In principle, they were all ready for the Cavendish to take on some of the thermo-nuclear work. Luke told them, though one or two knew beforehand, the minimal facts about it. It was peaceful, he said, no one need have any moral qualms. In fact, the reverse. The only people who need have moral qualms were those who in any way obstructed it. For this, if it came off, would meet the human race's need for energy for ever. If this country got it first, it would stay as a major power for a couple of generations. 'I'm not going to sell you something we haven't got,' said Luke. 'It's not in the bag yet. But if I were going to stick my neck out, I should say the chances weren't worse than evens.'

So far, so good. Everyone liked the sound of that. The first trouble was that, if any of the research came to a Cambridge laboratory, it would mean a special kind of security. 'You won't like it,' said Luke. 'I don't like it. No one in his senses likes it. It's mostly bloody nonsense, anyway. But we've got to have it. If you want to know why, you'd better ask Lewis Eliot.'

Some of them were uneasy. It wasn't that they were unused to security. But, as I had to explain what this special kind would mean, they thought it would be not only a nuisance inside the university, but something worse. The Vice-Chancellor and Crawford questioned me. I thought it was bad policy to gloss over the difficulties; I was ready to be as patient as they were, but Luke was getting restive.

'I can't credit that we're going to hold it up just because of a couple of flatfoots and a bit of vetting and the other thing—'

Towards six o'clock, negotiations adjourned until the next day, Crawford, Getliffe, Luke and I walked back to the college. Not willing, not able, to let the controversy fade out, Luke was saying that all these doubts and hesitations were anachronisms, they'd forgotten the time they were living in, the first thing we'd got to make sure was that 'this country can earn its living'. If this reaction came off, then the country could earn a living till our grandchildren's time or longer. Anything which got in its way was suicidal. Unless, Luke said, someone else was brighter than he was and could see another way to keep us 'a jump ahead'. Luke's voice rolled out unsubdued as we entered the first court.

In the bright and dramatic twilight, I looked at him. It was the kind of light which, after a brilliant day, suddenly gives shadows and moulding to faces – so that one has something like an optical illusion that the day, instead of darkening, is getting brighter. Luke's cheekbones stood out through flesh that was no longer full: his skin was matt, and the colour was washed out: his bristly, strong hair had gone quite grey. Although his backbone was ramrod stiff as he walked, he had a limp that had not left him since a radiation accident. He had aged more quickly than anyone I knew. When the college had first elected him – and it was only eighteen years before – he had been younger-looking than most men of twenty-four. He cheeks had been fresh and high-tinted; he had been surgent but self-restrained, determined to get on, certain that he would leave a great corpus of scientific work behind him.

It hadn't gone like that. War and the scientific revolution had played tricks on him. As a young man, he would never, not even in a fantasy, have imagined himself as he was that night, walking into his old college, possessed in his early forties of power, a title, a place among the decision-makers. Not that he disliked these things: people did not get what they didn't want. But he had expected quite different successes, and still valued them more. Compared with these two older men, Crawford and Getliffe, he knew that in natural talent he was their equal or superior. And yet, his creative work was slender by the side of theirs. In fifty years' time, when students read through the scientific textbooks, there would be pages about Crawford's discoveries; there would be descriptions of the Getliffe layer and the Getliffe effect; there would be a little, but only a very little, to keep alive Luke's name.

I did not know how much he regretted it. He was not an introspective man and, argumentative and articulate as he was, he did not often confide. All his imagination, vitality, crude and crackling force, seemed to have become canalised into the job he had set himself, what he called 'seeing that the country can earn a living'. Somehow his ambition, his scientific insight, his narrow and intense patriotism, had all fused into one.

When Francis had gone up to his rooms, Crawford asked Luke and me into the Lodge. There, in the study, after he had given us a drink, Crawford said, fingers together, gazing across the fireplace:

'I *think* I hope you get your way about this matter, Luke; I'm not certain, but I *think* I hope you get your way.'

'I should damned well hope you do,' said Luke.

'No, speaking as an old-fashioned man of science, I don't see it's as straightforward as that,' said Crawford imperturbably. With his usual respect both for ability and position, he approved of Luke: but he wasn't to be bullied when an idea was being talked about. Crawford didn't like disagreement on 'personalia', but when it came to an idea, he remembered that he was a son of the manse and became, at about half the speed, as disputatious as Luke himself.

As they argued (Crawford kept saying 'you *aver* that . . .' which I could not recall having heard anyone say before) they were enjoying themselves. I wasn't, for I had less taste for amateur metaphysics.

Just as we were getting ready to go, Crawford remarked:

'By the by, I'm afraid that I shan't be able to be with you tomorrow.'

I said that we shouldn't reach a decision anyway.

'As a matter of fact,' said Crawford, 'I have to attend to a rather troublesome piece of college business.'

'What's that?' Luke asked. 'The Howard flap, I suppose?'

For once, Crawford was taken aback, Buddha-smile dissolved into an astonished fretting stare.

'I really don't understand how you've heard that, Luke,' he cried.

'God love me,' Luke gave his harsh guffaw, 'it's all round the scientific world. Someone told me about it at the Ath. God knows how long ago.'

'Then I'm very distressed to hear it.'

'Never you mind.' Luke was still grinning. 'You couldn't have stopped it. Nothing's ever going to stop scientists talking, as you ought to know. Hell, that's what we've been chewing the rag about this afternoon! As soon as the boys in the Cavendish heard there was something fishy about Howard's paper, nothing could have stopped it going round. If you ask me, you've been bloody lucky that it's been kept as quiet as it has.'

'I should be very sorry to think,' said Crawford, 'that anyone in the college has spoken a word outside.'

'That's as may be,' Luke replied.

'I've never had the slightest indication,' Crawford went on, 'that anyone in the university outside this college knows anything of the unpleasantness we've been through.'

'Like a bet?' said Luke.

Crawford had recovered his equilibrium. He gave a smile, melon-lipped, contented with himself. 'Well,' he said, 'I don't want to say any more, but tomorrow I think there's every chance we shall have finished with this unfortunate business once for all.'

CHAPTER XX

A PIECE OF PAPER

AFTER another day of meetings, which had again been adjourned, without giving Luke and me what we were asking for, I went in the evening to Martin's rooms. Earlier in the day I had telephoned him, telling him what Crawford had said. The lights in the high eighteenth-century windows, late additions to the court, did not dominate it as they would when it was full dark: they just stood welcoming. I expected Martin to be waiting for me with the result.

What I did not expect was to enter the room and find not Martin, but Howard and his wife waiting there. Howard, who was reading an evening paper, looked up and said hallo. Laura said good-evening, addressing me in full, politely, formally, brightly.

'Martin let us know that the verdict was coming through tonight,' she explained.

'Nothing yet?'

'Not yet.' She remarked that Martin had gone out to see if he could 'pick up anything'. Both she and Howard seemed quite undisturbed.

Their nerves were steadier than mine, I thought. If I had been in their place, I couldn't have endured to plant myself in the college waiting, however certain I had been of what I was going to hear. In fact, the more certain I had been, the more I should have been impelled, by a streak of superstitious touching-wood, which they would both have despised, to make it a bit hard for the good news to catch up with me. In their place, I should have gone for a walk, away from telephones or messengers, and then returned home, hoping the news was there, still wishing that the envelope could stay unopened.

Not so these two. They were so brave that they seemed impervious. Howard had found in the paper something about an English soldier being killed on what he called 'one of *your* colonial adventures'. He would have liked to make me argue about politics. The curious thing was that, as he talked, protruding the Marxist labels, making them sound aggressive, he was also cross because the platoon had walked into an ambush. A cousin of his was serving with that brigade, and Howard suddenly slipped into a concern that I might have heard at Pratt's, irritated, paternal, patrician. One felt that, change his temperament by an inch, he would have made a good regimental officer.

There was a sound of footsteps on the staircase outside. I knew them for Martin's, though they might have sounded like a heavier man's. I stopped talking. Howard was looking towards the door.

Martin came in. He had a piece of paper in his hand. His eyes were so bright that, just for an instant, I thought that all was well. We were sitting round the chimney-piece, and he did not speak until he had reached the rug in front of us.

'I am sorry to be the one to tell you this,' he said to them in a hard voice. 'It's bad.'

Without another word he gave the note to Howard, who read it with an expression open and washed clean. He did not speak, passed the note to his wife, and once more picked up the evening paper. In a moment Laura, her colour dark, a single furrow running across her forehead, gave me the note. It carried the address of the college Lodge, and read:

'The Court of Seniors, at the request of the College, have reconsidered the case of Dr D. J. Howard, formerly a fellow. They have concluded that there is no sufficient reason for them to amend their previous decision.

> R. T. A. Crawford
> Master of the College.'

In a tone so quiet that it became a whisper, as though we were in a sick-room or a church, Martin told me that the notice had not yet gone round: it was just being duplicated in the college office, and he had collected a copy there. As he sat down, without saying any more, he looked at me, as if for once he did not know the etiquette, as if he was lost about what to say to these two or do for them. I hadn't any help to give. He and I sat there in silence, watching Laura gaze with protective love at Howard. He was holding the newspaper low, so as to catch the light from the reading-lamp. The only movement he made, the only movement in the whole room, was that of his eyes as they went down the page.

He did not turn over. I could not tell whether he had stopped reading, or whether he was reading at all.

All of a sudden he let the paper drop. As it fell, the front page drifted loose and we could see the headlines, bold and meaningless, upon the rug.

'I hope they're satisfied now,' he shouted. He began to swear, and the curses came out high and grating. 'Oh, yes,' he cried, 'I hope they're satisfied!' He went on shouting and cursing, as though Martin and I were not there. At last he sat up straight, looked at Martin, and said with a curious sneering politeness: 'If it comes to that, I hope you're satisfied too.'

'Don't speak like that to me!' Martin broke out. Then, getting back his usual tone, he said: 'Look, this isn't going to get us anywhere—'

'What I want to know is, why wasn't I asked to talk to that Court again, after they said they'd probably want me? I want to know, who stopped that? I suppose you're all pleased by the masterly way you've handled things. It's not important to be fair, all that matters is that everything should look fair.'

Howard did not seem to have noticed the flash of Martin's temper. For him, everyone was an enemy, everyone was a part of 'them', most of all those who had pretended to be working on his side. His voice changed. 'I'm positive, if I could explain how I wrote that paper, if I could explain quietly and sensibly and not get panicked, then the Court would see the point.' He was looking ingenuous and hopeful, as though the issue were still in the future and the Court could still be influenced. He was caught up by one of those moments of hope that come in the middle of disasters, when time gets jangled in the mind and it seems that one still has a chance and that with good management one is going to emerge scot-free and happy.

Another splinter of mood: he began to shout again. 'By God, they wanted to get me! I should like to have heard what they've been saying this last fortnight. I should like to know whether it's just a coincidence that *you* happened to be here,' he said to me, with the same jeering courtesy that he had used to Martin. 'But I don't suppose they wanted any extra help. They were determined to get me, and one's got to hand it to them, they've made a nice job of it.'

'It isn't finished yet,' said Laura. She had gone near to him; she was speaking with impatience and passion.

'They've made a very pretty job of it, I think they deserve to be congratulated,' cried Howard.

'For God's sake,' said Laura, 'you're not giving up like that!'

'I should like to know—'

'You're not giving up,' she said. 'We've got to start again, that's all.'

'You know nothing about it.'

He spoke to her roughly – but there was none of the suspiciousness with which he would have spoken to anyone else that night. Between them there flared up – so ardent as to make it out of place to watch – a bond of sensual warmth, of consolatory warmth.

'It's not finished yet, is it?' she appealed to Martin.

'No,' he said. He spoke to Howard. 'Laura's right. I suggest we cut the inquests and see about the next step.'

Martin's manner was businesslike but neither enthusiastic nor friendly. He was no saint. He had none of the self-effacingness of those who, in the presence of another's disaster, don't mind some of the sufferings being taken out on themselves. He didn't like being accused of treachery. He would gladly have got Howard out of sight and never seen him again. Martin had himself taken a rebuff, more than a rebuff, in the Seniors' verdict that night.

'You've got a formal method of appeal,' said Martin. 'You can appeal to the Visitor, of course.'

'Oh, that's pretty helpful,' said Howard. 'That's your best idea yet. Do you really think a bishop is going out of his way to do any good to me? And when I think of that particular bishop— Well, that ought to be the quickest way of finishing me off for good and all.' He said it with his paranoid sneer.

A bite in his voice, Martin replied:

'I said that it was the formal method. I mentioned it for one reason and one reason only. You're probably obliged to go through the whole formal machine before you bring an action for wrongful dismissal. I still hope we can get this straight for you without your bringing an action.'

'Do you?'

Martin's tone kept its edge, although he went on without being provoked: 'But after what's happened, I couldn't blame you if you went straight ahead. I don't think any of us could.'

Howard looked startled. He was startled enough to go in for a practical discussion: did Martin really advise him to see a solicitor straightaway? No, Martin replied patiently, but it was only fair to say that most men would think it justified. How did one start going about an appeal to the Visitor? Howard went on, beginning to look tired, confused, and absent-minded, his eyes straying to his wife, as though it was she only that he wanted.

Martin continued to reply, ready to bat on about procedure. It was Howard who said that he wasn't going 'to do anything in a hurry', that he had 'had enough for one night'. He left the room with his arm round Laura, and once more the two of us, watching them, felt like *voyeurs*.

After the door had closed behind them, Martin sat gazing into the grate. At last I said: 'Were you prepared for this—?' I pointed to the slip of paper with the Seniors' verdict.

'I wish I could say yes.'

He answered honestly, but also in a rage. Despite his caution and his warnings – or perhaps because of them – he had been totally surprised, as surprised as any of us. He was furious with himself for being so, and with the men who caused it.

'There'll have to be a spot of trouble now,' he said, able, since the Howards went, to let the anger show. People often thought that those who 'handled' others, 'managers' of Martin's kind, were passionless. They would have been no good at their job if they were. No, what made them effective was that they were capable of being infuriated on the one hand, and managerial on the other.

Vexed as he was, Martin did not lose his competence. There were two tasks in front of him straightaway, first to prevent any of his party doing anything silly, second to keep them together. Without wasting time, he said that we had better walk round and see Skeffington; he had heard him say that he was going to dine at home.

When we got to the bottom of the staircase, Martin looked across the court. The chapel door was open wide, a band of light poured on to the lawn; a few young men, gowns pulled round them, were hurrying away from evensong.

'It isn't anything special in the way of festivals, is it?' said Martin, nodding towards the chapel.

We paused for an instant. There was no sign of Skeffington coming round the path; there was only the chaplain, shutting the door behind him.

Not there, said Martin. We went through the screens, bustling and jostling with young men, some pushing early into hall, some swinging off with beer-bottles. In the second court there were lights in old Winslow's rooms.

'I wonder what *he* thinks he's doing,' I said.

'He's never had any judgment,' said Martin. 'He took you all in, but he never had much sense.'

I was thinking, as Martin unlocked the side door, how I had seen Winslow in his full power, a formidable man: and how the stock exchange of college reputations went up and down, so that Martin, nine years younger, saw him only as a failure. On that stock exchange, Brown's reputation had kept steady since my time, Crawford's had climbed a lot,

Nightingale's had rocketed – while men whose personalities filled the college when I was there, Winslow, Jago, had already been written off long before their deaths.

We crossed to the row of cottages and Martin pulled at the handbell on Skeffington's. There was no answer, although from the living-room, faintly lit, came a sound of voices. Martin pulled again. Suddenly lights sprang up behind the curtains, and substantial steps came to the door. It was Mrs Skeffington. As she opened the door, her face was reddened, her manner flustered. She said: 'Oh, it's you two, is it? I'm afraid you've caught me on the wrong foot.'

Martin asked if Julian was there.

No, she was alone, he had gone off for a meal at a pub.

Could we come in, since Martin wanted to leave a messge for him?

'You've caught me on the wrong foot,' Mrs Skeffington repeated, as we sat there in the living-room. I thought I knew why she was so embarrassed. It wasn't, or at least not immediately, because Julian had gone off alone. She had lived a long time with a marriage which had worn dry, so that she had forgotten how to conceal it, if indeed she had ever tried. No, it was something much sillier. She had been sitting by herself in that little parlour, with a tray in front of her, scrambled eggs on toast and a good stiff whisky: and the sounds of voices which we had heard in the lane outside came from the television set. It was now safely turned off, but Mrs Skeffington looked like a great, chapped-cheeked schoolgirl caught in the act: her hearty, brick-dropping, county assurance had dropped from her quite. She couldn't believe that men like Martin and me would have spent such an evening. She had an impression, which filled her with both ridicule and awe, that her husband's colleagues spent their entire existence at their books. She was certain that if we saw what she had been enjoying, we should despise her. With dazzled relief, she realised that we were not going to question her or comment. She poured out whiskies for us both, drank her own and helped herself to another. She drank, it seemed to me, exactly as her brothers would have done after a day's hunting.

Martin was set on getting her to understand his news. 'Look, Dora, this is important.' Next morning, by the first delivery, Julian would get the Court's decision. Martin told her the form of words.

'That's a slap in the eye for some of you, isn't it?' she said. 'They're as good as saying that old Uncle Cecil wasn't up to any monkey-business, aren't they?'

'Yes, they're certainly saying that.'

'Well,' said Dora Skeffington, 'I must say I'm rather glad. None of my family ever thought much of Cecil. My mother used to say that he was a bit common, though I never understood how she made that out. But still he did more than some of them and he was always decent to me when I was a little girl.'

She sat back, basking in the comfort of family piety and several drinks. But she was neither stupid nor, except when she felt it was due to herself, obtuse. She felt the absence of response. She said:

'What's the matter? Don't you believe the old man's all right?'

'Not for a minute. Nor will Julian. That's why I don't want him to fly off the handle—'

Martin told her that this meant that the affair had only got worse. None of the revisionists could accept this verdict, neither Julian, nor he, nor Francis, nor any of their followers. All it meant was that they were back where they started, with passions higher. The danger was, Julian might make things worse, if he insisted on behaving like a 'wild man'. Martin's plan was to call a meeting of the majority by the end of the week. Would she tell Julian to keep out of action until then?

'I'll tell him,' said Dora. 'Mind you, I don't know what good it'll do.'

She sounded both sad and jocular. Sad because it was a disappointment that old Palairet wasn't going to be left in peace, and sad too because she couldn't answer for her husband and spoke of him as one might speak of a not-very-close friend. And at the same time amused, because somehow she thought of her husband, not only as someone worth a certain kind of admiration, but also as a bit of an ass. Superb, handsome, high-minded, priggish, high-principled, extravagantly brave – that was how others saw him, but not she. Yet she was utterly loyal. Loyal partly because it was both her nature and training to be so: but also, oddly, just because their marriage had worn so thin and dry. Somehow that strengthened their knockabout, not-very-close friendship, instead of weakening it. They had become allies, neither of them humorous, each of them priding themselves on 'seeing the joke' in the other. It meant that, when she had to choose between Palairet's good name and her husband's principles, or even her husband's whims, there was no choice for her. She would make higher sacrifices than that for him. With her own kind of clumsy devotion, she was with him whatever he wanted to do. Others might admire him more, other women might long for the chance of admiring him, but she happened to be married to him.

CHAPTER XXI

TWO APPROACHES TO A STATESMAN

THE next evening, Walter Luke and I came back from a day of negotiations late but pleased with ourselves. It was too late to talk in our rooms: we went straight into the combination room, affable because, as Luke was saying, most of what we had come for was 'in the bag'. As soon as we entered the room, however, no one could have stayed affable. We had walked right into the hiss and ice of a quarrel. G. S. Clark was standing there, his useless leg braced against the table, Nightingale behind him. Two or three of the young scientists were talking angrily and did not lower their tone as we came in. Francis Getliffe was listening, with an expression fine-drawn, distressed, furious. One of the young men was saying that it was 'an outrage'.

'Aren't you going in for propaganda?' replied Clark.

'I've got to say,' Francis interrupted, 'that I've never seen anything worse handled.'

'What do you mean, worse handled?' said Nightingale, smiling, more in control than the others.

'Do you really think you can fob us off without an explanation?' said a scientist.

'Do you really think the Court didn't consider that?' G. S. Clark was asking.

'Do you know better than we do what they considered?'

'I'm prepared to trust them,' said Clark.

'I should like to know why.'

'I'm sorry,' said Clark, 'but that seems a little adolescent. I should have thought it reasonable to trust a Court of Seniors of this college to behave at least as responsibly as you would yourself.'

For some instants, Luke had been standing, for once looking stupefied and incapable of action, on the edge of the fracas. He asked: 'What is all this?'

'I don't know how much you ought to hear, Luke, not being a fellow—' Nightingale began.

Luke broke in:

'Oh, come off it, Alec. Is it the business I was talking to Crawford about two nights ago—?'

'I think you're bound to be told this some time,' said Nightingale. 'The Seniors have been sitting on an appeal on behalf of a man called

D. J. Howard. We've just informed the college that we've had to decide against him.'

Luke stared round at the angry faces.

'Well,' he said, 'I hope to God you've got it right.'

He was oddly at a loss. He had forgotten, if indeed he had ever paid much attention to it, how intense and open the emotions could show in a closed society like this. For fifteen years he had been used to high scientific affairs. He had seen great decisions taken, and had at least twice forced a great decision himself. He had been in the middle of a good deal of politics, but it had been controlled, official politics, with the feelings, the antagonisms, the hates and ambitions, kept some distance beneath the skin. It hadn't been different in kind from the college's politics, but there was a difference – Luke had forgotten how much – in nakedness and edge. The curious thing was, in terms of person-to-person conflict, when one moved from high affairs to the college one moved from a more sheltered life to a less.

It was the precise opposite of what most of us would have imagined. Just as, I thought, most of us would never have imagined another move, from a more sheltered life to a less. Observe the lives of tycoons, like my acquaintance Lord Lufkin, or boss administrators, like Hector Rose; they had much power, they carried responsibility, they were hard-working to an extent that the artists I knew could not begin to conceive. And yet, in a special sense, they were also sheltered. Neither Lufkin nor Rose had met a direct word of hostility for ten years: they did not have to listen to a breath of criticism of themselves as persons. While people whom they, the bosses, thought passed happy-go-lucky lives, the artists living right out of 'the world', had to take criticism, face to face, as straightforward as a school report, each week of their lives as part of the air they breathed. The artists were as exposed as much as the open politicians, the parliamentarians: those were the groups who were not sheltered at all.

As the butler announced dinner, Brown had walked into the combination room: President for the night, he took Luke and me into hall behind him. After grace, his eyes peered down the high table. Francis Getliffe and Martin were several places down from the President – and beyond them, having arrived late, was Skeffington, his head inches above any man's there.

From the head of the table, Brown watched the faces – and then, in his unfussed way, he talked to Luke and me as though it were a perfectly ordinary evening, as though, after his ten thousand dinners at the high table, this was just his ten thousand and first. The immemorial topics: new buildings: the flowers in the garden: which head of a house was retiring next. Walter Luke wasn't specially designed to meet that unflurried patter. Once Brown broke it, and asked us a question, wrapped up but shrewd, about the 'military side' of Luke's work. Brown did not approve of pacifism; if horrific bombs could be made, of course his country ought to make them. Then he returned to harmless talk, deliberately small beer, produced – since Brown was not afraid to seem boring – to damp down controversy, and to prevent anyone raising 'awkward subjects'.

It went on like that at our end of the table. It might have been a college evening at its most placid. To Luke, who went away immediately after dinner, it must have seemed that the excitement had died. When Brown took his seat in the combination room, he asked the junior fellow to see whether the company wanted wine, and himself called out to Francis and Martin – 'Won't you stay for a few minutes?' They were standing up: they glanced at each other, and Francis said that they had some business to attend to. Still speaking as though all were smooth, Brown said, 'Well, Julian, what about you?' Skeffington also had been standing up: but when he heard Brown's question, he dropped into a chair not far from Brown at the combination room table.

'That's right,' said Brown.

'No, Mr President,' Skeffington threw his head back, 'it's not right at all.'

'Can't you stay?'

'All I want to do is to tell you this is a bad show, and I for one am not prepared to sit down under it.'

'I'm sorry to hear you say that,' Brown said, playing for time. 'I suppose you must be talking about this decision, which the Seniors couldn't see any alternative to making—'

'There was a very simple alternative, Mr President.'

'What was that?'

'To admit that there'd been a crashing mistake. Then to make it up to the poor chap.'

'I'm sorry,' said Brown. 'We're all human and liable to error, but on this particular issue, speaking for myself, I've seldom been more certain that I was right.'

'Then it's time we had someone unprejudiced on this wretched Court—'

'Are you seriously suggesting that we should give up our places on the

Court of Seniors simply because we don't find ourselves able to accept your judgment?'

'No. Simply because you don't want to admit the facts when you see them.'

Brown said, dignified and still equable in tone: 'I think we'd better leave this for tonight. I don't think you will persuade us to abdicate our responsibility, you know. I fancy we'd better leave it for tonight and talk it over later, if you feel disposed.'

'No. I feel disposed for something which will bring results.'

At that, Martin, who had been standing behind us, said to Skeffington that it was time to go.

'I intend to have results and have them quickly,' cried Skeffington. 'I am not going to have this innocent chap left with a black mark against him while you put us off with one sidestep after another. If you can't give us a decent constitutional method of getting a bit of simple justice, then we shall have to try something else.'

'I'm not clear what else you can try,' Brown replied.

'I am ready to make the whole case public,' said Skeffington. 'I don't like it, it won't do much good to any of us or to this college. But it will do some good to the one chap who most needs it. The minute we've let a breath of fresh air into this wretched business, you haven't got a leg to stand on.'

'I hope I don't understand you, as I am afraid I do,' said Brown. 'Are you intending to say that you're prepared to get the college *into the papers*?'

'Certainly I am.'

'I'm obliged to tell you,' said Brown, 'that I'm astonished to hear the bare suggestion. All I can hope is that when you've slept on it you will realise how unforgivable all of us here would judge any such action to be.'

Skeffington replied, 'Don't you realise some of us here won't sleep at all? It's better than letting this chap be done down for ever.'

'I repeat,' said Brown, 'I hope you'll sleep on it.'

'Unless someone else can think up a nicer way, I'm ready to blow the whole thing wide open.'

'I should be surprised if you didn't think better of it.'

'I shan't.'

Skeffington's wild irritability seemed to have left him. He glanced over his shoulder at Francis and Martin, still waiting for him. He stood up, proud, vain, sure of himself. With the return of a naval officer's politeness – towering over the table, he appeared so theatrically handsome that he looked more like an actor playing a naval officer – he said, 'Good-night, Mr President', and the three of them went out.

Brown returned the good-night, but for a few moments he sat thinking, the decanter static before him in its silver runner. Two or three of the scientists had followed the others, and there were only half a dozen of us scattered around the long table. Of these Nightingale stayed until the decanter had gone round, and then, apologising to Brown, said that he had an hour's work to do before he went home. He spoke good-temperedly, not making any reference to the scene we had all witnessed. Neither did Clark, who departed soon after; he did mention, however, that he would be ringing Brown up that night or next morning, and it sounded like business. I hadn't much doubt that there would be other telephone calls about Skeffington's threat before the end of the night.

Soon Tom Orbell and I were left alone with Brown. He summoned Tom from the far end of the table, telling him to sit at his left hand. 'It's rather a small party for an April evening,' said Arthur Brown, and proceeded impassively to tell us how, as a junior fellow, he had found himself the only man dining at high table, one night in full term. But Brown's front was not impregnable. At the end of the story he became silent; just for an instant, he was too much preoccupied to be master of ceremonies; he turned to me and said, 'I know you are inclined to believe that the Seniors' judgment isn't the right one, Lewis.'

'I'm afraid I do,' I said.

'But you wouldn't deny that our friend Skeffington made an exhibition of himself, would you?'

For once Brown, the most solid of men, was asking for support. He was speaking to me not as an opponent, but as an old friend.

I could not help replying:

'I should have preferred him to do it in a different way, of course I should.'

'I thought you would,' said Brown, with a smile relieved, comradely, but still brooding, 'I thought we should agree on that.'

Just then Tom put in, deliberately innocent, his eyes wide open, as though he were exaggerating his youth: 'I wonder if you'd let me say something, Arthur?'

'My dear chap?'

'I think you know that, like Lewis, I don't see quite eye to eye with you over this. On this one single occasion, I do very sincerely think you're wrong.'

'I appreciate that,' said Brown.

'It's the only time since I've been here that, when it's come to a decision, I haven't felt you were incomparably righter than anyone else.'

'You're much too kind to me.'

Brown was watching Tom with care. He knew – it didn't take a wary man to know – that Tom was up to something. For what purpose Tom was trying to get round him, he couldn't foresee. I was thinking that Tom, quite apart from his hidden violence, was a subtle character. He was fluid, quick-moving, full of manœuvre, happy to play on other men. But, like other subtle characters, like R. S. Robinson, who had done mischief in my first marriage, he was under the illusion that his manœuvres were invisible. In fact, they were seen through, not only by people like Brown and me, but by the simplest. And that was true of most subtle men. As they went round, flattering, cajoling, misleading and promising, the only persons who found their disguise totally convincing were themselves.

'So I was wondering if you'd let me ask one question. Don't you think it might be a mistake to be too intransigent over this? I respect your attitude. I respect your opinion on the justness of the affair, though quite sincerely I can't agree with it. But don't you think it might be a mistake – well, one might call it a mistake in tactics, if you don't misunderstand me, to be too intransigent? Because there are several people like me who would follow your lead over anything else, who simply can't do it over this. And I do suggest it might be a mistake to put them off too much.'

Brown replied, 'I think I can speak for the other Seniors. Naturally we realised that the decision couldn't be a popular one.'

'I really wasn't thinking of the other Seniors. If I may say so, Arthur, I was thinking of you.'

'No,' said Brown. 'Again I'm not betraying a confidence, I think, when I say there is no difference between us on the Court.'

'There is one very important difference, if you'll allow me to say so.'

'What do you mean?'

'I mean, that none of the other Seniors is a candidate for the Mastership this autumn, and you most certainly are.'

Brown's face was heavy: 'I don't see where this is leading us.'

'There's something I've wanted to say for a long time. Perhaps I oughtn't to. I don't think you'll like it. It isn't my place to say it anyway.'

'I'd rather you did.'

Tom was put off by Brown's tone, formal and stern.

Would Tom realise, even at the last second, I was worrying, that he had misjudged his man?

He hesitated; then, once more acting the innocent, making his spontaneity into a technique, he cried:

'Yes, damn it, I will say it! Arthur, you know I want to see you get the Mastership. I want it more than anything in the college; I mean that most sincerely. And you know that some of us are working for you as hard as we can. Well, we've been a little anxious, or at least I have, about the effect your part in this affair is going to have. You see, it can't be helped, but everyone takes it for granted that you're the toughest obstacle to doing anything for Howard. If you hadn't been there, everyone assumes that something might have been patched up. That may or may not be fair, but it's what a lot of people are thinking. And, don't you see, it's bound to have a bad effect on some of those who ought to be your supporters. There's Taylor and one or two others. I've been counting on their votes, and now I can see us losing them unless we're careful. There's Martin Eliot. He's not committed to anyone. But I can't see that it would even be possible for him to vote for you if this affair goes much further. Arthur, I'm not asking you to change your mind. Of course, I know you can't. You believe what you believe, just as much as we do. But I am asking you to slip into the background and let people think you're being as fair-minded as they always expected you to be. I'm asking you to slip into the background, and let the others do the fighting.'

Brown had heard him out, but his own reply was prompt and hard. 'I should like to believe that you don't intend it.'

'I do, very sincerely'.

'You're asking me to alter my behaviour in a position of trust. I oughtn't to have to tell you that I can't consider it.'

Brown was plucking his gown round him, ready to get up from his chair. 'And it oughtn't to be necessary for me to tell you, which I will do now, since I don't wish the subject to be raised again, that during the whole course of this unfortunate business, I have not given a second's thought to any possible reactions on the Mastership election or on my chances in it.'

Brown stood up.

'I'm sorry to leave you a little earlier than I expected, Lewis,' he said. With steady steps he walked out of the room.

The interesting thing was, all Brown said was true. He had been manipulating the college for a generation. He was cunning, he knew all the ropes, he did not invent dilemmas of conscience for himself. He wanted the Mastership, and he would do anything within the rules to get it. But it had to be within the rules: and that was why men trusted him.

Those rules were set, not by conscience, but by a code of behaviour – a code of behaviour tempered by robustness and sense, but also surprisingly rigid, surprising, that is, to those who did not know men who were at the same time unidealistic, political, and upright. 'Decent behaviour', for Brown meant, among other things, not letting anyone interfere with one's integrity in a judicial process. On the Court of Seniors, he felt in the position of a judge, and so, automatically, without any examination of conscience, he fell into behaving as he thought a judge should behave. At the same time he was following, move by move, the campaign to get him votes for the autumn: but when he said that he had not so much as considered how many he would lose or gain by his judge-like stand, it sounded unrealistic for such a realistic man, but it was true.

That was a temptation which did not exist for him. It existed much less for him than for a more high-principled man like Francis Getliffe, who had wavered about Howard when he knew his duty was clear. Brown was under no such temptation; he believed that he had to condemn Howard, and guided by his code, he was not tempted to examine either his own motives or any price he might have to pay.

That was why men trusted him. His cunning, his personal skills, his behaviour, his mixture of good-nature and unbendingness, were all of a piece. As a young man, I believed, he had known unhappiness. He had known what it was like not to be loved; he always had sympathy, which came from a root deeper than good-nature, for those who had got lost in their sexual lives. But all that was long over. As an ageing man, he was utterly, sometimes maddeningly, unshakeably, at one.

Tom watched as the door closed behind Brown, utterly astonished. He could not conceive what he had done. What he had said, seemed to him quite innocuous. He was just giving legitimate political advice. It was unimaginable to him that it hit Brown as something like blackmail.

I was thinking – uncomfortably, for I had an affection for Tom and was getting concerned for him – that subtle men like him would be wiser not to play at politics.

CHAPTER XXII

'UNDER WHICH KING, BEZONIAN?'

SITTING in my room the following afternoon, I found myself with nothing to do. The bargain with the university was made, except for a formality which I could knock off next day: Laura had returned to London: I could stretch myself out on the sofa like an undergraduate, and read a novel. Just then, I hadn't my own writing to think about, for, despite the hours of leisure I had now carved out for myself in Whitehall, I had been abnormally occupied that spring and could not start another book. So, stretched on the sofa, I had nothing on my mind. I had the luxurious feeling that all time was spread out ahead. Did one feel that as a young man, and if so, did one chafe against it? Was it luxurious now just because it was the contradiction of the working life?

Before I lay down, the head porter had rung up to know if I was in my rooms. It seemed a little odd: I thought it might have to do with Arthur Brown's dinner party that night. At what he called 'shamefully short notice', Brown was organising a dinner in his rooms. For whom, and for what, I wasn't told, only that he needed me. It sounded as though he were acting fast, as though he were not glossing over the previous night.

I had not been reading for half an hour when I heard steps, a muttering of steps, outside. A tap on the door, and then the head porter, bowler hat in hand, unctuously calling out my name and announcing:

'Professor Gay!'

The old man was wrapped in a fur coat, with a silk muffler under his beard and round his neck. On his head he wore a wide-brimmed homburg, such as I had not seen for a generation. The head porter was supporting one arm, an assistant porter the other. Another college servant had been conscripted to follow behind, and so a phalanx of four entered the room.

'Ha, ha, my dear fellow! I've run you to earth, indeed I have!'

There was nothing for it but to get him into an armchair. He progressed in movements a few inches at a time, but neither embarrassed nor, so far as I could see, physically discomforted. His lungs did not seem to be troubling him, his breathing was easy. He dismissed the porters with a jaunty wave. 'Stay at your posts, men. We shall require you later. When we have conducted our business. We shall summon you by telephone. That's what we shall do.'

When they had gone, he informed me that he was going to continue to wear his hat – 'the draughts in these old rooms, one has to be careful of them nowadays.'

He looked at me, cheeks blooming, pupils white-rimmed but glance eager.

'Well, this is a surprise and a half for you, I'll be bound!'

It was.

'You can guess what's brought me here, I'll guarantee you can guess that.'

I could.

'But you couldn't guess that I should be able to find you, indeed you couldn't. Ha, ha. I have good spies. They keep me *au fait*, my spies do. I know more of what is going on than some people in this college realise. Why, you hadn't been in Cambridge half a day before I had you taped, my dear chap. Had you taped, indeed I had. That was the day before the special meeting of our so-called Court of Seniors. I knew you were here. I said to myself: "Young Eliot is here. A very promising lawyer, that young man is. He's well spoken of. He's got his name to make. Why, he might be the man for me!"'

He chuckled.

'You don't think I've come here just to make conversation, do you? Oh no. If you think that, you're vastly mistaken. No, my dear chap, I've come here for a purpose. I've come here for a purpose and a half. I wonder if you have any intimation what the purpose is?'

I had.

'Certain persons thought that I should forget,' said Gay. 'Not a bit of it. The psychological moment has arrived. I've given them every chance. If they had made amends in their last notification, even if they had mentioned my name, I should have been disposed to let them off. But no, it's no use looking back. Forward! Forward, that's the place to look. So now is the time that I bring my suit against the college.'

I was asking about his solicitors, but he interrupted me, his face shining with triumph, guile, and joy.

'Ah, my dear chap, this is where we help each other. This is a case of mutual help, if ever there was one. That's why I sought you out this afternoon. I don't mind telling you, I can do with a good cool legal head like yours, just to see that we bring all our guns to bear. Fine cool heads you lawyers have. But I don't intend to take advantage of you, my dear Eliot. Indeed I don't. I've come here with a proposition. If this case goes into court, I shall insist that you act for me. That will be a fine step in your career. Why, it will make your name! This is going to be a case and a half. It's a fine thing for a young man like you, to have his chance in a *cause célèbre*. After all, it isn't every day that a man of some little note in the learned world brings an action against his own college. I said to myself: "This will be a god-send to young Eliot. It will put his foot right on the ladder. There's no one who deserves to have his foot on the ladder more than young Eliot."'

Whether he was genuinely under delusions about me, I could not tell. Did he really think that I was still in my twenties? On the envelopes, when he wrote to me, he punctiliously put down style and decoration: had he forgotten what I was doing now, or was he just pretending? Of one thing I was certain. He was completely set in his monomania, and I did not see how we were going to distract him. He wasn't the first old man I had seen whose monomania kept him very happy. And also – what one had always forgotten in the presence of his preposterous and euphoric vanity – he had throughout his life been more tenacious than most of us. It wasn't for nothing, it wasn't simply because he was enthusiastic and vain, that he had made himself into a great scholar. There had been within him the kind of tenacity that could hold him at the same job for sixty years. It was that tenacity which I had walked into the teeth of now.

I repeated, because I could think of nothing better, what did his solicitors advise?

'Ha ha, ha ha!' said Gay. 'It's what you advise that I want to hear.'

No, I told him, he couldn't take the first step without his solicitors. He gave me a look sly and meaningful, what my mother would have called an 'old-fashioned' look.

'I'll be candid with you, my dear chap, indeed I will. My solicitors are not encouraging me to bring this action, that they're not. They're absolutely discouraging me from any such thing.'

'Well,' I said, 'that makes it very awkward.'

'Not a bit of it!' cried Gay. 'Why, you young men lose heart at the first check. Who are these solicitors of mine, after all? Just a firm of respectable professional men in Cambridge. What is Cambridge, after all? Just a small market town in the Fens. I strongly advise you young men to keep a sense of proportion. My dear Eliot, there is a world elsewhere.'

That did seem a bit cool, after he had lived in the place for over seventy years.

'If you're not satisfied with them,' I said, 'I'll gladly give you the names of some firms in London—'

'And who might these be?'

'Oh, they're as good as any in the country.'

'I suppose they'll take their time, my dear chap? I suppose they're good old stick-in-the-muds? *I suppose you might tip them the wink that there wasn't any special hurry about old Professor Gay?*'

Gay waved a finger at me, not in the slightest disturbed, and full of genial malice. 'Ah, you see, my dear chap, I know your little game. You're trying to play out time, indeed you are.'

I felt the joke was against me. I said:

'Oh no, I just need to be sure that the case is in good hands. After all, anything that concerns you is rather special. If it were anybody else, we shouldn't take such care—'

'Now I think you're *humouring* me,' said Gay, still triumphant. 'Don't humour me. That's not the point at all. I want to get down to business. To business, that's where I want to get.'

I tried another tack. Professionally, there was no business I could do, I explained. If I were a barrister taking his case, I could only receive instructions through a solicitor—

'Opportunity only knocks once! Remember that!' cried Gay. 'I shall soon be absolutely obliged to ask you a question, my dear Eliot. Yes, it's a question and a half. Which side of the fence are you coming down on, young man? I've told you, it's all very well to humour me. That's all very fine and large. But it's not enough, indeed it's not. We've got to make progress. I'm not the one to be content with marking time. So that's why I'm asking you the vital question. "Under which king, Bezonian?" '

Baffled, I said that he knew he had my sympathy—

'Not good enough, my dear chap. Not good enough for the needs of the moment. Time is not on our side. Indeed it isn't. You see, I've got a little surprise for you. You could absolutely never guess what my little surprise is, could you?'

I had an awkward feeling that I could.

'I'll put you out of suspense. Yes, indeed. It's no use talking to me about solicitors. I've already provided myself with one. A fine solicitor he is. Not the man to let the grass grow under his feet. If I tell him you're our man, you'll get a letter from him before you can say Jack Robinson. So I can't give you long to make up your mind. That's as plain as a pike-staff, isn't it?'

Triumphant, he seemed ready to go.

'This is the time for action,' he cried. 'Action, that's what I want to see!'

CHAPTER XXIII

BARGAINS AT A SMALL DINNER-PARTY

UNDER the chandeliers in Brown's room, eight of us sat at the dinner table. The names themselves would have had a simple eloquence for anyone inside the affair: Nightingale, Winslow, Clark, and Brown himself, on one side; Getliffe, Martin, me, and yes, though I hadn't expected it, Skeffington, on the other. It meant, and everyone present knew that it meant, some attempt at peace-making, it was a kind of response, almost instinctive and yet at the same time calculated, which all of us had seen before in the college when feeling ran high. Perhaps Brown had a point to score or a bargain to make: that was more likely than not. But also he wanted, unsentimentally but also unquestioningly, out of a desire for comfort as well as piety, to prevent 'the place getting unliveable-in', to ensure that it 'didn't come apart at the seams'.

On the other side, men like Francis Getliffe and Martin wanted the same thing. In bodies like the college, I was thinking, there was usually a core with a strong sense of group self-preservation. That had been true in the struggles I had seen there. Passions had gone from violence to violence, the group emotions were spinning wildly, and yet, from both sides of the quarrel, there had come into existence a kind of gyroscopic flywheel which brought the place into stability once more. This was the fiercest quarrel I had seen in the college. It was not accidental that Brown and the others, the bitterest of partisans, were behaving at dinner as though they were not partisans at all.

It was such a dinner as Brown liked to give his friends. Not lavish, but carefully chosen: only Brown could have persuaded the kitchens to produce that meal at twelve hours' notice. There was not, by business-men's standards, or writers', much to drink: but what there was was splendid. Brown was a self-indulgent man in a curious sense; he liked drinking often, but only a little, and he liked that little good. That night he brought out a couple of bottles of a '26 claret. Very rare, he said, but drinkable. Winslow made a civil remark as he drank. With most of them, I thought, it was going down uncomprehending crops. No one in the college nowadays, except Brown himself and Tom Orbell, cultivated a taste in wine.

As I ate my devils-on-horseback and drank the last of the claret, I was wondering whether, if he had not made his overture to Brown the night before, Tom Orbell might have been at this dinner. True, he was junior to everyone there. But still, he was committed in the affair, and yet in all other respects was a Brown man. I couldn't help feeling that Brown would have seen good reasons for having him along. Nightingale, Winslow and Skeffington had, so I had heard, attended the first Getliffe caucus; Clark was the only man present pledged to vote for Brown. Seeing them together, seeing how differently, while they were fighting out the affair, the alignment ran, I couldn't begin to prophesy how many of these allegiances were going to survive intact until the autumn.

While dinner went on, no one mentioned the Howard case. The nearest anyone came to it was myself, for, sitting next to Brown, I gave him a précis of my talk with Gay and said that in my view they had no choice but to placate the old man, and the sooner the safer. Brown asked Winslow if he had heard.

'No, my dear Senior Tutor, I have been sunk in inattention.'

Did he realise how often that happened to him now? Was he brazening it out?

'I think we may have to ask you to form a deputation of one and discuss terms with the Senior Fellow.'

Winslow roused himself.

'I have done a certain amount of service for this college, most of it quite undistinguished, in a misspent lifetime. But the one service I will not do for this college is expose myself to the conversation of M. H. L. Gay. It was jejune at the best of times. And now that what by courtesy one refers to as his mind appears to have given up the very unequal struggle, I find it bizarre but not rewarding.'

There were grins round the table, though not from Skeffington, who throughout the meal had sat stiffly, participating so little that he surrounded himself with an air of condescension. Winslow, encouraged because his tongue had not lost its bite, went on to speculate whether Gay was or was not the most egregious man who had ever been awarded fifteen honorary degrees. 'When I was first elected a fellow, and had quite a disproportionate respect for the merits of my seniors, he was in his early thirties, and I simply thought that he was vain and silly. It was only later, as the verities of life were borne in upon me, that I realised that he was also ignorant and dull.'

In an aside, Brown told me that Gay would have to be 'handled'. 'I blame myself,' he whispered, while the others laughed at another crack by Winslow, 'for having let it slide. After the first time you gave us the hint.'

Quietly, his voice conversational, he began talking to the party, when for an instant everyone was quiet. There did seem a need, said Brown, for a little discussion. He was glad to see them all round his table, and he had taken the liberty of asking Lewis Eliot for a reason that he might mention later in the evening. All sensible men were distressed, as he was, by the extent to which this 'unfortunate business' had 'split the college'.

Then Brown, with dignity and without apology, made an appeal. He said that the Court of Seniors had spent months of their time and had now reached the same decision twice. 'I needn't point out, and I know I am speaking for my two colleagues among the Seniors present tonight, that if we had felt able to modify our decision on Tuesday, we were well aware that we should make personal relations within the college considerably pleasanter for ourselves.' But they had felt obliged to reach the same decision, without seeing any way to soften it. They knew that others in the college – including some of their own closest friends – believed that they were wrong: 'It's even worse than voting on plans for a new building,' said Brown, with the one gibe that he permitted himself, 'for dividing brother from brother.' But still the decision was made. He didn't expect their critics to change their minds. Nevertheless, wasn't it time, in the interests of the college, for them to accept the decision at least in form? It had been a deplorable incident. No doubt some of the trouble could have been minimised if the Seniors had been more careful of their friends' sensibilities. He felt culpable himself on that score. Nevertheless, it wouldn't have affected the decision; that was made now. In the interests of the college, couldn't they agree to regard the chapter as closed?

Martin and Francis, who were sitting side by side, glanced at each other. Before either had spoken, Skeffington broke in. 'So far as I'm concerned, Senior Tutor, that's just not on.'

Brown pursed his lips and gazed at Skeffington.

'I hoped,' he said, 'that you would consider what I've just said.'

'It doesn't touch the issue,' said Skeffington.

'I'm afraid,' said Francis, 'that several of us can't let it go at this stage.'

'No, that's not acceptable, Arthur,' Martin put in. 'We didn't want to, but we've got to take it further.'

That meant, since he and Brown understood each other and spoke the same language, an appeal to the Visitor. Brown was considering, but again Skeffington was quick off the mark.

'You know, Martin, that's no good for me.' He turned to Brown with arrogant awkwardness. 'I spoke out of turn last night. I'm sorry. I oughtn't to have hit the ceiling. That was a bad show. But I stick to every word I said. If there's only one way to get this poor chap a square deal, then I've got no option.'

Brown did not hesitate any more. In a round, deliberate tone, as though he were dealing with a commonplace situation, he said, addressing himself to Martin and Francis: 'Well, I can see that you haven't lost your misgivings. In that case, I have a proposition to make which might ease your minds. Put it another way: it might show you that we on the Court of Seniors realise that you still have grave doubts on your consciences.'

There was no question that Arthur Brown had come equipped. If the first offer failed, as he expected it to, then he had the second ready. There was no doubt also why he was doing it, and why in the last few hours he had worked so fast. It wasn't because Francis and Martin stayed inflexible. Brown addressed his offer to them, but really all the time it was to Skeffington that he was speaking. Skeffington's threat had forced him, even while he thought it was an outrage.

To bring the college into the public light, to 'get it into the papers', was to Brown inadmissible and inexcusable. For Skeffington to threaten this took him out of the area of responsible men. From now on Skeffington could not be trusted in college affairs, nor could his opinion carry any weight. And yet, it was he who had broken through.

The curious thing was, Brown and Martin and all good performers in closed politics often exaggerated the importance of the shrewd, the astute, the men who knew the correct moves. At least as often as not, in a group like the college, the shrewd moves cancelled each other out and the only way to win was through the inadmissible and the inexcusable.

Brown's offer was well prepared. He said that he made it after consulting the other Seniors. Nightingale nodded his head, but Winslow was sleepy after dinner in the warm room. The proposal in essence was that the Seniors volunteered of their own free will and without pressure from the college to have a third and final enquiry. But, Brown said, it was pointless their doing this without some difference in procedure. Therefore the Seniors proposed, again of their own free will, one minor and one major change. The minor change was that, under the statutes, they had the power to co-opt other members: their suggestion was that they should ask Paul Jago to serve. If he had been willing in the first instance, he would have been one of the Court all through. 'Some of us know him well, though he's rather dropped out of things in late years,' said Brown, who used to be his closest friend. 'We feel that he would bring a fresh mind to our problems. And I don't think that his worst enemies would ever have said that he was lacking in human sympathy.'

'I'm sorry to say,' G. S. Clark remarked, 'that I've hardly spoken to him.'

'Oh, in the old days, G.S., he'd have done a lot for you,' said Brown, quick to meet the unspoken opposition.

'Could you give us a little information about him?'

'What do you want me to tell you? I think Lewis will agree, he was always very good about anyone in trouble—'

That was why I wanted him on the Court. He had more human resources than most men. But it did not satisfy Clark, who looked so sensible, so reasonable, so sweet-eyed, the knuckles of his bad hand purple-raw on the table, that I felt half-hypnotised and at a loss.

'Has he any strong attachments?' Clark persisted.

'I should have said, he had strong personal attachments, if that's what you mean—'

It wasn't.

'I meant rather, is he attached to causes?'

'I shouldn't have thought so,' Brown replied.

'Well then, is he a religious man?'

'No, I couldn't say that. His father was in orders, he was a fellow of Trinity, Dublin, but I always imagined Paul reacted against Papa pretty early on.'

Clark was looking troubled. Brown added, with the cheerful laugh of one man of sane opinions talking to another, 'Of course, Paul has always been a sound conservative. In fact, he sometimes went a bit further in the right direction than I was able to follow him. You know what these old Protestant Irish families are like.'

Clark had broken into a beautiful, acceptant smile. Now at last I had it. He had been suspicious in case Jago happened to be a man of progressive views. Paranoia didn't exist only on one side, I was thinking. Clark was ready to detect the sinister whenever he heard a radical word. And that air had blown round the college, more than Francis or Martin thought, living in it, right through the course of the affair. Even at this table, most of them felt a kind of group-content and group-safety, as they heard of a sound conservative. Certainly Skeffington did, the 'trouble-maker'.

Paranoia wasn't all on one side: and then by free association, the thought of Howard, staring blank-eyed, deluded with persecution mania, asking who could have removed the photograph, flickered through my mind.

It was agreed to ask Jago.

The second change – 'and this,' said Brown, 'is why I took it upon myself to bring Lewis Eliot into our exchange of views'—came as a surprise. It was that the Court should have two lawyers in attendance, 'one, to look after the interests of Howard, and the other, if I may say so, to give some help to the Seniors themselves'.

For the first, Brown said, at his most cordial and benign, he hoped that they might obtain 'the good offices of our old friend here' – he beamed at me. He knew that Lewis hadn't practised law for a long time, but this wasn't a formal trial. He felt sure that Francis Getliffe and Martin and the others would rest quieter if they knew that Lewis was there to give Howard guidance. As for the other lawyer, it meant letting someone else into the secret, but they had in mind 'a distinguished member of the college, known to the older people here, and someone who wouldn't be overweighted by Lewis, which I think we should all feel that the circumstances required'.

Brown finished by saying to Francis and Martin that he made the offer with the full authority of the Master. Just for an instant, he sounded like a shogun speaking formally of the Kyoto Emperor. The Seniors realised they couldn't make much claim on the lawyers' time; they believed that the entire re-hearing could be compressed into a few days.

Francis Getliffe was asking me if I could manage it. Running through my pocket-book, I said that I hadn't three consecutive weekdays free until the end of June.

'That's all right,' said Martin. 'So you'll do it, will you?'

'If you can wait that long—'

'Good.' Martin spoke suddenly, freshly, and with enthusiasm. For a second, across the dinner-table, we had gone back over the years. He was no longer the hard and independent man, more capable in so many ways than I was myself. He was a younger brother speaking to an older, investing in me, as when he was a child, greater faith than I deserved.

This would mean another two months' wasting time, Skeffington burst out.

'I'm sure we all regret that,' said Brown, steady but not cordial. 'But I hope we should all agree that it would be a mistake to spoil the ship for a ha'porth of tar.'

'I don't know that I can take it.'

'You'll have to take it,' Francis said. 'Brown has gone a long way to meet us. It's a fair offer, and we've got to make it work.' Francis said it with authority. Skeffington acquiesced with meekness because, as well as having an overweening sense of his duty, he had also a capacity for respect. He had a simple respect for eminence: to him, Francis was near the peak of eminence, and he both listened to him and was a little afraid of him.

Suddenly, however, Skeffington drew support from someone who had little respect for eminence and was afraid of no one. G. S. Clark, with his gentle, petulant smile, broke in: 'I must say, with due respect, that I've a lot of sympathy for Julian's view. I couldn't disagree with him more over the merits of this case, but heavens above, I think he's right to push on with it.'

'No,' said Nightingale, 'we've got to get the right answer.'

'You're preaching to the converted,' Clark replied. 'I'm sure we've already got the right answer, and we're going to get it again.'

'We'll see what happens,' Nightingale answered, with a smile open and confident.

'I'm sorry, I still support Julian on the timetable,' said Clark. 'I don't feel like accepting delay.'

'Then you'd better feel like it. Because that's the way it's going to be.'

Nightingale said it amiably enough, and, like Francis, with authority – though Francis's came from himself and Nightingale's from his office.

'The general opinion does appear to be against you, G.S.,' said Brown. Winslow roused himself and muttered, 'Hear, hear.'

Clark smiled across Winslow at Skeffington.

'We seem to be in a minority of two. If it were a meeting, we could have our names written in the minutes.'

There was a curious accord between them. They stood at the two extremes, both utterly recalcitrant. As often with extremists, they felt linked. They had a kinship, much more than with their own sides, the safe and sensible people in the middle.

Well then, said Brown, we were agreed. He was just putting a last question, when I slipped in one of my own. I had been thinking to myself over the chance of having Jago on the Court. Would Brown mind if I took a hand in persuading him to act? Brown, anxious to concede us any inessential point, agreed at once and went on with his question.

'I should like to ask everyone round the table, presuming that the Seniors reach a decision according to the methods we've agreed on tonight, whether they could see their way to pledge themselves to regard that as the finish. I'm not asking anyone to answer here and now. But I suggest to you that it wouldn't be unreasonable, if we're to get this place back on an even keel.'

'Content,' said Winslow, suddenly revivified.

'I am very happy,' said Nightingale.

'I'm not fond of hypothetical pledges,' said Francis, 'but, yes, I think it's reasonable.'

'I agree, this must be all or nothing,' said Martin.

Brown looked at Clark.

'What is your present feeling, G.S.?'

'Oh, it's bound to turn out right,' said Clark.

'And you?' Brown said to Skeffington.

'I shall try to accept what the Seniors decide,' Skeffington replied, after a long pause, his head high, staring at the wall. 'But I'm not making any promises tonight. And I don't see how I shall ever be able to.'

CHAPTER XXIV

HERMITAGE

NEXT morning, the clock on the Catholic church was striking eleven as I walked along by Fenner's to the Jagos' house. The trees were dense with blossom; the smell of blossom weighed down the air, the sky was heavy. I was coming unannounced, and I had no idea what reception I should get. All I knew was that Brown, wishing to clinch the bargain of the night before, had seen to it that the Master sent a letter to Jago by messenger.

In the dark morning the petals shone luminescent, the red-brick houses glowed. Jago's was at the corner of a side street. I had not been there before, as, when I knew him, they had been living in the Tutor's residence: but he had owned this house for forty years, since the time when, as a young don, he had married one of his pupils. They had lived there in the first years of the marriage, and when he retired they had gone back. It was ugly and cosy from the outside, late nineteenth-century decorated, with attic gables, and, through a patch of garden, a crazy pavement leading to the front door.

After I rang, the door was opened by Mrs Jago. She stood there massive, pallid and anxious. She looked at me as though she did not know whether to recognise me or not.

'Good-morning, Alice,' I said.

At her stateliest, she called me Sir Lewis.

I said that I was sorry to appear without warning, but could I have a quarter of an hour with Paul?

'I'm afraid my husband is much too busy to see visitors,' she said.

I said: 'It is fairly important—'

'On matters of business, I'm afraid my husband has nothing to say to anyone.'

'I should like you to tell him that I'm here.'

Once she had disliked me less than she had disliked most of Paul's colleagues. She stared at me. I did not know whether I should get the door slammed in my face.

'Please be good enough to come in,' she said.

Preceding me down a passage, she was apologising for the state of the house – 'not fit for *visitors*', she cried. In fact, it was burnished and spotless, and had a delicious smell. That, too, she had worked at, for it came from bowls of pot-pourri chosen to complement the smell of wood-fires. For anyone with a sharp nose, it was the most welcoming of houses. Not in other respects, however. When Alice Jago opened the study door and cried out that I had come to see him, Jago's voice did not express pleasure.

'This is unexpected,' he said to me.

'I shan't take much of your time.'

As he stood up to shake hands, he was watching me with eyes shrewd and restless in the fleshy face.

'Perhaps I have an idea what brings you here,' he said.

'Perhaps you have,' I replied.

'Ah well, sit you down,' said Jago. His natural kindness was fighting against irritability. He might have been a man essentially careless and good-natured, intolerably pressed by his job, not knowing what it was to have five minutes free, driven mad by this latest distraction.

The study could not have been more peaceful. Out of the french windows one saw the garden, with blossoming trees spreadeagled against the wall. The room was as light, as bright, as washed free from anxiety, as though it looked out to sea. They used it together. There was one chair and table and rack of books for him, the same for her, and another rack between them. Jago saw me examining the third rack. Realising that I was puzzled, quick to catch a feeling, he said:

'Ah, those are the books we're reading to each other just now. That was a good custom your generation didn't keep up, wasn't it?'

He was saying that one of them read to the other for an hour each evening, taking it in turns. That winter they had been 'going through' Mrs Gaskell. It all seemed serene. Perhaps, in spite of her neurosis, his pride, the damage she had done him and the sacrifice he had made for her, they truly were at peace together, more than most couples in retirement, provided that they were left alone.

I was not leaving them alone. Mrs Jago gazed at me, uncertain how to guard him, protect herself. With her most lofty inflection, she said:

'May I offer you a cup of coffee?'

I said that I would love one.

'It will be cold, needless to say.'

It was not cold. It was excellent. As I praised it, Alice Jago said with rancour:

'When I was obliged to entertain because of Paul's position, no one ever wanted to come to see *me*. So naturally I had to give them decent food.'

'Darling,' said Jago, 'that's all past history.'

'I expect,' said Alice Jago to me, 'that now you've had your coffee you'd like to talk to Paul alone.'

'I hope he doesn't expect to,' said Jago. He had not sat down again, and now he moved, on soft slippers, towards her.

'I think he'll appreciate that I don't see anyone alone nowadays. Anything he wants to say, I'm sure he'll be ready to say to us together.'

'Of course,' I said. To myself, I was wishing it wasn't so. While I was thinking about it again, I noticed the books on their two reading-racks. As with others who had waited a lifetime 'to catch up with their reading', Jago's didn't appear very serious. There were half a dozen detective stories, a few of the minor nineteenth-century novels, and a biography. On Mrs Jago's rack stood the Archer translations of Ibsen, together with a Norwegian edition and dictionary: it looked as though she were trying to slog through the originals. She used to be known in the college as 'that impossible woman'. She could still put one's teeth on edge. But it was she who had the intellectual interest and the tougher taste.

'I suppose,' I said, 'you did receive a letter from Crawford this morning?'

'Yes,' Jago replied, 'I received a letter from the Master.'

'Have you answered it?'

'Not yet.'

'I hope you won't,' I said, 'until you've listened to me.'

'Of course I'll listen to you, Lewis,' said Jago. 'You were always a very interesting talker, especially when the old Adam got the better of you and you didn't feel obliged to prove that there wasn't any malice in you at all, at all.' His eyes were sparkling with empathy, with his own kind of malice. He had scored a point, and I grinned. He went on:

'But I oughtn't to conceal from you that I don't feel inclined to accept the Master's kind invitation.'

'Don't make up your mind yet.'

'I'm very much afraid it is made up,' said Jago.

Mrs Jago was sitting in the chair next to mine, both of us looking out to the garden as to the sea. He was sitting on her chair-arm, with his hand on hers.

'I don't feel inclined,' he said, 'to get involved in college affairs again. I can't believe it's good for them, and it certainly isn't good for us.'

'I'm asking you to make one exception.'

'When I was looking forward to retiring,' he replied, 'I thought to myself that I would make just one exception. That is, I should have to drag myself away from here and set foot in the college once more. But not for this sort of reason, my dear Lewis.'

'What was it, then?'

'Oh, I think I shall have to cast my vote when they elect the next Master. This autumn. It would be misunderstood if I didn't do that.'

'Yes,' said Alice Jago. 'It's a pity, but you must do that.'

At first hearing it seemed strange. The last time those votes had been cast – that was the wound, which, except perhaps in this room, the two of them had not been able to get healed. And yet, it was the sort of strangeness one could, at least viscerally, understand. I had heard more than once that he was committed to vote, not for his old friend Arthur Brown, but for Francis – as though choosing the kind of distinction which he didn't possess and which had been thrown up against him. I thought of asking, and then let that pass.

'Look,' I said, 'this is a human situation.' I told him, flat out, why I wanted him on the Court of Seniors. He was much too shrewd a man to dissimulate with. I said that I believed Howard was innocent. Jago might not agree when he heard the complete story and studied the evidence – all his prejudices, I said, for I too knew how to dig in the knife of intimacy, would be against Howard. Nevertheless, Jago had more insight than any of them. I wanted to take the chance. If he happened to decide for Howard, that would make it easier for the others to change their minds than anything I could say.

'I don't see what claim you have on me,' said Jago. 'It would be different if I knew anything about this man already.'

'Don't you feel some responsibility?'

'Why should I feel responsibility for a man I don't know and a college I've had no control over for seventeen years?'

'Because you have more sympathy than most people.'

'I might have thought so once,' he replied simply and gravely, 'but now I doubt it.'

'You like people.'

'I used to think so,' said Jago, in the same unaffected tone, 'but now I believe that I was wrong.' He added, as though he were speaking out of new self-knowledge and as though I deserved the explanation:

'I was very much affected by people. That is true. I suppose I responded to them more than most men do. And of course that cuts both ways. It meant that they responded to one. But, looking back, I seriously doubt whether I genuinely liked many. I believe that, in any sense which means a human bond, the people I've liked you could count on the fingers of one hand. I've missed no one, no one now living in this world, since we thought we hadn't enough time left to waste, and so spent it all with each other.' He was speaking to his wife. It sounded like flattery, like the kind of extravagant compliment he used to give her to bring a touch of confidence back. I believed that it was sincere.

'Haven't you found,' he turned to me again, in a tone lighter but still reflective, 'that it's those who are very much affected by people who really want to make hermits of themselves? I don't think they need people. I certainly didn't, except for my own family and my wife. I've got an idea that those who respond as I responded finally get tired of all human relations but the deepest. So at the end of their lives, the only people they really want to see are those they have known their whole lives long.'

He glanced at me, his eyes candid, amused and searching.

'If your man has had the atrocious bad luck you think he has, I'm sure you'll persuade them, Lewis. But, as far as I'm concerned, I think you can see, can't you? – it would have to be something different to make me stir.'

It was no use arguing. I said goodbye almost without another word. I thanked Alice Jago for putting up with me.

'Not at all,' she said, with overwhelming grandeur.

I went out into the street, the blossom dazzling under the leaden clouds. I felt frustrated, no, I felt more than that: I felt sheer loneliness. I wasn't thinking of the affair: it would mean working out another technique, but there was time for that. Under the trees, the sweet smell all round me, I couldn't stay detached and reflect with interest on the Jagos. I just felt the loneliness.

PART FOUR

SUSPICION IN THE OPEN

CHAPTER XXV

ADDRESS FROM THE MODERATOR

IN the Fellows' Garden, the tea-roses, the white roses, the great pink cabbage-roses glowed like illuminations in the heavy light. The garden, when I entered it that afternoon, had looked like a steel-engraving in a Victorian magazine, the sky so boding, the roses bulbous. A week earlier, there would have been young men lying on the grass, staying in college to receive their degrees: but this was the last Friday in June, and as I strolled by the rose-bushes, scuffing petals over the turf, the garden was dead quiet, except for the humming by the beehives.

It was a cold day for midsummer, so cold that I could have done with a coat. I had seen no one since I arrived in Cambridge that lunch-time. In fact, I had taken care to see no one. This was my last chance to get my thoughts in order before tomorrow, the first day of the Seniors' hearing.

The college clock struck four. The time had gone faster than I wanted, the garden had a chilly, treacherous, rose-laden peace. It was irksome to be obliged to leave: but there had been an invitation waiting for me in the guest-room, asking me to tea with the Master to meet my 'opposite number', Dawson-Hill.

As I walked through the college it seemed deserted, and I could hear my own footsteps, metallic on the flagstones. The only signs of life in the second court were a couple of lights (Winslow's for one) in the palladian building. Once past the screens, though, and the first court was as welcoming as on a February afternoon, with windows lighted in the Bursary, in Brown's set, Martin's, the drawing-room and study in the Lodge. As I let myself into the Lodge and went upstairs, I could hear Crawford's laugh, cheerful, pawky and quite relaxed.

In the study, Dawson-Hill was in the middle of an anecdote. Crawford was contentedly chuckling as I came in. At once Dawson-Hill, slender and active as a young man, though he was a year my senior, was on his feet shaking my hand.

'My dear Lewis! How extremely nice to see you!'

He spoke as though he knew me very well. It was not precisely true, though we had been acquaintances on and off since we were pupils in the same Inn over twenty-five years before.

Looking at him, one found it hard to believe that he was fifty. He stood upright in his elegant blue suit, and with his Brigade tie discreetly shining he might have been an ensign paying a good-humoured, patronising visit to his old tutor. His face was smooth, as though it had been carved out of soapstone; his hair, sleekly immaculate, had neither thinned nor greyed. His eyes were watchful and amused. In repose, the corners of his mouth were drawn down in an expression – similar to that of someone who, out of curiosity, has volunteered to go on to the stage to assist in a conjuring trick – surprised, superior and acquiescently amiable.

He said:

'I was just telling the Master about last weekend at ——' He mentioned the name of a ducal house. Crawford chuckled. He might be an old-fashioned Edwardian liberal, but he wasn't above being soothed by a breath from the high life. The ostensible point of the story was the familiar English one, dear to the established upper-middle classes – the extreme physical discomfort of the grand. The real point was that Dawson-Hill had been there. Crawford chuckled again; he approved of Dawson-Hill for being there.

'*She* is rather sweet, though, isn't she, Lewis?' Dawson-Hill went on, appealing to me as though I knew them as well as he did. He wasn't greedy or exclusive about his social triumphs. He was ready to believe that nowadays I had them too. His own were genuine enough; he had been having them since he was a boy. He never boasted, he just knew the smart world, more so than any professional man I had met: and the smart world had taken him into themselves. Why, I had sometimes wondered? He had been born reasonably luckily, but not excessively so. His father was a modest country gentleman who had spent a little time in the army, but not in the kind of regiment Dawson-Hill found appropriate for himself in the war. Dawson-Hill had been to Eton; he had become a decently successful barrister. He had agreeable manners, but they were not at first sight the manners one would expect to make for social triumphs. He was no man-pleaser, and he wasn't over-given to respect. His humour was tart, sarcastic, and as his hosts must have known by now, not what they would describe as 'loyal'. And yet – to an extent different in order from that of any of the tycoons I knew, or the bureaucrats, or the grey eminences, or the literary people, or even the genuine aristocrats – he was acceptable everywhere and had become smart in his own right.

That must have been the reason, I thought, why, when Crawford and Brown were, out of the college's three or four Q.C.s, choosing one to advise them at the Court of Seniors, they had picked on him. At one time Herbert Getliffe, Francis's half-brother, would have been the automatic choice: but Brown was too shrewd not to have smelt the air of failure, not to have suspected, as I had heard Brown say, that 'the unfortunate chap does seem to be going down the hill'. Nevertheless, the college, usually pretty good judges of professional success, had over-estimated Dawson-Hill's – not very much, but still perceptibly. He was a competent silk, but not better. He was earning, so my old legal friends told me, about £9,000 a year at the Common Law bar, and they thought he'd gone as far as he was likely to. He was clever enough to have done more, but he seemed to have lacked the final reserve of energy, or ambition, or perhaps weight. Or conceivably, just as the college was dazzled by his social calendar, so too was he.

'Well,' said Crawford, loth to say goodbye to high life, 'I suppose we ought to have a few words about this wretched business.' He began asking whether we had been supplied with all the 'data'.

'I must say,' said Dawson-Hill, suddenly alert, 'it isn't like being briefed by a solicitor, Master. But I think I've got enough to go on with, thank you.'

'I fancy our friend Eliot, who has been in on the ground floor, so to speak, has the advantage of you there.'

'That's the luck of the draw.' Dawson-Hill gave a polite, arrogant smile.

'About procedure, now,' said Crawford. 'You'll appreciate that this isn't a court of law. You'll have to be patient with us. As for your own procedure,' he went on massively, 'we were hoping that you'd be able to agree at least in principle between yourselves.'

'We've had some talk on the telephone,' said Dawson-Hill.

I said that we proposed to spend the evening after hall working out a *modus operandi*.

Crawford nodded, Buddha-like. 'Good business,' he said. He went on to ask if he was correctly informed that Wednesday night, 30 June, five days hence, was the latest Dawson-Hill could spend in Cambridge. If that were so, we had already been told, had we not, that the Court was willing to sit on all the days between, including Sunday? We had already received the names of the fellows who wished to appear before the Court? We each said yes.

'Well, then,' said Crawford, 'my last word is for your ear particularly, Eliot. My colleagues and I have given much thought to the position.' He was speaking carefully, as though he had been coached time and time again by Arthur Brown. 'We feel that, in the circumstances of this hearing, the onus is on you, representing those not satisfied with the Seniors' previous and reiterated decision, to convince the Court. That is, we feel it is necessary for you to persuade a majority of the Court to reverse or modify that decision. There are, as you know, four members, and if we can't reach unanimity I shall be compelled to take a vote. I have to tell you that, according to precedents in the Court of Seniors, which so far as we can trace has only met three times this century, the Master does not possess a casting vote. Speaking not as Master but as an outside person, I'm not prepared to consider that that precedent is a wise one. But those are the conditions which we have to ask you to accept.'

All this I knew. The college had been seething for weeks. Minute-books, diaries of a nineteenth-century Master, had been taken out of the archives. I contented myself by saying: 'Of course I have to accept them. But it doesn't make it easy.'

'The only comfort is,' said Crawford, 'that, whatever rules one has, sensible men usually reach a sensible conclusion.'

Dawson-Hill caught my eye. He was deeply conservative, snobbish, perfectly content to accept the world he lived in: but, as he heard that sublime, Panglossian remark, I thought his expression was just a shade more like a conjuror's assistant's, just a shade more surprised.

'And now,' Crawford shrugged off the business and Arthur Brown's coaching, and became his impersonal, courteous self, 'I should like to say, speaking as Master, that the entire college is indebted to you two for giving us your time and energy. We know that we're asking a good deal of you without any return at all. I should like to thank you very much.'

'My dear Master,' said Dawson-Hill.

'I wish,' said Crawford, still with imperturbable dignity, 'that the next stage in the proceedings were not an extra tax on your good nature. But, as I expect you know, we have to reckon with a certain amount of *personalia* in these institutions. In any case, I think you have had due notice?'

Yes, we had had due notice. I felt irritably – for I was anxious enough about next day to have lost my taste for farce – that it was something we could have been spared. The college had had to buy old Gay off. The way they had found, the only way to placate him and prevent him from insisting upon his place on the Court, was to resurrect the eighteenth-century office of Moderator. This was an office I had never heard of, but the antiquaries had got busy. Apparently, in days when the fellows had been chronically litigious, one of the Seniors had been appointed to keep the ring. So solemnly in full college meeting, M. H. L. Gay, Senior Fellow, had been elected 'Moderator in the present proceedings before the Court of Seniors' – and that evening after tea, Crawford, Winslow and Nightingale in one taxi, Brown, Dawson-Hill and I in another, were travelling up the Madingley Road to Gay's to be instructed in our duties.

I said that this must be one of the more remarkable jaunts on record. Brown gave a pursed smile. He was not amused. Not that he was anxious; in times of trouble he slowed himself down, so that he became under the surface tougher and more difficult to shift. No, he was not anxious. But he was also not viewing the proceedings with irony. For Brown, when one was entering a formal occasion, even a formal occasion he had himself invented, the ceremonies had to be properly performed.

We filed, Crawford leading us, into the old man's study. Gay was sitting in his armchair, beard trimmed, shawl over his shoulders. He greeted us in a ringing voice.

'Good afternoon, gentlemen! Pray forgive me if I don't rise for the present. I need to husband my energies a little nowadays, indeed I do.' Then he said disconcertingly to Crawford: 'Tell me, my dear chap, what is your name?'

Just for a moment Crawford was at a loss. His mouth opened, the impassive moon of his face was clouded. He replied:

'I am Thomas Crawford, Master of the College.'

'I absolutely remember. I congratulate you, my dear chap,' said Gay, with panache. 'And what is more, I absolutely remember why you have attended on me here this very evening.'

He had not asked us to sit down. The room was dark. Out of the window, one saw, under the platinum sky, more roses. That day the town seemed to be full of them.

'I trust you had a comfortable journey out here, gentlemen?'

'Where from?' Crawford replied; he was still off his stroke.

'Why, from the college, to be sure.' Gay gave a loud, triumphant laugh. Someone said that it was a cold afternoon and an awful summer.

'Nonsense, my dear chap. Bad summer? You young men don't know what a bad summer is. Indeed you don't. Now, '88, that was a bad summer if ever there was one. Why, I was in Iceland that summer. I was just getting into the swim of what some critics have been kind enough to call my great work on the sagas. Great work – ah, indeed. Mind you, I've always disclaimed the word "great". I've always said, call the work distinguished if you like, but it's not for me to approve of the higher appellation. Certainly not. I was telling you, gentlemen, that I was in Iceland, that bitter summer of 1888. And do you know what I found when I got there? None of you will guess, I'll be bound. Why, they were having the best summer for a generation! It was fifteen degrees warmer than in our unfortunate Cambridge. Iceland – that country was very poor in those days. They were living hard lives, those poor people, like my saga-men. Do you know, that year they managed to grow some fresh vegetables? And for those poor people that was a luxury and a half. I remember sitting down to a meal with a dish of cabbage, I can taste it now, and I told myself, "Gay, my boy, this country is welcoming you. This country is giving you all it can." I'm not ashamed to say it seemed like an omen for my future work. And we should all agree that that was an omen which pointed true.'

We were still standing up. Crawford coughed and said:

'Perhaps I ought to introduce my colleagues to you—?'

'Quite unnecessary, my dear chap. Just because one has a slip of memory with your face, it doesn't mean that one forgets others. Indeed it doesn't. Welcome to you all.'

He waved magnanimously to Brown, Winslow and Nightingale, who were standing together on Crawford's left. None of us was certain whether he really knew who they were. 'In any case,' Crawford started again, 'I expect you don't remember our legal advisers here. May I present—?'

'Quite unnecessary once more. This is Eliot, who was a fellow of the College from 1933 until 1945, although he went out of residence during the war and then and subsequently did service to the state which has been publicly recognised. He has also written distinguished books, and I am glad to say that they have reached a wide public. Distinguished, yes; I never protested about people calling my own work that. It was when they insisted on saying "great" that I felt obliged to draw in my horns. And this must be Dawson-Hill, whom I don't recall having had the pleasure of meeting, but who was a scholar of the college from 1925 to 1928, took silk in 1939, became a major in the Welsh Guards in 1943, and is a member of the Athenæum, the Carlton, White's and Pratt's.'

The old man beamed, looking proud of himself.

'You see, I've done my homework, my dear—?' He gazed at Crawford with a smile, unabashed. 'I do apologise, but your name obstinately escapes me.'

'Crawford.'

'Ah, yes. Our present Master. Master, I'd better call you. I've done my homework, you see – Master. *Who's Who*, that's a fine book. That's a book and a half. My only criticism is that perhaps it could be more selective. Then some of us would feel at liberty to include slightly fuller particulars of ourselves.'

He turned in the direction of Dawson-Hill. 'I apologise for not welcoming you before.'

Dawson-Hill who, unlike Crawford, was quite at ease, went up and shook hands.

'I attended a lecture of yours once, Professor Gay,' he said.

'I congratulate you,' said Gay.

'It was a bit above my head,' said Dawson-Hill, with a mixture of deference and cheek.

Gay was disposed to track down which specific lecture it had been, but Winslow, who had managed to support himself by leaning on a chair, enquired: 'I confess I'm not quite clear about the purpose of this conference—'

'You're not quite clear, my dear chap? But I am. Indeed I am. But thank you for reminding me of my office. Yes, indeed. I must think about my responsibilities and the task in front of you all. Ah, we must look to the immediate future. That's the place to look.'

'Do you wish us to sit round the table?' Brown asked.

'No, I think not. I shall very shortly be addressing you about your mission. I shall be giving you your marching orders. This is a solemn occasion, and I shall make every effort to stand up for my work. Yes, I want to impress on you the gravity of the task you are engaged in.' He moved his head slowly from left to right, surveying us with satisfaction. 'I remember absolutely the nature of my office and its responsibilities. I remember absolutely the circumstances that have brought you to me this evening. Meanwhile, I've been refreshing myself by the aid of some notes.' From the side of his chair he pulled out a handful of sheets of paper, held them at arm's length, catching some light from the window, and studied them through a large magnifying glass. This took some time.

He announced: 'To what I have to say in the preliminary stages, I must request Eliot and Dawson-Hill to pay special attention. I should like to call them our Assessors. Assessors. That's a term and a half. But I find no warrant for the term. However. The Court of Seniors – as I hope you have been informed – it would be gross remissness on someone's part if you have not been so informed – has recently decided upon the deprivation of a fellow. That decision hasn't been received with confidence by a number of fellows. Whether they would have had more confidence if the Court of Seniors, as by right it should, had had an older head among them – it's not for me to say a wiser one – whether in those altered circumstances the fellows would have had more confidence, why, again, it's not for me to say. This isn't the time to cry over spilt milk.' Viewing his papers through the magnifying glass, he gave us a history of what had happened. It was a surprisingly competent history for a man his age, but again it took some time.

At last he said to Dawson-Hill and me: 'That's as much counsel as I'm able to give you. The details of this regrettable incident – why, that's the task you're obliged to put your minds to. It's a task and a half, I can tell you. Now I propose to give you all my parting words.'

He gripped the arms of his chair and tried to struggle to his feet.

'No, come, you needn't stand,' said Brown.

'Certainly I shall stand. I am capable of carrying out my office as I decide it should be carried out. Indeed I am. Will you give me an arm, Eliot? Will you give me an arm, Dawson-Hill?'

With some effort we got him to his feet.

'That's better,' cried Gay. 'That's much better. Pray listen to me. This is the last chance I shall have of addressing you before your decision. As Moderator in this case of a deprived fellow, being re-examined before the Court of Seniors, I give you my last words. To the Court of Seniors I have to say: This is a grave decision. Go now and do justice. If you can temper justice with mercy, do so. But go and do justice.'

He stopped for a breath, and went on, turning to Dawson-Hill and me: 'To these gentlemen, members of the college, experienced in the law, I have to say this. See that justice is done. Be bold. Let no man's feelings stand in your way. Justice is more important than any man's feelings. Speak your minds, and see that justice is done.'

Then he called to us, and we helped him back into his chair.

'Now I wish you all success in your tasks. And I wish you goodbye.'

He whispered to us, as the others began to leave the study:

'Was that well done?'

'Very well done,' I said.

Dawson-Hill and I had followed the others and were almost out of the room, when the old man called us all back.

'Ah! I had forgotten something essential. Indeed I had. I must insist on your all hearing it. This is positively my last instruction.' He looked at one of his pages of notes. 'You intend to reach a decision on or before Wednesday next, am I right?'

'That's what we hope. But, speaking as Master, I can't guarantee it,' said Crawford.

'Well spoken,' said Gay. 'That's a very proper caution. That's what I like to hear. In any case, the time's of no consequence. There will come a time when, I hope and pray, you'll be able to reach your decision. Stick to it, all of you, and you'll get there in the end. This is where my instruction comes in. I wish to be informed, before there is any question of your decision taking effect. As Moderator, I must be the first person to receive your decision. I do not feel inclined to insist on the whole Court of Seniors making this journey to my house again. It will meet my requirements if these gentlemen, Eliot and Dawson-Hill, are sent to me with the findings of the Court. Is that agreed?'

'Is that all right with you two?' Brown said under his breath.

'Agreed,' said Dawson-Hill. I said yes.

'Our two colleagues have undertaken to do that,' said Crawford.

'I shall be waiting for them day or night,' Gay cried with vigour. 'This is my last instruction.'

As we went out, he was repeating himself, and we could hear him until we were out on the step. All this time the taxis had been waiting. When Brown got into ours, he peered at the meter and whistled through his teeth.

That was the only comment Brown allowed himself. Otherwise, while the taxi jingled back over the bridge, he did not refer to the next day, or the reason why the three of us were bundled incongruously together, driving through the Cambridge streets. He just domesticated this situation as he had done others before it. He enquired roundly, affably, prosily, about my family as though there was nothing between us. With banal thoroughness he asked if I or Dawson-Hill would find the time to see any of the university match: he speculated about the merits of the teams. It was all as flat and easy as a man could reasonably manage. I wondered if Dawson-Hill saw through, or beneath, the cushioned prosiness of Brown.

There was nothing flat or easy about dinner in the combination room that night. There were eight fellows dining, besides Dawson-Hill and me. Those eight were split symmetrically, four for Howard, and four against. The sight of Dawson-Hill and me seemed to catalyse the clash of tempers. A harmless question by Tom Orbell – how many nights would they be dining in the combination room before they went 'back into hall' – brought a snub from Winslow. G. S. Clark was asking Skeffington, politely but with contempt – 'How can you possibly believe that? If you do, I suppose you're right to say so.' This was not over anything to do with the affair, but upon a matter of church government.

Someone made a reference to our visit. Winslow, who was presiding, said:

'Yes, I must say that this is a very remarkable occasion. But I suppose we oughtn't to ventilate our opinions while this business is what I believe in the singular language of our guests' profession is called *sub judice*.'

'It's all one to me,' said Dawson-Hill nonchalantly, 'and I'm sure I can speak for Lewis.'

'No, I suggest we'd better restrain ourselves for the time being,' said Winslow. 'Which, since I am credibly informed that some of our number are not now on speaking terms, may not be so difficult as might appear.'

The air was crackling. Dawson-Hill set himself to make the party go, but instead of getting less, the tension grew. At the end of the meal, I told Winslow that he would have to excuse the two of us, since we wanted to discuss the procedure. He seemed glad to see us go. As we left the combination room, I noticed that Winslow was lighting his pipe, and Skeffington reading a newspaper. No one was willing to sit round to talk and drink wine.

CHAPTER XXVI

DEFINITIONS BY A WINDOW

IN the court, as we walked to my rooms, the sky was lighter than it had been that afternoon. On the breeze came a smell of acacia, faint because the blossom was nearly over, faint because the evening was so cold and dry. Immediately we went into my sitting-room, Dawson-Hill said: 'I must say, they've given you the Number 1 dressing-room.'

It was true, they had given me the college's best spare set. Dawson-Hill, so he said, observing mine, had to put up with one much inferior. He observed it with a dash of surprise and no discernible rancour. In fact, he seemed to draw an obscure pleasure from changes of fortune, from the sheer worldliness of the world.

When we had first met, he had been the young man with the future, the brightest catch among young barristers. I had been a young provincial, said to be clever, but not in his swim. He had been polite, because that was his nature: he had laid himself out to amuse, because he had rather people round him were happy than unhappy: but he hadn't expected to see much of me again. Our acquaintanceship had gone on like that for years. Then I left the Bar, and he went on. He thought he had done pretty well. But he was a little surprised to find that, somehow, by processes which to him were pleasurably mysterious, I had become better known. He was surprised, but not in the least hipped. This was the world. Clever chaps bobbed up when you didn't expect them. It just showed that one often judged wrong. He was not an envious man, and nothing like so much a snob as he looked. He was ready to accept that I deserved what had happened to me. It made him like me more.

But, though he liked me more, he was as tough as he had ever been. He wasn't the opponent I should have chosen. Partly because he was in practice, and I had not done any real legal work for years. But much more because, though he sounded a playboy, he was hard-willed, the least suggestible of men.

As we sat in the window seat, gazing into the garden on the cloud-grey summer evening, chatting casually before we started business, I had only one advantage. It was not just that I knew the background of the case better: that didn't count for much against a lawyer of his class. But I also knew the people better. That might cut both ways: it wasn't all gain: but it was all I had to play with.

'Perhaps we'd better settle one or two things,' I said. We faced each other on the seat. It all looked slack, informal: it wasn't as informal as all that, and it went very quickly. 'We can't expect them to keep to the rules of evidence, can we?' said Dawson-Hill.

'That won't happen,' I said.

'We'd better tell them, when something wouldn't be evidence in court. Agreed?'

I nodded.

'Apart from that, it'll have to be catch as catch can. Agreed?'

Again I nodded.

'It's taken for granted we talk to members of the Court as and when they want us to? For instance, I am invited to dine with the Master on Monday night. I won't pretend the case isn't likely to crop up. Any objections?'

'None.' He needn't have asked. There wasn't any analogy in law that I could think of. He had been asked down to advise the Seniors, who were also the judges: what was to stop him talking to them?

'Well, then, Lewis, I think it's for you to start tomorrow.'

'What about your starting the case against Howard first?'

'No, no. You're arguing against a decision.' Dawson-Hill gave his superior, mouth-pulled-down smile. 'The Master made that clear at tea-time. And if he hadn't, it stands out a mile from the papers. No, no. You start tomorrow.'

I should have to give way in the end; I might as well give way quickly. But it was a point to him. In this case, I would much rather he had to make the running.

'So who are you going to bring in tomorrow?' he asked, after I had acquiesced. This wasn't mild curiosity. He wanted to know the schedule of my case, and he was within his rights.

'Howard.'

'You're starting with him, are you?' He was smiling. It was another point to him. He knew what it meant, the instant I said it – I was not confident of my chief witness.

'I fancy,' he went on, with a touch of neutral professional comment, 'that if I spend a bit of time on him, that might keep us most of to-morrow.'

'I fancy it might,' I replied. On Sunday, I reported, I should bring in Skeffington, Martin, Francis Getliffe. I didn't see why we shouldn't get them all into the morning session. Who was he going to call?

'Only one. The man Clark.'

'What's he going to say?'

Again this was a professional question, and this time it was I who was within my rights.

'Character-evidence. Character-evidence of a negative kind, I'm afraid. Reports of your chap Howard discussing his work.'

'Can you possibly think that that's admissible?'

'My dear Lewis, we've agreed, you can tell them what wouldn't be allowed in law.'

'It's going pretty far.'

'It's not going as far,' said Dawson-Hill, 'as Mr Howard and his supporters seem to have gone. Or am I wrong?'

Sitting there in the subdued light, his face even more unnaturally youthful because one could not see the etching beneath his eyes, he might have been asking me to have a drink. And yet, I suddenly realised that he was committed. He was not just acting like an eminent lawyer doing a good turn for his old college. That was true, but it wasn't all..

Up to that moment, I had been taking it for granted that, as a natural conservative, his feelings would be on the side of authority. I had also taken it for granted that, as a good professional, he would want the side that brought him down to win. Both these things were true – but they were nothing like all. Reasonable and off-hand as he sounded, he was as much engaged as I was. He was dead set against Howard, and perhaps even more against 'his supporters'. Another phrase which he used, in the same high, light, apparently careless tone, was 'the Howard faction'.

It was a warning. Now I had had it, I stopped that line of conversation.

Instead I said that it was time we defined what was 'common ground'. If we didn't, there was no chance of old Winslow keeping up with us, or even Crawford, and there would be no end to it.

'I can't for the life of me,' said Dawson-Hill, once more off-hand, professional, 'see how they're going to spin it out beyond Tuesday morning. And that's giving them all Monday to natter, bless them.'

'Tuesday morning?' I told him he had never lived in a college.

The spirit of personal feeling had passed. We were down to business again.

'All right,' said Dawson-Hill. 'Common ground?'

'Do we agree that the photograph in Howard's thesis, reproduced in his paper, was faked? That is, it was a deliberate fake by *someone*?'

'Agreed.' This was the photograph, with the expanded drawing-pin hole, which had set the affair going.

'Your line, of course, is that it was faked by Howard. Mine is that it was faked by old Palairet. Agreed?'

'Not within the area of common ground,' said Dawson-Hill, sharp on the draw. It was the way we were going to argue, he conceded, but he wouldn't agree to more. I hadn't expected him to.

'But I think this,' I said, 'must be common ground. The missing photograph in Palairet's note-book. The caption under that photograph refers, in the opinions of the scientists I'm calling, to a photograph similar to the one in Howard's thesis and by definition faked. I don't expect you to admit that the caption does necessarily bear that meaning. But assume that the photograph were not missing and that it was faked – then is it common ground that it must have been faked by Palairet?'

'I don't see any need to accept that.'

'I see great need.'

'I'm sorry, Lewis, I'm not playing.'

'If you don't, I shouldn't be able to leave it there. You see, the Court have listened to the college scientists often enough. I should have to insist on getting scientists from outside to examine Palairet's note-books—'

'You can't do that.'

'Can't I?'

He stared at me.

'You can't bring all this out in public, simply to prove a platitude? If there really had been a faked photograph stuck in the old man's notebook, then it wouldn't need outside scientists to tell us that in all reasonable probability he must have produced the photograph himself—'

'That's all I'm asking you to agree on.'

'It's extremely hypothetical and extremely academic.'

'Well, if necessary, I should want responsible scientists to confirm it.'

'The Seniors wouldn't be pleased if you brought them in.'

I was sure – and I was counting on it – that he had been warned by the Master and Brown that, whatever he did, none of the proceedings must leak outside.

'I shall have to bring them in,' I said, 'unless you and I agree on this as common ground.'

'Do you think the Court would dream for a moment of letting you?'

'In that case, I shall have to make myself more unpleasant than I want to.'

'You wouldn't do your case any good,' he said. 'You wouldn't do yourself any good, as far as that goes. And it's remarkably academic anyway. I'm sorry, but I don't believe you mean it.'

I replied, 'Yes, I mean it.'

Dawson-Hill was studying me, his eyes large, not as gay as the rest of the young-seeming face. He had met me as an acquaintance over nearly thirty years. Now he was trying to decide what I was like.

'Right,' he said lightly, without a change of expression. 'It's too trivial to argue over. Common ground.'

Each of us said he had no other point to raise. We smoked cigarettes, looking out into the garden. Soon afterwards, with a cheerful, social good-night, he left.

Through the window I caught the scent of syringa mixed with the late-night smell of grass. For an instant it pulled a trigger of memory, flooding me with feelings whose history that night I could not recall. Then my mind started working again in the here and now. I had not told Dawson-Hill that, over the missing photograph, I held a card whose value I was not certain of, and which I was still undecided whether or how to play. But I might have to.

One night a few weeks before, sitting with Martin, working up what I should say before the Seniors, I had asked – what I was sure he had asked himself too – just why that photograph happened to be missing. I had said that of course it could have been an accident. I had gone on to ask whether it could have been deliberate. Neither of us replied: but I believed the same answer was going through our heads.

It had been a half-suspicion of mine for months, ever since, perhaps before, Martin and I had listened to Howard's outburst, and Martin had threatened him that if anyone else heard him it would ruin his case. It was the kind of suspicion that others must have had, so fantastic, so paranoid, that one did not bring it to the surface. With me, it had flared up as I listened to G. S. Clark at Brown's dinner-party.

Last Christmas, before Palairet's notebooks reached Skeffington, there had been only one person with the chance to handle them. That was Nightingale. Was it credible that Nightingale had seen the photograph first, realised that it was a fake which proved Howard's story true, and pulled it out?

It didn't matter what I believed, but only what I could make others believe. If I were going to do the slightest good in front of the Court, I could not myself let out even the hint of a suspicion. That was simple tactics. To Crawford, Brown and Winslow, such a suspicion coming from me, as I acted as Howard's lawyer, doing my best with his case, would kill that case squalid dead.

And yet, that suspicion might have to be set to work within them. Staring sightlessly at the dark garden, I wasn't hopeful, I didn't see the way through. I couldn't do it. Who could, or would?

CHAPTER XXVII

COMBINATION ROOM IN THE MORNING

NEXT morning I had breakfast late, as I used to when I lived in college. The kidneys and bacon, the hard toast, the coffee: the sunlight through the low windows: the smell of flowers and stone: it gave me a sense of *déjà vu* and in the same instant sharpened the strangeness of the day. Under the speckled sunshine, I read my newspaper. I had asked Martin and the others to leave me alone this first morning before the Court. All I had to do was ring up the head porter and tell him to see that Howard was available in college from half-past ten. Then I went back to my newspaper, until the college bell began to toll.

The single note clanged out. It was five to ten, and we were due in the combination room on the hour. I walked through the fresh, empty, sunny court, the bell jangling and jarring through my skull. Through the door

939

which led to the combination room, Arthur Brown, gown flowing behind him, was just going in. Following after him, from the lobby inside the door I borrowed a gown myself.

The bell tolled away, but in the room the four Seniors and Dawson-Hill had all arrived and were standing between the table and the windows. At night, the table dominated the room: but not so in the morning sunlight. The high polish on the rosewood flashed the light back, while outside the lawn shone in the sun. Seven chairs were set at the table, four on the side near the windows, the others on the fireplace side. Before each chair, as at a college meeting, were grouped a blotter, a pile of quarto paper, a steel-nibbed pen, a set of pencils. In addition to the college statutes, in front of the Master's place loomed a leather-bound Victorian ledger with gold lettering on the back, a collection of Palairet's notebooks, a slimmer green book also with gold lettering, and at least three large folders stuffed out with papers.

Good-mornings sounded all round as I joined them. If these had been my business acquaintances, it crossed my mind, they would have shaken hands: but in the college one shook hands at the most once a year, on one's first appearance each Michaelmas term. Arthur Brown observed that it was a better day. Nightingale said that we *deserved* some good weather.

Suddenly, with an emptiness of silence, the bell stopped. Then, a few seconds later, the college clock began to chime ten, and in the distance, like echoes, chimed out other clocks of Cambridge.

'Well, gentlemen,' said Crawford, 'I think we must begin.'

Upright, soft-footed, he moved to the chair. On his right sat Winslow, on his left Brown; Nightingale was on the far right, beyond Winslow. They took up the places on the window side. Crawford pointed to the chair opposite Brown, across the table – 'Will you station yourself there, Eliot?' Dawson-Hill's place was opposite Nightingale and Winslow. The seventh chair, which was between Dawson-Hill's and mine, and which faced the Master's, was to be kept – so Crawford announced – 'for anyone you wish to bring before us'.

Crawford sat, solid, image-like, his eyes unblinking as though they had no lids. He said:

'I will ask the Bursar, as the Secretary of the Court of Seniors, to read the last Order.'

The leather-bound ledger was passed via Winslow to Nightingale, who received it with a smile. It was a pleased smile, the smile of someone who thoroughly enjoyed what he was doing, who liked being part of the ritual. Nightingale was wearing a bow-tie, a starched white shirt, and a new dark suit under his gown: he might have been dressed for a college wedding. He read: 'A meeting of the Court of Seniors was held on 22 April 1954. Present the Master, Mr Winslow, Mr Brown, Dr Nightingale. The following Order was passed: "*That, notwithstanding the decision reached in the Order of 15 April 1954, the Court of Seniors was prepared to hold a further enquiry into the deprivation of Dr D. J. Howard, in the presence of legal advisers.*" The Order was signed by all members of the Court.'

'That is all, Master,' said Nightingale.

'Thank you, Bursar,' said Crawford. 'I think it is self-explanatory. I also think that we are all seized of the circumstances. Speaking as Master, I have nothing to add at this stage. Our legal advisers are now sitting with us. I have explained to them, and I believe the point is taken, that it is for Eliot to show us grounds why we should consider overruling a decision already given to the college. Eliot, we are ready to hear from you now.'

I had expected more of a preamble, and I was starting cold. I hadn't the feel of them at all. I glanced at Brown. He gave me a smile of recognition, but his eyes were wary and piercing behind his spectacles. There was no give there. He was sitting back, his jowls swelling over his collar, as in a portrait of an eighteenth-century bishop on the linenfold, the bones of his chin hard among the flesh.

I began, carefully conciliatory. I said that, in this case, no one could hope to prove anything; the more one looked into it, the more puzzling it seemed. The only thing that was indisputable was that there had been a piece of scientific fraud; deliberate fraud, so far as one could give names to these things. No one would want to argue about that – I mentioned that it had been agreed on, the night before, by Dawson-Hill and me, as common ground.

'I confirm that, Master,' came a nonchalant murmur from Dawson-Hill along the table.

Of course, I said, this kind of fraud was a most unlikely event. Faced with this unlikely event, responsible members of the college, not only the Court, had been mystified. I had myself, and to an extent still was. The only genuine division between the Court and some of the others was the way in which one chose to make the unlikely seem explicable. Howard's own version, the first time I heard it, had sounded nonsense; but reluctantly, like others, I had found myself step by step forced to admit that it made some sort of sense, more sense than the alternative.

I was watching Brown, whose eyes had not left me. I hadn't made them more hostile, I thought: it was time to plunge. So suddenly I announced the second piece of common ground. If the photograph now missing from Palairet's Notebook V – I pointed to the pile in front of the Master – had been present there, and if that photograph had been a fraud, then that, for there would be no escape from it, would have to be a fraud by Palairet.

'No objection, Master,' said Dawson-Hill. 'But I'm slightly surprised that Eliot has used this curious hypothesis in the present context.'

'But you agree to what I've said? I haven't misrepresented you?' I asked him.

Dawson-Hill acquiesced, as I knew he would. Having given an undertaking, he would not be less than correct.

While he made his gibe about the 'curious hypothesis', I had glanced at Nightingale, who was writing notes for the minutes. Apart from the sarcastic twitch, his expression did not change; the waves of his hair, thick and lustrously fair for a man of sixty, seemed to generate light, down at the dark end of the table. Like a faithful functionary, he wrote away.

I went on: Who had done the fraud? Howard? or – we had all turned the suggestion down out of hand, but some of us couldn't go on doing so – Palairet? As I'd started by saying, I couldn't hope to prove, and possibly no one alive was in a position to, that Palairet had done it. The most I could hope to persuade them was that there existed a possibility they couldn't dismiss, at any rate not safely enough to justify them breaking another man's career. I should be able to prove nothing, I said. All I could reasonably set out to do before the Court was to ask a few questions and sharpen two or three doubts.

'Is that all for the present, Eliot?'

'I think it's enought to be going on with, Master,' I said. I had spoken for a bare ten minutes.

Crawford asked Dawson-Hill if he wished to address the Court next. No, said Dawson-Hill: he would reserve his remarks, if any, until the Court had heard testimony from the fellows that Eliot was bringing before them.

Crawford looked satisfied and bland. 'Well,' he said, 'at this rate it won't take too long before we put our business behind us.' Then he added: 'By the way, Eliot, there is one point I should like your opinion on. You repeated the suggestion which has of course been made to the Court before, and also to me in private – you repeated the suggestion, unless I misunderstood you, that it was Palairet who might have falsified his experiments. And you suggested it, again if I understood you correctly, not simply as a hypothesis or a trial balloon, but as something you thought probable. Or have I got you wrong?'

'No, Master,' I replied, 'I'm afraid that's so.'

'Then that's what I should like your opinion on,' he said. 'Speaking as a man of science, I find it difficult to give any credence to the idea. I oughtn't to conceal that from you. Let me remind you, Palairet. was moderately well known to some of the senior members of the college. I should be over-stating things if I said that he was the most distinguished man of science that the college has produced in our time—'

Just for an instant, I could not help reflecting that Crawford reserved that place for himself, and to one's irritation was entirely right.

'—but I have talked to men more familiar with his subject than I am, and I should not regard it as far wrong if we put him in the first six. He had been in the Royal Society for many years. He had been awarded the Rumford Medal of the Royal Society. Several of his researches, so I am informed on good authority, are classical beyond dispute. That is, they have been proved by time. The suggestion is now that, at the age of seventy-two, he went in for cooking his results.'

(Suddenly Crawford's Scottish accent, overlain by fifty years in Cambridge, broke through and we heard a long, emphatic 'cooking'.)

'You think he could possibly, or even probably, have produced fraudulent data? Where I should like you to give us your opinion, is this – what reason could such a man have for going in for a kind of fraud that made nonsense of the rest of his life?'

I hesitated. 'I didn't know him,' I said.

'I did know him,' Winslow put in.

He looked at me from under his lids. He had been staring at the table, his neck corded like an old bird's. But his hands, folded on his blotting-paper, stood out heavy-knuckled, the skin reddish, and neither freckled nor veined by age. 'I did know him. He came up the year after the college had the ill-judgment to elect me to a fellowship on the results of my tripos.'

'What was he like?' I said.

'Oh, I should have said that he was a very modest young man. I confess that I thought also that he had a good deal to be modest about.' Winslow was in early-morning form.

'What was he like afterwards?' I went on.

'I didn't find it necessary to see him often. With due respect to the Master, the men of science of my period were not specially apt for the purposes of conversation. I should have said that he remained a very modest man. Which appeared to inhibit his expressing an interesting view on almost anything. Yes, he was a modest and remarkably ordinary man. He was one of those men who achieve distinction, much to one's surprise, and carry ordinariness to the point of genius.'

I gazed at him. He had been a very clever person: in flashes he still was. Despite his disgruntlement and the revenges he took for his failure, he was at the core more decent than most of us. Yet he had never had any judgment of people at all. It was astonishing that anyone who had met so many, who had such mental bite, who had lived with such appetite, who had strong responses to almost anyone he met, should be so often wrong.

Nightingale raised his head from his notes.

'Eliot hasn't answered the Master's question, I think.'

'No—' I was beginning, but Nightingale went on:

'You've suggested, though of course we know the suggestion isn't your own invention, and we're none of us holding you to blame—'

He smiled quite openly, smoothing the lines from his face – 'But you've suggested that a distinguished old man has gone in for a bit of scientific forgery, so to speak. And mind you, and I want to stress this once again to everyone here, a very petty bit of scientific forgery at that. I mean, this work of Howard's, or the work that's referred to in Notebook V, is trivial compared with the old man's real contribution. Nothing of this kind could possibly have added one per cent to his reputation. You're asking us to believe that a man absolutely established, right at the top of his particular tree, is going to commit forgery for the sake of that? Putting it in its lowest terms, I'm sorry, but it just doesn't wash. I think it's up to you to answer the Master's question.'

Brown turned his head towards Nightingale. Crawford nodded.

Until then, I had not known how the Court worked among themselves. I had had no sense of the balance of power. It was clear, the instant one noticed the others listening to Nightingale, that we outside had underestimated him. He carried more weight than I liked. Not that he had been offensive to me; he was brisk, efficient, impersonal, speaking to me as though we were acquaintances doing a piece of business. That impersonal tone was a strength. And it was another strength, of course, that he was immersed in the detail. More than anyone there, he knew what he was talking about.

'I can't say anything very useful, as I didn't know Palairet,' I replied to Crawford. 'But do you want me to say why I don't think it's impossible?'

'We should be interested,' said Crawford.

I caught sight of Dawson-Hill along the table. His eyelids were pulled down in a half-smile of ridicule, or perhaps of professional sympathy. It seemed incredible to him, not used to academic meetings, that they should have rushed off in chase of this red herring. No rules, no relevance, in Dawson-Hill's terms, but instead they had obstinately got their heads down to the psychology of scientific fraud.

I did my best. I reproduced the names and anecdotes Francis Getliffe had told me, when we first talked about the affair, before the audit feast. Those frauds had happened. We knew nothing, or almost nothing, about the motives. In no case did money come in – in one, conceivably, the crude desire to get a job. The rest were quite mysterious. If one had known any of the men intimately, would one have understood?

Anyone's guess was as good as mine. But it didn't seem impossible to imagine what might have led some of them on, especially the more distinguished, those in positions comparable with Palairet's. Wasn't one of the motives a curious kind of vanity? 'I have been right so often. I know I'm right this time. This is the way the world was designed. If the evidence isn't forthcoming, then just for the present I'll produce the evidence. It will show everyone that I am right. Then no doubt, in the future, others will do experiments and prove how right I was.' The little I had picked up about Palairet – it didn't seem right out of his nature. I knew, I said to Winslow, that he gave one the impression of being a modest man. I should be prepared to believe that was true. But there was a kind of modesty and a kind of vanity which were hard to tell apart – and mightn't they, in fact, be one and the same thing? Reading the rubrics in his notebook, couldn't one at least think it possible that the aura of his personality had that particular tinge? Couldn't one at least imagine him getting old and impatient, knowing he hadn't much time, working on his last problem, not an important one, if you like, but one he was certain he knew the answer to? Certain that he knew how the world was designed? Almost as though it was the world designed by *him*. And mixed with that, perhaps, a spirit of mischief, such as one sometimes finds in the vain-and-modest – 'this is what I can get away with'.

Catching Brown's gaze, I knew that I had made a mistake. It was not just that his mind was made up against Howard. It was also that he didn't like or trust what I was saying. He was a man of genuine insight, the only one on the Court. He knew the people around him with accuracy, compassion and great realism. But, although he had that insight, he had no use for psychological imaginings. As a rule, even when we were on opposite sides, he thought me sensible about people. This time, he was dismissing me as too clever by half.

It had been an awkward situation, and I had mishandled it. Under

the pressure from Crawford and Nightingale I had had no option except
to take a risk, but I had shown bad judgment. Looking round the Court,
I had to recognise that I had done more harm than good.

CHAPTER XXVIII

THE SOUND OF FALSITY

AFTER the aside on Palairet, Crawford pushed the combination room bell,
and the butler carried in a tray, on which a coffee-pot and jug struck
sparks from the sunlight. He was followed by a servant, carrying cups
upon another of the massive college trays. The Court settled down to
drink their coffee. Dawson-Hill was interested in the silverware. What
was the date of the trays? he asked, and Brown, behaving as though this
were an unexacting party after hall, replied with care. Dawson-Hill
began asking about eighteenth-century silversmiths. Each appeared to
regard it as the most reasonable of conversations.

It was the kind of phlegm, oblivious of time, that I had met, chafed
against and envied, learned to imitate without truly possessing, all my
official life. Men of affairs weren't sprinters: they weren't tied to the
clock: if you hurried them when they didn't propose to be hurried, you
were not one of them.

The college clock was chiming a quarter past eleven before the trays
were taken away. Crawford, settled in his chair, addressed me:

'Well, Eliot, I understand this is the stage in our proceedings when you
would like to bring Howard in?'

I said yes. Crawford rang. After a wait of minutes, the door opened.
First the butler, with a figure behind him. At the first sight, entering at
the dark end of the room, Howard looked pale, ill-tempered, glowering.
With one hand he was pulling his gown across his chest.

'Good-morning,' said Crawford, 'do sit down.'

Howard stood still, undecided where he should go, although there was
only the one chair vacant in front of him.

'Won't you sit down?' said Crawford, as though standing up might be
a curious preference.

Polite, active, Dawson-Hill jumped up and guided Howard into the
chair. Once again, Crawford seemed disinclined to take part himself. He
merely asked Howard if he would mind answering questions put to him
by 'our colleagues', and then called on me to begin.

Turning half-left in my seat, trying to make Howard look at me – he was a yard away along the table – I could not get his eye. He was staring, and when I spoke to him he continued to stare, not at Brown but past him, into the corner of the room, where motes were jigging in parallel beams of sun. He was staring with mechanical concentration, as though he were watching a spider build its web.

All I could do with him, I had decided in cold blood weeks before, was to make everything sound as matter-of-fact as I could manage. So I started off on his career: he had come up to the college in 1939, hadn't he? and then he had joined the Army in '41? He could have stayed and gone on with his physics – how had he managed to avoid being kept as a scientist?

His reply, like his previous one, was slow.

'I knew someone who got me put down for his regiment.'

'Who was it?'

'As a matter of fact, one of my uncles.'

'Did he find it easy?'

'I expect he knew the ropes.'

Even then, he was ready to sneer at the influence which had always been within his reach. In a hurry I passed on. He had returned to the college in '45, taken Part II of the tripos in '46? Then he had gone off to Scotland to do research under Palairet? Why?

'I was interested in the subject.'

'Did you know him?'

'No.'

'You knew his name and reputation?'

'But of course I did.'

It would be fair to say that he had been impressed by Palairet's reputation and work? I had to force him. Just as young men are when they are looking for someone to do their research under? Was that fair? I had to press it. Reluctantly and sullenly, he said yes.

'When you arrived in his laboratory, who suggested your actual field of work?'

'I don't remember.'

'Can't you?'

Already I was feeling the sweat trickle on my temples. He was more remote and suspicious even than when I talked to him in private. 'Did you suggest it yourself?'

'I suppose not.'

'Well, then, did Palairet?'

'I suppose so.'

I persuaded him to agree that Palairet had, in fact, laid down his line of research in detail, and had supervised it day by day. More than a professor normally would? Maybe. Had he, Howard, found research easy?

'I shouldn't think anyone ever does,' he said.

Some of the results he, or they, had obtained were still perfectly valid, weren't they? A longer pause than usual – no one's criticised them yet, he said. But there was one photograph which was, beyond any doubt, a fraud? He did not reply, but nodded. Could he remember how that photograph got into the experimental data? Palairet must have brought it in, he said. But could he remember how, or when? No, he couldn't. Would he try to remember? No, he couldn't place it. There were a lot of photographs, he was trying to write his thesis and explain them.

'This was a more striking bit of experimental evidence than the rest, though, wasn't it?'

'But of course it was.'

'You can't remember Palairet first showing it to you?'

'No, I can't.'

It was no good. To the Court, he must have seemed deliberately to be refusing an answer. To me, trying to pull it out, he seemed not to want to remember – or else his whole memory was thinner-textured than most of ours, did not give him back any kind of picture. Didn't he preserve, I thought to myself, any sense of those days in the laboratory, the old man coming in, the time when they looked through the photographs together? This was only five years behind him. To most of us, intimations like that would have flickered in and out, often blurred, concertinaed, but nevertheless concrete, for a lifetime.

I tried to gloss it over. I asked him if he found the fraud hadn't come to him as a major shock? Yes. He gave me no help, but just said yes. I went through his actions after the first letters of criticism had come in from the American laboratories, doing my best to rationalise them. When he was first accused, I was leading him into saying, he had just denied it. Why should he do any more? Fraud had never crossed his mind: why should he invent explanations for something he had never imagined? The same was true the first two occasions he had appeared before the Court. He had simply said that he had faked nothing. It did not occur to him to think, much less to say, that Palairet had done the faking. It was only later, when he was compelled to recognise that there had been a fraud, that he began to think that only one person could have done it.

That was why, belatedly, so belatedly that it seemed an invention to save his skin, he had brought in the name of Palairet.

How much of this synoptic version I was managing to suggest – how much the Court took in, not as the truth, but as a possible story – I could not begin to tell. I had to suggest the whole story through my questions. His answers were always slow and strained, and sometimes equivocal. Once or twice he sounded plain paranoid, as in the public house with Martin, and I had to head him off.

All the time, I was thinking, another five minutes, a question which sets him going, and it might sound more credible. But that kind of hope was dangerous. This was tiring them; it was boring them. I was accomplishing nothing. If I went on, it could be less than nothing. I felt frustrated at having to surrender, but I gave it up.

Crawford looked at the grandfather clock in the corner of the room. It was nearly twenty-five to one.

'I am inclined to think,' he said, 'that is as far as we can go this morning. We shall have to trouble you' – he was speaking to Howard – 'to join us again this afternoon. I hope that doesn't upset any other arrangements?'

Howard shook his head. This automatic courtesy, such as he received from the Master or Brown, was too much for him.

When the door had closed behind him, Crawford invited us to lunch with him in the Lodge. I wanted to say no, but I daren't leave them. As usual, one couldn't afford to be absent. So I listened to Dawson-Hill entertaining the others at the Lodge dining-table. Someone mentioned that a couple of heads of houses would be retiring this next year. 'Which reminds me,' said Crawford, 'that I suppose my own successor will have to be elected at the end of the Michaelmas term. I take it there won't be any hitch about that, Brown?'

'I think it'll be looked after properly, Master,' said Brown. He gave no sign that he was himself involved. He spoke as though he were making arrangements for the appointment of the third gardener.

As we walked in the Master's garden after lunch, Crawford discussed his plans for moving out of the Lodge. All clear by Christmas: his old house would be waiting for him. 'Speaking as a husband,' he said, 'I shan't be sorry to get back. This' – he waved a short-fingered hand across the lawn, over which tortoiseshell butterflies were performing arabesques, towards the Lodge – 'is *not* a convenient house. Between ourselves, no one knew how to build a house until the nineteenth century, and moderately late in the nineteenth century at that.'

A butterfly traced out a re-entrant angle in front of us. On my face I felt the sun, hot and calming. We walked beside the long Georgian pond, the water-lilies squatting placidly on the water, and Crawford was saying:

'No, I don't know why anyone consents to come into the Lodge. As for any of you with a wife, I should advise very strongly against it.'

Back in the combination room at a quarter past two, the sun was beginning to stream into my eyes. Nightingale drew a blind, which up to then I had never noticed, so that the room took on the special mixture of radiance, dark and hush such as one meets in Mediterranean salons.

As soon as Howard was back in his chair, Dawson-Hill started in. The tone in his questions wasn't unfriendly; it had a good deal of edge just below the flah-flah, but so it had when he spoke to his friends. He kept at it for over two hours. His attack was sharp enough to hold them all, even Winslow, awake, alert, through the slumbrous afternoon. Dawson-Hill was having a smoother job than mine, I thought once or twice, as though I had been a young barrister again, with professional envy, professional judgment, resurrected. He was doing it well.

He limited himself to four groups of questions, and his line – any lawyer could have told – had been plotted out in advance. He sounded insouciant, but that was part of his stock-in-trade. There was nothing of the dilettante about his work that afternoon. He began by asking Nightingale to give him 'the thesis'.

This was a copy of Howard's fellowship thesis, which according to custom had been deposited in the college library. It was about a hundred and fifty pages long, typed – neatly typed, by a professional – on quarto paper. It was bound in stiff green covers, with the title and Howard's name in gold letters on the outside front cover and also on the spine.

'This does seem to be your thesis, doesn't it, Dr Howard?' said Dawson-Hill, handing it to him.

'But of course.'

Dawson-Hill asked how many copies there were in existence.

The answer was, three more. In the fellowship competition, the college asked for two copies. He had used the remaining two for other applications.

'This is the show copy, though?'

'You could call it that.'

'Then this' – there was a slip of paper protruding from the thesis and Dawson-Hill opened it at that page – 'might be your star print?'

It was the positive which everyone in that room knew. It was pasted in, with a figure 2 below it and no other rubric at all. It stood out, concentric rings of black and grey, like a target for a small-scale archery competition.

'It's a print, all right.'

'And this print is a fraud?'

I wished Howard would answer a straight question fast. Instead he hesitated, and only at last said, 'Yes.'

'That doesn't need proving, does it?' said Dawson-Hill. 'All the scientific opinion agrees that the drawing-pin hole is expanded? Isn't that true?'

'I suppose so.'

'That is, this print had been expanded, to make it look like something it wasn't?'

'I suppose so.'

'What about your other prints?'

'Which other prints?'

'You can't misunderstand me, Dr Howard. The prints in the other copies of your thesis?'

'I think I re-photographed them from this one.'

'You *think*?'

'I must have done.'

'And this one, this fake one, came from a negative which you've never produced? Where is it, do you know?'

'Of course I don't know.'

For once articulate, Howard explained that the whole point of what he had said before lunch was that he *couldn't* know. He had not seen the negative; Palairet must have made the print and the measurements and Howard had taken them over.

At that, Nightingale broke in.

'I've asked you this before, but I still can't get it straight. You mean to say that you used this print as experimental evidence without having the negative in your hands?'

'I've told you so, often enough.'

'It still seems to me a very curious story. I'm sorry, but I can't imagine anyone doing research like that.'

'I thought the print and the measurements were good enough.'

'That is,' I broke in, 'you took them on Palairet's authority?'

Howard nodded.

Nightingale, with a fresh, open look of incomprehension, was shaking his head.

'Let's leave this for a moment, if you don't mind,' said Dawson-Hill.

'I'm an ignoramus, of course, but I believe this particular print was regarded – before it was exposed as a fraud – as the most interesting feature of the thesis?'

'I shouldn't have said that,' said Howard. (I was thinking, why didn't the fool see the truth and tell it?) 'I should have said it was one interesting feature.'

'Very well. Let me be crude. Without that print, and the argument it was supposed to prove, do you believe, Dr Howard, that the thesis would have won you a fellowship?'

'I don't know about that.'

'Do you agree it couldn't have stood the slightest chance?'

Howard paused. (Why doesn't he say Yes, I thought?) 'I shouldn't say that.'

Nightingale again intervened: 'There's not a great deal of substance in the first half, is there?'

'There are those experiments—' Howard seized the thesis and began staring at some graphs.

'I shouldn't have thought that was very original work, by fellowship standards,' said Nightingale.

'It's useful,' said Howard.

'At any rate, you'd be prepared to agree that without this somewhat providential photograph your chances could hardly have been called rosy?' said Dawson-Hill.

This time Howard would not reply.

Dawson-Hill looked surprised, amused, and broke away into his second attack.

'I wonder if you'd mind giving us some illumination on a slightly different matter,' he said. 'This incident has somewhat, shall I say, disarranged your career?'

'What do you think?' Howard replied.

'Not to put too fine a point upon it, it's meant that you have to say good-bye to being a research scientist, and start again? Or is that putting it too high?'

'That's about the size of it.'

'And you must have realised that, as soon as this Court first deprived you of your fellowship?'

'But of course I did.'

'That was nearly eighteen months ago, seventeen months, to be precise?'

'You must have the date.' Howard's tone was savage.

'So far as my information goes, during that time, that quite appreciable time, you never took any legal action?'

It was the point Nightingale had challenged us to answer, at the Master's dinner-party after Christmas. I had no doubt that Nightingale had put Dawson-Hill up to it.

'No.'

'You've never been to see your solicitor?'

'Not as far as I remember.'

'You must remember? Have you been, or not?'

'No.'

'You never contemplated bringing an action for wrongful dismissal?'

'No.'

'I suggest you weren't willing to face a court of law?'

Howard sat, glowering at the table. I looked at Crawford; for an instant I was going to protest; then I believed that would make things worse.

'I always thought,' Howard replied at last, 'that the college would give me a square deal.'

'You thought they might give you much more of the benefit of the doubt?'

'I tell you,' Howard said, his voice strained and screeching, 'I didn't want to drag the college through the courts.'

To me this came quite new. When Martin and I had pressed him, he had never said so much. Could it be true, or part of the truth? It did not ring true, even to me.

'Surely that would be more magnanimous than any of us could conceive of being,' said Dawson-Hill, 'in the circumstances as revealed by you?'

'I didn't want to drag the college through the courts.'

'Forgive me, but have you really this extreme respect for institutions? I rather gathered that you had slightly less respect for existing institutions than most of us?'

For the first time that day, Howard answered with spirit.

'I've got less respect for existing society than most of you have, if that's what you mean. It's dying on its feet, and none of you realise how fast it's dying. But that doesn't mean I haven't got respect for some institutions inside it. I can see this university going on, and this college, as far as that goes, long after the system you're all trying to prop up is sunk without trace, except for a few jeers in the history books.'

Nightingale whispered to Winslow. Crawford, not put off by unplacatory statements, suddenly had his interest revived and was ready to argue, but Dawson-Hill got back to work. 'Yes, and your interesting attitude towards what I think you called – existing society, wasn't it ? – brings me to another question. What really were your relations with Professor Palairet ?'

'All right.'

'But you've given me the impression that they were slightly more intimate than one would naturally expect, between a very senior professor and, forgive me, a not yet remarkable research student. That is, the impression you've tried to give us is of someone coming in and out of your room, giving you pieces of experimental data and so on, very much as though he were a collaborator of your own standing. Does that sound likely ?'

'It's what happened.'

'But can you suggest any reason why we should think it likely ? Didn't you give Professor Palairet sufficient grounds to be less intimate with you than with other research students, not more ?'

'I don't know.'

'But you must know. Isn't it common knowledge that Professor Palairet was in ordinary terms a very conservative man ?'

'He was a conservative, yes.'

'Surely, actively so ?'

'If you put it that way.'

'Didn't he ask you to stop your open political activities while you were in his laboratory ?'

'He said something of the sort.'

'What did you say ?'

'I said I couldn't.'

'Didn't he object when you appeared as one of the backers of what I believe is called a "Front" organisation ? Scientists' World Peace Conference – wasn't that the eloquent name ?'

'I suppose he did.'

'You must know. Didn't he give you an ultimatum that, if you appeared in any such organisation again, you would have to leave his laboratory ?'

'I shouldn't have called it an ultimatum.'

'But that is substantially true ?'

'There's something in it.'

'Well, then, does all this correspond to the picture, the rather touching picture, I must say, of professor–student intimacy and bliss, on which your whole account of these incidents appears to depend ?'

Howard stared. Dawson-Hill went on: 'Further, I suggest to you that your whole account of these incidents doesn't make sense, whichever way one looks. If we assume, just for an instant, that Professor Palairet did perpetrate a ridiculous fraud, and we also assume the reality of this very touching picture of the professor–student intimacy, then we have to accept that he just gave you some experimental data and you quietly put them into your thesis and your papers as your own? Is that correct?'

It sounded like another point of Nightingale's. It was a valid one. From the start, Francis and Martin had been troubled by it.

'I made acknowledgements in everything I wrote.'

'But it would mean you were living on his work?'

'All the interpretations that I made were mine.'

'Does this sound likely behaviour on Professor Palairet's part – or on yours, as far as that goes?'

'I tell you, it's what happened.'

Dawson-Hill smoothed back his hair, already smooth.

'I shan't keep you much longer, Dr Howard. I know this must be rather irksome for you. And the Court has had a tiring day.' It was well past four. The sun, wheeling over the first court, had begun to leak into the further window behind Nightingale's back, and during the last questions he slipped away from the table and drew another blind.

'Just one final question: when your work was criticised, did you take the advice of any of your scientific colleagues here? Did you take any advice at all?'

'No.'

'You did nothing. You didn't produce the idea that Professor Palairet was in the habit of providing you with photographs. You didn't produce that idea for some weeks, if I'm not mistaken. My friend along the table' – Dawson-Hill smiled at me, superciliously, affably – 'has done his best to make that seem plausible. Tell me now, does it really seem plausible to *you*?'

'It's what happened.'

'Thank you, Master. I've nothing more to ask Dr Howard.'

Dawson-Hill leaned back in his chair, elegant, casual, as though he hadn't a thought or a care in the world.

'Well,' said Crawford, 'as has just been said, we've had a tiring day. Speaking as an elderly man, I think we should all do well to adjourn until tomorrow. The members of the Court of Seniors have all had opportunity to question Howard on previous occasions.' (Crawford had been punctilious throughout in calling Howard by his surname alone, as though he were still a colleague.) 'I don't know whether any Senior wishes to ask him anything further now?'

Winslow, eyes reddened, but surprisingly unjaded, said: 'I regard that as a question, Master, asked with the particle *num*.'

'What about you, Eliot?' Crawford said.

During Dawson-Hill's cross-examination, I had been framing a set of questions in reply. Suddenly, looking at Howard, I threw them out of mind.

'Just this, Master,' I said. I turned to Howard. 'Look here,' I said. 'There's been a fraud. You didn't do it?'

'No.'

'It must have been done, in your view, by Palairet?'

Even then he could not answer straight out. 'I suppose so,' he said at length.

'Of anything connected with this fraud you are quite innocent?'

He said, in a high, strangulated tone: 'But of course I am.'

As I signalled to Crawford that I had finished, Howard fell back in his chair, like an automaton. I felt – as on and off I had felt all day – something so strange as to be sinister. I had heard him speak like that when I believed him guilty. Now, so far as I was convinced of anything about another person, I was convinced that he wasn't. Yet, listening to him at that moment, I felt not conviction, but mistrust. What he said, although with my mind I knew it to be true, sounded as false as when I first heard it.

CHAPTER XXIX

DISSERVICE TO A FRIEND

BACK in my rooms after the day's session, I lay on the sofa. On the carpet the angle of the sunbeams sharpened, while I made up my mind. At last I put through two telephone calls: one to the kitchens, to say that I should not dine that evening: the other to Martin, asking him to collect the leaders of the pro-Howard party after hall.

'In my rooms?' said Martin, without other questions. For an instant I hesitated. In college, nothing went unobserved. The news would go round before we had finished talking. Then I thought, the more open the better. This wasn't a trial-at-law, where an advocate usually doesn't see his witnesses. The only tactics left to us were harsh. So, after eating alone, I went to Martin's rooms.

As I was going up the staircase, Francis Getliffe followed me, on his way across from the combination room. We entered Martin's sitting-room together. There Martin was waiting for us, with Skeffington and – to my surprise – Tom Orbell.

It was Tom who asked me first:

'How did it go?'

'Badly,' I said.

'How badly?' put in Martin.

'Disastrously,' I said.

As we brought chairs round by the windows, I told them that Howard was the worst witness in the world. I added that I had been pretty inept myself.

'I find that hard to believe,' said Francis.

'No,' I said. 'I wasn't much good.'

I went on:

'A lot of people would have done it better. But, and this is what I wanted to talk to you about, I'm not sure that anyone would have done the trick. I've got to tell you that, as things are and as they look like going, I don't believe that this man stands a chance.'

In the golden not-yet-sunset light, Skeffington's face shone effulgent, radiant, furious.

'That simply can't be true,' he cried.

'As far as I can judge, it is.'

Skeffington was in a rage, which did not discriminate clearly between Howard, the Seniors and myself. 'Are any of us going to wear this? Of course we're not.'

As for Howard, Skeffington was ready to abuse him too. In fact, I had noticed in Skeffington the process one often sees in his kind of zealot. He was still, as he had been from the day of his conversion, more integrally committed to getting Howard clear than anyone in the college. His passion for giving 'that chap' justice had got hotter, not more lukewarm. But as his passion for justice for Howard boiled up, his dislike for the man himself had only deepened. And there was something else, just as curious. For Howard's sake – or rather, for the sake of getting him fair play – Skeffington was prepared to quarrel with his natural associates in the college: the religious, the orthodox, the conservative. All this on behalf of a man whom Skeffington, not now able to bear him and not given to subtle political distinctions, had come to think of as the reddest of the red. The result was to make Skeffington, in everything outside the affair itself, more conservative than he had ever been before. He had taken on a rabid, an almost unbalanced, strain of anti-communism. It was said, I did not know how reliable the rumour was, that he was even having doubts about voting for Francis at the magisterial election – after all, Francis had been known to have a weakness for the left.

So he was lashing out at the Court, at Howard, and, somehow, projecting all his irritation, at me.

'I can't credit that you haven't got it wrong,' he cried.

'I wish I had,' I said.

'They can't help giving him his rights. Anything else – it's dead out.'

'Listen,' I said, 'this is the time that you must believe me.'

Francis said:

'We do.'

Martin nodded his head, so did Tom. I was sitting at the end of the semicircle, watching them as they faced the glowing cyclorama of the sky – Francis fine-featured and deep-orbited, Tom like a harvest moon, Martin composed, his eyes screwed up and hard. I looked at Skeffington, his head rearing handsomely above the others.

'You must believe me—' I said.

He said: 'Well, you've been in there all day.' It was an acquiescence, it occurred to me, about as graceful as one of Howard's.

Martin intervened:

'Right, then. Where do we go next?'

He knew that I had come with something to propose. What it was, he had not guessed.

Then I started. I wanted to shock them. It was no use going in for finesse. I said that the only question which might make the Court think twice was a question we had all thought about and kept to ourselves. That is, how had the photograph got removed from the old man's notebook? Could it have been removed deliberately? If so, by whom?

'The answer to that is simple,' I said. 'If it was removed deliberately, then it was by Nightingale.'

I looked at Martin and reminded him that we had asked ourselves those questions. I believed that, even to stand a chance of getting Howard off, it had to be asked in Court. I could not guarantee that it would work. It was risky, distasteful, and at the best would leave rancour behind for a long time. Nevertheless, for the short-term purpose of justice for Howard, I had to tell them that there was no alternative move at all.

The point was, were we justified in making it? It might do Nightingale harm – no, it was bound to do him harm, innocent or guilty. How certain were we of our own ground in suspecting him? Were we going to take the responsibility of harming a man who might be innocent?

The room was hushed. Martin looked at me, brilliant-eyed, without expression. Francis's face was dark.

It was Julian Skeffington who broke the silence.

'I've never been able to see how that photograph came unstuck,' he said, without his loftiness or confidence. 'I don't know what could make a chap do a thing like that. It's not a thing I expected to think of a chap doing. Especially when he's your senior and you're used to seeing him at dinner.'

'Well?' I asked him.

'I don't pretend to like it. I wish there was another way.'

'There's no other way of giving Howard a chance. Well?'

'If you put it to me like that,' said Skeffington, reluctant but straightforward, 'then I say we have to go ahead.'

'So do I,' said Tom Orbell. 'The trouble is, we've been too scrupulous all along!'

Francis cleared his throat. He disregarded Tom, and spoke straight to me.

'You were asking if we were justified, Lewis? I should like to say we weren't. But I can't do that.'

This startled me.

'You really think we're right to do it?' I said.

'I'm afraid I've had a suspicion, from very early days.'

'Since when?'

'I'm afraid – since the three of you came to see me in the lab. last Christmas.'

That was a shock. Then, an instant later, I had another, when Martin remarked:

'I'm sorry, but I disagree with you all.'

'Have you altered your mind?' I broke out.

'No, I thought about it when we last talked, but I came down on the other side.'

Mixed with my irritation, I was moved by sarcasm at my own expense. I had felt telepathically certain that we had agreed. It hadn't been necessary to say the words. It seemed bizarre to have been so wrong, about someone one knew so well. In the whole course of the affair, this was the first occasion when Martin and I had not been at one.

'What are you holding back for?' said Tom.

'I don't believe we're entitled to do it.'

'Don't you think it's possible that Nightingale pulled that photograph out—?' Skeffington's voice was raised.

'Don't you remember that it was Nightingale who had it in most for Howard?' Tom joined in.

'Yes, I think it's possible,' Martin replied to Skeffington. 'But I'm not convinced it happened.'

'I'm afraid I think it's ninety per cent probable,' said Francis.

'I don't,' said Martin. 'You've always distrusted Nightingale, I know. So have you, even more so,' he turned to me. 'From what you've told me, it would have been remarkable if you hadn't. I know Nightingale isn't everyone's cup of tea, let alone yours. He's close, he's narrow, he's not very fond of anyone except himself and his wife. Still, I should have thought he'd tried to become a decent member of society. I'm not prepared to kick him downstairs again unless I'm absolutely sure.'

Of these four, I was thinking, Martin was by a long way the most realistic. Yet it was the men of high principle, Skeffington and Francis, whom no one could imagine doing a shady act, who could themselves imagine Nightingale doing this. While Martin, who had rubbed about the world and been no better than his brother men, could not believe it. Was it that realistic men sometimes got lost when they met the sensational – as though they had seen a giraffe and found that they couldn't believe it? Or was it more personal? In being willing to defend Nightingale's change of heart, in showing a heat of feeling which came oddly from him, and which had surprised us all, was Martin really being tender to himself? For he, too, of course, had tried to make something different out of his life.

'I think there's substance in what Martin says,' said Francis, 'but still—'

'Look here,' cried Tom, eyes flat, face thrust forward, with the touch of cheerful hypomania which sometimes changed trigger-quick into temper, 'from what old Lewis tells us, you have this choice. Either you raise a doubt about Nightingale – which I must say seems to me a perfectly legitimate one, and it ought to have been brought out long ago – or else you leave Howard to be done down. What do you say, Martin? Is that all right?'

'It's a hard choice,' said Martin.

'Well, you must make it.'

'As far as I'm concerned,' Martin replied, without any cover at all, 'Howard's case will have to take its chance.'

'I can't and won't sit down under that,' said Skeffington.

'So that's what you'd let happen, is it?' said Tom.

'No,' said Francis, 'I'm afraid I've got to choose the other way. What about you, Lewis?'

'I'm with you,' I said.

So we settled it. Then I came to the harder part. Who was going to 'raise the doubt'? I told them that it would be useless for me to do it: I gave them the reasons I had thought over to myself the night before. And also, Nightingale and I had once been enemies. Though it was years ago, men like Brown would not have forgotten that. Did they agree?

There were frowns and heavy faces as they nodded. They had all seen where this must lead. 'So it's got to be one of us,' Tom said.

'Yes,' I replied: the doubt would have to come out in Court next day, while I examined one of them.

Tom Orbell said the one word:

'Who?'

There was a long pause. The sky in the west was a luminous apple-green shading into cobalt blue above the college.

'I'm damned if I like it,' said Skeffington, 'but I'd better do it.'

'I don't know enough about it, do I?' asked Tom. He was glad to be out of it, and yet half-disappointed.

Of them all, Skeffington was the last I should have selected. He did not carry weight. He had been so much the head and front of the Howard party that men did not listen to him any more. They would just dismiss this as another outburst, and the last.

I gazed at Martin. He would have been far more effective. He shook his head. 'No, I can't go back on what I said. I'll do anything else I can: but not that.'

Just as I was turning to Skeffington, resigned to making do with him, Francis said, in a tone strained, embittered and forced:

'No. I'm the best person to do it.'

Martin looked at him in consternation. They had never been specially fond of each other, but Martin said with a touch of affection, almost protectively:

'But it's not much in your line, you know.'

'Do you think I shall enjoy it?' Francis said. 'But they'll listen to me, and I'm the best person to do it.'

No man would more detest doing it. He was a man so thin-skinned that he didn't like the ordinary wear and tear of a college argument, much less this. He was less cushioned than the rest of us. Although he had played a part in scientific affairs, he had done so by force of will, not because he fitted in. He had never toughened his hide, as most men do for

961

self-protection, when they live in affairs. He had never acquired the sort of realistic acceptance which I, for example, could switch on, or pretend to. He continued to be upset when men behaved badly.

Yet, despite all that, or really because of it, he was, as he said himself, the man the Court would have to listen to. Not only for his name, his seniority, but also because he was a little purer than most men.

Martin asked him to think again, but Francis was impatient.

His decision was made. He didn't want any more talk. He wanted to do it and get it over. He knew, just as well as the politically minded Martin and Tom Orbell, what in practical terms he was losing. All of us knew that up to that night he had a clear lead in the magisterial election. By this time next day, he would have lost one vote for sure, possibly more.

In Martin's room, no one mentioned the election. But I did, later that night. As soon as Francis had said that he was 'the best person to do it', he got to his feet. All of us were constrained. There was some relief, certainly some expectancy in the air, but even a fluent man like Tom couldn't find any easy words. While they were saying good-night, Francis asked me if I would care to drive out with him and see his wife.

On our way out to their house, the same house I used to visit when we were young men, we scarcely spoke. I looked from the dashboard to the beautiful grape-dark dusk. Francis, silently driving, was both resentful at the prospect of next day, and also diffident. He had been in authority for so long, sometimes people disliked him for being overbearing, and yet he still curled up inside.

In the drawing-room, as soon as I went in, his wife Katherine cried out with pleasure. When I had first known her, nearly thirty years before, she had been a sturdy pony of a girl; now she was a matriarch. The clear, patrician Jewish features were still there, the sharp, intelligent grey eyes: but she sat statuesque in her chair, a big, heavy woman, her children grown up, massive, slow-moving, indolent, like those aunts of hers, other matriarchs, whom I had met at her father's dinner-parties when she and I were young. And yet, though the physical transformation was dramatic, though time had done its trick, and she sat there, a middle-aged woman filling her chair – I did not quite, at least not with photographic acceptance, see her so. I did not see her as I should have seen her if I had that night come into her house for the first time, and been confronted with her – as I had been confronted with those great matriarchs of aunts, having no pictures of their past. Somehow anyone whom one has known from youth one never sees quite straight: the picture has been doubly exposed;

something of themselves when young, the physical presence of themselves when young, lingers till they die.

We talked about our children. It seemed to her funny that her elder daughter should be married while my son was six years old. We talked of her brother, to whom she was, after a break of years, at last reconciled. We talked of her father, who had died the year before. Then I said, in the warmth of associations flowing back:

'Katherine, my dear, I've just done Francis a bad turn.'

'That's pretty gross, isn't it?' She glanced at her husband with her penetrating eyes. 'What have you been up to, Lewis?'

'No,' said Francis, 'we've all got trapped. It's not his fault.'

'In effect, I've done him a bad turn.'

I explained what had happened. She knew all about the affair: she was vehemently pro-Howard. Morally, she had not altered. She still kept the passion for justice, argumentative, repetitive, but quite incorruptible, that I remembered in her and her brother when they were young. At that time, that sharp-edged passion had seemed to me to be specifically Jewish: had I ever met non-Jews who felt for justice quite like that? But now I had lived with Margaret for years. She had the same passion, just as contemptuous of compromise, as any of my Jewish friends. If Margaret had been present that night, she would have judged the case precisely as Katherine did.

'You hadn't any option,' she said to Francis. 'Of course you hadn't. Don't you admit it?'

'No doubt that will comfort me a bit, when it comes to tomorrow afternoon.' Francis, who still loved her, made that gallows-joke as though with her he had managed to relax.

'But it's an intolerable nuisance. No, it's worse than that—' I began.

'It's monstrous to have to make yourself unpleasant in just that way, of course it is,' said Katherine to her husband.

'I meant something less refined,' I put in. The way I spoke recalled to her, as it was meant to recall, a private joke. When I had first entered the great houses in which she was brought up, I had been a poor young man determined to get on. I had had to play down my sensibilities, while she and her friends had been free to indulge and proliferate theirs. So they had made a legend of me, as a sort of Bazarov, unrecognisably monolithic, utterly different from what I really was, and from what they knew me to be. Somehow this legend had lasted half a lifetime: so that Katherine, whose nature was tougher than mine, sometimes pretended at odd moments that she was a delicate, fainéante relic of a dying class being attacked by someone implacable and raw.

'Much less refined,' I said. 'Look, Katherine, if Francis doesn't become Master next autumn, it will be because of what he's going to do tomorrow. Perhaps he'll still get it. But if he doesn't, it'll be on account of this business. I want you to realise that I am partly responsible.'

'Why, I suppose he is,' she said to Francis, in a tone I did not understand – angry? sarcastic?

'It's neither here nor there,' he replied.

'If I'd not spoken as I did tonight—'

'It would have added up to the same thing in the end.'

'Anyway,' I said to Katherine, 'I'm sorry it had to be through me.'

She had been gazing at me. Suddenly she laughed. It was a maternal laugh, a fat woman's laugh.

'You don't think I mind all that much, do you? I know the old thing wants it' – she grinned affectionately at Francis – 'and of course anything the old thing wants he ought to get. But between ourselves I've never really understood why he wants it. He hasn't done so badly anyway. And it would be an absolutely awful nuisance, don't you admit it? I don't mind telling you, I'm not panting to live in any beastly Lodge. Think of the people we should have to entertain. I'm not much good at entertaining. I'm getting too old to put up with being bored. Why should we put up with being bored? Answer me that.'

She chuckled. 'To tell you the truth,' she said, 'I've only got one ambition for the old thing now. That is, for him to retire. That's the only one.'

Francis smiled at her. It had been a good marriage. But just at that instant, as she said 'that's the only one', he couldn't lie to himself or even pretend to us that it was the only one for him.

CHAPTER XXX

THE WORD 'MISTAKE'

THE next morning, Sunday, the Court of Seniors were sitting at the combination room table waiting. They were waiting for Skeffington. He had been asked to be ready at half past ten. There was no sign of him.

Impatiently, I went to the window and gazed into the sunny court. Turning back to the table, I asked Crawford if he would like me to ring up Skeffington's house. Just as he was replying, the butler came in. He told the Master that Dr Skeffington was in the college; the head porter had seen him enter the chapel nearly half an hour before; he had still not reappeared.

'Thank you, Newby,' said Crawford. 'Bring him in as soon as he's available, if you don't mind.'

When e were alone again, Brown told us that there was no service in chapel between eight and eleven that day. 'He must be praying,' said Brown. 'That's what I get round to. He must be praying.'

He added:

'Well, God forbid that I should cause any of His little ones to stumble, but I wish the man weren't such an infernal time about it.'

'I'm very ignorant of these necromantic proceedings,' said Winslow, 'but I take it that Skeffington isn't attempting to bring supernatural influences to bear on our actions in this room? Or am I wrong?'

The old man was happy. He felt as though back in the Cambridge of the nineties, when unbelief, rude, positive unbelief, was fun. As he proceeded to inform the Court with relish, he still had exactly as much interest in 'religious exercises' as he had in the magic of savage tribes.

'I suppose Skeffington would like us to see a difference between his activities and rain-making. But I confess I think it's a major intellectual error to endow his activities with a sophistication that they don't inherently possess. I must say, praying before giving evidence does seem a singular example of sympathetic magic. I find it a very remarkable thing for a supposedly intelligent man to do.'

So, in private, did Crawford. Did Brown, who punctiliously attended college chapel, but, I often thought, out of social, not religious, piety, out of attachment to established things? It was neither they nor Nightingale who protested – but, from the opposite side of the table, Dawson-Hill, who said:

'I don't find it remarkable in the least, you know.'

'Really?'

'I should have thought it was entirely natural.'

Dawson-Hill smiled, self-possessed, unabashed. I should have remembered that he was a devout Catholic. I was ready for him to remind us that he had been to Mass that morning but at that moment the butler loudly called out Skeffington's name.

I cut my own examination short. Skeffington had nothing new to say, the Court had heard his opinion, fervent and lofty, times enough before. Everything fitted into place, once one saw Palairet had done it: the thing clicked, as it had clicked for him when he went through the notebooks: the missing photograph 'told its own story': Palairet had done it, and nothing else was 'on the cards'.

I passed him on to Dawson-Hill, expecting them to be easy with each other. From the first question and answer, they couldn't get on. It wasn't that Skeffington gave anything away; it wasn't that Dawson-Hill had thought of anything subtle. No, they just twitched a nerve of resentment in each other. Their eyes met only perfunctorily. Their handsome profiles were half-averted. Each of them was aware of his looks, I thought – to an extent which apparently irritated, not only more homely men, but also each other. Dawson-Hill took considerable care of his; his hair, that morning showing not a sliver of grey, was as burnished as an elegant undergraduate's. Was it the other's vanity each didn't like? They were both looking-glass vain.

There was more to it than that. Dawson-Hill saw someone 'out of the same stable' as himself, belonging to just the same pocket of the upper middle class, where smartness was making its last stand. That made the nerve of resentment quiver, when he found him hostile, in the enemy camp, in a case like this. Despite his tolerance, his free-and-easy sense of fairness – Dawson-Hill was not devoid of either – he could not help feeling that this man should be on his side.

Then I thought again what I had thought the night before. What made Skeffington resentful was that, in everything but his sense of honour, he felt it too. Speaking before the Court that morning, he would have liked not to have quarrelled with their ruling. He wanted to become one of them – or rather, he did not so much want it as think that was his proper place. One could hear that wish-to-accept in his voice; it made him angrier with Dawson-Hill, with the Court, with all who disagreed with him. It made his rebellion more peremptory.

Round the table the Seniors were listening to him with formal politeness, not attention. He hadn't made much effect that day, but such as it was, it had been negative.

I was relieved to see him go.

Martin, who came in next, said precisely what he had contracted to say. He did not speak about the missing photograph. On all other points, he was careful, considerate, and unbudging. For himself, he said, he was convinced an injustice had been done. He could understand why others were not convinced: but surely they didn't require that: wasn't it enough for them to see that an injustice might, conceivably might, have been done? He was too practised a committee man to overstate his case: but he was also too practised to seem compromising where he didn't intend to be.

Dawson-Hill tried a few sighting-shots of questions, but then left him alone, with the final word:

'What it boils down to, if I understand you, is that, in a matter which is full of room for different opinions, you are giving the Court yours?'

'I think,' said Martin, 'it is rather more than that.'

Crawford asked him the questions he had asked me, about Palairet and scientific fraud. Martin, more cautious than I had been, and a better judge of the Court, would not be drawn, except to say that he was forced to think Palairet had done it.

'Well, Martin,' said Crawford, with a cordiality not so impersonal as usual, 'that may be the point where we have to agree to differ.'

When Martin had gone, and the rest of us went into the Lodge for lunch, I was sure that Dawson-Hill believed it was all over. He showed me the teasing and slightly guilty kindness which one shows to a rival who has done his best, when the best isn't good enough. I was also sure that not one of the Court was ready to change his mind. It was true, Brown as well as Crawford had not been quite unaffected by Martin. The most Martin had done was to make Brown reflect that they hadn't 'handled the responsible chaps on the other side' too well. After they had 'dug in their heels about this case' – Brown felt immovably that that was his duty – then they would have to spend some time and care 'building bridges'.

Brown sipped a glass of hock with sober content, Dawson-Hill reminisced about travels down the Rhine, old Winslow put away three glasses. Then Brown noticed that I was not touching mine. 'You're not drinking, Lewis?' 'It's very fine,' Dawson-Hill said. 'You oughtn't to miss it, you really oughtn't to.' I said, not in the middle of the day. Brown was peering at me. He had noticed that I had been sitting silent. Did he suspect that I had not yet given up?

The Court regrouped itself in the combination room; the blind was pulled down; there was a smell of beeswax, furniture polish, Crawford's tobacco, honeysuckle from the terrace.

The butler cried out, as though rejoicing in the title:

'Sir Francis Getliffe!'

As Francis sat down, Crawford said:

'We are very sorry to drag you here on a Sunday afternoon.'

'I should be distressed if anyone worried about that, Master.'

'We know it's an infliction, but we hope you realise that we're grateful for your assistance.'

'It couldn't possibly be an infliction, Master, if I can be of the slightest help—'

It was some time since I had seen Francis at a meeting. I had forgotten that, especially when uneasy, he took on a curious, stylised courtesy like a Spaniard in a play by Calderón.

Looking at him, my eyes made fresh by the tension so that I might have been looking at him for the first time, I thought that his face, also, might have been a seventeenth-century Spaniard's. In shape, that is: long, thin, without much of a dome to the head. Not in colouring: the skin under the sunburn was pale and the eyes in the arched orbits were a kind of tawny yellow that I had seen only in Anglo-Saxons. They were splendid eyes, I suddenly realised, idealist's eyes, conceptualiser's eyes. Under them the skin was stained sepia and furrowed: those were the stains of anxious wear, the demands he had made upon himself, and they would not leave him now. The whole face was that of a man who had ridden himself hard, driven by purpose, amibition and conscience.

Examining him, I began slowly. I wanted to get the courtesy peeled away. It didn't matter whether the Court thought I was spinning out the routine, making the best of a bad job. As I went over the old history, asking when he had first heard of the scandal, whether he had looked at Howard's published papers, formal questions of no interest, I could see Dawson-Hill, lounging in his chair as though this was dull stuff.

'For some time you took it for granted that Howard had faked the photograph in his paper?'

'Certainly.'

'Accordingly, you accepted the verdict of the Court of Seniors, when they first deprived him?'

'In any circumstances I should want very strong reasons not to accept the verdict of the Court of Seniors of this college,' said Francis, inclining his head to the Master and Brown, 'and in these circumstances I thought their verdict was inevitable.'

'When did you begin to think otherwise?'

'Later than I should have done.'

That was better. His voice, light-toned and clear, had suddenly hardened.

'You began to think a mistake might have been made?'

'I should like to be clear about the word "mistake".'

'Let me ask you this instead. You began to think the Court had made a wrong decision?'

'I tried to explain that to them. Obviously I didn't go far enough.'

Francis was now speaking with full authority. This was it, I thought. I was just going in for the *coup*, when, maddened, I had to stop. There was one person who was not listening, either to full authority or anything else. Old Winslow, sedated by the heat and the glasses of hock, had nodded off, his nutcracker chin sunk low on his chest.

I stopped the question after the first word. Crawford enquired: 'Eliot?'

I pointed at Winslow.

'Ah,' said Crawford, without expression. 'None of us is as young as he used to be.' Gently he tugged at Winslow's gown.

The old man reluctantly, with saurian slowness, pulled up his head. Then he gave a smile rueful, red-lidded, curiously boyish.

'I apologise, Master,' he said.

Crawford asked with medical consideration if he was all right.

'Perfectly all right, I thank you,' said Winslow snappily, reaching out for the carafe of water in front of the Master's place. 'Please resume your remarkable proceedings,' he said to me.

With an eye on him, intent on keeping him awake, I asked Francis:

'You were saying that you hadn't gone far enough?'

'Certainly not.'

'What do you now think you should have done?'

Francis answered, clear and hard:

'You asked me just now about a "mistake". I didn't accept the word. I ought to have drawn the Seniors' attention to what may – I do not say it was, but I do say most seriously that it may have been worse than a mistake.'

There was no noise. Along the table I saw Nightingale, pen over the foolscap, in the middle of a note. He did not look up at Francis.

'I'm afraid I've not quite caught the drift of this,' said Crawford. 'Could you elucidate?'

'I'll try,' said Francis. 'I've been forced to form the view that throughout this business Howard has behaved like an innocent and not very intelligent man. I've told you before that I believe his account of what happened is substantially accurate. I believe that most scientists who studied the facts would come to the same conclusion. They would, of course, as a consequence, have to accept that Palairet did this fraud.'

'As the Master was saying to Martin Eliot before luncheon,' said Brown, 'that is just where we fundamentally disagree with you.'

'How can you?' Francis spoke in a quiet tone, brittle but inflexible. 'You've only been able to go on persuading yourselves because of one single fact. If that one photograph were present in Palairet's notebook, not one of you could even pretend to think that he wasn't responsible.'

'The photograph, however, is not present,' Crawford replied.

'That is what I meant by something possibly being worse than a mistake.'

'If I understand your innuendo correctly,' said Brown, 'you—'

'I am not making an innuendo. I am stating a possibility as clearly as I can. I believe the Court would be culpable if it did not take this possibility into account. It is: that the photograph now missing from Palairet's note-book was removed not by accident, but in order either to preserve Palairet's reputation or to continue justifying the dismissal of Howard.'

'That is a very grave thing to say,' said Arthur Brown. He was frowning, but not showing anger. I had no doubt that all the implications of what Francis had said were running through that cunning, politic mind – and at the same time outraging his feelings, because, tough and obstinate as he was, he was not willing that people should think he had done wrong or that he should think so himself.

'I know it,' said Francis.

Beyond Winslow, Nightingale was no longer writing and was gazing, together with the entire Court, at Francis. The lines on Nightingale's skin were visible, but no more than usual on a tiring day. The furrows ran across his forehead.

'I know it's a grave thing to say,' Francis repeated. 'I must ask the Court to remember that I've said it.'

CHAPTER XXXI

STATELINESS OF A MAN PRESIDING

WITHOUT another question, I told the Master that I had finished. Craw-ford turned to Dawson-Hill.

'Will you kindly proceed, then?'

Crawford's speech was as deliberate as usual, his moon-face took on its formal, meaningless smile: but behind his spectacles his eyes had a smeared, indecisive look.

Dawson-Hill was in a dilemma. He was too shrewd a man, too good a lawyer, not to have seen the crisis coming. It was not, however, the kind of crisis with which he had been trained to deal. Behind closed doors: the shut-in, senatorial faces: not an open word from any of the Court:

not a name mentioned. And yet the feeling in the room had tightened like a field of force. Without any guide he had to judge that feeling.

It seemed to me that he had two choices. Either take the risk, come right out with it, ask who could have touched the photograph: or else damp the whole thing down, be respectful and polite to Francis, but get him out of the way and assume this was just an incident, not a decisive one.

The instant Crawford called on him, he began speaking, quick on the uptake, sounding quite casual. 'This is extremely interesting, Sir Francis,' he said, allowing himself a few seconds to make up his mind. Then he went on as though he had decided to take the risk. The notebook – Dawson-Hill kept referring to it, eyebrows stretched as 'this *famous* notebook'. How much could Sir Francis help the Court about its history?

'I know no more than the Court does,' said Francis.

Did Francis know anything of Palairet's habits or about how he'd kept his notebooks?

'I never even visited his laboratory.'

Sensibly, Dawson-Hill was skipping the questions about legal proof. When the old man died, all his papers had been sorted out by his executor?

'So far as I know,' said Francis.

Dawson-Hill glanced at Nightingale, who nodded.

The executor was himself an old man, a clergyman? And he had sent them, with long intervals between, in batches to Palairet's solicitors? The famous notebook being in the last batch? And the solicitors had passed each batch in turn to the college?

As he asked these questions, Dawson-Hill was leaving gaps for the Seniors to break in. He was feeling his way, sensing how far he could safely go. If he gave them the lead, and one of them asked Francis just where and how he believed the photograph had been tampered with, then everything was in the open.

'And so the notebook arrived at the college?'

Francis said, 'Of course.'

Dawson-Hill looked across the table at the Court. Winslow was listening, hand propping up his jaw. Crawford sucked at his pipe. Brown sat back in his chair, firm and patient. Nightingale met Dawson-Hill's gaze. None of them volunteered a word.

Dawson-Hill had to make his decision. He could force the confrontation now – who had seen the notebook in the college? First Nightingale, then Skeffington, wasn't it? And so, what was Sir Francis Getliffe intending to say?

For any fighting lawyer, it was a temptation. But Dawson-Hill, trying to get the sense of the Court, felt that he mustn't fall into it. He drew back and went off on to an innocuous question. If I had been in his place I should have done just the same.

But, as he asked questions about Francis's opinion of Howard, he made what seemed to me a mistake in judgment, the first he had made since the hearing began. Francis had said that Howard's actions had been those of an 'innocent and not very intelligent man'. Dawson-Hill went in for some picador work. Was that really Francis's opinion? How long had it been so? Presumably he had not always thought Howard innocent? Not, in fact, until quite recently? Presumably also, he had not always thought him 'not very intelligent'? When he supported him for his fellowship, he could scarcely have considered him not very intelligent? Francis's estimates, both on character and ability, appeared to vary rather rapidly?

It would not have mattered that these questions were irrelevant. It did matter, or at least I thought it might, that Dawson-Hill let his temper show. Some of that temper came, of course, from pique. Until Francis spoke out that afternoon, Dawson-Hill had been certain that he had won. Now, looking round the uneloquent faces, he couldn't guess the end, but at least it was all to play for.

Yet there was something deeper than pique that made him more supercilious, sharpened the edge of his voice, drew him into addressing Francis with irritation as *Sir* Francis, with the accent on the title, as though Dawson-Hill had suddenly changed from an upper-class Englishman into a Maltese. It was deeper than pique, it was sheer dislike of Francis. For Dawson-Hill, despite his snobbisms and although he accepted the world, had a curious streak of emotional egalitarianism. He didn't like seeing people too miserable, and on the other hand he became irritated when he saw others in his view too well endowed. He got on better with sinners than with the high-principled. He liked men best who were battered by life, had some trouble on their minds, were still high-spirited and preferably short of money. To him, Francis was a living provocation. He was too scrupulous, too virtuous; he was too conscientious, too far from common clay; he had done altogether too well; he had had success in everything he touched; he had even married a rich wife and had abnormally gifted children. Dawson-Hill could not bear the sight of him.

So Dawson-Hill, for once in his suave career, lost his temper. There was also a perceptible surge of temper on Francis's side. Francis, much nearer common clay than Dawson-Hill supposed, had a good robust healthy appetite for disliking those who disliked him. Further, he had no use for men as elegant as Dawson-Hill, as beautifully dressed, as youthful-looking, men whom he dismissed as *flâneurs*.

Their exchanges became more caustically smooth from Dawson-Hill, more contemptuous and impatient from Francis. I saw Brown peering at them both. He began to write on the paper in front of him.

'Sir Francis,' Dawson-Hill was asking, 'don't you agree that Dr Howard, whose character you have praised so generously, showed a really rather surprising alacrity in accepting his professor's data?'

'I see nothing surprising in it.'

'Should you say it was specially admirable?'

'It was uncritical.'

'Shouldn't you say it was really so uncritical as perhaps to throw some doubt on his moral character?'

'Certainly not. A good many stupid research students would have done it.'

'Do you really think it specially creditable?'

'I didn't say it was creditable. I said it was uncritical.'

Just then Brown had finished writing his note. He placed it carefully on top of Crawford's pad. Crawford looked down, scrutinised the note, and, as Dawson-Hill was beginning another question, cleared his throat:

'I think there may be a measure of feeling among my colleagues,' he said, 'that this might be as far as we can usefully go this afternoon. Speaking as Master, I'm inclined to suggest that we adjourn.'

Winslow inclined his head. Crawford then asked Brown if he agreed, as though Brown's note had had no more effect on his, Crawford's, action than if it had been a love-poem in Portuguese.

'I am also inclined to suggest,' Crawford said, once more as though the idea had occurred to him out of a vacuum, 'that this is a point where the Seniors might spend a little time gathering the threads together. I think it might be convenient if you let me provide you with tea in the Lodge—' He looked along his side of the table, from Winslow to Nightingale. 'So shall we let Eliot and Dawson-Hill off for the rest of the afternoon?'

There was a murmur. There were ritual thanks from the Master to Francis Getliffe. Then the Seniors, led by Crawford, filed through the inner door of the combination room into the Lodge.

That left Dawson-Hill, Francis and me alone together. Not one of us could find a word to say. For an instant, Dawson-Hill's social emollience had left him quite. As for me, it was a long time since I had felt so awkward. Heavy-footedly, I asked if he would be dining in hall. 'Alas, no,' he said, getting back into his social stride, telling me the house where he was going.

Francis said to me that he would see me before I returned to London. Nodding to Dawson-Hill, he left the room. I went out after him, but I did not want to catch him up. I did not want to speak to anyone connected with the affair. I walked quickly through the court, beating it to the shelter of my rooms.

I knew well enough what I was doing. It did not look like it, but, as Leslie Ince in his mid-Atlantic moods might have said, I was keeping my fingers crossed. People thought that I was cautious and wary, easily darkened by the shadows of danger ahead. So I was. But also, all my life, I had been capable of being touched by too much hope, and in middle age I was so still. In fact, as I grew older, some of my inner weather reminded me more and more of my mother's. She too had been anxious and had over-insured: over-insured literally, in her case, so that years after her death I kept coming across pathetic benefits she had taken out in my name, with the Hearts of Oak and other insurance companies, into which she, like the poor of her time, paid her pennies a week.

While at the same time, more superstitious each year she lived (and I believed that at times the same was true of me), she invented formulae for good-luck every week, as she filled in her forms for the competitions in *John Bull*, *Titbits* and *Answers*. She had hours and days astrologically chosen, in which to write her great bold clumsy words: and another lucky hour in which to post the envelopes. She used to take me to the pillar-box when I was a child. I would hear the envelope flap-thud into the dark: and then she would look at me, and I knew that in her heart she had already won the prize. 'When our ship comes home,' she would say, and at once sternly warn me about 'counting our chickens before they were hatched'. With an air of harsh realism, she told me that we mustn't expect the first prize every week. Yet she not only expected it; as she warned and reproved me for too much hope, she was simultaneously working out the ways to spend it.

I was very like her. It sometimes seemed to me that it was the anxious, the far-sighted, the realistic, who were most susceptible to hope. Certainly I could still be drunk with it. And the word 'still' really had no meaning. In middle age I was invaded by hopes exactly as I had been as a young man. No one had learned more about the risks, the probabilities, the realistic expectations of careers: and yet, in secret moments, I had learned nothing. For a long time, as I came to know more about myself,

I had developed strategies to protect me and others from these surgent moments which – in their own existence, their own euphoria – I could not suppress.

By myself that evening, therefore, I would not allow a thought to stray towards the case. If I did so, I should just feel that it was safely won. Much more I wished to avoid meeting Martin or Skeffington, above all the Howards. If I did so, I should warn them how, in situations like this, anything could still happen. In the words I used, in the reasons I gave for staying in suspense, few people would be more guarded. And yet beneath the words there would be a feeling which completely contradicted them, and anyone who heard me would know it. It didn't take a perceptive person, as I had learned to my own and others' cost, to catch and believe the tone of irrepressible hope.

So I kept to myself, had a bath, took a book out into the garden and read till dinner time. When I arrived in the combination room I found, and was glad to find, that none of the principals was dining. Winslow, still in the Lodge, so the butler told me, had just sent word for them to strike his name off the list. Tom Orbell was the only partisan whose name was there. As soon as he entered he said, seeing me alone, 'How is it going now?'

'Oh, it's still early days,' I said in a judicious, reproving tone, the model of a middle-aged, responsible, experienced man, a man with a public face.

I did not let him say any more about the affair, and no one else wished to. It was a small party, and a very young one. When Tom picked up the list, and noticed that Lester Ince was presiding, he said:

'Now that isn't exactly my idea of the sweetness of life.'

Two or three of the young fellows came in, among them Ince, who, turning upon me a bland, benevolent and ceremonious gaze, said: 'I'm very pleased that you're able to be with us tonight. We're all very pleased.'

It might have been the Master or Brown speaking. For an instant, Tom Orbell and I were taken by surprise. It even occurred to me that Ince was mimicking. But he was just feeling his position as senior of those present. He addressed me in full: he did not feel it right to call me 'Lew'. He knew that he was in the chair, and he had set himself to make a proper job of it.

Dinner proceeded with decorum. After the meal was over he announced: 'I think I should like to present a bottle to mark the first time that I have presided in this room.'

Nothing could be more stately. On hot summer nights like this, it was a college custom to go on to the terrace outside the combination room, sit on a balustrade abutting the Master's garden, and drink white wine. In his less reverential moods, I had heard Lester Ince object to this practice, on the simple but severe grounds that sitting on stone gave him piles, and that white wine was better described as cat's piss. Not so that night. He led the way on to the terrace, planted a firm, masculine, Trollopian backside on the balustrade, proposed his first toast in Barsac and inclined his head gravely, with ceremonial pleasure, when Tom Orbell toasted him as donor of the wine.

The air was quiet. As five of us sat there on the terrace it was – especially to me, basking in it – the most placid of evenings.

Two of the young men got up to go.

'Must you leave us?' said Ince.

They said they had work to do.

'We shall miss you,' said Ince, as a kind of presidential blessing. With disappointment he looked at Tom Orbell, the only fellow left. 'I was going to ask them, I thought tonight was a good night for it, isn't it time we really began to think about this election?'

He meant, of course, the magisterial election. To Tom, who had been thinking of it for a couple of years past, the question seemed astonishingly cool.

'I suppose we ought to pay some attention to these things. It's our own fault if we're too lazy and then find that other people have been ganging up. It's a bore, but we probably ought to get hold of things and put some weight behind them. We'd better see that we get something sensible done.'

It appeared as though Ince had been preparing for this speech as soon as he found that he was President for the night. I was thinking how, like most apolitical men, he thought politics were very easy. He didn't see any complexities about them. For him, it was just the righteous but inert against the unrighteous but active. If only he and other men of good will applied themselves, all would come right.

It was an approach that could scarcely have been less endearing to Tom Orbell, who wrote about politics, whose dream-life was a politician's, and who, except in his persecuted moments, knew by instinct what the texture of politics was like.

Tom looked flushed and cross. In the warm evening, beads of sweat were standing out above his temples, where the hairline was going back.

'I think,' he said, at his most mellifluous, 'that there is something obviously sensible to be done. But then, I've always declared my interest.'

Sitting dignified between us, Ince did not pretend, as in his more intransigent turns, not to comprehend the phrase.

'Who are you thinking of, then?' he said.

'I've made it quite clear, I should have thought,' replied Tom Orbell. 'I'm voting for Arthur Brown.'

'No,' Ince reflected, 'I don't think I want him.'

'But why ever not? He's—'

'He's been here a bit too long,' said Ince. 'No, we've got to take some action before things go too far.'

'Don't you realise,' Tom asked, with an expression of 'God give me patience', 'that things have gone pretty far already? Don't you realise that it's a moral certainty that it's going to be either Brown or Getliffe—'

'No, I won't have Getliffe,' remarked Ince, as though that settled it.

'Why not?' I put in.

'I won't have a scientist,' said Lester Ince. 'I've got quite a different idea—'

'Who is it?' cried Tom.

Ince gave us a long, slow, subtle, satisfied smile. 'G. S. Clark.' He sat back, with the confidence of M. de Norpois mentioning the name of Giolitti, with the modest expression of an elder statesman who has produced the solution, obvious but so far concealed from others of less wisdom, out of his hat.

'God love my blasted soul!' Tom broke out. 'Hasn't it occurred to you that the man's a monster? Hasn't it occurred to you that he's a ridiculous monster? Look here, I'm a Tory and I suppose you'd say you weren't. I love my religion and, so far as I know, you haven't any. But do you want, any more than I do, a man who sees a communist under every bloody bed?'

'Everyone's got some bee in his bonnet,' said Ince, temperately.

'Well, please enlighten me as to what you *do* see in him,' Tom went on, beginning to show his silken, unstable courtesy and talking down his nose.

'He's independent.'

'With great respect, I doubt it.'

'I'm afraid,' said Ince, in his new, stately manner, 'I have to take people as I find them. I find him original. I find that he's not one of anyone's gang. And I'd like to tell you what a lot of people are thinking nowadays. It's time we got outside the gangs. We've got to keep our eyes open for men who stand on their own. And we shan't get a man in this college who stands on his own more than G. S. Clark does.'

'So that's what you think, is it?' said Tom.

'I should like to hear your opinion of him,' Ince turned to me.

I shook my head. 'If I'd been asked to imagine an improbable nomination,' I said, 'I couldn't have imagined one as improbable as that.'

'Look here,' Tom broke out furiously, 'I suppose you haven't given the faintest thought to the consequences, if you go ahead with this spectacular idea? I can tell you, and it's useless to deny it, things look pretty even just now between Brown and Getliffe. It looks like nine votes certain for Getliffe and seven for Brown, and the others not yet committed. If you go ahead with this spectacular idea, all you'll achieve is perhaps subtract a vote or two from Brown, including making Clark withhold his own vote. So with classical ingenuity, you will give Getliffe a long lead and probably let him in by default. Which is exactly the result you say you want the least. I suppose you hadn't thought of those consequences? Or I suppose that isn't the intention behind your spectacular idea?'

Tom was ready, as usual too ready, to smell out a conspiracy. Ince's face, up to that point rubbery, benevolent and composed, had taken on a frown.

'I've been listening to that kind of talk until I'm sick and tired,' he said. 'I'm just not prepared to play. All I'm prepared to do is to pick out the man I think best and say so and stick to it.'

'Thus cleverly producing the consequences that you say you don't want?'

'Damn the consequences. As for what you're telling me, there's only one answer to that.' Suddenly Ince's stateliness had dropped away. His presidential manners had got lost. He said: 'There's only one answer. Stuff it.'

As they were glaring at each other, the butler came out on to the terrace.

'Mr President,' he said to Ince, 'may I have permission to deliver a telephone message?'

'By all means,' replied Ince, shining with sedateness once again.

The butler came to my side, and in his clear confidential whisper said: 'Dr Nightingale's compliments, and he would much appreciate it if you could do him the favour of calling in his rooms as soon as you conveniently can tonight.'

CHAPTER XXXII

ONE ENEMY TO ANOTHER

WALKING through the third court to Nightingale's rooms, I was getting ready for a scene I did not like. I felt the mixture of combativeness, irritation and fear. My thoughts were all over the place: I even found myself thinking, with a childish sense of being ill-used, it's too nice a night to go and have a quarrel.

After the warm, flower-scented court, the staircase, not yet lighted, struck dank as a well. As I climbed to the third floor, the landing was bright, flooded by the sunset. My eyes were dazzled, coming up from the dark floors beneath, and I could scarcely read Nightingale's name above the door. When I knocked and went in, he had the curtains drawn and both the reading-lamp and an old-fashioned central chandelier switched on. He stood up, and in silence gave me an eager and charming smile.

He asked me to sit down, pointing to the one good armchair in the bare room. There was a church hush.

I was the first to make conversation. I said that I had glanced up at the Bursary, expecting to find him there.

'No,' said Nightingale, 'I don't believe in living over the shop.' He went on to say that he had occupied these present rooms ever since he was first elected and added: 'And that's longer ago than I'd care to think. If it comes to that,' he spoke to me civilly, as though we shared a rueful pleasure, 'it must be a long time since you were up here last. *That* must be longer ago than either of us care to think.'

It had, in fact, been before the war. I had only been inside that room twice during the time we were both fellows. Our relations had made it unlikely that I should visit him. And yet, Nightingale seemed to remember that period, when he was bitterly miserable, when he and I were barely on speaking terms, not sentimentally, not with affection, but with something like respect.

Perhaps he was one of those men, so self-absorbed that everything that has happened to them is precious, who don't want to dismiss an enemy from their minds, provided they have known him long enough. The bare fact of knowing him long enough gives him some claim upon them. Just then, he was speaking to me – whom he had always regarded as an enemy, that night with specific cause, and who in turn disliked him more than most men – as though we had something in common.

I looked round the room. It was as I dimly recalled it, bleak, less personal than most fellows' rooms. An oar, relic of undergraduate rowing, was hung along one wall. On his desk stood a large photograph of his wife, pudgy, amiable, full-eyed, which couldn't have been there in my time. I noticed on the walls photographs which must also have been recent, groups of officers in the desert. In one Nightingale sat in the middle wearing shorts and a beret. In another he was placed two from the left of a famous soldier, whom I happened to have met. I asked about him.

'Oh, they'd kicked me upstairs by then,' said Nightingale. 'They'd decided I was an old man, and no good for fighting any more.'

It occurred to me, he was oddly modest about his war. He had been a field officer in his mid-forties; I couldn't think of many amateurs who had done as much. I said that I knew his commander, Lord Gilbey. During the war, stories had collected in Whitehall, among officials not given to hero-worship, about his personal bravery. I asked Nightingale about this.

'Oh, he didn't much mind being shot at,' he said. He added, 'After all, he's been paid to be shot at all his life, hasn't he?'

'But still,' I said, 'he must have quite abnormal physical courage.'

'I suppose he has,' said Nightingale.

'I must say I envy it.'

'I don't think you need,' said Nightingale.

Suddenly I realised, what had been at the back of my mind all along, that I was talking of one very brave man to another. Like it or not, one had to admit that Nightingale's courage in both wars was absolute.

'I've seen too much of it to be impressed,' he remarked. 'I don't think you need envy it.' He said it with something like a sneer, but quite kindly. He was not a man with any interest in understanding others: he was too knotted in himself for that. Certainly he had no interest in me, except as one who filled him with resentment. Yet, just for an instant, he seemed to understand me better than if he had been fond of me. He spoke – it was bizarre, in the tension of that evening – as though he were reassuring me.

There was another, and a longer, church-like hush. We had finished all the conversation we could make. We had not, we had never had, a thought in common. We were both controlling ourselves, ready to wait.

At last Nightingale said:

'I wanted to talk to you about this afternoon.'

'Do you?' I replied.

'I should like to know why Getliffe said what he did.'

'He must have felt it was his duty,' I said.

'I take it you were responsible for this?' His voice was still controlled, but there was a strained, creaking note within it.

'I think that, for anything that concerns his actions, you'll have to ask Getliffe himself. Isn't that right?'

'Do you imagine for an instant that I can't see the power behind the scenes?'

'Do you imagine that I or anybody else could persuade Getliffe to say a word he didn't believe?'

'I want to know why he said this.'

'Now look,' I said, speaking as violently as he had done but more quietly, 'this will get you nowhere. The point is, Getliffe has said it. And what he says it's quite impossible for the Seniors to ignore. That's the brute fact—'

'Do you think we're trying to ignore it? What do you think we've been doing since we adjourned?'

He emphasised the 'we' as though, through being on the Court, he still drew not only strength but pride. I looked straight at him. The bones of his forehead, under the thick, wavy fair hair, were strong. He had crows' feet beneath his eyes, fine lines on his eyelids. The delicate etching of his skin seemed not to match the heavy, almost acromegalic, bones. His eyes stared full into mine – they were lustrous, innocent eyes, they held feeling but no insight. As we gazed at each other, the corners of his mouth stretched, as if he were using his muscles to master himself. He spoke in a voice which, though monotonous, was low, and said:

'I hope you'll listen to me, Eliot.'

I said yes.

'I know we haven't always seen eye to eye. I don't know how much I was to blame. I don't mind telling you this – if I had my time over again, I should try not to say some of the things I've said.'

It wasn't an intense statement. It didn't contain remorse. Yet it sounded sincere, and curiously businesslike.

Before I could reply, he asked me:

'I suppose there are some things you've said you'd like wiped off the record, aren't there?'

'Of course.'

That seemed to satisfy him.

'We haven't always seen eye to eye,' he repeated. 'That's agreed on both sides, but it oughtn't to affect the issue.'

'What do you mean?'

'You're no man's fool, Eliot,' he replied, still in the same level, businesslike fashion. 'You know as well as I do, and better, I shouldn't be surprised, that this afternoon got us into deep water.'

In contrast to his tone, his stare was illuminated.

'Now, I'm asking you to help us out of it,' he said. 'I'm asking you to put the past into cold storage and help us out of it.'

I was having to keep myself matter-of-fact. All his energy, his strained obsessive energy, was pouring out of him. His words were flat, yet one wasn't listening to them but to the force behind them. It made the air in the room seem denser, the light more dim.

'So far as I can see,' I said, 'there's only one conceivable way out.'

He took no notice of me.

'We've got into deep water,' he went off again. 'You know as well as I do, and a good deal better, that a suspicion was raised this afternoon. We're intended to suspect that someone may have falsified the books to do this man Howard down. We're intended to suspect someone. Someone? It might be me.'

I looked at him without speaking.

There was a pause.

He said:

'I don't expect you to worry about that. Why should you? But I tell you that it isn't the issue. It isn't what we think of one another. We've seen a lot of things happen to one another. I'm not talking about what might happen to either of us now. I don't expect you to worry about that. But I do expect you to worry about something else.'

He went on: 'If this goes on, what's the end of it going to be? If people begin suspecting as you want them to, then I can tell you the result, and I hope it's one you haven't thought of. They suspect someone. All right. I tell you, it might be me. Someone in this college. An officer of this college. What is going to be the effect on the place?'

He was speaking very fast, half-inarticulately, but with passion.

'I'd give a lot to keep the college out of danger, Eliot. I hope you would. I don't mind saying, it's done everything for me. I don't mean when I was a young man. A bright young man ought to be able to look after himself. No, it's done everything for me when I was afraid I was going to peter out. They trusted me. They gave me an office. It's the only thing anyone's ever elected me to. I've done my best not to let them down. I tell you, that office is the best thing that ever happened to me. Do you wonder that I'm not prepared to see anything bad happen to this place? That's why I'm talking to you. I'd give all I've got to keep it safe.'

I believed him. I believed him without the flicker of a doubt. It wasn't the easy-natured who were most seized by this kind of loyalty. It wasn't the successful: old Gay had as little as a man could reasonably have. It wasn't the self-sufficient. No, most of all it was those like Nightingale who were self-absorbed without being self-sufficient. For an instant, I wondered, was that also true of Howard? When I heard his mumbling statement that he was thinking of the college, I had thought he was confused, I had dismissed it. Was I being too sceptical, were these two alike in that one spot? Was it possible, when Howard gave his reason for not suing the college, a reason which he only half-admitted to himself, that it was true?

With Nightingale, the force of his feeling beat down on me. It was so strong that, not only recognising it but overcome, I lost all certainty of what he was like, much lesss what he had, or had not, done. I could not be sure at that moment whether I believed he had ripped out the photograph in cold blood. All I was sure of was his ferocious, self-bound loyalty. Whether I suspected him or not had become remote or indeed meaningless. And yet I could simultaneously and quite easily imagine that if the photograph had come his way, and if it seemed to threaten his idea of the college's honour, then he would have had it out – without his conscience being troubled, even though it meant victimising Howard, because this was an act of conscience too.

I had to struggle to keep detached, that is, detached enough not to give a point away.

I replied:

'No one wants to do the college the slightest harm.'

'I'm glad to hear you say it.'

'No one,' I said, picking out the words, 'would want to press the suspicion you mentioned further than he had to. But—'

'Yes?'

'As I said before, there's only one conceivable way out. If the Seniors can change their decision against Howard, then no one's going to cause any unnecessary trouble. But if the Seniors can't change their decision, then I'm afraid it would be very difficult to stop.'

He was waiting for me to continue, but I had finished. The telephone rang. I could hear him replying to the porter's lodge, saying that he wouldn't be long. He looked at me, his eyes shining:

'Is that all?'

'I can't say any more tonight.'

'Do you want to speak to your – friends?'

I said:

'That would make no difference.'

He acted as though exhilarated, and not disappointed. He seemed only to have heard the half of my reply, the anodyne half. He seemed not to have grasped what the reply meant. Or perhaps he was still borne up by the excitement of having spoken without constraint. Cheerfully, in a tone hearty and almost friendly, he said that he would have to go, his wife was waiting for him in the car outside the college. Together we walked down the stairs and through the courts. Nightingale looked up at the sky, where the first stars were coming out:

'Now I call this something like weather.'

We were walking as though I might never have left the college, as though we were a pair, not of friends exactly, but of friendly acquaintances who had been colleagues for twenty years, and were, without noticing it, getting old together.

Outside the main gate, the car was drawn up by the kerb, the door open, Mrs Nightingale looking out.

'Hullo,' she said, 'what have you boys been up to?'

'Oh, just talking a bit of shop,' said Nightingale.

She got out on to the pavement, so that Nightingale could climb in to drive. As he did so, she patted him affectionately and then stood chatting to me. She was as unselfconscious as anyone I had known. She was so easy that, though at sight she was not specially attractive, she took on an attraction of her own. And yet, the instant I heard her ask what we had been doing, and saw her great eyes glance at him, I was positive about two things. First, that she had known exactly what we had been talking about, and second, that, in the midst of the suspicion about him, she did not suspect but know. One way or the other, whichever was the truth, she knew. I was positive about something more. She was easy, she was good-natured. If he had not done what he was suspected of, she would be glad. But if he had done it, then she would not only know, she would talk about it with him, she would enjoy the complicity, and she would – for though she had good feelings, she had no kind of conscience – amiably approve.

PART FIVE

THE CURVES OF JUSTICE

CHAPTER XXXIII

THE SIGHT OF A BLANK SPACE

THE bell tolled, sunlight spotted the carpet, as I came into the combination room on the Monday morning. The Seniors were all there, standing by the fireplace. Even as we exchanged good-mornings, one could feel the strain in the air. It was not the specific kind of strain that one meets going into a group of acquaintances, when they are hiding bad news from one. I had no guide as to what had been said among themselves, either the night before or that morning; but I knew almost at once that they were split.

Dawson-Hill came in, not from the college door as I had done, but from the inner one which led to the Master's Lodge. I was wondering, how early did this conference begin? Dawson-Hill's hair was burnished, he smelled of shaving lotion: 'Good-morning, my dear Lewis,' he said, with his bright, indifferent smile.

We took our places at the table. Slowly, with neat fingers, Crawford packed and lit a pipe. He sat back in his chair, his face as unlined as ever, his body as still: and yet, as soon as he spoke, I was sure that for once his complacency was precarious.

'I'm inclined to think,' he said, 'that certain statements made by one of our colleagues involve us in some difficulty. I'm going to ask you to address your minds to the wisest way of removing the difficulty, remembering, of course, the responsibility before the Court.'

He sucked at his pipe.

'Eliot, these statements concern your side of the case. Are you able to give us a lead?'

Although I was looking at Crawford, I could feel Nightingale's gaze upon me. This had been pre-arranged, I thought. They were leaving the move with me. As for an instant I hesitated, a voice came from Crawford's right:

'With your permission, Master.'

Crawford turned, face and shoulders, to look at old Winslow.

'Do you wish to speak now?' Crawford asked him.

'If you please. *If* you please.'

Crawford held up his hand in my direction, as though I needed shutting up. Winslow bent his head down over the table, like a great battered bird investigating the ground for food; then, twitching his gown away from his collar, he stared up at us from that bent posture. His eyes were bold, unconcerned, almost mischievous.

'As you all know, Master,' he said, 'I speak as a complete ignoramus. When I hear the interesting subjects discussed so intelligently by everyone else on this Court, I marvel slightly at how remarkably little I know of these matters. However, there are limits even to my incapacity. Yesterday afternoon, of course I may delude myself, I thought I captured the general drift of what Francis Getliffe was trying to tell us. Unless I am considerably mistaken, he was trying to tell us something which is perhaps a shade out of the ordinary run. He appeared to be giving us, as his considered opinion, that the unfortunate Howard might conceivably have been what I believe is nowadays known as "framed". And that if this possibility should happen to be true, then it appears that one of the fellows, one of our singular and reputedly learned society, must have been guilty of *suppressio veri*. To put it with the maximum of charity, which is probably, as is usually the case, totally uncalled-for.

'I have been considering these rather unusual possibilities, but I see no reason to invent complexities where no complexities can reasonably exist. It seems to me impossible, much as one perhaps might wish it, to pretend that Getliffe did not mean what he said. It seems to me *a fortiori* impossible for this Court not to act accordingly. No, I have to correct myself. No doubt nothing is impossible for this Court, or for any other committee of our college. Shall I simply say that it is impossible for me? Of course, I know nothing of Getliffe's subject. But I have always understood that he is a man of great distinction. I have never heard anyone suggest that his character is not beyond reproach. For what little my opinion is worth, I have always thought very highly of him. Indeed, Master, may I bring it to a point?'

'Naturally.'

'Thank you, thank you. I need only remind you of what I think is common knowledge. Shortly, my dear Master, your remarkable reign is coming to a close and you will subside into obscurity with the rest of us. In the ensuing election, I have never so much as contemplated another candidate than Getliffe. If you will forgive the turn of phrase, I soon both expect and hope to see him in your place.'

Winslow gave a grim, nutcracker smile at Crawford, reminding him of supersession and mortality. He gave another smile past Crawford at Brown, reminding him of humiliation to come.

'I confess,' Winslow went on, 'I should find a certain inconsistency in supporting Getliffe as our next Master and not paying attention to his statement of yesterday afternoon. I do not propose to exhibit that inconsistency. I should therefore like to give notice, Master, that on this Court I intend to vote for the re-instatement of Howard, or if you prefer it, the quashing of his deprivation, whatever peculiar form of procedure we find it appropriate to use. I suggest that this is done forthwith. Of course,' said Winslow, 'it will make the Court of Seniors look slightly ridiculous. But then, the Court of Seniors *is* slightly ridiculous.'

Quiet. Whatever else had been talked about and decided, this hadn't, I was certain. No one there had expected Winslow's speech. Further, I was certain, after watching the others respond to Winslow, that among themselves much had been left unspoken. Was that because Nightingale had not left them? Hadn't Crawford and Brown talked by themselves?

'Is that all?' enquired Crawford, flatly but politely.

'Thank you, Master. That is all.'

It had sounded like an outburst, like a free, capricious act. Yet in fact, Winslow was running along an old groove: it wasn't often or for long that men of eighty could get out of the grooves their lives had worn, and despite his spirit, gusto and relish, Winslow had not done so that morning. He had always had a standard of suitable behaviour. His tongue made that standard sound odder than it was. Actually, it was as orthodox as Brown's, and in depth not so independent: for Winslow believed what responsible people told him, as now with Francis Getliffe, while Brown, however comfortably he spoke, in the long run believed no one but himself.

No, Winslow's standard of behaviour had nothing special about it. Nor, as far as that went, had the history of his life. It was not in those terms, but below them, that he was interesting.

His life had, of course, been by his own criteria a failure. He was fond of saying so. He explained how, of three inadequate bursars in succession, he had been the worst. He was prepared to expand on his 'lifetime of singular lack of achievement'. He believed he was telling the truth. In reality, except when he spoke of his son, living God knows how in Canada, nearly forty and without a job, taking his allowance and never sending a letter, he liked talking about his failure. 'I always felt I was slightly less crass than most of my colleagues. And indeed that was not making a superlative claim. Nevertheless, even compared with their modest efforts, I've done quite remarkably worse.' Speaking like that, he got the feeling of being unsparing and honest. Yet he wasn't. As he talked he believed he was a failure: but his whole physical being told him otherwise.

He had never been easy with men. He had never made close friends. He was both too arrogant and too diffident. And yet, at eighty, he still kept a kind of assurance that many disciplined, matey and, by his criteria, successful men, never attain at all. It was the kind of elemental assurance of someone who had after all lived according to his nature. It was the kind of assurance that one meets sometimes in the George Passants, in the rakes and down-and-outs – very likely, now I came to think of it, in his own son. It was the kind of assurance that both gave, and at the same time derived from, the strongest animal grip on life.

Crawford looked at Brown and said:

'I think we must take note that our senior colleague has declared his intentions.'

'If you please, Master,' said Winslow. '*If* you please.'

I too had been looking at Brown. He knew, both of us knew, that Winslow would from now on never budge.

'I suppose it is slightly premature for the Court to try to formulate its decision,' said Crawford. He said it with the faintest inflection of a question. From his left hand Brown, for once, did not help him out: Brown sat back, receptive, vigilant, without a word.

Without a word, we all sat there. For an instant I felt triumph. The case had cracked. Then, in a tone slightly harsh but businesslike, Nightingale said: 'I should regard it as premature, of course. I totally disagree with almost everything we've heard from Mr Winslow. I can't begin to accept that that is a basis for a decision. I move that proceedings continue.'

At last Brown spoke, steadily and with weight:

'I have to agree with the Bursar.'

'In that case,' said Crawford, in resignation, 'I'm afraid we come back to you, Eliot.'

Again, before I started speaking, I was interrupted: this time by Dawson-Hill.

'Master, with apologies to my colleague, may I—?'

Crawford, who was getting fretful, shut his eyes and nodded his head, like one of the mandarin toys of my childhood.

'I would like to make just one plea,' said Dawson-Hill. 'I haven't the slightest intention of depriving my colleague of an argument on his side of the case. I am sure he knows that I haven't the slightest intention.' He gave me his groomed, party smile. 'But I would like to ask if he can see his way to leaving Sir Francis Getliffe's statement as it stands. Naturally this statement can't be ignored by the Court. But with great respect and humility, I do suggest that if my colleague takes it further we face a prospect of getting into situations of some delicacy, without any gain either to his arguments or mine. I'm fully aware that anything said to this Court is privileged. Nevertheless, I do urge on my colleague that we avoid delicate situations where we can. I know he will agree with me, it is quite obviously incontrovertible, that none of Sir Francis Getliffe's speculations are provable in law. With great respect, I do suggest that we leave them now.'

Again, Nightingale was watching me. He was wearing a new butterfly bow, red with white spots, jaunty under the stern masculine jaw. In his eyes the pupils were large. This was the second version of his appeal to me.

I had made my choice long since. I said:

'I'm sorry, Master. I can't present a fair case for Howard with one hand tied behind my back.'

'All right!' It was Nightingale who said it, his voice gravelly. This was the first time violence, open violence, had broken into the room. He was furious, but furious not so much from a sense of danger as because he had been turned down. 'Put your cards on the table. That'd be a change for us all.'

'If you don't mind,' I said – I was playing to provoke him – 'I'd rather put Palairet's notebook on the table.'

'I should like a simple answer to a simple question,' Nightingale cried. 'How much of all this is intended for me?'

'I don't think,' I said, 'that the Bursar should conduct my case for me.'

'I'm afraid that's reasonable,' said Dawson-Hill, sounding both embarrassed and not used to being embarrassed, across the table to Nightingale.

But Nightingale was a daring man. Passions, long banked down, were breaking out of him. They were not, or only in part, the passions of the night before. Then he had spoken to me, an old enemy, with the intimacy that sometimes irradiates enmity. Now he wasn't speaking to me personally at all. He hated me, but only as one of many. He was speaking as though surrounded by enemies, with himself all set to hack his way out. He had lost his temper: but, as with some active men, having lost his temper made him more fit for action, more capable of looking after himself.

'I want to know,' he said, 'whether what Getliffe said yesterday was intended for me? Or what this man is telling us this morning?'

Deliberately I did not answer. I asked Crawford if he minded my having Palairet's notebook open on the table. 'Perhaps,' I said, 'the Bursar can help me find the place.' I got up from my seat, went round the table behind Crawford, took the notebook and stood with it at Nightingale's side.

'It's somewhere near halfway through,' I said. 'We ought to have had it tagged.'

Nightingale was watching the leaves as I furled them through. 'Later than that,' he said, not pretending that he was lost.

'There it is, isn't it?' I said.

'Yes,' said Nightingale, gazing carefully at the page but without expression.

Everyone was watching him as he studied the page.

I brought back the open notebook into the centre of the room, and set it on the table in front of Crawford's place. The right-hand page was numbered in ink, a hundred and twenty-one. The date, also in ink, stood on the left of the top line. Two-thirds of the page was empty, except for the trace of gummy paper marking out the sides of a rectangle, where the photograph had been. At the bottom of the rectangle, nearer the middle than the left-hand corner, was a scrap of the print, perhaps a quarter of an inch square. Getliffe and the rest had agreed that this scrap told nothing. Beneath the rectangle, in the bottom third of the page, the caption took up three lines of holograph, in the neat spiky Edwardian script. It was written in pencil, and looked fainter than when I had seen it before. It also looked insignificant, something domesticable that couldn't cause trouble.

'There, gentlemen,' I said.

I had judged my line by now. I began:

'You heard Getliffe give you his opinion yesterday. No one gives that kind of opinion lightly: and you all know Getliffe as well as I do. He said it was possible that the photograph which used to be on this page' – I had put a finger on the notebook – 'had been torn out. Not by chance.'

'I want to know whether that was intended for me.' Nightingale's voice swept across the room.

'Of course,' I said, not replying to him directly, 'Getliffe felt justified in saying that the photograph might have been torn out. Not by chance. But he didn't feel justified in speculating about – by whom? We can't know. I should think it quite likely that we shall never know. From the point of view of this case, or for those who have been convinced for so long of Howard's innocence, it doesn't matter. All that I need remind you of is that this notebook passed through several hands before it looked like *this*. It's not my function to attribute motives. I assume, as Getliffe does, as other physical scientists in the college do, but not the Bursar, that there was a faked photograph on that page. That faked photograph could have been seen by several people. As Getliffe said, someone who was pro-Palairet, or anti-Howard, might have desired that photograph out of the way. That is as much as anyone has any right to say. But I think I might remind you of the history of the notebook.'

Carefully, for I had a double purpose, since I had at once to keep the suspicion on Nightingale and simultaneously leave both him and the Court a tolerable way out, I went through the history step by step. The last entry was on 20 April 1951. Palairet had died after a long but not disabling illness, on 5 January 1952. He might – I said it casually, but I could feel a jolt – have ripped the photograph out himself. Why not? He might have got tired of being silly. If it were still there when he died, the notebook stayed in his laboratory for months: a laboratory assistant could have had access: would he have known or cared? Palairet was a solitary worker, but there were two or three research students about. No one had thought of talking to them.

'Red herrings,' said Nightingale.

Some time in the summer of 1953, a time probably impossible to define now, I said, the executor had moved the notebook, part of the last batch of scientific remains. The executor was a clergyman of eighty, quite unscientific. On 11 December 1953, the notebook and other papers had reached Palairet's solicitors. On 15 December 1953, it had arrived at the Bursary.

'And now,' I said to Crawford, 'may I ask the Bursar one or two questions?'

'Are you prepared for that, Nightingale?' Crawford asked.

'Of course I am.'

I spoke diagonally across the table. 'You were the first person in the college to see the notebook?'

'Of course I was.'

'Do you remember when?'

'Probably the day it arrived.'

'Do you remember – this page?'

'You'll be surprised to know I do.'

'What did it look like?'

'I might as well say, I hadn't much time to get down to Palairet's papers. I happened to be busy at the Bursary. Some of my predecessors managed to do the job in two hours a morning, but I've never been clever enough.'

His eyes rolled, so that I could only see crescents of dark against the whites. That was the kind of spite that one used to hear from him when he was a younger man, when everything had gone wrong. It was spite against Winslow, who had been a mediocre bursar while Nightingale was an exceptional one. It was revenge against Winslow for his speech that morning.

But Nightingale, though at his tensest, sounded matter-of-fact as he went on. 'I didn't have much time to get down to the papers. But I think I remember skimming through the notebook. I think I remember one or two things on the right-hand pages.'

He was speaking like a visualiser. I asked: 'You remember this page?'

'I think so. Yes.'

'What did it look like?'

'*Not like that.*'

Everyone there was taken right aback. Though I went straight on, I was as astonished as the rest.

'What then?'

'There was a photograph there, top half of the page.'

'What sort of photograph?'

'Nothing like the one in Howard's thesis. Nothing wrong with the pinhole. Nothing wrong with it at all.'

'What did you do?'

'I just glanced at it. It wasn't very interesting.'

'You say there was nothing faked in the photograph. What about the caption?'

'I was too busy to worry about that.'

'Too busy?'

'Yes, too busy.' His voice rose.

'You just looked at this photograph? The rest of the page was like this, was it?' I pushed the notebook towards him.

'Yes.'

'You looked at the photograph? Then, what did you do?'

He stared at me. In an instant he said:

'Just put the book back with the rest of the Palairet dossier, of course.'

The night before, in the violence of his feeling, I hadn't known what

I believed. So now, gazing at the empty page, I lost my sense of fact. I could see him, on a December morning, also gazing at the page: either at the photograph securely there, or at the gap after he had torn it out. Everything seemed equally probable or improbable. It was a sort of vertigo that I had felt as a young man, when I did some criminal law: and since, in the middle of official security: or dazzled by the brilliance of suspicion. Somehow, immersed in facts, in the simple, natural facts of a crime, one found them diminish, even take the meaning out of, the lives in which they played a part.

In the midst of the facts of the crime, there were times when one could believe anything. Facts were hypnotic, facts were neutral, facts were innocent. Just as they were for those who had done a crime. If Nightingale had ripped out this photograph, it could seem such a simple, such an innocent act. It might seem unfair that there was all this fuss about it. It was more than possible, it was easy – I had known many who had managed it, I had myself, when I had performed an act which damaged others – to forget, because the act itself was so innocuous, that one had done it at all.

'You put it back with the photograph still there, you mean?'

'Of course I mean that,' Nightingale cried violently.

'But the photograph had disappeared when the notebook was next opened?'

'That's what we've heard.'

Up to that point, Nightingale had given me nothing. Suddenly I saw him enraged, his eyes rolling with hostility again.

'I'm sorry,' I said, 'have I misunderstood? The next person to look at the notebook was Skeffington, wasn't it?'

'I've been told so.'

'Well, then, when he looked at the notebook the photograph was missing?'

'We've heard a lot,' said Nightingale, 'of no one making allegations against any particular person. Two can play at that game. I'm not going to make an allegation against any particular person. But why shouldn't one of Howard's friends have taken out the photograph? The perfectly genuine photograph? Just to get this started again? Not to make any bones about it, just to point their fingers at me?'

'But that could only be Skeffington?'

'You're saying that, I'm not.'

'Could anyone call him one of Howard's friends?'

'You can answer for them. I'm not going to.'

'Can you imagine Skeffington doing any such thing for any man or any purpose in the world?'

'Some of them have imagined things against me, haven't they?'

It was past one o'clock. There I left it. As soon as the afternoon sitting began, I knew that, though I hadn't broken through, I had done something. The last five minutes of the morning. Nightingale's accusation against Skeffington – those were what Dawson-Hill was trying to wipe out. The accusation was fantastic, Dawson-Hill was as good as telling Nightingale as he questioned him: wouldn't he reconsider and retract it?

For a long time Nightingale was obdurate. He had made no allegations against anyone, obstinately he repeated. Dawson-Hill handled him with gentleness and respect. Gradually one could see the lineaments of Nightingale's face changing in response. But Dawson-Hill did not get the retraction, the total return to the plane of efficiency and reason, that he was working for. Later, he was working for another answer which he did not get. He was anxious because Nightingale had admitted to seeing the photograph. How much could Nightingale trust his memory? Couldn't this particular recollection be wrong? Wasn't it possible, or even likely, that the photograph was already torn out when the notebook first came under Nightingale's eyes? Dawson-Hill wanted an open, easy yes. It took him all his time to make Nightingale tolerate the bare possibility.

The open, easy answers came at last, in reply to the last two questions.

'You see nothing to make you believe that Palairet faked any photograph at any time?'

'Of course I don't.'

'You still believe that Howard was guilty?'

'I believe that,' said Nightingale, in a fierce, daring and tireless tone, 'as much as I believe anything.'

Letting down the tightness in the room, Dawson-Hill then asked Crawford about the timetable for the next day, Tuesday. G. S. Clark had already been told to be ready first thing in the morning. After that, Dawson-Hill presumed, he and I would make our final remarks?

'That sounds reasonable to me,' said Crawford.

That afternoon he had wilted, much more so than Winslow, who spoke next:

'My dear Master, I confess the word "reasonable" doesn't seem to me to be specially appropriate. I seem to remember remarking this morning that, without further mummery, we should reinstate this man. With your permission, may I repeat that?'

'I'm afraid the consensus of opinion this morning was that the hearing should go on,' said Crawford.

'We hadn't the benefit, I might point out,' Winslow snapped, 'of today's interesting proceedings. I should like to hear others' views.'

Crawford was going through the motions of presiding.

Nightingale broke in:

'You know mine.'

'It is?' Crawford asked.

'It doesn't need saying. I stick to the Court's decision.'

'So the Bursar and you,' Crawford said to Winslow, 'appear to cancel each other out.'

'Very remarkable,' Winslow replied.

'Brown?'

Crawford turned to his left. All day long Brown had been quiet, quieter than I had ever seen him at a meeting. He had passed no notes to Crawford. Now he said, still sitting back, his expression heavy but his voice practised and level:

'I'm inclined to think that we're gone too far to try to short-circuit things now. As for my opinion, Master, I should like to reserve it until Wednesday.'

'Well then,' said Crawford, 'we meet tomorrow.' He had suddenly begun to look like an old man. In a tone sharp and petulant, he went on: 'I wish I could see more agreement among us. As far as my own opinion goes, I shall attempt to give some indication of it tomorrow afternoon.'

CHAPTER XXXIV

CRIPPLE WALKING ON THE LAWN

'HE's all man,' said Irene with glee. She was not talking of a lover, but of her son, away at his preparatory school. She and Martin and I were sitting on their lawn before dinner on the Monday evening. I had not long arrived. Martin, whose face had caught the sun, was lying back in his deck-chair, his hand to his eyes, squinnying towards the bottom of the garden.

Martin also was talking about the boy. He was out of comparison more protective than she was. In the weekly letter home Martin read undertones of trouble, concealed from parents, which she laughed off.

'He's all man,' she cried. 'He'll be as wild as a hawk, one day. That will be something.'

Martin smiled. Even he, the most cautious of men, did not find the idea unpleasant. As for her, she adored it. I was thinking, Martin's love for the boy was possessive, deep, more spontaneous than any other affection he had ever had. She loved the boy too, perhaps as much as Martin did, but in a way that was not in the ordinary sense maternal. She was a good mother; she was conscientious, to an extent that people who had known her in her raffish days could scarcely believe. And yet really she loved the boy looking upwards, not downwards, looking towards the time when he was a man, and would take her out and tell her what to do.

Once, when she was young and chasing a man twice her age, I had heard her squeal with delight and say that she was good at daughtering, not at mothering. It was truer than she thought. In the future, in her own family, when a bulky, ageing woman, she would feel younger than any of the men.

That was already so in her marriage. In calendar time she was a few months older than Martin: she looked older. But, now they had been married fifteen years, she had come to behave like a daughter to a father, who was wilful, capricious, but who was her one support: to whom under the teasing and the disrespect, she felt nothing but passionate respect.

It seemed to suit them both. Against all the prophecies, against the forecasts of wiseacres like myself, the marriage had worked. As she walked back into the house to put dinner on, stoop-shouldered, thickening, still active and light on her feet, from his chair Martin's eyes followed her. It was not till then that he asked me about Nightingale. He had kept from her, I felt sure, how he had been more scrupulous, more gentle, than the rest of us. Perhaps he knew that that was an aspect of him, surprising to his friends, surprising even to himself, that she would not wish to see.

'How did Nightingale take it?' As he asked the question, he was puzzled to see me grin. It just happened that his tone had not been at all gentle. Somehow it brought back to mind one of old Gay's saga men enquiring how some unfortunate hero had faced an ordeal, such as having his house burned over his head.

'Well, how did he take it?' Martin repeated.

I described the day. Martin listened with concentration. He was careful not to say whether he thought Nightingale's behaviour pointed to guilt or innocence. He was too experienced to worry me with doubts just then. I was in the middle of it; he was not going, even by a fraction, to weaken my will. As usual, he was leaving nothing to chance. It rested with Crawford and Brown now: what were they going to say?

'It ought to be all right,' I said.

Dawson-Hill was dining with Crawford that evening, wasn't he? Martin asked.

'I don't know that I like that,' he reflected. He insisted that I ought to see Brown alone on the following, Tuesday, night. After all, Brown was a friend and a good man. Despite all this faction, I could still talk to him as a friend. It might be worth doing. Martin was sure that it was worth doing. I was not eager, but Martin pressed me. Would I mind if he fixed it up straightaway? I said that anxiety was running away with him. 'Never mind,' said Martin, and went away to telephone.

He returned across the grass with a furtive smile.

'Uncle Arthur wasn't any keener on it than you are. But he'll see you in his rooms tomorrow night at nine o'clock.'

After dinner, the four of us were sitting near the window looking out over the wide lawn. On the further side, G. S. Clark had come down his own steps and was walking near the edge – so that he kept in the full evening sun, out of the shadow of the elms. He was walking slowly, dragging his useless leg. It took him minutes to reach the bottom of the garden, turn, go on with his exercise. Yet his locomotion, though it was painful and laborious, did not look so. There seemed a jaunty, almost wilful air, in the way he pulled up the bad leg and then set off for his next step, as though this wasn't a very good way to walk, but one that, out of eccentricity, he happened to prefer.

There was a murmur of voices from inside the house, and Irene left us. I heard her saying from the passage between her kitchen and the Clarks', 'Yes, he's here.'

'I know it,' came Hanna's voice, clear, the intonation off-English.

The two women came into the drawing-room and walked towards us, Hanna neat and catlike by Irene's side. The previous year, Hanna had been letting herself go: but now her hair, which had strayed grey and wispy, was glossy black again, trim on the shapely hamitic head. Despite her age she had preserved, or re-attained, something of the look of a student – an intelligent, well-groomed student, eager, argumentative, ratty.

'I can't stay long,' she said, refusing to sit down.

I pointed to her husband, doing another limp across the lawn.

'I know. He will tire himself.' For an instant she spoke like a nurse. Then she said:

'He appears before the Court tomorrow? You know that?'

I replied that of course I did.

'This is all beastly!' cried Hanna. 'This is rotten!' She was angry with me because she was having to be disloyal. Whatever feeling she had had for Clark had been corroded: but she was a woman who wanted to be loyal, who thought she would have been happy being loyal, and somehow luck and history had always tripped her up. She wanted to be loyal to a cause, to be loyal to a man. She did not like to lead a shabby life. Her politics were pure and unpersonal, she was not predatory in her human relations. And yet, for reasons which with all her intelligence she did not understand, she was constantly finding herself in traps like this.

'I thought you must be warned. *He* will say' – she glanced with black eyes on to the lawn – 'that Howard does not know what truth is. He will give examples about Howard talking of his scientific work.'

She went on:

'*He* believes that no one with Howard's opinions has any conception of truth at all. Or any other of the private virtues. He believes that. He means what he says. That is his strength.'

She cried:

'Are you ready for that, Lewis?'

'I think so.'

'Don't underestimate him.'

I said that I didn't, which was true. But Hanna would have liked a more fiery response. With an ill-tempered toss of her head she said:

'I never know where I am with you Anglo-Saxons. I never know when you're going to be soft and when you're going to be tough. Living your life, Lewis, I suppose your must have had to be tough in your time.'

Martin told her gently:

'He'll have it in hand.'

'Will he?' she asked.

Once more she refused to sit down. She could not stay long, she said, watching for Clark to begin his climb into the house. But she did stay just long enough to give a display of subtlety. How many of the younger fellows had I seen, said Hanna, mondaine, brimming with the sophistication of Central Europe, travelled, experienced, twice-married, since I arrived in the college? She didn't mean Howard, of course – for whom, being vixenish as well as subtle that night, she expressed contempt. 'The dullest sort of left-wing camp-follower.' She didn't mean Howard – but which of the others, she said with an inconsequence so airy that it knocked one down, had I managed to see?

It showed the subtlety of a schoolgirl of sixteen. I saw Irene's eyes, narrow and sly, glinting towards Martin. They were both amused, but they were amused with a touch of concern. For Martin and I were fond of Hanna, and so, more oddly, was Irene. And here Hanna was trying, by guile, to get us to talk of Tom Orbell.

When he had first begun to lavish worship on her, she hadn't paid much attention. Then she had come to like him. With her usual lack of instinct, she had let her imagination dwell on Tom. She was at a stage – perhaps for the first time in her life – when being loved could compel love. Maybe already the first crystal of feeling had become sharp within her. I hoped not. She was hard, she had a tongue like a viper, but she was also generous. She had never begrudged those she knew the good things that had come their way – not successes, which she didn't mind about, but the serenity and the children she had never had. I was afraid, I was sure Irene was afraid, that this was another of her boss-shots. Tom was a gifted man, and a man of force: but I believed it suited his nature to give his love without return. Once she responded, with a vulnerable, impatient, mature love, he might be frightened off. That would mean humiliation for him – but for her, it could be worse than that.

CHAPTER XXXV

THE INNER CONSISTENCIES

FROM the beginning of the Tuesday morning session, G. S. Clark was sitting opposite the Master, his face fresh, his eyes sky-blue, looking frail, like one of Dickens's saintly, crippled children in the midst of able-bodied men. As I listened to him, he did not seem either saintly or crippled. He was the best witness who had come before the Court. He knew exactly what he had come to say, and without fuss, qualification or misgiving, said it. He did not believe in Howard's honesty, he told Dawson-Hill; he made no bones about it; he did not believe he was straight either as a man or a scholar. That was true in general and in particular. Clark said he couldn't trust a scientist who said there might be 'something in' Lysenko, who went in for complicated apologetics when faced with attacks on the truth. To Clark that chimed with all he knew of Howard, and with one piece of evidence in particular.

This piece of evidence he wanted to give the Court. Clark did not claim much for it; but it did show, he said, what Howard thought about his science. The incident had happened four years before, while Howard was in the middle of his work with Palairet. Clark could date it precisely, because it took place on the first day of the Yorkshire match at Fenner's.

'I was walking across Parker's Piece,' said Clark. Listening, I remembered hearing that he never missed a match. He took a passionate, vicarious joy in the athletic life. 'And Howard caught me up. That's not very difficult, at the pace I have to go.' He gave his fresh smile, with the absence of self-pity so complete that it was embarrassing. 'I was surprised to see him, because I knew he was working up in Scotland. But he told me he was staying in college for the weekend. I asked him how his research was going. He said that he was fed up. I tried to encourage him a bit – I said that not even a scientist could expect a new discovery every day of the week. I don't want to put words into his mouth, but I think I remember how he replied. He said something very close to this: "I'm not interested in any damn' discoveries. All I'm interested in is cooking up a thesis. Then I can publish a paper or two, by hook or by crook. That's the way everyone's playing this game. And I'm going to play the same game too." '

It sounded the literal truth. As Clark spoke, he had the expression, open-eyed, credulous and observant, that I had seen in professional security officers. He was not the man to invent: and indeed, if anyone had wanted to invent evidence, they would have invented something more damaging than that. It did not seem very damaging. It was an anti-climax after all the preparation. Yet I felt that everyone there was trusting his word, and at the same time liking him.

Soon it was my turn. I asked at once:

'I accept the conversation you've reported, completely. But is it really significant?'

'Recalling it in the light of what's happened,' said Clark, 'I think it may be.'

'I should have thought,' I said, 'that those remarks are just what you might expect, from a young man disappointed, in a bad patch, with his work not coming out? I should have thought a lot of us at that age might have said very much the same?'

'With respect, and admitting that my own standards of behaviour haven't been what I should like – I don't think I should.'

'Have you forgotten,' I said, 'what it's like to be chafing because things aren't going right? Did you never make a cynical remark when you were in that state?'

'Not that kind of remark,' said Clark. He gave me a sweet smile. I had to keep my voice from getting rougher. He provoked me more than most men. Yet his manner towards me stayed benign and friendly.

'What's more,' he said, 'I've never heard a scientist talk like that about his scientific work.'

'You can't seriously believe that Howard announced to you – you've never been a special friend of his, have you? – that he was going in for fraud?'

'All I'm entitled to believe, on the strength of what he said that morning, is that he's not a man of good character.'

'What do you mean by good character?'

'Yes,' G. S. Clark replied, 'I was afraid that you and I might not see alike on that.'

'I'm sure we don't.' I spoke harshly and I made sure that the Court recognised the harshness. I had decided that my only tactics were to change my tone. With the same edge, I asked: 'Why did you want to appear here at all this morning?'

'I'm sorry,' he said, still equable, 'but I understood any fellow had a right to do so. Perhaps the Master will correct—'

'Of course you had a right to,' I said. 'But most fellows didn't exercise it. Why did you?'

'I can't answer for others' sense of their responsibility, can I?'

'I'm talking about your sense of your responsibility. Why did you want to come?'

'Under correction,' said Clark, 'I thought I had something to tell the Court.'

'Why did you think it was worth telling?'

My tone had hardened further. The Master was stirring, clearing his throat, ready to stop me. Clark stayed unbullied, obdurate.

'That is what,' he said, 'I've been trying to explain.'

'You didn't appear just through personal animus?'

'I'm sorry, Eliot—' Crawford was beginning, but Clark said:

'I'm quite prepared to answer, Master. I can honestly say that I have no personal animus whatsoever against this man.'

His confidence was unshaken. Brown was frowning; the Court was against me. But he was going where I wanted to lead him.

'I accept that. It might be less dangerous if you had,' I said. 'But you have political animus?'

'I don't approve of his political convictions.'

Still the Court was against me.

Still they felt – one could sense it in the room – that what he stood for, not always what he said, was right.

'I mean rather more than that,' I said. 'Don't you really think that a man of his convictions is a bad man?'

G. S. Clark was so set that he didn't hesitate. He said:

'I'm never quite happy at judging character outside the Christian framework.'

'You've got to. Don't you really believe that a man of Howard's convictions isn't to be trusted in any circumstances?'

'In many circumstances, I believe his convictions would be an obstacle to my giving him trust as I understand it.'

'Don't you really believe that he's not a man of the same kind as yourself?'

Clark gave a smile sweet and obstinate. 'I believe there are certain differences.'

'Don't you really believe that such men ought to be got rid of?'

'Really, Master,' Dawson-Hill protested, 'you can't permit that question—'

Clark was still smiling. I let it go at that.

In my last speech, which was a short one, but which was interrupted by lunch, I tried to make use of Clark's special kind of prejudice. Could the Court really give the faintest encouragement to the view that character and opinion went hand in hand? Wasn't this nonsense, and dangerous nonsense? Didn't we all know scientists – and I named one – whose opinions were indistinguishable from Howard's, and whose integrity was absolute? Wasn't it the chronic danger of our time, not only practical but intellectual, to let the world get divided into two halves? Hadn't this fog of prejudice – so thick that people on the two sides were ceasing to think of each other as belonging to the same species – obscured this case from the beginning? Hadn't it done harm to the college, to Howard himself, and to the chance of a just decision?

I said this without emollient words. G. S. Clark had given me the opening, and I was talking straight at Crawford, some of whose beliefs I thought I might still touch.

Then I said, and this time I was talking straight at Brown: 'As a matter of fact, I've come to know Howard moderately well on account of this business. I don't say that he would be my favourite holiday companion, but I think he's an honest man.'

It was then that we stopped for lunch, which was a sombre, creaking meal. Nightingale, alone of the four Seniors, did not look tired; he seemed buoyed up by the energy of strain, just as, in an unhappy love affair, one is as springy as though one had been taking benzedrine. Outside the Master's dining-room, the sunlight was brilliant. Crawford and Brown, not altering their habits by a single tick, drank their ritual glasses of wine, but I noticed that old Winslow, as though determined to keep his lids propped up, drank only water.

When we were back in the combination room I did not go on long. I said that, in the whole hearing, there had been just one critical piece of testimony – Francis Getliffe's. He hadn't produced a new fact: but he had produced a new and dangerous possibility. What he had said couldn't be unsaid. He had deliberately told the Seniors it mustn't be. No one wanted to bring up new suspicions, which would only fester because they couldn't be proved. No one wanted to institute new proceedings. Surely the best, and as far as that went the only course, was to declare a moratorium. Howard's innocence had to be officially recognised. Those I represented could not be content with less. But they were quite prepared to regard anything else that had been said or done as though it had not been. I finished, looking across the table:

'I don't believe there's any other course for the Court which is either prudent or just. If the Court doesn't do it, I can't see how the college will be worth living in for a decade. Just for policy's sake, even if there were a shade of doubt about Howard, I should try to persuade you to avoid that. But in my view there is no shade of doubt – so it isn't only policy or ordinary human sense that I'm asking you to act on. Those would be good reasons for altering your decision about Howard. But the best reason is that the decision – although most of us would have made it in your place – happened to be unjust.'

Dawson-Hill was quite unjaded. He had the stamina of a lawyer trained for trails. He showed less wear and tear than anyone present. Yet, like me, he chose to cut his speech short. Partly, I thought, he felt the older men were exhausted. Partly, like me, he couldn't get any response in that strained but deadened room. His tone throughout, under the casual mannerisms, was sharper than at any previous time, sometimes troubled, and often edged.

'Can Sir Francis Getliffe be wrong, I ask myself?' he demanded, at his most supercilious. 'I can only conclude that, just occasionally, in the world of mortal circumstances, the answer might conceivably be yes. Of course, I recognise that Sir Francis is most high-minded. Even those like myself who disagree with him on public issues recognise that he is more high-minded than is given to most of us. But I ask myself, can a man so high-minded, so eminent as a scientist, conceivably be wrong? Is it possible to be high-minded and at the same time rather curiously irresponsible?'

Dawson-Hill was sitting upright, with his head thrown back. 'I have to conclude that the answer may be yes. For, after all, his speculations before this Court – and with all my veneration, my heartfelt veneration for Sir Francis, I am not able to call them more than speculations – might involve the good name of others. They might, by a fantastic stretch of improbability, involve the good name of a most respected member of this Court. Dr Nightingale faced this issue plainly yesterday morning, and it would, I know, be going against his wishes, it would be less than fair to the respect that we all ought to bear him, if I didn't state it just as categorically now.' He inclined his head to Nightingale, whose eyes lit up. 'I put to you this possibility. It might be considered by some that, if this Court reverses its decision, if it reinstates Howard, then it is giving some weight to Sir Francis's speculations. It might even be considered by some that it indicated a lack of confidence in Dr Nightingale. Could one blame Dr Nightingale if he took that line himself? I am not authorised to say that he or others will take that line. I mention it only as a possibility. But I suggest that it exists.'

That was bold. Bolder than I counted on, or wanted. Afterwards, the rest of Dawson-Hill's speech went according to plan. Dismissing Getliffe's speculations, he said, he came back to the much more natural alternative, which sensible men had taken for granted all along, that the photograph had disappeared by accident, that probably it had disappeared before the Bursar saw the notebook, and that he had, to his own inconvenience, suffered a trick of memory, that it had been a genuine photograph, and that the caption was just an old man's ill-judged comment, 'perhaps a shade too optimistic, for his own private eye'. Surely that was the rational explanation, for rational men who weren't looking for plots and conspiracies and marvels?

'Which brings me to the very simple alternative with which the Court had to cope in the beginning,' he said. 'Regrettably, there has been a piece of scientific chicanery. We all know that, and it is a misfortune which the college didn't deserve. The Court previously had to choose, and still has to choose, between attributing this chicanery to one of two men. One was a man rightly honoured, an eminent scholar, dedicated and pious. The other is a man whom we can form our own opinions of. Master, I am a rather simple man. I don't possess the resources of my distinguished colleague. I don't find it easy to denigrate good old men, or to find virtues in those who have renounced all that most of us stand for. If I had been a member of the Court, I should have made the same choice as the Court has made before. I now suggest to the Court that, in spite of the painful circumstances, all it can do is repeat that same choice and reiterate that same decision.'

As he stopped, the grandfather clock in the corner racketed, coughed, whirred, and then gave a stroke just audible, like the creak of a door. It was a quarter past three. Crawford blinked, and said: 'Thank you, Dawson-Hill. Thank you both.' Staring straight in front of him he said: 'Well, that brings us to the last stage of our labours.'

'Master,' said Brown, quick off the mark, 'I wonder if I might make a suggestion.'

'Senior Tutor?'

'I don't know whether you or our other colleagues feel as I do,' said Brown, 'but as far as I'm concerned, listening to what to all of us have been difficult and distressing arguments, I think I've almost shot my bolt. I wonder whether you would consider breaking off for today, and then the Seniors could meet in private tomorrow morning when we're a little fresher?'

'In private?' Crawford looked a little bemused, listening, as he had done for so many years, to Brown's guidance.

'I don't think we need call on our legal friends. We have to reach a settlement on the basis of what they've said in front of us. Then we can perhaps discuss the terms of the settlement with them tomorrow, later in the day.'

For an instant Crawford sat without responding. Then he said: 'No, Senior Tutor. I gave notice yesterday that I should have something to say this afternoon. Speaking as Master, I wish to say it before we finish today's hearing.'

He said it with a mixture of dignity and querulousness. In exhaustion, he was letting something out. Right through his Mastership, for sixteen years Brown had held his hand, told him which letters to write, advised him whose feelings wanted soothing. He had used Brown as a confidential secretary: had he noticed how much he depended upon him? Until the affair, it had been a good Mastership. Did he know that he had Brown to thank for that? Now, when for once he asserted himself and upset Brown's protocol, one saw that he did know; but he didn't thank Brown for it. It was the kind of service which no one ever thanks a grey eminence for.

'As I've just told the Senior Tutor,' Crawford announced to the room at large, 'I wish to make a statement myself. But first of all, am I right in assuming' – he turned to Winslow – 'that you are of the same way of thinking as you were yesterday?'

Nightingale's voice came from beyond Winslow.

'I certainly am. I should like the Court to know that I agree with every word of Mr Dawson-Hill's.'

'You're continuing to vote against reinstatement?' said Crawford.

'Of course.'

Winslow leaned forward, hands clasped on the table, looking under his eyebrows with a subfusc pleasure:

'For myself, Master, I can only acknowledge the Bursar's most interesting observation. Like him, however, I find it remarkably difficult to change my mind. I think that answers your question, Master?'

Crawford sat back in his chair. His physical poise stayed with him, the poise of a man who had always been confident of his muscles. But his voice had lost its assurance altogether.

'Then we cannot avoid a disagreement. I think, as I thought yesterday, that it is time for me to speak.' He was looking straight in front of him past the chair, now empty, where the witnesses had sat. 'And speaking not as Master but as a man of science, I have to say that there are things in this hearing which have given me cause for much regret. Not only having to deal with this distasteful business of scientific cheating, which is, by its nature, a denial of all that a man of science lives for or ought to live for. But apart from that, there have been other things, straws in the wind maybe, which give reason to think that contemporary standards among a new scientific generation are in a process of decline. We have had a report this morning of this man Howard, whom we elected a fellow in a scientific subject in all good faith, expressing lack of interest in his research, as though that were a permissible attitude. It would not have been a permissible attitude in the laboratories here fifty years ago. When I was beginning my own research, I used to *run* to my laboratory. And before that, I used to *run* to my lectures. That was how *we* felt about our work.'

I had never heard Crawford reminisce, or show the slightest trace of sentimentality. For an instant, he was maundering. He jerked himself together: 'But we must give our minds to that decline in standards on another occasion. We now have to conclude the deplorable business for which we've been sitting here. I find it almost intolerable to have had to devote thought and attention to this deplorable business. There have been times, I confess, when it has seemed like asking bloodstock to draw a cart. But it has not been possible to escape. I cannot assess how much nearer we have been brought to wisdom. For myself, speaking as a member of the Court, all I know is that I can see my own course of action.'

Someone stirred. Crawford's face and body were quite still.

'I find it distressing not to have more factual certainty. I do not take the view, held apparently by some, that in matters of this kind one can usefully see into other people's minds. Speaking as a man of science, I do not apprehend the suggestions made why such and such a person may have done such and such. For myself, I have to fall back on first principles. My first principle is to discount what may have been happening in people's minds and to give weight to the man who knows most about the concrete phenomenon.'

He went on: 'That brings me straight away to our colleague, Getliffe. Here I might add something, from my own position, to what has been said by the senior fellow present. As he rightly told us, Getliffe is a distinguished man of science. He has served twice on the Council of the Royal Society, overlapping on one of those occasions with myself. He has not yet been awarded the Copley Medal' – said Crawford with satisfaction, who had – 'but in 1950 he won the only slightly less distinguished Royal Medal. I must say, I cannot find it within me to disregard a man of such credentials. We have known for some time, of course, that he was uneasy about the Court's original decision. I was never comfortable, as my colleagues will remember, that he was not altogether with us. But I was under the impression, which I believe was not completely false, that he was prepared to concede that there was a genuine margin for disagreement. Speaking both as Master and as a man of science, I feel that on Sunday, before the Court, he removed that impression. I have hoped all along that this wretched business could be settled without too much disturbance. But though nothing we can do now will please everybody, I think there is only one thing I for myself can say or do. I do not know that Getliffe convinced me that Howard was, beyond the possibility of doubt, innocent. He did convince me, however, that no body of sensible men, certainly no body of men of science, could say that he was guilty. Therefor I find myself obliged to believe that he has received less than fair treatment, and that he should be reinstated by this Court. I have to say so now.'

I lit a cigarette, looking across at Brown. Was it all right? I was thinking, Crawford, who for so long had been permanently middle-aged, had suddenly seemed old. I had seen the same change and the same symptoms in predecessors of his: men quite different from him except that they had just come to the critical point. He was thinking now only of the mainstay of his life: and for him, the mainstay had been his science, his position among scientists. Not that he was a man, one would have thought, who needed to buoy up his self-esteem: yet that had been the purpose, the meaning, the lustre of his life, and in his seventies, when he thought about it, as he did increasingly, it gave him happiness.

He had enjoyed being Master, just as he enjoyed any honour that came his way: although he had been in many ways a good one (we who had opposed his election had been wrong, I had long before admitted), to him it had really been an honour, not a job: his only ambition in the Lodge had been a quiet reign and no fuss. He had no involvement in other people, and very little feeling for them. Like many men whose human interests burn low, he was often, for that very reason, comfortable to be with, just because he made no demands. It was from the same source that he derived his dignity, his kind of impersonal tact. And yet, in the end, it had let him down. Throughout the affair, he hadn't been able to draw on enough reserves of feeling to give the college the leadership it needed. This was painful to him, it had aged him: not so much because he felt inadequate as because, step by step, he had found himself dragged into scenes of personal emotion. For, again like many men themselves not involved, he had a dread, superstitious or pathological, of feeling in others. The undertow of violence, of suspicion, of passion, had dragged at everyone in the Court: but he was the only one who had felt it like an old man's illness.

Without any hurry, as though he were discussing giving a grant of ten pounds to a choral exhibitioner, Brown said:

'Master, I'm afraid this puts me in a rather awkward position.'

He meant that the decision now rested with him. He said it without anxiety, for though he was far-sighted he was not anxious. He said it without drama, for no one was less histrionic. Yet his expression was full of care and feeling.

'I admit,' said Brown, still in a round, conciliatory tone, which contradicted his expression, 'that I am a little sorry that everyone has committed himself rather further than I should be prepared to do this afternoon. I am right in thinking, Master, that we shall have an opportunity to exchange views tomorrow? That is, when the Seniors meet in private?'

'If you wish it, Senior Tutor.'

'Thank you, Master. I don't feel able to come down finally one way or the other, until I've slept on it.'

Crawford was gathering his gown round him, ready to rise, when Brown went on:

'If you will allow me one last thought today. I have a feeling that it is only fair to Eliot, who has given us so much of his time and trouble.' He faced me with a slight smile. 'I have listened most carefully, as we all have, to his representations. We are all seized, as I am sure he knows, of the complexities of this case and its repercussions. Some of those repercussions, I am certain that he will recognise, are no fault of this Court. We have been given very pointed warnings by our other friend, Dawson-Hill. Of course Eliot will realise the responsibility those warnings put upon us. In most circumstances, as everyone in this room knows, I think, I should be the first person to look for a compromise. But I'm afraid I should have to stick in my heels against a compromise, if and when it might imply casting the slightest insinuation – the slightest insinuation that I was acquiescing in any suggestion of blame thrown against valued colleagues and innocent men.'

CHAPTER XXXVI

SPECIAL KIND OF IRRITATION

AT six o'clock, in the Howards' flat, as I listened to them talking to an Indian, I was preoccupied by the news which I had had no chance to break. If it had been good news, I should have somehow slipped in a word. Did they know that? They were both, Howard especially, more anxious than when they waited in Martin's room in April. Howard had taken two stiff drinks in a quarter of an hour.

The Indian, whose name was Pande, had been in the room when I arrived. He had a small, delicate, handsome head; by the side of the Howards he looked quiveringly fine-nerved. He was drinking orange-juice while the rest of us drank whisky. Laura was trying to persuade him to sign some protest. He was too polite to say that he did not want to, too polite even to change the conversation. As Laura got up to fill a glass, I noticed that she was pregnant. With her strong, comely figure, she carried the child lightly; she might be already four or five months gone. She saw my glance, and gave, to herself, not to me, a smile that was a mixture of triumph and modesty.

'You must see—' she said to the Indian, standing over him.

Very politely, Dr Pande did not quite see. I was thinking, he would have called himself as progressive as the Howards; but he was nothing like at home with them. They were too positive. With his nerves, at least, he would have been more at home with a quiet reactionary, like G. S. Clark. Once more the useless rat-race of anxiety went on in my mind: what words exactly had Brown used? Could they mean anything but their obvious meaning, that he had decided against us and that we had lost? Was he warning me that it was no use trying to move him that night?

The Howards, though they had not swerved from trying to persuade the Indian, kept slipping glances in my direction, making attempts to read my face. But they were so tough and disciplined that they stopped themselves trying to hurry Dr Pande out.

Howard was replying to one of his expressions of doubt.

'That's all very well. But objectively, it's holding up things. We haven't got time for that.'

Howard was a shade less pertinacious than his wife. Soon he was telling Pande that he needn't add his signature until next day. Pande gave a sigh, and with a jubilation of relief, looked round him.

'This is a jolly luxurious flat!' said Dr Pande.

'You'll sign tomorrow?' said Laura.

'I will talk to you. Perhaps on the telephone,' said Dr Pande, as, very light, very ectomorphic, he went out of the room.

We could hear his footsteps down the stairs. They looked at me.

'Is it all right?' asked Laura.

'No,' I said.

Laura flushed with shock. For the first time I saw tears in her eyes. While Howard stood there, his mouth open, not putting a face on it, not aggressive, for once undefiant. But I did not feel protective to either of them. For him I felt nothing at all, except a special kind of bitter irritation. It was the kind of irritation one feels only for someone for whom one has tried to do a good turn and failed: or for someone for whom one has tried to get a job, and who has been turned down.

Laura recovered herself. What had happened? I told them there had been a division on the Court. That was as far as I felt like going or could safely go. Howard pressed me for names, but I said that I couldn't give them. 'Damn it,' he said, 'are you an M.I.5 man?' It seemed to me that he was capable of believing that literally.

The Court would issue its finding the next day, I explained. Laura was back in action. So it wasn't all settled? So there were still things that might be done?

'Are you doing them?' she cried.

I said that I was doing all I could think of. I did not tell them that I was seeing Brown that night. Their hopes were reviving, despite anything I said. I repeated, I didn't believe anything I could do was relevant now: I had no support to offer them.

As soon as I left their flat and got down into the street, I felt an anger which couldn't find an outlet, a weight of anger and depression such as made the brilliant summer evening dark upon the eyes. I was not angry for Howard's sake: he remained more an object of anger than its cause. I didn't give a thought about injustice. No, the thought of Howard, the thought of Laura, the thought of seeing Brown, they were just tenebrous, as though they had added to my rage, but were looked at through smoked glass. There was nothing unselfish, nothing either abstract or idealistic about my anger, nothing in the slightest removed from the frets of self. I was just enraged because I hadn't got my way.

Slowly I walked by St Edward's Church and out into the Market Place. I bought a newspaper, as automatically as one of Pavlov's dogs, at the corner. I went into the Lion, drank a glass of beer, and was staring at the paper.

A thick, throaty voice came from over my shoulder.

'Why, it's the man himself!'

I looked up and saw Paul Jago, heavy, shabby, smiling.

He asked me to have another drink and, as he sat down beside me, explained that his wife had gone off to a sick relative. It was a long time, he said, since he had walked about the town alone in the evening, or been into a pub. He was studying me with eyes which, through the thick lenses, were still appraising, in the lined, self-indulgent face.

'Forgive me, old chap,' he said, 'am I wrong, or are you a bit under the weather?'

The quick sympathy shot out. Even when he was at his most selfish, one felt it latent in him. Now it was so sharp that I found myself admitting I was miserable. About the Howard case, I said.

'Oh, that,' Jago replied. Just for an instant his tone contained pride, malice, an edge of amusement. Then it softened again. 'I'm rather out of touch about that. Tell me about it, won't you?'

I did not mind being indiscreet, not with him. I did not even rationalise it by thinking that, as a fellow entitled to a place on the Court, he had a right to know. I let it all spill out. It seemed natural to be confiding in this ageing, seedy man, with the wings of white hair untrimmed over his ears, with the dandruff on the shoulders of his jacket. Yet we had never been intimates. Perhaps it seemed more natural just because he was seedy, because he had allowed himself to go to waste, had made a cult of failure and extracted out of it both a bizarre happiness and a way of life. It was not only his sympathy which led me on.

He soon grasped what had happened in the Court. His mind was as quick as his sympathy, and, although he had perversely misused it for so long, or not used it at all, it was still acute. About Getliffe's statement and Nightingale's answers the day after, he asked me to tell him again.

'I want to be sure,' he said. He gave a curious smile.

It was after half past seven, and I had already told him that I was calling on Brown at nine. He invited me to have dinner at an hotel. When I said that I didn't want much of a meal, he humoured me. He went back with me to the college, where we called at the buttery and, like undergraduates, came away with loaves of bread, a packet of butter and a large slab of cheese. In my room, Jago greedily buttered great hunks of crusty loaf. At the same time, his eyes lit up, he listened to me repeat in detail what Nightingale had said the day before and what Brown had said that day.

CHAPTER XXXVII

APPEAL

EATING a crust, butter sliding on to his fingers, Jago listened to me. He did not criticise or doubt. Once or twice he asked for an explication. He nodded. Suddenly he broke out:

'Say no if I'm imposing myself—'

'What do you mean?'

'Do you mind if I come with you to see Brown?'

It was a surprise and not a surprise. He was immersed in the drama. I had known that he was wanting to take a part. Was it just good-nature? He was a man of charm: maybe he still, just for an evening out, so to speak, liked proving that the charm wasn't lost. Or was it remorse, having turned me down before? Remorse, and the self-satisfaction that things would have gone better if the college had been in his hands?

'I've got a feeling,' said Jago, 'that Arthur Brown might pay some attention to me. We were close, once.'

On the stroke of nine, we walked together over the cobbles at the foot of Brown's staircase. After the week's heat, the smell from the wallflowers beneath the ground-floor windows was dusty and dry. When we had climbed the stairs, I went first into the room. Brown's greeting was friendly, but not open. When he saw Jago behind me, he grimaced with astonishment.

'My dear Paul!' he cried. He crossed the room and shook hands with Jago. 'How ever long is it since you've been in here?'

'Much too long,' said Jago lightly. 'And I mustn't come in now on false pretences, must I?'

'What's this?' But Brown had known as soon as he saw Jago.

'I'm afraid I've come to add my representations to Eliot's, you know.'

'Is that fair?' asked Brown.

'Don't you think it is?' said Jago, without self-consciousness.

'Anyway,' said Brown, 'it's very good to have you here, whatever you've come for.'

Brown's affection and pleasure were genuine. Tactically, he was on his guard. He did not need teaching that Jago would try to work on him; nor that, without a purpose, Jago would not have come. It was he who warmed to the reconciliation, if that was what it was, not Jago. And yet Brown had watched Jago let himself slip; he had watched him contract out of all human obligations, except one. To Brown, whatever his luck, any indulgence like that would have been outside his nature. He was stoic to the bones; whatever tragedy came his way, the King's government, the college, his relations with his friends, had to be carried on. He disapproved of Jago's abandonments; he scarcely understood them and in a sense he despised them. (Perhaps he also envied someone who could so totally let his emotions rip?) Further, he knew, no one better, that Jago had turned against him. But none of this, though it might have tinged Brown's affection for him, had uprooted it. Brown's affections, in spite of – or more truly, because of – their being so realistic, were more tenacious than any of ours. He could not change them as he did a suit of clothes or a set of tactics. It was a handicap to him, I used to think, as a politician: perhaps the only handicap he had.

Brown went through the ritual of drink-offering without hastening his pace.

'I've got a little white Burgundy waiting for you,' he said to me. 'I had an idea it might be rather restful after the work you've had to put in. Paul, unless my memory escapes me, you never cared much for it, did you?'

Brown's memory did not escape him. Jago asked for a sip of whisky.

'I don't think that's very difficult,' Brown replied, going out to his gyp-room and bringing back whisky bottle, siphon and jug of water to put by Jago's side.

'There we all are!' said Brown, settling into his chair. He told Jago that he was looking well. He asked after his garden. He was ready, just as though he were an American businessman, for an indefinite exchange of cordialities before getting to the point. Whoever first came to the point, it would not be he. But it was not really a battle of patience. Jago would have lost it anyway, but he was not playing. Very soon he gave a smile and said:

'I've been hearing a good deal about this case tonight.'

'Have you, Paul?'

'And about what's happened in the Court – of course, I don't question what Eliot's told me—'

'I'm sure,' said Brown, 'that you're right not to.'

All of a sudden, Jago's tone sharpened.

'Am I right, Arthur,' he leaned forward, 'that you've seen this case all along in terms of people? In terms of your summing-up of the people concerned?'

Brown's stonewall response did not come quite so pat. He said:

'That may be fair comment.'

'You have always seen everything that way.'

Jago spoke affectionately, but with weight of knowledge, as though drawing on their associations of the past and on history each could remember, as though he still possessed the moral leadership he had had when they were both young men. If I had used the same words to Brown, they would not have meant the same.

'I shouldn't regard that,' said Brown, 'as entirely unjust.'

'But for once, in this case, it may have made *you* entirely unjust.'

'You can't expect me to accept that, Paul.'

'I put it to you,' all Jago's reserves of force were coming out of him, together with a sadic spirt, 'that you've never been vain about much except your summing-up of people?'

'I shouldn't have thought that I claim much for myself in that respect.'

'Don't you?'

'I hope not,' said Brown.

'More than you think, Arthur, more than you think.'

'Only a fool,' said Brown, 'claims that he knows much about people.'

'Only a fool,' Jago darted in, 'claims it in the open. But I've known wise men, including you, who claim it to themselves.'

'I can only say again, I hope that isn't true.'

'Haven't you assumed all along that young Howard couldn't be innocent?'

'That's not quite fair,' said Brown steadily, 'but I don't want to shilly-shally. Put it another way: everything I know about the man makes me think that he could possibly be guilty.'

Jago had an intent, sharp smile.

'As for Nightingale. Haven't you assumed all along that Nightingale was above reproach? Haven't you closed your mind to what Getliffe said? Haven't you refused to believe it?'

'I should find it very hard to believe.'

'Why do you find it hard?'

Brown's high colour went higher still. He started in a burst of anger, his first that night.

'I regard it as abominably far-fetched.'

'Were you always so convinced that Nightingale was above reproach?' Jago spoke quietly, but again with weight and knowledge. When Brown had been his closest friend and had run him for the Mastership, it had been Nightingale, so they thought then, who had done them down.

After a pause Brown replied: 'You have good reason not to like him, Paul.' He paused again. 'But we should never, even then, have thought him capable of this—'

'I should have thought him capable of anything,' said Jago. 'And I still do.'

'No.' Brown had recovered his confidence and obstinacy. 'I can't see him like that.'

'You're being blinder than you used to be—'

'You mustn't think that I'm specially fond of him. I don't mind telling you, we haven't got much in common. But it sticks in my gullet not to do one's best for the chap with a record like that.'

A military record, Brown meant. Was this one of the reasons, I suddenly thought, for what had baffled me all along – Brown's loyalty to Nightingale and the origin of it? Brown, who on medical grounds missed the first war, had the veneration for physical courage of those who doubted their own. But, more than that, he had a kind of veneration for the military life. Tory, intensely patriotic, he believed, almost as simply as he might have done as a child, that, while he was sitting in his college rooms during two wars, men like Nightingale had kept him safe. He was one of those rare men who liked recognising their debts. Most of us were disposed to deny our gratitude. Arthur Brown was singular because he actually liked not denying his.

'I feel,' Brown said, 'a man like that deserves a bit of looking after.'

'You mean, that you won't let yourself see him as straight as you let yourself see anyone else?'

'I mean,' Brown replied, unmoved, 'that when I sit next to him in hall I am prepared to make a few allowances.'

'Arthur,' said Jago, 'do you realise how much you're evading me?'

'He's not an easy man. And I like an easy man,' said Brown, with impenetrable obstinacy. 'But I feel he's entitled to a bit of protection.'

'You mean, you won't let yourself entertain any suspicion of him, however reasonable?'

'I do not admit for a second that this is reasonable.'

'You won't even admit the possibility, not even the possibility, that he did this?' Jago said with violence.

'As I think I've told you, I should find it very hard to admit that.'

It was then I thought Jago had come to the end, and so had we all.

Jago switched again.

'I should like to tell you something about myself, Arthur.'

He had spoken intimately. Brown, still on guard, said yes.

'I should like to tell you something about my wife. I've never said it to anyone, and I never thought I should.'

'How is she, Paul?' asked Brown. He said it with warmth.

'You never liked her much, did you? No' – Jago was smiling brilliantly – 'none of my friends did. It's too late to pretend now. Oh, I can understand how you feel about her. And I hope you understand that I've loved her all my life and that she is the only woman I have ever loved.'

'I think I knew that,' Brown said.

'Then perhaps you'll know why I detest speaking of her to people who don't like her,' Jago flashed out, not only with love for his wife, but with intense pride. 'Perhaps you'll know why I detest speaking of her in the way I've got to this very moment.'

'Yes, I think I do.' Now it was Brown who spoke intimately.

'I've never spoken to you or anyone else about the last election. I suppose I've got to now.'

'It's better to let it lie,' said Brown.

'No. I suppose everyone still remembers that this man Nightingale sent round a note with a reference to my wife?'

'I hope that's all long forgotten,' said Brown, as though to him it really was a distant memory, one pushed for good sense's sake deep down.

'I can't believe that!' cried Jago.

'People don't remember these things as you think they do,' said Brown.

'Do you imagine I don't remember it? Do you think that many days have passed when I haven't had to remember every intolerable thing that happened to me at that time?'

'It's no use saying so, but I've always wished you wouldn't dwell on it.'

'It's no use saying so. Don't you think my wife remembers everything that happened? Most of all, the note that this man Nightingale sent round?'

Brown nodded.

'If it hadn't been for what Nightingale did then, she believed then and still believes things might have gone the other way. So she thinks she ruined me.'

'Looking back,' said Brown, 'for any comfort it may be worth, I don't believe it made a decisive difference—'

'That's neither here nor there,' said Jago, brilliant, set free. 'My wife does. She did so at the time. That is what I have to tell you. Do you know what she did, three months after the election was over?'

'I'm afraid I can guess,' said Brown.

'Yes, she tried to take her life. I found her one night with her bottle of sleeping-pills empty beside her. And a note. You can imagine what the note said.'

'I can.'

After an instant's pause, Jago glanced straight at Brown and said: 'And so I feel entitled to ask you not to rule out the possibility, the bare possibility, that this man Nightingale may have done something else. I admit there's no connection. So far as I know, he may have been spotless ever since. But still I feel entitled to ask you not to rule the possibility out.'

Brown said: 'You're not making this easy for either of us, are you?'

'Do you think,' cried Jago, 'that it's been easy for me to tell you this?'

Brown did not reply at once. I heard the hiss and tinkle as Jago refilled his glass.

Then suddenly Jago, as though in a flash he had seen Brown's trouble, made another switch.

'You won't admit the possibility, not even the possibility, that in any circumstances Howard might be innocent?'

For an instant Brown's face lightened, as though he welcomed Jago's question, put that way round.

He said:

'Will you repeat what you've just asked me?'

When Jago had done so, Brown sat without expression. Then he said, slowly and deliberately:

'No, I can't be as positive as that.'

'Then you do admit the possibility that the man's innocent?'

'The bare possibility. I think I shouldn't be comfortable with myself unless I do.'

I lit a cigarette. I felt the anti-climax of relief.

'Well, what action are you going to take?' Jago pressed him.

'Oh, that's going much too far. I shan't even have my own mind clear until tomorrow.'

With friendly roughness Jago went on:

'Never mind the formalities. There's some action you must take.

'I've still not decided what it is.'

'Then it's pretty near time you did.'

Jago drank some whisky, laughing, exhilarated because he had got home.

'An old dog can't change his tricks. I'm not as quick as some of you,' said Brown, domesticating the situation. 'You mustn't expect too much. Remember, both of you, I've only admitted the bare possibility. I'm not prepared to see other people blackguarded for the sake of that. And that's as far as I'm able to go tonight. Even that means eating more of my words than I like doing. I don't mind it with you, Paul, but it isn't so congenial elsewhere. Still, I've got this far. I think I shouldn't be entirely easy if we didn't make some accommodation for Howard.'

Brown did not like saying he had been wrong. He liked it less than vainer men: for, genuinely humble as he was, believing without flummery that many men were more gifted, he nevertheless had two sources of pride. One was, to use Jago's peculiar phrase, in his summing-up of people: the other was in what he himself would have called his judgment. He believed that half his colleagues were cleverer than he was, but he didn't doubt he had more sense. Now, for once, that modest conceit was deflated. And yet he seemed, not only resentful, but relieved. For days, I suspected, maybe for weeks, his stubbornness – which, as he grew older, was becoming something more than tenacity, something more like an obsession – had been fighting both with his realism and his conscience. Brown had had his doubts about the Howard case. Perhaps, as with many characters of exceptional firmness, he had them and did not have them. He didn't mind, in secret he half-welcomed, the call Jago had made on his affections. For Brown had been able to use it as an excuse. Just as Jago was not above working his charm, his intensity, for his own purposes (was this half-revenge, I had been thinking? had he exaggerated the story he had just told?), so Brown was not above working the strength of his own affections. He was really looking for an excuse inside himself for changing. The habit of stubbornness was becoming too strong for him. He was getting hypnotised by the technique of his nature. He was glad of an excuse to break out. His affection for Jago gave him precisely that. It allowed him, as a visit from me alone almost certainly would not have done, to set his conscience free.

There was another reason, though, not so lofty, why Brown welcomed an excuse to change. His own stubbornness, his own loyalties, had been getting in the way of his political sense. He knew as well as anyone that during the affair he had mismanaged the college. If he continued to 'stick in his heels', he would go on mismanaging it. In the end, since much of Brown's power depended on a special kind of trust, it would take his power away.

It had been astonishing to me, throughout the affair, how far stubbornness could take him. He was a supreme political manager. Nevertheless, his instincts had ridden him; they had ridden him right away from political wisdom; for the only time in his career as a college boss, he had not been sensible.

But now at last, triggered by that night, his conscience and his sense of management, which pulled in the same direction, were too strong.

In euphoria, Jago was talking about the college, rather as though he were visiting it, from the loftiest position in the great world outside, after a lapse of years. He mentioned Tom Orbell, who had been his last bright pupil. Brown was unbuttoned enough to say:

'Between ourselves, Paul, I hope that young man gets a very good job *elsewhere*.' None of us needed an explanation of that sinister old college phrase. It meant that a man, even though a permanency, as Tom was, would be under moral pressure to apply for other posts. It was getting late, and Jago and I stood up to say goodbye.

'Don't let it be so long before you come in again,' said Brown to Jago.

'It shan't be long!' Jago cried.

I wondered how long it would be.

'It shan't be long!' Jago hallooed back up the stairs.

When we got into the court, I realised that he was unsteady on his feet, on feet abnormally small and light for such a heavy man. I had not paid attention, but he had been drinking hard since we arrived. I should have liked to know how much he drank with his wife at home. Cheerfully he weaved his way at my side to the side gate.

The fine spell had broken. The sky was overcast, a bleak wind blew into our faces, but Jago did not notice.

'Beautiful night!' he cried. 'Beautiful night!'

He fumbled his key in the lock, until I took it from him and let him out.

'Shall you be all right?' I asked.

'Of course I shall be all right,' he said. 'It's a nice walk home. It's a beautiful walk home.' He put a hand on my shoulder. 'Go and sleep well,' he said.

CHAPTER XXXVIII

AN ORDER IN THE BOOK

OUT of the window, as I sat at breakfast next day, the garden was dark; the room struck cold. All the morning the room struck cold, while I waited for a message from the combination room, where the Seniors were having their last meeting. To myself, I had given them an hour or so to find a formula. By twelve o'clock there was still no news. I couldn't judge whether the delay was good or bad. I rang up Dawson-Hill, who also was waiting in his room: no, he had heard nothing.

There were no books in the guest-room. I had read the morning papers twice over. I ate the relics of the bread and cheese which Jago and I had brought in the night before. Between one and half-past I telephoned the porter's lodge. The head porter told me that the combination room lights, which had been on most of the morning, were now turned off. The Seniors must have gone to lunch.

As soon as I heard that, I went quickly through the courts to the college library, took out a couple of books, returned to my rooms. I was anxious enough to telephone the porter's lodge again: had there been a message during the minutes I had been away? When they said no, I settled down to read, trying to stop myself speculating: but I was ready to hear the college clock each time it struck.

It had just struck half past three, when there was a knock at my door. I looked for the college butler. It was Dawson-Hill.

'I must say, Lewis,' he said, 'the old boys are taking their time.'

He was not cross, not in the least worried, except that he had to catch the last train back to London.

'I suggest,' he said, 'that we both need a breath of fresh air.'

Leaving the window open on the garden side, we should, he said, be within earshot of the telephone. So we walked on the grass between the great chestnut and the palladian building. The wind was rough, the bushes seethed, but Dawson-Hill's glossy hair stayed untroubled. He set himself to entertain me with stories which he himself found perennially fascinating: of how the commanding officer of his regiment had mistaken X for Y, of how Lord Boscastle had remarked, of a family who were the height of fashion, 'Whatever made them think *they* were aristocrats?' He was setting himself to entertain me. His laugh, which sounded affected and wasn't, cachinnated cheerfully into the wind-swept March-like garden. By this time I was worrying like a machine that won't run down. I could have brained him.

At half past four his stories were still going on, but he had decided that we could do with a cup of tea. Back in my rooms, he rang up the kitchens: no one there yet, in the depth of vacation. He took me out to a café close by, leaving a message with the porter. No one had asked for us when we returned. It was after five when, sitting in my room, Dawson-Hill cachinnating, I heard another knock on the door. This time it was the butler.

'The Master's compliments, gentlemen, and he would be grateful if you would join him in the combination room.'

As he walked in front of us through the court, it occurred to me that this was how the news of my fellowship had come. I had been waiting in Francis Getliffe's rooms (without suspense, because it had been settled beforehand), the butler had knocked on the door, given me the Master's compliments, and led me in.

Again, this dark summer afternoon, the butler led us in. On the panels, the wall-sconces were shining rosily. The Seniors sat, Winslow with his head sunk over the table, Brown bolt upright, Nightingale with his arms crossed over his chest. Crawford gazed at us, face moonlike, back to his normal composure. When he spoke his voice was tired, but nothing like as jaded or spiky as on the day before.

'Pray be seated, gentlemen,' he said. 'We apologise for keeping you all this time. We have had a little difficulty in expressing our intention.'

In front of him and Brown were sheets of foolscap, written on, passages crossed out, pages of holograph with lines across them, attempts at drafting, discarded resolutions.

The butler was leaving the room, when Brown plucked at Crawford's gown and whispered in his ear.

'Before you go, Newby!' called Crawford.

'Thank you very much for reminding me, Senior Tutor,' he said. 'We are under pledge, as I think the Court will remember, to communicate our decision to Professor Gay, who was appointed by the college Moderator in this case. I believe it was agreed that our legal colleagues here would report our decision to the Moderator, as soon as it was signed and sealed. Is that correct?'

'Certainly, Master,' said Dawson-Hill.

'In that case,' Crawford said to the butler, 'I should be obliged if you would give a message to Professor Gay's house asking him to expect these two gentlemen this evening.'

No one was smiling. No one, except me, seemed to resent this final interruption.

The door closed.

'So that's all in train,' said Crawford, and Brown steadily nodded.

'Well, gentlemen,' said Crawford, 'perhaps now we can dispatch our business. I should like to make a preliminary observation. Speaking not as Master but as a member of the college, and as one who has spent half a century in academic life, I have often felt that our internal disagreements sometimes generate more heat than light. I seem to recall making a similar comment on other occasions. But, with deference to my colleagues, I doubt if that has ever been more true than in this present one, which, I am thankful to say, we are now concluding. Speaking as an academic man, I am sometimes inclined to believe in the existence of a special *furor academicus*. However, speaking now as Master about this special and unfortunate occasion, I have to say that it is one of our responsibilities to diminish the heat which it has generated. In the course of our very protracted and careful discussions in this Court, especially today, I need hardly remark that no one has ever entertained a thought that any fellow of the college – with the solitary exception of the man whom the Court originally deprived – could possibly have acted except with good intentions and according to the code of men devoted to science or other branches of learning.'

This wasn't hypocrisy. It was the kind of formal language in which Crawford had been brought up. It was not very different from the formal language of officials. It meant something like the opposite of what it said. It meant that such thoughts were in everyone's mind: and that for reasons of prudence, face-saving and perhaps a sort of corporate kindness, the thoughts had to be pushed away. Crawford went on. Maddened for him to come to the point, I heard phrases of Brown's put in for Nightingale's benefit. I heard the damping-down of crises, the explaining away of 'misunderstandings', the respectful domestication of Francis Getliffe.

At last Crawford said:

'I hope that conceivably these few superficial remarks may give our legal colleagues some idea of the difficulties we have found ourselves in, and of the way in which our minds have been working. I think it remains for me now, as Master of the college and President of the Court of Seniors, to let them know our finding. This finding has already been composed in the form of an Order. When we have heard any observations our legal colleagues may have to make, the Order will be inscribed in the Seniors' Order Book.'

He scrabbled among the papers in front of him. He picked up one sheet.

'No, Master, fortunately not,' said old Winslow. 'This is one of the resolutions, one of the considerable number of resolutions, if I may say so, that you and I didn't find altogether congenial.'

'This is it, Master,' said Arthur Brown, as unmoved as a good secretary.

'Thank you, Senior Tutor.' Crawford took off his glasses, replaced them with another pair, settled back in his chair, quite relaxed, and read:

'30 June 1954. At a Meeting of the Court of Seniors, held this day, present the Master, Mr Winslow, Mr Brown, Dr Nightingale, it was resolved with one dissentient; that, after the hearings on 26, 27, 28, 29 June, held in the presence of legal advisers, the testimony is not sufficient to support the Order for the Deprivation of D. J. Howard, dated 19 October 1952, and that the Order for such Deprivation is hereby quashed. It was further resolved that Dr Howard's fellowship should be presumed to have continued without interruption during the period of deprivation and that he should be paid dividends and commons allowance in full: and that his fellowship shall continue until it lapses by the effluxion of time.'

'Is that all right, Dawson-Hill?' Crawford asked, as he put down the paper.

Just for an instant, Dawson-Hill flushed. Then, nonchalantly, with his kind of patrician cheek, he said:

'I don't pretend to be entirely happy about it, Master.'

'If you have anything further to say—?'

'Would that be the slightest use?'

'We are very grateful to you both,' Brown put in, 'but I really think we've got as far as discussion can reasonably take us.'

'Are you satisfied, Eliot?' Crawford asked.

As I listened, I had felt nothing but elation, savage elation, the elation of victory. But it was a long time since I had heard the singular eloquence of college orders. It took me a moment to realise that it was not all victory. Like the other research fellows since the war, Howard had been elected for four years. We had assumed that, if he were reinstated, the period of deprivation wouldn't count against his term. They were counting it, by the simple method of paying him, so that he would slide out as early as the statutes allowed: this device had occurred to no one before.

'When does his fellowship run out?' I enquired.

Brown, who saw that I had taken the point, replied:

'December 13th this year.'

'Well,' I said, 'you're giving him half a loaf.'

'No, Lewis,' said Brown, 'we're giving him a reasonable deal according to our lights. We think we should be ill-advised to give him more.'

'He will, of course,' said Crawford, 'still be eligible for an official fellowship if and when a vacancy crops up. Though I doubt whether it would be in his own best interests to hold out much hope of that.'

Brown spoke to me: 'No, Lewis, he's getting more than half a loaf. He's getting the substance of what he wants. He won't have a black mark against him, his fellowship will have run its course. As for the way we've done it, we're entitled to consider ourselves.'

They all waited. The clock ticked in the silence, as I made up my mind.

'For myself,' I said, 'I think I can accept that. But I'm not certain that all the fellows I am representing will do.'

'They'll be seriously irresponsible if they don't,' Brown said. He added in a tone unusually simple and direct: 'This isn't altogether plain sailing, you know. You'll do your best to persuade them, won't you?'

Crawford, still relaxed in his chair, inclined his head, not his body, first to the right, then to the left. With a satisfied smile he said:

'Well then. That is agreed.'

He went on:

'I will now ask the Bursar to enter the Order in the book.'

The draft was passed along to Nightingale, who had the order-book already opened. He said, as though he were excited, but excited in a not unpleasurable way:

'I take it that I enter my own dissent. I don't know whether anyone's ever had the chance to do that before!'

Fair hair bent over the book, he dutifully wrote. Winslow, turning away from him, was making remarks sharp with mischief about the resolutions that Nightingale wouldn't have the 'trouble of inscribing'. I got the impression that much of the day Brown had been drawing up forms of words by which the Seniors ruled out most of the evidence, and by inference protected Nightingale: but that when they became specific, Winslow had said that he would enter his dissent; and when they were woolly, Winslow, with some aid from Crawford, had jeered them away. All his life Winslow had loved drafting. This had been his day.

Nevertheless, fighting Brown on those clauses, Winslow and Crawford had given way about Howard's tenure. That was a compromise, and the more one thought of it the more indefensible it seemed. It wasn't like Brown, even, though it was his work. He was both too shrewd and also too magnanimous not to know that, when one admitted being wrong, one ought to admit it altogether and be generous. I didn't believe that they were aiming at keeping Howard from voting at the election, though incidentally they would do just that. No, I believed that, in some fashion which, in the future, Brown himself would be hard put to it to disentangle, much less justify, this was an attempt to make a gesture in favour of Nightingale, against the man who, even if he were innocent, had caused the trouble.

Meanwhile, Winslow was expecting Nightingale to resign. Winslow had been brought up in a Cambridge stiff with punctilio, pique and private incomes, and where, when men were criticised, they had a knack of throwing resignations on to the table, as in fact Winslow had done himself. It seemed incredible to him that Nightingale should not resign. Each minute, with relish, the old man was expecting it. I was not. I didn't doubt that Nightingale, who had still four years to go as Bursar, would finish his term of office down to the last second of the last day. If there were coldness, or something like ostracism, from Winslow and others, he would take that, thickening his carapace, under which he would feel ill-used, perhaps at times persecuted, imagining attacks, becoming offensive in return.

Nightingale finished writing, and placed the book in front of Crawford. I got up, and when they had signed, stood behind them and studied the page. The order was as Crawford had read it, written in Nightingale's neat, school-mistressish hand. Underneath were the three signatures, R. T. A. Crawford, M.C., G. H. Winslow, A. Brown. At the bottom of the page ran two lines inserted by Nightingale before the others signed:

'Dr Nightingale, Bursar of the College and Secretary of the Court of Seniors, wished to have his dissent recorded. R. E. A. Nightingale.'

Everyone was standing up. Nightingale reverentially put a large piece of blotting-paper on top of the order and closed the book. Then he looked out of the window into the gloomy evening and said to no one in particular, with the meteorological interest that never seemed to leave him:

'Well, we've had the last of the summer.'

The Court, despite the day-long sitting, did not seem anxious to break up. It was the disinclination to part one sometimes sees in a group of men, gathered together for whatever purpose, never mind what the disagreements or inner wars have been. Crawford asked us all if we would like a glass of sherry. While the butler brought in decanter and glasses, Winslow was saying that, as soon as the Long Vacation term began, he must summon the first full pre-election meeting.

'You'll soon be vanishing into oblivion,' he said to Crawford, with an old man's triumph, prodding him with his retirement. 'You'll soon be no one at all!'

We stayed and talked. They went on about the timetable of the election, though no one mentioned the candidates' names. It was nearly seven, and I said that Dawson-Hill and I must soon be off on our mission to old Gay. As I said that, Brown, whom I could not remember ever having seen gesticulate, covered his face with his hands. He had just thought, he said, that under the statutes Gay, as senior fellow, still had the prescriptive right to convene the election and to preside at it. 'After our experience with him over this business,' said Brown, 'how are we going to dare to try and keep him out? How are we going to keep him out at all? I wish someone would answer me that.'

Dawson-Hill was shaking hands all round. As Brown saw us ready to leave, he had another thought. He spoke to Crawford: 'If our friends are going out to Gay's, then I think we ought to send a copy of the order to Howard himself. I have a feeling that it's only right and proper.'

It was the correct thing to do; but it was also good-natured. Brown detested Howard, he had behaved to him with extreme prejudice, but he was not the man to see him kept in unnecessary suspense.

CHAPTER XXXIX

VIEW OF AN OLD MAN ASLEEP

IN the taxi, along the Madingley Road, through the dense, grey, leafy evening, Dawson-Hill sat with an expression impatient and miffed. He did not like losing any more than most people; he was bored by having to visit Gay.

'Well, you've got away with it, Lewis,' he observed.

'Wasn't it right that I did?'

But Dawson-Hill would give no view about Howard's innocence. He went on talking in an irritated, professional tone.

'I must say,' he said, 'you played it very skilfully on Monday morning. I don't see how you could have got away with it unless you'd used that double-play. You'd obviously got to raise the dust about Nightingale and give them an escape-route at one and the same damned time. Of course, if you'd gone all out against Nightingale, it would have been absolutely fatal for your chap. That stood to sense. But still, I must say, you did it very neatly.'

He added: 'You've always been rather lucky, haven't you?'

'What do you mean?'

'My dear Lewis, people say you always have the luck.' He broke off: 'By the way, I confess I think Nightingale's had a rough deal. The one thing that sticks out a mile to my eye is that he's as blameless as a babe unborn.'

The trees, the garden hedges went by. I had been thinking, how odd it was if acquaintances thought one lucky. It was the last thing anyone ever thought about himself.

Then, sitting complacently back, tired and smug with winning, I heard what Dawson-Hill said of Nightingale. Could it be true? All my instincts told me the opposite. Sitting back, I let in only the trickle of the question, could it be true? If so, it was one of the sarcasms of justice. One started trying to get a wrong righted; one started, granted the human limits, with clean hands and good will; and one finished with the finite chance of having done a wrong to someone else. And yet, in the taxi, windows open to the chilly, summer-smelling wind, it was I who was smug, not Dawson-Hill.

He was enquiring what nonsense we should have to listen to from old Gay. How long would he keep us? Dawson-Hill could not miss his train, Gay or no Gay, senile old peacocks or no senile old peacocks. Dawson-Hill had to be in London for a late-night party. He told me the names of the guests: all very smart, all reported with that curious mixture, common to those who love the world, of debunking and being oneself beglamoured. It was remarkably tiresome, he said, to have to endure old Gay.

The taxi went up the drive. As Dawson-Hill and I stood on the steps of the house, he said, like the German officers on the night the war began: 'Nur fang es an.'

The housekeeper came to the door. Her first words were:

'I am so sorry.' She looked distressed, embarrassed, almost tearful. She said: 'I am so sorry, but the Professor is fast asleep.'

Dawson-Hill laughed out loud, and said, gently and politely: 'Never mind.'

She went on, in her energetic, Central European English, 'But he had been looking forward to it so much. He has been getting ready for you since tea-time. He was so pleased you were coming. He had his supper early, to be prepared. And then he goes to sleep.'

'Never mind,' said Dawson-Hill.

'But he will mind terribly. He will be so disappointed. And I dare not wake him.'

'Of course you mustn't,' said Dawson-Hill.

She asked if we would like to see him, and took us into the study. The room was so dark it was hard to see anything: but there Gay lay back in his chair, shawl over his shoulders, beard luminescent in the vestigial light, luminous white against the baby-clear skin. His head was leaned against the sidewing of the chair. His mouth was open, a dark hole, but he was not snoring. With all of us dead silent, we could hear his breaths, peaceful and soothing.

We tiptoed out into the hall. 'What is to be done?' said Dawson-Hill.

We could leave the copy of the order with a note signed by us both, I said.

'He will be so disappointed,' said the housekeeper. Tears were in her eyes. 'He will be heart-broken like a little child.'

'How long before he wakes?' asked Dawson-Hill.

'Who can tell? When he has what he calls his "naps" in the evening, it is sometimes one hour, sometimes two or three.'

'Don't worry, Mrs Nagelschmidt,' said Dawson-Hill, 'I will stay.'

She flushed with happiness. He had remembered her name, he was so polite, and all was well. I said it was very hard on him: I would volunteer myself, but I was dining with my brother, and afterwards might have to do some persuasion with the Howard faction.

'That's important,' said Dawson-Hill. 'No, you can't possibly stay. It's all right, I will.'

'And your party?'

'I suppose,' said Dawson-Hill to the housekeeper, 'I may telephone, mayn't I?'

'You shall have everything,' she cried. 'You shall sit in the drawing-room. I will make you a little dinner—'

I asked how he was going to get back to London. He said that he would have to hire a car.

It was pure good-nature. Half an hour before, we had seen Brown's good-nature; that one took for granted, it fitted deep into his flesh and bone. But Dawson-Hill's came as a shock. I remembered the stories of his good turns to young men at the Bar, done secretively, and with his name kept out. Those stories, whenever I met him and heard his prattle, I only half-believed. Now I broke out:

'You're a very kind man, aren't you?'

Dawson-Hill coloured from hairline to collar. He was delighted to be praised, and yet for once uncomfortably shy. His face seemed to change its shape. The lines, which as a rule ran downwards, giving him his air of superciliousness and faint surprise, suddenly went horizontal, broadening him out, destroying his handsomeness. He looked like a hamster which has just filled its cheek-pouches, shifty, but shining with chuff content. In a manner as gauche as an adolescent's, he said, in a hurry:

'Oh, I don't think we'd better talk about that.'

CHAPTER XL

WALKING OUT OF THE LODGE

WHEN I got to Martin's house, Margaret was there to welcome me. She had come up to take me home next day. She was bright-eyed because we had won; she wanted nothing except for us to be by ourselves. Irene was yelping with general irreverent glee: the room was warm, swept by currents of slapdash content.

But Margaret was bright-eyed, not only with joy, but with a kind of comic rage. Within five minutes of her arriving at the house – so they told me – Laura had been on to her by telephone. The Seniors' decision was an outrage: of course Donald's tenure ought to be prolonged by the entire period during which he had been deprived. Would Margaret see that that was done? and would she also sign a letter which, when Margaret mentioned it, I recognised as the one they had been forcing upon Dr Pande?

'It may be a perfectly reasonable letter,' cried Margaret. 'But I'm sick and tired of being pestered by that awful woman.'

'I thought you got on rather well with her?' said Martin, with a glint of malice.

'That's what you think,' Margaret said. 'I've had more of her than I can stand. What's more, I don't believe, as some of you do, that she's under her husband's thumb. I believe she's the bloodiest awful specimen of a party biddy, and I never want to see her again as long as I live.'

On the tenure of Howard's fellowship also, Margaret's conscience had worn thin. She would have struggled to the last to get him justice. But she did not see, she was saying happily, still pretending to be irascible, why he should get more. The way he had done his research, his lack of critical sense, his taking his professor's evidence – that wasn't even second-rate, it was tenth-rate. The man was no good. He ought to count himself lucky to get what the Seniors were giving him: he ought to count himself lucky and keep quiet.

Martin said that he hoped we could convince the others so. As he spoke, we were eating dinner.

'You haven't got to go out again tonight?' Margaret asked me. 'You've had a horrible day, you know you have.'

In fact, I was very tired. But I was not too tired to think, with the disrespect of love, that Margaret was not above a bit of rationalisation when she wanted something for herself. Was she really so sure that Howard had got his deserts? Was she really speaking as impartially as her academic relatives would have done? When she wanted to forget it all, stop them wearing me out, and be together?

Martin had already called a meeting. It would be dangerous, he said, not to 'tie up' the offer at once. By a quarter to nine we were back in college, sitting in Martin's rooms, cold that night after the house we had just left.

Francis Getliffe arrived soon after. We had brought our chairs round the table, by the side of which stood a standard lamp, leaving one end in shadow: Martin switched on a reading-light on a desk close by. As Francis sat down he said: 'Of course, we have to accept it.'

'I don't know whether there's going to be any trouble,' said Martin. 'But look—' he was speaking to Francis, 'you'd better let me run this. You've done enough already.'

He said it in a considerate tone. I believed he was speaking out of fairness. Though he had not told me, I still fancied that, when the election came, he intended to vote for Brown: but he knew, no one better, that, in saving Howard, Francis had done himself harm. Martin had, of course, foreseen it on the evening when Francis volunteered to speak out. Martin, with the fairness into which he was disciplining himself as he grew older, was not prepared to let him do more. Certainly Francis seemed to take it so, for he said: 'Good work.' It was the most friendly interchange between the two that I had seen.

Skeffington and Tom Orbell came in together, Tom with that air of being attached to balloons by invisible strings, which emanated from him when he had been drinking. He gave us a euphoric good-evening. Then Howard followed, with a nod, but without a word, and sat in the remaining chair, head bent on his chest, eyes glancing to the corner of the room.

'I couldn't collect any of the others who signed the memorandum,' said Martin. 'They're nearly all away, but this is a quorum. I suppose you all know the terms of the Seniors' decision?'

'I should think we do,' said Tom ebulliently.

'It seems to me to give you' – Martin was addressing himself down the table to Howard – 'eveything essential. What do you think?'

'I think,' said Howard, 'that it's pretty mingy.'

'It's a bad show,' said Skeffington, paying no attention to Howard, almost as though he were invisible. Loftily he bore down on me: 'It's a bad show. I can't understand how a man like you could let them give us a slap in the face like that.'

'Do you think it was quite as easy?' I said in temper. It occurred to me that I had not received a word of thanks, certainly not from the Howards. It occurred to me simultaneously that I did not remember seeing a group of people engaged in a cause they all thought good, who did not end in this kind of repartee.

'It ought to have been,' said Skeffington.

'You're not being realistic, Julian,' Martin said.

'If this is being realistic, then I'm all in favour of trying something else,' said Skeffington. 'What do you think?' he asked Francis.

'I agree with the Eliots,' said Francis.

'Really,' replied Skeffington, with astonishment, with outrage.

It was Francis's remark, made quietly and without assertion, that sent Tom Orbell over the hairline – the hairline which, when he was drunk, separated the diffuse and woofy benevolence from a suspicion of all mankind. He was not very drunk that night: he had come in exuding amiability and good will. Of all the young men in the college, he was the most interesting, if one had the patience. He had by a long way the most power of nature; he was built on a more abundant scale. Yet it was hard to see whether that power of nature would bring him through or wreck him. Suddenly as he heard Francis's remark, he once more saw the lie in life.

'So that's what you think, is it?' he said, talking down his nose.

'We've no option,' said Francis.

'That's all right. If you think so.' Tom thrust his great head forward. 'But some of us don't think so. We've got the old men on the run, and this is the time to make them behave decently for once. I don't know what Lewis was doing not to make them behave decently, except' – his suspicions fixed themselves on me – 'that's the way you've got on, isn't it, playing safe with the old men?'

'That's enough, Tom.' Martin spoke sharply.

'Who says it's enough? Haven't you done exactly the same? Isn't that the whole *raison d'être* behind this precious bargain? I don't like the Establishment. But I'm beginning to think the real menace is the Establishment behind the Establishment. That's what some of you' – he looked with hot eyes at Martin, at Francis, at me – 'are specialists in, isn't it?'

'Can it,' said Skeffington. He was the only man who could control Tom that night. 'What I want to know is, how are we going to set about it?'

'Set about what?' asked Martin.

'Getting this decision altered, of course.'

Gradually, as Tom sobered himself, the two of them began to shape a proposition. The time ticked by as we sat round the shadowed table. Only Howard, at the end removed from the rest of us, did not speak at all. The argument was bitter. Martin was speaking in the tone of reason, but even his composure grew frayed. Francis was getting imperative. I heard my own voice sounding harsher. While Skeffington would not budge from his incorruptibility. Somehow absolute and full recompense had to be given, pressed down and running over.

'We're going to have our pound of flesh,' cried Tom. 'We insist on complete reinstatement. Payment in full for the period of deprivation. And the fellowship to run from this day with the period of deprivation added on. We won't be fobbed off with less.'

'That's stretching it,' said Skeffington. 'We can't ask for payment for the deprivation if we get the period tagged on. That's the decent thing.'

'So that's what you think,' said Tom, turning on his ally.

'It's not on, to ask for money too.'

'Very well, then.' Tom lowered at us across the table. 'Julian Skeffington's willing to let you off lightly. I'd disown you first, but I'll come in. You'll have to go back to your friends and make them give us what he's pleased to call the decent thing.'

'You're seriously suggesting that we go back to the Master straightaway?' said Martin.

'What else do you think we're suggesting?' Tom burst out.

'Look here,' I intervened, 'I've sat through the whole of these proceedings. I know, and you don't know, what the feeling is. I tell you that we shouldn't stand a chance.'

'You want to make it easy for everyone, don't you?' Tom attacked me again.

'He's dead right,' said Francis.

'Now we listen to the voice of Science, disinterested and pure, the voice of Intellect at its highest, the voice that we shall always associate with Sir Francis Getliffe,' Tom declaimed.

'Hold it,' said Skeffington. 'You say,' he turned to me, angry with Tom as well as with us, stiff-necked, 'that if we go back to them we shan't get any change?'

'Not the slightest,' I said.

Tom was beginning another burst of eloquence, but Skeffington stopped him.

'I'll take that,' he said to me. 'We've got to take that. You know what's what. But that doesn't write us off—'

'What else can you do?' said Martin.

'It's pretty clear,' said Skeffington. 'We start all over again. We beat up a majority of the fellows, and we send the Court another memorandum. We accept their withdrawal, but we tell them we're not satisfied. We tell them they've got to do the decent thing. We'll put in the proper terms of reinstatement, just to leave no room for argy-bargy.'

'That's what I like to hear!' cried Tom.

There was a pause. Martin glanced at me, then at Francis, and began to speak:

'No. I'm sorry. You can't do it.'

'What do you mean, we can't do it?'

'How do you think you're going to get your majority?'

'We'll beat them up just as we did before.'

'You won't,' said Martin. 'Not to put too fine a point on it, you won't get me.' They were interrupting him, but he said sternly: 'Now listen for once. We've been in this too, every inch of the way. I haven't done much. But if it hadn't been for Lewis, I doubt if we'd have got any sort of satisfaction. If it hadn't been for Francis, I'm quite sure we shouldn't. Well, we've done our piece. And that's enough.'

Both Skeffington and Tom were speaking, the voices were jangling round the table, when there came an interruption. Howard, who after his first remark had not said a word, who had been sitting with jaw sunk into chest, noisily slammed his hand on the table and pushed back his chair.

He said, in a grating tone:

'I'm fed up.'

'What?' cried Tom.

'I'm fed up with being talked about. I'm not going to be talked about any more by any of you,' he said. He went on:

'They seem to have decided that I'm not a liar. I suppose that's something. I'm not having any more of it. You can go and tell them that it's all right by me.'

On heavy feet, he clumped out of the room.

He was innocent in this case, I had no doubt. And he had another kind of innocence. From it came his courage, his hope and his callousness. It would not have occurred to him to think what Skeffington and Tom had risked; and yet anyone used to small societies would have wondered whether Skeffington stood much chance of getting his fellowship renewed, or Tom, for years to come, any sort of office. Howard did not care. He still had his major hopes. They were indestructible. Men would become better, once people like him had set the scene. He stamped out of the room, puzzled by what had happened, angry but not cast down, still looking for, not finding, but hoping to find, justice in this world.

Martin, with face impassive, eyes sparkling, said:

'Well, that appears to settle it.'

Haughtily Skeffington announced:

'I shall write to the Master on my own.'

'I advise you not to, Julian,' said Martin.

'I shall have to,' Skeffington replied, obdurate and sea-green.

'But still,' said Martin, 'as far as we're concerned, that's settled it?'

Skeffington nodded. He said:

'It's all you can expect of a chap like that. He's got no guts.'

It was the first recognition of Howard's existence he had made all the evening. He did it seriously, his head uptilted, without a glint of humour, whereas Tom, his great frame shaking, his cheeks moist and roseate in the cool room, was billowing with laughter. He tried to speak, and emitted little squeals. All he could say was:

'Give me your hand, Martin. Give me your hand, Lewis.'

When we went down into the court, there was a light shining in the Master's study. 'We'd better get it over,' said Francis, and he, Martin and I walked across to the Lodge. The front door was unlocked, and we went in and climbed the stairs. As soon as I opened the study door, I saw Crawford on one side of the fireplace, Brown on the other.

'Good evening to you, gentlemen,' Crawford said. He offered us a nightcap of whisky, but I said that we had not come to stay.

'Perhaps I can act as spokesman,' I said. 'It's straightforward, Master. We've been talking to some of the signatories of the last memorandum. We've been talking about today's decision of the Court. All I need say is that it's been accepted.'

'Splendid,' said Brown. He got up, stood beside me, and took my arm. He had noticed what I had not said. Quietly, as Crawford was talking to the others, Brown said in my ear, 'You've done us all a service, you know.'

Crawford was saying at large:

'Well, I'm glad this business is settled without breaking too many bones.' He called to me as though he had never had a doubt in his life: 'I think I remember saying to you in this room last week, Eliot, perhaps we worry too much about forms of procedure. I think I remember saying that in my experience sensible men usually reach sensible conclusions.'

He said it with invincible content, with the reverence of one producing a new truth. The previous time, Dawson-Hill had seen the beauty of that statement. Now Martin, glancing at me, had to tighten the muscles of his jaw in order to keep his face impassive.

We went down the study stairs. Crawford pulled back the great oak door. Out in the court the chilly wind was blowing, so strong that the staircase lanterns sprayed and shook in the midsummer dark. Crawford walked out of the Lodge with Brown on his right hand, Getliffe on his left. Following after them, Martin once more glanced at me, eyes sharp, half-sarcastic, half-affectionate. Did he mean what I thought he meant? That, within six months, Crawford would be walking out of the Lodge for good, and one of those two would be walking in?